❧❧

I KNOW THAT GHOSTS HAVE WANDERED THE EARTH

❧❧

A Collection of Brontë-Inspired Ghost Stories, Local Legends, Paranormal Experiences, and Channelings
by
A Walk Around the Bronte Table Facebook Group

Edited by Kay Fairhurst Adkins

I KNOW THAT GHOSTS HAVE WANDERED THE EARTH

A Collection of Ghost Stories, Local Legends, Paranormal Experiences, and Channelings

A Walk Around The Bronte Table Facebook Group

Edited by Kay Fairhurst Adkins

Cover photo by Harry Hartley

Back Cover Illustration by Barb Tanke

To contact the publisher:
awalkaroundthebrontetable@aol.com

First edition

ISBN: 9798685334879

DEDICATION

To Barb Tanke and Harry Hartley.

Without one of Harry's photos I may never have imagined this book.
It was seeing his photo and considering it for the cover
of our COVID-19 poetry book that gave me the idea of putting
together a book of Ghost Stories. Additionally, his work
on the Local Legends and Folklore section is jaw-dropping.

I envisioned a book filled with illustrations for each
and every story and poem – a vision that would never have been
fulfilled without Barb's eager willingness to undertake
the illustration of story after story when others became overwhelmed
by the challenges of daily life during a pandemic.
She was never too busy to volunteer and her work is stunning.

These two individuals dedicated themselves to breathing life into
my vision for this book and I am grateful.

ACKNOWLEDGEMENTS

I am proud of each of our authors for creating such a delightfully spooky collection of tales. Some are true. Some are imagined. Some blur the line between.

I am equally proud of our illustrators for bringing more to life than they may have bargained for....

OTHER BOOKS
BY A WALK AROUND THE BRONTE TABLE

There Was No Possibility of Taking a Walk That Day
A Collection of Poems from the 2020 COVID-19 Lockdown

NOTE:

Enjoy the *Wuthering Heights* quotes used in the title and interspersed throughout this book. This book of ghost stories includes stories and poems written in American English and British English. You will also find Lithuanian and French punctuation in a few stories. I don't claim to be a perfect editor in any language. I may have inadvertently "corrected" spellings and punctuation that did not need correcting. This entire project has taken less than four months from conception to print date, so it is inevitable that there will be some regrettable errors. Please blame them on the poltergeist - his name is Weems. Though now that I've read the section on folklore, naming him may not have been the best idea....

MEET OUR VOLUNTEER ARTISTS

Barb Tanke can be contacted at bjtanke@gmail.com and will share her portfolio of work for anyone interested. Included in the portfolio is a Bronte website from 1999.

Catherine Rebecca creates from the very core of her childish self in the hope that she may help people tap into that element of themselves. She calls it her happy place. One of joy and innocence. A place to smile. A place where you can open your mind and free your spirit.

Christina Rauh Fishburne's art appears in tattoos, musical and literary collaboration projects, and her parents' refrigerator. Primarily a writer, most of her work can be found at smilewhenyousaythat.wordpress.com. She is also on Facebook and Instagram.

Debs Green-Jones lives in North Wales. She loves to write and illustrate books for very young children. She also enjoys painting in watercolour, classical music, reading, gardening and yoga. What a Week! is the first children's book she has both written and illustrated. Facebook: Debs Green-Jones, Twitter: @DebsGreenJones2

EmilyInGondal creates photographic and mixed media artwork inspired by the Brontës and their landscape. Find her on Etsy and social media under EmilyInGondal.

Emily Ross is an artist from Bedford, UK, who has been researching Brontë likenesses since 2014. She runs the Brontë Link which can be found at http://instagram.com/thebrontelink Her personal instagram is http://instagram.com/emilycharlotteross

JoJo Hughes is a mother of three, working as a teaching assistant in a beautiful corner of Cornwall, UK. She has always loved drawing for pleasure...when time allows!

Jon Beynon is a commissions artist/illustrator based in Gloucestershire, England. He specialises in portraits of pets, people and places. Contact via Facebook - Jon Beynon Portraits and Fine Art, or Instagram – jondbeynonart

Julie Rose is an artist and miniaturist inspired by the Brontës. Follow the Brontë Parsonage Dollhouse, art, books and crafts on Instagram - @miniaturebronteparsonage and Twitter - Julie Rose @R40JTR.

Nathalia Amorim is a librarian based in Rio de Janeiro, Brazil. In this project, she joined both of her passions: creating art and the Brontë sisters. She specializes in oil paintings, watercolors and other artistic techniques. Commissions are available at: nathalia.amorim18 @gmail.com

Rowan Coleman is a novelist, keen amateur artist, and author of The Brontë Mysteries writing as Bella Ellis. Twitter: @rowancoleman @brontemysteries Instagram: @rowanmcoleman @brontemysteries

Stephanie Rodriguez is an award-winning artist and educator. Stephanie's artwork has been published in various books and magazines and is seen on display in galleries and museums. To explore more of Stephanie's work, visit her website at: http://stephanie rodriguezart.com.

Yael Veitz is a New York-based poet, artist, and professional empath with a love of geographic diversity and animals. Her website is www.yaelveitz.com

Yvonne Solly lives in Canberra, Australia. She is learning to draw and paint during COVID-19 and from the looks of it, is making amazing progress.

CONTENTS

INTRODUCTION
October 2020

I would like to introduce this collection of ghost stories with a story of my own. One I have never told a soul – until now.

Before I morphed my tiny One Book Book Club Facebook group for *Wuthering Heights* into A Walk Around The Bronte Table I searched on Facebook to see if there was already an existing group that celebrated the Brontës in a manner that would satisfy my hunger for more Bronté-related discussion.

I didn't find it, but I did find something else. Something I have never been able to revisit since: A group, The Witches of Haworth.

Interesting, I thought...so I clicked on the group just to take a look... And immediately recoiled in horror!

They were planning a ceremony to bring Branwell back from the dead!

"Oh no!" I thought, "He wouldn't like that at all!"

For me, to bring someone back from the dead is taken very literally. It is reanimation, bringing someone back to life - as in digging up the remains, finding a new host for the spirit, or doing something equally creepy - and making the person come to life again until they are chased into a tower by a horde of angry villagers carrying torches.

I couldn't imagine Branwell happily embracing a new chance at living in a time so very different from his own. I couldn't imagine him being freed from his sorrows, or being able to live with the knowledge of the domino game of death his demise set off in the Brontë household.

I was never able to find the group again so I don't know how their adventure turned out. I believe they changed their privacy settings and became a secret group. For them, bringing someone back from the dead may be more a matter of talking to a disembodied spirit, in which case I am perfectly okay with that – as you'll find out later – and owe The Witches of Haworth an apology.

Perhaps you can pass it on for me...

11

If you are looking for page after page of blood, horror and gore, I'm afraid you won't find it here. We are writing these stories as we live out a real-life dystopian nightmare of pandemic, economic collapse, political mayhem, and rabid conspiracy theories. I live in the County with the second-highest COVID-19 death count in the State with the third-highest COVID-19 death count in the country with the most COVID-19 deaths in the world. Three of my husband's coworkers have been sick with COVID-19 and a dear friend who was presumably sick with COVID-19 in April 2020 (testing was not widely available in our country) is now in sudden and unexpected kidney failure – one of the many possible aftereffects of this novel disease.

Writing and illustrating ghost stories is one of the sanest things we can do right now. Our memories haunt us daily with pictures of the celebrations, travel, concerts, museum visits, family gatherings, and special moments with friends we once took for granted.

Every 2020 calendar mocks us.

Before I let you proceed into this cauldron of stories gathered from Brontë fans around the world, I must warn you: After reading just three of our tales the other evening, my husband had a nightmare.

Well done, authors, well done.

~Kay Fairhurst Adkins~
Founder of the A Walk Around The Bronte Table Facebook Group

The Vengeful Bride illustrated poem by Rowan Coleman, UK

13

You Said I Killed You
– Haunt Me, Then!

GHOST STORIES

The Saving of Branwell Brontë illustration by EmilyInGondal

THE SAVING OF BRANWELL BRONTË

By Mark Campbell
Tunbridge Wells, England

This ghost story is based on the day when Branwell was visited by the ghost of his dead sister Maria. This is an event which is supposed to have happened.

The wind roared wildly outside Branwell's window as he sat at his desk, hunched over the company ledger. He had held the position of clerk-in-charge of the Luddendenfoot Railway station for the previous three months. Moments later he heard a train pass by down below and entered something in the ledger.

"That will be the 2:45 express service from Bradford wending on its merry way to its next port of call." Branwell sighed as he rested his hands over his face. "Oh, how monotonous this life is. There never seems to be anything which happens to disturb the same routine in which I pass away every miserable day I serve this company. Why cannot something happen? Anything will do to disrupt the endless flow of mundane toil which I suffer each day. It is not as if..."

Just then, Branwell turned his head as though he had heard something. Not an everyday sound this, like a train passing by or a bird crying out: not even the roar of the wind. No, this was something else entirely. It had sounded like the voice of a child. But what would a child be doing in a deserted, out of the way station such as Luddendenfoot? On the face of it this did not make a modicum of sense.

Thinking at first that it was nothing but a figment of his imagination, Branwell returned once again to his ledger. However, barely had a few moments passed before he heard another sound much like the one which had reached him previously.

"What the deuce is that?" he asked his office in wide-eyed exasperation. He scratched his head, thinking a sojourn to the local tavern would be just the thing to drive this irritating diversion from his mind. "Why can I hear..."

"Branwell!" This time it was unmistakable. A young girl calling out to him to gain his attention. But which girl could it be? He looked around himself, exploring every square inch of his office but could find no sign of a mysterious girl. He was still quite alone. What was he to make of this strange development?

"Do not doubt your senses," urged the young voice as Branwell continued to walk around the room in a transport of confusion. "You have not lost your mind. I wish to speak to you, brother. Rest your book aside; we have much to discuss."

Despite the words which had reached him, words which had unnerved him a great deal, Branwell continued to look about himself as his sense of shock deepened further. "But what trick is this now?" he asked as he glanced first one way and then another in a state of fright.

"It is no trick, brother," came back the young voice which seemed awfully familiar to him, although at first he could not place it. "I am your sister Maria come back to you."

Branwell was aghast at this news. For while the sound of the voice sounded like his sister how could it really and truly be her?

"No," he railed at the disembodied voice. "This cannot be. Maria has been dead for ages past. A mere girl she was when her saintly soul was secreted off to heaven. So, I ask by all that's sacred in this world, how can I hear her now? How it is possible?"

"It is possible, brother: you must be assured on that point. And you hear me now because I have much to tell you."

Branwell stared at the empty office in disbelief. "To tell me? Why, what the deuce can *you* have to tell me? You have been dead to me for many years. Your memory is all that remains: that and a happy recollection of merry childhood days."

"Ah! But that is precisely why I have sought you out now." There was almost a mocking air about these words which made Branwell catch his breath. Whatever could the girl mean? he wondered. "The memories," she explained, "which you speak of have remained with me also, even into my spirit state. They have been a semblance of hope; a ray of sunshine, filling me up, in turn, with a desire that your regeneration may yet be effected. Given time and..."

"Wait a moment, oh dearest sister of my formative years. Why speak of my regeneration? I am not a lost cause, no dissolute soul, no..."

"Ah, but I beg to differ with you on that point, Branwell, and I do so with a great deal of urgency. For while it is true you are not in the completest sense of the word dissolute, you are nonetheless moving in that direction. I fear for you, brother, indeed I do, if you do not make your peace with God and alter your ways from this moment forward."

"What's this, sister? You take to chastising me, of bringing up the very question of religion which has made of me an outcast at home. This cannot be right. You belie me, Maria. Please say I have you amiss, I beg of you. I never thought that my guiding light, my shining star, my angelic vision of true belief could treat me so harshly. Why must you torment me?"

"I torment you, brother?" sneered Maria in a belittling tone. "Oh, no: that could never be. I love you now as much as ever I did. It is merely my intention to put you on the right track once more. For I do not believe you will ever amount to anything, will never reach the attainments which are within your powers unless your lifestyle is radically altered."

"My lifestyle?" sighed Branwell in exasperation. "Why, what the deuce has that got to do with my future prospects? I have done well enough for myself, have I not? I am in a responsible post, with a sterling income and my superiors assure me I could well go far in the railway industry."

"Pah!" scoffed a disdainful Maria. "This is not Branwell Brontë talking: he would not be so satisfied with mere crumbs of joy from a poor man's table. He would demand more for himself. But it would appear you are content with your present low station in life." There was a sarcastic tone to Maria as she uttered this remark. She followed it with a spurt of girlish giggling which pained Branwell. "Ah!" she continued. "What a shame it is you do not recall the dreams of your childhood..."

"But we never spoke of..."

"What brother? We not speak of the shining path of wonder which lay in front of us, not speak of the grand ascension which would raise us up on high? Oh, we did indeed speak of such things. We expressed it endlessly in our childhood. Ah! The jewels which were to be ours on growing into adulthood; we had only to reach out and they would be ours for the taking. How can you have forgotten?"

"I was young, sister," replied Branwell in a pitiful fashion. "You cannot expect me to..."

"Young?" remonstrated Maria. "We were both of us young, Branwell. How is it, then, that I can recall our plans for future prosperity, while you have no recollection of them?" Suddenly, Maria changed her attitude, as she began to speak in a more approving tone. "But let us conjecture no more: let us recollect the plans we made all those many years ago."

Branwell stared about him with an air of confusion. "But what do you mean, Maria? It is clear you can recollect these 'plans' as you term them, but I cannot. So..."

"But look, Branwell," commanded an urgent Maria. "Over there in the corner, next to the door. Do you not see us as we used to be, as we were all those years ago?"

Branwell quickly looked over to the corner of the room which Maria had indicated and let out an astonished cry. "Good grief! I cannot believe it. But how could..."

As if by magic, child versions of Branwell and Maria appeared next to the door. It soon transpired this was the Christmas of 1824, some 17 long years before; five short months before Maria's tragic death.

"What do you wish to be when you grow up, brother?" asked the child Maria, the one who at this point was still alive.

"I wish to be a great explorer or otherwise a statesman who is respected the country over for his integrity and high standing as a gentleman. And you, Maria? What do you wish to be?"

Maria stood in a reflective pose as she drew her palms together in front of her. "Ah! I would think it a good thing if I were to be a missionary. I could therefore carry out God's message to those who require his blessing and guidance the most. They being the poor unfortunates of this world, those who are uneducated, undernourished and destitute." She seemed to be in raptures at the idea. "Yes, indeed! I could do the Lord's work, and consider it a privilege to do so."

The present-day Branwell took the opportunity to approach closer to his child equivalent and the one who represented Maria. He was filled with stupefaction at what was unfolding in front of his eyes. However, it was not long before he recalled to his mind this childhood memory. He found he could remember it just as clearly and concisely as his sister.

Young Branwell scoffed at his sister's choice of occupation. "Pah! A missionary is a curious choice for you to make. It is hardly heroic. You cannot alter the world by being a missionary."

"Perhaps not. But it is not my intention to be heroic or to alter the manner in which civilization is run. Heroic endeavours should be left

20

to the men of this world. As to change: well, I feel sure living the life of a missionary will enable me to do good. If I can alter the life of just one poor underprivileged soul, I will derive a satisfaction which a hundred acts of heroism could not supersede."

"Oh, I cannot agree on that point, sister. But we will live grand lives, will we not?"

At this point, the adult Branwell took a more eager notice of the ongoing discussion between his former self and that of his sister. For this is precisely the point Maria had made to him before; the high aspirations they both had for themselves in childhood.

"We will indeed, Branwell," replied Maria. "You can count on it. We shall not stand on ceremony where that is concerned. We will rise to wonderous heights in our separate professions, ensuring that our names will stand out from the common herd."

The child Branwell erupted in an explosion of excitement which could not be contained. "Yes, we will, Maria: we will! I will discover new lands upon the horizon, while you will give a multitude of poor savages a new purpose in their lives..."

"Oh, tut! Tut! Do not speak so, Branwell. I do not care for the term 'savages.' These poor folk are not deserving of such a discourteous label. They require to be respected. They are not wild animals: merely persons who have lost their way through no fault of their own, but because they lacked the proper guidance. This I will provide, if God remains by my side."

"He will, sister. But we have good cause for rejoicing, have we not? For you will be a fine lady, a saintly figure who will command respect from man, woman and child from all walks of life, while I will be a respectable gentleman, well-thought of by an adoring public who will bow and curtsy to me as I move from one glorious adventure to the next."

Maria giggled at this. "Indeed, you speak rightly, brother. It is just as you say: the name of Brontë will be well thought of throughout the land once we have grown to adulthood. It will be a grand time: we have much to look forward to."

At this momentous stage, the children melted away from view. As they did so, Branwell moved over to the position where moments before his child self and that of Maria had been talking away so animatedly. There was an expression of bewilderment lining his features as he returned to his desk and sat with his head drooping down as if unable to take in all he had just seen.

However, he soon recovered himself and sat upright as he turned around. "Are you still with me?" he asked of the ghostly Maria. "If so, then speak without delay."

A whimsical Maria replied to his utterance. "Ah, yes indeed. It would appear this look into your past has rejuvenated your very soul. For you speak much more like the Branwell of old, the one I remember with such fondness, the playmate of my childhood years. You were ever impatient as a boy. You could never wait for events to unfold of their own accord. No, you desired your wishes to be granted overnight. How sad, then, to see you in your current plight."

Branwell stared ahead of him in annoyance. "My current plight? Why, you return to your former appraisal of my character which was cruel and unforgiving. This is not the Maria of my childhood, not the young missionary I have just looked onto: my angelic vision of true Christian virtue..."

"No, Branwell. You are wrong to say so. I am not changed: you are the one who has taken on a marked alteration in the way you view the world. Have you learnt nothing from the scene just played out? I showed that to you for a reason. I wished to open your eyes, to bring much-needed light into your life, to guide you onto a straighter, more purposeful course. But it appears my efforts have been in vain. You continue to stumble along much like a blind man would, with no direction, no Christian path to follow. It would seem you much prefer the debasement of your personal ideals to the pursuit of a worthy life. You place consorting with drunkards and rough youths above the striving after artistic attainments which formerly held such a prominent place in your heart.

Whatever happened to the boy Branwell, he who wished to become an explorer or a statesman? An artist or a writer you also desired to be. Instead what have you become? A clerk on a railway line, a man who prefers drinking with uneducated, brazen, foul-mouthed men to reaching out for a golden future which should have been his. You lost touch with your childhood ideals, Branwell. You failed to follow your dreams, and so here you are sitting in your station house regretting missed opportunities, wrestling with desires which remain unfulfilled.

A surge of anger rose up in Branwell as he listened to his sister's diatribe. "Why do you torment me in this way, Maria?" he asked her.

"You were ever kind to me beforetimes. I ever found in you a caring sister, a support to me when I needed you. When mamma died, you became much like a mother to me. I could always look to you for guidance. Yet now you speak coldly, belittling my efforts to make an honest living and questioning the company I keep. This is beyond all human endurance. And why should I sit here conversing with a ghost? You are dead, Maria: you are gone forever, never to return. I require not your spirit to erode all of the happy recollections I still hold close to my heart of a childhood spent in the comforting society of a dearly loved sister. Be gone, I say, ghost: be gone!"

"Bless me, brother," retorted Maria with some feeling. "You are swift enough in your pleas for my withdrawal from your society. And yet not much time has passed by since you were desperate for my company. Can you really be so forgetful of past times? Why, it is as if you are altered beyond all recall."

"Yes, but our childhood is long gone. Why do you remind me of..."

"No! You mistake me, brother. I do not allude to our childhood years. Much rather do I speak of some lines you wrote in my honour."

"Lines?" asked Branwell in confusion as to his sister's meaning. "What lines? I am afraid you have me at a disadvantage."

"Branwell! How can you plead indifference on this point? I speak of a series of poems you wrote a number of years past. I was the subject of these poems, or at least your memory of me was. Well, no matter: I am able to recall these same lines even if you are not. 'There was a light – but it is gone/There was a hope – but all is o'er/Where, Maria, where art thou!' There: does it sound familiar to you now?"

Branwell rose from his chair and begin to pace up and down the room in a ferment of emotion. "Ah yes, Maria," he told the ghost. "I understand you now, and yet at the same time I do not. I did indeed write those lines as a devotion to your blessed memory. I wrote them some five years past. But how did..."

"How was I acquainted with this poem when I had been dead some ten years before? Is that what you wished to say, brother?"

"Yes. How could you have..."

"Ah, but it was the simplest of matters to effect. For unbeknown to you, dear brother, I was in your presence when you set down those lines."

"What?" asked a startled Branwell. "You were there when I wrote that poem? You were in the same room?"

"Indeed I was. And not only on that occasion. I have looked over your shoulder many times in the past. 'There, then, her gentle cheek declined/All white her neck and shoulder gleamed/White as the bed where they reclined.' Do you recall composing that poem?"

Branwell paced the room in an even more frantic way than he had done moments before. Indeed, he seemed ready to explode as he cried out in exasperation. "Another poem! Yet one more of my poems have you witnessed me write. Why, this is intolerable. How can I ever again put pen to paper knowing as I do you could be looking over my shoulder?"

"Do not fret so, brother. It does not become you."

"Pray, Maria: it would be much to my preference if you desisted from teasing me. It never was in you to do so before. It would sadden me if you were to converse now in such a way that my memory of you will henceforth be obscured by cloud. Oh, how I wish you had not announced yourself. You have spoiled everything!"

"On the contrary, Branwell." It was an insistent Maria who now spoke. "I have given you the opportunity to redeem yourself, to make up to God for past sins committed and thereby prove yourself a worthy son. And as for this fear you have just expressed: well, there is no foundation in it. I am here now in the form of a 'guiding light' to show you the error of your ways and to make you see your life for what it truly is. But this visit will be my last..."

"What do you mean? The last time you speak to me? But it scarcely seems right that you should have been in my presence all these times and yet only now choose to converse with me. Why not..."

"No, brother. Once again you quite mistake my meaning. From this day on I will never again be in your presence, whether you be aware of it or not. My spirit will forever be distant from you. This meeting, brother, will be our last. Oh, that is to say until your death, at which time we will doubtless be reacquainted."

Branwell let out a melancholic sigh on hearing this. "So, this is to be the last time we are in communion, eh? That seems a harsh arrangement. I would so much have liked to..."

"Please, Branwell: time is short. I must say what I have to say and be gone."

"You wish to be out of my presence, then, sister. You have disowned me to such an extent?"

"No, it is not so. Why must you persist in this bleak outlook you have on life? I am not your accuser: I am your saviour. That is I wish to be, if you will allow me to lend a guiding hand instead of disputing my every word."

"But how can you guide me, Maria? You have long been dead, only your memory remains. And after this day never more will I be in your presence. All is lost for me..."

"No, Branwell. All is far from lost. You could direct yourself onto a straighter, more correct course if only you had the willpower to do so. But why, brother, did you lose your faith in God? I firmly believe you could still amount to something; you could still fulfill the expectations of your formative years if you placed your life in the Lord's hands. He could be the making of you. Instead you must disregard his love for you and so stumble along an uneven path to ultimate oblivion. Why, brother? Why must you forever wreck your ambitions? You could live a worthy life if you had a mind to. So why not grasp the chance you are given?"

"But Maria," replied a fervent Branwell. "My faith in God is undiminished. I retain my faith in him as always I have done. There is no relinquishment of my religious fervour, merely the form it takes."

"Ah yes! You said as much to your brother poet, did you not, but one short year ago? It was on a day's outing in the Lake District where you met..."

"Hartley Coleridge! Dear God: you were with me even then?"

"Indeed I was, brother. And how you angered that poor man with your irreligious stance. Not to take part in church services when your own father, my own that was, is a Reverend. Bless me! Is it any wonder he was put out of spirits? And yet you subscribed to the theory that it was not God you disowned but those men who preached his word. Illogical, brother: quite illogical."

"No, it is not so. I put much thought into my decision to abstain from church services. It was not a matter I took lightly. No, nothing could be further removed from the truth. I weighed up various conflicting viewpoints in my mind before arriving at the right course of action. It angered papa: it angered him a great deal. I was sorry for it. But there it is. One must stay true to one's ideals..."

"Ideals, brother?" returned a mocking Maria. "Why, you lost touch with your ideals a long time ago. Ever since reaching full manhood you have left behind any ideals you may have had. It is as if you became the explorer of your childhood, setting sail for a foreign land; a land of opportunity, of splendour, of divining grace. But in so doing, you bade farewell to the very ideals which formed your life, the very fibre of your being. You turned your back on religion, became a stranger at home and took to mingling with the baser and most dissolute facets the world has to offer. I say again, Branwell: you lost touch with your ideals; you did not stay true to them. Do not dare to justify your conduct to me, brother: I will not hear of it. I can only make one final plea to you..."

"What final plea may that be, Maria?"

"Simply that you place your life in God's hands. Listen to what he teaches us. Do not shut out the lessons he only too readily hands out to all of his children, whether they be lost sheep or devout followers. I make this final plea to you, Branwell, as a loving sister who wishes with all her being that you will raise yourself up from the unchristian practices you have of late times employed and reach out to take possession of the balm which the Lord is all too willing to offer up to you. But I leave that decision up to you: a life of saintly virtue, thereby reaping the rewards which then will be richly deserved, or a dissolute existence where drinking and carousing and intake of opium are your only supports and infamy and sad regrets the end result. Make your choice, brother: make your choice. I have given you a lifeline: the rest I leave to you. A fond farewell, then, playmate of my formative years: may you make good the promise of those years. Live well, brother!"

"Do not go, Maria!" beseeched Branwell in an ever more desperate vein. "Do not desert me so soon. I have much to discuss with you yet..."

Maria's final words to Branwell came out in a receding tone with each word being spoken quieter than the one before until the last one came out barely as a whisper.

"No, brother: our time together has passed. Be good, Branwell: the sanctity of your everlasting soul depends upon it."

"Maria! Maria! Please return: do not leave me on my own again. I cannot bear it. Pray, return."

There was no response to his despairing words. He slowly returned to his desk and collapsed into his chair. Lurching forward, he planted his elbows on the desk and rifled his hands through his hair.

Looking up, Branwell had the look quite of another world. "Dear Lord!" he cried out. "What course am I to take? How to find God when I have proved myself such an unworthy son? Is he an understanding God as Maria maintains, or even now am I cast out of heaven, a misdirected soul who can never be forgiven for past sins committed? Oh, how can I go on? How can ever I prove myself worthy in God's eyes? All is a black void, a chasm of unending misery, with no light, no shimmering angel to rescue me from oblivion. Oh, it is unendurable! It is unendurable!"

From this moment on, Branwell lived a life of contradictions. There were occasions when he seemed to take on board Maria's teachings but implementing them proved to be another thing altogether. The spirit in this instance was willing but the mind simply refused to follow. How to explain this apparent paradox?

Maria, though, never truly left him, even if he never sensed her presence again until the moment when he neared the end of his mortal existence. As he lay in his bed with his loving family around him, he blinked his eyes in wonder as a saintly vision settled a few yards from where he lay. This spirit hovered agonisingly close to his touch, but alas he had not the strength to raise his arms. He could see it was Maria, the same Maria he had remembered from his childhood.

There was no look of admonishment on her face as there had been in her voice when she had visited him in his station house seven years before. No, now there was only a welcoming smile as she motioned her arms towards him. As Branwell uttered a breathless 'Amen' to his father's final prayer by his bedside, he sank back on his pillow with a smile.

His family thought the smile may have signified a return to God's graces as Branwell's life came to an end or a sense of contentment at finally leaving his troubled existence behind him. But no, Maria knew the true cause of his smile. He had been returned to his beloved sister so they could once again explore their unfinished childhood dreams. They would roam around in heaven, running through the tall grass and the sweet-smelling flowers that reminded them of their beloved moors. Two souls joined together once more after years apart, never to be separated again. Theirs would be a celestial union with no end.

Leyland's Letter illustration by Jon Beynon

LEYLAND'S LETTER

by Elaine France-Sergeant
Wigan, England

Oh Branwell, my dearest friend.
You need your ways to mend
For time is passing by
And no one knows how long we live
And soon we have to die.

Cheer up my friend,
Think happy thoughts
For it's the novels you ought
To be writing
And not the world you are fighting.

Live long
Live free
Be the person you were meant to be.

Your friend,
Leyland

A Ghost Visits illustration by Barb Tanke

A GHOST VISITS

Janet Armstrong
Manchester, England

The darkness was creeping towards the house. Jane lay listening to the clattering of hooves and the soft admonishments of Edward as he coaxed the squealing horse into the horse box. The stallion's protests were out of character, he was usually so obedient. Barking twice in answer, Pilot went to the window before putting a soft paw against Jane's cheek. Edward had not wanted to leave, but Jane had been insistent. He had been training for months for this competition. The bundle in Jane's arms had stopped squalling and she allowed her eyes to rest.

A gleam of light dazzled her awake. The door groaned open to permit a tall and wide shadow to invade her bedroom. The shape of a woman, with thick, dark hair hanging long down her back, stood in the doorway. She did not see what dress the figure had on. It was white and straight, but whether it was a gown or a sheet, she could not tell. The body floated into the room; Jane tried to scream, but it came out silent.

To Jane's horror the figure took the baby in her arms. Tears began to fall down the figure's face as she caressed the infant's cheek with a charred finger. She handed the baby gently back to Jane and faded into nothing.

Timetable illustration by Jon Beynon

TIMETABLE

by Claire Shepherd
Keighley, UK
*I was inspired to write this story after hearing the Keighley and
Worth Valley steam train during Lockdown in April 2020,
when the rest of the world was silent.*

A whining wind and rain hammered against my attic window, a
rude awakening as it found the leak awaiting fixing. Ironically, the
weather had been too awful for the builders to come. My starlight view
was not such a joy in a storm; once the dripping began, it would not
cease until the rain did also, the rhythmic plop into a strategically
placed bowl cancelling any notion of sleep. Groping for my phone, it
told me that it was a little past four AM, and as I shoved both it and my
head back under the pillow, I heard the shriek of the steam train as it
chuffed along the old Keighley and Worth Valley Line which runs
behind our house. Apparently, if you paid a premium it could be hired
for weddings and parties. It seemed a strange hour though, even for a
Hen Party, and what a hideous night for it.

I must have dozed a little but by six o'clock the bowl needed
emptying, as did my bladder, so I gave up on bed for the night. I had
promised to walk the Labrador of a friend who had travelled up to
Scotland for the weekend and, observing the elements outside, was
seriously regretting it. Deciding that then was as good a time as any, for
according to my app the weather was supposed to deteriorate
throughout the day - unbelievable as that seemed - I splashed my face
then threw on as many layers as I comfortably could. I didn't know a
great deal about dogs, but if they were anything like humans, then
Roger (what a name) would be bursting for his first toilet of the day.

Wind and rain slammed into my face as Roger, who didn't seem at
all perturbed by the weather, bounded ahead of me straining at the
lead. There was just enough light to pick out the old stony pathway
linking Haworth to Oakworth as day struggled to overthrow night and
once off the road I let the dog loose, whereby he immediately raced
around in random directions, delighted with everything his nose
located. A few withered blackberries still clung to the hedgerows and
the floor was slick with soggy leaves making for slippery progress.

Rain drummed on my hood and blurred the view rendering me both deaf and blind, the icy wind stinging my face and hands as Roger almost knocked me off balance before streaking off again, reassured that I was still there. I would have to towel him down before allowing him back indoors.

The only way to keep warm was to up my pace, so hands pressed into pockets, head down against the wind, I pushed on, and it was in this stance that I collided with another walker marching in the opposite direction.

Both of us lurching backwards in surprise, I realised at once that she was crying. Barely out of childhood, her hair hung in sodden clumps, her clothes offering no protection against the barrage of the storm. Her shoes were submerged beneath the mud, her dress so filthy that she appeared to have risen from the earth itself and the soaking garment was trying its best to return her to whence she had come, hanging heavily off her delicate frame.

"I'm sorry," she mumbled, her voice taken by the wind as, resuming her purpose, she almost ran past me.

"Are you okay?" I had to shout to be heard. "Excuse me! Are you alright?"

Pivoting, I changed direction to pursue her inelegantly through the boggy ground. How could she manage to move so lightly?

"Miss?"

Abruptly she turned so that we almost collided again.

"Forgive me, I cannot stop."

"But you look upset. Can I help?"

"Please, I must continue. How much further to Haworth Station?"

"You're about twenty minutes away. Less, if you continue at that pace."

"Good. I need to catch the next train. There is one on the hour." Her purple-ringed eyes kept glancing in the direction from which she had come.

"I don't think so. They only run about four times a day at the most. You've got loads of time."

"Really? But I need to go now! It said there was a train at seven. I checked!"

Her voice was desperate but her shoulders slumped, her constantly darting eyes giving her a hunted expression that reminded me so much of Roger who burst through the hedge at that moment, fur on end and growling.

"Roger, stop that! I'm sorry, he's normally so friendly."

As if to prove me a liar, he began to bark fiercely, his teeth bared like some feral wolf.

"Roger, what has got into you? Come here!" Grabbing him by the collar, it took all my strength to detain him, his growling, snarling weight dragging against my hold. "I'm so sorry, this isn't like him at all."

"I must go." She turned, almost running in the direction of Haworth, the rain by now slicing the sky, gushing in rivulets down the track, her hem trailing in the mud.

"Miss! You don't have a coat! Can I lend you mine?"

She didn't turn.

"Miss, what's your name?" The urge to know something about her, just in case, was strong. A young girl should not be out alone in this weather. At least I had Roger for company and protection.

She stopped and looked straight at me then, her hollow eyes meeting mine through the rain. Scanning my face, she hesitated as if fighting an internal battle, then relented.

"Catherine. I am Cathy and if anybody asks, please would you say you saw me walking that way?" She pointed in my direction, from whence she had come, her eyes pleading.

I knew nothing about her. She could have committed a crime, been high on drugs or absconding into unknown danger, but something in her desperation tugged at my conscience.

"Are you in some kind of trouble?"

"I cannot say. I am sorry. But will you do this for me? Please?"

I made a secret vow to myself that I would tell the truth later if necessary. I would be watching the local news carefully for the next few days, but right now she needed my help.

"Okay"

For the first time she smiled. "Thank you."

And then she was gone. I blinked the rain out of my eyes, but all I could see was the flooded track and Roger, calm again, at my side. The dog and I tacitly agreed that we had had enough and, the wind behind us now, started towards home.

Back in my own kitchen, I once again heard the whistle of the train as it departed Haworth and wondered if Catherine was upon it, starting the next phase of her story, whatever that may be. I hoped she would be okay. The kettle whistled its welcome signal at almost exactly the same moment and, grabbing a mug, I settled down for a warming cup of tea.

Yesterday's paper lay open where my dad had left it the previous evening. Flicking through it, my eyes landed upon a picture of the Keighley and Worth Valley steam train. Above the picture ran the headline TRAINS RAINED OFF. Puzzled, I scanned the article which explained that all trains had been cancelled until further notice due to damage caused by flooding to the track. This made no sense, for in the lull between gusts and lashings of rain, I could clearly hear the chuff-chuffing of its engine, followed by one final blast of the whistle as it faded across the moors into the arms of the storm.

I Have To Remind Myself To Breathe

You Will Know Me illustration by Yvonne Solly

YOU WILL KNOW ME

by Charlie Rauh
New York, USA
William comforting Anne through the scenery of Scarborough

It is the first of the year.
I will breathe with you through the wind from the sea.
In just over two weeks' time
I will gift you the finest jewels embedded in golden ribbons
when the afternoon clouds give way during your walk.
When you wake tomorrow, I will be with you.
You will know me by the stillness of the sky,
the laughter of the waves,
and the embrace of the setting sun.

The Mice of Marston Moor illustration by Yvonne Solly

THE MICE OF MARSTON MOOR

By Sebastian Chamorro
Connecticut, USA

I wish I had chosen someplace other than Whitefield Hall. Anyplace. Even a house just a few miles away would do. But Whitefield Hall is where my choice has taken me. A choice I must live with so long as I can.

It was not long ago, not long ago at all, that Grandfather passed away, leaving myself and my sister a plentiful fortune built up by generations of master shipbuilders. With no wife nor child of my own there was little for me to do with my half of this wealth but indulge in my nostalgic sentimentalities. I'd always held a fascination with the past, with the deeds and events surrounding my old and soon to be extinguished lineage. A particularly noteworthy ancestor - the founder of our shipbuilding tradition - was a Roundhead lieutenant under Cromwell who emigrated to the Massachusetts colony after being left lame by musket-fire at Marston Moor.

It was to Marston Moor, then, that I set my sights. After a lengthy process of inquiry, I at last settled on purchasing Whitefield Hall, a somewhat unkempt but otherwise quite imposing manor tucked away in the Yorkshire fenns to the northeast of the famed battle-site.

I moved in - some small advance - luggage in hand and unaccompanied by the staff whose contracts were to begin in the new year - towards the middle of October, a few weeks before the unexpected coming of the late-autumn snows, which in turn began ten days before I set pen to paper tonight. I have not left the manor in these past ten days - my vehicle unable to make it through the snowbanks and the Hall well-provisioned by some foresightful stockpiling on my part.

It began on the first night of my isolation. The mice. From my bedchamber I heard them, heard them scurrying about behind the walls as I settled into bed. Scurrying always downwards. Irate at the realtors for neglecting to inform me of an infestation, I shook off my annoyance and slept for the night, the snowy wind battering at the window-panes.

I awoke to silence, blessed silence. I searched around my chamber and could find no evidence of the vermin and as the hours passed by and the sun shone weakly above the snowdrifts, I convinced myself that it had been only a dream.

This comforting illusion did not last the night. Again they scurried, ever-downwards - louder now than they had been the night before. Nothing stopped their mad scramble; rapping my cane against the wall in the hopes of momentarily scaring them away affected them not one bit.

Unable to return to sleep, I lit a candle and crept downstairs, hoping to find whatever it was these vermin were scurrying towards.

Stopping and listening in near-every room at the bottom storey of the manor, I found myself before a small, unobtrusive trap-door in a forgotten linen closet. The movements of the mice seemed to culminate at this point; following their trajectory would mean descending below. As the door seemed heavy and the drowsiness that had been held at bay by curiosity crept back into me, I decided to investigate further on the morrow.

Then the nightmares came. Strange visages entered my dreams: a dark grotto, putrid and full of decay; a hand, made not of flesh, grasping out blindly in the darkness. And everywhere the chittering of mice. An unseen mouth behind me whispered into my ear - in what language I do not know, for I cannot recall a word of it; but the intent behind it was absolute. It was a warning. A warning expressed so utterly that I had no doubt as to its veracity even after awakening into the weak morning light.

* * *

Thus was a cycle born, which has repeated itself every night, even tonight. During the day I go about my business, solitary within this snow-bound prison, avoiding the linen closet with a leaden dread. During the night, as the mice resume their circuit - a surge of curiosity. Any attempt to will myself to sleep has proven futile: soon enough I would be awake again with but the chilling memory of the same nightmare to show for it.

By dawn's break the mice quieten, and I am able to sleep in peace. But each passing day it has proved harder and harder to reach that point. In the first night I felt no curiosity at all, and the second night I could return to my chambers after having come to the trap-door, by the third I found myself drawn irrepressibly to follow the mice downwards, only stopping myself as I was about to descend the stairwell.

By the fourth night, I bolted my chamber door.

By the fifth, I unlocked the bolt, and made it down the hall before turning back.

By the sixth, I was at the first storey landing before I was able to force myself to return to bed.

On the seventh night, I wrote this letter for the first time. That was three nights ago.

On the eighth, I was able to force myself to write this letter ten times before slipping away from bed; after dragging myself back, I wrote it twenty times over.

On the ninth night - yesterday night - I lost count of the number of times I wrote, tossed aside, and rewrote this letter.

Tonight is the same. I must write. As I cannot avoid thinking of the trap-door, and whatever horrors lurk beckoningly below, reflecting on the path that led me to this fate is the only way to keep my body from wandering without me. I must write. I must not stop writing. If I cannot write more, I must destroy and start again. And again. And again till dawn breaks and the curse lifts till nightfall.

The urge to lay aside my pen and hurtle down to where the mice gather edges closer and closer to overwhelming me. It is only an hour till dawn. If I leave my post I am lost. The mice grow ever louder. Each word is a struggle against that infernal curiosity. I could not hope to last another night like this.

I will take my chances against the storm once the morrow breaks. It is the only way out of this hell.

I need only outlast the night. I need only stay in my room.

Perhaps a small peek won't hurt.

Oh God! It Is Unutterable!

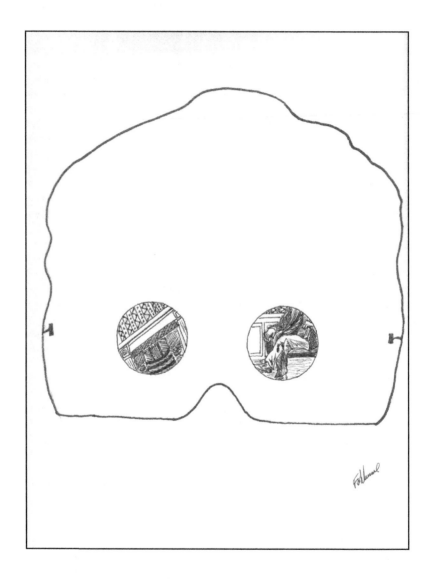

The Repair Woman illustration by Christina Rauh Fishburne

THE REPAIR WOMAN

by Christina Rauh Fishburne
An American in England

Cecile imagined the luminous bride stepping through cobbled streets, clipping white ribbons held across the chapel road by children. She imagined the groom waiting, happy, in a multicolored sunbeam. In her mind, she saw obstacles dropping beneath the bride's tiny silver blades, her flashing brilliant teeth catching the sunlight between her lips.

Cecile imagined sweat sliding around the outline of her own lips, joining a tear, more salty evidence of the body's way to solve problems. She did not imagine the tears. Those were real enough.

* * *

Later, Cecile mended shirts in the stifling Paris apartment after sweeping the returned unopened note and problematic wedding gift aside. Desolate, she wrote no letters. Excluded, she needed no confidence. She bit thread from buttons.

The newspapers flowed with news of defeat, casualties, illness, the victory of inches obliterated by a buttonhole's measure. The words built impenetrable walls of image first in her sleeping mind and then throughout the day. Cecile drowned in mud. She lost limbs to gangrene. Her empty eyes reflected clouds and the edge of a helmet shaped like the dish she had washed that morning. But then she blinked and her apartment refocused. She held a shirt. A needle. A torch.

She did not imagine the bride anymore, separated as surely as Cecile. Her face did not factor. Her irrelevant arms and muted sighs became vapor in Cecile's account of injustice. Everyone was alone. She could not allow for empathy. The man was now a soldier, a cog in a great machine. Cogs felt more hopeful than pawns. It was necessary to feel purpose. It was an impossible contest.

He would never know Cecile battled him to live longest.

Every morning the open window asked, *why can he not love you?*

At 7:00 she closed the door with one hand, the woven basket looped over the crook of her other arm, the golden clouds and pinkening light answered: *Because you are ugly, Cecile.*

43

The 24 stone steps down to the street: *Because you are fat, Cecile.*

The cats, calico, black, gray and slinking around corners: *Because you are stupid, Cecile.*

The canvas market tents and awnings: *Because you are very ordinary, Cecile.*

She imagined ornamental scissors (the Somme's ribbon: purple, Dullness: pale blue, Ignorance: unspooled nameless iridescence), and him awaiting her instead.

She had planned to include the mask in her gift. It was to be an olive branch. A thick paper half-face, small blank eyes, swooping cheeks with a notch spaced for a nose. Golden exotic skin tone and a rust, brown, and green illustrated turban looped with flat one-dimensional pearls and feathers at the top where the wearer's forehead met scalp. Two torn pinprick holes at the sides where a string no longer tied. At the last moment she changed her mind. They would not understand it. They would laugh. Perhaps tear it in two, from one already torn pinprick to the other. Cecile could not allow that. Even the idea disturbed her. Cecile knew the ways of needle. She was acquainted with the strength of thread.

A desperate rain fell against her window in ribbons, the lashes of a punishing pirate captain. The lamplight threw her own face against the glass and tossed her image in the waves of darkening twilight. Thunder rolled in the east. Paris was next. It put her in mind of the visit to Brussels she made two summers before. Of a shop that smelled of dust and coffee. Of surprise and sudden shelter. It was there she found the mask.

* * *

The insufferable heat of the third floor was an ocean current against her. Slicing bread and pulling cold beef from the icebox was exhausting. The rain moved west and left thick heavy air in its wake. A trick of nature and science and all expectation. Sitting as she was at her wooden table on her single chair, she watched the clouds move outside the now open window. The panes sparkled after being drenched, twinkling in the sunlight now darting in and out of the clouds. A cold front. A warm front. A western front.

Her face was damp with sweat but her eyes were dry. She was eyeless.

Her fingers raised the paper face to her own. The eyeless. Closer. Closer...

Her chair, the walls, the table, the air all dropped away as her shoulders were drawn back, her chin pulled up as her throat followed the invisible, the inaudible instruction to *rise*. Gooseflesh and winter-filled lungs. Her hands held the paper half-face ear to ear with no regard for her wish to lower them. Her dry eyes now burned feverishly as smoke and lingering roasted meat filled her nose. She was freezing. She was suddenly very hungry.

A glow clarified before her as she rushed toward it, shot through a tunnel of pale maroon and faded pattern. A plain wooden frame. A shining center table. The pleasant musty scent of books and crackle of burning wood. Her heartbeat alarmed her. She could no longer breathe.

"What do you want most...?"

Cecile tore the mask from her face and sent it slicing through the air to the ground.

* * *

The gift remained wrapped in brown paper, careful, attentive, self-conscious. It rested on the narrow sideboard. It waited, crushed into the corner with the newspapers. *He may be in that crowd, in that ditch.* How could she light her stove with the last image of him she may ever see? The papers were a sad oracle. He would die in the muddy open wound of exploded ground. The guns would tear him apart and the earth would suck him into herself and seal him beneath her liquified injuries. She imagined him blown apart. His arms flung high, his legs splintered, his blood the deep rich red of wine and meat. But his face was always clean and whole and as it was the last time she had seen him—smiling at her father, shaking his hand with the one not wrapped around her little sister. The last time she had hoped. The last time she had a little sister.

* * *

Cecile made her deliveries, accepted payment, and took in new work: shirts worn too thin, undergarments snatched by branches from drying lines, stockings caught on garden thorns, skirts torn by animals. She never expected explanations but they were sometimes provided. Guilt was something fascinating to Cecile, something that should have a color. To spoil a beautiful work of embroidery while gardening felt a pale-yellow sort of guilt. A childish guilt. An accidental disaster of

45

nature. The repair cost very little. It was the red guilt, the rending of hopes, that cost more. It caused hiding. Red guilt had consequences.

She had not picked up the mask since the other day. It lay on the floor, a half-face on the edge of a tasseled rug where it touched the floorboards. The morning was already warm. Her own face felt very exposed. She wanted cover.

Eyeless. Sightless. Closer. Closer...

Blasted into the icy tunnel, she chased her breath but could not catch it. She so focused on filling her lungs with the burning, splintering, freeze, that she missed the question. A deep voice asked her something she did not understand, something about dealing with *him.* It was not her voice that answered, "*Reason. But if not, the whip.*" The reply echoed in her ribs, confirmed in the bones of her arms. Perhaps it was her voice after all.

* * *

Cecile walked home from the market. She gripped the woven basket tighter and patted the handle where it rested between the soft parts of her arm. The mask lay at the bottom of the heavy linen. She felt like a spy. When she was younger and had a sister, Cecile would play games with her. Her sister was small-boned, lithe, petite. The hiding games were never as fun for Cecile. She could not fit in the smallest, the unrecognizable, the best places. A knee always betrayed. A backside revealed. Her sister slid between walls. Her sister diminished beside bookcases. Shadows partnered with her. A cup cannot hold a piano; Cecile was relegated to the most obvious. Cecile always lost.

At school, the boys played war and threw sticks and rocks at each other and then they called her sister *Belle.* It was not her real name. They never found another name for Cecile. She was too obviously herself. After school, her sister took her new name; in fact, the name came for her. Beauty took her. It did not ask. Cecile watched it happen with interest. She waited, but it never came for her.

She had the mask with her. Outside. On the street.

Before turning onto Rue—, Cecile half-smiled as she slipped into an alley. She pulled the paper mask from beneath the linen and pressed it eagerly to her face. Instantly, her back pushed against the stone building's wall and her lungs were pulled down the narrowing tunnel to the maroon swirled room, the crackling fire, the gleaming wooden table, and the man's voice. The deep Irish voice asked, "What is the best way to know the difference between intellects of men and women?"

Cecile felt the roll and switch of tides; she was pulled back toward the alley but dug her heels, willed her eyeless face to remain, clung to the sides of the mask with fingernails suddenly vicious as talons. The frame around her sight sharpened and through the cut eyes a figure, sat patiently in a chair. Cecile opened her mouth. She knew the answer. It's in our bodies. The frame blurred and darkness bled into the holes, sucking her backwards and dropping her, gasping, back in the alley. The mask fluttered to the basket and rested on the linen as gently as a baby's breath.

* * *

In her apartment, Cecile swept the floor. The casualties were countless as the stars and just as unfathomable. Pinpricks in a page. Miniscule. Dust covered the sideboard now and she wiped it clean. The problematic wedding gift, still wrapped in brown paper, still tied tightly with twine, sat still. The sunlight painted its portrait. Cecile rested the broom against the wall.

She took her mending basket from the couch and looped the scissors in her fingers.

She cut the twine.

She unwrapped the gift.

There was no more wedding to celebrate and no more blows to soften. She stood the gift up, spine straight and facing the world, insides closed up safe, face to the sideboard's edge. Feeling better, breathing easier, Cecile seated herself on the couch and took up her needle. Pinpricks in skin bleed first in beads and then in rivers if left unattended.

* * *

Cecile woke, sweating, thirsty, and irritated. It was not yet morning. She reached for the small glass beside her bed but found the mask instead. She balanced it on her face and fell both down a deep endlessly swirling maroon patterned chasm and down into a deep dreamless sleep, the low humming question, "*what is the best book in all the world?*" weaving through her thoughts and drawing her brain tightly into a package until morning opened it.

On Tuesday she received a letter. The handwriting was so sloppy it became beautiful in a hidden, buried, layered way. In her hand, the letter looked small. Propped against the straight and free spine of

Practical Sewing and Dressmaking by S Allington on the sideboard, it looked young and teachable. She did not open it until Friday, until checking the casualty lists, and before she slit the top of the envelope with her blade, she reached for the mask.

The black rimmed frames breathed frost over her eyes, making her want to close them. The paper cut into the ridge of her nose and found the notch slowly built for it to fit into. The fire crackled and spit in its metal grate to her left. She leaned into it, searched for the voice. She had the feeling she had missed the question, or she had been passed over, or worse: forgotten altogether. Turning her eyeless face to the polished wooden table, she saw no one. The dark green empty couch stared at her. The door lay open to a cold gray hall. Behind her, a window, a church beyond and a cemetery between.

"Where are you?" she called from behind her face. No sound came.

She made a full circle of her space and the black rims sifted through the frozen air to find the white mantle, the fireplace. Her breath was fast and loud in her uncovered ears and when she looked up, he was there.

"What is the best mode of education for a woman?"

Cecile dropped beneath the floor; her arms flung straight up with the force of her plunge. A trap door. A trap. As the icy rush ran up her legs, her stomach, her arms, her fingertips fluttering with the plummet, the reply came from high above, "That which would make her rule her house well..." It is the nature of a trap to contain. To catch. To retain with no exit. It is expected to pair with a trick.

* * *

Cecile woke on the floor of her apartment. Someone was knocking at her door. She grasped the table leg, the surface, then pulled herself up. Straightening her skirt, smoothing her hair, adjusting her face, Cecile opened the door.

Belle stood between the door jambs and casings, where she fit. A tissue, a telegram curled crushed in her small white hand. Red rimmed eyes bore into Cecile's.

"What is the best mode of spending time?"

48

Cecile watched her through the black outlines of an empty hole. She was suddenly very interested in how it would happen. Her breathing was steady. Her mouth relaxed. She folded her hands before her and heard a soft voice say, *"Laying it out in preparation for a happy eternity."*

Someone screamed from very far away.

A Sister's Kiss illustration by JoJo Hughes

A SISTER'S KISS

by JoJo Hughes
Cornwall, UK

Dearest Charlotte,
Let us in.
The bells toll loud;
Tis such a din!
The stone is cold
The tomb so still.
We must shake off sepulchral chill
So lift the sash and stoke the fire
And give us what our souls desire
Just one last kiss to see us on
The road we'll walk so hard upon
The Host of Kingdoms waits our tread
Yet we have felt our way with dread
Without Papa to hold our hand
How will we reach that hallowed land?
Our dear Mama is waiting there
Yet we are slowed with earthly care
If we leave you, I know not how
You'll manage there without us now.
So let us stay
We'll make no sound
Our feet step gentle on the ground.

Come, sister, let me dry your eyes,
Don't think we cannot hear your cries,
Your blinding rage, your broken heart
Because we are thus ripped apart.
We'll stay with you and calm your breast
So let us hold you close, dear. Rest.
And I will whisper in your ear
That song which always gave you cheer
About the captain on his ship...
Though mast were down and mainsail ripp'd
He breasted out the swelling main
And brought his crew back home again
As waves upon the restless deep
I'll rock you till you fall asleep
I'll kiss your lids and say a prayer
That God will thee, my darling, spare,
And one day our whole family
Will rest in one Eternity.

And now you're still,
In calm repose
We'll leave to walk the path He chose.
(Lord, keep these four in Thy embrace
And give Papa Thy strength and grace).
And though we leave the way we came
O Lottie, we'll be back again
So do not close the sash too tight,
Pray, leave for us a guiding light
So we may pause from Heaven's bliss
To briefly steal a sister's kiss.

The Haunting of Hannah Brown illustration by Debs Green Jones

THE HAUNTING OF HANNAH BROWN

A GHOST STORY FOR CHRISTMAS
by Elaine France-Sergeant
Wigan, England

My name is Emelia Clark,

So let's start at the beginning.

I have always been fascinated by the lives of the Brontë family and the town of Haworth, their home. I had travelled down to the village of Haworth. I was staying at a little cottage in the town. It was a very cold winter's day. Snow was on the ground. I have always collected old books so when I saw an old book shop on the cobbled main street I went in hoping to find another old book to do with the Brontë's.

It has always been my greatest dream to one day own a 1st edition of the Brontë sisters' book of poetry; not easy as it is very rare. Well, I can dream, can't I?

This was my favorite kind of shop. There is something special about the smell of old books. All that history. Have you ever wondered who owned them and what they were like? So many books to choose from.

"Can I help you?" said the old man behind the desk. He was a tall, thin man with grey hair balding at the sides. He looked rather bored.

"I just love old books and I'm just very much interested in any Brontë books you may have."

He said "We have some old books, just come in, at the back of the shop." Off he went and came back with a box full of old books. Some of the books I already had, but at the bottom of the box was an old black leather book with a brass clasp.

I opened it and found it was a diary, or so I thought. The name on the front was Hannah Brown. The diary was old and battered and had seen better days. I can't explain why I wanted it, but I did. So I asked the bored shop assistant how much he wanted for it. He said "It is old £20 pounds."

I said "Will you take £15 for it?"

"Yes," the assistant replied, so I bought it, put it into my bag, and left the shop.

I had a lovely time visiting the church and Parsonage, but was always at home on the moors. If there was anywhere on earth the Brontë's would be, it would be there. It was like entering their world, their time. They were so close, you could almost see them.

As I made my way up to the cottage, I couldn't wait to read the diary. I wondered what she was like, this Hannah Brown, or what she had written. When I got back, I sat down in the comfy chair and took out the book to read it.

On the front it said: Hannah Brown 1889 Haworth.

It began:

I would like to tell my story so at least someone may find this and make some sense of it some how. I'm not too sure what I saw but I know one thing: The things I saw were real, as solid as you or I.

I'm finding it really hard to believe that they were ghosts. Memories, maybe, of a time long ago or a time slip or ghosts. You decide. Who am I to say so? This is my story, written to remind myself and to remember that strange night.

A while ago I moved into an old cottage at the end of the lane in Haworth. My aunt had died and left me the cottage, It was small, but had a homely atmosphere. I have always liked the countryside, with its large open spaces and couldn't wait to go for a walk on the moors of Haworth.

It was just after tea. The weather was fine for this time of year. It was the 24th December, a cold day, but fine when I made my way to the moors along the path. I spent several hours happily taking in all that I saw. When it started to rain and I realised that it was getting quite dark, I decided to make my way back. By now it had gone quite misty, like a fog. I couldn't see anything in front of me. By then I began to realise that I was lost on the moors. The mist got worse and I couldn't see which way to go.

I shivered as I remembered the tales of people lost on the moors, then I saw a light in the distance. It was a farmhouse. There were two large trees and a stone wall. I could just about see them. There was a light in the strange window, reminding me more of a castle than a farmhouse. I knocked loudly on the door.

A tall girl came to the door. She looked surprised to see me.

"I'm sorry to disturb you at this hour but I seem to have lost my way."

54

"What possessed you to come out on the moors in this weather?" she said. "Come in or it will be the death of you if you stay outside."

It seemed I had no choice but to do just that. "I am sorry to drop in on you uninvited, but the weather turned so quickly, I had not time to get back. I hope you don't mind me knocking at your door."

"I may mind," said the girl, "depending on you being good company or not."

This girl was nothing but direct and a little shy. I had noticed as she sat in the corner of the room. She was writing in a book.

"I'm writing a novel," she said.

"Oh, I love novels. Can I read a little of it, if it is convenient?"

"Convenient!" she said staring oddly in my direction, "Well I won't let anyone inconvenience me if I can help it. I'd rather not, if you don't mind. I like to keep myself to myself. We don't get many visitors. It is a long time since we had any or I would not be talking to you now."

"Why, then, did you let me in?"' I asked.

"There are too many lost souls wondering the moors," she then asked, "Do you believe in ghosts?"

"Yes," I replied, "It's rather out of the way here."

"Oh, I don't live here," she said, "I just visit from time to time. I live in Haworth."

"But it is so peaceful here," I said.

"Peace can be good in small measures, but you tire of it. I'm going home in a while. I don't want to stay out too long, as my father would be looking for me. Come along, if you've a mind to."

All this time I have not told you what the girl looked like. She was wearing an old fashioned green dress, a shawl tied over her shoulder with a broach. Her hair was tied in a bun with two curls hanging down on her pale face. I thought it rather odd to be out in this weather with only a shawl and no coat and I told her so.

"No, I'm not cold. The weather doesn't bother me, I'm used to it. I have long since ceased to worry about such things. Silly, really, what the mind will fuss over when we ought to be concerned about the matters of our souls. My father is a parson, you see. I'm not in the habit of saving strange girls in the moors, but for the sake of my father I have done so tonight because he would not leave a person in need.

"We had better be off." She opened the door, "I will get my dog," she said. A large dog with a brass collar came out of the back room. He was no friendlier than his owner. "Oh don't worry about him. He won't eat you, he's not hungry," she laughed.

The mist outside was like a fog. You couldn't see in front of you, but the girl seemed to know where she was going.

There was a kind of light in front. "Not that way, that's Peg's Lantern, you don't want to go that way. You should come in the summertime, Miss, the moors are carpeted in a sea of heather. There is no place on earth so divine and the mist is like the breath of a thousand lost souls."

I found myself liking this girl; she had a way with words. No doubt she was sometimes rather sharp in her choice of words, but that was just her way. She was rather shy and, like she said, she didn't get to meet many people.

Soon we saw a light in the distance.

"My brother has left a light on for me. Would you like to meet my family?" she asked. She knocked on the door. There was a large lion knocker on the door. It made a loud noise, like it was echoing across the silence.

A small lady came to the door. She was wearing a long brown dress and had very small gold glasses which made her eyes look bigger than they probably were.

"This is my sister," the girl said, "I found this lady on the moors quite lost."

"It's not the first time my sister has found lost things out on the moors. Come in!" the sister invited me, "You are most welcome to sit for a while and tell us your adventures, as we don't get many visitors and my sister seems to have taken a liking to you. If you knew her real nature you would be as surprised as I am that she brought you here tonight. Come into the parlour."

The parlour had a large table at which a girl sat reading a book. She was slim and was wearing a grey dress with a white collar. A small string of coral beads hung around her neck. Her hair was a mass of small light curls, her eyes of the clearest blue. In contrast to the other girls, she was quite pretty.

"Look what our sister has found on the moors."

"Oh, you poor thing, you look so cold, come sit by the fire," she said, "I must apologise for my sisters. We don't get many visitors and it is a long time since we have had company. We are only visiting, you see, sort of passing through. Though we shall always call this place home, we have to be on our way by morning. We meet here every year at Christmastime."

Just then an old man came in the room. He was tall with a dark coat and trousers. Around his neck was a large white collar.

"You are most welcome my dear" he said. "This is my son."

A boy with came in. He had a mane of red unkempt hair. He was wearing small glasses, and he had brown eyes, rather small, lost behind the glasses he wore.

"This is indeed fortunate!" said the boy, "I have written some poems. Would you like to hear them?"

"Perhaps one," said the father, "I must leave you in the company of my son and his sisters. They will entertain you, no doubt." And with that, he was gone.

"Would you like to hear my poems?" asked the boy.

"Yes," said I, "I love poems."

He looked rather pleased and began to read from the piece of paper he had in his hand. The poem read,

> *They do tell of long ago,*
> *Knights of old were very bold.*
> *Rode out to rescue the damsel fair,*
> *On a steed of white, with flaming red hair,*
> *I rode to rescue my lady fair.*

"That's very good," said I.

"I would like to give it to you, if I may."

"Thank you," said I, putting the paper into my pocket, "Thank you for all you have done for me, but I really must be going."

"Of course," said the boy, "have a safe journey home and if you ever pass this way again, we always meet at Christmastime. You are always welcome to call."

"I will," said I, as I walked out the door and began my way down the path to the town.

As I looked back, the light had gone out from the window. The cold had set in so I hurried home. I opened the door of the cottage and went quietly to bed, thinking what a day and how glad I was to be back and safe.

The next day I returned to the Parsonage, but the knocker on the door had gone, and the place looked oddly different. A man came to the door in answer to my knock.

"Is the lady of the house in?" I asked, realising that I did not know their names.

"No lady here. I have no wife," he said.

"But what of the people who were here last night?"

"There were no people here last night. I live alone," he said as he shut the door, thinking I must be a little mad.

I was beginning to think it, myself, then I remembered the poem.

Yes, it was there, yellow and dull looking - but wait! The strange boy had signed it.

'Patrick Branwell Brontë'

So my friends, you decide. I leave you the poem in this book. This was no daydream. Best wishes, Hannah.

P.S. By the way, I have been back to the place every year at Christmastime, but it is always the same. They are not there. I hope they know I called to say hello and to thank them for their help so long ago.

At the back of the book, there was an address Hannah Brown, Raven Cottage, Haworth.

This gave me a shock as Raven Cottage was the very cottage I was staying in! Had Hannah in some way led me to this book?

I will never know.

Had she been here all along? I decided to go back to the book shop. The old man was at the counter.

"Excuse me please, can you tell me where you got this book that I purchased from you the other day?"

"Yes," said the old man, "a lady came in with a box of books. She said she had found them in the attic of an old cottage in the town."

"Thank you," I said as I turned to go. I realised I was meant to find that book and as for the poem, I believe it to be real, as I believe Hannah's story.

Well, my friends, I must leave my tale there. It is for you to decide. The mystery is told. I hope that one day you will visit Haworth. There is something about the place. I have been back several times. You can say the place haunts me. Goodbye my friends, safe journey home. For you have, indeed, been on a strange journey which I hope you have enjoyed.

I Broke My Heart
With Weeping
to Come Back to Earth

The Dreamers and the Walking illustrations by JoJo Hughes

THE DREAMERS AND THE WALKING

By JoJo Hughes,
Cornwall, UK

Mama, stay awhile longer.
Do not fade.
The birds still sleep.
See here, this I have made.
It is for you.
You are no shade.
I smell your skin.
Wild thyme and sea.
Hold my hand.
Stay here with me.
Your smile is mine.
Your eyes, the deepest, greenest brine.
A sea of salt tears I have cried
Since the morning that you died.
Sweet Mother,
Hold me tight.
Dear Mama.
Ignore the cruel dawn's light.
In loving arms, O wrap me fast
And stay here till this pain has passed.
I vow I shall not let you go
To distant realms, dear lady, so
I shall cling to that dear heart
Which none shall henceforth from me part.

Sister, my soul's darling, stay.
Have you come at last to play?
I've made some room in here for you.
Forget the glint of morning dew.
Kick old Keeper off the bed
And warm your toes on me instead.
He sees you too, he feels your touch
He's missed you, Em, so very much.
Rest your cheek on mine, so wet.
These tears are joy. You don't regret
Man's paradise, so proudly spurned?
My heart is filled that you're returned.

Heaven is here, just next to me.
We always talked how it should be.
Let's make a tale.
Read me to sleep
And this our secret I will keep
Hold me close and promise then
You'll never go away again.

My little child, how is it so
I hear no tread
Though you are walking round my bed?
How can it be that I may see
Each auburn curl upon your head
Though light is low
There's yet a glow in eyes so dear belovéd
My bonny girl
What do you here?
Why came you back?
You cannot fear to rest in heavenly embrace?
And yet...to look upon that face,
Once more so lit with radiant grace
Is joy divine.
That chin is mine, thy mother's brow
Thy maimeó's smile...
I know not why He spared you now
To come to me whilst I here rest,
To lean your head upon my breast
(But I will not regret these tears.
I've held them in these long hard years.
To feel her once more in my arms
To know that she is safe from harm
To kiss her curls and smell her hair
Though mist she is and breathes not air
I bless the Lord for this embrace
And for the smile upon her face).

Brother, is it you who hides in yon dark place?
Come out from shadow! Show your face.
Now Brany, let the moonlight fall
On features I loved best of all
So. There you are. Where did you go?
I never gave up hope, you know.
And though 'tis good to see you grin

I could whip thee for thy cruel sin!
But fear me not...I will not chide.
Though from now on you must abide.
Hush, do not laugh! You'll wake Papa.
Do not you know the Young Men are
So battle-sore, in need of us?
Our foes we will their spirits crush!
Hurry, imp! Our thoughts must bend.
To new campaigns. You must attend.
For I have found a treasured land
And you must take up full command
Stand before the Men and see
A world I made for none but thee!
A continent we'll make our home
And nevermore we'll need to roam
This time you'll come. You will be brave
And lead us both to glory.
Now, brother, sit still. Come. Behave.
Let's make out one more story.

Why don't they come as I lay here?
I'm sure that I would feel no fear
To see them pass through yonder door
And look upon them all once more
Why am I left alone to fade
Without discourse with dearest shade?
When moon is high and I lay weak
I see dust stir, I hear stairs creak
I know they're moving just outside
They do not even come to chide
Their wretched brother, hopeless son
Though I was once the golden one.
This restless thirst I cannot slake
Yet numbness does not cure the shake
My heart is starved of loving smile
And I grow thin this torturous while
My forehead burns
My bones are chill
Does no one care that I am ill?
There's only one I would see now
She'd put her hand upon my brow
(Though when we were last left alone
Her own forehead was cold as stone)

One night she'll come
She'll visit me
She'll smile and love me tenderly
She'll dry my eyes and stroke my hair
I'll give myself into her care
And in those arms I'll gladly sleep
Till beams across the floorboards creep
And I'll be calmer for the day
Because Maria with me did stay.

The stars have died.
The sun has won.
The dreamers sleep.
The walkers, gone.

The Miniature Brontë Parsonage illustration by Julie Rose

THE MINIATURE BRONTË PARSONAGE

By Julie Rose

England

You can follow the miniature world behind the doors of the Brontë Parsonage Dollhouse on Instagram @miniaturebronteparsonage.

Daylight was fading as I found myself standing on the steps of the Miniature Brontë Parsonage. I glanced down, surprised to see that I was wearing a long silk dress, a shawl around my shoulders and carrying a lace bonnet. Am I dreaming? I thought to myself, feeling very strange and peculiar. My pride and joy is my Brontë dollhouse and I have spent many an hour furnishing it, attempting to replicate the atmosphere of the actual Parsonage in Haworth. Now it appeared to be a feature of my dream.

I looked slowly around and shivered as the wind howled through the surrounding trees. I could see a faint light coming from the window to my left as I contemplated my next move. "I have to go inside," I thought, "the opportunity is too great to miss." Decision made, I moved tentatively forward up the steps, and was about to knock on the door when it slowly opened of its own accord.

The hallway ahead appeared familiar, but somehow different. I entered cautiously, almost falling over a large brown paper parcel, the contents of which were strewn across the sandstone floor. I looked down to find a large pile of handwritten papers. The words 'Dear Currer Bell, we thank you for your manuscript but unfortunately...' revealed at the top of one page. A fleeting shadow on the stairway suddenly caught my eye, and my heart skipped a beat as the long case clock chimed loudly...1, 2, 3, 4, 5, 6, 7, 8, 9 times.

I wondered if that could be Mr. Brontë on his way upstairs to bed, pausing to wind the clock? The sound of laughter suddenly rang out from the room to my left. I was familiar with the Parsonage layout and knew it to be the dining room, where the sisters would write and walk around the table, discussing their ideas and thoughts.

"Hello," I stuttered nervously, "Is there anybody there?" Regretting my choice of words as soon as they escaped from my mouth and hoping that I hadn't awoken any mischievous spirits. The laughter immediately stopped.

I removed my shawl and bonnet and drew closer to the room. "Hi, I'm sorry to disturb you," I continued, "but your front door was open and I thought I heard voices."

There was no response.

I took another step forward, my ear to the door. I could detect a distant noise that sounded like tiny footsteps and whispering voices. The laughter resumed.

"Be quiet Emily, Papa will hear us." A voice cried out.

I paused with my hand on the doorknob, wondering whether to make an attempt to open the door. The voices continued.

"Oh Charlotte, I think Papa has already guessed our little secret. And I'm sure Branwell has his suspicions."

"But we need to be very careful, Emily. Our manuscripts have to be sent to the next publishing house on my list and not left carelessly in the hallway where they are in danger of being discovered."

"Do you think anyone will ever publish our novels, Charlotte? Our Poems were hardly a success. Are we good enough?"

"You are, you are!" I wanted to shout as I continued to eavesdrop on their conversation.

"I hope so, Emily, but I fear The Professor is lacking somewhat and holding you and Anne back. I have a new idea for a story about the life of a poor unwanted child who grows up to be a governess before meeting the man of her dreams, falling in love, and finally living happily ever after!"

"Oh Charlotte it sounds so perfect, if a little unbelievable! I am beginning to have similar doubts about Wuthering Heights. Will the reader think it wild and offensive, and Heathcliff too violent? What do you think Anne?"

"Perhaps people will be shocked at the content of our writing, Emily, especially if they realise that we are women. But we must take courage and have faith in our work and one day we could all be famous in our own right."

"I agree Anne. Ill-success fails to crush us. We must pursue our dreams."

I listened a little longer, intrigued, yet fearful of breaking the spell. I suddenly heard a sound coming from upstairs.

"Oh no I'm going to be discovered," I thought, quickly seeking a place to hide. The noise grew louder as, suddenly, a large mastiff dog came bounding towards me at a galloping pace.

"Shush, Keeper, stay quiet," I whispered, trying to keep him calm, "I hope you've not been on that bed again! Emily won't be happy."

Looking dejected, he waddled off in the direction of the kitchen, whilst I resumed my position at the dining room door. The conversation appeared to be over.

I slowly moved forward, eager to reveal what lay behind the door. Should I keep quiet and listen a little longer? But the temptation proved too great, and I slowly opened the door, uncertain of what I would discover.

The cramped room was just as I had furnished it. My Charlotte, Emily and Anne figurines stood motionless around the table. Porcelain Flossy was asleep on the chair by the fire, the handmade books stacked neatly on the shelves; the black sofa remained empty. Everything was in its correct place. Or was it?

I realised that Charlotte's writing slope lay open on the table, when I always kept it shut. I examined it closer. The contents appeared to be correct, with the exception of one miniature envelope that I found concealed in the drawer. I picked it up, unable to recall seeing it before. One single word was handwritten on the front – 'Reader' it said. The rear of the envelope was complete with an authentic red wax seal.

A candle flickered on the mantelpiece and I feared that I was going to awaken before disclosing the envelope's contents. The candle flickered again and then died, as the room was quickly plunged into darkness. Time to leave, I thought, as I stumbled around blindly, knocking my leg on a chair. In my panic to escape I forgot about the manuscript papers left outside the door and I lurched forward, dropping the envelope and tumbling down the miniature Parsonage steps.

I struggled to open my eyes, feeling most disoriented. There appeared to be someone watching me from the open doorway. As my head spun, the figure slowly came into focus. It was Branwell, laughing at me from the steps.

"Have you forgotten something?" he asked ominously, holding up the small envelope in his hand.

As I tried to stand, desperately reaching for the envelope, he slowly disappeared and I suddenly awoke to find myself back in my bed, heart pounding and the dream sadly over.

No, no, no! What was in the envelope? What did it say? What did it say? Disappointment enveloped me as I realised that the secret would never be revealed.

Several days later, my dream forgotten, I was writing an article for my Miniature Brontë Parsonage account. I opened the miniature doors of the dollhouse, seeking inspiration and peered inside the dining room. I immediately noticed that my figurine of Charlotte was standing in a different position, her writing slope open on the table. I carefully placed her back near the bookshelf and as I did so a miniature envelope fluttered to the floor.

Thoughts of my dream suddenly returned.

I picked up the envelope. 'Reader' it said in tiny writing on the front. Would the charm be broken if revealed, I wondered? Deciding to take a chance, I enthusiastically broke the seal and unfolded the paper within.

I couldn't help but smile as I read the words — 'Thank you for keeping our spirit alive'

Spirit illustration by Julie Rose

SPIRIT

By Julie Rose
UK

All hushed and still within the house,
Without - the rain is falling.
Yet voices echo through the walls,
The Sisters' spirit is calling.

Cold in the earth, yet still alive,
Through many a wild December.
Perhaps forgotten over the years,
Though I will always remember.

I love the silent hour of night,
When I can hear their laughter.
A time they believed in hopes and dreams,
And a happy ever after.

Come walk with me across the moors,
And sense their ghosts together
With Heathcliff, Cathy, Agnes and Jane,
And bluebells, and blossom, and heather.

Though the night is darkening round me now,
And the howling winds do blow.
I'll surround you with warmth and gratitude,
And a love you will never know.

So farewell to thee! But not farewell,
My respect for you will survive.
Your books, your poems, will live forever,
And I'll keep your spirit alive.

The Moccasin Mystery illustration by Amy Turner

THE MOCCASIN MYSTERY

by Donna Turner
Halifax, West Yorkshire

Darren, my husband of 28 years, had a very annoying habit of losing his car keys and had spent the last 15 minutes tearing around the house looking for them, getting more and more harangued.

Having been ready for the last half hour, I was now doing my best to help locate the keys whilst at the same time trying not to get stressed. I'd had this evening booked for several weeks and didn't want anything to spoil it.

"Which coat did you wear last?" I asked

I heard him rummaging through coat pockets in the hall "At last! Found them!" he exclaimed with relief.

"Thank Goodness." I sighed.

"What time does this thing start tonight?" he asked.

"7pm." I replied. "I hope it's not going to rain, the weather forecast this morning mentioned we could get thunder storms tonight, too." The sun was shining, but a few dark clouds had started to appear.

"It needs it, it's too stuffy, it needs to clear the air." Darren checked his phone. "If we set off now, you're going to be far too early, you know."

"Better that than being late or failing to turn up at all. You know how bad the traffic can be sometimes through Queensbury on a Friday tea time. Are we ready to set off?"

My punctuality drove Darren insane at times; I was one of those people who liked to arrive early for everything.

The date was Friday 26th June, and I had booked myself a place on an after hours' event being held at the Brontë Parsonage in Haworth. The evening was listed as 'The Unexpected Moccasins of Charlotte Brontë'.

This was the first event I had attended and although I wasn't sure what to expect, I was beyond excited. My favourite place in the world was Haworth and the Parsonage Museum. Certainly, Charlotte Brontë's moccasins were a mystery to me. They were not the type of footwear you would normally associate with her. I was intrigued to learn as to how they came to be in her possession in the first place.

I had been looking forward to this evening for weeks now. I was actually going to see something up close - and possibly get to handle - an item of clothing that Charlotte Brontë had actually worn. My obsession with the Brontës, especially Charlotte, began in my teens when I studied Jane Eyre for my English language O level. Since then I have read all of the sister's novels numerous times, joined the Brontë Society and try to visit the Museum as often as I can. I feel extremely lucky that this piece of history is here practically on my doorstep. I've also joined numerous Facebook groups, who all share the same fascination as me with the children of an Irish clergyman, who lived in a remote village in West Yorkshire.

It was 6.20 pm when we pulled into the carpark at Haworth. The traffic had been kind to us and, as Darren pointed out several times, I was far too early.

"Looks like you're the first one here. I told you we would be too early. What are you going to do? Do you want to come and wait with me in the Black Bull?" asked Darren

"No, I'll hang around and see if anyone else turns up," I replied scanning the deserted lane.

"See you at 8ish then." And with that Darren strolled along the cobbles towards the pub.

The gate into the Parsonage Museum garden, which was usually kept locked when the Museum was shut, was open. As I entered the garden there was no one else around. The sun that had been shining gloriously suddenly hid behind a very large, grey, ominous looking cloud, casting a dark shadow over the garden. There was a distant rumble of thunder in the distance. "Oh no, I hope it doesn't start raining," I thought, pulling my cardigan around me. I suddenly felt chilly.

I strolled around the garden enjoying the peace and quiet when it suddenly struck me that the birds were not singing as usual. I shivered and got an eerie feeling that I was being observed. I turned abruptly and stared across the graveyard, but it was unoccupied apart from the poor souls slumbering in the cold earth. Something out of the corner of my eye made me turn around and look towards the front of the Parsonage; I thought I saw what looked like a small female figure walking around the parlour with a book in her hand. The figure unexpectedly stopped walking and looked directly at me.

I raised my hand to wave at the lady. It must have started already, I reasoned. I looked at my watch, the time showed as 6 pm. I held the watch to my ear, I could still hear the familiar ticking. That's odd I thought as I began to walk to the front door. I tried to wind the watch, but found it was fully wound. I hoped it wasn't broken, as it had belonged to my late grandmother.

I was just about to knock on the door when the lady, I presumed a volunteer at the Parsonage, opened it.

The lady was the same person I had seen walking around in the parlour. She was beautifully dressed as Charlotte Brontë, her dark hair was plaited and wound around her head, and she wore the little spectacles we all associate with Charlotte due to her poor eyesight. The dress was adorned with tiny blue flowers, it looked to be the one usually on display upstairs in the glass cabinet in Charlotte's old bedroom. She was so petite. Her dress, the spectacles and hair certainly were impressive, she looked very authentic. I was trying not to appear rude, but I was unable to stop staring at her, I couldn't believe how much she resembled the portrait of Charlotte drawn by George Richmond in 1850. I silently congratulated the Brontë Parsonage Museum, on how realistic the costume was; I believed this was going to be an interesting evening.

"Hello, I'm Charlotte, please enter." She smiled and beckoned me in. She spoke so quietly, I could barely hear her.

"Hello, pleased to meet you, I'm Donna. I thought I would be far too early, but it looks like you've started already."

I followed Charlotte down the passage. She glided silently along the stone passageway turning into the parlour. I could smell freshly baked bread and the smouldering of a coal fire.

The parlour looked and felt so different with the oil lamps and candles lit and a small fire glowing in the grate. It was so warm and inviting. The rope that usually held Brontë enthusiasts at bay had also been removed. I felt light headed. I couldn't believe I was actually standing in the parlour, where the girls had sat and written their novels. Charlotte's writing box was on the table with papers, ink bottle and pen strewn across it; she hastily gathered up the items and closed the box.

I had to pinch myself. "This is charming," I thought. I wasn't expecting anything like this when I had booked the event. So far it had exceeded my expectations.

Without warning, the room suddenly appeared darker and the rumble of thunder could be heard getting nearer. The wind must have started up too, as the fire crackled and hissed, and the candle flames sputtered. Although, when I looked across at the graveyard the trees were quite still.

"I hate thunderstorms, don't you?" I asked.

Charlotte nodded in agreement and beckoned for me to sit on one of the dark wood dining chairs.

I could see the little pair of moccasins set out on display on a small table in one of the alcoves together with other Brontë artifacts.

Charlotte picked the moccasins up and offered them to me. "You've come to see these." It was more of a statement than a question.

My hands trembled as she passed them to me. As her hands brushed mine, I noticed they were icy cold.

I couldn't believe it, the shoes were so small and exquisitely made with what appeared to be a soft, buttery leather. Charlotte sat next to me and pointed out the embroidered beaded floral motif. The glass beads looked beautiful, sparkling in the candlelight.

"See how pleasing the needlework is." She remarked. "Do you also see the initials 'CB' I stitched on the right shoe?"

"They are beautiful." I exclaimed. I couldn't believe I was actually holding something that Charlotte Brontë had worn.

While I continued to admire the shoes, Charlotte explained how the moccasins had come into her possession. They were sent to her as a gift from her publisher in New York, Harper and Brothers. She had taken them with her when she and her friend, Ellen Nussey, and her very ill sister, Anne, visited Scarborough. Her voice trembled when she told me they thought the sea air would revive Anne as she was so weak, but alas, sadly not. Her eyes filled with tears as she revealed the sad story to me. As I went to put my hand on her arm to comfort her, she briskly moved away and stood before the fire. They must have hired an actress I thought; she was very convincing. Another loud clap of thunder boomed directly overhead. The candles and the fire blew out, and the room was plunged into semi darkness.

74

I made my way over to the alcove and placed the shoes back on the table, but when I turned to thank Charlotte the room was empty.

I went out into the hall and called her, but there was no answer. I tried Patrick's study door, but that was locked. The kitchen was empty. I ran to the bottom of the stairs and could hear a shuffling sound moving in one of the rooms above. "Hello," I called "are you there?" Thunder boomed overhead.

The temperature in the Parsonage plummeted and the clock began to strike continuously. I began to feel frightened and ran quickly to the door. The door was locked. I struggled with it and began frantically pulling on the handle. I began to panic, my heart was hammering, the blood rushing in my ears.

A loud, dull thud could be heard on the stairs, I turned and could see a dark shadow slowly descending. I pulled again at the door as hard as I could, blind panic was coursing through me now.

The door suddenly gave way and flew open, I heard Charlotte whisper, "Go quickly." I flew out of the Parsonage tripping down the steps and the door slammed closed behind me.

I could see a group of about 8 people by the gate, one I recognised as Ann Dinsdale, the Museum curator. I was so relieved to be out of the Parsonage and with other people.

"Oh, thank goodness!" I called out shakily.

The group fell silent and everyone stared at me.

"Hello, are you Donna?" asked Ann, looking at me quizzically, "Are you feeling alright?"

I just nodded my head, I couldn't speak. What had just happened inside the Parsonage? I looked up at the bedroom window above the study and could see a dark shadowy figure staring at me. "Branwell!" I shouted and pointed up at the window. Everyone turned to look, but when I looked back, there was no one there.

The group looked at me in bewilderment and followed Ann to the Parsonage. She began unlocking the door.

"Wait!" I called. "I've already been inside. I've seen the moccasins."

It was the group's turn to look confused now. I had eight pairs of eyes staring blankly at me. They looked as though they thought I was mad.

"I don't understand. The museum is locked. I have the keys here." Ann held up the bunch of keys. "There is no one in the Museum, you couldn't possibly have been inside, as you would have set the alarm off."

Ann unlocked the door and group began to follow her inside. I stayed outside on the lawn, the thunder rolling in the distance now and the sun was making a reappearance, peeping out from behind the clouds.

Without warning, Charlotte appeared at the parlour window. She waved goodbye to me, before vanishing into thin air.

Ann came to the door. "Are you coming in Donna? You've gone dreadfully pale. You look like you've just seen a ghost."

With Me Always photo by Emma Langan

With Me Always photo by Emma Langan

WITH ME ALWAYS

Emma Langan
UK
(Dedicated to my late mother, Glynis)

You are with me always
And hath taken many forms
From the stare in the black cat's eyes
To the hope and longing in my heart
And the limpets in my thoughts.

I am not completely alone in this abyss
But never again will I find another like you
Life at times has often been unutterable
But I have to live without the source of my life and soul
Knowing you are not far away.

Grief has bled my countenance grey
The ghosts of your dying breaths
Hath breathed life back into my soul to carry on
And my soul keeps you alive.

The Night I Left illustration by Yvonne Solly

THE NIGHT I LEFT

By Emma Langan
UK
(Dedicated to my late mother, Glynis)

I know I am not the only traveler
Who is stuck in this present limbo
I have been trying to let go of regrets
Take me back to the night I left.

And then I would know what to do
And maybe my actions could've saved you
And then I wouldn't be living this life without you
Take me back to the night I left.

Alone I went home in silence on a ghost train
And I left you in the cold
Now tell me what I'm supposed to do
Now that I'm haunted by the ghost of you
Take me back to the night I left.

Followed was a Tuesday filled with worry
Then a Wednesday filled with dread
Then came the Thursday filled with terrors
And a police officer who didn't know what to say
The night before was the night you left.

Ever since that day I've been trying to do good by you
But now tell me what I'm supposed to do
Now that I'm haunted by the ghost of you
Take me back to the night you left.

Sounds From the Silent Country illustration by Jon Beynon

SOUNDS FROM THE SILENT COUNTRY

By Emmeline Burdett
London, England

'Sleep, O cluster of friends,
Sleep! – or only, when May,
Brought by the West Wind, returns
Back to your native heaths,
And the plover is heard on the moors,
Yearly awake, to behold
The opening summer, the sky,
The shining moorland – to hear
The drowsy bee, as of old,
Hum o'er the thyme, the grouse
Call from the heather in bloom!
Sleep, or only for this
Break your united repose!'

-Matthew Arnold, 'Haworth Churchyard' (1855)

Charlotte stooped and picked up the small round object from where it lay in the flowerbed. If the sun hadn't caught it, she might not have seen it at all. She rubbed the soil off it and, after some peering, could make out that it was a badge proudly bearing the statement 'I've been to the Brontë Parsonage Museum!' What the badge's former owner's impressions of her home had been, Charlotte could only guess, but given that the badge appeared to have been carelessly discarded in the garden, she thought that further speculation would be unlikely to prove particularly fruitful.

Though Charlotte had always hoped that she and her sisters would live on through their novels and poetry, she had to admit that there were some disadvantages to the fact that Haworth, and in particular the Parsonage, had become a place of pilgrimage. In particular, she objected to the hordes of strangers who trooped through the Parsonage daily, sitting on Emily's sofa, trying to wind the clock on the staircase, and expressing surprise that there had been not two Brontë sisters, but three. Indeed, Charlotte wondered whether many of those visitors really knew much about her and her family at all. That had certainly been her suspicion when, not so long ago, she and her siblings had taken advantage of their non-corporeal state to attend a screening of a strange film called *To Walk Invisible,* which had been shown at West Lane Baptist Church. The film, which purported to tell the life-story of Charlotte and her family, had endowed each Brontë with, as far as Charlotte could tell, one characteristic – her own being ambition. Or rather, she thought bitterly, Emily, Anne and herself had each had one characteristic, but Branwell, needless to say, had been given two – addiction and unrealised promise.

Sadly, though, neither of those two qualities were at all inaccurate, and now that all four of them inhabited what Matthew Arnold had referred to as 'the silent country', Branwell's tradition of unrealised promise was continuing apace. He had left the screening of *To Walk Invisible* early – so early, in fact, that he never found out what happened to him in the end – to resume his favourite occupation of frightening the drinkers in the Black Bull public house by moving their glasses, tilting their chairs, and playing the piano when, as far as most people were concerned, there was no-one there.

Charlotte might complain that Branwell was, yet again, failing to fulfil his potential, but really, what could he do? What could *any* of them do? 'Yearly awake, to behold' was all very well, but it *did* mean that one's power to influence anything was rather limited. In fact, Charlotte and her siblings always seemed to arrive right in the middle of something – in 1915, for example, they had found that everyone in Haworth was discussing 'The Great War', and they had had distinct feelings of *déjà vu*, when this happened again in 1916, 1917, and 1918.

They always tried to meet in the same place and up until recently this had been under the pine tree planted by Charlotte and Arthur, but now, of course, this possibility was no longer open to them. Branwell had suggested that they take turns standing guard by the tree, making spooky noises whenever anyone came near. In this way, he had said, they could prevent the tree being felled, but Charlotte had rolled her eyes and tutted to demonstrate her opposition to what she considered to be a very childish suggestion indeed. Still, there was no denying that the loss of the tree had been a blow. What was worse, though, was that she could no longer recall exactly where they had planted it, and without it as a marker, she had also lost the location of the box that lay beneath it.

It was while Charlotte was examining the badge and wondering sadly about her box that she had first become aware of someone standing behind her watching what she was doing. Her initial reaction was annoyance – surely one was entitled to stand in one's own garden without all and sundry coming along to observe what one was doing??

On further reflection, though, she was at first alarmed, and then intrigued. She had never quite been able to work out why it was that while most people could not see her, a few undoubtedly could. It appeared that this person – a rather anxious-looking woman with untidy brown hair – was one such. Charlotte hoped that the woman might realise that she did not want any company and leave her alone, but sadly, the woman approached her looking decidedly enthusiastic and inclined for conversation. Charlotte sighed.

"Excuse me, but I've been watching you for a while now. Are you Charlotte Brontë? My name is Hannah, and I've been doing some research in the Parsonage library. I'm writing a book about you. Are you here alone?"

Charlotte gave a non-committal smile. Whilst she was unwilling to be actively rude, the last thing she wanted to do was to give encouragement to this 'Hannah', who would presumably regard a face-to-face meeting with the subject of her book as something of a coup – especially given that the subject in question had been dead for over one hundred and fifty years. Charlotte remembered all too well how Mr Thackeray had taken great pleasure in showing her off and intro-ducing her to his friends as 'Jane Eyre'. It was not only the disrespect and flippancy which Charlotte had felt that this entailed, but it seemed also to suggest that Thackeray was accusing her of a lack of imagination and saying that in writing the novel Charlotte had done nothing more than simply recording her own feelings. She had had this suspicion about other people, too, such as when she had seen a poster for a film of 'Jane Eyre' starring one Susannah York –on the poster, York had been shown looking exactly like a portrait of Charlotte, herself! Charlotte was roused from these rather less-than-pleasant reflections by the sound of Hannah enquiring where her siblings were.

Charlotte resisted the temptation to retort that the Brontës did not travel in herds, and that anyway she was quite mature enough to be out by herself, *in the grounds of her father's house*, and replied that she believed that Emily and Anne had gone to Ponden Hall, whilst Branwell was no doubt somewhere in Haworth. Charlotte knew that Branwell was probably in the Black Bull, but she felt a sense of shame in acknowledging the fact and decided that it was better to be discreet. Accepting that Emily and Anne had gone to Ponden Hall without her was in some ways equally difficult, but at least the claim that she had chosen to stay behind in the hopes of finding her box was not wholly untrue.

More to drive away her painful thoughts about her siblings than because she was actually particularly interested, Charlotte decided to ask Hannah about the book she was writing – it might at least be amusing to discover what strange creature Hannah had managed to conjure up to masquerade as 'Charlotte Brontë'. Charlotte certainly had a low opinion of most of the biographers who had claimed to portray her and her family.

"Well," began Hannah, "I know it sounds really arrogant, but none of the Brontë biographers has ever really 'done it' for me. Do you know what I mean?"

Without waiting to hear whether or not Charlotte did indeed 'know what she meant', Hannah continued;

"I mean, obviously the biographies are fascinating – I've learnt so many things that I wouldn't otherwise have known. Things about your childhood, about the nineteenth century, about letters you wrote, about what happened when you went to Belgium...but there's always something missing, no matter how thorough the biographer has been."

Interested in spite of herself, Charlotte enquired "What do you think is missing?"

Hannah considered. "Well, I don't really know how to describe it. It's nothing I can really put my finger on, but when I read your books and your poetry, I can sort of feel you with me. When I read a biography, of course it's very interesting, but that feeling just isn't there. A biography tells me how you feel, but it doesn't tell me how you know how *I* feel. It doesn't tell me why, when you call me 'Reader', I feel all gooey."

Charlotte realised – in reality, she had always known – that this was why she had written. Of course, her ambition to be published had been a part of it – and an important part, especially given that opportunities for women had been so limited – but it had not been everything. 'The secret and deeply-felt wish to be more than a self-seeker' – that's what it had been. And now, apparently, her wish had come true. Nevertheless, Charlotte was unwilling to place too much confidence in Hannah, no matter how tempting it might seem. She had tried that before, and it had brought her nothing but misery.

As though she was able to read Charlotte's thoughts, Hannah suddenly enquired why Charlotte had been standing alone in the garden. "Have you lost something?" she asked. "Maybe I can help you look for it?"

Charlotte hesitated. Her own attempts at searching had come to nothing, but that did not mean that she wanted to share her secret with Hannah. The point of burying things was to keep them for oneself, and so not to have to share them with everyone. Charlotte had also decided that marrying Arthur would have to mean placing her memories of Monsieur Heger firmly in the past. She could not bring herself to destroy the things he had given her, so, in the manner of Lucy Snowe, she had decided to bury them – both literally and metaphorically.

'Old Jews' selling suitable glass tubes being conspicuous by their absence in Haworth, she had found an old metal box, sealed it to stop the damp earth soiling its contents, and buried it underneath the tree that she and Arthur had just planted. Now that the tree was gone, though, she could no longer remember exactly where it had stood.

"Would it help if I brought my metal detector?" suggested Hannah gently. "And I'll bring a couple of spades. It sounds like we might have to dig up whatever it is you've lost. Meet me here early tomorrow morning. If we can find it before anyone sees what we're doing, no-one will be any the wiser."

Charlotte turned to ask Hannah something, but there was no sign of her. She had vanished.

* * *

The following morning, when it was barely light, Charlotte was somewhat surprised to find herself again standing in the Parsonage garden, waiting impatiently to see if Hannah would keep her promise. She was relieved when she saw Hannah coming towards her, struggling under the weight of what was presumably the promised 'metal detector'.

Hannah laid the spades down beside her, and brandished the metal detector gleefully. "This should save us a bit of time," she said, "If you can tell me a bit more about the object we're actually looking for."

Charlotte had spent most of the preceding evening anticipating this question, and worrying about how she should answer it. Whilst she did not want to rise to Emily-like levels of evasiveness, neither was she particularly keen to show Hannah how excited she was and how much the box and its contents meant to her.

"It's just a metal box," she explained, "Its contents are precious to me. I have been looking everywhere for it, but I cannot find it. I buried it under the tree that Arthur and I planted when we married, but that is gone now."

Hannah looked thoughtful. "The pine tree?" she asked, "I watched it being felled. I think I can remember where it stood. It was awful to see it go, but it had become diseased, and I think they were worried that it would suddenly fall on someone and squash them!"

Charlotte shuddered, but Hannah appeared not to notice, and gestured to a patch of ground not far from where they were standing.

"I think it was about there," she said, "Let's have a look, anyway, and see if anything turns up. If you buried it quite near the surface, the metal detector should have no trouble picking it up."

Charlotte looked around. They did not have time to 'see if anything turned up'. And yet, what on earth were they actually doing wrong? It was the Brontës' own garden, for heavens' sake! Though Charlotte herself could be reasonably confident of remaining unseen, she felt that the same could not be said of Hannah, and still less of all the paraphernalia that she had brought with her.

Hannah switched the metal detector on, and moved it slowly over the patch of earth where she had suggested they were most likely to find what they were looking for – or rather, what Charlotte was looking for; Hannah was really none the wiser.

Charlotte had never used a metal detector. She did not know what would happen if Hannah found anything, but she assumed that there would be some sort of indication that their search had been successful. She watched anxiously as Hannah moved the detector over the patch of ground she had selected. At first nothing happened, but after a few minutes the detector began to beep. Charlotte almost pushed Hannah out of the way in her eagerness to discover what was there, and they both began scrabbling at the patch of earth. Charlotte's fingers almost immediately closed over a small metal object, and she pulled it out of the ground to take a closer look at it. She brushed some of the earth off it, and stared at it in dismay. Hannah looked at it over her shoulder.

"Oh dear! Well, that sometimes happens – quite frequently, actually" laughed Hannah, "It's a ring-pull from a drink can. Detect-orists are always finding those. Never mind – let's see if we can turn up anything more promising."

Charlotte – who had not drunk anything for over a century and a half – would normally have enquired what a 'drink can' was, but, lost in her disappointment, she did not care.

Hannah rummaged around in the soil that they had already disturbed and soon brought out a rusty metal box. Looking at it, however, it was soon clear that Charlotte's precautionary seal had been insufficient – it must have rotted away long ago, for there was no sign of it. Charlotte was almost afraid to look at the box's contents, seeing how the seal had fared. Taking a deep breath, though, she took the box from Hannah but she found that, though the seal was missing, the box was still impossible to open.

"Here, let me," said Hannah, who seemed to have come prepared for every eventuality. She took from her pocket a rather lethal-looking tool with lots of blades attached to it. Hannah looked at the tool and chuckled. "My dad gave me this for my eighteenth birthday. I think he still couldn't accept that I wasn't a boy. It has been useful over the years, though."

She opened one of the blades on her tool and tried to slide it underneath the lid of the box, but it took a lot of persuasion before it would actually fit. All of a sudden, the blade slipped under the lid, which flew off and landed with a clatter some little way away.

Charlotte and Hannah both peered inside the box. Perhaps because the lid had been so securely attached, whatever was in there seemed to be relatively unscathed. It proved to be a small bound book and something wrapped in fragile-looking paper. Charlotte took them out of the box and examined them tenderly. Hannah sat down beside her and watched.

"Monsieur bought this book and he had it bound for me," explained Charlotte.

She stroked the binding and opened the book. Though some of the pages were stuck together, Hannah could make out that the book was entitled 'The Field of Waterloo', by Walter Scott', and was dated 1815. Though she knew that Charlotte had loved Sir Walter Scott, she had never heard of this particular publication. At least she presumed that this 'Walter Scott' and the better-known 'Sir Walter' were one and the same person.

"Is it a poem?" she asked, "I suppose it has something to do with whatever's wrapped up in the paper?"

"Well, yes," said Charlotte, "As you might imagine, it's about the Battle of Waterloo."

Hannah could hear the implied criticism in Charlotte's voice and was reminded of what a poor teacher she must have been, given her impatience with people who were not as knowledgeable as she was. She'd always thought, though, that Charlotte's faults made her human, which surely made her easier to identify with than if she'd been the paragon that some Brontë fans appeared to want. Hannah decided to risk asking Charlotte what was wrapped in the paper.

Charlotte laid the book back in the box, and picked up the other object that was in there. As she started to unwrap it, the paper disintegrated, and Hannah could see that it looked like a piece of wood that had once belonged to a tree.

"Monsieur gave me this at the same time as he gave me the book," said Charlotte, "It's from the Waterloo battlefield, and is said to be a part of the tree from which the Duke of Wellington directed the battle. Walter Scott brought back two knots from the tree, but this is just a little cross-section from one of its branches. I imagine it must have been treated with something, or it would probably have gone the same way as the paper!"

She laughed rather ruefully.

"These were not the only gifts which Monsieur gave me, but even so I found them special. I always thought that he could see me for who I really was and these seemed to prove it. I loved Wellington; I loved his victories. I loved Sir Walter Scott. When Arthur seemed to see someone entirely different, I felt that that period of my life was over."

The feminist in Hannah was rather unhappy with Charlotte apparently having been so willing to be defined by other people, and to define her own life by what they thought. Still, it was hardly an observation that no-one had made before.

"What do you want to do with these things?" asked Hannah. "Now that we've found them, do you really want to put them back in the ground?"

Of course Charlotte didn't want that, but she had been so focused on wondering where her box was that she had never really considered what might happen once she found it.

"What about giving it to the Museum? They do have other things that Monsieur Heger gave to you. I can imagine it being the centrepiece of an exhibition. Maybe about Waterloo, or about your Brussels experience. I'm afraid this story really won't belong to you anymore."

"How do you suggest we bring it to their attention?" asked Charlotte rather caustically, "Leave it on the window-ledge and hope someone notices it? Or maybe you'd prefer to go to them and explain that a ghost told you about the box, and you helped her find it again? No – did you not say that you were writing a book?"

"Well, yes," said Hannah, "but you didn't seem very happy with the idea of helping me with it."

"That was true," agreed Charlotte, "but you helped me find the box, and I know that I can no longer do this alone. After today, I cannot return until next year, but could you try to think of how we might use these objects to tell a story? I will do the same. On this day next year, meet me here and we can decide what to do. Meanwhile, carry on writing your own book. It sounds as though it could be very interesting."

"I will," agreed Hannah, trying to disguise her excitement.

She looked round, but this time it was Charlotte who had vanished.

* * *

That evening in her hotel room, Hannah read through her chapter plans for her book, and thought wistfully how well 'Strange Meeting in the Parsonage Garden' would fit into what was, after all, a personal response to Charlotte Brontë. She had made a promise, though, and she could not go back on it. She would just have to wait a year, and then discuss it with her co-author. Her co-author, Charlotte Brontë!

Unquiet souls! In the dark fermentation of earth,
In the never-idle workshop of nature,
In the eternal movement.
Ye shall find yourselves again!

-Matthew Arnold, 'Haworth Churchyard' Epilogue

A Wild, Wicked Slip She Was

The Bonnet illustration by Yael Veitz

THE BONNET

Arthur Li
California, USA

A friend had told me, years ago, about Charlotte's traveling dress, brown silk with plain skirt and bodice, carefully preserved and displayed in the Brontë Parsonage. I walk a circle around the dress, taking pictures with my phone.

A friend had told me about the juvenile drawings Charlotte made, of flowers and human noses, of a boy taking shelter under a crooked tree. Beautiful and delightful renderings, behind plexiglass.

I had wanted to see these things. Dragged my family in a jumbo jet across the Atlantic to be here now among these artifacts.

Nobody had told me about the baby's bonnet. Here, displayed in the corner of Charlotte's bedroom in a red velvet-lined case. A white woolen head wrap, miniaturized for a newborn, resting on a wooden knob, two strings loosely tied dangling at the chin. Looks scratchy, but would have been adorable framing a sleeping babe's face under its ruffled brim. The card below said a friend knitted it for the child Charlotte was expecting.

The bonnet was never used.

I think about the unborn child who perished with her mother. I allow myself to wonder. How formed and close to life the child might have been when the mother died.

In the dark of Charlotte's bedroom, I hear a baby cry.

I see candle light flicker on a man's face. Craggy nose, oversized mouth, and two thick sideburns that meet in the middle of his chin. The man wears a pale long sleeve nightshirt that falls from his collar to his ankles in one piece. He lifts a crying baby girl, a newborn, onto his shoulder, a baby wearing a white woolen bonnet. The baby nearly fits into the palm of the man's hand, as he rocks her back and forth, singing a hymn, moisture at the corner of his eyes. This baby is the only living extension of the woman he loved, the wife he had just buried. He could not entrust this girl to anyone else's care. He grabs the glass bottle, cradles his daughter across his chest, and brings the bottle to the baby's lips. The baby drinks. Tiny eyes slowly close in the candlelight. He sets her down in the wooden crib. Then he slides gently onto the floor, leaning against the wall, and follows his baby to sleep.

I hear people talking below the floorboards. A deep voiced man, and a confident young girl, reciting numbers. I peer down the stairs toward the parlor. It is daylight, and I see the bearded man with his daughter at a rounded table, with paper and feather pen at hand.

"Ten plus three..." he says.

"Thirteen" she says, without pause.

He scribbles more numbers, bigger numbers on the paper and hands it to her.

The man's father in law, bespectacled and gray, reclines on the sofa behind them and grumbles. "It's a dereliction of duty for any man, a curate no less, to ignore his God-given duties," he says, " just so he can teach his child arithmetic. Now send her to a school before the Church trustees vote you out!"

But this daughter *is* this man's God-given duty. And he knows Charlotte would have never considered boarding her at a school.

In leather boots and a child's blue walking dress, hair brushed and parted in the middle, the girl waits for him at the door. He takes her hand and they depart under the portico and onto the moors behind the Parsonage. I follow them outside. Grey clouds, cool wind, lush green all around. I watch them while keeping a slight distance. The girl may be little, but she attacks the steep climbs and descents of the hills, pulling her father with her.

They pause before a modest stream of water trickling under a flat granite bridge. He sits her atop a large stone shaped like a chair. He plucks strands of heather from the thicket, and presents her with an exploding purple bouquet wriggling in the wind. She laughs. He pulls himself up on the rock beside her and puts his hand in his chin, gazing together with his daughter at the water. "Your mother," he says. "She loved it here like no other place in the world."

The girl cocks her head to the side and squints. I have not kept enough distance. She sees me. She waves at me. Uncertain of what to do, I wave back.

The man sees me now, too. He motions me to come.

So I walk with this girl and her father. A child's soft steps flitting across wild grass, and the more deliberate clomping of men crushing

92

the greens beneath their boots. Dirt and prickly shrubs and piles of heavy rocks winding across the moors, separating sheep and cows. Three farmhouses connect the dots along the course of a rising hill. We climb it. The girl breathes hard, the father hums a song. They hold hands and swing their arms together in wide arcs with each step.

We reach the farmhouse at the top. I turn around and see orange streaks of sun through a hole in the clouds, reflecting off the windswept waves of tall green fields rolling around in the valley below.

This man, I have read about him before. He is supposed to be a grave, serious fellow. Yet he is hoisting his happy daughter upon his shoulders, and bounding between and around mounds of sheep droppings, laughing and twirling his girl up in the air and catching her, and bringing her in to his sturdy chest for a hug. He chortles and she screams and then grins. They turn their heads to look at the valley. We breathe in the air, crisp and pure enough to cleanse any lung or cure any affliction.

"To Ponden Hall," he says, "The library."

"New books!" she says, eyes widening, "How I love reading!"

He turns to m, "Are you coming?"

I stare at the man's double buttoned grey frock coat, the vest underneath, and the white cravat covering his neck.

"Are you ghosts?" I say.

"Father, this man is strange," the girl says.

* * *

Upon returning to the Parsonage, I search for my family. In the foyer, a young creature with flying black hair skitters across the floor and wraps herself around my leg. She is not an apparition. She is my daughter. She is real and she is mine, though I blink twice and pat her head to make sure.

"Daddy!" she says. "I saw these teensy tiny books upstairs." She raises her hand in front of her face, squints, and holds her thumb and index finger a millimeter apart. "The words on the page were *this* small! They gave you a magnifying glass to read them!"

My wife emerges from Patrick's study. "I'm glad we came," she says. "I never knew the author of Pride and Prejudice had such a tragic history."

I laugh. My wife, hopeless. I love her anyway.

Inside the church, we hold hands before the sign engraved into the stone pillar. "Maria and Patrick, Maria," reads my daughter, out loud. "Elizabeth, Branwell, Emily Jane, Charlotte." She glances to the left and to the right of the pillar. "Are they all buried...underneath us?"

"Yup," my wife says. "Right below our feet."

"Eww," my daughter says.

And Charlotte's unborn child, too, still inside of her, I think to myself.

I look around the church for more ghosts. But the pews are empty at present.

"OK guys," I say. "What y'all think about taking that walk to Top Withins now?"

Branwell's Carousel illustration by Yael Veitz

BRANWELL'S CAROUSEL

By Emma Langan
UK

"I sit, this evening, far away,
From all I used to know,
And naught reminds my soul to-day
Of happy long ago."

I mourn this eve of dear souls pass'd
And deliberate how my life has changed so fast
Scorned by selfish lover's lust
As I pick at the feeble embers of my trust.

I gaze back upon a blacken'd toilsome trail
Once was prosperous, now besieged with fail
I sip another bead of life's mortal sin
And yearn over the un-numbed feelings within.

Years gone by and I look upon a soul who has taken my place
And naught has changed but a fairer face
Life has changed, but hers is parallel
The life that is Branwell's carousel.

The Spirit of the Moor illustration by Julie Rose

THE SPIRIT OF THE MOOR

By Jenny Courtney Fidgeon
West Yorkshire, England

Tears well in my eyes as I see what they would have seen
I wish time would snare me in his wrath
It's where they were and always have been
The wind blows fierce up here
The clouds hang low and grey
The air sounds desperate and angry
But I have no fear today
I can almost see Emily's ghostly form
She strides across the open land
The heath trembles before me
Her wayward spirit seems close at hand

I Beheld the Wretch illustration by Barb Tanke

I BEHELD THE WRETCH

by Kay Fairhurst Adkins
Palm Springs, California, USA

Just a figment of the imagination, a trick of the fog. No man could
be that large. A blink of the eye, a shake of the head, and it was gone.
Gone, it's true; not gone into vapor, but gone far along its way. Gone
closer to its shrouded destination.

The fog partly obscured the large man-like form as he... as it...
moved swiftly up the cobbled road, expertly blending into doorways
and shadows with the careful practice of miscreant decades. Nearly
empty, the road may as well have been deserted for all the notice
anyone gave the figure as its huge strides ate up the distance. One look
and it was gone, gone at long last to crouch among the graves, rheumy
yellow eyes peering intently at its desired end. Great hands grasped the
roughness of stone as its nose, such as it was, twitched, sniffing like a
dog to gather information before the creature slowly, slowly crept
around the quiet Parsonage, making an intent examination of every
door, every window.

Quietly, hesitatingly, it made its way to the back door and hovered
for achingly long minutes. It had heard so much, traveled so far. Hope
tried to spring in its breast, but decades of harsh experience beat hope
soundly back. This time, it was sure, would be no different. The
rumors, it was sure, were true for others but not for him. Never could
kindness exist for an abomination such as he. He began to turn away,
to slink back to his pointless and endless wanderings before turning
abruptly and rapping on the kitchen door. Hope, it turned out,
was bloodied but not yet annihilated. He crouched.

A bit of a bustle and then the door swung open to reveal a tall
raven-haired woman.

"Emily, lass," Tabby called from her chair, "Who's it treck'n rahnd
a' this hour?"

Emily Brontë, eyes widened with surprise at the hulking form
before her, kept her composure, for she recognized and cared deeply
for every wounded animal that crossed her path and the cringing giant
before her showed unmistakable signs of long neglect. Long grey hair
that still retained some sign of its former blackness hung lank alongside
his shriveled complexion, watery eyes, and black lips. Yellow skin
tautly covered his form, which was clothed in an odd assortment of

rags, regular-sized clothing being far too small for the well-proportioned eight-foot human-ish thing.

She greeted the creature with a nod and a kindly "Good evening. How can I assist you, sir?"

Tears spring to the creature's eyes and he covered his face with outsized hands, fighting to control the sobs that threatened to wrack his body for all eternity.

"Sir...," he muttered with a voice scraped from the very bottom of the quarry at Penistone Hill, "You called me sir..."

"Indeed I did." she affirmed, beginning to suspect that the singular shape before her had sprung straight from the pages of fiction, impossible though it seemed, "It is an honor to have you here." Emily Brontë glared straight at Tabby with a meaningful look and said, pointedly, "Tabby, I would like you to prepare yourself to meet my new friend. At first glance I believed it to be Adam Hinchliffe, but if I am correct, it is someone I read about many years ago. Please welcome Mister...." Here she paused, beckoning him to enter the house, unable to recall a Christian name for the being at the door.

"You are far too kind to such a miserable wretch as myself," the creation sniffed. As he stepped inside, becoming fully visible in the kitchen's candlelight, Tabby muffled a quick scream, her initial horror-struck response at his startling appearance mitigated by Emily's timely forewarning. Two years prior, good Adam Hinchliffe had been hideously mutilated in a mill accident and survived yet to limp and drag his malformed body along the streets of Haworth, but this! This was far worse than the deformed face and figure of the hardworking townsman.

"Hsst!" Tabby motioned Emily to her, "Ye canna allow that ghastly thing inta th'house! The Reverend ud just a'soon have gytrash in his kitchun!"

"Hush yourself!" Emily commanded in an urgent whisper, "He will hear you! Papa could just as well quote Hebrews and say "Do not neglect to show hospitality to strangers, for thereby some have entertained angels unawares."

Tabby sniffed derisively, "That, o'er there?! Some Angel!"

"Well, even if he were gytrash I would not send him away. There is something in his eyes that begs for care and comfort and I say we are the ones to provide it. Besides, who are you to pass up the chance to be part of a new legend to tell by the fireside?" And with that, the tall girl turned her attention back to her hideous guest.

Head ducked, the giant shuffled in embarrassment, never having been welcomed into company before in all the years of his wretched existence. Hesitantly made his request, the elegant phrases he had practiced over and over again in his mind failing him completely, "I....I wonder if I....I have heard such things about...," then blurting abruptly, "Is the Reverend Brontë available? I should very much like to speak with him."

Emily gave a small curtsey, saying "Just a moment, let me see if he is free to see you."

This was just like a play worthy of Glass Town and Gondal and all the rest! Emily popped her head into her father's study and quickly explained the situation with no equivocation. Odd and absurd as her statements seemed, Reverend Patrick Brontë took it all in stride. His many years as counselor and advisor to his parishioners had exposed him to the unexpected so often the unconventional had ceased to be notable. All who came to confer with him were children of God; this extraordinary giant who came to fill his study was no exception.

The creature's moments spent silently fidgeting in the kitchen with an astounded Tabby had brought some semblance of composure back into his battered heart; composure he nearly lost completely at Reverend Brontë's first welcoming words.

"Good morning, my child. I understand you wished to see me?"

"Ah, good sir," the creature shook his head in despair, "That is my greatest woe, my most heinous curse. I am not now and never have been a child. Once you know my story you will never again call me child. I am the sole being living on this earth who has never been a child."

Reverend Brontë nodded, "My daughter's suspicions are correct, then? You are the creation of Victor Frankenstein whom most would call a monster? If so, I am familiar with your story as told in the novel *Frankenstein*, provided Mrs. Shelley's account is true to your experience. You see, we are a well-read family in this house."

"Yes," the creature nodded sadly, "It is true. All of it. I am that lamentable and despised being."

"Curious," Reverend Brontë stroked his chin thoughtfully, "If I recall correctly, the novel ends with your intention to head to the northernmost regions of the world and end your life in a self-made conflagration. The fact of your presence here this morning shows that particular detail to be fiction rather than fact."

"Oh! How I longed to end my life of loneliness and torment! But I could not..." the giant buried his face in his hands, "...I could not. Suicide cannot be a sin for one such as I, one who should never have seen life, but I – I who have found life to be anything but precious – I discovered that I could not be the instrument of my own end."

Full knowing the value of silence, Patrick reached a hand forward to rest upon the giant's shoulder waiting a full five heartbeats before asking gently, "And what has your life been these many long years since the last pages of the novel?"

The creature drew a long shuddering breath and raised his face to look into the nearsighted eyes of his counselor, "At first I did not know how to live without my creator trailing me with plans for my death and destruction in his heart, plans which sorely afflicted his brain. It had become a kind of game with me. A game of watching out for him, of caring for him. It gave me purpose. Without him," he spread his hands expressively, emptily, "I had no life. Neither did I know how I could live with myself. Contrary to my true nature, I had been the monster, the..." he paused to whisper, "murderer, he desired – no, demanded – that I be. I had destroyed his brother, his friend, his beloved with these, my own hands. I had caused his father to die of grief. I even caused my creator, himself, to teeter on the edge of sanity well before his own death.

"What life could I have? I, who am loved by no man, befriended by none, welcome in no home, contributor to no society? Wracked with guilt and remorse I did what I could to absolve my conscience, to make amends and atone for my sins; if one such as I, created not by God but by man, can be held accountable to the same measure of sin as a man. I returned to Geneva, to the sole remaining member of the Frankenstein family and covertly devoted my life to his service.

"Working in the shadows, never seen throughout the decades, I ensured that Ernest Frankenstein was well cared for, well loved, well educated, well married, and well employed in managing his fortune. With well-placed whispers and surreptitious acts I made doors open for him that wiped away much of his grief. I changed the narrative of his family's downfall so that the lamentable deaths at my hand – deaths which had become warped in public opinion to be considered heinous acts of Victor Frankenstein and his deranged mind - are now believed to be the result of a strange, strangulating blood disorder. His proud lineage is assured for the future and he loves his many children as his true wealth. Ernest Frankenstein is as happy as a man can be and has no further need for my intervention.

Patrick adjusted his glasses on his nose and nodded, "I see. And what brings you to me?"

The creature sat up straighter and focused his swimming yellow eyes on the Reverend, "I have heard that you are a good man, a fair man, who does not rush to judgment, but considers well the realities and practicalities of each situation. I have heard that you are a well-educated man of deep thought and feeling. I want to know if there is hope for one such as I to live out my remaining years in a way that can bring peace to my heart. Have I any chance at forgiveness and joy? I, an abomination whose very life is an affront to God?"

Patrick smiled and said gently, "When I read your story years ago it gave me much to think on. God alone has the power to grant life to flesh. I feel certain that without God's agreement, your form could not have become animate, regardless of Victor Frankenstein's brilliance."

The creature started at these words and shook his head in disbelief, "But I have never been loved. Surely God would not agree to a life such as mine."

"I believe God had a purpose in allowing you to live. A purpose of emphasizing the importance of bringing needed boundaries of humanity and conscience to science. Because man *can* is not reason enough for the doing. Yet, it is not God who led to your neglect. That tragedy lies at the feet of Frankenstein alone."

"You blame him," the giant asked, "as he blamed himself, for my unwise creation?"

"I blame him for running away from his creation. Just as every parent is responsible for his child, so was Frankenstein responsible for you. Yes, there was a lesson for him to learn, but there was also a responsibility for him to shoulder. He failed you, wholly and completely."

The beast swallowed hard before asking the question that had plagued him his entire existence, "Why... why could he not love me?"

"Although I cannot know for certain, I do believe he realized at your first breath that you were always going to be discriminated against every moment of your life; that he allowed you to be birthed into the very situation which created that. You would grow to know he was the sole creator of your inevitable misery," the Reverend Brontë cleared his throat briefly, giving his snowy cravat a slight tug before continuing, "Truly, how can one cope with that? There is no coping. There is no intellectual way to make it right.

"Fortunately, God has not failed you. Your Heavenly Father is more willing to give His Holy Spirit to them that ask him than parents are to give good gifts to their children. Do not be afraid to ask for God's gifts. Do not be afraid to come to Jesus, for He says, 'Him that cometh unto Me, I will nowise cast out.' Ask Jesus to come into your heart and teach you, for 'He is exalted to give repentance and remission of sins' and if you ask Him, He will gladly give them to you. You have done well to do good acts on behalf of Ernest Frankenstein, but it is your relationship to God alone that has the power to give you the release of forgiveness and to fill your spirit with joy."

The creature nodded solemnly in answer to the Reverend's simple question, "Will you pray with me?"

The two sat in quiet peace, heads bowed and hands clasped together as Reverend Brontë murmured inspired words of humility and supplication, guiding the being whose great hands he held to the glory that exists for all who would accept it. As their heads rose after the final "Amen," a new glow appeared to light the giant's shriveled complexion.

"I would have spoken your name in our prayer," the Reverend confessed, "but I am afraid I don't recall it from the novel and I have rudely neglected to ask it. Pray tell me what is your name, friend?"

"Name? I have no name. As something that was never supposed to exist, I was never given a name. With Victor Frankenstein dead, who is there left to give me a name?"

A smile broadly creased Patrick Brontë's face as he spread his hands wide and announced, "You see here before you a man who began life as Padraig Brunty. We make our own names. Let us choose one for you now. I seem to recall there was a family who helped you learn speech and much more as you secretly observed them. What was their name?"

"De Lacey."

"It would seem to be a good surname for you, since they reared you, as it were. Is that acceptable?"

"...yesss" the being spoke slowly, thoughtfully, "The De Laceys denied me upon seeing my form and hurt me most terribly, but with the passage of time I have gained the wisdom to forgive them for destroying my dreams of happiness within their circle. Yes, the name that once caused me such pain is an acceptable surname now."

"And now for a first name. Is there any name you wish to be called?"

"For the span of my years spent in misery, I would choose the name Jonah."

"Bah! That is no fit name for you now. Your past is forgiven and you are made anew; your new name should reflect the promise of God.... Yes, of course! Matthew, Gift of God. That is a fit name for you, my friend."

A visible change seemed to come over the being as he felt himself being christened with the new identity being handed him.

"Matthew De Lacey...Matthew De Lacey... It is a good name, is it not? What can a man not do with such a name, despite the circumstances of his birth? What can a man not do with such a friend?"

And so the destitute of Haworth and its surroundings began to find wood chopped, water carried and gifts of food at their doors some mornings, as though a compassionate angel had appeared in the darkness of night to relieve their suffering. Patrick had an irregular and welcome evening visitor on moonless nights for long and thoughtful discussions. And Emily had a new friend and companion who could easily keep up with her long strides across the wild and remote places of the moors.

Matthew De Lacey lived quietly among the ruins of the Withens until the day Emily came upon his lifeless body, the strange, long-cursed gift of his creator finally drained from his form. They buried him where he lay, the dozen or so privileged souls who had come to know and love him, in a long and peaty grave; and as he lay, slowly becoming one with the earth through the benevolent actions of worm and beetle, Matthew finally achieved his lifelong goal and became embraced as part of the natural cycle of life.

Author's Note: Reading Mary Shelley's groundbreaking 1818 novel, Frankenstein, I was surprised to see how far pop culture has taken us away from the depths of her masterpiece. Pity.

An Angel by the Cradle illustration by JoJo Hughes

AN ANGEL BY THE CRADLE

by JoJo Hughes
Cornwall, UK

"Papa!" she called, "You must come here!"
Although she shook, she showed no fear
I leapt the stairs, two at a time.
She put her little hand in mine
And led me to the nursery room
Now darkening with evening's gloom
Her sweet, small face was full and bright
As though she'd just seen Heaven's light
"O dear Papa, it stood just there,
And placed its hand on Annie's hair!"
She said she thought a choir she heard
Though understood she not a word.
She told me then, with large grey eyes,
"An angel flew down from the skies!
St Michael sent one of his host
to bless that babe we love the most"

My children know I abhor lies
But this true avouch of her own eyes
Was wondrous strange
It made me weep
And though I must this secret keep
I never will forget, I pray,
My daughter's joy that gloaming day.

At Bridlington Beach illustration by EmilyInGondal

AT BRIDLINGTON BEACH

by Richard and Sally Sneddon
Harrogate, North Yorkshire, UK

High summer yet the wind was cold and malign, the moon hid in dark clouds. Seeking human warmth, I walked to the fun fair area by the harbour, seeking the flashing lights. Exchanging pleasantries, I bought some doughnuts and went down to the beach for a last look at the sea before going back to the guest house. The gloom was pierced by the flashes from the lighthouse across the bay, the tide in-coming.

Funny, I thought, these days a place for trippers, but in yesteryear so different. Fishing vessels drawn up on the beach, an American buccaneer sinking British vessels off the headland, U-boats slithering under the sea, serpent like, seeking for prey. I stared at the dark, advancing sea. This was also the location where in the nineteenth century Charlotte Bronte and her friend Ellen Nussey stayed on holiday. No funfairs then!

My reverie ceased, an object in the water attracted my attention. I stepped forward to see better. A body - I noted in disgusted fascination - strangely dressed as a sailor of long ago. Then I observed another bobbing in the sea. Then a whole number. I kept staring. Soon there were scores of bodies washed up where the tide meets the sand.

With sudden resolve I turned to leave the beach but my way was barred by a circle of bloated bodies, their eyeless, fish-chewed faces turned towards me.....

The Ghost That I Remember illustration by Nathalia Amorim

THE GHOST THAT I REMEMBER

Arthur Li
California, USA

The official 25th Reunion schedule says it's time to go to an expert alumni talk about machine learning, but instead I take a stroll across campus to visit my old dorm.

I peek into the windows of the dorm's dining hall, recently shuttered for the summer. I see the tables where we would gather to eat and share each other's company decades ago. All those lively and meaningful conversations over barely palatable college food.

I gaze at the red brick exterior façade, and the blue capped cupola rising from it toward the sky. I study the rows and rows of windows, looking for the one I remember.

A straggler student carrying boxes emerges from the front door, and I hold it open for him before sneaking inside. He's preoccupied with moving out and doesn't notice that I'm too paunchy and weathered to properly belong in the dormitory foyer. So before anyone has a chance to call campus security on me, I make a quiet dash for the room. Not my old room, but hers. The one she used to live in.

In front of her door, I take a breath, and knock. No answer. I fish in my pocket for the universal key card I stole from the reunion registration desk. I swipe the lock with it, and push through the door.

Her room is barren and vacant, emptied of all furnishings and ornaments.

I see the rusted coils of the radiator under the double hung windows. Next to the fireplace with the cracked tiled hearth. Unchanged for 25 years.

I step lightly across creaking wooden floors, and comfort my toes on her red Tibetan throw rug.

There's the Tori Amos and Kate Bush CDs, scattered on her dresser. The poster of Gustav Klimt's Golden Kiss on the wall. The black lacquered chair where she sits at her desk, tapping away at a boxy Macintosh keyboard, the curled ends of her long chestnut hair grazing the backs of her fingers.

I am on her couch, working through biostatistics problem sets while she types her English Literature senior thesis, the one about lone wandering women in Victorian England. Scribbled notes and heavily annotated maps are spread out across her desk.

"I've been thinking about the intersection between independence and desire in *Jane Eyre*," she tells me, during an evening study break. We are outside on the footbridge, three red brick arches stretching over the Charles River, across from the dorm. Our elbows lean against the stone railing. "My idea is that when independence and desire conflict, a long wandering ensues."

Her crimson wool scarf flaps in the crisp night wind and the silvery clouds glide swiftly across the black sky above us. The moon shimmers on the water flowing beneath us. The Boston skyline glows in the distance.

"When I was in England researching my thesis," she says, "I visited all the places, every manor, every church and school in the novel. I walked Jane's painful journey from Cowan Bridge School to the church in Tunstall. I went to Norton Conyers, an estate so old that it is listed in the Doomsday Book, and I paced around in the attic where the real madwoman had lived. I walked the moors in the rain at night for so many miles that I could barely stand anymore. I wondered if I'd have to build a nest in the grass for shelter until daybreak. I'd grown such a kinship to Charlotte. I felt I'd earned the right and authority to speak on her behalf."

Her youthful face is spirited and alive in the moonlight. Wide eyes and supple cheeks. Pale, silken skin with a little bit of peach fuzz.

"You are incredible," I say. "Do you think, after your adventures, that you will ever be the same again?"

"No, I never will," she says. "If wandering was always a whisper in my soul, it is now a living breathing force."

Back in her dorm room, we set a Duraflame wax starter log in the fire place and strike a match to light it ablaze. We lie down together on the red Tibetan rug and embrace, while the radiator clicks and hisses warmth into the room. The starry night screensaver flickers on her Macintosh.

"I want to be a Literature professor," she says. "But it's near impossible. Even the PhDs from the most prestigious schools can't find tenure track jobs." Her eyes flicker with the reflection of the fire light. "But English literature is the most beautiful thing I've ever come across. I will not give it up."

"I love your ambition, your courageous dreams," I say.

"That's sweet," she says, reaching over to hold my hand. "What about you, what are your dreams?"

"Oh, my dreams?" I say. "I just want to go to medical school and survive it. Eventually settle down with someone I love. Bounce a kid on my knee and read him Hans Christian Anderson." I pull in closer to her and lay my head on top of her chest. "When I feel down on myself, the thought of someday being a father gives me comfort." I feel her tighten her grip on my hand. "But those things are all so mundane, I guess."

"No, those are nice things," she says.

When dawn arrives, we hold each other in a sleep deprived haze in front of the double-hung windows while we watch the sun rise over the Charles.

"Everything is so perfect right now," I say.

* * *

I wake up alone on cold, bare hardwood planks. The rug is gone. The black chair and the desk are not here. The fireplace is scrubbed clean. The harsh daylight streaming through the windows makes me cover my eyes. My hip hurts and I need to pee. As I make my way to her bathroom, the thud of my feet echoes throughout her empty suite.

The sink faucet hardware in the bathroom looks new. I miss seeing her toothbrush and rolled up tube of toothpaste resting in the divot where the soap should be. I glance into the mirror above the sink. In my memories of her, she has not aged. Yet in the mirror I see my sagging face and the furrows in my brow, the pitted skin on my nose and the dark sunspots everywhere.

I glance down at my phone. There's a text from my wife saying that she loves me and hopes I'm enjoying catching up with old friends at the reunion. I must have been asleep and missed it. Seeking this room out, spending the night in it, feeling the presence of another even if while alone, feels wrong.

Before leaving the room, I notice a scrap of wrinkled paper peeking out from under the radiator. I reach in, grab it, and unfurl it. The paper is yellowed and faded, mostly blank except for a miniature portrait stamped at the top of the four Brontë siblings gathered around a table. The brother holds a rifle, while the sisters gaze solemnly in various directions. I suddenly remember. Her effusive letters she wrote to me during the summer between semesters when we were apart, in which she confessed her feelings for me, all of it handwritten on pages of the engraved Brontë stationery she had brought back from her trip to Haworth. She had scribbled "The Brontë Bunch" caption on the paper, with an arrow pointing to the tiny portrait of the siblings. Apparently, a renegade sheet from her stash had survived under the radiator all these years.

I carefully fold up the scrap and slip it into my pocket.

* * *

Breakfast service for reunion attendees across campus at Memorial Hall is just getting underway. In yesterday's clothes, with my hair uncombed, I go through the self-service food line and take my tray with scrambled eggs and toast to one of the long wooden tables. Only a handful of early rising alumni drift about the airy, walnut-paneled hall.

A former classmate pulls up a chair opposite me. "Michael," she says. "It's so good to see you."

I squint for a moment at this middle aged woman, then I remember she was a political science major in my dorm, a friend of a friend. "Frieda!" I say. "It's great to see you, too!"

We briefly go through the perfunctory reunion roll call, exchanging data on the number and ages of our kids, what our spouses do, our current home towns and jobs, being sure to say *congratulations,* or *that's so cool,* at the appropriate times.

When we have both finished giving our personal updates, we settle back down and enjoy a peaceful moment of silence.

"There are ghosts here," I say. "I think I was haunted by one last night."

"I know what you mean," she says.

"Really?" I say. "Didn't you marry your ghost?"

"Yes," she laughs. "But he doesn't much resemble anymore the ghost that I remember." She takes a sip of orange juice from her glass, then pauses. "We're actually in kind of a rough patch right now."

"I'm sorry to hear that," I say.

114

"It's really difficult being here," she says. "So many pleasant memories of our time here together. It reminds me how sheltered college love is, like in a bubble. Marriage really exposes you. It's longer and way harder. So many more moving parts that can wear out and break."

"Marriage can be tough," I say. "But I think trying to overcome the rough stretches together is what can make it stronger. Hopefully you two can work through it."

"I hope so," she says. "What about your ghost? What happened to her?"

"I'm not sure," I say. "She decided not to come to the reunion. And I haven't seen her since we broke up just before graduation."

"I remember your girlfriend," she says. "I remember she was sweet and quiet, and that she was very passionate about her work. She was the Brontë scholar, right? And you were the studious pre-med." She cuts up an apple and tosses it into her oatmeal. "You two were a really cute couple. Total opposites, but you seemed to fit well together."

I start to well up, tears forming in the corner of my eyes. "We were so different. She would've grown restless and bored with me. No way it would've worked out long term."

"Yet, even though you know that," she says, "her ghost still haunts you." She rests her elbows on the table and places her chin on the back of her folded hands. "When you make a meaningful connection like that, it's hard to forget."

"I know." I say. "What I need is an exorcism." I tear the pieces of crust off my toast and toss them onto the tray. "I think about my wife, whom I love dearly. I know my wife is at home right now, probably stressing out, cooking breakfast for our kids and getting ready to drive them to school before she goes to work. We've raised these children together, grown middle aged and overweight together, been through so much. My wife would be rightfully pissed if she knew I was here thinking about my ex whom I haven't seen in 25 years."

"Yes, it's so unfair, right?"

* * *

When the plane lands, and the bars on my phone alert me that I have service again, I text my wife to let her know I'm back in San Francisco. *Can't wait to see you*, she texts back. As the other passengers queue up in the aisle, I grab my suitcase from the overhead compartment. The line begins to trickle forward.

I see a flight attendant moving between the emptying seats, sticking her latex gloved hand into the seat pockets. She pulls out used plastic cups and wadded up napkins, and pitches them into the white garbage bag she is holding.

Before leaving my row, I reach into my pants pocket and extract the folded piece of salvaged stationery that I had rescued from under the radiator. I look at it one last time. Then I stuff the Brontë Bunch into the seat pocket in front of me, next to the safety instructions card. I set my rolling suitcase on the ground, step into the line, and exit the plane.

Do Not Leave Me In This Abyss, Where I Cannot Find You!

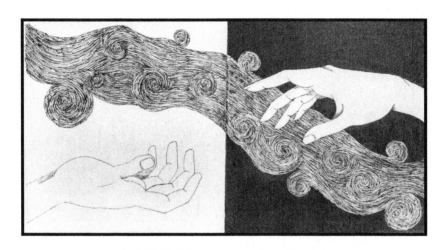

Reanimation illustration by Nathalia Amorim

REANIMATION

By Kay Fairhurst Adkins
California, USA

You would raise Branwell from the dead?
Please don't, he would not thank you
His pain so real, too much to feel
Please don't, he would not thank you.

You would bring Charlotte back to life?
Please don't, she would not like it
She's far too shy, her time's gone by
Please don't, she would not like it

You would bring back dear Emily?
Please don't, she's far too busy
Like wind, she's free, so let her be
Please don't, she's far too busy

You would lift Anne to live again?
Yes please, I hear her calling
Her heart rings true, there's work to do
Yes, please, I hear her calling

Footsteps at the Parsonage illustration by Rowan Coleman

FOOTSTEPS AT THE PARSONAGE

by Maria van Mastrigt
Netherlands

Late 1977 – It had been a long, pleasant summer, which was now steadily coming to an end. I had travelled to several very warm places this year and was now ready to come to the place of my dreams, the Brontë Parsonage Museum in Haworth, as I had been a fan of this family ever since my mother introduced me to their literature some ten years earlier. It felt very cold that morning as I had only just arrived from my journey to California a few days earlier, where I had stayed with some old English hippie friends of mine who now lived there.

I checked myself in at a B&B on West Lane. I cannot for the world remember which cottage it was, as it is so long ago, but it is probably no longer a B&B these days, as I'm sure the old woman who owned the place will most likely no longer be part of this life by now. The old lady kindly invited me to have a cup of tea with her, so I spent the first couple of hours in her cosy living room listening with great interest to all the local stories she could think of from the past, of course the Brontës being at the centre of all of them. She knew quite a few of the old locals who were grandsons and granddaughters of people who had known our beloved family and by gum, they knew a thing or two by the sounds of it.

The lady also told me that the Parsonage was now a haunted place and that there had been many sightings of the Brontës (presumably) in and about the place. People had seen unexplainable shadows or experienced sudden chills while working or visiting the Museum. Mysterious muddy footsteps in the hall and kitchen were once spotted by one of the employees when she opened the Museum in the morning, though this person was sure there weren't any the night before when she locked up and there had been no sign whatsoever that somebody had broken into the building.[x]

"It would be a wonderful place for a séance," my landlady said. She knew that somebody had once tried to organise such a meeting, but the curator at the time had not allowed it.[xx] Perhaps wisely so, even if out of respect for the dead. After our lovely chat I went up to my bedroom to unpack my rucksack and have a ten minute rest on my lovely clean bed, before I would go out on my first exploratory walk around the village.

My room was simple, but clean. There were no luxuries at all. I put my own little transistor radio, which had traveled the world with me, on the bedside table so I could listen to some music and the news as I always liked to stay informed about the goings on in the world, more than that I did not need. The bed was lovely and warm. I had not bothered to undress, as I felt so very tired and it would only be for a few minutes. Though as soon as I lay down I started to feel a bit drowsy and the last thing I remembered was that I wondered if there had been something in my tea? Before I knew it, I fell into a deep slumber.

After my little rest I came down and told the woman I was going out for a walk. She was sitting in her chair by the fireplace doing some knitting. "There's been a note for you come through the letterbox", she said. A note for me? That was very strange, as I knew nobody at all in this part of the world. She handed me the little envelope with my name written on it. I opened it and within was a little purple card with black letters saying nothing more and nothing less then the following words: 'You've been invited to come to the Brontë Parsonage tonight at 11 pm sharp'. Was this some kind of prank? I looked at the woman, but she just shrugged her shoulders and was clearly as puzzled about the mysterious note as I was.

I did go out for a little walk that afternoon, but my mind was not with it at all. I was just too preoccupied with the note. I did go up to the Museum to ask for an explanation, but unfortunately it had just closed and all had gone home by the time I reached the gate to the front garden. I went on for a short walk on the moors and I could feel the cool wind in my hair which was lovely and soothing, just what I needed that moment in time.

The evening came and from my bedroom I could hear people passing by on their way to the local pubs. I was just sitting on the bed staring at my note and wondering what to do. Who had invited me and why? The little purple card gave me an unsettled feeling. Was I scared? No, but maybe yes! Was I intrigued? For sure! Was I going out to the Museum at the time requested? Who knows...I mean yes, of course I was going out to the Museum. Too curious not to go and see what was behind all this.

It was time to go! I left the cottage. My landlady had already gone to bed and had given me a key to the door so I could let myself in and out as I pleased. There I was, making my way to the Museum, choosing to go via the church steps on Main Street and just as I reached the top of the steps I could hear the church bells strike eleven. It sounded so ominous, I could feel a shiver down my spine.

Pub goers were now leaving for home and it was quite busy around the Kings Arms, Black Bull and White Lion. That was quite pleasant for me as I felt I was not alone. However, that all changed as I was walking past the church onto Church Street. Suddenly, there was no one there. It was dark. The church looked very big now, black and eerie, and the graveyard just looked even worse, like graveyards tend to do, I supposed, but it gave me the creeps all the same.

A cold wind had struck up and occasionally I could hear the screeching of a crow living in the trees in the graveyard. I sensed some dark shadow rushing by at the side of me. I will never know what that was, if indeed it was anything, but it felt like the ghost of a dog or something similar. The word gytrash sprang to mind. In the not-so-far distance, I saw a shimmering light. Lo and behold...it was at the Parsonage!

There was a woman standing in the doorway, which was wide open. She was holding a lantern or a candle in her hand and she seemed to be waiting for someone to arrive. It was an elderly lady, dressed in an old long frock and apron of an era long gone. She looked kind enough and I didn't feel too scared as I finally reached her and she held up the lantern to my face to see who I was. I was going to introduce myself and wanted to shake hands, but as I was about to touch her she backed off. It only occurred to me then that she was not a real person at all but a ghost!

She spoke to me in a strong old fashioned Yorkshire accent which I wasn't familiar with at all, but I could make out that she told me that "they're all through there" and she turned around and showed me the way. Could this possibly be the ghost of Tabby?

I followed her in, wondering what was going to happen next? My body was shaking all over and I was thinking to myself 'this could be heaven or this could be hell!' She took me to the back of the house, to the kitchen and offered me a chair. The warm smell of freshly baked bread, roasted meat and vegetables was filling the room.

She asked me what I would like to drink and I answered that I wouldn't mind a glass of wine. "We haven't had that spirit here since 1849," she said and she gave me a glass with something that looked like water, but by Jove...I don't know what the hell it was, but water it was not! The woman summoned me to drink it all at once and so I did. It was very strong and it gave me a very warm feeling around my chest. My legs started to feel numb, my head grew heavy and my sight grew dim. All I can remember is that I could hear some voices coming from down the hall. I could hear a gentle voice calling, "Tabby, Tabby...where are you?" Laughter followed and a second voice, slightly heavier than the one before called for Tabby again, "Tabby come quick, the feast will be starting in Papa's room when the clock strikes twelve. Hurry up with the food and bring in our guest."

I could hear footsteps running up and down the stone steps of the hall and still those voices kept calling, now also joined by male voices, and I could hear a clock strike once which meant that it was now half past eleven.

I could not move. I was totally paralysed. Was it the drink, or was it my own fear? It was clear by now that I was the invited guest for a feast around the Brontë table, so to speak. Why...why was I there at all? I had been a fan of the Brontës for many years now, but this was weird. This was so very freaky that no one would ever believe me if I told them.

Then I could see out the corner of my eye that a small woman with a plain but gentle face and beautiful eyes was entering the kitchen. She spoke to me in a soft voice. "Don't be afraid" she said "we want you to join us as it is just so nice to have a guest around from another era to our own. We are all spirits now and you're still flesh and blood. We are all just prisoners here of our own device. The Parsonage is our home and you are welcome to stay with us in this lovely place."

She wanted to say more, but suddenly I managed to stand up and gave the woman one last look. She was, after all, Charlotte Brontë, my heroine! I loved her, but she was of another world to mine. Part of me wanted to stay, sure, but I also wanted to get the hell out of there. I wanted to say something kind to her, but I could not...my voice had given up on me. Last thing I remember, I was running for the door. I had to find the passage back to the place I was before.

Suddenly a shock! I opened my eyes and I woke up, I woke up in my bedroom at the B&B and I could hear my own little radio and the Eagles singing: "Relax said the nightman, we are programmed to receive, you can check out any time you like, but you can never leave."

Had it all been nothing but a bizarre dream? Part of me was relieved, but there was also some disappointment. That face, that face of Charlotte I will never forget to this day. It was there, so realistic, so strong. How could this have been a dream? I got up from the bed, my body still shaking. I reached for my walking boots as I thought it a good idea to go for a little stroll. Perhaps I should also put on a new

jumper as I noticed that the jumper I was still wearing smelt like...
freshly baked bread, roasted meat and vegetables?!

Here pause: pause at once. There's enough said. Trouble no quiet,
kind heart; leave sunny imaginations hope. Let it be theirs to conceive
the delight of joy born again fresh out of great terror. Let them picture
union and a happy succeeding [after] life. I leave it to you, the reader,
to decide whether this was a dream or a real event. Whatever you decide, let this story also be a warning to you, as one thing at least is so
totally true! Once you're smitten with this family, there's no way back!
You can check out any time you like, but you can never leave...nor
would we want to!

On that note I left my B&B and went for a long walk on the moors,
cool wind in my hair!

* * *

[x] *The story of the muddy footsteps is based on an allegedly true story.*

[xx]*Former curator Joanna Hutton had indeed once refused such a meeting.*

*With thanks to some of the words borrowed from that wonderful song
Hotel California by the Eagles.*

*With thanks to some of the final words borrowed from that wonderful
book Villette by Charlotte Brontë.*

Let Me In! Let Me In!
I'm Come Home

The Midnight Bride illustration by JoJo Hughes

MIDNIGHT BRIDE

By JoJo Hughes
Cornwall, UK

Who are you here in my dark room?
What shadow slides in midnight gloom?
What figure walks with dreadful creep
And tears me from my fitful sleep?
It's searching now
What does it see?
I do believe it is a she.
It's not Adele
Too thin for Grace
I have no wish to see her face.
She's reaching out
With dirty claw
To open up my dresser drawer.
She takes my veil
Like one to wed
She places it upon her head.
The moon shines full upon the gauze
And by the glass I watch her pause
The darkest eyes I see within
I hear the laugh
I see the grin
Her mist reflection darkens now
Those eyes are gone 'neath angry brow
Her breath it quickens
Her hands now shake
Can this be real?
Am I awake?
The woman growls in angry pain
And pulls the veil back off again
Her nails are long; it's ripped apart
(I'm sure she hears my pounding heart).
She stamps on it. I watch her stride
Towards my bed, this midnight bride.
She bends her face down close to me
And in her eyes the pain I see,
I smell her breath upon my cheek
I feel her spit, she tries to speak
And just as I begin to see
The darkness comes and swallows me.

A Butterfly in Winter illustration by Luna

A BUTTERFLY IN WINTER

by Luna
Lithuania

The sun was high up, everything around seemed to dazzle and sparkle. A small breeze played in the air and all seemed to dance and celebrate.

It was the middle of summer, the very zenith of light. Ellen Nussey walked hand in hand with Charlotte. They chatted about something, with Ellen's eyes gleaming mischievously. She prattled something about the sun shining so pleasantly, still she swore she could see three suns in the sky instead of just one.

-Oh, quit it- Charlotte playfully nudged her- you know my sisters' reluctance to talk about such matters. One of them especially.

They both looked back at Emily and Anne walking behind them. Anne was very interested in the view. Emily walked in her usual fashion, with her head cast down and her hands behind her.

-Doesn't Emily look a bit worse for wear? Or is it just an impression?

- Indeed, we are all a bit tired. Branwell is completely insufferable and then the fiasco with, well, the person I talked about in my letter. – She nervously glanced over her sisters.

- Did the esteemed George Smith send you more books? – Ellen playfully laughed.

Charlotte rolled her eyes, knowing Ellen would now have amusement for many years to come.

They found a lovely spot to rest, where they would be veiled by the shade and among the most beautiful heather. Green branches, jeweled with white, purple and pink were like the most expensive palace décor.

-What marvelous books appeared this season- Ellen was at it again- took me a few days of little sleep, till I finished them. All so different, but equally good.

Anne smiled shyly and cast her gaze down. Charlotte looked at Ellen with a quizzical expression. Emily just lay among the heather, with her hands supporting her head.

-You know I sent you my new one before going to London? - Anne whispered to Ellen. She nodded- Well, me and Emily had quite a discussion about it the other day.

-Oh? And what did she say

-We just talked about the nature of art. Should art serve some purpose? Or should art be just for art's sake? She saw no use in writing about what already is.

-And you?

-I'm afraid I saw no use in living only in her fantasy land. Isn't it selfish, when there is so much real suffering to be addressed? - Anne picked some springs of heather without thinking about it- What do you think, Miss Nussey?

-I believe I never thought about such things. I always believed in working to help our neighbor, but never really believed a world could be rid of all sufferings. An ability to read about better things has always been a great consolation.

Anne sighed and just shook her head.

Ellen forwarded those springs of heather that Anne picked to Emily, but to her surprise, Emily didn't even look; she just fixed her gaze on the clouds and looked at them with such eagerness, Ellen was sure she even forgot to blink.

-I'm glad I've read your book. Truly.

Emily now was scratching the ground with her foot- like many nervous people do.

-Ellen, please tell me, what is the use of writing about perishable worldly things, when you can gaze and see the immortal and endless?

-Because the earth is a reflection of heaven- Ellen said after thinking- Because we all have to work for the good of the neighbor. I remember the saying: earth is in turmoil, but heaven is still.

-I would like to bathe in the vast sea of heaven and forget, oh forget everything. To drink at the rich rivers and never thirst, to rest in the long sleep of dreams...-Emily sighed- wouldn't you sometimes?

-I believe I still have much to accomplish and so do you. Haven't you started that second book of yours? Because, Charlotte said... I probably shouldn't mention this to you- Ellen quickly caught herself, but Emily didn't seem to mind now. Even if Ellen shouted the name

Ellis Bell over those moors and valleys, she wasn't sure Emily would mind in this sort of mood.

Emily just shook her head.

-I have a strange dream still. To love in art. We love our creation as they are. Not to censure them to appear as they should be. Didn't they teach you in Sunday school that the love of Creator is unconditional? And such is his righteousness? Then why should your beliefs be measured by how you exclude people who don't measure up to your standards? Why should I be held immoral because I choose to walk with those creations of mine whom "your moral and polite society would shun"? I have a dream to depict both the Divine law and the sinner. I must admit, I failed to depict the law that much in my last...- she laughed- but there's still time. And anyway, isn't the Divine law reflected in one word?: love.

-Well, this speech seems rather hedonist and heretical...- Ellen didn't wish to go into details- you aren't God.

- But aren't we all *in* God? Don't we exist in God? And were we annihilated here on earth, we wouldn't be destroyed because we are all engraved in the eternal memory of God? Don't we mirror God in our ability to love? - She now was out of breath and buried her face in her knees.

-Look, look, - Emily gestured Ellen to take a look- The grass beneath your feet, the sun above your head. All is the law of Divine. He put both light and shadow on this earth, both sun and moon. It has suffering and joy all in perfect balance. Human beings are weak by nature, so they also need some guides to show the way, both sitting with them in dark nights and celebrating bright days. When I'm older or more mature, I will create balance between those two, I'm sure. Look, what a lovely little caterpillar, crawling through branches- she smiled. Then her gaze appeared tired again, more lifeless.

-But, you see, I'm not sure if I could... I'm too much of a coward to try a second time. The world and I never saw each other eye to eye and I have a difficulty expressing myself in all its limited ways. And don't say that I'm exceedingly brave, Nelly. You are all wrong about me. I mind what people say- She rested her head on Ellen's knees. – But I promise to write that book for you. I'll read it to you when you come. It would be a long story, I would gather all of my imaginary children...there will be more of them, mind you... but promise to come...

129

- I will try to come at Christmas. We will all be merry then, I'm sure.

Emily just nodded.

* * *

Ellen stood in her house and watched the snow fall. The whole month had been very cold and damp, with just one day more beautiful than the others. On the 19th the sun finally appeared in the sky more brightly, the air was clearer and more pleasurable. She remembered taking the walk that afternoon and wondering at how calm and peaceful it all was.

Now she remembered her promise to Emily to come and visit, but their family had been through much during the months leading from summer. Branwell had unexpectedly died, leaving all the family bereft. Charlotte had been ill, then Anne and Emily all had their share. She had just gotten Charlotte's letter saying that Emily doesn't appear to get better, but Charlotte was always one prone to hysterics, not like phlegmatic even-tempered Ellen.

So the promise had to be postponed until they all felt better. She just now sat at her desk to write a few words to Emily, herself, and she would add some treats, some cake. Ellen was sure they would all feel better afterwards.

Near her feet, her little niece was playing with her dolls. She appeared happy, chatting with someone very merrily.

-And how is the play going? - She asked her niece, winking.

-Very good. We now play with a lovely lady. We play a game of some woman tlaveling flom a dalk folest to a lovely castle.

-Well, every child your age should have an imaginary friend- Ellen laughed.

-She came just yestelday. I love my new fliend. She has good ideas how to play with dolls. Tomolow, she offeled to teach me how to make buttelflies flom papel, she loves butteflies. She said she nevel finished making them, but now she says she's happy thele ale always someone who'd finish.

Ellen laughed heartily, but was distracted by her maid coming in.

-A letter for you, Miss Nussey.

-Oh, I'm sure it's from Emily, I'll read it later.

-No, it's not, Miss. It's from Miss Charlotte again.

-Will you read it?

-*Dear Ellen,*

Emily suffers no more either from pain of weakness now. She will never suffer more in this world- She is gone after a short, hard conflict. - Ellen dropped her pen- She died on Tuesday, the very day I wrote to you...She has died in a time of promise- but it's God's will and the place where she is gone is better than that she has left.

Try to come- I never so much needed the consolation of a friend's presence...

With tears in her eyes, Ellen looked around the room. For a moment, it appeared to her that she caught a glimpse of Emily's bright eyes and a mischievous smile, but just shook her head and turning to Mary said,

-Please, find out when the earliest train to Keighley leaves.

-Oh, Miss, you cannot leave your family, it's Christmas soon...

In the murmur of their voices, the little girl lifted her eyes to the window and saw a butterfly flying, just near the window. Aunt Ellen always said that there can be no butterflies in winter, but this one landed just on the girl's nose as if greeting her and then flew up and up, as if searching for a warmer clime.

My Fingers Closed On The Fingers Of A Little, Ice-Cold Hand!

From M. Paul's Ghost to Lucy Snowe illustration by JoJo Hughes

FROM M. PAUL'S GHOST TO LUCY SNOWE

By Jessa Fabiano
Rhode Island, USA

The sea swallows our ship and fills my ears
with water from a time before birth.
Thunder pulverizes, deafens, silences,
and in silence I hear you turn pages of your book,
one I left on your bench,
one I placed with tenderness
with hope within my breast that
you might feel a caress of light
and not know darkness, pain, or fright.

You'll know my gentle ghost,
in the persistent rustle of your skirts,
in whispering leaves in spring,
and at night stars will shift and sigh,
as I furl my shadow into your small shape.
The summer breeze of my story will tickle your ears
in subtle crinkles as you turn, turn, pages.
Your fingers- oh such slender ladies in dance,
know me now without confines, revel in gossamer spirit.

Can you sense the pungent smoke of my cigar
curl a crown around your hair?
On your hard seat, you wearily wait,
drop your head into your arms,
weep and wonder if my lips will grace your knuckles again,
or if death's devilish grip choked our chance at dance.
You would not deign gift flowers for a living friend,
allow not now plump, dewy blooms to linger
over chilly vaults, no matter how sunny the day,
no matter how lusty the waxing, gibbous moon.

Shall I disclose my innermost secret?
My heart beat an entire life seeing you high colored and proud,
dressed in crimson (pink pink, you say!),
admiring art without shame,
how I longed to hear you cry my Christian name,
to feel a tremble in your arms
as my lips assured you protection from mortal harm.

In love, I drown and fly to you,
I vow sweet things, taunts and teases,
and learn my final lesson,
the lightness of bodies born on saltwater,
adrift on sanctity of movement without music.
As ears and eyes close,
we find freedom to love in deepest repose.

The Walk Around The Table illustration
by Holly May Walker Dunseith

THE WALK AROUND THE TABLE

by Holly May Walker-Dunseith
Todmorden, West Yorkshire, England

Holly May Walker-Dunseith BA(Hons), MA, PGCE (Distinction), QTS is an English Literature PhD candidate at University College Cork in Ireland. She has also achieved a Masters Degree in Gaelic Literature from University College Cork, and is a published author and poet. She holds a PGCE with QTS, and is a fully qualified teacher of English for both GCSE and A Level education. She completed her BA(Honours) English Language and Literature degree at the University of Leeds. Her professional memberships include The Brontë Society and the British Association of Irish Studies.

In the nineteenth century, Holly's family lived in Thornton (Yorkshire) at the same time as the Brontë family. Her fifth great grandad, Thomas Thornton, was born in Thornton on the 1st March 1798. Her fifth great grandma was called Ellen Bradley, and she was also born in Thornton on the 25th March 1801. Thomas and Ellen married each other on the 18th May 1820. Email: hmwd@outlook.com.

ROUND ONE

In our home, on Yorkshire ground,
We walk around, and round, and round,
Our table that we all can see,
I, Charlotte, and my sisters three.
We've walked this walk many a time,
To give our hearts a beat and our tongues a rhyme,
We've marched around here many a mile,
It will be a while, it will be a while,
Before we again sit and write some more,
And our father comes to open the door,
To remind us of the hour late,
Our minds will therefore have to wait,
Until tomorrow morning or afternoon,
When we can again return to this very room,
Where our three hearts beat as one,
And life's troubles feel as though they are gone.
About our ideas we then talk,
And resume our daily walk.

ROUND TWO

But this is no ordinary table,
It is used to create many a fable,
On this surface we all write,
And walk a circle every single night.
No matter where we are in life's fight,
We always return right here to write,
And all of a sudden there is a light,
Shining from the darkness of the cold graves below,
Just outside our dining room window,
I wonder, do the walking souls out there,
Watch us as we walk, oh do they glare?
Through the window at our stroll
But we again hear our clock's strong toll,
Our quills' ink now must dry,
And to our work we say goodbye,
Until the next chapter, and the next day
And for many years it carries on this way.

ROUND THREE

Today, I walk in front; we are aligned
In a circle for our traditional walk,
Emily and Anne standing behind,
And then to them I talk:
"Sisters, we walk every day the same,
To inspire our special writing,
One day, we may rise to fame,
Our words may come out fighting.
I hope my *Villette* and *Jane Eyre* see famous sights,
Anne, your *Tenant of Wildfell Hall,*
And Emily, your *Wuthering Heights,*
And we could all print the tales of Gondal,
We could even publish our poetry when,
We write as women, but print as men,
Currer, Ellis, and Acton are we three,
Ellis and Acton for you two, and Currer for me.

And this we all three achieved,
Our printed novels lay on the table before me – bereaved,
As I sit now, oh so very grieved,
For my two sisters have from this world departed,
Leaving me to walk heavy hearted
Around our table that still stands here,
It has witnessed our happiness; it has seen our fear
We have walked around this table in flesh at most,
But we will walk round this table in the form of a ghost,
Our souls, our spirits, we three ghosts in death,
Walk around the table with stories in our breath.
And, oh look! We *are* being watched! Oh sisters three!
Not by the ghosts, but by faces of glee,
That look at our table, in our museum of a home,
Our writing must have walked to a fame known,
I did not know that as we walked around the table,
And in a circle whirled
That many hearts would read our fable
And our writing would walk around the world.

The Soldiers illustration by Holly May Walker Dunseith

THE SOLDIERS

by Holly May Walker-Dunseith
Todmorden, West Yorkshire, England

Twelve soldiers have marched in from the city,
From our father's trip to Leeds,
We create stories that are witty,
About captains, and generals, and steeds,
And now we must choose a soldier each,
To fight in battle and also to reach
Our newspaper headlines that tell of wartime glories,
The soldiers will also feature in our stories,
Written in little books with tiny writing,
About how those twelve soldiers are fighting.

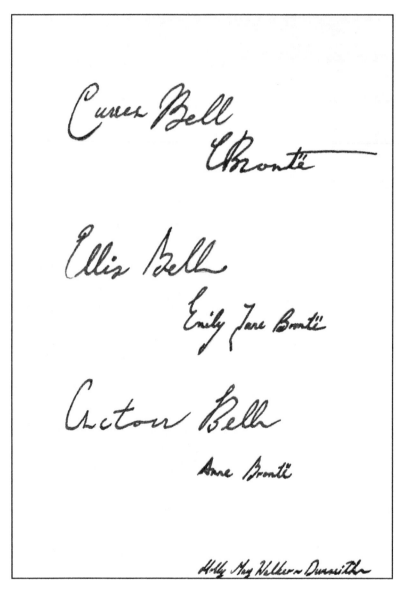

The Pseudonyms illustration by Holly May Walker Dunseith

THE PSEUDONYMS

by Holly May Walker-Dunseith
Todmorden, West Yorkshire, England

Back in the 1800s, in a world of men,
Women could not publish, only when
They hid their names under a façade,
Using pseudonyms as a mask to guard

Against the prejudice of the contemporary day,
Yet the Brontë sisters found a way,
To make their strong voices heard,
And to share their literary word.

For a time, Charlotte wrote as Currer Bell,
Emily as Ellis, and Acton for Anne,
Until it was time to tell,
That the three names usually given to a man,
Were three sisters who,
To themselves stayed true,
So that Bell could be Brontë again
And they could write as women, and not as men.

On Elizabeth Gaskell's visit to the
Brontë Parsonage in Haworth in
September 1853, Martha Brown stated:

'For as long as I can remember ~ Tabby says
since they were little bairns, Miss Brontë
& Miss Emily & Miss Anne used to put
away their sewing after prayers, & walk
all three one after the other round the
table in the parlour till near eleven o'
clock. Miss Emily walked on as long as
she could; & when she died Miss Anne
& Miss Brontë took it up, — and now my
heart aches to hear Miss Brontë
walking, walking on alone'.

HOLLY MAY WALKER-DUNSEITH.

The Brontë Table: A Ghost Story illustration by Holly May Walker Dunseith

142

THE BRONTË TABLE: A GHOST STORY

by Holly May Walker-Dunseith
Todmorden, West Yorkshire, England

A table. I suppose that is all that I am. Yet, not many tables have witnessed the supernatural, and still experience the paranormal realms. Indeed, my role in the Brontë family's life is sometimes forgotten. I belong to that wonderful family. In fact, I still remain in their dining room, following my return in 2015. Unfortunately, Patrick Brontë died in 1861, and I dearly miss him as well as the Brontë siblings. Patrick was the last surviving Brontë family member, and it was after his death that the family's possessions were then sold on and therefore taken away from the Parsonage home.

Yes, I have been away from Haworth for one hundred and fifty-four years, and I never thought that I would see this place ever again. I had given up and relinquished all hope of return. Following on from the dispersion of the Brontë's household items, I was passed down through the generations of a different family. Undoubtedly, I was looked after well, and I visited the Parsonage again in 1997 in order to celebrate both Charlotte Brontë's *Jane Eyre* and Emily Brontë's *Wuthering Heights*, which had been published one hundred and fifty years since. Of course, I had never forgotten where I came from. As soon as I resumed my rightful place, a cascade of memories flooded back and fresh feelings of nostalgia were suddenly present. In 2015, the Brontë Society was successful at an auction, and I was brought back to my home.

Amazing! Emily must have felt this way when she returned home from Brussels. My heart is at home also, and time spent away from Haworth has confirmed this contention. Now, at this moment, I sit in the Brontë's dining room, expecting the sisters to walk in through the door at any minute.

The dining room! Ultimately, it was heaven for the Brontë sisters. Although the room is very accurately replicated in modern times, I will describe what I remember from the nineteenth century. There was a black couch that stood next to the wall at the right-hand side of the room. Books of differing magnitudes covered the adjacent back wall and filled the shelves that were lined up next to a marble fireplace that was situated at the centre of the wall. This fireplace carries beautiful, aesthetic ornaments, and is responsible for ensuring that the room is light and warm. Without doubt, the Parsonage was almost always freezing, especially in the winter. The floor was made of stone and felt like ice. The Brontë sisters would always have to wear their tiny shoes and warm shawls. Otherwise, they were at risk of catching cold that could turn into pneumonia. The sisters always took great care of themselves and each other. After all, they were not distant from grief, or bereavement, or the effects of ill health. Their mother was called Maria Brontë, and she died from cancer in 1821. Their eldest siblings, Maria and Elizabeth, died due to consumption (tuberculosis) in 1825. Therefore, the remaining siblings were fully aware of the futility and fragility of human life.

Directly beside the fireplace, on either side of the back wall, there were two miniscule mahogany tables that held little books, candles, and teacups and saucers. The candlelight accompanied the illustrious light that emanated from the fire and would guide the sisters' eyesight. Poor Charlotte was often concerned about her eyes,[1] and she always placed her tiny glasses beside her wooden, portable desk. On this desk, there was an inkwell, a feather quill, and paper that contained Charlotte's beautiful, decorative, and calligraphic handwriting. I carried Charlotte's writing desk – her beloved possession – on my grand, mahogany surface. Indeed, I carried more than their possessions. I shared their burdens, their emotions, and I listened to their genius ideas and fascinating conversations. I, being their table, carried their books, their manuscripts, their sewing material, their paintbrushes, their cutlery, their inkwells, and their quills. It was an honour, and I enjoyed the time that I spent with them even though I was always the observer in the room – the silent table.

As I was located at the heart of the dining room, I could oversee the view from the window, which constituted an array of graves. Indeed, the Parsonage was situated next to a graveyard; it was a constant reminder of death... a constant reminder to live whilst we have the chance. Hauntingly and eerily, nighttime at the Parsonage could be summarised in three words: supernatural, preternatural, and paranormal.

Enchanted and enthralled by their writing, the sisters would work as late as possible into the evening. However, when the hour grew too late, Patrick would remind them to get some sleep in order to maintain their health. His entrance into the dining room would coincide with

---

[1] Elizabeth Gaskell, *The Life of Charlotte Brontë*, 2 vols (London: Smith, Elder, and Co., 1857), I, p. 322.

the heavy chiming from the substantial grandfather clock that lived just above the first flight of stairs.

Following this, I would be left alone. Until the next day, no more would the sisters walk around the table and recite their great works. The works that would one day walk farther than their circular route and pilgrimage around the dining room. In complete solitude and loneliness, similar to the feeling that exists now that they have left this world (and therefore this dining room as well), I now sit in the darkness. The fire is no longer brightly burning, and the candle flames are no longer jumping and dancing with life. They are extinguished for this moment; but that does not mean that they will not shine again... perhaps they will shine even more brightly when they are lit again tomorrow evening. It was the absence of light, as well as the overwhelming darkness, that characterised the night hours here at the Parsonage.

The only source of light was the reflection from the moon that loomed above the church facing the graveyard. It was incredibly clear that this graveyard was not at rest, but restless. Emily must have noticed this as well, because the resolution to her Bildungsroman novel, Wuthering Heights, encapsulates this experience perfectly: Lockwood 'wondered how anyone could ever imagine unquiet slumbers, for the sleepers in that quiet earth'.2 This was not the only feature that inspired the hearts and minds of the sisters that would write the world into their novels. As expected in the northern town of Haworth, the weather consisted of rain, wind, and a damp atmosphere. Nevertheless, at exactly twelve o'clock every night, at exactly when the

---

2 Emily Brontë, *Wuthering Heights*, ed. by Paul Nestor (London: Penguin, 2003), p. 337.
3 Emily Brontë, *Wuthering Heights*, ed. by Paul Nestor (London: Penguin, 2003), p. 25.
4 Holly May Walker-Dunseith, 'Reason forbids, but passion urges strongly' (*The Tenant of Wildfell Hall*): The Relationship between Passion and Violence in *Wuthering Heights* and *The Tenant of Wildfell Hall*', *Ad Alta: The Birmingham Journal of Literature*, 11 (2019), 51-60 (p. 52) <https://www.birmingham.ac.uk/Documents/college-artslaw/english/ad-alta/AdAlta-Volume-XI-Communities.pdf> [accessed 15 July 2020].

old day would pass into a new day; there was always an event that could not be explained in rational terms.

Trees surrounded the Parsonage, and their branches were wild and unruly. They would hit the latticed windows of the house, as if they were knocking on the window in order to demand entrance into the Parsonage. Does this sound familiar? Of course, this is again reminiscent of Wuthering Heights. In Chapter Three, 'the branch of a fir-tree' that hit the window becomes a supernatural phenomenon or dream in which Cathy creates a sound at the window in order for Lockwood to 'let [her] in!' to Wuthering Heights.3 Emily engineered her supernatural character, Cathy's ghost, to walk on the earth in death with lost dreams that were unattained and unfulfilled in human life ('to return to Wuthering Heights').4 What if there are souls that walk the earth in a ghostly form instead of a human form? I hope that the Brontë family are happy and at peace. Not a day goes by when they are not in my thoughts.

When morning arrived, I would look forward to them running into the dining room and conversing about their narratives over their breakfast. Every day, the three sisters would sit down and resume their work: Charlotte, Emily, and Anne Brontë. Of course, they had other commitments, too. They had housework to attend to, and they often baked beautiful, fresh bread that would fill the house with the smell of home. Also, they often worked at the village school, where they would use their outstanding and exceptional knowledge to teach the next generation. Although they were very good at teaching, their hearts longed to return to their writing. The best moment was when their work had been published, and their writing therefore had an opportunity to walk into the world. Both *Jane Eyre* and *Wuthering Height* were published in 1847. Charlotte's *Jane Eyre* was released into print on the 16th October 1847, and Emily's publication date for *Wuthering Heights* was in December 1847. Anne's *The Tenant of Wildfell Hall* was published in June 1848.

On these publication days, and also when they discovered that they were all going to become published authors, they danced across the dining room in celebration and continued to recite their now published creations that were soon to be transformed into printed editions.

Every morning, the three sisters would walk around the dining room, and it carried on this way for many years. The first death that entered both the Parsonage and the conversation in the dining room was Branwell Brontë, who died on the 24th September 1848. Not only did I carry the abundant amount of papers that the sisters had been writing upon, I also carried their tears that day and for many days to come. A few months later, it was almost Christmas, but it was not the Christmas time that usually took place here at the Parsonage. The sisters did not happily paint or write at this time and, when they did resume their creations, it was with life's pain. This was a wound that would undoubtedly influence their great works and would make the feelings that they described even more poignant. Although Christmas is a time for celebrating the birth of Jesus Christ, and the tradition of giving and receiving gifts, this Christmas was very different for the Brontë family.

Although they were given gifts, their main gift was taken away from them that year. On the 19th December 1848, Emily was collapsed on the couch in the dining room.[5] Emily's fatal illness began back in early October 1848, which was approximately seven days after the funeral of Branwell. She had been suffering for some time, and she was denying medical help. Of course, Patrick and the sisters ensured that she received some medical attention, and they arranged a visit from a doctor in order to help her. However, at two o'clock that day, Emily died from consumption (tuberculosis). Leaving her two remaining sisters on this earth, Emily departed into the afterlife. I missed Emily's presence and her writing. She had carved a letter into my mahogany, shiny surface: 'E' for Emily. I could never forget her, even if she had not carved her initial in this permanent way.

On the 24th May 1849, Charlotte and Anne departed to the seaside town of Scarborough with Ellen Nussey. Prior to this, just like Branwell and Emily, Anne had fallen ill and the doctor told her that sea air may aid her health and breathing. I waited at home for their return. No one walked around the dining room. No one recited their stories. No one spilt ink on me, or accidently dropped the candle again, causing a burn mark to blemish the polished, mahogany surface. The room was empty; the room was lonely.

BANG! The Parsonage door opened and shut in a moment. The noise was quiet yet loud at the same time, yet the feeling of loudness came from the meaning that was carried through the sound of the closing door. Indeed, it symbolised a closed door in a metaphorical sense. I was expecting both Charlotte and Anne to walk into the dining room. Perhaps they would invite Ellen Nussey into the house for a cup

[5] Agnes Mary Frances Robinson, *Emily Brontë* (Boston: Roberts Brothers, 1883), p. 308.

of tea? However, Charlotte walked into the room alone, and tears were falling from her eyes. At once, I knew what had happened to Anne, and I knew that she would not be returning to the Parsonage in human form. It was clear that Charlotte was now the only remaining sibling. She sat down and began to write in her diary and, simultaneously, she spoke her words out loud. I could hear that Anne had died from consumption (tuberculosis) on the 28th May 1849 and, like Emily, she also died at two o'clock. Anne instructed Charlotte to have courage,[6] and I knew that Charlotte would honour this advice.

The courageous Charlotte continued to write... alone. It was not the same; she could not ask her sisters for their opinion on her work, nor could she walk around the dining room with them anymore.

Alone.

Alone.

Alone.

Charlotte continued to write in a ghostly solitude.

Here, each of these abstract nouns – 'alone' – represents a Brontë sibling, and the longer sentence mirrors how Charlotte still lived on in the human world.

However, the sentence of Charlotte's life also began to grow shorter, and led to me being left alone again...

On the 31st March 1855, Charlotte was taken away from this world. I heard that her cause of death was consumption (tuberculosis) and perhaps typhoid fever. However, since then, it has been suggested that she died from hyperemesis gravidarum. Her child, as yet unborn, also died on this day. Patrick was therefore the longest surviving Brontë family member. He died on the 7th June 1861. After Patrick's death, Charlotte's widowed husband - Arthur Bell Nicholls - travelled back to Banagher (County Offaly) in 1861. Alone.

Alone.

Alone.

Alone.

Alone.

[6] Elizabeth Gaskell, *The Life of Charlotte Brontë*, 2 vols (London: Smith, Elder, and Co., 1857), II, p. 109.

Alone.

Yet, I was never alone.

The Brontë family lived on in more ways than one.

Firstly, not only did their books walk around the dining room; they walked around the world. The family are famous. Although I, myself, lived away for a while, I returned home to the Parsonage. Furthermore... the day that I returned, the Brontë family welcomed me back into their dining room. Yes, that's right. They were ghosts, and they were all completely happy and at perfect peace. They were all there: Patrick, Maria (mother), Maria (daughter), Elizabeth, Charlotte, Branwell, Emily, Anne, and Arthur Bell Nicholls. Charlotte held her baby in her arms... the genius that was never born. These wonderful ghosts accompany me, as I remain in the human world, as an onlooker, observer, and communicator of the supernatural.

Secondly, people visit the Parsonage every day, and they are readers of the Brontë novels. The house is now a landmark; a landmark that people visit from all around the world. The family are so very pleased with the legacy that they have left, and they bestow happiness on every visitor that walks through the door.

Indeed, their writing walked around the world, and their ghosts again walk around the table. I am never alone.

List of References

Brontë, Emily, *Wuthering Heights*, ed. by Paul Nestor (London: Penguin, 2003)

Gaskell, Elizabeth, *The Life of Charlotte Brontë*, 2 vols (London: Smith, Elder, and Co., 1857), I

The Life of Charlotte Brontë, 2 vols (London: Smith, Elder, and Co., 1857), II

Robinson, Agnes Mary Frances, *Emily Brontë* (Boston: Roberts Brothers, 1883)

Walker-Dunseith, Holly May, 'Reason forbids, but passion urges strongly' (*The Tenant of Wildfell Hall*): The Relationship between Passion and Violence in *Wuthering Heights* and *The Tenant of Wildfell Hall*, Ad Alta: The Birmingham Journal of Literature, 11 (2019), 51-60 <https://www.birmingham.ac.uk/Documents/college-artslaw/english/ad-alta/AdAlta-Volume-XI-Communities.pdf> [accessed 15 July 2020].

The Most Haunted illustration by Debs Green -Jones

THE MOST HAUNTED

By E A France-Sergeant
Wigan, England

Most Haunted, I watch it all
Ghost at the window
Scratching on the wall
The wailing of the banshee call
Is this a ghost or are you crazy?
Did you really see the white lady?
Footsteps on the stairs when there's no one there.
Who's that rocking in the rocking chair?
Heathcliff and Cathy on the moors do walk.
A little girl who likes to talk,
At the Black Bull you won't find a screaming skull.
There is more body then spirit there
Is Branwell sitting in his favourite chair?
Bell ringing when there's no one there.
Walk the church yard at night,
It gave the Most Haunted team a proper fright
So go to Haworth if you dare
And give yourself a proper scare
So I send you this poem for all to share
If you see a ghost, please don't stare
For it's only the people of Haworth.
Who have always been there

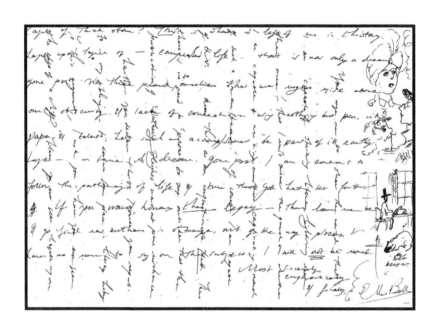

What If? Illustration by Emily Ross

WHAT IF?

by Kay Fairhurst Adkins
Palm Springs, California, USA

Thomas Cautley Newby, Publisher

30th June, 1850

My Dear Mr. Newby,

I am in receipt of your letter of the 18th, your letter of the 11th and your letter of the 3rd, as well as the dozen or so letters prior and I must sincerely tell you that this is the first and last communication you can expect from me. I have no interest or intent to allow for a re-publication of Wuthering Heights, Agnes Grey, Tenant of Wildfell Hall, or Jane Eyre at this time or any future time.

Your arguments in favor of publication are many and varied, yet I tell you plainly, each argument is invalid so far as concerns me, and as I am the only surviving Bell sibling and thus, the holder of all copy-rights, my word is final. Your many pleading words tell me that you yearn to overlook my plain speech and dismiss me as an emotional and changeable creature so I will address your tiresome pleas to reinforce the steel of my unwavering point.

You tell me the public clamors for more from the Bells. Do those who claimed us to be "coarse and disagreeable", "wild, confused, disjointed, and improbable", "a compound of vulgar depravity and unnatural horrors" clamor for more? Do they wish to feel again as if they have "come fresh from a pest house"? Let us spare them that, clamor though they might. It is none of my concern. I reply that the Bells are no more, so there can be no more from the Bells.

You insist that the volumes will sell extremely well, bringing me wealth beyond imagining. I say that the original publications sold extremely well, leaving me with all I will ever need. You dangle fame and travel before me. I have no use for either. In point of fact, the very idea of traveling to far flung places in order to be fawned over by people I neither know nor care about repels me. I can imagine no proposal more noxious and insipid.

You urge me to show the world I am capable of striking literary lightning more than once - that I must answer the question whether I

153

am capable of writing another captivating novel of such rare breed. Of course I am capable of this. I know this as an unquestionable truth, thus there is no need to prove to any outsider that the publication of Wuthering Heights was not pure mischance.

Lastly, you declare that I owe this republication to my siblings to ensure their place in literary history. To this argument, I ask you, have you ever seen the edge of a cliff? Have you ever seen layer upon layer of thick stone? This is what is left of us in history. Layer upon layer of compressed life that is only a dream gone past. We three proved to ourselves that we could rise above our obscurity and lack of connections using nothing but pen, ink, paper, and talent. Let our accomplishment be part of its earthly layer in time. A dream gone past. I am content to follow the pathways of life and time that God has set forth.

If you would honor their legacy, then leave me be and go find new authors in strange, out of the way places. I have no more to say on the subject and I will NOT be moved.

Most sincerely, emphatically, and finally,

Ellis Bell

Emily sat back and admired her signature, blotting carefully before folding and addressing her letter so it would be ready for the morning's post and free from prying eyes, an outdated force of habit since there were few eyes about anymore to do any prying.

Keeper, stiff and grey, sighed from his place on the rug by the fire. Emily rose from her writing desk to kneel and rub his ears. Flossy, alert and watchful from her place on the sofa – the exact spot where she had often sat on dear Anne's lap – hopped down to keep Emily's other hand occupied in the silkiness of floppy ears.

"Good old friends," Emily said with a smile, "I'm so glad you're here."

It had been so very difficult at the beginning, first losing Branwell to his own tragic downfall, then Charlotte, her weakness from grief and heartache opening the door to insidious infection, then finally little Anne fading gently away, her warrior soul no match for her consumptive body. It still seemed odd on wash day to have no blood stains to scrub out of the handkerchiefs. Only Emily had remained strong though it all.

Then, only Emily remained.

The last remaining Brontë sibling stood up and stretched. With no need to observe propriety, she scratched an itch or two before beginning her slow walk around the dining table. She thought out loud. Just because there were no fleshly human ears to hear her didn't mean she had to give up the practice of years. Dutifully, Flossy followed, prepared to stop suddenly when inspiration struck her dead mistress' beloved sister, as it always inevitably did.

"What shall we do next?" she mused as she began her walk and the room began to fill.

Northangerland, sulking in the corner, raised an eyebrow and cleared his throat while the Duke of Wellington glowered at him from across the room and Louisa Vernon begged for release from her prison in the fireplace. Julius Brenzaida appeased his wife and queen, Rosina, by the doorway while his mistress Geraldine Sidonia looked on and the ghost of Gerald, King of Exina laughed at his enemy's discomfort.

"No, not yet," Emily decided. It wasn't time for Angria, Glass Town, and Gondal in their new, combined form. Waiting Boy, Augusta Geraldine Almeda, Lord Charles, Gravey, Mary Percy, and so many others in the room gave a collected sigh of disappointment, consigned to wait a bit longer before their next bout of battles, imprisonments, executions, and torrid love affairs.

Emily returned to her writing desk, getting out a fresh sheet of paper. Personal correspondence of a more agreeable kind needed to be finished first.

"Let's see...." she said, tapping the end of her pen on her teeth as she thought, "I am overdue for a letter from Branwell." Pen poised, she began writing slowly, hesitantly at first, steadily gaining speed as the persona of her brother overlaid her soul.

Letters from her brother and sisters were so much more interesting since they had died.

Charlotte was in Brussels raising M. Heger's love child as her own and reveling in the excitement of life under a hidden identity. Anne, governess to a lovely family of four, was traveling with that family in an exotic land of turbans and veils, only just becoming aware that her employer, Mr. Walden, had ingested a water wolf shortly before their departure and was beginning to exhibit disturbing symptoms. And Branwell...

Branwell had been gifted a small legacy by the infamous Lydia Robinson upon her death, along with a note from her dying hand filled with claims of devoted love and laments of the long-reaching legal machinations of her departed husband which had kept her silent and apart from her true love in life. At this same time, the culprit of the missing funds at Luddenden Foot had come forward to admit his guilt and Branwell had been reinstated in his position with the railway. This combination had reformed him enough to improve his health, but not enough to make him uninteresting.

As her pen scribbled, Branwell wrote to her of a horribly gruesome accident. Luddenden Foot's leading solicitor, a Jonas Hargrieve, had been run over by the 4 am train, slicing him in two. But was it an accident? Whispers hinted at suicide, while the space between the whispers spoke of murder. Branwell, this new and improved Branwell, was determined to ferret out the truth, with Emily the captivated observer of his pursuits.

Emily smiled to herself as her hand continued its dip and scratch, with pen moving swiftly from inkwell to page.

She looked forward to receiving Branwell's letter tomorrow. Next week maybe Charlotte would write....

Bertha illustration by Catherine Rebecca

BERTHA

By Alexa Hardy
Stretham near Ely in Cambridgeshire

*I wrote this thinking of Bertha's ghost always wandering the halls,
still with her anger and fear.*

When will the calm come after the storm
When the light returns and quiets the seas
You can't hear the rumblings so distant
But they are ever present.

When they grow and gain ground you forget to hear
Until it rages and swells again in its strength
This never ending storm presses on
It cannot be hushed

It tears and Rips with no regard for us
Weakening what was strong and unyielding
Then as it seems to burn itself out
It's anger spent, it lulls you
Yet it remains deep down, silently waiting

To swell and roar once again,
        when it finally breaks against the defences.

A Tale of Two Glass Towns illustration by Jon Beynon

A TALE OF TWO GLASS TOWNS

By Nicola Friar
Northwest England

Nicola Friar, Brontë lover and book blogger writes often about the Brontës and other authors in her Bronte Babe Blog at https://brontebabeblog.wordpress.com

It all began with a set of six wooden toy soldiers that Aunt Nina picked up at a car boot sale. They reminded her of the ones given to her when she was a little girl, the ones she had played with all day and all night. She had actually had twelve of them and remembered the fun she'd once had with them. She thought they'd make an excellent present for Theo once she had cleaned them up a bit. Aunt Nina worried that being so far from home wasn't proving to be much fun for Theo.

His stay was meant to be for a few weeks at the start of the year but had quietly stretched on into the summer and that was when she remembered the soldiers she'd stored in the attic. The red paint on their once glorious coats was dull and peeling, the black of their trousers grey, and their faces washed out and expressionless. However, she thought that with a bit of attention they'd help to cheer up her nephew; even in 2020, seven year old boys still enjoyed playing with toy soldiers, and so she set to work secretly restoring them every night when Theo had gone to bed.

When Aunt Nina finally presented Theo with the soldiers, they were almost unrecognisable from when she had bought them. Their paint work was now fresh and gleaming; their red coats shone brilliantly, the black of their trousers was like shining coal, and their faces wore jolly expressions, their cheeks rosy and their eyes sparkling blue. Theo loved them, and when not doing his home school lessons or playing in Aunt Nina's garden, he was usually to be found curled up reading a book with one of the soldiers for company. His favourite was the biggest, the one he had named Wellington, a name suggested by Aunt Nina as there had once been a real and very famous soldier with this name.

Theo was away from everything he knew, and the difference between the big city in Norfolk he normally lived in and the small Lancashire town he now found himself in was huge. Still, it was hopefully short term, until Theo's parents had recovered from the illness that was sweeping through the world. There was nothing Aunt

159

Nina wouldn't do for her nephew and so when it became clear he'd need somewhere to stay for a few months as his grandparents were also recovering, her cottage was the obvious choice. Theo's temporary home was barely more than a village, the internet connection was practically non-existent, and there were no other children for miles around. He supposed it didn't matter much anyway as he wouldn't have been able to play with them due to the Prime Minister's new rules on keeping a distance from others.

As the schools had been closed before he could be enrolled in the nearest one he had not even met anyone his own age. However, it wasn't all bad; Aunt Nina's cottage looked old on the outside but inside everything was modern, she had a big garden, and so many books Theo wondered how she found time to read them all. She lived next door to the vicarage which was itself next door to a small church called St Michael's with an old churchyard, and beyond that, just across the little stretch of road that ran in front of the cottage garden, was an even older graveyard.

The graveyard across the street occupied a square patch of land that had become overgrown and rundown. At first Theo had been alarmed at sleeping so close to the ghosts until Aunt Nina pointed out that there was no need to be scared of the people who were buried there; whether they were ghosts or not, they couldn't possibly harm him. Theo learned not to look on the place as spooky or scary, but instead as a peaceful place for people to rest. Every weekend a small team of volunteers, who Theo thought were all old enough to be his grandparents' grandparents, assisted by the vicar of St Michaels', Reverend Grey, all pitched in to help to keep the graves neat and tidy.

Nobody had been buried there for over seventy years but Aunt Nina said there was no excuse for letting them become rundown; the people in the graves had been loved by someone when they were alive and should be respected. Theo enjoyed getting to know the volunteers who told him stories about the games they played in the graveyard as children. Hide and seek in the derelict building in the middle of the plot had been a favourite; it was what remained of the chantry which was the very first church to be built in the area hundreds of years ago.

Theo wasn't sure exactly how his Aunt Nina had come to be living next door to a church in the middle of nowhere helping some very old people to look after even older graves. He thought maybe it was to do with her job; he knew she wrote things which she said helped her to pay the bills. Whenever he had asked her she had told him she lived in the cottage for inspiration. He did not really know what she meant

160

by this. When he had asked Reverend Grey after church one Sunday why Aunt Nina lived in the cottage next to his in the middle of nowhere, his ears had gone slightly pink and he'd become very interested in the umbrella he was holding.

Reverend Grey tended to the churchyard graves, but, like school, playtime, and even church, the work in the old graveyard had eventually had to stop due to the Prime Minister's new rules; instead Theo watched as the weeds crept back in, working their way up through the ground as the unchecked ivy stole along and wound itself around the iron gate and railings, the bluebells grew out of control, and the moss obscured the names on the big tombs in middle. Aunt Nina told Theo that one good thing to come out of the new rules was that people had stopped sneaking into the graveyard to smash up the headstones and take bricks from the old church. Although Theo had been free to walk around the graveyard whenever he wanted (Aunt Nina had Reverend Grey's spare key), it just wasn't the same without Arthur, Ned, Bill, Jean, John, and Eliza chatting over tea, biscuits, shovels, and spades.

One day when he was especially restless he asked for the key and went for a stroll around the plot with Aunt Nina watching from the cottage garden gate as she chatted over the fence to Reverend Grey. Theo marvelled at the changes that had come over the graveyard. Although he had watched things spring up and spread out from his bedroom window, everything seemed so much wilder from up close, and he was a little spooked by it. The worst affected grave was the biggest; it was a tomb right in the middle, and Ned had once told him that this was where the Glass Man was buried. Theo thought it was the most interesting one of all as not only was it so much bigger and grander than the rest, but it also had its own set of railings around it, and the writing on it was not in English. Ned had told him the Glass Man had come to live in the town from Belgium over a hundred years ago. He had been a very rich man, and had eventually opened up a glass making business and built a big factory on the outskirts of town. When he died his family had paid for the big tomb to be built so that people could remember the good things he had done for the local people in what had become known as Glass Town.

Back in 2020, the Prime Minister had begun to talk about letting people go back to school and opening up some of the shops again, and Theo wondered if that meant the volunteers would be coming back to tidy the graveyard. Unfortunately, as they washed up the dishes one night, Aunt Nina sadly pointed out that it still wasn't safe for them all to be mixing with people from other households just in case they became ill. Theo thought of his parents and grandparents and hoped they would get better soon. He hated the germs and just wanted everything to get back to normal, but deep down, something was whispering to him that things would never quite be the same again. Aunt Nina tried to take his mind off things and suggested that they could both do a bit of gardening if he liked, and plant some new seeds, which was something Theo enjoyed. He asked whether they could also tidy up the old graveyard a little at the weekend. Aunt Nina agreed and Theo decided they could ask Reverend Grey to help as he had also been sticking to the Prime Minister's rules, and although they shouted over the garden fence to him, he thought he might be lonely without all of the people coming to see him in church every week. Aunt Nina agreed but Theo noticed that her cheeks had gone slightly red and she had become unusually interested in the dish cloth she was holding.

That weekend Theo, Aunt Nina, and Reverend Grey (who now formed part of what the prime minister had called a bubble; Theo hadn't really understood what he had meant by this) headed across the road, unlocked the gate, and entered the graveyard together. They worked all day pulling up the leaves, planting the new flowers which Reverend Grey had brought over from the vicarage garden, and carefully scraping the moss from the gravestones so that you could read that the Marias, Patricks, Williams, and Johns buried there were resting in peace once more. They also worked together to clean the Glass Man's tomb, and Theo could once again read the strange writing and trace the words, "Ville de Verre". He remembered Ned had told him that this translated as Glass Town.

They returned the following day and toiled away until the twilight surrounded them and they locked everything up once again. As Theo looked out over the graveyard from his bedroom window that night, he saw a garden coming back to life with the big tomb in the middle dwarfing everything around it. He settled down in his bed with a book and Wellington, falling asleep before he had even turned the page.

He dreamt that night of a glittering city with huge buildings built entirely of sparkling glass and scores of people walking around dressed in their finest, and to him, most unusual clothes. They chattered away in what sounded like many different languages as Theo made his way through the bustling streets full of horses, carts, and stalls, before coming to a halt in front of a tower that seemed to stretch all the way up to the sky. A young red-haired boy caught him staring with astonishment and smiled at him as he approached the tower. Startling Theo, the boy told him that it was called The Tower of All Nations. Before he could ask about this glorious building though, the boy had disappeared along with the rest of his magnificent dream city as Wellington fell with a crash onto Theo's bedroom floor, waking him and thrusting him back to reality. It wasn't until the next morning that Theo realised that Wellington had been damaged in the fall; distraught, he rushed to Aunt Nina who promised to fix his favourite solider. With a man down, Aunt Nina suggested that Theo should play with another of the soldiers until Wellington could be properly repaired.

The following week saw Wellington restored, but Theo was hesitant to play with him due to his recent injuries so instead Wellington took pride of place on the bedside table in Theo's bedroom. That weekend some of the volunteers returned to the graveyard, each wearing their face masks whenever they could not keep their distance from one another. Their spirits seemed to have drooped a little since they had all last been together, and the tea and biscuits had been put on hold for a while, but Theo was pleased to see them all again. He loved to walk around as everyone worked, helping where he could, and watching and listening where he couldn't. The first Saturday back, he helped Jean plant some new flowers by the gate, and looked on as Arthur and Dave pieced together the remains of a broken gravestone like a jigsaw puzzle.

Theo found Ned inside the old chantry building staring around at the names on the gravestones that now lay on their floor at his feet. The bluebells were still growing free here. Ned was pleased to see him, and Theo was able to ask him some more about the Glass Man and the town's history, as well as telling him all about his fantastic dream city where everything had been made of glass. Ned chuckled and noting the new soldier in Theo's hand, asked about Wellington and who had defeated him in battle.

When Theo had finished telling the story of his favourite soldier's downfall and restoration, he realised he hadn't bothered to name his replacement. Ned said he thought Napoleon might be a good name. He stayed to chat with Ned for a while until he heard Aunt Nina calling him, a worried tone in her voice. He said goodbye to Ned, and came out into the sunlight where he bumped into a relived Aunt Nina. She scolded him a little for going out of sight but Theo insisted he was safe and wasn't alone. A ruffle of his sandy hair told him that he was forgiven and they said their goodbyes to everyone and made their way back to the cottage to get washed up before tea.

That night, an exhausted Theo returned to the glittering city with the sparkling glass buildings after falling asleep. He walked around the same bustling streets filled with the people in their finest clothes but this time, he walked on further, past the Tower of All Nations, and towards the outskirts of the city where the crowds thinned and he could see the woods in the distance. Perched in between the city and trees was a small building named Bravey's Inn which looked like a pub. Theo could see soldiers, real life soldiers, passing in and out, their red coats vibrant, buttons shining, and trousers as black as coal. He stood and watched for a few minutes before he caught sight of a red haired boy sneaking around the side of the building. Theo followed him quietly and turned the corner to see him peeking in at the window, his face pressed against the glass. His clothing was clean but old fashioned; he wore brown trousers, a shirt which had once been white but had seen better days, and a brown jacket that had clearly been repaired and stitched several times. His hair was sticking up at all angles as though it had never seen a comb.

Theo stepped on a twig which startled the boy, and as he turned Theo realised it was the same boy he'd seen by the Tower. The boy, too, seemed to recognise Theo and smiled, beckoning Theo to join him by the window. Creeping up alongside him, Theo turned his gaze to the inside of the pub where he saw many soldiers, talking and laughing; they seemed to be celebrating something. And then the ground felt like it had fallen away beneath him when he spotted, right in the middle of the room with what seemed like a small army of admirers listening to him, Wellington himself. Theo gasped. The boy laughed. As Theo looked he realised that the soldiers nearest to him were the ones he had in his bedroom back home. There was one exception; Napoleon was nowhere to be seen. That was because Napoleon had been left behind with Ned in the graveyard. As he realised this, the world around him vanished once again and he woke up in his bed back in Aunt Nina's cottage.

The next day, Theo went with Aunt Nina to retrieve Napoleon. They looked everywhere; all around the graveyard, inside the old church building, in the cottage and garden, and even the churchyard next door. Napoleon had vanished just as the glittering city had done from Theo's dream. However, Theo thought that if the magnificent dream city had returned, then there was no reason why Napoleon should not.

As he made his way back to the cottage with Aunt Nina, they spotted Reverend Grey opening up the church doors and pinning up some notices. The church had been shut for months; Reverend Grey had tried to do services on the internet because the Prime Minister had said that the churches all had to shut, but the internet had been too bad. Theo missed the people who came to the services every Sunday and he knew that Reverend Grey did, too. Theo saw that there was a list featuring prayers for local people. As Aunt Nina spoke with Reverend Grey, Theo took a moment to read every name and say a little prayer for Agnes Smith, Florence Clark, Mary Percy, Edward Laury, Graham Gilbert, Henry Hastings, Herbert Moore, Jack Archer, and Oliver Burns.

Theo returned to Aunt Nina's side to hear Reverend Grey say that he was going to be very busy over the next week or so. With a sad smile he returned to the church. Aunt Nina explained to Theo that the prayers he had been reading were for the people who had died, and that their funerals were going to be held the next week. She said they could send some flowers if he liked. Theo thought this was a nice idea and she seemed relieved. Over the next few days, the rain poured down on the small groups of people dressed in black who arrived at the church for the funerals. Reverend Grey had posted several leaflets and booklets through Aunt Nina's door; they were prayers and funeral books for the people whose names Theo had read on the list in the church. As she looked through them, Aunt Nina told Theo that the volunteers wouldn't be going to tidy up the graveyard as they would attending the funeral taking place on the Saturday and the weather continued to be wet and windy.

When Saturday arrived, Theo watched the last group of mourners dressed in black through the rain streaked windows. Their figures were blurred but he knew that in the midst of the rain and umbrellas were Arthur, Ned, Bill, Jean, John, and Eliza. A sense of sadness swept over Theo as he watched them disappear into the church and he thought of the people he was missing back home. With his eyes fixed on the church, he prayed that they would all be OK. He also thought again of Napoleon and wondered about his fate.

When the volunteers next came to the graveyard they were not their usual cheerful selves, although they were trying to put on brave faces. Wandering past the tomb of the Glass Man, Theo found himself inside the chantry with Ned who looked slightly troubled. Theo tried to cheer him up by talking of his soldiers, the missing Napoleon, and his wonderful dream city. Remembering the funerals, Theo realised that Ned must have lost someone important to him. Seized by a sudden idea, Theo sprinted through the graveyard, past the volunteers and Aunt Nina, and back across the road into the cottage. He was running out again with a solider in his hand as Aunt Nina came to look for him. She looked torn between being cross and relieved again. Satisfied he was back within the view of the volunteers, she resumed her work with Reverend Grey.

Back inside the chantry, Theo presented Ned with a toy soldier with a slightly damaged leg that Aunt Nina had said was called Stumps. He offered it to Ned to cheer him up whenever he was sad. Ned promised to return him when he felt slightly more cheerful. They sat in peaceful silence for a while, listening to the birds calling to one another from the treetops. Eventually, Theo heard Aunt Nina calling for him and he said goodbye to Ned.

Over tea that night, Aunt Nina asked him if he was OK after being in the graveyard again with the volunteers. She talked about how different it had seemed, and how different it would be from then on. Theo told her he could see how sad everyone was and wanted to cheer them all up. He said he would give them all a soldier to help but he'd lost Napoleon so there weren't enough to go around. Aunt Nina pointed out that he still had five; one each for Arthur, Bill, Jean, John, and Eliza.

Theo shook his head and said he didn't have enough because she'd forgotten Ned, and he only had four now because he'd already given one to Ned that afternoon. Aunt Nina went very pale when he said this, but then shook her head as if to clear it and smiled. She asked if Theo had left the soldier in the churchyard with Ned's flowers when he'd run across the road earlier. Theo was puzzled and asked why there were flowers in the churchyard for Ned. Aunt Nina told him the volunteers had paid for some flowers for Ned's grave, and that she had also sent some across for his funeral just as she had suggested.

Theo's world began to spin. Ned couldn't be dead; he'd been talking to him in the chantry that afternoon. Running out of the cottage and into the churchyard next door, he looked for fresh flowers on the graves. He spotted some and went amongst the headstones looking for Ned's name. He couldn't find it anywhere. Turning around, he found Aunt Nina looking at him sadly. She had one of the booklets in her hand that Reverend Grey had pushed through the letterbox; as she passed it to Theo he could see the name "Edward Laury" on the front. He was confused but opening the booklet he saw Ned's face smiling up at him from a photograph. Theo gasped. Aunt Nina then took him to a spot which had a small wooden cross in the ground with the name "Edward Laury" engraved on it. She explained that Edward was Ned's full name and that the volunteers had attended his funeral last week. Ned's death was the reason they had all been so sad.

Theo began to cry as the shock and realisation hit him. Aunt Nina hugged him and took him back to the cottage. They sat for a while and talked about illness, death, loss, and separation. Aunt Nina told him she believed that loved ones were always with you no matter where they actually were and reassured him that his parents and grandparents were on the mend, and he could go home soon. Theo cried even more and when Aunt Nina asked why he said it was because he would miss her so much when he returned home. She told him that she'd always be with him no matter where they were, and so would Ned.

As Theo lay in bed that night he thought about his dream city, his missing solider, and his lost friend. He curled up with Wellington after placing the remaining soldiers on his bedside table. A spark of hope came to him in the dark; if the dream city and the red-haired boy could re-appear, then so could Ned. In fact, he already had. He did not tell Aunt Nina about his conversation with Ned that afternoon. Although she was right when she said that loved ones never really left, he thought it best to keep that information to himself. He would find Ned again and talk to him to try to understand what had happened; a big part of him thought that it just couldn't be true.

Theo's mind then wandered to his parents and grandparents; although he had talked to them on the phone, the internet connection was too poor to allow him to video call them. He'd thought of them every day since arriving in the cottage, and every Sunday (when church had been open) he had said a prayer for them all. A part of him hoped he could go home soon, and back to normality, but another part of him would miss Aunt Nina and Glass Town so much.

The following day, Reverend Grey arrived at the door with some flowers and suggested they could put them on Ned's grave. Theo agreed and they walked into the churchyard to place the small tribute at the foot of Ned's grave. They stood in silence for a moment, with Theo still half-believing, and hoping, that none of it was true. The sun dazzled in the sky and the birds sang to one another from the treetops. Theo then asked if he could gather up some of the bluebells from the chantry to give to Ned. Reverend Grey hesitated as he knew they weren't really supposed to touch the bluebells but eventually, and reluctantly, he gave in to Theo's plea as he could see how much it meant to him.

Reverend Grey unlocked the gate and Theo jogged over towards the chantry. To his surprise when he reached it, there was already someone there. It was not Ned, nor any of the volunteers; it was the red-haired boy from his fantastic dream city, and in his hand was Napoleon. The boy turned at the sound of Theo's approach and clutched the solider tight to his chest. He looked frightened. Theo smiled and reassured the boy that he was safe in Glass Town. Recognising Theo he relaxed slightly. In the shadowy ruins, the boy and his old-fashioned clothing didn't look out of place. Theo told him he could keep the soldier if he wanted to.

"His name is –" began Theo.

"Napoleon," finished the boy.

Theo didn't have to ask how the boy knew Napoleon's name. He wasn't entirely sure, but he knew that the connection lay in Glass Town. Theo explained that he had come to pick some bluebells for his friend's grave as he had recently died. The boy explained how, back home, he picked them with his sisters on the moors in memory of their mum and their two eldest sisters. The bluebells were particular favourites of his two younger sisters. Without speaking, they began to gather the best of the bunch growing inside the ruins. When they had finished, they split the bunch with Theo pressing some onto the boy to take home.

"I hope your sisters like them," said Theo, smiling and extending a hand to the boy. "Tell them they're a present from Glass Town. I'm Theo Ellrington. What's your name?"

"Branwell Brontë," replied the boy, returning the smile.

The sound of Reverend Grey's footsteps cut short the conversation and his smiling face came into view in the doorway. Turning back, Theo saw that Branwell was gone. On the ground lay Napoleon. He picked him up and examined him, realising as he did so the bluebells he had given to Branwell had vanished. Branwell had taken them but left the soldier for Theo. On the way out of the graveyard he paused on reaching the Glass Man's tomb. There, placed on top, was Stumps. Picking him up carefully, he clutched him tightly along with Napoleon. Ned was gone, just as Branwell's mum and sisters were. Theo knew in that instant he would never see his friend again, but also that Ned would always be with him.

He returned to Aunt Nina after leaving the bluebells for Ned. She seemed down and whilst she busied herself writing, Theo read Ned's funeral booklet and was astonished to discover so many things about him. He had thought that Ned's family were from Glass Town, but they actually came from much further afield. His dad had grown up in a small village called Haworth in Yorkshire, and although his mum was from Glass Town, her granddad had come all the way from Belgium and was none other than the Glass Man himself. Theo went to bed that night with his mind full of the day's events but his slumber was dreamless.

The next day Aunt Nina told Theo he was going home in two weeks. He was happy to see his mum and dad again but his heart was aching at the thought of leaving Aunt Nina. Theo left the soldiers behind to keep her company. He didn't have to worry about her, though, because a few weeks later she moved into the vicarage with Reverend Grey who assured Theo they would carry on helping the volunteers and take care of Ned's grave. When workmen finally came to fix the village's internet problem he video called Aunt Nina and she told him that a new family had moved into her cottage and that there was a boy who was the same age as Theo. Sadly his granddad had died just before they'd moved and he was still adjusting to his new school so he was feeling a bit lonely. Theo told Aunt Nina to give the soldiers to the boy. He'd enjoyed playing with them and they'd kept him company through a confusing time in his life, but he thought they might now help someone else. Theo didn't need physical reminders; Glass Town would be in his heart forever, and in his heart he would forever be in Glass Town.

'Come in! Come in!' He Sobbed, 'Cathy, Do Come. Oh, Do – Once More!'

Cathy illustration by Debs Green-Jones

CATHY

by Debs Green-Jones
Wales, UK

Oh Cathy I've lost you,
my soul lingers on,
Oh Cathy I've found you but still
you are gone.

Oh Cathy come back to me,
hold me once more,
Oh Cathy forgive me,
my heart is so sore.

My mind beats against me
my life is in two,
my hopes and my wishes
were buried with you.

Oh Cathy, my Cathy
my soul lingers on
but Cathy, my Cathy
I wish it were gone.

Heathcliff illustration by Debs Green-Jones

HEATHCLIFF

by Debs Green-Jones
Wales U.K.

I see him now, upon the moor,
His black eyes shine for ever more

I wish that I could touch his face,
I know this time, I know this place.

He haunts the Heights and looks for passion,
she's in his sights but cannot fashion his need of her.

And so he dies,
who never lived
save in her sighs..

A Wind Like That illustration by Emily Ross

A WIND LIKE THAT

by Jenna Gareis
Seattle, Washington, USA

It was a quiet morning as she slipped into the bench by the window to drink her coffee in the cafe. She'd risen early...or had she even slept? The bed had sagged in the middle and the clawfoot tub - although a cute touch aesthetically, dripped all night. Her bed and breakfast at the foot of the main cobbled Haworth climb had offered a huge traditional breakfast spread, but the dining room was small and crowded and she felt impatient, although impatient for what she did not know. Her train from Leeds back to London didn't leave until well into the afternoon. Plenty of time to wander through the moors behind the Parsonage as she'd planned to do since she first envisioned this trip from her sofa in her sparse Seattle apartment on the other side of the sea.

She'd checked out early. Too early, really, and no one was about. She was glad of this. When she'd arrived yesterday afternoon, she'd disembarked from the steam train with a gaggle of tourists. She'd had to endure holding her tongue as the people in the conversation seats across the aisle from her spoke ignorant nonsense to each other about the Brontë family and who they were, even what they had written. She'd almost been compelled to speak when the older woman claimed *Rebecca* was Emily Brontë's greatest work, but she'd refrained. Pearls before swine...to try to correct strangers would almost always be like throwing pearls before swine. And anyway, she'd placed herself on this tourist steam train. She didn't consider herself a tourist, more like a devotee. This was a pilgrimage, not a vacation stop.

She didn't really have an agenda. She only wanted to be in space they had been in. She only wanted to see what they might have seen. To hear what they might have heard. Of course, she wasn't delusional. She didn't underestimate the effects of time and progress. Nor did she anticipate that she would be able to commune with them, as she saw others claim on social media. She was just seeking an immersion. What that would feel like she didn't even pretend to anticipate know-ing. As she progressed through this trip though, she was becoming more and more certain of what that immersion did *not* feel like. It did not feel like this.

So she wanted to escape from society. She would head into the wild, untamed, moors behind the Parsonage for the morning, and then board that steam train back to Leeds and London beyond. Yet, to her dismay, she'd trekked back to the Museum and along the path that skirted the cemetery, through the gate and following the wooden signs in English and Japanese along alleys between private homes, she'd found herself in a glorified dog park. Clearly marked trails, a parking lot, and people - so many people. Spread out, to be sure, but still so many people. Walking their dogs.

Trying to shrug off disappointment at finding not what she was looking for, she began a ginger walk along one of the paths, more mud than solid. The wind was fierce and the colors were muted by the morning light as it struggled to break through the clouds. She could see rain in cylindrical sheets falling and feel drops travel on the wind to pelt her in the face like ocean spray, although it was not actually raining where she stood. Stopping to pull her windbreaker from her bag she was astonished to be completely bowled over by a huge grey beast of a dog. It had come barreling toward her through the wet foliage at full speed and tackled her in joyous and muddy abandon. It was a gentleman, this dog, and stopped abruptly in its stride to return to her and ensure she was alright. He stuck his wet muzzle into her face and she couldn't help but laugh. She audibly thanked him for allowing himself to be used as a stabilizing element while she righted herself. She was now covered in grime but didn't care in the least.

She surveyed the area for the dog's owner but weirdly saw no one whereas, just before the tackle, there had been whole populations of people. "Where'd everyone go?" she asked her new companion and was tremendously grateful that he didn't respond. She slipped her windbreaker on over her muddy clothes, making a mental plan to change at the train station before heading back to Leeds, and continued her walk.

The huge dog lopped along with her - alternately running ahead and waiting for her to catch up. Occasionally he'd divert from the path and into the scrub, sending a flock of blackbirds flying and squawking into the weather. The further they walked, the further she became concerned about this dog finding his owner. "Don't you want to head home?" She'd ask him occasionally. He didn't seem to be interested in that line of conversation. They crested a small slope and she turned to see the way they'd come from. The view before her was a breathtaking mingle of greens and browns. She wanted to capture it. She pulled her phone from her pocket to snap a picture and share it across her social media accounts only to realize she had no cell coverage. It made sense she supposed, although she had only been walking for a little over an hour; she had to guess at that as the time on her phone didn't seem to be working properly either.

"We should head back," she said to her companion. And they did begin to walk back along the way they had come but it wasn't long, maybe thirty or forty steps, when a long whistle came from out of nowhere and the dog began to whine with anticipation. His ears perked up and his nose raised into the air. "Who was that? Is someone calling you?" The skin along his ribs was twitching with excitement. No doubt about it, this was a familiar whistle. So why didn't he go? She expected to see his owner stride along the path toward them any moment now, headed back the way they had both obviously come - them much earlier than she. So they waited. And waited. And waited. No one came.

The dog grew only more excited. It was unnerving, this waiting, this anticipation - unfulfilled. That feeling of impatience that she had been struck with upon waking this morning, but which had slipped off her the further she had walked into this wilderness, came over her again on the path. She had to move. She had to make progress. Toward what, she did not know. If she could have seen the skin upon her ribs, she was sure it too was twitching with excitement.

After a time, out of sheer compulsion, she began her return walk again. The wind was still whipping around with a ferocity she had only experienced on the plains of Tibet. A wind like that, she reminded herself, carried sounds. A wind like that, she reminded herself, confused a listener. The eye is a more faithful companion in a wind like that. So she looked, but the wind and the rain and colors created an odd mirage effect and everything looked like something it wasn't and there appeared to be people where there were not people and water where there was not water and birds where there, it would turn out, were no birds. It was like trying to see through a glare but the sunlight now, muted as it was by clouds, was giving off no glare.

"We should head back," she said, again, to her companion. And they did, again, begin to walk back along the way they had come but it wasn't long again, maybe twenty or thirty steps, when the long whistle came from out of nowhere and the dog began to whine with anticipation. His ears perked up, listening this way and that, and he pawed the ground and whined. "Who *is* that? Is that your someone? Calling you?" Again, she expected to see his owner stride along the path toward them any moment now, headed back the way they had both obviously come - them much earlier than she. So, again they waited. And waited. And waited. No one came.

The dog grew only more excited. It was even more unnerving, this waiting, this anticipation - unfulfilled. It was ominous, really. She began to have that feeling one gets on the stairs sometimes, that there is someone barreling up or down behind you. That feeling that you are not alone. She had to move. She had to make progress. Toward what was not as important as away from what. Out of sheer compulsion, she began her return walk again - this time at a quickened pace. The wind was still whipping around with a ferocity she had only experienced on the plains of Tibet. A wind like that, she reminded herself again, carried sounds. A wind like that, she reminded herself again, confused a listener. "That's it!" She said with a brightness, to her companion, that she definitely did not feel. "It's the wind. Your master is out there whistling for you but we don't know where to find them because the wind is throwing the sounds around. That's it. Isn't it?" The dog did not respond.

"We should head back," she said to her companion. And they did begin to walk back along the way they had come very quickly, and with many looks over her shoulder to be sure that who or whatever it was that she was certain was following them couldn't be seen. It wasn't long, maybe ten or twenty steps, when that long whistle came from out of nowhere and the dog began to howl with anticipation. "Who are you? Where are you?" she yelled into the wind, knowing it would play with the sounds of her voice like a game of keep away. She spun around and around to see but saw nothing comprehensible. Just browns and greens and blacks and blues and greys. She expected to see something careening along the path toward them any moment now. It was unnerving, this waiting, this anticipation - unfulfilled. She had to move. She had to make progress. The wind was still whipping around. A wind like that, she reminded herself, carried sounds. A wind like that, she reminded herself, confused a listener.

"Where *is* everyone?" she asked herself as she took off in a sprint along the path she'd followed. She felt that unseen something gaining on her, breathing on her neck, running its fingers along her back. There it was, the whistle, loud this time, right beside her, right at her left ear. Terror made her gasp and choke, her eyes filled with water. There was a pressure change that made her ears stop up and a misstep caused her to fall, thudding to the ground. She slid along the path on her side and stomach for a body length or more. Dread made her stay where she lay. She shook and trembled and waited with her eyes shut tight. She felt the dog's wet muzzle on her cheek and neck but she remained coiled on the ground and waited for that something or someone to overtake her.

"You alright? I saw you take that tumble." Gasped a red-faced, middle-aged man as he jogged toward her. "Let me help you up." He said, grabbing her hands. "My, my you look a fright," he said, taking in the mud and muck that gleamed along her person. She misunderstood him though. She thought he said she'd *had* a fright. "I have," she said shakily. "Where's the dog?"

"Dog?" he asked.

"Yes. I was walking with a dog. Big grey thing. Where's he got to?"

"I didn't see a dog, miss. Just you and that woman running after you down the path. Now, where's she got to, I wonder?"

Be With Me Always
– Take Any Form –
Drive Me Mad!

Emily's Ghost illustration by Becky Clayton

EMILY'S GHOST

by Becky Clayton
Derbyshire, England

The dust green sky
A mirror of the heath
Asks, denies nothing
In its silence

Footsteps – an echo, a shadowing

"A little, ice-cold hand"

Footsteps have no aim
Beyond life and death wanderings
Creatures – furtive
Sharp bitten, wild

A thin cry – rising

"I'd lost my way on the moor!"

There is no intent
Only the great presence of the land,
The light – a drifting between shadows,
Rain on the edge of the wind

"And to be always there,
Not seeing it dimly through tears"

Your leather boots – well worn
As weathered stone
Striding now – become
Shreds of skin caught in the roots

"We've dared each other
To stand among the graves"

And you delight in the great cycle
The great solitude,
In the knowledge that we are

No more, no less

Than hawk, lapwing
Viper, the thorny
Gorse, the knotted heath.
For all come to their end.

"It was far in the night
And the bairnies grat"

Alone, in the limitless landscape

"Only do not leave me alone
In this abyss where I cannot find you! "

And it is others who are lost
Clinging and craving.

"We saw its nest in winter
Full of little skeletons."

Full of little skeletons.

The Gift illustration by Yvonne Solly

THE GIFT

by Kay Fairhurst Adkins
Palm Springs, California, USA

The door blew open with a gust like a hurricane, "Girls! Girls! Wake up! Wake up! You'll never guess what has happened!" the boy twisted his head nearly backwards to call over his shoulder, "Baby, wake up! Get in here!"

Rubbing sleep from their eyes, the two girls roused out of bed to gather around their brother, the erstwhile leader of their small, but devoted, group. He held something tantalizingly behind his back, refusing to reveal the secret until after Baby toddled in, her tawny hair slumber-mussed into a perfect halo.

"Wha...at?" she yawned, curling her toes tightly against the chill of the floorboards.

"Come," he ordered, brandishing his arm in a perfect arc to show his sisters where to sit on the floor as befitted the perfect audience of his command performance, "Sit!"

Curiosity rising with each moment, the girls sat quickly, crossing their legs and leaning forward with mounting excitement. They knew their flame-haired brother well enough to keep mum until he had made his presentation. An interruption at this point could make him shut his lips firmly, exact a military turnabout, and march straight out of their room in a silent snit that no amount of pleading could atone for.

"Papa has returned from his trip and he has brought home this!" His hand whipped around and he proudly displayed in the palm of his hand a brightly painted egg-shaped....person.

The girls looked at each other, daring each sister to be the one to speak first. A significant look from eldest to youngest sealed the decision and Baby squeaked out a rather timid, "It's lovely, but...what is it?"

With all the aplomb of a practiced magician, the boy held firmly to the bottom of the egg and twisted off the torso! "This...," he paused for maximum drama to fix each of the girls in turn with his shining eye, "This is what is called," he paused again simply to be infuriating, "a Nesting Doll."

He quickly unscrewed each descending component of the doll, reattaching matching torsos and bases until five separate roly-poly little dolls were spread before them. Magnanimously, the boy told his sisters that he was willing to share his toy and they could each choose a doll for their own. His father had made it very clear that the gift was for all of them, but the girls didn't have to know that.

"*I*," he swooped his hands down to grab two of the figures, "shall take these two. Because," he held up one palm to stave off their protests, "I am the only boy and they are both boys. Well, a man and a boy," he amended quickly before his eldest sister could begin to argue.

"No!"

His quick correction hadn't helped.

"There are five dolls. We each get one and the man is the father. We will take turns playing with the father." She said it as if there would be no argument and there wasn't. She looked around, assuming leadership because she was the eldest and because she couldn't help it.

"They are a family, just like us."

The two oldest girls reached out for the two biggest girl dolls, but Baby would have none of that.

"No!" she pouted, "I always get left with the littlest one. Every time. It's not fair!"

The sight of impending tears and the possibility of a high-pitched post-toddler scream prompted the eldest sister to quick action.

"Here, you take this one," she said, plopping her girl doll into Baby's lap and grabbing up the littlest oval person. "But," she said meaningfully, peering at the little doll in her palm, "even though she's the littlest, she is still going to be the eldest."

The middle sister held tight to her prize - the biggest girl doll - but as she held tight, a tiny gaze of admiration escaped her and she looked with awe at the tiny doll, murmuring "she's fairy-sized."

"We shall name our dolls and give them adventures!"

"Yes! Mine shall be Emily Jane!" cried the middle girl, letting the name she had always secretly wished to have for her own finally be spoken aloud for other ears to hear.

"Mine is Anne," Baby cooed, hugging her doll closely.

The oldest thought a moment and with a brief nod of firm decision announced, "My doll is named Charlotte."

"MINE," the boy spoke significantly, ready to take back the lead as he often did in their playtime, "is Branwell. And the Papa is to be called Patrick."

"But there is no Mama," Baby sighed.

There *was* a Mama," the middle girl's eyes lit with dramatic possibilities, "but she *died* a most long and painful death! Her name was...her name was Maria! She grew up in a beautiful sunny land by the seashore, with flowers and friends all around her...then, when she married, she was forced to live in a dreary, out-of-the-way little town like...like a prisoner! Her only joy was her four children."

"Six!" the boy nearly shouted. "Six! She had six children, but the first two died horrible deaths after being *tortured* in a...a school that's supposed to be a good place, but turns out to be ghastly!"

"They're hungry and cold at school and they get punished all the time for practically no reason at all," Baby added, getting caught up in the fun.

"And then," the oldest of them all leaned in and lowered her voice, eyes wide with dramatic possibilities, "they get consumption and wither away to almost...nothing!"

I Wish They May Shovel In The Earth Over Us Both!

Lucy and Paul illustration by Christina Rauh Fishburne

LUCY AND PAUL

by Crystal McFarland
Maine, USA

The ghost follows me everywhere,
She is neither here nor there.
She threatens the love inside my heart,
Tries with all her might to tear me apart.

Is she real or only an illusion?
Either way she is an unwelcome intrusion.
I want desperately to send her away,
Tell her that only I can stay.

But wait, there she goes,
Leaving behind all her clothes.
Now only one stands in my way,
But it is not her who has the final say.

He's come back to me again,
My dearest, dearest friend.
The choice was always ours to make,
And in the end it's his hand I take.

The Haunted Ring illustration by Barb Tanke

THE HAUNTED RING

by E A France-Sergeant
Wigan, England

The ring was a small gold ring with ornate gold leaves and flowers on the shoulders of the ring, a pretty little ring, Victorian I would say.

How it got where it was, I don't know as one day I was walking in Haworth's old cemetery when I saw it on the path at the far end of the cemetery. It was very dirty. I picked it up and put it in my pocket to take it back to my cottage to clean it; it was a dainty little ring that was the trouble. I thought it very pretty and tried it on my second finger of my right hand. It fit very well but when I tried to get off again, that was a different matter. For try as I could, I couldn't get the ring off. It was at this time that strange things began to happen to me and when I first saw Susanna Woods. She was standing outside the Black Bull. She was a tall, thin, dark haired girl wearing a white dress. I thought she was a ghost and I told her so. She laughed.

"I'm waiting for my father," she said.

"I'm going for a walk on the moor," I said.

"It's pretty this time of year," she said. "Do you like heather?" she said.

"Yes I do," I said.

"There is lots of heather on the moors at this time of year. Maybe I will see you later," she said.

"Yes," said I, "Goodbye."

As I was making my way past the graveyard, I saw a small lady in Victorian clothes, a black dress and black bonnet walking up the path alongside the Parsonage, the one leading to the moors.

I was surprised to see her, so I followed her onto the moors to a small body of water with large rocks. She had a metal box in her hands and it looked to me like she was burying it, then she walked back the same way as she had come.

When a lady came out of the church, they spoke.

"Miss Charlotte,'" the woman said, "how is your father today?"

"Very well thank you," she replied.

"Tell Mr. Brontë, we hope to see him in church this Sunday."

"I will," said the lady as she made her way to the Parsonage, then I saw the girl dressed in white again sitting near the church.

"What is your name?" I asked.

"'Susanna Woods," she said, "I live in Haworth."

"Mine is Sarah Green," I said, "What year is this?"

She looked at me with a strange expression upon her face.

"It's 1847," She said, "Don't you know the date?"

"No," said I. She must have known by the look on my face that something was wrong, but she didn't say anything.

"I have to go," I said.

"I hope to see you again. Maybe in church on Sunday. Goodbye," she said.

As I came to the Parsonage I saw a tall girl sitting on a stool reading from a book. It all seemed so real, but how could it be? Was it really 1847? Was it even possible to walk into the past, hundreds of years ago? In my time these people were ghosts, but in their time they were just people...but then what was I?

Was I the ghost as I had not yet been born?

My clothes must have looked as strange to Susanna as her clothes were to me. Would I wake up in a while? Could it be all a dream? How do I even get back to my own time? Would I be in 1847 forever?

It was then that I saw her again at the end of the cemetery. I went to see what she was doing, as she was bending down looking at something. As I got near, she had gone. Where was she? It was then that I came to the grave. On the headstone it said "Susanna Woods, died 1847. In her 18th year." On the stone it said,

"Time is but a grain of sand,

Come take my hand,

We will meet again,

The ring will bind us together"

Was it possible that the ring was hers? I tried to get it off; it was getting smaller. I pulled and pulled and finally managed to get it off my finger. I saw a crack in the gravestone. Placing the ring inside, I filled the crack with dirt as I had seen Charlotte bury her box earlier out on the moors. What was in that box? Letters? Papers? I would never know.

That was a mystery for another day. The church bells rang. The time was 12.

As I came out of the cemetery I saw a girl. "What year is this?" I asked.

She looked back at me with a smile upon her face. "2020," she said, "don't you know the date?"

"Just checking," said I. "Have a good day," I said. Glad to be back in my own time. No more hauntings by the ghosts of the past - or was I the ghost? It makes you think...Are they the ghosts in our time or are we the ghosts in their time?

The ring is in a safe place now. Maybe one day I will return to 1847, for after all it is the ring that binds us together.

It's strange to think you could get so attached to a ring that you would return from the grave to find it. So if you find a ring or object, you may have found more than you think. I must leave you with this thought.

Farewell, my friends.

The Heights illustration by EmilyInGondal

THE HEIGHTS

by Crystal McFarland
Maine, USA

Heathcliff and Cathy are everywhere here,
They traverse the earth without fear.
They walk through the streets, they walk through the moors,
Sometimes at night I hear them walking the floors.

I've seen them here at the Heights,
Perhaps they see the lights.
They come back to their childhood home,
And up and down the halls they roam.

They're not haunting the living,
Nothing to us would they be giving.
They're haunting themselves, you know,
If they thought we knew, they would go.

The Kindness of Mr. Roddie Top Withins illustration by Jon Beynon

THE KINDNESS OF MR. RODDIE

by Jon Beynon
Gloucesterschire, England

The tall man appeared in the lane ahead of me, as if from nowhere. He was motionless and held a lantern, which illuminated half of his face but threw the rest into deep shadow.

"Oh, my goodness, you startled me!" I exclaimed. He neither moved nor spoke, so I continued:

"Could you please tell me the name of this place? I seem to be lost."

"Yer right late to be stuck 'ere," he said, in a strong local accent. I attempted a self-deprecating laugh in response.

"Ha! Yes, indeed. I... I'm on my way to Leeds for a business meeting tomorrow. But I've run out of fuel." Rather vaguely, I gestured along the village lane behind me to indicate the location of my vehicle. The man with the lantern stared for a while, then said,

"Aye, well. Leeds is a fair step from 'ere. You'll no get theer tonight."

"Really? Where am I, then? I... I must have taken a wrong turning somewhere and ended up driving over the moors. Way off course by now, I should think! Um... I have a hotel booked in Leeds and I..."

A sudden gust of wind rendered me silent for a moment. The stranger, perhaps twelve or fifteen feet away, remained still and quiet. I heard the shriek of an owl and what sounded like a shed door banging as the wind rose. A dog barked somewhere, and the man spoke again.

"This is t'village of Stanbury. 'Tis late now, so you'll get nowt 'til morning. Yud best follow me."

With this, he turned and began walking away. I glanced around me at the dark buildings lining the street. All shutters and curtains were closed and there was no sign of life. To my left, a row of low, terraced cottages. To the right, a small, single-storey, detached structure behind a gated wall - perhaps a little chapel, or a tiny school. The wind strengthened again and I shouted above its noise.

"But I must get to Leeds tonight! They're holding my room at the hotel!"

The moving glow from his light swiveled and stopped. My coat flapped in the wind. I pulled it tighter around me and tugged up the collar.

"Ye canna do owt now. It'll soart in t'morning." He turned again and moved off along the street. I watched him go, wondering what my options were. Stanbury, he called it. A silent, sleeping village, miles from anywhere. No fuel - not tonight anyway. A storm coming, probably. And this stranger with his lantern. "A light in the darkness, literally!" I said to myself and started to follow him.

He turned left onto a stony track that led slightly uphill. I had to break into a trot - he was walking quickly and I needed to catch up.

"Do you live in Stanbury, then?" I called. He continued walking, but shouted over his shoulder.

"A little way off. Come on."

We soon passed a house, its dark bulk looming into view on my right. There were trees, dimly silhouetted against the sky, with bare limbs shuddering in the breeze. This fellow seems decent enough, I thought. If he can provide me with somewhere to spend the night and maybe give me some assistance in the morning, it would be a great help. My meeting is not until one o'clock tomorrow, so I should have time. If he has a telephone, I could speak to the hotel and apologise for not turning up. It'll be fine. *I'll* be fine. Stop worrying!

I kept my eyes fixed ahead on the pale circle of light emanating from the stranger's lantern. I could no longer really see the man himself – his shifting form in its dark clothes seemed totally lost in the darkness.

When we came to a fork in the track, he took the left-hand route, which was narrower and rockier and bordered by stone walls. It became steeper for a while but didn't seem to slow him down. I had to half-walk, half-run to keep up, and still he remained twenty or thirty feet ahead of me. Every now and then, he and his light seemed to disappear completely.

The landscape, although difficult to see, gradually changed. When the moonlight broke through a gap in the clouds, it was possible to make out – just for a moment or two – a great wilderness of exposed moorland, stretching for miles around in every direction. Before long, there were no more trees, no more dry-stone walls, just this rough track under the wide night sky. The wind was strong and cold up here. Where on Earth are we going? I began to feel reckless and vulnerable, increasingly fearful of this wild, desolate place and the stranger I was following.

"Is it much further?" I called out, but my voice was snatched away by the wind and he didn't hear me.

* * *

I have no idea how long we had been walking or how far we had come, but it must have been a good few miles when eventually we came to a derelict farmhouse. In the moonlight I could see that the windows had lost their glass and the door was missing. There were small paddocks enclosed by broken walls. A little further on, my new acquaintance paused, waiting for me at what turned out to be a stone stile. I could just make out three stunted trees waving restlessly in the shadows and a steep downward slope to the left of the path. At the foot of this little incline stood the ruins of a large outbuilding.

"Watch yuh feet, mind," he said, as I approached. "Step over."

"Thank you!" He lowered the lamp to help me see, and I climbed through the stile. "This is certainly an isolated place!" I exclaimed.

"Aye," he replied with a wry smile. "God's own country, they call it. Come on, before t'light guz out."

He continued along the undulating path, seemingly without effort. I followed, wondering at his rapid pace and finding myself short of breath.

Before long, we came to the wreck of another, larger, house with a partially ruined barn at its side. Again, these buildings were dilapidated; broken windows and large holes in the roof. I stopped walking for a moment, to catch my breath and take it all in. My legs were beginning to ache. The wind moaned through the void of the farm's interior and I began to fear that my new friend might be some kind of hermit, leading me for miles across inhospitable desert, only to spend the night in a similarly tumbledown place with no roof and gaping windows. Then, suddenly, the sound of a sheep bleating close by startled me. I glanced around, but could see nothing. Trembling, I peered into the darkness and felt a wave of dread; the glint of the man's lantern was nowhere to be seen. Wind howled through the buildings behind me and another sheep called, louder and closer than before. I felt the heavy splash of rain on my face and had to suppress an urge to scream.

Without the point of lamplight to guide me, I could see nothing, not even the path, and had no idea where to go or what to do.

Then, mercifully, I spotted the moving light again. It was much further away now, and in the pitchy blackness of the night, seemed to be rising impossibly above ground level. "Thank God!" I cried aloud, my heart thumping in my chest.

"Wait for me!" I shouted pointlessly into the wind.

As I began to run forward, the rain began in earnest, soaking my hair and stinging my face. I moved as quickly as I could, but progress was more difficult now; the path was less well defined, winding left or right and dipping or rising without warning. I stumbled a few times, tripping on stubborn tussocks of grass or bracken. Once I lost my balance completely and fell sideways into a ditch of running water.

I struggled to my feet, cursing under my breath, and started forward again. My right hand and coat sleeve felt sodden and muddy. Wet hair fell over my eyes. With some relief, I noted that the spot of light – many yards away now – had stopped moving. He's waiting for me, I thought. Thank the Lord!

The path ahead of me appeared to widen now and began to rise steeply. I paced up it as quickly as I could, trying to ignore the aching fatigue in my thighs. The higher I went, the rougher the weather became. We seemed to have reached the top of the world; the powerful wind lashed rain painfully into my face. Squinting into the wet darkness, I noticed that my guiding light had disappeared again. Panic rose in my belly, but I was able to see – silhouetted in the silvery moonlight – the shape of what appeared to be a barn or perhaps another farmhouse. Sincerely, I hoped that this would be the end of our journey. I approached with some trepidation, as my friend with the lamp was still invisible. The high, windowless gable end of the building rose to my right, a slab-laid walkway lay along its base. A low wall curved away to the left and I sensed the great open moor sloping off beyond it. I reached the far corner of the house and, looking round it, immediately saw the lantern glowing.

"Ah!" I called. "There you are! That was quite a hike! How far have we come? I take it this is your home?"

I moved towards him, waiting for replies, but none came. A gentle slope led past a huge barn porch and then to the house door, where the man stood waiting, the candle in his lantern guttering and almost spent.

In the flickering glow of candlelight, I could see him clearly for the first time; his face was lined and ruddy with an unkempt, dark moustache flecked with grey – older than I, perhaps in his forties. He wore a dark woolen hat, pulled securely over his ears, a thick black or brown jacket buttoned high, and a scarf wrapped tightly around his neck and chin. I noticed he was pressing his free hand against his stomach. Standing before him here, I had the weather driving directly into my face and I longed to get inside.

"We've arrived at last, then," I exclaimed, blinking against the rain. "This is where you live?"

With an unmistakable glint of the eye, he studied me for a moment. Then he held the lantern toward the open door.

"Welcome to Wuthering Heights," he said.

* * *

I stepped into the warm darkness. He followed. The lantern threw dim, trembling light into the space. Then, a sudden flare as he lit a match. A small, blackish brown dog jumped up at his legs, its little tail wagging so furiously the whole of his rump moved too.

"Dahn, Jerry!" he said, then laughed. "Nobbut a cross 'tween a lamp-poast an' a walkin' stick!"

I stood awkwardly in the middle of the room, waiting. At a table by the window, he placed a new, lighted candle in the lantern. He blew out the match, then gathered two further lamps and a candlestick. These he lit using two more matches.

" Nivver use a match moar than twice," he said. "They'll shoot off yer 'ead."

He arranged the lights around the room, revealing its modest size. Without hall or lobby, the main door opened straight into what was obviously the main living space. I noticed a pervasive odour – hot, pungent, earthy and sweet. The floor was paved with old stone flags and the ceiling was heavily beamed and smoke-stained. He removed his hat and scarf.

" Well, doan't jes stand theer like a flighted callant. Ye'd best tek off yer cooat."

" Oh, yes – thank you..."

197

I did so and placed it over the back of a plain chair near the table. I pushed the wet hair from my face and watched as he moved to the fireplace.

"Nah, come on, lad, set ye dahn. Ye mun be fair beaten wi' clomping all that way."

He gestured to a comfortable-looking armchair by the fire. I sat down and watched as he pokered the fire and threw a lump of something onto it. The little mongrel curled up in front of the hearth.

"Nowt like t'smell of a peat fire," said the man.

"Oh, that's what it is! You're burning peat!"

He regarded me with a look of puzzlement.

"Aye, o' course. Cut it out off t'moor oop behind t'house. There's nivver a chance o' getting' logs or cooal this far owt."

"Er... No, I suppose not." I indicated the lamps and candlestick with a slightly defeated flap of my arms. "And, obviously... no electricity either?"

"Nay, nay! Not all this way up." He chuckled and removed his coat and scarf. "Doan't want it, doan't need it."

My heart sank. I had been hoping to make a telephone call. Anxiety tugged at my chest. He dragged another chair from the table and joined me by the fire.

"Anyroad up, t'name's Roddie. Ernest Roddie." He announced a little formally.

I answered with my name and added, "I'm very pleased to meet you. Thank you so much for helping..."

He interrupted me with a little dismissive wave and said: "Best get these off..."

He busied himself with untying the laces of his boots, grunting at the effort of leaning forward.

Glancing subtly around, I tried to absorb my surroundings. The walls were roughly plastered and coated for the most part with a flaking blue wash. In places, especially lower down and in corners, this had been thinly overpainted in white. A redecoration still in progress, it seemed. To the right of the stone fireplace was a slim grandfather clock and, next to that, a wooden door. At the back of the room, opposite the mullioned front window, stood a dresser covered in piles of books. A few of these had paper covers but most were leather-bound volumes in brown, green and wine-red. Among this muddle of reading matter, there were pots, bowls and copper pans.

" Aye, that'll be moar like," he breathed and started pulling at the boots to get them off.

* * *

Behind me, above the book-laden dresser, a range of shelves contained plates – both pewter and china - held in place by dowel rods. A worn, stone staircase led to the upper floor and, at its side, stood a black settle, like something out of an old country pub. Upon it, I noticed for the first time, two sleeping cats curled up on a knitted blanket.

"Tha'd best tek off them shoon," he said, pointing to my feet.

"Sorry?"

"Let 'em dry," he replied, still pointing.

"Oh, my shoes! Of course – yes. Thank you!" I kicked them off. We watched the peat burn and listened to the ticking of the clock. The wind wailed mournfully around the house, and I could feel an icy draught blowing under the door. Rain clattered at the windowpanes. Steam was beginning to rise gently from my trousers and socks.

"Are you a farmer here?" I asked, feeling a need to make conversation even though I was tired and starting to long for sleep.

" Aye, of a soart. Poultry," he chuckled. "Allus jawked I'd live up 'ere somedeah. A kind o' dream sin' ah were nobbut a lad. And now 'ere I am at last"

"But why here, particularly? It seems very remote. The winters must be dreadful!"

"Aye, well", he replied, and leaned closer. "Tha sees...this auld farm is a reet feamous place."

"Oh, really?"

His eyes narrowed. He lowered his voice and said with a slow nodding of the head, "yer in Brontë Country now."

"Ah! Brontë Country," I said, feigning polite interest. I failed to understand why this information seemed so significant to him. I was vaguely aware that someone called Brontë had written books a long time ago. I've heard of Charles Dickens as well and had to read *Emma*

199

by Jane Austen in literature lessons at school, and some Shakespeare, which I hated.

"Tell me more," I said, not really wishing to encourage this turn in the conversation. I've never had much interest in novels and poetry, especially the old stuff. Roddie reached onto the mantelpiece for his pipe and began pushing tobacco into it, which he took from a soft leather pouch.

"Well," he said, and I braced myself. "The Brontë village is jes' four mile from 'ere. Down t'Sladen Valley theer. Haworth. Where they lived 'most all their lives and wrote all them books."

" 'They'? Was there more than one? I'm sorry, I..."

"Aye!" he answered with great vehemence. "There were four on 'em: Charlotte, t'little squinty one – near blind as a bat; Emily – very tall an offish, cross-looking; pretty young Anne who wu'nt go boo at a goose; and the kittle madling, their daft ginger brother. 'Course, they all died young, one after t'other..."

He held a match to the bowl of his pipe. I watched as he lit it and began puffing smoke. I found myself wondering what the time was and whether I would get any sleep. I felt exhausted and rather preoccupied with how I would manage to get to Leeds in the morning.

"I were born and bred in Haworth, me faither were a drill sergeant in t'local volunteers. When I were a lad, there wuh folks still living who remembered all t' Brontës, and the town were reet proud of all t'clever books and poems they writ. Happen ye've read 'em?"

"Er, no, I'm afraid not." I tried to laugh it off.

"Aye, well, *Wuthering Heights* were allus my fav'rit. It's a reet strange, mystical tale of passion an' hatred an' fightin' an' cruelty an' death. Restless spirits glidin' abaht on t'moors."

He crossed to the dresser and picked up a slim volume, bound in red leather, which he passed to me. I opened it and looked at the title page: *Wuthering Heights* by Emily Brontë. Roddie crossed to the uncurtained window, which was still spattered and running with rain. He gazed out, and said quietly,

"The desp'rate little ghooast of a bairn', Catherine, beating at t' window and screaming to come in. An' Heathcliff, like a divil with his sharp teeth an' 'is fierce black eyes, diggin' in her grave with nobbut 'is bare hands and huggin' and kissin' with her dead body."

200

I glanced down with some distaste at the book in my hands. Mr. Roddie drew on his pipe and exhaled a cloud of grey smoke. The sweet smell of his tobacco blended pleasantly with that of the smoldering fire. The clock ticked on and I began to feel almost drugged with tiredness. Roddie moved away from the window and stood at the foot of the stairs.

"And that gaumless young thing, all ringlets and frills, kept prisoner 'ere. An' that gypsy lyin' dead in t'bed up theer wi' t'window open and the weather comin' in..."

He gazed up the stairs and nodded at the ceiling as he said this. I turned in my chair a little.

"Here?" I said. "All this happened here?' I raised the book and waved it. " I thought this was a novel – you know, fiction." Then I remembered something he had said earlier, when we first arrived at the house. "Ah! You said 'welcome to Wuthering Heights'!"

He returned to his chair, laughing.

"Nay, nay!! That were jes' me larking. This place is Top Withins, or High Withins. Sometimes, Upper Withins. They call it all soarts. Happen With*ins* or With*ens*. Way back, it were allus called Top o' t'Witherns. Them we passed on t'way, goin' to ruin, that's Lower Withins and Middle Withins. Been empty for years now. This were empty long time 'for I got 'ere. Needed a bit o' fixin' up, o' coarse."

"Of course."

"The point is, lad," he said, leaning forward again and fixing me a knowing look, "Theer's folks as reckon this place is what Emily had in mind when she writ *Wuthering Heights*. That this house is what she were thinkin' on."

He nodded and sat back in his chair.

"Oh, I see, " I said, too sleepy to muster much enthusiasm. He puffed at his pipe.

"People come 'ere from all over t'world. Just to see. Even America! They clomp all t'way up from Haworth – four mile – and stand owt theer gawping. Near ev'ry day they come."

"Goodness me!" I shifted in my seat in the hope that I could fend off the need for sleep.

"Aye," he continued, with a short, reflective laugh. "Some on 'em even reckon to come inside, so I tek 'em to the back window up theer," he pointed at the beamed ceiling, " and tell 'em 'bout Cathy's wailin' ghoast. Then into t'barn and mistal to show where Heathcliff were made to sleep. Hehe! Their maws drop open and they smile and gawp! O' 'course, I allus tell folks the place is 'aunted."

"Haunted? And is it?" I asked.

He paused, inhaling smoke, which he then exhaled in a long, soft cloud. The clock tick-tocked away. Outside, it seemed the wind had dropped and the sound of rain on the window had ceased. The little dog at our feet suddenly yelped, still asleep. His paws twitched. Chasing rabbits, I thought, drowsily.

"Well, theer's more things in 'eaven an' Earth, tha knaws," he said. "Messter Shekspeare said that." Another pull on the pipe. "I allus tell folks about t'ghoast of Emily Brontë passin' by."

"Really?

"Aye!" He pointed a thumb back over his shoulder, toward the door and the moors beyond. "Striding out wi' noa bonnet and t'wind in 'er hair, off to Ponden Kirk or the Stones up yonder. Or comin' back agin. No cloak on an' mud on 'er frock, an' that greeat beast of a dog clompin' along at 'er side. Hehe! They likes that."

I felt my head nodding and my eyelids trying to close. Mr. Roddie's voice droned on.

"An' in these parts, I says to 'em, there's the Hunter's Wind: allus tells of a death comin'. Blows over t'top wi' t'sound of gallopin' hooves. Ah heered it one evenin' – me brother were 'ere that day – an' t'next moarnin' we found me auld hoss, Tommy, lying dead down theer in t'field. Jes' back theer in t'Rough, we call it."

He continued with his stories, but the drag of sleep became irresistible. I remember only snatches of his commentary after this.

" An' a strange bird buzzes o'er... sound like t'mosquitoes I heered when I were overseas in t'war... not a lark or a linnet... not grouse or lapwing... Nivver sin it though... Top Withins is a-waitin', he said to me... crystal clear, the water in t'spring up theer"

* * *

I slept but felt I was spinning restlessly under a huge empty sky. My dreams were filled with flickering, fragmentary visions; the fuel gauge in my car edging into the red; a lamp swinging in the dark; a child's white hand bleeding on the shattered pane of a window; I could hear the rhythmic thud of a horse's hooves and saw a dark rider glide swiftly past, his black cloak flying behind; the corpse of a young woman in an open coffin with its side torn away, her pale eyes suddenly opening and staring into mine; moonlight; a drift of white feathers dancing in the air and turning into heavy snowflakes, driven by a screaming wind. I looked down at roofless old buildings and heard a distant muffled screaming that changed into the bleating of sheep. A peaty odour and the soft scratch of coarse grass against my cheek. A sensation of walking, walking. A slow, cool dawn.

* * *

Back in Stanbury, I checked that all was well with my car and set off along the street in search of help. Soon, I arrived at a pub with green and gold signage: "The Wuthering Heights". I banged on the door, hoping to convey polite urgency. There was no response. I walked to the back of the building, where a woman was shaking a duster from an upstairs window.

"Hello, there!" she called and then, a little apprehensively: "I'm afraid we're not open yet – can I help at all?"

"Oh, good morning!" I smiled up at her. "Thank you so much. I'm afraid I'm in a bit of a fix…"

I explained my predicament to her as briefly as I could, and she listened sympathetically.

"Hang on, then. Wait there. I'll give my husband a shout."

She disappeared from the window and I soon heard her muffled shouts from within. I brushed at the dried mud on my coat sleeve and noticed water stains on my trousers. Not the best impression to give at an important meeting, I thought. My shoes were caked in mud, too.

The back door opened with the sound of heavy bolts sliding free and the woman appeared and beckoned to me.

"Come on in. My husband's just coming down. We can let you have some petrol, no problem. We always keep a bit spare in case. Are you alright? Come in and have a sit."

I followed her inside. The bar was full of mahogany tables and dark, hard chairs. A high rail displayed decorative china plates. The red walls were covered in pictures and mirrors in gilt frames. Polished horse brasses hung on old black beams. There was a chalkboard with a hand-written lunch menu hanging above the fireplace. I perceived the sharp smell of stale beer and disinfectant combined.

A smiling man came into the room and asked for my car keys.

"I've spare fuel out in the shed," he said. "I can top you up."

"You're so kind, thank you very much. Let me know what I owe..."

He waved a hand in dismissal and said "Make the man a coffee, then! He looks like he's had a rough night."

He left the room, shaking my keys as he went. His wife went behind the bar and busied herself at the coffee machine.

"Lovely place you've got here," I said. "The Wuthering Heights!"

"Oh, I know!" She rolled her eyes. "You can't get away from it round here – it's all Brontë this and Brontë that! Means good trade for us though. You know... We do lunches and evening meals and all that. Nice beer garden out the back in the summer."

She raised her voice over the loud gurgling of the milk frother. "And we've a couple of nice B&B rooms too. Well worth it, you know, because people come from all over the world to do the Brontë Country thing!"

"Yes, yes – I know," I said, thinking of Mr. Roddie regaling his visitors with tales of the supernatural.

"We get a lot of people all year round. Lots of walkers, especially – some lovely walks round here. You know, they maybe come to Haworth, or stay here for a few days so they can trek up to Top Withins and that." She pointed casually at an old framed photograph on the wall, then brought my coffee.

"Thank you."

"Because," she continued, "Top Withins is the original of the building in the book, so people like to see it."

"Yes, indeed. I've heard all about that – in fact, Top Withins is where I spent the night."

I stirred my coffee. The woman stopped on her way back to the bar and turned to face me.

"Top Withins?"

"Yes."

Her face crinkled into a good-humoured grimace and, after a pause, she laughed and shook her head.

"Must have been somewhere else. Top Withins has been in ruins for years and years and years. There's nothing much of it left now. You know, you traipse all the way up there in your sturdy boots with your backpack full of sandwiches, just to find there's nothing to see except rubble and sheep poo."

I put down my cup and stared at her. Something in my belly churned. She took the picture from the wall and brought it for me to see.

"This is how it used to look."

It was a print of an old, sepia-toned photograph. I recognized the building immediately even though I had only seen it in the dark; the huge barn porch, the row of mullioned windows, the partially collapsed wall running along the front, a solitary chimney.

"Yes! That's it! I was there last night!"

The woman had taken her phone from her pocket and was tapping and swiping.

"I was looked after by the man who lives there. Ernest Roddie..."

She held out her phone, showing me an image of a derelict building – low walls, no roof, no windows, the high gable standing proud. "That's how it looks now," she said, and then, "hang on a minute..."

She tapped and scrolled again.

"Ernest what?"

"Roddie..."

"Ah yes. Here we are, look..." She started reading aloud from the screen in little bursts.

"Um... 'Last inhabited by Ernest Roddy in 1926...' Blah blah...Ah! 'Withins came back to life in the 1920s, its chickens farmed by a Mr. Ernest Roddie, but he gave it up...' Uh... 'Ernest Roddy,' (spelt different), 'a tall, affable man lived there...'"

"Yes, quite tall..." I could hardly speak. "Very kind... he... had a lantern..."

The landlord returned with my keys.

"All sorted," he smiled. On his way out, he said, "I'm going to bring them barrels in."

The woman considered me for a moment and looked again at her phone.

"It says here that 'John Ernest Bagnall Roddie died in 1950 at the age of seventy-seven.' Seventy years ago, pretty much."

I lifted my eyes and searched hers as though, somehow, she could answer all the questions I wanted to stammer out. She looked away.

"Drink your coffee," she said.

The Meeting illustration by Lisa Dambrough

THE MEETING

by Lisa Darnbrough
Cottingham in East Yorkshire, currently living in Leicester

She watched them from a distance
Entranced, captivated, mesmerised
By these lovers, lost in time
Cold pale skin oblivious to the wild withering wind
Flakes of fresh snow dancing around them playfully,
Dark shadows against the snow-kissed heather
Excluded, remote and alienated from the Earth
The world having almost forgotten them
Transported into old wives tales and fire-side stories
Of their bitter struggles, lost and won

Miseries were forgotten
Their own heaven reconciled, solidified

For an instant the ghosts looked over at her
A glimmer of recognition, a bond formed

She wrapped her shawl around her tighter
Watched them silently, slowly move on

At home her candle flickered and bowed
She picked up her quill
She had her tale, their tale
The words formed on the blank page
'1801 ...'

Les Perles illustration by Maud Servignat

LES PERLES

by Maud Servignat
Orléans, France

« Je vois bien que nous ne sommes, nous tous qui vivons ici, rien de plus que des fantômes ou que des ombres légères ».

-Sophocle

Fantôme : sa seule évocation inspire, terrifie, ou est simplement sujette à moquerie.

Peut-on ne jurer de rien ? Qu'y a-t-il à voir au-delà des apparences ? Nos morts ont-ils réellement disparu pour toujours ?

L'histoire que je vais vous conter maintenant est la mienne mais pourrait tout aussi bien être la vôtre.

Orléans - France 20 février 2020 - 20 heures

Je vis dans une petite ville française dont le passé historique et sa figure tutélaire hantent encore ses charmantes petites rues médiévales. La vie y est agitée, bruyante, parfois violente, chacun étant absorbé par ses obligations et difficultés du quotidien, oubliant les beautés alentours. Pour moi, la beauté se trouve dans l'art, la littérature, et la découverte de leurs mondes infinis et stimulants. Ce soir, après une dure journée de travail, je suis heureuse d'avoir enfin le temps de commencer à lire « *The Tenant of Wildfell Hall* » que j'avais délaissé depuis plusieurs années au profit de lectures plus divertissantes.

Dans mon lit, bien calée contre mon oreiller, je commence ma lecture. Les hurlements du vent et les bruits de la ville semblent s'éloigner doucement de moi comme un train quittant une gare bondée de voyageurs. Petit à petit, le sommeil m'envahit.

Silence...

Cling, cling, cling, Cling, Cling, Cling !!!!

Un son, de plus en plus fort, résonne en moi, me réveille brusquement et me fait prendre conscience que je me trouve dans mon lit avec, entre les mains, le livre ouvert à la page 20.

Tendue, en éveil, j'écoute. *Cling, cling, cling !* On dirait des perles dévalant les marches de l'escalier en bois de la maison. Le chat est-il en train de faire rouler son jouet favori ? Les félins vivent la nuit, ces petits chenapans ! Afin de me rassurer, je saute précipitamment du lit mais trébuche sur le tapis. Quelle maladroite je suis par moments ! Mes pieds sont nus sur les lattes du vieux parquet en chêne. Le sol est glacé en ce mois de février. Une soudaine rafale de vent secoue violemment la vitre au-dessus de l'escalier me frappant d'effroi. Le cœur battant, les doigts agrippés à la balustrade, je scrute le palier du bas plongé dans la pénombre... rien ! Avec courage, j'entame ma descente. Chaque marche craque sous mes pas, je suis seule dans cette grande maison. Au rez-de-chaussée, je trouve le chat tendrement lové sur une chaise du hall d'entrée près du radiateur. Il n'est donc pas à l'origine de cet étrange bruit. D'où provient-il alors ? Je décide d'aller explorer la cuisine... rien ! Je me dirige ensuite, à pas feutrés, en direction du salon... toujours rien ! Soudain, j'entends un fort craquement suivi d'un *Cling, cling, cling !* Terrorisée, je fais demi-tour, retourne dans la cuisine, et me saisis d'un rouleau à pâtisserie abandonné sur la table. Courageusement, je suis prête à défendre mon bien mais lutte contre mon sentiment d'insécurité grandissant...

Cling, cling, cling ! Le son provient désormais du hall d'entrée.

Les mains raidies sur le rouleau, la gorge sèche, je me dirige vers le hall. Figée, je suis sous le choc : une trentaine de petites sphères orange lumineuses tournoient au pied de l'escalier. Elles se rapprochent et s'éloignent de moi en un va et vient incessant puis se dirigent vers le seuil de ma chambre. Tremblante, je reste prostrée, comme dans un mauvais rêve...

Combien de minutes, d'heures, suis-je restée là, immobile sous le charme de cette apparition ?

Après que les sphères aient disparues, je retrouve mes esprits et rejoins ma chambre pour tenter de trouver le sommeil. Pluie et tonnerre envahissent l'atmosphère, semblables aux griffes acérées d'un prédateur affamé désirant entraîner sa proie vers les ténèbres.

Orléans – la semaine suivante

Une semaine comme toutes les précédentes.

Les heures s'écoulent lentement à exercer un travail dénué de sens en compagnie de collègues pour lesquels je n'ai guère d'affinité. La pluie ne cesse de tomber et métamorphose le jour en nuit. Me pressant et luttant contre le vent qui me fouette le visage, je rentre chez moi en rêvant d'un bon bain chaud relaxant accompagné d'une tisane à la lavande. J'ai très peu repensé à cette étrange expérience du 20, pensant que seule la fatigue était responsable de ce phénomène inexpliqué.

L'eau coule avec vigueur. La vapeur commence à envahir la salle de bain. Le chat, fasciné comme à son habitude, parcourt le rebord en faïence de la baignoire. Subitement, il se contracte, et en un bon, saute sur le sol puis s'échappe en faisant violemment claquer la porte. Surprise par sa réaction, je ferme immédiatement le robinet et reste immobile, à l'affût du moindre bruit. Je perçois de très faibles rires qui deviennent de plus en plus envahissants, suivis de pas rapides dans l'escalier. Mon Dieu, ça recommence ! Des inconnus ont pénétré dans la maison ! Je sors en courant mais personne sur le palier. Je descends les escaliers et aperçois au loin le chat assis devant la bibliothèque du salon. Je me rapproche et remarque, à ses pieds, un livre retourné sur le parquet. Comment un livre enserré parmi d'autres dans une bibliothèque surchargée a-t-il pu tomber sur le sol ? Son titre : **Charlotte et Emily Brontë - Le Palais de la Mort.** Je me saisis du livre et reste stupéfaite en lisant les premières lignes de la page sur laquelle il s'est ouvert :

Emily J Brontë 15 mai 1842

Le Chat

« Je puis le dire avec sincérité, que j'aime les chats ; aussi sais-je donner de très bonnes raisons, pourquoi ceux qui les haïssent, ont tort. Un chat est un animal qui a plus de sentiments humains que presque tout autre être ».

Mon chat, toujours à mes côtés, ronronne de bien-être et semble acquiescé, me fixant de son regard bleu azur. Que vient-il de se passer ? Paradoxalement, un sentiment étrange d'apaisement m'envahit. Ces évènements ne devraient-ils pas, au contraire, me faire perdre la raison ? Ma maison serait-elle hantée ? Aux aguets, je prête l'oreille. Plus aucun bruit ; le calme est revenu. Dans la salle de bain, malgré la tiédeur de l'eau, je peux enfin me détendre.

Le lendemain, au bureau

Malgré l'effet apaisant du bain, je suis restée éveillée toute la nuit, essayant de trouver une explication rationnelle à ces étranges phénomènes. Je me sens frustrée, épuisée et décide de prendre un peu de repos pour profiter d'un moment de tranquillité. Mais dans la salle de pause, je croise une collègue. Après quelques banalités échangées, la conversation commence à prendre une étrange tournure :

Ma collègue : « *J'ai regardé hier un documentaire à la télé sur Charlotte Brontë. Tu savais qu'elle était amoureuse de son professeur en Belgique et qu'elle lui envoyait régulièrement des lettres enflammées en Français auxquelles il n'a jamais répondu ?* »

Moi : « *Oui bien sû ! Je suis, si je puis dire, une grande admiratrice de la famille Brontë* ».

Le temps d'un instant, il me semble curieux qu'elle mentionne Charlotte puis... brusquement, comme habitée par une âme étrangère, j'énonce la phrase suivante :

« *Quand je prononce des mots français, il me semble que je vous parle* »

Troublée, j'écourte la conversation pour rejoindre mon poste de travail, oubliant mon café déjà froid.

Avec l'impossibilité de me concentrer, la journée se transforme en véritable torture mentale. Les propos de Charlotte sortant de ma bouche à la manière d'un esprit qui s'empare de ma volonté... je deviens folle ! Je m'isole, épuisée, et fonds en larmes. N'y tenant plus, je prétexte une migraine et rentre chez moi.

De retour

Enfin à la maison ! je retire mes chaussures et me jette sur le canapé. Le chat s'étend sur moi, heureux de trouver une source de chaleur dans cette grande demeure froide et sombre. Je ferme les yeux et... subitement reprends conscience, inquiète. J'ai dû m'assoupir un moment. Je suis frigorifiée, un courant d'air froid me frôle le visage. Tout semble calme dans la maison. Le livre tombé de la bibliothèque est resté sur la table. Je décide de le ranger dans son emplacement. Je le saisis et, baissant le regard vers le chat qui se frotte contre mes jambes, il me semble voir passer furtivement, du coin de l'œil, une ombre blanche. Brusquement, un frisson glacé me parcourt le corps. Je suspends mon mouvement... une main gelée vient de se poser sur la mienne. Je lâche le livre qui tombe sur le sol. Mon cœur est prêt à éclater. Je fais volte-face, terrorisée, mais ne vois pas âme qui vive. J'entends, une fois de plus, de faibles rires provenant de l'escalier. Je me déplace prudemment dans leur direction...personne ; l'atmosphère est redevenue silencieuse.

La soirée approche, j'allume le téléviseur et augmente le volume sonore pour me rassurer en prenant bien soin de fermer à double tour toutes les portes de la maison. Je me fais couler un bain et prépare un rapide repas pour le soir.

Soirée

Assise sur le canapé, serrant fortement ma tasse entre mes mains pour les réchauffer, je bois les dernières gorgées de ma camomille. A l'extérieur, de grandes rafales de pluie menaçantes cinglent les fenêtres. Je ne prête pas attention aux deux protagonistes qui s'époumonent en agitant les bras dans l'écran de télévision. Mon esprit est complètement accaparé par ces étranges expériences et une sensation diffuse d'être observée par un ennemi invisible me pénètre.

Fatiguée, je ferme les yeux. Je dois me reposer, j'en ai *besoin*...

Un léger fléchissement de lumière me fait rouvrir les yeux.

Le lampadaire placé à côté du canapé clignote de manière irrégulière comme s'il émettait un message en Morse. Tout est calme, pourtant, règne toujours cette sensation de ne pas être seule. Tout en réadaptant petit à petit ma vision à la lumière naturelle, je suis éblouie ...

Les petites sphères orange apparues une semaine auparavant tournoient dans le salon au-dessus de la table basse puis près de la bibliothèque. Elles se regroupent puis se séparent comme pour m'inviter à les accompagner dans leur joyeuse sarabande. L'environnement, jusque-là glacial, semble s'emplir d'une douce chaleur optimisante. Je me sens littéralement absorbée par cette vision, surprise de ne pas être plus effrayée. Mon impression de ne plus être seule dans la maison se transforme en certitude. L'agitation monte. Les rires... ils sont de retour, plus précis, plus nets, plus imposants... dans l'escalier. Des enfants... ce sont des rires d'enfants. Ils semblent trouver un écho dans toute la maison. Une horloge sonne comme une confirmation. Je suis toujours assise sur le canapé, incapable de bouger, pétrifiée. Je me surprends à sourire malgré un frisson qui me parcourt le corps. Ma curiosité l'emporte sur ma peur. Je me lève en direction des sphères qui m'invitent à les suivre. Arrivée au pied de l'escalier, je les retrouve, tournoyantes devant la porte de ma chambre au premier étage. Je monte très lentement les marches, ma main droite, très légèrement crispée, glisse sur la rambarde. Les rires qui semblent s'être déplacés proviennent désormais de ma chambre. Le palier est plongé dans la pénombre. Je distingue une faible lumière blanche à travers la porte entre-ouverte. J'étais pourtant sûre de l'avoir fermée, comme toutes les autres de la maison ! Soudain, les sphères maintenant regroupées en un unique globe semblable à un disque solaire, s'introduisent par l'entrebâillement de la porte et me laissent éblouie par leur intensité. « *Suis-nous* », semblent-elles me chanter. Je pousse la porte, ma vision toujours altérée. Mon cœur cogne fort dans ma poitrine. A l'intérieur, une douce chaleur bienfaisante m'envahit.

L'extraordinaire disque orange me donne l'impression d'avoir investi tout l'espace. Soudain, il se divise en trois sphères de tailles plus modestes ; une lumière éclatante jaillit de chacune d'elles. Je suis totalement aveuglée et, reculant, je tombe sur le sol contre le mur attenant à la porte. Je tente d'ouvrir les yeux en dépit de la douloureuse luminosité. Puis, les yeux mi-clos, j'observe, se dressant devant moi, trois petites silhouettes fragiles, épousant par moment la forme d'un seul et même nuage blanc mais toujours entourées des trois sphères flamboyantes.

La lumière émise est désormais beaucoup plus supportable. Elle me permet d'admirer ce qui se déroule sous mes yeux, toujours assise au sol : le nuage semble hésiter, il tente de se scinder en quatre parties distinctes mais, cet équilibre instable ne semblant pas lui convenir, se stabilise à trois. Trois silhouettes pour trois sphères solaires. Elles sont au départ, semblables à de la brume blanche impalpable mais après quelques instants suspendus, j'observe nettement leurs contours. Comme encerclées de néons blancs, de volumineuses robes nuageuses prennent forme. De la même manière, des visages flous entourés de bonnets désuets complètent ces silhouettes féminines.

La suite de cette incident surnaturel m'est encore très difficile à décrire. Je me sens envahie par une émotion si intense que mes larmes coulent, tombent et s'infiltrent entre les touches de mon clavier d'ordinateur... mais je dois achever mon récit.

Toujours assise au sol, je n'ose pas bouger, émerveillée. Comment les décrire ? des spectres, des apparitions, des illusions d'optique ? Elles ne sont, en tout cas, pas ce que l'on décrit dans les romans d'épouvante. Elles sont bienveillantes, chaleureuses, pleines d'un amour que l'on décrirait comme inconditionnel. Cette étrange énergie, mélange de persévérance, d'amour de la vie et de confiance en soi, m'est transmise à cet instant même. Une douce mais impérieuse sensation prend corps en moi, celle de savoir désormais qui je suis, d'être pleinement maîtresse de ma vie.

Au moment même où je suis investie par ce nouveau pouvoir, les trois sphères orange semblent également se métamorphoser. Elles se fondent avec les silhouettes nuageuses pour laisser place à une boule d'énergie si éblouissante que cette dernière m'oblige à fermer les yeux et me recroqueviller sur moi-même. Après quelques secondes, elle s'évapore, rendant la clarté de la pièce beaucoup plus tolérable. Enfin... je peux rouvrir les yeux. Il me faut encore quelques secondes pour m'acclimater à la luminosité ambiante et ne plus voir de traces blanches se déplacer autour moi.

Près de la table de chevet, sur laquelle repose le roman d'Anne Brontë, la trentaine de petites sphères orange tourbillonne, diffusant toujours cette très légère chaleur nourrissante. Puis, en l'espace d'un éclair, elles disparaissent, laissant derrière elles, délicatement posé sur le livre ... *un collier de perles de Cornaline.*

Depuis cette soirée de février, le calme est revenu dans ma vieille maison. Mais une chose est sûre cher lecteur, je peux vous l'affirmer... les fantômes existent.

La pierre de Cornaline redonne vitalité et énergie, transmet l'amour de la vie, éloigne la peur de la mort, favorise la résolution, la réussite, entretient la créativité et donne confiance aux timides.

Honest People Don't Hide Their Deeds

The Beads Illustration by Maud Servignat

THE BEADS

by Maud Servignat
Orléans, France

"For I see that those of us alive are nothing more than ghosts or empty shadows."

-Sophocles

Ghost: his invocation alone inspires, terrifies, or is just prone to mockery.

There is not very much to be sure about? Is there something to see through the shallow layer of illusion? Have our dead really disappeared forever?

The story I am going to tell you now is mine, but could be yours just as well.

Orléans - France February 20th 2020 - 20 hours PM

I live in a small French town whose historic past and tutelary figure still haunt its charming medieval streets. Life is hectic, noisy, sometimes violent, everybody remaining absorbed by their obligations and daily difficulties, forgetting the surrounding beauties. For me, beauty can be found in art, literature and the discovery of their infinite and stimulating worlds. Tonight, after a hard day work, I'm happy to finally have time to start reading "The Tenant of Wildfell Hall" which I had left behind for several years in favor of more entertaining readings.

In my bed, snugged against my pillow, I start reading. The howling of the wind and the sounds of the city seem to slowly move away from me like a train leaving a crowded station. Little by little, sleep invades me.

Silence...

Cling, cling, cling, Cling, Cling, Cling!!!!

Growing louder, the sound resonates in me, wakes me suddenly from sleep, and makes me realize that I am in bed with the book in my hands opened on page twenty.

Tense, on alert, I listen. *Cling, cling, cling!* It sounds like beads running down the steps of the house's wooden staircase. Is the cat rolling his favorite toy? Felines live at night, these little rascals! To reassure myself, I hastily jump out of bed but trip over the carpet. How awkward I can be at times! My feet are bare on the old oak parquet's slats. The ground is icy in February. A sudden gust of wind violently shakes the staircase window, hitting me in terror. With my heart beating, fingers gripped at the railing, I scrutinize the bottom landing plunged into darkness... nothing! With courage, I begin my descent. Each step creaks under my feet; I'm alone in this big house. On the ground floor, in the entrance hall, I find the cat near the heater, tenderly curled up on a chair. So, he is not the source of this strange noise. Where does it come from then?

I decide to go and explore the kitchen...nothing! I then quietly walk towards the living room...still nothing! Suddenly, I hear a loud crack followed by a *"cling, cling, cling"* sound. Terrorized, I turn around and, back in the kitchen, grab a rolling pin left on the table. Courageously, I am ready to defend my property, but have to fight against my growing insecurity feeling...

Cling, cling, cling! The sound comes from the entrance hall.

Hands stiffened on the rolling pin, throat dry, I walk towards the hall. I'm in shock, frozen: thirty bright small orange orbs rotate around the bottom of the stairs. In a constant back and forth they approach and retreat from me to finally move towards my bedroom's threshold. Trembling, I remain powerless, as in a bad dream...

How many minutes, hours, have I been there, motionless under the spell of this apparition?

After the orbs have disappeared, I regain my senses and reach my bedroom to try to find some sleep. Rain and thunder invade the atmosphere, like the sharp claws of a hungry predator wishing to lead its prey into darkness.

Orléans – the next week

A week like all the previous ones.

The time passes slowly, doing meaningless work in the company of colleagues for whom I have little affinity. The rain never stops falling, turning day into night. Hurrying and fighting against the wind that whips my face, I go home dreaming of a good relaxing hot bath, accompanied by a lavender herbal tea. I thought very little about the strange experience of the 20th, incriminating fatigue as the only responsible cause of this unexplained phenomenon.

The water flows vigorously. Steam begins to invade the bathroom. The cat, as usual fascinated, crosses the bathtub's earthenware ledge. Suddenly, he shrinks and, in a leap, jumps on the floor and escapes by violently slamming the door. Surprised by his reaction, I immediately close the tap and stay still, on the lookout for the slightest noise. I hear very weak laughter becoming more and more invasive, followed by brisk steps in the stairs. My God, it starts all over again! Strangers have entered the house! I run out, but find no one on the landing. I go down the stairs and see in the distance, the cat sitting in front of the living room's bookshelf. I get closer and notice, at his feet, a book turned over on the wooden floor. How could a book tightly packed among others in an overcrowded bookshelf fall? Its title: ***Charlotte et Emily Brontë - Le Palais de la Mort*** (Charlotte and Emily Brontë – The Palace of Death). I grab the book and I am stunned when I read the first lines of the page where it opened:

Emily J Brontë 15 mai 1842

Le Chat

« Je puis le dire avec sincérité, que j'aime les chats ; aussi sais-je donner de très bonnes raisons, pourquoi ceux qui les haïssent, ont tort. Un chat est un animal qui a plus de sentiments humains que presque tout autre être ».

(Emily J Brontë May 15, 1842

The Cat

"I can say it with sincerity, that I love cats; also I know how to give very good reasons, why those who hate them, are wrong. A cat is an animal that has more human feelings than almost any other being.")

My cat, still by my side, purrs with delight and seems to nod, staring at me with his azure blue eyes. What just happened? Paradoxically, a strange quietude invades me. On the contrary, shouldn't these events make me lose my mind? Is my house haunted? Vigilant, I'm listening. No more noise; quiet is restored. In the bathroom, despite the luke-warm water, I can finally relax.

The next day, at the office

Despite the bath's soothing effect, I stayed awake all night, trying to find a rational explanation for this strange occurrence. I feel frustrated, exhausted, and decide to take some rest to enjoy a moment of tranquility. But, in the break room, I run into a colleague. After some shared trivialities, the conversation begins to take a strange turn:

My colleague: *"Yesterday I watched a documentary about Charlotte Brontë on TV. Did you know that she was in love with her teacher in Belgium and that she regularly sent him fiery letters in French to which he never replied?"*

Me: *"Yes of course! I am, if I may say so, a great admirer of the Brontë family".*

For a moment, it seems strange to me that she mentions Charlotte, and... suddenly, as if inhabited by a stranger soul, I enunciate the following sentence:

« *Quand je prononce des mots français, il me semble que je vous parle* »

("When I say French words, it seems to me that I speak to you")

Troubled, I cut short the conversation to reach my workstation, forgetting my already cold coffee.

Impossible to concentrate; day turns into real mental torture. Charlotte's words coming out of my mouth like a spirit taking hold of my will... I am going insane! I isolate myself, exhausted, and burst into tears. I can't take it any longer; I pretend a migraine and go home.

Back home

Finally, I'm home! I take off my shoes and throw myself on the sofa. The cat lies on top of me, happy to find a heat source in this dark and cold big house. I close my eyes and ... suddenly regain consciousness, worried. I must have dozed off for a while. I'm freezing, a cold breeze brushes my face. Everything seems calm in the house. The book that fell from the bookshelf is still on the table. I decide to store it back in its location. I grab it, looking down at the cat rubbing himself against my legs. From the corner of my eyes, I seem to see a white shadow passing by. Suddenly, an icy shiver runs through my body. I suspend my movement...a frozen hand has just laid on mine. I drop

220

the book to the ground. My heart is about to burst. I turn around, terrorized, but do not see any living soul around. I can hear, once again, faint laughs coming from the stairs. I move carefully in their direction but find nobody. The atmosphere has become silent again.

The evening is approaching, I turn the television on and increase the volume to reassure myself, taking care to bar all of the house's doors. I run a bath and prepare a quick meal for the evening.

Evening

Sitting on the sofa, squeezing my mug tightly between my hands to warm them, I drink the last sips of my chamomile. Outside, great threatening gusts of rain lash the windows. I do not pay attention to the two protagonists running out of breath while waving their arms on the television screen. My mind is completely captured by my strange experiences and a diffuse feeling of being observed by an invisible enemy penetrates me.

Tired, I close my eyes. I need to rest, *I need it...*

A slight decrease of light makes me open my eyes.

The floor lamp placed next to the sofa flashes irregularly as if it is transmitting a message in Morse code. Everything is calm; however, there still exists this feeling of not being alone. While gradually adapting my vision to natural light, I am dazzled ...

The small orange orbs that appeared a week earlier spin in the living room above the coffee table and then, near the bookshelf. They regroup and separate as if to invite me to accompany them in their joyful saraband. The environment, so far icy, seems to be warming with a gentle optimizing heat. I literally feel absorbed by this vision, surprised I am not more afraid. My feeling of no longer being alone in the house turns into certainty. The agitation rises. The laughs ... they are back, more precise, sharper, more imposing ... in the stairs. Children... these are children's laughs. They seem to resonate throughout the house.

A clock rings like a confirmation. I'm still sitting on the couch, unable to move, petrified. I find myself smiling despite a shiver running through my body. My curiosity prevails over my fear. I get up in the direction of the orbs which invite me to follow them. Arriving at the bottom of the stairs, I find them spinning in front of my bedroom door on the first floor. I climb the steps very slowly. My right hand, slightly tense, slides on the railing. The laughter seems to have moved. It comes now from my bedroom. The landing is plunged into darkness. I can see a faint white light through the half-open door. Like all the other doors in the house, I was sure I had closed it! Suddenly, the orbs join together into a single ball looking like a solar disk, break into the half-opening door, and leave me dazzled by their intensity. "*Follow us*", they seem to be singing to me. I push the door, my vision still altered. My heart bangs hard into my chest. As I enter the room, a gentle warmth invades me.

The extraordinary orange disc seems to totally fill the space. Suddenly, it divides into three spheres of more modest sizes, a bright light springing from each one of them. I am totally blinded, and while stepping back, I fall on the floor against the wall adjoining the door. I try to open my eyes despite the painful light. Then, eyes half-closed, I observe standing in front of me, three small fragile silhouettes regaining, at times, the appearance of a single white cloud surrounded by the three flamboyant spheres.

The light emitted is now much more bearable. Still sitting on the ground, it allows me to admire what is happening before my eyes: the cloud seems to hesitate, it tries to split into four distinct parts but this unstable balance not seeming to suit it, stabilizes at three. Three silhouettes for three solar spheres. They are initially like impalpable white mist, but after a few suspended moments, I can clearly see their contours. As if surrounded by white neon lights, voluminous cloudy dresses take shape. In the same way, blurred faces surrounded by old-fashioned bonnets complete these feminine figures.

The rest of this unearthly incident is still very difficult for me to describe. I feel overwhelmed by an emotion so intense that my tears flow, fall and infiltrate the keys of my computer keyboard... but I have to finish my story.

Still sitting on the ground, I do not dare moving, amazed. How to describe them? Wraiths, Apparitions, Optical illusions? In any case, they are not what we describe in Horror Novels. They are compasssionate, warm, full of a love that one could describe as unconditional. This strange energy, a mixture of perseverance, love of life and self-confidence, is transmitted to me at this very moment. A sweet but imperious feeling takes shape in me, that of figuring out now who I am, of being fully in control of my life.

At the same moment that I am invested with this new power, the three orange spheres also seem to be metamorphosing. They blend with the cloudy silhouettes to make room for a ball of energy so dazzling that it forces me to close my eyes and curl up on myself. After a few seconds, it evaporates, making the clarity of the room much more bearable. Finally, I can open my eyes again. I still need a few seconds to acclimatize myself to the ambient light and no longer see white traces moving around me.

Near Anne Brontë's novel on the bedside table the thirty small orange orbs swirl, always diffusing this very light, nurturing heat. Then, at lightning speed, they disappear, leaving behind them, delicately placed on the book ... a Carnelian bead necklace.

Since that February evening, calm has returned in my old house. But one thing is certain dear reader, I can tell you... ghosts exist.

The Carnelian gemstone restores vitality and energy, transmits the love of life, removes the fear of death, promotes resolution, success, maintains creativity and gives confidence to the timid.

May She Wake In Torment

A Halloween for Miss Nussey illustration by Luna

A HALLOWEEN FOR MISS NUSSEY

By Luna
Lithuania

*Tale of a lady's adventure, where she helped a good cause using her wit and imagination.

PART 1: VARIOUS INTERESTS AND ANXIETIES OF MISS NUSSEY

Ellen was sitting with some girls in her dining room. As it was October, the fire place was lit up and the whole place appeared as cozy as could be. She gave the girls some of her baked treats and a few books that she thought the girls might enjoy.

-Miss Nussey, please won't you come this evening and read some stories to us, making voices like only you can, oh please Miss Nussey...

-Girls, what have I told you? You must not rely too much on others in this world- She let them go with a stern stare- now, run along, because I have too many matters of other sorts. I acted a little while in school, but forgot all about it now, I'm sure.

When the girls left, she resumed her work at poor Billy's shirt. Billy was the son of her maid's sister- a poor woman, who worked diligently to support her son and sick husband but could not make enough. She kept on sewing, but her mind was elsewhere. She kept glaring at the letter she got this morning from a certain gentleman.

Dear Miss Nussey,

I should have replied to your note sooner, but I was much preoccupied by matters of other sorts. To your persistent inquiries I can answer only this: the rights to publish letters of Miss Brontë belong to her husband and indeed, if your presumptions are correct, it would be against his wishes to make them publicly known. While I agree with you that were those letters published, the character of Charlotte Brontë and her sisters would be better known and understood, still we must heed Mr. Nicholl's feelings in this matter.

As for your enquiries about possible donations to ladies' charities- we have so many requests of that sort that we have decided to decline any participation in such activities for the present.

Thank you for enquiring about my own health, I'm glad to inform you that I am considerably well, and can only complain of overwork and too little spare time, but I'm happy to sign,

Yours truly obliged,

G. Smith

-So, indeed, -she decided to herself while cutting the thread- I can expect no help in that quarter. It's up to Mr. Reid and I.

She kept sewing, thinking all the time, these two activities got along marvelously.

Her musings got interrupted by a person who walked into the room.

-Miss Nussey? I hope I'm not interrupting? You appear at work?

-Mr. Reid? I was just sewing a shirt for little Billy, but I hope to finish soon. Please, take a seat.

He sat down in a comfortable armchair (a really beautiful one as well; Miss Nussey liked to surround herself with aesthetic things). Some time passed until he was ready to speak.

-I came with two little problems, well, maybe not so little- he kept playing with his hat in his hands- the first one could be framed like this: Mr. Nicholls has just read our little article and wrote me in the worst of tempers. I'm afraid he's quite determined to visit...

- To visit you, Mr. Reid? -Miss Ellen enquired

-No, I'm afraid he is to visit you, Miss Nussey. He wrote me a very curt letter as he was on the verge of leaving...calling you many names I'm afraid that could hardly be uttered in polite society, but one of them was what you would call a female dog.

-Indeed, Mr. Reid, this cross of mine would never be lifted I'm afraid, but I hope to meet him politely nevertheless...

She rang for her maid and told her that should Mr. Nicholls come for a visit while she was not at home, she should send him to meet her at the Christian Ladies' Society in a nearby church, where she spent most of her time.

-Another matter that requires your attention would be the questions about the Brontë family that many people admiring the family have sent to my humble person. - Miss Nussey lifted her head from work and prepared to listen- I have one about Mr. Branwell: When Mr.

Branwell had an affair with Mr. Robinson, how had his wife reacted and why did she agree to be a scapegoat in this whole situation?

-Excuse me?

Mr. Reid appeared very inconvenienced and proceeded to a second question.

-It's about Miss Emily. Did she know any other languages apart from dog and why was she so glad to die?

-I cannot imagine. I just think that slowly suffocating from mortal illness at the age of 30 is what mostly people dream of. She was just so happy about the possibility of dying that she was in denial about it until the last and then went out with a horrible struggle, because, you know, every person who wants to die holds on to hope that they are not dying till the last.

-There are a few other questions about Anne and Charlotte, for example was the depression Charlotte had after the death of her siblings caused by her unrequited love of Mr. Nicholls?

Ellen visibly shivered by the mention of this name.

-Mr. Reid, I believe that it is in your professional capabilities to answer those questions. I have told you most things I knew myself and you have read every letter that I have from them. I wish to be alone for a while to think about what could be done with the situation. If you'll excuse me- Ellen got up and went to open a window to get some fresh air.

Mr. Wemyss Reid, thought for a minute and decided not to pursue the matter further. He turned to go, but before he left, he asked Miss Nussey what to do with a certain George Smith that she hoped to visit.

-I'm still planning on paying him a visit, of course, but if I don't succeed I would like you to speak with him also.

As soon as Mr. Reid left, Ellen went to her writing table and started a new letter, not in English, but in French. She dipped her pen in ink and scribbled a few lines before she was interrupted again, this time by a lady visitor. The lady wished for Ellen to come and see the new church decorations from those flowers that bloom in autumn and to give her opinion in said matters.

The church was beautifully decorated. A bouquet of asters was put near the altar, a handful of last summer roses decorated the table along with prayer books. Ellen was always calmed when being there. Such beauty on earth was definitely just a poor shadow of the splendor of Heaven's and yet even such shadow reminded her of the unchangeable principle of love and devotion; that this world with all its pride and foolishness was fragile as a near broken glass at the doors of eternity.

Her schoolgirl's dreams (some would say unbecoming of woman of her age) were rudely interrupted by the church door opening and a voice: -Your servant said I would find you here, Miss Nussey.

Already irritated, Ellen turned with the brightest of smiles to greet Mr. Nicholls.

-Mr. Nicholls, I'm surprised to see you here.

-And I'm not surprised by any of your acts. In fact, I came here today...- he made no effort to hide his irritation.

- I already know... it's because of little Lotte isn't it?

-About what? – he screamed louder

-I apologize- she took out her handkerchief- yes, I took some food and...and medicine to poor Lotte... she is sick, her parents are hard-working people, but cannot provide all she needs in life...

-What are you rambling about?

Ellen appeared to shiver and still kept her handkerchief close to her eyes, sniffing demonstratively.

-I know how angry you are that the girl was christened by your wife's name...like you wouldn't christen the baby whom parents wanted to call Brontë... but to allow that little girl to starve to death...

Mr. Nicholls expression turned to almost fury.

-I...I... I didn't come for this!

- Mr. Nicholls- now one woman from the parish couldn't manage to stay out of it- stop screaming at Miss Ellen!

-I'm trying to keep calm, and to somehow communicate why I came in the first place! It's because of what she wrote...

-Yes- Ellen tried to speak in between sniffs and sobs- we all know you dislike literate people.

He stood completely astounded for a minute or two.

-Indeed Mr. Nicholls- the other woman noticed- This is completely unfit behavior for a clergyman.

-I'm not a clergyman anymore, Ellen chased me out of there!

Ellen just shook her head and buried her face in a handkerchief, blowing her nose in the most exaggerated manner.

-It's...it's because you practically imprisoned old Mr. Brontë at his home... treated him...horribly... but I'm sure you ought to find forgiveness in church...I forgive you Mr. Nicholls...I truly do...

He almost groaned.

-Now, now- a more sensible lady stood at the end of the church, well dressed, and mostly amused by the whole spectacle- Mr. Nicholls, are you a clergyman here?

-I am not! - he screamed.

-There's no need to shout. I just wanted to offer you a holiday proposal for a few days. I'm a landlady, I rent little houses near the forest; it's also near the seaside. Miss Nussey knows me, and indeed she's rented a house one or two times. Think about it, and please write if you'd wish to take lodgings.

Mr. Nicholls just stood there dumbstruck.

At Miss Nussey's home, her cook and a maid were having a tete a tete. They enjoyed their freedom while mistress was away and drank coffee sitting in her armchairs near the table.

-Is it long day for you today?

-No, mistress asked me to post one letter for her today and said I could go home to visit my ma and pa. Thought it an interesting letter, this one. Some foreign address Rue d'Isabelle or something like that. Anyway, I always love to have a bit of strong coffee at mid-day and I'm so lucky that mistress is away.

The cook couldn't agree more, though the sensible lady wasn't at all so calm; she couldn't decide between beef and codfish for dinner.

PART 2: MISS ELLEN GOES TO LONDON

George Smith sat at his office, utterly perplexed, as it seemed. He stared at the envelope and at the letter in his hands.

Mr. Williams just returned to their shared office from a break, eating his sandwich with ham and lettuce, blissfully unaware of his young superior's state of mind.

He dropped into his chair and phlegmatically viewed a few documents.

-And how is your gathering tomorrow? I trust the charming Mrs. Smith will greet us just as always.

-Yes, my wife is better, but you will ask her yourself that evening I have no doubt. Williams, I need your advice about the letter I've just received...

-And how is little Dolly? Still the little princess?

-Yes, I'm afraid I spoil her too much, but...

-And how does she like her new little brother?

-Not well. She wanted another sister, because apparently, she doesn't get along with the ones she already has. Williams, can you read this letter? It's been bothering me since morning. Advise me what can be done with the mater.

Mr. Williams was in a happy slumber after eating lunch and had no wish to discuss further business problems, but since his superior was so insistent he slowly got up to have a look.

(The letter was written in French but the author will present all such conversations in English, both for readers' convenience and author's limited knowledge of such language)

Mr. Smith,

I'm writing to you, because of a little problem I now have. A certain Miss Nussey constantly harasses me, asking to publish such letters which only the husband of Miss Brontë has the right to publish.

I would very much like to visit London and to somehow get this delicate matter settled; with Miss Brontë's husband or at least with her publisher.

I apologize for the inconvenience my letter might have created, but I knew Mrs. Gaskell and she advised me to apply to you, should such problems arise.

With best wishes,

C. Heger

Mr. Williams lifted his eyebrows in amazement.

-Indeed, it's a complication...

- As I'm not Miss Brontë's husband, I shouldn't burden myself with such decisions it seems to me. I will write to Mr. Nicholls and invite him to my party tomorrow, offer him to stay with me and my wife should he wish so, and if M. Heger has already reached London (as I received the letter later than usual thanks to some incompetent boy), I'll invite him as well. It's annoying that all of late Miss Brontë's acquaintances should apply to me. – he frowned.

He took some paper and pen and began writing.

Dear Mr. Nicholls,

As your late wife's publisher, many matters regarding publication of her personal life, I'm afraid, have fallen into my hands. Right now, I have been contacted by Miss Brontë's teacher while she was in Brussels, who has some letters written by her and is pressured (or so it appears) by Miss Nussey to have them published. He wishes to discuss this matter with you.

I'm holding a small gathering in my house tomorrow, and I plan on inviting M. Heger if he has already reached London. If it is comfortable, I would like to extend my invitation to you. Please let me know should the plan suit you. I remain, my dear Sir,

Yours very respectfully and truly,

G. Smith

Mr. Smith hoped that it would set the matter right and told one of his clerks to post it.

The next morning as he was eating breakfast (egg with bacon), a maid brought two letters, one signed by Mr. Nicholls, the other by M. Heger.

-Heger has agreed and thinks it's the best solution. -He informed his wife, glaring over the letter and eating with his spare hand. - Now only to know what Mr. Nicholls will say.

My dear Sir,

I am much obliged for your help, as I think my late wife would be as well. I'm not naturally inclined to London life, but for an important matter I could make an exception. I believe the faster it is settled the better. As you probably know by now, I have no communication with Miss Nussey and her plans are altogether unknown to me.

I wish it to be agreed on quickly, because I plan on going for a rest for a bit at the seaside.

231

Yours respectfully,

A.B. Nicholls

-So, that settles it then- he murmured – they will settle this between them.

-Ah, I almost forgot- his wife interrupted- Guess who I invited for tomorrow?

- Minny Thackeray? – He automatically assumed, still lost in his thoughts.

-No, you goose. A very lovely woman, your acquaintance. She came to London for just a short visit, but I'm sure... Are you listening? -She asked again

-I'm sorry dear, I'm too preoccupied about the whole situation. As my wife, please invite who you will. If you'll excuse me, I need to be at the office.

Tomorrow's evening arrived sooner than expected. A great hall was lit up, many tables were set with food and the food was already inspected by many great ladies and gentlemen. The street nearby was lit by the lights from the windows and the whole street gave the appearance of strange warmness even to strangers who walked by. One of them just arrived by cab stared, mesmerized by the sight of another guest, this one coming on foot.

-Mr. Nicholls, so glad you could come- the host standing by the door greeted him- I'm sure your trip was pleasant?

-What the damn is that woman doing here? – was his greeting and Smith turned to look, just in time to notice his wife greeting Ellen Nussey.

-Alas, yes, I had to walk. As you know, most of my money now goes to impoverished children and I cannot afford carriage rides for myself. It's the gentlemen who can do such a thing, we ladies have to look after the well-being of those less fortunate then us, I'm sure you'll agree Mr. Nicholls? - She said handing her fur coat to the servant who came to collect them.

He grumbled and turned away, walking inside and finding a spot as far from her as he could.

-Miss Nussey? - a few people came to her asking something: Mr. Smith was too far away to hear what they said, but she was already chatting pleasantly.

-It's so rude of you to order a cab for Mr. Nicholls and offer him accommodations while making Miss Nussey walk here only to throw her into a cold, black night again, whence the party is over. - His wife scolded him.

-Well, it's you who invited her in the first place. So, I'm sure you'll find her a more comfortable means of travel if her legs don't work anymore. I'm sure our broom would do the trick. Not sure she would agree, though. I think making a martyr of herself is one of her charitable undertakings.

His wife rolled her eyes, but her husband's attention was already at the banquet table. There was one particular type of sandwich that many found equal to the great works of Raphael or Miss Brontë. It was a plain bread, cut in squares with a bit of sauce on it and a piece of chicken, coated in some black bread crumbs. It was disappearing quickly and Mr. Smith had to help his guests with this.

Ellen was speaking rather loudly about something and the whole assembly with her was listening in great interest.

Mr. Smith was still at the banquet table. M. Heger came to him and greeted him.

-Ah, M. Heger. We were just waiting for you. Could I escort you to Mr. Nicholls? So, you could speak about the letters or indeed anything you wished to discuss.

-What? (said in French)

-I said I will lead you to M. Nicholls...

-Mon anglish est no god... Do you speak French?

-Well, my knowledge of French is quite limited, but I'm sure it's not with me you'll be holding most conversations.

M. Heger nodded and let himself be led by Smith to the corner where Mr. Nicholls was guarding his territory to be at least 5 metres from Miss Nussey.

-Mr. Nicholls, could I introduce you to M. Heger?

-M Heger, Mr. Nicholls- he gestured to him.

- (in French) Ah, that's nice. It appears you were that youth that my beloved student so admired as to marry.

-What?

- (in French) I just hope you are not in close understanding with that annoying mademoiselle, who constantly harasses me to have the secrets of your wife's heart revealed?

-What?

Mr. Smith began to see the problem here.

-I believe M. Heger isn't fluent in English. He says that he has no wish to publish those letters and that Miss Nussey is harassing him, so he hopes you would support him in this matter.

-I'd wring her neck should the occasion arise!

Mr. Smith translated to M Heger this in a more decent manner.

A few other guests began to show interest in M. Heger.

-M. Heger I believe? Were you the teacher of Miss Brontë in Brussels?

Smith translated.

- (in French) Oh yes, a brilliant student. Such talent and genius, of course, and dedication to her craft...What interesting essays would she write... you know, it sometimes seemed like our souls understood each other without words. Like she wrote, something like: "an invisible thread coming from my heart connected with a similar thread in his". It's such a tragedy the poor girls died so young.

-What is he saying Mr. Smith? –

Mr. Smith didn't appear as genial as before.

-That she was a student of his, but he had a heart operation and almost died, so he is sad he couldn't know her very well.

-Is it true, that you were an inspiration of M. Paul Emmanuel?

Smith translated through gritted teeth.

- (in French) Yes, yes, like I said, we had a special connection like Lucy and Paul Emmanuel.

Smith translated again.

-Do you think it would be better for Lucy to end up with Paul Emmanuel when Dr. John was implied in the first part of the book? - one of the ladies asked.

Smith translated this as: Do you sometimes think that Paul Emanuel should have ended with Dr. John's wife?"

- (in French) No, no. She had to be with the doctor. They are both shallow and not very educated. Paul Emmanuel would very soon grow tired of her.

Smith translated this correctly.

-M Heger I would like to ask...

-I'm sorry- Mr. Nicholls interrupted, whispering to Smith - but Ellen Nussey is speaking about somebody proposing to Charlotte and she's probably talking about Mr. Taylor, which we agreed not to mention. I would have interrupted, but as you are the host, I believe this is your responsibility. I would probably drag her out by physical force.

Not wanting the public spectacle, Smith quickly sprang to his feet and approached the scene.

-So, of course, it was 1853 winter... I got alarmed when...

-Miss Nussey? - Smith interrupted- wouldn't you like something to eat? I'm sure the servants just announced that dinner is ready.

-No, I was actually...

-I believe Mr. Nicholls requires your presence. He has something of utmost importance to say. – He didn't appear to be backing down.

- I... well, - she got up- Ladies, gentlemen. -She was fanning herself quite vigorously. -Dinner is announced.

Smith took her seat once she was gone.

-Pray, tell us, what's for dinner? I believe you were obsessed with that menu for weeks- one of the ladies asked.

-Well, I like to be meticulous about such matters- he played with his cufflinks. – I believe chicken sautéed in French sauce would satisfy... I believe Miss Nussey was telling one of her delightful stories for you. Though sometimes she can be a bit lost at distinguishing facts from imagination, which annoys such a precise man as Mr. Nicholls. – he tried very hard not to chuckle or show merriment, but the twinkle in his eyes betrayed the opposite.

-Yes, we heard many interesting stories...Can I ask you plainly- a rather forceful looking lady played with her fan- what was that strange relationship between you and Miss Brontë?

He chuckled.

-I'm amused. The kind lady- he gestured at Ellen- who is now having the most pleasant conversation with Mr. Nicholls (indeed, his growling can be heard even here) will no doubt have acquainted you with the legend that I've proposed to Charlotte Brontë- his eyes twinkled with a silent laugh.

-So that's why we were wondering...

-No, for my own part I was never in love with Charlotte Brontë. I never could have loved any woman who, how do you put it, didn't have certain qualities of grace and charm of a person, and alas she had none, though she would have given all of her genius to have beauty. I'm afraid this answer will not raise me in your estimation, but I cannot be but frank. – he shrugged his shoulders. - Though my mother was at one time alarmed she might be in love with me. Though of course, I was never a coxcomb enough to believe such nonsense...- he waited a bit, playing with his cuffs.

- I believe that Charlotte was in love with you, Mr. Smith- one of the ladies, a very polite one, finally said.

-No, indeed, I would not...- he was interrupted by Mr. Nicholls again, storming to him.

- Please, somehow make her go away. Also, I cannot comprehend a word that Frenchman says, he and that Nussey apparently found a common language, because she is showing him something and he nods his head. I also nod, because I don't know what else to do.

George Smith sighed, for the previous conversation had much charm to him, but proceeded nevertheless.

-Also, Mr. Nicholls, Ellen was really talking about Mr. Taylor and his proposal...

-I abhor the man.

-Yes, yes, I as well. That's why I sent him to India. When Charlotte... Miss Brontë was in London, she would speak hours about you, even more than about her father...

-Really? -Mr. Nicholls stared at him in disbelief.

-Yes, yes, really. And Taylor was really annoying, much like Ellen, and Miss Brontë disliked him at first sight, but might have grown fond of him in time. So, I interfered on your behalf. Of course, I speak about these matters in a strictly confidential manner. I wouldn't like anyone knowing.

-Yes, I am very private person myself. That's why I disliked that my wife disclosed her secrets so openly in her letters to Miss Nussey. - Nicholls shared his grievances.

-Yes, I cannot applaud her for sharing anything with Miss Nussey either. Although I wouldn't worry too much about her. I don't think that many would believe her- She was indeed talking about a proposal from Mr. Taylor, but somehow got the years wrong. It was 1851, not 1853. Also, the name. His name was James, not George. As a matter of fact, Taylor's mother couldn't have opposed it as his mother is dead. So, pay no attention.

When they reached M Heger, Ellen Nussey was in a really happy mood. She was looking over some advertisement and M Heger was smiling nearby.

-You seem in a happy mood. – Smith noticed.

-Indeed. M Heger was looking forward to spending a few more days in England. It's so lovely that Mr. Nicholls promised to take M Heger with him.

-I promised what?

-You shouldn't have nodded... – Mr. Smith added gloomily

Utterly perplexed Nicholls stared at Ellen.

George Smith was faster and almost dragged him away saying

-How lovely to get to know such a marvelous person! Thank you for organizing this little holiday for us, Miss Nussey, for I too would be escorting Mr. Nicholls. Mr. William! Indeed, Miss Nussey could you call him here? I would like to have a word.

-If you refuse now, I'm sure Nussey will invite him somewhere -he whispered to Nicholls – we need to be the ones he'll confide in, otherwise he'll publish those letters and needless to say they won't do a great credit to your wife's character...

-Ah, Williams, there you are? Do you fancy a small holiday?

-Me- the old man seemed utterly perplexed.

-Yes, consider it traveling on business purpose, I'll explain to you later. -He just saw Mr. Nicholls screaming something at Ellen, and her grabbing her handkerchief and almost fainting at the couch, with his wife standing there in utter confusion.

-I'm surely not wanted here- Ellen rubbed her eyes, 'till they turned red -I'll probably go.

-Now- Mrs. Smith asked- but surely, there's still a cake to be tasted...

-No, no, it's alright

-Let me give you our carriage...

-It's fine.

-Mrs. Smith- George came to them- I'm sure Miss Nussey has a lot of her business to attend to, and knowing her dislike of carriages, I wouldn't deter her any longer. It was pleasure meeting you, Miss Nussey, and I hope to work together in future- he shook her hand. – James, give Miss Nussey her coat, will you?

Ellen was in the worst of spirits, being exiled from the party, even without tasting a bit of cake, into coldness and darkness.

-Well at least you'll amuse yourself most pleasantly on your holiday... so much so that you'll remember it 'till your last.

-What is it, Miss Nussey? - Asked George Smith

-Nothing indeed, Mr. Smith, just wished Mr. Nicholls a good holiday... Oh, some sweets, how kind of you, Mrs. Smith...

-Like a 13th fairy uninvited to the king's ball- commented Mr. Williams

-What is it Williams? – George brought him a glass of Nelson sherry

-Nothing. I was reminded of a fairytale my mother read to me when I was little...

-Oh, quit with those fairy tales and help me. My rare free day to be spent with Paul Drownmanual -soon-to-be and that man who looks like he's eaten a stick for breakfast and probably flogs himself to sleep with it, in a house Nussey recommended. Admirable holiday! - he said dropping on a couch with his glass of sherry

PART 3: HOW THE GENTELMEN FOUND THEIR HOUSE AND ABOUT A LOVELY NIGHT SPENT THERE

It was a bright and lovely morning for traveling. Arthur Bell Nicholls already patrolled the hall since 8 o'clock and Mr. Williams arrived around 9 with M Heger, whom he found lost in a main street.

He said that he doesn't know London, doesn't know English, so got lost among many strange streets.

Finally, Smith came down and it seems everything was ready.

-I apologize if I made you wait. Not used to rising so early on Saturdays -he yawned.

M Heger in French: What a beautiful vase. I would like to have such at home!

-What did he say? – Nicholls took interest- Something to me?

- No, I believe he wants to take Mr. Smith's vases home with him. - whispered Mr. Smith Williams

George Smith went to the yard, and had a few words with his coachmen. One of them showed them the way and they got in.

-Your luggage, sir- one approached Arthur.

-I'd like to have it with me, thank you very much. My food is in here and I sometimes get hungry during travels, even though it is my fasting week.

Mr. Smith Williams tried not to smile and cast his gaze down. It's sure to be an interesting trip.

Mr. Smith tapped with his cane on the roof and the carriage began moving. Overall, it was a pleasant trip. The changing scenery was a treat in itself- watching city life changing and diminishing. Hills and valleys emerged, replacing buildings and city halls. The Sun was now high in the sky and the day appeared clear and bright. The trees wore coats of many colors this time of the year and the ground was covered in red, orange and brown. Overall, Octobers tend to be warm, still they say that candles burn the brightest before extinguishing all together.

When they drove through uninhabited wild fields of nature, with only a few farm houses far away from one another, Smith turned to Nicholls

-Perhaps some of you would like something to eat. As I didn't have breakfast, I'm quite famished. Mr. Nicholls promised to take us something to eat, I think.

-Yes, indeed- he took out a handkerchief from his bag. Something was wrapped in it. M Heger understood the word eat and also looked with interest.

Mr. Nicholls carefully unfolded the handkerchief and inside were 4 pieces of bread. He also took a bottle with something in it. They later saw it was water.

-A good, simple meal for the start of the day.

Three other men were less then amused. Mr. Smith was hungry and in bad spirits.

-I believe we could at first try to find something to eat, what say you? - He asked first thing when they arrived.

Mr. Williams agreed wholeheartedly. M Heger understood nothing, so he had no opinion. Mr. Nicholls kept snacking on his piece of bread like he did the whole way.

The sea was uneasy- roaring and breaking unto the shore. It was windy, nothing like the sunny air in London. A few people walked near the beach; it was mostly wild and solitary.

Mr. Smith noticed a restaurant near the sea, called "The Port". As they had no better option, the gentlemen decided to dine there, after eating such a strong, fine breakfast.

Looking over the menu M Heger asked in his native language:

-What dish would you recommend? I would like to try the most popular one.

-A gentleman here would like the most unusual dish that you could find. Something that nobody orders? - Smith asked the waiter

-Well, there's a pork roast with mushroom sauce. It was one of the reasons we were closed for a season by a health inspection. – They explained to M Heger in English

- (in French) Excellent. As long as a lot of people liked it it's going to be good.

- And I would like a simple piece of bread, with a glass of water- calmly explained Mr. Nicholls. – As I'm dinning out, maybe spread some butter on the bread.

- I would like those pancakes with crab meat- Mr. Smith closed his menu- as they look tasty, please one and a half portion.

-Excuse me, sir, you'll have to wait a bit for that.

-It's alright, I'll wait. Mr. Williams? What about you?

Mr. Williams ordered a salade de jour and they waited. "Hey, -they heard screaming from the kitchens- some rich looking idiot ordered those pancakes with crabs, boy run to the store, see if they have any. I'm sure they didn't sell all last year."

It's strange, but Mr. Williams and M Heger got their dishes at around the same time. Mr. Williams had no complaints except that they looked like somebody's uneaten side dish from yesterday. M Heger started eating his dish. Someone didn't eat bread with their soup, so the abandoned bread quickly made its way to Mr. Nicholls table.

-Why does my bread look chewed on?

-Is everything to your satisfaction, gentlemen? - the waiter appeared. – I apologize, but maybe we could put something else on your pancakes, sir? Like some marmalade or syrup? Or if you want sea food maybe shrimps?

-Marmalade, thank you. What is it Heger? - He asked in French.

- (in French) I'm sure my pork is raw...- he began getting angry, and his whole face flashed red.

-How can it be raw? Don't scream.

He showed it blood-running-from-the inside raw.

-Is everything to the French gentleman's liking?

-Well, he can be very meticulous about food. In his native land he never ate pork so well cooked. He imagined the dish more like uncooked minced pork meat with raw mushrooms. – Smith said in English- so it's quite unacceptable.

-I'm sorry sir, I'll change the dish right away. - he took Heger's plate.

His second dish appeared very quickly together with George's pancakes. He took to them right away. Heger looked at his new plate with inexpressible despair. He began twitching.

Some man on the other table also ordered that unfortunate pork and now was complaining as well. Professor Heger, when seeing this began to desperately gesture to his dish as well.

-We only got bread for breakfast and now this nonsense- Smith murmured.

-Well, someone would benefit from eating less, I'm sure- a voice from the other table reached them and George Smith turned his head just to see James Taylor.

Mr. Williams gulped- apparently, they didn't part on good terms.

-It's James Taylor- whispered Smith to Nicholls.

-What does he want from us- Nicholls asked chewing his bread in very bad spirits.

-Sir, - George Smith nodded.

-I'm just saying that some gentlemen would benefit from fasting on bread- he joked again.

-Excuse me? – Mr. Nicholls has taken this compliment as to himself.

-Who the hell are you?

-Mr. Nicholls. I'm sure Miss Brontë mentioned me many times in London.

-Never heard of you. Well, -he continued his litany- I'm sure we are all glad that the person in question also wasn't successful in his romantic attempts...

-Sir, please stop your insults or you'll have to answer. - said Mr. Nicholls, raising

-I'm not even sure who you are. Go back to your farm.

This was the last straw as Mr. Nicholls dealt him a blow that would turn some men off their feet. Mr. Taylor collapsed on the table.

-I offer bets. Ask me for the odds – Smith began screaming, standing on their table- Who casts their bets on Mr. Nicholls? Bet for Mr. Taylor?

Waiters appeared in the greatest hurry.

M Heger still tried to talk with someone about his dish (in French obviously)

-What a horror is this! I would like to see the chef! In Belgium we would never... how horrid!

They were soon kicked out of there and went to see their Villa in the forest.

A few people whispered in low voices when they walked by: Yes, I'm glad the restaurant is working again. After one person died from that crab last year, I was sure they would close for good.

Mr. Smith complained about feeling bad from his pancakes. Mr. Nicholls noted that when a person feels that the food is bad, he doesn't eat two portions of it.

They finally saw their Villa.

-What witched lived and died in there? - was first utterance of Mr. Williams.

They opened the door with a strange sound, "like a live-buried child screaming"- observed Mr. Williams. And this is what they saw. The toilet was the most spacious room in the house with a fancy bath and a lot of space.

In another room, there was a table and a sofa in decent condition, along with a two-story bed. The second story was so near the ceiling that a person would have a trouble crawling into it, there was no question about sitting. The first story bed appeared alright, but was so old, that the person from second story could very well just fall and crush the first person.

The stairs were of such a strange form as if someone chewed them. The attic was so small that George Smith couldn't stand straight. The beds were ancient and with mattresses that appeared to be inherited from a 1700s' mad house.

-No. Just no- George Smith picked up his things and headed down almost falling from the chewed staircase.

-Maybe... if someone sleeps on the sofa...- Williams was trying to be diplomatic.

Running through the door, Smith almost fell on an old lady.

-Who are you? – he asked when he got a better look at her. She was old and appeared crooked with a long nose and grey hair.

-I'm your landlady, of course. Although you should be thankful I'm letting you stay after you beat my other tenant so badly.

-The point is that we are not staying. Or at least not in this house. The mattresses look to be from a mad house and smell like somebody died and rotted on them.

-Wait, Smith. -Nicholls approached- I'm staying. It's a lovely house- he said to the lady- thank you for letting us rent it. It's really popular, all the other houses are already taken.

-Nicholls, are you out of your mind?

-I kind of like it too- Mr. Williams confessed. - can we have the keys.

-Sure enough, dear boys. – Mr. Smith didn't feel easier when she licked her lips- here are your keys, your house number is 55. Have a nice night.

Smith was too overcome to speak.

-Well, you and Heger will sleep on that cupboard. Heger on the second shelf.

Mr. Williams murmured something about it being a good enough bed and back they went to the beach.

Smith tried to hold them as long as he could on the beach. The sun finally disappeared over the horizon, the waves kept crashing without anyone seeing them and the stars appeared in the sky. It was time to go back to their house.

-So, you mean you want to go back to that hell house as soon as possible? - Smith lay happily on the sand- because I'm quite comfortable here.

-Then sleep here. -Nicholls offered- I always go to sleep about 10 o'clock and I'm not changing my decision.

The first question M. Heger asked about sleeping arrangements was why he had to sleep on the upper bed. Smith answered that is because he's so light and short. Another person would surely crash on Mr. Williams.

The men finally settled in their beds and M Heger and Arthur took to sleeping because they were tired. Mr. Williams read some book. Mr. Smith tried to sleep, but couldn't help staring at the floor. There were some scratch marks, like someone dragged somebody through the floor or some lunatic was kept inside. To him the bed smelled like a dead person. Arthur slept soundly.

He checked the time; it was about 12. Suddenly, some steps could be heard in the first floor. "It's probably Mr. Williams going to the loo" -he thought to himself. Let's sleep. He kept a candle by the bed- side just in case, but noticed that the light disappeared on the first floor. Then light appeared again, like a night candle, and some steps. "Probably Williams cannot sleep, like I". Still, it was hard to sleep, because of how hot and damp the attic was- there was almost no air and no windows.

Suddenly some voice appeared "Nicholls...Nicholls..." Very quickly Smith got up on his feet.

-Did you hear?

-What? - Nicholls murmured- let me sleep...

- What the... -Smith watched in disbelief.

He saw Nicholls' bed moving from its place. Little by little. This was enough for him, he dashed down the stairs and decided to sleep on the sofa.

-At least no one had died on it.

The sofa was quite comfortable, actually, and probably the newest thing in the house, because Smith felt himself drifting asleep and attributed all his experiences to some strange half-sleep state.

To Mr. Williams and M Heger, however, the fun was just beginning. To begin with, Mr. Williams didn't sleep so soundly. His sleep was more of a nervous kind, to be awakened by a single sound. At first, he believed he only imagined it and decided to sleep. However, in time, the sound got louder and louder, something like swings moving in motion. He would have decided to sleep again, but he believed he saw some figure at the window. He quickly got up and heard the voice

-Who sleeps in this bed? Who sleeps in this bed? We slept on this bed!

-What? - the professor was awake too- what?

-We died on this bed. The bed broke...My sister hit her head on the ceiling and fell on me. We both died...

-What? What? - the professor tried to rise, but he hit his head on the ceiling and fell on his bed, motionless.

Mr. Williams, fearing that prophecy or whatever, got up from the bed and ran quickly, searching for a place to hide.

-We were both orphans... but you hate orphans...

-No, no, I love orphans... I really do...

-If you loved orphans you would help Miss Nussey with her charity.... you would help Miss Nussey...

He hid in the fire place as it was the only place...

-I'm just an editor...- He hid his head, but the voice, apparently, stopped talking. He promised never to get out of this safe space.

From the running sound, George Smith awoke as well. He heard somebody flushing the toilet.

-Williams? Is that you?

-No... it's not Williams... it's Olivia...

Flushing toilet again.

-Olivia who?

-I once rented this house... I died on the sofa that you sleep on... from dysentery...I ate the crab... I ate the crab...

-Then why are you talking to me? - He tried to make sense of it all.

-Because, I knew Miss Nussey... You are harming her now... Oh, she simply asked for your help for her orphans, nothing more. You used her for Brontë knowledge and then left her...And it was so easy for you to die too... I waited for that crab that you didn't get today... Life is giving you another chance. Give the money to Miss Nussey's charity, don't spend them on pancakes...

The ghost stopped talking and Smith just sat there on that sofa.

Mr. Nicholls was having his own problems. The sounds of a screaming Mr. Williams and flushing toilets ruined his sleep. The voice that once was trying to reach him finally caught him awake and started its tirade.

-Mr. Nicholls... Mr. Nicholls... my brother and I died here. We died here.

-So, why are you talking and why do you sound like Ellen if you died? - he was skeptical.

-We suffocated from the lack of air here... we weren't rich...We just wanted a holiday... I tried to get downstairs, my brother didn't make it... do you see the scratches on the floor? That's his nails... it was such a hot night, we tried to climb down, but he didn't make it. I left him dying and suffocating here and tried to climb those strange stairs...But I didn't watch my steps and dashed my head on that floor... please

246

publish Miss Brontë's letters... let Ellen publish her letters...- there was some banging on the roof to intensify the scene.

Arthur looked around, uneasy

-What does this have to do with those letters and that Nussey?

- We died happy after we read her biography by Mrs. Gaskell... We were happy to die, because we read it.

-Well, I'm sure Gaskell will be happy. She was a bit sour, when she lost her reputation as "The most annoying woman in the world" to that Nussey.

-Share Charlotte with the world...make others happy...- Then there was this strange sound that Williams heard.

When the voice stopped talking, Mr. Nicholls stopped appearing calm and dashed downstairs. He found only Smith.

-Maybe you know where Mr. William is? - He asked when he saw Nicholls.

-I hate to tell this, but from the sound of it, flushed into the toilet. Why is Heger lying like that?

- When I awoke, he was already like that. I'm sure they carried his soul away.

-It's that Nussey woman and her orphans... I'm sure she hexed us- Nicholls appeared in fury.

- I wasn't talking with orphans, I was talking with some rich Olivia who died from dysentery. – Smith screamed and got up, because dysenteric sofa wasn't on his list of most comfortable beds.

-I don't like you being in our house- the voice said again- go outside, go outside, into the cold, dark night, like you turned out poor Ellen...

Flushing toilet again.

They screamed and ran outside, hiding in some kid's playground house that was built nearby.

About 7 it was beginning to grow light and they heard a rooster crow. Some kids came out to play. They stared at the men wide-eyed and ran to their mothers.

-Those houses are cursed! Haunted! - screamed Nicholls at the kids.

-It's alright child, the asylum is nearby, I'm sure they missed their inmates.

Smith cleared his throat.

-Maybe... Let's go inside- he offered- I'm sure ghosts are less active during the day.

Just then they saw Mr. Williams coming from that house, all covered with ashes, like a little ash-boy from a fairytale.

- I was never gladder to see you in the morning- Smith ran to him- Where were you?

- Some voices started to scream at me about some pancakes so I hid in a fireplace. They went silent for a while, so I made my way here. M Heger is now just recovering.

-So, Nussey didn't take his spirit away? - Nicholls appeared surprised.

-No, he hit his head on the ceiling, but I'm sure he didn't fracture his skull. He is now drinking tea in the house and relaxing. – Both Nicholls and Smith stared at Williams in disbelief. – Well, those ghosts speak English and he doesn't understand English.

-Gentlemen, - a voice startled them. They saw a young woman approaching- So, you made yourselves welcome last evening? I'm so sorry, I had to be with my ill father and couldn't show you around, but I left the doors unlocked and key in the door. Your house number was 2, wasn't it?

-Wait, and who was the elderly lady that let us in yesterday?

-I don't know about what lady are you talking about. Over here lives old Alice, but she can barely move from rheumatism. She had the keys? With your house number on it?

-No, with 55 number on it- Nicholls blurred out.

-Well, I'm very sorry for any inconvenience you had and I can only offer you to stay another night, free of charge...

-So, I go to pack my stuff- Smith decided- the sooner we leave the better.

-It's strange -Mr. Williams observed the ladder near their house- why did those ghosts need a ladder to get to the roof?

PART 4: AFTERMATH

Mr. Smith Williams, Mr. Smith and Arthur Bell Nicholls sat in a café. It was a pleasant day and they all looked rested after their adventure.

-Mr. Nicholls, I'm glad you decided to extend your stay in London by a few days. – Mr. Smith said.

Mr. Williams preferred to drink his coffee in silence.

-I, myself, have undertaken a few new projects...- he admitted- and Mr. Williams also joins me.

-Yes, with half of my salary and my wife's savings- he admitted.

- We will send a bit of help to that charitable institution Miss Nussey runs -Smith added

-And I also thought about her words myself- Mr. Nicholls was playing with his watch – Maybe she was right about me sharing Charlotte's possessions with the world and inspiring people. I'm planning on working with the best experts in this field to preserve her legacy. I'm sure it's a wise choice as one of them is called Wise. Maybe you would like to gift your letters as well.

-No, I would like to keep Miss Brontë's letters to myself- Smith quickly added- I believe charity is enough for me.

Ellen was walking down the street when she was approached by her partner in caring for the orphans.

-Miss Nussey it's so good to have you back. I hope you have rested well during your short holiday?

-Oh, magnificently. I also bought a souvenir which may help to draw luck and funds to our orphanage. - She showed her friend a key with number 55 engraved on it.

-Do you really believe in those things?

-Oh, the ways of luck are mysterious. And those who have good intentions at heart always succeed in their undertakings.

The Curse of Bertha Mason illustration by Barb Tanke

THE CURSE OF BERTHA MASON

by Kay Fairhurst Adkins
Palm Springs, California, USA
Bertha Mason's last wish for her husband, Mr. Rochester

Wherever You Wander
In Groups or Alone
Long May You Falter
And Never Find Home
Long May You Lose
Everything You Desire
For You Have Dared Anger
The Essence of Fire

An Interesting Interlude illustration by Rowan Coleman

AN INTERESTING INTERLUDE –

by Laurie Mangru
London, Ontario, Canada

*For those three incredible ladies at Ponden Hall, who made that
evening so special and for my mom, who always praises my writing.*

That night the wind howled a death knell,
For one that was lost in the dark.
If we listen we'll hear the lone church bell,
Ring for one who ne'er left his mark.

Four women gathered in a room with a flagstone floor that was, in
fact, the original floor of the home when it was first built. It was said
that a litter of puppies was born on this very floor at the feet of Emily
Brontë, while being entertained by Robert Heaton. The women
chatted happily together around the large stone hearth and there was
such an apparent camaraderie among these four women that each one
of them felt the special sensation steal across them silently, leaving
them with a strong sense of "belonging". They were so comfortable
with each other and more than once the thought, "they are more
myself than I am" had crossed the minds of each of the women, yet
they had only known each other less than a day!

And here they were talking long into the night, all not wanting the
moment to end. There was magic in the air that evening and often
when Laurie looked back on that night she smiled to herself as she
recalled the perfect evening spent with three complete strangers. And
while they shared their stories and talked about literature, with an
emphasis on the Brontës, Laurie did keep one secret to herself. That
night there were five sitting around the large fireplace, not four. She
had watched silently the form that had appeared before her. It was a
young man who was very subdued and seemed to be lost in his own
thoughts. His head was bowed down to the floor except for one
moment when he suddenly looked up towards the ceiling and stared
intently at something above their heads. He stared without blinking for
so long that Laurie found herself tilting her head upwards to spot what
was of so much interest to this unexpected visitor.

"You have noticed the meat hooks!" Josie said suddenly, bringing
Laurie out of her reverie.

"Meat hooks? Is that what they are?"

"Yes, they were used to hang meat for drying and smoking by the fire. They are the original hooks and would have been familiar to the Brontës." Josie pointed upwards to the great meat hooks well above her head in the wooden beams. One could hardly imagine slabs of meat smoking by the fireplace in an age gone by. Out of the corner of her eye Laurie saw the young man glance up once more and then reach into his pocket for a piece of paper. She looked away and joined in with the conversation again, but she couldn't stop herself from stealing a glance now and then at the contemplative young man. He leaned back into the sofa that was adjacent to the sofa she was sitting upon as he sketched something on the paper balanced awkwardly on his knee. Every now-and-then he would glance up at the hooks and then look back down to his paper. He paid no attention to the women who sat chatting throughout the evening. Laurie wondered if he could hear them. He seemed lost to another world and time and was certainly deep in his own thoughts. He wore clothing that clearly spoke of another century – possibly mid-19th century, Laurie thought.

Just after her arrival, Laurie had been walked through Ponden Hall by her host and given a tour of the home that dated back to the 1500's. Outside stood the sad remains of what was once a pear tree said to have been planted for Emily by Robert. Nothing remains today of the tree, save for small a stump set down in the ground, barely visible unless one is specifically searching for the stump. It was a sad story of unrequited love, Laurie sighed, as she bent down to touch the withered bit of stump that protruded from the grass.

She could hardly believe she was here. This was a place she had read about and thought often of, but never had she dreamed of ever visiting, and yet now she was standing in a home hundreds of years old and she would be sleeping in the room with the small window, said to be the window where Cathy's ghost appeared. She had no fear of ghosts, not in this place, at least. They would be welcome to invade her space if desired. She had walked on the moors when she had first arrived in Haworth and had felt many ghosts around her, whispering over her shoulder and floating on the wind beside her as her feet carried her along the same paths that the Brontës had once walked. She had a quiet picnic at the Brontë Bridge and was lucky to find herself completely alone in this oasis. She beckoned the ghosts to come to her and almost dared them to show themselves to her in this magical place. No ghosts did she see, but magic was certainly in the air. She laid back on the grass and let the warmth of the sun beat down on her face. In just a few minutes she was sound asleep in this lovely, protective dell, surrounded by hills and purple heather. She smelled the heather in the air and later when she would return that day she would catch the scent of heather in her hair – "Just like Cathy," she told herself. She was a romantic and knew by heart many popular passages from her beloved Brontë books; books that were now well-worn with handling and perusing over many years.

She slept peacefully at the Brontë Bridge listening to the water babble happily on its way until she was awakened by the barking of a dog and two visitors who had entered her quiet nook. She sat up quickly, surprised to see the sun so low in the sky. She had been asleep for a few hours and though the intruders apologized for disturbing her peaceful slumber she thanked them for their intrusion. It would not have been fun to wake up in the middle of a moor in the pitch black. As she made her way back across the moor she wondered if the Brontës had often been intruded upon by unwelcome guests while they sat reading or writing or just daydreaming and talking. She had only ever envisioned the Brontës here and no one else. This spot was theirs during their time and it still belongs to them. That will never change.

Laurie was pulled out of her silent reverie when the young man suddenly shifted position on the couch. He was now bent solemnly over his drawing as he continued to sketch with rapid strokes. He wore small round spectacles that sat on the end of his nose, and now that he had leaned forward and was directly under an overhead light, Laurie noticed that he had a mop of fiery, red hair that was disheveled.

"Laurie, I'm just admiring your brooch," Josie said. "Is that heather?"

"Yes. I actually didn't buy it here, but in Canada in an antique shop. The heather on the brooch reminded me of the moors in Yorkshire."

"It's lovely! It looks like the heather has been hand-painted. I have a bracelet with heather on it, but it is not as intricately detailed as this."

Laurie reached up to her brooch and unpinned it, so that Josie could have a closer look at the heather. "It's adorable. I like the shape being square. It's very unique." She handed the brooch back to Laurie and Laurie pinned it safely onto her blouse again. She suddenly felt another pair of eyes on her and glanced up quickly at the young man. His eyes darted from her back to the paper. Had he been looking at her? Could he see her and the others? He sat unmoving, staring down at that bit of crumpled paper. The only movement that returned was the quick, abrupt strokes his hand made as he continued to sketch his picture.

"What are your plans for tomorrow?" Angie asked.

"I had planned to meet with the curator tomorrow to look at some of the artifacts. I saw your book in the shop when I was there the other day!" Laurie said turning to Shannon. "I had no idea that you would be at Ponden the same time as myself."

Shannon smiled, "It was meant to be," she said simply.

"I really wish now that I had bought your book when I was at the Parsonage. I planned to buy it after my return home only because my suitcase is packed with 28 other books."

Without hesitating Shannon extended her hand towards Laurie with her book held in it. They had been talking about it earlier that evening. It was a biography about one of the Brontës.

"Have this copy. I'm sorry it isn't in pristine condition."

Laurie at first refused politely, but Shannon insisted she take the book to remember the evening – not that she would be likely to ever forget this evening. She accepted the book gratefully and Shannon even signed the copy for her – "For our lovely Ponden evening!" That summed it up perfectly. How short the evening hours were. Before she knew it, the time had sped on and it was nearly 1 am. She had an enchanting room waiting for her with the infamous box-bed and window. A fire had been lit in her room that evening and would be dying down by now. The glow of the embers would still be welcoming, she thought.

They all got up and stretched, then moved from the room towards the stairs. Just before leaving the room Laurie looked back over her shoulder at the fireplace. He still sat on the couch unmoving. He was oblivious to the departure of the four women. He continued to hold the pencil in his hand and glanced upwards every now and then.

"Out you go before I turn off the light," Josie urged. Laurie stepped out of the room quickly with one final glance at the young man. She saw him hunch over his drawing again just as the light flickered off and the room fell into darkness.

The next morning Laurie awoke in her bed that was enclosed on all sides by wood paneling. The foot of the bed had doors that slid open and the length of the bed that was not against the wall, also had sliding wood panels. Laurie had left the doors at the foot of the bed open, so that she could see if any ghostly presence might appear in the night. At first she feared that leaving the doors open would allow intruders to tug at her exposed feet, but then she decided it was better to be able to see the approach of someone or something rather than sensing there was something lurking in the room with her on the other side of the closed panels.

She turned on her right shoulder and looked out the quaint window where the little ghostly hand had reached desperately for Mr. Lockwood's. She could almost hear that thin, wispy voice on the wind – "Let me in! Let me in!" it cried out to anyone who would hear. Laurie's thoughts moved away from Wuthering Heights for a moment as she watched the night fall away and dawn appeared. The morning was grey and damp and the window became slightly fogged. She wondered what her response would be if a voice had implored, "Let me in!" She couldn't imagine being as violent as Lockwood had been. She wouldn't have dragged the pale arm across the shards of broken glass, in a saw-like motion, out of terror to free herself from its grip. Laurie peered at the tiny window – a single paned window that was just large enough for a person to put a hand through.

She thought there was something out there in the mist and she drew closer to the tiny window to get a closer look. She liked believing there was "something" out there. It gave her such a pleasant, eerie sensation while she held the bed sheets tightly around her for comfort. There was nothing to be seen outside the window. Laurie's thoughts turned to the young man she had seen last night. Last night seemed so far away now. She wondered if he still sat on that sofa sketching on that small piece of crumpled paper. There was something so melancholy about him. The other women hadn't mentioned seeing him and so she assumed she had been the only one. With questions about the young man still lingering in her mind, Laurie got up to get ready for breakfast. She showered and dressed still thinking of the young man. She thought she knew who he was, but wouldn't say anything to anyone just yet. She hesitated about mentioning "him" to the other women simply because nobody else had seemed to have seen him. She opened the door to her room to head down to breakfast, but then stopped and stood in quiet contemplation for a moment. Had he seen them? There was only that fleeting moment when Laurie had thought she'd caught him looking at her, but she couldn't be sure.

"Coming to breakfast?" Laurie jumped at the sudden voice that pulled her from her meditation on the young man. "I'm sorry, dear. Didn't mean to startle you," Shannon apologized.

"That's okay! I was just on my way down." The delicious sense of mystery and the unknown washed away from her as she reached for her purse.

The two women headed downstairs together and enjoyed a full-English breakfast. As Josie set the plates of steaming food down in front of her guests, she had remarked how rare it was for English people to partake in a full-English breakfast. Tourists seemed to enjoy it though and so she always served a full English. Angie was already eating and the other two women sat down to join her. Once everyone was served Josie joined the group with a cup of tea.

"I hope you all slept well last night," Josie asked her guests. They all smiled and made the appropriate comments. "I will be heading into Haworth this morning, so if any of you would like to ride with me you are more than welcome to join," Josie offered.

Laurie did not have a car and quickly accepted Josie's offer. Shannon and Angie had plans of their own that day and would be heading off in their own cars.

Josie dropped Laurie off at the Parsonage where she waited with growing excitement to be taken into the Parsonage library, which had been added onto the Parsonage by Reverend John Wade who moved in after Patrick Brontë died. Laurie waited outside in the garden, leaning against a tree that overlooked the cemetery beyond the garden wall. She was told that it had been planted there by Charlotte Brontë on her wedding day. She patted the bark of the great tree and looked up into its strong limbs. She breathed in her surroundings and closed her eyes imagining the gentle rustle of the long dresses and stiff fabrics. She could hear the sound of horses' hooves on the cobblestones and even imagined the animals having a difficult time climbing up the steep main street of Haworth. Hooves would slip and lose their grip in wet weather and when the ice and snow came it would have been near impossible to drive a horse up the street. She thought of the faithful servant, Tabby, who had slipped on the ice one winter on Haworth's main street and broken her leg.

"Come on in. We are ready for you," a voice called out from the doorway of the Parsonage. Laurie looked up and quickly hurried forward. She was taken down the hall and into the kitchen. The rope that served to keep visitors out of the kitchen area was removed and to Laurie's surprise a door she had never noticed before was opened. She stepped through the doorway into a secret room beyond full of books by the Brontës and biographies about the Brontës. It was as though she had stepped into another world. An academic one! Around the rectangular room sat a few people at two long tables. All were examining artifacts very scrupulously.

One lady had several pen nibs aligned on a black velvet stand. She was holding one up to a light for closer inspection. She couldn't believe those were the pen nibs of the Brontës. She wondered which Brontë they had once belonged to. Laurie was guided to a chair opposite the lady with the nibs and was shown a great many artifacts of the Brontës. She saw the original letters and drawings that she knew so well and even saw up-close small circles of hair that were pinned delicately to a board. She wanted to reach out and stroke the locks with her baby finger. There was something so unhappy about them. Perhaps it was knowing that this was all that now existed of the Brontës. This was as close as she would ever come to "seeing" them.

Everything moved her very much emotionally, but it wasn't until she was presented with one drawing that her heart ceased momentarily. She stared in numbness at the drawing as the curator provided an explanation of the piece.

"Branwell Brontë sketched this drawing just a year before he died. We are certain that this is the living room at Ponden Hall. The large fireplace in the background suggests this. Added confirmation for this supposition is the hooks in the beams around the fireplace. You can clearly see the beams around the fireplace and the hooks that have been nailed into the beams for drying meat." Laurie continued to stare at the drawing in disbelief. It was most certainly the room she had been in last evening. It was the same room in which she and the three other women had passed an enchanting night. This drawing was created from the perspective of someone standing back surveying the room from the dining room. The entire room was in view and hanging from the hooks in the picture were great slabs of meat. The large slabs of raw flesh were the only items that had not been present that evening. Laurie still had not made any comment, but continued to stare in silence at the picture.

"You stayed at Ponden Hall last night, didn't you?" Laurie nodded. The woman looked at Laurie and frowned slightly, "You must have seen this room. Surely you recognize it. It is quite a good likeness of the Ponden Hall living room."

"Yes, I know the room well."

"It certainly has character. There is always a special kind of magic in the air at Ponden," the curator said, smiling as she carefully put the drawing down on the protective mat on the table. "Now," she continued, "This drawing is interesting not only because of the room, but because of the shady, almost ghostly outlines of three people sitting around the fireplace in conversation. Their features are indistinct, but we can see they are three women. We wonder who they are. Many have speculated that Branwell was most likely sketching his sisters, but others argue that the women don't remotely resemble the sisters in body size. Remember, Charlotte was a very petite woman. Even in her time many often remarked about her diminutive size. Perhaps Branwell was merely drawing from his imagination. Unfortunately, we're never likely to know the answers to these questions. These three women will forever remain a mystery."

Laurie leaned towards the sketch for a closer look. She focused on the woman who sat in the same place Laurie had last night. And there it was! Pinned to the woman's shirt was a small, square brooch.

"Isn't it interesting that the faces of the women are not discernible, but this piece of jewelry on this woman is very distinct. You can see every bit of heather on that brooch and can almost see the purple hue of the heather, even though this is a black and white sketch."

Laurie remained silent, but slowly reached up and touched the brooch that was pinned to her blouse. She didn't look at it, but just felt the shape of the brooch silently with her fingers as she gazed at the sketch before her. Outside the window the sound of a church bell could be heard.

> Judge not a man's "mark" left to time,
> Lest his soul rise up from the grave
> And to greatness he will boldly climb,
> For success will wait for the brave.

I Cannot Continue In This Condition!

Emily's Diary illustration by Yvonne Solly

EMILY'S DIARY

by Elaine France-Sergeant,
Wigan, England
*During a recent examination of Emily's writing desk, an undated diary
paper was discovered tucked deeply into a hidden nook.
Here you see it published for the first time:*

Old Tabby, shes just not well because on the cobbled road she slipped
and fell.
We girls are writing poems all three and father, well, he just cant see.
Branwell is running here and there, hes drinking gin and he dont care.
For hes out and about. If you want a good night give him a shout,
a good tale he is not without.
Marther has got a lot to do, for Keepers started the shoes to chew.
He got mud all over his head and he put paw marks on the bed.
My Aunt Branwell, shes going crazy. She dont like keeper, says hes fat
and lazy.
Heathcliff and Cathy haunt each other. He says he will never love
another.
They're giving everyone a terrible fright, wandering the moors at night.
Thats all for now. I wonder where we will be in 4 years time.

*The Ghost of the House illustration
by James Marshall Fynn Masterson*

THE GHOST OF THE HOUSE

Chelsealee Gibbons-Crangle
Liverpool, England

The ghost of the house
walks among us like she belongs here.
Walk, is a strong word.
She floats, almost ballet like, through the house.
She stares out the window,
       longing for something in the dark moor.
Her gaze adrift with painful scorns.
Thorn in her side,
she aches with every move.

Midnight.
The strike of the clock at twelve is her heartbeat,
howl of the wind, her cry,
sting of freshly boiled water, her touch.
I ask her why she won't let me help her.
She simply looks through me,
       with empty eyes and white sheet expression.

Is there blood in your heart?
The squeal of the kettle, her scream,
creek of the floorboards, her footsteps,
chirp of the birds, her singing.

Her soul and mine,
cut from the same cloth,
entangled,
forevermore.

The Staircase illustration by DM Denton

THE STAIRCASE
by DM Denton
USA
*Author of Without the Veil Between, Anne Brontë:
A Fine and Subtle Spirit*

Who?

At first, I didn't think the question was directed at me. I didn't want to be seen. If by some unintended wish I was, I didn't feel inclined to answer, to reveal more than I had already.

I didn't want to be rude, either, the manners Aunt Elizabeth had instilled in me continuing to influence my judgment.

It was the staircase I meant to be present for as I moved out of the shadows and onto its wide bottom step, Queen Anne in its demeanor and mine. Would there be the smell of polish and creaking on certain steps, its handrail smooth, cold, and substantial beneath my small hand? It was a miracle that I had found it again, and myself as eager and expectant as when the journey to my independent future packed more illusions—especially of the juvenile variety—than clothes.

The staircase had darkened with age but in its afterlife had been restored for a brighter environment. Gone was the eighteenth-century oak paneling of its first home that eclipsed the rare beauty of its burred yew unless a candle was held near. Now surrounded by white-washed walls and ceilings, and light-fixtures with flames that didn't flicker, the imperfections of the staircase's wood glowed.

Once again it seemed I was alone, or, at least, without anyone realizing my presence pretending to be other than it was. The first time I stepped onto the staircase I was still in awe of Blake Hall's magnificence and certain I was at the threshold of an exciting time in my young life. In terms of my own actions, maintenance, faculties, and possibilities, I was just beginning.

I intended to make the most of an opportunity for refinement and worthiness.

It was April 1839. I was taken up a back way to a small but comfortable bedroom to briefly revive with refreshment and rest, leaving little time to tidy my appearance before I emerged less than an hour later. I walked along a paneled and papered hallway to a grander way down to

265

meet new responsibilities, convinced the society below would put my shyness and insecurities at ease and improve and cultivate me. Lifting the mud-splattered hem of my skirt, I wished it clean and my petti-coats, too, although I was wearing only one. I saw skimpy slippers on my feet rather than sensible boots. Somewhere, probably the drawing room, a piano was being played and there was singing, the latter much less in tune, but, as a young female child's voice often was, sweet and pretty.

My optimism in being entrusted with the care and education of children was enthused until I heard mockery and crying.

A door slammed.

A rude boy, no more than six or seven, bounded up past me, while the same stately woman who had met my arrival earlier with nothing more than was necessary to say, stood at the bottom of the stairs expressionless.

I could go no further in that disagreeable direction.

I hadn't followed the fate of the staircase to revisit the pomposity, unpleasantness, and worst of the Inghams, or my own wickedness that I wasn't proud of but seemed necessary at the time. I closed my eyes, counted to ten, opened them, and all that remained was my flight of fancy on those stairs.

* * *

My faith had prepared me to settle in heavenly peace where I was reunited with those I loved, one in particular even more agreeable in the hereafter. I was rarely nostalgic for the life I had abandoned too soon, especially once Charlotte and Flossy were with me again. I have to— affectionately—blame Emily, who was still into haunting, for alerting me to the demolition of Blake Hall after what was salvaged of its character and worth had been auctioned off. That was as far as Emily was willing to go with the news, while Charlotte had long ago grown disillusioned with London, so I made a second trip there on my own.

Of course, I could do nothing but watch the dealings that started at a Kensington antiques fair, continued miles away in a damp, dusty warehouse, and culminated in the staircase's sale and a plan to send it to be reassembled even farther away from fitting in.

By then, I was curious about the couple who had crossed the Atlantic to flaunt their money and steal a little of the old world to the new. Giving into the temptation to eavesdrop on Allen and Gladys Topping during their return voyage, I meant to limit my spying to their discussions about "the English treasures" purchased for their new house on a "long island". Instead, my fascination with their engaging if sometimes vulgar speech and mannerisms and Gladys' spontaneous operatic singing, which made her husband's eyes shine, became an inexcusable intrusion upon their privacy.

No sooner I returned to time without measure than Allen Topping was there. I wanted to ask him about the staircase but decided not to because he didn't know me. He was greeted by a crowd of condolences for the loss of his wife. I often wondered if William ever felt bereaved over what might have been between us, but I was still too shy to ask him. Heaven, like earth, was full of unfinished love stories. I knew Allen would be all right.

Gladys would be, too, for, as my dearest Flossy told me, Allen had left her with a special gift.

* * *

"Mr. Wyk, what is it?"

Mr. Wyk reminded me of Emily's Keeper, intimidating until he wagged his tail and nuzzled my hand for a treat he wasn't supposed to have. I was sure he was a comfort to his mistress who, unlike Emily, had no rules that kept him off her bed or from roaming anywhere in the house. Not that Emily and Keeper were less devoted to each other, their reunion as intensely emotional as mine had been with Flossy.

"Mr. Wyk?"

The young Doberman Pincher ran up the stairs to the first landing, his snout down on his front paws and his spine rising as he resumed growling.

I began to ascend, thinking to put him at ease again, but he backed away whining and turned to Gladys. She had one hand over her mouth while the other lifted a chamber stick that illuminated the fear and curiosity in her eyes.

I waited for the question I didn't want to answer.

Who? it came, although it wasn't spoken.

Quickly, once and for all, in a whisper meant to be an impression, I told her.

I was surprised she had heard of me, also of my sisters and brother, and had even seen the lovely moors.

"Ah, she's gone." Gladys stroked Mr. Wyk's ears and went down the stairs. I moved aside, forgetting I didn't need to. The faithful dog wanted to follow her but waited for me to gesture him to. "You must be hungry, Mr. Wyk. Will anyone believe we saw her? I wonder if she'll be back."

I have been, but not so Gladys has actually observed me again. It's hard to be sure about Mr. Wyk; perhaps he no longer sees anything unusual in my visits.

I often make a detour to catch a sunrise over the ocean from one of Quoque's beaches, before returning to Sanderling where I like to go up and down the staircase, rather like a madwoman, which I would never have done in life, or, hopefully, put in a novel. Sometimes, I offer little noises and other signs that get Gladys' attention but don't disturb her too much or give away more than I have already.

If The Little Fiend Had Got In At The Window, She Probably Would Have Strangled Me!

Last Breath illustration by EmilyInGondal

LAST BREATH

By Emma Wellman
Adelaide, South Australia

Heathcliff's eyes closed as he drew his last shuddering breath. A smile on his lips at last. Her ghost had haunted him for many years. For too long he could feel her spirit, forever tormenting his soul, not allowing him to rest. Heathcliff could see her standing there, arms outstretched, the sweetest smile playing on her lips. He walked into those arms and then together, their ghosts floated towards the moors of their childhood. Whatever their souls were made of, they were the same...

Leatherman illustration by Barb Tanke

LEATHERMAN

by Maria Johnson
Connecticut, USA

"Busted flat in Baton Rouge, waitin' for a train, feelin' near as faded as my jeans..." Janis Joplin's soulful voice came over the radio as Dave started up the car, SuSu singing along as they pulled out of the parking lot. "Freedom is just another word for nothin' left to lose..."

"Wanna drive around for a bit? It's just eight-thirty and still pretty light out. No school tomorrow, no school for awhile!" As usual, Dave would leave it up to his best friend SuSu to decide.

She nodded her assent as she sang along until the end of the song.

"It's been a couple of years now, but I still can't believe that Janis is gone," she sighed. "What a voice!"

They drove along Route 6, still a fairly busy road connecting Danbury, Connecticut with Brewster, New York, but not yet the commercial and dining area it would become. Dotted with the occasional farm stand or other small shop, the miniature golf course afforded about the only entertainment to be found. Dave took a turn off to the right near a small deli onto Joe's Hill Road. SuSu sat bolt upright and protested. "Dave, what are you doing? I didn't think you'd drive down Joe's Hill!"

"What are you talking about? It's a nice, scenic road. Not much traffic. Perfect for a drive on a summer's evening." And so it would seem as they drove along, the overhanging branches of maple and elm providing a welcome respite after the heat and humidity of the fast-ending day.

SuSu looked at him in disbelief. "You know what I'm talking about! Strange things go on here. Satan worshippers, the Jesus Tree, ghosts, the White Lady..."

"Have *you* ever seen anything? I mean, we've all seen the Jesus Tree, it's just a bit farther along from here. But what about the rest?"

"It's not so much what I've seen, but what I've *heard*," she said in a quiet voice.

"Ooh, sounds interesting!" Dave was intrigued now. "Let's pull over and you can tell me all about it."

Dave found a fairly wide spot on the right hand side of the road and pulled over. Heavily wooded on either side, the upper branches nearly met over the middle of the road to form a tunnel, but there was still a bit of sky to be seen. A short distance ahead on the left, they could just make out the surface of the pond from between the trunks of the trees.

"Spill!" Dave demanded. "Who, or what, did you hear?"

SuSu took a deep breath, "The Creaky Man - the Leatherman. Well, it was over ten years ago, when I was a little kid going to nursery school here on this very road. One day, Miss Nancy took us on a walk to visit what she said had been a hermit's cave nearby. It was no longer occupied, of course, but had served as a shelter for the Leatherman whenever he passed through town on his regular tramp through New York and Connecticut a hundred years ago."

"Why did you call him the Creaky Man?" Dave asked. "I thought he was just the Leatherman."

"Well, I mean, he was always dressed in leather. No matter the weather, he wore a handmade suit of leather clothes and you could hear the leather creak as he walked by. In fact, we heard the creaking sound the very day that we visited the cave. It was really loud and spooky, but that was probably Miss Nancy's tag-along brother Eddie trying to scare us from a hiding place near the cave, but, anyway, it scared the heck out of all of us and we ran back to school right away. I don't want to go near there!"

Dave smiled. "You were a kid then and Eddie was pulling a prank. I should think you'd be over it by now. Anyway, I don't think that people are even sure if the Leatherman had a cave around here."

Daylight was nearly gone now, but Dave could tell that something was wrong. SuSu's face was pale and her eyes twitched nervously. "Oh, he did! I saw it! I saw him!"

"What?"

Her eyes, no longer twitching, seemed almost round with wonder. "I haven't thought about this in a while, but a few years ago, my friend Jen - you know Jen - and I liked to ride our bikes around here. We'd each bring a snack and a book and we'd look around for a quiet place to read. We could spend hours reading in some leafy nook in the quiet of the woods. There were so many cool, shady places to go to around here and we would try to visit as many likely spots as we could." She began to feel more confident as the memories came back to her. "Anyhow, one day we stopped near here, where we are now, over on the left-hand side, a little bit before reaching the pond. The area had become a bit more overgrown from what I remembered as a kid. Well, we walked our bikes into the woods a little way, found a nice spot, and began to hang out and read. After a while, Jen got up to stretch her legs and, after only a few minutes, came running back excitedly. 'Look what I found, SuSu! A cave! It looks like someone used to live there!'

"Now, I hadn't thought about the hermit's cave since I was very small, but at first glance I knew that it was the very same one. I remembered how the slabs of rock had formed a kind of triangle at the entrance, which was large and open enough that you could see in a little way. We could see signs of a campfire and even some old sticks of very crumbly-looking firewood piled up inside, as if whoever had been using the cave expected to return and build a fire someday." She paused, "Then it happened!"

"What happened?" Dave leaned forward intently.

"All of a sudden, a feeling came over me, like a really thick blanket of muggy air. The weight of it was oppressive." Her breathing was becoming as rapid as the words spilling out of her mouth. "I started to hear the creaking of leather - Jen heard it, too, it was that loud - from deep inside the cave. Hearts pounding, we stood stock still as someone called out something... 'kee el la', it sounded like. It was dark inside the cave, but I was able to make out his face somewhat: with hair disheveled, and staring, penetrating eyes, looking out almost crazily from beneath the brim of his leather hat.

"We high-tailed it out of there, grabbed our bikes from where we'd left them, and pedaled toward home as fast as we could. We couldn't get out of there fast enough! It wasn't until we were well onto the main road that we realized that we had left our food and stuff behind us near the cave when we'd dropped everything to make our escape. I was really bummed too since I'd left behind my copy of Jane Eyre - my all-time favorite book - and Jen was none too pleased to lose her new Lord of the Rings trilogy set, but there was no way that we were going back there to get them. No way!"

SuSu leaned back on the car seat. She had filed these memories away as there was no explanation for what had happened, and now she was scared. Dredging them up again was taking her to a place that she would rather not visit. Sensing this, Dave thought it best to try a logical approach.

"I don't know what you saw, SuSu, but it couldn't have been the Leatherman - we both know he died, like, a hundred years ago!"

SuSu would not be swayed. "Maybe it was his ghost or his spirit or something. I told you, this area is creepy and there are a lot of un-explained things that go on here. Maybe he got angry at Jen and me disturbing his rest when we got near his cave and decided to scare us off. Maybe he couldn't 'rest in peace' because of us."

Logical Dave tried again, "I thought he was buried in New York somewhere, so how could you be disturbing his rest here? I know that he wandered around, but he does have a grave somewhere and I suppose that he would haunt people from there. Anyway, what was his story? It's common knowledge that he wandered around between Connecticut and New York, but why did he do it? Do you know?"

"Like you, I know that he used to walk a continuous loop from the Hudson River through New York and into Connecticut over to the Connecticut River, then down to the coast and back west through New

York to the Hudson again, sleeping in caves along the way. He did this over and over again. I also know that the whole loop he walked took him thirty-four days. They say that his arrival was so predictable that folks would leave food out for him. He would never come inside their houses, though, no matter how bad the weather, or even speak much with any of them. Just a few words in broken English, nothing more."

"He didn't speak English?" Dave asked.

"Not much, I guess," SuSu replied. "He spoke French. The only people he would ever talk to were people who spoke French - and even then, he didn't talk much."

"But why the hell did he wander around like that?" Dave wanted to know. "You seem to be such an expert, what made him do that? What was his name?"

SuSu began, "Well, no one really knows that much for sure, but what I know I learned from my grandmother. She heard it from her mother who used to actually see him when he passed near her house. Grandma told me that his name was Jules and that he was from France. He fell in love with a young lady there and, somehow or other, got into some sort of financial trouble and lost his money and that of his girlfriend's family. Needless to say, he lost his girlfriend, too. "Eventually, he ended up in this area, although some say he went to Canada first, and that he wanders around, sleeping rough in handmade clothes made of leather as a sort of penance. I mean, I don't know if any of this is true, but I kinda like the romantic angle of it, and I don't see why it can't be true.

"At any rate, he wandered around a very large area - and I think he wanders still!"

Dave smiled. "I seriously doubt it. Anyway, I've gotta go answer Nature's call. Will you be okay here for a few minutes? I'll be right back."

SuSu looked nervously around. "Fine, but make it quick, please. This place gives me the creeps!"

He headed off into the woods on SuSu's side of the car. The full moon had risen, lighting the way for Dave to find a suitable spot nearby, and giving SuSu a little bit of confidence as she sat alone waiting for him to return.

A cloud briefly obscured the moon, and SuSu began to feel a chill. She was beginning to get creeped out when she heard something, perhaps the rustling of leaves or the creaking of branches, coming from the other side of the road. It seemed to be getting nearer. "Maybe it's a raccoon or something", she thought, "Or maybe Dave just wants to freak me out - that would be just like him!"

As suddenly as the sound started, it stopped. She looked up, expecting to see Dave by the driver's side of the car, but he wasn't there. There was no one there. "Dave," she called out, "where are you?"

"Right here, silly!" he said from a few feet away from the passenger side door.

"Well, you took long enough!" SuSu scolded him. "What are you doing over there? I heard you crashing about on the other side."

"C'mon, SuSu, didn't you see me head off in this direction? I guess you just weren't paying attention. Besides, I didn't hear anything 'crashing about'. I was trying to be very quiet on the way back so I could give you a scare, but then you ruined it by calling out to me," Dave harrumphed. "You must have heard an animal or something,"

"Maybe, but I don't think so. God, this place is creepy! Let's get out of here!"

"It's really not all that creepy. It's just because of the full moon tonight. Spooky energy, you know?" His face grew animated. "I have an idea! Why don't we come back here tomorrow and check things out in the light of day? I'm sure you won't think it's so creepy then."

SuSu looked at him doubtfully, "I don't know..."

"I'll pick you up tomorrow before it gets too hot and we can stop at that little deli on Route 6 to pick up some sandwiches, make a picnic of it. A nice un-spooky, un-creepy picnic."

"Well, okay, Dave, but don't pick me up too late. I have to babysit later on."

"Deal!"

* * *

The next day, Dave arrived, radio blasting, to pick up SuSu for their un-creepy picnic.

"Great! I love Stevie Wonder! 'Very superstitious, writing on the wall...'" she sang along.

"Very appropriate," said Dave, singing along "but wait: 'When you believe in things that you don't understand, you will suffer...'"

"Ha! Like the ghost of the Leatherman, you mean?"

"To quote the great Lennon and McCartney 'Let it Be'!"

275

"Okay, you got me. We're almost to the place where we were parked last night. Why don't we just go there?" asked SuSu, determined to be brave, but not quite able to convince herself...

Dave pulled the car off to the side of the road, very near the same spot as the night before. They grabbed their bag of sandwiches and headed off into the woods across from where they were parked. They decided to have their lunch in a small clearing they found perhaps a hundred yards into the woods. Clearing though it was, very little sun penetrated the leafy canopy, keeping out the ever-increasing heat and humidity as well as the sound of the traffic from the interstate nearby.

"It really is peaceful here," SuSu said. "The trees really muffle the sounds from the highway, don't they? I can see why the old Leatherman would have sought shelter around here."

"There was no highway here back then," Dave reminded her.

"Of course not! But there were some important roads nearby. No matter what, this place is off the beaten path."

"Damn, I forgot to bring my portable radio. We could have been listening to some tunes!"

"I'm glad you forgot it, Dave. I would hate to disturb this peace and quiet with 'Crocodile Rock', and who knows who else we might disturb..."

"It's daylight, SuSu," Dave laughed. "He wouldn't be in his cave now anyway. Wouldn't he be walking on his way to the next cave?"

"Good point."

Dave reached for SuSu's sandwich wrapper, balled it up, and placed it in the bag from the deli. "If you're done eating, why don't we go look for the cave? Would you recognize it?"

"Of course I would! Let's go!"

* * *

Dave went on ahead as they walked further into the woods. "I think I've found it! You said it had a triangular opening, right?"

New Englanders are accustomed to seeing lots of rocks. The glaciers seeded the area quite generously with their geologic detritus. Slabs upon slabs, seemingly precarious, formed natural shelters for all members of animal kind - humans included.

Soon they came upon a triangular formation, the opening of which was a yard or more in height, very sturdy looking, and very dark. The cave - let's call it that - extended a good four or five yards under a small mound of earth and stone.

"That's it!" she said.

"I'm going in!" he said.

"Dave, don't..."

"Nothing's going to happen to me, SuSu, it's just an opening in an outcropping of rocks. Are you feeling any weird sensations so close to the hermit's cave?"

"Actually, Dave, I'm kinda surprised, and a bit disappointed. Must be because it's daytime and the Leatherman would have been long gone by now."

"Exactly! I brought a flashlight - I'm gonna check it out!"

Before she could make any further protest, he was crawling into the cave. After a few minutes, he crawled back out, brushing spiderwebs and leaves, and possibly some less attractive items, off of his clothes.

"Well, that was gross! Lots of animals have been using this cave, that's for sure! I did see a really old pile of wood and some smoke marks, but that's about it." He took another moment to brush himself off. "Do you think we should head home? I've gotta get washed up and you said that you had a babysitting gig."

"You're right, Dave, let's go. Man, I can't wait to get my license. My exam is in a couple of weeks. Do you think that I could practice-drive on the way back?"

"Sure, SuSu! You know how to drive a stick, right?"

"Yep! My brother taught me."

They walked back to the car, and SuSu got behind the wheel. As she started up the car she said to Dave, "I'm still kinda disappointed that I didn't see the old Leatherman... Oh, well, let's hear some tunes!"

Janis Joplin came on again as SuSu put the car into reverse: "Freedom's just another word for nothin' left to lose/Nothin' don't mean nothin' hon' if it ain't free, no, no..." As she backed up the car, she felt the car go over something. She got nervous and the car stalled. Dave and SuSu got out to see what they'd run over.

"What is it, SuSu?"

"No! Oh my god!"

"What is it?"

SuSu picked up a small, filthy, rectangular object. She carefully brushed away the grime. "Oh my god!"

Dave stared at her, waiting for an explanation.

"It's a book! *My* book!"

"Your book?" he asked.

"The book I lost when I was here with Jen. Jane Eyre! And look! There's something inside it, maybe a bookmark? Between chapters thirty-five and thirty-six. Let me look at it. It's an old photo. Three ladies from long ago!"

"Does it say anything on it, SuSu?"

She carefully turned over the photo. "It says something in French, but I see the word 'Brontë'."

Dave was puzzled. "What does this all mean?"

To Dave, SuSu replied, "I have absolutely no idea!" But to her heart she said "Merci, Jules."

Ghost Written illustration by Barb Tanke

GHOST WRITTEN

By Jessa Fabiano
Rhode Island, USA

Spiteful spirit,
you taught me well,
no haunt's as savage
as love who won't forgive.
Stern as a nun,
you seek sanctuary
in the attic of my dreams, and
refuse to leave me.

Furious phantom, your icicle fingers,
touch my cheek as I sleep,
insist our inclination was fabrication,
a mirrored glimmer made of paste.
Dancing away with my breath's ragged rhythm,
your spectral laugh gnashes my bones,
gnaws my marrow, leaves me hollow.

Haunt me harder-
I'll offer my neck, my blood- drain me until
I become light enough to follow you
on bleak journeys toward horizons,
liminal with loss.
Let's fly from cliffs, swirl on storms
while people below wonder at heaven's strange tenants.

Terrorizing teacher, your dreary lesson
lends no escape,
but you do not cage me in the bars of your bones,
do you?
You slide like smoke through my embrace
as night draws darkness across sky,
over my eyes- a heavy, velvet cloak.

Little ghost, even blind, I seek sweet curves of shadow,
beg your presence in the smallest flake of snow,
or delicate grain of fallen feather.
Fire no longer warms,
yet you exist in the salt of my skin,
and refuse to leave me.

Emily Alone illustration by Emily Ross

EMILY ALONE

by Joanne Dalton,
Ripon, North Yorkshire, UK.

The day is almost over and the Parsonage is quiet at last. I hear the front door close and the turn of a key in the lock. The people have all gone now; so many of them all day, every day wandering through my home without a care. I wish they would all leave and not return! What place do they have here and why do they come? Who lets them in? I do not know, it can only be Charlotte's doing. She brought fame upon us, so noisy and unwelcome when all I want is peace and solitude.

Sometimes I wander the house when the people are here, but they do not see or hear me. Occasionally I will stand behind some person and they will look over their shoulder, but they do not acknowledge me and for this I am grateful.

Now I am alone, certainly, but *they* are always with me. I wander past my Father's study. There he sits, reading a newspaper silently. I see him but momentarily, then his figure fades and he disappears before me. Always it is the same.

I hear the dogs bark and run by in the hall but I do not see them. I hear the pounding of little feet and childish giggles that remind me of my long dead sisters, Maria and Elizabeth. I call after but they never reply.

I approach the kitchen and I can hear Tabby muttering something under her breath in her strong dialect, almost imperceptible. I imagine she wants the girls to help her peel the vegetables for dinner. I look and see her at the kitchen table but she does not see me, then she too is gone. Why can I not speak to her?

I climb the stairs but it feels like I am floating. Branwell pushes past me with blind eyes and an irritated tone, addressed not to me but perhaps our Father. "Damn it! I'm off to the Bull and you will not stop me!" He blusters down the hall and walks through the closed, locked front door. Oh, Dear Branwell! You never will change; it is not possible now.

As I step onto the landing, I hear a baby crying and I see Charlotte holding a tiny, tiny bundle. "Hush, hush" she says to it as she drifts into her bedroom and disappears from my view. Are you happy now

Charlotte? When did this happen and where was I? It is as if I was sleeping at the time. So many things confuse me now. I do not understand how Charlotte can have married and had a baby when all she wanted was to be a writer. I think the baby is a ghost and I am not sure about Charlotte, poor Charlotte.

Always I wonder, where is Anne? She is not here, I never see her in my wanderings amidst the house, the churchyard, the moors. I dream she is at the seaside, strolling sadly along the seafront amongst crowds of people, bright flashing lights and noise. In my mind's eye, I see her standing in a different churchyard looking sadly at a grave. These images haunt my days and nights. How I miss Dearest Anne!

I can hear my Mother's voice coming from her bedchamber. I peer in and see her lying there, holding Aunt Branwell's hand. Her voice is weak and filled with pain. "Take care of them for me, dear Elizabeth! Look after Patrick, you will, I know you will!" My Aunt nods sadly; I cannot bear this scene, it breaks my heart and I am glad when the scene fades and is gone.

So now I am truly alone. The people have gone, those strange people who come and go each day, gazing at my family's things, some with reverent awe and others with disinterest. I am glad they are gone and happy for them never to return, but what of my family? They are here but not here and I see them only as ghosts, fleeting and remote; with me yet also gone forever.

Am I a ghost too, like Cathy rapping at the window, except no one hears me? I know I am dead and my family are too, so what else can I be? I will leave here now and go out to the moors. I am a spirit as gauzy and intangible as Cathy and Heathcliff and I feel they are out there, somewhere, waiting for me.

Maybe they will speak to me.

He's More Myself Than I Am

Buried by the Moor Flower illustration by Stephanie Rodriguez

BURIED BY THE MOOR FLOWER

by Paige Campey-Dean
Nottinghamshire, England

Blooming moor flower, spring is nigh,
Shades of pale lavender and beauty is high,
But it is what is beneath the soil,
That encompasses the earthly turmoil.

Many years ago, a couple fled,
Straight out onto Haworth moor did they tread,
And what this story does not say,
Is what happened after that fateful day.

Time passes, as it does,
And people were still no closer to the cause.
Townsfolk fretted and then all too soon,
The flowers began to bloom.

One would gaze upon the flowers and say that her wildness is
apparent;
And that his bitter nature was also inherent.
But when the autumn falls,
All beauty in the moor flower crumbles.

The West Yorkshire wind carries the laughter and tears of that couple,
Among which, the cackles would grapple.
But how sure I was that I saw the two that day,
And clearer than clear, the couple ran away.

Alas, it cannot be them, and so it must be a daydream,
Something that physically cannot be,
But I say something was there,
Amongst the pale and grave moor flower.

One may make comment upon that fateful day,
When two young lovers were blinded by array.
But what the town did not know,
Was that the two were closer than they would ever know.

Many years were spent pushing daisies, or so was thought,
When people began to consider something more fraught.
What if their souls had left their human bodies?
And now live a life they wish they had embodied.

After leaving their beautiful death site, it was time to move on,
To keep witnessing life, akin to the birdsong.
But what shall never be forgot,
Is the beauty that their death begot.

Life carries on past these mere earthly years,
And an eternity awaits you and your peers.
I dearly hope that the couple who fled,
Can be together, at peace, after their toxic earthly tread.

Death becomes life, and life becomes death,
A cycle that leaves many bereft,
But when you hear merriment and laughter on Haworth moor,
Turn to the flower, and remember life's law.

Elsie illustration by Barb Tanke

ELSIE

by Abi Daly
England

She opened her eyes, straining to see her surroundings against the overpowering darkness. An almost doll-like finger brushed against her cheek softly, the pressure so light it was barely there. Elsie turned, dazed and confused. Looking to her right she saw nine tiny figures, their heads cocked slightly to one side watching her. Elsie attempted to sit up but a sudden violent pressure forced her head back down to the floor. "Not yet child," a chilling voice spoke. "It's not your time."

* * *

Elsie Carpenter was 16 years old, middle height with vibrant copper hair and startling, piercing blue eyes. She felt distinctly different to other people she knew, not just physically, either. Elsie almost felt like she didn't belong. These streets, this town, it didn't feel like her world at all.

Elsie had always felt this way as long as she could remember. Everything about her life was disconnected from her, even her parents.

285

There was nothing but an empty space longing to be filled. When she was small, Elsie used to tell her parents this, she tried to explain as best as a young child could but the words never formed quite what she wanted to say. At first Helen and Edward brushed it off as one of those bizarre things children say and eventually grow out of, but the longer it continued the more distressing it became, especially for Helen.

Helen had always wanted children, but by the time she married Edward she had been considered too old to conceive. After visiting several specialists and being told it would never happen Helen became desperate and began praying, but not to God. Never to God. Helen prayed to something else entirely and amazingly it had worked - she got her much longed for child, but at a price. No one could know the toll she would have to pay, not even Edward. It was a dark secret that Helen would take to her grave, after all that's what she had promised them.

* * *

Elsie had learnt fairly quickly to keep her complex and unusual feelings locked away deep inside herself. Instead she took her frustrations out on long walks across the barren moors. She had a few favourite haunts, particularly the Alcomden Stones where very few people ever went. That wasn't Elsie's preferred place, though. A little way beyond the stones, over the boggy, wild ground, a set of large rocks jutted out from the side of the steep valley. Standing on the rocks and looking at the drop below was enough to make your stomach churn, but Elsie felt no fear, only comfort. This was where she belonged, on this craggy outcrop in this uncivilised environment. This was home.

Elsie gently picked her way over to the stones carefully avoiding placing her feet on any of the wildflowers that crept silently out of the soft ground. She headed over to the large, flat top of the stones. Standing as close to the edge as she dared, Elsie stretched her arms out wide, the wind rushing and pulling at her body, tangling her hair. Laughing, she sat down admiring the breath-taking view in front of her. In the distance Ponden Reservoir gleamed and shone in the early morning sunlight, the blue cloudless sky only helping to create the diamond like shimmer below. Closer by, the wind whipped through the heather, moving it like waves in the sea. Then there were the variety of colours, not just brown and green but deep pinks, purples, blues and greys. Elsie inhaled deeply and closed her eyes. Yes, this was definitely home.

Just below where Elsie sat in the base of the rocks was a small opening just big enough for an adult to lie in. It was open at both ends and was only accessible via a short, steep, treacherous climb down the side of the rocks. There were no real hand or foot holds, you just had to use what you could and hope for the best.

Within the dark confines of the cave - the best word anyone had to describe it - lived an unusual group of beings. You wouldn't think that this hole was big enough to house anything comfortably except the tiniest animals, but these creatures were the perfect size.

If you were to hold your thumb up against one then they would be ever so slightly taller, barely big enough to see over the top of your fingernail. Their bodies are lithe and clothed in natural materials scavenged from the moors. Fallen leaves, Lapwing feathers and sprigs of heather all used cleverly to create an elaborate miniature wardrobe. They wear no shoes, preferring instead to feel the cold earth between their toes. Their hair comes in the most vibrant hues and their eyes are a startling, piercing blue. To stare into them is to feel as if your soul is being ripped from your body.

These creatures are commonly known as faeries; however, they are far removed from the cute, smiling images you may be thinking of, for in reality faeries are manipulative, scheming beings with fiery tempers and dispositions to match. They are cunning and at times violent, especially if threatened. Occasionally, though, they offer up their help to those who ask, but only for a price. There was always a price.

Now in this cave resided ten of these faeries. They had lived on this land for millennia, fighting an ever-bitter battle against humans and their destructive tendencies. The faeries used to number in the hundreds, but over time they had been killed in the ongoing war or forced to flee, until just this small band of ten remained sheltered in the remote cave on the moors, the only safety they had left. They had watched as their beautiful world was slowly destroyed by noisy roads and the huge, smog-belching factories that sprang up around them, creeping across the land, encroaching on their sacred sites. Understandably they were incensed and this is what led them to devise their most ambitious plan to date. One that would end the war with humans forever.

* * *

As Elsie lay in the warm sun above the cave, the faeries convened below. Their treasure was back and they knew it, all their senses alerted them to the fact. Unbeknownst to Elsie, she was the treasure the faeries longed for. She was how they would win this war. Elsie had been watched, manipulated and formed to their pattern since the day she was created. They knew her every thought, her every move, they even knew how many of those vibrant copper hairs there were on her head. After all, they had put them there.

As Elsie lay unwittingly above this tiny war council, the wind suddenly began to tear violently across the valley and deep grey clouds loomed overhead. A storm was coming. Almost instantaneously large drops of rain began streaming from above, pelting Elsie and stinging her skin with their ferocity. She was miles from shelter and would be soaked before she could make it back to town. It was then that Elsie made her fateful choice to climb down to the cave. She had only ventured there once before, where she had briefly peered inside expecting just an empty hole, but instead had heard tiny whispers and seen flitting shadows move quickly against the rocks. Convinced that the cave was haunted, Elsie had never gone back, believing that she was safe at the top. Now, however, it seemed she had no choice; she had to go into the cave or get soaked to the skin.

As the storm continued unrelentingly, Elsie clambered down the steep pass between the rocks and the edge of the moors. Each footstep was considered carefully. She didn't want this to be how she ended her days. Elsie hesitated at the bottom. The cave entrance beckoned invitingly. It wouldn't be comfortable, but it would be dry and right now that mattered more.

From within the cave the faeries watched Elsie approaching with an increasing delight. This is what they had waited for, sixteen long years and their plan was nearing its end. They made themselves as small as possible, hiding in the cracks and crevices of the rocks. They needed Elsie to come right in, to feel comfortable and above all, safe. If she became scared or suspicious in any way then all their hard work and patience would be for nothing. They were determined never to fail again.

By now Elsie was at the entrance. She took a moment to peer into the semi darkness inside, "there's nothing there," she told herself repeatedly. If something was within then surely she would be able to see it? Elsie placed a hand gingerly into the cave, it felt surprisingly warm like a bed that had just been vacated. She moved slowly and carefully until she was completely enclosed by the walls. Breathing a sigh of relief Elsie twisted, shuffled and contorted herself until she was lying on her back. The rain sounded like a thousand tiny cannon balls pummeling at the stone outside but at least in here it was dry.

A good twenty minutes passed and the rain carried on as strongly as before. Elsie continued to lie on her back in the cramped space, staring at the non-descript ceiling wondering when she could leave, whilst unnoticed around her the faeries began to implement the final stages of their plan. The smallest - yet bravest - of them crept out from her hiding place towards Elsie's cheek. As she neared Elsie, she drew a miniscule knife from behind her back. As quick as a flash, so quick as to be imperceptible to the human eye, she struck. The knife, laced with various concoctions, was brutally plunged into Elsie's neck. Behind the assailant another faery winced at what he perceived to be immense pain, however all Elsie felt was a small pin prick. Within seconds the combination of potions seeped into her blood stream and she steadily passed into unconsciousness.

As Elsie floated between the realms of the living and the dead the faeries gathered round her. First, they bound her with rope made from grasses and interweaved with their magic. They then used all their combined power to continue the storm with even more ferocity so they would not be disturbed. Finally, they fetched their Queen.

Through a secret door, hidden deep in the ancient stone, emerged the Queen. She rarely left her private apartments, only when she deemed it to be of the upmost importance. The Queen looked resplendent in the finest materials a faery could wish for. Downy feathers plucked straight from the backs of moorland birds created a sweeping floor-length dress. Hollowed out pebbles from the shores of the reservoir made a pair of surprisingly delicate shoes, and freshly collected morning dew formed a crown that glittered in what little light there was. She stepped forwards and gracefully glided up onto Elsie's forehead. "Your Majesty, she's ready," another faery spoke as she pulled herself down into a deep curtsey. The Queen simply nodded in response. At long last, it was time.

The Queen peered down at Elsie. So this was the one they had waited for all this time. She certainly looked the part, at least the magic had worked in that sense. Now they would find out if the magic had worked completely. The Queen bent down and lifted a strand of Elsie's copper hair plucking it clean out. She then passed it to her assistant who hurriedly began to roll it into a small ball before placing it into a miniscule pestle and mortar. Next, he selected a bottle of clear liquid from a bag that looked an awful lot like a much smaller version of one that would belong to a Victorian Doctor. The faery assistant then poured half the liquid into the mortar, added some herb-like flakes and began to mix the ingredients together. As he worked the

Queen continued to stare down at Elsie, patiently waiting for the next step.

Finally, the mixture was ready. The mortar was handed up to the Queen who passed a delicate doll-like hand across it whilst murmuring an enchantment. She then knelt down on Elsie's forehead as two other faeries glided up towards Elsie's eyes. They gently lifted her left eyelid first. The Queen poured some of the mixture directly onto the piercing blue iris letting it settle before moving onto the right eye. When the same actions had been repeated, the Queen then carefully moved her way down to Elsie's mouth, the two faeries following. This time they parted Elsie's lips slightly and the Queen poured what remained of the mixture into Elsie's mouth.

Now all they had to do was wait.

It felt like an eternity. The only noises that could be heard were the sound of the driving rain outside and ten tiny hearts beating loudly in their equally tiny chests. Each of the faeries waited tensely hoping beyond all hope that this would work. They couldn't afford to try this again. Suddenly Elsie began to shiver, her body rippling with the effects of the potion as it bound itself to each individual cell within her. Her eyelids fluttered briefly but wouldn't open, she tried to cry out but could not open her mouth to do so. Elsie terrifyingly felt as though she was trapped in her own body. Although she was completely unaware of all that had passed before, Elsie knew that something was horrifically wrong. She could feel a series of strange sensations coursing through her as, unbeknownst to Elsie, her body slowly surrendered to the magic that was growing stronger inside her as every second passed by.

As she lay there unable to move, Elsie became aware of voices surrounding her. They had an eerie quality to them that made her feel even more unsettled. Trying not to let the rising panic overcome her, Elsie began to imagine everything she loved. The moors, the rushing wind against her skin, the sound of the stream as it crashed down the valley, her parents. As remote as she felt from them, she did love them. She wished they were here beside her. These thoughts comforted Elsie bringing a sense of calm which helped her to slowly begin to gain back some control over her body.

She opened her eyes, straining to see her surroundings against the overpowering darkness. An almost doll-like finger brushed against her cheek softly, the pressure so light it was barely there. Elsie turned, dazed and confused. Looking to her right she saw nine tiny figures, their heads cocked slightly to one side watching her. Elsie attempted to sit up but a sudden violent pressure forced her head back down to the floor. "Not yet child," a chilling voice spoke. "It's not your time."

Her heart pounding, Elsie managed to utter, "Who are you?" so quietly she thought it went unheard. A small cackle bounced off the cave walls in response, "You mean you don't know? Who do you think we are?" Elsie stared at the figures. There was something so familiar about them, yet also very sinister. A face suddenly dropped into view above her right eye. It wore a hideous smile that wouldn't look out of place on a cartoon villain. Elsie jumped slightly making the face laugh. "I'd thought you recognise us, at least," it spoke. "Look closer." Elsie felt her head being turned back towards the figures. At first she struggled to see anything familiar, but then Elsie began to notice their features. They had startling piercing blue eyes the same as her own, and their hair was the most vibrant she had ever seen, just like her own.

"I don't understand," Elsie stuttered. "You look like me. How can you look like me!" The Queen hopped off Elsie's head and joined her subjects on the ground, "actually I think you'll find it's you that looks like us," she replied. "Your Mother, Helen, isn't it? She wanted a baby so badly she'd do anything to get her wish. She came to us to ask for our help and we said yes. Obviously, we couldn't give our services for free. Helen knew that, so she made a teeny promise to us that if we created a baby for her then that baby would become ours one day for whatever purpose we wished. We couldn't tell her when we'd take you though, that would spoil the surprise." The Queen smiled triumphantly at Elsie, "So we made you in our image, our very own weapon."

"Weapon?" Elsie stammered.

"Hmm," the Queen responded. She was beginning to lose interest in the conversation. "Yes, we created you as a weapon against the humans. They need stopping and you will do that perfectly. Now then, enough talking. We haven't got all day."

The Queen clicked her fingers and Elsie felt one final surge of power flood through her body. The sensation was almost overwhelming. The other faeries began to untie Elsie, working swiftly as the Queen made her way to the entrance of the cave. She stamped her elegant foot and the rain suddenly ceased. The dark clouds evaporated and the brilliant sun shone through the bright blue sky once more. The Queen smiled to herself, hands on hips. Perfect weather for a perfect day.

The Queen stepped out of the cave first and was quickly followed by her nine subjects, each of whom was pulling Elsie out with them. As the sudden sunlight fell on her face it caused Elsie to screw her eyes up tight. When she reopened them, she found she had somehow made it back up the top of the Kirk. She sat up still extremely confused. The Queen glided over and levitated up so that she was level with Elsie's face, "Now then, here's what happens next," she said.

"At exactly midday, when the sun is at her peak, you will feel a rising within you. In just a few minutes it will have overpowered you and all this will be over." The Queen smiled triumphantly as she spoke.

"What do you mean by overpowered me? I don't understand," Elsie cried.

Sighing impatiently the Queen responded, "It means that the magic within you will have taken control, you will no longer be in charge of your body or mind. The magic will burst out of your very soul and spread across the land destroying every human in its path ending their disgusting invasion of *OUR LANDS*!" The final words were screamed at such a volume that they echoed around the valley. Elsie's terrified face only caused mirth amongst the other faeries, "Oh don't worry, it will take you too," the Queen snarled. "We have no more use for you after this."

Elsie looked around her in utter shock. In just a few short hours everything and everyone she knew and loved would be gone and she would be the catalyst. She couldn't let this happen, there had to be a way to stop them, to stop the magic working. But she couldn't see a way out. This was it, the end of everything.

As the Queen sauntered around the rock, Elsie broke down in tears. She wouldn't even get to say goodbye to her parents, to say sorry for ever hurting them. As she sat there in complete despair a thought, a voice, female, soft and ethereal, spoke in her head, "You can stop this," it said. "but you can't survive."

Elsie slowly looked around her. No one was speaking, the faeries stood a few metres away, too busy celebrating their epic victory to care about her.

In her head Elsie responded to the voice by thought, "How? How do I stop them? Tell me."

"I can't block them for long," the voice replied urgently, "so listen carefully. Just before midday they will ask you to stand on the rock, you must do what they say however you will need to stand much closer to the edge than is safe to do so. As the time nears you will need to make your move. You need to jump from the rock."

"But that will kill me!" Elsie's fear was heard clearly, "I can't jump!"

"I said you wouldn't survive. If you die, the magic dies. It's the only way," the voice responded sadly. "I'm sorry, but it is your life or everyone's. One life to save billions. Don't you think it is worth it?"

Elsie knew the voice was right. The faeries said she would die anyway, so why not die stopping them? "But my parents, how will they know? I won't see them again!" Fresh tears streamed down Elsie's face at the thought.

"Hush, you will. I guarantee this isn't the end of your story, far from it." The voice soothed. "I can't hold them back anymore. Please trust me. Please!"

The mysterious voice evaporated into the wind just as the Queen strutted over to Elsie, "Aw, poor thing crying," she mocked cruelly. The others laughed manically and for longer than was necessary. "Nearly time, little one," the Queen cooed as she scraped her delicate finger across Elsie's cheek.

The resolve hit Elsie harder than she thought, "I can do this."

A sudden sharp noise signaled the time. The faeries came towards Elsie and began to pull her up, "I can stand by myself," she snapped at them.

The Queen looked amused by this; a small smile lingered on her face. "I am glad to see you are so willing. It makes things much easier," she said with a hint of triumph. Elsie stood on the rock staring directly ahead down the valley. She slowly shuffled her feet towards the edge, her heart pounding violently in her chest.

She turned to face the faeries, "You think you've won, don't you?" Elsie spoke with more confidence than she felt. "You underestimate us humans, though. We might do stupid things and realise too late what we're doing to the world, but we would do anything to save the ones we love." At those words Elsie leaned back as far as she could causing her to topple from the rock. The last thing she saw was the look of pure horror on the Queen's face.

Elsie tumbled for what felt like an eternity. The wind rushed past her, pulling at her body and tangling her hair as she fell silently towards the earth. A thud. Darkness. Quiet. Still. A voice. The voice. "Didn't you do well?"

* * *

As promised, that was not the end of Elsie's story. She bravely defeated the faeries when she left the earthly planes that day, but Elsie didn't die. Instead her soul lives on, wandering the moors and the streets, protecting and caring for those she knew and loved in life. If you listen carefully to the wind as it rushes by your ears, you may hear her voice calling out to you either in greeting or warning. Take note of what she says!

As for the faeries, they grew disconsolate with their Queen who became more malicious and bitter with every passing day. Eventually the nine drifted away to find a more remote, peaceful home away from their vengeful leader. The Queen, however, remained. Still intent on ending the humans, she wanders the moors looking for unsuspecting victims. She'll pick them off one by one if she has to.

So, if you find yourself out on the moors alone, be aware of what's around you. For you could come across a bloodthirsty faerie Queen out for revenge or maybe even the soul of a girl who silently sacrificed herself to save the world.

Elsie illustration by Barb Tanke

Little Jane York Illustration by JoJo Hughes

LITTLE JANE YORK
by Robin A. Sparks
San Francisco, California, USA

Did you hear the story about the woman who was haunted by the ghost of Emily Brontë? Her name was Little Jane York and it all started late one October evening on a dark cold day with the wuthering winds determined to uproot everything in its path; jack-o-lanterns rolled down the unpaved streets like tumbleweeds. Little Jane York stood inside her cottage at the oval window near the front door and watched the small town blow by, then pulled her woolen shawl close over her shoulders and returned to her desk next to the fireplace.

Little Jane was often found at her small green desk, scrolling through Facebook looking for new posts on her favorite page, A Walk Around The Bronte Table. Oh, she loved the Brontë sisters' unique yet gloomy view of the small world in which they lived, and the endless discussions and observations found on A Walk Around The Bronte Table stoked her curiosity about them.

She directed her attention to their latest post: "Which Bronte wrote the best poetry?" The fireplace crackled. She glanced at the hearth on the lookout for stray sparks. Satisfied that none emerged, she returned her attention to her laptop and read the responding posts:

Ellen Rollins: Branwell, of course, the un-sung hero

Tony Jesse: No, Emily was the best poet in the family

Lucy Gaskell: Did Charlotte write poetry?

Peter Dunbar: What about the father? Didn't he publish a book of poems?

Little Jane composed her own post while the winds outside blew through the Aspen tree that grew in her front yard; its willowy branches bending and waving, making scratching sounds on the roof of her house.

"I vote for Emily" she posted.

Three dots undulated on the screen indicating a new comment about to post.

Emjay: *Why won't you open the door?*

Then, suddenly, the post disappeared.

Now the tree branches seemed to be clawing at the front door as if the tree wanted shelter from the weather. Little Jane rose and walked over to the window near the door. She wanted to see if the wind would finally take down the old fence separating her property from the vicar's next door. But the fence stood tall and fearless against the gales that scooped up the leaves in a cyclone before dispersing them.

The sky was obscured by thick black clouds and the rain descended with purpose. As Little Jane turned from the window, she caught sight of something crouched down by her front door, something furry. "My gosh, that's a dog! It must be lost and frightened." Slowly she opened the door, allowing the light from the fireplace to illuminate the cur: a large brown damp dog wearing a leather collar. "Well, this is some-body's dog, and he's probably lost." she decided as she widened the door to allow the dog entrance into her home.

The well-mannered dog slowly and quietly strode past Little Jane York and curled up on the worn throw-rug next to the fireplace. Little Jane stooped to caress the dog's head and noticed a tattered metal tag hanging from the collar, so old and decrepit it could hardly be read. By the light of the fire, it appeared that the dog's name was Kenny.

296

"Don't' worry, Kenny. I'll find your master". The tired wet cur went fast asleep, and Little Jane returned to her desk.

In her absence, Facebook posts populated her screen. The latest was from her friend from college, Daniel, a journalist living in Manhattan who posted a link to his recent interview with the Poetry Chair at Syracuse University. Little Jane read the posted reviews and accolades:

Mike Moraga: Dan the man! Great interview with Professor Karr!!

Laura Smyrl: Are you still with the New York Times?

Little Jane scrolled through the responses looking for posts by fellow peers from college until she saw:

Emjay: *watch for me tonight at midnight, in the moonlight under the bright shining stars*

Then, the post disappeared.

Little Jane looked up at the clock over her desk which read 11pm. I must be tired, she thought as she rubbed her eyes. I'm seeing things, she thought. Strange posts appearing and disappearing were tricks the weariness was playing on her. Little Jane shut-down her laptop, blew out candles, and prepared to ascend the steps to her bedroom. Kenny was still fast asleep by the fireplace, it didn't seem like he'd moved an inch. Little Jane stooped and stroked the top of his head with the back of her hand, "Don't worry, Kenny, we'll find your owner." Little Jane climbed the steps to her bedroom went to bed.

The rain beat down, the winds howled, and Little Jane tossed and turned in bed, trying to quiet her mind to find comfort in sleep. When she finally released her thoughts, sleep came, and with sleep came dreams. In her dreams came visions of dry stone walls that pointed to the dark sky, rolling green hills in patchwork design, Alder trees and heather; a feeling of freedom, a feeling of being alive and sharing that life with the grass under her feet, the wetness in the air, the eminence of the sky.

Little Jane rolled over in her sleep and drew her legs close to her chest; she was cold, especially her feet. She wanted to stay in her sweet dreams but her feet were ice-cold. Little Jane rolled over again and rubbed her numb feet against each other, her toes stiff and foreign. As she drifted back to visions of Haworth, she felt the sensation of her bedding creeping slowly over her lower legs. The motion brought her out of her reverie. She opened her eyes and lifted her head to scan the room. "Who's there?" Had Kenny come upstairs seeking human comfort? The room was still, the clock ticked away the seconds, she was alone in her room. Satisfied that nothing was amiss, she succumbed to somnolence.

But, Little Jane was not alone in her room.

Once again, she felt her bed quilt moving. The quilt she kept at the foot of her bed was slowly unfolding and spreading across the bed... inching towards her shoulders, wrapping around her shoulders as if... as if someone were tucking her in. Her eyes popped open but she remained still, observant.

"Am I dreaming? ...Am I awake?"

She heard a sound, she saw a shadow, a large shadow that slowly took the shape of a woman. It was a woman with a chignon wearing a long bell-shaped dress with puffy sleeves. The shadow was leaning over her, fussing over the quilt, and attending to her comfort. Little Jane did not know if she was asleep and dreaming, or if an actual ghost was in her room. But she was not frightened by the apparition in her room, or perhaps in her dream. Little Jane closed her eyes and relapsed back into a deep sleep, warm and cozy in her small bed.

The next morning, Little Jane awoke feeling completely refreshed and eager to greet the day and tackle her chores. She peeked out of her bedroom window and saw sunshine, the storm now a memory, the trees resting their branches on the stillness of the day. A monarch flitted over the blooms in her front yard, and two brown linnets perched on the shrub tops and chirped. The pumpkin sitting on the neighbor's porch smiled at her. Today, she decided, I'll pop into the shops and post flyers asking if anyone has lost a dog.

Downstairs at her desk, Little Jane York fired up her laptop. But, before creating the lost dog flyer, she irresistibly logged onto Facebook and navigated to the A Walk Around The Bronte Table page. There, she viewed a post from the previous evening that contained a collage of sketches drawn by the Brontës. As she clicked through the pencil sketches of Anne and Charlotte, she stopped on a drawing of a dog's head resting submissively on his paw, his one eye slightly open and stealing a glance at the grass just under his nose. Little Jane leaned in to the screen to read the words above the dog's head: "Keeper from life, April 24, 1838 – Emily Jane Brontë". Three dots undulated indicating a post, a comment on this sketch of Keeper:

Emjay: *Thank you for sheltering Keeper from the storm*

Emjay: *He'd gotten away after Tabby left the cellar door ajar*

Little Jane bolted back from the screen, her heart racing, knowing and not knowing at the same time. "What Keeper?" was the first flash. She turned her head to the rug by the fireplace; Kenny was gone! She scanned the room. Nothing was out of order, the front door closed with its deadbolt in place. The flashes came like paparazzi aiming cameras: *Pop!* The stray dog's tag read 'Kenny', or did it? Maybe it read 'Keeper'? *Pop!* The disappearing Facebook posts by 'Emjay'. Could Emjay be Emily Jane? *Pop!* The shadowy figure tucking her in during the night. *Pop!* Was there a shadowy figure, or was she dreaming? Did the entire previous evening with the wind and the storm and the stray dog even happen? Or was it all a strange dream?

I ask you, Dear Reader, did Little Jane York have a nightmare? Or, OR, was she haunted by the ghost of Emily Brontë and her dog?

You Know That I Could As Soon Forget You As My Existence!

The Plea illustration by Nathalia Amorim

THE PLEA

by M. J. Holmes
Hagerstown, Maryland, USA

If only you had lingered a moment longer.
Rap on the glass once more
break the damn window
bloody your knuckles.
Wrench my wrist and wrap your peat-cool fingers around my hand.

If only you had lingered a moment longer.
Catherine, Cathy. "Wild, wick slip" of a girl.
Earnshaw or Linton or Heathcliff?
I've called every name of yours: waif, witch, ghost, spirit of these
moors.
Haunt me like my own dark shadow.

If only you had lingered a moment longer.
Torment me. Drive me mad or drive me to hell.
Let me sink into a bog at night
dream-like.
Let the wind bend my body
like a tree whose branches reach for you.

If only you had lingered a moment longer.
I'd tell you Cathy grates on my tongue
gnashes my teeth.
Capricious spirit—I'll dash your name upon the rocks and rid the world
of it.
Linger, Catherine, please.

If only you had lingered a moment longer.
Leave your grave-scent on the windowsill
mud and moss
the moors have preserved you.
Never return to those bones and tenant
my soul instead.

If only you had lingered a moment longer.
You've left me mired here
with a forgery of yourself. If her laugh carries to
me—so much it reminds me of you!—I'll strangle your
voice from her throat.

Sotto voce, Catherine, for my ears only.

If only you had lingered a moment longer.
I'd make you stay
soul-same
bright-burning girl.
Come back to Wuthering Heights
once more.

An Encounter illustration by Barb Tanke

AN ENCOUNTER

By Sally Sneddon
Harrogate, North Yorkshire, UK

That day I was visiting the village of Birstall in West Yorkshire with my husband Richard. This visit was prompted by my interest in family history research. Birstall is only about an hour's drive by car from where we live and I was interested to visit the village and area as the place where some of my ancestors lived in the eighteenth and nineteenth centuries. It appears that they were weavers who eventually worked in the mills which sprung up all around the area. I was also interested to visit the grave of a historic local character, John Nelson, a Stonemason who became a Methodist preacher of some note and whom I suspected may be related to my Birstall ancestors.

The day was pleasant in summer and we walked around the churchyard. We found the grave of John Nelson easily and removed some of the ivy growing thickly over it.

Having spent some time at John Nelson's grave, I wandered further around the churchyard looking at the other graves. Soon I espied the Nussey's family grave and recognised this as the resting place of Ellen Nussey, the close friend of Charlotte Brontë. I knew this as I have an interest in the Brontë family and their novels. I knew that Birstall was said to have been used as a setting for the novel Shirley, written by Charlotte Brontë.

I mused about my ancestors and what life would have been like in Birstall at the time when the novel Shirley was written and whether my ancestors might have been involved in the Luddite riots featured in the novel. I noticed some wildflowers growing nearby and, on a whim, picked a small posy to lay by Ellen Nussey's name on the gravestone.

Having laid the posy, I was idly standing when I sensed a movement behind me. I quickly looked round and saw a small female person behind me, strangely dressed. I did not want to be rude so I didn't look too closely, but she appeared to be dressed eccentrically in old-fashioned clothing. I then decided I should be polite and say a quick "hello". She then spoke a question.

"Did you know her?"

I was taken aback by this and felt nervous. I replied, slowly ..."No but I know she was a friend of the author, Charlotte Brontë.

There was some delay, then she spoke again.

"I am Charlotte Brontë."

I was lost for words. She started to walk away, leaving me feeling confused.

I saw Richard walking towards me. "Charlotte" walked away over the grass, then faded and disappeared.

"Did you see her?" I asked.

"The lady you were speaking to?" He said.

"Yes" I replied. I wasn't sure how to explain .... "Can ghosts talk?"

Although I asked the question, in my heart I knew the answer.

A Kind of Haunting illustration by Julia Ogden

A KIND OF HAUNTING

by Michelle Wright
Cardiff, UK

Emily and Anne Diary Papers, November the 24 1834.
Anne and I say I wonder what we shall we be like and what we shall be
and where we shall be if all goes on well in the year 1874 - in which
year I shall be in my 57th year, Anne will be going in her 55th year,
Branwell will be in his 58th year and Charlotte in her 59th year hoping
we shall all be well at that time we close our paper

Anne, Diary Paper; Haworth, 31 July 1845
I wonder how we shall all be and where and how situated on the
thirtyeth of July 1848 when if we are all alive Emily will be just 30 I
shall be in my 29th year and Charlotte in her 33rd and Branwell in his
32nd and what changes shall we have seen and known and shall we be
much changed ourselves?

What shall we be? Where shall we be?
What changes shall we have seen and known?
Wondering the future, now past, shifting
Drifting between tenses and ages,
Writing yourself backwards and forwards
You have exited time,
Exploded its dimensions
Infinite versions of you, alive and dead.
Refracted mirror images, apparitions
Inscribed in shadow lives.

You will find me in the margins
You will find me between the lines
Charlotte, Emily, Anne distilled into ink
Channeled through quill to paper,
Letter by letter three souls enshrined,
Blotted manuscript; set in type.
The ghostly figure of the author
Forever present, paradox of time,
A disembodied voice, a breath in the text
Familiar, stranger, phantom guest.

We're the wrong side of the window
Let us in, let us in! We've come home

Spectres and stories the sisters saw come alive,
As they walked around the dining table
Where still their presence presides.
Jane Eyre, Heathcliff, Cathy, Agnes Grey,
The readers run to meet them,
Wandering the wild moors
Where still their energy rests,
Otherworldly, elemental, rest-less.

I am no bird; and no net ensnares me!
I shall be forever now, forever known
Possessed by imaginary landscapes
Inner worlds too big to hold,
Words flowed through their fingers
Cast from the pen like prophecy.
The hand is spun, exhaled
Runes of self become other,
Bound between pages, covers, spine
Boundless in time.

Behold, a kind of haunting,
Bewitching readers' minds:
Currer, Ellis, Acton – ghost writers,
Intermediaries, actors, ciphers.

A Source of Little Visible Pleasure Illustrations by JoJo Hughes

A SOURCE OF LITTLE VISIBLE PLEASURE

By JoJo Hughes
Cornwall, UK

I received the first chill pang that something was wrong as I walked up the drive. Hastening past the climbing roses that still gave off the sweet, sherbet perfume I remember inhaling deeply as a child, I noticed he wasn't in his usual bay window seat, looking out for my arrival from above a newspaper. My fingers fumbled with the keys as I tried to unlock the door. Inside the hall was dark and cool, silent as if holding its breath, so that I fancied I could still hear the delayed echoes of my hurried, crunching steps on the gravel behind me. As I wondered which room to try first, my heart gave a painful leap to hear my name called from behind the panelled door to my left. The voice sounded as relieved as I felt, and I burst into the room, delirious as a happy child to see my grandfather, so dignified and timeless in his high back chair. He lowered The Times noisily, his anxious face breaking into a broad, warm smile that made his tanned temples as crumpled as the paper now on his lap.

I kissed his thick, silver mane of hair and sat opposite, watching him pour the tea from the old teapot with the mismatched lid. Relaxing at last, I sank back into the old sun-bleached cushions, breathing in the familiar comforting scent of book leather, roses and gingerbread.

We lazily exchanged family gossip and parish matters and when we finished giggling helplessly at the memory of a recent play, so awful that it was good, my grandfather's face suddenly seemed to give way, his eyes cast themselves around the room as if searching for something and I wondered if all our happy chat had been an affectation, a delay in the build-up to this moment. Maybe my initial unease had not been so misplaced after all.

He raised his misty blue eyes from the steeple of slim, tanned fingers before him and held me fast with a gaze I had never seen before. At length he spoke, low and hurried, almost conspiratorial:

"You should understand that what I share with you now must remain here in this house. Swear to me that you'll not repeat what follows to another living soul. Your grandmother took the secret to her grave and I never told your father, (though I confess that was more due to fear of his scorn than of wider exposure).

"Ah. You're smiling. You are more like your grandmother than you know. She could always reassure me with a smile and calm the trembling that still plagues me after all these years. I entrust myself to your sympathy and discretion completely.

"I won't give you my personal testimony of what happened that summer. We have Arthur's diary; he'll be our narrator. The immediacy of his thoughts and his frank recount of the events as they happened will guard against melodrama. And I say we have it, because soon this diary and the item to which it refers will be your responsibility, though I might better say burden. There. My lecture is over. I will continue".

Ill at ease but curious, I kicked off my shoes and crossed my legs beneath me as I used to. The sun had crept past the cluttered mantelpiece and now inky shadows began to appear in the corners behind him. The silence was profound, save for his urgent voice and the chatter of a wren outside in the hedge.

"Arthur and I met during our second term at Cambridge. We had much in common. Both hailing from Cornwall, even the same part, as it goes - that secret southeast corner, cobwebbed with narrow, sunken

308

lanes, millstreams and standing stones. We'd both lost elder brothers during the War and had contributed to the general effort by helping our fathers plough the clifftop fields, whilst the naval ships jostled for space amongst the trawlers and screaming gulls down in the bay.

"We both studied English Literature and had a very real desire to leave our lush, hedge-bound idyll and to teach in a big city. As fellow Celts we had an innate love of story and back in those halcyon days we wanted to share the world of legend and literature with a generation of children sadly prosaic in their outlook after an early education in air raids, bombsites, rationing and loss.

"When not studying or rushing to attend the incessant seminars and lectures, Arthur and I would haunt antiquarian bookshops and house clearances around the city, spending our meagre allowances on tattered first editions, rejoicing in the smell of book dust and the faded pencilled margin-notes of students long since graduated.

"Arthur introduced me to his deep interest in the Brontë family, his passion so infectious that I soon became a devoted acolyte and accompanied him through much of East Anglia, either on bike or by train, on the trail of a particular edition of Clement Shorter or some new transcriptions of juvenilia. Furthermore, Arthur's maternal side was a notable Penwith family who claimed kinship with the Branwells of Penzance, from whose branches the Haworth children were descended.

"We stayed up into the early hours poring over any scraps we could find during our trips, arguing over whether Jane Eyre or Villette were the better novel, trying to pinpoint the origins of Branwell's decline and whether Anne was actually the strongest Brontë after all and most like her father. I became a true Reverend Brontë devotee. My respect for the man and awe at his journey from humble origins in Ireland, grew with everything I read about him. In short, for a time, I made him my idol, and - though I'm sure he would have baulked at being thus placed - he was a guiding light to me from his pulpit which rapidly turned into a pedestal.

"I was particularly impressed by his easy ability to communicate with all classes, his love of learning and his passion for reform in favour of the poor. It goes without adding that I also revelled in our shared Celtic blood; I felt I understood his deeply ingrained love of a good tale, inherited from his father, just as I had from mine.

"Although it wasn't my college, I would cycle over to St John's, wander about the quad and imagine him studying there as sizar, alongside such illustrious students as the future Lord Palmerston. I was even permitted to see the registrar's ink-smeared entry in the admissions' book, fancying I could hear Patrick's Irish brogue repeat his name behind my shoulder as I read the words: Patrick Branty.

"I set myself a goal to work hard, to strive, to achieve as he had achieved, though I had no religious calling. I would teach. I would make changes for good and inspire those under my tutelage".

My grandfather sighed wistfully. Then he shook off his reverie.

"Such was my dream during those terms at Cambridge, but the story does not progress beyond the last summer and ends in the final pages of this notebook.

"Take it. I shall leave you alone in here with Arthur and his words. You'll find me on the rose terrace with my crossword. I have no wish to relive what you are about to read, though each entry echoes, verbatim, in my heart.

During this final sentence, he was rising from his chair and, having taken his cane, he loomed above me, fixing me with a look of such concern and, I thought, something like guilt, that I was all for tossing the book to the corner of the sofa and joining him outside to help decipher 7 across. He recognised my hesitation at once and turned quickly away. Leaning heavily on his stick, he walked slowly but purposefully through the garden doors, to be bathed in the afternoon sun yet shining on the terrace. The study seemed to darken with his leaving and I went to sit in his bay window for better light.

In my hands lay a thin journal, of medium size. Its pages were well thumbed, giving the impression that the events and thoughts recorded inside had been revisited and reread out of chronological sequence. The leather binding was not of any great quality or age, but had a pleasing tooled pattern bordering a central embossed monogram which consisted of the initials ART.

Arthur Toms. I knew very little about Grandfather's friend, other than there had been "a bit of a do" as my grandmother had called it, after his Finals and that he'd suddenly ceased all contact with his erstwhile best friend. The reaction of my grandfather, who'd suffered the withdrawal of such a long friendship with a bewildered but calm resignation, suggested, said my grandmother, that he knew more than he wished to discuss.

There was a photograph of Arthur which my grandfather kept on his baby grand. I rose and, balancing the diary on the edge of the midnight glossed wood, sat down on the piano stool. As my eyes searched the dusty, shadowed frames for the picture, they passed over the music score my grandfather must have been playing recently, the lid being, unusually, still open. It was his beloved Allegretto, the second movement of Beethoven's Seventh Symphony. I smiled. Grandfather had no need to practise this. Its chords made the sweet, melancholy soundtrack to my childhood and just a few bars had the ability to transport me as an adult, back to this very stool, on Grandfather's knee, my fat childish fingers attempting, without success, to replicate the enchanting world rising from beneath the dark lid in front of us. With my grandfather's arms around me, I would instead place my hands on his as they crawled calmly down the key changes.

Now my fingers were as tapered as his and, though my piano playing years were not half so long, I shared his deep love of Beethoven, of painting dark and light with ivory and ebony keys and slowly yielding brass pedals. The fact that the black dots and lines on the white page in front of me meant nothing didn't hinder me in wrapping those chords around my heart. I had learned in this very study to replicate the sounds my grandfather played, or indeed any music I heard and loved. For many years I feigned a technical understanding of quaver and stave, until it finally came to my first formal music examination, where I was tested on my sight-reading skills and was unmasked as the guileless impostor I'd felt for years. Still, I achieved distinctions in all my performance pieces.

I now placed my fingers in their familiar position and heard the whispered tones begin to lift from the strings as the light fell outside.

Lost in visions, I had no recollection of how long I sat there or whether Grandfather had now returned indoors, until my trance was shattered by what I irrationally thought were pistol shots let off in rapid succession. Waking quickly, I saw the cause of the sounds was the almost simultaneous clattering to the wooden floor of two objects from the piano top.

The French doors to the terrace were closed and there was no draught. I could only ascribe the incident to Sleeping Ludwig, a childish story Grandfather told to explain the violent reverberations he made when in the throes of a particularly resonant piece of music, which sometimes made the photograph frames dance and shimmy along the lid, as they had just now done. This was caused, Grandfather used to whisper, by the composer himself who lived amongst the strings inside the piano, stirring himself to rage to hear his compositions so horribly mutilated.

One of the fallen items was an old photograph, silver frame now dented and glass cracked, of two young men in slacks and pullovers, sitting on a huge boulder fringed with heather, smoking pipes as they shared a small book held in my grandfather's hand. His downturned face was hidden from view, yet I knew by the way my grandfather's cheeks were arranged that he was grinning. The other figure was not so engrossed in their shared reading material, neither was he smiling. He seemed distracted, looking out ahead as if he'd heard or noticed something the moment the picture was taken. His heavy brow was knitted above dark eyes that searched the space behind the photographer. The handsome jaw was clenched around his pipe, making his full sensual mouth pout slightly and not unbecomingly. Where my flaxen-haired grandfather appeared to be bathed in moorland sun - judging from the glare off his Brylcream - his earnest companion was in shadow, an effect no doubt compounded by his mop of raven black hair which did not shine.

My grandfather always told the legend of Arthur's Mousehole forebears being the product of Spanish raids on the Cornish coast and his handsome Iberian lineage was plain to see in this photograph.

The other object on the floor was Arthur's journal, spread wide with several pages cast about. With a gasp of horror I bent to pick up the book and pages and found a very old yellowed letter, so aged and folded so that the creases were in danger of becoming cracks were it to be too much opened. On one of the foxed faces was a neat sloping hand of surely over a century ago, spelling out just two words:

"Être brûlé"

Turning on the lamp, I childishly pocketed the photograph and frame - mortified - promising to have it repaired the next day, and carried the diary and letter over to the chair by a fire long since expired. I turned on a lamp. Feeling like a crass interloper, and with silent shaking, fingers, I unfolded the letter, which cracked ominously, like old bones in tired joints.

Dearest Polly

> *Before you perform that small service I asked of you in my last letter (N.B. keep back NOT ONE and let none see what you are about; ensure the night is cool to avoid suspicion as to why you should need a blaze - mayhap you will have a chill?), I have one last bundle of kindling for you to read before the Grand Conflagration.*

It is done. Your entreaties came too late and the pages are gone. Consigned to the peat and lapwing nests. It was the last duty I could perform for her and now I am sadly free. In strange expiation for my traitorous act four years ago, when I discovered her unearthly verses and hungrily exposed that hidden heart to the dubious world of Light and Men, now her words remain, as they ever should have done, hidden from the day, planted in the richest soil in which no tree will grow, but where they will moulder and enrich, to become part of her moor.

And I swear to you, Pol, though I weep to write it, she has truly left me now. The burial of the pages was so necessary, (though I fancy I hear your voice across the miles in vehement disagreement). But though their interment has saved my beloved sister's memory from further censure by a dullard world, it has also taken from me that tall, slender phantom, whose flashing eyes and clenched fists were transgressions of all God's natural laws, yet which were a vestigial presence of a physical life so beloved. She is no longer by my side when I walk, behind my shoulder when I write or in the corner of the room when I slumber. I feel I have lost her again. And my gritstone heart could split with the grieving.

There. I am recovered. As her Heathcliff says, "I know that ghosts have walked the earth" and like him I have begged her to stay. But she is gone. She sleeps up beyond Withins in the peaty embrace of her eternal lover as words that will never be read by another living soul. I'm sure that in burying the box, she has forgiven me. I confess I had not the heart to consign them to those same flames I now demand of you. A compulsion beyond my reason made me wrap the precious bundle, like a babe, in waxed linen and enclose it in a modest tin box of Papa's. With Keeper and I the cortège and curlew the lych bell, our procession followed the lengthening shadows westward until we found the place. Just as she had said, there was the hollow beneath the stone in the centre of the circle. The western wind mourned and gave the eulogy as I covered the box with earth. The stones will be the guardians of her soul now. And that strange body of words will lie beneath the high altar until worms take it.

I know, dearest Pag, you will sigh and furrow that great forehead of yours and claim it was wrong and that I bury more

313

than a story. You are in the right. But you know a sister's devotion. And you remember Em. And you will understand.

So now, take a poker and stoke that fire you've built and lay me there amongst the flames. Do it without delay. For this must be FORGOT.

Write to me with ink made from the ashes and give me an account of your bunions.

CB

Two hours ago, this letter would have meant very little to me. And yet my recent conversation with Grandfather had allowed me to decode the references in the letter, as if I was suddenly able to read musical notation for the first time. With a pounding heart I believe I knew who Em was and who had signed the letter, although what was wrapped in waxen cloth "like a babe" and buried beneath a rock with such pagan ceremony, I couldn't imagine.

I realised the rest of the room was suddenly quite dark and very chill. My thoughts rushed before my legs could keep up with them, to the rose terrace, where I found Grandfather asleep, a tartan blanket over his knees, no doubt placed there by an ever-solicitous Maddie who was, at this moment, frying onions and minced lamb for Grandfather's Wednesday shepherd's pie. I noticed his crossword hadn't even been started. Instead he'd doodled a face on the margin of the page, the gaunt, handsome face of a young woman. A few tremulous but skilled lines of ink had rendered the anger in the expressive eyes, in the lines of the mouth and brow. It bore no resemblance to my grandmother but I thought no more about it, as I gently woke him and helped him inside. Fortified by a whisky and water, we silently made our way to the dining room.

Replete after a long meal, where no mention of Arthur or the diary was made, I now sat up in my old bed, wide awake, with the diary beside me on the candlewick bedspread. I traced my fingers over the initials and looked again at the swarthy, pensive figure in the photograph. I now fancied I perceived an entreaty in his expression. Or perhaps it was the claret. But I felt an intense urgency on me to read palpable around me. So I adjusted the bedside lamp for better reading and opened the first page, praying that I hadn't replaced the loose pages out of chronological order.

The first ten pages or so were a collection of scribbles, which on closer examination turned out to be excerpts from various sources:

314

quotes, transcriptions of private correspondence and publishers'
letters. One was transcribed in a pen pressed so hard that the paper
was nearly scratched through by the nib and ink was spattered around
the letters:

Dear Sir

*I am much obliged by your kind note & shall have great
pleasure in making arrangements for your next novel. I would
not hurry its completion, for I think you are quite right not to
let it go before the world until well satisfied with it, for much
depends on your new work. If it be an improvement on your
first you will have established yourself as a first rate novelist,
but if it falls short the Critics will be too apt to say that you
have expended your talent in your first novel. I shall therefore,
have pleasure in accepting it upon the understanding that its
completion be at your own time.*

Believe me

My dear Sir

Yrs sincerely

C Newby

There were copied diary papers, dates, journal titles and periodical
numbers. Arthur had written extra notes in the margins which seem to
cross-reference other resources. There were hastily penned questions
and to-do lists. I was astonished at the disorder and untidiness of it all -
I had always imagined research by a student of Oxbridge calibre to be
more methodical or at the very least legible. But here seemed to be the
urgent, hurried, compacted scrawl of a fevered mind. A mind
obsessed, with little time and, it seemed, paper. Every spare space was
filled in whichever orientation best fitted. I had to turn the book
around to read some entries.

Another double page showed an admirably rendered copy of a
section of a large scale map, drawn with a much more steady hand and
head than the rest; this was evidently of great importance to Arthur.
Every contour line, field boundary and feature was delineated with a
draughtsman's precision. The only element lacking was text. It was
obviously an Ordnance Survey from the early years of this century. To
the east, there were small enclosed fields rising either side of winding
water courses. There were no main centres of habitation but there
were houses or farmsteads scattered across the area on higher, dryer
ground. Moving west, the fields disappeared and gave way to treeless

315

moor, denoted by the familiar row of short strokes which still represent heath, moor and grassland today. The winding streams in the east narrowed as the eye followed them west, until they fanned out and stopped, reminding me of creases on an aged palm.

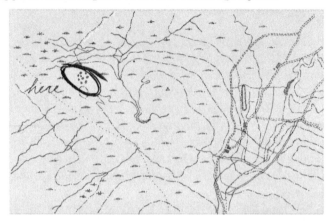

The contour lines, like tide marks on the sand, broadened and disappeared as they climbed the high ground. The very centre of the map was featureless, devoid of all symbols, apart from a cluster of ten or so tiny circles, near the very top of the hill. Here this small area of brow and boulder was ringed heavily by the fevered hand again, several times, in red ink, by which were the only words written on the whole map "*Here*".

I turned the page.

Wednesday 25th July

To Barker and Shackleton's Saleroom

It's mine. I got it. Beat them all. No-one knew. Dragged poor Tris along. He had other plans but when I explained what I'd noticed in one of the lots he became as obsessed as me. It's cleared me out but I'm ecstatic beyond words. We searched the other books in the box for any other such letters but none were found. Just this one. My hands shook to open it for a second time - now away from prying eyes and potential rivals. I've stuck it in the back pro tem but will get Tom to work his magic and do a bit of paper conservation at the lab.

Thursday 26th July

Tristan and I have amassed our collection of Brontëana together which we'll pore over tomorrow. Trip up to Yorkshire next week. Everything is in place. Beyond excited. Tris phoned the Lion. Twin booked for three days. Half board. Tickets bought. Reading matter for the journey packed. I suppose I should think about clothes. Father's going to sub me and says I can repay when I start the job at Devonport in September. So much prep to do although my class isn't so large. The head's a brick. Mixed feelings about going back southwest for good. So close to the Olds and yet so far. A river in between. Tris says there's talk of bridging the Tamar one day for automobiles. That really will be the end, says Gran, whose own grandfather regarded Brunel's bridge as a harbinger of doom. But no doomy talk now. This is my last summer with Tris, who starts up in Edinburgh in the autumn. I intend to enjoy my last quest. Quest! Ha! What portentous names we have! Can hardly put into words the thing we may be on the trail of but it could be big. Sally's for tea. Tristan eats too much.

Friday 27th July

Little sleep. Up at sparrowfart. Arthur restless too. Found me knee-deep in travel guides and OS Maps. Spilt my coffee over Ilkley Moor but don't think I need it. JH Turner quotes Lewis. A "Druidical" stone circle? Natural outcropping? Glacial action? Hm. We'll see.

Charlotte says they walked west. Following the setting sun...up beyond Withins. Without any shadow of a doubt I know she's talking about the Alcomden Stones (I prefer that name to Oakenden. Sounds like a Tube station). Dear God, is that where it is? Tris seemed irritable at lunch. He says we should just go hiking, try the beers, relax and soak up some sun after all our hours shut up swatting indoors. He's taking his paint box and I can't help but wonder where his fire has suddenly gone. Unless it's Elizabeth, but she's never tied him down or tried to divide us. She's a good girl. As far as girls go. Though not enough fire for me. I'll speak to her about Tris.

Saturday 28th July

Lizzie's worried too. Tristan won't talk to her about the trip and spends hours playing her father's piano. Always Beethoven. No jazz anymore. He never smiles now. Has got to me. Couldn't prep today. Feel strangely flat after another bloody awful dream. Seemed so real. Have moved the chest of drawers but the shadow's still there. Last night it was stood there again, glaring angrily. It stalked quickly out of the corner over to where I lay and bent its face down to me.

A woman. A girl. A handsome boy. God knows. But the eyes stared into mine as it leaned over the bed. If it'd had breath I'd have felt it on my cheek. Couldn't open my mouth. Think I fainted. Woke up hours later with a thick head. Christ, I'm cold. Almost August and I'm shivering. Hope I'm not ill.

Sunday 29th July 7

It didn't come last night. An evening out with Tris and several whiskies put paid to that. Perhaps it doesn't approve of drink. I probably exhaled enough spirit vapours to compete with the most tenacious night visitor. Head pounding now but no chills. Oddly, I've just discovered my suitcase all in disarray. I must have been rummaging for something in my stupor last night but nothing's missing. Tristan seemed much better too. I may buy him a hip flask.

Some pages were torn out here.

Thursday 3rd August

We're here. Room clean and snug. We can hear the bells of St Michael and all his Angels ring the hours as well as the rooks heckling each other through their interminable parliaments. Good journey but so long. Saw my shadow figure at Euston. It's definitely a she. Ever the gent, Tris held the door for her, only to realise there was no one there. I can't tell him. I couldn't describe the shadow in the seat in the corner of the carriage staring at us. The anger from those eyes that stayed on mine up to Leeds. She's got a simmering energy that made other passengers, seeing the spare seats, suddenly smile uneasily, slide the door closed again and hurry away in search of another compartment. At least she's got her uses. Tris put his feet up, staring through the summer storm and lapsed into one of his silences again. He hardly said a word on the train from Keighley. Still, he likes the hip flask. I heard him refilling it as I washed off the soot smuts in the bathroom before dinner.

Friday 4th August

Splendid breakfast. Am in love with black pudding. Tris in good spirits. Possibly literally. What troubles him? He surely revels in our imminent discovery.

We pushed our way through the visitors and souvenir hunters buzzing around the headstones, staring at the Parsonage, (emmets, Gran would call them) to get to the path beyond the kissing gate on the other side of the graveyard that climbs up to Sowdens. Saw old Grimshaw's barn as we climbed higher and higher up to Penistone. Am sat on a rock writing this looking across the heather towards Rombald's Moor. Ominous dark clouds. Are they coming this way? It's strange but I feel...tailed is the only word. Like someone's on our trail, just as we follow someone else's. A fellow walker saw my camera and offered to take a photo. Nice chap. He didn't see her stood behind him. I did.

More torn out pages.

Saturday 5th August

We have it. I have it. The storm, which suddenly rushed in from the north and soaked us to the bone as we dug, was glorious. The lightning made the wet boulders flash like photographers bulbs. I could smell the electricity and taste the earth. I laughed at the deafening rolls of thunder, just as my spade struck metal. What a consummation! Devoutly to be wished! Tristan's hands trembled like the very ground beneath us as he passed me my box. MY grail.

* * *

I've slept through breakfast and Tris has gone God knows where. But I have it. It's there on the table. Right now. I'm looking at it. So is she. Every so often she glances at me. In the shadows, I see the white in her eyes move. And I know it's a challenge. A dare. "Open it, then".

Tris knows I plan to open it. That's why he's disappeared. He's finally seen her, too. She strode out of her corner and leaned right over him last night. He got into an awful state. Tangled in his blanket, he fell on the floor and by the time I'd switched the light on, he was gulping from his flask like a baby with a bottle. Dear Tris. I'll make it up to you one day.

Well, my bonny cousin with the flashing eyes. I accept your challenge but I won't open it yet. I'm going to find my friend. You stay here and guard your precious babe.

* * *

We're back. Arthur's sleeping now. He doesn't remember anything and I'm relieved. The staff at the Parsonage Museum were awfully nice; I suspect they think he's a little touched. By the time I'd got up and out, it was a dark, gloomy mid-morning that threatened more rain so I sauntered up the wet cobbles on Church Street to see if Arthur had already gone into the Parsonage. I bought a ticket from a young lady who seemed not to notice me, but was craning her neck around to look into Patrick's study on the right. Although still early, a small crowd was crammed into the hall and doorway of the room, all eagerly looking, or rather listening to some kind of recital being given within.

Only, it all seemed a bit impromptu...most of the staff seemed to be at a loss as to what to do. They kept looking at each other and shrugging.

I pushed through the small mêlée to see who was giving the recital on Emily's cottage piano. Whoever it was, they were jolly good. I'd never heard Beethoven's Allegretto played with such quiet, grave authority; it was mesmerising. The slow heartbeat of the tempo never wavered. It slowly walked like a procession, shouldering the chords, carrying them like a precious burden, ever downwards. The volume attempted to rise and climb with the octaves and yet the effort seemed futile as, inexorably, the entire structure, quietened again and receded back to the lower keys. I stood entranced and felt the earth pulling me down. I stared at the grey flags and smelled peaty moorland soil. I tasted spicy mulch. And there, suddenly, I felt the first metallic stab of regret. Yes, even of shame.

I was shaken from this sobering reverie by the sudden giggle of a woman next to me: "I say, I do believe he's still in his pyjamas!" I pushed forward and nearly tripped on the scarlet rope which was supposed to prevent further access into the room. One person had stepped over this barrier, however. The intruder was now sat at the small piano, the tears streaming down ashen cheeks from glazed eyes that stared unblinking, unseeing, at the grey silk folds in front of his face. Beneath his tweed jacket, Arthur sat in his pyjamas, lost in worlds. Horrified, I stepped forward and slid a hand under the leather elbow patch of his jacket and, with a feeble attempt at jollity, said "That will do extremely well, old boy. You have delighted us long enough. Let the other young ladies have time to exhibit".

Accompanied by the silent curator, I guided him past the stunned faces of visitors down the hall to the front steps. After apologising profusely to her and offering to pay for any damages incurred, I breezily commented "You have to admit, though, he was pretty good on the old ivories". She smiled and said sympathetically "Your poor friend was clearly lost in a very moving piece of music. Alas, he was the only one to hear it. One day we hope to restore Emily's piano, and then, perhaps we may invite him back to allow us to enjoy what he evidently heard so clearly in his head".

Reeling, the pair of us somehow staggered back to The Lion, looking for all the world like a couple of student reprobates. As I half expected, the room was in complete disarray, the journal in which I now write was splayed open on the floor, clothes, tobacco, shaving equipment and bedlinen thrown about with what must have been some force. Only the rusting, earth-crusted box stood untouched, just where I had left it on the table. I took off Tristan's jacket, lay him in his

320

tangled bedsheets, gave him a swig from his flask, whereupon he closed his red, swollen eyes and slept.

Sitting down on my bed, I picked up my journal and sorted the pages. I took a swig and wrote the above, Tristan's exquisite, non-existent chords still descending through my head. Only once did I look up. This time, I could tell by the eyes in the shadow by the dresser that she was smiling in triumphant scorn. Ashamed, I couldn't hold her gaze, but looked back down to write.

* * *

It is mid-afternoon. I must have fallen asleep. The storm woke me. In my dream the rain spattering on the window which overlooks the top of Main Street, sounded like fingernails tapping on the glass. I sat bolt up to see, for a sleep-addled second, a pair of eyes beyond the small panes, looking in at me, but when I rubbed my own, I saw only my shocked reflection. The flask beside me is empty. And so is Arthur's bed.

All three have gone. My friend. My box. My shadow. I am all alone. And it is a terrible thing. I can see a note, lying on the low table where Arthur's bag stood".

I then found a final note, pasted into the journal, and recognised my grandfather's writing at once.

> *My dear friend*
>
> *I hope you'll forgive me. By the time you read this, I shall have caught the next Keighley train. I have taken the box. I hope you'll be able to understand. I hope that reading back through these pages you'll see how this obsession changed you. This is not who you are. This was not a quest. She was not your grail. We are contemptible resurrectionists, hungry to examine and probe, to exhume and expose that which should be left to sleep. Not King Arthur and his loyal knight. Merely grave-robbers...Burke and Hare....*
>
> *She will follow me up to Edinburgh, I've no doubt and I cannot blame her. It is hers and we did a despicable thing. When you have gone, when we are both recovered and working, marking English essays and arithmetic, buried in house scores and team lists, I will return and lay her to rest once more, somewhere you'll never find her. Don't ask for it.*

It will consume you once and for all. And do not ask me to open it. I swear on my life to you and to her that I never shall.

T.

Oddly, after all the packed pages, the rest were blank, save for what looked like doodles, mostly of faces in profile. One sketch however, was of a face looking directly out at me from the thick, cream paper. I had seen that face once before today. The beautiful eyes were staring out intently into mine, the fine brows slightly gathered in question. Her strong O'Prunty nose led down to an intelligent, expressive mouth, the closed lips curled sardonically at the corners, the chin raised in challenge and defiance. She was beautiful..

I closed the book and smiled at the shadow I'd been aware of in the opposite corner, watching me read. Waiting. She knew the promise I made right in that moment. The promise to catch the next day's train from Edinburgh to Leeds, to take another to Bradford, thence on to Keighley and Haworth. I would carry few clothes up the steep, cobbled hill, as well as a map, a spade and a small rusting tin box. I would follow the lengthening shadows westward across the coconut-scented gorse and purpling heather, up behind Withins Height and I would find the stones.

I smiled again at the shadow, unafraid. A faint light seemed to glow for a moment in the dark corner, and I saw she nodded slowly and smiled back.

I Wish I Were A Girl Again, Half-Savage And Hardy, And Free

The Ghosts of Those We Knew illustration by Luna

THE GHOSTS OF THOSE WE KNEW

By Luna
Lithuania

It was beginning to grow dark. The man sitting in a chair lit a candle and resumed his seat. The firelight was burning in his room and fire gave a cozy light, not sufficient to illuminate the object clearly, but mainly to transfer an idea of things. The moon rose, a bright, crescent moon, leading the way in darkness and making the garden and the streets seem too far away, like in another place and time. The clock ticked slowly- tick, tock, tick tock. Everything appeared fanciful, like the manuscript he was reading. So strange- thoughts of the minute, a passing of a soul, preserved carefully by an ink, a pen, a symbol.

He was glad to have a minute to himself. To examine himself (though some may say that was one characteristic he lacked) and know himself as he really was. The night gave ample time for this anyway.

He was not at all startled to see a familiar figure in his room. He just smiled sadly and with a little bit of tenderness and said

-So, it's you.

The vision, ghost, spectral illusion, call it whatever you may, smiled elusively and turned around the room.

-Well, you weren't the most believing in such things while I was here, were you. Am I a figment of your imagination?

-It's hard not to believe, now, when... I have lived more and gained more and lost more... Anyway- he shook his head- life must go on and it's always better to think what is to be done now, then to fret about what was or could have been, or that sort of thing.

-Are you still angry with me or are we to be friends?

-We always were good friends, though, I must admit there was a moment I was angry with you, but I was happy to have you for a friend and I'm sorry that we didn't part as such – he reached out his hand to her. The sprite shook it in good terms.

- I was afraid you were a little angry with me, but you see, I could not do it another way then. - she looked at him through the rims of her spectacles- I saw how your life was to turn out long before you yourself. As you may have noticed I used a lot of dream material in my writings. Though I must say I was saddened by how quickly you fulfilled it- her gaze was now quite strict.

- And of course, this never concerned me in the least! – he shouted in amazement -You just decided that with your spirit friends, probably your greatest friend the nun. Was she so angry with me that I held her a figment of your imagination?

The dusk has now turned to pitch black night- During these last February days it wasn't as dark as mid-winter, but the nights were long and dense.

-I don't think it is possible to choose a different course than you are capable of choosing. And yet, there is that wonderful thing called change and movement. The whole universe sometimes reminds me of an eternal dance of leaves rustling in the wind, upheld by one ever-lasting pillar of love, the only universal rock and pillar to hold onto.

However, you seemed little grieved for how things turned out- you seemed very merry and mischievous over the whole situation.

-I was the most miserable wretch! Still, I'll admit it's not above me to have a little laugh at the expense of some...very particular people. And I spoke with them in earnest; it wasn't my fault that they are so bent on misunderstanding me! – humorous, kindling fires now played in his eyes.

-That's the problem, you always seemed joking when you were earnest and earnest when you were joking.

-You yourself would have had a good laugh with me, were you here. Also, you did surpass me with your jokes, on one occasion especially and indeed, you had a good laugh at my expense then, admit it. – he was now beginning to grow sullen, and kept playing with a pen in his hand.

- That's why I came. You have already lived how you had to. You'll soon go where you'll have to separate from what you're used to. From beauty of the matter, to the beauty of the inconceivable. Even, though, I admit- your pink bonnet with a drooping ostrich feather suits you so fine-

He grew red and started tapping his leg in annoyance.

-Don't fret - you know that in this earth pink bonnets are not to be despised. You'd have grown tired of old shabby grey in about two months, and exchanged it for pink I'm sure. I'm glad to have given you the chance.

But now the time is coming when you will leave those old clutches and shadows, the part of you that held them a necessity. The transformation is coming and your other longings will guide you, for now it's the time for them to be fulfilled.

His gaze was cast down and he was deep in thought. Finally, he asked: -Will it be painful?

-Like a wished-for sleep after a long day of work.

-When?

- The funeral day was yesterday, the death will be tomorrow, And what was buried when came such day, death will revive by morrow.

- Will you guide me through it? Since most of my life you aided me in crucial matters, could you gratify me this last time? Give me your hand, for it was a generous one, for me, always.

The vision nodded. The bell rang announcing dinner was served. The figure began to vanish with a small smile, when he said with a small tear running down his cheeks

-You know that no surprises can deter me from a good dinner.

The Loving Heart Illustration by Debs Green-Jones

THE LOVING HEART

By Debs Green-Jones
Wales, UK

She tries to sleep,
instead she weeps.

She lies in wait
for him to come

Her heart is torn
her soul is numb.

She waits in vain
he cannot claim
her now, or blame her.

She tries to sleep
but sleep won't come.

Death's torn apart
her loving heart

And waits with him
who cannot come
whose heart is torn
whose soul is numb

Who waits for her
who tries to sleep
to come to him
and not to weep.

The Legacy illustration by JoJo Hughes

THE LEGACY

By Nathalia Amorim
Brazil

Deep in the wild moors
Not only the heather grew,
Three sisters: bold, shy and obscure
Carried a whole different view.

Since childhood creativity was their partner
Along with loneliness and sorrow,
And through difficult times,
They began to write a new tomorrow.

Three sisters, which indeed took courage
To deal with their pain,
And as we write this homage,
Their legacies will remain.

Two hundred years after their existence
Readers still crave for their words
Through their books, living spirits,
As free, cageless birds

And today, in the fields their spirits wander
Flying along with the birds
And still, after so many years,
Their voices can be heard.

The Last Ghost illustration by EmilyInGondal

THE LAST GHOST
By EmilyInGondal
England

The mist shimmered with promise, half solidified into a slender shape then, with a soft exhale, evaporated. Sighing, Charlotte turned away from the bare, square paned window, uncomfortable on the narrow bed, wondering how Emily could have slept with the sash window ajar. The wind did not seem like a friend while it nipped and snapped at her face and feet.

'Nor does it speak of freedom when laughing at me and snatching at my hair,' she grumbled.

Every night the mist came, promising shape and substance, each time disappointing, drifting away, leaving her alone.

'Where are you? Where *are* you?' Charlotte called into the freezing night air. The room remained empty, the moonlight had lost all value, midnight offered no poetry, stars offered no solace, flinging herself onto her back she stared at the white ceiling, stoically waiting for daybreak, ignoring the rustling and murmuring sounds of children at play, for she knew they were in her mind only.

* * *

Charlotte sat on a boulder on the heath, she did not seem to be able to roam far from the house, its grey roof echoed the grey sky, the sheep were silent, the clouds drearily rainless, the wind absent, saving itself for midnight.

'I am neither tired nor hungry,' she thought wonderingly. Tiredness had been her constant companion for the last seven years, dragging at her heels and leeching the colours from her days. There had been cliffs at Scarborough and the blustery heights of Ponden Kirk, temptresses offering to end her pain, but each time she had trudged away half mad with grief, singing childhood songs, a half burnt comb and garnet-red seastones in her pocket.

'The heath looks like our dining room on a cold day,' she thought. Crags, hills and heather nestling alongside the furniture, books and floorboards. 'Why does the world suddenly seem so fluid?' she thought. Time was not behaving as it should. There was no set length to either night or day. She was finding herself in places she had not walked to and in noon or midnight without the hours in-between having passed. 'It is too much,' she thought, 'too much to carry in my heart.'

* * *

Charlotte woke in the narrow bed, stark with the stiff white cotton sheets that Emily had painfully hemmed while dying, refusing to let go of the routine of sewing each evening until seven o'clock when they would put down their needles and pick up their quills. Wincing against the imagined cold, Charlotte dressed hurriedly, the pale dawn light keeping her secret of not washing. Smoothing down her hair she stepped onto the landing of the strangely quiet house.

The Parsonage had never been quiet. The Grandfather clock had filled all the cracks between clinking dishes, doors opening and closing, meows, barks, feathers rustling, the iron clang of the oven door, fires being stoked, the thump of bread being kneaded, light footsteps up and down the stairs followed by claws clicking on stone of eager dog paws.

'I thought at least Tabby would be here to greet me.' Charlotte whispered to herself gliding down the graceful stone stairs, past the stopped Grandfather clock. Not once in her life had she known that sonorous tick to be silent, her father had wound it faithfully every night on his way up to bed. Reaching the bottom, standing hesitantly in the wide stone flagged hallway she debated turning left into her father's study or right into the dining room.

'If anywhere they must be in there.' Charlotte said out loud. The words did not unsettle the air, dust motes hovered undisturbed, nobody answered or listened. Opening the dining room door, quickly, fearfully, she stepped inside, shut the door and leant back against it, hands behind her, still clutching the door knob.

The room was cold. The fire grate swept clean, the books on the shelves in the recesses either side of the fireplace seemed huddled and shrunken, the familiar mahogany table, its leaves always outstretched occupying almost all the space, was empty. There were no books, papers, ink wells, quills or desk-boxes, not even a candle. Charlotte had never seen it like this, their writing and drawing things had only ever been removed for meal times and then the table had been swiftly filled with cutlery and crockery. She shut her eyes against the memory of Emily's white christening mug and the way coffee could be seen through its thin white china, like Emily's throat at the end - thin, white, and transparent. She dragged her thoughts to the dainty pink and green

Faith, Hope and Charity tea-cups the rest of the family would drink from, Anne always choosing Hope.

The church bells chimed two o'clock. A breeze began, touching Charlotte's cheek, teasing her to open her eyes. As she did the pretty patterned wallpaper she had so recently hung began to dissolve until the stained plaster underneath showed through. The walls then started to shimmer, twisted tree branches took their place, the air became alive with ravens croaking, sheep bleating, cats yowling, geese honking, hawks shrieking, dogs barking, a lapwing's 'peewit!', a skylark's panicked jumbled song as it climbed to the sky and an owl's surprised hoot at being woken so early.

The trees were winter black and bare, they rattled their fingers against the ceiling as if a storm was coming. The wooden floorboards flickered and summer-time heather alive with the buzz of bees slowly carpeted the spotless floor, which, gazing up at the trees, encouraged the lime-green leaves of Spring to leap out, softening the rattle into soft sighs.

As if wanting to join in the jubilee of seasons, the silky plaster of the ceiling began to snow. Charlotte's normally dim eyes were able to detect the unique pattern of each snowflake, touching the bridge of her nose she wondered where her little round spectacles had gone and why she could see without them. The seasons played with each other framed by the shadowy dining room, as if when weathers and landscapes had been poured out in ink they had become part of the room for eternity.

The soft seasons started to turn, feathery snowflakes became stinging ice spikes, hail threw itself at Charlotte, the horizons hardened as unfriendly winds howled over them, clouds amassed in dirty yellows and blues like bruises, so heavy they forced her to her knees under their weight, yet she kept her eyes unwaveringly fixed on the horizon, willing a familiar figure to come striding over it.

Lightning struck the dining table splitting it in two, running along the floorboards and blackening the toes of her tiny dove-grey boots. Night fell, a full moon rose steadily, its silver surface bubbling and writhing under a pale, round face hovering in and out of sight within the moon-shape, its gaze was pitiless, a prim rosebud mouth unsmiling, but its presence was so longed for, Charlotte reached achingly forward, rising to her feet then running, running, running through the table, through fireplace and brick chimney behind it. Through moss-stained, leaf-wet graves, through dry-stone walls and onto the heath behind the house where the lightning struck the ground again and again as if warning her to stay away, scorching the dusty stone-strewn paths, coming closer and closer, yet never quite reaching her, as if angry but unable to actually hurt her.

Unafraid, looking past the lightning up to the wrathful moon she watched its pale blue eyes blink at her like eclipsed planets.

'Emily! Oh, oh, Emily!' Charlotte cried. The flames that had begun welling at the ends of the lightning forks became big, soft, round raindrops, which pattered down on the bonnet Charlotte suddenly wore like tears.

* * *

Charlotte woke on the narrow bed beside the square paned sash window. Sighing, she tried to remember what the wind had been telling her, its voice had wrapped around her ears while she slept, making her dreams hard to remember and her memories useless.

'What did I want most in the world?' she asked herself, shaking her clouded head, wispy hair still kinked from the harsh bun she wore in the daylight hours. 'I wanted to die,' she whispered back to herself, clapping her hands over her mouth to stifle the shocking sentiment.

'No, no, not to die, but just to see them, my sisters, once again.' She placed her hands over her heart as if it hurt beyond bearing. 'Was it wrong? To crawl up to Ponden Kirk, high up on the moor, on trembling legs, to tuck myself into the fairy cave, the little hollow at its base and imagine myself curled there forever, until my spirit was freed and my little white bones were left behind for shepherds to wonder over.

'Why was I, the smallest, the least significant sibling, left to carry on alone? Surely gifted Maria, wonderful Elizabeth, vivacious Branwell, ferocious Emily or faithful Anne were more worthy of life?' Charlotte lay back down on the narrow bed exhausted by her own thoughts.

She sat up suddenly.

'Gondal! Yes! They must be in Gondal...But how do I get there?' Emily and Anne must be in their imaginary land. It must be somewhere in the horizons and the house, for Emily would have made a home for her mind in such materials as were to be found at hand.

'In the dining room, she must be there for that is where the strongest living went on.' And down the stairs she ran, unaware that she had done this every morning for a year.

Charlotte stood at the bottom, paralysed, both afraid that she would and she wouldn't see them. She crept forward softly, even though her feet made no sound, holding her breath even though her fear and anticipation could not be heard. Papers rustling to her left, behind her Father's study door distracted her for a moment but she decided to ignore the sound for surely he was sitting in there alone, facing the window that overlooked the garden where once his six children had played, his back to the piano his daughters would play for him; Handel and Bach on light summer evenings, merry voices on the warm air, pleasure in each other's company. No. She could not look at his dear lined face emerging from its snowy white cravat, sure more lines would have emerged now he was alone, having outlived his wife, sister-in-law, the faithful, taciturn servant Tabby and his six beloved children. No, that was a solitude she could not bear. For if she saw him she would never leave his side, would never find Anne or Emily, would never find out why she was the last and only ghost.

Opening the dining room door a playful Spring wind rushed at her like a welcoming puppy. The trees and walls and skies were still there, hovering over a gentle afternoon. Jane Eyre sat on the wide, white windowsill, reading. Helen Graham walked pensively around the dining table, her elegant bonnet hiding her face, clutching her silk shawl tightly with long pale fingers. Catherine Earnshaw stood on the mahogany table pulling feathers from a pillow, throwing handfuls in the air.

Delighted, Charlotte stepped inside hoping these characters would step aside and reveal their creators. The 'snick' of the door closing behind her startled them, like little garden birds they vanished leaving only a lapwing feather hanging on the air and a discarded book on the windowsill.

The wind turned cold, hooting mournfully, whipping her skirts behind her and dismantling her hair. The ceiling sky lowered with threatening slate-grey clouds that began to spit stinging ice-chips at her. Momentarily blinded she grasped the door-knob behind her. Blood-curdling, the hissing and howling turned into a lunatic song, for along with the violent wind sang Bertha Mason crouched in the corner behind the tattered black sofa, in a filthy nightdress with hooded, malevolent eyes.

A boot heel tapping alerted Charlotte to Arthur Huntingdon sitting beside Jane's book, the window lighting into ruby rays the glass of red wine he held, a sardonic sneer twisting his features as he looked her up and down, clearly finding her wanting. A creaking floorboard betrayed

Heathcliff's presence, his hands to either side of the window case as he leant deeply into it, his nose almost on the glass, oblivious to the scene behind him, scanning, scouring with his black eyes the moorland beyond the garden. Moorland that had now entirely surrounded the house, all that remained of the village and church were a few ancient table graves with worn carvings, and beyond them only heather, bilberries, scrub grass and endless lines of distance as if the Parsonage floated in nowhere.

The mad, coarse and brutal three rose and turned, glowering with sharp teeth and claw-like hands, advancing on her as death had advanced on Branwell, Emily and Anne, with no time to absorb or heal; she had watched helplessly and guiltily as they had faded away, broken and lost like the little wooden soldiers they had once lived through so vividly.

Charlotte shut her eyes, still stood with her back against the closed door, glad that she should be brought to account for surviving and continuing to write when they could not. Refusing Zamorna, her old imaginary hero, who tugged at her mind, demanding she allow him to come charging in on his steed and whisk her away in a romantic rescue. Perhaps if she let these fiends take her she would be able to join her siblings to live on with them in an eternal sunny web, having earned heaven with sorrow, grief and loneliness.

Thunder rolled in across the velvety curves of the ominous fur-grey clouds, lightning bolts hurled themselves down in frenzied spite, scattering the chairs and books, exposing the characters transparency and ephemeral ineffectiveness to hurt her as they broke into evaporating mist leaving her alone with the elements.

The dining room broke into fragments, the balance of inside and out veered wildly towards outside, like an avalanche of peat-bog mud and iron-brown water, leaving her unprotected on the very tops of the moor, beside the old deserted farmhouse at Top Withens. She curled into a ball on the tattered grass, under the stinging rain and the lightning shattering in hot white sparks around her tiny, foetal form, crying wretchedly, more from loneliness than fear.

'Emily! Emily! Emily! Emily!' she called out as persistently as she had called for angels in her childhood, 'Michael! Gabriel! Uriel! Raphael!' in the terrible months after they had lost the first two sisters, Maria and Elizabeth, reasoning an angel for each remaining child, herself, Branwell, Emily and baby Anne would stop this dreadful march of mortality.

The angel names comforted her. As her desperation calmed the lightning stopped, the rain lessened and the sun peeped out behind the clearing clouds, a breath-held silence covering the whole like a feather-down quilt. A bumblebee, striped and fuzzy, circled her head on its silly, impossible wings, its buzzing brought back the moor-sounds. A sheep's bleat, a thrush song, a pheasant's rusty cry, a crow's 'caw' from the farmhouse roof. The brightened skies highlighted a small, feathered form circling the blue with a melancholy cry, wheeling and diving with a wayward freedom, so fast she could barely keep her eyes on it.

'A merlin! A merlin! Nero, Emily's bird!' Charlotte gasped. She stood up, head thrown back, hair streaming down her spine, drenched dress steaming in the hot sun. The bird of prey on its angular wings circled lower and lower until she could see the slate-blue back, striped tail feathers, the speckled red-brown breast, white throat and surprising yellow talons. Its big eyes fixed on her. With a shrill cry it darted down in a death dive, clipped her head, ascended, descended, ascended then descended into a clump of tall, coarse grass, a hunting method designed to scare small birds into the sky to their doom.

The grass remained divided with the hole punched into it, the small circle wavered and grew and where the bird had been, finally flickering into existence, a slender girl in a lank slate-blue dress with a long white throat, yellow boots and fierce, dark, kindling eyes rose tall above the grass and looked down on Charlotte who sank to her knees.

'Emily!' Charlotte shouted angry with relief, 'Oh where have you been?'

Emily turned fierce falcon eyes on her sister. 'I have struggled to reach you.' She said stepping out of the grass clutching at her legs. She walked over to Charlotte and knelt beside her, putting a long white finger on Charlotte's cheek. 'How long has it been?'

'Six years, three months and twelve days, I think, time has been moving so strangely, that is the last count I made. Why did you never come to visit me?'

'Because you betrayed me Talli.'

'Never, my bonnie love, never!'

'You did not listen to me and I have paid dearly for it.'

'How? How?'

'I was very clear how I needed to be buried, I wrote quite clearly in Wuthering Heights; 'The place of Catherine's interment, to the surprise of the villagers, was neither in the chapel, under the carved monument of the Lintons, nor yet by the tombs of her own relations outside. It was dug on a green slope in a corner of the kirkyard, where the wall is so low that heath and bilberry plants have climbed over it from the moor; and peat mould almost buries it'

'But you are not Catherine!'

'I am everything and everyone in that book, it could not exist unless I had poured every atom of my being into it.'

'But it was fiction.'

'When have you known my fictions and my realities to be divided? You buried me inside a church, in a vault, under stone flags. My soul was pinned down, unable to visit you or roam unfettered, unable to disintegrate, ride the wind and disappear into delighted fragments, as I should have. I have only been ripped free now in the tornado of your despair.'

Charlotte hung her head, remembering her own imaginary land of Angria, how it had invaded the school room where once she had been teaching, becoming more real than the children who sat before her.

'I meant you no harm. I wanted you to be safe with our mother, aunt and sisters. Where are they now? Are they with you?' She peeped eagerly around Emily as if a family picnic might have sprung up behind her.

'No. Mother and Aunt returned to Cornwall, their childhood home. Mother will only return to fetch father when he dies, they will probably go to Ireland together, where faeries, sprites and ghosts are accepted among the living, no exorcisms or sage burnings there. Maria and Elizabeth were too young to be alone, so are cared for in heaven, it is the purest of places and they belong there, no doubt they will be reborn when they are ready. Branwell was so traumatised and exhausted he did not have the energy to return and rests in peace. Anne, Anne is still in Scarborough where you left her, she walks beside the sea and can be seen whenever the sunrise or sunset have violet and blue tints.

'Have you seen her?'

'No, I told you, I have been trapped, my wrath leaking from my coffin, cursing you, unable to wander the hills or dance in the heather,

338

sour with resentment ensuring you would be the last ghost, alone for eternity.'

'The last ghost? Emily what have you done?' Charlotte whispered, remembering Emily's hot temper in life. Emily's looked beyond Charlotte, her face pinched with regret that her words did not express.

'Where is Keeper?'

'I thought he would be with you by now, he died on the anniversary of your death three years later.'

'Where did you bury him?'

'Should I keep that to myself until you free me?'

Emily turned a look of vexation, which softened into love at Charlotte's familiar, penny-round face.

'We always did try to contain each other didn't we?' Emily said softly.

'What now?'

'I don't know, you were always the one who solved the problems, forced us forward.'

'Even when you were running in the opposite direction!' Charlotte laughed.

'Nothing could have saved me, Nothing could have prevented my death. I refused a doctor because I knew that. You were trying to hold water in your fingers, impossible and fruitless, I wanted you to be able to let go.'

'I never did though, I never did.' Charlotte's heartsick face tugged at Emily's heart, making her ashamed of her vengeful ways. She wrapped her long body around her tiny sister. The bilberry plants, knolls of heather and branches of fern stirred. Dusk rendered the forlorn ghosts, curled up together on the moortop, almost invisible, like little piles of soft grey velvet, only the stardrops of their tears twinkling on the earth.

* * *

'Charlotte...Charlotte...Charlotte...' Emily's voice spoke from a great distance, its very quietness pulling Charlotte into wakefulness. Sitting up on the warming dawn earth she had a sense of peace as if she were made of feathery air and sunrays, calm and balmy. Emily stood on a nearby hill looking down on Charlotte. A huge tawny dog with a black muzzle and grim expression stood close by her side, leaning into her skirts.

'Keeper! You found him!' Charlotte called out, standing up. "Come down, let me hold him.'

'I can't. Everything is flying apart. You have released me from the vault as I had wished but I was surely dust in my coffin, only my fury and your love holding me together, now as dust I am streaming apart on the wind.'

'No! Emily, don't leave me here alone in this comfortless nether-world, undo my isolation!'

'I cannot, I am powerless in death as I was in life. I am so sorry Talli...'

Emily and Keeper were becoming transparent, the moors behind them pushing through.

'But there is no-one here for me. What shall I do?'

'Wait...Can you wait for Ellen? Your oldest and best friend, she loves you like a sister and would likely search for you on her death.'

'Nell, my dearest Nell, yes. But for how long?'

Emily's face became transfixed as if she were searching for an answer.

'Nearly forty three years Talli.'

'Forty three years...Alone?'

'Yes...' The 'yes' was uttered so softly, little more than a murmur on the breeze, from the idea of a shape rather than Emily's complete likeness.

'I will be all elements, all plants, all clouds, all horizons, all weathers; everything that touches you will be me. You will only want for faces and conversations, everything else that exists around you will be me. You will be alone in name only.'

'I don't think I can do it, Emily. Purple heather symbolizes solitude and it is everywhere here.' Charlotte sank to her knees, face in her hands.

With a gradual sizzle all around her, the colour in the purple heather grew fainter and fainter until a glowing snowy white carpet crept up to Charlotte and cradled her like divine sprigs of angel feathers.

'White heather...for protection, good luck and wishes coming true...white heather for you...' Emily's voice was just a suggestion in Charlotte's mind now, unable to look up and see the void where Emily had once stood, Charlotte kept her face hidden.

'I can give you one more thing Talli, just one...'

'What? What could you possibly give me that would ease this pain?' Charlotte sobbed through her fingers.

'Sleep...Talli...Sleep...You will sleep dreamlessly and contentedly, here on this little moortop heath under the heather. No-one mortal will know you are here. And one day, when she is ready, Nell will walk up the hill, over that brow where in happy summers we all walked together during her visits, Branwell chattering, instructing us all in much embellished folklore. Anne and I, arms around each other's waists, lagging behind, whispering poetry to each other. And you arm in arm with Nell, who loved and admired you so, looking into your face with astonishment as you would tease and teach her all the unladylike things she did not know. Dear loyal, fussy, funny Nell, sixth sister, who will bring you home to us all...'

As Emily and her faithful dog vanished back into the gloaming, becoming all shadows and sprites in the corner of an eye forever on that desolate moor, Charlotte curled up in the white heather which had been springy and unforgiving in her lifetime yet now was as soft and welcoming as the family she missed so ferociously. And on her tiny curled up form soft snowflakes fell thickly and silently until she was entirely covered up and sleeping, a small smile on her smooth, flushed little face.

The Intense Horror Of My Nighmare Came Over Me

341

HAWORTH PARSONAGE

Local Legend and Folklore illustration by Jon Beynon

LOCAL LEGEND AND FOLKLORE

The Moon Will Never Shine On Their Revels More
illustation by JoJo Hughes

THE MOON WILL NEVER SHINE
ON THEIR REVELS MORE

By JoJo Hughes
Cornwall, UK

"We are the fairish
Have a careish
Don't go nearish
Please bewareish
Never stareish
Or we will perish!"

In every shire
We looked the same,
Though you'd give us a different name
We danced on moor, in woodland dell,
In becks of green we wove our spell.
Until you made our sacred burn
Round giant wheels its flow to turn
And now we have at last forsook
The valleys you so greedy took
You drove us out with hissing train
You'll never hear our song again
Your chimneys blotted out the sun
The smoke it choked us, every one.
Your preachers cried we were the past
That our great race would never last
Your church bells rang our sad death knell
Such sweet demise you knew full well
Your miners knew our secret caves
But hungrily they made our graves
You blamed us when your milk turned sour
And for the weevils in your flour
And though you thought our ways were wild
We never took a human child
The bairns they were the last to see
They understood our misery
They begged us, sobbing, for to stay
They loved to join us in our play.
They met us down the leafy dell
And watched us sadly bid farewell
We dance no more in moonlight glade
We are no more.
You've watched us fade.
Look to yourselves and do not blame
us little folk
Yours is the shame.

Haworth Local Legend & Folklore Associations with Death
photo by Harry Hartley

HAWORTH LOCAL LEGEND & FOLKLORE
by Harry Hartley and Leah Helliwell
Haworth, England

ASSOCIATIONS WITH DEATH

In the Brontë's time, Haworth was not the picturesque, charming village it is today. The village was overpopulated for the housing available with reports of families of seven in a cellar dwelling sharing two beds between them. Most houses would not have had a water supply or WC, with most houses using communal privies and water supply outside their houses. The water supplies were usually wells with a pump tap to fill water vessels. Chamber pots, water used in wash bowls and drainage from houses was disposed into the open channels and gutters which ran down the streets, as there were no sewers in Haworth.

Privy's were ECs (earth closets, not WCs, water closets). These were simply containers in outhouses that were filled with human waste, emptied and taken away by the night soil men. The Public Health Act was not passed in England until 1875, which mandated one outhouse per household; therefore these privies were used by four or five households. There are reports of more than twenty households using one privy and these privies or cess pits often overflowed with accounts of them bursting open to flow down the street, or soil seeping through walls and running across the floors of adjoining houses. The privies barely fulfilled the rules of decency and were exposed to the gaze of passersby with one privy perched up high, almost having a view of the whole of the main street.

Many people kept pigs in the village, adding to the swill in the open gutters and the unsanitary conditions. Midden-steads, refuse and manure heaps were also scattered about the village. The midden-steads contained a potent mix of household waste, human waste, waste from the slaughterhouses, animal waste and who knows what else. They were very large containers filled over time with the rotting waste, causing much the same problem as the privies and cess pits; overflowing, foul smelling and extremely capable of causing disease.

Taps or wells for water supplies to houses were sometimes located next to privies, cesspits, midden-steads or pig stys which would per-colate the ground to contaminate water supplies and, to quote local historian Ian Dewhirst MBE, "the room for contagion was absolutely mind boggling". There was also no clean air act. People still burned refuse, most homes had fireplaces, some burned peat, wool combers always had fires going to obtain temperatures required for the task and Haworth was an industrial village with over twenty mills, so not only was the air foul smelling it was also polluted.

This life threatening mix had devastating consequences for Haworth's inhabitants, massively impacting their health and making Haworth a place very familiar with death. Conditions were so bad that the villagers of Haworth took action and sent a petition to the General Board of Health in London in October 1849, requesting an inspector be sent to Haworth to inspect the water supply. Benjamin Herschel Babbage (son of Charles Babbage) began his three day inspection in April 1850, culminating with the Babbage Report, a condemning report of Haworth's ill health and the remedial actions needed.

The average life expectancy was 24 to 28 years, 41.6% of babies born would never reach the age of six. Funerals were frequent and the lines of this life and the next were blurred in Haworth. The graveyard of St Michael And All Angels Church which surrounds the Parsonage contains over 40,000 bodies, with graves containing entire families literally stacked on top of each other with burial records dating back to 1645. A walk through the graveyard and a look at the gravestone inscriptions tell this sad story of loss and the common place of death in Haworth.

One particular beautifully sculpted gravestone of a baby sleeping shows this sad story intimately through the eyes of one family, the Heaton's. Joseph Heaton was an extremely talented and skilled stone mason who carved this memorial for his family. The gravestone is adorned with decoration and is clearly a labour of love with great devotion poured into its craft. The sleeping baby at the base of the gravestone is said to be James Whitham Heaton, one of Joseph's infant children. The inscription on the memorial shows Joseph Heaton tragically had seven of his infant children die, possibly due to the poor living conditions of Haworth, who are all buried in this family grave. A story common across many of the gravestones at St Michael And All Angels, with some graves containing over fifteen children from one family. The Heaton family grave inscription reads:

Sacred

To

The Memory Of

James William
Son Of
Joseph & Elizabeth Heaton
Of Haworth
Who died
February 1st 1871
In the 1st year of his age
Also three infants of theirs
Also James Whitham
Their son died July 19th 1878
In the second year of his age
Also Elizabeth their daughter
Who died July 19th 1885
Aged six weeks
Also an infant son of theirs
Also of the above named
Joseph Heaton
Who died March 18th 1914
In his 69th year
Also Elizabeth his wife
Who died April 22nd 1917
In her 71st year
Sweet rest at last

The blurred lines of life and death in Haworth inspired the Brontës in their somewhat gothic fiction, with the everyday crossing of lines and strong spirituality of Haworth being echoed in their works with moments of necromance and a closeness to the other side. This time of mass crossing in Haworth's history has left an indelible mark on the landscape, impressions on the minds of all who live in or visit the area, a constant reminder of the fragility of mortality, a deep spiritual connection and a belief in something more.

As if living conditions were not bad enough, there were also occupational hazards in Haworth, some of which resulted in fatalities. Working conditions in the mills were harsh and some mills employed children as young as six, as they were cheap labour. If the children did not do a good enough job they may have been disciplined or had wages stopped and were often savagely treated by some of the over lookers. They worked sometimes 16 hours a day to exhaustion, with little time for meals, instead of the 1819 Factory Act limit of 12 hours for children. The long hours of work would make the children sleepy, lethargic and unalert resulting in sometimes fatal accidents as they were caught up in machinery. Some locals today have reported hearing looms running in Griffe Mill. As a young boy I spent many hours in the abandoned mills, which now are nearly all gone, where I certainly could feel a presence of the buzzing hive of activity that once was.

Richard Oastler, aka The Factory King, who was born at Leeds in 1789 campaigned during the 1830s to decrease the work hours children had to endure in the mills. Twelve thousand of the Factory King's supporters marched to York in 1832 in protest of the overworking of children. A Leeds Civic Trust Blue Plaque on the wall of The Wardrobe, 6 St. Peter's Square in Leeds, commemorates Richard Oastler, The Factory King

Other jobs for children could include stone getters or even coal miners. Penistone Hill, now a country park in Haworth, was comprised of several quarries. Stone from this quarry has been used to pave the streets of London and build Morecambe's old stone jetty and is a highly prized good quality sandstone. On one part of Penistone Hill there is an old pump just below a large sandstone platform where a windmill once stood to power the pump below via a belt to pump the water out of Haworth's only coal seam. The other end of the shaft is visible from Lower Laithe waterworks bridle path.

One particularly windy day the windmill was spinning too fast. A gentleman went up to shut it down. His scarf got caught in the blades and he was strangled to death.

DAREDEVIL OF HAWORTH

On the side of Penistone Hill there is the new Haworth Cemetery, accessible quite obviously from Cemetery Road. Enter the main gates of the cemetery and on the path immediately to the right you will find a gravestone with an air balloon on it. This is the grave of Lily Cove. Her gravestone inscription reads:

In
Loving memory
Of
Elizabeth Mary,
(Miss Lilly Cove,
Parachutest;)
Daughter of

Thomas Charles Cove
of London,
who died June 11th 1906,
Aged 21 years.

The star attraction of the 1906 Haworth Gala held on the 9th of
June at the West Lane Football Field (now cricket pitch) was Lily
Cove, with her air balloon ascent and parachute descent. Lily Cove was
a young daredevil air balloon parachutist from East London who
toured the country with Captain Bidmead, her employer of two years
also from London and a fellow daredevil boasting 400 balloon ascents.

Captain Bidmead performed at the Keighley Gala of 1898 where
his parachute cord had failed to snap, leaving him hanging onto his
balloon traveling twenty-seven miles before coming down near
Pontefract. At the Haworth Gala of 1906 a crowd of 6,000 gathered to
watch Lily Cove, but the conditions were bad and Haworth's town gas
used to inflate the balloon had poor lifting power, so the event was
postponed until Monday the 11th of June. On this day Miss Cove,
wearing black knee-length trousers and a white blouse, took her seat
under the large brown balloon swaying above the crowd in the netting.

She was hooked onto the balloon, at 19:40. Miss Cove asked for a
handkerchief and the balloon rose steadily into the air, with Miss Cove
waving her handkerchief to the cheering crowd below. She drifted
away across the Stanbury Valley as Captain Bidmead climbed to his
watching post. Miss Cove was seen floating over Stanbury towards
Ponden, swinging her legs happily. Captain Bidmead, back at his
watching post, watched Miss Cove drift off into the distance to a speck
over a mile before he saw the balloon, nine minutes later, shoot up as
Miss Cove jumped and the balloon lightened.

In Stanbury, Mr. Robert Rushworth caught sight of the descending
parachute. He thought he saw Miss Cove shrugging her shoulders,
coming detached from the parachute and falling nearly head first. Mr.
Cowling Heaton's account was the parachute burst open above him,
Miss Cove and the parachute parted company and she fell turning over
and over and landed on the grass with Mr. Heaton running towards the
spot. The balloon was nearby; Miss Cove was still wearing her belt to
attach to the parachute. She was unconscious, bleeding at the nose and
mouth, and died on the spot.

The crowd waiting in Haworth for Lily's triumphant return had an abrupt end to their gala celebrations as they saw the vehicle conveying her body past the field from which the ascent had been made. There was speculation of a suicide. However, Captain Bidmead said at the inquest his opinion was Miss Cove saw she was approaching Ponden Reservoir and, as she could not swim, she wanted to avoid it, so she left the parachute thinking it was lower than it really was.

After examination of the equipment used on that fateful day the jury saw this as the most likely turn of events, giving the verdict of death by misadventure. Miss Cove was taken to the White Lion Hotel on Main Street where she and Captain Bidmead had been staying and on the 14th of June she was carried in her coffin, shoulder high, to the cemetery by the members of the Gala Committee with several hundred people walking alongside. It is said 1,500 people gathered at the grave while workmen stood with their caps in their hands in the quarry behind as she was laid to rest amid the landscape of her last performance.

GUINEAS AND FOWLS

In St Michael And All Angels Graveyard at the side of the Black Bull, there is a mysterious gravestone with a story forbidden to be told. Brush aside decaying leaf mulch and you will uncover a gravestone with no epitaph or memorial, just two small simple initials, JS, and the year of interment, 1796. This is the grave of Mr. James Sutcliffe, aka James Freeman, aka James Smith, a highway man and violent professional thief who was buried here in secret.

Mr. John Wignall was traveling along Halifax Road near Keighley (the town closest to Haworth) where he was assaulted by the highwayman Mr. Sutcliffe, who put him in fear of his life. He then stole a parcel from Mr. Wignall containing sixty guineas and several notes and bills worth two hundred pounds.

The Highwayman did not get far, though, as he was apprehended and imprisoned at York Castle on the 5th of March, 1796. He was charged upon the oath of Mr. Wignall and sentenced to death by hanging on Saturday the 2nd of April, 1796, at the gallows in Knavesmire, just outside of York; the same place Highwaymen Dick Turpin and John Stead were hung.

James Sutcliffe's charge sheet read:

> James Sutcliffe alias Freeman alias Smith
> for having feloniously assaulted Mr. John Wignall

on the Kings Highway, on Halifax Road near Keighley in the West
Riding
putting him in bodily fear of his life and feloniously stealing from his
person a parcel
containing 60 guineas and several notes and bills.

This may seem a harsh punishment to us today, but back then you could get a death sentence for stealing a loaf of bread and one of the people being hung on the same day as the Haworth highwayman, James Sutcliffe, was Thomas Birch, an army private who was so hungry he stole a hen.

On the day of the Haworth highwayman's punishment, Reverend George Brown spoke the words to Mr. Sutcliffe "let us, who are of the day, be sober, putting on the breastplate of love, and for a helmet the hope of salvation. For God has not appointed us to wrath, but to obtain salvation by our lord Jesus Christ." He then left York Castle Jail to go to the gallows at Knavesmire where he accepted his guilt and gave a confession before the rope slipped tight.

Relatives and friends claimed his remains and carted his body on a day and night-long journey back to St Michael And All Angels Church in Haworth where he was immediately and quietly buried in a corner of the graveyard.

Back then it was legal for doctors to cut up criminals corpses for anatomical examinations and research. This could be the reason for the indistinct markings on his gravestone, or it may be the case it was to set an example of non-condolence for such actions by the church. Both are speculation, but possible. As a boy my granddad would show me the grave and tell me a thief was executed by hanging and buried here. I am still learning new things about the Haworth highwayman and the mystery keeps unravelling.

MAID OF THE SEA / HAWORTH'S TITANIC

Next to the Parsonage garden wall there is a tabletop gravestone that can only provide a memorial to one of the family members inscribed who remains missing, but not forgotten. William Hartley was Haworth's postmaster who sat on the committee of the Haworth Operative Conservative Society with Branwell Bronte and John Brown, the church sexton. They were also friends and enjoyed a drink together. In fact, William Hartley and his family are buried next to John Brown and his family.

Reading the inscription on William Hartley's gravestone gives an insight into a harrowing story of the time.

His daughter Elizabeth Hartley worked as a maid for the Thomas family from Huddersfield. Her job as a maid offered up new and exciting opportunities as her employers, the Thomas family, were going to Australia and Elizabeth was invited to join them to continue her duties as maid or possibly for a holiday. She accepted the offer and on the 13th of December, 1865, they boarded the Steam Ship London at the Gravesend Thames Estuary in Kent destined for Melbourne, Australia, and a new life.

The Steam Ship London was a vessel of its time when technology moved in nautical engineering from wind power to engine power. This is evident in the ship's design, as it was a hybrid of both steam power and wind power, combining three masts rigged with sails and a two hundred horsepower steam engine that alone could propel the ship at 9 knots. This made the ship fuel efficient as well as more reliable. The ship, delayed by bad weather, left England late on the 5th of January, 1866, with 345 tons of iron for the railways, 263 passengers and crew onboard, including six stowaways, with the experienced Australian navigator, Captain Martin, at the helm.

For the next two days the SS London encountered heavy seas and bad weather. So bad that on the 7th of January a divine service was cancelled. For the next couple of days the SS London ploughed into a gale under the power of steam at two knots in the Bay of Biscay. On January the 9th the ship taking crashing seas over the bows had a lifeboat washed away, forcing the captain to turn around and return to England. Captain Martin was now unknowingly heading into the eye of a storm and on January the 10th, still in the Bay of Biscay, the sea carried away another lifeboat, the jib-boom, the fore topmast, all the rigs and gear, leaving the SS London with steam power only.

On January the 11th an immense wave crashed on deck leaving water pouring down the hatches and extinguishing the fires. The ship was now rolling badly and wallowing helplessly and the captain made the decision to abandon ship. The remaining lifeboats launched were immediately swamped, bar one saved for crew members. Their efforts to cover up the engine room hatches with anything they could and bail the water with pumps failed and as the water level in the engine compartment was still rising, Captain Martin told his men "Boys, you may say your prayers".

Soon the SS London was sinking rapidly, and Captain Martin ordered Mr. Greenhill, the ship's engineer, and eighteen others into the last lifeboat telling him "your duty is done, mine is to remain here". The captain was asked again to board the lifeboat, but he replied "NO! I will go down with the passengers, but I wish you Godspeed," he then threw a compass into the boat and shouted their course "North North East to Brest!"

Maid of the Sea/Haworth's Titanic illustration by Barb Tanke

The lifeboat drew away from the SS London as the passengers stood on deck singing the hymn Rock Of Ages and when the lifeboat got about 70 metres away, the stern (back) of the SS London went under and the bow (front) rose high until the ship's keel was visible, throwing the passengers on deck into the water to be dragged down with the ship by the vortex.

Greenhill and the eighteen others onboard the lifeboat were finally rescued by an Italian vessel, the Marianopole, and taken back to England. There were just 19 survivors from the 263 passengers onboard with a death toll of 244, including Mr. James Thomas, Mrs. Sarah Anne Thomas, their two children, Annie Mary Thomas and William Bradbury Thomas and their maid Elizabeth Hartley of Haworth. Other passengers onboard included Gustavus Vaughan

Brooke, a famous Irish Actor, John Debenham, the son of the founder of Debenham department stores, the wife and three children of Henry Brewer Chapman, an attorney general who introduced the secret ballot, and John Woolley, the first principal of the University of Sydney, Australia. Frederick Chapman whose mother, brother and sisters were onboard the SS London when it sank to the depths in the Bay of Biscay, wrote of his mother having just inherited "a mass of diamonds" from his Great Aunt Fanny that were with her on that fateful day.

An inquest found that the SS London was overloaded with heavy cargo that blocked the scupper holes, preventing drainage of seawater and making the ship too low in the water. The disaster received global publicity in its time with numerous accounts, survivor testaments, newspaper articles, a poem by William Mcgonagll and some artistic interpretations. The case drew the attention of Samuel Plimsoll, who campaigned for compulsory standards in marine safety and in 1876 had the Plimsoll Line (a marking on the ships side specifying the maximum load) made compulsory for British ships. Samuel Plimsoll's campaigning for the compulsory provision of lifeboats, however, was not introduced until the Titanic catastrophe of 1912, after Samuel Plimsoll's death in 1898.

The newspaper *Liverpool Mercury* printed the following obituary on Tuesday the 25th of January, 1866:

THOMAS, HARTLEY, Jan 11th, lost at sea on board the steam ship London, James Thomas Esq., late of London, formally of Huddersfield, Yorkshire, together with Sarah Anne his wife and two children Annie Mary and William Bradbury, also Elizabeth Hartley, for many years a most faithful and devoted servant of the above.

Elizabeth Hartley's memorial inscription on her family's gravestone next to the Parsonage garden wall in St Michael And All Angels graveyard Haworth reads:

Also the memory of Elizabeth their daughter who was lost in the Steamship London which was bound from London to Australia and foundered in the Bay of Biscay January 11th 1866 aged 37 years.

LAD OR SCARR ON CROW HILL

Up on the outer reaches of the windy moors of Haworth, past Top Withens and Alcomden Stones on the Yorkshire Lancashire border at Crow Hill where the Bronte children were reportedly caught in a bog burst, there is a mysterious stone with the inscription Lad or Scarr on

Crow Hill. The stone most likely dates from a boundary dispute of 1788 and is a marker stone for a boundary erected by Henry Cunliffe in 1788.

The stone is also said to be the resting place of an unfortunate unknown boy who was lost in a snowstorm and died here on the border of the two parishes. When the lad's remains were discovered neither parish would accept responsibility for the boy. Eventually Trawden Parish agreed to pay the expenses for burying the lad where he still lay on the moor side, after which they demanded the boundary be changed to bring the grave within their parish.

LONELY ON THE DESERT MOOR

Many people get lost on the moors that surround Haworth. The weather can change rapidly and the blanket of heather makes some hillsides indistinguishable from others. There are lots of stories of people losing their path and perishing, but two particular stories coincidentally share some incredible similarities. In 1801 a farmer from the area called Thomas Helliwell set out on a walk over the moor unaware of his son, Joseph, following him. Joseph soon lost his father, froze to death and was found the next day near Harbour Lodge. Emily Bronte wrote the following poem, *Redbreast, Early in the morning,* about this Haworth tragedy.

Redbreast,
early in the morning dank and cold and cloudy grey,
Wildly tender is thy music,
Chasing angry thought away.
My heart is not enraptured now,
My eyes are full of tears,
And constant sorrow on my brow,
Has done the work of years.
It was not hope that wrecked at once
the spirit's calm in the storm,
But a long life of solitude,
Hopes quenched and rising thoughts subdued,
A bleak November's calm.
What woke it then? A little child,
Strayed from its father's cottage door,
And in the hour of moonlight wild,
Laid lonely on the desert moor.

I heard it then,
You heard it too,
And seraph sweet it sang to you
But like the shriek of misery
That wild, wild music wailed to me

Half a century later, in 1851, another farmer's child from the area, also called Joseph Helliwell, went missing on the same stretch of moorland and was found three days later by John Kitson who also wrote a poem called The Dead Boy for this incredibly similar Haworth tragedy.

A HIGH MOORLAND PASS

The A6033 Hebden Bridge Road between Oxenhope and Pecket Well near Haworth is a high moorland pass over Cockhill Moor which in bad weather is notoriously dangerous, even today.

On the 30th of October, 1920, the day before Halloween, 37 people boarded an open topped charabanc at the Robin Hood Inn, Pecket Well, for an outing across the stretch of moorland. On the decent from Cockhill to Oxenhope, coming down too fast the charabanc's brakes failed, sending it hurtling through a wall at a sharp left turn, throwing out some passengers, killing five people and seriously injuring four.

Foster's: W. & H. Foster were manufacturers of worsted wool products who moved to Denholme around 1830. Because of a shortage of local weavers, Fosters would employ weavers from Wadsworth & Crimsworth, both near Pecket Well, and therefore would have to cross this stretch of moorland often to collect the pieces required. Benjamin Foster was a 22 year old junior member of Fosters who on the 4th of February, 1831, was making this journey to collect the family firm's products. After collecting the required pieces, it was nearly dark and snowing badly. Benjamin's friends asked him to stay the night, but he refused and set off into the snow over the moor with his dog Shep, horse and cart in the darkness. His horse and cart got stuck on the edge of the moor. He then decided to leave the horse and cart possibly to find help or carry on without, but he did not get far.

Benjamin fell into a bog and injured himself. Unable to carry on he lay in the snow and froze to death. Benjamin Foster was found the next day covered in snow with his dog Shep still at his side. Benjamin was buried on the 10th of February at Denholme Wesleyan Chapel. After this tragedy 185 stone stoops were erected along the roadside by the Fosters to show the way and prevent such a tragedy happening again. The stones were painted white with black tops to make them visible in the snow. Some of the stones remain along the side of the road today, minus the deteriorated paint. The infamous Shep went on to become Fosters trademark. Work at Fosters Mill Denholme stopped in 2005 and the building has since been demolished, just like many of the grand historic mills of the area.

GUYTRASH

Guytrash, also referred to as Guytresh, Gytrash, Trash, Padfoot, Shagfoal, Hellhound, the black dog, the big dog, the Gurt dog, Shriker, Skriker, Barghest or Barguest, is a malevolent shape-shifting ghost known to take the form of a dog or horse. The legendary Guytrash is said to haunt the lonely roads, lanes, and paths around Haworth where it leads travellers astray. Most commonly in the shape of a large dog, guytrash is said to have large glowing eyes like saucers, long hair and a huge head.

Guytrash illustration by Barb Tanke

Its presence was said to spell disaster or the possibility of a looming forthcoming death of a loved one. Locals believed any attempts to interfere with Guytrash or its domain could have fatal results, and some feared to cross his territory. Upon the death of some people the Barguest is said to howl, followed by the dogs in the vicinity joining in. As well as being able to shape-shift, the spectre can also wander in invisibility, making the sounds of rattling chains or the tramping of soggy footsteps.

Charlotte Brontë mentions Guytrash in chapter twelve of her 1847 novel, *Jane Eyre,* where the title character mistakes Mr. Rochester's dog for Guytrash. Branwell Brontë also mentions Guytrash in his Angrian narrative story Thurstons of Darkwall so the Brontës were fully aware of the local spectre, with it having a noticeable influence on their works.

Was it Guytrash that led the many missing people around Haworth to their demise? We will never know, but the spirit lives on with visitors and locals still speaking of sightings of what is quite possibly Haworth's most famous ghost.

There are also stories of Guytrash guiding travellers over the moor and showing the way, so maybe it is not the fearsome nasty creature it has been branded. My own personal opinion on Guytrash is that you are entering its domain and if you treat the moorland with disrespect Guytrash may not forgive it, but if you treat the moorland with respect you will be welcomed in.

Other Yorkshire accounts of large dog-like creatures include the Guytresh of Goathland, the Guytresh of Horton, the headless black dog of Ivelet Bridge and the Barguest of Troller's Gill

THE WATER WOLF

Another piece of folklore from the area involving a dog-like creature is the Haworth Water Wolf. It is said that people sometimes swallow a Water Wolf when drinking from some wells, troughs or streams, which then live and grow in the stomach. The Water Wolf would consume the food they ate, move about in the host's stomach and sleep on their heart at night.

The Keighley Herrald reported an occurrence of the Water Wolf in 1909. The Water Wolf's host was Miss Maria Judson of 7 Prospect Street, Haworth, who stated she has had the Water Wolf in her stomach for a few years. Miss Judson explained that she had drunk from a spring while living at Leeshaw and one day while having a drink she felt something slip down her throat. The Water Wolf she had swallowed six years previously grew and moved about in her stomach, consuming the food she ate.

One evening Miss Judson was making some food and had it cooking on the fire at home. Miss Judson stated she could feel the thing moving up her throat with the smell of the cooking food lingering in the air. She went to take the food off the heat, opened her mouth and something fell out lopping over twice, burning itself on the fire. Miss Judson shut her mouth, grabbed the pan of cooked food, and shooed it outside slamming the door on it. The Water Wolf was said to have been grey, rough, and the size of a frog. Miss Judson was happy to be finally rid of the wolf as she was then able to eat anything she liked.

THE OLD SILENT INN

The Old Silent Inn Stanbury, formally known as The Eagle Inn and the New Inn before that, is over 400 years old, but was not used as an Inn until the early 1800s. The pub has been featured in many literary works including Ricroft of Withens by Halliwell Sutcliffe. The Old Silent Inn Stanbury and then-owner Joseph Narey and his son Mark won the Pub of the Year contest in 1999. Poet Alfred Holdsworth lived in Hob cottage next to the Silent Inn during the mid 1900s

There have been numerous reportings of ghosts at the Old Silent Inn by visitors, locals, staff and owners, including feelings of ghosts watching, coldness, a ghost of a man, the ghost of a tall man with a long coat and big hat that usually appears downstairs to women, a large man with a bag over his shoulder walking up the stairs stopping at the top to turn around and vanish, conversations with the ghost of a young girl, items being moved, items being thrown and broken, rocking chairs moving, curtains opening, paintings sliding across the room, disturbed sleep, hair stroked while lying in bed, bells ringing and even shaking rooms.

A former landlady of the Old Silent Inn was said to have had many cats and when it was time for their feeding, she would alert the cats by ringing a bell. The cats would flock to the sound of the bell for their feeding and the ringing of bells followed by sounds of cats can still be heard during the night, sometimes waking up people who are staying at the Inn.

Another version of the story says the landlady of the Old Silent Inn would often walk around the Inn on the moors late at night, calling her many cats that each had a bell round its neck.

A visiting couple staying at the Inn gave an extraordinary account of their night's stay, claiming to be woken in the night by the room beginning to shake and a glass flying across the room and smashing. The couple ran out of the room and woke the pub manager, whose room they spent the remainder of the night in. The manager and couple then saw a painting shaking on the wall, falling off and then sliding across the floor. The curtains flung open and furniture fell over as objects were floating round the room.

The Old Silent Inn illustration by Jon Beynon

A night vigil was performed by UK Ghost investigators in 2003 where they heard voices, footsteps, ringing bells, had feelings of cats brushing past, two presences, and found a handprint in room ten. Telegraph & Argus rated the pub as one of Bradford's top 10 haunted pubs

The Pub has an 1834 moon dial on the exterior of the building. Perhaps this could be an indication of when such ghosts may be present and if you are in Haworth looking for ghosts, this may be your best place to start as it tells of more ghostly presences than any other.

PAGAN TRADITIONS

St Michael And All Angels church in Haworth dates back to the 14th century with the current building being the third to stand at this site. It is said to be an old place of Pagan worship before the first chapel was built on the site; however, this is just speculation and lacks any real concrete evidence to back the claim. Haworth does hold one particular seasonal ceremony that has a link back to Pagan worship, although the event is a modern conception and is aimed at Christianity, not Paganism.

Scroggling The Holly is an annual event usually held in late November or early December to mark to start of the Christmas festive season in Haworth. Scroggling is an old word meaning gathering, therefore scroggling the holly means gathering the holly. Local children usually dressed in Victorian attire to suit the scene welcome the Christmas spirit to Haworth by gathering baskets of holly and carrying them up the main street, followed by a procession of Morris Men, musicians and merry makers to the St Michael And All Angels church steps. Here one lucky girl will be crowned The Holly Queen. She will then have to provide for her subjects by unlocking the church gates to allow the Christmas spirit to enter the village.

The Holly King is the Pagan personification of the winter who is locked in an eternal battle with the Pagan personification of summer, the Oak King. These two seasonal kings were traditionally worshiped on the day of their total dominance over the land, namely the summer and winter solstices, reflecting the seasonal cycles. The winter solstice is on the 21st or 22nd of December and therefore does not correlate with Haworth's Scroggling The Holly event, however it is held close to the date of the winter solstice.

The tradition has connections in both Paganism and Christianity, as John The Baptist and Jesus have been said to be a variant of the holly and oak king. Some neopagans also consider Father Christmas to be a variant of the Holly King. The Oak King is said to sacrificially mate with the great mother, die in her arms and be resurrected, similar to Jesus who sacrificially dies and is resurrected. Scroggling the holly has no connection with Wiccan traditions, as their depiction of the battle of seasons is the horned god Herne and it has no connection to witchcraft, only the appreciation for nature.

Carving from York Minster photo by Harry Hartley

The Cowthorpe Oak was an oak tree at Cowthorpe near Wetherby in North Yorkshire, once famous for being the largest and oldest oak tree in the UK. The tree was said to have been 45 feet high, and 60 feet in circumference. It had branches 50 feet in length with a canopy that covered 0.5 acres and a hollow trunk able to fit forty people. This famous oak dated to the era of the Norman Conquest or possibly even early Roman times.

The artist Turner made three sketches of The Cowthorpe Oak in 1816 while on one of his grand tours of Yorkshire. The Scottish physician, writer and editor, Alexander Hunter, wrote in his 1776 edition of John Evelyn's *Sylva or A Discourse Of Forest Trees and the Propagation of Timber in His Majesty's Dominions*, "The dimensions are almost incredible and when compared to this, all other trees are but children of the forest."

Hopefully Haworth will continue this seemingly old English tradition in its old time setting, maybe even expanding the celebrations to also accommodate for scroggling the oak and an appreciation of the summer season.

THUNDER STONES

Ponden Kirk is a sandstone outcrop overlooking Ponden and much of the Worth Valley. The word kirk means church in Yorkshire Dialect and this may give an indication of the historical uses of this site. The Kirk has a hole large enough to crawl through in the lower part of the rock that is used for a local tradition. Locals believe if a couple was to pass through the hole together they would be blessed with a happy life, however if an unmarried couple passed through they would have to marry within a year or spend their days alone and would die if they married someone else, having to haunt the kirk for an eternity.

The Brontë's knew Ponden Kirk well and it is believed that the Penistone Crags in Emily Brontë's novel *Wuthering Heights* is based on Ponden Kirk. Pennistone Crags is described in *Wuthering Heights* by one of the lead characters, Catherine Earnshaw, as having a fairy cave underneath the crag, just like Ponden Kirk.

"This bed is the fairy cave under Penistone Crag, and you are gathering elf bolts to hurt our heifers; pretending, while I am near, that they are only locks of wool. That's what you'll come to fifty years hence; I know you are not so now. I'm not wandering, you're mistaken, or I should you really were that withered hag, and I should think I was under Penistone Crag."

Elf bolts are also called fairy arrows or thunder stones. These are flint arrowhead-shaped tools usually turned up by farmers. It's possible the Brontës knew about elf bolts due to their alternative name, thunder stones, as bronte means the sound of thunder in ancient Greek and they had quite a fascination with thunder and lightning. Astrape and Bronte are the twin goddesses of lightning and thunder in Greek mythology.

The local folklore of Ponden Kirk runs throughout Emily Brontë's novel *Wuthering Heights* and the knowledge of the kirk's traditions help to understand the book better by giving an insight into the writer's thoughts.

The Brontë's Nanny and Housekeeper, Tabitha Aykroyd, told the Brontë children many stories about Haworth folklore and the creatures that inhabit the surrounding landscape. Tabitha would tell the children of fairies that once inhabited the valley but were scared away by the development of the mills and industrialisation. It is believed by locals that some of the fairies still reside around Haworth in the quieter parts of the moorland, and with patience you may be able to see them. One possible way to see the fairies, according to English folklore, is to fall asleep under an elder tree in full bloom. This would enable one to see the fairies, however there is a great danger of being transported into the underworld never to return.

In Cottingley, about 6 miles away from Haworth, fairies were photographed in 1918. Arthur Wright was a keen amateur photographer who lived next to Cottingley Beck where the photographs were taken by his daughter, Elsie Wright, and her cousin, Frances Griffiths who both feature in the photographs meeting the fairies. The cousins maintained the fairies were real throughout intense media speculation over their lives until 1983 when Elsie Wright confessed they were all fakes. Frances Griffiths, however, maintained all her life that the Cottingley Fairies were real, and it is possible that Elsie Wright gave her statement just to end the intense scrutiny she had endured most of her life.

WYCOLLER

Although Haworth is undoubtedly proud of being part of Yorkshire, it is very close to the county boundary. Wycoller is a ten mile journey over the border into Lancashire on the Brontë Way footpath or by road and is well worth the visit. The hamlet is nestled in a quiet valley on the side of the moor and consists of a handful of charming houses gathered round Wycoller Beck, its old bridges and the ruins of the once great Wycoller Hall.

The settlement is said to date back before 1000 BC and Wycoller's clam bridge is believed to be 6000 years old. Wycoller Hall was built in 1550 by Piers Hartley; the Hall was passed through marriage from the Hartley family to the Cunliffe family in the early seventeenth century, who extended the building in the eighteenth century. In 1818 Wycoller Hall's estate was sold due to debts and the building passed to distant relatives, the Oldham family, who partly demolished the building for the stone to be reused in the construction of a cotton mill at Trawden.

Wycoller Hall is believed to be the inspiration for Ferndean Manor in Charlotte Brontë's 1847 novel, *Jane Eyre*. Elizabeth Cunliffe of Wycoller Hall married Thomas Eyre of North Lees Hall in Hathersage, Derbyshire. North Lees Hall is believed to be the inspiration for Thornfield and Hathersage is believed to be the inspiration for Morton in Charlotte Brontë's novel, *Jane Eyre*.

If you are at Wycoller Hall in the dead of the night you may be spooked by the horseman of Wycoller. A ghostly apparition of a previous resident of the Hall who frequently returns to replay a fateful night in Wycoller Hall's History.

Wycoller illustration by Jon Beynon

Simon Cunliffe was believed to have been a squire of the Hall during the reign of King Charles II. One day, the squire and his hunt were in pursuit of a fox which ran inside the Hall and up the stairs. The then squire rode his horse into the Hall and up the stairs, chasing the fox with his hounds. Mr. Cunliffe's hounds attacked the fox and his unexpecting wife was given a huge shock as the hounds, horse, and Mr. Cunliffe came thundering up the stairs. The squire cursed his terrified wife's cowardice and raised his crop to strike her when she died of fright, literally scared to death.

Some nights the horseman can be seen dressed in the attire of the Stuart era, returning to the Hall. The horse's hoofs clatter across the bridge, into the Hall and up the steps followed by a woman's bloodcurdling screams that reverberate throughout the hamlet. The ghost then comes hurtling down the steps, out of the Hall with the cracking sound of a riding crop, over the bridge and disappears into the night. The horseman is said to return once a year and his wife, named Black Bess, still haunts the Hall with multiple accounts of sightings of a woman wearing a black silk dress with some people claiming to have talked to her.

Another version of the story of the Wycoller horseman is that his wife was having an affair. On hearing the news, the horseman returned home raging mad, dismounted his horse at the door and stormed up the stairs where he mercilessly murdered his wife. He then fled the scene of the crime on horseback and these events are echoed again every year by the ghosts of the Cunliffe's.

Paranormal investigators recorded the sound of a riding crop in 1996 and many ghost hunters still visit the area hoping to catch a glimpse of the horseman of Wycoller. There is no record of a Simon Cunliffe or these events ever happening at Wycoller Hall, however with so many accounts of sightings by visitors and locals I will still be looking out for the horseman and his unfortunate wife in the dark of the night in Wycoller.

Other ghosts reported in Wycoller include the blue lady who floats through walls of adjoining houses that once were one property next to the tea rooms on the other side of the beck.

WITCHCRAFT

If you walk to Top Withens in Haworth and carry on up to the bog at the top of the hill, you will be able to see over a vast expanse of moorland. Far in the distance is the ominous Pendle Hill jolting into the sky on one side with a comparatively gentle slope down the other.

The Brontë children did play on this part of moorland under the gaze of Pendle Hill, so I am sure they would have known about some of its history.

In 1612 the hill gave its name to one of the most famous witch trials in history, the Pendle Hill witch trials, where twelve inhabitants of its surrounding area were accused of murdering ten people by the use of witchcraft.

Pendle Hill Witch Trials illustration by Barb Tanke

In 1562 the Act Against Conjurations Enchantments And Witch-crafts was passed which demanded the death penalty for anyone using witchcraft to harm others. The act was expanded in 1604 to also give a death penalty to anyone who invoked evil spirits or communed with familiar spirits. People found guilty of minor witchcraft offences were now punished with one year in prison and second offences were punishable by death. These laws took the jurisdiction away from the ecclesiastical courts, therefore providing an ordinary court procedure and eliminating the punishment of being burnt at the stake.

In 1612 the Justice of the Peace for Pendle, Mr. Roger Nowell of Reed Hall, was ordered to compile a list of people in the area who refused to attend Anglican Church. This, and the practice of Catholicism, was a criminal offence at the time exasperated to the point of repudiation due to Guy Fawkes of York and the Gunpowder Plot of 1605.

A complaint was made by Mr. John Law to Pendle's Justice of the Peace, claiming to have been injured by witchcraft. Mr. Law was a peddler from Halifax who claimed he had encountered Alizon Device while passing through Trawden Forest. Alizon Device had asked Mr. Law for some pins, but he refused to give any to Alizon. When he was walking away from Alizon he heard her mutter and he fell to the ground, possibly having a mild heart attack or a stroke from which he recovered.

Alizon Device claimed she was trying to buy the pins and Mr. Law refused to open his pack for such a small transaction. Mr. Law's family claimed she did not have enough money and was begging for the pins. Pins were known to be frequently used for magical purposes and it is also possible, therefore Mr. Law refused to give any pins to Alizon Device. Mr. Law's son took Alizon to see his father a few days later where she confessed to being a witch and cursing him for his refusal to give her the pins.

Alizon Device is said to have strongly believed she was a witch, possibly because she was the granddaughter of a local witch, Elizabeth Southerns aka Demdike. Alizon's elderly Grandmother Demdike was suspected of being a witch for decades. People posing as witches could make a living from casting spells, healing, extortion and begging, so it is possible that the elderly witch Demdike made her living this way. After Alizon's confession of using witchcraft to Mr. Law he made the complaint to Pendle's Justice of The Peace.

Alizon Device, her brother James and her mother Elizabeth were then all summoned to a meeting with Pendle's Justice of The Peace on the 30th of March where Alizon confessed to selling her soul to the Devil and asking him to hurt John Law after he had insulted her. Alizon's brother James also stated that his sister had bewitched a local child and Alizon's mother Elizabeth stated Alizon's grandmother, the infamous witch Demdike, had a mark on her body which then was widely regarded as a mark left by the Devil. Alizon, while being questioned, also accused another local woman, Anne Whittle, of murdering five people by the use of witchcraft, including her father, who Anne Whittle had extorted with threats. Alizon's father, John, claimed on his deathbed in 1601 that his sickness was caused by Anne Whittle because he had not paid for his yearly protection.

Anne Whittle, aka Chattox, was another local witch very much like Alizon's grandmother Demdike, in her eighties making a living posing as a witch. One of Chattox's family members had also previously broken into the home of the Device family's Malkin Tower and stolen goods of small value. It is possible Alizon Device accused Chattox of using witchcraft to harm people because she wanted revenge, or she wanted to eradicate the competition of another rival local witch.

Chattox, her daughter Anne Redferne, and Alizon's grandmother Demdike were then summoned to a meeting with Pendle's Justice of the Peace where even more confessions of witchcraft were made. Chattox claimed she had sold her soul to "a thing" that promised any revenge that she desired. Demdike claimed to have seen Chattox's daughter Anne making clay figures and another witness claimed her brother died after a disagreement with Anne. Demdike also claimed to have sold her own soul to the Devil.

Anne Chattox Clay Figure illustration by Barb Tanke

As a result of these two conferences and confessions given, Alizon Device, her grandmother Demdike, Chattox and her daughter Anne were all committed to trial for causing harm by the use of witchcraft.

Alizon's mother, Elizabeth Device, then held a private meeting at the Device family home, Malkin Tower, where some friends and family attended to give their sympathy. The meeting was held on Good Friday, a day on which everybody should attend church and this caught the attention of Pendle's Justice of The Peace who investigated the meeting further. This led to eight more people accused of witchcraft being committed to trial. Alice Nutter, Katherine Hewitt, Alice Grey, John Bulcock, Jane Bulcock, James Device and Elizabeth Device were sent to join the four already imprisoned. Jannet Preston, another accused, was sent to York for her trial as she lived just across the border at Gisburn in Yorkshire.

Janet Preston was charged with the murder of Thomas Lister by witchcraft. It was also her second time appearing at York Assizes (court) accused of murder by the use of witchcraft, for which she had previously been found not guilty. Janet Preston, who pleaded her innocence, was found guilty of murdering Thomas Lister by the use of witchcraft and executed by hanging on the 29th of July, 1612, at the gallows in Knavesmire just outside of York.

Alizon Device's nine year old sister Jennet Device was brought in as a witness at the Lancaster Assizes where the rest were tried. Jennet Device identified the people who attended the Malkin Tower meeting and gave evidence against her sister Alizon, her brother James and her mother Elizabeth. Alice Nutter, Demdike and Elizabeth Device were charged with the murder of Henry Mitton. Elizabeth Device was also charged with the murder of John Robinson and James Robinson. When Elizabeth's daughter Jennet was called to give a statement, Elizabeth started to shout and curse at her daughter and had to be removed from the courtroom. Jennet then stated her mother had been a witch for years and had a familiar in the form of a brown dog called Ball that her mother asked to commit murders.

James Device was charged with the murder of John Duckworth and Anne Townley after his statement to the Justice of the Peace was read out in court and his sister Jennet claimed her brother had conjured a black dog to kill Anne Townley.

Alizon Device was charged with causing harm by witchcraft after John Law, her alleged victim, was brought into court and Alizon burst into tears confessing her guilt.

Chattox was accused of murdering Robert Nutter and pleaded not guilty to the charge, however the damming confessions she gave to the Justice of the Peace were read out in court. A previous lodger at the Chattox house stated that Chattox was indeed a witch. Chattox then broke down, asked God for forgiveness and admitted her guilt.

Anne Redferne was charged with the murder of Cristopher Nutter after Demdike's statement of Anne making clay figures was read out in court and Anne was branded a witch more dangerous than her mother Chattox.

Alice Nutter was charged with the murder of Henry Mitton. Two members of the Nutter family had previously been executed as Catholic Priests and Jennet Device's statement that Alice Nutter attended the Malkin Tower meeting must have marked Alice as a nonconformist.

Jane Bulcock and John Bulcock were charged with the murder of Jennet Deane. Jennet Device's statement they had been at the Malkin Tower meeting must not have helped.

Katherine Hewitt was charged with the murder of Anne Foulds and was identified by Jennet Device as having attended the Malkin Tower meeting. James Device stated that Katherine Hewitt had mentioned the murder at the Malkin Tower meeting.

Alice Grey was also accused of assisting in the murder of Anne Foulds, however she was found not guilty.

It was also alleged that the Pendle witches were planning to blow up Lancaster Castle in their own gunpowder plot.

As a result of the court proceedings Elizabeth Southerns aka Demdike, Elizabeth Device, James Device, Alizon Device, Anne Whittle aka Chattox, Anne Redferne, Jane Bulcock, John Bulcock, Alice Nutter, and Katherine Hewitt were found guilty and sentenced to death by hanging on the 20th of August, 1612, at Gallows Hill in Lancaster.

Execution illustration by Barb Tanke

Of the twelve convicted, ten were executed by hanging. Between the 15th and 18th centuries there were fewer than 500 executions of accused witches making the 10 people executed in the Pendle Hill witch trials accountable for two percent of all the accused witches executed during this time period. Only Alice Gray was found not guilty and Elizabeth Southerns aka Demdike is said to have died while being held in prison. Some locals believe Demdike did not die in prison as she broke free using her witchcraft and she still resides under the shadow of Pendle Hill to this day.

Ursula Sontheil aka Mother Shipton aka The Witch of York is arguably Yorkshire's most famous witch said to have been born in 1488 during a thunderstorm in a cave near the River Nidd at Knaresborough. Her teenage mother, Agatha, who never revealed the father's name, raised Ursula in the cave for years until a local Abbot took pity arranging for Agatha to be taken away to a nunnery and a local family to take Ursula in. Other stories state Ursula's mother died in childbirth and that Ursula was found by the Abbot the next day.

As a child Ursula was called the devils daughter or hag face on account of her apparently grotesque appearance and she was said to have been able to push, pull or pinch her school friends from a distance. Later in life Ursula married Tobias Shipton from York who died a few years after, therefore becoming Ursula Shipton. As an elderly woman Ursula became known as Mother Shipton and was widely regarded as a prophetess or soothsayer as well as a healer and maker of remedies.

She is said to have foretold the great fire of London, the defeat of the Spanish Armada, the invention of iron ships, the death of Cardinal Wolsey, the English civil war, Oliver Cromwell's rise to power and the fates of rulers. She is said to have lived in the forests near to the cave in which she was born and she died at the age of 73 in 1561. Mother Shipton's Cave near Knaresborough in North Yorkshire is now a tourist destination. The cave features a sulphate carbonate-rich well in which various objects are petrified and displayed for visitors.

St Robert is another mythical character who resided in a cave near the River Nidd at Knaresborough. The twelfth century hermit born in York had miraculous healing powers and was even visited by King John. The Trinitarian Priory of St Robert is said to have been built on the lands given by King John to St Robert.

Other famous witches from Yorkshire include Awd Nan of Sexhow, the Barrow Witch of Driffield, Sally Cary of Kirby Hill, Peggy Flaunders of Marske, Nan Hardwick of Spittal Houses and the Witches of Pocklington, Danby Dale and Fewston.

A witch stone is a stone with a naturally formed hole through it. These witch stones can be hung with string or rope to keep witches at bay. Witch posts are sometimes seen in the older houses of Yorkshire. A witch post is usually a stone next to a door, window, or fireplace which is decorated with an X symbol to prevent witches from entering the house. Planting rowan trees or mountain ash will also protect against evil spirits or witchcraft. Rowan branches collected on the 18th of August (St. Helens Day which celebrates Helena Augusta the Roman empress who discovered the True Cross) are also placed around windows, doorways, or fireplaces to ward off witches and evil spirits.

Witch Stone illustration by Barb Tanke

Elder trees also have an association with witches, as it is said that witches can turn themselves into an elder tree. Its wood is used for making magic wands and burning elder wood will raise the Devil, bringing about death and destruction. It is also believed that an elder tree will never be struck by lightning. The Elder Mother is the guardian of the elder trees and when taking wood from the tree one has to ask the Elder Mother for permission first as follows, "Elder Mother, give me some of thy wood and I will give thee some of mine when I grow into a tree." I do enjoy a glass of elderflower champagne every now and then and when I collect the sprays of elderflowers to make it, I always ask the Elder Mother for permission.

GIANTS OF FOLKLORE

The giant of Yorkshire folklore is, of course, the giant Rombald. Rombald's Moor, named after the giant who once ruled the land is an area which includes Addingham High Moor, Morton Moor, Bingley

Moor, Baildon Moor, Hawksworth Moor, Burley Moor and Ilkley Moor. Romuald's Moor is an ancient landscape with many visible marks left by past civilizations. There are standing stones and over 400 cup and ring or other prehistoric markings across Rombald's gigantic stretch of moorland.

The Hitching stone is a large square block of gritstone about the size of a small house on Keighley moor near the village of Cowling. The stone has a quite deep rectangular hole in the side of it and a three-foot-deep basin on the top, about four by eight foot wide, that is usually filled with rainwater. The boulder, which is supposed to be one of the largest in Yorkshire and weighs over a thousand tons, was said to have been thrown from Rombald's Moor by Rombald's wife while she was tidying up the moorland. Rombald's wife was said to have struck the handle of her broom into the side of the rock, hitched it up into the air and slung it off the moorland to its current position. This story explains the hole in the side of the stone as this is possibly where Rombald's wife struck her broom handle in and it explains the name of the stone as Rombald's wife hitched it into the air with her broom to throw it out of her way.

Geologists think that the stone's unusual indentations and fractures are due to a tree that once grew on the stone. Evidence of the tree that once inhabited it can be seen inside the hole on the side of the stone as a fissure or tube running through the gritstone that was formed by a Lepidodendron tree. The hole in the side of the Hitching Stone is commonly known as the druids chair or the priest's chair as it is supposed that ceremonies may have taken place at the stone and also that Baptists may have performed baptisms in the pond on top of the stone.

The Cow and Calf are two large boulders next to each other on Ilkley Moor, so named because one is larger than the other, therefore resembling a cow and its calf. It is believed that the Cow and Calf were once one stone that was split in half when Rombald slipped on it after taking a gigantic stride from Almscliffe Crag, near North Rigton at the other side of the valley.

The nearby Skirtful stones or Great Skirtful of Stones, also on Ilkley Moor, are said to have been dropped there by Rombald's wife who was carrying them in her skirt while on another one of her evidently epic cleaning sessions. Remains of a Bronze Age cairn can be found at the stones, although it has been greatly disturbed.

In Keighley's Airedale Shopping Centre stands a twelve foot high bronze statue of Rombald lifting a piece of stone. The statue was sculpted by John Bridgeman and first installed in 1968. Unfortunately, Rombald's wife remains nameless, even though it is fairly obvious she did much of the work.

William Bradley (1787-1820) was a 27 stone, 7 foot nine inch tall man from Market Weighton who was said to be the tallest Englishman ever recorded and was nicknamed the Market Weighton Giant. William Bradley was exhibited at fairs up and down the country and even met King George IV, who gave him a gold chain for his notoriety as the Yorkshire giant.

Other Yorkshire giants include the Penhill Giant, who is said to have lived in a castle on Penhill in Wensleydale and was a descendant of the Viking god, Thor; the Sessay Giant, who was said to have had one eye and the mouth of a lion; Wade the Giant, the Anglian chieftain who is said to have formed the Devil's Punchbowl on the North York Moors when he scooped up some earth to throw at his wife, Bell, during an argument. Wade the giant also built Wade's Causeway and with his wife, Bell, built the castles of Mulgrove and Pickering at the same time with one hammer.

Ilkley Moor, which is part of Rombald's Moor, is the birthplace of the famous Yorkshire anthem On Ilkla Mooar Baht 'at shines a light on Yorkshire's view of death and its chin up, keep laughing attitude. On Ilkla mooar baht 'at translates from Yorkshire Dialect to English as on Ilkley Moor Without A Hat. There is some mystery regarding the origin of the lyrics set to Thomas Clark's 1805 tune, Cranbrook, however it is believed it was created by a choir on an outing across Ilkley Moor. When the choir stopped for lunch one of the boys was said to have slipped away for some quiet time with a girl called Mary Jane. When he re-joined the group he must have been given a good telling off and given his hat back. It is thought that one, or some, of his fellow choir members made the song to pull his leg and have a laugh. The lyrics and translation are as follows:

Where wor ta bahn when ah saw thee
(where were you going when I saw you)
On Ilkla Mooar baht 'at
(on Ilkley moor without a hat)
Tha has been courtin Mary Jane
(you have been courting Mary Jane)
On Ilkla Mooar baht 'at

Tha's bahn ter catch t' death o' a cold

(you're going to catch the death of a cold)

On Ilkla Mooar baht 'at

Then we sh'll 'ave ter bury thee

(then we shall have to bury you)

On Ilkla Mooar baht 'at

Then t' worms 'ill come an' eat thee up

(then the worms will come and eat you up)

On Ilkla Mooar baht 'at

Then t' ducks 'ill come an' eat up t' worms

(then the ducks will come and eat up the worms)

On Ilkla Mooar baht 'at

Then we 'ill come an' eat up t' ducks

(then we will come and eat up the ducks)

On Ilkla Mooar baht 'at

Then we shall all 'ave etten thee

(then we will all have eaten you)

On Ilkla Mooar baht 'at

Let this song be a warning to all those walking on Rombald's or any of Yorkshire's moors to take a hat and be prepared, otherwise you may be eaten by the locals.

YORKSHIRE WELCOMES THE BRONTËS

Dewsbury was the first place in Yorkshire where Patrick Brontë lived. In December of 1809 he was made curate at the then All Saints Church (now Dewsbury Minster) where he eagerly took on additional responsibilities in the church, Sunday school, and parish. He took a leading role in the newly built Sunday school, opened in 1810, where he taught reading and writing. As a supporter of the Christian Mission Society the vicar would enroll Patrick to attend meetings on his behalf two evenings a week.

Some parts of the grade II listed Dewsbury Minster date back to 1220 and the area has been a place of worship since St Paulinus preached at the crossing point of the river Calder at Dewsbury in AD 627. Along with housing the oldest stone representation of Christ In Majesty, circa 850, the Minster tower also houses an infamous bell called Black Tom. The bell was given by Thomas Soothill to the church in penance for murdering a servant boy. Patrick Brontë would have been accustomed with a tradition called The Devil's Knell, dating back to the 15th century where each Christmas Eve the bell is tolled once for every year since the birth of Christ. The Devil's Knell tradition was commemorated on a 1986 Royal mail postage stamp

Yorkshire Welcomes the Brontës illustration by Jon Beynon

Patrick relaxed by taking walks along the banks of the River Calder which flows through the centre of Dewsbury. On one such occasion he met a group of young boys, one of which had fallen into the water. Patrick jumped into the river and rescued him from being swept away by the strong fast-flowing currents of the Calder.

On the 1810 Whit Walk, Patrick led the procession and a drunk who would not let the procession pass confronted leader Patrick Brontë. Patrick took hold of the drunk by the collar and threw him into a ditch, much to the amusement of all the children on the walk.

A memorial plaque to Patrick Brontë can be found on the south aisle wall of the Minster, which reads:

> In memory of the Reverend Patrick Bronte, B.A. S Johns College Cambridge,
> Born at Emdale County Down, St Patrick's Day 1777
> Died at Haworth Parsonage 1861,
> Curate at Weatherfield Essex 1806-1809, Wellington 1809, Dewsbury 1809-1811,
> Incumbent of Hartshead 1811-1815, Thornton near Bradford 1815-1820, Haworth 1820-1841,
> Erected by admirers of him and his talented daughters Charlotte, Emily and Anne Bronte.

WORSTEDOPOLIS

Haworth's nearest city, Bradford, is the once-capital of the woollen industry. It is also called Worstedopolis, Woolopolis, or Wool City for this reason (worsted is a type of wool) and has many tales of folklore and ghosts. It is believed to be a Saxon settlement. The name Bradford is supposed to be old English for 'broad ford'. This probably refers to a crossing over Bradford Beck that the city eventually grew around. It is possible that Bradford is a Brigantian settlement now over two thousand years old.

When Bradford was still a small settlement during medieval times it was said to have been terrorised by a wild boar - later to become known as The Bradford Boar - that lived in nearby Cliffe Wood. The boar would attack people and restrict access to a much needed well by drinking there frequently, therefore scaring off the people of Bradford. A reward was offered by the lord of the manor for killing the boar and the proof of its death. A huntsman called John Northrop went to the nearby well and waited with his bow and spear for the boar to return to its regular drinking hole. When the boar eventually appeared, Mr. Northrop shot it with his arrows through the heart and made sure of the kill by running forward and thrusting his spear into the boar. He then cut out the boar's tongue to prove he had killed the malevolent beast. Another huntsman must have been either watching or he turned up afterwards to find the boar, minus a tongue, at the well. The second huntsman then cut off the boar's head and took it into Bradford where he claimed he had killed the animal only to be discredited moments later when John Northrop appeared with the boar's missing tongue. The Bradford coat of arms features a boar with no tongue and there are countless carvings of and references to boars throughout the city.

After the Harrying of the North in 1070, the Manor Of Bradford, which had been valued at four pounds troy weight of silver just four years prior, was laid to waste and given to Ilbert de Lacy for his services to William The Conqueror, thereby becoming part of the Honour of Pontefract. The Norman, Ilbert de Lacy, who replaced the local Anglo-Danish lords to rule the region from Pontefract Castle is said to have fought at William The Conqueror's side during the Battle of Hastings.

The 1086 Doomsday Book records the area as "Ilbert hath it – it is a waste". The lands passed down the de Lacy family until 1311 when it passed to the Earls of Lincoln through marriage. In 1359 the Manor of Bradford passed to the English prince John of Gaunt, who was considered one of the richest men of his era and the ancestor of all English monarchs. John of Gaunt was a successful military leader and statesman who gained vast amounts of land due to advantageous marriages and his royal lineage, therefore receiving the titles Earl of Richmond, Earl of Leicester, Earl of Lancaster, Earl of Derby, Duke of Lancaster, Duke of Aquitaine, King of Galicia, King of Castile and King of Leon.

In his spare time John of Gaunt enjoyed hunting and one of his favourite hunting grounds was "Broad Ford Dale" (the area around Bradford). Doe Park at Denholme near Bradford was stocked with game, as it name suggests, and was a favoured hunting ground of the prince. It is believed John of Gaunt was the lord of the manor associated with the infamous Bradford Boar.

On one occasion John of Gaunt was said to have been hunting in the nearby Yorkshire Dales where he and his party brought down a stag. An old man approached the hunting party begging for food and money and John of Gaunt pushed the man away. At that moment he realised the old beggar had only one leg and looked to be in bad health. The beggar then fell to John of Gaunt's feet swearing allegiance to him and asking "My lord you have so much. I have nothing. Could you not spare a little of your wealth for me and my family." The hunting party mocked the old man until John of Gaunt told them to stop and told the old beggar, "Old man, I believe you are a loyal subject and we need support in these lands." John of Gaunt then told the old one-legged beggar to come back to the field at dawn when he could have as much land as he could hop round without the aid of his sticks, for him and his family forever.

In the morning the old one-legged beggar came back to the field where John of Gaunt and his hunting party had set up camp. The party was surprised to see the beggar as they thought he would not return and joked that he wouldn't last an hour. When the old one legged beggar started hopping, the party laughed at the spectacle unfolding before them. Their laughter must have subsided as the old one legged beggar hopped out of the field and down to a nearby town. The beggar hopped all day using up all his energy eagerly trying to gain as much land as he could until he fell down at sunset. When word of the beggar's accomplishment came back to the hunting party at the field, John of Gaunt praised the beggar for his loyalty and being a man of his word granted the old one-legged beggar, called Malham, the town he had hopped around. It still bears his name today. Malham is a small town in the Craven District of North Yorkshire with many beauty spots such as Malham Cove, Malham Tarn, Gordale Scar and Janet's Foss.

It is believed that John of Gaunt had a hunting lodge, the remains of which can be found at Haverah Park Beaver Dyke Reservoirs, Harrogate, called John O' Gaunt's Castle. The Royal Hunting Lodge acquired by John of Gaunt in 1372 was a tower on a square platform surrounded by a moat with a hall, chapel, and queen's chamber. The foundations can still be found; however the tower no longer stands at the lodge.

Bolling Hall in Bradford is one of the city's oldest buildings that was first mentioned in the 1086 doomsday book as owned by a person called Sindi. After the Harrying of the North, the Hall passed to the de Lacy family mentioned above. They owned the Hall for over two hundred years. In the 1300s the Bolling family - who the Hall was subsequently named after - acquired the property. In the 1500s the Hall passed to the Tempest family who owned it into the 1600s when King Charles I was on the throne.

King Charles believed in the divine right of kings and many thought he wanted to make England Catholic again. The Protestant Puritans opposed the king, believing the Church of England should completely remove themselves from the Roman Catholic Church and that it was the responsibility of the government to establish religious worship. Many of the Puritans were Roundhead supporters during the English Civil War who also sought a constitutional monarchy instead of King Charles I's supposed absolute monarchy.

In 1642 the Earl of Newcastle gathered a Royalist army in Bradford as he was angry that Bradford, being mostly Puritan and completely defenceless, had not yet fallen. The night before the Earl of Newcastle attacked Bradford with his army, he stayed with Richard Tempest at Bolling Hall. Sir Richard Tempest of Bolling Hall was a Royalist supporter who believed that the King appointed by God should rule as he saw fit. The Earl of Newcastle went to bed that night vowing to kill every man, woman, and child in Bradford. During the night the Earl was woken by his bedsheets being pulled away from him. A ghostly figure of a woman stood at the side of his bed sobbing and pleading with the Earl to "pity poor Bradford". The next day the Earl of Newcastle attacked Bradford with his army, however only ten deaths were recorded.

The White Lady of Bolling Hill illustration by Barb Tanke

The ghostly figure of the sobbing woman that would come to be known as the white lady is frequently seen in the Hall. Bolling Hall has had many accounts of ghostly presences such as sounds of banging doors, sounds of footsteps, sounds of breathing, sounds of voices, feelings of being pushed near the main staircase, figures walking past and disappearing in the main hall, Victorian figures watching in the blue room, a child's crib rocking as people enter the room and a lady dressed in white floating across the room to disappear into the fireplace.

The Equinox Paranormal Research UK team photographed a ghost known as the woman in black. The Most Haunted team from Living TV captured the child's crib rocking of its own accord. In recent years, a local newspaper offered a reward to anyone who could stay at Bolling Hall overnight however the challenge was never taken up. Bolling Hall has had many overnight ghost hunts and vigils and it is possible to organise a ghost hunt of your own on one of their haunted evening events.

Bolling Hall is now a museum and education centre open to the public. On display are some photos of ghosts taken at the Hall as well as some English Civil War relics, and even Cromwell's death mask. The Hall has many references to the folklore of the Bradford Boar such as a Jacobean plaster ceiling featuring a boar, and a boar's head on the wall. Bolling Hall attracts many paranormal investigators and ghost hunters and has become known as one of the most haunted places in England.

MAD WOMAN OF NORTON CONYERS

Norton Conyers is a medieval manor house at Wath near Ripon in North Yorkshire. The building has had later additions and has recently been restored, winning the Historic Houses Association & Sotheby's Restoration Award in 2014. Since 1624, the house has belonged to the Graham family, who had strong connections to the Royals. Sir Richard Graham fought for King Charles I at the Battle of Marston Moor where over four thousand Royalists were killed. Sir Richard, who fought until the battle was over, was badly wounded and chased on horseback by Oliver Cromwell and a troop of cavalry back to Norton Conyers. On arrival Sir Richard was carried to bed where he soon died, after which Oliver Cromwell arrived to find the dead body of Sir Richard Graham and ordered his men to ransack the house. Charles I stayed at Norton Conyers in 1633 and James II stayed at the house in 1679. Charlotte Bronte also visited Norton Conyers in 1839 while she was in the area with the Sidgwick family who employed her as a governess.

Thornfield Hall in Charlotte Brontë's 1847 novel, *Jane Eyre*, is based on Norton Conyers and some of the house's history also inspired the novel. Charlotte was very interested in the Graham family legend of a mad woman who was held in an attic room during the 1700s. The woman was said to be imprisoned in an upstairs attic room at Norton Conyers which was only accessible from a hidden door and staircase on the first floor. The discovery of a blocked staircase at Norton Conyers in 2004 from the first floor to the attic confirmed that the house was the inspiration for *Jane Eyre*. It is believed that the character Bertha Antoinetta Mason in the novel, *Jane Eyre*, is based on the mad woman of Norton Conyers.

Mad Woman of Norton Conyers illustration by Jon Beynon

It is possible the insane woman held at Norton Conyers was a member of the Graham family or maybe somebody they gave pity, as insane asylums at the time were basically prisons. People suffering from mental illness were often treated unfairly as it was not recognised as a condition; however progress was being made, as people generally believed it was a medical matter and not a supernatural event as in previous years. Family members would confine mentally ill people to, prevent them from being humiliated in public by others, to protect them from harm, to protect others from harm and to keep the afflicted person out of the prison-like insane asylums where they would be treated harshly. Under these circumstances we can sympathise with the Graham family and *Jane Eyre's* Mr. Rochester as keeping someone in an attic may have been the most humane option available at the time.

Norton Conyers is open to the public 28 days a year. Other nearby places to visit on a day out around Ripon include Ripon Cathedral, Marmion Tower, the Victorian Workhouse Museum, the Prison And Police Museum, the Courthouse Museum, Thornborough Henge, and even Lightwater Valley Theme Park.

BOGGART

A boggart is a mischievous elf or imp that inhabits the homes of unfortunate families and causes mischief. There is very little description of a boggart as it spends most of its time cloaked in invisibility, however the few descriptions of an unveiled boggart given through English history describe it as a small hairy humanlike figure with long thick arms and a grotesque beast-like appearance. The boggarts are believed to have once been helpful household spirits, such as brownies or silkies that were ill treated, turning them into mischievous and sometimes malevolent boggarts. The name boggart is believed to be derived from the middle English word 'bugge' meaning a frightening thing or the old welsh word 'bwg' meaning evil spirit; the name bogyman or boogieman is also believed to be similarly derived. Possibly the most common name for this mischievous little imp is a Hob or Hobgoblin. Other names include bugbear, boggle, house elf and poltergeist.

Household hobs, brownies, silkies, imps or elves can be a positive presence as they help with household chores. However, if they are mistreated, they may become a nuisance. The ill-treated alter ego boggart, hobgoblin, bugge, bogyman, bugbear or boggle are said to cause things to be misplaced, snatch away objects, knock over objects, throw objects at people, sour milk, play pranks, shake beds, strip off bedsheets, and sit on people as they sleep.

A helpful household hob does not like praise or reward for its work and the best way to keep one happy is to leave it alone. To name or reward a boggart or hob would displease it and would also provoke the boggart to play more pranks. Leaving clothes out for either a hob or boggart would be the greatest insult, causing it to leave the house. In fact, leaving clothes out for a boggart to wear is said to be the only way to get rid of a one, as hobs and boggarts are not tied to one specific place and can follow a family to new homes. If the boggart does not leave the house insulted by the clothes laid out for it, it could become a serious problem as you are left with a very angry boggart wanting revenge. Leaving a pile of salt outside your bedroom or hanging a horseshoe on the door of the house are other methods of keeping a boggart away. On the other hand, with time and perseverance a boggart can be made to feel welcome, therefore restoring some of its helpful house elf qualities. Not naming the boggart or hob, giving it space and laughing at its pranks may turn the mischievous boggart into a helpful household hob who helps to find items or does cleaning.

Boggarts are often confused with barguests, which are not household elves, but instead are shapeshifting animals found roaming outdoors, ogres that live outdoors under bridges and in caves, or gremlins that are large-eyed, sharp-toothed small creatures with claws and spiked backs that cause mischief, usually by causing machinery to malfunction, hence their other name machine gremlin.

GRINDYLOW

A Grindylow is a creature that lives in the bogs on the moorland and sometimes can be found in lakes and ponds. They are said to grab people who come too close to the edge of the bogs, and pull them down into the water to drown them. Grindylows are described as pale bluey green or brown, small in size with long spindly arms, long fingers, sharp teeth, gills, webbed feet, long fingernails and small horns.

This Aquatic demon especially targets children who walk near the edge of bogs. It grabs them with its long arms, pulls them down into the bog to drown and then eat them. Some people believe grindylows take their victims to their underwater villages where they are held captive.

Peg Powler is a water spirit who inhabits the River Tees which forms the boundary between Yorkshire and Durham. The green-haired hag with a voracious desire for human life is similarly said to drag children into the water if they get too close. Froth or foam which forms on the river has been given the name Peg Powler's Suds. The

River Skerne, which is a tributary of the Tees River, is inhabited by a similar spirit called Nanny Powler who is said to be the daughter of Peg Powler.

At the start of the track to Harbour Lodge, on the edge of Penistone in Haworth, there is a small bog. This bog is rumoured to have had a horse and cart stray into it and sink never to be seen again.

A little girl playing one day in the River Worth at the bottom of Lord Lane was sucked down a water supply pipe for the nearby mill and found several days later. Are these occurrences due to encounters with a grindylow? We will never know, but we can assure our safety by staying away from the waters' edge and avoiding the many bogs that blanket the moorland around Haworth.

She Burned Too Bright
For This World

Dragon photo by Weems

DRAGONS

by Harry Hartley and Leah Helliwell
Haworth, England

DRAGON OF WANTLEY

Wharncliffe Crags is a Gritstone escarpment six miles from Sheffield in the West Riding of Yorkshire, much of which is a steep rock face that runs for over two miles in length. The crags have a long history of rock climbing, but they are most famous as the scene of an epic battle between West Yorkshire's most famous dragon, the Dragon of Wantley and the dragon slaying knight, Moore of More Hall. The Dragon was said to be as big as a Trojan Horse and had wings, a sting in its tail, claws and forty four teeth of iron. The dragon would devour anything, even buildings, and was said to have eaten cattle as well as three children.

389

The dragon was clearing the woodland by consuming the trees and drinking from local wells. The dragon was reputed to fly across the valley to Allman Well on the Waldershelf Ridge above Deepcar to have a drink. Allman Well is also known as Dragon's Well and its waters are said to have special healing qualities, possibly from its repeated visits from the dragon.

Wortley is a village nearby and the name of a local family whose head rose to become the Earl of Wharncliffe. The Earl of Wharncliffe's lands included Wharncliffe Crags and Wantley is believed to be derived from either the name Wharncliffe or Wortley. The knight's residence, More Hall, lay beneath the crags and he must have been very familiar with the dragon that lived above his home on the clifftops.

Dragon of Wantley silhouette by Weems

The locals came to More Hall pleading with the knight to save them all and slay the dragon. Moor had a bespoke suit of spiked Sheffield armour made for the battle and this gave him an advantage as Sheffield is famous for its metalwork and metal production. Moor was said to have looked like a porcupine or a hedgehog in his spikey suit of armour. The knight then downed six pints of ale and had a shot of malt spirit before marching unarmed up the crag, where he lay in hiding. When the Dragon appeared, he jumped out and kicked it in the mouth. Moore then delivered a fatal kick to the dragons "arse gut" it's only vulnerable spot, as it explained with its dying breath. The dragon of Wantley was recounted in a 1685 ballad and later included in the 1767 Reliques of Ancient English Poetry by Thomas Percy.

SLINGSBY SERPENT

Most of the other Yorkshire dragons were different from their usual depiction and were usually worm or serpent-like creatures. The antiquary Rodger Dodsworth (1585-1654) gave an account of the dragon that lived between Malton and Helmsley saying that it "lived upon the pray of passengers". The Wyvill family had six generations of knights live in Slingsby. The most famous of these was the fourteenth century knight Willian de Wyvill, who was said to have slayed the serpent with help from his dog. An effigy of a knight and a dog in All Saints Church at Slingsby is believed to be a depiction of the fourteenth century serpent-slaying knight, Sir William Wyvill.

HANDALE SERPENT

Another Yorkshire serpent was the Handale Serpent. Handale is a hamlet two miles south of Loftus in north Yorkshire where the serpent was said to have lived in the local woods. The Serpent had the power to control young women. It would bewitch young maidens, causing them to leave their homes and enter the woods where the serpent would devour them. A knight called Scaw had a friend killed by the serpent and swore he would slay the beast or die trying.

The enraged Scaw put on his armour and made his way to the serpent's cave in the woods where he struck a rock with his sword to alert the Serpent of his presence. The Serpent came out spitting fire and brandishing its sting, however Scaw, hell bent on vengeance, fought hard and killed the serpent. Scaw then found the Earl's daughter still alive in the cave and returned her home safely. The Earl rewarded Scaw with land and the local woods at Handale still bear his name. Others say Scaw fell in love with and married the Earl's daughter, therefore inheriting the lands.

Handale Priory was founded in 1133 and dissolved during the dissolution of the monasteries in 1539. Very little remains of the Benedictine Priory and the Handale Abbey walled garden marks the location where Handale Priory once stood. In 1830 there were 16 skeletons, a pedestal for a cross or font, and a stone coffin with a skeleton clutching a sword inside it found at the site. The skeleton in the stone coffin is believed to be the serpent-slaying knight, Skaw. The sword has since been lost or, hopefully, been taken away to be looked after; however the stone coffin and cross base can still be found at Handale Priory.

SOCKBURN WORM

The Sockburn Worm was a different kind of beast with a venomous bite and poisonous breath. The Worm was said to be sixteen feet in length, to have lived in the region for seven years, to have laid waste to the village of Sockburn, and to have devoured more than 1,000 people. Sockburn Hall is a privately owned house beautifully located on a loop of the River Tees at Sockburn near Darlington in County Durham.

The Manor was for many years the home of the Conyers family, who were related to the Conyers that once owned the lands Norton Conyers (one of the houses that inspired *Jane Eyre*) was built on. At the time of the Sockburn Worm, Sockburn Hall was the home of John Conyers who was a noble brave knight who wielded a mighty sword called the Conyers Falchion. A falchion is a European one-handed single edged sword.

Wrapped in a coat of chainmail and armed with his trusty sword, John Conyers slew the worm which had killed so many. He then buried the worm beneath a grey stone which is thought to be a glacial boulder made of sharp granite that can still be found at Sockburn. The mighty sword Conyers Falchion is now kept at one of Britain's most impressive buildings, Durham Cathedral. The Cathedral also houses relics of Saint Cuthbert, the head of Saint Oswald, the remains of Venerable Bede, one of the most complete sets of early printed books in England, and three copies of the Magna Carta.

Sockburn Worm silhouette by Weems

The Conyers Falchion, which was given to the cathedral by Sir John, is presented to every new bishop of Durham who would then return it to its keepers. The Lord of Sockburn would read the words "My lord bishop, I hereby present you with the falchion wherewith the champion Conyers slew the worm, dragon or fiery flying serpent which destroyed man, woman and child; in memory of which the king then reigning gave him the manor of Sockburn, to hold by this tenure, that upon the first entrance of every bishop into the county the falchion should be presented." The sword, weighs 1300g, is 890mm in length, has a 734mm long 109mm wide blade, has a handle made of ash, has bronze pommel on the handle with heraldic arms motifs and has a bronze cross on the handle decorated with dragon motifs.

The Durham Cathedral Conyers Falchion tradition was continued until 1771, after which the sword was kept at Sockburn Hall. In 1947 it was presented to Durham Cathedral by Mr. Arthur Edward Blackett and the ceremony was revived in 1994. The Sockburn Worm is widely believed to have inspired Lewis Carroll's poem *Jabberwocky*.

NUNNINGTON WORM

Nunnington is a small village and civil parish in North Yorkshire. The river Rye flows through the village which is home to a grade I listed mansion that is open to the public. The parish church is also a grade I listed building that houses the supposed tomb of Peter Loschy or Loschi who was a local knight and member of King Arthur's court.

The villagers of Nunnington were celebrating their annual harvest of hay with a procession and traditional crowning of a local girl who would become that year's harvest queen. The eighteen year old queen was being ceremoniously paraded on the cart carrying the symbolic final load of hay when a fire-breathing dragon descended from the sky, snatched the queen and took her back to its lair on top of the hill. The beast that would become known as the Nunnington Worm was said to have had the head of a dragon, the body of a serpent, the ability to quickly heal itself and breathed toxic fumes. This description sounds much more like a wyvern, which are winged dragons with two legs, no arms and arrow tipped tails; however most wyverns do not breathe fire.

The gallant knight, Sir Peter Loschy, then set out to kill the dragon and rescue the villagers' harvest queen. He had a suit of armour made that was covered with razor sharp blades. Protected by his razor armour, armed with his Damascene sword similar to King Arthur's Excalibur, and with his faithful mastiff dog at his side, he ventured up the hill to the dragon's lair. On arrival the dragon instantly went for Sir Peter and wrapped its body around him to constrict its prey, but the dragon let go as the razor-sharp armour cut deeper and deeper the more it tightened its grip.

Sir Peter hit back and began to lunge at the dragon while his dog was biting its legs. Every time the beast was injured it would quickly heal itself, but the beast could not coil itself around the knight to restrain him therefore the battle raged on and on. Sir Peter sliced away at the dragon until the end of its tail was cut off. His dog grabbed the tail in its mouth and ran away with it before it could heal again. Sir Peter then lashed out with his mighty Damascene sword until every piece of the dragon had been cut off and carried away by his cooperative and rather useful mastiff dog. The sound of a final hiss signified the kill and the knight's trusty dog celebrated with its master by licking his face. Unknown to Sir Peter, the dog had poison on its teeth and breath from the dragon which it had bit and carried away. Tragically the would-be hero knight and his faithful dog died in the moment of victory on the hillside that now bears the knight's name and the villager's harvest queen was never found.

SEXHOW WORM

Sexhow is a hamlet on the River Leven five miles west of Stokesley in North Yorkshire where a legendary dragon, called the Sexhow Worm, coiled itself around a local hill. The worm plagued the area by extorting the local farmers and laying waste to their produce. The Sexhow Worm did not eat humans or cattle and only drank milk. It was said to have required the milk of nine cows to satisfy its appetite and if the local farmers did not deliver the milk then the worm would breathe across the fields killing livestock and crops with its toxic breath. An unnamed knight arrived at the hamlet one day, possibly sent by the lord of the manor. To the delight of the farmers, he killed the toxic milk-loving worm that had tormented them for so long. The courageous knight then rode on and left Sexhow, scorning praise and thanks from the locals. The farmers then skinned the worm and displayed its scaly skin in the nearby church. The skin of the Sexhow Worm was said to have been destroyed during the reformation.

RALPH PARKIN AND THE FILEY BRIGG DRAGON

Filey Brigg is a peninsula about five miles north of Filey in North Yorkshire. Its steep cliffs are a site of special scientific interest and the fields on top of the Brigg are now the nine-acre Brigg Country Park. The waters below the clifftops were once home to the Dragon of Filey Brigg. This sea monster was said to be an air breathing serpent that was nearly a mile long.

Ralph Parkin was a local fisherman who went to enjoy a spot of lunch down by the sea. The dragon was lurking in the sea nearby and caught a whiff of Ralph's wife's homemade sticky treacle ginger oatmeal cake which made its belly rumble with hunger. The dragon raised its head out of the water in front of Ralph, who was scared half to death and jumped back dropping his sticky ginger cake, which the dragon snatched up.

The dragon bit into the delicious cake in great satisfaction. However, the sticky treacle and oatmeal stuck its teeth together and the dragon dunked its head under the water trying to unstick its sharp teeth. Ralph Parkin then saw his chance and jumped onto the dragon's head to drown the beast by pushing it under the water. His weight was not enough to push the dragons head down and he called for his friends, who came running to help. They all jumped on the dragon and, with their combined weight, managed to drown the beast.

It is said that the bones of the gigantic dragon lie where it was killed and form the impressive clifftops which became known as Filey Brigg. To this day, the irresistible sticky treacle ginger oatmeal cake that is much loved by the folk of Yorkshire is known as Parkin in honor of Ralph and his wife.

The only dragons to be found in Yorkshire now are dragonflies and many of Yorkshire's dragon stories are thought to be accounts of battles with or raids by Vikings who had dragons carved onto the front of their boats and regularly used dragon motifs.

Viking Boat illustration by Weems

Home of the Gothic illustration by Barb Tanke

HOME OF THE GOTHIC

by Harry Hartley and Leah Helliwell
Haworth, England

The Whitby Goth Weekend, founded in 1994, is a biannual
alternative festival held in Whitby, Yorkshire, that incorporates the
Bizarre Bazaar, an alternative market. Whitby has since attracted many
contemporary Goths, however Whitby has long before had an association with the gothic and the macabre.

Bram Stoker visited Whitby in late July 1890 and stayed in the
guesthouse at 6 Royal Crescent. Mr. Stoker was manager for the actor
Henry Irving and had just completed a tour of Scotland with him.
Bram Stoker, who would become known as one of the world's greatest
gothic fiction authors, would take walks to the Abbey while staying in
Whitby. Whitby Abbey was founded in the eleventh century and stood
on the site of a much earlier monastery founded in 657 by Princess
Hild. The once-great Abbey, which now stands in ruin, looms over the
town infusing the air with gothic thoughts. On the 8th of August, Stoker
visited Whitby's public library and found William Wilkinson's 1820
book *An Account of the principalities of Wallachia and Moldavia*. The
book gave an account of a 15th century prince, known as Vlad Tepes,
Vlad The Impaler, or Dracula, who impaled his enemies on stakes.

Dracula is believed to be a Romanian name meaning son of the
dragon or the Wallachian word for Devil. Bram Stoker used the name
Dracula for his eponymous blood sucking character in his 1897 novel.
While at Whitby he also wrote down names from the gravestones to
use in the book. He was also inspired by the local shipwreck of the
Dmitry a few years earlier, which he renamed the Demeter in his
novel. In the novel Dracula shape shifts into a large dog which is
reminiscent of the local folklore of barguests (as mentioned in the
Guytrash section) that inhabited the moors surrounding Whitby. In
Bram Stoker's novel *Dracula*, the title character travels to England
where the ship runs aground on the shores of Whitby and Dracula's
English solicitor's fiancée holidays in Whitby.

This leisurely visit to Whitby planted the seeds for one of the
world's best gothic horror fiction novels. It took six more years of
research and writing to complete the work which was first intended as a
play with his holiday chum Henry Irving playing the lead role. The

play was redrafted as a novel and went on to become known as one of the greatest books ever written.

Bram Stoker illustration by Barb Tanke

Charlotte Brontë's 1847 novel, *Jane Eyre,* mentions vampires. During the Brontës time, depictions of vampires were different from today's pale looking vampire. They were often described as having a ruddy, dark looking face or countenance. In Charlotte Brontë's novel the lead character, Jane Eyre, describes Bertha Mason as savage, purple with swelled dark lips, and compares her to a vampire. Mr. Rochester implies Bertha Mason is foreign in the novel and he describes Bertha as having a discoloured black face similar to the current depictions of vampires.

In the novel, Bertha Mason also bit her brother while he was visiting. It is very easy to see that Charlotte knew of vampires and it is possible to surmise that Bertha Mason was, herself, a vampire. The idea of vampirism has existed for millennia; however the name vampire came from eighteenth century Eastern Europe. Vampires had already been written about in European literature and the name vampire is thought to be derived from the French vampyre or German vampir. John William Polidori, who wrote the 1819 short story

Vampyre (after a bet with lord Byron, Mary Shelly, Percy Shelly that also created the novel *Frankenstein*), is credited by some as the English language creator of the vampire genre, however Bram Stoker's *Dracula* is still considered to be the preeminent vampire novel.

Vampire killing kit at Leeds Royal Armouries photo by Harry Hartley

Queen Victoria was arguably the most fashionable Goth. After Prince Albert died in 1861 Queen Victoria wore black in mourning of her much loved husband. This was the custom of the time, however most mourners would wear black for a few months after the passing of a loved one, whereas Queen Victoria wore black for the remaining forty years of her life. Jewelry was no exception to her eternal mourning and her most liked gemstone was jet, as the black gemstone suited her dark gothic attire.

Unlike most gemstones, jet is organic as it has been formed from prehistoric wood and is a mineraloid. Queen Victoria particularly desired Whitby Jet, as the jet mined in Whitby has a deep black lustre, is smooth, lightweight, hard and will not fade over time. Jet from other places could be brown in colour and the expression 'jet black' is thought to derive from the deep black of Whitby Jet. Queen Victoria made Whitby Jet and mourning jewelry very fashionable during her era. The Brontës had much mourning jewelry that is usually on display at Haworth Parsonage, though none are as grand as Queen Victoria's Royal Whitby Jet-studded treasures and trinkets.

Whitby is haunted by many ghosts, but possibly one of most renowned ghosts is that of a phantom carriage. If you walk up the 199 steps to St Mary's Church next to the Abbey on a cold dark night you may hear the sound of galloping horses hastily approaching. The phantom coach is then said to appear hurtling towards the church with the driver furiously whipping. As the carriage draws up outside St Mary's the horses rear up on their hind legs and barely visible figures at the entrance to the church board the coach before it disappears. Other ghosts of Whitby include The Oyster Man, The Brave Lighthouse Keeper and the Ghost of Grape Lane.

The Hand of Glory is a gristly device used by burglars to bring them luck. The hand was a real hand taken from the corpse of a criminal while they still hung at the gallows. The fingers were bent to hold a candle made from human fat, then the hand was dried in the sun and embalmed. Some Hands of Glory have their fingers fully stretched out and the actual fingers of the hand would be lit.

Lighting the gruesome candle was thought to send people sleeping in the house into a coma from which they could not wake. If the candle would not light it was a sign that somebody in the house was still awake. The light of the hand had to be extinguished by pouring blood or skimmed milk over the flame. Yorkshire accounts of the Hand of Glory include Spital Inn on Stainmore in 1797 and the Oak Tree Inn, Leeming, 1824. In 1935 a Hand of Glory was given to Whitby Museum and is thought to be the only hand to have survived.

EAST RIDDLESDEN HALL

East Riddlesden Hall is a grand manor house in Keighley (Haworth's nearest town) that was built in 1642 and is now open to the public. The Hall is reputed as being one of the most haunted places in the Worth Valley, with numerous sightings of ghosts.

East Riddlesden Hall's most famous ghost is the Grey Lady who lived at the house during the civil war. It is said that the man of the house returned from battle to find that his wife, the Grey Lady, had been having an affair and he murdered his wife's lover. The man of the house then punished his wife by bricking her up behind a wall and leaving her to die a slow death. The Grey Lady's ghost can be seen roaming the corridors searching for her lover.

Other ghosts at East Riddlesden Hall include the Blue Lady who was said to have been drowned in the fishpond, a coachman who was said to have been dragged into the lake by a horse, and a Scottish merchant who was murdered while he slept.

There have been countless sightings of ghosts at East Riddlesden Hall and even photos and films of ghosts caught by visitors. When people who live in the Worth Valley are asked where to find ghosts, most people would give the answer East Riddlesden Hall as this is famously the place where most ghosts in the valley that includes Haworth are sighted.

CALVERLEY HALL

Walter Calverley was an English squire and murderer who died in 1605 and lived at Calverley Hall, a medieval manor house at Calverley, West Yorkshire, England, about twelve miles from Haworth. Walter was to marry for love and got engaged to his chosen match. His guardian, however, insisted that he break the engagement and marry Philippa Brooke, a granddaughter of Lord Cobham and a woman of good standing. Walter married Philippa, whom he disliked, and spiralled into a life of heavy drinking and gambling.

On the 23rd of April, 1605, Walter heard of a relative who was arrested for a debt Walter was responsible for. In a crazed drunken madness, Walter took out his anger on his two sons, aged four and eighteen months, killing them both. He then stabbed his wife, Philippa, who survived. He ran out of the house to ride to the next village where his third son was with the nanny, intent on killing him, too. Before Walter could reach his third son, he was apprehended on the road and taken to Wakefield prison. When he was brought to trial at York he declined to plea and was sentenced to death by crushing. Walter Calverley was then pressed to death by stones in York where he pleaded for more weight and a faster death by shouting "A pund more weight!! Lig on!! Lig on!!"

This was to become one of Yorkshire's best known murders which inspired the 1607 play, *Miseries Of Enforced Marriage,* by George Wilkins and the 1608 Jacobean stage play, *A Yorkshire Tragedy,* by Thomas Middleton.

The ghost of Walter Calverley is said to haunt Calverley Hall and can be seen in the form of an angry figure covered in blood, holding a dagger and sometimes riding a headless horse.

The Landmark Trust now owns the property and runs it as a holiday let, details of which are found on their website.

WHITE DOE OF RYLSTONE

Emily Norton lived at Rylstone Hall in the Craven District of North Yorkshire. She was the last of her family, as the rest of her family had been removed due to their involvement in the uprising of the north. Emily made the journey to Bolton Priory Church, under ten miles away, to attend Sunday service every week. On her journey to Bolton Abbey she was accompanied by a white doe (female deer). After Emily's death the white doe continued to make the journey from Rylstone to Bolton Abbey.

White Doe of Rylstone illustration by Barb Tanke

The River Wharfe which flows through Bolton Abbey is considered to be extremely dangerous. The river narrows at a point called the Strid. The fast flowing water, strong currents, and the rocky bed of the Strid makes it the most dangerous place along the stretch of river. Some foolhardy people attempt to jump across this part of the river; however falling in at the Strid would guarantee death. In 1154 a young man called Romilly was out on a solo hunting trip around the river. He attempted to jump across the Strid, but was held back by his dog, fell in the water and was swept away by the unconquerable currents, never to be seen again. It is said that young Romilly's grief-stricken mother donated the surrounding land to the Augustinian monks that founded Bolton Abbey so they would pray for her son.

William Wordsworth wrote about the folklore of Bolton Abbey in his poems *The White Doe Of Rylstone* and *The Force Of Prayer.*

Ponden Kirk illustration by Jon Benyon

PONDEN KIRK

By Jenny Courtney Fidgeon
West Yorkshire, England

*This poem is about a stone near to Ponden Kirk and Ponden Hall
with the inscription 'LAD ORSCARR ON CROW HILL'
One story goes that a boy died near here in a snowstorm on the border
of two parishes and neither parish would accept responsibility for the
burial. The upshot was that he was buried where he was found.*

Climbing higher
Until I can't hear a thing
No sound, no tread of tyre
Just the sigh of the wind
It blows over the moorland top
Heath surrounds me
Jagged crags on the moorside
No creature anywhere to see
I come across a grave
Someone's brother, someone's son
That lad, no soul could save

I'd Lost My Way On The
Moor!

Alcomden the Great photo by Harry Hartley

ALCOMDEN THE GREAT

By Harry Hartley
Haworth, England

Alcomden the Viking lord flew to the furthest thriding
on his Wyvern that spat fire
And there he landed in Haworth carrying the thunder stone
gifted to him by Thor
He walked up the heather covered hillside until
he could not get any higher
And under the grey black clouds descending above
planted the seed on the moor
The Grindylow built their villages round the place where he planted it
But the black faced sheep sent from the three graces shouted words
Stood on top of the altar stone in mist and in rain with three flames lit
The thunder stone shone down on Haworth
and the light was split into thirds
Thunder and thunder and thunder and words

The Redemption of Ceit Mhor illustration by Stephanie Rodriguez

THE REDEMPTION OF CEIT MHOR

by Kay Fairhurst Adkins

Palm Springs, California, USA

This story was originally published in the Fall 2014 edition of The Searcher, a publication of the Southern California Genealogical Society. While not specifically Brontë-related, it is a true story of my family and I like to think it is the kind of tale Tabby would have enjoyed telling.

* * *

Gather round the fire, me kith and kin, an' I will tell ye a story. As ye noticed, there were an extra plate at table tonight, as there will be every nicht during this week o' the full moon, for November is the month o' the Mourning Moon, a time to remember those who came afore us.

Tonight, we will right a wrong done long ago to ain of our very own. A wrong that has placed unwonted shame deep into the bones of our line from Ceit Mhor, of whom I will speak, down through her son Alexander MacKenzie, tae his son, Alistair Og MacKenzie, tae his daughter Isabella MacKenzie, tae her daughter Mary Matheson, tae her daughter Mary McRae, tae her daughter Elizabeth Raymond, tae her daughter Alice Megaw, and on tae me. As the line ends with no cradle ever gracing my home, the wrong will die out here as well, but not without first having the full light of truth shone upon it so it may shrivel an' die of it's ain falseness.

I have seen photographs of the eternal resting places of both Reverend Lachlan Mackenzie and of Ceit Mhor. A great stone slab tells all who come that the late Minister of Lochcarron died on the 20th of April, 1819, in the 37th year of his ministry. His simplicity of manners, his vivid imagination, and his holy unction in his ministrations are praised. At the end of his life, he is praised in the churches and mourned by his parish.

It tells nothing of his cruel use of that imagination to hound and persecute, as he did to our very own Ceit Mhor. Her resting place has no headstone or formal marker to honor her life and mourn her death. Buried in a ruined churchyard, there is a modern signpost over her grave with her name. Better that the site remain unmarked both by headstone and by the visitors who come to gawk at the resting place of the wicked sinner brought to God through the godly Minister of Lochcarron.

For that is the tale they celebrate even today as "The Wonderful Conversion of Muckle Kate", for Muckle Kate she was, or Big Kate as some would call her. As recently as March 2013, this tale shows up in print as an example that even the worst of sinners can be saved by God's grace. The Reverend Mr. Lachlan called her "An ill-looking woman without any beauty in the sight of God and man." She is touted as having "very masculine dimensions" and is accused of having 'been guilty of every forbidden crime in the Law of God, except for murder." This Muckle Kate they speak of is fearsome indeed and none of the Minister's appeals can reach her.

But the Reverend Lachlan is uncommonly canny and devises a plan to reach her conscience. A pamphlet called 'Muckle Kate, or Sovereign Grace: Much More Abounding' first promulgated the story. So far as I can tell, the original pamphlet is lost to us, but the damage caused by it and by Mr. Lachlan carries on.

The author of 'Muckle Kate' explains "It was customary among the Highlander to meet at nightfall in each other's houses, and spend the long evenings in singing Gaelic melodies. The women brought with them their distaffs and spindles, while the men mended their brogues or weaved baskets and creels. This was called 'going on ceilidh'."

So far as we know, this is the only sin she is directly accused of. Going on ceilidh. All other sins are merely hinted at. The Reverend Lachlan, "knowing this, and having a turn for rhyming, composed a Gaelic song in which all Kate's known sins were enumerated and lashed with all the severity of which the composer was capable. This song Mr. Lachlan set to music, and sending for some persons who were known to 'go on ceilidh' with Kate he taught them the song and instructed them to sing it in her hearing on the first opportunity.'"

The legend states that Kate was stricken upon hearing the song when it was first sung in her hearing, leading immediately to agony. Full awareness of her sins came upon her as God "drove the truth right home to her heart". The words of the Reverend's song are lost, but according to the story, Muckle Kate acquires a conscience. In remorse over her many alleged sins, she takes to wandering, goes blind, and is driven mad by guilt. The pamphlet states that "She was a "wonder to many," as well she might be, for at her age, between 80 and 90, it is rare to see a person called by grace."

Aye, Ceit Mhor was well into her 80's when Reverend Lachlan turned his satiric wit to torment her by training the young folk of the village to taunt her with his hateful song.

The way they tell it, it all fits nicely into a pamphlet and makes a fine story for the Church Gazette. But that is not the whole story. For most folk, second sight is not a mystical gift, but the ability to look farther than most people bother to set their gaze. So I ask, what would make an 80 year old woman such a target for Reverend Lachlan's vitriol?

This information is obtained from Christopher & Donald MacKenzie and their niece Cathie MacRae of Ardelve, Scotland. They are descendents of Ceit Mhor's grandson Alistair Og MacKenzie whose croft, Craigmhore, still stands. They are descended from his son, Christopher, while my descent is through Alistair Og's daughter Isabella MacKenzie. In a letter dated 20 June 1985, they tell that Ceit Mhor was widowed early in life and left with two sons.

They write of a Mrs. MacRae whose uncle was neighbor to a niece of Reverend Lachlan Mackenzie. This niece lived in the Manse for some years during Mr. Lachlan's time and knew Ceit Mhor. She recalled Ceit Mhor as "a patient, intelligent, kind-hearted, tall, large featured woman, who was independent in her ways and manner. Loneliness, sorrow, and poverty were her lot for much of her life."

That is the woman ridiculed by a Minister of God and set forth as the wickedest sinner. It seems that his niece knew more of Christian charity than did he.

So why did the Minister Lachlan, so loved and admired by the time of his death in 1819, hound poor, widowed Ceit Mhor?

Being born in 1754, Lachlan Mackenzie only knew life in the Highlands as it was well after the Jacobite Risings ended in 1746, but Ceit Mhor's long life took her through most of the turbulent 18th Century. We don't know the exact dates of Ceit Mhor's birth or death, but a wee bit of figuring can give us an idea. Reverend Lachlan's gravestone states that he died in 1819 in the 37th year of his ministry, so his ministry lasted from 1782 to 1819. All are agreed that Ceit Mhor was in her mid eighties at the time of this conversion. Thus, she was likely born sometime between 1697 and 1734. We know her grandson Alistair Og was born in 1877 and have a statement that Ceit Mhor was widowed young. That leads us to the likelihood that she was born around 1730. There is a possibility that we are missing a generation and that Alistair Og was actually her great grandson. This would put her birth closer to 1710.

The Jacobite risings attempted to return King James and the House of Stuart to the throne, and pitted the Highland supporters of the rightful King against the English and the Lowland English sympathizers. In the wake of the uprisings came punitive laws to break the Highlander of his ways and to bring peace – a peace enforced by armed soldiers who disparaged the old ways of the Highlands.

Jacobites who had raised arms against the King of England were imprisoned or executed. Their estates were forfeited, and their land and money went to the King. The clan system was dismantled and weapons were confiscated. England knew she needed to break the back of the Highland culture if she wanted to end the threat of Jacobite risings once and for all. The signature Tartan cloth of the clans was outlawed along with playing of pipes, unauthorized gatherings, teaching Gaelic, and singing traditional songs. The first offense of wearing Highland garb meant imprisonment for six months without bail; a second offense could lead to transportation to the colonies.

But is this cultural changing of the guard reason enough to harass a poor aged woman? No. With her advanced years, patience alone would see Ceit Mhor to her grave. There was something more. Something beyond the regular ministerial zeal to save souls, though a reading of "The Wonderful Conversion of Muckle Kate" would not lead you to that conclusion.

In that pamphlet, Revered Lachlan takes Muckle Kate "kindly by the hand," leading her through the crowd to the Communion Table. Family lore, as passed verbally to my mother during a visit to Craigmore, says otherwise. At roughly 85 years of age, blind Ceit Mhor was forced by Reverend Lachlan to crawl on her knees down the crowded aisle of the church to publicly beg forgiveness at the altar, demeaning herself before him in front of his entire congregation.

Reverend Lachlan was known to despise moderates among ministers, saying that "there would be streets in Hell paved with the heads of graceless ministers". In fact, three members of the Presbytery of Lochcarron recognized the danger of his zealotry and held back his license for over a year. As written in the "Brief Memoir of the Rev. Lachlan Mackenzie, composed by his sister, Anne Mackenzie", the ministers who stood in her brother's way did so out of jealousy. Only after their unexpected deaths was Reverend Lachlan licensed as a

Minister, with people of the neighborhood feeling that they had better not cross him lest they meet with an untimely end themselves.

Reverend Lachlan intensely desired to put an end to the "barbarous practices" which prevailed in the Highlands, and made his parishioners sign a list of rules to ensure that they be "more orderly in going to church and returning home on the Sabbath, as well as at burials." Rules to abstain from drinking at burials, rules to inform against anyone suspected of drinking at meeting, rules to go home immediately after sermon without any conversations in the churchyard, rules to suppress any habit or practice contrary to the word of God.

Rule 5 stands out. "That if any of us, through slavish fear or a desire to gratify an appetite, shall break through any of these resolutions, he shall be reckoned infamous." And that is precisely what he did through his song of Muckle Kate. He took the large, kind, independent woman who had already lived through a lifetime of repressive rules designed to crush her beloved Highland culture, a woman who freely enjoyed going on ceilidh and celebrating the culture that had been outlawed through much of her life, and made of her an example. For if he wouldn't hesitate to crush a poor, blind, elderly woman, what wouldn't he do to the other parishioners?

An' now, my darlin's, 'tis time for bed. My tale is told an' a long buried truth has seen the light o' day. For the first time in many a long year, our ain Ceit Mhor lies peaceably at rest in her grave while the Reverend Lachlan is beginnin' to squirm in his. I feel it in me bones.

Terror Made Me Cruel

The Lonely Ghost illustration by Julie Rose

THE LONELY GHOST

By E A France-Sergeant
Wigan, England

The thunder roars,
The lightning strikes,
The dead awake
In the unquiet earth that night
A lonely girl all alone,
Awakes and thinks of home
Where is my mother dear?
How did I get here?

It is the end of October and she only has one night.
On the road she wanders in front of the car headlights
If you take this girl home,
She will never get there
1 mile before Haworth she will disappear

She can get no further than the place she died,
forever bound to wander
An unquiet spirit is she
On the 31st of October, All Hallows Eve,
On the road to Haworth a ghost you will see.

PARANORMAL EXPERIENCES

The Dutch Don't Believe in Ghosts illustration by Barb Tanke

THE DUTCH DON'T BELIEVE IN GHOSTS

(A TRUE STORY)
by Maria van Mastrigt
Netherlands

It was the spring of 1985...after my divorce I had made up my mind to follow my heart and finally move to the 'Land of Hope and Glory', having been inspired by this Vera Lynn song since time and memory began for me, somewhere during the early sixties. Always this fascination with England. Added to that was my love and passion for Jane Eyre, which I read for the first time some years later when I was about eleven years of age, followed by everything Brontë related. I read from then on, with Mrs. Gaskell's *Life of Charlotte Brontë* being my main guide.

I had visited Haworth and the Parsonage once in the winter of 1983. I did not know what to expect at all, but I certainly had not expected to fall head over heels in love with the place the way I did! The Parsonage, the village, the moors and the people - everything about it had me in its grip and still has till this very day. It was a strange sensation and I did not quite know what to do with it, till shortly after my divorce a year later. I made up my mind...I was going to Haworth to start a new life!

And so I arrived...on the 4th of April 1985. I knew no one, had no connections at all in the UK. The only thing I had was a little room I'd booked for a long period at Keeper's Cottage, a B&B just off Main Street, directly behind the Kings Arms in a place called The Fold. It was a tiny place, one up one down, with one loo and one shower to share between me and the woman living downstairs, named Loraine. She and I became friends soon enough and she was a wonderful introduction to Haworth for me as she knew quite a few of the locals and had plenty of stories to tell. Sadly, we failed to keep in touch later on in life as we both moved away and did our own thing. It just goes like that sometimes, but I often wonder where she is and how she is getting on these days.

The cottage we shared is the last in a row of centuries-old cottages, tucked away in a narrow cul de sac and overlooking the terrace at the back of the Kings Arms pub. The gable end is only a few yards away from St Michael and All Angels church, where all the Brontës, bar one (Anne) lay buried beneath one of the pillars inside the church. Inside

415

my little antiquated room you could hear the church bells every hour and every half an hour, loud and clear. Normally that would have made me want to leave the place before long as I like my peace and quiet, but as it was our much worshipped Brontë church, I just loved it and it made me want to stay there forever. Though at night those bells would sometimes sound so eerie, it could easily speak to the imagination, if you were that way inclined.

Haworth is a very old place as you know. I believe it goes back to the 13th century. As we have learned in this book, there are plenty of ghosts and ghost stories to be had. Now the Dutch in general like a good spooky story, but we don't necessarily believe in them. I for one certainly didn't live my life in fear of ever seeing one. I loved my new environment and soon felt at ease in this ancient village stroke town and in that tiny old cottage which had been built long before the Brontës ever set foot in the place. That cottage was now called after Emily's dog Keeper, like so many other places in Haworth these days are called after or make reference to the Brontës, their books or their pets. It truly felt like a safe haven...at least it did for the first few months of my stay!

Now I knew there were quite a few folkloristic ghost stories around Haworth and its surroundings. The Gytrash for instance, a legendary big black dog which can take on various shapes, waiting for lonely travelers on gloomy and desolate moorland paths being the most famous one, since it was mentioned in *Jane Eyre*. That highly gothic yet romantic scene, when dog Pilot rushes past, horse Mesrour slips and Rochester and Jane clap eyes on each other for the very first time. Okay, I'm telling it a bit tongue in cheek, but it really is one of the finest moments in this book of books to my mind.

Another, perhaps less well known ghost story with a link to *Jane Eyre* is the one where a man on horseback is heard or seen approximately once a year at Wycoller Hall, which is just short of an eight mile walk from Haworth. Nowadays a ruin, the late 16th century manor house in the village of Wycoller, just over the Yorkshire/ Lancashire border, is said to be the inspiration for Ferndean Hall. Also of interest is that one of the former occupants, Elizabeth Cunliffe, became Elizabeth Eyre through marriage.

I'm hoping that other authors of this book with much more local knowledge than I, will take on these stories in much greater detail as they are certainly of interest to the history of the area and so much part of the Brontë novels. I'm only writing them down as these were the first stories I became familiar with during these first months of my moving to Haworth. It seems to me however, but please correct me if I'm wrong, that in modern days the Gytrash has lost ground altogether, whereas the Wycoller ghost is still going strong, or at least it was in those days, the mid eighties of the last century. These are certainly not the only stories, though...I learned of plenty more later on....the area is riddled with spirits, good and bad! Some stories may be forgotten; others survived and still speak to the imagination of the locals.

Reader (!), I hope you feel the tension building up now, as I'm reaching the part where I will be telling you my own personal story with a meeting of an energy from another time, from another sphere and matter to our own.

I spent my days looking for jobs mainly, but there was also plenty of time left to do as I pleased, to go and explore my new surroundings. That particular day started so well, with beautiful sunshine and the promise that it would stay like that all day long. I had written some application letters and made my way to the bookshop on top of Main Street to ask if I could stay at their B&B the next week for a fortnight or so. When I had booked my room at The Fold I was told that I could not stay those weeks due to an earlier reservation, so I needed to move out for that short period. I managed to book the room, not realising at that moment in time what an important move that would turn out to be and how that place and the people living there would later become the centre of my universe for the rest of my life spent living in Haworth... Anyway, we move on!

Later that morning I decided to go for one of my long walks. Top Withens being my aim that day, I packed some lunch and a bottle of water bought at Southams (some of you will remember) and off I toodled. Well, I made it to the famous Brontë Falls and Bridge. The sky had been radiant blue with only a few little white clouds here and there, but by the time I reached the waterfall the sky had changed altogether. Looking towards Top Withens and Lancashire beyond there, I could see dark clouds had started to form and they would definitely be heading my way. So I decided not to go over the Brontë Bridge and started on my way back to the village instead. I could hear the rumbling in the distance and I got quite scared of the approaching thunderstorm as it started to rain. There was nowhere to hide. Any moment now I could be struck by lightning, which had always been one of my fears. Now, I'm not a natural runner, but for the first time in my life I ran all the way to the safety of Haworth and my sweet little room at Keeper's Cottage.

It had been quite an eventful day, finished off over a beer at the Kings together with Loraine, but not more than one as neither of us could afford it and I wasn't a great beer drinker then, anyway. When I eventually went to bed, I felt exhausted but happy and before I knew it, I fell into a wonderful deep sleep. I don't remember dreaming or even hearing the 'eerie' church bells, as I was just too tired.

It must have been way after midnight when all of a sudden I seemed to feel something tugging at my blanket. I will never know if I really felt that or if it was just a sensation, a spiritual warning that something was going on that shouldn't be going on. It all happened in a few seconds, but the brain can do an awful lot in a short amount of time when in a dangerous situation. I woke up immediately and became aware that there was someone in my room!!! I turned around and saw...I just really saw this oval shape hovering next to my bed. A grey, misty, hazy, transparent oval shape, with the face of an old woman in the centre, just like a portrait in an oval frame. The face was just as grey and transparent as the oval shape surrounding it. She had long grey hair hanging down over her shoulders. It all happened so quickly, but I can still see this image now. I believe, nay I'm *certain* I screamed at it and reached for the switch of my bedside light. The moment I turned it on the ghost was poof, gone! WHAT ON EARTH WAS THAT ALL ABOUT? You can imagine that the light stayed on after that and that there was no way of me going back to sleep again that night.

I did not know what to make of it at all! Was it just a dream? A figment of my imagination? To me it was very, very real. The only little fantasy I had was that I wondered for a short while if it was Charlotte, herself, my heroine...but no, the woman I saw was too old to be any of the Brontës. It was just a silly little notion, plain wishful thinking. If it had been her, I would for the rest of my life utterly regret that I had switched on that light, as I'm sure you can all imagine.

The next morning I could not wait to tell my friend Loraine about the events of that night. Over coffee I told her what had happened. Much to my surprise, she told me that this was not the first time things had gone bump in the night upstairs, but that she had not told me about it before as she did not want to frighten me. Oh my God! It meant that my experience was now definitely not a dream, but my little lovely room was a haunted room?! Would I ever be safe again? It turned out that the adult son of our landlady never dared to go up to that room at all, as he was highly sensitive to anything supernatural and he felt there was something going on upstairs.

Loraine also told me a story of a woman who had left the room in the middle of the night and gone home because of a similar experience to mine. Holy guacamole, what to do with that piece of information? The only little bit of light relief was that, according to Loraine, it only happened about once a year and...if it happened again I could wake her up. That made all the difference, of course (though I'm not sure why!) and I decided to stay a while longer. Only I never dared to sleep again with the lights off for the rest of my stay there and I never saw the ghost again.

* * *

Three years or so later I lived with my new partner at Lumbfoot, a little hamlet between Haworth and Stanbury. One evening we got a visit from Sue, our friend and neighbour there, and she asked me if I wanted to meet a friend who was staying with her. As by total chance, this woman had just told her a very similar story to mine when she once stayed at Keeper's Cottage. More proof for me that my ghost was real! She had indeed seen the ghost of a woman sitting in a chair in the corner of the room. I can't sadly remember any specifics, only that she was not the same person Loraine told me about who had once left the room in the middle of the night.

You may all wonder who this ghost of a woman was? Well, so do I! I cannot tell you much about her, only that I learned from another befriended local person at the time, an elderly lady named Rachel who lived just above the White Lion and opposite The Fold, that there used to be a washerwoman living there and it was supposed to be her ghost. According to Rachel it was that long ago, that she might even have known the Brontës. Now, whether or not that is true? I don't know....I leave it with you! As for me, I quite like the idea.

I hope you enjoyed my story and if you ever stay at this cottage and meet my ghost, please let me know.

He'd Crush You Like A Sparrow's Egg

Haunted Homestead illustration by Barb Tanke

HAUNTED HOMESTEAD

by Barb Tanke Regency
Western New York, USA

"Hey Dad, why are all these books laying here in the middle of the floor?"

"You know Barb, I just saw the damndest thing. They were flying off the bookshelf on their own."

I had just come home from school and walking towards the center room of our house noticed a pile of books in the middle of the room on the carpet. Our bookshelves covered the main wall. As I walked through that room and around the corner into the living room questioning my dad, I found him as white as a ghost; which was a bit unnerving for a teenager at the time. Several weeks later, my sister was studying and sitting on a small couch in front of the bookcase in the same room. She was startled when each encyclopedia started to fall off the shelf one at a time. These were heavy books. She stood up and looked at the shelving, thinking it was collapsing. It wasn't. We could not figure out what was happening.

These were just two incidents of odd activity in our house while growing up back in the 1960s/70s. We lived in a two-story farmhouse built in 1890 on what was originally Native American Indian land. The gravel road in front of our house had been an Indian path. My father and aunt had also grown up in the same house and my grandparents worked the land with hired farmhands with land below the house that bordered a creek. My father repurchased his homestead as an adult in 1961 where we lived until 1977. Because it was original farmland, my grandfather would hire young men in need of work and one of these men was Hans, a man from Denmark. He was only planning to stay a short season, but ended up staying with my grandparents until the day he died at age 40 and is buried next to them in our church cemetery. As was customary at the time, funerals/wakes were held inside the home. In this case, the central room of our house or living room was where Hans was laid out for his wake when he passed away. So after the bookcase incidents, we just laughed it off as "It must be Hans" whenever we couldn't explain something.

In 1974, we held a large 50th anniversary party for my grandparents on the property. I was away at college getting my art degree, and my mom and sister asked me to design an invitation. I decided to draw the house as it appeared in 1924 for the front of the invitation. I sent my mom and sister two copies and much to my dismay, they thought one copy should be colorized and got out their color pencils (I wasn't too happy about that). They placed the invitations on the bookcase and stepped back to get a better look to help decide. Immediately one of the invitations shot right off the shelf past them. Surprised and bewildered, they looked to see if the window was open or a possible incoming draft. Nothing. It was as if someone slapped the invitation with the back of their hand. "Ok Hans. I guess he likes this one" and shrugged it off.

Off the central room was the staircase leading upstairs to three bedrooms. My bedroom was the first room at the top of the stairs on the right. Sometimes at night I would hear creaking, footsteps, or some strange noise that always unnerved me. No one else seemed to hear anything. One night I had an odd dream of something active, like energy, circling around the ceiling of my room past my head, which made a whooshing sound. I could see it – it was white-ish in color. Honestly, I don't know what it was. My sister's room was across the hallway and with our doors open, she woke one night to see me stand straight up on my bed, and walk off the end. I woke with a bruise the next morning with no memory of doing it.

One night my parents and my sister and I were returning from dinner. As we came into the kitchen area, we heard the washing machine running. The washer was behind louvered doors off the kitchen. My dad opened the doors and turned the machine off. He said "That's funny. How could it be running without the water turned on?"

Fast forward to 2012. New owners had now been in the house since 1978. I drove by the house one day and noticed that the huge tree on the front lawn was being taken down. I got very emotional. I used to play with my Barbie doll at the base of that tree as a child. When I saw the tree being cut down, I decided to write the new owner a note. She responded saying that it also upset her to have to make the decision to take it down, as it had been struck by lightning and rotted out. From that point, she and I kept up a steady stream of communication and one day she invited my sister and I to return to the homestead to see it again. We sat in our old kitchen reminiscing, and then the topic got back to activity in the house and "ghosts". She told us several instances of her dog growling and not staying in the central room or kitchen area; a daylight photo of a large orb on her outer porch; and her son's memory of waking (in my old bedroom) as if someone was choking

422

him. I asked "Ever hear anything on the stairs?" She said "Yes, I would wake to hear sounds of movement on the stairway at night." We both agreed on that activity and then to make light of her son's memory, I said "Well, maybe it is a pissed off Indian that doesn't like men" who was choking her son. We agreed and laughed it off.

As my sister and I walked through the house after so many years, it all appeared so much smaller. Strange to see how your perception changes from childhood to adulthood. She took us upstairs and I noticed the antique hinge on my bedroom door. It was so amazing to see that again. Memories started flooding in. My room looked the same, despite the change in bed location. As she and my sister walked around the corner to my parent's old room, I decided to just snap a photo of the staircase descending down to the central room, and went in to join the girls. "Wow! There is the original wallpaper!" I gasped. The owner mentioned she could never get it off the wall and left it. Down in the corner was the small door to the attic, which would vibrate each time anyone would go into the room. "Hans is hiding" we would laugh. When we finished and headed downstairs to leave, I walked out of the central room and turned and yelled "Goodbye ghosts!" and laughed.

When I got home and looked through my digitals, something caught my eye. The photo of the staircase showed a solid white orb at the bottom of the stairs. Shocked, I sent the photo to the owner. Maybe Hans wanted to see me again?

During the same time, I happened to run into the owner's husband at the post office. Before leaving, I asked "Any activity?" He said "Well, Yeah. One night my wife was out of town and about 11:30, I woke to hear a loud noise in the central room. I yelled "Who's there?! Get out of here!! The master bedroom is downstairs where they sleep and just off the central room and through their bedroom is a doorway that leads into another living area (what was originally an apartment built on). He continued and said "I thought someone was in the house, and then it was as if a person was actually walking into the bedroom and I felt a strong breeze go past me and through the apartment door."

As of 2020, the owners and I have remained friends. Just recently during the pandemic, she mentioned how she was on her back porch and her dog, being outside, started barking and growling at her while she stood there. He had never done that before. Her husband also mentioned that when their daughter recently visited and slept downstairs on the sofa, she was uneasy at night hearing creaking footsteps and felt someone was in the room walking back and forth past her, into the central room.

To date, the house has not been investigated nor do the owners want it made public. Perhaps they may sell the house one day, and as they have lived in peace it isn't worth digging into further and they just shrug off any activity. One note I forgot to mention was that another farmhand had died in the well on the property when it was a working farm. Maybe he and Hans and the Indian just want someone's attention?

The Nursery Window Photo by Maggie Gardiner

THE NURSERY WINDOW
MY STRANGE GHOSTLY ENCOUNTERS
WITH THE BRONTËS
A True Story by Maggie Gardiner
Haworth, UK

It was a cold, dark and damp December evening when I ventured up Haworths' famous cobblestones on my way to the Parsonage. The rain was lashing down, the wind wrestling for control of my umbrella as I sidestepped the emerging puddles.

I decided to cut through the churchyard and as I walked up the slippery stone steps, I noticed a single spotlight creating an eerie glow across the ancient tombstones. Moths danced, mesmerized by the light. The Parsonage twinkled in the background as it waited patiently to welcome its evening visitors.

Jackdaws chattering on the naked ebony branches suddenly started squawking, annoyed perhaps that I interrupted their bedtime stories. I quickly moved on. I had really been looking forward to this weekend, an early Christmas present to myself, a treat, a Brontë Treasures evening followed by a candlelit walk around the Parsonage.

Prosecco supped, the visitors were ushered into the library. We listened intently to the passionate tones of the curator, excited that we were able to experience a myriad of items with connections to the Brontës. I peppered the curator with questions; patiently and gracefully she answered all.

Throughout the evening I found myself easily distracted by the haunting sounds of the whistling wind and, from the corner of my eye, the spindly, ebony tree branches swaying against the library window. It made me think of Emily alone on the wintery moors.

When the talk came to an end, we were all released to experience the Parsonage by candlelight. It was quite an experience. With the main lights dimmed and the artificial candlelight flickering, I walked into the Kitchen.

Immediately I felt a cold chill seep deep into my bones and an icy draft as if someone had walked straight through me.

It was a very unnerving feeling as I walked on through the rest of the house. The bedroom window shutters were open and we could all appreciate the magnificent view of St Michael and All Angels, its ghostly churchyard glowing mysteriously. Within the house the clicking sound of lots of photographs being taken and the distant murmurings from satisfied visitors could be heard.

I was the first and only person on the upper floor level, yet I could hear footsteps in the main exhibition room. I followed the sound to see who was there. When I looked into the room it was empty.

I had a feeling it was going to be one of those strange nights, something was happening that just couldn't be explained away.

I went back to the nursery and took a photograph of the room looking out of the window and onto the Churchyard. At the time, I hadn't noticed anything unusual in the children's room, but later that evening I would be astonished.

After the obligatory thank you's and goodbyes, I made my way back down the cobblestones to the guest house. Once I was in my room, happily reminiscing, I started to look through my photographs to choose which ones would end up on Facebook. When I came across the photograph of the nursery I was shocked and amazed to see a number of blurry faces in the window panes, both male and female.

The most prominent was a side profile of what looked like the fragment from the destroyed gun portrait (either Emily or Anne depending on whose research you believe). On closer look there were other shadowy female images as well as grainy male features.

I couldn't quite believe what I was seeing. Surely it must be a reflection of an image from either a portrait hanging in the nursery or on the upstairs landing? I would have to go back to the Parsonage in the morning to investigate.

I then placed the photograph on Facebook and asked people to comment on what they could see. The response was overwhelming, confirming it wasn't just a figment of my overactive imagination. The next morning I visited the Parsonage and went upstairs to the nursery. There were no portraits or any items which could have accounted for the faces in the window.

I spoke to staff and told them about my experiences of the night before and showed them my photograph. They were all very excited to view it.

So, this is my story. Did the Brontës show their presence that evening or was it all just a trick of the light? Reader, you must decide.

Our Night at the Black Bull Photos by Jacqueline Ploeg

OUR NIGHT AT THE BLACK BULL

by Jacqueline Ploeg
Brisbane, Queensland, Australia

When I went to Haworth with my husband (Theo) and daughter (Maleea) in 2017, we stayed at Branwell's old stomping ground: The Black Bull Pub/Hotel on the Main Street. We had a lovely night and it wasn't very busy so the owners had time to chat to us about everything Brontë-related. At about 11pm we thought it was time to go to bed and upstairs there are 3 rooms. One room they didn't use at that moment so it was perfect for us that we could use the 2 other rooms available. We checked out the rooms to see what they were like and when we walked into one of them, Theo said: 'Maleea, which room would you like to stay in?' and she decided that the one we were standing in was okay, so we chose the other one. So far so good.

The next morning Theo and I came down for breakfast in the pub and Maleea was already there. Her face was white as a sheet, so we asked her what was the matter, didn't she sleep well, etc. She said that she was watching TV in bed last night and all of a sudden the back of her neck and shoulders went really cold and she couldn't move. She sat in her bed like a statue and she could hear a scream in her head. She didn't know what to do and didn't want to leave the bed to come to us and didn't want to make a sound. So she sat there until the uncomfortable feeling and the cold went away. She tried to relax and eventually dozed off a few times, but as soon as it became daylight, she got up.

She is quite a 'no-nonsense and down to earth' person and didn't panic but she was pretty scared. So when we told the lady who owns the pub the story, she said: 'Well, I didn't want to tell you last night but the story goes that apparently a maid was murdered in room 3 (Maleea's room) upstairs hundreds of years ago and people have heard voices or have seen a shadow, etc.'

Lots of people who hear these stories don't believe it, but Maleea thought it was quite an experience. She found it interesting as well, but would not want to stay there again. Her room was facing the graveyard and the church and further up there was the Parsonage. People say that, because of the elements over the years, hundreds of bodies from the graveyard may have slipped down the hill and now lie under the pub (keep in mind that there are about 40.000 bodies in the graveyard).

Later, Theo said that when he entered that room the night before, "Something made me feel uncomfortable, so I was much happier to stay in the other room." Our room was great, nice atmosphere and facing the Main Street. We slept well and it was really comfortable. Poor Maleea.

We would love to go back to Haworth, but I think we will be staying in a different B&B next time .....

The Murdered Do Haunt Their Murderers

Ghostly Experiences illustration by JoJo Hughes

GHOSTLY EXPERIENCES

by Leonore Blacklock.

UK

I fell in love with Haworth at a very early age and ever after would persuade my parents to go there for day trips or holidays. You can therefore imagine my delight when they announced we were going to move there.

We were living in Norfolk at the time and drove up one weekend, armed with property details from various estate agents. They were all lovely properties but not what we wanted. Feeling despondent we headed back to the car; it was then we noticed a Victorian terrace cottage with a 'for sale' sign. We made enquiries and were told it had just gone on the market, would we like a viewing? We fell in love with it instantly and set the wheels in motion to purchase it.

Our plan was to get everything delivered to the new property and to stay with relatives in Lancashire, travelling over daily to unpack, assemble furniture etc. So at the end of a long and tiring day we waved goodbye to the removal men and headed over the border.

Next day we arrived back at the house for an early start, but no sooner had we entered the dining room, when my Mother stopped dead and said something was wrong - the boxes had been moved. My Father and I were not too sure, but he changed all the locks just in case.

By the end of the week we were ready to move in and the last item to be assembled was my pride and joy - a cabin bed. That night I pulled the curtains closed and settled down for a good night's sleep.

I awoke in the early hours to hear someone in bare feet running along the landing and a girlish giggle. It sounded too young for my Mother, but I made a mental note to ask her about it in the morning and went back to sleep.

It wasn't my Mother! Perhaps I'd been dreaming? That night I slept soundly but Mother was kept awake by someone running along the landing and going up the attic stairs.

Our nocturnal visitor came most nights and during the day it sounded like a dog running up the stairs to the first floor. Then things started to escalate! Being keen on crafts I always had some project on the go - if I put my scissors down they would disappear for days and turn up in odd places. Dad would be doing some DIY project round the house and his tools would also go AWOL. We just learnt to have spares to hand!

A few months later I bought a German Shepherd dog I named Max and he would sleep in my room at night. One morning the curtains of the bed gently parted and I reached down and felt Max's wet nose and furry muzzle. "Morning Max" I said as I threw open the curtains - only Max wasn't there. He was fast asleep by the door!

Max had the run of the house but he never ventured into the attic bedroom. I had to go up there one day and somehow persuaded him to follow. As soon as he reached the top of the stairs his hackles rose and he started growling at the corner of the room. The growls turned to snarls and he broke into to a sweat, absolutely terrified by whatever he could see. I couldn't call him away so I had to drag him down the stairs by the collar.

Mother would hang her necklaces from the dressing table mirror - one day she found them all tied together in knots, it took us ages to separate them. Then my late Grandmother's earrings went missing - pretty, blue china flowers which Mum kept in a little box. We practically turned the bedroom upside down looking for them and I was on my hands and knees checking under the furniture - no sign. A few months later they turned up broken in the middle of the bedroom floor.

I think that was the last straw for Mother and we went along to 'Spooks' on the Main Street to ask if anyone could help. The chap said he could recommend a medium, but when we told Dad he was against it as he didn't want to make matters worse.

A few years later Dad had a mild heart attack on the moors and Max guided him home. The hills were now too much for him and it was decided to put the house up for sale and leave Haworth.

On our last day in the house we all sat discussing the ghostly goings on when Dad dropped a bombshell - he'd seen the figure of a man standing outside my bedroom door! Quite tall in stature, the figure was dark with no discernible facial features but wearing a top hat and had a large white collar like a vicar.

Once unpacked in our new home I found my Brontë books and a picture of the Reverend Patrick. I showed it to my Father who was stunned - that looked like the figure he saw, especially the large white collar (cravat). I should point out that my Father was in no way interested in the Brontës and I don't think had ever ventured into the Museum.

I'm not saying it was Patrick he saw, but as the cottage was built in 1855 he could have visited there on parochial duties. Maybe it could have been Arthur Nicolls or a fellow curate?

A few years ago I became acquainted with the present owner of our old house. I hadn't even mentioned our ghostly experiences when she told me of the ghostly children who ran up and down the stairs at night!

May You Not Rest As Long As I Am Living!

Keepers of the Truth illustration by Barb Tanke

KEEPERS OF THE TRUTH

by Danette Eggleston Camponeschi
Maryland, USA

Halloween, Halloween,
Apples a-bob,
Elves at the key-hole
And Imps at the hob.

Bolt and bar the door,
Draw the curtains tight.
Wise folk are in before
The moon-rise tonight!
~Molly Capes

I believe that much of what was told by the fireside in the oral tradition was true. I know that this story -- my ghost story -- is true. *I know that ghosts have wandered the earth.*

This is a story for the fireside on a cold, dark night. It should be told in late autumn, as the chill begins to creep through the cracks and we shiver for scary delights. Or it might be told in the dead of winter, when the darkness is thick and the frosty air envelops our brains so we're driven inside to seek warmth and diversion.

It's best told when the wind is tap, tap, tapping on the window like a cold, stiff finger begging to get in; a reminder of a tortured soul reaching out from beyond the grave. When shadows from the fire in a dark room are flickering and dancing like little evil men, inebriated and ready for mischief. When every sound sparks the imagination until we're sure that somewhere (just above, in the attic, perhaps?) there's a crazy inmate struggling to get out and wreak havoc.

This tale is best told in an old cottage. It should, perhaps, be set in a bleak and forbidding expanse where the wind whistles and howls around the windows and the night is blacker than pitch, no other humans for miles and only the moorland creatures for company. Or, perhaps, the old cottage is set amongst the graves of old; a constant reminder of mortality where a mournful, decaying whisper seeps into anything within reach.

This story is best told by an old woman who is work-weary, grateful for time to sit and rest her bones in a snug kitchen deep in the recesses of that old cottage. A scrubbed pine table sits atop cold, stone floors and the odors of the evening meal and the hearth smoke linger. In the shadows of the room crockery sits atop shelves like sentinels keeping watch; the back door is shut tight against whatever may lurk on the other side. The bread-kneading and clothes-scrubbing and rug-beating are done for another day.

The old woman should be like Tabby, telling tales that are older than anyone would believe. Tales that should be savored and retold, and then -- because they are worthy -- repeated down through generations. Like Tabby, the old woman should believe that she knows folks who have seen fairies. She is a Christian and yet a believer of the ancient ways.

These old women were keepers of the truth, embellishers of the truth and, ultimately, they were entertainers on those long, dark evenings. They told tall tales, folklore, bits of wisdom, and, yes, ghost stories. They told the stories that were told to them. They had long memories, and they knew how to speak so listeners were drawn in and then mesmerized. This tale, my frightful ghost story, should be told like this.

And while our time of horror might look very different from theirs, we are getting a glimpse into what many generations before us felt in times of isolation, times of dread, times of terror of the unknown and of transmitted disease. When shut inside during our own time of horror -- while the world sleeps and waits and holds its collective breath -- we continue the tradition of storytelling in our own way, keeping the truth alive and the imagination flourishing. We pass the time and turn inward. With our own stories and poems, created during this time of human separation, this time of pause and fright, we're coming together to honor the old women, the truth-keepers.

So here is my little story, my contribution. This tale is true; it really did happen to me. I know that ghosts have wandered the earth.

This time I can be the old woman telling the story by the fire...

* * *

It was a chilly autumn day two decades ago in Gettysburg, Pennsylvania, USA. The weekend of October 6th, to be exact. Visiting this historic place where one of the bloodiest battles of the United States Civil War was fought, I was awed and humbled as I thought about all that had happened here during those hot July days in 1863. Because I know my ancestors fought at Gettysburg, serving alongside their comrades-in-arms for the Co. H., 24th Virginia Infantry, I felt a strange kinship with this place. And, despite what happened to me there, I know I always will.

It was a trip (only 45 minutes from home) for my husband and I to celebrate our tenth wedding anniversary. A weekend away to explore, relax and be pampered in a Gettysburg inn. That Saturday evening, as we weren't far from home, my long-time friend and her husband met us for dinner in the old, quaint inn where we were staying. The inn existed in Gettysburg at the time of that fateful battle. Its walls, indeed its very atmosphere, saturated with the past and that horrific battle.

As the dinner hour was winding down, perhaps around 10 o'clock, our hostess approached the tables which held the last, lingering guests and asked if any of us would like to see the attic. "We offer tours to guests if you would like to go up with me. I can show you the bullet holes that are still in the stone walls there. During the battle, Confederate sharpshooters commandeered the attic, shooting out of

436

the windows and killing Union soldiers. Eventually, Union soldiers stormed the attic and shot them all and that's why there are bullet holes in the walls. We find there's often haunting activity up there," she added.

That had our attention!

As a group of perhaps twelve people from the dining room assembled to take the tour our little group of four joined them, all eager for a fright. What might be in the attic? What would happen? Although it was totally unreasonable, the image of Bertha popped in my head. After all, we were going to explore the attic!

As we mounted the stairs I asked the hostess why she took a small oil lamp from one of the dining tables. "Oh, just in case the light either doesn't come on or it does come on, but then goes out...if the spirits don't want any of us there that sometimes happens," she matter-of-factly replied. Hmmmm...

We ascended the three flights of old, creaky stairs to the landing just outside the attic door. The hostess was talking about the inn's role in the battle and how it was used as a makeshift hospital. And, listener, don't worry. I'm completely aware that many of the "tourist" places in areas such as this play up the "ghost" angle. Still, I was willing to go along for fun. After all, it was October, so it was the perfect time for a little fright. She opened the door, switched on the overhead light, and...hurray! It came on! So far, so good.

My friend was beside me as we were ushered into the long, narrow attic space, our husbands following behind. The others -- who we didn't know -- followed suit. I remember thinking, "Okay, since we're the first ones in, we're stuck all the way in the backspace of the attic. This might not be such a good idea!" Then, just about the time we were all shuffling into the backspace... DARKNESS! The light went out! We were so far from the door that the tiny oil lamp held by the hostess did nothing to reach us. Because the space was so long and narrow, even the faint light from the landing didn't penetrate to where we were standing. Everyone's breath did an intake and muffled cries were heard. The flustered hostess tried flipping the light switch on and off, on and off, to no avail. "Okay, it looks like the spirits don't want us here tonight for some reason!" she said, a bit of panic in her voice.

At just that precise moment, to my complete amazement and terror, I saw IT. IT was the most horrifying sight I've ever seen and I was chilled to my very marrow. IT was a head, disembodied, floating in the air. A head hardened by time. Grizzled. Sunken. Evil grin.

Unkempt white hair and a white shaggy beard. A hat. An old soldier hat. And...ANGER!

I've never felt so much hate, anger and total destruction from anything in my life! And IT was looking straight at me. In the blink of an eye, before I even had time to react except to suck in my breath, IT moved with an eerie speed, yet with grace. IT sped around the attic in a circular fashion, all the time keeping IT'S evil eyes trained on me. This happened in just a matter of seconds. Then all of a sudden IT stopped, moved upwards just a bit and then shot straight towards my face! All that hate, rage, and anger directed at me! I truly felt like it wanted me to die!

This entire encounter lasted maybe 4-5 seconds, but I assure you, listener, that it DID happen.

As soon as the head shot towards me I screamed at the top of my lungs, at the same time grabbing onto my friend and we both fell to the floor (me dropping to escape IT and her because I pulled her down with me!). At that instance (I'm sure I shut my eyes just as IT was going to collide with me) the head vanished! I was still breathless when the light suddenly -- at the moment IT vanished -- came back on. Believe me, listener, I would never act in such a way in a room of people I didn't know (or even ones I do know!) unless I had no choice. I am an introvert by nature and, to say the least, I was extremely embarrassed and confused!

All at once everyone began asking what happened. My friend was the first to ask, with her arm around me and concern on her face, as the others chimed in with questions. I was shaking and trying to breathe and trying to explain. I could see the looks of disbelief on their faces. My friend genuinely didn't know what happened, and she knew I wasn't one for theatrics. Her confusion was my first hint. As we all tried to slowly make our way towards the door the hostess also asked what happened. This is when I slowly began to realize that NO ONE ELSE IN THE ROOM saw what I saw! IT wasn't a projected image, an elaborate hoax by the proprietor of the inn to drum up businesses. NO ONE ELSE saw IT. Not even my friend, who was right beside me, or our husbands. What could this mean?

Well, listener, after this frightful experience guess where I had to sleep that night? Yes, my husband (who, I might add, does not believe in spirits of any kind!) and I had a room in the inn and we had to sleep under that roof, under that attic. That night was the second most terrifying time of my life, next only to what had occurred in that attic. I lay in bed, hiding my head under the covers (childish, I know, but I didn't care!) and refusing to look, refusing to even open my eyes. After all, I reasoned, if I didn't look I wouldn't see! Terrifyingly, all night I could hear the very real sounds of footsteps which seemed to slowly circle around our bed. Back and forth, back and forth...

While my husband refused to talk about it back then, all these years later he does admit, begrudgingly, to also hearing the footsteps. But, being ever stubborn, he absolutely refuses to attribute it to anything unearthly. "There's always an explanation," he says. But what that could be he cannot say.

Just as an aside, listener, our room in that old inn was called the "Jennie Wade" room. Mary Virginia "Jennie" Wade was the only civilian casualty of the battle of Gettysburg. She was shot by a stray bullet while she was in her sister's home, a little way down the street from the inn, kneading bread. There was even an old picture of her -- you know the kind, where the eyes seem to follow you -- in our room. Did she pace around the bed all through the night, a sentinel to keep me safe from IT? Or perhaps the night-pacer was the spirit of a Confederate soldier who was killed in the attic, keeping me safe from IT (for I intuitively sensed that IT was the spirit of a Union soldier)?

The next morning, grateful to survive the night, the whole episode in the attic kept bothering me. Maybe someone in the group managed to pull the trick on me somehow? I asked the hostess at breakfast if we could see the attic in the daylight. I wanted to see how open of a space it was, since in my brain the space was all muddled from the confusion and darkness of the previous night.

Once I saw the attic in the daylight, however, I was convinced that no mortal being could have tricked me. I know that ghosts have wandered the earth.

The attic, while having one somewhat narrow and open path, also contained old pieces of large and small furniture here and there that would have made it impossible for someone to navigate in the dark! Also, listener, I know that the head floated far and above the height that any human could reach unaided. These truths, and the fact that I was the ONLY one to see the ghastly head, convinced me that IT was no earthly thing I encountered that night. This encounter chilled me so much I've never returned to that inn, much less that attic!

Could it be that because I'm Virginia born and bred and am descended from soldiers who fought FOR THE CONFEDERACY, that the spirit of a long dead Union soldier decided to take his anger out on me? Me - "a Confederate" - had once again invaded that attic space and he wanted to drive "the Confederate" away (or worse)?

I'll never know, but this is my true ghost story. Let me tell you, listener, that ghosts ARE real. I know that ghosts have wandered the earth.

Tabby knew that, and so much more. Tabby was the keeper of the truth, embellisher, entertainer, and -- in her own way – the protector of every ghostly, clever, bone-chilling and spine-tingling reference in "her childers'" novels that we all enjoy today. One might say she was the spark that lit their imaginations; a model, too, although of this she would most likely be unaware. I wonder, even, if she was even aware of her influence on them at all.

Generations upon generations ahead of us will enjoy her "childers'" stories because we, all of us, are the keepers of the truth. We know -- ghostly or otherwise -- that their stories are brilliant. We love them and want to share them with others. We know the importance of keeping the "Tabby tradition" alive by sharing our own stories. In this way we show our gratitude to all the "Tabbys" of the past.

I hope you enjoyed my true ghost story told by the fireside as much as I enjoyed being the old woman telling it. Thank you, Tabby, and all the wise old women throughout the ages who knew that ghosts have wandered the earth...the keepers of the truth.

I Love My Murderer – But Yours! How Can I?

The First Night photo by Weems

THE FIRST NIGHT

by Don Adkins
California, USA

Excited to be spending my first night in my newly rented home in the mountains, I lit a fire in the fireplace. As I laid back to gaze at the light and shadows dancing on the walls, I noticed the incredible variety of rocks that made up the fireplace. So many different kinds of rocks and minerals, some shining, some sparkling. I realized that the original owners of the house must have collected the colorful rocks from their various travels in a true labor of love for the home they built.

Long after I went to bed, I awoke suddenly from a sound sleep. There had been no noise, so why was I awake? Then I felt it. The bottom edge of my mattress was pressed down as if someone was sitting there. I moved my leg, trying to feel the edge of the mattress with my foot, but I kept pressing up against something unseen. I could not get my foot to the edge of the mattress.

I lay back, staring at the nothing on the foot of my bed. Then it moved. I felt the mattress rise back up to normal as whatever it was stood up...or left. In time - a long time - I was able to get back to sleep.

The Illustration illustration by JoJo Hughes

THE ILLUSTRATION

by JoJo Hughes
Cornwall, UK

I thought I'd share this as it was quite recent and it felt very real (although I remain skeptical as, apart from one other incident in the house, I don't tend to experience paranormal things). This happened last Monday. I've been writing some ghost poems and a short story for *I Know That Ghosts Have Wandered The Earth.* Having three children on summer holidays has made it hard to get in the zone during the day so I normally try to write at night. This seems to have had the effect of making me sleep-compose, where ideas and sentences come to me when I'm fast asleep.

Anyway, the story I was writing involved a shadow figure, constantly observing the narrator from a corner of the bedroom or railway carriage etc. Last week, the ending was writing itself in my head at about 4 am and, knowing it would all be forgotten by the morning, I threw myself out of bed to go to the bathroom and then come back to write it all down. Just before I entered the bathroom down the hall, I looked back at the dark bedroom and saw a tallish figure framed by the dim moonlight/dawn coming through the curtains.

It moved and I calmly assumed it was my husband, who I must have woken up and who also now needed to go. The odd thing is he seemed to dither and move towards the bed. I shouted his name, to ask if he was OK, and heard him answer and appear in a hurry from the other side of the door. He'd been fast asleep and woke in a panic when he heard me, thinking that something was wrong. I told him everything was fine and related what I saw. Weirdly, I was very calm and merely shrugged. Of course it could've been my poor old brain playing tricks, although I was wide awake.

At any rate, I got the story finished once back in bed, with some degree of relief as it was evidently having a rather spooky effect on me!

My illustration is what I saw down the hall from the bathroom.

I Cannot Live Without My Life! I Cannot Live Without My Soul!

CHANNELINGS

Ghosts in the Night illustration by Catherine Rebecca

GHOSTS IN THE NIGHT

by Catherine Rebecca
Isle of Wight, UK

*This did actually happen whilst I was living in a house back in 2013.
I live on the isle of Wight - at the time I lived in what once was
an old railway - the house was called Station House*

Nothing could prepare for what I encountered in the still of the night,
On that cold October evening,
Never to be the same again,
An experience so chilling,
or was it....

Woken in the dead of the night by a dark shadow towering over me,
Enchanting, yet some would say intimidating,
I wipe my eyes to clear my vision.
Perhaps expecting my visitor to be gone.

I sat up in my bed,
And stared at the silhouetted figure that stood before me,
"Please help me"
My heart was pounding yet I felt so calm.
Now was not the time to be afraid.

They spoke once more,
"Please help me"
I stared into the heart of the being looking for a clue
What was expected of me,
What could I do to help.

As I connected soul to soul,
There appeared a void within this person,
So empty and yet so full,
An overwhelming sense of sadness.
So enveloped by loss.

Images flashed before me
of times gone by,
When the house I lived in was once a working railway station,
Busy with bodies,
Scurrying figures moving this
way and that.

Saying hello, Waving farewell.
Some saying goodbye
Not knowing there were to be...

No more reunions.

As I gazed at the being before me
Her form took shape.
A lady in her twenties, wearing a long dress and a frilly bonnet.
Empty eyes, no sparkle, no hope.
I looked down to her feet...
She was floating three foot above the carpet.

She spoke no more words yet she said so much,
The visions she instilled within my head were so vivid.
Showing her waving goodbye to her loved one.
Chasing the train as it departed from the station.
Inconsolable tears cascading down her grey, ashen face.

I closed my eyes, lost with her in that moment.

Eyes wide open once more,
I see a second figure stood before me.
Her man. Her lost lover.
A tall dark handsome soldier.
He told me how he had left for war
Killed in action, died a hero.
As the life was seeping rapidly from his body
All he could think of was her.

I implored him to take opportunity and tell her what she means to
him.
To remind her they can now be together once more.

He turned to his long lost love.
Took her hand softly in his
And gently led her away,
Drifting off into the night.

Reunited in their new realm of existence.

Ghosts brought together by their love.

Whatever Our Souls

Are Made Of,

His And Mine Are The Same

*There Is More To This World Than You Think illustration
by Julie Rose*

THERE IS MORE TO THIS WORLD THAN YOU THINK

by Kay Fairhurst Adkins
Palm Springs, California, USA

It's true. There is more to this world than you think. There are things you can't see with your eyes, things you can't touch with your skin, but they're there. I always *thought* I believed this, but *living* it is a different experience altogether. Once I learned Reiki - a Japanese form of energy healing - and started to live my life intertwined with the world of life force energy, impossibilities suddenly became possible.

How could it really be possible that bringing energy from Source through my crown to my heart and sending it out from the palms of my hands changed my Mother in Law's emergency hospital stay from what doctors said would be a week-long ordeal to an overnight stay, less than 24 hours? How did my brother go from a coma in Intensive Care with expected brain damage to leaving the hospital about a week later with an MRI showing only an old, healed scar on his brain? How did I get that small bone in my foot to move back into place after over a year of discomfort by simply laying my hands on it for a few minutes a day for two weeks only to have it click back into place with a step or two? How could the restaurant worker who felt and *heard* her finger sizzle on the grill be pain-free after I held my Reiki-infused hands near her finger for five minutes? Could miracles really happen?

Maybe it's all just coincidence. Maybe I'm just making this all up. Maybe I'm imagining things. Maybe I'm crazy.

As you read this tale – a true tale for those ready to accept that there is far, far more to this world than what we think – you may comfort yourself with the conviction that I am just making this all up, with the assurance that I am crazy. But you'd be wrong.

Most Reiki practitioners take clients and do hands on healing at spas and alternative health centers, but I've never been drawn to that kind of work beyond helping friends and family and volunteering as a Reiki Master at the local Cancer Center and Stroke Recovery Center. Instead, in addition to teaching Reiki, I like to explore the possibilities of doing energy work in other ways. I've helped people cross over after natural disasters, horrific accidents, and severe seizures that brought on heart attacks. I've cleared lonely spirits from roadside memorials that

451

kept them tied to their death spots. I've brought messages of forgiveness from the higher selves of people killed in accidents to the individuals who brought about their cause of death. I've held mass healings for pedophiles so the chain of abuse can weaken and break, helping possible future victims of abuse avoid attack and victimhood entirely.

This is all possible because Distance Reiki goes beyond time and space.

One day, thinking about Branwell Brontë, I wondered if I could send healing back in time to him. I settled in and began the flow of energy. Reaching out with the energy, I connected with the tortured soul of Branwell Brontë. A Branwell filled with regret, filled with frustration. A Branwell of sobs and self-destruction. A Branwell you may think was ripe for healing, but as I attempted to send the energy it simply wouldn't *go*.

This was curious.

It is true that healing cannot be forced on anyone. A person doesn't have to believe in Reiki or other forms of energy work in order for them to be effective – it's not faith healing – but they do have to be open at a spiritual level to accepting the energy. That kind of barrier to flow is something I've experienced before, but this time was different. I leaned into the energy connection to learn more.

Suddenly, I found myself connected with a *different* Branwell Brontë, a higher level Branwell Brontë. A Branwell Brontë of wisdom and gravitas.

"No, my dear. You can't send healing this time."

Energetically, I asked for clarification. I was willing to accept "No" for an answer, but there was something else here I needed to understand. I had never before reached a soul at two different levels – the hurt and broken level and the raised, healed, ascended version, both existing concurrently and revealing themselves to me. I had heard that all time exists all in one NOW moment, but now I was experiencing it in a way that went far beyond occasional déjà vu.

"Ah," he responded, understanding my unspoken "why?", "The healing took place the moment I died. I knew I had served my purpose on earth and lived my life as best I could within that human frame. What you perceive as weaknesses in my lifetime were precisely what was needed to spur my sisters to write and publish. But the Branwell you see over there," he motioned towards the sniveling wreck, "exists as he is because he is needed by people who are currently living. He is serving a purpose.

"People feel a kinship, a comfort, from the unhealed Branwell that they are not yet ready to experience from me. The broken-hearted, the unfulfilled dreamers, those with addictions, those whose lives are littered with perceived failures, they *need* the Branwell Brontë of sobs as a form of reassurance that they are not alone. They need the Branwell Brontë of a pint and a laugh and a good time to know that they are good enough.

"In time, as they grow in Spirit, they will come to know what you have already discovered: That we are none of us failures. We are all servants to the lifting of humanity's conjoined soul, slowly moving ourselves in a pre-ordained upwards spiral. They will know that there are no failures, only lessons to help us learn and grow. There are no failures, only service to God through roles that help others learn and grow."

Meeting Emily Brontë at a later date gave me another perspective of the many layers one soul can take.

When I was in college I kept a diary. A friend used that diary to betray me, reading it aloud to others in our dormitory to laugh and deride me. I had been long aware that my roommate had read my diary, herself, but it was only a few years ago that I learned about the public betrayal and humiliation. I sat over lunch with a smile plastered on my face and pretended I knew about it all along, while an old college aquaintance talked about the daily reading of my diary as a real laugh riot.

Looking at those diaries brought me no pleasure, only pain. Should I let go of that past and destroy the diaries?

Unable to make a decision, I meditated and called in Emily Brontë to advise me. So many of her papers had been destroyed, she seemed like the perfect person to give me perspective.

Reaching Emily is not easy. She is more of an element than a spirit, so it is difficult for her to communicate with human words and concepts. She would much rather be the wind. I couldn't "see" her with my mind's eye, but I could feel her energy and uncover the advice her energy represented. She was very clear that I was the only person concerned in the matter and didn't need any advice from anyone. I felt the truth of this, but still wanted more guidance.

Emily left her windspace and lowered her energy to be able to speak to me more clearly, "As they have never been a pleasure for you to re-read, they do not fulfill their intended purpose, so it is acceptable to let them go into the ether. Trust that you will remember the things you want or need to remember and let go of the rest. The person you were is inconsequential. The person you are now is what matters."

I shredded most of the diaries and felt freer. I felt cleansed by the wind.

Sometime later as I was doing yardwork and thinking about the Brontës – not an unusual thing for many of us in A Walk Around The Bronte Table – Emily Brontë appeared to me again. But this wasn't Emily of the wind and outdoor spaces, this was a domestic Emily.

I could "see" her back as she sat or stood in the kitchen. Piles of half-peeled potatoes and carrots were on the edges of the table in front of her while she kneaded dough in the center. Her back heaved repeatedly. At first I thought she was sobbing, but I was wrong. She was snickering.

"What's so funny?" I asked.

"How you and so many other people think you know us. You have a few fragments of writing, a house and some artifacts and you imagine that you know everything about us. It's comical."

"Are we really that far off base?"

"Oh, you get some things right."

"Which things?"

"Do you think I'm going to tell you and spoil my fun? Imagine that after you die people take a few scraps of your life – some drawings, some poetry, a story or two, some images of you, a childhood toy, a few bits of clothing – and come up with what they imagine to be a fully-fleshed version of you. How close do you think they'd be?" she scoffed.

"I see your point."

"People are multifaceted beings. When we write about them we have to boil them down to a few points to create a character. The reader fills in the rest. You'll never know all of their thoughts, their feelings, their experiences, their relationships. But you'll keep convincing yourself that you do. And it's quite entertaining. None of you will ever really know me, the true me. And that suits me completely."

Charlotte is another person who came to me in the backyard as I was doing yardwork and thinking about the Brontës. I had recently finished reading The Professor for the first time and was thinking sadly about her marriage to Arthur Bell Nicholls. I couldn't "see" Charlotte, but she made herself heard as she stood up firmly for her husband.

"Why does everyone think I am to be pitied in my choice of a husband?" she asked expressively.

"Well, I know Ellen didn't like him very much." I answered.

"Of course she didn't like him! You've lived in this world long enough to know how single women feel about their best friends getting married and leaving them behind while the bride invests all her time and energy in her new household. It is no surprise that she felt replaced by him and betrayed by me."

"You're right about that. But you wanted someone passionately devoted to you."

"And that's exactly what I received," Charlotte avowed, "Arthur waited for me for years. He nearly broke his heart being apart from me. He pursued me with a love that few women have ever had the grace to experience."

I raised my next point, "But he was always telling you what to do and what not to do. He was too controlling."

"You have read Jane Eyre and The Professor, so you know something of my ideal model for a man," Charlotte pointed out gently, "but you have not lived in my time. We did not have your freedoms ingrained in us. In earning my own living, I had a degree of freedom that many women did not possess, but in my heart I craved to be loved and cared for. I wanted a strong man who could be my master, and in Arthur I had that. Like women immemorial, I had many subtle methods at my disposal to manage him so I could have my own way in areas that really mattered to me, but oh! It was such bliss to please him after so many sad, sick, lonely years on my own."

"He kept you from writing."

"He saved me from the *need* to write. He took heavy burdens from me. He cared for my father as a devoted son, despite the painful separation my father had enforced between us. As my father's curate, he opened the possibility of securing the living after my father's death

455

so the threat of being evicted from the home I knew abated. He gave me rest and peace. He gave me the ability to travel without fear and shyness. He shielded me from unwanted crowds and attention. I have no doubt I would have returned to writing in time, had I lived long enough, but to be a wife and mother was the new desire of my heart. To assist Arthur and Papa, to live as a newly formed family was a joy. I had already fulfilled my desire to write and be published. I wanted to *be* my own story and *live* my life. I wanted to exist."

"He destroyed so much after your death."

"I destroyed so much before my death, too. Writings, scribblings, drawings. Bits and pieces. Mine and my sisters'. Branwell's, too. There was nothing unusual in it. You use shredders and garbage cans, thrift stores and estate sales to clear out the belongings of your loved ones when they die. We used flames and conflagration. As authors we wanted to be remembered, it's true, but we never expected to be remembered as individuals to this degree. When I was destroying the bits and pieces of my sibling's lives I had no inkling I would ever marry, much less have a child. I was alone with no expectation of a future generation to act as a tender and loving caretaker. Saying farewell and removing the ghosts of the ephemera that surrounded me was how I began, in fits and starts, to crawl out of the depths of the grief that consumed me. Arthur did the same after both my father and I were dead. It was normal. Your desire to have our entire household complete after nearly 200 years is what is abnormal."

"He wasn't very exciting."

"He didn't need to be. He was something far more valuable to me. He was someone who *knew* me, who knew *us*. To live with a man who could talk of Emily and Anne and Branwell, who knew their mannerisms and their voices...who else could give me that? Why, oh why won't people believe my dying words? "We have been so happy." We *had* been so happy together. Together, we shared tenderness, we shared passion. Arthur may not have been Byronic in looks and temperament, but he was my hero and I loved him."

And now we come to Anne Brontë. I didn't have to call to her or seek her out with energy. She felt my need and came to me. She offered help and came regularly to be by my side as I worked on expanding my capabilities. She was a true friend.

After becoming a Reiki Master, Spirit made it clear to me that I would be writing a book. It would be called <u>Community Reiki: The Reiki Practitioner's Guide to Healing the World</u> and it would combine my knowledge of Reiki with my career as a Health Education Specialist. Sounds simple enough, but when you've never written a book before and are starting from scratch it is quite daunting. I sat down at my computer, terrified. Could I do it? Would it be good enough? How would I ever get it published? Who was I to tell people how to heal the world? I was nothing. I was nobody.

Anne's spirit came gently to me to buoy me up and give me confidence. She told me that she and Charlotte often speak to authors, though the authors themselves aren't always aware of it. Read DM Denton's book, Without the Veil Between, Anne Brontë: A Fine and Subtle Spirit and you'll hear Anne's influence. (Anne cautions me that I must make it clear that the novel is completely Denton's work; Anne and Charlotte simply nudge and influence. Some parts are very much true to their lives, but they, like Emily, aren't about to "spoil the fun" and let us know where they've gone beyond nudging.)

Anne Brontë led me through the writing process and helped me to grow, bit by bit. I didn't "see" her with my mind's eye, but I felt her presence. If I reached out my right hand, I could actually touch it and feel the vibration of her energy with my fingertips. She helped me create a structure for the book and break down the sections into small, easy pieces for me to write; things I knew well and could write easily. She helped me move forward slowly, revealing each piece as it was needed so I wouldn't be overwhelmed and give up. She helped me through the hurdles of formatting the book and self publishing through Amazon's print-on-demand arm. She guided me through rewrite after rewrite. She helped me emotionally to become a person who felt herself worthy of having something to say that would benefit others.

While Anne Brontë helped me, she also shared with me a few things about her life.

Anne told me that the girls from Thorpe Green and she had a vibrant correspondence. Each letter had to be consigned to the flames immediately after it was read out of consideration for Branwell. She would have loved to keep them, but it was more important to spare Branwell a portion of his pain. In her letters she endeavored to train the girls away from gossip and sensationalism and hoped she did some good by them. Their visit to her at the Parsonage was not out of the blue, although it took some doing and subterfuge to keep Branwell away and ignorant of the visit. Anne cared for her grown students deeply. This was a feeling and relationship Charlotte was not able or not willing to comprehend.

Anne is proud of a number of the accomplishments she achieved in life. She was the first to earn her own keep for an extended period of time, relieving her father of the burden of supporting her. She did not quail under the pressures, loneliness, and disappointment of being a governess, but did her duty to the best of her ability by the grace of God. She is the only sister who was able to get Branwell employed in a position that suited his talents and abilities, although it ultimately ended badly. The fact that the Robinsons were willing to employ Branwell and maintain him in employment for roughly two years proves that both she and her brother proved satisfactory.

Feeling her energy give a little half-smile, Anne allowed her competitive nature to peek out, mentioning with arched eyebrow that she had two books published at a younger age and in quicker succession than either of her sisters.

I asked why she stayed with Newby for Publishing <u>The Tenant of Wildfell Hall</u> after seeing how poorly his business performed in comparison with Charlotte's publisher, Smith, Elder and Co. She answered thusly:

"We three sisters shared much more about our novels as we wrote them than most of you imagine. Each work is truly the effort of its author, but we supported each other in choosing the right words, forming the best sentences, and conjuring the best plotlines and characters. It was obvious from the start that Charlotte was strongly against nearly every aspect of Tenant. Charlotte and George Smith had such a strong relationship, I feared she would influence him to require major changes to my novel that would gut both its spirit and intent. Charlotte was very forceful when her mind was set. Staying with Thomas Newby maintained my independence and preserved my voice. When it came to the possibility of republishing <u>The Tenant of Wildfell Hall</u> under George Smith, you see my concerns were valid, as it never again saw the light of day while Charlotte lived."

When asked about her position as the youngest in the family, she said this:

"All performers need an audience. By being the youngest, I was always behind the others in development, making me the defacto audience. It is not unexpected that my input was viewed as immature and often left unheard. In addition to being a result of my shyness and sense of inadequacy amongst my brilliant siblings, my stutter was a means to enter into conversations and be heard. It was only by leaving my home that I could break away from the bonds familiarity created for me. This is why I am quite content to rest in Scarborough. I can be myself."

"To understand me is to look at the original title of my notes for Agnes Grey, "Passages in the Life of an Individual." It is exactly what I have been saying again and again throughout my adult life: I EXIST! I AM!"

Thanks to Anne Brontë's support, I was able to complete Community Reiki. I was also able to use the skills she helped me develop to publish a memoir of my father-in-law's experiences growing up on Catalina Island and, in January 2021, a book about the new Nova Gaia energies on earth, written by myself and two dear friends somewhat anonymously as The Cartographers of the New World. Thanks to Anne, I was able to conceive the idea of our first book project for A Walk Around The Bronte Table and know that I could execute not only There Was No Possibility of Taking A Walk That Day, our collection of Bronte-inspired COVID-19 Lockdown poems, but any and all future book projects we may undertake as a group.

Yes, Reader, the very book you hold in your hands exists only because of the love, strength, and persistence of Anne Brontë.

Birth Daze illustration by Stephanie Rodriguez

BIRTH DAZE

by Laurel Hausman
Centreville, Virginia, USA

I was destined to be haunted.

My maternal grandmother was born on April 21, 1906, my mother on July 30, 1930. I entered the world on January 17th, 1954. It would be many years before I understood the significance of these dates: Charlotte, Emily, and Anne Bronte's birthdays, respectively. Coincidence? Perhaps. But the mathematical probability of three generations of birthdays coinciding with those of the Bronte sisters is approximately one out of 500-billion.* I prefer to believe it was destiny.

My introduction to the Brontes began when I was 15 years old. The small private high school I attended held a "Movie Day" as a reward for sitting through a week of mid-term exams. The 1939 version of Wuthering Heights, with Merle Oberon as Cathy, and Sir Laurence Olivier as Heathcliff, was displayed from a reel-to-reel projector (in glorious black and white) and emitted a crackling sound on the portable movie screen. As an American, I was not familiar with manor houses and moors, desolate places seemingly inhabited by spectres. Nonetheless, my classmates and I sobbed as we watched Cathy die in Heathcliff's arms, promising to meet him in the afterlife on Penistone Crag. My adolescent heart was enraptured by a love so strong it could defy the grave. (Later, when I read the book and discovered the movie ended in the middle of the plot, omitting an entire generation, I seethed at the indignation committed against Emily Bronte's masterpiece.) Her story haunted me; I could not get it out of my mind. I was crushed to learn Wuthering Heights was Emily's only novel and that she died soon after it was published. When my English teacher mentioned that Emily had had sisters who also wrote books, it was as if I had discovered family members about whose existence I had previously known nothing. I set out to read more Bronte literature.

I do not recall how I came to acquire a copy of Jane Eyre, a small inexpensive paperback I still possess (perhaps Charlotte Bronte placed it under my pillow as I slept), but I vividly remember devouring every word she penned. Once again, the description of the wild moors stirred something in me. Despite the 3,000 miles of ocean "come broad between us," I felt a connection, a kinship if you will, that I could not explain.

Many years later, after rereading Wuthering Heights and Jane Eyre twice more, and after becoming an English teacher, I decided to introduce the novels to my literature students. Before that, however, in order to foster in them a deeper appreciation of Bronte literature, I determined to learn more about the lives of the Bronte sisters, for while I had read much written by them, I had never read anything about them. By this time the internet was readily available and I perused it eagerly, learning all I could about the Bronte family. It was then that I discovered Charlotte shared a birthday with my grandmother, but at the time I thought it nothing more than an interesting coincidence. Further research disclosed Emily's birthday as a match for that of my mother. Intrigued, I clicked on an image of Anne's grave and read the birth date engraved on the headstone: January 17, 1820. My heart quickened. Three consecutive generations of women who share the sisters' birthdays. Was this an explanation for the kinship I felt toward the Brontes? Was this the reason I was fascinated with their novels and with their lives? I determined to visit the Bronte home as soon as possible.

August 4th, 2016 was the day I first laid eyes on the village of Haworth and the surrounding moors; the day I first walked to Top Withins and listened to the wind rustle the heather, the sheep bleating on the hillsides; the day on which I shed tears upon seeing the dining room table where my favorite novels had been written. On that day, the spirits of Charlotte, Emily, and Anne settled fully in the marrow of my being, where they would both inspire and haunt me from that day forward. Like Cathy knocking on the window at Wuthering Heights, the sisters continue to knock on the window of my soul.

* The probability of being born on any given date is 1 out of 365 days. The probability of being born on April 21st and July 30th and January 17th is $1/365 \times 1/365 \times 1/365 = 1/48,627,125 = 0.00000002$ or one out of 500-billion.

I Don't Like Being Out In The Dark Now

Young Maria Brontë Illustration by EmilyInGondal

YOUNG MARIA BRONTË

by Rachel Maria Bell
West Yorkshire, England

Reader, I trawled through over 500 diary entries and an 80,000 word book on my communication with the Brontës, wondering what to share with you!

I'm sure you, too, will have written journals on portions of your life, perhaps even a memoir.

I never expected mine would go this way.

Back in August 2000 I ran away from the Parsonage and shut out the entire Brontë family and Haworth after witnessing Emily's death in broad daylight whilst crammed into a busy bank holiday Parsonage. Perhaps you, too, were there that day? Perhaps you saw a tall woman legging it fast out past the church and onto the moors, where the sky promptly turned black.

"Whatever the Brontës want with me, I'm done with them!" I said with vehemence, throwing myself down on the ground in the rain. "I'll NEVER return to that place".

Well, "never" turned out to be 16 years later. In summer 2016 I did not know what was coming next in my life, nor how I was set to spend those Brontë bicentenary years. I was at an extremely low point emotionally and had recently been through a stressful court drama. The Brontës were not on my mind, rather tucked away in an inner box marked "weird things I don't talk about," after all, I'd been seeing Charlotte and Emily since I was nine years old after a school trip to Haworth.

Then one unremarkable day in Scarborough, sitting on a bench right beside Anne Brontë's grave, I had a truly awe-inspiring awakening. The sky opened and light appeared. Anne beamed out from her own grave. I could not believe my eyes and my heart beat so fast I thought it might pop out of my chest.

Channels of light beamed in a triangle between my own heart, Anne and the sky. The word Biblical came to mind. What on earth was going on? There was no one else around.

My fast heartbeat at the appearance of Anne told me in an instant I was personally involved with the Brontë family. Something was different this time: there was not going to be any turning back or running away. Someone seemed to speak to me. Anne? Is it you, Anne?

A voice told me to read The Tenant of Wildfell Hall just like I'd been "told" to read Wuthering Heights in 1998. These spirits were very clear with their reading instructions.

The appearance of Anne in my life set me on a new path altogether, one of recovery and discovery in equal measure. Following this moment, I began having a series of new events popping up in my mind's eye, always diverting my attention right back to Haworth and to the Brontës.

I could see into the past and my analytical mind would run riot pondering the meaning. It was all so very real. I seemed to be able to see what was happening in another timeframe but it was exactly like memory. I could see the past! This was not something I expected to be able to see, let alone for it to be so very specific.

Frequently I was at the back of Anne's head while she wrote and I started to wonder whether these were actually memories, because that's definitely how it felt. But who on earth would Anne have allowed to be hovering around the back of her curly locks? Whoever I was, perhaps I was very nosey, but I cared for the whole family so much and loved them dearly.

There began a trail, with twists and turns, dreams and voices, sounds, waking visions and increasing synchronicities. Patterns in family events, dates and names between then and now would crop up. Events I remembered from my childhood and adolescence suddenly seemed to have already been written in Brontë books in the 1840s. This frequently got rather weird as you might imagine.

The skills I'd had as a child returned with vigour, and this time I wasn't for suppressing them. I had seen Charlotte when she was alone in the hallway fetching a tray with Patrick's supper. I heard her clompy little boots on the hard stone floor as though the sound was in my bedroom in 2016. When she saw me, she stumbled and nearly dropped the tray. Poor Charlotte. She looked sad, and I wished I could comfort her, but I just stood there looking at her and wishing I could reach out and cuddle her. Who on earth was I, hanging round the dark hallway on a winter's night?

This possibility of me having had a past life with the Brontës was a feature dominating my thoughts, and I felt I had to work it out. Now if I'd been there in the 1850s this narrowed it down somewhat. Male or female? Arthur Bell Nicholls? No! Ellen Nussey? No! Margaret Wooler? No!

No matter who I considered, it never felt right at all.

Then November 2017 came. In the process of attempting to buy a house in real life, one night in a dream I dreamt of signing the deeds of the property. I took up my quill (!) and signed the scroll "Bronte" but without the diaresis: I'd written more of a squiggly line above the e. In an instant I was awake and sitting upright in bed. Think Miss Marchmont's final night in Villette where she becomes entirely lucid!

My name was Bronte! Oh my God I was actually a Bronte!

After all those months of daily communication with a whole gang load of spirits, I had finally reached the point of truly being ready to know.

I asked out loud, implored the ether above my head, "If you can hear me now, come and tell me. I need to know and I promise it will be okay. I'm ready."

My right hand girl was there: Charlotte appeared by my side and I laid my head down dead calm on the pillow with her beside me. She talked me through a scene, a waking vision that we co-created. Around 12 people sat at a long table. I announced my return and declared who I was, although I didn't know myself. I trusted her. Charlotte had left me an envelope on the piano with a clue. Very soon after I discovered, or rather remembered, that I had once lived as Maria Brontë.

No wonder I was always at the back of everyone's heads or tucked in behind the door. I wasn't actually in a body! The joy inside my heart from the knowing was incredible. My moment of enlightenment was one of pure joy and freedom and gratitude that I was able to be brought to this point in this lifetime. It's something I will never forget.

Finally, all of my memories made sense. And at the age of 39, I'd lived my Old Testament and was about to create my new one.

Only after this did my memories go back further and I could now see myself from within as Maria. Only fragments would appear from time to time: kitchen or dining room scenes – and the garden was so bright without all the big trees and so many graves. It brings me great joy to recollect all of the memories I have recalled and been gifted with in this life, many of which I share in my book, Waking Up With the Brontes. (There are no timescales for publication other than to say it will be with you on God's schedule. If you ever feel compelled to read it, then I'd be honoured to call you my Reader.)

We are only ever shown what we need to know from a past life to retrieve an important aspect or emotion or lesson that needs to be understood and integrated within the current life. I don't travel there for entertainment and in fact some of the memories have been quite sad, particularly around Branwell's grief as a child.

He has also been the source of much joy and entertainment for me: often Charlotte, Branwell and I have played together in dreams, co-creating our realities both from within our childlike states in the 1820s and bringing valuable insights back into the here and now.

At last, I could re-form proper relationships with all of the Brontës based on our existing family relationship spanning back to that time. There seemed to be rather a lot to resolve. My healing journey in this life – the becoming of myself, often led back to healing of the soul family line in the Brontë times.

At last I understood why I tended to see Anne as a baby – I can assure you this does not happen with other authors! But it's clear to me that I mended Maria's grief of bereavement when we lost our mother by showering my affection onto baby Anne.

Don't get me wrong, I'm no quantum physicist: I'm a regular single mum who worked as a Business Lecturer and who was suffering from a chronic pain condition with a story to tell that may be of benefit for other people. My awakening has allowed me to open up to my psychic skills and to feel increasingly comfortable with operating in extra dimensions.

Certainly my past life experience has made me realise the enormous value of connecting with our eternal souls by retrieving unresolved and unhealed aspects of our souls via our past life healing journey. Only the soul of the individual truly knows the meaning and growth potential for them.

Unfortunately I lost many relationships through people not understanding or being able to accept my experiences, which has been challenging but not a surprise. The changes occurring in me could only be contained by people who were willing to be open to exploring infinite possibilities of the human mind and imaginary realm experiences.

It's important for me to be clear that I underwent no past life regression, hypnosis, no near-death experience and no drug-taking, all of which can activate past life or in between life states of memory. I was strongly guided not to visit psychic mediums nor to have intervention from others so that I may record the truth of what came through to me alone, so that you may know that this can happen to you or those around you.

I firmly believe we all have psychic capabilities, but the extent to which we have blocked them varies, both due to societal and cultural conventions, customs, upbringing and on whether it is in our personal skillset and lifepath to bring these skills through during this particular lifetime.

I will leave you with one of my memories now, of my day of transition from life to the afterlife as Maria Brontë.

6th May 1825

A lovely bright morning
And I think Tabby was downstairs baking bread in the kitchen
Perhaps I could smell it
Everyone was just going about their business around the house as normal
Branwell, Anne, Aunt Branwell and Papa were downstairs
And I got out of bed
(I should not have been out of bed, I was dying)
I could hear music
And I wanted to hear the music
I wanted to go to Branwell
Maybe it was a flute
I got to the top of the stairs
There was nothing in me and I was barely breathing
But something had taken me over
Perhaps it was the knowledge that I was about to die and didn't want to do it alone
I could barely feel my body anymore
I knew I was going somewhere else
But I didn't want to be alone
I wanted my family and in that moment, I wanted to be with Branwell
But I only had the strength to walk down a couple of stairs
Before I fell
On the top staircase
Someone screamed at the bottom of the stairs, outside the kitchen door
It took me until I went back to the Parsonage in 2018 to know it was Tabby

Tabby saw me fall and yelled for Patrick
She must have been astounded to see me out of bed
He ran so fast and bounded up the stairs 2 at a time
Patrick was a nimble man
He knew my time had come
And this was goodbye
He scooped up my wasted little frame in his arms
As gently as possible
Lovingly, tenderly
He carried me back into the bedroom
And laid me down
He never stopped praying and crying
It was not very long before I started seeing things from the ceiling
It must have been very smooth to leave my little body behind
No effort at all to let go
And I was free!
Poor Papa was crying over me, still praying non-stop
But I was already on the ceiling!
I wished he could see me to know I was alright
I could do this!
Wheeeee, I could move anywhere so freely!
I could breathe again
Papa, don't cry! I'm right here above your head!
And then the room filled with light
I don't know how Papa didn't see it all aglow!
Such bright, glorious light
All around, filling every inch of the room
And marvellous beings appeared
They were ever so tall, much taller than tall adults
They stood around
They were looking towards Patrick who was sitting over my little body
on the bed
I was already up in the room
Everything had changed so quickly
It wouldn't be quite right to say these beings were dressed in white
But they were definitely glowing white
Long robes that glowed, as did their entire beings
How was Papa not seeing this?!
One main being spoke with me
He didn't speak in English so I can't repeat it to you now, but I
understood what he was saying
Whatever this language was, it made sense at the time

And to give you the gist
He said something about how I had fulfilled something
My part of this life – he seemed to be congratulating me on a job well
done!
He also explained my choices about what would happen next
I was worried because I could see a golden ladder
I thought if I went up it, I might not come down
And then I got very worried about leaving my family behind
There was a strong pull back towards them
About not wanting to leave
He sensed this and explained that I could travel between different
places
And I could spend time further up wherever the golden ladder went
(who knows?)
Or I could also exist here very close to the earth plane
What, with my family, here in the Parsonage?
Yes, here in the Parsonage
Okay, cool
So that's what I did
I travelled various places during my time in between
And I felt very close to my human state when I was back in the
Parsonage hanging around on the ceiling and behind the front door
Loving them, watching them, hearing them, seeing them, generally
hanging out just like we used to, but without a body
And often I was outside with them, too
Say on the street or on the moors or flying at the back of their carriages
I even attended my own funeral
But I also lived someplace else that I could return to
A light place that I can't really remember, somewhere very high up
Perhaps the place you go back to, to restore bliss
To get re-charged with everything and everybody in the light
The only word I know is Heaven
And when you want to travel down to earth from the light place
(For example if someone you love is in distress and you just get called)
You know, like "somebody" coming out of the Black Bull
Well it's such a cool ride
Like a really exciting fast ride at the seaside
That makes your tummy go all funny inside
But faster, and with far more gliding and grace
So my memory of the in between life state around the Brontës started
on May 6th 1825

And it ended on March 31st 1855 when my little sister Charlotte passed over
None were alone
No one ever is xxx

———

I hope you enjoyed these little extracts into my past life awakening as Maria Brontë. Remember, there is every possibility. Particularly when you lay out your time in preparation for a happy eternity.

I am Maria Brontë.

Zombie photo by Maria Johnson

Would You Like To Live With Your Soul In the Grave?

This book is dedicated to my darling wife Danielle—a wonderful woman.

Contents at a Glance

Contents

About the Author

Peter Carter is a SQL Server expert with over a decade of experience in developing, administering, and architecting SQL Server platforms, data-tier applications, and ETL solutions. Peter has a passion for SQL Server and hopes that his enthusiasm for this technology helps or inspires others.

About the Technical Reviewers

Louis Davidson has been in the IT industry for more than 15 years as a corporate database developer and architect. He has spent the majority of his career working with Microsoft SQL Server, beginning in the early days of version 1.0. He has a bachelor's degree from the University of Tennessee at Chattanooga in computer science, with a minor in mathematics. Louis is the data architect for Compass Technology (Compass.net) in Chesapeake, Virginia, leading database development on their suite of nonprofit-oriented customer relationship management (CRM) products, which are built on the Microsoft CRM platform and SQL Server technologies.

Alex Grinberg is a senior SQL Server database administrator (DBA) with more than 20 years of IT experience. He has been working on Microsoft SQL Server products since version 6.5. Alex currently works in the Pennsylvania branch of Cox Automotive, headquartered in Atlanta, GA. His primary duties are to provide architecture, tuning, optimization, analysis, operational, and development services; to create new applications; to convert legacy technologies (SQL Server, VB.NET, and C#); and to provide on-site training with the latest Microsoft technologies including .NET (VB and C#), SSRS, and SSIS. Alex is a frequent speaker at professional IT events, including SQLSaturdays, Code Camps, SQL Server User Groups, and other industry seminars, where he shares his cumulative knowledge. He is the guest author for SQLServerSentral.com and is also the cofounder of HexaArt Inc., an IT consulting services company for small and mid-size corporations. For any questions or consulting needs, Alex can be reached at hexaart@gmail.com.

## PART I

Installing and Configuring SQL Server

CHAPTER 1

■ ■ ■

Planning the Deployment

Planning a deployment of SQL Server 2014, in order to best support the business's needs, can be a complicated task. You should make sure to consider many areas—edition and licensing requirements, on-premises vs. cloud hosting, hardware considerations, and software configuration. And all of this is before you even start to consider which features of SQL Server you may need to install to support the application.

This chapter will guide you through the key decisions that you should make when you are planning your deployment. You will also learn how to perform some essential operating system configurations. This chapter will also give you an overview of the top-level features that you can choose to install and discuss why selecting the appropriate features is important.

Editions and License Models

Choosing the edition of SQL Server 2014 to support your data-tier application may sound like a simple task, but in fact, you should spend a large amount of time thinking about this decision and consulting with both business stakeholders and other IT departments to bring their opinions into this decision. The first thing to consider is that there are six editions of SQL Server. These editions not only have different levels of functionality, but they also have different license considerations. Additionally, from an operational support perspective, you may find that the TCO (total cost of ownership) of the estate increases if you allow data-tier applications to be hosted on versions of SQL Server that are not deployed strategically within your estate.

A full discussion of feature and licensing considerations is beyond the scope of this book, however, Table 1-1 details the available licensing models for each edition of SQL Server, whereas Table 1-2 highlights the primary purpose of each edition.

Table 1-1. *SQL Server Edition License Models*

Edition	License Models	Comments
Enterprise	Per-core, volume, and third-party hosting	--
Business Intelligence	Server + CAL, volume, third-party hosting	--
Standard	Per-core, server + CAL, volume, retail, third-party hosting	--
Web	Per-core, third-party hosting	--
Developer	Per-user, volume, retail	Not for use in a production environment
Express	Free edition of SQL Server	Limited functionality and small capacity limits, such as a 10GB database size, a 1GB limit on RAM, and a CPU limit of one socket, or four cores

Table 1-2. *SQL Server Edition Overview*

Edition	Edition Overview
Enterprise	Fully featured edition of SQL Server for Enterprise systems and critical apps.
Business Intelligence	Aimed at large, scalable business intelligence (BI) environments. It has a full suite of BI product functionality, but limited Database Engine functionality.
Standard	Core database and BI functionality, aimed at departmental level systems and non-critical apps.
Web	Is only available for service providers hosting public websites that use SQL Server.
Developer	A fully featured edition, to the level of Enterprise edition, but meant for development use and not allowed for use on production systems.
Express	A free, entry-level version of SQL Server geared toward small applications with local data requirements.

A CAL is a client access license, where a client can refer to either a user or a device. You can choose whether to purchase user or device licenses based on which will be cheapest for your environment.

For example, if your organization had a SQL server that was supporting a call center that had 100 computers, and it ran 24/7 with three eight-hour shifts, then you would have 100 devices and 300 users, so device CALs would be the most sensible option for you to choose.

On the flip side, if your organization had a SQL server that was supporting a sales team of 25 who all connected to the sales application not only via their laptops, but also via their iPads, then you would have 25 users, but 50 devices, and therefore choosing user CALs would be the more sensible option.

To summarize, if you have more users than devices, then you should choose device CALs. If you have more devices than users, on the other hand, you should choose user CALs. Microsoft also supplies a tool called Microsoft Assessment and Planning (MAP) Toolkit for SQL Server, which will help you plan your licensing requirements.

The version(s) of SQL Server that you choose to support in your Enterprise applications will vary depending on the project's requirements, your organization's requirements, and the underlying infrastructure. For example, if your organization hosts its entire SQL Server estate within a private cloud, then you are likely to only support the Enterprise edition, since you will be licensing the underlying infrastructure.

Alternatively, if your organization is predominantly utilizing physical boxes, then you most likely need to support a mix of SQL Server versions, such as Enterprise and Standard editions. This will give projects the flexibility to reduce their costs if they only require a subset of features and are not expecting high volume workloads, and hence can live with the caps that Standard edition imposes on RAM and CPU.

Assuming that Enterprise is the edition that you choose to support your application, then you should be aware of a common misconception that is not well documented by Microsoft. I was caught out by this myself the first time that I designed a platform for SQL Server 2012, and the same applies to SQL Server 2014.

In SQL Server 2012 and SQL Server 2014, Enterprise edition has been split into two separate SKUs (stock keeping units); Enterprise and Enterprise Core. Many people believe that Enterprise Core is for the installation of SQL Server in a Windows Core environment (discussed momentarily) and many others believe that the only difference in the two products is the licensing model. Both of these beliefs are incorrect.

In SQL Server 2012, Microsoft removed the server + CAL licensing model for Enterprise edition, but in order to allow customers time to prepare and transition, they retained Enterprise with the intention of this being a short-term transitional edition. Therefore, if you are not upgrading your server from an older version of SQL Server where you utilized the server + CAL model, don't use Enterprise edition; you should always use Enterprise Core instead. This is not only for licensing, but also because Enterprise edition has a technical limitation that Enterprise Core does not.

The limitation is for large systems that have more than 20 cores. If your system has more than 20 cores, and you use Enterprise edition, then SQL Server will only utilize 20 of the cores in your server. SQL Server enforces this by only allowing a maximum of 20 schedulers to be online (or a maximum of 40 schedulers in hyperthreaded systems).

You can witness this behavior for yourself on a server that has more than 20 cores by running the code in Listing 1-1.

Listing 1-1. How Many Schedulers Are in Use?

```
SELECT COUNT(*)
FROM sys.dm_os_schedulers
WHERE status = 'VISIBLE ONLINE'
```

On a server with 24 hyperthreaded cores, the query in Listing 1-1 would return 40, as opposed to the expected value of 48.

The next thing you should consider before choosing which version you will use is whether or not you will use a Windows Server Core installation of SQL Server. Installations on Server Core can help improve security by reducing the attack surface of your server. Server Core is a minimal installation, so there is less surface to attack and fewer security vulnerabilities. It can also improve performance, because you do not have the overhead of the GUI and because many resource-intensive applications cannot be installed. If you do decide to use Server Core, then it is also important to understand the impacts of doing so.

From the SQL Server perspective, the following features cannot be used:

- Reporting Services

- SQL Server Data Tools (SSDT)

- Client Tools Backward Compatibility

- Client Tools SDK

- SQL Server Books Online

- Distributed Replay Controller

- Master Data Services (MDS)

- Data Quality Services (DQS)

The following features can be used, but only from a remote server:

- Management Tools

- Distributed Replay Client

From the broader perspective of operational support, you will need to ensure that all of your operational teams (DBAs, Windows Operations, and so on) are in a position to support Server Core. For example, if your DBA team relies heavily on a third-party graphical tool for interrogating execution plans, does this need to be installed locally on the server? Is there an alternative tool that would meet their needs? From a Windows Ops perspective, does the team have the tools in place for remotely monitoring and managing the server? Are there any third-party tools they rely on that would need to be replaced?

You should also consider if your operations team has the skill set to manage systems using predominantly command-line processes. If it does not, then you should consider what training or up-skilling may be required.

Hardware Considerations

When you are planning the hardware requirements for your server, ideally, you will implement a full capacity planning exercise so you can estimate the hardware requirements of the application(s) that the server will support. When conducting this exercise, make sure you take your company's standard hardware lifecycle into account, rather than planning just for today. Depending on your organization, this could be between one and five years, but will generally be three years.

This is important in order to avoid under sizing or oversizing your server. Project teams will generally want to oversize their servers in order to ensure performance. Not only is this approach costly when scaled through the enterprise, but in some environments, it can actually have a detrimental effect on performance. An example of this would be a private cloud infrastructure with shared resources. In this scenario, oversizing servers can have a negative impact on the entire environment, including the oversized server itself.

Specifying Strategic Minimum Requirements

When specifying the minimum hardware requirements for SQL Server within your environment, you may choose to specify the minimum requirements for installing SQL Server—4GB RAM and a single 2GHz CPU (based on Enterprise edition). However, you may be better served to think about operational supportability within your enterprise.

For example, if your environment consists predominantly of a private cloud infrastructure, then you may wish to specify a minimum of 2 vCores and 4GB RAM + (number of cores * 1GB) since this may be in line with your enterprise standards.

On the other hand, if you have a highly dispersed enterprise, which has grown organically, and you wish to help persuade projects to use a shared SQL Server farm, you may choose to enforce much higher minimum specifications, such as 32GB RAM and 2 sockets/4 cores. The reasoning here is that any projects without large throughput requirements would be "forced" to use your shared farm to avoid the heavy costs associated with an unnecessarily large system.

Storage

Storage is a very important consideration for any SQL Server installation. The following sections will discuss locally attached storage and SAN storage, as well as considerations for file placement.

Locally Attached Storage

If your server will use locally attached storage, then you should carefully consider file layout. By its very nature, SQL Server is often input/output (IO) bound, and therefore, configuring the IO subsystem is one of the critical aspects for performance. You first need to separate your user databases' data files and log files onto separate disks or arrays and also to separate TempDB, which is the most heavily used system database. If all of these files reside on a single volume, then you are likely to experience disk contention while SQL Server attempts to write to all of them at the same time.

Typically, locally attached storage will be presented to your server as RAID (Redundant Array of Inexpensive Disks) arrays and various RAID levels are available. There are many RAID levels available, but the most common are outlined in the following pages.

RAID 0

A RAID 0 volume consists of between two and n spindles, and the data bits are striped across all of the disks within the array. This provides excellent performance; however, it provides no fault tolerance. The loss of any disk within the array means that the whole array will fail. This is illustrated in Figure 1-1.

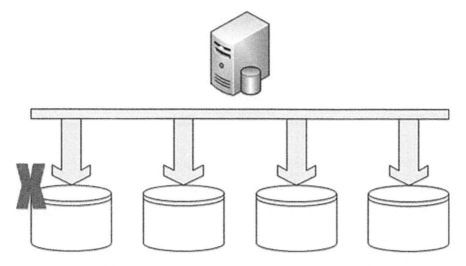

Figure 1-1. *The RAID 0 array provides no redundancy*

■ **Caution**   Because RAID 0 provides no redundancy, it should not be used for production systems.

RAID 1

A RAID 1 volume will consist of two spindles, working together as a mirrored pair. This provides redundancy in the event of failure of one of the spindles, but it comes at the expense of write performance, because every write to the volume needs to be made twice. This method of redundancy is illustrated in Figure 1-2.

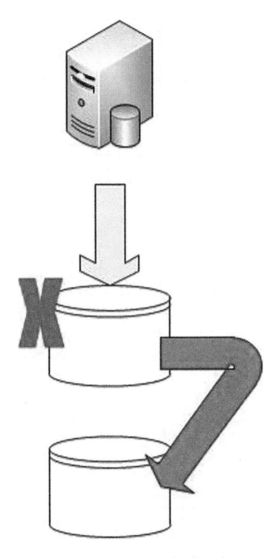

Figure 1-2. *RAID 1 provides redundancy by mirroring the disk*

___

■ **Note**   The formula for calculating the total IOPS (Input/output per second) against a RAID 1 array is as follows: IOPS = Reads + (Writes * 2).

___

RAID 5

A RAID 5 volume will consist of between three and *n* spindles and provides redundancy of exactly one disk within the array. Because the blocks of data are striped across multiple spindles, read performance of the volume will be very good, but again, this is at the expense of write performance. Write performance is impaired because redundancy is achieved by distributing parity bits across all spindles in the array. This means that there is a performance penalty of four writes for every one write to the volume. This is regardless of the number of disks in the array. The reason for this arbitrary penalty is because the parity bits are striped in the same way the data is. The controller will read the original data and the original parity and then write the new data and the new parity, without needing to read all of the other disks in the array. This method of redundancy is illustrated in Figure 1-3.

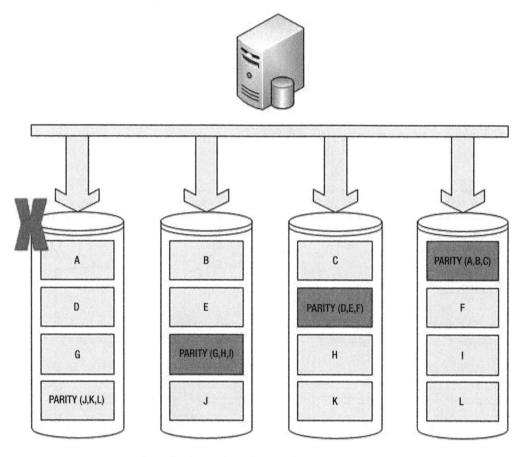

Figure 1-3. *RAID 5 provides redundancy through parity bits*

It is worthy of note, however, that should a spindle within the array fail, performance will be noticeably impaired. It is also worthy of note, that rebuilding a disk from the parity bits contained on its peers can take an extended amount of time, especially for a disk with a large capacity.

■ **Note**   The formula for calculating total IOPS against a RAID 5 array is as follows: IOPS = Read + (Writes * 4). To calculate the expected IOPS per spindle, you can divide this value for IOPS by the number of disks in the array. This can help you calculate the minimum number of disks that should be in the array to achieve your performance goals.

RAID 10

A RAID 10 volume will consist of four to *n* disks, but it will always be an even number. It provides the best combination of redundancy and performance. It works by creating a stripe of mirrors. The bits are striped, without parity, across half of the disks within the array, as they are for RAID 0, but they are then mirrored to the other half of the disks in the array.

This is known as a nested, or hybrid RAID level, and it means that half of the disks within the array can be lost, providing that none of the failed disks are within the same mirrored pair. This is illustrated in Figure 1-4.

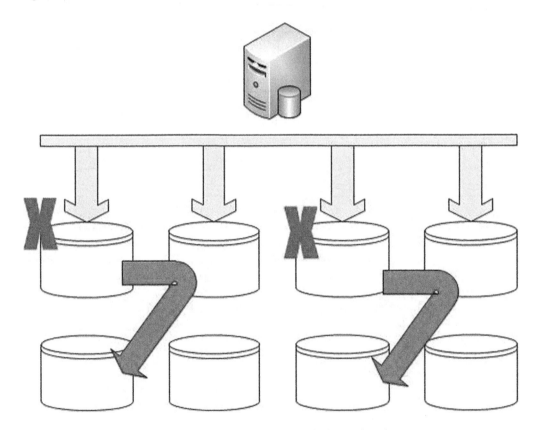

Figure 1-4. *RAID 10 provides redundancy by mirroring each disk within the stripe*

■ **Note**   The formula for calculating total IOPS against a RAID 10 array is as follows: IOPS = Read + (Writes * 2). In the same way as for RAID 5, in order to calculate the expected IOPS per spindle, you can divide the value for IOPS by the number of disks in the array. This can help you calculate the minimum number of disks that should be in the array to achieve your performance goals.

File Placement

It is generally accepted that RAID 0 should not be used for any SQL Server files. I have known people to suggest that RAID 0 may be acceptable for TempDB files. The rational here, is that a heavily used TempDB often requires very fast performance, and because it is re-created every time the instance restarts, it does not require redundancy. This sounds perfectly reasonable, but if you think in terms of uptime, you may realize why I disagree with this opinion.

Your SQL Server instance requires TempDB in order to function. If you lose TempDB, then your instance will go down, and if TempDB cannot be re-created, then you will not be able to bring your instance back up. Therefore, if you host TempDB on a RAID 0 array and one of the disks within that array fails, you will not be able to bring the instance back up until you have performed one of the following actions:

1. Wait for the storage team to bring the RAID 0 array back online.

2. Start the instance in "minimal configuration mode" and use SQLCMD to change the location of TempDB.

By the time either of these steps are complete, you may find that stakeholders are jumping up and down, so you may find it best to avoid this option. For this reason, TempDB is generally best placed on a RAID 10 array, whenever possible. This will provide the best level of performance for the database, and because its size is significantly smaller than the user database files, you do not have the same level of cost implication.

In an ideal world, where money is no object, the data files of your user databases will be stored on RAID 10 arrays, since RAID 10 provides the best combination of redundancy and performance. In the real world, however, if the applications you are supporting are not mission critical, this may not be justifiable. If this is the situation, then RAID 5 can be a good choice, as long as your applications have a fairly high ratio of reads to writes. I would normally use a ratio of three to one in favor of reads as being a good baseline, but of course, it can vary in every scenario.

If your databases are only using basic features of SQL Server, then you will likely find that RAID 1 is a good choice for your log files. RAID 5 is not generally suitable, because of the write-intensive nature of the transaction log. In some cases, I have even known RAID 1 to perform better than RAID 10 for the transaction log. This is because of the sequential nature of the write activity.

However, some features of SQL Server can generate substantial read activity from the transaction log. If this is the case, then you may find that RAID 10 is a requirement for your transaction log as well as your data files. Features that cause transaction log reads include the following:

*   AlwaysOn availability groups

*   Database mirroring

*   Snapshot creation

*   Backups

*   DBCC CHECKDB

*   Change data capture

*   Log shipping (both backups, and also if restoring logs WITH STANDBY)

Solid State Drives (SSDs)

One common reason to use locally attached storage, as opposed to a storage area network (SAN), is to optimize the performance of SQL Server components, which require extremely fast IO. These components include TempDB and buffer cache extensions. It is not uncommon to find that a database's data and log files are stored on a SAN, but TempDB and buffer cache extensions are stored on locally attached storage.

In this example, it would make good sense to use SSDs in the locally attached array. Solid state drives (SSDs) can offer very high IO rates, but at a higher cost, compared to traditional disks. SSDs are also not a "magic bullet". Although they offer a very high number of IOPS for random disk access, they can be less efficient for sequential scan activities, which are common in certain database workload profiles, such as data warehouses. SSDs are also prone to sudden failure, as opposed to the gradual decline of a traditional disk. Therefore, having a fault tolerant RAID level and hot spares in the array is a very good idea.

Working with a SAN

Storage area network are three words that can strike fear into the heart of a database administrator (DBA). The modern DBA must embrace concepts such as SAN and virtualization; however, although they pose fundamental change, they also ease the overall manageability of the estate and reduce the total cost of ownership (TCO).

The most important thing for a DBA to remember about a SAN is that it changes the fundamental principles of the IO subsystem, and DBAs must change their thinking accordingly. For example, in the world of locally attached storage, the most fundamental principle is to separate you data files, log files, and TempDB, and to ensure that they are all hosted on the most appropriate RAID level.

In the world of the SAN, however, you may initially be alarmed to find that your SAN administrators do not offer a choice of RAID level, and if they do, they may not offer RAID 10. If you find this to be the case, it is likely because the SAN is, behind the scenes, actually stripping the data across every disk in the array. This means, that although the RAID level can still have some impact on throughput, the more important consideration is which storage tier to choose.

Many organizations choose to tier the storage on their SAN, offering three or more tiers. Tier 1 will be the highest tier and may well consist of a combination of SSDs and small, highly performing Fibre Channel drives. Tier 2 will normally consist of larger drives—potentially SATA (Serial Advanced Technology Attachment)—and Tier 3 will often use nearline storage. Nearline storage consists of a large number of inexpensive disks, such as SATA disks, which are usually stopped. The disks only spin up when there is a requirement to access the data that they contain. As you have probably guessed, you will want to ensure that any applications that require good performance will need to be located on Tier 1 of your SAN. Tier 2 could possibly be an option for small, rarely used databases with little or no concurrency, and Tier 3 should rarely, if ever, be used to store SQL Server databases or logs.

Your real throughput will be determined by these factors, but also many others, such as the number of networks paths between your server and the SAN, how many servers are concurrently accessing the SAN, and so on. Another interesting quirk of a SAN is that you will often find that your write performance is far superior to your read performance. This is because some SANs use a battery-backed write cache, but when reading, they need to retrieve the data from the spindles.

Next, consider that because all of your data may well be striped across all of the spindles in the array— and even if it isn't, the likelihood is that all files on a single server will probably all reside on the same CPG (Common Provisioning Group)—you should not expect to see an instant performance improvement from separating your data, log, and TempDB files. Many DBAs, however, still choose to place their data, log, and TempDB files on separate volumes for logical separation and consistency with other servers that use locally attached storage. In some cases, however, if you are using SAN snapshots or SAN replication for redundancy, you may be required to have the data and log files of a database on the same volume. You should check this with your storage team.

Disk Block Size

Another thing to consider for disk configuration, whether it is locally attached, or on a SAN, is the disk block size. Depending on your storage, it is likely that the default NTFS (New Technology File System) allocation unit size will be set as 4KB. The issue is that SQL Server organizes data into eight continuous 8KB pages, known as an *extent*. To get optimum performance for SQL Server, the block sizes of the volumes hosting data, logs, and TempDB should be aligned with this and set to 64KB.

You can check the disk block size by running the Windows PowerShell script in Listing 1-2, which uses fsutil to gather the NTFS properties of the volume. The script assumes that f: is the volume whose block size you wish to determine. Be sure to change this to the drive letter that you wish to check. Also ensure that the script is run as Administrator.

Listing 1-2. Determine Disk Block Size

```
# Populate the drive letter you want to check

$drive = "f:"

# Initialize outputarray

$outputarray = new-object PSObject

$outputarray | add-member NoteProperty Drive $drive

# Initialize output

$output = (fsutil fsinfo ntfsinfo $drive)

# Split each line of fsutil into a seperate array value

foreach ($line in $output) {

    $info = $line.split(':')

    $outputarray | add-member NoteProperty $info[0].trim().Replace(' ','_') $info[1].trim()

    $info = $null

}

# Format and display results

$results = 'Disk Block Size for ' + $drive + ' ' + $outputarray.Bytes_Per_Cluster/1024 + 'KB'

$results
```

Operating Systems Considerations

SQL Server has support for many operating systems. For example, the 64-bit version of SQL Server 2014 Enterprise edition is supported on the following versions of Windows:

Windows Server 2012 R2 Datacenter 64-bit

Windows Server 2012 R2 Standard 64-bit

Windows Server 2012 R2 Essentials 64-bit

Windows Server 2012 R2 Foundation 64-bit

Windows Server 2012 Datacenter 64-bit

Windows Server 2012 Standard 64-bit

Windows Server 2012 Essentials 64-bit

Windows Server 2012 Foundation 64-bit

Windows Server 2008 R2 SP1 Datacenter 64-bit

Windows Server 2008 R2 SP1 Enterprise 64-bit

Windows Server 2008 R2 SP1 Standard 64-bit

Windows Server 2008 R2 SP1 Web 64-bit

Windows Server 2008 SP2 Datacenter 64-bit

Windows Server 2008 SP2 Enterprise 64-bit

Windows Server 2008 SP2 Standard 64-bit

Windows Server 2008 SP2 Web 64-bit

In contrast, SQL Server 2014 Standard edition can be installed on all of the following versions of Windows Server:

Windows Server 2012 R2 Datacenter 64-bit

Windows Server 2012 R2 Standard 64-bit

Windows Server 2012 R2 Essentials 64-bit

Windows Server 2012 R2 Foundation 64-bit

Windows Server 2012 Datacenter 64-bit

Windows Server 2012 Standard 64-bit

Windows Server 2012 Essentials 64-bit

Windows Server 2012 Foundation 64-bit

Windows Server 2008 R2 SP1 Datacenter 64-bit

Windows Server 2008 R2 SP1 Enterprise 64-bit

Windows Server 2008 R2 SP1 Standard 64-bit

Windows Server 2008 R2 SP1 Foundation 64-bit

Windows Server 2008 R2 SP1 Web 64-bit

Windows Server 2008 SP2 Datacenter 64-bit

Windows Server 2008 SP2 Enterprise 64-bit

Windows Server 2008 SP2 Standard 64-bit

Windows Server 2008 SP2 Foundation 64-bit

Windows Server 2008 SP2 Web 64-bit

If you choose to use a Windows Core environment, then the following operating systems can be used for Enterprise edition:

Windows Server 2012 R2 Datacenter 64-bit

Windows Server 2012 R2 Standard 64-bit

Windows Server 2012 Datacenter 64-bit

Windows Server 2012 Standard 64-bit

Windows Server 2008 R2 SP1 Datacenter 64-bit

Windows Server 2008 R2 SP1 Enterprise 64-bit

Windows Server 2008 R2 SP1 Standard 64-bit

Windows Server 2008 R2 SP1 Web 64-bit

It is unlikely, however, that you will want to allow SQL Server to be installed on any operating system that is supported. It is advisable to align a version of SQL Server with a specific version of Windows. This gives you two benefits.

First, it drastically reduces the amount of testing that you need to perform to sign off your build. For example, imagine that you decide you will only allow Enterprise edition within your environment. In theory, you would still need to gain operational sign-off on 16 different operating systems. In contrast, if you allow both SQL Server Enterprise and Standard editions of SQL Server, but you align Enterprise edition with Windows Server 2012 R2 Datacenter and Standard edition with Windows Server 2012 R2 Standard, then you would only require sign-off once for each of your supported editions of SQL Server.

The second benefit is related to end of life cycle (EOL) for your platforms. If you allow SQL Server 2014 to be installed on Windows Server 2008, the end of mainstream support for Windows is January 2015, as opposed to September 2019 for SQL. At best, this will cause complexity and outage while you upgrade Windows, and at worst, it could lead to extended support costs that you could have avoided.

Configuring the Operating System

It is probable that your Windows administration team will have a "gold build" for Windows Server 2012, but even if they do, is it optimized for SQL Server? Unless they have produced a separate build just for the purposes of hosting SQL Server, then the chances are that it will not be. The exact customizations that you will need to make are dependent on how the Windows build is configured, your environmental requirements, and the requirements of the data-tier application that your server will be hosting. The following sections highlight some of the changes that are often required.

■ **Note**   A *gold build* is a predefined template for the operating system that can be easily installed on new servers to reduce deployment time and enforce consistency.

Setting the Power Plan

It is important that you set your server to use the High Performance power plan. This is because if the Balanced power plan is used, then your CPU may be throttled back during a period of inactivity. When activity on the server kicks in again, you may experience a performance issue.

You can set the power plan through the Windows GUI by opening the Power Options console in Control Panel and selecting the High Performance radio button, as illustrated in Figure 1-5.

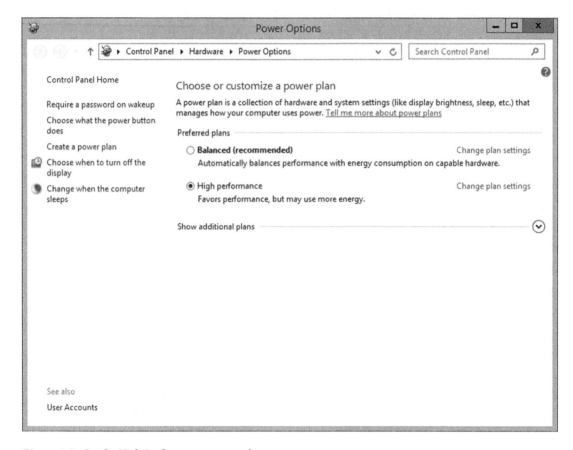

Figure 1-5. *Set the High Performance power plan*

The High Performance power plan can also be set by using PowerShell. Listing 1-3 illustrates this by passing in the GUID of the High Performance power plan as a value for the -setactive parameter of the powercfg executable.

Listing 1-3. Set High Performance Power Plan with PowerShell

```
powercfg -setactive 8c5e7fda-e8bf-4a96-9a85-a6e23a8c635c
```

Optimizing for Background Services

It is good practice to ensure that your server is configured to prioritize background services over foreground applications. In practice, this means that Windows will adapt its context-switching algorithm to allow background services, including those used by SQL Server, to have more time on the processor than foreground applications have.

To ensure that Optimize for Background Service is turned on, enter the System console in Control Panel and choose Advanced System Settings. In the System Properties dialog box, select Settings within the Performance section. These screens are illustrated in Figure 1-6.

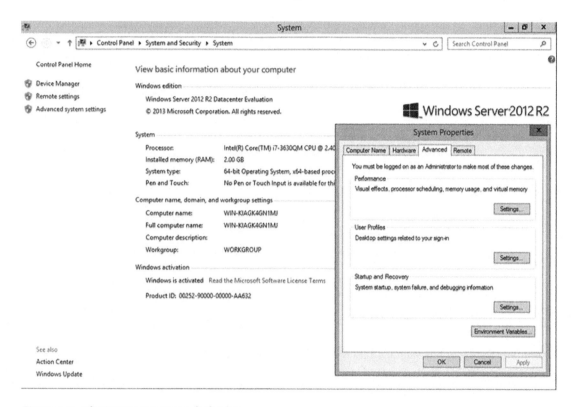

Figure 1-6. *The System Properties dialog box*

In the Performance Options screen, illustrated in Figure 1-7, ensure that the Background Services radio button is selected and click OK.

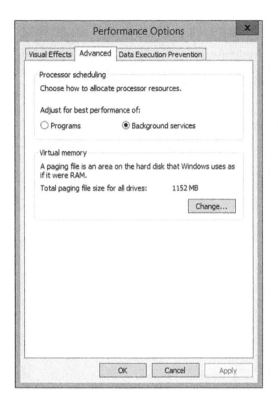

Figure 1-7. *Performance Options*

Optimizing for background services can also be set by using PowerShell. Listing 1-4 demonstrates using the set-property command to update the Win32PrioritySeperation key in the Registry. The script must be run as Administrator.

Listing 1-4. Setting Optimize for Background Services with Powershell

```
Set-ItemProperty -path HKLM:\SYSTEM\CurrentControlSet\Control\PriorityControl -name
Win32PrioritySeparation -Type DWORD -Value 24
```

Assigning User Rights

Depending on the features of SQL Server that you wish to use, you may need to grant the service account that will be running the SQL Server service user rights assignments. These assignments allow security principles to perform tasks on a computer. In the case of the SQL Server service account, they provide the permissions for enabling some SQL Server functionality where that functionality interacts with the operating system. The three most common user rights assignments, which are not automatically granted to the service account during installation, are discussed in the following pages.

Initializing the Instant File

By default, when you create or expand a file, the file is filled with 0s. This is a process known as "zeroing out" the file, and it overwrites any data that previously occupied the same disk space. The issue with this is that it can take some time, especially for large files.

It is possible to override this behavior, however, so that the files are not zeroed out. This introduces a very small security risk, in the respect that the data that previously existed within that disc location could still theoretically be discovered, but this risk is so small that it is generally thought to be far outweighed by the performance benefits.

In order to use instant file initialization, the Perform Volume Maintenance Tasks User Rights Assignment must be granted to the service account that is running the SQL Server Database Engine. Once this has been granted, SQL Server will automatically use instant file initialization. No other configuration is required.

To grant the assignment through Windows GUI, open the local security policy from Control Panel | System and Security | Administrative Tools, before drilling through Local Policies | User Rights Assignment. This will display a full list of assignments. Scroll down until you find Perform Volume Maintenance Tasks. This is illustrated in Figure 1-8.

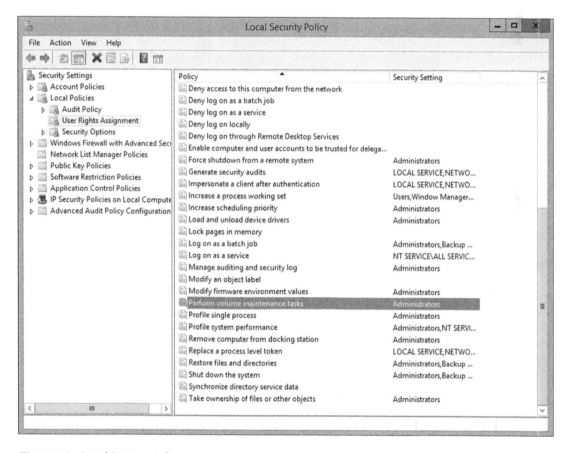

Figure 1-8. *Local Security Policy*

Right-clicking on the assignment and entering its properties will allow you to add your service account, via the Add User Or Group button, as illustrated in Figure 1-9.

Figure 1-9. *Perform Volume Maintenance Tasks Properties*

Locking Pages in Memory

If Windows is experiencing memory pressure, it will attempt to page data from RAM into virtual memory on disk. This can cause an issue within SQL Server. In order to provide acceptable performance, SQL Server caches recently used data pages in the buffer cache, which is an area of memory reserved by the Database Engine. In fact, all data pages are read from the buffer cache, even if they need to be read from disk first. If Windows decides to move pages from the buffer cache out to disk, the performance of your instance will be severely impaired.

In order to avoid this occurrence, it is possible to lock the pages of the buffer cache in memory, as long as you are using the Enterprise, Business Intelligence, or Standard edition of SQL Server 2014. To do this, you simply need to grant the service account that is running the Database Engine the Lock Pages In Memory assignment using the same method as for Perform Volume Maintenance Tasks.

▓ **Caution** If you are installing SQL Server on a virtual machine, depending on the configuration of your virtual platform, you may not be able to set Lock Pages In Memory, because it may interfere with the balloon driver. The balloon driver is used by the virtualization platform to reclaim memory from the guest operating system. You should discuss this with your virtual platform administrator.

SQL Audit to the Event Log

If you are planning to use SQL Audit to capture activity within your instance, you will have the option of saving the generated events to a file, to the security log, or to the application log. The security log will be the most appropriate location if your enterprise has high security requirements.

In order to allow generated events to be written to the security log, the service account that runs the Database Engine must be granted the Generate Security Audits User Rights Assignment. This can be achieved through the Local Security Policy console.

An additional step, in order for SQL Server to be able to write audit events to the security log, is to configure the Audit Application Generated setting. This can be located in the Local Security Policy console, by drilling through Advanced Audit Policy Configuration | System Audit Policies | Object Access. The properties of the Audit Application Generated event can then be modified as illustrated in Figure 1-10.

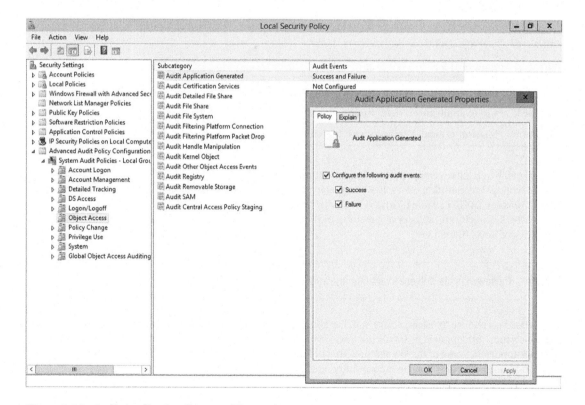

Figure 1-10. *Audit Application Generated Properties*

■ **Caution**   You need to ensure that your policies are not overridden by policies implemented at the GPO level. If this is the case, you should ask your AD (Active Directory) administrator to move your servers into a separate OU (Organizational Unit) with a less restrictive policy.

Azure Options

If you are planning to host your database(s) in the cloud, then you have many different options. The main decision that you need to make is if you should use an Azure SQL Database or if you need an Azure Virtual Machine (VM) that hosts SQL Server.

Azure SQL Database

If you choose the option of an Azure SQL Database, then the main advantage is that it is a DBaaS (Database as a Service) offering, which will require little or no infrastructure maintenance on your part. For example, software updates will be applied automatically. It is also simple to scale your databases up through the service tiers as required. There are currently three service tiers on offer from Microsoft, which are listed in Table 1-3.

Table 1-3. *Azure SQL Database Service Tiers*

Tier	Designed for
Basic	Small databases with no concurrency requirements
Standard	Cloud applications that require concurrency
Premium	Mission-critical databases with high throughput and concurrency

All of the tiers offer varying levels of capacity and DR (Disaster Recovery) facilities. For example, at the time of writing, Basic edition offers 2GB of capacity, with a self-service restore for the last 7 days, whereas Standard offers 250GB of capacity and self-service restore for the last 14 days, and the Premium tier offers 500GB capacity and self-service restore for the last 35 days. All of the tiers offer a 99.99% uptime SLA (Service Level Agreement).

■ **Note**   These levels are subject to change and you should check the current values at `azure.microsoft.com`.

When you choose to use an Azure SQL Database, the most important thing to remember is that you do not have a fully functional SQL Server instance as you would with an on-premises option. Many features are not supported. Some of the key features that are not supported at the time of writing are as listed here. Support for these features may be incorporated at a later date.

- CDC (Change Data Capture)
- Data compression
- Partitioning

- FILESTREAM data

- Policy-based management

- Resource Governor

- Replication

- Database mirroring

- Service Broker

- Server Agent jobs

- Extended stored procedures

- Typed XML

Azure SQL Server Virtual Machine

The alternative to an Azure SQL Database is a cloud-based virtual machine (VM). There are several offerings available from companies such as Microsoft and Amazon. If you choose Microsoft as a provider, then you will purchase an Azure SQL VM. In this case, you can choose one of a number of virtual machine images that have been configured by the SQL Server product team and build out an entire VM.

It is possible to build your virtual machine with 1, 2, 4, 8, or 16 virtual cores; auto-scaling options are also available. Additionally, you are able to select between Web, Standard, or Enterprise versions of SQL Server. These versions are the same as their on-premise equivalents. A special image has also been built around Enterprise edition and it is configured specifically for data warehousing. Additional instances of SQL Server can also be installed on the VMs, but these may be subject to additional licensing requirements.

■ **Note**   The images available are correct at the time of writing, but are subject to change. You should check the currently available images on Azure Marketplace.

The Azure SQL VM offers much more flexibility, in terms of functionality, than the Azure SQL Database option, with the majority of SQL Server functionality being available out-of-the-box:

- Integration Services

- Analysis Services

- Reporting Services

- Data Quality Services

Other features, such as the following, may require additional configuration steps, however:

- Distributed Replay Client

- Master Data Services

- PowerPivot for SharePoint

Selecting Features

When installing SQL Server, it may be tempting to install every feature in case you need it at some point. For the performance, manageability, and security of your environment, however, you should always adhere to the YAGNI (you aren't going to need it) principle. The YAGNI principle derives from extreme programming methodology, but it also holds true for the platform. The premise is that you do the simplest thing that will work. This will save you from issues related to complexity. Remember that additional features can be installed later. The following sections provide an overview of the main features you can selected during an installation of SQL Server 2014 Enterprise edition.

Database Engine Service

The Database Engine is the core service within the SQL Server suite. It contains the SQLOS, the Storage Engine, and the Relational Engine, as illustrated in Figure 1-11. It is responsible for securing, processing, and optimizing access to relational data. It also contains replication components and the DQS Server features, which can be selected optionally. Replication is a set of tools that allows you to disperse data. DQS Server is a tool that allows you to easily find and cleanse inconsistent data. This book focuses primarily on the Database Engine.

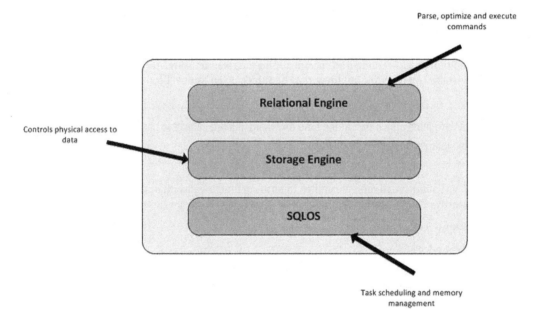

Figure 1-11. *Database Engine arcitecture*

Analysis Services

SSAS (SQL Server Analysis Services) is a set of tools that can be harnessed for the analytical processing and data mining of data. It can be installed in one of three modes:

- Multidimensional and Data Mining

- Tabular

- PowerPivot for SharePoint

Multidimensional and Data Mining mode will provide the capability to host multidimensional cubes. Cubes offer the ability to store aggregated data, known as *measures*, that can be sliced and diced across multiple dimensions, and provide the basis of responsive, intuitive, and complex reports and pivot tables. Developers can query the cubes by using the multidimensional expressions (MDX) language.

Tabular mode gives users the ability to host data in Microsoft's BI semantic model. This model uses xVelocity to provide in-memory analytics, offering integration between relational and nonrelational data sources and provides KPIs (Key Performance Indicators), calculations, multilevel hierarchies, and calculations. Instead of using dimensions and measures, the tabular model uses tables, columns, and relationships.

PowerPivot is an extension for Excel, which like the tabular model, uses xVelocity to perform in-memory analytics and can be used for datasets up to 2GB in size. The PowerPivot for SharePoint installation expands on this by running Analysis Services in SharePoint mode, and it offers both server-side processing and browser-based interaction with PowerPivot workbooks; it also supports Power View reports and Excel workbooks through SharePoint Excel Services.

Reporting Services

Reporting Services is a set of server and client components that can be used for the hosting, management, and delivery of reports in a variety of formats. Reporting Services can be installed in two different modes:

- Native

- SharePoint

When installed in Native mode, Reporting Services uses its own Web interface, called Report Manager, to host reports and data source connections. This interface is exposed via a Web Service and implements its own security model.

When installed in SharePoint mode, reports and data source connections are hosted in a SharePoint site. For this reason, Report Manager is not installed.

Reporting Services Add-in for SharePoint Products

The Reporting Services add-in for SharePoint provides a set of Reporting Services features on SharePoint. This includes Power View, which is a data visualization tool that provides end users with drag-and-drop reporting. It also includes features such as a report viewer web part and the ability to open Report Builder reports from SharePoint.

Data Quality Client

The Data Quality Server is installed as an optional component of the Database Engine, as mentioned earlier. The Data Quality Client, however, can be installed as a shared feature. A shared feature is installed only once on a server and is shared by all instances of SQL Server on that machine. The Client is a GUI that allows you to administer DQS, as well as perform data-matching and data-cleansing activities.

Client Connectivity Tools

Client Connectivity Tools is a set of components for client/server communication. This includes the OLEDB, ODBC, ADODB, and OLAP network libraries.

Integration Services

Integration Services is a very powerful, graphical ETL (extract, transform, and load) tool provided with SQL Server. From SQL Server 2012 onward, Integration Services is incorporated into the Database Engine. Despite this, the Integration Services option still needs to be installed for the functionality to work correctly, because it includes binaries that the functionality relies on.

Integration Services packages comprise a *control flow*, which is responsible for management and flow operations, including bulk inserts, loops, and transactions. The control flow also contains zero or more data flows. A *data flow* is a set of data sources, transformations, and destinations, which provides a powerful framework for merging, dispersing, and transforming data.

Client Tools Backward Compatibility

Client Tools Backwards Compatibility provides support for discontinued features of SQL Server. Installing this feature will install SQL Distributed Management Objects and Decision Support Objects.

Client Tools SDK

Installing the Client Tools SDK provides the SMO (server management objects) assemblies. This allows you to programmatically control SQL Server and Integration Services from within .NET applications.

Documentation Components

The Documentation Components do not include the product documentation. The product documentation does not ship with the media. Installing this feature will install the Help Viewer and the Help Management tools. After this feature is installed, you will be able to use the Help Viewer to view online product documentation, or you can download a local copy of the documentation and then install this by using the Help Library Manager.

Management Tools

When installing the Management Tools, there are two options to choose from, either Basic or Complete. If you select the basic option, the following features will be installed:

- SQL Server Management studio (the GUI used for managing SQL Server instances)
- SQLCMD (the command line interface for querying SQL Server)
- SQL Server PowerShell provider (the libraries for PowerShell, which allow it to interact with SQL Server)

If you select the Complete option, then in addition to the features just listed, the following will also be installed:

- Management Studio extensions that provide support for SSRS, SSAS, and SSIS

- Profiler (a graphical tool for tracing SQL Server activity)

- Utility Management (a tool that provides a holistic view of SQL Server health throughout the enterprise)

- Database Engine Tuning Advisor (a graphical tool that samples a workload and provides guidance on indexes, indexed views, and partitioning)

Distributed Replay Controller

Distributed Replay is a feature that allows you to capture a trace and then replay it on another server. This allows you to test the impact of performance tuning or software upgrades. If this sounds familiar to functionality in Profiler that you may be used to, then you are correct, there is some overlap. Distributed Replay has the following advantages, however:

1. Distributed Replay has a lower impact on resources than Profiler, meaning that the servers you are tracing run less risk of suffering performance issues while the trace is running.

2. Distributed Replay allows you to capture workloads from multiple servers (clients) and replay them on a single host.

Within a Distributed Replay topology, you need to configure one server as the controller. It is the controller that will orchestrate the work against the client(s) and the target server.

Distributed Replay Client

As described earlier, multiple client servers can work together to create a workload to be replayed against the target server. The Distributed Replay Client should be installed on any servers that you wish to capture traces from using Distributed Replay.

SQL Client Connectivity SDK

The Client Connectivity SDK provides a SDK for SQL Native Client to support application development. It also provides other interfaces, such as support for stack tracing in client applications.

Master Data Services

Master Data Services is a tool for managing master data within the enterprise. It allows you to model data domains that map to business entities, and it helps you manage these with hierarchies, business rules, and data versioning. When you select this feature, several components are installed:

- A web console to provide administrative capability

- A configuration tool to allow you to configure your MDM databases and the Web console

- A web service, which provides extensibility for developers

- An Excel add-in, for creating new entities and attributes

Summary

Planning a deployment can be a complicated task that involves discussions with business and technical stakeholders to ensure that your platform will meet the applications requirements, and ultimately the business needs. There are many factors that you should take into account.

Make sure you consider which is the appropriate version of SQL Server to install and the associated licensing considerations for that version. You should consider the holistic supportability of the estate when making this decision and not just the needs of the specific application. You should also consider if an Azure hosting option may be right for your application, or potentially even a hybrid approach, involving both on-premise and cloud hosting. SQL Azure will be discussed in further detail in *Section V: Managing Hybrid Cloud Environments*.

When planning a deployment, make sure to carry out thorough capacity planning. Also think about the hardware requirements of the application. How much RAM and how many processor cores you will need are important considerations, but perhaps the main consideration is storage. SQL Server is usually an IO-bound application, so storage can often prove to be the bottleneck.

You should also consider requirements for the operating system. This should not be limited to the most appropriate version of Windows, but also to the configuration of the operating system. Just because there is a Windows gold build available, does this mean that it is configured optimally for your SQL Server installation?

Finally, consider which features you should select to install. Most applications require only a small subset of features, and by carefully selecting which features you require, you can reduce the security footprint of the installation and also reduce management overheads.

CHAPTER 2

■ ■ ■

GUI Installation

You can invoke SQL Server's Installation Center by running SQL Server's setup.exe application. The Installation Center provides many utilities that will help you install an instance; these include links and tools to assist you with planning your deployment, stand-alone and clustered installation capability, and advanced tools, which will allow you to build instances using configuration files or based upon preprepared images.

This chapter will provide an overview of the options available to you in the Installation Center before guiding you through the process of installing SQL Server using the graphical user interface (GUI). It will also offer real-world advice on decisions that are critical to the ongoing supportability of your instance.

Installation Center

The SQL Server Installation Center is a one-stop shop for all activity that relates to planning, installing, and upgrading a SQL Server instance. It is the application that you are greeted with when you run the SQL Server installation media. Installation Center consists of seven tabs, and the following sections will describe the content of those tabs.

The Planning Tab

The Planning tab is illustrated in Figure 2-1 and consists of numerous links to MSDN (Microsoft Developer Network) pages, which provide you with important documentation on SQL Server, such as a complete set of hardware and software requirements and documentation for SQL Server's security model.

Figure 2-1. *The Planning tab*

In addition to accessing documentation with the links provided, you can also access two tools. The first of these is the System Configuration Checker. This tool runs during the installation process to determine if there are any conditions that will prevent SQL Server from being installed. These checks include ensuring that the server is not already configured as a domain controller and checking that the WMI (Windows Management Instrumentation) Service is running. When you run this tool before you begin installing SQL Server, it can prewarn you of any issues that may cause the installation to fail so that you can fix them before you begin installation. The System Configuration Checker is also available on the Tools tab on the Installation Center.

The second tool is the Install Upgrade Advisor. You can use this tool to analyze any instances of SQL Server 2005 or higher that already exist on the server to ensure that you will have no issues upgrading those instances to SQL Server 2014.

The Installation Tab

As illustrated in Figure 2-2, the Installation tab of the Installation Center contains the tools that you will use for installing a new instance of SQL Server, adding new features to an existing instance, or upgrading an instance from SQL Server 2005, 2008, or 2012. In order to install a stand-alone instance of SQL Server, you would select the New SQL Server Stand-Alone Instance Or Add New Features To An Existing Instance option.

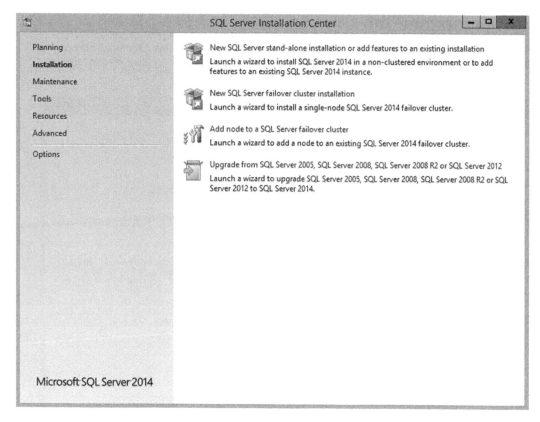

Figure 2-2. *The Installation tab*

In addition to installing a stand-alone instance, adding new features to an instance, and upgrading an existing instance to the latest version, there are also options on this screen for installing a SQL Server failover clustered instance and for adding a new node to an existing failover cluster. A *failover cluster* is a system where between 2 and 64 servers work together to provide redundancy and protect against a failure that stops one or more of the servers from functioning. Each server that participates in the cluster is known as a *node*.

The SQL Server Database Engine and the SQL Server Analysis Services are both "cluster-aware" applications, meaning that they can be installed on a Windows cluster and can make use of its failover capabilities. When installed on a failover cluster, databases and transaction logs are located on shared storage, which any node in the cluster can use, but the binaries are installed locally on each of the nodes. Failover clustering will be discussed in detail in Chapter 12.

The Maintenance Tab

The Maintenance tab contains tools for performing an edition upgrade, repairing a corrupt instance, and removing a node from a cluster; it also contains a link to run Windows Update, as illustrated in Figure 2-3.

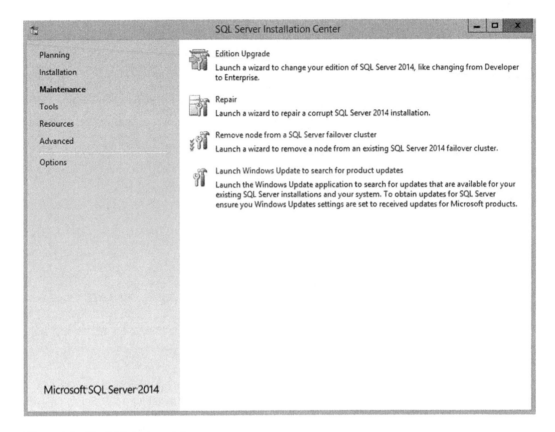

Figure 2-3. *The Maintenance tab*

You can use the Edition Upgrade option to upgrade an existing SQL Server 2014 instance from one edition to another; so for example, you may wish to upgrade an instance installed as Developer edition to Enterprise edition. You may remember that in Chapter 1, I spoke about a situation in which you may have mistakenly installed Enterprise edition as opposed to Enterprise Core edition. You can use the Edition Upgrade option to fix that issue.

You can use the Repair option to attempt to resolve issues with a corrupt installation of SQL Server. For example, you can use this tool if the Registry entries are corrupt or if the data files of the Master database have become corrupted, preventing the instance from starting.

Use the Remove Node From A SQL Server Failover Cluster option to remove SQL Server from a node within a failover cluster. You can use this option as part of the process for evicting a node. Unfortunately, the Installation Center has no functionality for uninstalling an instance. You must do this through the Control Panel.

Not surprisingly, you can use the Launch Windows Update To Search For Product Updates option to launch Windows Update. You can then choose to install the updates and fixes that are available for SQL Server.

The Tools Tab

The Tools tab contains a selection of tools that will assist you in installing SQL Server, as illustrated in Figure 2-4. This includes the System Configuration Checker, which I introduced earlier in this chapter; a discovery tool for SQL Server components already installed on the local server; the Microsoft Assessment and Planning (MAP) tool; a link for downloading SQL Server Data Tools for Business Intelligence; and the PowerPivot Configuration Tool.

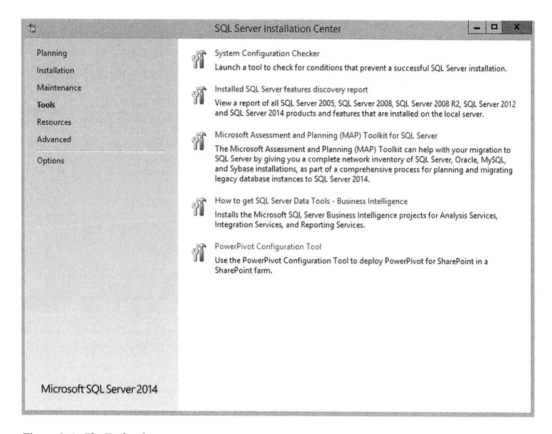

Figure 2-4. *The Tools tab*

Choose the Installed SQL Server Features Discovery Report option to analyze the local server and return a list of all SQL Server features and components that are installed. This will include features from all versions, from SQL Server 2005 on.

The Microsoft Assessment And Planning (MAP) Toolkit For SQL Server option will provide you with a link from which you can download the MAP for SQL Server tool. When you run this tool, it will perform a network-wide search for SQL Server, Oracle, and MySQL installations. It will produce a detailed report, which, for SQL Server, will include the name, version, and edition of the component. For Oracle, it will include the size and usage of each schema, including complexity estimates for migration. You can also use this tool to plan migration and consolidation strategies and to audit license requirements across the enterprise.

The How To Get SQL Server Data Tools - Business Intelligence option provides you with a link for downloading SQL Server Data Tools. Data Tools provides an IDE (integrated development environment) and project templates that allow developers to build components across the SQL Server BI stack, including SSIS (SQL Server Integration Services), SSRS (SQL Server Reporting Services), and SSAS (SQL Server Analysis Services), within a Visual Studio shell. T-SQL project templates are also available for Data Tools, taking away developers' dependency on SQL Server Management Studio.

You can use the PowerPivot Configuration Tool to remove, upgrade, repair, or configure PowerPivot within a SharePoint 2010 or 2013 farm. The configuration options included allow you to specify the account that will run PowerPivot's Internet Information Services (IIS) application pool, select a port number for the Central Administration web app, and specify the local instance of SQL Server that will run PowerPivot. This option is required if you are using a named instance.

The Resources Tab

As illustrated in Figure 2-5, the Resources tab contains links to useful information regarding SQL Server. This includes a link to SQL Server Books Online, the Developer Center, and the SQL Server product evaluation site. Additionally, on this tab, you will also find links to Microsoft's privacy statement and the full SQL Server license agreement. Another very useful link is one that directs you to the CodePlex samples site. From this site, you can download the AdventureWorks databases, which will aid you in testing features of SQL Server with a precreated database.

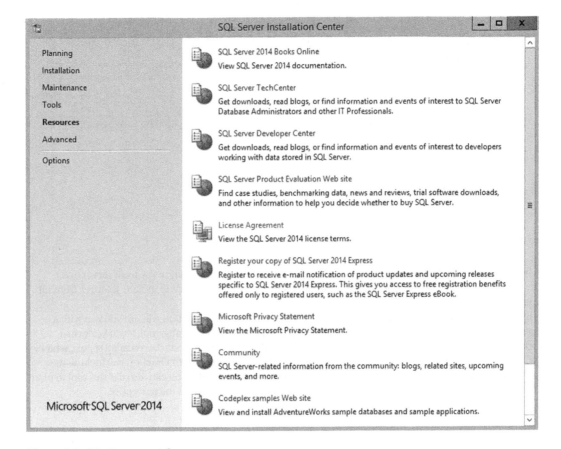

Figure 2-5. *The Resources tab*

The Advanced Tab

On the Advanced tab, illustrated in Figure 2-6, you will find tools for performing advanced installations of SQL Server, both as a stand-alone instance and also as a cluster. These tools include Install Based On Configuration File, Advanced Cluster Preparation, Advanced Cluster Completion, Image Preparation Of A Stand-Alone Instance Of SQL Server, and Image Completion Of A Stand-Alone Instance Of SQL Server.

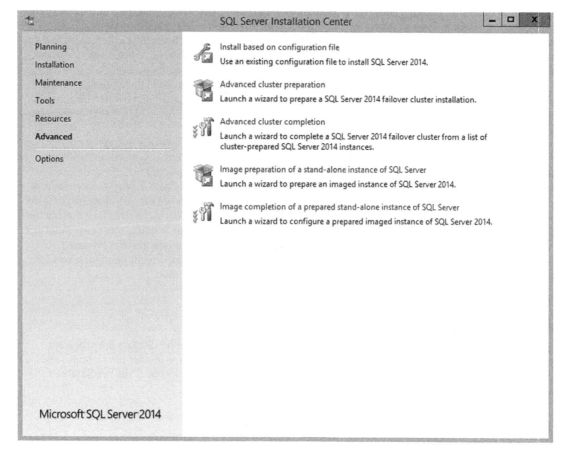

Figure 2-6. *The Advanced tab*

When you are installing SQL Server, a configuration file will automatically be created. It is also possible to create this configuration file manually. You can then use this configuration file to install other instances of SQL Server with an identical configuration. This can be useful for promoting consistency across the enterprise. Once this configuration file has been created, you can use the Install Based On Configuration File option to install further instances based on the precreated configuration. Configuration files can also be useful for command-line installs, which will be discussed in Chapter 3. Additionally, you can also use a configuration file for cluster preparation.

If you wish to use a configuration file for cluster preparation, then instead of choosing to install the cluster via the New SQL Server Failover Cluster Installation and Add Node To A SQL Server Failover Cluster wizards, which are available on the Installation tab, you should choose the Advanced Cluster Preparation option on the Advanced tab. You will initially run this on one of the cluster nodes that can be a possible owner of the SQL Server instance, and a configuration file will be generated. Subsequently running the Advanced Cluster Preparation wizard on all other nodes of the cluster that can be possible owners will result in the configuration file being used to ensure consistency of installation across the cluster. This approach will even work for multi-subnet clusters (also known as geoclusters), since SQL Server will automatically detect the relationship between the subnets and you will be prompted to select an IP address for each subnet. The installation will then add each of the IP addresses as dependencies to the cluster role, using the OR constraint, where each node cannot be the possible owner of every IP address. Alternatively, it will use the AND constraint, where each node can be the possible owner of every IP address.

Once you have run the Advanced Cluster Preparation wizard on every node that is a possible owner of the clustered instance, you can run the Advanced Cluster Completion wizard. You only have to run this wizard once and you can run it on any of the nodes that are possible owners. After this wizard has completed successfully, the clustered instance will be fully functioning.

The Image Preparation Of A Stand-Alone Instance Of SQL Server option will use Sysprep for SQL Server to install a vanilla instance of SQL Server, which is not configured with account-, computer-, or network-specific information. It can be used in conjunction with Windows Sysprep to build a complete template of Windows with prepared SQL Server instances, which can then be used for deployments across the enterprise. This helps enforce consistency. In SQL Server 2014, all features of a stand-alone instance are supported by Sysprep; however, repairing an installation is not supported. This means that if an installation fails during either the prepare phase or the complete phase of the process, the instance must be uninstalled.

To finish the installation of a prepared image, you can use the Image Completion Of A Prepared Stand-Alone Instance Of SQL Server option. This option will allow you to complete the configuration of the instance by inputting the account-, computer-, and network-specific information.

The Options Tab

As illustrated in Figure 2-7, the Options tab of the SQL Server Installation Center displays the processor architecture that you can use to install SQL Server, based on the processor type in your server. It also allows you to specify a path to the installation media. This can be useful if you have a copy of the media stored locally on the server.

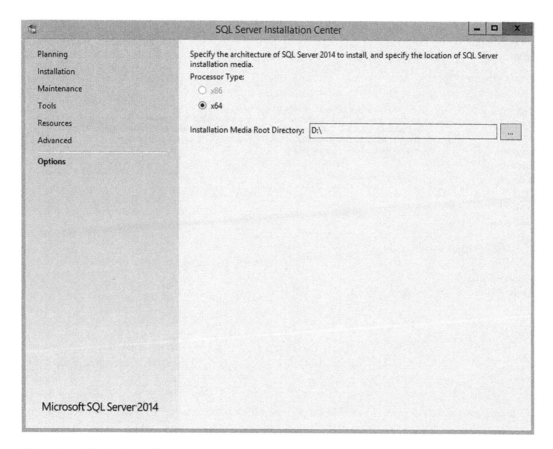

Figure 2-7. *The Options tab*

Installing a Stand-Alone Database Engine Instance

As discussed in the preceding section, an instance of SQL Server can be installed in various ways, including via the command line, by using Sysprep with an advanced installation using a configuration file, or by using the New SQL Server Stand-Alone Installation Or Add Features To An Existing Installation option on the Installation tab. It is the last of these options that we will use to install SQL Server in the following demonstration. In the following sections, we will install a Database Engine instance with features that will be examined in further detail throughout this book, including FILESTREAM and Distributed Replay. We will also take an in-depth look at choosing the correct collation and service account for the instance.

Preparation Steps

When you choose to install a new instance of SQL Server, the first screen of the wizard that you are presented with will prompt you to enter the product key for SQL Server, as illustrated in Figure 2-8.

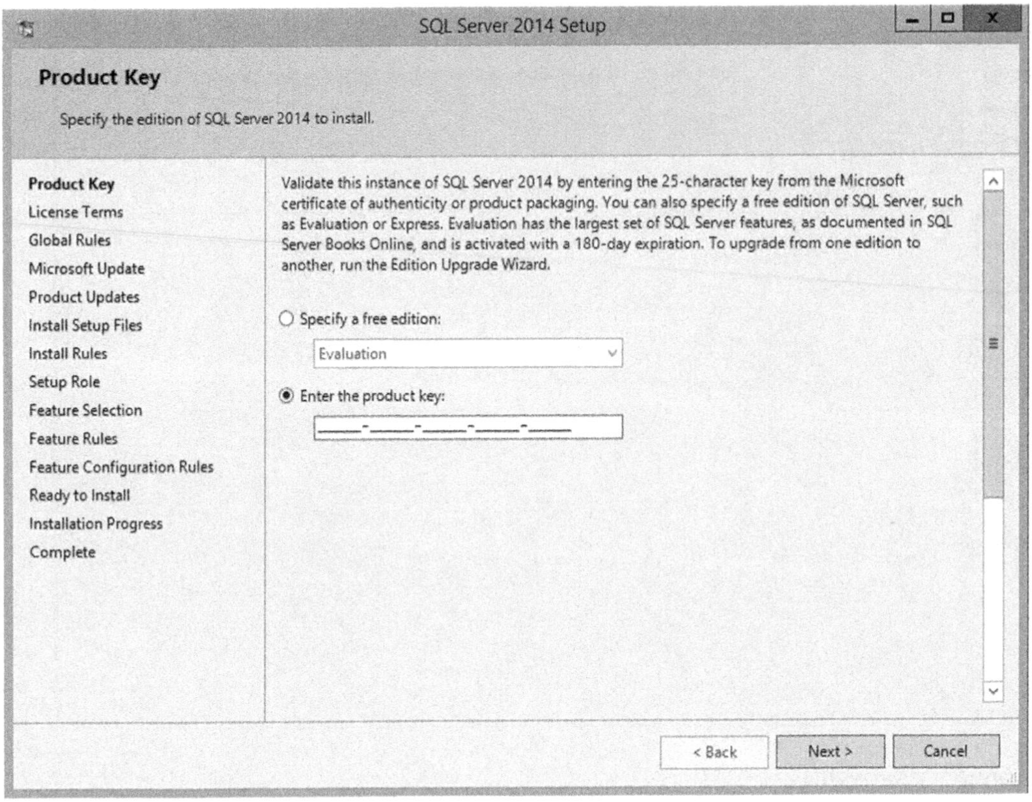

Figure 2-8. *Product Key page*

If you do not enter a product key on this screen, you will only be able to install either the Express edition of SQL Server or the Evaluation edition. The Evaluation edition has the same level of functionality as the Enterprise edition, but it expires after 180 days.

The next screen of the wizard will ask you to read and accept the license terms of SQL Server, as illustrated in Figure 2-9. Additionally, you will need to specify if you wish to participate in Microsoft's Customer Experience Improvement Program. If you select this option, then error reporting will be captured and sent to Microsoft. A link provided on this screen will give you further details of Microsoft's privacy policy in relation to this error reporting. You should always read the statement carefully, to ensure acceptance aligns with you company policy, but in general, it is a good thing to participate in the program because it helps Microsoft improve the platform and generally, no personal data is collected.

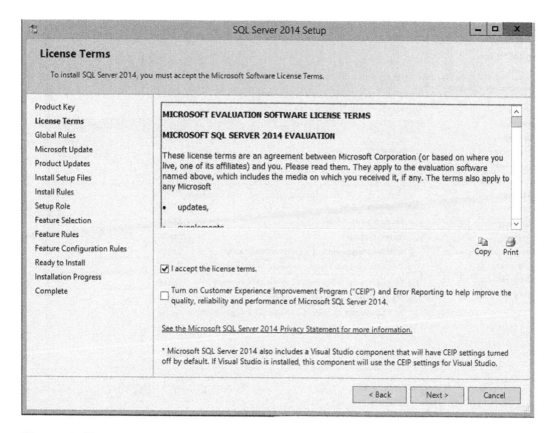

Figure 2-9. *License Terms page*

After you accept the license terms, SQL Server setup will run a rules check to ensure that it can continue with the installation, as illustrated in Figure 2-10. This is the same configuration check that you can run independently from the Planning tab of SQL Server Installation Center, as discussed earlier in this chapter.

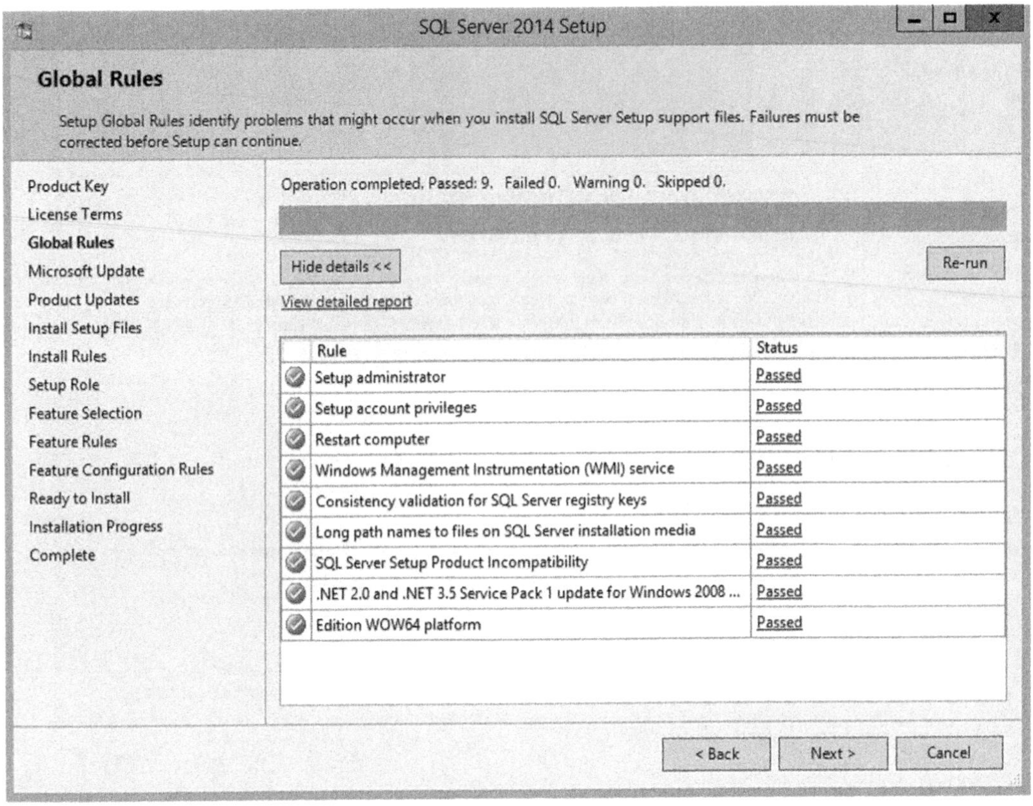

Figure 2-10. *Global Rules page*

Assuming that all checks pass successfully, the screen of the wizard illustrated in Figure 2-11 will prompt you to choose if you want Windows Update to check for SQL Server patches and hotfixes. The choice here will depend on your organization's patching policy. Some organizations implement a ridged patching regime for the testing and acceptance of patches, followed by a patching cycle, which is often supported with software such as WSUS (Windows Server Update Services). If such a regime exists in your organization, then you should not select this option.

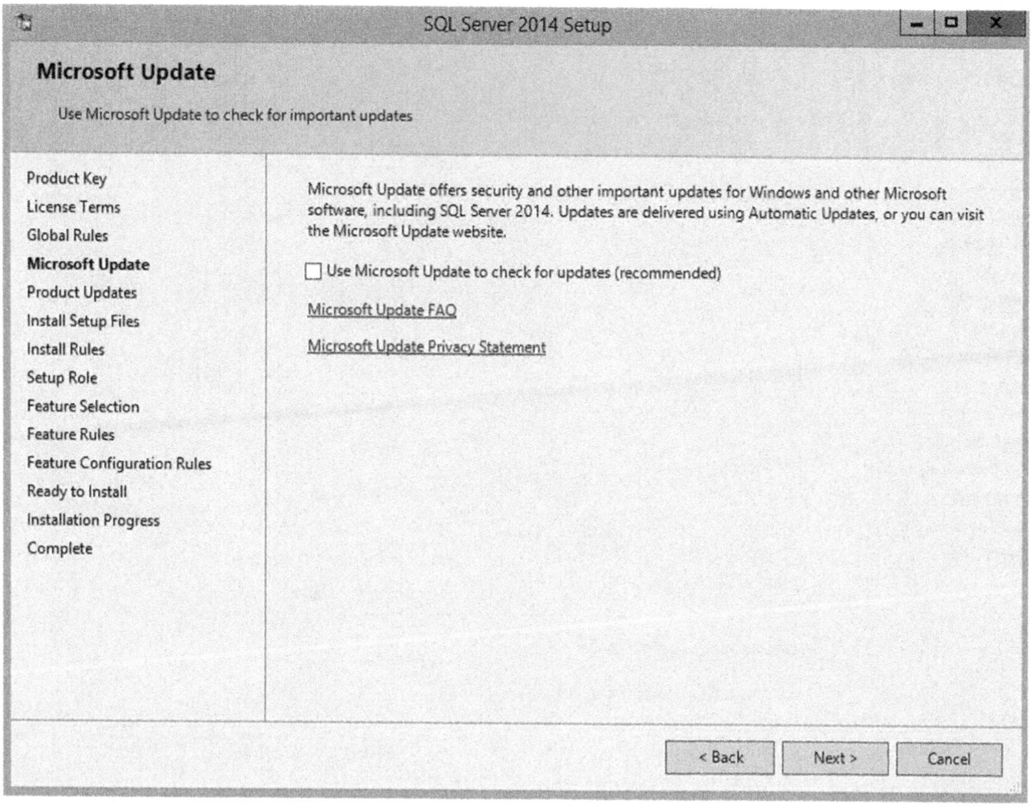

Figure 2-11. Microsoft Update page

▦ **Note**   This screen will only appear if your server is not already configured to receive product updates for SQL Server.

The next screen of the wizard, illustrated in Figure 2-12, will attempt to scan for SQL Server updates to ensure that you install the latest CUs (cumulative updates) and SPs (service packs) with your installation. It will check the Microsoft Update service on the local server for these updates and list any that are available. This is an extension of slipstream installation functionality, which allows you to install updates at the same time as the installation of the base binaries by specifying their location for setup, but it has now been deprecated. The Product Updates page can also be configured to look for updates in local folders or network locations. This functionality will be discussed in further detail in Chapter 3.

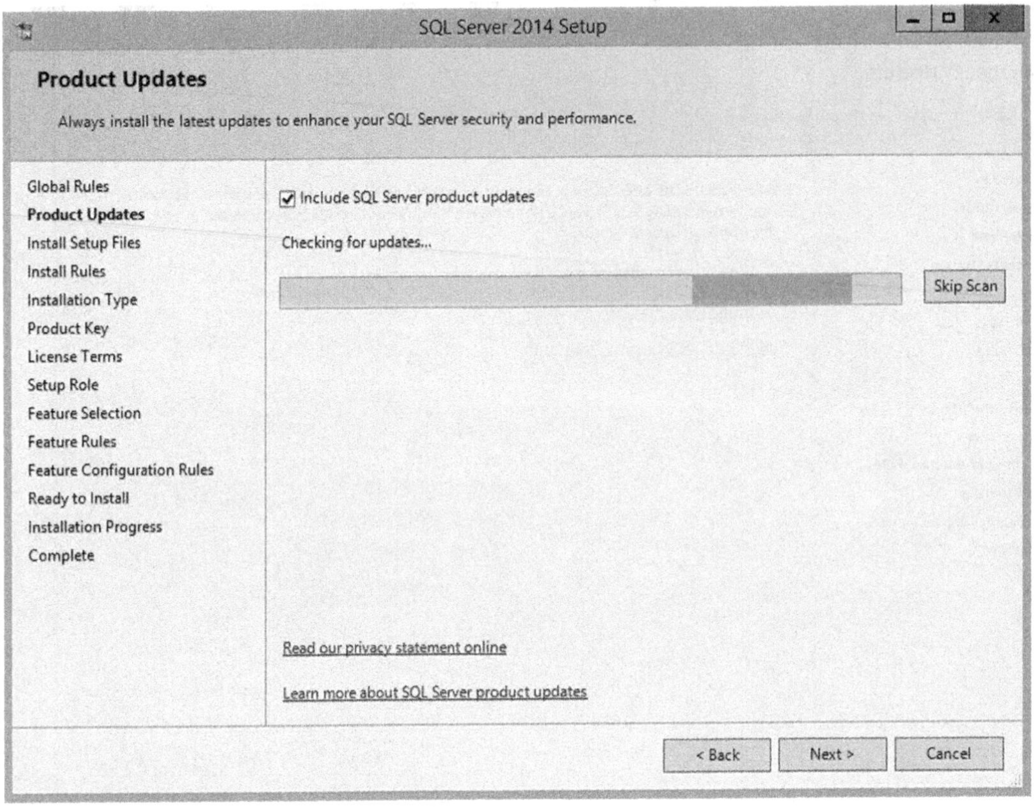

Figure 2-12. *Product Updates page*

■ **Note**   This screen will not appear if product updates are not found.

As setup moves to the next page of the wizard, which is illustrated in Figure 2-13, the extraction and installation of the files required for SQL Server setup begins, and the progress displays. This screen also displays the progress of the download and extraction of any update packages that were found by Product Updates.

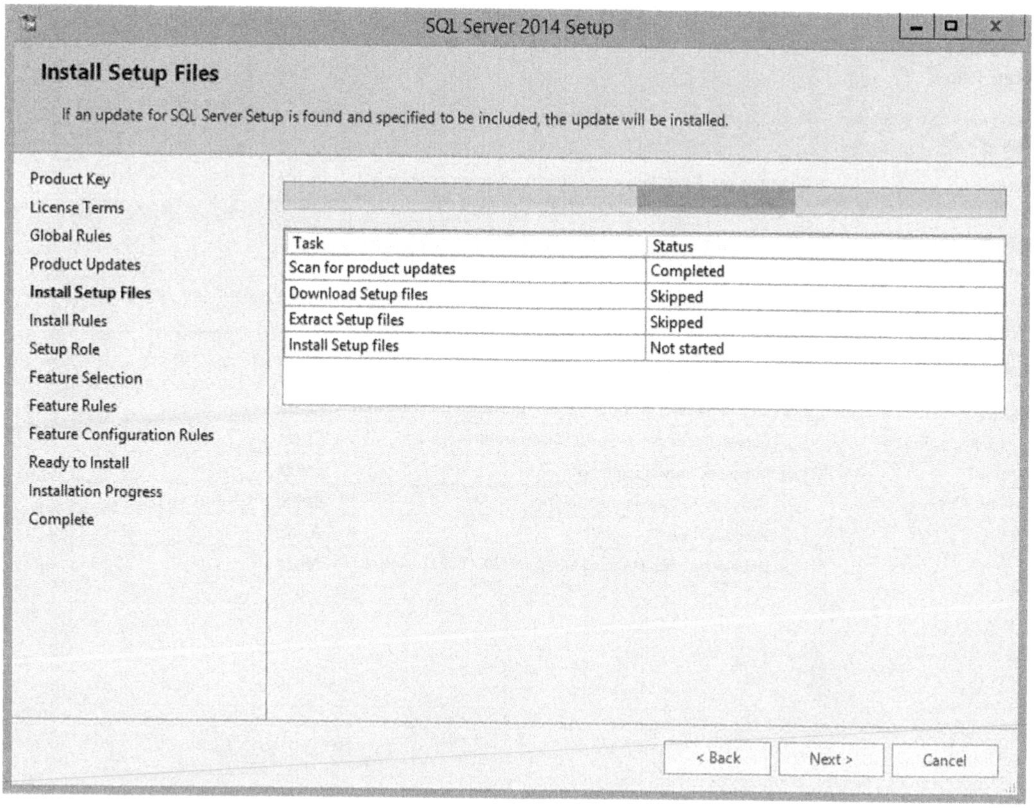

Figure 2-13. *Install Setup Files page*

As illustrated in Figure 2-14, the next screen of the wizard runs an installation rule check and displays and errors or warnings that you may need to address before installation begins.

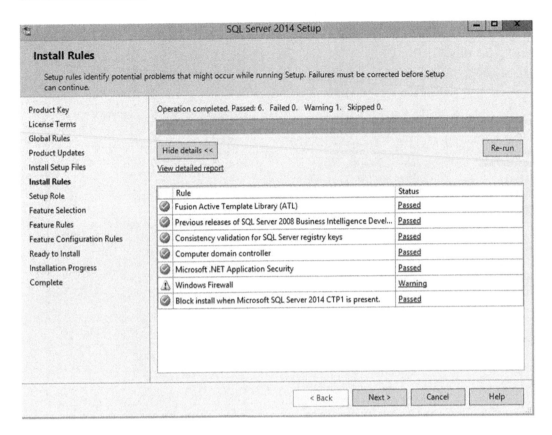

Figure 2-14. *Install Rules page*

In Figure 2-14, notice the warning being displayed for Windows Firewall. This will not stop the installation from proceeding, but it does warn you that the server has Windows Firewall switched on. By default, Windows Firewall is not configured to allow SQL Server traffic, so rules must be created in order for client applications to be able to communicate with the instance that you are installing. We will discuss SQL Server ports and Firewall configuration in detail in Chapter 4.

Assuming no errors are discovered that need to be addressed before you continue, the next page of the wizard will ask you to decide if you want to perform a SQL Server Feature Installation, a SQL Server PowerPoint for SharePoint installation, or All Features With Default Values for service accounts. This screen is illustrated in Figure 2-15.

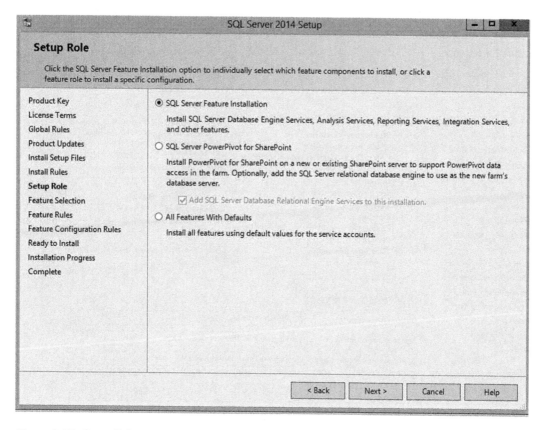

Figure 2-15. *Setup Role page*

The Feature Selection Page

If you select the SQL Server Feature Installation option, when you move to the feature selection page of the wizard, none of the feature options will be selected, and you can select each option you require. If you choose the All Features With Defaults option, and then all features on the feature selection page, the reverse will be true. Every available option will be checked and you will need to uncheck any options that you do not require. Also, as you move through the setup wizard, you will find that all options have been prepopulated with default values. However, this includes options such as adding the current user as an instance administrator, which you may not want to do in all scenarios, so be extremely careful when you use this approach.

The SQL Server PowerPivot For SharePoint option can be used to install PowerPivot within a SharePoint farm. A full discussion of PowerPivot administration is beyond the scope of this book.

Choosing the SQL Server Feature Installation option will cause the Feature Installation page of the setup wizard to display. This will allow you to select the options that you wish to install. An overview of each of the available options can be found in Chapter 1. The Feature Selection page is illustrated in Figure 2-16.

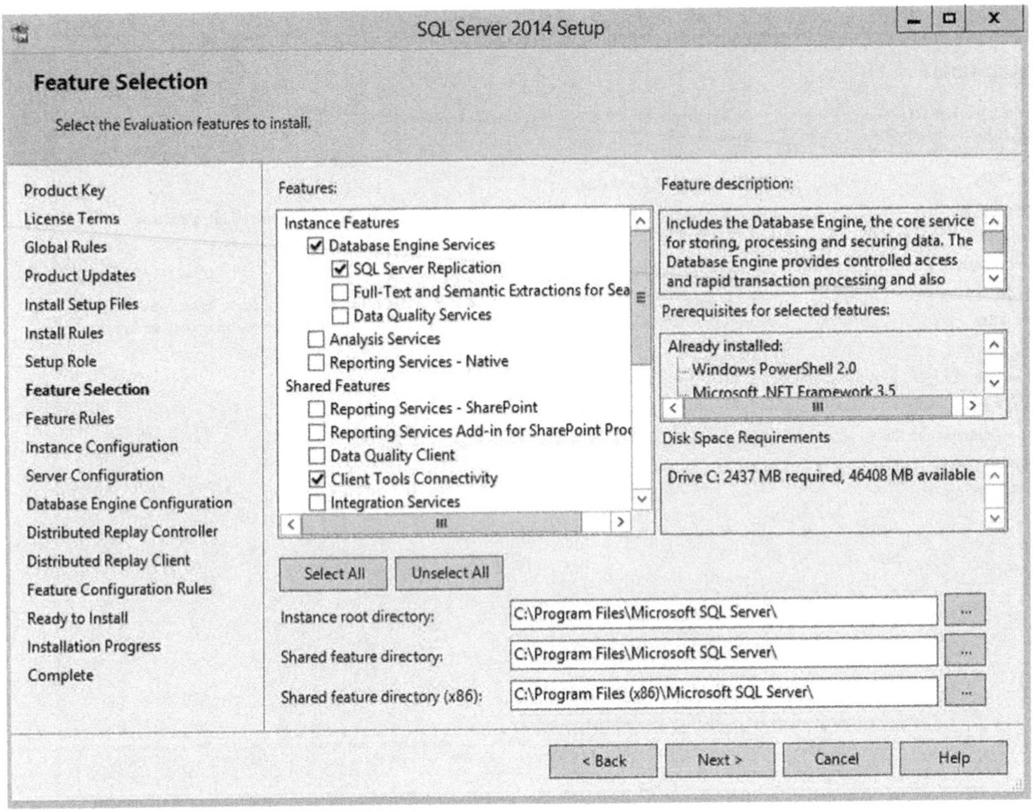

Figure 2-16. *Feature Selection page*

We will select the following features, since they will be used for demonstrations and discussions throughout this book.

- Database Engine Services
  - SQL Server Replication
- Client Tools Connectivity
- Management Tools - Basic
  - Management Tools - Complete
- Distributed Replay Controller
- Distributed Replay Client

Additionally, this page of the wizard requires you to specify folder locations for the instance root directory and the shared features directory. You may want to move these to a different drive in order to leave the C:\ drive for the operating system. You may want to do this for space reasons, or just to isolate the SQL Server binaries from other applications. The instance root directory will typically contain a folder for each instance that you create on the server, and there will be separate folders for the Database Engine, SSAS, and SSRS installations. A folder associated with the Database Engine will be called MSSQL12.[InstanceName], where instance name is either the name of your instance, or MSSQLSERVER for a default instance. The number 12 in this folder name relates to the version of SQL Server, which is 12 for SQL Server 2014. This folder will contain a subfolder called MSSQL, which in turn will contain folders that will be home to the files associated with your instance, including a folder called Binn, which will contain the application files, application extensions, and XML configurations associated with your instance; a folder called Backup, which will be the default location for backups of databases; and a folder called Data, which will be the default location of the system databases. The default folders for TempDB, user databases, and backups can be modified later in the installation process, and splitting these databases onto separate volumes is almost always good practice, as discussed in Chapter 1. Other folders will also be created here, including a folder called LOGS, which will be the default location for the files for both the Error Logs and the default Extended Event health trace.

If you are installing SQL Server in a 64-bit environment, you will be asked to enter folders for both 32- and 64-bit versions of the shared features directory. This is because some SQL Server components are always installed as 32-bit processes. The 32- and 64-bit components cannot share a directory, so for installation to continue, you must specify different folders for each of these options. The Shared Features directory becomes a root level directory for features that are shared by all instances of SQL Server, such as SDKs and management tools.

On the next page of the wizard, illustrated in Figure 2-17, an additional rules check will be carried out to ensure that the features that you have selected can be installed.

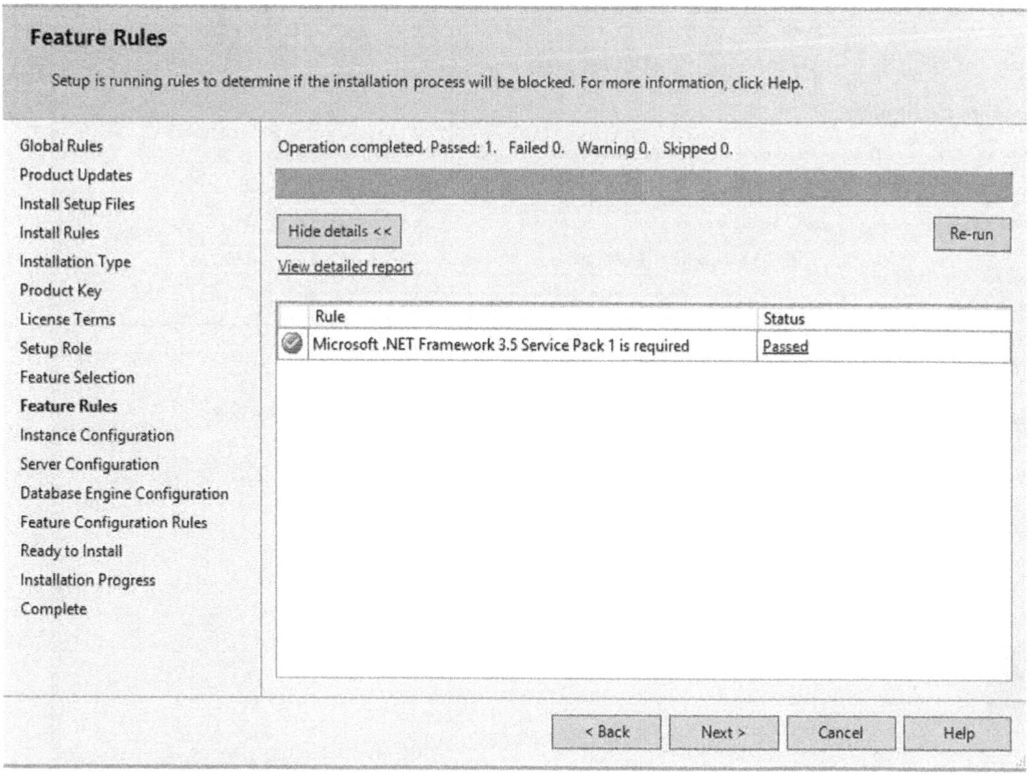

Figure 2-17. *Feature Rules page*

The rules that are checked will vary depending on the features that you have selected, but a common gotcha is that, if the .NET Framework 3.5 is missing, it may only be discovered at this point. It is sound advice to install the .NET Framework 3.5 before beginning the installation of SQL Server, since the Database Engine relies on its availability.

■ **Tip** For Windows Server, the installation of the .NET Framework 3.5 involves using Server Manager to add the .NET Framework 3.5 feature. This feature also includes .NET Framework 2.0 and .NET Framework 3.0 in Windows Server 2012.

The Instance Configuration Page

After successful completion of the rules check, the following screen of the wizard will allow you to specify if you would like to install a default instance or a named instance, as illustrated in Figure 2-18. The box in the lower half of the screen will give you details of any other instances or shared features that are already installed on the server.

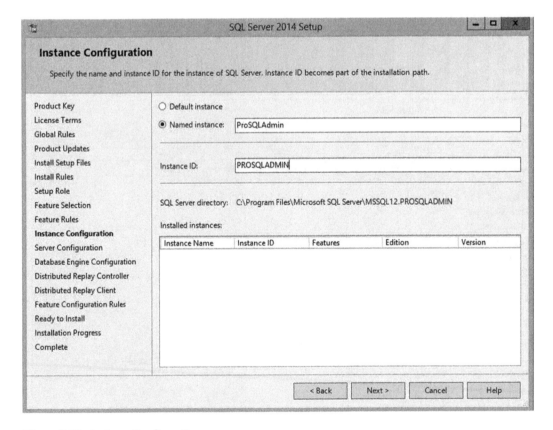

Figure 2-18. Instance Configuration page

The difference between a default instance and a named instance is that a default instance takes the name of the server that it is installed on, whereas a named instance is given an extended name. This has the obvious side effect that it is only possible to have a single default instance of SQL Server on a server, but you can have multiple named instances. With SQL Server 2014, up to 50 stand-alone instances can be hosted on a single server. For failover clusters, this number stays the same if your data is hosted on an SMB file share, but it reduces to 25 if you use a shared cluster disk for storage.

You are not required to install a default instance before installing a named instance. It is a perfectly valid configuration to have only named instances on a server with no default instance. Many DBA teams choose to only support named instances in their environments so that they can enforce naming conventions that are meaningful at the SQL Server layer, as opposed to relying on the naming conventions imposed by the infrastructure teams who build the servers or VMs. The maximum length of an instance name is 16 characters. By default, the InstanceID will be set to the instance name, or MSSQLSERVER for a default instance. Although it is possible to change this ID, it is bad practice to do so, because this ID is used to identify Registry keys and installation directories.

Selecting Service Accounts

The next screen of the wizard is separated into two tabs. The first tab will allow you to specify service accounts for each of the SQL Server services, as illustrated in Figure 2-19, and the second tab will allow you to specify the collation of your instance.

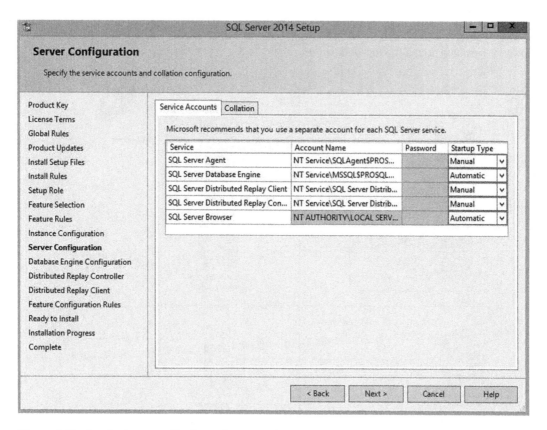

Figure 2-19. *Service Accounts Configuration page*

SQL Server 2014 supports the use of local and domain accounts, built-in accounts, virtual accounts, and MSAs (managed service accounts) as the security context used to run a service. The service account model that you choose is key to both the security and manageability of your environment.

Different organizations have different requirements for service account models, and you may be constrained by compliance requirements and many other factors. Essentially, the choice that you make is a trade-off between the security and operational supportability of your environment. For example, the Microsoft best practice is to use a separate service account for every service and to ensure that every server in your environment uses a discrete set of service accounts, since this fully enforces the principle of least privilege. The *principle of least privilege* states that each security context will be granted the minimum set of permissions required for it to carry out its day-to-day activities.

In reality, however, you will find that this approach introduces significant complexity into your SQL Server estate, and it can increase the cost of operational support, while also risking increasing outage windows in disaster scenarios. On the flip side, I have worked in organizations where the service account model is very coarse, to the point where there is only a single set of SQL Server service accounts for each region. This approach can also cause significant issues. Imagine that you have a large estate and the whole estate uses the same service account. Now imagine that you have a compliance requirement to change service account passwords on a 90-day basis. This means that you would cause an outage to your entire SQL Server estate at the same time. This simply is not practical.

There is no right or wrong answer to this problem, and the solution will depend on the requirements and constraints of individual organizations. For organizations that use domain accounts as service accounts, however, I tend to recommend a distinct set of service accounts for each data-tier application. So if you imagine an environment, as shown in Figure 2-20, where your data-tier application consists of a two-node cluster and an ETL server in a primary site, and two DR servers in a secondary site, this design would involve a common set of service accounts used by all of these instances, but other data-tier applications would not be allowed to use these accounts and would require their own set.

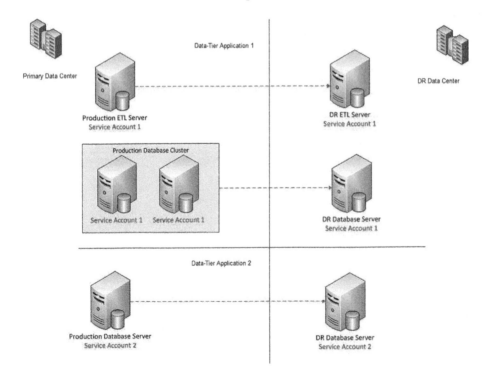

Figure 2-20. Service account model by data-tier application

Of course, this model poses its own challenges. For example, you would need to review and amend this policy if you were to start a process of consolidation. Because of the challenges surrounding service account management, Microsoft introduced virtual accounts and MSAs. *Virtual accounts* are local accounts that have no password management requirements. They can access the domain by using the computer identity of the server on which they have been created. *Managed service accounts*, on the other hand, are domain-level accounts. They provide automatic password management within AD (Active Directory) and also automatically maintain their Kerberos SPNs (service principal names), as long as your domain is running at the functional level of Windows Server 2008 R2 or higher.

Both of these types of account have a limitation, however. They can only be used on a single server. As discussed earlier, this can introduce complexity into your SQL Server estate, especially for highly available, multiserver applications. This issue has been resolved by the introduction of group MSAs, which give you the ability to associate an MSA with multiple servers within the domain. In order to use this functionality, however, your forest needs to be running at the functional level of Windows Server 2012 or higher.

Choosing the Collation

The second tab of the Server Configuration page will allow you to customize your collation, as illustrated in Figure 2-21.

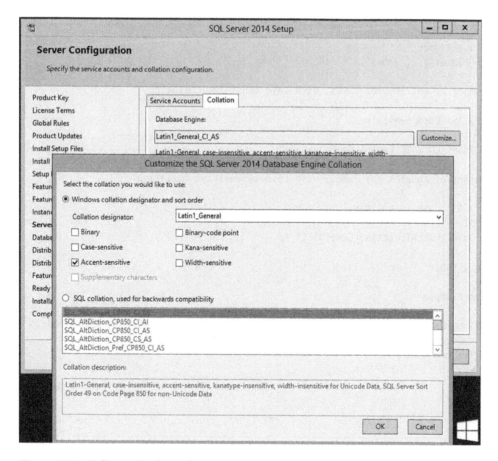

Figure 2-21. *Collation Configuration page*

Collations determine how SQL Server will sort data and also define SQL Server's matching behavior, with regard to accents, kana, width, and case. You can also specify that sorting and matching should be carried out on the binary or binary code point representations.

If your collation is accent sensitive, then in comparisons, SQL Server does not regard è as the same character as e, whereas it will treat these characters as equal, if accent insensitivity is specified. Kana sensitivity defines if the Japanese Hiragana character set is equal to the Katakana character set. Width sensitivity defines if a single byte representation of a character is equal to its two-byte equivalent.

Case sensitivity defines if a capital letter is equal to its lowercase equivalent during comparison. For example, the code in Listing 2-1 will create and populate a temporary table and then run the same query, but using two different collations.

Listing 2-1. Effect of Case Sensitivity of Matching

```
--Create a local temporary table

CREATE TABLE #CaseExample
(
        Name          VARCHAR(20)
)

--Populate values

INSERT INTO #CaseExample
        VALUES('James'), ('james'), ('John'), ('john')

--Count the number of entries for James, with case sensitive collation

SELECT COUNT(*) AS 'Case Sensitive'
FROM #CaseExample
WHERE Name = 'John' COLLATE Latin1_General_CS_AI

--Count the number of entries for James, with case insensitive collation

SELECT COUNT(*) AS 'Case Insensitive'
FROM #CaseExample
WHERE Name = 'John' COLLATE Latin1_General_CI_AI

--DROP temporary table

DROP TABLE #CaseExample
```

You can see from the results in Figure 2-22, that the first query only found one example of the word John, because it used a case-sensitive collation, but because the second query uses a case-insensitive collation, it matched two results.

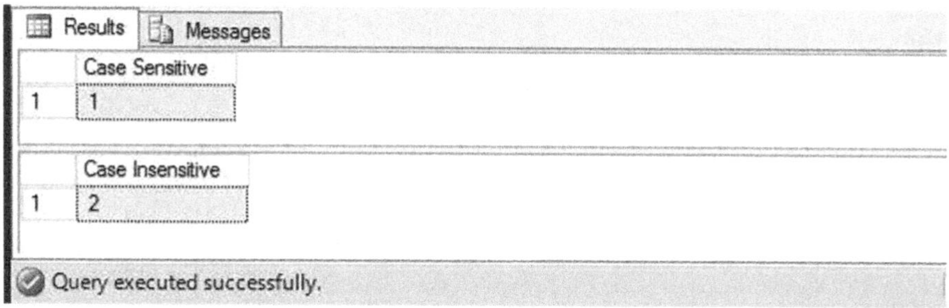

Figure 2-22. *Results of case sensitivity example*

Although the effects of the various collation sensitivities may be fairly straightforward, a slightly more confusing aspect is how collations can affect sort order. Surely there is only one correct way to order data? Well, the answer to this question is no. There are various ways that data can be correctly ordered. For example, while some collations order data alphabetically, other collations may use nonalphabetic writing systems, such as Chinese, which can be ordered using a method called radical and stroke sorting. This system will identify common character components and then order them by the number of strokes. An example of how collations can affect sort order is demonstrated in Listing 2-2.

Listing 2-2. Effect of Collations on Sort Order

```
--Create a temporary table

CREATE TABLE #SortOrderExample
(
        Food            VARCHAR(20)
)

--Populate the table

INSERT INTO #SortOrderExample
VALUES ('Coke'), ('Chips'), ('Crisps'), ('Cake')

--Select food using Latin1_General collation

SELECT Food AS 'Latin1_General collation'
FROM #SortOrderExample
ORDER BY Food
COLLATE Latin1_General_CI_AI

--Select food using Traditional_Spanish collation

SELECT Food AS 'Traditional_Spanish colation'
FROM #SortOrderExample
ORDER BY Food
COLLATE Traditional_Spanish_CI_AI
```

The results in Figure 2-23 show that the value Chips has been sorted differently using the two collations. This is because in traditional Spanish, ch is regarded as a separate character, and is sorted after cz.

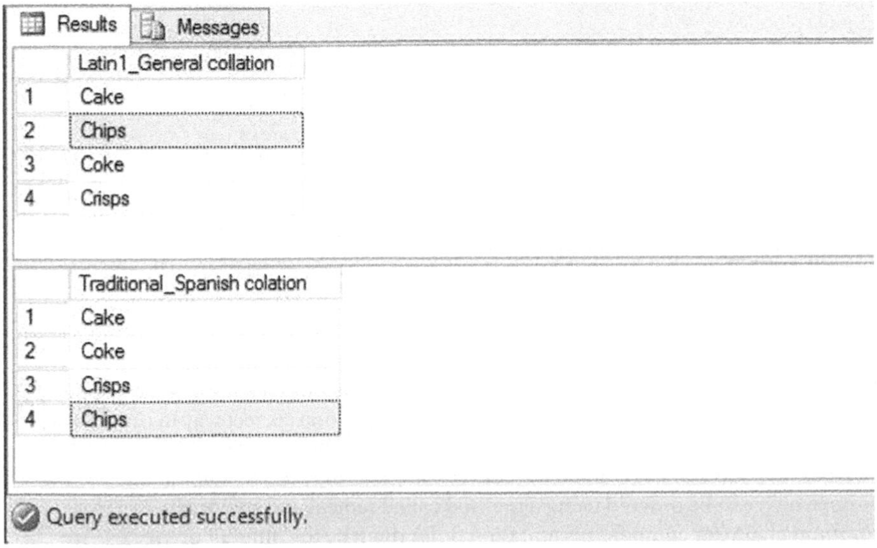

Figure 2-23. *Results of sort order example*

There are two types of binary collation to choose from. The older style binary collations are included for backward compatibility only and are identified with the BIN suffix. If you choose to choose this type of binary collation, then characters will be matched and sorted based on the bit patterns of each character. If you choose the modern binary collations, which can be identified with a BIN2 suffix, then data will be sorted and matched based on Unicode code points for Unicode data and the code point of the relevant ANSI code page, for non-Unicode data. The example in Listing 2-3 demonstrates the behavior of a binary (BIN2) collation, compared to case-sensitive and case-insensitive collations.

Listing 2-3. Binary Collation Sort Order

```
CREATE TABLE #CaseExample
(
        Name          VARCHAR(20)
)

--Populate values

INSERT INTO #CaseExample
        VALUES('James'), ('james'), ('John'), ('john')

--Select all rows with a case sensitive collation

SELECT name as [Case Sensitive]
FROM #CaseExample
Order by Name COLLATE Latin1_General_CS_AI

--Select all rows, with a case insensitive collation

SELECT name as [Case Insensitive]
FROM #CaseExample
Order by Name COLLATE  Latin1_General_CI_AI
```

```
SELECT name as [binary]
FROM #CaseExample
Order by Name COLLATE  Latin1_General_BIN2

--DROP temporary table

DROP TABLE #CaseExample
```

The results in Figure 2-24 show that because the data is ordered by code point rather than alphabetically, the values beginning with capital letters are ordered before those beginning with lowercase letters, since this matches the code points of the characters.

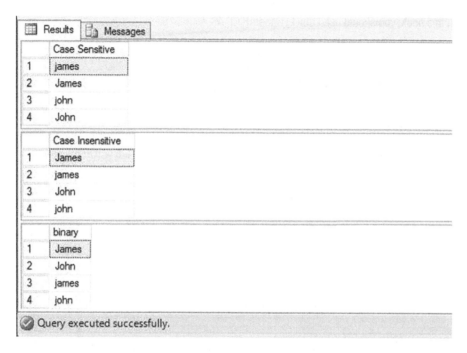

Figure 2-24. *Binary collation sort order*

Collations can be challenging, and ideally you will maintain consistent collations across the enterprise. This is not always possible in today's global organizations, but you should aspire to it. You should also be careful to select the correct collation for the instance at the point of installation. Changing the collation afterward can be challenging, because databases and columns within tables have their own collations, and a collation cannot be changed if other objects depend on it. At a high level, a worst-case scenario will involve the following actions to change your collation at a later date:

1. Re-create all databases.

2. Export all data into the newly created copies of the databases.

3. Drop the original databases.

4. Rebuild the Master database with the desired collation.

5. Re-create the databases.

6. Import the data back into you database from the copies that you created.

7. Drop the copies of the databases.

Unless you have a specific backward compatibility requirement, you should avoid using SQL collations and only use Windows collations. It is best practice to use Windows collations because SQL collations are deprecated and are not all fully compatible with Windows collations. Additionally, you should be mindful when selecting newer collations, such as Norwegian or Bosnian_Latin. Although this new family of collations map to code pages in Windows Server 2008 or above, they do not map to code pages in older operating systems. So if you were to run a SELECT * query, against your instance from an older operating system, such as Windows XP, the code page would not match, and an exception would be thrown.

■ **Note**   Examples in this book, you should use Latin1_General_CI_AS.

Provisioning Instance Security

The next page of the setup wizard allows you to configure the Database Engine. It consists of three tabs. In the first tab, you can specify the authentication mode of the instance and instance administrators, as illustrated in Figure 2-25. The second tab allows you to specify the folder that will be used as the default data directory, as well as specific locations for user databases and TempDB. The third tab will allow you to configure FILESTREAM.

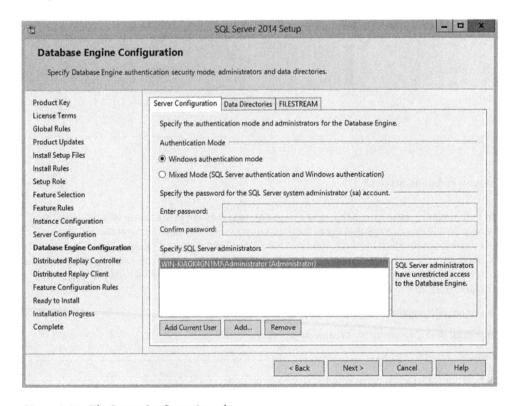

Figure 2-25. *The Server Configuration tab*

Windows Authentication Mode means that the credentials that a user supplies when logging into Windows will be passed to SQL Server, and the user does not require any additional credentials to gain access to the instance. With Mixed Mode, although Windows credentials can still be used to access the instance, users can also be given second tier credentials. If this option is selected, then SQL Server will hold its own user names and passwords for users inside the instance, and users can supply these, in order to gain access, even if their Windows identity does not have permissions.

For security best practice, it is a good idea to only allow Windows authentication to your instance. This is for two reasons. First, with Windows authentication only, if an attacker were to gain access to your network, then they would still not be able to access SQL Server, since they would not have a valid Windows account with the correct permissions. With mixed-mode authentication however, once inside the network, attackers could use brute force attacks or other hacking methodologies to attempt to gain access via a second tier user account. Second, if you specify mixed-mode authentication, then you are required to create an SA account. The SA account is a SQL Server user account that has administrative privileges over the instance. If the password for this account became compromised, then an attacker could gain administrative control over SQL Server.

Mixed-mode authentication is a necessity in some cases, however. For example, you may have a legacy application that does not support Windows authentication, or a third party application that has a hard-coded connection that uses second tier authentication. These would be two valid reasons why mixed mode authentication may be required. Another valid reason would be if you have users that need to access the instance from a non-trusted domain.

■ **Caution** Use mixed-mode authentication by exception only in order to reduce the security footprint of SQL Server.

Configuring the Instance

On the Server Configuration tab, you will also need to enter at least one instance administrator. You can use the Add Current User button to add your current Windows security context, or the Add button to search for Windows security principles, such as users or groups. Ideally, you should select a Windows group, which contains all DBAs that will require administrative access to the instance, since this simplifies security.

The Data Directories tab of Database Engine Configuration page is illustrated in Figure 2-26.

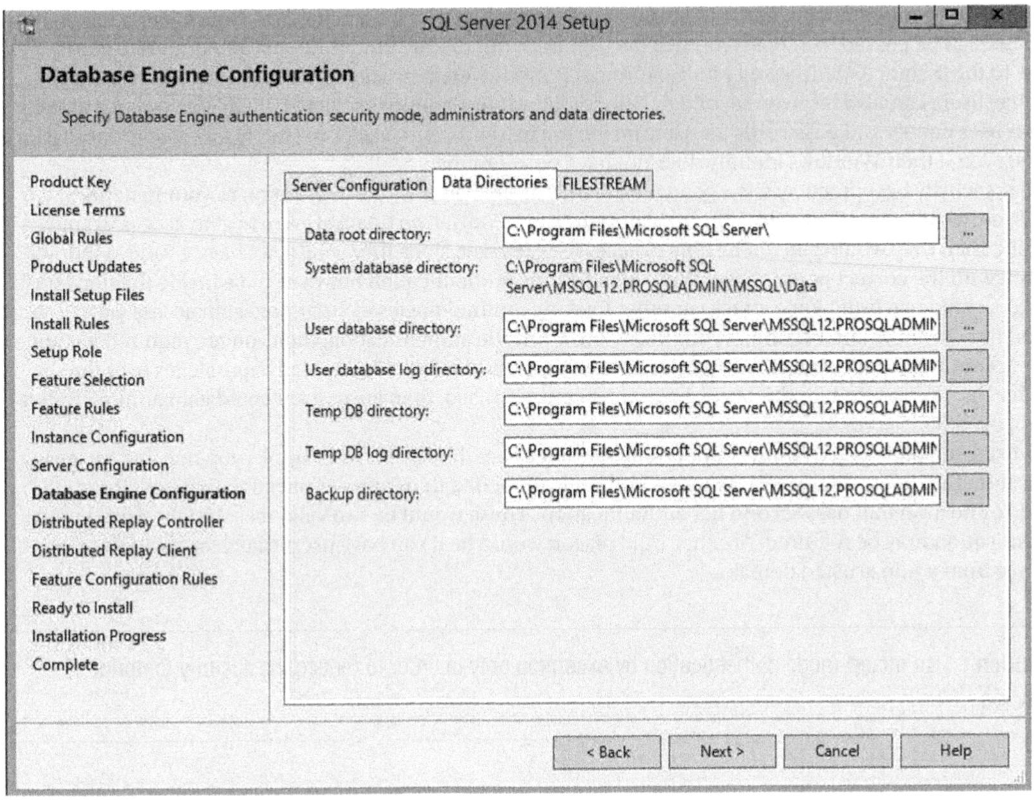

Figure 2-26. *The Data Directories tab*

The Data Directories tab allows you to alter the default location of the data root directory. On this screen, you can also change the default location for user databases and their log files, as well as specify where TempDB data and log files should be created. As you may recall from Chapter 1, this is particularly important, because you will probably wish to separate user data files from their logs and also from TempDB. Finally, this tab allows you to specify a default location for backups of databases that will be taken.

The FILESTREAM tab of the Database Engine Configuration page allows you to enable and configure the level of access for SQL Server FILESTREAM functionality, as illustrated in Figure 2-27. FILESTREAM must also be enabled if you wish to use the FileTable feature of SQL Server. FILESTREAM and FileTable provide the ability to store data in an unstructured manner within the Windows folder structure, while retaining the ability to manage and interrogate this data from SQL Server.

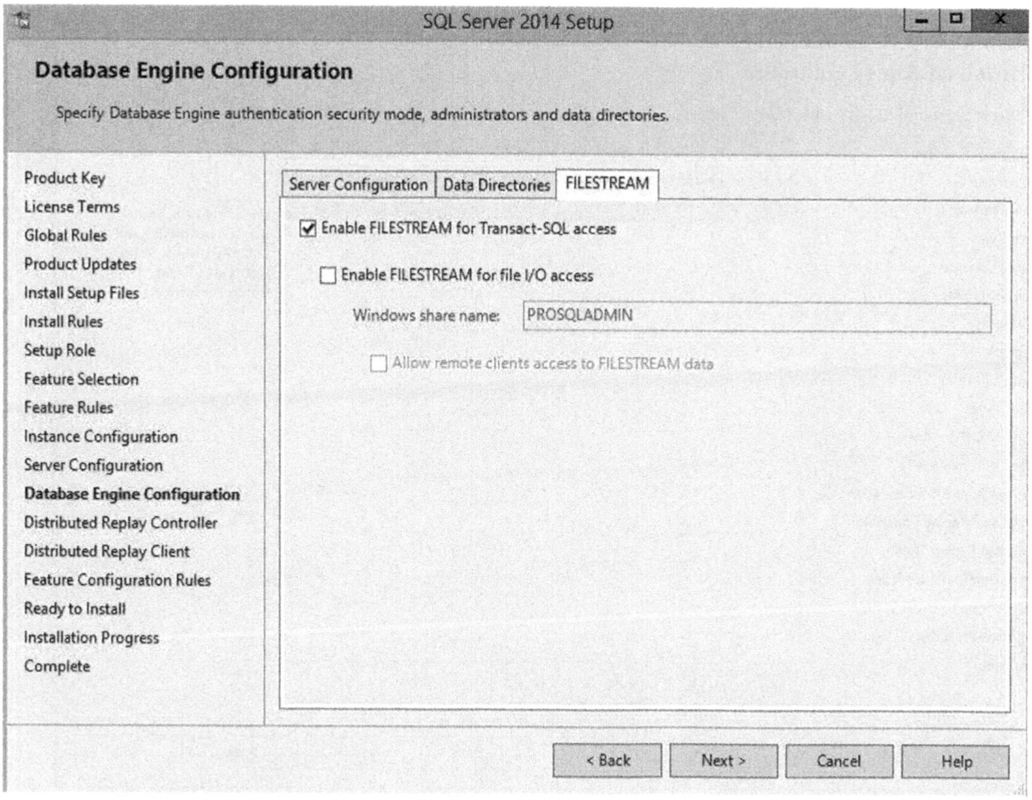

Figure 2-27. *The FILESTREAM Tab*

Selecting Enable FILESTREAM For Transact-SQL Access will enable FILESTREAM, but the data can only be accessed from inside SQL Server. Additionally, selecting Enable FILESTREAM For File I/O Access enables applications to access the data directly from the operating system, bypassing SQL Server. If this option is selected, then you will also need to provide the name of a preexisting file share, which will be used for direct application access. The Allow Remote Clients Access To FILESTREAM Data option makes the data available to remote applications. The three options build on top of each other, so it is not possible to select Enable FILESTREAM For File I/O Access without fist selecting Enable FILESTREAM For Transact-SQL Access, for example. FILESTREAM and FileTable will be discussed further in Chapter 5.

Configuring Distributed Replay

As illustrated in Figure 2-28, the next page of the wizard will prompt you to specify the users who will be given access to the Distributed Replay Controller service. In the same fashion that you grant administrative permissions to the instance, you can use the Add Current User button to add your current security context or you can use the Add button to browse for Windows users and groups.

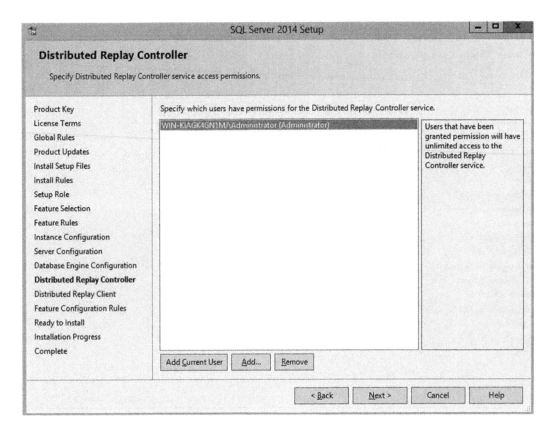

Figure 2-28. *The Distributed Replay Controller page*

On the next page of the wizard, you can configure the Distributed Replay client, as illustrated in Figure 2-29. The Working Directory is the folder on the client where the dispatch files are saved. The Results Directory is the folder on the client where the trace file will be saved. The files in both of these locations will be overwritten each time a trace is run. If you have an existing Distributed Replay Controller configured, then you should enter its name in the Controller Name field. However, if you are configuring a new controller, then this field should be left blank and then amended later in the DReplyClient.config configuration file. The configuration and use of Distributed Replay will be discussed in Chapter 20.

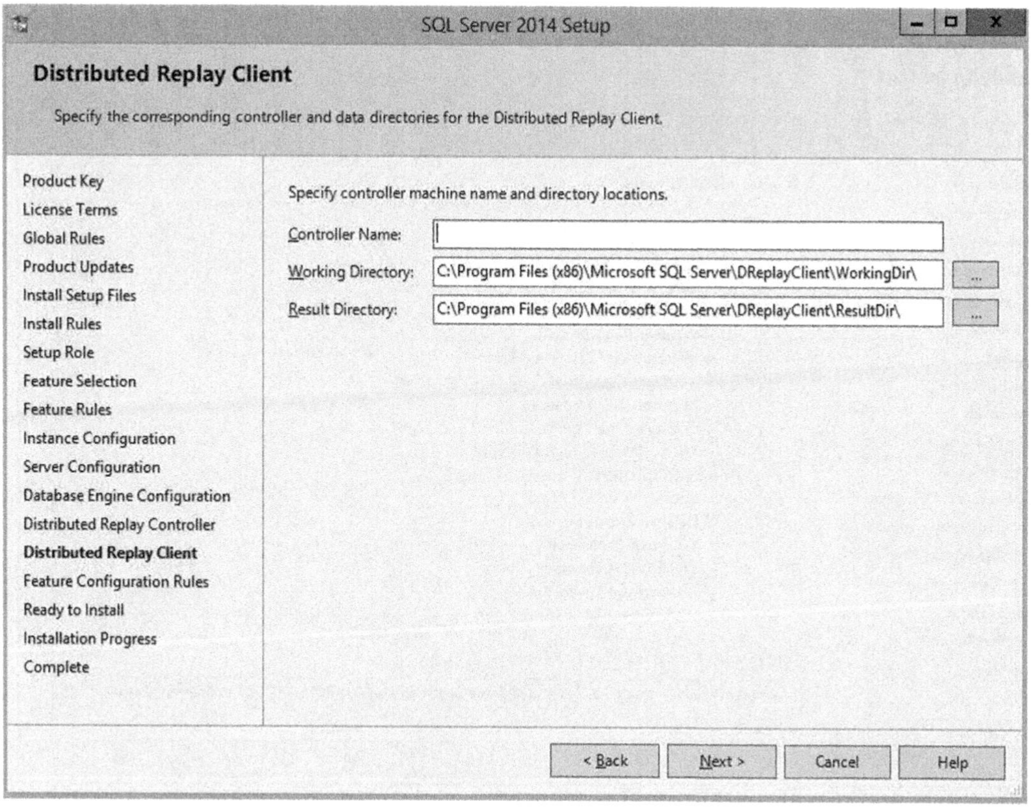

Figure 2-29. *The Distributed Replay Client page*

Completing the Installation

The Ready to Install page of the wizard is the final page before installation commences, and it is illustrated in Figure 2-30. This screen gives you a summary of the features that will be installed, but possibly the most interesting component of this page is the Configuration File Path section. This gives you the path to a configuration file that you are able to reuse to install further instances with an identical configuration. Configuration files will be discussed further, in Chapter 2.

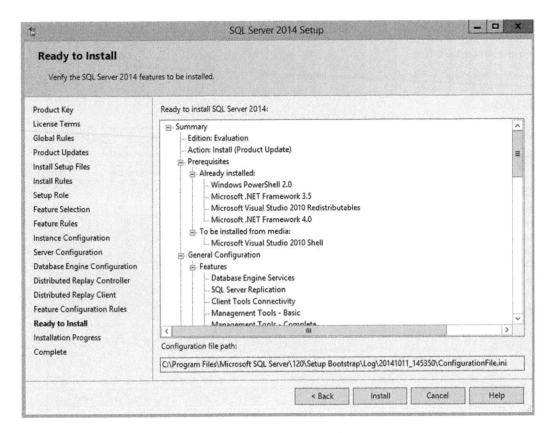

Figure 2-30. *The Ready to Install page*

The setup wizard will display a progress bar during the installation. When installation is complete, a summary screen will be displayed, as shown in Figure 2-31. You should check to ensure that each of the components being installed has a status of Succeeded. The SQL Server installation is then complete.

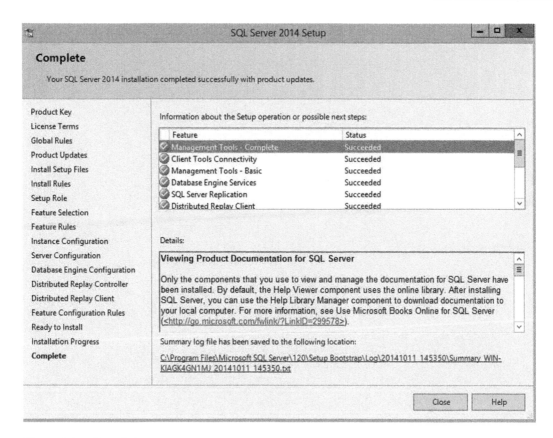

Figure 2-31. *Completion page*

Summary

SQL Server's Installation Center provides many useful tools and links for guiding and assisting you in the installation process. You can use the Installation Center to install failover clustered instances as well as stand-alone instances of SQL Server. There are also tools to assist in advanced installation requirements, such as preprepared images of SQL Server and installations based on configuration files.

In addition to using the SQL Server 2014 Setup wizard to install an instance of the Database Engine, you can also use the same tool to install the tools within the BI and ETL suite, such as Analysis Services, Integration Service, Reporting Service, Data Quality Services, and Master Data Services. If you use the wizard to install Analysis Services, then the tool can be configured with the multidimensional model, the tabular model, or installed to SharePoint in order to support PowerPivot and Power View.

Although you can install SQL Server successfully using default values, for the ongoing supportability of your instance, and indeed your estate, make sure you consider many aspects of the installation. This applies especially to collations, service accounts, and other security considerations, such as the most appropriate administrators group to add and the authentication model to implement.

CHAPTER 3

■ ■ ■

Server Core Installation

Because SQL Server does not support remote installations and because Windows Server Core provides only a command line interface (CLI) and no graphical user interface (GUI), you must perform installation of SQL Server on Windows Server Core as a command line operation. You can also use a configuration file to produce consistent, repeatable installations.

In this chapter, we will review the considerations for installing SQL Server on Windows Server Core before demonstrating how to perform an installation on this platform. We will also discuss using configuration files and how you can use them to simplify future installations and enforce consistency.

Considerations for Server Core Installations

In Chapter 1, you may remember that we discussed the limitations of SQL Server on Windows Server Core and how some features, such as Reporting Services, Master Data Services, and Data Quality Services, are not supported, whereas other features, such as Management Tools and Distributed Replay Client, are only supported remotely.

In addition to considering the features available within Windows Server Core and ensuring operational supportability across various competencies within your organization, including proficiency in PowerShell, you should also think about the prerequisites for installing SQL Server on Windows Core. In order to successfully install SQL Server, the following software prerequisites must be in place:

- Windows Installer 4.5

- Windows PowerShell 2.0

- .NET Framework 2.0 SP2

- .NET Framework 4 Server Core Profile

- .NET Framework 3.5 SP1 Full Profile

If you are planning to install SQL Server on Windows Server 2012 Core, then the first four of these prerequisites are shipped with the product by default and the SQL Server installation will enable them if the features being installed require them. This means that the only prerequisite that may require action is .NET Framework 3.5 SP1 Full Profile. Of course, if your Windows team members have a Windows Server Core build designed specifically for SQL Server, then they may have this already installed. You can check by running the PowerShell command in Listing 3-1.

Listing 3-1. Checking .NET 3.5 Installation on Server Core

```
Get-windowsfeature
```

Figure 3-1 shows part of the output from running this command when .NET Framework 3.5 SP1 Full Profile has not been installed. As you can see, .NET Framework 4.5 has an x beside it, indicating that it is installed. .NET Framework 3.5, however, does not have an x beside it, which means that the prerequisite has not been met.

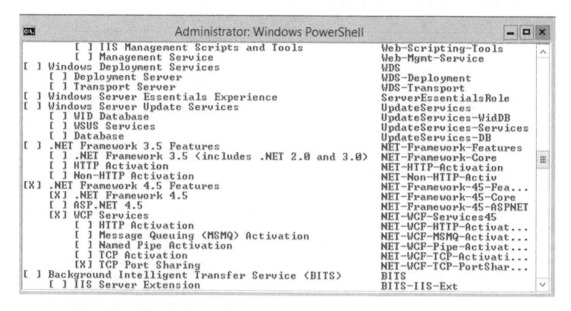

Figure 3-1. *Results of get-WindowsFeature*

Because Server Core has no GUI and therefore no web browser and no server manager with which to install .NET Framework 3.5, you will need to use the command line to install the feature. You can find the package in the \sources\sxs folder of the Windows Server 2012 installation media. The PowerShell command in Listing 3-2 demonstrates how to install the .NET Framework 3.5 SP1 Full Profile. In this case, the -source parameter points to a share on a file server where the .NET Framework 3.5 full package is located.

Listing 3-2. Installing .NET Framework 3.5 SP1 Full Profile

```
Install-WindowsFeature Net-Framework-Core -source \\192.168.183.1\netsp35sp1\
```

■ **Note** Ensure that the account you are using has permissions to the file share.

Following the installation, you will see the message that is displayed in Figure 3-2. This informs you that the installation has succeeded and that there is no requirement to restart the server.

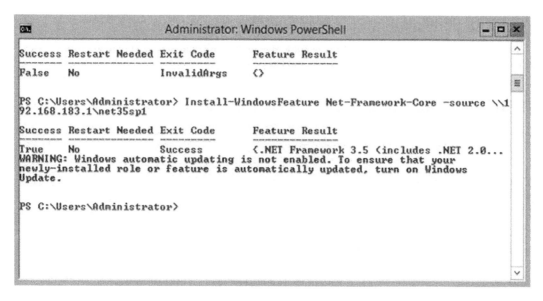

Figure 3-2. Successful installation of .NET Framework 3.5

Installing an Instance

Installing SQL Server in Windows Server Core involves running setup.exe from the command line. Setup.exe can be found in the root directory of the SQL Server installation media. When running setup.exe from the command line, you can use switches and parameters to pass in values, which will be used to configure the instance.

■ **Note**   You can follow the same process to install SQL Server on a GUI-based version of Windows, if required.

Required Parameters

Although many switches and parameters are optional, some must always be included. When you are installing a stand-alone instance of the Database Engine, the parameters listed in Table 3-1 are always required.

Table 3-1. Required Parameters

Parameter	Usage
/IACCEPTSQLSERVERLICENSETERMS	Confirms that you accept the SQL Server license terms
/ACTION	Specifies the action that you want to perform, such as Install or Upgrade
/FEATURES	Specifies the features that you wish to install
/INSTANCENAME	The name to be assigned to the instance
/SQLSYSADMINACCOUNTS	The Windows security context(s) that will be given administrative permissions in the instance of the Database Engine
/qs	Performs an unattended install. This is required on Windows Server Core since the installation wizard is not supported.

IACCEPTSQLSERVERLICENSETERMS Switch

Because /IACCEPTSQLSERVERLICENSETERMS is a simple switch that indicates your acceptance of the license terms, it does not require any parameter value be passed.

ACTION Parameter

When you perform a basic installation of a stand-alone instance, the value passed to the /ACTION parameter will be install, however a complete list of possible values for the /ACTION parameter are listed in Table 3-2.

Table 3-2. *Values Accepted by the* /ACTION *Parameter*

Value	Usage
install	Installs a stand-alone instance
PrepareImage	Prepares a vanilla stand-alone image, with no account-, computer-, or network-specific details
CompleteImage	Completes the installation of a prepared stand-alone image by adding account, computer, and network details
Upgrade	Upgrades an instance from SQL Server 2005, 2008, or 2012
EditonUpgrade	Upgrades a SQL Server 2014 from a lower edition (such as Developer edition) to a higher edition (such as Enterprise)
Repair	Repairs a corrupt instance
RebuildDatabase	Rebuilds corrupted system databases
Uninstall	Uninstalls a stand-alone instance
InstallFailoverCluster	Installs a failover clustered instance
PrepareFailoverCluster	Prepares a vanilla clustered image with no account-, computer-, or network-specific details
CompleteFailoverCluster	Completes the installation of a prepared clustered image by adding account, computer, and network details
AddNode	Adds a node to a failover cluster
RemoveNode	Removes a node from a failover cluster

FEATURES Parameter

As shown in Table 3-3, the /FEATURES parameter is used to specify a comma delimited list of features that will be installed by setup, but not all features can be used on Windows Server Core.

Table 3-3. *Acceptable Values of the /FEATURES Parameter*

Parameter Value	Use on Windows Core	Description
SQL	NO	Full SQL Engine, including Full Text, Replication, and Data Quality Server
SQLEngine	YES	Database Engine
FullText	YES	Full Text search
Replication	YES	Replication components
DQ	NO	Data Quality Server
AS	YES	Analysis Services
RS	NO	Reporting Services
DQC	NO	Data Quality Client
IS	YES	Integration Services
MDS	NO	Master Data Services
Tools	NO	All client tools and Books Online
BC	NO	Backward compatibility components
BOL	NO	Books Online
Conn	YES	Connectivity components
SSMS	NO	SQL Server Management Studio (SSMS), SQLCMD, and the SQL Server PowerShell provider
Adv_SSMS	NO	As SSMS, plus SSMS support for AS, RS, and IS, Profiler, Database Engine, Tuning Advisor, and Utility management
DREPLAY_CTLR	NO	Distributed Replay Controller
DREPLAY_CLT	NO	Distributed Replay Client
SNAC_SDK	NO	Client connectivity SDK
SDK	NO	Client tools SDK

■ **Note** If you choose to install other SQL Server features, such as Analysis Services or Integration Services, then other parameters will also become required.

Basic Installation

When you are working with command line parameters for setup.exe, you should observe the rules outlined in Table 3-4 with regard to syntax.

Table 3-4. *Syntax Rules for Command Line Parameters*

Parameter Type	Syntax
Simple switch	`/SWITCH`
True/False	`/PARAMETER=true/false`
Boolean	`/PARAMETER=0/1`
Text	`/PARAMETER="Value"`
Multi-valued text	`/PARAMETER="Value1" "Value2"`
/FEATURES parameter	`/FEATURES=Feature1,Feature2`

■ **Tip**   For text parameters, the quotation marks are only required if the value contains spaces. However, it is considered good practice to always include them.

Asuming that you have already navigated to the root directory of the installation media, then the command in Listing 3-3 provides PowerShell syntax for installing the Database Engine, Replication, and client connectivity components. It uses default values for all optional parameters, with the exception of the collation, which we will set to the Windows collation Latin1_General_CI_AS.

Listing 3-3. Installing SQL Server from the Command Line

```
.\SETUP.EXE /IACCEPTSQLSERVERLICENSETERMS /ACTION="Install" /FEATURES=SQLEngine,Replication,
Conn /INSTANCENAME="PROSQLADMINCORE2" /SQLSYSADMINACCOUNTS="Administrator"
/SQLCOLLATION="Latin1_General_CI_AS" /qs
```

■ **Note**   This syntax will work from the command prompt as well as PowerShell.

In this example, a SQL Server instance named PROSQLADMINCORE will be installed. Both the Database Engine and the SQL Agent services will run under the SQLServiceAccount1 account, and the Windows group called SQLDBA will be made administrator.

When installation begins, a pared down, noninteractive version of the installation wizard will appear to keep you updated on progress. The first screen that displays will show the progress of downloading product updates and unpacking the SQL Server setup files, as shown in Figure 3-3.

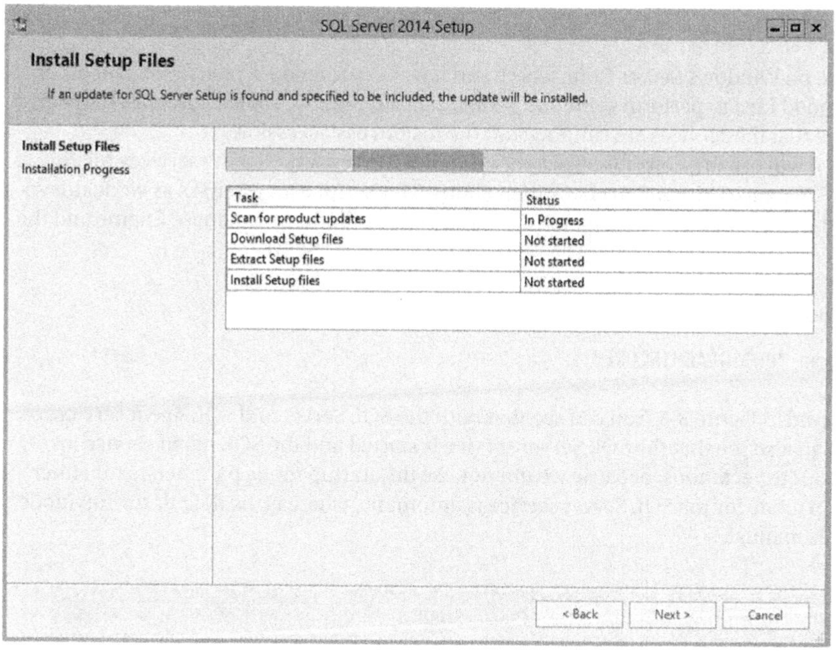

Figure 3-3. *Install Setup Files progress*

Once this stage has been completed, an installation progress screen will display as the instance is installed. This screen is illustrated in Figure 3-4.

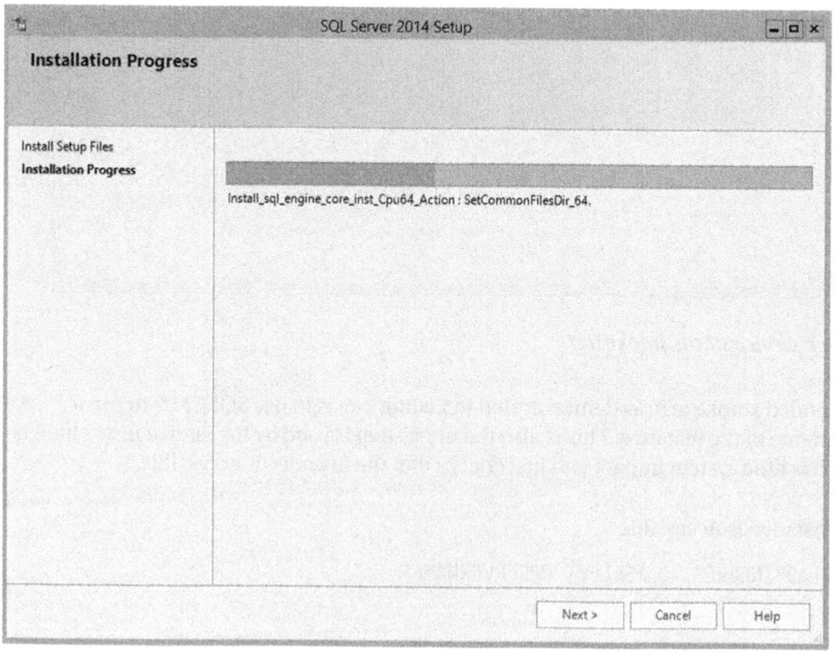

Figure 3-4. *Installation progress*

Smoke Tests

After installing an instance on Windows Server Core, where you have no summary screen at the end of installation, it is always a good idea to perform some smoke tests. In this context, *smoke tests* refer to quick, high-level tests that ensure that the services are running and the instance is accessible.

The code in Listing 3-4 will use the PowerShell get-service cmdlet, to ensure that the services relating to the PROSQLADMINCORE instance exist and to check their status. This script uses asterisks as wildcards so that we only need to run the command once, as opposed to running it for both the Database Engine and the SQL Agent service.

Listing 3-4. Checking Status of Services

```
Get-service -displayname *PROSQLADMINCORE*
```

The results are displayed in Figure 3-5. You can see that both the SQL Server and SQL Agent services have been installed. You can also see that the SQL Server service is started and the SQL Agent service is stopped. This aligns with our expectations, because we did not use the startup mode parameters for either service. The default startup mode for the SQL Server service is automatic, whereas the default startup mode for the SQL Agent service is manual.

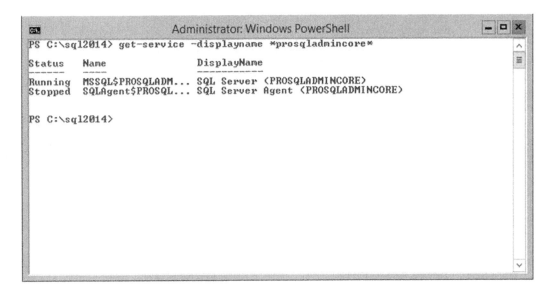

Figure 3-5. *Results of check service status smoke test*

The second recommended smoke test, as demonstrated in Listing 3-5, is to use SQLCMD to run a query that will return the name of the instance. This is also the query that is used by the IsAlive test, which is performed by a cluster. It has little system impact and just checks that the instance is accessible.

Listing 3-5. Checking if Instance Is Accessible

```
sqlcmd.exe -S ".\PROSQLADMINCORE" -Q "SELECT @@SERVERNAME"
```

In this example, the -S switch is used to specify the instance name that you will connect to, and the -Q switch specifies the query that will be run and also tells SQLCMD to exit when the query completes. If we used the -q switch instead, then we would remain inside the SQLCMD application, after query execution. We would then need to use the exit command to manually exit the application. The results of this smoke test are illustrated in Figure 3-6. As you can see, the query resolved successfully and returned the name of the instance.

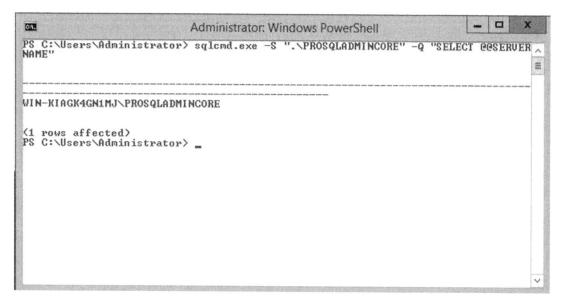

Figure 3-6. *Results of check instance accessible smoke test*

Troubleshooting the Installation

If an error occurs during the installation of the instance, or if your smoke tests fail, then you will need to troubleshoot the installation. With no GUI, this may seem like a daunting task, but luckily the SQL Server installation process provides a full set of verbose logs, which you can use to identify the issue. The most useful of these logs are listed in Table 3-5.

Table 3-5. *SQL Server Installation Logs*

Log File	Location
Summary.txt	%programfiles%\Microsoft SQL Server\120\Setup Bootstrap\Log\
Detail.txt	%programfiles%\Microsoft SQL Server\120\Setup\ Bootstrap\Log\<YYYYMMDD_HHMM>\
SystemConfigurationCheck_Report.htm	%programfiles%\Microsoft SQL Server\120\Setup Bootstrap\Log\<YYYYMMDD_HHMM>\

Summary.txt

Summary.txt will normally be your first point of call when you troubleshoot SQL Server installation issues. It provides basic information regarding the installation and can often be used to determine the issue. The sample in Figure 3-7, for example, clearly shows in Exit Message that the installation of an instance failed because the instance name specified was too long.

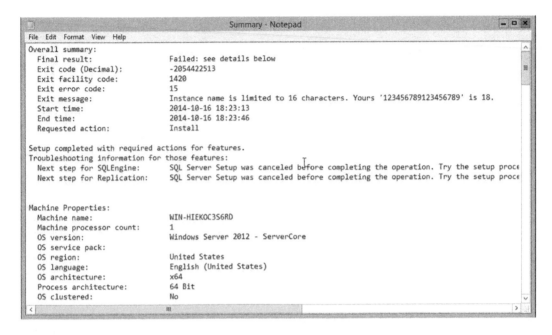

Figure 3-7. *Summary.txt*

In addition to returning high-level information, such as the exit code, exit message, and start and end time of the installation, summary.txt will also provide you with details about the OS environment. Additionally, it will detail the components that setup tried to install with the status of each MSI (Microsoft Installer) that was executed, and it will list any command line parameters that were specified. At the end of the file, you will also find an exception summary, which includes a stack trace.

You can use Notepad to open a text file in Windows Server Core. So, assuming that you had already navigated to the %programfiles%\Microsoft SQL Server\120\Setup Bootstrap\Log\ folder, you could use the command notepad summary.txt to open this file.

Detail.txt

If summary.txt does not provide the granular detail that you need, then your next stop will be detail.txt. This is a verbose log of actions performed by the installation, which are organized by the time at which the execution occurred, rather than by the component that executed them. To find errors in this log, you should search for the strings *error* and *exception*.

SystemConfigurationCheck_Report.htm

The SystemConfigurationCheck_Report.htm file provides a description and the status of each of the rule checks that happened during the installation in a web page format. Unfortunately, Windows Server Core has no support for rendering HTML. Therefore, in order to view this file, you have two options. The first is to view it in Notepad, which will give you the detail you are looking for, but it will be buried in-between HTML tags, with no intuitive formatting. This pretty much misses the point of Microsoft providing the information in a user friendly format.

The second option is to open the file remotely from a machine that has a GUI installed. This sounds like a much better option, and indeed it is, as long as you have a share created on the server that you can drop the file into and from which you can access it quickly. If this is not the case, however, and if your environment does not provide the capability to quickly move this file onto another machine, you may not want to spend too much time on this. Especially since the only reason you would normally be accessing it is because your installation has just failed and you are likely to have project teams requesting that you resolve the issue quickly.

Other Log Files

Many additional log files are produced by the SQL Server setup routine, including a folder named Datastore, which contains a series of XML files, each of which represent individual settings that have been configured. Also of interest, you will find a copy on the configuration file that setup generated and a file called settings. xml. This file defines the metadata for the configuration options, including the source of where the value of the configuration was contained, such as a default value, or user specified.

A verbose log will also be created for every MSI that was run during the setup process. The quantity of these logs will of course depend on the features that you have chosen to install. On Windows Server Core, as long as you are not performing an SSAS-only installation, at a minimum, there will be a .log file relating to the SQL Engine. These .log files can provide even more granular detail regarding their specific MSI, which can assist you in troubleshooting.

Using the MSI logs is not totally straightforward, however, since you may find many errors that are caused by a preceding error, as opposed to being the root cause of the issue. To use these log files, you should order them by the time that they were created. You can then work through them backwards. The last error that you find will be the root cause issue. To search these files for errors, search for the string *Return value 3*. It can get even more complicated, however, because not all *Return value 3* occurrences will relate to unexpected errors. Some of them may be expected results.

Optional Parameters

There are many switches and parameters that can optionally be used to customize the configuration of the instance that you are installing. The optional switches and parameters that you can use for the installation of the Database Engine are listed in Table 3-6.

Table 3-6. *Optional Parameters*

Parameter	Usage
/AGTSVCSTARTUPTYPE	Specifies the start-up mode of the SQL Agent Service. This can be set to Automatic, Manual, or Disabled.
/BROWSERSVCSTARTUPTYPE	Specifies the start-up mode of the SQL Browser Service. This can be set to Automatic, Manual, or Disabled.
/SQLSVCACCOUNT	The service account that will be used to run the Database Engine. If this parameter is not specified, a virtual account will be created. This account will access the network using the computer account of the server.
/SQLSVCPASSWORD	The password of the service account that will be used to run the Database Engine. This parameter will become required if the /AGTSVCACCOUNT parameter is specified.
/AGTSVCACCOUNT	The service account that will be used to run SQL Agent. If this parameter is not specified, a virtual account will be created. This account will access the network using the computer account of the server.
/AGTSVCPASSWORD	The password of the service account that will be used to run SQL Agent. This parameter will become required if the /AGTSVCACCOUNT parameter is specified.
/CONFIGURATIONFILE	Specifies the path to a configuration file, which contains a list of switches and parameters so that they do not have to be specified inline, when running setup.
/ENU	Dictates that the English version of SQL Server will be used. Use this switch if you are installing the English version of SQL Server on a server with localized settings and the media contains language packs for both English and the localized operating system.
/ERRORREPORTING	Determines if error reporting will be set to Microsoft. Set to 0 for off or 1 for on.
/FILESTREAMLEVEL	Used to enable FILESTREAM and set the required level of access. This can be set to 0 to disable FIESTREAM, 1 to allow connections via SQL Server only, 2 to allow IO streaming, or 3 to allow remote streaming. The options from 1 to 3 build on each other, so by specifying level 3, you are implicitly specifying levels 1 and 2 as well.
/FILESTREAMSHARENAME	Specify the name of the Windows file share where FILESTREAM data will be stored. This parameter becomes required, when /FILESTREAMLEVEL is set to a value of 2 or 3.
/INDICATEPROGRESS	When this switch is used, the setup log is piped to the screen during installation.
/INSTANCEDIR	Specifies a folder location for the instance.
/INSTANCEID	Specifies an ID for the instance. It is considered bad practice to use this parameter, as discussed in Chapter 2.
/INSTALLSHAREDDIR	Specifies a folder location for 64-bit components that are shared between instances.
/INSTALLSHAREDWOWDIR	Specifies a folder location for 32-bit components that are shared between instances. This location cannot be the same as the location for 64-bit shared components.
/INSTALLSQLDATADIR	Specifies the default folder location for instance data.

(continued)

Table 3-6. (*continued*)

Parameter	Usage
/NPENABLED	Specifies if Named Pipes should be enabled. This can be set to 0 for disabled or 1 for enabled.
/PID	Specifies the PID for SQL Server. Unless the media is pre-pidded, failure to specify this parameter will cause Evaluation edition to be installed.
/SAPWD	Specifies the password for the SA account. This parameter is used when /SECURITYMODE is used to configure the instance as mixed-mode authentication. This parameter becomes required if /SECURITYMODE is set to SQL.
/SECURITYMODE	Use this parameter, with a value of SQL, to specify mixed mode. If you do not use this parameter, then Windows authentication will be used.
/SQLBACKUPDIR	Specifies the default location for SQL Server backups.
/SQLCOLLATION	Specifies the collation the instance will use.
/SQLSVCSTARTUPTYPE	Specifies the start-up mode of the Database Engine Service. This can be set to Automatic, Manual, or Disabled.
/SQLTEMPDBDIR	Specifies a folder location for TempDB data files.
/SQLTEMPDBLOGDIR	Specifies a folder location for TempDB Log files.
/SQLUSERDBDIR	Specifies a default location for the data files or user databases.
/SQLUSERDBLOGDIR	Specifies the default folder location for log files or user databases.
/SQMREPORTING	Specifies if SQL Reporting will be enabled. Use a value of 0 to disable or 1 to enable.
/TCPENABLED	Specifies if TCP will be enabled. Use a value of 0 to disable, or 1 to enable.
/UPDATEENABLED	Specifies if Product Update functionality will be used. Pass a value of 0 to disable or 1 to enable.
/UPDATESOURCE	Specify a location for Product Update to search for updates. A value of MU will search Windows Update, but you can also pass a file share or UNC.

Product Update

The Product Update functionality replaces the deprecated slipstream installation functionality of SQL Server and provides you with the ability to install the latest SP (service pack) or CU (cumulative update) at the same time you are installing the SQL Server base binaries. This functionality can save DBAs the time and effort associated with installing the latest update immediately after installing a SQL Server instance and can also help provide consistent patching levels across new builds.

In order to use this functionality, you must use two parameters during the command line install. The first of these is the /UPDATEENABLED parameter. You should specify this parameter with a value of 1 or True. The second is the /UPDATESOURCE parameter. This parameter will tell setup where to look for the product update. If you pass a value of MU into this parameter, then setup will check Microsoft Update, or a WSUS service, or alternatively, you can supply a relative path to a folder or the UNC (Uniform Naming Convention) of a network share.

In the following example, we will examine how to use this functionality to install SQL Server 2014, with CU2 for RTM included, which will be located in a network share. When you download a SP or CU, they will arrive as an executable, which is wrapped in a zipped, self-extracting executable. This executable must be extracted before you can use it with Product Update functionality, and the /UPDATESOURCE parameter must point to the extracted application. This is extremely useful, because even if WSUS is not in use in your environment, once you have signed off on a new patching level, you can simply replace the SP or CU within your network share; when you do, all new builds can receive the latest update, without you needing to change the PowerShell script that you use for building new instances.

The PowerShell command in Listing 3-6 will install an instance of SQL Server, named PROSQLADMINCU2, with the same configuration as PROSQLADMINCORE, except that CU2, which is located on a file server, will be installed at the same time.

Listing 3-6. Installing CU During Setup

```
.\SETUP.EXE / IACCEPTSQLSERVERLICENSETERMS /ACTION="Install" /FEATURES=SQLEngine,Replic
ation,Conn /INSTANCENAME="PROSQLADMINCU2" /SQLSVCACCOUNT="MyDomain\SQLServiceAccount1"
/SQLSVCPASSWORD="Pa$$w0rd" /AGTSVCACCOUNT="MyDomain\SQLServiceAccount1" /
AGTSVCPASSWORD="Pa$$w0rd" /SQLSYSADMINACCOUNTS="MyDomain\SQLDBA" /UPDATEENABLED=1 /
UPDATESOURCE="\\192.168.183.1\SQL2014_CU2\" /qs
```

■ **Note** The account that you are using to run the installation will require permissions to the file share.

The code in Listing 3-7 demonstrates how you can interrogate the difference between the two instances. The code uses SQLCMD to connect to each of the instances in turn and return the systems variable that contains the full version details of the instance, including the build number. The name of the instance is also included to help us easily identify the results.

Listing 3-7. Determining Build Version of Each Instance

```
.\sqlcmd.exe -S ".\PROSQLADMINCORE" -Q "SELECT @@SERVERNAME, @@VERSION"
```

```
.\sqlcmd.exe -S ".\PROSQLADMINCU2" -Q "SELECT @@SERVERNAME, @@VERSION"
```

In this example, the -S parameter specifies the name of the instance we will connect to, and the -Q parameter specifies the query that we want to run and also that we wish to exit SQLCMD on completion. Because we have not specified the -u (user name) or -p (password) parameters, SQLCMD will automatically use Windows authentication. The results of the first of SQLCMD query are shown in Figure 3-8.

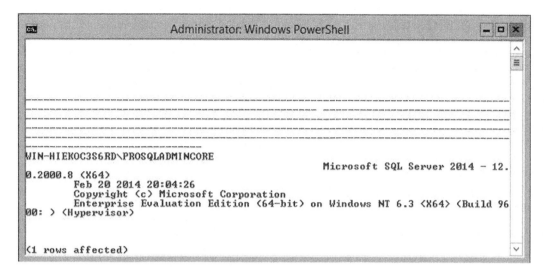

Figure 3-8. PROSQLADMINCORE version details

The results of the second SQLCMD query are shown in Figure 3-9.

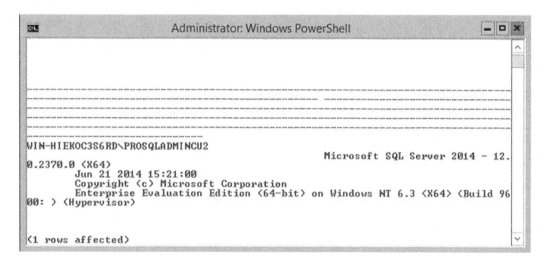

Figure 3-9. PROSQLADMINCU2 version details

We can see from the results that PROSQLADMINCORE is running on SQL Server build version 12.0.2000.0, which is the build number of SQL Server 2014 RTM, whereas PROSQLADMINCU2 is running on build version 12.0.2370.0, which is the build number of SQL Server 2014 RTM, CU2.

Using a Config File

We have touched on using configuration files to produce consistent builds at several points already in this book. The sample in Listing 3-8 is the content of a configuration file, which has been populated with all of the required parameters that are needed to install an instance named PROSQLADMINCONF1 on Windows Server Core. It also contains the optional parameters to enable named pipes and TCP/IP, enables FILESTREAM at the access level where it can only be accessed via T-SQL, sets the SQL Agent service to start automatically, and configures the collation to be Latin1_General_CI_AS. In this .ini file, comments are defined with a semicolon at the beginning of the line.

Listing 3-8. Configuration File for SQLPROSQLADMINCONF1

```
; SQL Server 2014 Configuration File
[OPTIONS]

; Accept the SQL Server License Agreement

IACCEPTSQLSERVERLICENSETERMS

; Specifies a Setup work flow, like INSTALL, UNINSTALL, or UPGRADE.
; This is a required parameter.

ACTION="Install"

; Setup will display progress only, without any user interaction.

QUIETSIMPLE="True"

; Specifies features to install, uninstall, or upgrade. The list of top-level
; features include SQL, AS, RS, IS, MDS, and Tools. The SQL feature will
; install the Database Engine, Replication, Full-Text, and Data Quality
; Services (DQS) server. The Tools feature will install Management Tools, Books
; online components, SQL Server Data Tools, and other shared components.

FEATURES=SQLENGINE,REPLICATION,CONN

; Specify a default or named instance. MSSQLSERVER is the default instance for
; non-Express editions and SQLExpress is for Express editions. This parameter is
; required when installing the SQL Server Database Engine (SQL), Analysis
; Services (AS), or Reporting Services (RS).

INSTANCENAME="PROSQLADMINCONF1"

; Agent account name

AGTSVCACCOUNT="MyDomain\SQLServiceAccount1"

; Agent account password

AGTSVCPASSWORD="Pa$$w0rd"
```

```
; Auto-start service after installation.

AGTSVCSTARTUPTYPE="Automatic"

; Level to enable FILESTREAM feature at (0, 1, 2 or 3).

FILESTREAMLEVEL="1"

; Specifies a Windows collation or an SQL collation to use for the Database
; Engine.

SQLCOLLATION="Latin1_General_CI_AS"

; Account for SQL Server service: Domain\User or system account.

SQLSVCACCOUNT="MyDomain\SQLServiceAccount1"

; Password for the SQL Server service account.

SQLSVCPASSWORD="Pa$$w0rd"

; Windows account(s) to provision as SQL Server system administrators.

SQLSYSADMINACCOUNTS="MyDomain\SQLDBA"

; Specify 0 to disable or 1 to enable the TCP/IP protocol.

TCPENABLED="1"

; Specify 0 to disable or 1 to enable the Named Pipes protocol.

NPENABLED="1"
```

■ **Tip**   If you use a configuration file created by a previous SQL Server installation as a template for your own config file, you will notice that the following parameters are specified: MATRIXCMBRICKCOMMPORT, MATRIXCMSERVERNAME, MATRIXNAME, COMMFABRICENCRYPTION, COMMFABRICNETWORKLEVEL, and COMMFABRICPORT. These parameters are intended for internal use by Microsoft only and should be ignored. They have no effect on the build.

Assuming that this configuration file had been saved as c:\SQL2014\configuration1.ini, then the code in Listing 3-9 could be used to run setup.exe from PowerShell.

Listing 3-9. Intsalling SQL Server Using a Configuration File

```
.\setup.exe /CONFIGURATIONFILE="c:\SQL2014\Configuration1.ini"
```

Although this is a perfectly valid use of a configuration file, you can actually be a little bit more sophisticated and use this approach to create a reusable script, which can be run on any server, to help you introduce a consistent build process. Essentially, you are using a scripted version of a prepared stand-alone image for Windows Server Core. This is particularly useful if your Windows operational teams have not adopted the use of Sysprep or use other methods to build servers.

In Listing 3-10, you will see another configuration file. This time, however, it only includes the static parameters that you expect to be consistent across your estate. Parameters that will vary for each installation, such as instance name and service account details, have been omitted.

Listing 3-10. Configuration File for PROSQLADMINCONF2

```
;SQL Server 2014 Configuration File
[OPTIONS]

; Accept the SQL Server License Agreement

IACCEPTSQLSERVERLICENSETERMS

; Specifies a Setup work flow, like INSTALL, UNINSTALL, or UPGRADE.
; This is a required parameter.

ACTION="Install"

; Setup will display progress only, without any user interaction.

QUIETSIMPLE="True"

; Specifies features to install, uninstall, or upgrade. The list of top-level features
include SQL, AS, RS, IS, MDS, and Tools. The SQL feature will install the Database Engine,
Replication, Full-Text, and Data Quality Services (DQS) server. The Tools feature will
install Management Tools, Books online components, SQL Server Data Tools, and other shared
components.

FEATURES=SQLENGINE,REPLICATION,CONN

; Auto-start service after installation.

AGTSVCSTARTUPTYPE="Automatic"

; Level to enable FILESTREAM feature at (0, 1, 2 or 3).

FILESTREAMLEVEL="1"

; Specifies a Windows collation or an SQL collation to use for the Database Engine.

SQLCOLLATION="Latin1_General_CI_AS"

; Windows account(s) to provision as SQL Server system administrators.

SQLSYSADMINACCOUNTS="MyDomain\SQLDBA"
```

```
; Specify 0 to disable or 1 to enable the TCP/IP protocol.

TCPENABLED="1"

; Specify 0 to disable or 1 to enable the Named Pipes protocol.

NPENABLED="1"
```

This means that to successfully install the instance, you will need to use a mix of parameters from the configuration file and also inline with the command that runs setup.exe, as demonstrated in Listing 3-11. This example assumes that the configuration in Listing 3-10 has been saved as C:\SQL2014\Configuration2.ini and will install an instance named PROSQLADMINCONF2.

Listing 3-11. Installing SQL Server Using a Mix of Parameters and a Configuration File

```
.\SETUP.EXE /INSTANCENAME="PROSQLADMINCONF2" /SQLSVCACCOUNT="MyDomain\SQLServiceAccount1"
/SQLSVCPASSWORD="Pa$$w0rd" /AGTSVCACCOUNT="MyDomain\SQLServiceAccount1" /
AGTSVCPASSWORD="Pa$$w0rd" /CONFIGURATIONFILE="C:\SQL2014\Configuration2.ini"
```

Automatic Installation Routines

This approach gives us the benefit of having a consistent configuration file that we do not need to modify every time we build out a new instance. This idea can be taken even further, however. If we were to save our PowerShell command as a PowerShell script, then we could run the script and pass in parameters, rather than rewrite the command each time. This will give a consistent script for building new instances, which we can place under change control. The code in Listing 3-12 demonstrates how to construct a parameterized PowerShell script, which will use the same configuration file. The script assumes D:\ is the root folder of the installation media.

Listing 3-12. PowerShell Script for Auto-install

```
param(
[string] $InstanceName,
[string] $SQLServiceAccount,
[string] $SQLServiceAccountPassword,
[string] $AgentServiceAccount,
[string] $AgentServiceAccountPassword
)

D:\SETUP.EXE /INSTANCENAME=$InstanceName /SQLSVCACCOUNT=$SQLServiceAccount /SQLSVCPASSWORD=
$SQLServiceAccountPassword /AGTSVCACCOUNT=$AgentServiceAccount /AGTSVCPASSWORD=$AgentService
AccountPassword /CONFIGURATIONFILE="C:\SQL2014\Configuration2.ini"
```

Assuming that this script is saved as SQLAutoInstall1.ps1, the command in Listing 3-13 can be used to build an instance named PROSQLADMINAUTO1. This command runs the PowerShell script, passing in parameters, which are then used in the setup.exe command.

Listing 3-13. Running SQLAutoInstall.ps1

```
./SQLAutoInstall.ps1 -InstanceName 'PROSQLADMIN1' -SQLServiceAccount 'MyDomain\
SQLServiceAccount1' -SQLServiceAccountPassword 'Pa$$w0rd' -AgentServiceAccount 'MyDomain\
SQLServiceAccount1' -AgentServiceAccountPassword 'Pa$$w0rd'
```

Enhancing the Installation Routine

You could also extend the SQLAutoInstall.ps1 script further and use it to incorporate the techniques that you learned in Chapter 1 for the configuration of operating system components and the techniques that you learned earlier in this chapter for performing smoke tests.

After installing an instance, the amended script in Listing 3-14, which we will refer to as SQLAutoInstall2.ps1, uses powercfg to set the High Performance power plan and set-ItemProperty to prioritize background services over foreground applications. It then runs smoke tests to ensure that the SQL Server and SQL Agent services are both running and that the instance is accessible.

Listing 3-14. Enhanced PowerShell Auto-install Script

```
param(
[string] $InstanceName,
[string] $SQLServiceAccount,
[string] $SQLServiceAccountPassword,
[string] $AgentServiceAccount,
[string] $AgentServiceAccountPassword
)

# Initialize ConnectionString variable

$ServerName = $env:computername
$ConnectionString = $ServerName + '\' + $InstanceName

#Install the instance

./SETUP.EXE /INSTANCENAME=$InstanceName /SQLSVCACCOUNT=$SQLServiceAccount /SQLSVCPASSWORD=
$SQLServiceAccountPassword /AGTSVCACCOUNT=$AgentServiceAccount /AGTSVCPASSWORD=$AgentService
AccountPassword /CONFIGURATIONFILE="C:\SQL2014\Configuration2.ini"

# Configure OS settings

powercfg -setactive 8c5e7fda-e8bf-4a96-9a85-a6e23a8c635c

Set-ItemProperty -path HKLM:\SYSTEM\CurrentControlSet\Control\PriorityControl -name
Win32PrioritySeparation -Type DWORD -Value 24

# Run smoke tests

Get-service -displayname *$InstanceName*

sqlcmd.exe -S $ConnectionString -Q "SELECT @@SERVERNAME"
```

As well as passing variables into the setup.exe command, this script also uses the $InstanceName parameter as input for the smoke tests. The parameter can be passed straight into to get-service cmdlet, with wildcards on either side. For SQLCMD, however, we need to do a little extra work. SQLCMD requires the full name of the instance, including the server name, or (local), assuming that the script is always run locally. The script pulls the name of the server from the ComputerName environmental variable and then concatenates this with the $InstanceName variable, placing a \ between the two. This concatenated value populates the $ConnectionString variable, which can then be passed into -S switch SQLCMD.

The results of this script being used to install an instance named PROSQLADMINAUTO2 are displayed in Figure 3-10. As you can see, after installing the instance, the console will display the results of the smoke tests.

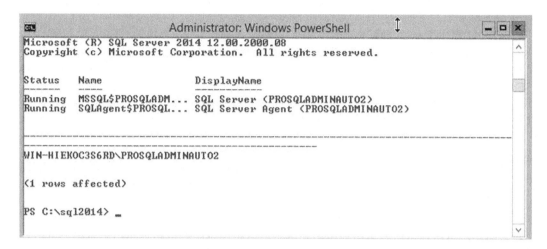

Figure 3-10. *Results of enhanced auto-install script*

Production Readiness

Finally, you may wish to add some defensive coding to your script in order to make it production ready. Although PowerShell has try/catch functionality due to setup.exe being an external application, which will generate its own messages and errors, the most effective technique for ensuring the smooth running of this script is to enforce mandatory parameters.

The code in Listing 3-15 is a modified version of the script, which we will refer to as SQLAutoInstall3. ps1. This version of the script uses the Parameter keyword to set the Mandatory attribute to true for each of the parameters. This is important, because if the person running this script were to omit any of the parameters, or if there was a typo in the parameter name, the installation would fail. This provides a fail-safe by ensuring that all of the parameters have been entered before allowing the script to run. The additional change that we have made in this script is to add annotations before and after each step, so that if the script does fail, we can easily see where the error occurred.

Listing 3-15. Auto-install Script with Defensive Code

```
param(
[Parameter(Mandatory=$true)]
[string] $InstanceName,
[Parameter(Mandatory=$true)]
[string] $SQLServiceAccount,
[Parameter(Mandatory=$true)]
[string] $SQLServiceAccountPassword,
[Parameter(Mandatory=$true)]
[string] $AgentServiceAccount,
[Parameter(Mandatory=$true)]
[string] $AgentServiceAccountPassword
)
```

```
# Initialize ConnectionString variable

$ServerName = $env:computername
$ConnectionString = $ServerName + '\' + $InstanceName

"Initialize variables complete..."

#Install the instance

./SETUP.EXE /INSTANCENAME=$InstanceName /SQLSVCACCOUNT=$SQLServiceAccount /SQLSVCPASSWORD=
$SQLServiceAccountPassword /AGTSVCACCOUNT=$AgentServiceAccount /AGTSVCPASSWORD=$AgentService
AccountPassword /CONFIGURATIONFILE="C:\SQL2014\Configuration2.ini"

"Instance installation complete..."

# Configure OS settings

powercfg -setactive 8c5e7fda-e8bf-4a96-9a85-a6e23a8c635c

"High Performance power plan configured..."

Set-ItemProperty -path HKLM:\SYSTEM\CurrentControlSet\Control\PriorityControl -name
Win32PrioritySeparation -Type DWORD -Value 24

"Optimize for background services configured..."

# Run smoke tests

Get-service -displayname *$InstanceName* -ErrorAction Stop

"Service running check complete..."

sqlcmd.exe -S $ConnectionString -Q "SELECT @@SERVERNAME"

"Instance accessibility check complete..."
```

In Figure 3-11, the SQLAutoInstall3.ps1 script has been run, but without any parameters specified. In previous versions of the script, PowerShell would have gone ahead and executed the code, only for setup.exe to fail, since no values were specified for the required parameters. In this version, however, you can see that you will be prompted to enter a value for each parameter in turn.

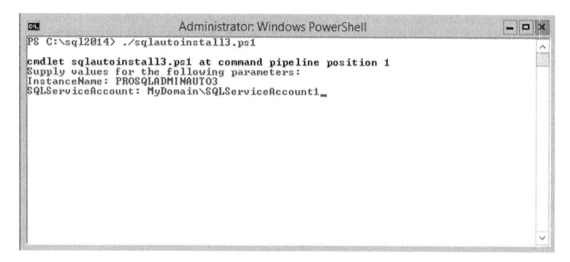

Figure 3-11. SQLAutoInstall3.ps1 prompts for each missing paramter

In Figure 3-12, you will notice that after each phase of the script execution, our annotations are shown. This can aid you in responding to errors, because you can easily see which command caused an issue before you even begin to decipher any error messages that may be displayed.

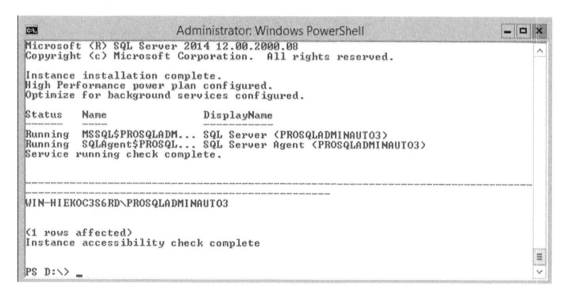

Figure 3-12. Annotations displayed in script

Summary

Ensuring that the prerequisites are in place is key to a successful build. When you are installing on Windows Server 2012 Core, this will normally involve obtaining the full .NET Framework 3.5 package and installing it on the Server. The other SQL Server prerequisites are supplied by default as part of a Windows Server Core build and if required, will be enabled automatically by the SQL Server installation process.

Installing SQL Server on Windows Server Core can be as simple as running a single command from PowerShell and passing in the appropriate parameters. However, for consistency across the enterprise and to reduce manual effort, you may wish to automate your build process. You can do this by using a configuration file, but you can also expand this process out to fully automate the installation, including OS configuration. You will then be able to keep a PowerShell script under change control and simply run it, passing parameters, every time you wish to build a new instance.

After installing an instance, you should run smoke tests to ensure that the services are running and that the instance is accessible. This will highlight any show-stopping issues. If you do need to troubleshoot a build, then your starting point should be to check the Summary.txt log file and if you need to, the Detail.txt log file.

In addition to installing the base binaries, you can use SQL Server's Product Update functionality to install the latest service pack or cumulative update at the same time. Product Update can be configured to check Microsoft Update, a folder location, or network folder. If you store the latest fully tested update on a network share, then you can use this when installing any instance on the network, and when you wish to increase the level of update that you support, you can simply replace the update file on the network share.

CHAPTER 4

■ ■ ■

Configuring the Instance

The installation and configuration of your SQL Server instance does not end when setup successfully completes. There are many other considerations that you should take into account, both inside the database engine and outside of it, using tools such as SQL Server Configuration Manager. In this chapter, we will discuss many of the most important instance-level configuration options, including SQL Server's new buffer pool extension technology and important configuration choices for system databases. We will also look at how your instance can communicate through a firewall before finally demonstrating how to uninstall an instance, both from Windows Server Core and through the GUI.

Instance Configuration

At the instance level, there countless settings and flags that can be configured. In the following sections, we will look at viewing and configuring these settings using tools such as sp_configure, sys.configurations, DBCC TRACEON, and ALTER SERVER.

Using sp_configure

You can change many of the settings that you can configure at the instance level using the system stored procedure sp_configure. You can use the sp_configure procedure to both view and change instance level settings. This procedure will be used in many examples throughout this book, so it is important that you understand how it works. If a procedure is the first statement in the batch, you can run it without the EXEC keyword, but you must use the EXEC keyword if there are any preceding statements. If the procedure is run with no parameters, then it will return a five-column result set. The meaning of these columns is detailed in Table 4-1.

Table 4-1. *Result Set Returned by sp_configure*

Column	Description
Name	The name of the instance level setting.
Minimum	The minimum value that is acceptable for this setting.
Maximum	The maximum value that is accepted for this setting.
Config_value	The value that has been configured for this value. If this value differs from the value in the Run_value column, then the instance will need to be either restarted or reconfigured for this configuration to take effect.
Run_value	The value that is currently being used for this setting.

If you wish to use sp_configure to change the value of a setting, as opposed to just viewing it, then you must run the procedure with two parameters being passed in. The first of these parameters is called configname and is defined with a VARCHAR(35) data type. This parameter is used to pass the name of the setting that you wish to change. The second parameter is called configvalue and is defined as an integer. This parameter is used to pass the new value for the setting. After you have changed an instance level setting using sp_configure, it will not immediately take effect. To activate the setting, you will need to either restart the Database Engine Service, or reconfigure the instance.

There are two options for reconfiguring the instance. The first is a command called RECONFIGURE. The second is a command called RECONFIGURE WITH OVERRIDE. The RECONFIGURE command will change the running value of the setting as long as the newly configured value is regarded as "sensible" by SQL Server. For example, RECONFIGURE will not allow you to disable contained databases when they exist on the instance. If you use the RECONFIGURE WITH OVERRIDE command, however, this action would be allowed, even though your contained databases will no longer be accessible. Even with this command, however, SQL Server will still run checks to ensure that the value you have entered is between the Min and Max values for the setting. It will also not allow you to perform any operations that will cause serious errors. For example, it will not allow you to configure the Min Server Memory (MB) setting to be higher than the Max Server Memory (MB) setting, since this would cause a fatal error in the Database Engine.

The first time you run the sp_configure stored procedure with no parameters in SQL Server 2014, it will return 18 rows. These rows contain the basic configuration options for the instance. One of the options is called Show Advanced Options. If you turn on this option and then reconfigure the instance, as demonstrated is Listing 4-1, then an additional 52 advanced settings will be displayed when you run the procedure. If you try to change the value of one of the advanced options before turning on the Show Advanced Options setting, then the command will fail.

Listing 4-1. Showing Advanced Options

```
EXEC sp_configure 'show advanced options', 1
RECONFIGURE
```

As an alternative to viewing these settings with sp_configure, you can also retrieve the same information by querying sys.configurations. If you use sys.configurations to return the information, then two additional columns will be returned. One of these columns is called is_dynamic and it designates if the option can be configured with the RECONFIGURE command (1), or if the instance needs to be restarted (0). The other column is called is_Advanced, and it indicates if the setting is configurable without Show Advanced Options being turned on.

Processor and Memory Configuration

When configuring your instance, one of your first considerations should be the configuration of processor and memory resources. There are two main considerations that you should give to the processor. One is processor affinity and the other is MAXDOP (maximum degree of parallelism).

Processor Affinity

By default, your instance will be able to use all of the processor cores within your server. If you use Processor affinity, however, specific processor cores will be aligned with your instance and these will be the only cores that the instance has access to. There are two main reasons for limiting your instance in this way. The first is when you have multiple instances running on the same server. With this configuration, you may find that the instances are competing for the same processor resources and therefore blocking each other. Processor affinity is controlled via a setting called *affinity mask*.

Imagine you had a server with four physical processors, each of which had two cores. Assuming that hyperthreading is turned off for the purpose of this example, there would be a total of eight cores available to SQL Server. If you had four instances on the server, then to avoid the instances competing for resources, you could align cores 0 and 1 with instance 1, cores 2 and 3 with instance 2, cores 4 and 5 with instance 3, and cores 6 and 7 with instance 4.

If you have other services running on the server, such as SQL Server Integration Services (SSIS), you may wish to leave a core available for Windows and other applications, which cannot be used by any of the instances. In this case, you may have identified that instance 4 uses less processor resources than the other instances. It may be an instance dedicated to ETL (extract, transform, and load), for example, and be used primarily for hosting the SSIS Catalog. In this case, you may align instance 4 with core 6 only. This would leave core 7 free for other purposes. This design is illustrated in Figure 4-1.

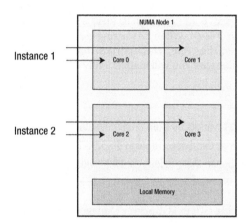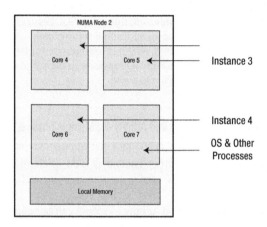

Figure 4-1. *Processor afinity diagram*

■ **Note**   SSIS is incorporated into the Database Engine. However, when SSIS packages run, they run in a separate DTSHost process and are, therefore, not aligned with the processor and memory configuration of the instance.

When using processor affinity, it is important for performance to align an instance with cores on the same NUMA (non-uniform memory access) node. This is because, if a processor needs to remotely access the memory of a different NUMA node, it needs to go via an interconnect, which is a lot slower than accessing the local NUMA node. In the example shown in Figure 4-1, if we had aligned instance 1 with cores 0 and 7, then we would have breached the NUMA boundary and performance would have been impaired.

■ **Caution**   Although it is not recommended for SQL Server, some virtual environments use a technique called *over-subscribed processors*. This means that more cores are allocated to guests than actually exist on the physical hosts. When this is the case, you should not use processor affinity because NUMA boundaries will not be respected.

The affinity mask reducing contention also holds true for clustered environments. Imagine you have a two-node cluster with an Active/Active configuration. Each node of the cluster is hosting a single instance. It may be important for your business that you can guarantee consistent performance in the event of a failover. In this case, assuming that each of your nodes has eight cores, then on node 1, you could configure instance 1 to use cores 0, 1, 2, and 3. On node 2, you could configure instance 2 to use cores 4, 5, 6, and 7. Now, in the event of failover, your instances will continue to use the same processor cores and not fight for resources.

The second reason for using processor affinity is to avoid the overhead associated with threads being moved between processors at the operating system level. When your instance is under heavy load, you may see a performance improvement by aligning SQL Server threads with specific cores. In this scenario, it would be possible to separate standard SQL Server tasks from SQL Server IO related tasks.

Imagine that you have a server with a single processor, which has two cores. Hyperthreading is turned off and you have a single instance installed. You may choose to align tasks associated with IO affinity, such as Lazy Writer, with core 0, while aligning other SQL Server threads with core 1. To align IO tasks with specific processors, you need to use an additional setting, called *Affinity I/O Mask*. When this setting is enabled, a hidden scheduler is created, which is used purely for Lazy Writer. Therefore, it is important that you do not align the affinity and affinity IO masks with the same core. Otherwise you will inadvertently create the contention that you are trying to avoid.

■ **Caution**   It is very rare that Affinity I/O Mask is required. To align workloads from multiple instances, Affinity Mask is sufficient. It is normally only appropriate for very large databases running on 32-bit systems. With 64-bit systems with larger amounts of RAM, IO churn is less, hence there is less context switching.

Both Affinity Mask and Affinity I/O Mask can be set through the GUI in SQL Server Management Studio by selecting the Processors tab in the Instance Properties dialog box, as shown in Figure 4-2.

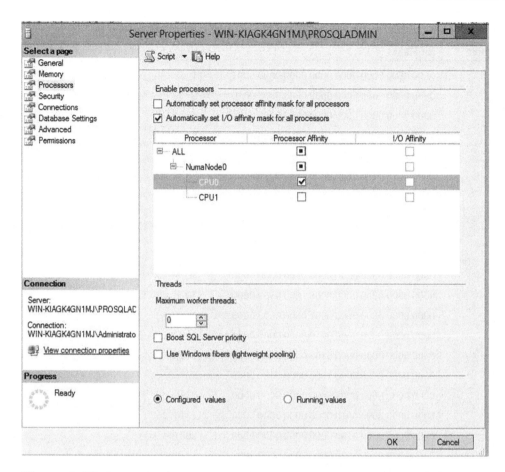

Figure 4-2. *The Processors tab*

Processor affinity works based on bit maps. Therefore, if you wish to use sp_configure to set processor affinity, then you first need to calculate the integer representation of the bit map value. This is made more complex because the INT data type is a 32-bit signed integer, meaning that some of the representations will be negative numbers. The value assigned to each processor is listed in Table 4-2.

Table 4-2. Processor Affinity Bit Maps

Processor Number	Bit Mask	Signed Integer Representation
0	0000 0000 0000 0000 0000 0000 0000 0001	1
1	0000 0000 0000 0000 0000 0000 0000 0010	2
2	0000 0000 0000 0000 0000 0000 0000 0100	4
3	0000 0000 0000 0000 0000 0000 0000 1000	8
4	0000 0000 0000 0000 0000 0000 0001 0000	16
5	0000 0000 0000 0000 0000 0000 0010 0000	32
6	0000 0000 0000 0000 0000 0000 0100 0000	64
7	0000 0000 0000 0000 0000 0000 1000 0000	128
8	0000 0000 0000 0000 0000 0001 0000 0000	256
9	0000 0000 0000 0000 0000 0010 0000 0000	512
10	0000 0000 0000 0000 0000 0100 0000 0000	1024
11	0000 0000 0000 0000 0000 1000 0000 0000	2028
12	0000 0000 0000 0000 0001 0000 0000 0000	4096
13	0000 0000 0000 0000 0010 0000 0000 0000	8192
14	0000 0000 0000 0000 0100 0000 0000 0000	16384
15	0000 0000 0000 0000 1000 0000 0000 0000	32768
16	0000 0000 0000 0001 0000 0000 0000 0000	65536
17	0000 0000 0000 0010 0000 0000 0000 0000	131072
18	0000 0000 0000 0100 0000 0000 0000 0000	262144
19	0000 0000 0000 1000 0000 0000 0000 0000	524288
20	0000 0000 0001 0000 0000 0000 0000 0000	1048576
21	0000 0000 0010 0000 0000 0000 0000 0000	2097152
22	0000 0000 0100 0000 0000 0000 0000 0000	4194304
23	0000 0000 1000 0000 0000 0000 0000 0000	8388608
24	0000 0001 0000 0000 0000 0000 0000 0000	16777216
25	0000 0010 0000 0000 0000 0000 0000 0000	33554432
26	0000 0100 0000 0000 0000 0000 0000 0000	67108864
27	0000 1000 0000 0000 0000 0000 0000 0000	134217728
28	0001 0000 0000 0000 0000 0000 0000 0000	268435456
29	0010 0000 0000 0000 0000 0000 0000 0000	536870912
30	0100 0000 0000 0000 0000 0000 0000 0000	1073741824
31	1000 0000 0000 0000 0000 0000 0000 0000	-2147483648

■ **Tip** Many free calculators are available on the Internet that will assist you in converting binary to signed integer.

On a 32-core server, there are 2.631308369336935e+35 possible combinations for processor affinity, but a few examples are included in Table 4-3.

Table 4-3. Examples of Affinity Masks

Aligned Processors	Bit Mask	Signed Integer Representation
0 and 1	0000 0000 0000 0000 0000 0000 0000 0011	3
0, 1, 2, and 3	0000 0000 0000 0000 0000 0000 0000 1111	15
8 and 9	0000 0000 0000 0000 0000 0011 0000 0000	768
8, 9, 10, and 11	0000 0000 0000 0000 0000 1111 0000 0000	3840
30 and 31	1100 0000 0000 0000 0000 0000 0000 0000	-1073741824
28, 29, 30, and 31	1111 0000 0000 0000 0000 0000 0000 0000	-268435456

Because of the nature of the affinity mask and the integer data type having a maximum range of 2^32, if your server has between 33 and 64 processors, then you will also need to set the Affinity64 Mask and Affinity64 I/O Mask settings. These will provide the masks for the additional processors.

The settings discussed in this section can all be configured using sp_configure. The example in Listing 4-2 demonstrates aligning the instance with cores 0 to 3.

Listing 4-2. Setting Processor Affinity

```
EXEC sp_configure 'affinity mask', 15
RECONFIGURE
```

Even with the 64-bit masks, there is still a limitation of aligning the first 64 cores using this method, and SQL Server will support up to 256 logical processors. For this reason, newer versions of SQL Server have introduced an enhanced method of setting processor affinity. This is through a command called ALTER SERVER CONFIGURATION. Listing 4-3 demonstrated two ways that this command can be used. The first aligns the instance with specific processors in the way that we have seen up until now. In this example, the alignment is with CPUs 0, 1, 2, and 3. The second aligns the instance with all processors within two NUMA nodes, in this case, nodes 0 and 4. Just as when you make changes using sp_configure, changes made using ALTER SERVER CONFIGURATION will be reflected in sys.configurations.

Listing 4-3. ALTER SERVER CONFIGURATION

```
ALTER SERVER CONFIGURATION
    SET PROCESS AFFINITY CPU=0 TO 3

ALTER SERVER CONFIGURATION
    SET PROCESS AFFINITY NUMANODE=0, 4
```

MAXDOP

MAXDOP will set the maximum number of cores that will be made available to each individual execution of a query. The thought of this may initially sound counterintuitive. Surely you would want every query to be parallelized as much as possible? Well, this is not always the case.

Although some data warehousing queries may benefit from high levels of parallelization, many OLTP (Online Transaction Processing) workloads may perform better with a lower degree of parallelization. This is because if a query executes over many parallel threads, and one thread takes much longer than the others to complete, then the other threads may sit waiting for the final thread to finish so that their streams can be synchronized. If this is occurring, you are likely to see a high number of waits with the wait type CXPACKET.

In many OLTP systems, high levels of parallelization being chosen by the Query Optimizer actually indicate issues such as missing or highly fragmented indexes. Resolving these issues will improve performance far more than running queries with a high degree of parallelism.

For instances that support heavy data warehousing workloads, different MAXDOP configurations should be tested and set accordingly, with the understanding that MAXDOP can also be set at the query level, through the use of a Query Hint, if a handful of queries would benefit from a different setting to the majority of the instance's workload. In the vast majority of cases, however, the instance level setting for MAXDOP should be configured to the lowest of the following three values:

- 8

- Number of cores available to the instance (the default value for MAXDOP)

- The number of cores within a NUMA node

The default value for MAXDOP is 0, which means that queries are only limited by the number of cores that are visible to the instance. You can configure MAXDOP via the GUI by configuring the Max Degree of Parallelism setting on the Advanced tab of the Server Properties. Figure 4-3 illustrates this setting being configured to 8.

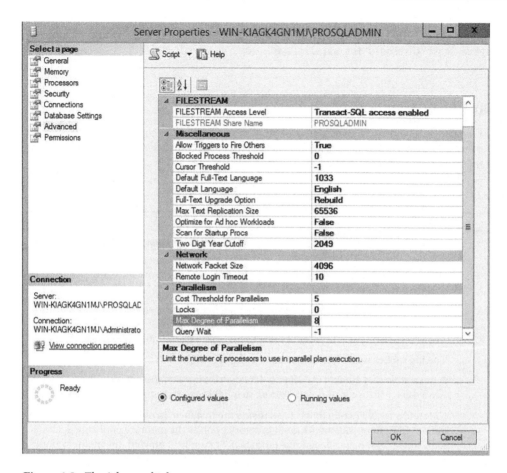

Figure 4-3. *The Advanced tab*

You can also configure MAXDOP using `sp_configure`. Listing 4-4 demonstrates using `sp_configure` to set MAXDOP to a value of 8.

Listing 4-4. Configuring MAXDOP with sp_configure

```
EXEC sys.sp_configure max degree of parallelism', 8
RECONFIGURE
```

An alternative to lowering the MAXDOP setting is to increase the threshold at which the Query Optimizer will choose a parallel plan over a serial plan. The default setting for this is an estimated serial execution time of 5 seconds, but you can configure this to anything between 0 and 32767 seconds. The cost threshold for the parallelism option will be ignored, however, if you have MAXDOP configured to 1, or if there is only one core available to the instance. The script in Listing 4-5 will increase the cost threshold for parallelism to 10 seconds.

Listing 4-5. Configuring Cost Threshold for Parallelism

```
EXEC sp_configure 'cost threshold for parallelism', 10
RECONFIGURE
```

Min and Max Server Memory

The Min Server Memory (MB) and Max Server Memory (MB) settings are used to control how much memory SQL Server has available for its memory pool. The memory pool contains many components. Some of the largest components are detailed in Table 4-4.

Table 4-4. *SQL Server Memory Pool*

Component	Description
Buffer cache	The buffer cache stores data and index pages before and after being read from or written to disk. Even if the pages your query requires are not in the cache, they will still be written to the buffer cache first and then retrieved from memory, as opposed to been written directly from disk.
Procedure cache	The procedure cache contains execution plans, not just for stored procedures, but also for ad-hoc queries, prepared statements, and triggers. When SQL Server begins to optimize a query, it first checks this cache to see if a suitable plan already exists.
Log cache	The log caches stores log records before they are written to the transaction log.
Log pool	A hash table that allows HA/DR and data distribution technologies, such as AlwaysOn, Mirroring, and Replication, to quickly access required log records.
CLR	CLR refers to .NET code that is used inside the instance. In older versions of SQL Server, CLR sat outside of the main memory pool, as the memory pool only dealt with single, 8KB page allocations. From SQL Server 2012 onward, the memory pool now deals with both single and multipage allocations, so CLR has been brought in.

In many environments, it is likely that you will want to provide the same value, for both Min and Max Server Memory. This will avoid the overhead of SQL Server dynamically managing the amount of memory it has reserved.

If you have multiple instances, however, then dynamic memory management may be beneficial so that the instance with the heaviest workload at any given time can consume the most resources. You must give extra consideration if your instances are hosted on an Active/Active cluster. I have seen one example of a client turning on Lock Pages In Memory and then configuring the min and max memory for the instances on each node as if they were stand-alone boxes. At the point of failover, the remaining node crashed, because there was not enough RAM to support the memory requirements of all instances on one box.

No matter how your environment is configured, you will always want to leave enough memory for the operating system. Assuming that you have one instance and no other applications, such as SSIS packages, running on the server, you would normally set both the min and max memory setting to be the lowest value from the following:

- RAM - 2GB

- (RAM / 8) * 7

If you have multiple instances, you would, of course, divide this number appropriately between the instances, depending on their requirements. If you have other applications running on the server, then you must also take their memory requirements into account and add those to the operating system requirements.

Min Server Memory (MB) and Max Server Memory (MB) can both be configured by using the Memory tab in the Server Properties dialog box, as shown in Figure 4-4.

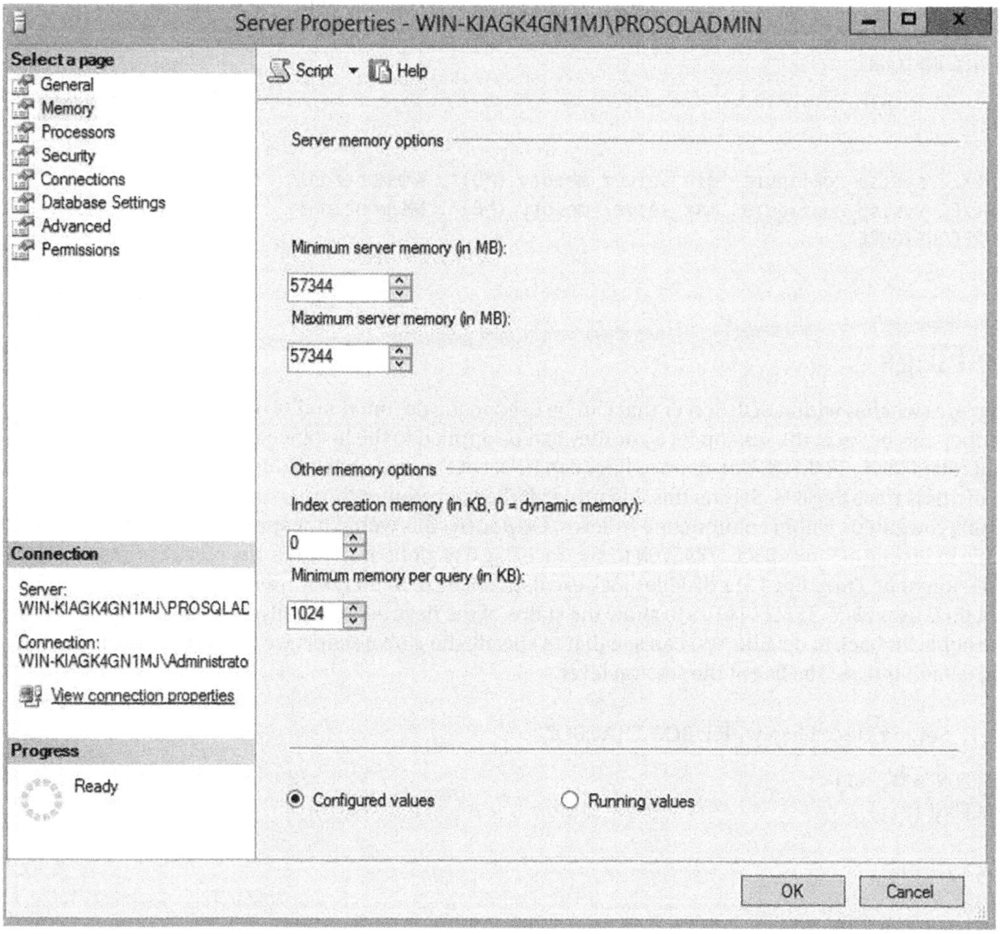

Figure 4-4. *The Memory tab*

You can also configure both the settings through T-SQL by using the `sp_configure` stored procedure. Listing 4-6 demonstrates this.

Listing 4-6. Configuring Min and Max Server Memory

```
DECLARE @MemOption1 INT = (SELECT physical_memory_kb/1024 - 2048 FROM sys.dm_os_sys_info)
DECLARE @MemOption2 INT = (SELECT ((physical_Memory_kb/1024)/8) * 7 FROM sys.dm_os_sys_info)

IF @MemOption1 <= 0
BEGIN
        EXEC sys.sp_configure 'min server memory (MB)', @MemOption2
        EXEC sys.sp_configure 'max server memory (MB)', @MemOption2
        RECONFIGURE
```

```
END
ELSE IF @MemOption2 < @MemOption1
BEGIN
        EXEC sys.sp_configure 'min server memory (MB)', @MemOption2
        EXEC sys.sp_configure 'max server memory (MB)', @MemOption2
        RECONFIGURE
END
ELSE
BEGIN
        EXEC sys.sp_configure 'min server memory (MB)', @MemOption1
        EXEC sys.sp_configure 'max server memory (MB)', @MemOption1
        RECONFIGURE
END
```

Trace Flags

Trace flags are switches within SQL Server that can be used to toggle functionality on and off. Within the instance, they can be set at the session level, or they can be applied to the instance globally, using a DBCC command called DBCC TRACEON. Not all trace flags can be set at the session level due to their nature. An example of this is trace flag 634. Setting this flag turns off the background thread responsible for periodically compressing rowgroups within columnstore indexes. Obviously, this would not apply to a specific session. The sample in Listing 4-7 uses DBCC TRACEON to set trace flag 634 globally. It also turns on 1211 for the current session only. Trace flag 1211 disables lock escalation based on memory pressure or number of locks. The script then uses DBCC TRACESTATUS to show the status of the flags before finally using DBCC TRACEOFF to toggle the behavior back to default. You can see that to specify the global scope, we use a second parameter of -1. The default is to set the flag at the session level.

Listing 4-7. Setting Trace Flags with DBCC TRACEON

```
DBCC TRACEON(634, -1)
DBCC TRACEON(1211)

DBCC TRACESTATUS

DBCC TRACEOFF(634, -1)
DBCC TRACEOFF(1211)
```

■ **Caution** Trace flag 1211 is used here for the purpose of demonstrating DBCC TRACEON. However, it may cause an excessive number of locks and should be used with extreme caution. It may even cause SQL Server to throw errors due to lack of memory for allocating locks.

Figure 4-5 shows the results screen that is produced from running this script, assuming that no other trace flags have currently been toggled away from their default setting. There are no results to display from the DBCC TRACEON and DBCC TRACEOFF commands. The messages windows, however, will display execution completed messages or inform you of any errors.

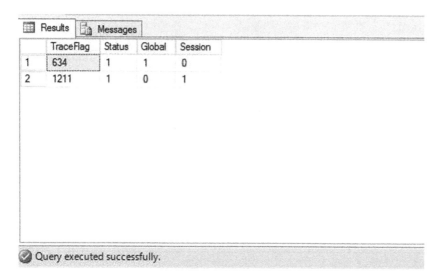

Figure 4-5. *DBCC TRACESTATUS results*

The limitation of using DBCC TRACEON, even with a global scope, is that the settings are transient and will not be persisted after the instance has been restarted. Therefore, if you wish to make permanent configuration changes to your instance, then you must use the -T startup parameter on the SQL Server service.

Startup parameters can be configured in SQL Server Configuration Manager. Expanding Service in the left hand window will display a list of all SQL Server–related services on the server. Entering the properties for the Database Engine service and selecting the Startup Parameters tab will then allow you to add or remove startup parameters. Figure 4-6 illustrates setting trace flag 1118.

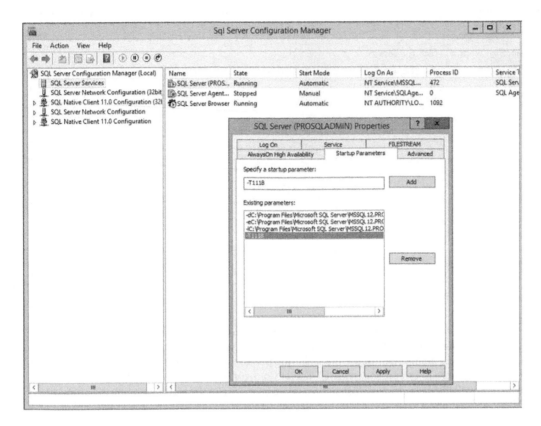

Figure 4-6. *Startup parameters*

If your instance is running on Windows Server Core, or if you want to script the configuration on a GUI-based server, then you could achieve the same results by running the PowerShell script in Listing 4-8. This script allows you to specify the instance name and trace flag to be configured in the top two variables. These could also be parameterized if you wish to create a reusable script. Similarly, the script could be added to the automatic installation script that we created in Chapter 2.

The PowerShell script works by determining the Registry path to the startup parameters and then by counting the number of arguments that already exist. Counting the arguments allows the next argument number in sequence to be determined. It then adds the new argument, specifying the required trace flag.

Listing 4-8. Configuring Trace Flags on Windows Server Core

```
# Define initial variables

$InstanceName = "PROSQLADMINCORE"
$TraceFlag = "1117"

# Configure full service name to be inserted into Registry path

$Instance = "MSSQL12.$InstanceName"

#Create full registry path
```

```
$RegistryPath = "HKLM:\SOFTWARE\Microsoft\Microsoft SQL Server\MSSQL12.$InstanceName\
MSSQLServer\Parameters"

# Gather all properties from the Registry path

$Properties = Get-ItemProperty $RegistryPath

# Count the number of SQLArg properties that already exist so that the next number in
sequence can be determined

$Arguments = $Properties.psobject.properties | ?{$_.Name -like 'SQLArg*'} | select Name,
Value

# Create the name of the new argument based on the next argument number in sequence

$NewArgument = "SQLArg"+($Arguments.Count)

# Construct the complete value of the argument

$FullTraceFlag = "-T$TraceFlag"

# Set the trace flag
Set-ItemProperty -Path $RegistryPath -Name $NewArgument -Value $FullTraceFlag
```

Many trace flags can be specified as startup parameters and the vast majority of them are only helpful in very specific circumstances. There are a few that stand out, however, as having the potential for more widespread use. These trace flags are detailed in the following sections.

Trace Flag 1118

SQL Server stores data in 8KB chunks, known as *pages*. These pages are organized into *extents*. An extent is eight continuous pages and is the smallest amount of data that SQL Server ever reads or writes to disk. There are two types of extent: mixed and uniform. A *mixed extent* holds data from multiple objects. These objects could include tables and indexes. A *uniform extent*, on the other hand, only stores data from a single object. Every new table is initially created on a mixed extent. When the size of the table grows to more than 64K, then the table begins to use uniform extents, even if row deletion or table truncation brings it back down below 64K. When you create a new index, if the initial size of the index is less than 64K, then the same rules will apply. If the initial size is greater than 64K, however, it will immediately be placed in uniform extents.

SQL Server keeps track of which extents are in use and if they are mixed or uniform with the use of GAM (Global Allocation Map) and SGAM (Shared Global Allocation Map) pages. These are special data pages, stored with the data files of each database, that store one bit for every extent in their range, and flip this bit, depending on the usage of a specific extent. If you have a database where many objects are created and dropped, such as TempDB, then these GAM and SGAM pages can become a bottleneck, due to multiple processes needing to access them simultaneously in order for space to be allocated for new objects.

Trace flag 1118 will turn off the use of mixed extents. This means that all new objects will be placed onto uniform extents. This can help reduce the contention on systems pages. It is important to note, however, that this flag will apply to all databases on the instance, not just TempDB. This means that the trade-off is less efficient storage if you have databases that contain many very small tables (less than 64KB).

■ **Caution**   Although well-known and well documented, even by Microsoft, this trace flag does not appear in Books Online. This means that it is regarded as an undocumented feature. This is important, because if you open a support ticket with Microsoft, they may ask you to turn this off before continuing an investigation.

Trace Flag 1117

When there are multiple files within a filegroup, SQL Server uses a proportional fill algorithm to assign extents to the file with the most available space. This works well, but when a file becomes full, it will grow, whereas the other files in the filegroup stay the same size. This skews the proportional fill algorithm.

If your instance is hosting certain types of database, such as a large data warehouse with large sequential scans, then this can cause a performance issue because the IO will not be evenly distributed. In order to avoid this problem, you can turn on trace flag 1117. Doing so will cause all of the files with a filegroup to grow at the same time.

The trade-off is that without proper configuration, you will use up free space on disk more quickly. However, if you think ahead about your initial file configuration, you can easily resolve this. For example, if you have four files within a filegroup and you would normally set an auto growth increment of 2048MB, you would simply alter the auto growth increment to be 512MB, if you wish to use this trace flag,

Of course, it is always beneficial to initially size all of you data files so that they will be the correct size and never have to grow. With even the best capacity planning, however, this is often not possible. Imagine a scenario where you anticipate, based upon natural growth, that your Sales data warehouse will grow to 2TB within five years, which is the anticipated lifecycle of the application. A year after, however, your company buys out two smaller firms. Suddenly, your capacity planning will be way out of sync with reality. Therefore, it always pays to have auto growth enabled as a fail-safe.

■ **Caution**   Although well-known and even specifically recommended in some of Microsoft's reference architectures, Trace Flag 1117 is not official documented by Microsoft. This is important, because if you open a support ticket with Microsoft, they may ask you to turn this off before continuing an investigation.

Trace Flag 3042

When you are performing backups using backup compression in SQL Server, a preallocation algorithm is used to allocate a defined percentage of the database size to the backup file. This gives you a performance advantage, over growing the size of the backup file, as required, on the fly. On the flip side, however, if you need to preserve disk space on your backup volume and use only the minimum amount of space required, then you can use trace flag 3042 to turn off this behavior and grow the file as required.

Trace Flag 3226

By default, every time you take a backup, a message will be recorded in the SQL Server log. If you take frequent log backups, however, then this can very quickly cause so much "noise" in the log, that troubleshooting issues can become more difficult and time consuming. If this is the case, then you can turn on trace flag 3226. This will cause successful backup messages to be suppressed in the log, resulting in a smaller, more manageable log.

Trace Flag 3625

SQL Server enforces tight controls on the visibility of metadata. Users can only view metadata for objects they own, or where they have explicitly been granted permissions to view metadata. This method of protection is still fallible, however, and a skilled attacker could still gain information. One way in which they could achieve this is by manipulating the order of precedence in queries in order to produce error messages.

In order to mitigate this risk, you can set trace flag 3625. This trace flag will limit the amount of metadata visible in error messages by masking certain data with asterisks. The downside of this defensive tactic, however, is that error messages become less meaningful and harder to understand. This can make troubleshooting issues more difficult.

Ports and Firewalls

In modern enterprise topologies, it is likely that your SQL Server instance will need to communicate through at least two firewalls. One of these will be a hardware firewall and the other will be the Windows Firewall, also known as the local firewall. In order for your instance to communicate with other interfaces—whether those are applications or other instances on the network—while still maintaining the security provided by a firewall, ports will need to be opened so that SQL Server can communicate through those ports.

Process of Communication

In order to understand which ports will need to be opened to allow SQL Server traffic, you must first understand how clients communicate with SQL Server. Figure 4-7 illustrates the process flow for TCP/IP connections. This example assumes that the instance is listening on Port 1433—this will be discussed in more detail later in this chapter. It also assumes that the client is running on Windows Vista/Windows Server 2008 or higher.

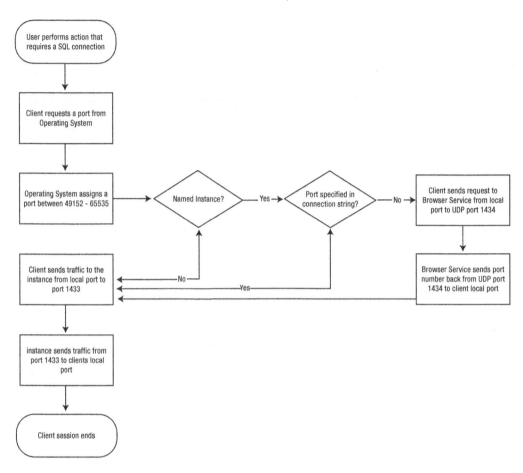

Figure 4-7. *Communication process flow*

If you wish clients to access the instance via named pipes, as opposed to TCP/IP, then SQL Server will communicate over port 445. This is the same port used by file and printer sharing.

Ports Required By SQL Server

If you install a default instance of SQL Server, then setup will automatically assign port 1433, which is the port registered for SQL Server in IANA (Internet Assigned Numbers Authority). Many DBAs choose to change this port number, however, for enhanced security. An attacker will know that you are likely to have instances running on port 1433 and will therefore know which port to attack. In smaller estates, unless you are confident of the security of your network, using nonstandard port numbers may be a good idea to add an extra layer of obfuscation. In larger enterprises, however, you will need to consider the impact on operational supportability. For example, if each instance has a different port number, you will need a method of recording and very quickly obtaining the port number for a given instance in case of failure of the browser service. This will be less of a concern in environments where multiple named instances are permitted on each server, since you will already have the inventory tooling for recording these port numbers.

■ **Note** IANA, the Internet Assigned Numbers Authority, is responsible for coordinating the allocation of Internet protocol resources, such as IP addresses, domain names, protocol parameters, and port numbers of network services. Its website is `www.internetassignednumbersauthority.org/`.

If you install a named instance of SQL Server, then setup will configure the instance to use dynamic ports. When dynamic ports are configured, then every time the instance starts, it will request a port number from the operating system. The OS will then assign it a random available port from the dynamic range, which is from 49152 to 65535, assuming that you are running on Windows Server 2008 or above. In earlier versions of Windows, the dynamic port range was from 1024–5000, but Microsoft changed this in Windows Vista and Windows Server 2008 to comply with IANA.

If your instance is configured to use dynamic ports, then configuring firewalls can be challenging. At the Windows Firewall level, it is possible to configure a specific service to communicate on any port, but this can be hard to replicate at the hardware firewall level. Alternatively, you need to keep the full dynamic port range open bidirectionally. Therefore, I recommend that the instance is configured to use a specific port.

It is important to remember that SQL Server uses many other ports for various features. The full set of ports that may be required by the Database Engine is listed in Table 4-5. If you install features outside of the Database Engine, such as SSAS or SSRS, then additional ports will be required. There will also be additional requirements if you plan to use additional services with your instance, such as IPSec for encryption, MSDTC (Microsoft Distributed Transaction Coordinator) distributed transactions, or SCOM (System Centre Operations Manager) for monitoring.

Table 4-5. *Ports Required by the Database Engine*

Feature	Port
Browser Service	UDP 1433.
Instance over TCP/IP	TCP 1433, dynamic or static configured.
Instance over named pipes	TCP 445.
DAC (Dedicated Administrator Connection)	TCP 1434. If TCP 1434 already in use, the port will be printed to the SQL Server log during instance startup.
Service Broker	TCP 4022 or as per configuration.
AlwaysOn Availability Groups	TCP 5022 or as per configuration.
Database Mirroring	TCP 7022 or as per configuration.
Merge Replication with Web Sync	TCP 21, TCP 80, UDP 137, UDP 138, TCP 139, TCP 445.
T-SQL Debugger	TCP 135.

Configuring the Port That the Instance Will Listen On

As mentioned earlier in this chapter, if you have a named instance, then before configuring your firewall, it is likely that you will want to configure a static port for the instance. The port can be configured within the TCP/IP Properties dialog box of the TCP/IP protocol in SQL Server Configuration Manager. To navigate to this dialog box, drill down through SQL Server Network Configuration | Protocols for *INSTANCENAME* (where *INSTANCENAME* is the name of your instance) in the left hand pane of SQL Server Configuration Manager. Entering TCP/IP in the right hand pane will display the dialog box.

On the Protocol tab, you will notice a setting named *Listen All*, which has a default value of Yes, as shown in Figure 4-8. The significance of this setting will become apparent shortly.

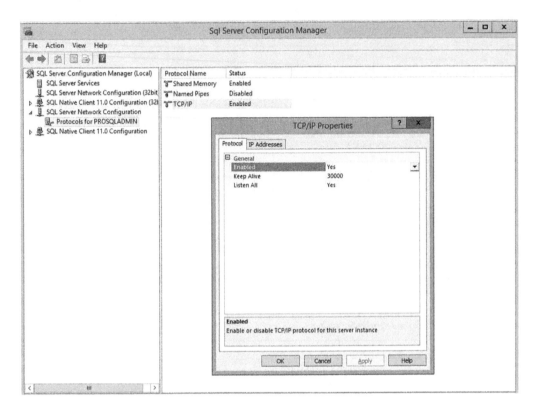

Figure 4-8. *The Protocol tab*

In the IP Addresses tab, you will notice that there are configuration details for multiple IP addresses. Because the Listen All setting is set to Yes, however, SQL Server will ignore all of these configurations. Instead, it will look solely at the settings specified for IP All at the very bottom of the dialog box. The TCP dynamic ports field will display the random port that has been assigned by the operating system and the TCP Port field will be blank, as illustrated in Figure 4-9. To assign a static port number, we need to flip this around. We will need to clear the TCP Dynamic Port field and populate the TCP Port field with 1433, which is our chosen port number. The SQL Server service will need to be restarted before this change can take effect.

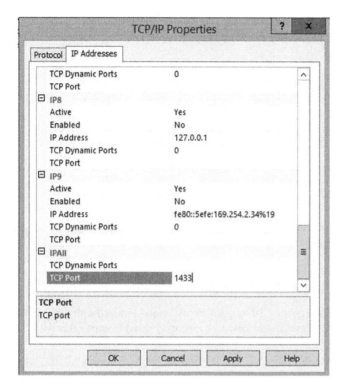

Figure 4-9. *IP Addresses tab*

■ **Tip**   Remember that the Default instance will take port 1433 by default. Therefore, if a Default instance already exists on the server, when you create the named instance, you must use a different port.

We could achieve the same result from PowerShell by running the script in Listing 4-9. This script has two variables at the top where you should insert the name of your instance and the port number you want to assign. These could also be parameterized to create a reusable script. The script loads the relevant SMO Assembly. It then creates a new SMO object and connects to the TCP properties of the object to configure the port. The script must be run As Administrator.

Listing 4-9. Assigning a Static Port

```
# Initialize variables

$Instance = "PROSQLADMIN"
$Port = "1433"

# Load SMO Wmi.ManagedComputer assembly
[System.Reflection.Assembly]::LoadWithPartialName("Microsoft.SqlServer.SqlWmiManagement") |
out-null
```

```
# Create a new smo object
$m = New-Object ('Microsoft.SqlServer.Management.Smo.Wmi.ManagedComputer')

#Disable dynamic ports

$m.ServerInstances[$Instance].ServerProtocols['Tcp'].IPAddresses['IPAll'].IPAddressPropertie
s['TcpDynamicPorts'].Value = ""

# Set static port

$m.ServerInstances[$Instance].ServerProtocols['Tcp'].IPAddresses['IPAll'].
IPAddressProperties['TcpPort'].Value = "$Port"

# Reconfigure TCP

$m.ServerInstances[$Instance].ServerProtocols['Tcp'].Alter()
```

Implementing Windows Firewall Rules

Windows Firewall rules can be implemented through the GUI by using the Windows Firewall with Advanced Security console, which can be found in Control Panel. In the following example, we will assume that we have an instance that will connect on port 1433 and that we also plan to use AlwaysOn Availability Groups. We will also assume that the browser service will be disabled and applications will be specifying a port number in the connection string.

This means that we will need to create a new inbound rule for dynamic ports TCP 1433 and TCP 5022. We will also need a new outbound rule for ports TCP 1433 and TCP 5022. When you choose to create a new inbound rule, the New Inbound Rule Wizard will be displayed. You should select Port as the rule type, as shown in Figure 4-10.

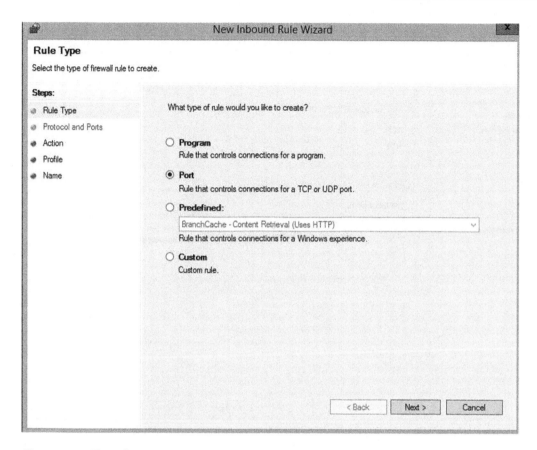

Figure 4-10. *The Rule Type page*

On the next screen of the wizard, ensure that TCP is selected and enter the required port numbers and range, as shown in Figure 4-11.

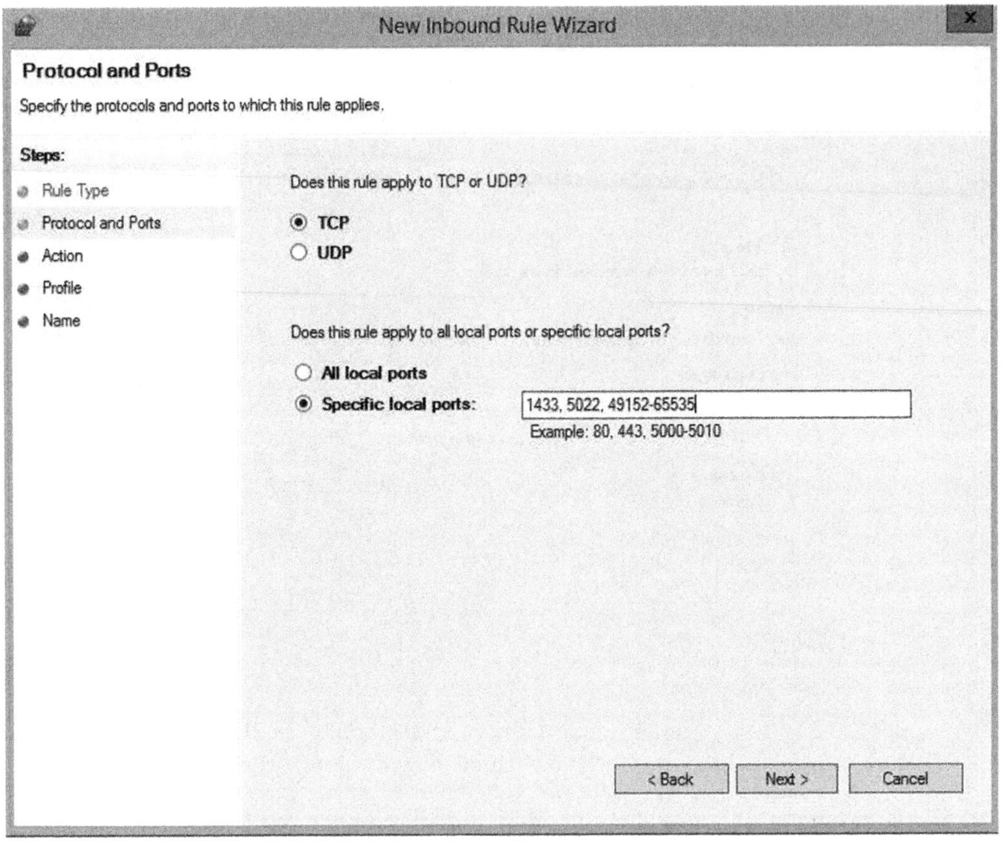

Figure 4-11. The Protocols And Ports page

On the Action page of the wizard, we will ensure that the Allow The Connection option is selected, as illustrated in Figure 4-12, and click Next to move on.

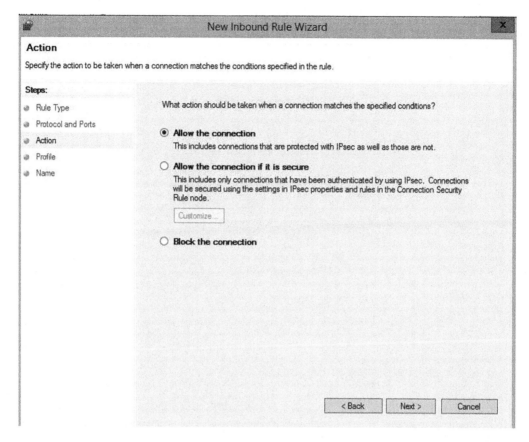

Figure 4-12. *The Action page*

As illustrated in Figure 4-13, the Profile page of the wizard will allow us to select which type of network connection our rule will apply to. In most environments, we would only want domain authenticated users connecting to our instance, so we will deselect the options for Private and Public networks.

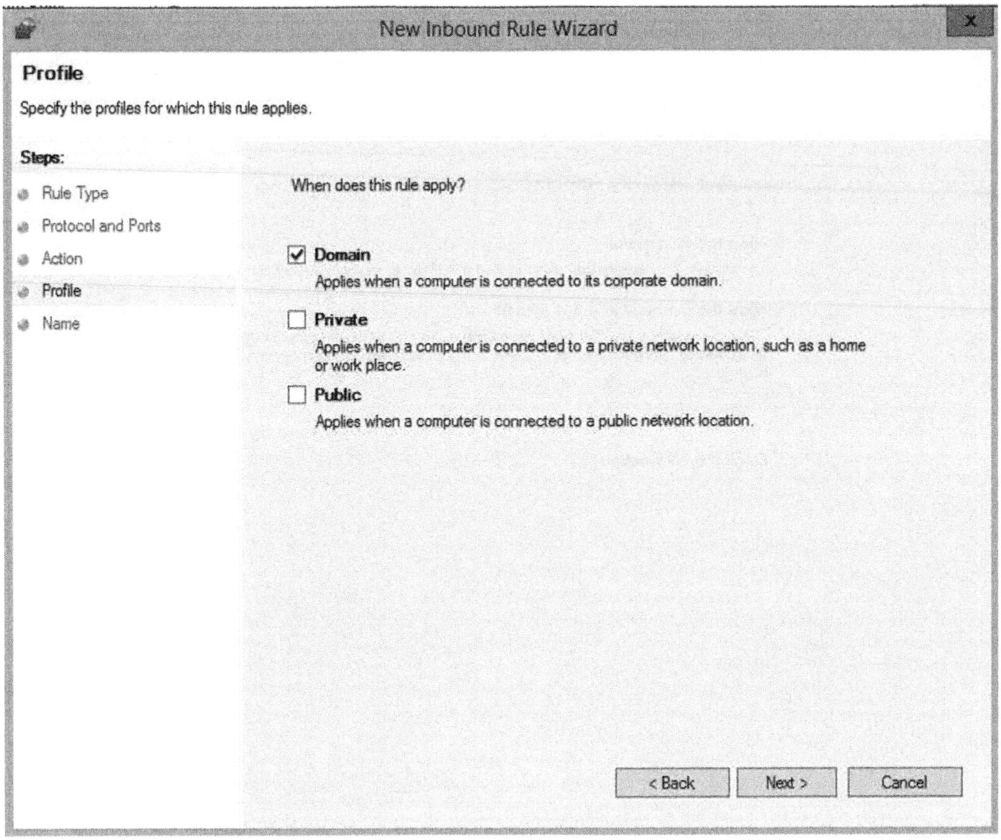

Figure 4-13. *The Profile page*

On the final page of the wizard, we will specify the name of our rule. This name should be descriptive and you should also add a description, specifying the ports that you are opening. This is illustrated in Figure 4-14.

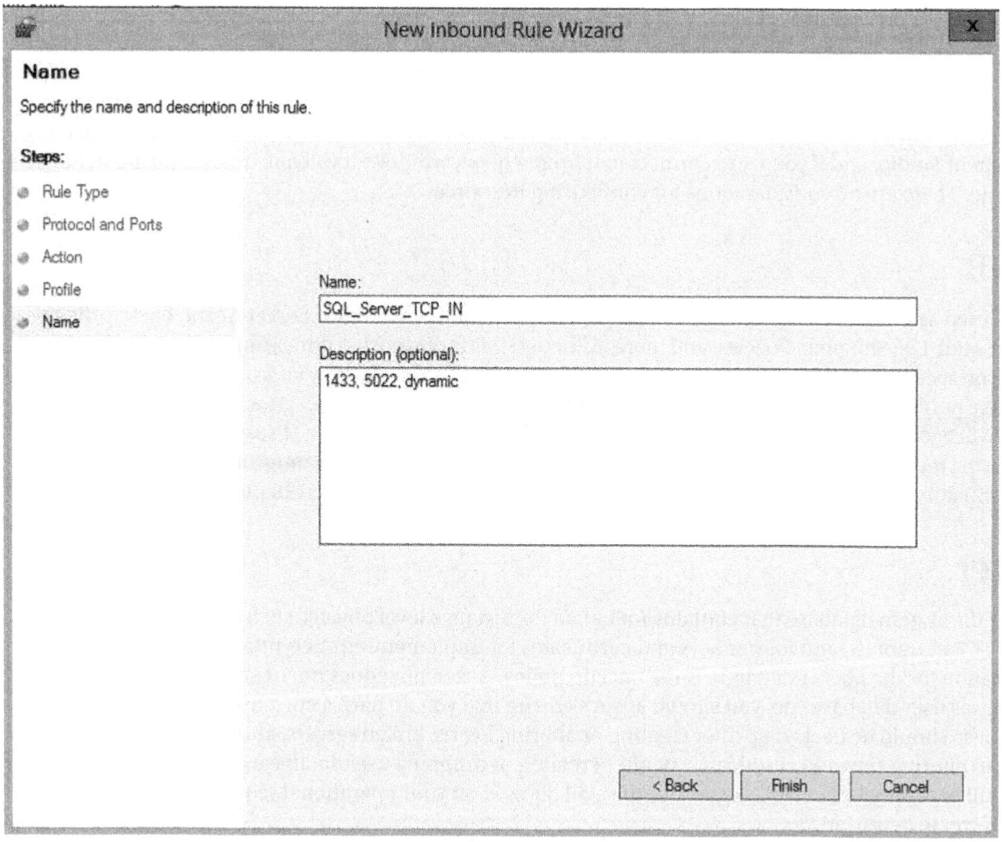

Figure 4-14. *The Name page*

After creating the inbound rule, you would need to repeat the process for an outbound rule. Following our example, we would need to specify ports TCP 1433 and TCP 5022. There would be no need to specify dynamic ports. If we decided to use the browser service, we would need to create additional rules for the UDP 1434 Port.

The inbound rule just demonstrated could also be created by using the PowerShell script in Listing 4-10.

Listing 4-10. Creating an Inbound Firewall Rule

```
New-NetFirewallRule -DisplayName "SQL_Server_TCP_IN " -Description "1433, 5022, Dynamic"
-Direction Inbound -Profile Domain -Action Allow -Protocol TCP -RemotePort 1433,5022,
49152-65535
```

System Databases

SQL Server maintains five system databases, each of which is important to the efficient running of your instance. The following sections describe each of these databases and details any special considerations for configuring them.

mssqlsystemresource (Resource)

Although referred to as Resource, the full name of the Resource database is `mssqlsystemresource`. It is the physical repository used to store the system objects that appear within the `sys` schema of every database. It is read-only and should never be modified, except under guidance from Microsoft. It is not visible within Management Studio, and if you try to connect to it from a query window, it will fail, unless you are in Single User Mode. There are no considerations for configuring Resource.

MSDB

MSDB is used as a metadata repository for many SQL Server features, including Server Agent, Backup/Restore, Database Mail, Log Shipping, Policies, and more. Although this is obviously a critical and useful database, there are no specific configuration options to consider. That being said, in a very large instance consisting of a very large number of databases, all with frequent log backups, the database can grow very large. This means that you will need to purge old data and sometimes consider indexing strategies. Historic backup data can be purged using the `sp_deletebackuphistory` stored procedure or the History Cleanup Task in a Maintenance Plan. Automating routine maintenance tasks will be discussed in more detail, in Chapter 21.

Master

Master is the system database that contains metadata for instance level objects, such as Logins, Linked Servers, TCP endpoints, and master keys and certificates for implementing encryption. The biggest consideration for the Master database is the backup policy. Although it does not need to be backed up as frequently as user databases do, you should always ensure that you do have a current backup. At a minimum, the database should be backed up after creating or altering logins, linked servers, and system configurations; creating or altering keys and certificates; or after creating or dropping user databases. Many people select a weekly, full backup schedule for Master, but this will depend on your operational requirements, such as how often you create new users.

■ **Note**   Logins and users will be discussed in Chapter 9, backups will be discussed in Chapter 15, and keys and certificates will be discussed in Chapter 10.

Although technically possible, it is considered bad practice to store user objects in the Master database. I have seen clients implement this for stored procedures that need to be shared by all databases on the instance, but it adds complexity, because they are fragmenting the storage of user objects and also increasing the frequency with which they must backup Master.

Model

Model is used as a template for all new databases that are created on the instance. This means that spending some time configuring this database can save you time and reduce human error when you are creating user databases. For example, if you set the Recovery Model to be *Full* on the Model database, then all new user databases will automatically be configured in the same way. You still have the option to override this in your `CREATE DATABASE` statement. Additionally, if you need a specific object to exist in all databases, such as a maintenance-stored procedure or a database role, then creating this in Model will mean that the object will automatically be created inside every new database. Model is also used for creating TempDB every time the instance starts. This means that if you create objects in the Model database, they will automatically be added to TempDB when the instance restarts.

■ **Tip** When you are configuring or adding new objects to Model, existing databases will not be updated. Changes will only apply to new databases that you create subsequently.

TempDB

TempDB is a workspace used by SQL Server when it needs to create temporary objects. This applies to temporary tables created by users, and less commonly known, it also applies to table variables. Table variables always cause an object to be created in TempDB, but data is only spooled to disk if it breaches size thresholds. There are also many internal reasons why SQL Server will require temporary objects to be created. Some of the key reasons are as follows:

- Sorting and spooling data

- Hashing data, such as for joins and aggregate grouping

- Online index operations

- Index operations where results are sorted in TempDB

- Triggers

- DBCC commands

- The OUTPUT clause of a DML statement

- Row versioning for snapshot isolation, read-committed snapshot isolation, queries over MARS, and so on

Because TempDB is responsible for so many tasks, in high-volume instances, it is likely to have a very high throughput. For this reason, it is the system database that you should spend the most time configuring in order to ensure the best performance for your data-tier applications.

The first thing you should consider is the size of TempDB. Ideally, TempDB will be subject to capacity planning for large or highly transactional instances. A full discussion of capacity planning is beyond the scope of this book, but ideally, this will involve using a test server to expand all of the user databases on the instance out, to the size that they are expected to grow to, discovered through their own capacity planning exercises. You would then run representative workloads through those databases and monitor the usage of TempDB. Additionally, you should also perform administrative tasks against the databases that you have expanded to their expected size. Specifically, this would include activities such as rebuilding indexes so that you can examine the usage profile of TempDB during these activities. There are a number of DMVs (dynamic management views) that can help you with this planning. Some of the most useful are described in Table 4-6.

Table 4-6. DMVs for TempDB Capacity Planning

DMV	Description
sys.dm_db_session_space:usage	Displays the number of pages allocated for each current session. This will include page counts for the following objects: • User and system tables • User and system indexes • Temporary tables • Temporary indexes • Table variables • Tables returned by functions • Internal objects for sorting and hashing operations • Internal objects for spools and large object operations
sys.dm_db_task_space:usage	Displays the number of pages allocated by tasks. This will include page counts from the same object types as sys.dm_db_session_space:usage.
sys_dm_db_file_space:usage	Displays full usage information for all files in the database, including page counts and extent counts. To return data for TempDB, you must query this DMV from the context of the TempDB database, since it can also return data from user databases.
sys.dm_tran_version_store	Returns a row for every record within the version store. You can view this data raw or aggregate it to get size totals.
sys.dm_tran_active_snapshot_database_transactions	Returns a row for every current transaction that may need to access the version store, due to isolation level, triggers, MARS (Multiple Active Results Sets), or online index operations.

In addition to the size of TempDB, you should also carefully consider the number of files that you will require. This is important, because due to the nature of many objects being very rapidly created and dropped, if you have too few files, then you can suffer contention of the GAM and SGAM pages, even with trace flag 1118 turned on. If you have too many files, on the other hand, you may experience increased overhead. This is because SQL Server allocates pages to each file within the filegroup in turn in order to maintain proportional fill. With a large number of files, there will be an extra synchronization effort to determine if the allocation weighting for each file should be altered.

The current, general recommendation is that you should have one TempDB file for every core available to the instance, with a minimum of two files and a maximum of eight files. You should only add more than eight files if you specifically witness GAM/SGAM contention. This will manifest itself as PAGELATCH waits occurring against TempDB. You will find a discussion of how to add files and alter their size in Chapter 5.

▪ **Tip** PAGEIOLATCH waits indicate a different issue than PAGELATCH waits. If you see PAGEIOLATCH waits against TempDB, this indicates that the underlying storage is the bottleneck. Wait types will be discussed in more detail in Chapter 17.

Buffer Pool Extension

As already mentioned, the buffer pool is an area of memory that SQL Server uses to cache pages before they are written to disk and after they have been read from disk. There are two distinct types of pages that exist in the buffer cache: clean pages and dirty pages. A *clean page* is a page to which no modifications have been made. Clean pages usually exist in the cache because they have been accessed by read operations, such as SELECT statements. Once in the cache, they can support all statements. For example, a DML statement can access the clean page, modify it, and then update its dirty page marker.

Dirty pages are pages that have been modified by statements such as INSERT, UPDATE, and DELETE among others. These pages need to have their associated log record written to disk and subsequently, the dirty pages themselves will be flushed to disk, before they are regarded as clean. The process of writing the log record first is known as WAL (write-ahead logging), and it is how SQL Server ensures that no committed data can ever be lost, even in the event of a system failure.

Dirty pages are always kept in the cache until they are flushed to disk. Clean pages, on the other hand, are kept in cache for as long as possible, but are removed when space is required for new pages to be cached. SQL Server evicts pages based on a least-recently-used policy. This means that read-intensive workloads can rapidly start to suffer from memory pressure if the buffer cache is not correctly sized.

The issue here is that RAM is expensive and it may not be possible to keep throwing more and more memory at the problem. In order to address this, Microsoft has introduced a new technology in SQL Server 2014 called buffer pool extensions.

A buffer pool extension is designed to be used with very fast SSDs, which will normally be locally attached to the server, as opposed to being located on a SAN. In short, the storage needs to operate as fast as possible. The extension will then become a secondary cache for clean pages only. When clean pages are evicted from the cache, they will be moved to the buffer pool extension, where they can be retrieved faster than by going back to the main IO subsystem.

This is a very useful feature, but it is not a magic bullet. First, it is important to remember that the buffer pool extension will never be able to provide the same performance improvement as a correctly sized buffer cache will without an extension. Second, the performance gain that you will experience from using a buffer pool extension is workload specific. For example, a read-intensive OLTP workload will probably benefit substantially from buffer pool extensions, whereas a write-intensive workload will see little benefit at all. This is because dirty pages cannot be flushed to the extension. Large data warehouses are also unlikely to benefit dramatically from buffer pool extensions. This is because the tables are likely to be so large that a full table scan, which is common with this workload scenario, is likely to consume the majority of the both the cache and the extension. This means that it will wipe out other data from the extension and will be unlikely to benefit subsequent queries.

It is sensible to use a resilient SSD volume such as a RAID 10 stripe. This is because if the volume were to fail, with no resilience, your server would immediately see a drop in performance. In the event that the SSD drive that your extension is stored on fails, SQL Server will automatically disable the extension. It can be re-enabled manually, or it will automatically attempt to re-enable itself when the instance is restarted.

I also recommend that you size the extension between four and eight times the size of your Max Server Memory setting in order to obtain optimum performance. The maximum possible size of the extension is thirty-two times the size of the Max Server Memory setting.

Buffer pool extension can be enabled using the statement shown in Listing 4-11. This script assumes that the SSD drive that you wish to use is mapped as the S:\ volume. It also assumes that we have 32GB set as the Max Server Memory setting, so we will configure the extension to be 128GB, which is four times the size.

Listing 4-11. Enable Buffer Pool Extension

```
ALTER SERVER CONFIGURATION
SET BUFFER POOL EXTENSION ON
(FILENAME = 'S:\SSDCache.BPE', SIZE = 128 GB )
```

If required, the buffer pool extension can be disabled by using the command in Listing 4-12. Be warned, however, that removing a buffer pool extension is likely to result in a sudden drop in performance.

Listing 4-12. Disable Buffer Pool Extension

```
ALTER SERVER CONFIGURATION
SET BUFFER POOL EXTENSION OFF
```

Uninstall an Instance

SQL Server Installation Center has no option for uninstalling an instance. This means that if you wish to remove either an instance or shared features from your server, you will need to use either Control Panel or the command line. The following sections will demonstrate how to remove SQL Server using both of these methods.

Uninstall from Control Panel

To uninstall SQL Server from the GUI, you should open the Programs And Features console in Control Panel. The program that we will initially be removing is Microsoft SQL Server 2014 (64-bit). When you select this application, you are prompted to Add, Repair, or Remove the program, as show in Figure 4-15. You should select the option to Remove.

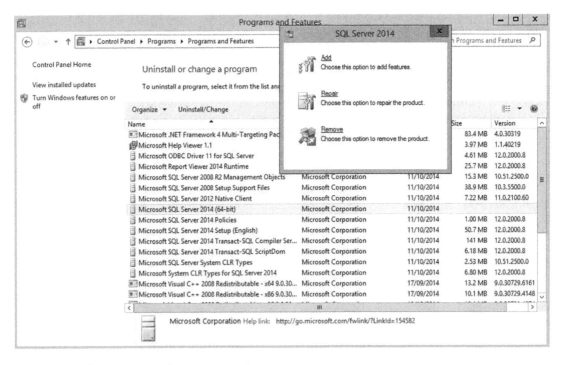

Figure 4-15. *The Programs And Features console*

After choosing to remove the program, SQL Server will run the Global Rules check to ensure that it will be able to complete the action. You should review the rules check and ensure that there are no issues. The Global Rules screen is illustrated in Figure 4-16.

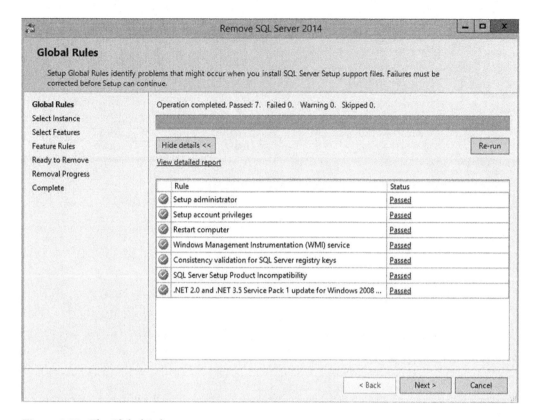

Figure 4-16. *The Global Rules page*

After the rules have been checked, you will need to select which instance you want to remove. In this example, we will be uninstalling an instance called PROSQLADMINREM, so we should ensure that this instance is selected, as shown in Figure 4-17; then we click Next to move on.

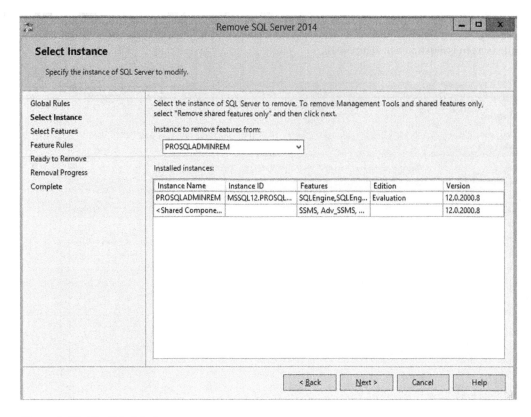

Figure 4-17. *The Select Instance page*

Our next task is to select specifically which features we want to remove from the instance. We can also select individual shared features to remove on this screen, as illustrated in Figure 4-18. In this example, however, we plan to remove all aspects of SQL Server, so we have selected all shared features as well as all features of the instance.

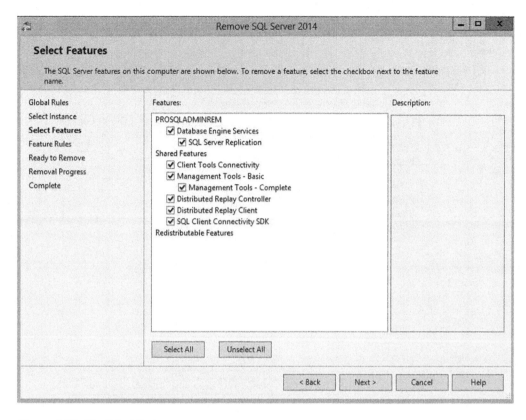

Figure 4-18. *The Select Features page*

Setup will now run an additional rules check for the specific features that you will be uninstalling. You should ensure that there are no issues identified before you continue. The Feature Rules screen is illustrated in Figure 4-19.

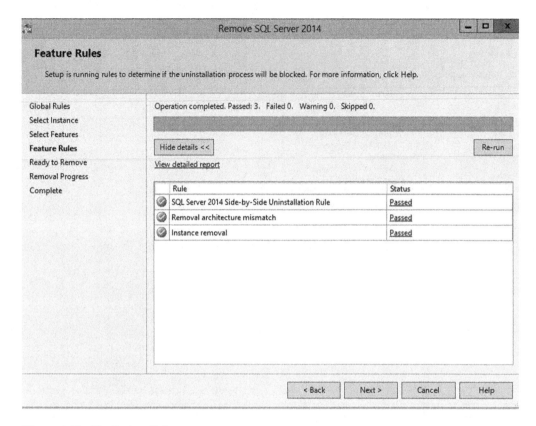

Figure 4-19. *The Feature Rules page*

Finally, setup will provide you with a summary of the features that will be removed. Just like it does when you are installing an instance, setup will also provide a link to a configuration file that it will use during the uninstall process. This screen is illustrated in Figure 4-20.

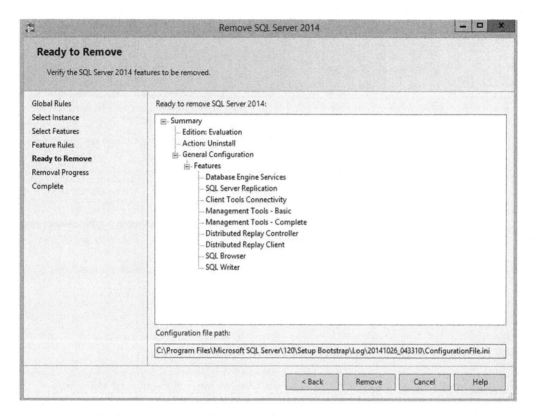

Figure 4-20. *The Read To Remove page*

After completing the removal process of SQL Server, you may diskover that when you refresh the Programs And Features console in Control Panel, there are still elements of SQL Server that have not been uninstalled. Figure 4-21 shows that, in our example, Microsoft ODBC Driver 11 for SQL Server, Microsoft SQL Server 2008R2 Management Objects, SQL Server 2012 Native Client, and Microsoft SQL Server CLR Types still exist on the Server. These need to be removed manually.

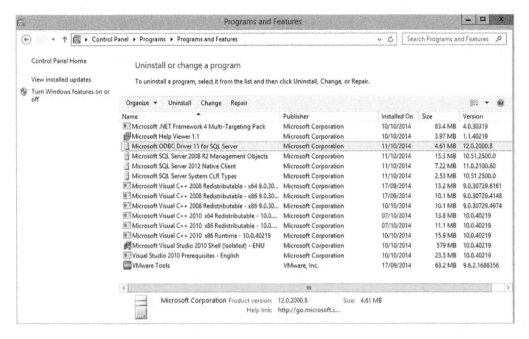

Figure 4-21. *Remaining features*

If you navigate to the root directory of the instance, you will also notice that some of the instance's folder structure also still exists. This is because setup does not remove the error logs, health traces, and so on. If you do not need these logs, you should manually delete the instance directory structure. You may also find that the instance is still referenced within the Registry. Many generic SQL Server references will remain, but your instance will still be referenced by name in the following areas of the Registry.

- AutoRecoverMOFs

- Installer Folders

- ProfileImagePath

- EventLog | Application

Uninstall from PowerShell

Removing a SQL Server instance on Windows Server Core is a relatively straightforward process. You can run setup.exe from the root of the installation media, specifying an action of Uninstall. To perform an uninstall from an instance on Windows Server Core, which has the Database Engine, Replication, and connectivity components installed, you would run the PowerShell command in Listing 4-13. The command could also be used to script the uninstall process on GUI-based servers.

Listing 4-13. Uninstalling an Instance

```
./SETUP.EXE /ACTION="Uninstall" /FEATURES=SQLEngine,Replication,Conn /INSTANCENAME=
"PROSQLADMINREM" /qs
```

Summary

You should consider how you should configure your processor and memory for the instance. With regard to the processor, these considerations should include affinity mask settings for multiple instances, or avoiding context switching during IO operations. You should also consider the appropriate settings for MAXDOP in your environment.

With regard to memory, you should consider the most appropriate usage of Min and Max Server Memory and if it is appropriate to configure these to the same value. You should also consider if buffer pool extensions would help your system performance and if so, you should use Max Server Memory as the base for calculating the correct size of this warm cache.

Trace flags toggle settings on and off, and adding them as startup parameters will ensure that your instance is always configured as you require it to be. Many trace flags are for very specific purposes, but some have more generic usage, such as 1118, which will force uniform extents, which can help optimize TempDB.

For your SQL Server instance to be able to communicate with applications and other instances on the network, you should configure the instance port and local firewall appropriately. It is generally considered bad practice to use a dynamic port for SQL Server connections, so you should configure the instance to use a specific TCP port.

All five of the system databases are critical to the proper functioning of the instance. In terms of configuration, however, you should give most consideration to TempDB. TempDB is heavily used by many SQL Server features, and therefore it can quickly become a bottleneck in busy systems. You should ensure that you have the correct number of files and that they are sized correctly.

Uninstalling an instance or removing features from an instance can be done either from Control Panel, or from the command line. You should be mindful of the fact that even after an instance is uninstalled, there will still be a residue left in the file system and also in the Registry.

## PART II

Database Administration

CHAPTER 5

■ ■ ■

Files and Filegroups

Within a database, data is stored in one or more data files. These files are grouped into logical containers called filegroups. Every database also has at least one log file. Log files sit outside of filegroup containers and do not follow the same rules as data files. This chapter begins by discussing filegroup strategies that database administrators (DBAs) can adopt before it looks at how DBAs can maintain data and log files.

Data Storage

Before considering which filegroup strategies to adopt, it is important that you understand how SQL Server stores data. The diagram in Figure 5-1 illustrates the storage hierarchy within a database.

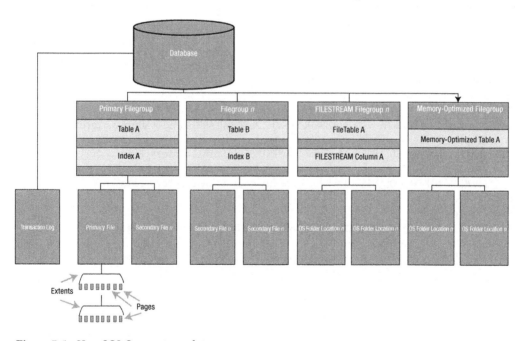

Figure 5-1. *How SQL Server stores data*

A database always consists of at least one filegroup, which contains a minimum of one file. The first file in the database is known as the *primary file*. This file is given an .mdf file extension by default. You can, however, change this extension if you wish. This file can be used to store data, but it is also used to store metadata that provides database startup information and pointers to other files within the database. The filegroup that contains the primary file is called the *primary filegroup*.

If additional files are created within the database, they are known as *secondary files* and are given the .ndf extension by default. You can, however, change this extension if you wish. These files can be created in the primary filegroup and/or in secondary filegroups. Secondary files and filegroups are optional, but they can prove very useful to database administrators, as we will discuss later in this chapter.

Filegroups

Tables and indexes are stored on a filegroup, as opposed to a specific file within the container. This means that for filegroups containing more than one file, you have no control over which file is used to store the object. In fact, because SQL Server allocates data to files using a round-robin approach, each object stored in the filegroup has a very high chance of being split over every file within the filegroup.

To witness this behavior, run the script in Listing 5-1. This script creates a database that has a single filegroup that contains three files. A table is then created on the filegroup and populated. Finally, %%physloc%% is used to determine where each of the rows within the table is stored. The script then counts the number of rows in each file. You should modify this script to use your own file locations.

Listing 5-1. SQL Server Round-Robin Allocation

```
USE Master
GO

--Create a database with three files in the primary filegroup.

CREATE DATABASE [Chapter5]
 CONTAINMENT = NONE
 ON  PRIMARY
( NAME = N'Chapter5', FILENAME = N'F:\MSSQL\MSSQL12.PROSQLADMIN\MSSQL\DATA\Chapter5.mdf'),
( NAME = N'Chapter5_File2',
        FILENAME = N'F:\MSSQL\MSSQL12.PROSQLADMIN\MSSQL\DATA\Chapter5_File2.ndf'),
( NAME = N'Chapter5_File3',
        FILENAME = N'F:\MSSQL\MSSQL12.PROSQLADMIN\MSSQL\DATA\Chapter5_File3.ndf')
 LOG ON
( NAME = N'Chapter5_log',
        FILENAME = N'E:\MSSQL\MSSQL12.PROSQLADMIN\MSSQL\DATA\Chapter5_log.ldf');
GO
IF NOT EXISTS (SELECT name FROM sys.filegroups WHERE is_default=1 AND name = N'PRIMARY')
        ALTER DATABASE [Chapter5] MODIFY FILEGROUP [PRIMARY] DEFAULT;
GO

USE Chapter5
GO

--Create a table in the new database. The table contains a wide, fixed-length column
--to increase the number of allocations.
```

```
CREATE TABLE dbo.RoundRobinTable
(
        ID              INT             IDENTITY        PRIMARY KEY,
        DummyTxt        NCHAR(1000),
);
GO

--Create a Numbers table that will be used to assist the population of the table.

DECLARE @Numbers TABLE
(
        Number          INT
)

--Populate the Numbers table.

;WITH CTE(Number)
AS
(
        SELECT 1 Number

        UNION ALL
        SELECT Number +1
        FROM CTE
        WHERE Number <= 99
)
INSERT INTO @Numbers
SELECT *
FROM CTE;

--Populate the example table with 100 rows of dummy text.

INSERT INTO dbo.RoundRobinTable
SELECT 'DummyText'
FROM @Numbers a
CROSS JOIN @Numbers b;

--Select all the data from the table, plus the details of the row's physical location.
--Then group the row count.
--by file ID

SELECT b.file_id, COUNT(*)
FROM
(
        SELECT ID, DummyTxt, a.file_id
        FROM dbo.RoundRobinTable
        CROSS APPLY sys.fn_PhysLocCracker(%%physloc%%) a
) b
GROUP BY b.file_id;
```

The results displayed in Figure 5-2 show that the rows have been distributed evenly over the three files within the filegroup. If the files are different sizes, then the file with the most space receives more of the rows due to the proportional fill algorithm, which attempts to weigh the allocations to each file in order to evenly distribute data across each of the files.

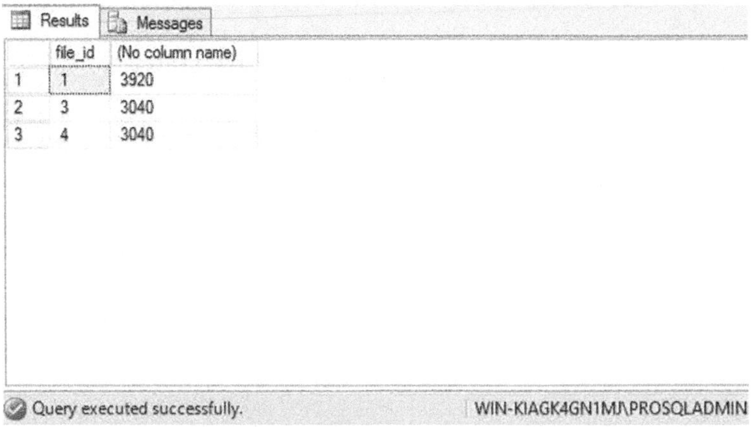

	file_id	(No column name)
1	1	3920
2	3	3040
3	4	3040

Query executed successfully.   WIN-KIAGK4GN1MJ\PROSQLADMIN

Figure 5-2. Evenly distributed rows

■ **Tip**   You may notice that there are no rows returned for File 2. This is because file_id 2 is always the transaction log file (or first transaction log file if you have more than one). file_id 1 is always the primary database file.

■ **Caution**   The physloc functions are undocumented. Therefore, Microsoft will not provide support for their use.

Standard data and indexes are stored in a series of 8KB pages; these are made up of a 96-byte header that contains metadata about the page and 8096 bytes for storing the data itself. These 8KB pages are then organized into units of eight continuous pages, which together are called an extent. An *extent* is the smallest unit the SQL Server can read from disk. The structure of pages is discussed in more detail in Chapter 6.

FILESTREAM Filegroups

FILESTREAM is a technology that allows you to store binary data in an unstructured manner. Binary data is often stored in the operating system, as opposed to the database, and FILESTREAM gives you the ability to continue this, while at the same time offering transactional consistency between this unstructured data and the structured metadata stored in the database. Using this technology will allow you to overcome SQL Server's 2GB maximum size limitation for a single object. You will also see a performance improvement for large binary objects over storing them in the database. If files are over 1MB in size, the read performance is likely to be faster with FILESTREAM.

You do need to bear in mind, however, that objects stored with FILESTREAM use Windows cache instead of the SQL Server buffer cache. This has the advantage that you do not have large files filling up your buffer cache causing other data to be flushed to either the buffer cache extension or to disk. On the flip side, it means that when you are configuring the Max Server Memory setting for the instance, you should remember that Windows requires extra memory if you plan to cache the objects, because the binary cache in Windows is used, as opposed to SQL Server's buffer cache.

Separate filegroups are required for FILESTREAM data. Instead of containing files, these filegroups point to folder locations in the operating system. Each of these locations is called a *container*. FILESTREAM must be enabled on the instance in order to create a FILESTREAM filegroup. You can do this during the setup of the instance, as discussed in Chapter 2, or you can configure it in the properties of the instance in SQL Server Management Studio.

We can add a FILESTREAM filegroup to our Chapter 5 database by using the Add Filegroup button on the Filegroups tab of the Database Properties dialog box and then adding a name for the filegroup in the Name field, as shown in Figure 5-3.

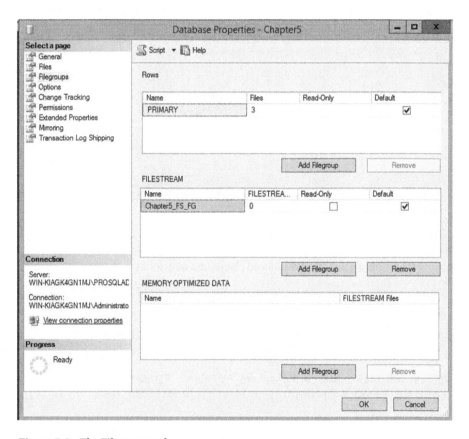

Figure 5-3. *The Filegroups tab*

We can then use the Files tab of the Database Properties dialog box to add the container. Here, we need to enter a name for the container and specify the file type as FILESTEAM data. We are then able to select our FILESTREAM filegroup from the Filegroup drop-down box, as illustrated in Figure 5-4.

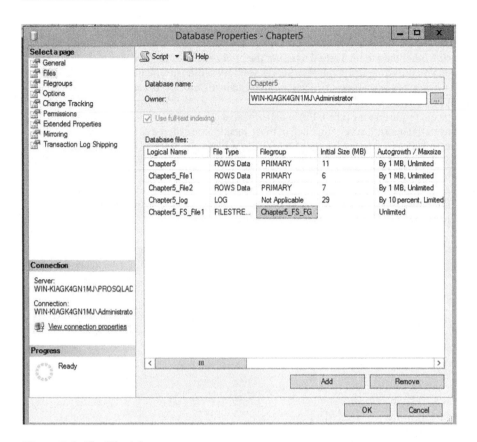

Figure 5-4. *The Files tab*

We can achieve the same results by running the T-SQL commands in Listing 5-2. The script creates a FILESTREAM filegroup and then adds a container. You should change the directories in the script to match your own configuration.

Listing 5-2. Adding a FILESTREAM Filegroup

```
ALTER DATABASE [Chapter5] ADD FILEGROUP [Chapter5_FS_FG] CONTAINS FILESTREAM;
GO

ALTER DATABASE [Chapter5] ADD FILE ( NAME = N'Chapter5_FA_File1', FILENAME =
N'F:\MSSQL\MSSQL12.PROSQLADMIN\MSSQL\DATA\Chapter5_FA_File1' ) TO FILEGROUP [Chapter5_FS_FG];
GO
```

In order to explore the folder structure of a FILESTREAM container, we first need to create a table and populate it with data. The script in Listing 5-3 creates a table, which consists of a unique identifier—which is required for all tables that contain FILESTREAM data—a text description of the binary object, and a VARBINARY(MAX) column that we will use to store the illustration from Figure 5-1, earlier in this chapter. The file that we have used is unimportant, so to run the script yourself, change the name and location of the file being imported to a file on your system.

Listing 5-3. Creating a Table with FILESTREAM Data

```
USE Chapter5
GO

CREATE TABLE dbo.FilestreamExample
(
        ID                      UNIQUEIDENTIFIER ROWGUIDCOL NOT NULL UNIQUE,
        PictureDescription      NVARCHAR(500),
        Picture                     VARBINARY(MAX) FILESTREAM
);
GO

INSERT INTO FilestreamExample
    SELECT NEWID(), 'Figure 5-1. Diagram showing the SQL Server storage hierachy.', * FROM
    OPENROWSET(BULK N'c:\Figure_5-1.jpg', SINGLE_BLOB) AS import;
```

■ **Note**   We have used a UNIQUE constraint, as opposed to a primary key, since a GUID is not usually a good choice as a primary key. If the table must have a primary key, it may be more sensible to add an additional integer column with the IDENTITY property specified. We have used a GUID and set the ROWGUIDCOL property, since this is required by SQL Server to map to the FILESTREAM objects.

If we now open the location of the container in the file system, we can see that we have a folder, which has a GUID as its name. This represents the table that we created. Inside this folder is another folder that also has a GUID as its name. This folder represents the FILESTREAM column that we created. Inside this folder, we will find a file, which is the picture that we inserted into the column. This file's name is the log sequence number from when the file was created. It is theoretically possible to change the extension of this file to its original extension and then open it. This is certainly not recommended, however, because it may have undesirable effects within SQL Server. At the root level of the container you will also find a file called filestream.hdr, which contains the metadata for the container and a folder called $FSLog. This folder contains a series of files that make up the FILESTREAM equivalent of the transaction log. This folder hierarchy is illustrated in Figure 5-5.

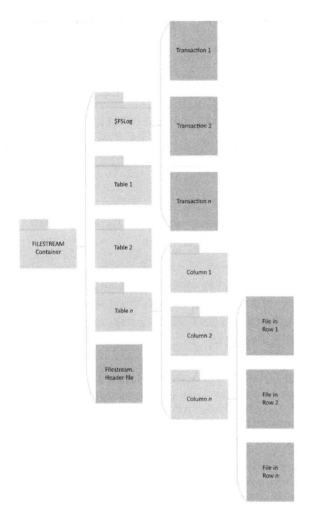

Figure 5-5. *FILESTREAM folder hierarchy*

■ **Tip** The SQL Server Service account is automatically be granted file system permissions on the FILESTREAM container. It is considered bad practice to grant any other users permissions to this folder structure. If you try to access the folder with a Windows Administrator account, you are given a permissions warning, stating that if you continue, you will be permanently granting yourself permissions to the folder.

FileTable is a technology that builds on top of FILESTREAM and allows data to be stored in the file system. Therefore, to use it, you must enable FILESTREAM with streaming access. Unlike FILESTREAM, however, FileTable allows nontransactional access to the data. This means that you can move data so it is stored in the SQL Engine rather than in the operating system without needing to modify existing applications. You can also open and modify the files through Windows Explorer like any other files in the operating system.

To achieve this, SQL Server enables Windows applications to request a file handle without having a transaction. Because of this functionality, you need to specify, at the database level, what level of nontransactional access applications may request. You can configure the following access levels:

- NONE (Default—Only transactional access is permitted.)

- READ_ONLY (The object in the file system can be viewed but not modified.)

- FULL (The object in the file system can be viewed and modified.)

- IN_TRANSITION_TO_READ_ONLY (Transitioning to READ_ONLY)

- IN_TRANSITION_TO_OFF (Transitioning to NONE)

You also need to specify the root directory for the FileTable container. Both of these tasks can be performed with the same ALTER DATABASE statement, as demonstrated in Listing 5-4.

Listing 5-4. Setting the Nontransactional Access Level

```
ALTER DATABASE Chapter5
    SET FILESTREAM ( NON_TRANSACTED_ACCESS = FULL, DIRECTORY_NAME = N'Chapter5_FileTable' );
```

SQL Server now creates a share, which has the same name as your instance. Inside this share, you will find a folder with the name you specified. When you create a FileTable, you can again specify a directory name. This creates a subfolder with the name you specify. Because FileTables do not have a relational schema, and the metadata that is stored about the files is fixed, the syntax for created them includes only the name of the table, the directory, and the collation to use. The code in Listing 5-5 demonstrates how to create a FileTable called Chapter5_FileTable.

Listing 5-5. Creating a FieTable

```
USE Chapter5
GO

CREATE TABLE dbo.ch05_test AS FILETABLE
  WITH
  (
    FILETABLE_DIRECTORY = 'Chapter5_FileTable',
    FILETABLE_COLLATE_FILENAME = database_default
  );
GO
```

To load files into the table, you can simply copy or move them into the folder location, or developers can use the System.IO namespace within their applications. SQL Server will update the metadata columns of the FileTable accordingly. In our example, the file path to the container where the FileTable files can be found is \\127.0.0.1\prosqladmin\Chapter5_FileTable\Chapter5_FileTable. Here, 127.0.0.1 is the loopback address of our server, prosqladmin is the share that was created based on our instance name, and Chapter5_FileTable\Chapter5_Filetable FILESTREAM\FileTable is the container.

Memory-Optimized Filegroups

SQL Server 2014 introduced a new feature called *memory-optimized tables*. These tables are stored entirely in memory; however, the data is also written to files on disk. This is for durability. Transactions against in-memory tables have the same ACID (Atomic, Consistent, Isolated and Durable) properties as traditional disk-based tables. We will discuss in-memory tables further in Chapter 6 and in-memory transactions in Chapter 18.

Because in-memory tables require a copy of the data to be stored on disk, in order to be durable, SQL Server 2014 introduces the memory-optimized filegroup. This type of filegroup is similar to a FILESTREAM filegroup but with some subtle differences. First, you can only create one memory-optimized filegroup per database. Second, you do not need to explicitly enable FILESTREAM unless you are planning to use both features.

In-memory data is persisted on disk through the use of two file types. One is a Data file and the other a Delta file. These two file types always operate in pairs and cover a specific range of transactions, so you should always have the same amount. The Data file is used to track inserts that are made to in-memory tables and the Delta file is used to track deletions. Update statements are tracked via a combination of the two files. The files are written sequentially and are table agnostic, meaning that each file may contain data for multiple tables.

We can add an in-memory optimized filegroup to our database in the Filegroups tab of the Database Properties dialog box by using the Add Filegroup button in the Memory Optimized Data area of the screen and by specifying a name for the filegroup. This is illustrated in Figure 5-6.

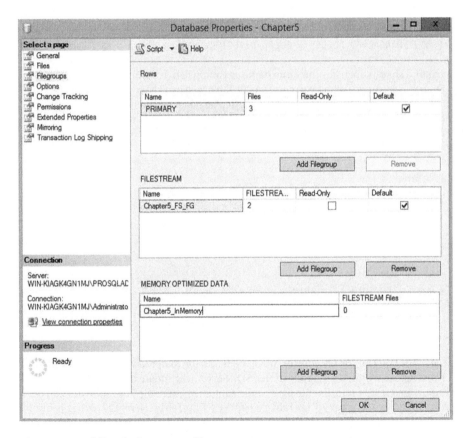

Figure 5-6. *Adding the in-memory filegroup*

We can then add the container to the filegroup by using the Add File button in the Files tab of the Database Properties Dialog box. Here we need to specify the logical name of our file and select the FILESTREAM file type. We will then be able to choose to add the file to our in-memory filegroup by using the drop-down box, as shown in Figure 5-7.

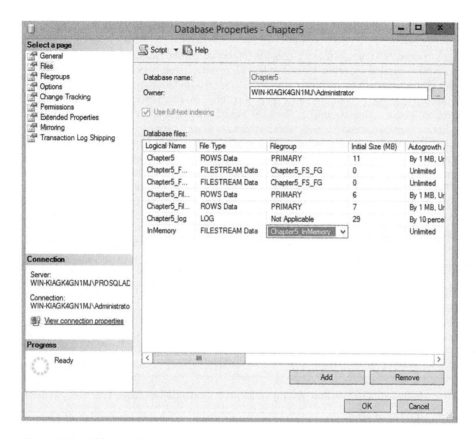

Figure 5-7. *Adding an in-memory container*

Alternatively, we can achieve the same results by using the T-SQL script in Listing 5-6. Make sure to change the file location to match your directory structure.

Listing 5-6. Adding an In-memory Filegroup and Container

```
ALTER DATABASE [Chapter5] ADD FILEGROUP [Chapter5_InMemory] CONTAINS MEMORY_OPTIMIZED_DATA;
GO

ALTER DATABASE [Chapter5] ADD FILE ( NAME = N'InMemory', FILENAME =
N'F:\MSSQL\MSSQL12.PROSQLADMIN\MSSQL\DATA\InMemory' ) TO FILEGROUP [Chapter5_InMemory];
GO
```

Strategies for Structured Filegroups

A DBA can adopt different filegroup strategies to assist with requirements such as performance, backup time, recovery time objectives, and tiered storage offerings. The following sections explore those strategies.

Performance Strategies

When designing a filegroup strategy for performance, consider object placement in relation to joins performed by the application's queries. Imagine, for example, a large data warehouse. You have a wide fact table, with hundreds of thousands of rows, which joins to two dimension tables, each with millions of rows. If you placed all three of these objects on the same filegroup, then you can distribute the IO by using multiple files, placing each file on a different spindle. The issue here, however, is that even though the IO can be distributed, you do not have granular control over which tables are placed on which LUNs (Logical Unit Numbers). As demonstrated earlier in this chapter, all objects will be stripped evenly, using a combination of round-robin and proportional fill algorithms, across each of the files. Therefore, it is possible to gain a performance advantage by splitting these tables onto three separate filegroups, each of which would be created on separate LUNs. This may allow SQL Server to improve the parallelization of the table scans.

Alternatively, another scenario may be that you have a massive data warehouse, in the tens of terabytes (TBs), and a very large server, with a balanced throughput, such as a server built using the Fast Track Data Warehouse Reference Architecture (details of which can be found on the MSDB library); in this case, you may get the best performance by creating filegroups over every single disk available. This gives the server the best performance in terms of IO throughput and helps prevent the IO subsystem from becoming the bottleneck.

Also consider the placement of tables that are subject to horizontal partitioning. Imagine a very large table where data is partitioned by month. If your application's workload means that several months of data are often being read at the same time, then you may see a performance improvement if you split each month out into separate filegroups, each of which uses a discrete set of spindles, in a similar way to the join example, mentioned earlier. There will be a full discussion on partitioning in Chapter 6.

■ **Caution**   The downside to this approach is that placing partitions on separate filegroups prevents you from using partitioning functions, such as SWITCH.

Backup and Restore Strategies

SQL Server allows you to back up at the file and filegroup level as well as at the database level. You are subsequently able to perform what is known as a *piecemeal restore*. A piecemeal restore allows you to bring your database online in stages. This can be very useful for large databases that have a very low recovery time objective.

Imagine that you have a large database that contains a small amount of very critical data that the business cannot be without for more than a maximum of two hours. The database also contains a large amount of historic data that the business requires access to on a daily basis for the purpose of reporting, but it is not critical that it is restored within the two-hour window. In this scenario, it is good practice to have two secondary filegroups. The first contains the critical data and the second contains the historic data. In the event of a disaster, you can then restore the primary filegroup and the first secondary filegroup. At this point, you can bring the database online and the business will have access to this data. Subsequently, the filegroup containing the historic reporting data could be brought online.

Filegroups can also assist with backup strategies. Imagine a scenario where you have a large database that takes two hours to back up. Unfortunately, you have a long-running ETL process and only a one-hour window in which the database can be backed up nightly. If this is the case, then you can split the data between two filegroups. The first filegroup can be backed up on Monday, Wednesday, and Friday, and the second filegroup can be backed up on Tuesday, Thursday, and Saturday. Backups and restores are discussed fully in Chapter 15.

Storage-Tiering Strategies

Some organizations may decide that they want to implement storage tiering for large databases. If this is the case, then you will often need to implement this by using partitioning. For example, imagine that a table contains six years' worth of data. The data for the current year is accessed and updated many times a day. Data for the previous three years is accessed in monthly reports, but other than that is rarely touched. Data as far back as six years must be available instantly, if it is needed for regulatory reasons, but in practice, it is rarely accessed.

In the scenario just described, partitioning could be used with yearly partitions. The filegroup containing the current year's data could consist of files on locally attached RAID 10 LUNs for optimum performance. The partitions holding data for years 2 and 3 could be placed on the premium tier of the corporate SAN device. Partitions for data older than three years could be placed on near-line storage within the SAN, thus satisfying regulatory requirements in the most cost-effective manner.

Some organizations have also introduced automated storage tiering, such as AO (Adaptive Optimization). Although automated storage tiering technology works extremely well in some environments, its implementation for SQL Server can sometimes prove problematic. This is because it works in two phases. The first is an analysis phase, which decides which tier each block or file should reside on for the best tradeoff between cost and expense. The second phase will actually move the data to the most appropriate tier.

The issue is that the window where data is being moved tends to reduce the performance of the SAN. Therefore, running analysis followed by moving the data frequently (i.e., hourly) can cause unacceptable performance degradation. On the flip side, however, running analysis less frequently (such as during business hours) and moving data overnight sometimes does not tally with SQL Server usage profiles. For example, imagine a reporting application that needs optimum performance, but where the weekly reports are generated on a Friday. Because the last analysis window before this peak period was Thursday, when not a lot was happening, the data is likely to reside on a slower, more cost-effective tier, meaning that performance will be impaired. When Saturday arrives, however, and the application is virtually idle again, the data will reside on the premium tier, because of the analysis window, during Friday's peak usage. For this reason, automated storage tiering often works best in environments where databases have set hours of operation, with little day-to-day variance in usage profiles.

Strategies for Memory-Optimized Filegroups

Just like structured filegroups, memory-optimized filegroups will use a round-robin approach to allocating data between containers. It is common practice to place these multiple containers on separate spindles in order to maximize IO throughput. The issue is, however, that if you place one container on spindle A and one container on spindle B, then the round-robin approach will place all of the Data files on one volume and all of the Delta files on the other volume.

To avoid this issue, it is good practice to place two containers on each of the volumes that you wish to use for your memory-optimized filegroup. This will ensure that you get a balanced distribution of IO, as illustrated in Figure 5-8. This is in line with Microsoft's recommended best practice.

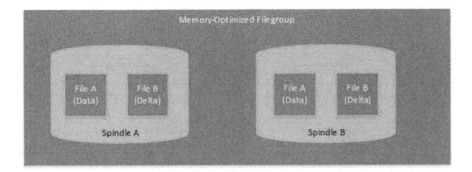

Figure 5-8. Balanced IO distribution for memory-optimized filegroups

File and Filegroup Maintenance

During the lifecycle of a data tier application, at times you may need to perform maintenance activities on your database files and filegroups for reasons such as performance or capacity management. The following sections will describe how to add, expand, and shrink files.

Adding Files

You may need to add files to a filegroup for both capacity and performance reasons. If your database grows past your capacity estimates and the volume that hosts your data files cannot be resized, then you can add additional files to the filegroup, which is hosted on different LUNs.

You may also need to add additional files to the filegroup in order to increase the IO throughput if the storage subsystem becomes a bottleneck for your application. As illustrated in Figure 5-9, we could add an additional file to our Chapter5 database by using the Files tab of the Database Properties dialog box. Here, we will use the Add button and then specify the logical name of the file, the filegroup that we want the file to reside in, the initial size of the file, the autogrowth settings, the maximum size of the file, and the physical path to where the file will be stored.

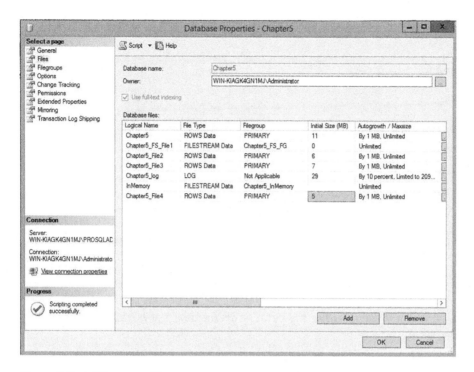

Figure 5-9. *Adding a new file*

Alternatively, we could use the script in Listing 5-7 to achieve the same results. You should change the directory path in the script to match your own directory structure.

Listing 5-7. Adding a New File Using T-SQL

```
ALTER DATABASE [Chapter5] ADD FILE ( NAME = N'Chapter5_File4', FILENAME =
N'G:\DATA\Chapter5_File4.ndf' , SIZE = 5120KB , FILEGROWTH = 1024KB ) TO FILEGROUP [PRIMARY];
GO
```

In this scenario, however, it is important to remember the proportional fill algorithm. If you add files to a filegroup, then SQL Server will target the empty files first, until they have the same amount of free space remaining as the original files. This means that if you create them with the same size as the original files, you may not receive the benefit that you are expecting. You can witness this behavior by running the script in Listing 5-8. This script uses the same technique we used when we initially created and populated the RoundRobin table to generate an additional 10,000 rows and then identify how many rows are in each file.

Listing 5-8. Adding Additional Rows to the RoundRobin table

```
--Create a Numbers table that will be used to assit the population of the table

DECLARE @Numbers TABLE
(
        Number          INT
)

--Populate the Numbers table
```

```
;WITH CTE(Number)
AS
(
        SELECT 1 Number
        UNION ALL
        SELECT Number +1
        FROM CTE
        WHERE Number <= 99
)
INSERT INTO @Numbers
SELECT *
FROM CTE;

--Populate the example table with 10000 rows of dummy text

INSERT INTO dbo.RoundRobinTable
SELECT 'DummyText'
FROM @Numbers a
CROSS JOIN @Numbers b;

--Select all the data from the table, plus the details of the rows' physical location.
--Then group the row count
--by file ID
SELECT b.file_id, COUNT(*)
FROM
(
        SELECT ID, DummyTxt, a.file_id
        FROM dbo.RoundRobinTable
        CROSS APPLY sys.fn_PhysLocCracker(%%physloc%%) a
) b
GROUP BY b.file_id;
```

You can see from the results in Figure 5-10, that the proportional fill algorithm used the new file exclusively until it was full and then restarted the round-robin allocation between each file.

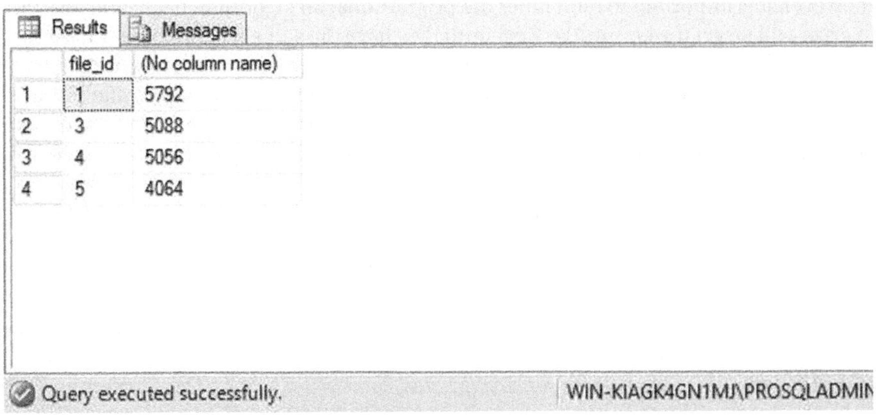

Figure 5-10. *Row allocations to new file*

The workaround here would be to either create smaller files or increase the size of the existing files. Either of these approaches would level out the amount of free space left in each file and make SQL Server distribute the writes evenly.

Expanding Files

In Figure 5-9, the eagle-eyed may have noticed that the initial size of our files were 11MB, 6MB, and 7MB, respectively, as opposed to the 5MB that we configured for them earlier in this chapter. This is because a more accurate name for the Initial Size field would actually be Current Size. Because we have configured autogrowth for the files, as they have become full, SQL Server has automatically grown the files for us.

This is a very useful fail-safe feature, but ideally we should use it as just that—a fail-safe. Growing files uses resources and also causes locks to be taken out, blocking other processes. It is therefore advisable to presize the database files in line with capacity estimates, as opposed to starting with a small file and relying on autogrow.

For the same reason, when specifying a file's autogrowth settings, you should shy away from the default value of 1MB and specify a much larger value. If you don't, if your file becomes full and autogrowth kicks in, your files will grow in very tiny increments, which is likely to impair performance, even if you are using instant file initialization. The value that you should set your files to grow by will depend on your environment. You should take into account, for example, the amount of free space that is available on the volume and the number of other databases that share the volume. You can see how much space is left in a file by using the `sys.dm_db_file_space:usage` dynamic management view (DMV). This DMV will return a column named `unallocated_extent_page_count`, which will tell us how many free pages there are left to be allocated. We can use this to calculate the remaining free space in each file, as demonstrated in Listing 5-9.

Listing 5-9. Calculating Free Space in Each File

```
SELECT
    file_id
    ,unallocated_extent_page_count * 1.0 / 128 'Free Space (MB)'
FROM sys.dm_db_file_space:usage;
```

If we want to expand a file, we do not need to wait for autogrowth to kick in. We can expand the file manually by changing the value of the Initial Size field in the Files tab of the Database Properties dialog box, or by using the `ALTER DATABASE` command. The command in Listing 5-10 will resize the newest file in our `Chapter5` database to be 20MB.

Listing 5-10. Expanding a File

```
ALTER DATABASE [Chapter5] MODIFY FILE ( NAME = N'Chapter5_File4', SIZE = 20480KB );
```

Shrinking Files

Just as you can expand database files, you can also shrink them. There are various methods for achieving this, including shrinking a single file, shrinking all files within a database including the log, or even setting an Auto Shrink option at the database level.

To shrink an individual file, you need to use the `DBCC SHRINKFILE` command. When you use this option, you can specify either the target size of the file or you can specify the `EMPTYFILE` option. The `EMPTYFILE` option will move all data within the file to other files within the same filegroup. This means that you can subsequently remove the file from the database.

If you specify a target size for the database then you can choose to specify either TRUNCATEONLY or NOTRUNCATE. If you select the former, then SQL Server will start at the end of the file and reclaim space until it reaches the last allocated extent. If you choose the latter, then beginning at the end of the file, SQL Server will begin a process of moving allocated extents to the first free space at the start of the file.

To remove the unused space at the end of our expanded Chapter5_File4 file, we could use the Shrink File screen in SQL Server Management Studio, which can be found by right-clicking the database and drilling through Tasks | Shrink | Files. In the Shrink File screen, we can select the appropriate file from the File Name drop-down box and then ensure that the Release Unused Space radio button is selected. This option enforces TRUNCATEONLY. This process is illustrated in Figure 5-11.

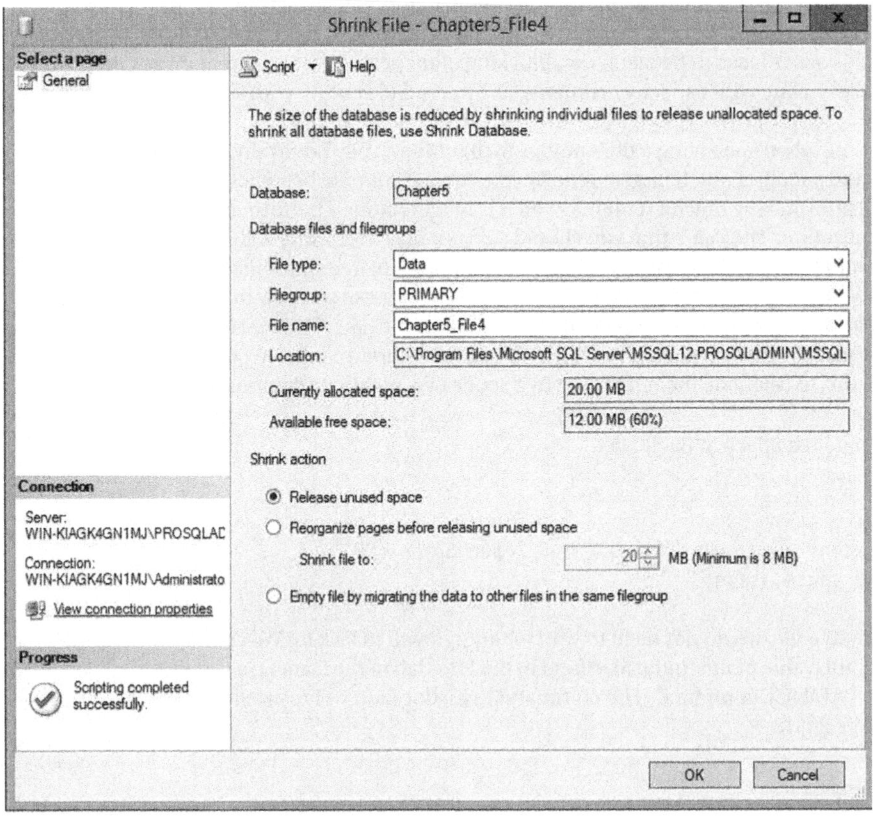

Figure 5-11. *Shrinking a file*

We could also achieve the same result by running the command in Listing 5-11.

Listing 5-11. Shrinking a File with TRUNCATEONLY

```
USE [Chapter5]
GO

DBCC SHRINKFILE (N'Chapter5_File4' , 0, TRUNCATEONLY);
```

If we wanted to reclaim the unused space at the end of all files in the database, we could right-click the database and drill down through Tasks | Shrink | Database. We would then ensure that the Reorganize Files Before Releasing Unused Space option is not selected and click OK, as illustrated in Figure 5-12.

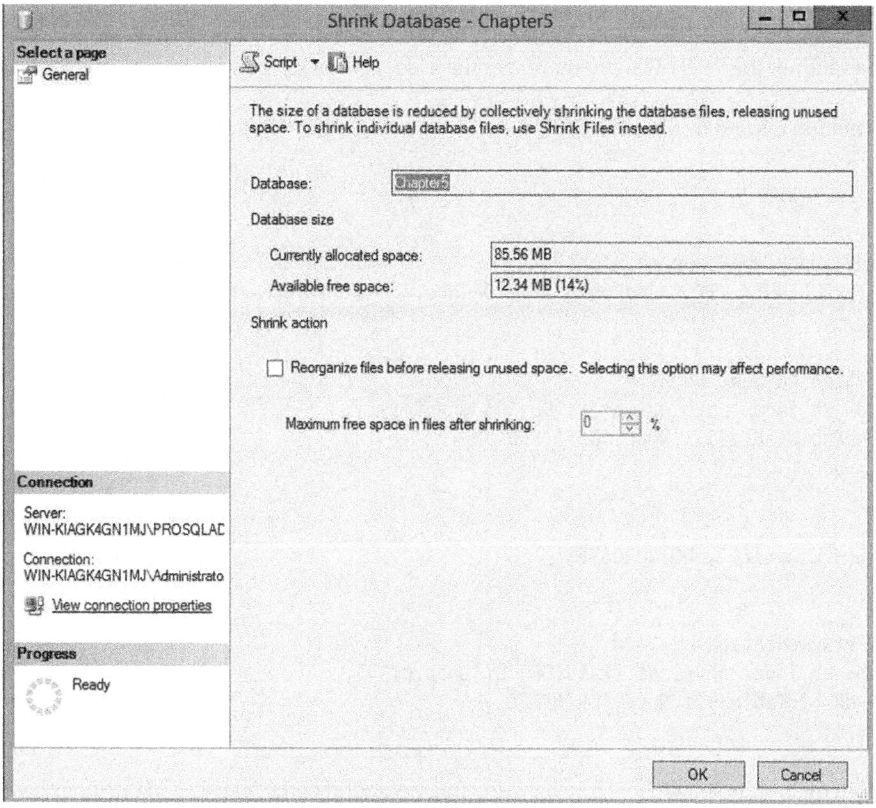

Figure 5-12. *Shrinking a database*

We could achieve the same result via T-SQL by running the command in Listing 5-12.

Listing 5-12. Shrinking a Database via T-SQL

```
USE [Chapter5]
GO

DBCC SHRINKDATABASE(N'Chapter5' );
```

There are very few occasions when it is acceptable to shrink a database, or even an individual file. There is a misconception that large, empty files take longer to backup, but this is a fallacy. In fact, I have had only one occasion in my career when I needed to shrink data files. This instance happened after we removed several hundred gigabytes of archive data from a database and were approaching our 2TB LUN limit, but this was an exceptional circumstance. Generally speaking, you should not look to shrink your database files, and you should certainly never, ever use the Auto Shrink option on a database.

In the event that you do have to shrink a database, be prepared for the process to be slow. It is a single-threaded operation and will consume resources while running. You should also never consider using the NOTRUNCATE option. As described earlier, this will cause extents to be moved around inside the file and will lead to massive fragmentation issues like those you can see using the script in Listing 5-13. This script first creates a clustered index on our RoundRobin table. It then uses the sys.dm_db_index_physical_stats DMV to examine the level of fragmentation at the leaf level of the clustered index. Subsequently, it shrinks the database and then re-examines the level of fragmentation of the leaf level of our clustered index.

Listing 5-13. Fragmentation Caused by Shrinking

```
USE Chapter5
GO

--Create a clustered index on RoundRobinTable
CREATE UNIQUE CLUSTERED INDEX CIX_RoundRobinTable ON dbo.RoundRobinTable(ID);
GO

--Examine Fragmentation on new index
SELECT * FROM sys.dm_db_index_physical_stats(DB_ID('Chapter5'),
OBJECT_ID('dbo.RoundRobinTable'),1,NULL,'DETAILED')
WHERE index_level = 0;

--Shrink the database
DBCC SHRINKDATABASE(N'Chapter5', NOTRUNCATE);
GO

--Re-examine index fragmentation
SELECT * FROM sys.dm_db_index_physical_stats(DB_ID('Chapter5'),
OBJECT_ID('dbo.RoundRobinTable'),1,NULL,'DETAILED')
WHERE index_level = 0;
GO
```

As you can see from the results shown in Figure 5-13, the fragmentation of the leaf level of the index has increased from 0.08 percent to a massive 71.64 percent, which will severely impact queries run against the index. Indexes and fragmentation will be discussed in detail in Chapter 7.

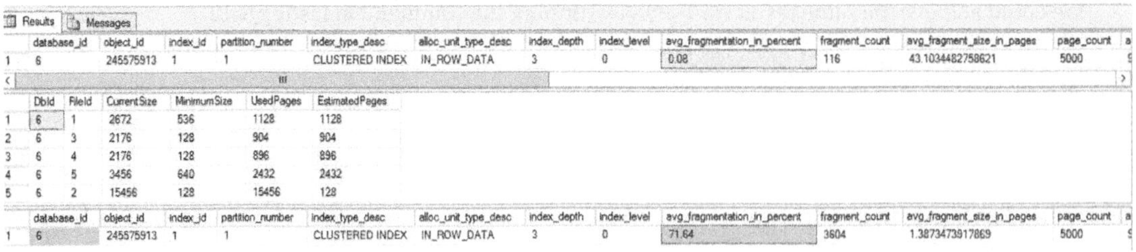

	database_id	object_id	index_id	partition_number	index_type_desc	alloc_unit_type_desc	index_depth	index_level	avg_fragmentation_in_percent	fragment_count	avg_fragment_size_in_pages	page_count	a
1	6	245575913	1	1	CLUSTERED INDEX	IN_ROW_DATA	3	0	0.08	116	43.1034482758621	5000	

	DbId	FieId	Current Size	Minimum Size	Used Pages	Estimated Pages
1	6	1	2672	536	1128	1128
2	6	3	2176	128	904	904
3	6	4	2176	128	896	896
4	6	5	3456	640	2432	2432
5	6	2	15456	128	15456	128

	database_id	object_id	index_id	partition_number	index_type_desc	alloc_unit_type_desc	index_depth	index_level	avg_fragmentation_in_percent	fragment_count	avg_fragment_size_in_pages	page_count	a
1	6	245575913	1	1	CLUSTERED INDEX	IN_ROW_DATA	3	0	71.64	3604	1.3873473917869	5000	

Figure 5-13. *Results of fragmentation*

■ **Note** The fragmentation level may vary depending on layout of extents within your file(s).

Log Maintenance

The transaction log is a vital tool in SQL Server's armory; it provides recovery functionality but also supports many features, such as AlwaysOn Availability Groups, Transactional Replication, Change Data Capture, and many more.

Internally, the log file is split down into a series of VLFs (virtual log files). When the final VLF in the log file becomes full, SQL Server will attempt to wrap around to the first VLF at the beginning of the log. If this VLF has not been truncated and cannot be reused, then SQL Server will attempt to grow the log file. If it is not able to expand the file due to lack of disk space or max size settings, then a 9002 error will be thrown and the transaction will be rolled back. Figure 5-14 illustrates the structure of the log file and its circular usage.

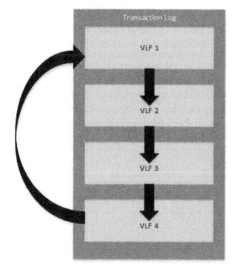

Figure 5-14. *Log file structure*

The amount of VLFs inside a log file is determined by the size of the log when it was initially created and also the size that it is expanded by each time it grows. If the log file is created at or grows in increments of less than 64MB, then 4 VLFs will be added to the file. If it is created at or grows in increments between 64MB and 1GB, then 8 VLFs will be added to the file. If it is created at or grows by more than 1GB, then 16 VLFs will be added.

The transaction log is a fairly low-maintenance component of the SQL Server stack. There will be times, however, when maintenance scenarios occur; these are discussed in the following sections.

Recovery Model

The *recovery model* is a database-level property that controls how transactions are logged and, therefore, it has an impact on transaction log maintenance. The three recovery models within SQL Server are described in Table 5-1.

Table 5-1. *Recovery Models*

Recovery Model	Description
SIMPLE	In the SIMPLE recovery model, it is not possible to back up the transaction log. Transactions are minimally logged and the log will automatically be truncated. It is incompatible with several HADR (High Availability/Disaster Recovery) technologies, such as AlwaysOn Availability Groups, Log Shipping, and Database Mirroring. This model is appropriate for reporting databases where updates only occur on an infrequent basis. This is because point-in-time recovery is not possible. The Recovery Point Objective will be the time of the last FULL or DIFFERENTIAL backup.
FULL	In the FULL recovery model, transaction log backups must be taken. The log will only be truncated during the log backup process. Transactions are fully logged and this means that point-in-time recovery is possible. It also means that you must have a complete chain of log file backups to restore a database to the most recent point.
BULK LOGGED	The BULK_LOGGED recovery model is meant to be used on a temporary basis when you are using the FULL recovery model but need to perform a large BULK INSERT operation. When you switch to this mode, BULK INSERT operations are minimally logged. You then switch back to FULL recovery model when the import is complete. In this recovery model, you can restore to the end of any backup, but not to a specific point in time between backups.

■ **Note**   Recovery models will be discussed further in Chapter 15.

Log File Count

Several times I have witnessed a misconception that having multiple log files can improve the performance of a database. This is a fallacy. The idea is driven by the belief that if you have multiple log files on separate drives, you can distribute IO and relieve the log as a bottleneck.

The truth is that the transaction log is sequential, and even if you add multiple log files, SQL Server treats them as if they are a single file. This means that the second file will only be used after the first file becomes full. As a result, no performance benefit can be gained from this practice. In fact, the only possible reason that you would ever need more than one transaction log file is if you ran out of space on the LUN that was hosting the log, and for some reason it cannot be moved elsewhere and the volume can't be expanded. In my professional career, although I have encountered multiple log files on several occasions, I have never encountered a valid reason for having them.

Shrinking the Log

Shrinking your log file should never be part of your standard maintenance routines. There is no benefit to adopting this policy. There are some occasions, however, when you may have to shrink a log file, and, thankfully, it does not come with the same hazards as shrinking a data file.

The usual reason for needing to shrink your log file is when an atypical activity occurs in your database, such as an initial data population or a one-time ETL load. If this is the case, and your log file expands past the point where space thresholds on your volume are being breached, then reducing the size of the file is likely to be the best course of action, as opposed to expanding the volume that is hosting it. In this eventuality, however, you should carefully analyze the situation to ensure that it really is an atypical event. If it seems like it could occur again, then you should consider increasing capacity to deal with it.

To shrink a log file, you can use the Shrink File dialog box, as illustrated in Figure 5-15. Here, select Log in the File Type drop-down box. This causes the Filegroup drop-down box to be grayed out and, assuming you only have one log file, it will automatically be selected in the File Name drop-down. If you have multiple transaction log files, you will be able to select the appropriate file from the drop-down list. As with shrinking a data file, choosing the Release Unused Space option will cause TRUNCATEONLY to be used.

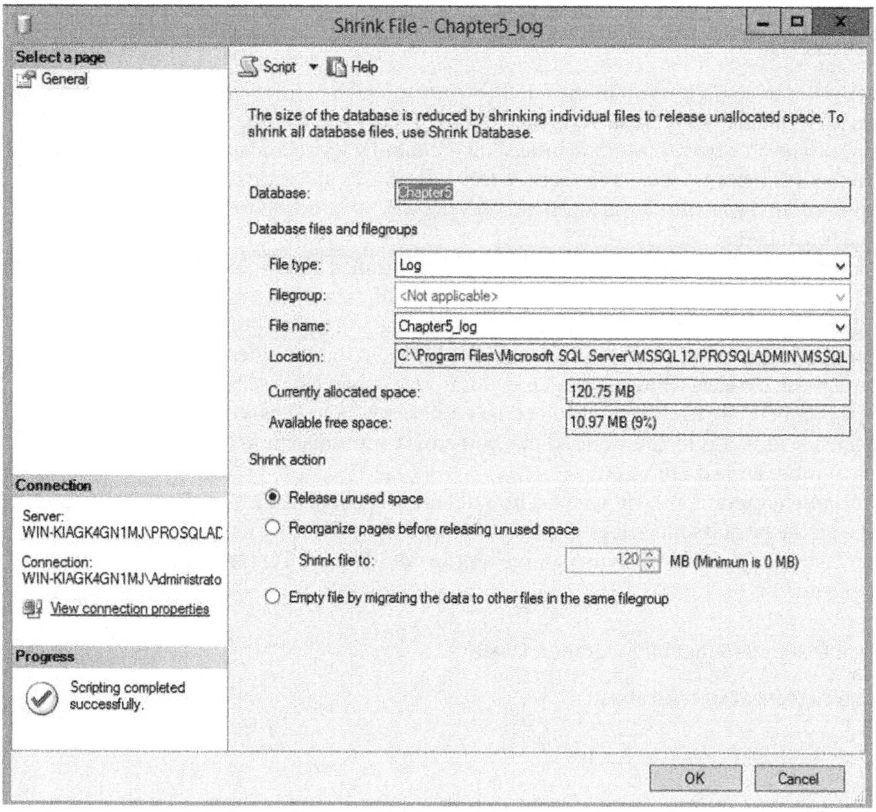

Figure 5-15. *Shrinking a log file*

Alternatively, you can use the script in Listing 5-14 to achieve the same results. It is important to note, however, that shrinking the log file may not actually result in any space being reclaimed. This happens if the last VLF in the file cannot be reused. A full list of reasons why it may not be possible to reuse a VLF is included later in this chapter.

Listing 5-14. Shrinking a Log with TRUNCATEONLY

```
USE [Chapter5]
GO


DBCC SHRINKFILE (N'Chapter5_log' , 0, TRUNCATEONLY);
GO
```

▪ **Tip**   Because shrinking the transaction log always involves reclaiming space from the end of the log, until the first active VLF is reached, it is sensible to take a log backup and place the database in single user mode before performing this activity.

Log Fragmentation

When the log is truncated because of a backup in the Full Recovery model or a Checkpoint operation in the Simple Recovery model, what actually happens is that any VLFs that can be reused are truncated. Reasons why a VLF may not be able to be reused include VLFs containing log records associated with active transactions, or transactions that have not yet been sent to other databases in Replication or AlwaysOn topologies. In a similar fashion, if you shrink the log file, then VLFs will be removed from the end of the file until the first active VLF is reached.

There is no hard and fast rule for the optimum number of VLFs inside a log file, but I try to maintain approximately two VLFs per GB for large transaction logs, in the tens-of-gigabytes range. For smaller transaction logs, it is likely the ratio will be higher. If you have too many VLFs, then you may witness performance degradation of any activity that uses the transaction log. On the flip side, having too few VLFs can also pose a problem. In such a case where each VLF is GBs in size, when each VLF is truncated, it will take a substantial amount of time to clear, and you could witness a system slowdown while this takes place. Therefore, for large log files, it is recommended that you grow your transaction log in 8GB chunks to maintain the optimum number and size of VLFs.

To demonstrate this phenomenon, we will create a new database called Chapter5LogFragmentation, which has a single table on the primary filegroup, called Inserts, and then populate it with one million rows using the script in Listing 5-15. This will cause a large number of VLFs to be created, which will have a negative impact on performance.

Listing 5-15.   Creating the Chapter5LogFragmentation Database

```
--Create Chapter5LogFragmentation database

CREATE DATABASE [Chapter5LogFragmentation]
 CONTAINMENT = NONE
 ON  PRIMARY
( NAME = N'Chapter5LogFragmentation', FILENAME = N'F:\MSSQL\MSSQL12.PROSQLADMIN\MSSQL\DATA\
Chapter5LogFragmentation.mdf' , SIZE = 5120KB , FILEGROWTH = 1024KB )
 LOG ON
( NAME = N'Chapter5LogFragmentation_log', FILENAME = N'E:\MSSQL\MSSQL12.PROSQLADMIN\MSSQL\
DATA\Chapter5LogFragmentation_log.ldf' , SIZE = 1024KB , FILEGROWTH = 10%);
GO

USE Chapter5LogFragmentation
GO

--Create Inserts table

CREATE TABLE dbo.Inserts
(ID              INT                IDENTITY,
DummyText        NVARCHAR(50)
);
```

```
--Create a Numbers table that will be used to assit the population of the table

DECLARE @Numbers TABLE
(
        Number  INT
)

--Populate the Numbers table

;WITH CTE(Number)
AS
(
        SELECT 1 Number

        UNION ALL
        SELECT Number +1
        FROM CTE
        WHERE Number <= 99
)
INSERT INTO @Numbers
SELECT *
FROM CTE;

--Populate the example table with 100 rows of dummy text

INSERT INTO dbo.Inserts
SELECT 'DummyText'
FROM @Numbers a
CROSS JOIN @Numbers b
CROSS JOIN @Numbers c;
```

You can review the size of your transaction log and see how many VLFs are in your log by running the script in Listing 5-16.

Listing 5-16. Size of Log and Number of VLFs

```
--Create a variable to store the results of DBCC LOGINFO

DECLARE @DBCCLogInfo TABLE
(
RecoveryUnitID        TINYINT
,FieldID              TINYINT
,FileSize             BIGINT
,StartOffset      BIGINT
,FseqNo           INT
,Status           TINYINT
,Parity           TINYINT
,CreateLSN      NUMERIC
);

--Populate the table variable with the results of DBCC LOGINFO
```

```
INSERT INTO @DBCCLogInfo
EXEC('DBCC LOGINFO');

--Display the size of the log file, combined with the number of VLFs and a VLFs to GB ratio

SELECT
         name
        ,[Size in MBs]
        ,[Number of VLFs]
        ,[Number of VLFs] / ([Size in MBs] / 1024) 'VLFs per GB'
FROM
(
        SELECT
                 name
                ,size * 1.0 / 128 'Size in MBs'
                ,(SELECT COUNT(*)
                          FROM @DBCCLogInfo) 'Number of VLFs'
        FROM sys.database_files
        WHERE type = 1
 ) a;
```

The results of running this script inside the Chapter5LogFragmentation database are displayed in Figure 5-16. You can see that there are 61 VLFs, which is an excessive amount given the log size is 345MB.

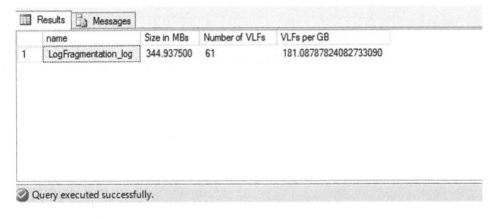

Figure 5-16. *VLFs per GB*

■ **Caution**   DBCC LOGINFO is undocumented, so it will not be supported by Microsoft. For example, in SQL Server 2012, Microsoft added a column to the output named RecoverUnitID, but they have never made its description public.

The full results of running DBCC LOGINFO in the Chapter5LogFragmentation database are shown here:

RecoveryUnitId	FileId	FileSize	StartOffset	FSeqNo	Status	Parity	CreateLSN
0	2	253952	8192	33	2	64	0
0	2	253952	262144	34	2	64	0
0	2	253952	516096	35	2	64	0
0	2	278528	770048	36	2	64	0
0	2	262144	1048576	37	2	64	34000000013600447
0	2	262144	1310720	38	2	64	34000000026100298
0	2	262144	1572864	39	2	64	34000000046900106
0	2	262144	1835008	40	2	64	35000000014900478
0	2	262144	2097152	41	2	64	35000000040200375
0	2	262144	2359296	42	2	64	36000000015500018
0	2	262144	2621440	43	2	64	36000000028500056
0	2	327680	2883584	44	2	64	37000000013600203
0	2	327680	3211264	45	2	64	37000000018400001
0	2	393216	3538944	46	2	64	37000000043400161
0	2	393216	3932160	47	2	64	38000000013600510
0	2	458752	4325376	48	2	64	38000000050100045
0	2	524288	4784128	49	2	64	39000000026100511
0	2	524288	5308416	50	2	64	40000000037600511
0	2	589824	5832704	51	2	64	41000000007200135
0	2	655360	6422528	52	2	64	41000000046900001
0	2	720896	7077888	53	2	64	42000000049600031
0	2	786432	7798784	54	2	64	43000000049600066
0	2	851968	8585216	55	2	64	44000000062100046
0	2	983040	9437184	56	2	64	45000000061600027
0	2	1048576	10420224	57	2	64	46000000071000245
0	2	1179648	11468800	58	2	64	47000000074600091
0	2	1310720	12648448	59	2	64	49000000001600032
0	2	1441792	13959168	60	2	64	49000000088700512
0	2	1572864	15400960	61	2	64	51000000001600001
0	2	1703936	16973824	62	2	64	52000000001600067
0	2	1900544	18677760	63	2	64	52000000125500104
0	2	2097152	20578304	64	2	64	54000000001600374
0	2	2293760	22675456	65	2	64	55000000001600510
0	2	2490368	24969216	66	2	64	56000000013600408
0	2	2752512	27459584	67	2	64	57000000005600099
0	2	3014656	30212096	68	2	64	58000000001600372
0	2	3342336	33226752	69	2	64	58000000227700001
0	2	3670016	36569088	70	2	64	59000000244900472
0	2	4063232	40239104	71	2	64	60000000257300510
0	2	4456448	44302336	72	2	64	61000000277600511
0	2	4915200	48758784	73	2	64	62000000303100510
0	2	5373952	53673984	74	2	64	63000000337600510
0	2	5898240	59047936	75	2	64	64000000367700510
0	2	6488064	64946176	76	2	64	65000000397600140
0	2	7143424	71434240	77	2	64	66000000433600476
0	2	7864320	78577664	78	2	64	67000000479900001
0	2	8650752	86441984	79	2	64	68000000519600510

0	2	9502720	95092736	80	2	64	69000000577700224
0	2	10485760	104595456	81	2	64	70000000625600320
0	2	11534336	115081216	82	2	64	71000000685700511
0	2	12713984	126615552	83	2	64	72000000758200041
0	2	13959168	139329536	0	0	0	73000000824700510
0	2	15335424	153288704	0	0	0	74000000905100001
0	2	16908288	168624128	0	0	0	75000000983600510
0	2	18546688	185532416	0	0	0	76000001094400272
0	2	20447232	204079104	0	0	0	77000001200500072
0	2	22478848	224526336	0	0	0	78000001324300191
0	2	24707072	247005184	0	0	0	79000001446800510
0	2	27197440	271712256	0	0	0	80000001587500512
0	2	29884416	298909696	0	0	0	81000001757000195
0	2	32899072	328794112	0	0	0	82000001916400510

The meaning of each column is identified in Table 5-2.

Table 5-2. *DBCC LOGINFO Columns*

Column	Description
FileID	The ID of the physical file. Assuming that you only have one file, this should always return the same value.
FileSize	The size of the VLF in bytes.
StartOffset	How many bytes there are from the beginning of the physical file until the start of the VLF.
FSeqNo	Defines the current usage order of the VLFs. The highest FSeqNo indicates the VLF that is currently being written to.
Status	A status of 2 means that the VLF is currently active. A status of 0 means that it is not and can therefore be reused.
Parity	Parity starts at 0. When a VLF is initially used, it is set to 64. Subsequently, it can be set to either 64 or 128. Each time a VLF is reused, this flag is switched to the opposite value.
CreateLSN	CreateLSN indicates the log sequence number that was used to create the VLF.

With an understanding of the columns, we can identify several interesting facts about the results shown earlier. First, because the first 4 VLFs have a CreateLSN value of 0, we know that these were the VLFs that were initially created when the log file itself was generated. The rest have been created by the log expanding, rather than cycling. We can also see that the final 10 VLFs in the results have not yet been used, because they have a Parity of 0. The VLF with an FSeqNo of 83 is the VLF where records are currently being written, since it has the highest FSeqNo.

Most interestingly, for the purpose of this example, we can see that the first 51 VLFs are marked as active, meaning that they cannot be reused. This means that if we attempt to shrink our log file, only 10 VLFs can be removed and the file would only shrink by the sum of their file sizes.

The reason that our log was growing and could not be cycled was because all the space was used during the course of a single transaction and, of course, our log has not been backed up. The query in Listing 5-17 will enable you to determine if there is any other reasons why you transaction log is growing. The query interrogates the sys.databases catalog view and returns the last reason that a VLF could not be reused.

Listing 5-17. sys.databases

```
SELECT log_reuse_wait_desc
FROM sys.databases
WHERE name = 'Chapter5LogFragmentation';
```

The log reuse waits that are still used in SQL Server 2014 and that are not for Microsoft's internal use only are described in Table 5-3. It is important to understand that the log reuse wait applies to the point when the log attempts to cycle and may still not be valid at the point you query sys.databases. For example, if there was an active transaction at the point that the last log cycle was attempted, it will be reflected in sys.databases, even though you may not currently have any active transactions at the point when you query sys.databases.

Table 5-3. *Log Reuse Waits*

Log_reuse_wait	Log_reuse_wait_description	Description
0	NOTHING	The log was able to cycle on its last attempt.
1	CHECKPOINT	Normally indicates that a CHECKPOINT has not occurred since the last time the log was truncated.
2	LOG_BACKUP	The log cannot be truncated until a log backup has been taken.
3	ACTIVE_BACKUP_OR_RESTORE	A backup or restore operation is currently in progress on the database.
4	ACTIVE_TRANSACTION	There is a long running or deferred transaction. Deferred transactions will be discussed in Chapter 18.
5	DATABASE_MIRRORING	Either an asynchronous replica is still synchronizing, or mirroring has been paused.
6	REPLICATION	There are transactions in the log that have not yet been received by the distributor. Replication will be discussed in Chapter 16.
7	DATABASE_SNAPSHOT_CREATION	A database snapshot is currently being created. Database snapshots will be discussed in Chapter 16.
8	LOG_SCAN	A log scan operation is in progress.
9	AVAILABILITY_REPLICA	Secondary replicas are not fully synchronized or the availability group has been paused.
13	OLDEST_PAGE	The oldest page of the database is older than the checkpoint LSN. This occurs when indirect checkpoints are being used.
16	XPT_CHECKPOINT	A memory-optimized CHECKPOINT is required before the log can be truncated.

In our scenario, in order to mark the VLFs as reusable, we need to back up our transaction log. Theoretically, we could also switch to the SIMPLE recovery model, but this would break our log chain. Before we do this, we need to take a full backup. This is because all backup sequences must begin with a full backup. (Backups and restores will be discussed in Chapter 15.) This will leave only the VLF with an FSeqNo of 83 as active and the others will be marked as reusable.

In order to improve log fragmentation, we need to shrink the log file and then expand it again, with a larger increment. So in our case, we would shrink the log as far as possible, which will be to VLF FSeqNo 83, because this is the last active VLF in the file. We then expand it back to 500MB. We can perform these tasks with the script in Listing 5-18.

Listing 5-18. Defragmenting the Transaction Log

```
USE [Chapter5]
GO

DBCC SHRINKFILE (N'Chapter5_log' , 0, TRUNCATEONLY);
GO

ALTER DATABASE [Chapter5] MODIFY FILE ( NAME = N'Chapter5_log', SIZE = 512000KB );
GO
```

Finally, we run the query in Listing 5-16 again so that we can examine the differences. Figure 5-17 shows that despite growing the log by around 155GB, we have fewer VLFs than we started with.

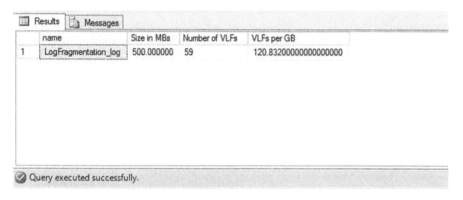

Figure 5-17. *Log fragmentation after shrinking and expanding*

Summary

Filegroups are logical containers for data files. Special filegroups also exist for FILESTREAM/FileTable data and for memory-optimized data. When tables and indexes are created, they are created on a filegroup as opposed to a file, and the data in the object is distributed evenly across the files within that filegroup.

You can adopt various strategies for filegroups to assist with performance, backup/restore activities, or even storage tiering. For performance, you can either choose to place frequently joined objects into separate filegroups, or you can distribute all objects across all spindles on the server in order to maximize IO throughput.

To support backups of very large databases when there is a limited maintenance window, you can split data across filegroups and you can back up those filegroups on alternate nights. To improve recovery times for critical data, you can isolate critical data in a separate filegroup and then restore it before other filegroups.

To support manual storage tiering, implement table partitioning so that each partition is stored on a separate filegroup. You can then place the files within each filegroup on an appropriate storage device.

Both FILESTREAM and memory-optimized filegroups point to folders in the operating system, as opposed to containing files. Each folder location is known as a container. For memory-optimized filegroups, consider having two containers for each disk array you use in order to evenly distribute IO.

You can expand and shrink data files. Shrinking files, especially auto-shrink, however, is considered bad practice and can results in serious fragmentation issues, which lead to performance problems. When expanding files, you should use larger increments to reduce repeated overhead.

You can also expand and shrink log files, although it is rare that you need to shrink them. Expanding log files in small increments can lead to log fragmentation, which is where your log file contains a vast amount of VLFs. You can resolve log fragmentation by shrinking the log and then growing it again in larger increments.

■ ■ ■

## CHAPTER 6

Configuring Tables

During the lifecycle of you data-tier applications, you may need to perform a number of maintenance tasks and performance optimizations against the tables that hold your application's data. These operations may include partitioning a table, compressing a table, or migrating data to a memory-optimized table. In this chapter, we will explore these three concepts in detail.

Table Partitioning

Partitioning is a performance optimization for large tables and indexes that splits the object horizontally into smaller units. When the tables or indexes are subsequently accessed, SQL Server can perform an optimization called *partition elimination*, which allows only the required partitions to be read, as opposed to the entire table. Additionally, each partition can be stored on a separate filegroup; this allows you to store different partitions on different storage tiers. For example, you can store older, less frequently accessed data on less expensive storage. Figure 6-1 illustrates how a large Orders table may be structured.

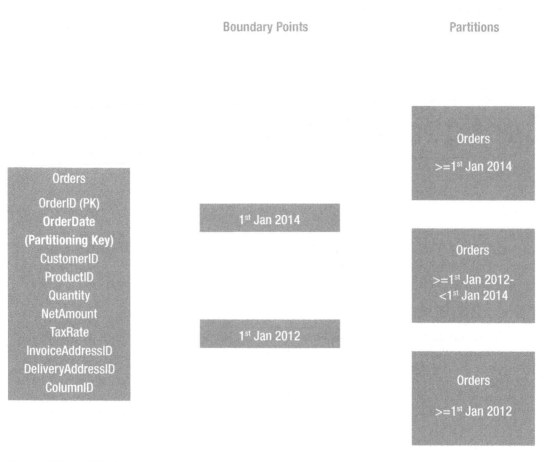

Figure 6-1. *Partitioning structure*

Partitioning Concepts

Before drilling into the technical implementation of partitioning, it helps if you understand the concepts, such as partitioning keys, partition functions, partition schemes, and partition alignment. These concepts are discussed in the following sections.

Partitioning Key

The *partitioning key* is used to determine in which partition each row of the table should be placed. If your table has a clustered index, then the partitioning key must be a subset of the clustered index key. All other UNIQUE indexes on the table, including the primary key (if this differs from the clustered index), also need to include the partitioning key. The partitioning key can consist of any data type, with the exception of TEXT, NTEXT, IMAGE, XML, TIMESTAMP, VARCHAR(MAX), NVARCHAR(MAX), and VARBINARY(MAX). It also cannot be a user-defined CLR Type column or a column with an alias data type. It can, however, be a computed column, as long as this column is persisted. Many scenarios will use a date or datetime column as the partitioning key. This allows you to implement sliding windows based on time. We discuss sliding windows later in this chapter. In Figure 6-1, the OrderData column is being used as the partitioning key.

Because the column is used to distribute rows between partitions, you should use a column that will enable an even distribution of rows in order to gain the most benefit from the solution. The column you select should also be a column that queries will use as a filter criteria. This will allow you to achieve partition elimination.

Partition Function

You use boundary points to set the upper and lower limits of each partition. In Figure 6-1, you can see that the boundary points are set as 1st Jan 2014 and 1st Jan 2012. These boundary points are configured in a database object called the *partition function*. When creating the partition function, you can specify if the range should be left or right. If you align the range to the left, then any values that are exactly equal to a boundary point value will be stored in the partition to the left of that boundary point. If you align the range with the right, then values exactly equal to the boundary point value will be placed in the partition to the right of that boundary point. The partition function also dictates the data type of the partitioning key.

Partition Scheme

Each partition can be stored on a separate filegroup. The *partition scheme* is an object that you create to specify which filegroup each partition will be stored on. As you can see from Figure 6-1, there is always one more partition than there is boundary point. When you create a partition scheme, however, it is possible to specify an "extra" filegroup. This will define the next filegroup that should be used if an additional boundary point is added. It is also possible to specify the ALL keyword, as opposed to specifying individual filegroups. This will force all partitions to be stored on the same filegroup.

Index Alignment

An index is considered aligned with the table if it is built on the same partition function as the table. It is also considered aligned if it is built on a different partition function, but the two functions are identical, in that they share the same data type, the same number of partitions, and the same boundary point values.

Because the leaf level of a clustered index consists of the actual data pages of the table, a clustered index is always aligned with the table. A nonclustered index, however, can be stored on a separate filegroup to the heap, or clustered index. This extends to partitioning, where either the base table or nonclustered indexes can be independently partitioned. If nonclustered indexes are stored on the same partition scheme or an identical partition scheme, then they are aligned. If this is not the case, then they are nonaligned.

Aligning indexes with the base table is good practice unless you have a specific reason not to. This is because aligning indexes can assist with partition elimination. Index alignment is also required for operations such as SWITCH, which will be discussed later in this chapter.

Partitioning Hierarchy

Objects involved in partitioning work in a one-to-many hierarchy, so multiple tables can share a partition scheme and multiple partition schemes can share a partition function, as illustrated in Figure 6-2.

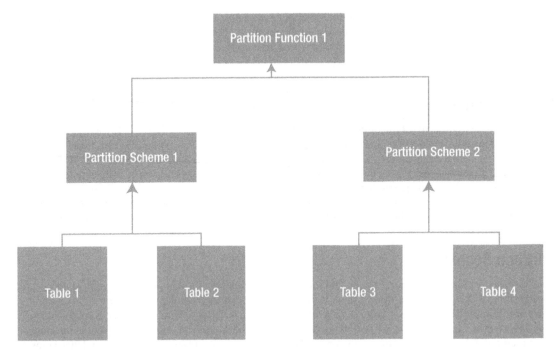

Figure 6-2. *Partitioning hierachy*

Implementing Partitioning

Implementing partitioning involves creating the partition function and partition scheme and then creating the table on the partition scheme. If the table already exists, then you will need to drop and re-create the table's clustered index. These tasks are discussed in the following sections.

Creating the Partitioning Objects

The first object that you will need to create is the partition function. This can be created using the CREATE PARTITION FUNCTION statement, as demonstrated in Listing 6-1. This script creates a database called Chapter6 and then creates a partition function called PartFunc. The function specifies a data type for partitioning keys of DATE and sets boundary points for 1st Jan 2014 and 1st Jan 2012. Table 6-1 details how dates will be distributed between partitions.

Table 6-1. *Distribution of Dates*

Date	Partition	Notes
6th June 2011	1	
1st Jan 2012	1	If we had used RANGE RIGHT, this value would be in Partition 2.
11th October 2013	2	
1st Jan 2014	2	If we had used RANGE RIGHT, this value would be in Partition 3.
9th May 2015	3	

Listing 6-1. Creating the Partition Function

```
USE Master
GO

--Create Database Chapter 6 using default settings from Model

CREATE DATABASE Chapter6 ;
GO

USE Chapter6
GO

--Create Partition Function

CREATE PARTITION FUNCTION PartFunc(Date)
AS RANGE LEFT
FOR VALUES('2012-01-01', '2014-01-01') ;
```

The next object that we need to create is a partition scheme. This can be created using the CREATE PARTITION SCHEME statement, as demonstrated in Listing 6-2. This script creates a partition scheme called PartScheme against the PartFunc partition function and specifies that all partitions will be stored on the PRIMARY filegroup. Although storing all partitions on the same filegroup does not allow us to implement storage tiering, it does enable us to automate sliding windows.

Listing 6-2. Creating the Partition Scheme

```
CREATE PARTITION SCHEME PartScheme
AS PARTITION PartFunc
ALL TO ([PRIMARY]) ;
```

Creating a New Partitioned Table

Now that we have a partition function and partition scheme in place, all that remains is to create our partitioned table. The script in Listing 6-3 creates a table called Orders and partitions it based on the OrderDate column. Even though OrderNumber provides a natural primary key for our table, we need to include OrderDate in the key so that it can be used as our partitioning column. Obviously, the OrderDate column is not be suitable for the primary key on its own, since it is not guaranteed to be unique.

Listing 6-3. Creating the Partition Table

```
CREATE TABLE dbo.Orders
        (
        OrderNumber int         NOT NULL,
        OrderDate date          NOT NULL,
        CustomerID int          NOT NULL,
        ProductID int           NOT NULL,
        Quantity int            NOT NULL,
        NetAmount money         NOT NULL,
        TaxAmount money         NOT NULL,
        InvoiceAddressID int    NOT NULL,
        DeliveryAddressID int   NOT NULL,
```

```
            DeliveryDate date        NULL
       )  ON PartScheme(OrderDate)  ;
GO


ALTER TABLE dbo.Orders ADD CONSTRAINT
       PK_Orders PRIMARY KEY CLUSTERED
        (
       OrderNumber,
       OrderDate
       ) WITH( STATISTICS_NORECOMPUTE = OFF, IGNORE_DUP_KEY = OFF,
                 ALLOW_ROW_LOCKS = ON, ALLOW_PAGE_LOCKS = ON) ON PartScheme(OrderDate) ;


GO
```

The important thing to notice in this script is the ON clause. Normally, you would create a table "on" a filegroup, but in this case, we are creating the table "on" the partition scheme and passing in the name of the column that will be used as the partitioning key. The data type of the partitioning key must match the data type specified in the partition function.

Partitioning an Existing Table

Because the clustered index is always aligned with the base table, the process of moving a table to a partition scheme is as simple as dropping the clustered index and then re-creating the clustered index on the partition scheme. The script in Listing 6-4 creates a table called ExistingOrders and populates it with data.

Listing 6-4. Creating a New Table and Populating It with Data

```
--Create the ExistingOrders table

CREATE TABLE dbo.ExistingOrders
        (
        OrderNumber int          IDENTITY       NOT NULL,
        OrderDate date          NOT NULL,
        CustomerID int           NOT NULL,
        ProductID int            NOT NULL,
        Quantity int              NOT NULL,
        NetAmount money      NOT NULL,
        TaxAmount money      NOT NULL,
        InvoiceAddressID int    NOT NULL,
        DeliveryAddressID int   NOT NULL,
        DeliveryDate date        NULL
        )  ON [PRIMARY] ;
GO


ALTER TABLE dbo.ExistingOrders ADD CONSTRAINT
        PK_ExistingOrders PRIMARY KEY CLUSTERED
         (
        OrderNumber,
        OrderDate
        ) WITH( STATISTICS_NORECOMPUTE = OFF, IGNORE_DUP_KEY = OFF,
                  ALLOW_ROW_LOCKS = ON, ALLOW_PAGE_LOCKS = ON) ON [PRIMARY] ;
```

```
GO

--We will now populate the data with data so that we can view the storage properties
--and then partition the table when the data already exists.

--Build a numbers table for the data population

DECLARE @Numbers TABLE
(
        Number          INT
)

;WITH CTE(Number)
AS
(
        SELECT 1 Number
        UNION ALL
        SELECT Number + 1
        FROM CTE
        WHERE Number < 20
)
INSERT INTO @Numbers
SELECT Number FROM CTE ;

--Populate ExistingOrders with data

INSERT INTO dbo.ExistingOrders
SELECT
        (SELECT CAST(DATEADD(dd,(SELECT TOP 1 Number
                                FROM @Numbers
                                ORDER BY NEWID()),getdate())as DATE)),
        (SELECT TOP 1 Number -10 FROM @Numbers ORDER BY NEWID()),
        (SELECT TOP 1 Number FROM @Numbers ORDER BY NEWID()),
        (SELECT TOP 1 Number FROM @Numbers ORDER BY NEWID()),
        500,
        100,
        (SELECT TOP 1 Number FROM @Numbers ORDER BY NEWID()),
        (SELECT TOP 1 Number FROM @Numbers ORDER BY NEWID()),
        (SELECT CAST(DATEADD(dd,(SELECT TOP 1 Number - 10
                                FROM @Numbers
                                ORDER BY NEWID()),getdate()) as DATE))
FROM @Numbers a
CROSS JOIN @Numbers b ;
```

As shown in Figure 6-3, by looking at the Storage tab of the Table Properties dialog box, we can see that the table has been created on the PRIMARY filegroup and is not partitioned.

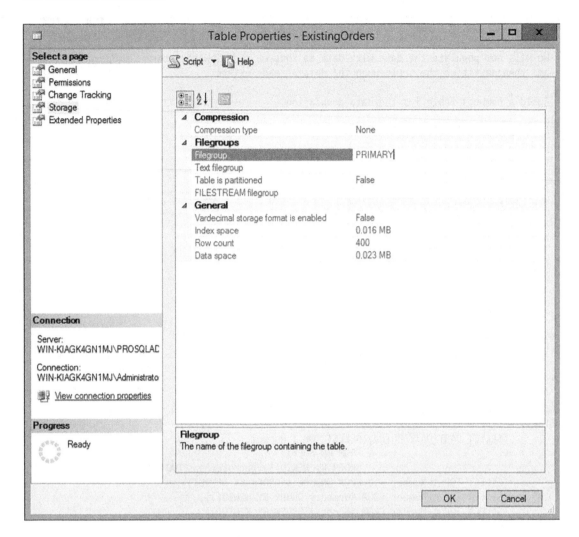

Figure 6-3. *Table properties nonpartitioned*

The script in Listing 6-5 now drops the clustered index of the ExistingOrders table and re-creates it on the PartScheme partition scheme. Again, the key line to note is the ON clause, which specifies PartScheme as the target partition function and passes in OrderDate as the partitioning key.

Listing 6-5. *Moving the Existing Table onto the Partition Scheme*

```
--Drop Clustered Index

ALTER TABLE dbo.ExistingOrders DROP CONSTRAINT PK_ExistingOrders ;
GO

--Re-created clustered index on PartScheme
```

```
ALTER TABLE dbo.ExistingOrders ADD  CONSTRAINT PK_ExistingOrders PRIMARY KEY CLUSTERED
(
        OrderNumber ASC,
        OrderDate ASC
)WITH (PAD_INDEX = OFF, STATISTICS_NORECOMPUTE = OFF, SORT_IN_TEMPDB = OFF,
          IGNORE_DUP_KEY = OFF, ONLINE = OFF, ALLOW_ROW_LOCKS = ON,
          ALLOW_PAGE_LOCKS = ON) ON PartScheme(OrderDate) ;
GO
```

In Figure 6-4, you can see that if you look again at the Storage tab of the Table Properties dialog box, you find that the table is now partitioned against the PartScheme partition scheme.

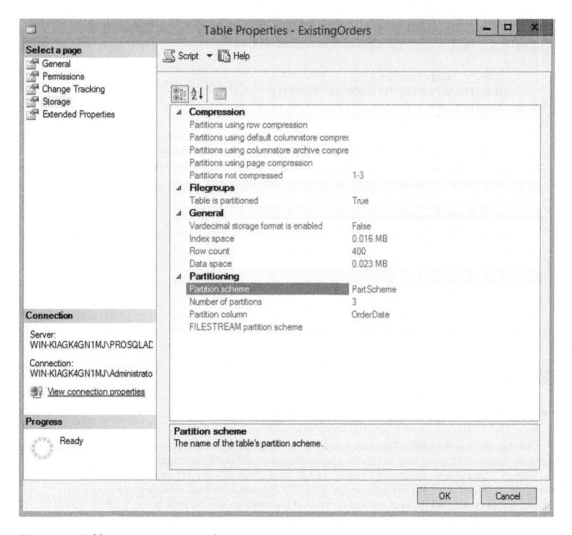

Figure 6-4. *Table properties partitioned*

Monitoring Partitioned Tables

You may wish to keep track of the number of rows in each partition of your table. Doing so allows you to ensure that your rows are being distributed evenly. If they are not, then you may wish to reassess you partitioning strategy to ensure you get the full benefit from the technology. There are two methods that you can use for this: the $PARTITION function and the Disk Usage by Partition SSMS Report.

$PARTITION Function

You can determine how many rows are in each partition of your table by using the $PARTITION function. When you run this function against the partition function, it accepts the column name of your partitioning key as a parameter, as demonstrated in Listing 6-6.

Listing 6-6. Using the $PARTITION Function

```
SELECT
        COUNT(*) 'Number of Rows'
        ,$PARTITION.PartFunc(OrderDate) 'Partition'
FROM dbo.ExistingOrders
GROUP BY $PARTITION.PartFunc(OrderDate) ;
```

From the results in Figure 6-5, you can see that all of the rows in our table sit in the same partition, which pretty much defies the point of partitioning and means that we should reassess our strategy.

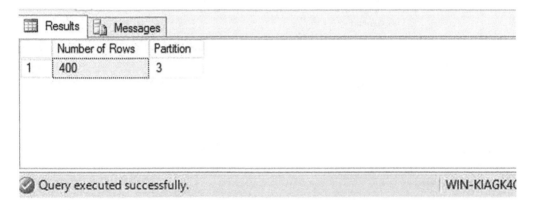

Figure 6-5. *The $PARTITION function run against a partitioned table*

We can also use the $PARTITION function to assess how a table would be partitioned against a different partition function. This can help us plan to resolve the issue with our ExistingOrders table. The script in Listing 6-7 creates a new partition function, called PartFuncWeek, which creates weekly partitions for the month of November 2014. It then uses the $PARTITION function to determine how the rows of our ExistingOrders table will be split if we implemented this strategy. For the time being, we do not need to create a partition scheme or repartition the table. Before running the script, change the boundary point values so they are based upon the date when you run the script. This is because the data in the table is generated using the GETDATE() function.

Listing 6-7. $PARTITION Function Against a New Partition Function

```
--Create new partition function
CREATE PARTITION FUNCTION PartFuncWeek(DATE)
AS RANGE LEFT
FOR VALUES ('2014-11-7','2014-11-14','2014-11-21','2014-11-28') ;

--Assess spread of rows
SELECT
        COUNT(*) 'Number of Rows'
        ,$PARTITION.PartFuncWeek(OrderDate) 'Partition'
FROM dbo.ExistingOrders
GROUP BY $PARTITION.PartFuncWeek(OrderDate) ;
```

The results in Figure 6-6 show that the rows of the ExistingOrders table are fairly evenly distributed among the weekly partitions, so this may provide a suitable strategy for our table.

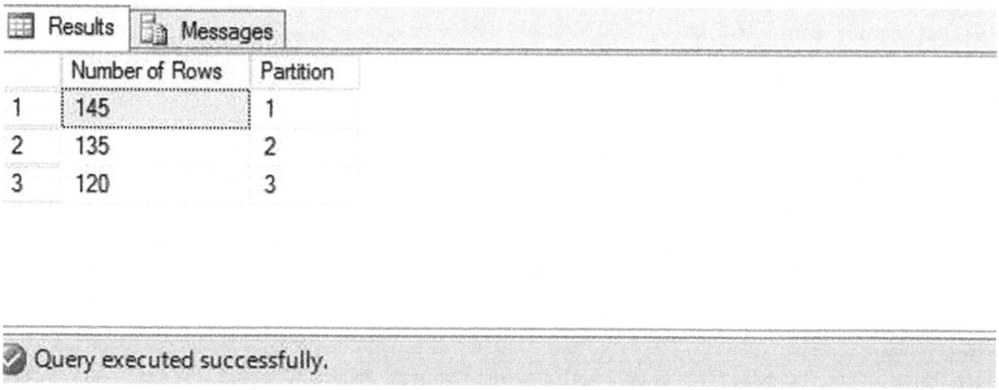

	Number of Rows	Partition
1	145	1
2	135	2
3	120	3

Query executed successfully.

Figure 6-6. *$PARTITION function against a new partition function*

Sliding Windows

Our weekly partitioning strategy seems to work well, but what about when we reach December? As it currently stands, all new order placed after 28th November 2014 will all end up in the same partition, which will just grow and grow. To combat this issue, SQL Server provides us with the tools to create sliding windows. In our case, this means that each week, a new partition will be created for the following week and the earliest partition will be removed.

To achieve this, we can use the SPLIT, MERGE, and SWITCH operations. The SPLIT operation adds a new boundary point, thus creating a new partition. The MERGE operation removes a boundary point, thus merging two partitions together. The SWITCH operation moves a partition into an empty table or partition.

In our scenario, we create a staging table, called OldOrdersStaging. We use this table as a staging area to hold the data from our earliest partition. Once in the staging table, you can perform whatever operations or transformation may be required. For example, your developers may wish to create a script, to roll the data up, and to transfer it to a historical Orders table. Even though the OldOrdersStaging table is designed as a temporary object, it is important to note that you cannot use a temporary table. Instead, you must use a permanent table and *drop* it at the end. This is because temporary tables reside in TempDB, which means that they will be on a different filegroup, and SWITCH will not work. SWITCH is a metadata operation, and therefore, both partitions involved must reside on the same filegroup.

The script in Listing 6-8 implements a sliding window. First, it creates a staging table for the older orders. The indexes and constraints of this table must be the same as those of the partitioned table. The table must also reside on the same filegroup in order for the SWITCH operation to succeed. It then determines the highest and lowest boundary point values in the partitioned table, which it will use as parameters for the SPLIT and MERGE operations. It then uses the ALTER PARTITION FUNCTION command to remove the lowest boundary point value and add in the new boundary point. Finally, it reruns the $PARTITION function to display the new distribution of rows and interrogates the sys.partition_functions and sys.partition_range_values catalog views to display the new boundary point values for the PartFuncWeek partition function. The script assumes that the PartSchemeWeek partition scheme has been created and the ExistingOrders table has been moved to this partition scheme.

Listing 6-8. Implementing a Sliding Window

```
--Create the OldOrders table

CREATE TABLE dbo.OldOrdersStaging(
        [OrderNumber] [int] IDENTITY(1,1) NOT NULL,
        [OrderDate] [date] NOT NULL,
        [CustomerID] [int] NOT NULL,
        [ProductID] [int] NOT NULL,
        [Quantity] [int] NOT NULL,
        [NetAmount] [money] NOT NULL,
        [TaxAmount] [money] NOT NULL,
        [InvoiceAddressID] [int] NOT NULL,
        [DeliveryAddressID] [int] NOT NULL,
        [DeliveryDate] [date] NULL,
 CONSTRAINT PK_OldOrdersStaging PRIMARY KEY CLUSTERED
(
        OrderNumber ASC,
        OrderDate ASC
)WITH (PAD_INDEX = OFF, STATISTICS_NORECOMPUTE = OFF, IGNORE_DUP_KEY = OFF,
        ALLOW_ROW_LOCKS = ON, ALLOW_PAGE_LOCKS = ON)
) ;
GO


--Calculate the lowest boundary point value

DECLARE @LowestBoundaryPoint DATE = (
        SELECT TOP 1 CAST(value  AS DATE)
        FROM sys.partition_functions pf
        INNER JOIN sys.partition_range_values prv
                ON pf.function_id = prv.function_id
        WHERE pf.name = 'PartFuncWeek'
        ORDER BY value ASC) ;

--Calculate the newest boundary point value

DECLARE @HighestboundaryPoint DATE = (
SELECT TOP 1 CAST(value  AS DATE)
        FROM sys.partition_functions pf
        INNER JOIN sys.partition_range_values prv
                ON pf.function_id = prv.function_id
```

```
            WHERE pf.name = 'PartFuncWeek'
            ORDER BY value DESC) ;

--Add 7 days to the newest boundary point value to determine the new boundary point

DECLARE @NewSplitRange DATE = (
            SELECT DATEADD(dd,7,@HighestboundaryPoint)) ;

--Switch the oldest partition to the OldOrders table

ALTER TABLE ExistingOrders
            SWITCH PARTITION 1 TO OldOrdersStaging PARTITION 2 ;

--Remove the oldest partition

ALTER PARTITION FUNCTION PartFuncWeek()
            MERGE RANGE(@LowestBoundaryPoint) ;

--Create the new partition

ALTER PARTITION FUNCTION PartFuncWeek()
            SPLIT RANGE(@NewSplitRange) ;
GO

--Re-run $PARTITION to assess new spread of rows

SELECT
            COUNT(*) 'Number of Rows'
            ,$PARTITION.PartFuncWeek(OrderDate) 'Partition'
FROM dbo.ExistingOrders
GROUP BY $PARTITION.PartFuncWeek(OrderDate) ;

SELECT name, value FROM SYS.partition_functions PF
INNER JOIN SYS.partition_range_values PFR ON PF.function_id = PFR.function_id
WHERE name = 'PARTFUNCWEEK' ;
```

The results displayed in Figure 6-7 show how the partitions have been realigned.

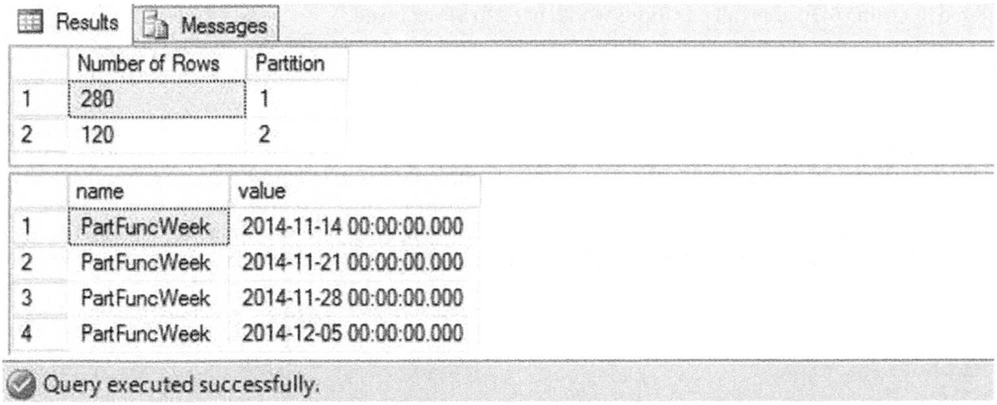

	Number of Rows	Partition
1	280	1
2	120	2

	name	value
1	PartFuncWeek	2014-11-14 00:00:00.000
2	PartFuncWeek	2014-11-21 00:00:00.000
3	PartFuncWeek	2014-11-28 00:00:00.000
4	PartFuncWeek	2014-12-05 00:00:00.000

Query executed successfully.

Figure 6-7. New partition alignment

175

When you are using the SWITCH function, there are several limitations. First, all nonclustered indexes of the table must be aligned with the base table. Also, the empty table or partition that you move the data into must have the same indexing structure. It must also reside on the same filegroup as the partition that you are switching out. This is because the SWITCH function does not actually move any data. It is a metadata operation that changes the pointers of the pages that make up the partition.

You can use MERGE and SPLIT with different filegroups, but there will be a performance impediment. Like SWITCH, MERGE and SPLIT can be performed as metadata operations if all partitions involved reside on the same filegroup. If they are on different filegroups, however, then physical data moves need to be performed by SQL Server, which can take substantially longer.

Partition Elimination

One of the key benefits of partitioning is that the Query Optimizer is able to access only the partitions require to satisfy the results of a query, instead of the entire table. For partition elimination to be successful, the partitioning key must be included as a filter in the WHERE clause. We can witness this functionality by running the query in Listing 6-9 against our ExistingOrders table and choosing the option to include the actual execution plan.

Listing 6-9. Query Using Partition Elimination

```
SELECT OrderNumber, OrderDate
FROM dbo.ExistingOrders
WHERE OrderDate BETWEEN '2014-11-01' AND '2014-11-14' ;
```

If we now view the execution plan and examine the properties of the Index Scan operator through Management Studio 2014, we see that only one partition has been accessed, as shown in Figure 6-8.

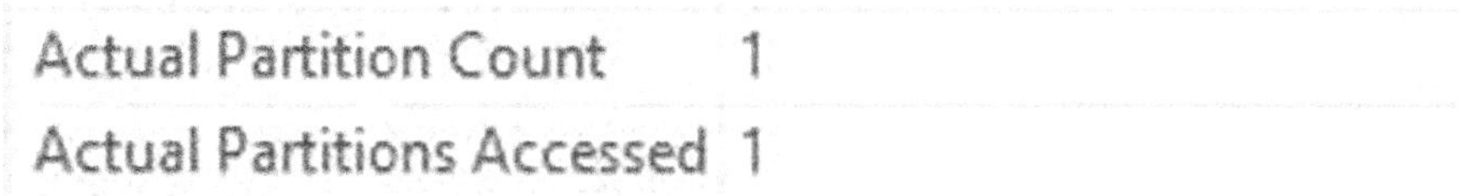

| Actual Partition Count | 1 |
| Actual Partitions Accessed | 1 |

Figure 6-8. *Index Scan operator properties with partition elimination*

The partition elimination functionality can be a little fragile, however. For example, if you are manipulating the OrderDate column in any way, as opposed to just using it for evaluation, then partition elimination cannot occur. For example, if you cast the OrderDate column to the DATETIME2 data type, as demonstrated in Listing 6-10, then all partitions would need to be accessed.

Listing 6-10. Query Not Using Partition Elimination

```
SELECT OrderNumber, OrderDate
FROM dbo.ExistingOrders
WHERE CAST(OrderDate AS DATETIME2) BETWEEN '2014-11-01' AND '2014-11-14' ;
```

Figure 6-9 illustrates the same properties of the Index Scan operator, viewed through Management Studio 2014. Here you can see that all partitions have been accessed, as opposed to just one.

| Actual Partition Count | 3 |
| Actual Partitions Accessed | 1..3 |

Figure 6-9. *Index Scan properties, no partition elimination*

Table Compression

When you think of compression, it is natural to think of saving space at the expense of performance. However, this does not always hold true for SQL Server table compression. Compression in SQL Server can actually offer a performance benefit. This is because SQL Server is usually an IO-bound application, as opposed to being CPU bound. This means that if SQL Server needs to read dramatically fewer pages from disk, then performance will increase, even if this is at the expense of CPU cycles. Of course, if your database is, in fact, CPU bound because you have very fast disks and only a single CPU core, for example, then compression could have a negative impact, but this is atypical. In order to understand table compression, it helps to have insight into how SQL Server stores data within a page. Although a full discussion of page internals is beyond the scope of this book, Figure 6-10 gives you a high-level view of the default structure of an on-disk page and row.

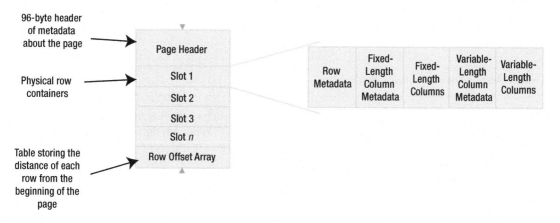

Figure 6-10. *Structure of a page*

Within the row, the row metadata contains details such as whether or not versioning information exists for the row and if the row has NULL values. The fixed-length column metadata records the length of the fixed-length portion of the page. The variable-length metadata includes a column offset array for the variable-length columns so that SQL Server can track where each column begins in relation to the beginning of the row.

Row Compression

On an uncompressed page, as just described, SQL Server stores fixed-length columns first, followed by variable-length columns. The only columns that can be variable length are columns with a variable-length data type, such as VARCHAR or VARBINARY. When row compression is implemented for a table, SQL Server uses the minimum amount of storage for other data types as well. For example, if you have an integer column that contains a NULL value in row 1, a value of 50 in row 2, and a value of 40,000 in row 3, then in row 1, the column does not use any space at all; it uses 1 byte in row 2, because it will store this value as a TINYINT; and it uses 4 bytes in row 3, because it will need to store this value as an INT. This is opposed to an uncompressed table using 4 bytes for every row, including row 1.

In addition, SQL Server also compresses Unicode columns so that characters that can be stored as a single byte only use a single byte, as opposed to 2 bytes, as they would in an uncompressed page. In order to achieve these optimizations, SQL Server has to use a different page format, which is outlined in Figure 6-11.

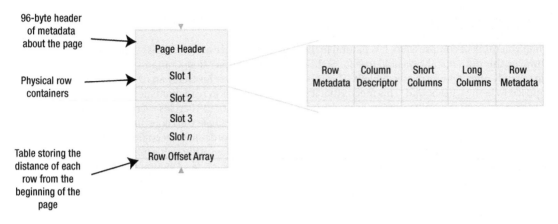

96-byte header of metadata about the page →

Physical row containers →

Table storing the distance of each row from the beginning of the page →

Figure 6-11. *Page structure with row compression*

■ **Note**   A short column is 8 bytes or less.

In Figure 6-11, the first area of row metadata contains details such as whether or not there is versioning information about the row and if any long data columns exist. The column descriptor contains the number of short columns and the length of each long column. The second area of metadata contains details such as versioning information and forwarding pointers for heaps.

Page Compression

When you implement page compression, row compression is implemented first. Page compression itself is actually comprised of two different forms of compression. The first is *prefix compression* and the second is *dictionary compression*. These compression types are outlined in the following sections.

Prefix Compression

Prefix compression works by establishing a common prefix for a column across rows within a page. Once the best prefix value has been established, SQL Server chooses the longest value that contains the full prefix as the anchor row and stores all other values within the column, as a differential of the anchor row, as opposed to storing the values themselves. For example, Table 6-2 details the values that are being stored within a column and follows this with a description of how SQL Server will store the values using prefix compression. The value Postfreeze has been chosen as the anchor value, since it is the longest value that contains the full prefix of Post, which has been identified. The number in <> is a marker of how many characters of the prefix are used.

Table 6-2. *Prefix Compression Differentials*

Column A Value	Column A Storage	Column B Value	Column B Storage
Postcode	<4>code	Teethings (Anchor)	—
Postfreeze (Anchor)	—	Teacher	<2>acher
Postpones	<4>pones	Teenager	<3>nager
Postilion	<4>ilion	Teeth	<5>
Imposters	<0>Imposters	Tent	<2>nt
Poacher	<2>acher	Rent	<0>Rent

Dictionary Compression

Dictionary compression is performed after all columns have been compressed using prefix compression. It looks across all columns within a page and finds values that match. The matching is performed using the binary representation of a value, which makes the process data-type agnostic. When it finds duplicate values, it adds them to a special dictionary at the top of the page, and in the row, it simply stores a pointer to the value's location in the dictionary. Table 6-3 expands on the previous table to give you an overview of this.

Table 6-3. *Dictionary Compression Pointers*

Column A Value	Column A Storage	Column B Value	Column B Storage
Postcode	<4>code	Teethings (Anchor)	—
Postfreeze (Anchor)	—	Teacher	[Pointer1]
Postpones	<4>pones	Teenager	<3>nager
Postilion	<4>ilion	Teeth	<5>
Imposters	<0>Imposters	Tent	<2>nt
Poacher	[Pointer1]	Rent	<0>Rent

Here, you can see that the value <2>acher, which appeared in both columns in the previous table, has been replaced with a pointer to the dictionary where the value is stored.

Page Compression Structure

In order to facilitate page compression, a special row is inserted in the page immediately after the page header, which contains the information regarding the anchor record and dictionary. This row is called the compression information record, and it is illustrated in Figure 6-12.

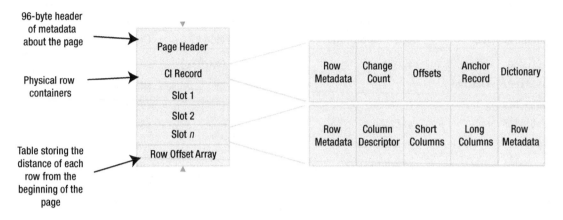

Figure 6-12. *Page structure with page compression*

The row metadata for the compression information record specifies if the record contains an anchor record and a dictionary. The change count records how many changes have been made to the page, which may affect the usefulness of the anchor and dictionary. When a table is rebuilt, SQL Server can use this information to determine if the page should be rebuilt. The offsets contain the start and end locations of the dictionary, from the beginning of the page. The anchor record contains each column's prefix value and the dictionary contains the duplicate values for which pointers have been created.

Columnstore Compression

Columnstore indexes are always compressed, automatically. This means that if you create a clustered columnstore index on your table, your table is also compressed, and this cannot be combined with row or page compression. There are two types of columnstore compression available to you; COLUMNSTORE, which was introduced in SQL Server 2012, and COLUMNSTORE_ARCHIVE, which was introduced in SQL Server 2014.

You can think of COLUMNSTORE as the standard compression type for columnstore indexes and you should only use the COLUMNSTORE_ARCHIVE algorithm for data that is infrequently accessed. This is because this new compression algorithm in SQL Server 2014 breaks the rules for SQL Server data compression as far as performance goes. If you implement this algorithm, expect a very high compression ratio, but prepare for it to be at the expense of query performance.

Implementing Compression

The planning and implementation of row and page compression is a fairly straightforward process, and it is discussed in the following sections.

Selecting the Compression Level

As you probably realized from the earlier descriptions of row and page compression, page compression offers a higher compression ratio than row compression, which means better IO performance. However, this is at the expense of CPU cycles, both when the table is being compressed, and again when it is being accessed. Therefore, before you start compressing your tables, make sure you understand how much each of these compression types will reduce the size of your table by so that you can assess how much IO efficiency you can achieve.

You can accomplish this by using a system stored procedure called sp_estimate_data_compression_savings. This procedure estimates the amount of space that you could save by implementing compression. It accepts the parameters listed in Table 6-4.

Table 6-4. *sp_estimate_data_compression_savings Parameters*

Parameter	Comments
@schema_name	The name of the schema, which contains the table that you want to run the procedure against.
@object_name	The name of the table that you want to run the procedure against.
@index_ID	Pass in NULL for all indexes. For a heap, the index ID is always 0 and a clustered index always has an ID of 1.
@partition_number	Pass in NULL for all partitions.
@data_compression	Pass in ROW, PAGE, or NONE if you want to assess the impact of removing compression from a table that is already compressed.

The two executions of the sp_estimate_data_compression_savings stored procedure in Listing 6-11 assess the impact of row and page compression, respectively, on all partitions of our ExistingOrders table.

Listing 6-11. Sp_ estimate_data_compression_savings

```
EXEC sp_estimate_data_compression_savings @schema_name = 'dbo', @object_name = 'ExistingOrders',
     @index_id = NULL, @partition_number = NULL, @data_compression ='ROW' ;

EXEC sp_estimate_data_compression_savings @schema_name = 'dbo', @object_name = 'ExistingOrders',
     @index_id = NULL, @partition_number = NULL, @data_compression ='PAGE' ;
```

The results in Figure 6-13 show that for the two partitions that are currently in use, page compression will have no additional benefit over row compression. Therefore, it is pointless to add the extra CPU overhead associated with page compression. This is because row compression is always implemented on every row of every page in the table. Page compression, on the other hand, is assessed on a page-by-page basis, and only pages that will benefit from being compressed are rebuilt. Because of the random nature of the largely numeric data that we inserted into this table, SQL Server has determined that the pages of our table will not benefit from page compression.

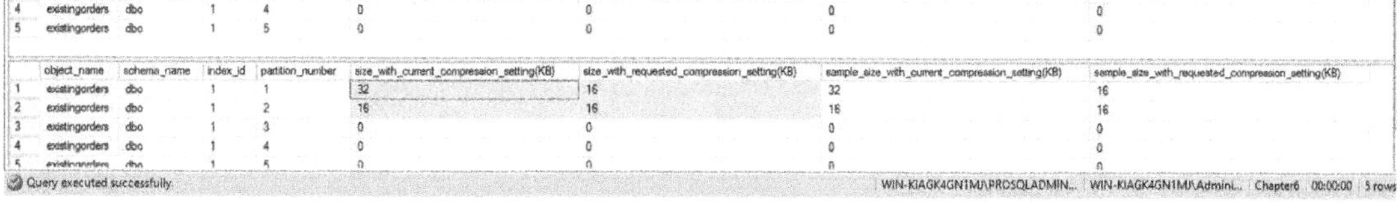

	object_name	schema_name	index_id	partition_number	size_with_current_compression_setting(KB)	size_with_requested_compression_setting(KB)	sample_size_with_current_compression_setting(KB)	sample_size_with_requested_compression_setting(KB)
1	existingorders	dbo	1	1	32	16	32	16
2	existingorders	dbo	1	2	16	16	16	16
3	existingorders	dbo	1	3	0	0	0	0
4	existingorders	dbo	1	4	0	0	0	0
5	existingorders	dbo	1	5	0	0	0	0

	object_name	schema_name	index_id	partition_number	size_with_current_compression_setting(KB)	size_with_requested_compression_setting(KB)	sample_size_with_current_compression_setting(KB)	sample_size_with_requested_compression_setting(KB)
1	existingorders	dbo	1	1	32	16	32	16
2	existingorders	dbo	1	2	16	16	16	16
3	existingorders	dbo	1	3	0	0	0	0
4	existingorders	dbo	1	4	0	0	0	0
5	existingorders	dbo	1	5	0	0	0	0

Query executed successfully. WIN-KIAGK4GN1MJ\PROSQLADMIN... WIN-KIAGK4GN1MJ\Admini... Chapter6 00:00:00 5 rows

Figure 6-13. *Resuts of sp_estimate_data_compression_savings*

Compressing Tables and Partitions

We determined that row compression reduces the size of our table, but we can't gain any further benefits by implementing page compression. Therefore, we can compress our entire table using the command in Listing 6-12.

Listing 6-12. Implementing Row Compression on the Entire Table

```
ALTER TABLE ExistingOrders
    REBUILD WITH (DATA_COMPRESSION = ROW) ;
```

If we look more closely at the results, however, we can see that, in fact, only partition 1 benefits from row compression. Partition 2 remains the same size. Therefore, it is not worth the overhead to compress partition 2. Running the ALTER TABLE statement in Listing 6-13 will rebuild only partition 1. It will then remove compression from the entire table by rebuilding it with DATA_COMPRESSION = NONE.

Listing 6-13. Implementing Row Compression for Specific Partitions

```
--Compress partition 1 with ROW compression

ALTER TABLE ExistingOrders
    REBUILD PARTITION = 1 WITH (DATA_COMPRESSION = ROW) ;
GO

--Remove compression from the whole table

ALTER TABLE ExistingOrders
    REBUILD WITH (DATA_COMPRESSION = NONE) ;
```

Data Compression Wizard

The Data Compression Wizard can be reached via the context menu of a table by drilling down through Storage | Manage Compression. It provides a graphical user interface (GUI) for managing compression. The main page of the wizard is illustrated in Figure 6-14. On this screen, you can utilize the Use Same Compression Type For All Partitions option to implement one type of compression uniformly across the table. Alternatively, you can specify different compression types for each individual partition. The Calculate button runs the sp_estimate_data_compression_savings stored procedure and displays the current and estimated results for each partition.

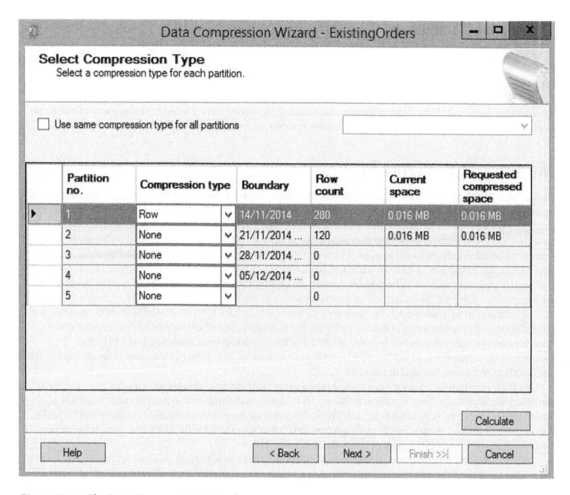

Figure 6-14. The Data Compression Wizard

On the final page of the wizard, you can choose to run the process immediately, script the action, or schedule it to run using SQL Server Agent.

Maintaining Compression on Heaps

When new pages are added to a heap (a table without a Clustered Index), they are not automatically compressed with page compression. This means that rebuilding a compressed table should be part of your standard maintenance routines when it does not have a clustered index. To rebuild the compression on a table, you should remove compression and then re-implement it.

■ **Tip** New heap pages will be compressed if they are inserted using INSERT INTO...WITH (TABLOCK) or if they are inserted as part of a bulk insert where optimizations have been enabled.

Maintaining Compressed Partitions

In order to use the SWITCH operation with partitions, both partitions must have the same level of compression selected. If you use MERGE, then the compression level of the destination partition is used. When you use SPLIT, the new partition inherits its compression level from the original partition.

Just like with a non-partitioned table, if you drop the clustered index of a table, then the heap inherits the compression level of the clustered index. However, if you drop the clustered index as part of an exercise to modify the partition scheme, then compression is removed from the table.

Memory-Optimized Tables

In-Memory OLTP is a new feature of SQL Server 2014 that can offer significant performance improvements by storing all of the table's data in memory. This, of course, can dramatically reduce IO, despite the fact that the tables are also saved to disk for durability. This is because the disk-based version of the tables is stored in an unstructured format, outside of the database engine, using a FILESTREAM-based technology. Also, memory-optimized checkpoints happen a lot more frequently. An automatic checkpoint is taken after the transaction log has grown by 512MB since the last time an automatic checkpoint occurred. This removes IO spikes that are associated with checkpoint activity. IO contention on transaction logs can also be reduced with memory optimized tables since less data is logged.

In addition to minimizing IO, In-Memory OLTP can also reduce CPU overhead. This is because natively compiled stored procedures can be used to access the data, as opposed to traditional, interpreted code. Natively compiled stored procedures use significantly fewer instructions, meaning less CPU time. Memory-optimized tables do not help reduce network overhead, however, because the same amount of data still needs to be communicated to the client.

By their very nature, memory-optimized tables increase memory pressure as opposed to reducing it, because even if you never use the data, it still sits in memory, reducing the amount of space available in which traditional resources can be cached. This means that in-memory functionality is designed for OLTP workloads as opposed to data warehousing workloads. The expectation is that fact and dimension tables within a data warehouse are too large to reside in memory.

As well as lower resource usage, memory-optimized tables can also help reduce contention. When you access data in a memory-optimized table, SQL Server does not take out a latch. This means that both latch and spinlock contention is automatically removed. Blocking between read and write transactions can also be reduced because of a new optimistic concurrency method for implementing isolation levels. Transactions and isolation levels, including memory optimized, are discussed in Chapter 18.

■ **Caution**   In the RTM version of SQL Server 2014, using memory-optimized tables may cause the log reuse wait to be incorrectly identified as XPT_CHECKPOINT, when there is, in fact, an entirely different reason for why the log could not be cycled. This can cause operational supportability issues for your databases. Further details of this issue can be found at connect.microsoft.com.

Durability

When creating memory optimized tables, you can specify either SCHEMA_AND_DATA or SCHEMA_ONLY as the durability setting. If you select SCHEMA_AND_DATA, then all of the table's data is persisted to disk and transactions are logged. If you select SCHEMA_ONLY, however, then data is not persisted, and transactions are not logged. This means that after the SQL Server service is restarted, the structure of the table will remain intact, but it will contain no data. This can be useful for transient processes, such as data staging during an ETL load.

Creating and Managing Memory-Optimized Tables

■ **Tip** At first glance, it may be tempting to use memory-optimized tables throughout your database. They have many limitations, however, and, in fact, you should only use them on an exception basis. These limitations will be discussed later in this section.

Before you can create a memory-optimized table, a memory-optimized filegroup must already exist. Memory optimized filegroups are discussed in Chapter 5.

You create memory-optimized tables using the CREATE TABLE T-SQL statement, as you would for a disk-based table. The difference is that you must specify a WITH clause, which specifies that the table will be memory optimized. The WITH clause is also used to indicate the level of durability that you require.

Memory-optimized tables must also include an index. We fully discuss indexes, including indexes for memory-optimized tables, in Chapter 7, but for now, you should know that memory-optimized tables support the following types of indexes:

- Nonclustered hash index

- Nonclustered index

Hash indexes are organized into buckets, and when you create them, you must specify a bucket count using the BUCKET_COUNT parameter. Ideally, your bucket count should be two times the number of distinct values within the index key. You will not always know how many distinct values you have; in such cases, you may wish to significantly increase the BUCKET_COUNT. The tradeoff is that the more buckets you have, the more memory the index consumes. Once you have created the table, the index will be a fixed size and it is not possible to alter the table or its indexes.

The script in Listing 6-14 creates a memory-optimized table called OrdersMem with full durability and populates it with data. It creates a nonclustered hash index on the ID column with a bucket count of 2,000,000, since we will be inserting 1,000,000 rows. The script assumes that the memory-optimized filegroup has already been created.

Listing 6-14. Creating a Memory-Optimized Table

```
USE [Chapter6]
GO

CREATE TABLE dbo.OrdersMem(
        OrderNumber int IDENTITY(1,1) NOT NULL PRIMARY KEY NONCLUSTERED HASH
                                                WITH (BUCKET_COUNT= 2000000),
        OrderDate date NOT NULL,
        CustomerID int NOT NULL,
        ProductID int NOT NULL,
        Quantity int NOT NULL,
        NetAmount money NOT NULL,
        TaxAmount money NOT NULL,
        InvoiceAddressID int NOT NULL,
        DeliveryAddressID int NOT NULL,
        DeliveryDate date NULL,
)WITH (MEMORY_OPTIMIZED = ON, DURABILITY = SCHEMA_AND_DATA) ;
```

```
DECLARE @Numbers TABLE
(
        Number          INT
)

;WITH CTE(Number)
AS
(
        SELECT 1 Number
        UNION ALL
        SELECT Number + 1
        FROM CTE
        WHERE Number < 100
)
INSERT INTO @Numbers
SELECT Number FROM CTE ;

--Populate ExistingOrders with data

INSERT INTO dbo.OrdersMem
SELECT
        (SELECT CAST(DATEADD(dd,(SELECT TOP 1 Number
                                FROM @Numbers
                                ORDER BY NEWID()),getdate())as DATE)),
        (SELECT TOP 1 Number -10 FROM @Numbers ORDER BY NEWID()),
        (SELECT TOP 1 Number FROM @Numbers ORDER BY NEWID()),
        (SELECT TOP 1 Number FROM @Numbers ORDER BY NEWID()),
        500,
        100,
        (SELECT TOP 1 Number FROM @Numbers ORDER BY NEWID()),
        (SELECT TOP 1 Number FROM @Numbers ORDER BY NEWID()),
        (SELECT CAST(DATEADD(dd,(SELECT TOP 1 Number - 10
                                FROM @Numbers
                                ORDER BY NEWID()),getdate()) as DATE))
FROM @Numbers a
CROSS JOIN @Numbers b
CROSS JOIN @Numbers c ;
```

Performance Profile

While memory-optimized tables were in development, they were known as *Hekaton*, which is a play on words, meaning 100 times faster. So let's see how performance compares for different query types between in-memory and disk-based tables. The code in Listing 6-15 creates a new table, called OrdersDisc, and populates it with the data from OrdersMem so that you can run fair tests against the two tables.

■ **Note**   For this benchmarking, the tests are running on a VM, with 2×2 Core vCPUs, 8GB RAM, and a hybrid SSHD (Solid State Hybrid Technology) SATA disk.

Listing 6-15. Creating a Disk-based Table and Populating It with Data

```
USE [Chapter6]
GO

CREATE TABLE dbo.OrdersDisc(
        OrderNumber int NOT NULL,
        OrderDate date NOT NULL,
        CustomerID int NOT NULL,
        ProductID int NOT NULL,
        Quantity int NOT NULL,
        NetAmount money NOT NULL,
        TaxAmount money NOT NULL,
        InvoiceAddressID int NOT NULL,
        DeliveryAddressID int NOT NULL,
        DeliveryDate date NULL,
 CONSTRAINT [PK_OrdersDisc] PRIMARY KEY CLUSTERED
(
        [OrderNumber] ASC,
        [OrderDate] ASC
)
) ;

INSERT INTO dbo.OrdersDisc
        SELECT *
        FROM dbo.OrdersMem ;
```

First, we will run the most basic test—a SELECT * query from each table. The script in Listing 6-16 runs these queries after tearing down the plan cache and the buffer cache to ensure a fair test.

Listing 6-16. The SELECT * Benchmark

```
SET STATISTICS TIME ON

--Tear down the plan cache

DBCC FREEPROCCACHE

--Tear down the buffer cache

DBCC DROPCLEANBUFFERS

--Run the benchmarks

SELECT *
FROM dbo.OrdersMem ;

SELECT *
FROM dbo.OrdersDisc ;
```

From the results in Figure 6-15, you can see that the memory-optimized table returned the results just under 4.5 percent faster.

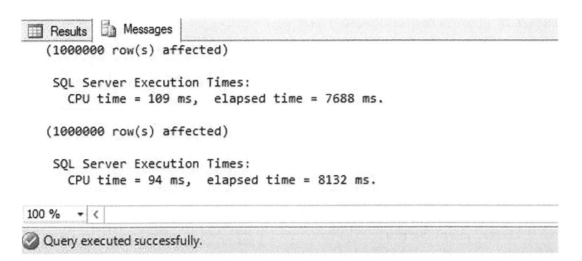

Figure 6-15. *SELECT * benchmark results*

■ **Tip** Naturally, the results you see may vary based on the system on which you run the scripts.
For example, if you have SSDs, then the queries against the disk-based tables may be more comparable.
Also, be aware that this test uses cold data (not in the buffer cache). If the data in the disk-based tables is warm
(in the buffer cache), then you can expect the results to be comparable, or in some cases, the query against the
disk-based table may even be slightly faster.

In the next test, we see what happens if we add in an aggregation. The script in Listing 6-17 runs
COUNT(*) queries against each of the tables.

Listing 6-17. The COUNT(*) Benchmark

```
SET STATISTICS TIME ON

--Tear down the plan cache

DBCC FREEPROCCACHE

--Tear down the buffer cache

DBCC DROPCLEANBUFFERS

--Run the benchmarks

SELECT COUNT(*)
FROM dbo.OrdersMem ;

SELECT COUNT(*)
FROM dbo.OrdersDisc ;
```

From the results in Figure 6-16, we can see that this time, the memory-optimized tabled performed considerably better than the disk-based table, offering us a 340-percent performance improvement over the disk-based table.

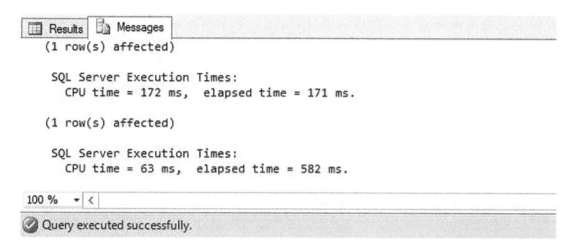

Figure 6-16. *COUNT(*) benchmark results*

It is also interesting to see how memory-optimized tables compare to disk-based tables when there is a filter on the OrderNumber column, since this column is cover by an index on both tables. The script in Listing 6-18 adds the data in the NetAmount column, but it also filters on the OrderNumber column so that only OrderNumbers over 950,000 are considered.

Listing 6-18. Primary Key Filter Benchmark

```
SET STATISTICS TIME ON

--Tear down the plan cache

DBCC FREEPROCCACHE

--Tear down the buffer cache

DBCC DROPCLEANBUFFERS

--Run the benchmarks

SELECT SUM(NetAmount)
FROM dbo.OrdersMem
WHERE OrderNumber > 950000 ;

SELECT SUM(NetAmount)
FROM dbo.OrdersDisc
WHERE OrderNumber > 950000 ;
```

In this instance, because the memory-optimized table was scanned but the clustered index on the disk-based table was able to perform an index seek, the disk-based table performed approximately ten times faster than the memory-optimized table. This is illustrated in Figure 6-17.

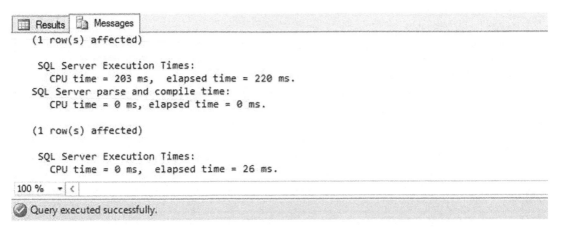

Figure 6-17. SUM filtering on primary key benchmark results

■ **Note**   We would have received a far superior performance for the final query on the memory-optimized table if we had implemented a nonclustered index as opposed to a nonclustered hash index. We completely discuss the impact of indexes in Chapter 7.

Table Memory Optimization Advisor

The Table Memory Optimization Advisor is a wizard that can run against an existing disk-based table and it will walk you through the process of migration. The first page of the wizard checks your table for incompatible features, such as sparse columns and foreign key constraints, as illustrated in Figure 6-18.

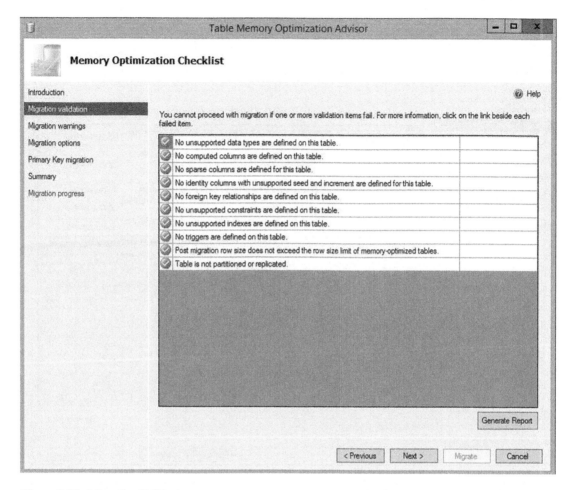

Figure 6-18. *Migration Validation page*

The following page provides you with a warning having to do with which features are not available for memory-optimized tables, such as cross database transaction and TRUNCATE TABLE statements, as shown in Figure 6-19.

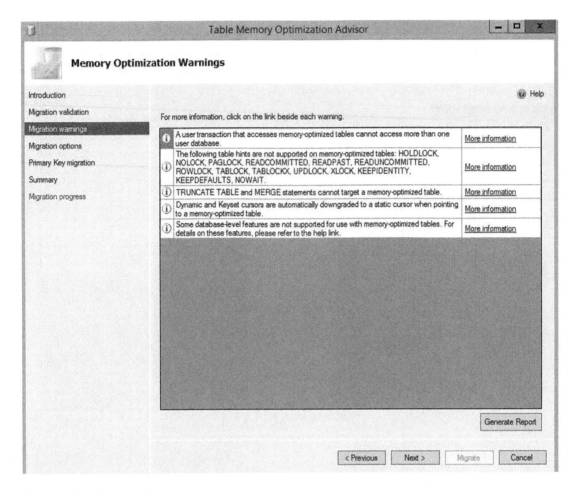

Figure 6-19. *Migration Warnings page*

The Migration Options page of the wizard allows you to specify the durability level of the table. Checking the box causes the table to be created with DURABILITY = SCHEMA_ONLY. On this screen, you can also choose a new name for the disk-based table that you are migrating, since obviously, the new object cannot share the name of the existing object. Finally, you can use the check box to specify if you want the data from the existing table to be copied to the new table. This page of the wizard is illustrated in Figure 6-20.

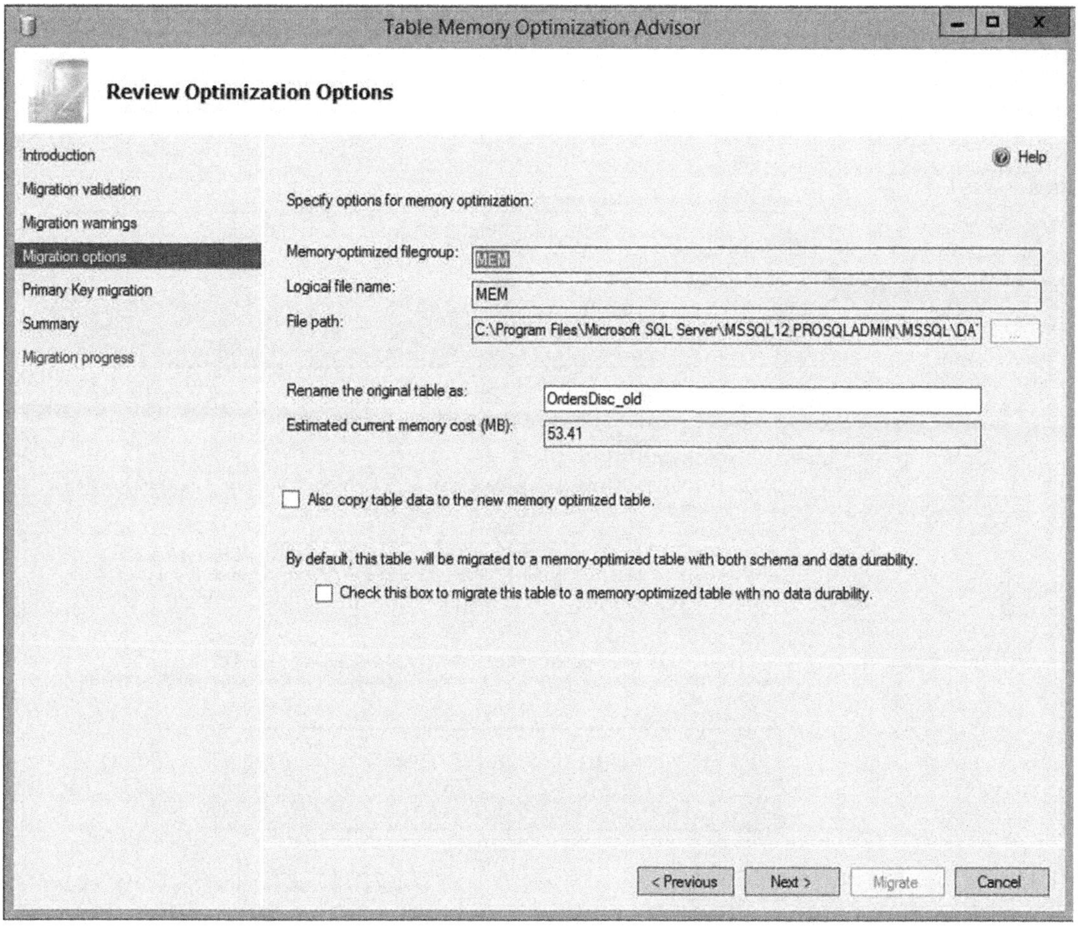

Figure 6-20. *Migration Options page*

The Primary Key Migration page allows you to select the columns that you wish to use to form the primary key of the table as well as the index that you want to create on your table. If you choose a nonclustered hash index, you need to specify the bucket count, whereas if you choose a nonclustered index, you need to specify the columns and order. The Primary Key Migration screen is shown in Figure 6-21.

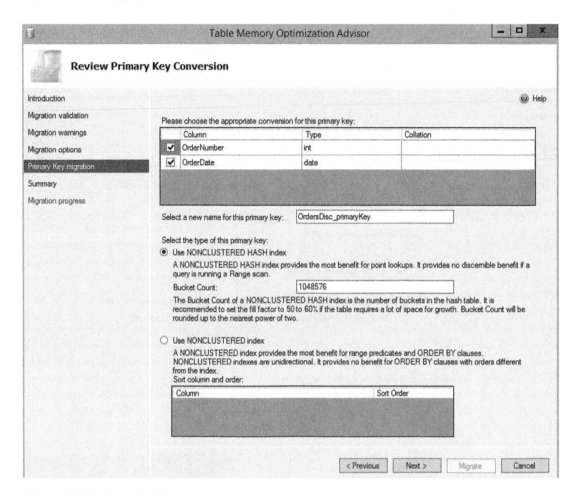

Figure 6-21. *Primary Key Migration screen*

The Summary screen of the wizard provides an overview of the activities that will be performed. Clicking the Migrate button causes the table to be migrated.

Limitations of Memory-Optimized Tables

Not all features are compatible with memory-optimized tables. The following lists the data types that cannot be used with memory-optimized tables:

- DATETIMEOFFSET
- HIERARCHYID
- SQL_VARIANT
- GEOGRAPHY
- GEOMETRY
- ROWVERSION

- `(N)VARCHAR(MAX)`
- `VARBINARY(MAX)`
- `IMAGE`
- `(N)TEXT`
- `XML`

Other table features that are not compatible with memory-optimized tables include the following:

- Computed columns
- Sparse columns
- Foreign key constraints
- Check constraints
- Unique constraints
- `ROWGUIDCOL`
- Altering or rebuilding a table

Also, not all database features and operations are compatible with memory-optimized tables. For example, the following cannot be used against in memory tables:

- Replication (It can still be used against other tables, as long as `sync_method` is not via `database_snapshot`.)
- `DBCC CHECKTABLE`
- `DBCC CHECKDB` (This can still be run in the database, but it will skip memory-optimized tables.)
- Database snapshots
- `MARS`
- `TRUNCATE TABLE`
- `MERGE`
- `AUTO_CLOSE`
- Event notifications
- `UPDATE` statements that change the primary key
- Triggers
- Dynamic and keyset cursors
- Partitioning
- Mirroring
- Transparent Data Encryption (TDE)
- Linked servers
- Change tracking

- Change Data Capture (CDC)

- Policy-based management

- Bulk logged recovery mode

- Some query hints, including HOLDLOCK, NOLOCK, PAGLOCK, READCOMMITTED, READPAST, READUNCOMMITTED, ROWLOCK, TABLOCK, TABLOCKX, UPDLOCK, XLOCK, KEEPIDENTITY, KEEPDEFAULTS, and NOWAIT.

Natively Compiled Objects

In-Memory OLTP introduces native compilation, for both memory-optimized tables and for stored procedures. The following sections discuss these concepts.

Natively Compiled Tables

When you create a memory-optimized table, SQL Server compiles the table to a DLL (dynamic link library) using native code and loads the DLL into memory. You can examine these DLLs by running the query in Listing 6-19. The script examines the dm_os_loaded_modules DMV and then joins to sys.tables using the object_id of the table, which is embedded in the file name of the DLL. This allows the query to return the name of the table.

Listing 6-19. Viewing DLLs for Memory-Optimized Tables

```
SELECT
        m.name DLL
        ,t.name TableName
        ,description
FROM sys.dm_os_loaded_modules m
INNER JOIN sys.tables t
        ON t.object_id =
(SELECT SUBSTRING(m.name, LEN(m.name) + 2 - CHARINDEX('_', REVERSE(m.name)),
len(m.name) - (LEN(m.name) + 2 - CHARINDEX('_', REVERSE(m.name)) + 3) ))
WHERE m.name like '%xtp_t_' + cast(db_id() as varchar(10)) + '%' ;
```

For security reasons, these files are recompiled based on database metadata every time the SQL Server service starts. This means that if the DLLs are tampered with, the changes made will not persist. Additionally, the files are linked to the SQL Server process to prevent them from being modified.

SQL Server automatically removes the DLLs when they are no longer needed. After a table has been dropped and a checkpoint has subsequently been issued, the DLLs are unloaded from memory and physically deleted from the file system, either when the instance is restarted or when the databases are taken offline, or dropped.

Natively Compiled Stored Procedures

In addition to natively compiled memory-optimized tables, SQL Server 2014 also introduces natively compiled stored procedures. As mentioned earlier in this chapter, these procedures can reduce CPU overhead and offer a performance benefit over traditionally interpreted stored procedures because fewer CPU cycles are required during their execution.

The syntax for creating a natively compiled stored procedure is similar to the syntax for creating an interpreted stored procedure, but there are some subtle differences. First, the procedure must start with a BEGIN ATOMIC clause. The body of the procedure must include precisely one BEGIN ATOMIC clause. The transaction within this block will commit when the block ends. The block must terminate with an END statement. When you begin the atomic block, you *must* specify the isolation level and the language to use.

You will also notice that the WITH clause contains NATIVE_COMPILATION, SCHEMABINDING, and EXECUTE AS options. SCHEMABINDING must be specified for natively compiled procedures. This prevents the objects on which it depends from being altered. You must also specify the EXECUTE AS clause because the default value for EXECUTE AS is Caller, but this is not a supported option for native compilation. This has implications if you are looking to migrate your existing interpreted SQL to natively compiled procedures, and it means that you should reassess your security policy as a prerequisite to code migration. The option is fairly self-explanatory.

You can see an example of creating a natively compiled stored procedure in Listing 6-20. This procedure can be used to update the OrdersMem table.

Listing 6-20. Creating a Natively Compiled Stored Procedure

```
CREATE PROCEDURE UpdateOrdersMem
        WITH NATIVE_COMPILATION, SCHEMABINDING, EXECUTE AS OWNER
AS
BEGIN ATOMIC WITH (TRANSACTION ISOLATION LEVEL = SNAPSHOT, LANGUAGE = 'English')
        UPDATE dbo.OrdersMem
                SET DeliveryDate = DATEADD(dd,1,DeliveryDate)
        WHERE DeliveryDate < GETDATE()
END ;
```

When planning a code migration to natively compiled procedures, you should advise your development teams that there are many limitations, and they will not be able to use features including table variables, CTEs (Common Table Expressions), subqueries, the OR operator in WHERE clauses, and UNION.

Like memory-optimized tables, DLLs are also created for natively compiled stored procedures. The modified script in Listing 6-21 displays a list of DLLs associated with natively compiled procedures.

Listing 6-21. Viewing DLLs for Natively Compiled Procedures

```
SELECT
        m.name DLL
        ,o.name ProcedureName
        ,description
FROM sys.dm_os_loaded_modules m
INNER JOIN sys.objects o
        ON o.object_id =
(SELECT SUBSTRING(m.name, LEN(m.name) + 2 - CHARINDEX('_', REVERSE(m.name)),
len(m.name) - (LEN(m.name) + 2 - CHARINDEX('_', REVERSE(m.name)) + 3) ))
WHERE m.name like '%xtp_p_' + cast(db_id() as varchar(10)) + '%' ;
```

197

Summary

SQL Server offers many features for optimizing tables. Partitioning allows tables to be split down into smaller structures, which means that SQL Server can read fewer pages in order to locate the rows that it needs to return. This process is called partition elimination. Partitioning also allows you to perform storage tiering by storing older, less frequently accessed data on inexpensive storage.

SWITCH, SPLIT, and MERGE operations will help you implement sliding windows for your partitioned tables. SWITCH allows you to move data from its current partition to an empty partition or table as a metadata operation. SPLIT and MERGE allow you to insert and remove boundary points in a partition function.

Two compression options are available for row-based tables. These types of compression are designed as a performance enhancement, because they allow SQL Server to reduce the amount of IO it needs to read all of the required rows from a table. Row compression works by storing numeric and Unicode values in the smallest space required, rather than the largest space required, for any acceptable value. Page compression implements row compression, and also prefix and dictionary compression. This provides a higher compression ratio, meaning even less IO, but at the expense of CPU.

Memory-optimized tables are a new feature of SQL Server 2014, which enable massive performance gains by keeping an entire table resident in memory. This can significantly reduce IO pressure. You can use such tables in conjunction with natively compiled stored procedures, which can also increase performance, by interacting directly with the natively compiled DLLs of the memory-optimized tables and by reducing the CPU cycles required, as compared to interpreted code.

CHAPTER 7

■ ■ ■

Indexes and Statistics

Recent versions of SQL Server support many different types of index that are used to enhance query performance. These include traditional clustered and nonclustered indexes, which are built on B-tree (balanced-tree) structures and enhance read performance on disk-based tables. There are also indexes that support complex data types, such as XML. DBAs can also create Columnstore indexes to support data warehouse–style queries, where analysis is performed on very large tables. SQL Server 2014 also introduces in-memory indexes, which enhance the performance of tables that are stored using In-Memory OLTP. This chapter discusses many of the available index types inside the Database Engine.

SQL Server maintains statistics on index and table columns to enhance query performance by improving cardinality estimates. This allows the Query Optimizer to choose the most efficient query plan. This chapter also discusses how to use and maintain statistics.

Clustered Indexes

A *B-tree* is a data structure you can use to organize key values so a user can search for the data they are looking for much more quickly than if they had to read the entire table. It is a tree-based structure where each node is allowed more than two child nodes.

A *clustered index* is a B-tree structure that causes the data pages of a table to be logically stored in the order of the clustered index key. The clustered index key can be a single column, or a set of columns that enforce uniqueness of each row in the table. This key is often the table's primary key, and although this is the most typical usage, in some circumstances, you will want to use a different column. This is discussed in more detail later in this chapter.

Tables without a Clustered Index

When a table exists without a clustered index, it is known as a *heap*. A heap consists of an IAM (index allocation map) page(s) and a series of data pages that are not linked together or stored in order. The only way SQL Server can determine the pages of the table is by reading the IAM page(s). When a table is stored as a heap, without an index, then every time the table is accessed, SQL Server must read every single page in the table, even if you only want to return one row. The diagram in Figure 7-1 illustrates how a heap is structured.

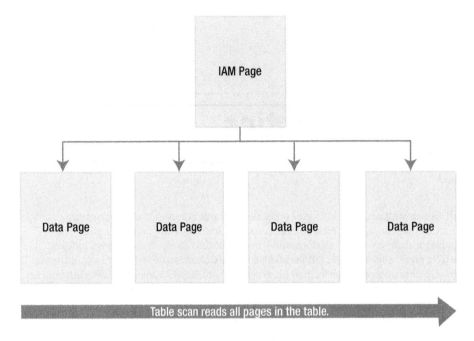

Figure 7-1. *Heap structure*

When data is stored on a heap, SQL Server needs to maintain a unique identifier for each row. It does this by creating a RID (row identifier). A RID has a format of `FileID: Page ID: Slot Number`, which is a physical location. Even if a table has nonclustered indexes, it is still stored as a heap, unless there is a clustered index. When nonclustered indexes are created on a heap, the RID is used as a pointer so that nonclustered indexes can link back to the correct row in the base table.

Tables with a Clustered Index

When you create a clustered index on a table, a B-tree structure is created. This B-tree is based on the values of the clustered key, and if the clustered index is not unique, it also includes a uniquifier. A *uniquifier* is a value used to identify rows if their key values are the same. This allows SQL Server to perform more efficient search operations by creating a tiered set of pointers to the data, as illustrated in Figure 7-2. The page at the top level of this hierarchy is called the *root node*. The bottom level of the structure is called the *leaf level*, and with a clustered index, the leaf level consists of the actual data pages of the table. B-tree structures can have one or more intermediate levels, depending on the size of the table.

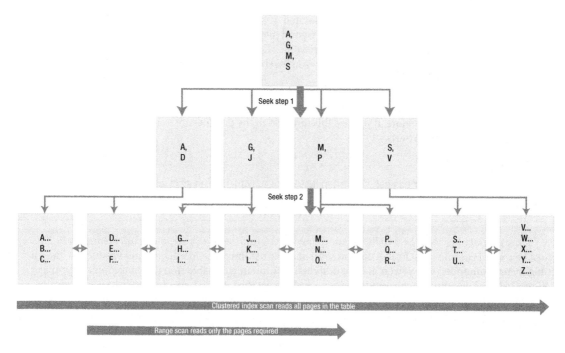

Figure 7-2. *Clustered index structure*

Figure 7-2 shows that although the leaf level is the data itself, the levels above contain pointers to the pages below them in the tree. This allows SQL Server to perform a seek operation, which is a very efficient method of returning a small number of rows. It works by navigating its way down the B-tree, using the pointers, to find the row(s) it requires. In this figure, we can see that, if required, SQL Server can still scan all pages of the table in order to retrieve the required rows—this is known as a *clustered index scan*. Alternatively, SQL Server may decide to combine these two methods to perform a range scan. Here, SQL Server seeks the first value of the required range and then scans the leaf level until it encounters the first value that is not required. SQL Server can do this, because the table is ordered by the index key, which means that it can guarantee that no other matching values appear later in the table.

Clustering the Primary Key

The primary key of a table is often the natural choice for the clustered index, because many OLTP applications access 99 percent of data through the primary key. In fact, by default, unless you specify otherwise, or unless a clustered index already exists on the table, creating a primary key automatically generates a clustered index on that key. There are circumstances when the primary key is not the correct choice for the clustered index. An example of this that I have witnessed is a third-party application that requires the primary key of the table to be a GUID.

Creating a clustered index on a GUID introduces two major problems if the clustered index is to be built on the primary key. The first is size. A GUID is 16 bytes long. When a table has nonclustered indexes, the clustered index key is stored in every nonclustered index. For unique nonclustered indexes, it is stored for every row at the leaf level, and for nonunique nonclustered indexes, it is also stored at every row in the root and intermediate levels of the index. When you multiple 16 bytes by millions of rows, this drastically increases the size of the indexes, making them less efficient.

The second issue is that when a GUID is generated, it is a random value. Because the data in your table is stored in the order of the clustered index key for good performance, you need the values of this key to be generated in sequential order. Generating random values for your clustered index key results in the index becoming more and more fragmented every time you insert a new row. Fragmentation is discussed later in this chapter.

There is a workaround for the second issue, however. SQL Server has a function called NEWSEQUENTIALID(). This function always generates a GUID value that is higher than previous values generated on the server. Therefore, if you use this function in the default constraint of your primary key, you can enforce sequential inserts.

■ **Caution**　After the server has been restarted, NEWSEQUENTIALID() can start with a lower value. This may lead to fragmentation.

If the primary key must be a GUID or another wide column, such as a Social Security Number, or if it must be a set of columns that form a natural key, such as Customer ID, Order Date, and Product ID, then it is highly recommended that you create an additional column in your table. You can make this column an INT or BIGINT, depending on the number of rows you expect the table to have, and you can use either the IDENTITY property or a SEQUENCE in order to create a narrow, sequential key for your clustered index.

■ **Tip**　Remember a narrow clustered key is important because it will be included in all other indexes on the table.

Performance Considerations for Clustered Indexes

Because an IAM page lists the extents of a heap table in the order in which they are stored in the data file, as opposed to the order of the index key, a table scan of a heap may prove to be slightly faster than a clustered index scan. Exceptions to this would be if the clustered index has zero-percent fragmentation, or if the heap has many forwarding pointers.

You can witness this behavior by running the script in Listing 7-1. This script creates two temporary tables. The first is a heap, and the second has a primary key, which has forced a clustered index to be created implicitly. STATISTICS TIME is then turned on, and a SELECT * query is run against each of the tables, which causes a table scan of the heap and a clustered index scan of the second table.

Listing 7-1. Benchmarking a Table Scan against a Clustered Index Scan

```
--Create the OrdersHeap table

CREATE TABLE #OrdersHeap
        (
        OrderNumber int         NOT NULL    IDENTITY,
        OrderDate date          NOT NULL,
        CustomerID int          NOT NULL,
        ProductID int           NOT NULL,
        Quantity int            NOT NULL,
        NetAmount money         NOT NULL,
```

```
        TaxAmount money            NOT NULL,
        InvoiceAddressID int       NOT NULL,
        DeliveryAddressID int      NOT NULL,
        DeliveryDate date          NULL
        )  ON [PRIMARY] ;
GO

--Build a numbers table for the data population

DECLARE @Numbers TABLE
(
        Number          INT
)

;WITH CTE(Number)
AS
(
        SELECT 1 Number
        UNION ALL
        SELECT Number + 1
        FROM CTE
        WHERE Number < 20
)
INSERT INTO @Numbers
SELECT Number FROM CTE ;

--Populate OrdersHeap with data

INSERT INTO #OrdersHeap
SELECT
        (SELECT CAST(DATEADD(dd,(SELECT TOP 1 Number
                            FROM @Numbers
                            ORDER BY NEWID()),GETDATE())as DATE)),
        (SELECT TOP 1 Number -10 FROM @Numbers ORDER BY NEWID()),
        (SELECT TOP 1 Number FROM @Numbers ORDER BY NEWID()),
        (SELECT TOP 1 Number FROM @Numbers ORDER BY NEWID()),
        500,
        100,
        (SELECT TOP 1 Number FROM @Numbers ORDER BY NEWID()),
        (SELECT TOP 1 Number FROM @Numbers ORDER BY NEWID()),
        (SELECT CAST(DATEADD(dd,(SELECT TOP 1 Number - 10
                            FROM @Numbers
                            ORDER BY NEWID()),GETDATE()) as DATE))
FROM @Numbers a
CROSS JOIN @Numbers b ;

--Create the OrdersCI table
```

```
CREATE TABLE #OrdersCI
        (
        OrderNumber int         NOT NULL    IDENTITY,
        OrderDate date          NOT NULL,
        CustomerID int          NOT NULL,
        ProductID int           NOT NULL,
        Quantity int            NOT NULL,
        NetAmount money         NOT NULL,
        TaxAmount money         NOT NULL,
        InvoiceAddressID int    NOT NULL,
        DeliveryAddressID int   NOT NULL,
        DeliveryDate date       NULL
        ) ON [PRIMARY] ;


--Populate OrdersCI with data
--The NEWID() function is used to select a random row

INSERT INTO #OrdersCI
SELECT
        (SELECT CAST(DATEADD(dd,(SELECT TOP 1 Number
                                FROM @Numbers
                                ORDER BY NEWID()),GETDATE()) as DATE)),
        (SELECT TOP 1 Number -10 FROM @Numbers ORDER BY NEWID()),
        (SELECT TOP 1 Number FROM @Numbers ORDER BY NEWID()),
        (SELECT TOP 1 Number FROM @Numbers ORDER BY NEWID()),
        500,
        100,
        (SELECT TOP 1 Number FROM @Numbers ORDER BY NEWID()),
        (SELECT TOP 1 Number FROM @Numbers ORDER BY NEWID()),
        (SELECT CAST(DATEADD(dd,(SELECT TOP 1 Number - 10
                                FROM @Numbers
                                ORDER BY NEWID()),GETDATE()) as DATE))
FROM @Numbers a
CROSS JOIN @Numbers b ;

--Run Benchmarks

SET STATISTICS TIME ON

SELECT * FROM #OrdersHeap ;

SELECT * FROM #OrdersCI ;
```

The results pictured in Figure 7-3 show that the scan of the heap was faster than the scan of the clustered index. This is as expected.

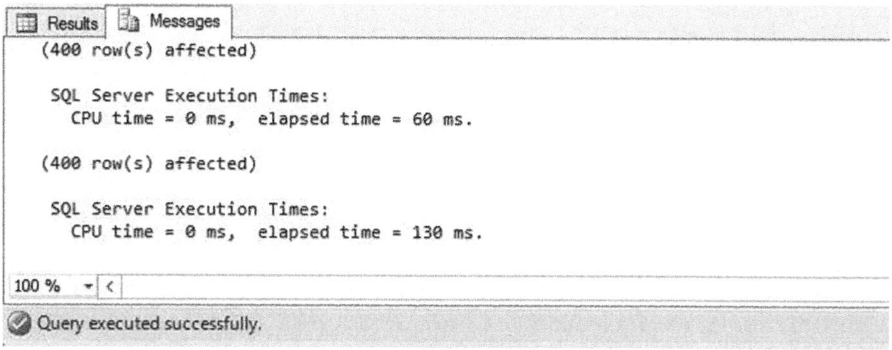

Figure 7-3. *Results of table scan verses clustered index scan bechmark*

Inserts into a clustered index may be faster than inserts into a heap when the clustered index key is ever-increasing. This is especially true when multiple inserts are happening in parallel, because a heap experiences more contention on system pages (GAM/SGAM/PFS) when the database engine is looking for spaces to place the new data. If the clustered index key is not ever-increasing, however, then inserts lead to page splits and fragmentation. The effect of this, is that inserts into a heap are faster. A large insert into a heap may also be faster if you take out a table lock and take advantage of minimally logged inserts. This is because of reduced IO to the transaction log.

Updates that cause a row to relocate due to a change in size are faster when performed against a clustered index, as opposed to a heap. This is for the same reason as mentioned earlier for insert operations, where there is more contention against the system pages. Rows may change in size when updated for reasons such as updating a varchar column with a longer string. If the update to the row can be made in-place (without relocating the row), then there is likely to be little difference in performance. Deletes may also be slightly faster into a clustered index than they are into a heap, but the difference is less noticeable than it is for update operations.

▪ **Tip** If a row in a heap has to relocate, then a forwarding pointer is left in the original page. Many forwarding pointers can have a very detrimental impact on performance.

Administering Clustered Indexes

You can create a clustered index by using the CREATE CLUSTERED INDEX statement, as shown in Listing 7-2. Other methods you can use to create a clustered index are using the ALTER TABLE statement with a PRIMARY KEY clause and using the INDEX clause in the CREATE TABLE statement, as long as you are using SQL Server 2014 or higher. This script creates a database called Chapter7 and then a table called CIDemo. Finally, it creates a clustered index on the ID column of this table.

■ **Note**   Remember to change the file locations to match your own configuration.

Listing 7-2. Creating a Clustered Index

```
--Create Chapter7 Database

CREATE DATABASE Chapter7
 ON  PRIMARY
( NAME = N'Chapter7', FILENAME =
    N'F:\Program Files\Microsoft SQL Server\MSSQL12.PROSQLADMIN\MSSQL\DATA\Chapter7.mdf'),
 FILEGROUP [MEM] CONTAINS MEMORY_OPTIMIZED_DATA  DEFAULT
( NAME = N'MEM', FILENAME = N'H:\DATA\CH07')
 LOG ON
( NAME = N'Chapter7_log', FILENAME =
    N'E:\Program Files\Microsoft SQL Server\MSSQL12.PROSQLADMIN\MSSQL\DATA\Chapter7_log.ldf') ;
GO

USE Chapter7
GO

--Create CIDemo table

CREATE TABLE dbo.CIDemo
(
        ID              INT                 IDENTITY,
        DummyText       VARCHAR(30)
) ;
GO

--Create clustered index

CREATE UNIQUE CLUSTERED INDEX dbo.CI_CIDemo ON dbo.CIDemo([ID]) ;
GO
```

When creating an index, you have a number of WITH options that you can specify. These options are outlined in Table 7-1.

Table 7-1. *Clustered Index WITH Options*

Option	Description
MAXDOP	Specifies how many cores are used to build the index. Each core that is used builds its own portion of the index. The tradeoff is that a higher MAXOP builds the index faster, but a lower MAXDOP means the index is built with less fragmentation.
FILLFACTOR	Specifies how much free space should be left in each page of the leaf level of the index. This can help reduce fragmentation caused by inserts at the expense of having a wider index, which requires more IO to read. For a clustered index, with a non-changing, ever-increasing key, always set this to 0, which means 100-percent full minus enough space for one row.
PAD_INDEX	Applies the fill factor percentage to the intermediate levels of the B-tree.
STATISTICS_NORECOMPUTE	Turns on or off the automatic updating of distribution statistics. Statistics are discussed later in this chapter.
SORT_IN_TEMPDB	Specifies that the intermediate sort results of the index should be stored in TempDB. When you use this option, you can offload IO to the spindles hosting TempDB, but this is at the expense of using more disk space.
STATISTICS_INCREMENTAL	Specifies if statistics should be created per partition. Limitations to this are discussed later in this chapter.
DROP_EXISTING	Used to drop and rebuild the existing index with the same name.
IGNORE_DUP_KEY	When you enable this option, an insert statement that tries to insert a duplicate key value into a unique index will not fail. Instead, a warning is generated and only the rows that break the unique constraint fail.
ONLINE = OFF	Specifies that the entire table and indexes should not be locked for the duration of the index build or rebuild. This means that queries are still able to access the table during the operation. This is at the expense of the time it takes to build the index. For clustered indexes, this option is not available if the table contains LOB data.*
ALLOW_ROW_LOCKS	Specifies that you can take row locks out when accessing the table. This does not means that they definitely will be taken.
ALLOW_PAGE_LOCKS	Specifies that you can take page locks out when accessing the table. This does not means that they definitely will be taken.

Spatial data is regarded as LOB data.

As mentioned earlier in this chapter, if you create a primary key on a table, then unless you specify the NONCLUSTERED keyword, or a clustered index already exists, a clustered index is created automatically to cover the column(s) of the primary key. Also, remember that at times you may wish to move the clustered index to a more suitable column if the primary key is wide or if it is not ever-increasing.

In order to achieve this, you need to drop the primary key constraint and then re-create it using the NONCLUSTERED keyword. This forces SQL Server to cover the primary key with a unique nonclustered index. Once this is complete, you are able to create the clustered index on the column of your choosing.

If you need to remove a clustered index that is not covering a primary key, you can do so by using the DROP INDEX statement, as demonstrated in Listing 7-3, which drops the clustered index that we created in the previous example.

Listing 7-3. Dropping the Index

```
DROP INDEX dbo.CI_CIDemo ON CIDemo ;
```

Nonclustered Indexes

A nonclustered index is based on a B-tree structure in the same way that a clustered index is. The difference is that the leaf level of a nonclustered index contains pointers to the data pages of the table, as opposed to being the data pages of the table, as illustrated in Figure 7-4. This means that a table can have multiple nonclustered indexes to support query performance.

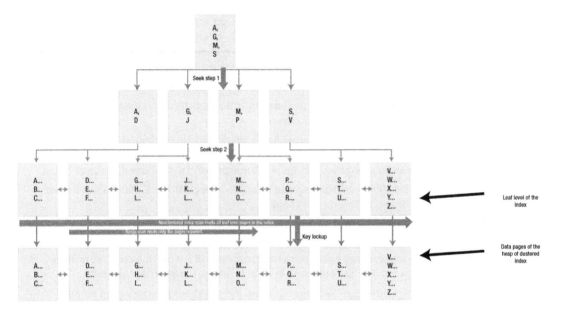

Figure 7-4. *Nonclustered index structure*

Just like a clustered index, a nonclustered index supports seek, scan, and range scan operations in order to find the required data. If the index key of the nonclustered index includes all columns that need to be accessed during a query, then you do not need for SQL Server to access the underlying table. This also holds true if the only columns accessed are in the nonclustered index and the clustered index key. This is because the leaf level of a nonclustered index always contains the clustered index key. This is referred to as an index *covering the query*, which is discussed in the next section.

If the query needs to returns columns that are not included in the nonclustered index or clustered index key, SQL Server needs to find the matching rows in the base table. This is done through a process called a *key lookup*. A key lookup operation accesses the rows required from the base table using either the clustered index key value or the RID if the table does not have a clustered index.

This can be efficient for a small number of rows, but it quickly becomes expensive if many rows are returned by the query. This means that if many rows will be returned, SQL Server may decide that it is less expensive to ignore the nonclustered index and use the clustered index or heap instead. This decision is known as *the tipping point* of the index. The tipping point varies from table to table, but it is generally between 0.5 percent and 2 percent of the table.

Covering Indexes

Although having all required columns within the nonclustered index means that you do not have to retrieve data from the underlying table, the tradeoff is that having many columns within a nonclustered index can lead to very wide, inefficient indexes. In order to gain a better balance, SQL Server offers you the option of included columns.

Included columns are included at the leaf level of the index only, as opposed to the index key values, which continue to be included at every level of the B-tree. This feature can help you cover your queries, while maintaining the narrowest index keys possible. This concept is illustrated in Figure 7-5. This diagram illustrates that the index has been built using Balance as the index key, but the FirstName and LastName columns have also been included at the leaf level. You can see that CustomerID has also been included at all levels; this is because CustomerID is the clustered index key. Because the clustered index key is included at all levels, this implies that the index is not unique. If it is unique, then the clustered key is only included at the leaf level of the B-tree. This means that unique, nonclustered indexes are always narrower than their nonunique equivalents. This index is perfect for a query that filters on Balance in the WHERE clause and returns the FirstName and LastName columns. It also covers queries that returned CustomerID in the results.

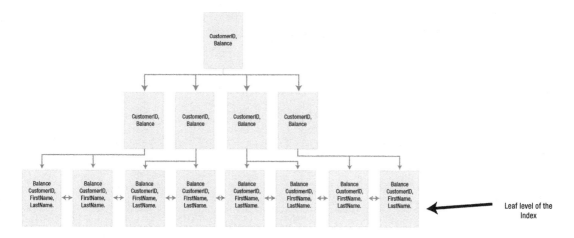

Figure 7-5. *Nonclustered index with included columns*

■ **Tip** If both the clustered and nonclustered indexes are nonunique, each level of the nonclustered B-tree includes the clustering uniquifier, as well as the clustered key.

You can also use the index illustrated in Figure 7-5 to cover queries that filter on FirstName or LastName in the WHERE clause providing that other columns from the table are not returned. To process the query, however, SQL Server needs to perform an index scan, as opposed to an index seek or range scan, which is, of course, less efficient.

Administering Nonclustered Indexes

You can create nonclustered indexes using the CREATE NONCLUSTERED INDEX T-SQL statement. The script in Listing 7-4 creates a table called Customers and a table called Orders within the Chapter7 database. It then creates a foreign key constraint on the CustomerID column. Finally, a nonclustered index is created on the Balance column of the Customers table. Clustered indexes are created automatically on the primary key columns of each table.

■ **Caution**   Due to the nature of Listing 7-4, it may take a very long time to execute. The exact execution time varies depending on your system's performance, but it is likely to take at least several hours.

Listing 7-4. Creating Tables and Then Adding a Nonclustered Index

```
USE Chapter7
GO

--Create and populate numbers table

DECLARE @Numbers TABLE
(
        Number          INT
)

;WITH CTE(Number)
AS
(
        SELECT 1 Number
        UNION ALL
        SELECT Number + 1
        FROM CTE
        WHERE Number < 100
)
INSERT INTO @Numbers
SELECT Number FROM CTE ;

--Create and populate name pieces

DECLARE @Names TABLE
(
        FirstName       VARCHAR(30),
        LastName        VARCHAR(30)
) ;

INSERT INTO @Names
VALUES('Peter', 'Carter'),
                ('Michael', 'Smith'),
                ('Danielle', 'Mead'),
                ('Reuben', 'Roberts'),
```

```
                    ('Iris', 'Jones'),
                    ('Sylvia', 'Davies'),
                    ('Finola', 'Wright'),
                    ('Edward', 'James'),
                    ('Marie', 'Andrews'),
                    ('Jennifer', 'Abraham') ;

--Create and populate Customers table

CREATE TABLE dbo.CustomersDisc
(
        CustomerID          INT                 NOT NULL    IDENTITY    PRIMARY KEY,
        FirstName           VARCHAR(30)         NOT NULL,
        LastName            VARCHAR(30)         NOT NULL,
        BillingAddressID    INT                 NOT NULL,
        DeliveryAddressID   INT                 NOT NULL,
        CreditLimit         MONEY               NOT NULL,
        Balance             MONEY               NOT NULL
) ;

SELECT * INTO #CustomersDisc
FROM
        (SELECT
                (SELECT TOP 1 FirstName FROM @Names ORDER BY NEWID()) FirstName,
                (SELECT TOP 1 LastName FROM @Names ORDER BY NEWID()) LastName,
                (SELECT TOP 1 Number FROM @Numbers ORDER BY NEWID()) BillingAddressID,
                (SELECT TOP 1 Number FROM @Numbers ORDER BY NEWID()) DeliveryAddressID,
                (SELECT TOP 1
                    CAST(RAND() * Number AS INT) * 10000
                    FROM @Numbers
                    ORDER BY NEWID()) CreditLimit,
                (SELECT TOP 1
                    CAST(RAND() * Number AS INT) * 9000
                    FROM @Numbers
                    ORDER BY NEWID()) Balance
        FROM @Numbers a
        CROSS JOIN @Numbers b
) a ;

INSERT INTO dbo.CustomersDisc
SELECT * FROM #CustomersDisc ;
GO

--Create Numbers table

DECLARE @Numbers TABLE
(
        Number          INT
)
```

```
;WITH CTE(Number)
AS
(
        SELECT 1 Number
        UNION ALL
        SELECT Number + 1
        FROM CTE
        WHERE Number < 100
)
INSERT INTO @Numbers
SELECT Number FROM CTE ;

--Create the Orders table

CREATE TABLE dbo.OrdersDisc
        (
        OrderNumber     INT      NOT NULL        IDENTITY        PRIMARY KEY,
        OrderDate       DATE     NOT NULL,
        CustomerID      INT      NOT NULL,
        ProductID       INT      NOT NULL,
        Quantity        INT      NOT NULL,
        NetAmount       MONEY    NOT NULL,
        DeliveryDate    DATE         NULL
        ) ON [PRIMARY] ;

--Populate Orders with data

SELECT * INTO #OrdersDisc
FROM
        (SELECT
                (SELECT CAST(DATEADD(dd,(SELECT TOP 1 Number
                                        FROM @Numbers
                                        ORDER BY NEWID()),GETDATE())as DATE))
                                        OrderDate,
                (SELECT TOP 1 CustomerID FROM CustomersDisc ORDER BY NEWID()) CustomerID,
                (SELECT TOP 1 Number FROM @Numbers ORDER BY NEWID()) ProductID,
                (SELECT TOP 1 Number FROM @Numbers ORDER BY NEWID()) Quantity,
                (SELECT TOP 1 CAST(RAND() * Number AS INT) +10 * 100
                    FROM @Numbers
                    ORDER BY NEWID()) NetAmount,
                (SELECT CAST(DATEADD(dd,(SELECT TOP 1 Number - 10
                                        FROM @Numbers
                                        ORDER BY NEWID()),GETDATE()) as DATE))
                                        DeliveryDate
        FROM @Numbers a
        CROSS JOIN @Numbers b
        CROSS JOIN @Numbers c
) a ;
```

```
INSERT INTO OrdersDisc
SELECT * FROM #OrdersDisc ;

--Clean-up Temp Tables

DROP TABLE #CustomersDisc ;

DROP TABLE #OrdersDisc ;

--Add foreign key on CustomerID

ALTER TABLE dbo.OrdersDisc ADD CONSTRAINT
     FK_OrdersDisc_CustomersDisc FOREIGN KEY
      (
     CustomerID
     ) REFERENCES dbo.CustomersDisc
      (
     CustomerID
     ) ON UPDATE  NO ACTION
      ON DELETE  NO ACTION ;

--Create a nonclustered index on Balance

CREATE NONCLUSTERED INDEX NCI_Balance ON dbo.CustomersDisc(Balance) ;
```

We can change the definition of the NCI_Balance index to include the FirstName and LastName columns by using the CREATE NONCLUSTERED INDEX statement and specifying the DROP_EXISTING option as demonstrated in Listing 7-5.

Listing 7-5. Altering the Index to Include Columns

```
CREATE NONCLUSTERED INDEX NCI_Balance ON dbo.CustomersDisc(Balance)
    INCLUDE(LastName, FirstName)
    WITH(DROP_EXISTING = ON) ;
```

You can drop the index in the same way that we dropped the clustered index earlier in this chapter—using a DROP INDEX statement. In this case, the full statement would be DROP INDEX NCI_Balance ON dbo.CustomersDisc.

Performance Considerations

Although nonclustered indexes can dramatically improve the performance of SELECT queries, at the same time, they can have a negative impact on INSERT operations. This is because an insert never benefits from a search on the index key, because the value does not yet exist. At the same time, while adding the new row(s) to the base table, SQL Server also has to modify all of the nonclustered indexes on the table to add a pointer to the new row. Therefore, the more nonclustered indexes are on the table, the more overhead there is.

Nonclustered indexes can have either a negative or positive impact on UPDATE and DELETE operations. When an UPDATE or DELETE operation is performed, you need to make changes in the nonclustered indexes; this increases the overhead. If you imagine a table with one million rows, however, and you wish to delete or update a single row in that table, if you can find the row by using a nonclustered index seek, as opposed to a table scan, then the operation will be faster when using the supporting index.

213

So we know that nonclustered indexes can dramatically improve query performance, but exactly how much difference can the correct indexes make? Well, our OrdersDisc table is fairly substantial, with one million rows. Assuming that at this point, the only index on the OrdersDisc table is the clustered index on the OrderID column, we can run the query in Listing 7-6 to gain a baseline of performance. As with all benchmarking queries in this book, we start by tearing down the procedure cache and removing clean pages from the buffer cache to ensure a fair test. In this case, in addition to turning on STATISTICS TIME, we also turn on STATISTICS IO so that we can see how many pages are being read.

■ **Note**   For this benchmarking, note that the tests are running on a VM with 2×2 Core vCPUs and 8GB RAM.

Listing 7-6. OrdersDisc Table Baseline Performance

```
USE Chapter7
GO

DBCC FREEPROCCACHE
DBCC DROPCLEANBUFFERS

SET STATISTICS TIME ON
SET STATISTICS IO ON

SELECT CustomerID, ProductID, Quantity
FROM dbo.OrdersDisc
WHERE CustomerID = 88 ;
```

The results in Figure 7-6 show that 4484 pages were read from disk (3 physical and 4481 read-ahead) and that the query completed in 852ms. Because we have no nonclustered indexes, SQL Server has no other option than to perform a clustered index scan.

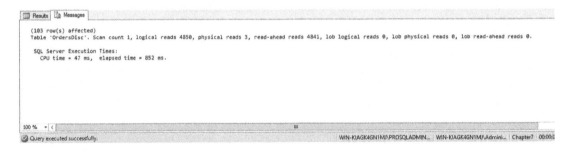

Figure 7-6. Table baseline results

■ **Note**   In my test, 103 records returned, but due to the random data that is generated, this number can be different if you run the code samples in this chapter.

Let's now create a nonclustered index on the `CustomerID` column. Because `CustomerID` is in the `WHERE` clause, SQL Server is able to use this index to perform a seek operation on `CustomerID` 88. It then needs to perform a key lookup operation against the clustered index in order to retrieve the `ProductID` and `Quantity` columns. Listing 7-7 creates the index and runs the test.

Listing 7-7. Benchmarking a Nonclustered Index

```
USE Chapter7
GO

--Create nonclustered index

CREATE NONCLUSTERED INDEX NCI_CustomerID ON dbo.OrdersDisc(CustomerID) ;
GO

--Drop cache

DBCC FREEPROCCACHE
DBCC DROPCLEANBUFFERS

--Turn on statistics capture

SET STATISTICS TIME ON
SET STATISTICS IO ON

--Run the benchmark
SELECT CustomerID, ProductID, Quantity
FROM dbo.OrdersDisc
WHERE CustomerID = 88 ;
```

The results in Figure 7-7 show that this time, the query took only 85ms to execute. This is 10 percent of the time of the baseline test. This is because only 875 pages needed to be read from disk.

Figure 7-7. *Benchmark with nonclustered index results*

Figure 7-8 shows the execution plan for this query; it demonstrates the seek of the nonclustered index, followed by the key lookup to the clustered index.

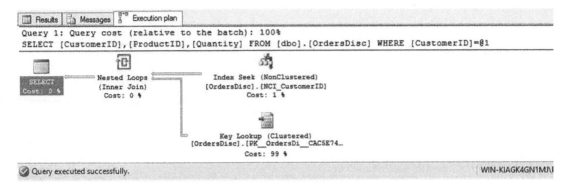

Figure 7-8. *Benchmark with nonclustered index execution plan*

The next test is to alter the nonclustered index to include the ProductID and Quantity columns. This allows SQL Server to satisfy the entire query from the nonclustered index without accessing the base table at all. The script in Listing 7-8 makes this change to the index before rerunning the benchmark query.

Listing 7-8. Bechmark with Nonclustered Index, Containing Included Columns

```
USE Chapter7
GO

--Create nonclustered index

CREATE NONCLUSTERED INDEX NCI_CustomerID ON dbo.OrdersDisc(CustomerID)
    INCLUDE (ProductID, Quantity)
    WITH(DROP_EXISTING = ON) ;
GO

--Drop cache

DBCC FREEPROCCACHE
DBCC DROPCLEANBUFFERS

--Turn on statistics capture

SET STATISTICS TIME ON
SET STATISTICS IO ON

--Run the benchmark
SELECT CustomerID, ProductID, Quantity
FROM dbo.OrdersDisc
WHERE CustomerID = 88 ;
```

The results in Figure 7-9 show that we have now brought the pages that need to be read from disk down to just two, and the execution time has reduced down to a mere 3ms.

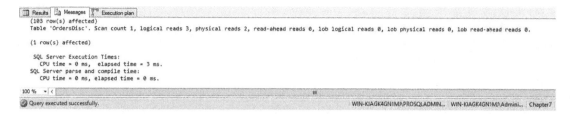

Figure 7-9. *Benchmark with nonclustered index, containing included columns results*

The execution plan for this query is shown in Figure 7-10. As you can see, the Query Optimizer is able to perform a nonclustered index seek without performing a key lookup to the clustered index.

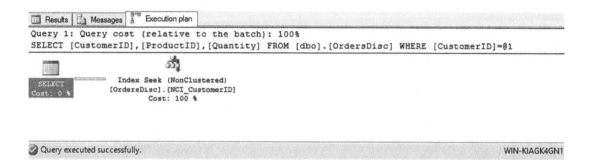

Figure 7-10. *Benchmark with nonclustered index, containing included columns execution plan*

When you create covering indexes, if you are only concerned with read performance, you want columns that are included in the WHERE clause, the JOIN clause, or the GROUP BY clause, or those that are involved in aggregations to be in the index key. You then want any columns that are returned with the query results but are not involved in these operations to be added as included columns. If any of the included columns are involved in the operations just mentioned, SQL Server may still be able to use the index, but only with a nonclustered index scan, as opposed to a nonclustered index seek. As you have seen in this section, a scan operation is less efficient than a seek operation, because it involves additional IO.

Because nonclustered indexes improve query performance but can have a negative impact on DML operations, it is sensible for DBAs to remove indexes that are infrequently used. You can identify indexes that are not being used by using the sys.dm_db_index_usage_stats DMV. The query in Listing 7-9 demonstrates using this DMV to find indexes that are infrequently used.

Listing 7-9. Sys.dm_db_index_usage_stats

```
SELECT
--The name of the database in which the index resides
DB_NAME(database_id) 'Database'
--The name of the table on which the index was created
,OBJECT_NAME(i.object_id) TableName
--The ID of the index
,i.index_id
--The name of the index (unique within a table)
,i.name
--The number of seeks performed against the index by user queries
```

217

```
,user_seeks
--The last time a user query performed a seek against the index
,last_user_seek
--The number of scans performed against the index by user queries
,user_scans
--The last time that a user query performed a scan of the index
,last_user_scan
--The number of lookup operations performed on the index by user queries
,user_lookups
--The last time that a user query performed a lookup against the index
,last_user_lookup
--The number of user queries that have performed updates by using the index
,user_updates
--The last time a user query performed an update by using the index
,last_user_update
FROM sys.dm_db_index_usage_stats ius
INNER JOIN sys.indexes i
ON ius.object_id = I.object_id
        AND ius.index_id = i.index_id
ORDER BY user_updates - (user_seeks + user_scans + user_lookups) DESC ;
```

Indexes that have few scans or seeks, or indexes that have not been used for a significant amount of time, may be candidates for removal. This is even more important if the value for user_updates is high. This column increments every time the index needs to be modified because of DML statements in the base table.

■ **Caution**   There is no substitute for business knowledge, and just because you identify an index that has not been used for nearly a month does not necessarily mean that you should remove it. What if the index is used to support a time-critical business function that happens on a monthly basis? Always look deeper and never remove indexes without thought and consideration.

Filtered Indexes

A filtered index is an index built on a subset of the data stored within a table, as opposed to one that is built on all of the data in the table. Because the indexes are smaller, they can lead to improved query performance and reduced storage cost. They also have the potential to cause less overhead for DML operations, since they only need to be updated if the DML operation affects the data within the index. For example, if an index was filtered on OrderDate >= '2014-01-01' AND OrderDate <= '2014-12-31' and subsequently updated all rows in the table where the OrderDate >= '2015-01-01', then the performance of the update would be the same as if the index did not exist.

Filtered indexes are constructed by using a WHERE clause on index creation. There are many things that you can do in the WHERE clause, such as filter on NULL or NOT NULL values; use equality and inequality operators, such as =, >, <, and IN; and use logical operators, such as AND and OR. There are also limitations, however. For example, you cannot use BETWEEN, CASE, or NOT IN. Also, you can only use simple predicates so, for example, using a date/time function is prohibited, so creating a rolling filter is not possible. You also cannot compare a column to other columns.

The statement in Listing 7-10 creates a filtered index on DelieveryDate, where the value is NULL. This allows you to make performance improvements on queries that are run to determine which orders are yet to have their delivery scheduled.

Listing 7-10. Creating Filtered Index

```
CREATE NONCLUSTERED INDEX NonDeliveredItems ON dbo.OrdersDisc(DeliveryDate)
      WHERE DeliveryDate IS NULL ;
```

Indexes for Specialized Application

In addition to traditional B-tree indexes, SQL Server also provides several types of special indexes to help query performance against memory-optimized tables and against special data types within SQL Server, such as XML. The following sections discuss these special indexes. Although beyond the scope of this book, SQL Server also offers special indexes for geospatial data.

Columnstore Indexes

As you have seen, traditional indexes store rows of data on data pages. This is known as a *rowstore*. SQL Server also supports *columnstore* indexes. These indexes flip data around and use a page to store a column, as opposed to a set of rows. This is illustrated in Figure 7-11.

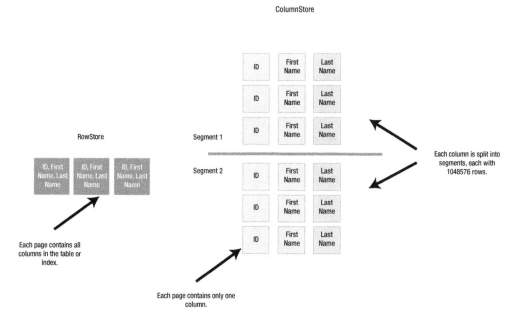

Figure 7-11. *Colunstore index structure*

A columnstore index slices the rows of a table into chunks of between 102,400 and 1,048,576 rows each. Each slice is called a *rowgroup*. Data in each rowgroup is then split down into columns and compressed using VertiPaq technology. Each column within a rowgroup is called a *column segment*.

Columnstore indexes offer several benefits over traditional indexes, given appropriate usage scenarios. First, because they are highly compressed, they can improve IO efficiency and reduce memory overhead. They can achieve such a high compression rate because data within a single column is often very similar between rows. Also, because a query is able to retrieve just the data pages of the column it requires, IO can again be reduced. This is helped even further by the fact that each column segment contains a header with

219

metadata about the data within the segment. This means that SQL Server can access just the segments it needs, as opposed to the whole column. A new query execution mechanism has also been introduced to support columnstore indexes. It is called batch execution mode, and it allows data to be processed in chunks of 1000 rows, as opposed to on a row-by-row basis. This means that CPU usage is much more efficient. Columnstore indexes are not a magic bullet, however, and are designed to be optimal for data-warehouse style queries that perform read-only operations on very large tables. OLTP-style queries are not likely to see any benefit, and in some cases, may actually execute slower. SQL Server 2014 supports both clustered and nonclustered columnstore indexes, and these are discussed in the following sections.

Clustered Columnstore Indexes

Clustered columnstore indexes are new in SQL Server 2014 and cause the entire table to be stored in a columnstore format. There is no traditional rowstore storage for a table with a clustered columnstore index; however, new rows that are inserted into the table may temporarily be placed into a rowstore table, called a *deltastore*. This is to prevent the columnstore index from becoming fragmented and to enhance performance for DML operations. The diagram in Figure 7-12 illustrates this.

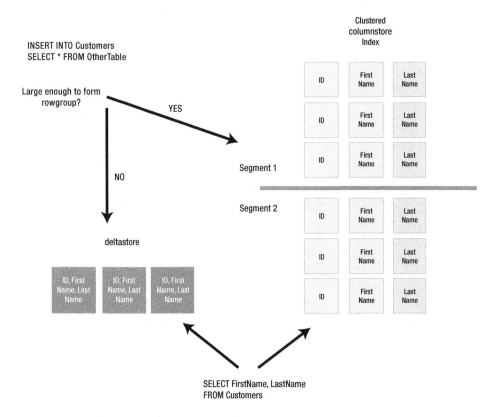

Figure 7-12. *Clustered columnstore index with deltastores*

The diagram shows that when data is inserted into a clustered columnstore index, SQL Server assesses the number of rows. If the number of rows is high enough to achieve a good compression rate, SQL Server treats them as a rowgroup or rowgroups and immediately compresses them and adds them to the columnstore index. If there are too few rows however, SQL Server inserts them into the internal deltastore structure. When you run a query against the table, the database engine seamlessly joins the structures together and returns the results as one. Once there are enough rows, the deltastore is marked as closed and a background process called the *tuple* compresses the rows into a rowgroup in the columnstore index.

There can be multiple deltastores for each clustered columnstore index. This is because, when SQL Server determines that an insert warrants using a deltastore, it attempts to access the existing deltastores. If all existing deltastores are locked, however, then a new one is created, instead of the query being forced to wait for a lock to be released.

When a row is deleted in a clustered columnstore index, then the row is only logically removed. The data still physically stays in the rowgroup until the next time the index is rebuilt. SQL Server maintains a B-tree structure of pointers to deleted rows in order to easily identify them. If the row being deleted is located in a deltastore, as opposed to the index itself, then it is immediately deleted, both logically and physically. When you update a row in a clustered columnstore index, then SQL Server marks the row as being logically deleted and inserts a new row into a deltastore, which contains the new values for the row.

You can create clustered columnstore indexes using a `CREATE CLUSTERED COLUMNSTORE INDEX` statement. Although a clustered columnstore index cannot coexist with traditional indexes, if a traditional clustered index already exists on the table, then you can create the clustered columnstore index using the `DROP_EXISTING` option. The script in Listing 7-11 copies the contents of the `OrdersDisc` table to a new table called `OrdersColumnstore` and then creates a clustered columnstore index on the table. When you create the index, you do not need to specify a key column; this is because all of the columns are added to column segments within the columnstore index. Your queries can then use the index to search on whichever column(s) it needs to satisfy the query. The clustered columnstore index is the only index on the table. You are not able to create traditional nonclustered indexes or a nonclustered columnstore index. Additionally, the table must not have primary key, foreign key, or unique constraints.

Listing 7-11. Creating a Clustered Columnstore Index

```
SELECT * INTO dbo.OrdersColumnstore
FROM dbo.OrdersDisc ;
GO

CREATE CLUSTERED COLUMNSTORE INDEX CCI_OrdersColumnstore ON dbo.OrdersColumnstore ;
```

Not all data types are supported when you are using columnstore indexes. It is not possible to create a clustered columnstore index on tables that contain the following data types:

- TEXT
- NTEXT
- IMAGE
- VARCHAR(MAX)
- NVARCHAR(MAX)
- ROWVERSION
- SQL_VARIANT
- HIERARCHYID
- GEOGRAPHY
- GEOMETRY
- XML

Nonclustered Columnstore Indexes

Nonclustered columnstore indexes are not updateable. This means that if you create a nonclustered columnstore index on a table, that table becomes read only. The only way you can update or delete data from that table is to first drop or disable the columnstore index, and then re-create it once the DML process has completed. To insert data into a table with a nonclustered columnstore index, you must first either drop or disable the columnstore index or, alternatively, use partition switching to bring the data in. Partition switching is discussed in Chapter 6.

It is appropriate to use a nonclustered columnstore index instead of a clustered columnstore index when the table supports multiple workload profiles. In this scenario, the nonclustered columnstore index supports real-time analytics, whereas OLTP-style queries can make use of a traditional clustered index.

The statement in Listing 7-12 creates a nonclustered columnstore index on the FirstName, LastName, Balance, and CustomerID columns of the CustomersDisc table. You can see from our creation of this index that unlike clustered columnstore indexes, nonclustered columnstore indexes can coexist with traditional indexes and, in this case, we even cover some of the same columns.

Listing 7-12. Creating Nonclustered Columnstore Indexes

```
CREATE NONCLUSTERED COLUMNSTORE INDEX NCCI_FirstName_LastName_Balance_CustomerID
    ON dbo.CustomersDisc(FirstName,LastName,Balance,CustomerID) ;
```

Performance Considerations for Columnstore Indexes

In this section, we examine how different types of query perform when they are able to use a columnstore index, as opposed to a traditional index. We start with a simple SELECT * query, which uses a clustered index scan on the OrdersDisc table and a columnstore index scan on the OrdersColumnstore table, which of course, hold the same data. The script in Listing 7-13 runs this benchmark.

Listing 7-13. Clustered Index Scan against Columnstore Index Scan

```
DBCC FREEPROCCACHE
DBCC DROPCLEANBUFFERS

SET STATISTICS TIME ON
SET STATISTICS IO ON

SELECT * FROM OrdersDisc ;

SELECT * FROM OrdersColumnstore ;
```

As you can see from the results in Figure 7-13, the clustered index actually performs better than the columnstore index.

```
Results   Messages   Execution plan
(1000000 row(s) affected)
Table 'OrdersDisc'. Scan count 1, logical reads 4850, physical reads 3, read-ahead reads 4841, lob logical reads 0, lob physical reads 0, lob read-ahead reads 0.

(1 row(s) affected)

 SQL Server Execution Times:
   CPU time = 140 ms,  elapsed time = 5051 ms.

(1000000 row(s) affected)
Table 'OrdersColumnstore'. Scan count 1, logical reads 1923, physical reads 6, read-ahead reads 5483, lob logical reads 0, lob physical reads 0, lob read-ahead reads 0.

(1 row(s) affected)

 SQL Server Execution Times:
   CPU time = 235 ms,  elapsed time = 6298 ms.
100 %
 Query executed successfully.                                    WIN-KIAGK4GN1MJ\PROSQLADMIN...  WIN-KIAGK4GN1MJ\Admini...  Chapter7  00:00:12  2000
```

Figure 7-13. *Clustered index scan against columnstore index scan results*

When we start to perform analysis on large datasets, we start to see the benefits of the columnstore index. The script in Listing 7-14 creates a nonclustered index to cover the CustomerID and NetAmount columns of the OrdersDisc table before it runs a benchmark test, which adds the data in the NetAmount column and groups by the CustomerID.

Listing 7-14. Columnstore Index against Traditional Nonclustered Index for Aggregation

```
CREATE INDEX NCI_CustomerID_NetAmount ON dbo.OrdersDisc(CustomerID, NetAmount) ;

DBCC FREEPROCCACHE
DBCC DROPCLEANBUFFERS

SET STATISTICS TIME ON
SET STATISTICS IO ON

SELECT SUM(netamount), CustomerID
FROM dbo.OrdersDisc
GROUP BY CustomerID ;

SELECT SUM(netamount), CustomerID
FROM dbo.OrdersColumnstore
GROUP BY CustomerID ;
```

From the results in Figure 7-14, you can see that this time, the tables have turned and the columnstore index has outperformed the nonclustered index with an execution time over six times faster, which is pretty impressive.

```
Results   Messages   Execution plan
(10000 row(s) affected)
Table 'OrdersDisc'. Scan count 1, logical reads 2730, physical reads 0, read-ahead reads 186, lob logical reads 0, lob physical reads 0, lob read-ahead reads 0.

(1 row(s) affected)

 SQL Server Execution Times:
   CPU time = 125 ms,  elapsed time = 419 ms.

(10000 row(s) affected)
Table 'OrdersColumnstore'. Scan count 2, logical reads 4628, physical reads 1, read-ahead reads 1612, lob logical reads 0, lob physical reads 0, lob read-ahead reads 0.
Table 'Worktable'. Scan count 0, logical reads 0, physical reads 0, read-ahead reads 0, lob logical reads 0, lob physical reads 0, lob read-ahead reads 0.
Table 'Workfile'. Scan count 0, logical reads 0, physical reads 0, read-ahead reads 0, lob logical reads 0, lob physical reads 0, lob read-ahead reads 0.

(1 row(s) affected)

 SQL Server Execution Times:
   CPU time = 31 ms,  elapsed time = 67 ms.
100 %
 Query executed successfully.                                    WIN-KIAGK4GN1MJ\PROSQLADMIN...  WIN-KIAGK4GN1MJ\Admini...  Chapter7  00:00:04  20
```

Figure 7-14. *Columnstore index against traditional nonclustered index for aggregation results*

Figure 7-15 shows the execution plan for the two queries. We can see that the Query Optimizer is able to parallelize the query against the columnstore index. The query against the OrdersDisc table is run sequentially.

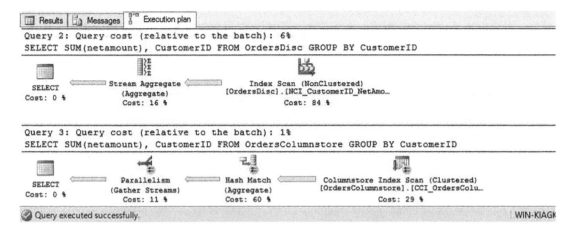

Figure 7-15. *Execution plans*

Also of interest, are the properties of the Columnstore Index Scan and the Hash Match operators, shown in Figure 7-16. Here we can see that SQL Server is able to use batch mode execution for both of these operators, which explains why the CPU time for the query against the columnstore index is 31ms as opposed to the 125ms for the query against the nonclustered index.

Columnstore Index Scan (Clustered)
Scan a columnstore index, entirely or only a range.

Physical Operation	Columnstore Index Scan
Logical Operation	Clustered Index Scan
Actual Execution Mode	Batch
Estimated Execution Mode	Batch
Storage	ColumnStore
Actual Number of Rows	1000000
Actual Number of Batches	1153
Estimated I/O Cost	0.0623843
Estimated Operator Cost	0.117392 (29%)
Estimated Subtree Cost	0.117392
Estimated CPU Cost	0.0550079
Estimated Number of Executions	1
Number of Executions	2
Estimated Number of Rows	1000000
Estimated Row Size	19 B
Actual Rebinds	0
Actual Rewinds	0
Ordered	False
Node ID	2

Object
[Chapter7].[dbo].[OrdersColumnstore].
[CCI_OrdersColumnstore]

Output List
[Chapter7].[dbo].[OrdersColumnstore].CustomerID, [Chapter7].
[dbo].[OrdersColumnstore].NetAmount

Hash Match
Use each row from the top input to build a hash table, and each row from the bottom input to probe into the hash table, outputting all matching rows.

Physical Operation	Hash Match
Logical Operation	Aggregate
Actual Execution Mode	Batch
Estimated Execution Mode	Batch
Actual Number of Rows	10000
Actual Number of Batches	12
Estimated I/O Cost	0
Estimated Operator Cost	0.248046 (60%)
Estimated Subtree Cost	0.365438
Estimated CPU Cost	0.248046
Number of Executions	2
Estimated Number of Executions	1
Estimated Number of Rows	10000
Estimated Row Size	19 B
Actual Rebinds	0
Actual Rewinds	0
Node ID	1

Output List
[Chapter7].[dbo].[OrdersColumnstore].CustomerID,
Expr1003

Figure 7-16. *Execution plan properties*

In-memory Indexes

As we saw in Chapter 6, SQL Server provides two types of index for memory-optimized tables: nonclustered and nonclustered hash. Every memory-optimized table must have a minimum of one index and can support a maximum of eight. All in-memory indexes cover all columns in the table, because they use a memory pointer to link to the data row.

Indexes on memory-optimized tables must be created in the CREATE TABLE statement. There is no CREATE INDEX statement for in-memory indexes. Indexes built on memory-optimized tables are always stored in memory only and are never persisted to disk, regardless of your table's durability setting. They are then re-created after the instance restarts. You do not need to worry about fragmentation of in-memory indexes, since they never have a disk-based structure.

In-memory Nonclustered Hash Indexes

A nonclustered hash index consists of an array of buckets. A hash function is run on each of the index keys, and then the hashed key values are placed into the buckets. The hashing algorithm used is deterministic, meaning that index keys with the same value always have the same hash value. This is important, because repeated hash values are always placed in the same hash bucket. When many keys are in the same hash bucket, performance of the index can degrade, because the whole chain of duplicates needs to be scanned to find the correct key. Therefore, if you are building a hash index on a nonunique column with many repeated keys, you should create the index with a much larger number of buckets. This should be in the realm of 20 to 100 times the number of distinct key values, as opposed to 2 times the number of unique keys that is usually recommended for unique indexes. Alternatively, using a nonclustered index on a nonunique column may offer a better solution. The second consequence of the hash function being deterministic is that different versions of the same row are always stored in the same hash bucket.

Even in the case of a unique index where only a single, current row version exits, the distribution of hashed values into buckets is not even, and if there are an equal number of buckets to unique key values, then approximately one third of the buckets is empty, one third contains a single value, and one third contains multiple values. When multiple values share a bucket, it is known as a *hash collision*, and a large number of hash collisions can lead to reduced performance. Hence the recommendation for the number of buckets in a unique index being twice the number of unique values expected in the table.

■ **Tip** When you have a unique nonclustered hash index, in some cases, many unique values may hash to the same bucket. If you experience this, then increasing the number of buckets helps, in the same way that a nonunique index does.

As an example, if your table has one million rows, and the indexed column is unique, the optimum number of buckets, known as the BUCKET_COUNT is 2 million. If you know that you expect your table to grow to 2 million rows, however, then it may be prudent to create 4 million hash buckets. This number of buckets is low enough to not have an impact on memory. It also still allows for the expected increase in rows, without there being too few buckets, which would impair performance. An illustration of potential mappings between index values and hash buckets is illustrated in Figure 7-17.

■ **Tip** The amount of memory used by a nonclustered hash index always remains static, since the number of buckets does not change.

Unique Key Values   Hash Buckets

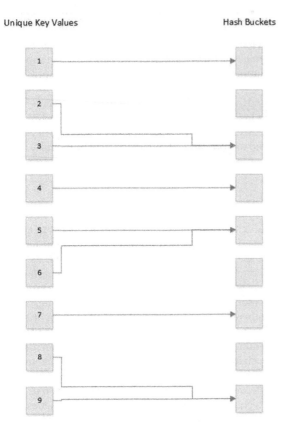

Figure 7-17. *Mappings to a nonclustered hash index*

Hash indexes are optimized for seek operations with the = predicate. For the seek operation, however, the full index key must be present in the predicate evaluation. If it is not, a full index scan is required. An index scan is also required if inequality predicates, such as < or > are used. Also, because the index is not ordered, the index cannot return the data in the sort order of the index key.

■ **Note**   You may remember that in Chapter 6, we witnessed superior performance from a disk-based table than from a memory-optimized table. This is explain by us using the > predicate in our query; this meant that although the disk-based index was able to perform an index seek, our memory-optimized hash index had to perform an index scan.

Let's now create a memory-optimized version of our OrdersDisc table, which includes a nonclustered hash index on the OrderID column, using the script in Listing 7-15. Initially, this row has 1 million rows, but we expect the number to grow to 2 million, so we use a BUCKET_COUNT of 4 million.

Listing 7-15. Creating a Table with a Nonclustered Hash Index

```
CREATE TABLE dbo.OrdersMemHash
(
        OrderNumber     INT    NOT NULL    IDENTITY    PRIMARY KEY
                                NONCLUSTERED HASH WITH(BUCKET_COUNT = 4000000),
        OrderDate       DATE    NOT NULL,
        CustomerID      INT     NOT NULL,
        ProductID       INT     NOT NULL,
        Quantity        INT     NOT NULL,
        NetAmount       MONEY   NOT NULL,
        DeliveryDate    DATE     NULL,
) WITH(MEMORY_OPTIMIZED = ON, DURABILITY = SCHEMA_AND_DATA) ;

INSERT INTO dbo.OrdersMemHash(OrderDate,CustomerID,ProductID,Quantity,NetAmount,DeliveryDate)
SELECT OrderDate
        ,CustomerID
        ,ProductID
        ,Quantity
        ,NetAmount
        ,DeliveryDate
FROM dbo.OrdersDisc ;
```

If we now wish to add an additional index to the table, we need to drop and re-create it. We already have data in the table, however, so we first need to create a temp table and copy the data in so that we can drop and re-create the memory-optimized table. The script in Listing 7-16 adds a nonclustered index to the OrderDate column.

Listing 7-16. Adding an Index to a Memory-Optimized Table

```
--Create and populate temp table

SELECT * INTO #OrdersMemHash
FROM dbo.OrdersMemHash ;

--Drop existing table

DROP TABLE dbo.OrdersMemHash ;

--Re-create the table with the new index

CREATE TABLE dbo.OrdersMemHash
(
        OrderNumber     INT    NOT NULL    IDENTITY    PRIMARY KEY
                                NONCLUSTERED HASH WITH(BUCKET_COUNT = 4000000),
        OrderDate       DATE    NOT NULL         INDEX NCI_OrderDate NONCLUSTERED,
        CustomerID      INT     NOT NULL,
        ProductID       INT     NOT NULL,
        Quantity        INT     NOT NULL,
        NetAmount       MONEY   NOT NULL,
        DeliveryDate    DATE     NULL,
```

```
) WITH(MEMORY_OPTIMIZED = ON, DURABILITY = SCHEMA_AND_DATA) ;
GO

--Allow values to be inserted into the identity column

SET IDENTITY_INSERT OrdersMemHash ON ;
GO

--Repopulate the table

INSERT INTO
dbo.OrdersMemHash(OrderNumber,OrderDate,CustomerID,ProductID,Quantity,NetAmount,DeliveryDate)
SELECT *
FROM #OrdersMemHash ;

--Stop further inserts to the identity column and clean up temp table

SET IDENTITY_INSERT OrdersMemHash OFF ;

DROP TABLE #OrdersMemHash ;
```

We can examine the distribution of the values in our hash index by interrogating the sys.dm_db_xtp_hash_index_stats DMV. The query in Listing 7-17 demonstrates using this DMV to view the number of hash collisions and calculate the percentage of empty buckets.

Listing 7-17. sys.dm_db_xtp_hash_index_stats

```
SELECT
    OBJECT_SCHEMA_NAME(HIS.OBJECT_ID) + '.' + OBJECT_NAME(HIS.OBJECT_ID) 'Table Name',
    I.name as 'Index Name',
    HIS.total_bucket_count,
    HIS.empty_bucket_count,
    FLOOR((CAST(empty_bucket_count AS FLOAT)/total_bucket_count) * 100) 'Empty Bucket
    Percentage',
    total_bucket_count - empty_bucket_count 'Used Bucket Count',
    HIS.avg_chain_length,
    HIS.max_chain_length
FROM sys.dm_db_xtp_hash_index_stats AS HIS
INNER JOIN sys.indexes AS I
        ON HIS.object_id = I.object_id
                AND HIS.index_id = I.index_id ;
```

From the results in Figure 7-18, we can see that for our hash index, 78 percent of the buckets are empty. The percentage is this high because we specified a large BUCKET_COUNT with table growth in mind. If the percentage was less than 33 percent, we would want to specify a higher number of buckets to avoid hash collisions. We can also see that we have an average chain length of 1, with a maximum chain length of 5. This is healthy. If the average chain count increases, then performance begins to tail off, since SQL Server has to scan multiple values to find the correct key. If the average chain length reaches 10 or higher, then the implication is that the key is nonunique and there are too many duplicate values in the key to make a hash index viable. At this point, we should either drop and re-create the table with a higher bucket count for the index or, ideally, look to implement a nonclustered index instead.

Figure 7-18. *sys.dm_db_xtp_hash_index_stats results*

In-memory Nonclustered Indexes

In-memory nonclustered indexes have a similar structure to a disk-based nonclustered index called a *bw-tree*. This structure uses a page-mapping table, as opposed to pointers, and is traversed using less than, as opposed to greater than, which is used when traversing disk-based indexes. The leaf level of the index is a singly linked list. Nonclustered indexes perform better than nonclustered hash indexes where a query uses inequality predicates, such as BETWEEN, >, or <. In-memory nonclustered indexes also perform better than a nonclustered hash index, where the = predicate is used, but not all of the columns in the key are used in the filter. Nonclustered indexes can also return the data in the sort order of the index key. Unlike disk-based indexes, however, these indexes cannot return the results in the reverse order of the index key.

Performance Considerations for In-memory Indexes

In Chapter 6, we saw that a memory-optimized table with a nonclustered hash index can offer significant performance gains over a disk-based table with a clustered index, as long as the correct query pattern is used. We also saw that results can be less favorable if inequality operators are used against a hash index. In this section, we evaluate the performance considerations when choosing between in-memory nonclustered indexes and nonclustered hash indexes.

The script in Listing 7-18 creates a new memory-optimized table, called OrdersMemNonClust. It then runs a query using an equality operator against the OrdersMemHash table, the OrdersMemNonClust table, and also the OrdersDisc table to generate a disk-based benchmark against a clustered index.

Listing 7-18. Equality Operator Benchmark

```
CREATE TABLE dbo.OrdersMemNonClust
(
        OrderNumber    INT      NOT NULL    IDENTITY    PRIMARY KEY    NONCLUSTERED,
        OrderDate      DATE     NOT NULL,
        CustomerID     INT      NOT NULL,
        ProductID      INT      NOT NULL,
        Quantity       INT      NOT NULL,
        NetAmount      MONEY    NOT NULL,
        DeliveryDate   DATE     NULL,
) WITH(MEMORY_OPTIMIZED = ON, DURABILITY = SCHEMA_AND_DATA) ;
GO

INSERT INTO
    dbo.OrdersMemNonClust(OrderDate,CustomerID,ProductID,Quantity,NetAmount,DeliveryDate)
SELECT OrderDate
```

```
        ,CustomerID
        ,ProductID
        ,Quantity
        ,NetAmount
        ,DeliveryDate
FROM dbo.OrdersDisc ;
GO

DBCC FREEPROCCACHE
DBCC DROPCLEANBUFFERS

SET STATISTICS TIME ON
SET STATISTICS IO ON

SELECT OrderNumber
FROM dbo.OrdersMemHash
WHERE OrderNumber  IN(78,88,98) ;

SELECT OrderNumber
FROM dbo.OrdersMemNonClust
WHERE OrderNumber IN(78,88,98) ;

SELECT OrderNumber
FROM dbo.OrdersDisc
WHERE OrderNumber  IN(78,88,98) ;
```

From the results in Figure 7-19, we can see that although the nonclustered index outperforms the disk-based table, by far the best results come from the nonclustered hash index, which takes less than a ms to complete.

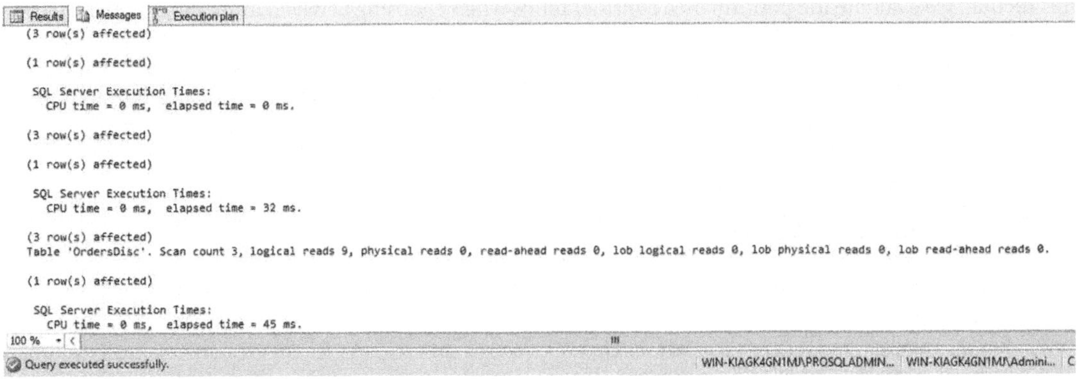

Figure 7-19. *Equality operator benchmark results*

■ **Note**   Physical IO stats are of no use against memory-optimized tables.

For our next test, we use an inequality operator. The script in Listing 7-19 queries all three of our orders tables, but this time it uses the BETWEEN operator as opposed to the IN operator.

Listing 7-19. Inequality Operator Benchmark

```
DBCC FREEPROCCACHE
DBCC DROPCLEANBUFFERS

SET STATISTICS TIME ON
SET STATISTICS IO ON

SELECT OrderNumber
FROM dbo.OrdersMemHash
WHERE OrderNumber  BETWEEN 78 AND 98 ;

SELECT OrderNumber
FROM dbo.OrdersMemNonClust
WHERE OrderNumber BETWEEN 78 AND 98 ;

SELECT OrderNumber
FROM dbo.OrdersDisc
WHERE OrderNumber  BETWEEN 78 AND 98 ;
```

From the results in Figure 7-20, we can see that this time, the nonclustered index on the memory-optimized table offers by far the best performance. The nonclustered hash index is actually outperformed by the disk-based table. This is because a full scan of the nonclustered hash index is required, whereas an index seek is possible on the other two tables.

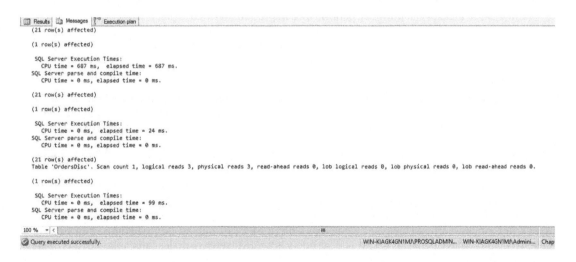

Figure 7-20. Inequality operator benchmark results

XML Indexes

SQL Server allows you to store data in tables, in a native XML format, using the XML data type. Like other large object types, it can store up to 2GB per tuple. Although you can use standard operators such as = and LIKE against XML columns, you also have the option of using XQuery expressions. They can be rather inefficient unless you create XML indexes, however. XML indexes outperform full-text indexes for most queries against XML columns. SQL Server offers support for primary XML indexes and three types of secondary XML index; PATH, VALUE, and PROPERTY. Each of these indexes is discussed in the following sections.

Primary XML Indexes

A primary XML index is actually a multicolumn clustered index on an internal system table called the node table. This table stores a shredded representation of the XML objects within an XML column, along with the clustered index key of the base table. This means that a table must have a clustered index before a primary XML index can be created.

■ **Tip**   XML shredding is the process of extracting values from an XML document and using them to build a relational data set

---

The system table stores enough information that the scalar or XML subtrees that a query must have can be reconstructed from the index itself. This information includes the node ID and name, the tag name and URI, a tokenized version of the node's data type, the first position of the node value in the document, pointers to the long node value and binary value, the nullability of the node, and the value of the base table's clustered index key for the corresponding row.

Primary XML indexes can provide a performance improvement when a query needs to shred scalar values from an XML document(s) or return a subset of nodes from an XML document(s).

Secondary XML Indexes

You can only create secondary XML indexes on XML columns that already have a primary XML index. Behind the scenes, secondary XML indexes are actually nonclustered indexes on the internal node table. Secondary XML indexes can improve query performance for queries that use specific types of XQuery processing.

A PATH secondary XML index is built on the NodeID and Value columns of the node table. This type of index offers performance improvements to queries that use path expressions, such as the exists() XQuery method. A VALUE secondary XML index is the reverse of this, and it is built on the VALUE and NodeID columns. This type of index offers gains to queries that search for values without knowing the name of the XML element or attribute that contains the value the query is searching for. Finally, a PROPERTY secondary XML index is built on the clustered index key of the base table, the NodeID and the Value columns of the nodes table. This type of index performs very well if the query is trying to retrieve nodes from multiple rows of the base table.

Performance Considerations for XML Indexes

In order to discuss the performance considerations for XML indexes, we first need to create and populate a table that has an XML column. The script in Listing 7-20 creates a table with an XML column called OrderSummary. Next, it populates this table by using a FOR XML query against the OrdersDisc and CustomersDisc tables within our Chapter7 database, and it creates a primary XML index on the column. It then runs a query against the table in order to benchmark the results with just a primary XML index.

Listing 7-20. Benchmarking a Primary XML Index

```
CREATE TABLE dbo.OrderSummary
(
        CustomerID        INT       PRIMARY KEY       CLUSTERED,
        OrderSummary XML
) ;

INSERT INTO dbo.OrderSummary
SELECT CustomerID,
(SELECT
        CustomerDetails.FirstName FirstName
        ,CustomerDetails.LastName LastName
        ,CustomerDetails.CreditLimit CreditLimit
        ,Orders.ProductID ProductID
        ,Orders.Quantity Quantity
        ,Orders.NetAmount NetAmount
FROM dbo.CustomersDisc CustomerDetails
INNER JOIN OrdersDisc Orders
        ON CustomerDetails.CustomerID = Orders.CustomerID
WHERE CustomerDetails.CustomerID = a.CustomerID
ORDER BY CustomerDetails.CustomerID
FOR XML AUTO, ROOT('OrderSummary')) OrderSummary
FROM dbo.CustomersDisc a ;

CREATE PRIMARY XML INDEX PXI_OrderSummary ON dbo.OrderSummary(OrderSummary) ;

DBCC FREEPROCCACHE
DBCC DROPCLEANBUFFERS

SET STATISTICS TIME ON

SELECT *
FROM dbo.OrderSummary
WHERE OrderSummary.exist('/OrderSummary/CustomerDetails/.[@CreditLimit = 0]') = 1 ;
```

▪ **Tip**   Details of the FOR XML query can be found at msdn.microsoft.com/en-GB/library/
ms178107(v=sql.120).aspx and details of the XQuery exist method can be found at
msdn.microsoft.com/en-us/library/ms189869.aspx.

From the results in Figure 7-21, we can see that with just a primary XML index on the column, the query took over four seconds to complete.

Figure 7-21. Benchmark primary XML index results

The next test involves adding a secondary XML index. Because we are running a query with the exist() XQuery method, the most suitable secondary index to create is a PATH index. The script in Listing 7-21 creates a PATH index and then reruns the benchmark query.

Listing 7-21. PATH Index Benchmark

```
CREATE XML INDEX SXI_OrderSummary_PATH ON dbo.OrderSummary(OrderSummary)
USING XML INDEX PXI_OrderSummary
FOR PATH ;
GO

DBCC FREEPROCCACHE
DBCC DROPCLEANBUFFERS

SET STATISTICS TIME ON

SELECT *
FROM dbo.OrderSummary
WHERE OrderSummary.exist('/OrderSummary/CustomerDetails/.[@CreditLimit = 0]') = 1 ;
```

The results in Figure 7-22 show that adding the PATH secondary XML index reduces the query time by over 800ms.

```
 Results    Messages

   (191 row(s) affected)

   SQL Server Execution Times:
     CPU time = 436 ms,  elapsed time = 3793 ms.
 100 %   ▾ <
  Query executed successfully.
```

Figure 7-22. PATH index benchmark results

Administering XML Indexes

As you can see from the code examples in the previous section, primary XML indexes are created using the CREATE PRIMARY XML INDEX syntax. You use the ON clause to specify the name of the table and column as you would for a traditional index.

When we create the PATH secondary XML index in the preceding code samples, we use the CREATE XML INDEX syntax. We then use the USING XML INDEX line to specify the name of the primary XML index on which the secondary index is built. The final line of the statement uses the FOR clause to specify that we want it to be built as a PATH index. Alternatively, we could have stated FOR PROPERTY or FOR VALUE, to build PROPERTY or VALUE secondary XML indexes instead.

XML indexes can be dropped with the DROP INDEX statement, specifying the table and index name to be removed. Dropping a primary XML index also drops any secondary XML indexes that are associated with it.

Maintaining Indexes

Once indexes have been created, a DBAs work is not complete. Indexes need to be maintained on an ongoing basis. The following sections discuss considerations for index maintenance.

Index Fragmentation

Disk-based indexes are subject to fragmentation. Two forms of fragmentation can occur in B-trees: internal fragmentation and external fragmentation. *Internal fragmentation* refers to pages having lots of free space. If pages have lots of free space, then SQL Server needs to read more pages than is necessary to return all of the required rows for a query. *External fragmentation* refers to the pages of the index becoming out of physical order. This can reduce performance, since the data cannot be read sequentially from disk.

For example, imagine that you have a table with 1 million rows of data, and that all of these data rows fit into 5000 pages when the data pages are 100-percent full. This means that SQL Server needs to read just over 39MB of data in order to scan the entire table (8KB * 5000). If the pages of the table are only 50 percent full, however, this increases the number of pages in use to 10,000, which also increases the amount of data that needs to be read to 78MB. This is internal fragmentation.

Internal fragmentation can occur naturally when DELETE statements are issued and when DML statements occur, such as when a key value that is not ever-increasing is inserted. This is because SQL Server may respond to this situation by performing a *page split*. A page split creates a new page, moves half of the data from the existing page to the new page, and leaves the other half on the existing page, thus creating 50 percent free space on both pages. They can also occur artificially, however, through the misuse of the FILLFACTOR and PAD_INDEX settings.

FILLFACTOR controls how much free space is left on each leaf level page of an index when it is created or rebuilt. By default, the FILLFACTOR is set to 0, which means that it leaves enough space on the page for exactly one row. In some cases, however, when a high number of page splits is occurring due to DML operations, a DBA may be able to reduce fragmentation by altering the FILLFACTOR. Setting a FILLFACTOR of 80, for example, leaves 20-percent free space in the page, meaning that new rows can be added to the page without page splits occurring. Many DBAs change the FILLFACTOR when they are not required to, however, which automatically causes internal fragmentation as soon as the index is built. PAD_INDEX can be applied only when FILLFACTOR is used, and it applies the same percentage of free space to the intermediate levels of the B-tree.

External fragmentation is also caused by page splits and refers to the logical order of pages, as ordered by the index key, being out of sequence when compared to the physical order of pages on disk. External fragmentation makes it so SQL Server is less able to perform scan operations using a sequential read, because the head needs to move backward and forward over the disk to locate the pages within the file.

■ **Note**　This is not the same as fragmentation at the file system level where a data file can be split over multiple, unordered disk sectors.

Detecting Fragmentation

You can identify fragmentation of indexes by using the sys.dm_db_index_physical_stats DMF. This function accepts the parameters listed in Table 7-2.

Table 7-2. *sys.dm_db_index_physical_stats Parameters*

Parameter	Description
Database_ID	The ID of the database that you want to run the function against. If you do not know it, you can pass in DB_ID('MyDatabase') where MyDatabase is the name of your database.
Object_ID	The Object ID of the table that you want to run the function against. If you do not know it, pass in OBJECT_ID('MyTable') where MyTable is the name of your table. Pass in NULL to run the function against all tables in the database.
Index_ID	The index ID of the index you want to run the function against. This is always 1 for a clustered index. Pass in NULL to run the function against all indexes on the table.
Partition_Number	The ID of the partition that you want to run the function against. Pass in NULL if you want to run the function against all partitions, or if the table is not partitioned.
Mode	Choose LIMITED, SAMPLED, or DETAILED. LIMITED only scans the non-leaf levels of an index. SAMPLED scans 1 percent of pages in the table, unless the table has 10,000 pages or less, in which case DETAILED mode is used. DETAILED mode scans 100 percent of the pages in the table. For very large tables, SAMPLED is often preferred due to the length of time it can take to return data in DETAILED mode.

Listing 7-22 demonstrates how we can use sys.dm_db_index_physical_stats to check the fragmentation levels of our OrdersDisc table.

Listing 7-22.　sys.dm_db_index_physical_stats

```
USE Chapter7
GO

SELECT
i.name
,IPS.index_type_desc
,IPS.index_level
,IPS.avg_fragmentation_in_percent
,IPS.avg_page_space_used_in_percent
,i.fill_factor
,CASE
    WHEN i.fill_factor = 0
        THEN 100-IPS.avg_page_space_used_in_percent
```

```
    ELSE i.fill_factor-ips.avg_page_space_used_in_percent
END Internal_Frag_With_Fillfactor_Offset
,IPS.fragment_count
,IPS.avg_fragment_size_in_pages
FROM sys.dm_db_index_physical_stats(DB_ID('Chapter7'),OBJECT_ID('dbo.OrdersDisc'),NULL,NULL
,'DETAILED') IPS
INNER JOIN sys.indexes i
        ON IPS.Object_id = i.object_id
                AND IPS.index_id = i.index_id ;
```

The output of this query is shown in Figure 7-23. You can see that one row is returned for every level of each B-tree. If the table was partitioned, this would also be broken down by partition. The index_level column indicates which level of the B-tree is represented by the row. Level 0 implies the leaf level of the B-tree, whereas Level 1 is either the lowest intermediate level or the root level if no intermediate levels exist, and so on, with the highest number always reflecting the root node. The avg_fragmentation_in_percent column tells us how much external fragmentation is present. We want this value to be as close to zero as possible. The avg_page_space_used_in_percent tells us how much internal fragmentation is present, so we want this value to be as close to 100 as possible. The Internal_Frag_With_FillFactor_Offset column also tells us how much internal fragmentation is present, but this time, it applies an offset to allow for the fill factor that has been applied to the index. The fragment_count column indicates how many chucks of continuous pages exist for the index level, so we want this value to be as low as possible. The avg_fragment_size_in_pages column tells the average size of each fragment, so obviously this number should also be as high as possible.

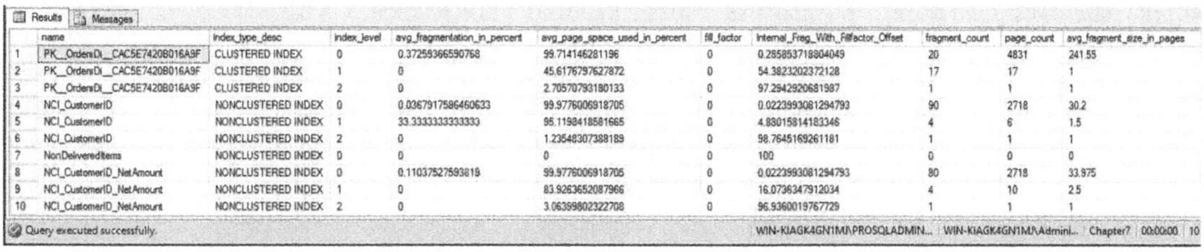

	name	index_type_desc	index_level	avg_fragmentation_in_percent	avg_page_space_used_in_percent	fill_factor	Internal_Frag_With_FillFactor_Offset	fragment_count	page_count	avg_fragment_size_in_pages
1	PK__OrdersDi__CAC5E74208016A9F	CLUSTERED INDEX	0	0.37259366590768	99.714146281196	0	0.285853718904049	20	4831	241.55
2	PK__OrdersDi__CAC5E74208016A9F	CLUSTERED INDEX	1	0	45.6176797627872	0	54.3823202372128	17	17	1
3	PK__OrdersDi__CAC5E74208016A9F	CLUSTERED INDEX	2	0	2.70570793180133	0	97.2942920681987	1	1	1
4	NCI_CustomerID	NONCLUSTERED INDEX	0	0.0367917586460633	99.9776006918705	0	0.0223993081294793	90	2718	30.2
5	NCI_CustomerID	NONCLUSTERED INDEX	1	33.3333333333333	95.1198418581665	0	4.83015814183346	4	6	1.5
6	NCI_CustomerID	NONCLUSTERED INDEX	2	0	1.23548307388189	0	98.7645169261181	1	1	1
7	NonDeliveredItems	NONCLUSTERED INDEX	0	0	0	0	100	0	0	0
8	NCI_CustomerID_NetAmount	NONCLUSTERED INDEX	0	0.11037527593818	99.9776006918705	0	0.0223993081294793	80	2718	33.975
9	NCI_CustomerID_NetAmount	NONCLUSTERED INDEX	1	0	83.9263652087966	0	16.0736347912034	4	10	2.5
10	NCI_CustomerID_NetAmount	NONCLUSTERED INDEX	2	0	3.06399802322708	0	96.9360019767729	1	1	1

Query executed successfully.   WIN-KIAGK4GN1MA\PROSQLADMIN...   WIN-KIAGK4GN1MA\Admini...   Chapter7   00:00:00   10

Figure 7-23. *sys.dm_db_index_physical_stats results*

Removing Fragmentation

You can remove fragmentation by either reorganizing or rebuilding an index. When you reorganize an index, SQL Server reorganizes the data within the leaf level of the index. It looks to see if there is free space on a page that it can use. If there is, then it moves rows from the next page, onto this page. If there are empty pages at the end of this process, then they are removed. SQL Server only fills pages to the level of the FillFactor specified. Once this is complete, the data within the leaf level pages is shuffled so that their physical order is a closer match to their logical, key order. Reorganizing an index is always an ONLINE operation, meaning that the index can still be used by other processes while the operation is in progress. Where it is always an ONLINE operation, it will fail if the ALLOW_PAGE_LOCKS option is turned off. The process of reorganizing an index is suitable for removing internal fragmentation and low levels of external fragmentation of 30 percent or less. However, it makes no guarantees, even with this usage profile, that there will not be fragmentation left after the operation completes.

The script in Listing 7-23 demonstrates how we can reorganize the NCI_CustomerID_NetAmount index on the OrdersDisc table.

Listing 7-23. Reorganizing an Index

```
ALTER INDEX NCI_CustomerID_NetAmount ON dbo.OrdersDisc REORGANIZE ;
```

When you rebuild an index, the existing index is dropped and then completely rebuilt. This, by definition, removes internal and external fragmentation, since the index is built from scratch. It is important to note, however, that you are still not guaranteed to be 100-percent fragmentation free after this operation. This is because SQL Server assigns different chunks of the index to each CPU core that is involved in the rebuild. Each CPU core should build its own section in the perfect sequence, but when the pieces are synchronized, there may be a small amount of fragmentation. You can minimize this issue by specifying MAXDOP = 1. Even when you set this option, you may still encounter fragmentation in some cases. For example, if ALLOW_PAGES_LOCKS is configured as OFF, then the workers share the allocation cache, which can cause fragmentation. Additionally, when you set MAXDOP = 1 it is at the expense of the time it takes to rebuild the index.

You can rebuild an index by performing either an ONLINE or OFFLINE operation. If you choose to rebuild the index as an ONLINE operation, then the original version of the index is still accessible, whilst the operation takes place. The ONLINE operation comes at the expense of both time and resource utilization. You need to enable ALLOW_PAGE_LOCKS to make your ONLINE rebuild successful.

The script in Listing 7-24 demonstrates how we can rebuild the NCI_CustomerID index on the OrdersDisc table. Because we have not specified ONLINE = ON, it uses the default setting of ONLINE = OFF, and the index is locked for the entire operation. Because we specify MAXDOP = 1, the operation is slower, but has no fragmentation.

Listing 7-24. Rebuilding an Index

```
ALTER INDEX NCI_CustomerID ON dbo.OrdersDisc REBUILD WITH(MAXDOP = 1) ;
```

If you create a maintenance plan to rebuild or reorganize indexes, then all indexes within the specified database are rebuilt, regardless of whether they need to be—this can be time consuming and eat resources. You can resolve this issue by using the sys.dm_db_index_physical_stats DMF to create an intelligent script that you can run from SQL Server Agent and use to reorganize or rebuild only those indexes that require it. This is discussed in more detail in Chapter 17.

■ **Tip** There is a myth that using SSDs removes the issue of index fragmentation. This is not correct. Although SSDs reduce the performance impact of out-of-order pages, they do not remove it. They also have no impact on internal fragmentation.

Missing Indexes

When you run queries, the Database Engine keeps track of any indexes that it would like to use when building a plan to aid your query performance. When you view an execution plan in SSMS, you are provided with advice on missing indexes, but the data is also available later through DMVs.

■ **Tip** Because the suggestions are based on a single plan, you should review them as opposed to implementing them blindly.

In order to demonstrate this functionality, we drop all of the nonclustered indexes on the OrdersDisc and CustomersDisc tables. We can then execute the query in Listing 7-25 and choose to include the actual execution plan.

■ **Tip**   You can see missing index information by viewing the estimated query plan.

Listing 7-25. Generating Missing Index Details

```
SELECT SUM(c.creditlimit) TotalExposure, SUM(o.netamount) 'TotalOrdersValue'
FROM dbo.CustomersDisc c
INNER JOIN dbo.OrdersDisc o
        ON c.CustomerID = o.CustomerID ;
```

Once we have run this query, we can examine the execution plan and see what it tells us. The execution plan for this query is shown in Figure 7-24.

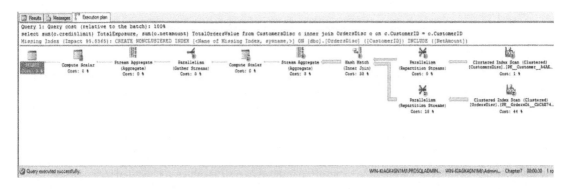

Figure 7-24. *Execution plan showing missing indexes*

At the top of the execution plan in Figure 7-24, you can see that SQL Server is recommending that we create an index on the CustomerID column of the OrdersDisc table and include the NetAmount column at the leaf level. We are also advised that this should provide a 95-percent performance improvement to the query.

As mentioned, SQL Server also makes this information available through DMVs. The sys.dm_db_missing_index_details DMV joins to the sys.dm_db_missing_index_group_stats through the intermediate DMV sys.dm_db_missing_index_groups, which avoids a many-to-many relationship. The script in Listing 7-26 demonstrates how we can use these DMVs to return details on missing indexes.

Listing 7-26. Missing Index DMVs

```
SELECT
        mid.statement TableName
        ,ISNULL(mid.equality_columns, '')
            + ','
            + ISNULL(mid.inequality_columns, '') IndexKeyColumns
        ,mid.included_columns
        ,migs.unique_compiles
        ,migs.user_seeks
```

```
        ,migs.user_scans
        ,migs.avg_total_user_cost
        ,migs.avg_user_impact
FROM sys.dm_db_missing_index_details mid
INNER JOIN sys.dm_db_missing_index_groups mig
        ON mid.index_handle = mig.index_handle
        INNER JOIN sys.dm_db_missing_index_group_stats migs
                ON mig.index_group_handle = migs.group_handle ;
```

The results of this query are shown in Figure 7-25. They show the following: the name of the table with the missing index; the column(s) that SQL Server recommends should form the index key; the columns that SQL Server recommends should be added as included columns at the leaf level of the B-tree; the number of times that queries that would have benefited from the index have been compiled; how many seeks would have been performed against the index, if it existed; the number of times that the index has been scanned if it existed; the average cost that would have been saved by using the index; and the average percentage cost that would have been saved by using the index. In our case, we can see that the query would have been 95 percent less expensive if the index existed when we ran our query.

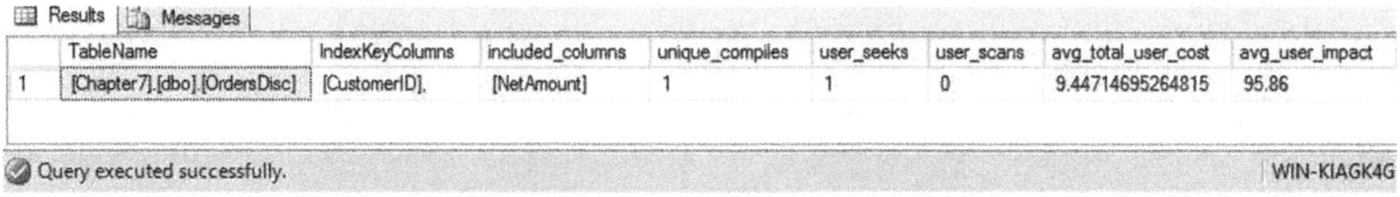

	TableName	IndexKeyColumns	included_columns	unique_compiles	user_seeks	user_scans	avg_total_user_cost	avg_user_impact
1	[Chapter7].[dbo].[OrdersDisc]	[CustomerID],	[NetAmount]	1	1	0	9.44714695264815	95.86

Query executed successfully.   WIN-KIAGK4G

Figure 7-25. *Missing index results*

Partitioned Indexes

As mentioned in Chapter 6, it is possible to partition indexes as well as tables. A clustered index always shares the same partition scheme as the underlying table, because the leaf level of the clustered index is made up of the actual data pages of the table. Nonclustered indexes, on the other hand, can either be aligned with the table or not. Indexes are aligned if they share the same partition scheme or if they are created on an identical partition scheme.

In most cases, it is good practice to align nonclustered indexes with the base table, but on occasion, you may wish to deviate from this strategy. For example, if the base table is not partitioned, you can still partition an index for performance. Also, if you index key is unique and does not contain the partitioning key, then it needs to be unaligned. There is also an opportunity to gain a performance boost from unaligned nonclustered indexes if the table is involved in collated joins with other tables on different columns.

You can create a partitioned index by using the ON clause to specify the partition scheme in the same way that you create a partitioned table. If the index already exists, you can rebuild it, specifying the partition scheme in the ON clause. The script in Listing 7-27 creates a partition function and a partition scheme. It then rebuilds the clustered index of the OrdersDisc table to move it to the new partition scheme. Finally, it creates a new nonclustered index, which is partition aligned with the table.

■ **Tip**   Before running the script, change the name of the primary key to match your own.

240

Listing 7-27. Rebuilding and Creating Partitioned Indexes

```
--Create partition function

CREATE PARTITION FUNCTION OrdersPartFunc(int)
AS RANGE LEFT
FOR VALUES(250000,500000,750000) ;
GO

--Create partition scheme

CREATE PARTITION SCHEME OrdersPartScheme
AS PARTITION OrdersPartFunc
ALL TO([PRIMARY]) ;
GO

--Partition OrdersDisc table

ALTER TABLE dbo.OrdersDisc DROP CONSTRAINT PK__OrdersDi__CAC5E7420B016A9F ;
GO

ALTER TABLE dbo.OrdersDisc
ADD PRIMARY KEY CLUSTERED(OrderNumber) ON OrdersPartScheme(OrderNumber) ;
GO

--Create partition aligned nonclustered index

CREATE NONCLUSTERED INDEX NCI_Part_CustID ON dbo.OrdersDisc(CustomerID, OrderNumber)
    ON OrdersPartScheme(OrderNumber) ;
```

When you rebuild an index, you can also specify that only a certain partition is rebuilt. The example in Listing 7-28 rebuilds only Partition 1 of the NCI_Part_CustID index.

Listing 7-28. Rebuilding a Specific Partition

```
ALTER INDEX NCI_Part_CustID ON dbo.OrdersDisc REBUILD PARTITION = 1 ;
```

Statistics

SQL Server maintains statistics regarding the distribution of data within a column or set of columns. These columns can either be within a table or a nonclustered index. When the statistics are built on a set of columns, then they also include correlation statistics between the distributions of values in those columns. The Query Optimizer can then use these statistics to build efficient query plans based on the number of rows that it expects a query to return. A lack of statistics can lead to inefficient plans being generated. For example, the Query Optimizer may decide to perform an index scan when a seek operation would be more efficient.

You can allow SQL Server to manage statistics automatically. A database level option called AUTO_CREATE_STATISTICS automatically generates single column statistics, where SQL Server believes better cardinality estimates will help query performance. There are limitations to this however. For example, filtered statistics or multicolumn statistics cannot be created automatically.

■ **Tip** The only exception to this is when an index is created. When you create an index, statistics are always generated, even multicolumn statistics, to cover the index key. It also includes filtered statistics on filtered indexes. This is regardless of the AUTO_CREATE_STATS setting.

Auto Create Incremental Stats causes statistics on partitioned tables to be automatically created on a per-partition basis, as opposed to being generated for the whole table. This can reduce contention by stopping a scan of the full table from being required. This is a new feature in SQL Server 2014.

Statistics become out of date as DML operations are performed against a table. The database level option, AUTO_UPDATE_STATISTICS, rebuilds statistics when they become outdated. The rules in Table 7-3 are used to determine if statistics are out of date.

Table 7-3. *Statistics Update Algorithms*

No of Rows in Table	Rule
0	Table has greater than 0 rows.
<= 500	500 or more values in the first column of the statistics object have changed.
> 500	500 + 20 percent or more values in the first column of the statistics object have changed.
Partitioned table with INCREMENTAL statistics	20 percent or more of values in the first column of the statistics object for a specific partition have changed.

The AUTO_UPDATE_STATISTICS process is very useful and it is normally a good idea to use it. An issue can arise, however, because the process is synchronous and blocking. Therefore, if a query is run, SQL Server checks to see if the statistics need to be updated. If they do, SQL Server updates them, but this blocks the query and any other queries that require the same statistics, until the operation completes. During times of high read/write load, such as an ETL process against very large tables, this can cause performance problems. The workaround for this is another database level option, called AUTO_UPDATE_STATISTICS_ASYNC. Even when this option is turned on, it only takes effect if AUTO_UPDATE_STATISTICS is also turned on. When enabled, AUTO_UPDATE_STATS_ASYNC forces the update of the statistics object to run as an asynchronous background process. This means that the query that caused it to run and other queries are not blocked. The tradeoff, however, is that these queries do not benefit from the updated statistics.

The options mentioned earlier can be configured on the Options page of the Database Properties dialog box. This is illustrated in Figure 7-26.

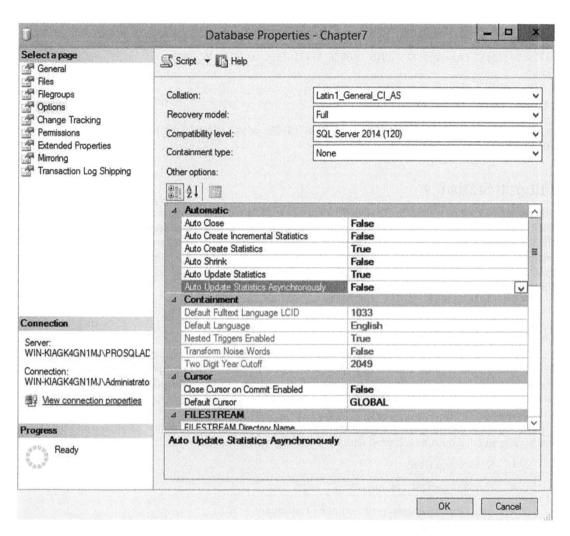

Figure 7-26. *The Options page*

Alternatively, you can configure them using ALTER DATABASE commands, as demonstrated in Listing 7-29.

Listing 7-29. Toggling Automatic Statistics Options

```
--Turn on Auto_Create_Stats

ALTER DATABASE Chapter7 SET AUTO_CREATE_STATISTICS ON ;
GO

--Turn on Auto_Create_Incremental_Stats

ALTER DATABASE Chapter7 SET AUTO_CREATE_STATISTICS ON  (INCREMENTAL=ON) ;
GO
```

```
--Turn on Auto_Update_Stats_Async

ALTER DATABASE Chapter7 SET AUTO_UPDATE_STATISTICS ON WITH NO_WAIT ;
GO

--Turn on Auto_Update_Stats_Async

ALTER DATABASE Chapter7 SET AUTO_UPDATE_STATISTICS_ASYNC ON WITH NO_WAIT ;
GO
```

Filtered Statistics

Filtered statistics allow you to create statistics on a subset of data within a column through the use of a WHERE clause in the statistic creation. This allows the Query Optimizer to generate an even better plan, since the statistics only contain the distribution of values within the well-defined subset of data. For example, if we create filtered statistics on the NetAmount column of our OrdersDisc table filtered by OrderDate being greater than 1 Jan 2014, then the statistics will not include rows that contain old orders, allowing us to search for large, recent orders more efficiently.

Incremental Statistics

Incremental statistics can help reduce table scans caused by statistics updates on large partitioned tables. When enabled, statistics are created and updated on a per-partition basis, as opposed to globally, for the entire table. This can significantly reduce the amount of time you need to update statistics on large partitioned tables, since partitions where the statistics are not outdated are not touched, therefore reducing unnecessary overhead.

Incremental statistics are not supported in all scenarios, however. A warning is generated and the setting is ignored, if the option is used with the following types of statistics:

- Statistics on views

- Statistics on XML columns

- Statistics on Geography or Geometry columns

- Statistics on filtered indexes

- Statistics for indexes that are not partition aligned

Additionally, you cannot use incremental statistics on read-only databases or on databases that are participating in an AlwaysOn Availability Group as a readable secondary replica.

Managing Statistics

In addition to being automatically created and updated by SQL Server, you can also create and update statistics manually using the CREATE STATISTICS statement. If you wish to create filtered statistics, add a WHERE clause at the end of the statement. The script in Listing 7-30 creates a multicolumn statistic on the FirstName and LastName columns of the CustomersDisc table. It then creates a filtered statistic on the NetAmount column of the OrdersDisc table, built only on rows where the OrderDate is greater than 1st Jan 2014.

Listing 7-30. Creating Statistics

```
USE Chapter7
GO

--Create multicolumn statistic on FirstName and LastName

CREATE STATISTICS Stat_FirstName_LastName ON dbo.CustomersDisc(FirstName, LastName) ;
GO

--Create filtered statistic on NetAmount

CREATE STATISTICS Stat_NetAmount_Filter_OrderDate ON dbo.OrdersDisc(NetAmount)
WHERE OrderDate > '2014-01-01' ;
GO
```

When creating statistics, you can use the options detailed in Table 7-4.

Table 7-4. *Creating Statistics Options*

Option	Description
FULLSCAN	Creates the statistic object on a sample of 100 percent of rows in the table. This option creates the most accurate statistics but takes the longest time to generate.
SAMPLE	Specifies the number of rows or percentage of rows you need to use to build the statistic object. The larger the sample, the more accurate the statistic, but the longer it takes to generate. Specifying 0 creates the statistic but does not populate it.
NORECOMPUTE	Excludes the statistic object from being automatically updated with AUTO_UPDATE_STATISTICS.
INCREMENTAL	Overrides the database-level setting for incremental statistics.

Individual statistics, or all statistics on an individual table, can be updated by using the UPDATE STATISTICS statement. The script in Listing 7-31 first updates the Stat_NetAmount_Filter_OrderDate statistics object that we created on the OrdersDisc table and then updates all statistics on the CustomersDisc table.

Listing 7-31. Updating Statistics

```
--Update a single statistics object

UPDATE STATISTICS dbo.OrdersDisc Stat_NetAmount_Filter_OrderDate ;
GO

--Update all statistics on a table

UPDATE STATISTICS dbo.CustomersDisc ;
GO
```

When using UPDATE STATISTICS, in addition to the options specified in Table 7-4 for creating statistics, which are all valid when updating statistics, the options detailed in Table 7-5 are also available.

Table 7-5. *Updating Statistics Options*

Option	Description
RESAMPLE	Uses the most recent sample rate to update the statistics.
ON PARTITIONS	Causes statistics to be generated for the partitions listed and then merges them together to create global statistics.
ALL | COLUMNS | INDEX	Specifies if statistics should be updated for just columns, just indexes, or both. The default is ALL.

You can also update statistics for an entire database by using the sp_updatestats system stored procedure. This procedure updates out-of-date statistics on disk-based tables and all statistics on memory-optimized tables regardless of whether they are out of date or not. Listing 7-32 demonstrates this system stored procedure's usage to update statistics in the Chapter7 database. Passing in the RESAMPLE parameter causes the most recent sample rate to be used. Omitting this parameter causes the default sample rate to be used.

Listing 7-32. Sp_updatestats

```
EXEC sp_updatestats 'RESAMPLE' ;
```

■ **Note**   Updating statistics causes queries that use those statistics to be recompiled the next time they run. The only time this is not the case is if there is only one possible plan for the tables and indexes referenced. For example, SELECT * FROM MyTable always performs a clustered index scan, assuming that the table has a clustered index.

Summary

A table that does not have a clustered index is called a heap and the data pages of the table are stored in no particular order. Clustered indexes build a B-tree structure, based on the clustered index key, and cause the data within the table to be ordered by that key. There can only ever be one clustered index on a table because the leaf level of the clustered index is the actual data pages of the table, and the pages can only be physically ordered in one way. The natural choice of key for a clustered index is the primary key of the table and, by default, SQL Server automatically creates a clustered index on the primary key. There are situations, however, when you may choose to use a different column as the clustered index key. This is usually when the primary key of the table is very wide, is updateable, or is not ever-increasing.

Nonclustered indexes are also B-tree structures built on other columns within a table. The difference is that the leaf level of a nonclustered index contains pointers to the data pages of the table, as opposed to the data pages themselves. Because a nonclustered index does not order the actual data pages of a table, you can create multiple nonclustered indexes. These can improve query performance when you create them on columns that are used in WHERE, JOIN, and GROUP BY clauses. You can also include other columns at the leaf level of the B-tree of a nonclustered index in order to cover a query. A query is covered by a nonclustered index, when you do not need to read the data from the underlying table. You can also filter a nonclustered index by adding a WHERE clause to the definition. This allows for improved query performance for queries that use a well-defined subset of data.

Columnstore indexes compress data and store each column in a distinct set of pages. This can significantly improve the performance of data-warehouse–style queries, which perform analysis on large data sets, since only the required columns need to be accessed, as opposed to the entire row. Each column is also split into segments, with each segment containing a header with metadata about the data, in order to further improve performance by allowing SQL Server to only access the relevant segments, in order to satisfy a query. Nonclustered columnstore indexes are not updatable, meaning that you must disable or drop the index before DML statements can occur on the base table. You can, on the other hand, update clustered columnstore indexes. Clustered columnstore indexes are a new feature of SQL Server 2014.

You can create two types of index on memory-optimized tables: nonclustered indexes and nonclustered hash indexes. Nonclustered hash indexes are very efficient for point lookups, but they can be much less efficient when you must perform a range scan. Nonclustered indexes perform better for operations such as inequality comparisons, and they are also able to return the data in the sort order of the index key.

You can create XML indexes on columns with the XML data type in order to improve query performance. You can only create a primary XML index if a clustered index already exists on the table and it works by creating a clustered index on an internal nodes table, which stores metadata and shredded node values. When you then need XML fragments or scalar values, you can use this data to reconstruct the nodes. Secondary XML indexes can further improve performance by creating nonclustered indexes on the internal nodes table. A PATH index can improve performance for XQuery methods such as exists(). A VALUE index can improve performance for XQuery expressions that search for values without knowing the name of the element. A PROPERTY index improves performance for queries that return nodes from multiple rows within a table, since a PROPERTY includes the clustered index key.

Indexes need to be maintained over time. They become fragmented due to DML statements causing page splits and can be reorganized or rebuilt to reduce or remove fragmentation. When pages become out of sequence, this is known as external fragmentation, and when pages have lots of free space, this is known as internal fragmentation. SQL Server stores metadata regarding index fragmentation and can display this through a DMF called sys.dm_db_index_physical_stats. SQL Server also maintains information on indexes that it regards as missing. A missing index is an index that does not exist in the database but would improve query performance if it were created. DBAs can use this data help them improve their indexing strategies.

SQL Server maintains statistics about the distribution of values within a column or set of columns to help improve the quality of query plans. Without good-quality statistics, SQL Server may make the wrong choice about which index or index operator to use in order to satisfy a query. For example, it may choose to perform an index scan when an index seek would have been more appropriate. You can update statistics manually or automatically, but either way causes queries to be recompiled. SQL Server 2014 also introduces incremental statistics, which allow statistics to be created on a per-partition basis, as opposed to globally for an entire table.

■ ■ ■

## CHAPTER 8

Database Consistency

Databases involve lots of IO. When you have a lot of IO, you inherently run the risk of corruption. Your primary defense against database corruption is to take regular backups of your database and to periodically test that these backups can be restored. You need to look out for database corruption, however, and SQL Server provides tools you can use to check the consistency of your database, as well as to resolve consistency issues if backups are not available. This chapter will look at the options you have for both checking and fixing consistency issues.

Consistency Errors

Consistency errors can occur in user databases or system databases, leaving tables, databases, or even the entire instances in an inaccessible state. Consistency errors can occur for many reasons, including hardware failures and issues with the Database Engine. The following sections discuss the types of error that can occur, how to detect these errors, and what to do if your system databases become corrupt.

Understand Consistency Errors

Different database consistency errors can occur; these cause a query to fail or a session to be disconnected and a message to be written to the SQL Server error log. The most common errors are detailed in the following sections.

605 Error

A 605 error can point to one of two issues, depending on the error severity. If the severity is level 12, then it indicates a dirty read. A *dirty read* is a transactional anomaly that occurs when you are using the Read Uncommitted isolation level or the NOLOCK query hint. It occurs when a transaction reads a row that never existed in the database, due to another transaction being rolled back. Transactional anomalies will be discussed in more detail, in Chapter 18. To resolve this issue, either rerun the query until it succeeds or rewrite the query to avoid the use of the Read Uncommitted isolation level or the NOLOCK query hint.

The 605 error may indicate a more serious issue, however, and often it indicates a hardware failure. If the severity level is 21, then the page may be damaged, or the incorrect page may be being served up from the operating system. If this is the case, then you need to either restore from a backup or use DBCC CHECKDB to fix the issue. (DBCC CHECKDB is discussed later in this chapter.) Additionally, you should also have the Windows administrators and storage team check for possible hardware or disk-level issues.

823 Error

An 823 error occurs when SQL Server attempts to perform an IO operation and the Windows API that it uses to perform this action returns an error to the Database Engine. An 823 error is almost always associated with a hardware or driver issue.

If an 823 error occurs, then you should use DBCC CHECKDB to check the consistency of the rest of the database and any other databases that reside on the same volume. You should liaise with your storage team to resolve the issue with the storage. Your Windows administrator should also check the Windows event log for correlated error messages. Finally, you should either restore the database from a backup or use DBCC CHECKDB to fix the issue.

824 Error

If the call to the Windows API succeeds but there are logical consistency issues with the data returned, then an 824 error is generated. Just like an 823 error, an 824 error usually means that there is an issue with the storage subsystem. If an 824 error is generated, then you should follow the same course of action as you do when an 823 error is generated.

5180 Error

A 5180 error occurs when a file ID is discovered that is not valid. File IDs are stored in page pointers, as well as in system pages at the beginning of each file. This error is usually caused by a corrupt pointer within a page, but it can potentially also indicate an issue with the Database Engine. If you experience this error, you should restore from a backup or run DBCC CHECKDB to fix the error.

7105 Error

A 7105 error occurs when a row within a table references an LOB (Large Object Block) structure that does not exist. This can happen because of a dirty read in the same manner as a 605 severity 12 error, or it can happen as the result of a corrupt page. The corruption can either be in the data page that points to the LOB structure or it in a page of the LOB structure itself.

If you encounter a 7105 error, then you should run DBCC CHECKDB to check for errors. If you don't find any, then the error is likely the result of a dirty read. If you find errors, however, then either restore the database from a backup or use DBCC CHECKDB to fix the issue.

Detecting Consistency Errors

SQL Server provides mechanisms for verifying the integrity of pages as they are read from and written to disk. It also provides a log of corrupt pages that helps you identify the type of error that has occurred, how many times it has occurred, and the current status of the page that has become corrupt. These features are discussed in the following sections.

Page Verify Option

A database-level option called Page Verify determines how SQL Server checks for page corruption that the IO subsystem causes when it is reading and writing pages to disk. It can be configured as CHECKSUM, which is the default option, TORN_PAGE_DETECTION, or NONE.

The recommended setting for Page Verify is CHECKSUM. When this option is selected, every time a page is written, a CHECKSUM value is created against the entire page and saved in the page header. A CHECKSUM value is a hash sum, which is deterministic and unique based on the value that the hashing function is run against. This value is then recalculated when a page is read into the buffer cache and compared to the original value.

When TORN_PAGE_DETECTION is specified, whenever a page is written to disk, the first 2 bytes of every 512-byte sector of the page are written to the page's header. When the page is subsequently read into memory, these values are checked to ensure that they are the same. The flaw here is obvious; it is perfectly possible for a page to be corrupt, and for this corruption not to be noticed, because it is not within the bytes that are checked. TORN_PAGE_DETECTION is a deprecated feature of SQL Server, which means that it will not be available in future versions. You should avoid using it. If Page Verify is set to NONE, then SQL Server performs no page verification whatsoever. This is not good practice.

If all of your databases have been created in a SQL Server 2014 instance, then they are all configured to use CHECKSUM by default. If you have migrated your databases from a previous version of SQL Server, however, then they may be configured to use TORN_PAGE_DETECTION. You can check the Page Verify setting of your databases by using the script in Listing 8-1.

Listing 8-1. Checking the Page Verify Option

```
SELECT
        name
        ,page_verify_option_desc
FROM sys.databases ;
```

If you find that a database is using TORN_PAGE_DETECTION, or worse, was set to NONE, then you can resolve the issue by altering the setting in the Options page of the Database Properties dialog box, as shown in Figure 8-1.

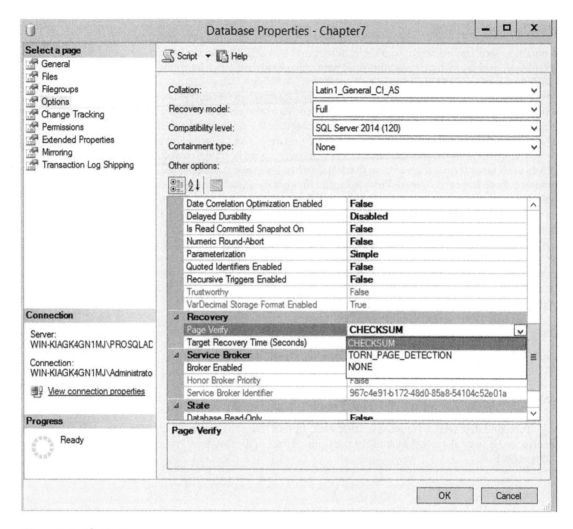

Figure 8-1. *The Options page*

■ **Note**   Changing the Page Verify option does not cause the CHECKSUM to be created against the data pages immediately. The CHECKSUM is only generated when the pages are written back to disk after being modified.

Alternatively, you can achieve the same results using T-SQL by using an ALTER DATABASE <DatabaseName> SET PAGE_VERIFY CHECKSUM WITH NO_WAIT statement. The script in Listing 8-2 causes all databases that are currently set to either NONE or TORN_PAGE_DETECTION to be reconfigured to use CHECKSUM. The script uses the XQuery data() function to avoid the need for a cursor. The script works by building the statement required for every row in the table. It flips the data for each row into XML, but the tags are then striped out using the Data() function, leaving only the statement. It is then flipped back to a relational string and passed into a Unicode variable, which is then executed as dynamic SQL.

Listing 8-2. Reconfiguring All Databases to Use CHECKSUM

```
DECLARE @SQL NVARCHAR(MAX)

SELECT @SQL =
(
SELECT
        'ALTER DATABASE ' + QUOTENAME(Name) +
                        ' SET PAGE_VERIFY CHECKSUM WITH NO_WAIT; ' AS [data()]
FROM sys.databases
WHERE page_verify_option_desc <> 'CHECKSUM'
FOR XML PATH('')
) ;

BEGIN TRY
    EXEC(@SQL) ;
END TRY
BEGIN CATCH
    SELECT 'Failure executing the following SQL statement ' + CHAR(13) +CHAR(10) + @SQL ;
END CATCH
```

■ **Tip**   You can use this technique any time you require a script to perform an operation against multiple databases. The code is far more efficient than using a cursor and promotes good practice by allowing DBAs to lead by example. You are always telling your developers not to use the cursor, right?

Suspect Pages

If SQL Server discovers a page with a bad checksum or a torn page, then it records the pages in the MSDB database in a table called dbo.suspect_pages. It also records any pages that encounter an 823 or 824 error in this table. The table consists of six columns, as described in Table 8-1.

Table 8-1. *suspect_pages Columns*

Column	Description
Database_id	The ID of the database that contains the suspect page
File_id	The ID of the file that contains the suspect page
Page_id	The ID of the page that is suspect
Event_Type	The nature of the event that caused the suspect pages to be updated
Error_count	An incremental counter that records the number of times that the event has occurred
Last_updated_date	The last time the row was updated

The possible values for the event_type column are explained in Table 8-2.

Table 8-2. *Event Types*

Event_type	Description
1	823 or 824 error
2	Bad checksum
3	Torn page
4	Restored
5	Repaired
7	Deallocated by DBCC CHECKDB

After recording the suspect page in the suspect_pages table, SQL Server updates the row after you have fixed the issue by either restoring the page from a backup or by using DBCC CHECKDB. It also increments the error count every time an error with the same event_type is encountered. You should monitor this table for new and updated entries and you should also periodically delete rows from this table, which have an event_type of 4 or 5, to stop the table from becoming full.

■ **Note**   Page restores will be discussed in Chapter 15.

The script in Listing 8-3 creates a new database called Chapter8, with a single table, called CorruptTable, which is then populated with data. It then causes one of the table's pages to become corrupt.

Listing 8-3. Corrupting a Page

```
--Create the Chapter8 database

CREATE DATABASE Chapter8 ;
GO

USE Chapter8
GO

--Create the table that we will corrupt

CREATE TABLE dbo.CorruptTable
(
ID    INT    NOT NULL    PRIMARY KEY CLUSTERED    IDENTITY,
SampleText NVARCHAR(50)
) ;

--Populate the table

DECLARE @Numbers TABLE
(ID        INT)
```

```
;WITH CTE(Num)
AS
(
SELECT 1 Num
UNION ALL
SELECT Num + 1
FROM CTE
WHERE Num <= 100
)
INSERT INTO @Numbers
SELECT Num
FROM CTE ;

INSERT INTO dbo.CorruptTable
SELECT 'SampleText'
FROM @Numbers a
CROSS JOIN @Numbers b ;

--DBCC WRITEPAGE will be used to corrupt a page in the table. This requires the
--database to be placed in single user mode.
--THIS IS VERY DANGEROUS - DO NOT EVER USE THIS IN A PRODUCTION ENVIRONMENT

ALTER DATABASE Chapter8 SET  SINGLE_USER WITH NO_WAIT ;
GO

DECLARE @SQL NVARCHAR(MAX) ;

SELECT @SQL = 'DBCC WRITEPAGE(' +
(
        SELECT CAST(DB_ID('Chapter8') AS NVARCHAR)
) +
', 1, ' +
(
        SELECT TOP 1 CAST(page_id AS NVARCHAR)
        FROM dbo.CorruptTable
        CROSS APPLY sys.fn_PhysLocCracker(%%physloc%%)
) +
', 2000, 1, 0x61, 1)' ;

EXEC(@SQL) ;

ALTER DATABASE Chapter8 SET  MULTI_USER WITH NO_WAIT ;
GO

SELECT *
FROM dbo.CorruptTable ;
```

The results in Figure 8-2 show that the final query in the script, which tried to read the data from the table, failed because one of the pages is corrupt, and therefore, there is a bad checksum.

Figure 8-2. Bad checksum error

■ **Caution**   DBCC WRITEPAGE is used here for educational purposes only. It is undocumented and also extremely dangerous. It should *never* be used on a production system and should only be used on any database with extreme caution.

You can use the query in Listing 8-4 to generate a friendly output from the msdb.dbo.suspect_pages table. This query uses the DB_NAME() function to find the name of the database, joins to the sys.master_files system table to find the name of the file involved, and uses a CASE statement to translate the event_type into an event type description.

Listing 8-4. Querying suspect_pages

```
SELECT
    DB_NAME(sp.database_id) [Database]
    ,mf.name
    ,sp.page_id
    ,CASE sp.event_type
        WHEN 1 THEN '823 or 824 or Torn Page'
        WHEN 2 THEN 'Bad Checksum'
        WHEN 3 THEN 'Torn Page'
        WHEN 4 THEN 'Restored'
        WHEN 5 THEN 'Repaired (DBCC)'
        WHEN 7 THEN 'Deallocated (DBCC)'
    END AS [Event]
    ,sp.error_count
    ,sp.last_update_date
FROM msdb.dbo.suspect_pages sp
INNER JOIN sys.master_files mf
        ON sp.database_id = mf.database_id
                AND sp.file_id = mf.file_id ;
```

After corrupting a page of our CorruptTable table, running this query will produce the results in Figure 8-3. Obviously, the page_id is likely to be different if you were to run the scripts on your own system, since the Database Engine is likely to have allocated different pages to the table that you created.

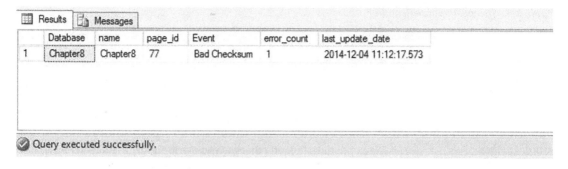

Figure 8-3. *Results of querying suspect_pages*

■ **Note**   We will fix the error later in this chapter, but that involves loosing data that was stored on the page. If a backup is available, then a page restore is a better option than a repair in this scenario.

Consistency Issues for Memory-Optimized Tables

Corruption usually occurs during a physical IO operation, so you can be forgiven for thinking that memory-optimized tables are immune to corruption, but this is a fallacy. As you may remember from Chapter 6, although memory-optimized tables reside in memory, a copy of the tables—and depending on your durability settings, a copy of your data—is kept in physical files. This is to ensure that the tables and data are still available after a restart of the instance. These files can be subject to corruption. It is also possible for data to become corrupt in memory, due to issues such as a faulty RAM chip.

Unfortunately, the repair options of DBCC CHECKDB are not supported against memory tables. However, when you take a backup of a database that contains a memory-optimized filegroup, a checksum validation is performed against the files within this filegroup. It is therefore imperative that you not only take regular backups, but that you also check that they can be restored successfully, on a regular basis. This is because your only option, in the event of a corrupted memory-optimized table, is to restore from the last known good backup.

System Database Corruption

If system databases become corrupt, your instance can be left in an inaccessible state. The following sections discuss how to respond to corruption in the Master database and the Resource database.

Corruption of the Master Database

If the Master database becomes corrupted, it is possible that your instance will be unable to start. If this is the case, then you need to rebuild the system databases and then restore the latest copies from backups. Chapter 15 discusses strategies for database backups in more detail, but this highlights why backing up your system databases is important. In the event that you need to rebuild your system databases, you will lose all instance-level information, such as Logins, SQL Server Agent jobs, Linked Servers, and so on, if you are not able to restore from a backup. Even knowledge of the user databases within the instance will be lost and you will need to reattach the databases.

In order to rebuild the system databases, you need to run setup. When you are rebuilding system databases using setup, the parameters described in Table 8-3 are available.

Table 8-3. *System Database Rebuild Parameters*

Parameter	Description
/ACTION	Specify Rebuilddatabase for the action parameter.
/INSTANCENAME	Specifies the instance name of the instance that contains the corrupt system database.
/Q	This parameter stands for options. Use this to run setup without any user interaction.
/SQLCOLLATION	This is an optional parameter that you can use to specify a collation for the instance. If you omit it, the collation of the Windows OS is used.
/SAPWD	If your instance uses mixed-mode authentication, then use this parameter to specify the password for the SA account.
/SQLSYSADMINACCOUNTS	Use this parameter to specify which accounts should be made sysadmins of the instance.

The PowerShell command in Listing 8-5 rebuilds the system databases of the PROSQLADMIN instance.

Listing 8-5. Rebuilding System Databases

```
.\setup.exe /ACTION=rebuilddatabase /INSTANCENAME=PROSQLADMIN /SQLSYSADMINACCOUNTS=
SQLAdministrator
```

As mentioned, when this action is complete, ideally we restore the latest copy of the Master database from a backup. Since we do not have one, we need to reattach our Chapter8 database in order to continue. Additionally, the detail of the corrupt page within the suspect_pages table will also be lost. Attempting to read the CorruptTable table in the Chapter8 database causes this data to be repopulated, however. The script in Listing 8-6 reattaches the Chapter8 database. You should change the file paths to match you own configuration before you run the script.

Listing 8-6. Reattaching a Database

```
CREATE DATABASE Chapter8 ON
( FILENAME = N'F:\MSSQL\DATA\Chapter8.mdf' ),
( FILENAME = N'F:\MSSQL\DATA\Chapter8_log.ldf' )
 FOR ATTACH ;
```

Corruption of the Resource Database or Binaries

It is possible for the instance itself to become corrupt. This can include corrupt Registry keys or the Resource database becoming corrupt. If this happens, then find the repair utility that ships with the SQL Server installation media. To invoke this tool, select Repair from the Maintenance tab of the SQL Server Installation Center.

After the wizard has run the appropriate rule checks, you are presented with the Select Instance page, as illustrated in Figure 8-4.

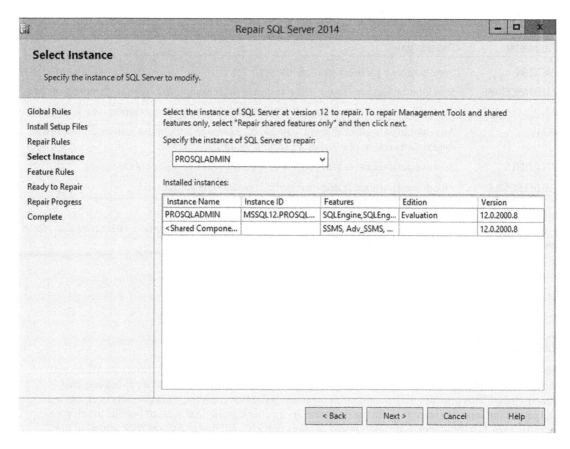

Figure 8-4. *The Select Instance page*

After you select the instance that needs to be repaired, the following page of the wizard runs an additional rules check to ensure that the required features can be repaired. Finally, on the Ready To Repair page, you see a summary of the actions that are to be performed. After choosing to repair, you see the repair progress report. Once the repair completes, a Summary page displays, which provides you with the status of each operation that was performed and also a link to a log file that you may wish to review if you need to perform troubleshooting.

As an alternative to using SQL Server Installation Center, you can achieve the same rebuild from the command line. This is useful if your instance is running on Windows Server Core. When you are repairing an instance from the command line, the parameters available to you, are those listed in Table 8-4. Because the Master database is not being rebuilt when you are repairing an instance, you do not need to specify a collation or Administrator details.

Table 8-4. *Instance Repair Parameters*

Parameter	Description
/ACTION	Specify Repair for the action parameter.
/INSTANCENAME	Specifies the instance name of the instance that contains the corrupt system database.
/Q	This parameter is options. Use this to run without any user interaction.
/ENU	An optional parameter that you can use on a localized operating system to specify that the English version of SQL Server should be used.
/FEATURES	An optional parameter you can use to specify a list of components to repair.
/HIDECONSOLE	An optional parameter that causes the console to be suppressed.

The PowerShell command in Listing 8-7 also rebuilds the PPROSQLADMIN instance. This script also works for instances hosted on Windows Server Core.

Listing 8-7. Repairing an Instance

```
.\setup.exe /ACTION=repair /INSTANCENAME=PROSQLADMIN /q
```

DBCC CHECKDB

DBCC CHECKDB is a utility that can be used to both discover corruption and also fix the errors. When you run DBCC CHECKDB, by default it creates a database snapshot and runs the consistency checks against this snapshot. This provides a transactionally consistent point from which the checks can occur, while at the same time reducing contention in the database. It can check multiple objects in parallel to improve performance, but this depends on the number of cores that are available and the MAXDOP setting of the instance.

Checking for Errors

When you run DBCC CHECKDB for the purpose of discovering corruption only, then you can specify the arguments, detailed in Table 8-5.

Table 8-5. *DBCC CHECKDB Arguments*

Argument	Description
NOINDEX	Specifies that that integrity checks should be performed on heap and clustered index structures but not on nonclustered indexes.
EXTENDED_LOGICAL_CHECKS	Forces the logical consistency of XML indexes, indexed views, and spatial indexes to be performed.
NO_INFOMSGS	Prevents informational messages from being returned in the results. This can reduce noise when you are searching for an issue, since only errors and warnings with a severity level greater than 10 are returned.

(continued)

Table 8-5. (*continued*)

Argument	Description
TABLOCK	DBCC CHECKDB creates a database snapshot and runs its consistency checks against this structure to avoid taking out locks in the database, which cause contention. Specifying this option changes that behavior so that instead of creating a snapshot, SQL Server takes out a temporary exclusive lock on the database, followed by exclusive locks on the structures that it is checking. In the event of high write load, this can reduce the time it takes to run DBCC CHECKDB, but at the expense of contention with other processes that may be running. It also causes the system table metadata validation and service broker validation to be skipped.
ESTIMATEONLY	When this argument is specified, no checks are performed. The only thing that happens is that the space required in TempDB to perform the checks is calculated based on the other arguments specified.
PHYSICAL_ONLY	When this argument is used, DBCC CHECKDB is limited to performing allocation consistency checks on the database, consistency checks on system catalogs, and validation on each page of every table within the database. This option cannot be used in conjunction with DATA_PURITY.
DATA_PURITY	Specifies that column integrity checks are carried out, such as ensuring that values are within their data type boundaries. For use with databases that have been upgraded from SQL Server 2000 or below only. For any newer databases, or SQL Server 2000 databases that have already been scanned with DATA_PURITY, the checks happen by default.
ALL_ERRORMSGS	For backward compatibility only. Has no effect on SQL 2014 databases.

DBCC CHECKDB is a very intensive process that can consume many CPU and IO resources. Therefore, it is advisable to run it during a maintenance window to avoid performance issues for applications. The Database Engine automatically decides how many CPU cores to assign the DBCC CHECKDB based on the Instance level setting for MAXDOP and the amount of throughput to the sever when the process begins. If you expect load to increase during the window when DBCC CHECKDB will be running, however, then you can throttle the process to a single core by turning on Trace Flag 2528. This flag should be used with caution, however, because it causes DBC CHECKDB to take much longer to complete. If a snapshot is not generated, either because you have specified TABLOCK or because there was not enough space on disk to generate a snapshot, then it also causes each table to be locked for a much longer period.

The sample in Listing 8-8 does not perform any checks but calculates the amount of space required in TempDB in order for DBCC CHECKDB to run successfully against the Chapter8 database.

Listing 8-8. Checking TempDB Space Required for DBCC CHECKDB

```
USE Chapter8
GO

DBCC CHECKDB WITH ESTIMATEONLY ;
```

Because our Chapter8 database is tiny, we only require less than half a megabyte of space in TempDB. This is reflected in the results, shown in Figure 8-5.

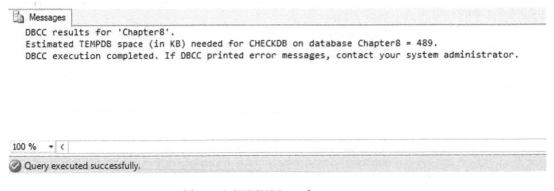

Figure 8-5. *TempDB space required for DBC CHECKDB results*

The script in Listing 8-9 uses DBCC CHECKDB to perform consistency checks across the entire Chapter8 database.

Listing 8-9. Running DBCC CHECKDB

```
USE Chapter8
GO

DBCC CHECKDB ;
```

Figure 8-6 displays a fragment of the results of running this command. As you can see, the issue with the corrupt page in the CorruptTable table has been identified.

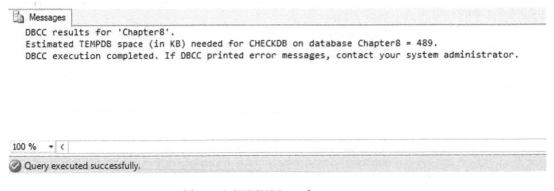

Figure 8-6. *DBCC CHECKDB identifies corrupt page*

In real life, unless you are troubleshooting a specific error, you are unlikely to be running DBCC CHECKDB manually. It is normally scheduled to run with SQL Server Agent or a maintenance plan. So how do you know when it encounters an error? Simply, the SQL Server Agent job step fails. Figure 8-7 shows the error message being displayed in the history of the failed job. The output from DBCC CHECKDB is also written to the SQL Server Error log. This is regardless of whether or not it was invoked manually or through a SQL Server Agent job.

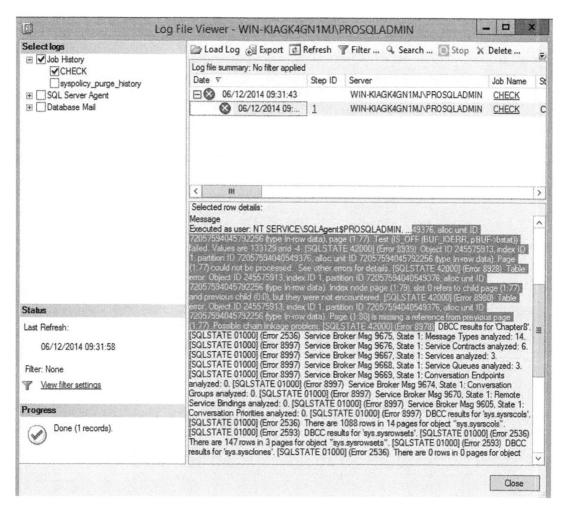

Figure 8-7. *Errors in job history*

Because DBCC CHECKDB finding errors causes the job to fail, you can set-up a notification so that a DBA receives an alert. Assuming that Database Mail is configured on the sever, you can create a new operator that receives e-mails by selecting New Operator from the context menu of the Operators folder under the SQL Server Agent folder in SQL Server Management Studio, as illustrated in Figure 8-8.

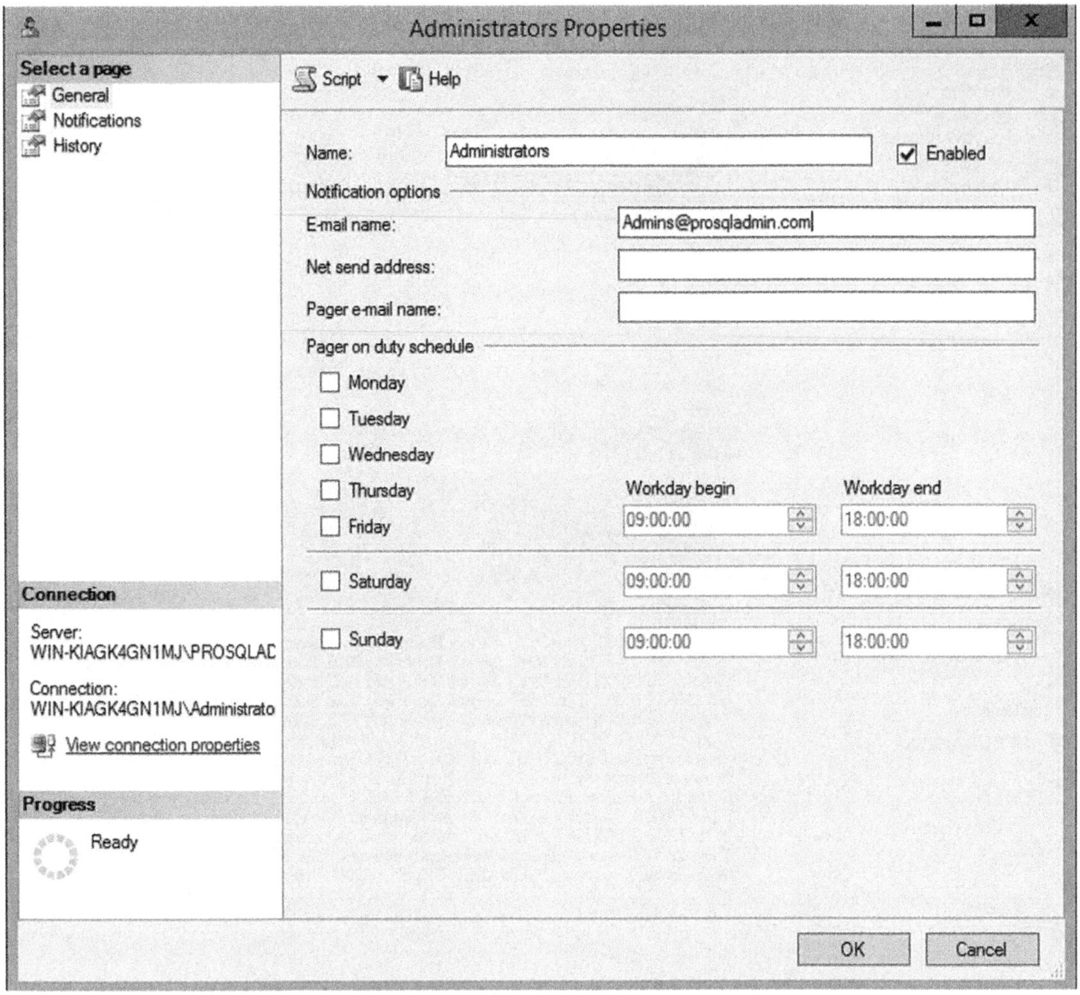

Figure 8-8. *Create a new operator*

Once you have create the operator, you are able to specify that operator in the Notifications tab of the Job Properties page of the SQL Server Agent job. This is illustrated in Figure 8-9.

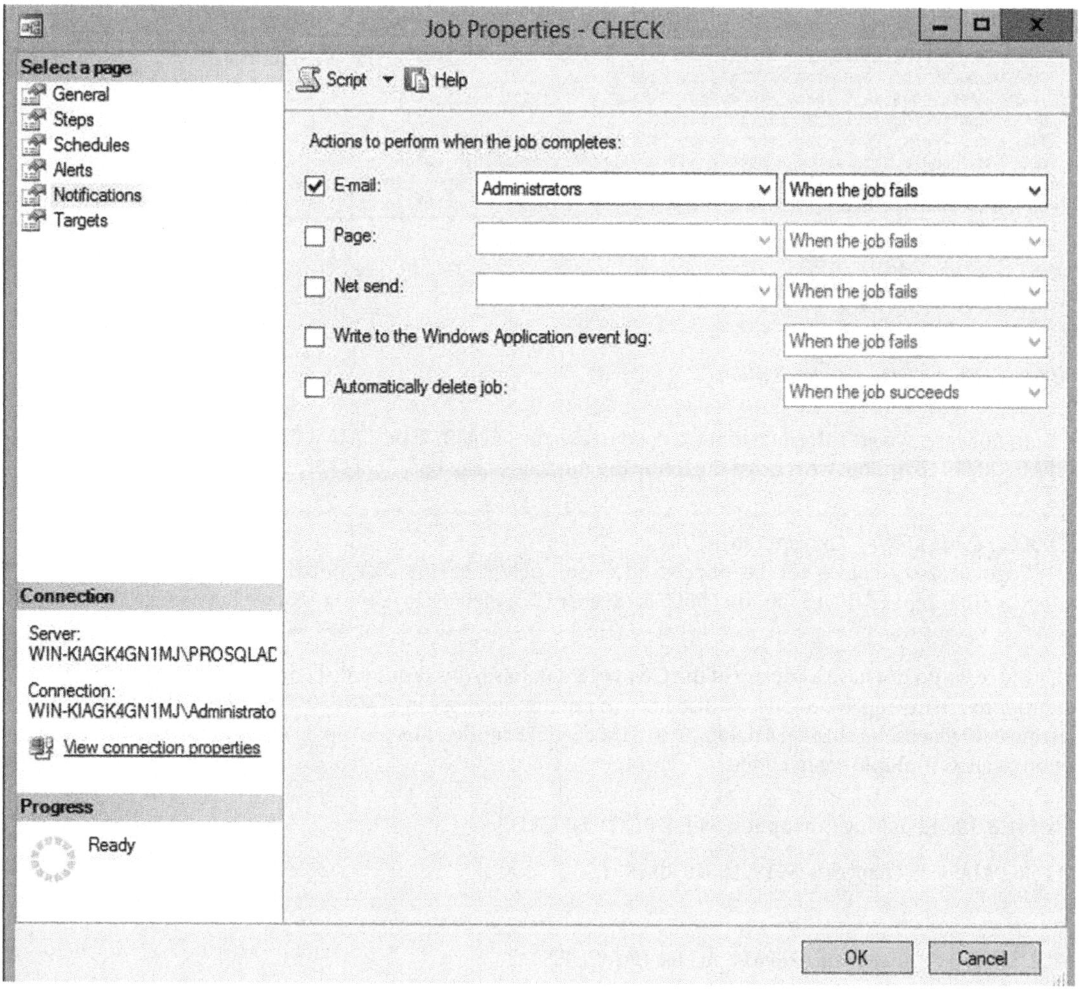

Figure 8-9. *Configure notification*

SQL Server Agent jobs are discussed fully in Chapter 21.

Fixing Errors

When we use DBCC CHECKDB to repair a corruption in the database, we need to specify an additional argument that determines the repair level to use. The options available are REPAIR_REBUILD or REPAIR_ALLOW_DATA_LOSS. REPAIR_REBUILD is, of course, the preferred option, and it can be used to resolve issues that will not cause data loss, such as bad page pointers, or corruption inside a nonclustered index. REPAIR_ALLOW_DATA_LOSS attempts to fix all errors it encounters, but as its name suggests, this may involve data being lost. You should only use this option to restore the data if no backup is available.

Before specifying a repair option for DBCC CHECKDB, always run it without a repair option first. This is because when you do so, it will tell you the minimum repair option that you can use to resolve the errors. If we look again at the output of the run against the Chapter8 database, then we can see that the end of the output advises the most appropriate repair option to use. This is illustrated in Figure 8-10.

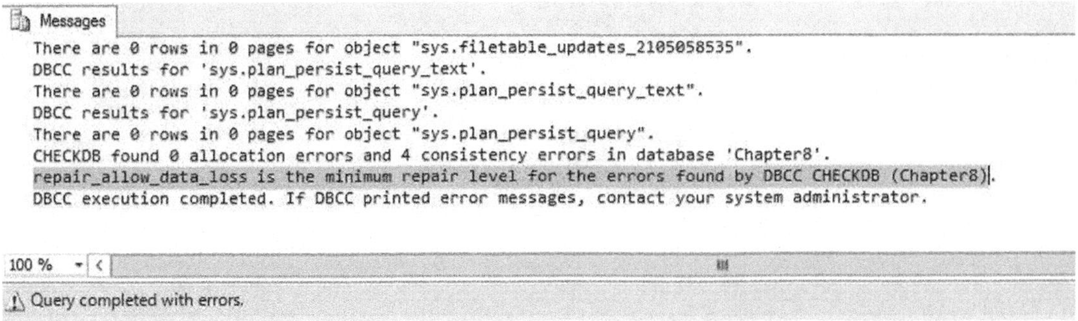

> ▣ Messages
>
> ```
> There are 0 rows in 0 pages for object "sys.filetable_updates_2105058535".
> DBCC results for 'sys.plan_persist_query_text'.
> There are 0 rows in 0 pages for object "sys.plan_persist_query_text".
> DBCC results for 'sys.plan_persist_query'.
> There are 0 rows in 0 pages for object "sys.plan_persist_query".
> CHECKDB found 0 allocation errors and 4 consistency errors in database 'Chapter8'.
> repair_allow_data_loss is the minimum repair level for the errors found by DBCC CHECKDB (Chapter8).
> DBCC execution completed. If DBCC printed error messages, contact your system administrator.
> ```
>
> 100 % ▾ <
>
> ⚠ Query completed with errors.

Figure 8-10. *Suggested repair option*

In our case, we are informed that we need to use the REPAIR_ALOW_DATA_LOSS option. If we try to use the REPAIR_REBUILD option, we receive the following message, from DBCC CHECKDB:

```
"DBCC results for 'CorruptTable'.
... Page (1:292) could not be processed.  See other errors for details.
      The repair level on the DBCC statement caused this repair to be bypassed.""
```

Since we do not have a backup of the Chapter8 database, this is our only chance of fixing the corruption. In order to use the repair options, we also have to put our database in SINGLE_USER mode. The script in Listing 8-10 places the Chapter8 database in SINGLE_USER mode, runs the repair, and then alters the database again to allow multiple connections.

Listing 8-10. Repairing Corruption with DBCC CHECKDB

```
ALTER DATABASE Chapter8 SET SINGLE_USER ;
GO


DBCC CHECKDB (Chapter8, REPAIR_ALLOW_DATA_LOSS) ;
GO


ALTER DATABASE Chapter8 SET MULTI_USER ;
GO
```

The partial results in Figure 8-11 show that the errors in CorruptTable have been fixed. It also shows that the page has been deallocated. This means that we have lost all data on the page.

Figure 8-11. *Results of repairing corruption with DBCC CHECKDB*

If we query the MSDB.dbo.suspect_pages table again using the same query as demonstrated in Listing 8-4, we see that the Event column has been updated to state that the page has been deallocated. We can also see that the error_count column has been incremented every time we accessed the page, through either SELECT statements or DBCC CHECKDB. These results are displayed in Figure 8-12.

Figure 8-12. *Suspect_pages table, following repair*

Emergency Mode

If your database files are damaged to the extent that your database is inaccessible and unrecoverable, even by using the REPAIR_ALLOW_DATA_LOSS option, and you do not have usable backups, then your last resort is to run DBCC CHECKDB in emergency mode using the REPAIR_ALLOW_DATA_LOSS option. Remember, emergency mode is a last resort option for repairing your databases, and if you cannot access them through this mode, you will not be able to access them via any other means. When you perform this action with the database in emergency mode, DBCC CHECKDB treats pages that are inaccessible due to corruption as if they do not have errors in an attempt to recover data.

This operation can also backup databases that are inaccessible due to log corruption. This is because it attempts to force the transaction log to recover, even if it encounters errors. If this fails, it rebuilds the transaction log. Of course, this may lead to transaction inconsistencies, but as mentioned, this is an option of last resort.

As an example, we will delete the transaction log file for the Chapter8 database in the operating system. You can find the operating system location of the transaction log file by running the query in Listing 8-11.

Listing 8-11. Finding the Transaction Log Path

```
SELECT physical_name
FROM sys.master_files
WHERE database_id = DB_ID('Chapter8')
    AND type_desc = 'Log' ;
```

Because data and log files are locked by the SQL Server process, we first need to stop the instance. After starting the instance again, we can see that our Chapter8 database has been marked as Recovery Pending, as shown in Figure 8-13.

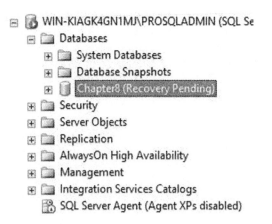

Figure 8-13. *Database in Recovery Pending*

Since we have no backup available for the Chapter8 database, the only option that we have is to use DBCC CHECKDB in emergency mode. The script in Listing 8-12 puts the Chapter8 database in emergency mode and then use DBCC CHECKDB with the REPAIR_ALLOW_DATA_LOSS option to fix the error.

Listing 8-12. DBCC CHECKDB in Emergency Mode

```
ALTER DATABASE Chapter8 SET EMERGENCY ;
GO

ALTER DATABASE Chapter8 SET SINGLE_USER ;
GO

DBCC CHECKDB (Chapter8, REPAIR_ALLOW_DATA_LOSS) ;
GO

ALTER DATABASE Chapter8 SET MULTI_USER ;
GO
```

The partial results, displayed in Figure 8-14, show that SQL Server was able to bring the database online by rebuilding the transaction log. However, it also shows that this means that transactional consistency has been lost and the restore chain has been broken. Because we have lost transactional consistency, we should now run DBCC CHECKCONSTRAINTS to find errors in foreign key constraints, and CHECK constraints. DBCC CHECKCONSTRINTS is covered later in this chapter.

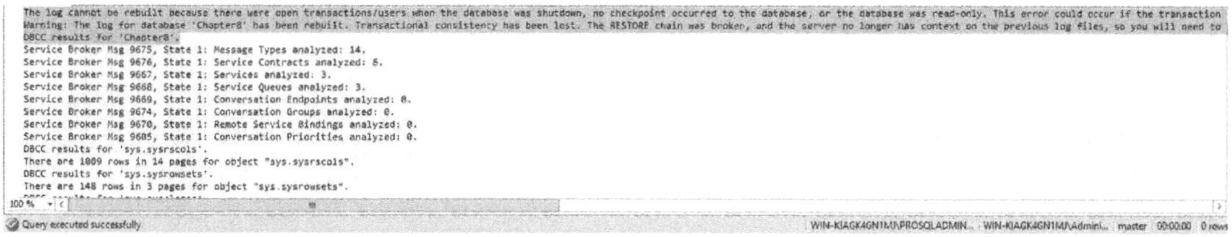

The log cannot be rebuilt because there were open transactions/users when the database was shutdown, no checkpoint occurred to the database, or the database was read-only. This error could occur if the transaction
Warning: The log for database 'Chapter8' has been rebuilt. Transactional consistency has been lost. The RESTORE chain was broken, and the server no longer has context on the previous log files, so you will need to
DBCC results for 'Chapter8'.
Service Broker Msg 9675, State 1: Message Types analyzed: 14.
Service Broker Msg 9676, State 1: Service Contracts analyzed: 6.
Service Broker Msg 9667, State 1: Services analyzed: 3.
Service Broker Msg 9668, State 1: Service Queues analyzed: 3.
Service Broker Msg 9669, State 1: Conversation Endpoints analyzed: 0.
Service Broker Msg 9674, State 1: Conversation Groups analyzed: 0.
Service Broker Msg 9670, State 1: Remote Service Bindings analyzed: 0.
Service Broker Msg 9605, State 1: Conversation Priorities analyzed: 0.
DBCC results for 'sys.sysrscols'.
There are 1009 rows in 14 pages for object "sys.sysrscols".
DBCC results for 'sys.sysrowsets'.
There are 148 rows in 3 pages for object "sys.sysrowsets".
100 %
Query executed successfully.
WIN-KIAGK4GN1MJ\PROSQLADMIN...
WIN-KIAGK4GN1MJ\Admini...
master
00:00:00
0 rows

Figure 8-14. *Results of DBCC CHECKDB in emergency mode*

■ **Note** If running `DBCC CHECKDB` in emergency mode fails, then there is no other way that the database can be repaired.

Other DBCC Commands for Corruption

A number of other DBCC commands perform a subset of the work carried out by `DBCC CHECKDB`. These are discussed in the following sections.

DBCC CHECKCATALOG

In SQL Server the system catalog is a collection of metadata that describes the database and data held within it. When `DBCC CHECKCATALOG` is run, it perform consistency checks on this catalog. This command is run as part of `DBCC CHECKDB` but can also run as a command in its own right. When run in its own right, it accepts the same arguments as `DBCC CHECKDB`, with the exception of `PHYSICAL_ONLY` and `DATA_PURITY`, which are not available for this command.

DBCC CHECKALLOC

`DBCC CHECKALLOC` performs consistency checks against the disk allocation structures within a database. It is run as part of `DBCC CHECKDB` but can also be run as a command in its own right. When run in its own right, it accepts many of the same arguments as `DBCC CHECKDB`, with the exception of `PHYSICAL_ONLY`, `DATA_PURITY`, and `REPAIR_REBUILD`, which are not available for this command. The output is by table, index, and partition.

DBCC CHECKTABLE

`DBCC CHECKTABLE` is run against every table and indexed view in a database, as part of `DBCC CHECKDB`. However, it can also be run as a separate command in its own right against a specific table and the indexes of that table. It performs consistency checks against that specific table, and if any indexed views reference the table, it also performs cross table consistency checks. It accepts the same arguments as `DBCC CHECKDB`, but with it, you also need to specify the name or ID of the table that you want to check.

> ■ **Caution** I have witnessed people split their tables into two buckets and replace DBCC CHECKDB with a
> run DBCC CHECKTABLE against half of their tables on alternate nights. This not only leaves gaps in what is
> being checked, but a new database snapshot is generated for every table that is checked, as opposed to one
> snapshot being generated for all checks to be performed. This can lead to longer run times, per table.

DBCC CHECKFILEGROUP

DBCC CHECKFILEGROUP performs consistency checks on the system catalog, the allocation structures, tables, and indexed views within a specified filegroup. There are some limitations to this, however, when a table has indexes that are stored on a different filegroup. In this scenario, the indexes are not checked for consistency. This still applies if it is the indexes that are stored on the filegroup that you are checking, but the corresponding base table is on a different filegroup.

If you have a partitioned table, which is stored on multiple filegroups, DBCC CHECKFILEGROUP only checks the consistency of the partition(s) that are stored on the filegroup being checked. The arguments for DBCC CHECKFILEGROUP are the same as those for DBCC CHECKDB, with the exception of DATA_PURITY, which is not valid and you cannot specify any repair options. You also need to specify the filegroup name or ID.

DBCC CHECKIDENT

DBCC CHECKIDENT scans all rows within a specified table to find the highest value in the IDENTITY column. It then checks to ensure that the next IDENTITY value, which is stored in a table's metadata, is higher than the highest value in the IDENTITY column of the table. DBCC CHECKIDENT accepts the arguments detailed in Table 8-6.

Table 8-6. DBCC CHECKIDENT Arguments

Argument	Description
Table Name	The name of the table to be checked.
NORESEEED	Returns the maximum value of the IDENTITY column and the current IDENITY value, but will not reseed the column, even if required.
RESEED	Reseeds the current IDENTITY value to that of the maximum IDENTITY value in the table.
New Reseed Value	Used with RESEED, specifies a seed for the IDENTITY value. This should be used with caution, since setting the IDENTITY value to lower than the maximum value in the table can cause errors to be generated, if there is a primary key or unique constraint on the IDENTITY column.
WITH NO_INFOMSGS	Causes informational messages to be suppressed.

We could check the IDENTITY value against the maximum IDENTITY value in our CorruptTable table by using the command in Listing 8-13.

Listing 8-13. DBCC CHECKIDENT

```
DBCC CHECKIDENT('CorruptTable',NORESEED) ;
```

The results, displayed in Figure 8-15, show that both the maximum value in the IDENTITY column, and the current IDENTITY value are both 10201, meaning that there is not currently an issue with the IDENTTY value in our table.

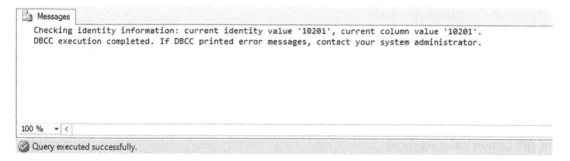

Figure 8-15. *DBCC CHECKIDENT results*

DBCC CHECKCONSTRAINTS

DBCC CHECKCONSTRAINTS can check the integrity of a specific foreign key or check constraint within a table, check all constraints on a single table, or check all constraints on all tables of a database. DBCC CHECKCONSTRAINTS accepts the arguments detailed in Table 8-7.

Table 8-7. *DBCC CHECKCONSTRAINTS Arguments*

Argument	Description
Table or Constraint	Specifies either the name or ID of the constraint you wish to check, or specifies the name or ID of a table to check all enabled constraints on that table. Omitting this argument causes all enabled constraints on all tables within the database to be checked.
ALL_CONSTRAINTS	If DBCC CHECKCONSTRAINTS is being run against an entire table or entire database, then this option forces disabled constraints to be checked as well as enabled ones.
ALL_ERRORMSGS	By default, if DBCC CHECKCONSTRAINTS finds rows that violate a constraint, it returns the first 200 of these rows. Specifying ALL_ERRORMSGS causes all rows violating the constraint to be returned, even if this number exceeds 200.
NO_INFOMSGS	Causes informational messages to be suppressed

The script in Listing 8-14 creates a table called BadConstraint and inserts a single row. It then creates a check constraint on the table, with the NOCHECK option specified, which allows us to create a constraint that is immediately violated by the existing row that we have already added. Finally, we run DBCC CHECKCONSTRAINTS against the table.

271

Listing 8-14. DBCC CHECKCONSTRAINTS

```
USE Chapter8
GO

--Create the BadConstraint table

CREATE TABLE dbo.BadConstraint
(
ID          INT PRIMARY KEY
) ;

--Insert a negative value into the BadConstraint table

INSERT INTO dbo.BadConstraint
VALUES(-1) ;

--Create a CHECK constraint, which enforces positive values in the ID column

ALTER TABLE dbo.BadConstraint WITH NOCHECK ADD CONSTRAINT chkBadConstraint CHECK (ID > 0) ;
GO

--Run DBCC CHECKCONSTRAINTS against the table

DBCC CHECKCONSTRAINTS('dbo.BadConstraint') ;
```

The results of running this script are shown in Figure 8-16. You can see that DBCC CHECKCONSTRAINTS has returned the details of the row that breaches the constraint.

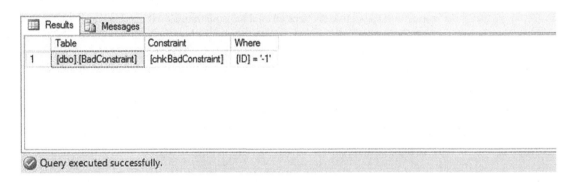

Figure 8-16. DBCC CHECKCONSTRAINTS results

▪ **Tip** After running DBCC CHECKDB, or other DBCC commands to repair corruption, it is good practice to run DBCC CHECKCONSTRAINTS. This is because the repair options of the DBCC commands do not take constraint integrity into account.

Even if `DBCC CHECKCONSTRAINTS` does not find any bad data, it still does not mark the constraint as trusted. You must do this manually. The script in Listing 8-15 first runs a query to see if the constraint is trusted and then manually marks it as trusted.

Listing 8-15. Marking a Constraint as Trusted

```
SELECT
    is_not_trusted
FROM sys.check_constraints
WHERE name = 'chkBadConstraint' ;

ALTER TABLE dbo.BadConstraint WITH CHECK CHECK CONSTRAINT chkDadConstraint ;
```

Consistency Checks on VLDBs

If you have VLDBs (very large databases), then it may be difficult to find a maintenance window long enough to run `DBCC CHECKDB`, and running it while users or ETL processes are connected is likely to cause performance issues. You may also encounter a similar issue if you have a large estate of smaller databases that are using a common infrastructure, such as a SAN or a private cloud. Ensuring that your databases are consistent, however, should be a priority near the top of your agenda, so you should try and find a strategy that achieves both your maintenance and performance goals. The following sections discuss strategies that you may choose to adopt to achieve this balance.

DBCC CHECKDB with PHYSICAL_ONLY

One strategy that you can adopt is to run `DBCC CHECKDB` regularly, ideally nightly, using the `PHYSICAL_ONLY` option, and then run a complete check on a periodic, but less-frequent basis, ideally weekly. When you run `DBCC CHECKDB` with the `PHYSICAL_ONLY` option, consistency checks are carried out of system catalogs and allocation structures and each page of every table is scanned and validated. The net result of this is that corruption caused by IO errors is trapped, but other issues, such as logical consistency errors are identified. This is why it is important to still run a full scan weekly.

Backing Up WITH CHECKSUM and DBCC CHECKALLOC

If you are in a position where all of your databases have a full backup every night and all are configured with a `PAGE_VERIFY` option of `CHECKSUM`, then an alternative approach to the one mentioned in the previous section, is to add the `WITH CHECKSUM` option to your full backups, followed by a `DBCC CHECKALLOC`, to replace the `DBCC CHECKDB`, with the `PHYSICAL_ONLY` option specified on a nightly basis. The `DBCC CHECKALLOC` command, which is actually a subset of the `DBCC CHECKDB` command, validates the allocation structures within the database. When the full backups are taken `WITH CHECKSUM`, then this fulfills the requirement to scan and verify each page of every table for IO errors. Just like running `DBCC CHECKDB`, with the `PHYSICAL_ONLY` option specified, this identifies any corruption caused by IO operations and identifies any bad checksums. Any page errors that occurred in memory, however, are not identified. This means, that like the `PHYSICAL_ONLY` strategy, you still require a full run of `DBCC CHECKDB` once a week to trap logical consistency errors or corruptions that occurred in memory. This option is very useful if you have an environment with common infrastructure and you are performing full nightly backups of all databases, since you will reduce the overall amount of IO on a nightly basis. This is at the expense of the duration of your backup window, however, and it increases the resources used during this time.

Splitting the Workload

Another strategy for VLDBs may be to split the load of DBCC CHECKDB over multiple nights. For example, if your VLDB has multiple filegroups, then you could run DBCC CHECKFILEGROUP against half of the filegroups on Monday, Wednesday, and Friday, and against the other half of the filegroups on Tuesday, Thursday, and Saturday. You could reserve Sunday for a full run of DBCC CHECKDB. A full run of DBCC CHECKDB is still advised on a weekly basis, since DBCC CHECKFILEGROUP does not perform checks, such as validating Service Broker objects.

If your issue is common infrastructure, as opposed to VLDBs, then you can adapt the concept just described so that you run DBCC CHECKDB on a subset of databases on alternate nights. This can be a little complex, since the approach here, in order to avoid swamping the SAN, is to segregate the databases intelligently, and based on size, as opposed to a random 50/50 split. You can find details of how to achieve this in Chapter 17.

Offloading to a Secondary Server

The final strategy for reducing the load on production systems caused by DBCC CHECKDB is to offload the work to a secondary server. If you decide to take this approach, it involves taking a full backup of the VLDB and then restoring it on a secondary server before you run DBCC CHECKDB on the secondary server. This approach has several disadvantages, however. First, and most obviously, it means that you have the expense of procuring and maintaining a secondary server, just for the purpose of running consistency checks. This makes it the most expensive of the options discussed. Also, if you find corruption, you will not know if the corruption was generated on the production system and copied over in the backup or if the corruption was actually generated on the secondary server. This means that if errors are found, you still have to run DBCC CHECKDB on the production server.

Summary

Many types of corruption can occur in SQL Server. These include pages that have been damaged at the file system level, logical consistency errors, and corrupt pages that have a bad checksum. Pages can also be damaged in memory, which would not be identified through a checksum.

Three page verification options can be selected for a database. The NONE option leaves you totally exposed to issues and is regarded as bad practice. The TORN_PAGE_DETECTION option is deprecated and should not be used, since it only checks the first 2 bytes in every 512-byte sector. The final option is CHECKSUM. This is the default option and should always be selected.

Pages that are damaged are stored in a table called dbo.suspect_pages in the MSDB database. Here, the error count is increased every time the error is encountered and the event type of the page is updated to indicate that it has been repaired or restored as appropriate.

If a system database, especially Master, becomes corrupt, you may be unable to start your instance. If this is the case, then you can rectify the issue by running setup with the ACTION parameter set to Rebuilddatabases. Alternatively, if the instance itself has become corrupt, then you can run setup with the ACTION parameter set to repair. This resolves issues such as corrupt Registry keys or corruption to the Resource database.

DBCC CHECKDB is a command that you should run on a regular basis to check for corruption. If you find corruption, then you can also use this command to fix the issue. There are two repair modes that are available, depending on the nature of the corruption: REPAIR_REBUILD or REPAIR_ALLOW_DATA_LOSS. You should only use the REPAIR_ALLOW_DATA_LOSS option as a last resort in the event that no backup is available from which to restore the database or corrupt pages. This is because the REPAIR_ALLOW_DATA_LOSS option is liable to deallocate the corrupt pages, causing all data on these pages to be lost.

Other DBCC commands can be used to perform a subset of DBCC CHECKDB functionality. These include DBCC CHECKTABLE, which can validate the integrity of a specific table, and DBCC CONSTRAINTS, which you can use to verify the integrity of foreign keys and check constraints, especially after you run DBCC CHECKDB with a repair option.

For VLDBs or estates that share infrastructure, running DBCC CHECKDB can be an issue because of performance impact and resource utilization. You can mitigate this by adopting a strategy that offers a trade-off between maintenance and performance goals. These strategies include splitting the workload, offloading the workload to a secondary server, or running only subsets of the checking functionality on a nightly basis and then performing a full check on a weekly basis.

## PART III

Security, Resilience, and Scaling

CHAPTER 9

■ ■ ■

SQL Server Security Model

SQL Server 2014 offers a complex security model with overlapping layers of security that help database administrators (DBAs) counter the risks and threats in a manageable way. It is important for DBAs to understand the SQL Server security model so that they can implement the technologies in the way that best fits the needs of their organization and applications. This chapter discusses the SQL Server security hierarchy before demonstrating how to implement security at the instance, database, and object levels.

Security Hierarchy

The security hierarchy for SQL Server begins at the Windows domain level and cascades down through the local server, the SQL Server instance, the databases, and right on down to the object level. The model is based on the concept of principals, securables, and permissions. *Principals* are entities to which permissions are granted, denied, or revoked. Revoking a permission means deleting an existing grant or deny assignment. Groups and roles are principals that contain zero or more security principals and simplify the management of security by allowing you to assign permissions to similar principals as a single unit.

Securables are objects that can have permissions granted on them—for example, an endpoint at the instance level, or a table within a database. Therefore, you grant a permission on a securable to a principal. The diagram in Figure 9-1 provides an overview of each level of the security hierarchy and how principals are layered.

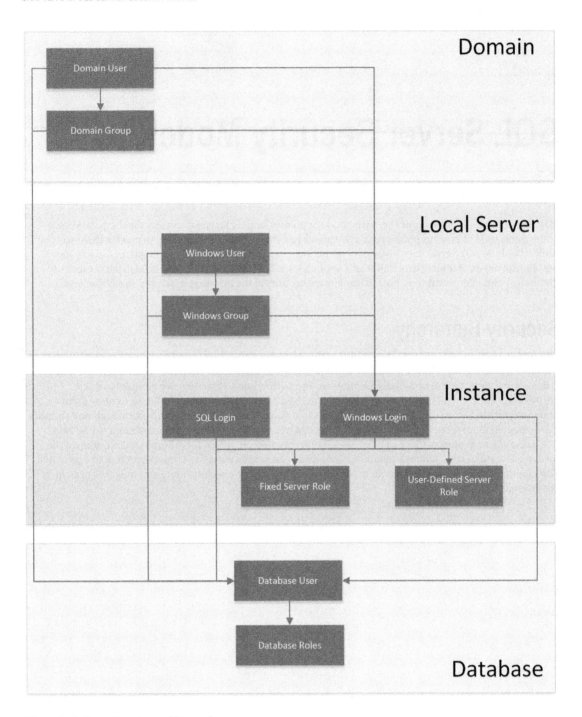

Figure 9-1. *Security principal hierarchy*

The diagram shows that a login, created within the SQL Server instance, can be mapped to a local Windows user or group or to a domain user or group. Usually, in an Enterprise environment, this is a domain user or group. (A *group* is a collection of users that are granted permissions as a unit.) This eases the administration of security. Imagine that a new person joins the sales team. When he is added to the domain group called SalesTeam—which already has all of the required permissions to file system locations, SQL Server databases, and so on—he immediately inherits all required permissions to perform his role.

The diagram also shows that local server or domain-level users and groups can be mapped to a login at the database level. This is part of the contained database functionality that was introduced in SQL Server 2012. Contained database authentication is discussed later in this chapter.

You can then add the Windows login, which you create at the SQL Server instance level or at a second tier SQL Server login (if you are using mixed-mode authentication), to fixed server roles and user-defined server roles at the instance level. Doing this allows you to grant the user common sets of permissions to instance-level objects, such as linked servers and endpoints. You can also map logins to database users.

Database users sit at the database level of the hierarchy. You can grant them permissions directly on schemas and objects within the database, or you can add them to database roles. Database roles are similar to server roles, except they are granted a common set of permissions on objects that sit inside the database, such as schemas, tables, views, stored procedures, and so on.

Implementing Instance-Level Security

Unless you are using contained databases, all users must be authenticated at the instance level. You can use two authentication modes with SQL Server: Windows authentication and mixed-mode authentication. When you select Windows authentication, a login at the instance level is created and mapped to a Windows user or group, which exists either at the domain level or at the local server level.

For example, let's say you have two users, Pete and Danielle. Both users have domain accounts, PROSQLADMIN\Pete and PROSQLADMIN\Danielle. Both users are also part of a Windows group called PROSQLADMIN\SQLUsers. Creating two logins, one mapped to Pete's account and one mapped to Danielle's account, is functionally equivalent to creating one login, mapped to the SQLUsers group, as long as you grant the exact same set of permissions. Creating two separate logins provides more granular control over the permissions, however.

When you create a login mapped to a Windows user or group, SQL Server records the SID (security identifier) of this principal and stores it in the Master database. It then uses this SID to identify users who are attempting to connect, from the context that they have used, to log in to the server or domain.

In addition to creating a login mapped to a Windows user or group, you can also map a login to a certificate or an asymmetric key. Doing so does not allow a user to authenticate to the instance by using a certificate, but it does allow for code signing so that permissions to procedures can be abstracted, rather than granted directly to a login. This helps when you are using dynamic SQL, which breaks the ownership chain; in this scenario, when you run the procedure, SQL Server combines the permissions from the user who called the procedure and the user who maps to the certificate. Ownership chains are discussed later in this chapter.

If you select mixed-mode authentication for your instance, however, then in addition to using Windows authentication, as described earlier, users can also connect by using second tier authentication. When you use second tier authentication, you create a SQL login, which has a user name and password. This user name and password is stored in the Master database with its own SID. When a user attempts to authenticate to the instance, she supplies the user name and password, and this is validated against the credentials stored.

When you are using mixed-mode authentication, there will be a special user, called the SA. This is the System Administrator account, and it has administrative rights to the entire instance. This can be a security vulnerability, because anybody looking to hack into a SQL Server instance will first try to crack the password for the SA account. Because of this, it is imperative that you use a very strong password for this account.

An additional security tip is to rename the SA account. This means that a potential hacker will not know the name of the administrative account, which makes it a lot harder to break into the instance. You can rename the SA account by using the command in Listing 9-1.

Listing 9-1. Renaming the SA Account

```
ALTER LOGIN sa WITH NAME = PROSQLADMINSA ;
```

By its very nature, Windows authentication is more secure than second tier authentication. Therefore, it is good practice to configure your instance to use Windows authentication only, unless you have a specific need to use second tier authentication. You can set the authentication mode in SQL Server Management Studio within the Security tab of the Server Properties dialog box, as illustrated in Figure 9-2. You will need to restart the SQL Server service for the change to take effect.

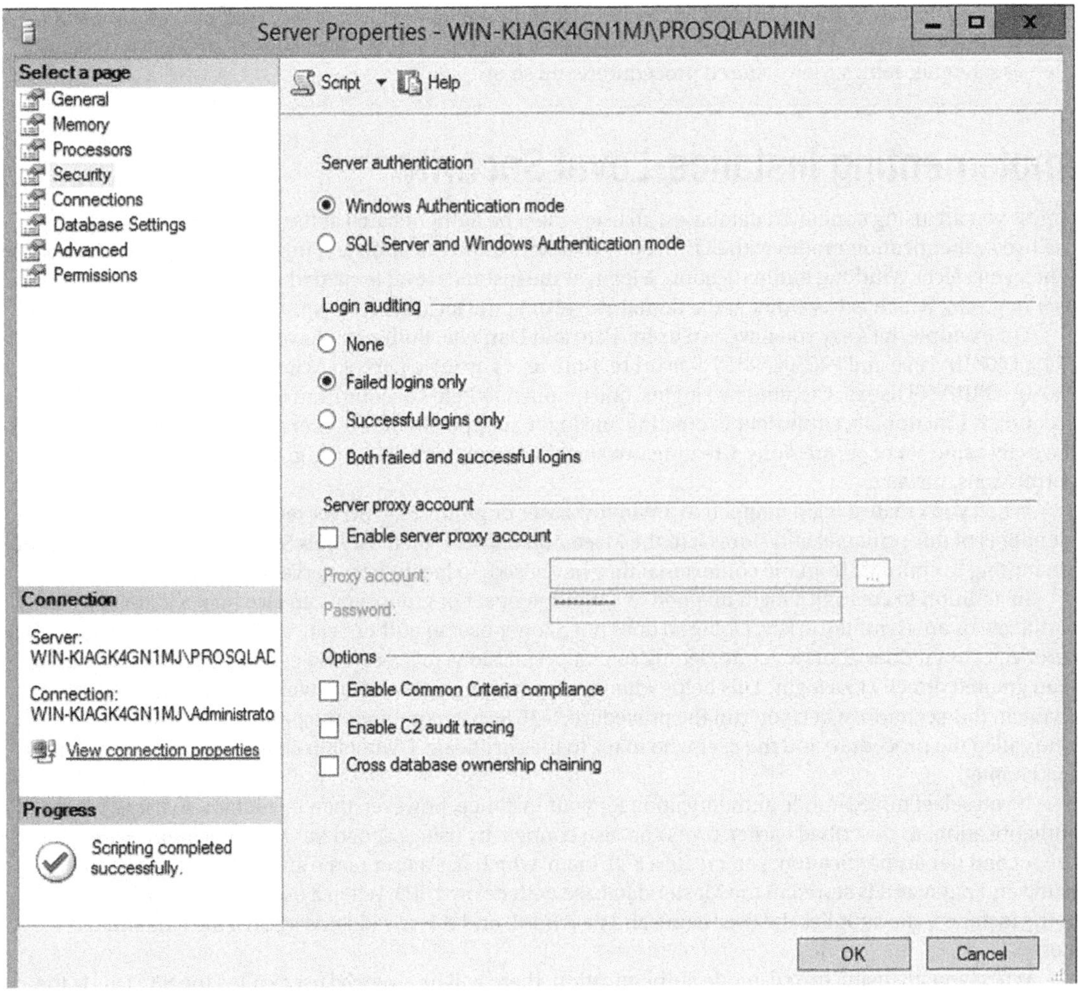

Figure 9-2. The Security tab

■ **Tip** It can be helpful to use mixed-mode authentication in development environments to make testing security easier.

Alternatively, you can change the authentication mode through T-SQL by executing the command in Listing 9-2. This command updates the value of LoginMode in the Registry. Update it to 1 to set it to Windows authentication or to 2 for mixed-mode authentication. Again, you need to restart the service for the change to take effect. The xp_instance_regwrite procedure is undocumented, despite it being the method SQL Server Management Studio uses to change the authentication mode. The advantage of using xp_instance_regwrite over xp_regwrite is that the code you write is transferrable to other instances. This is because it abstracts the full path of the Registry key, which includes the instance name.

Listing 9-2. Configuring Windows Authentication

```
USE Master
GO

EXEC xp_instance_regwrite
    @rootkey = N'HKEY_LOCAL_MACHINE'
    ,@key = N'Software\Microsoft\MSSQLServer\MSSQLServer'
    ,@value_name = N'LoginMode'
    ,@type = N'REG_DWORD'
    ,@value = 1 ;
GO
```

Server Roles

SQL Server provides a set of server roles, out of the box, that allow you to assign instance-level permissions to logins that map to common requirements. These are called *fixed server roles*, and you cannot change the permissions that are assigned to them; you can only add and remove logins. Table 9-1 describes each of these fixed server roles.

Table 9-1. Fixed Server Roles

Role	Description
sysadmin	The sysadmin role gives administrative permissions to the entire instance. A member of the sysadmin role can perform any action within the instance of the SQL Server relational engine.
blkadmin	In conjunction with the INSERT permission on the target table within a database, the bulkadmin role allows a user to import data from a file using the BULK INSERT statement. This role is normally given to service accounts that run ETL processes.
dcreator	The dbcreator role allows its members to create new databases within the instance. Once a user creates a database, he is automatically the owner of that database and is able to perform any action inside it.
diskadmin	The diskadmin role gives its members the permissions to manage backup devices within SQL Server.

(continued)

Table 9-1. (*continued*)

Role	Description
processadmin	Members of the processadmin role are able to stop the instance from T-SQL or SSMS. They are also able to kill running processes.
public	All SQL Server logins are added to the public role. Although you can assign permissions to the public role, this does not fit with the principle of least privilege. This role is normally only used for internal SQL Server operations, such as authentication to TempDB.
securityadmin	Members of the securityadmin role are able to manage logins at the instance level. For example, members may add a login to a server role (except sysadmin) or assign permissions to an instance-level resource, such as an endpoint. However, they cannot assign permissions within a database to database users.
serveradmin	serveradmin combines the diskadmin and processadmin roles. As well as being able to start or stop the instance, however, members of this role can also shut down the instance using the SHUTDOWN T-SQL command. The subtle difference here is that the SHUTDOWN command gives you the option of not running a CHECKPOINT in each database if you use it with the NOWAIT option. Additionally, members of this role can alter endpoints and view all instance metadata.
setupadmin	Members of the setupadmin role are able to create and manage linked servers.

You can also create your own server roles, which group users who need a common set of permissions that are tailored to your environment. For example, if you have a highly available environment that relies on availability groups, then you may wish to create a server role called AOAG and grant this group the following permissions:

- Alter any availability group

- Alter any endpoint

- Create availability group

- Create endpoint

You can then add the junior DBAs, who are not authorized to have full sysadmin permissions, but who you want to manage the high availability of the instance, to this role. You can create this server role by selecting New Server Role from the context menu of Security | Server Roles in SSMS. The General tab of the New Server Role dialog box is illustrated in Figure 9-3.

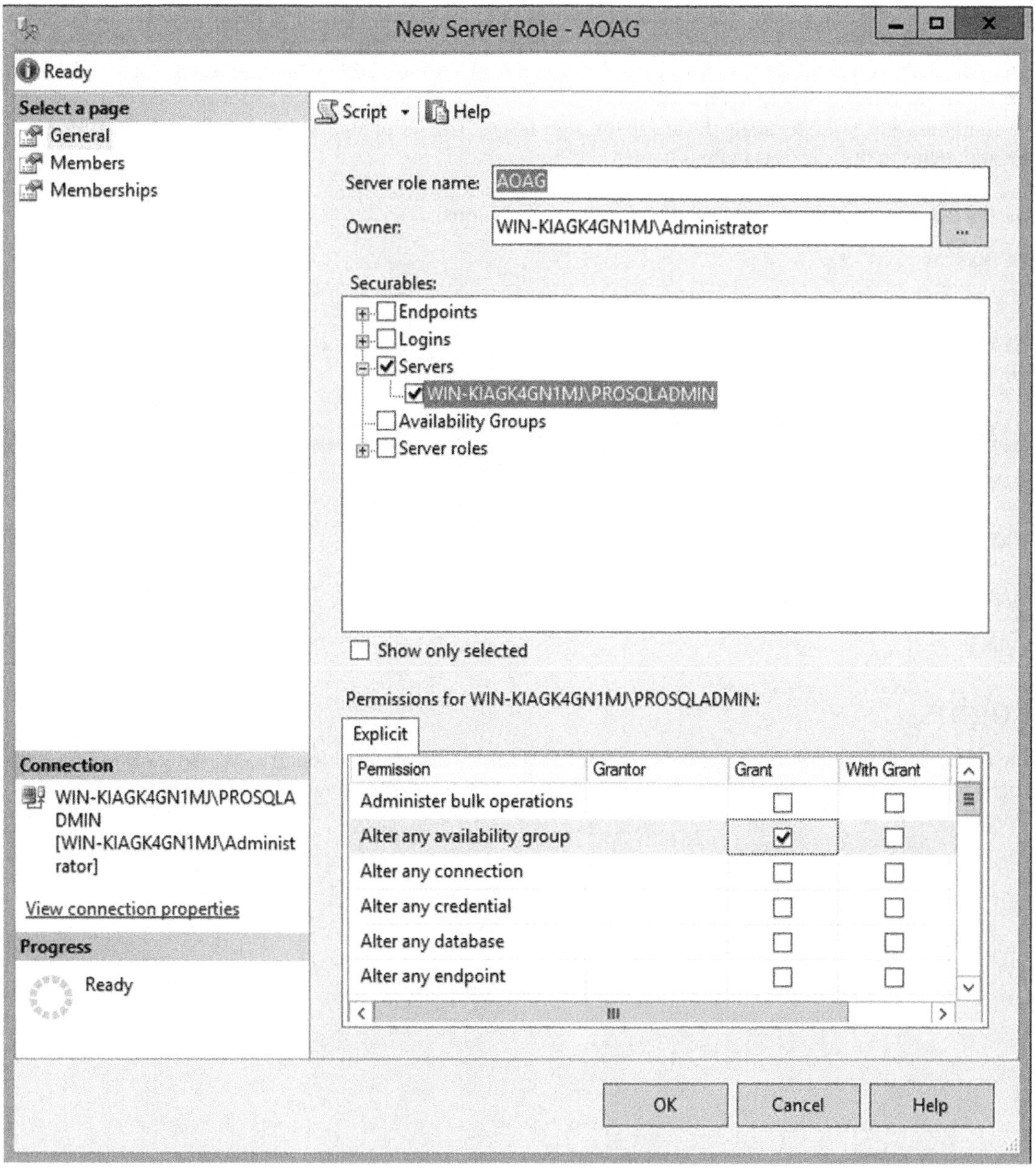

Figure 9-3. *The General tab*

You can see that we have assigned the name of the role as AOAG, we have specified an owner for the role, and we have selected the permissions required under the instance that we are configuring. On the Members tab of the dialog box, we can search for preexisting logins that we will add to the role, and in the Membership tab, we can optionally choose to nest the role inside another server role.

Alternatively, you can create the group through T-SQL. The script in Listing 9-3 also creates this group. We add logins to the role later in this chapter.

Listing 9-3. Creating a Server Role and Assigning Permissions

```
USE Master
GO

CREATE SERVER ROLE AOAG AUTHORIZATION [WIN-KIAGK4GN1MJ\Administrator] ;
GO

GRANT ALTER ANY AVAILABILITY GROUP TO AOAG ;

GRANT ALTER ANY ENDPOINT TO AOAG ;

GRANT CREATE AVAILABILITY GROUP TO AOAG ;

GRANT CREATE ENDPOINT TO AOAG ;
GO
```

Logins

You can create a login through SSMS or through T-SQL. To create a login through SSMS, select New Login from the context menu of Security | Logins. Figure 9-4 shows the General tab of the Login-New dialog box.

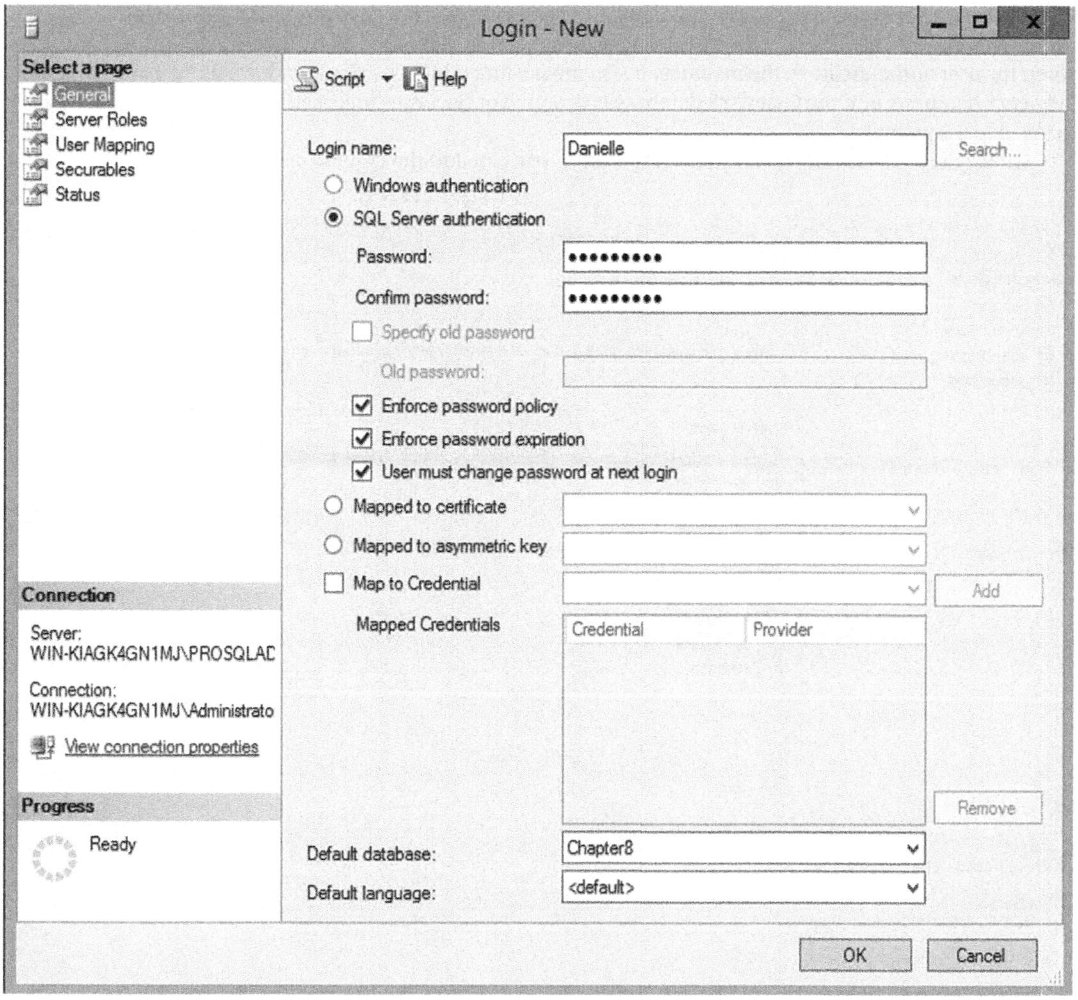

Figure 9-4. *The General tab*

You can see that we have named the login Danielle, and we have specified SQL Server authentication as opposed to Windows authentication. This means that we have also had to specify a password and then confirm it. You may also note that three boxes are checked: Enforce Password Policy, Enforce Password Expiration, and User Must Change Password At Next Login. These three options are cumulative, meaning that you cannot select Enforce Password Expiration without also having Enforce Password Policy selected. You also cannot select User Must Change Password At Next Login without also selecting the Enforce Password Expiration option.

When you select the Enforce Password Policy option, SQL Server checks the password policies for Windows users at the domain level and applies them to SQL Server logins as well. So, for example, if you have a domain policy that enforces that network user's passwords are eight characters or longer, then the same applies to the SQL Server login. If you do not select this option, then no password policies are enforced against the login's password. In a similar vein, if you select the option to enforce password expiration, the expiration period is taken from the domain policies.

We have also set the login's default database to be Chapter8. This does not assign the user any permissions to the Chapter8 database, but it specifies that this database will be the login's landing zone, when the user authenticate to the instance. It also means that if the user does not have permissions to the Chapter8 database, or if the Chapter8 database is dropped or becomes inaccessible, the user will not be able to log in to the instance.

On the Server Roles tab, illustrated in Figure 9-5, you can add the login to server roles.

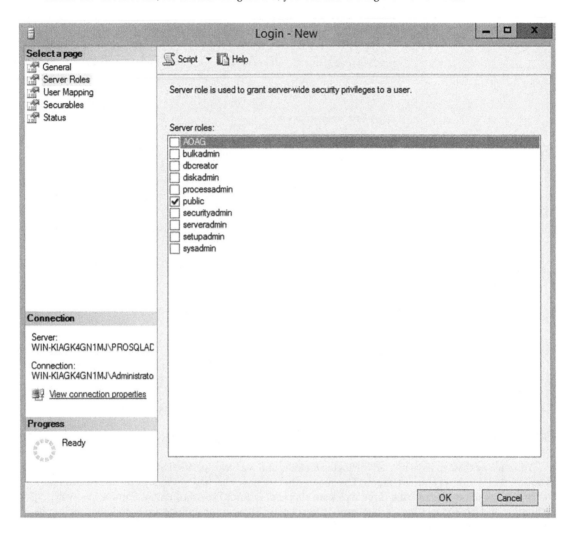

Figure 9-5. *The Server Roles tab*

In our case, we have chosen not to add the login to any additional server roles. Adding logins to server roles is discussed in the next section of this chapter.

On the User Mapping tab, illustrated in Figure 9-6, we can map the login to users at the database level.

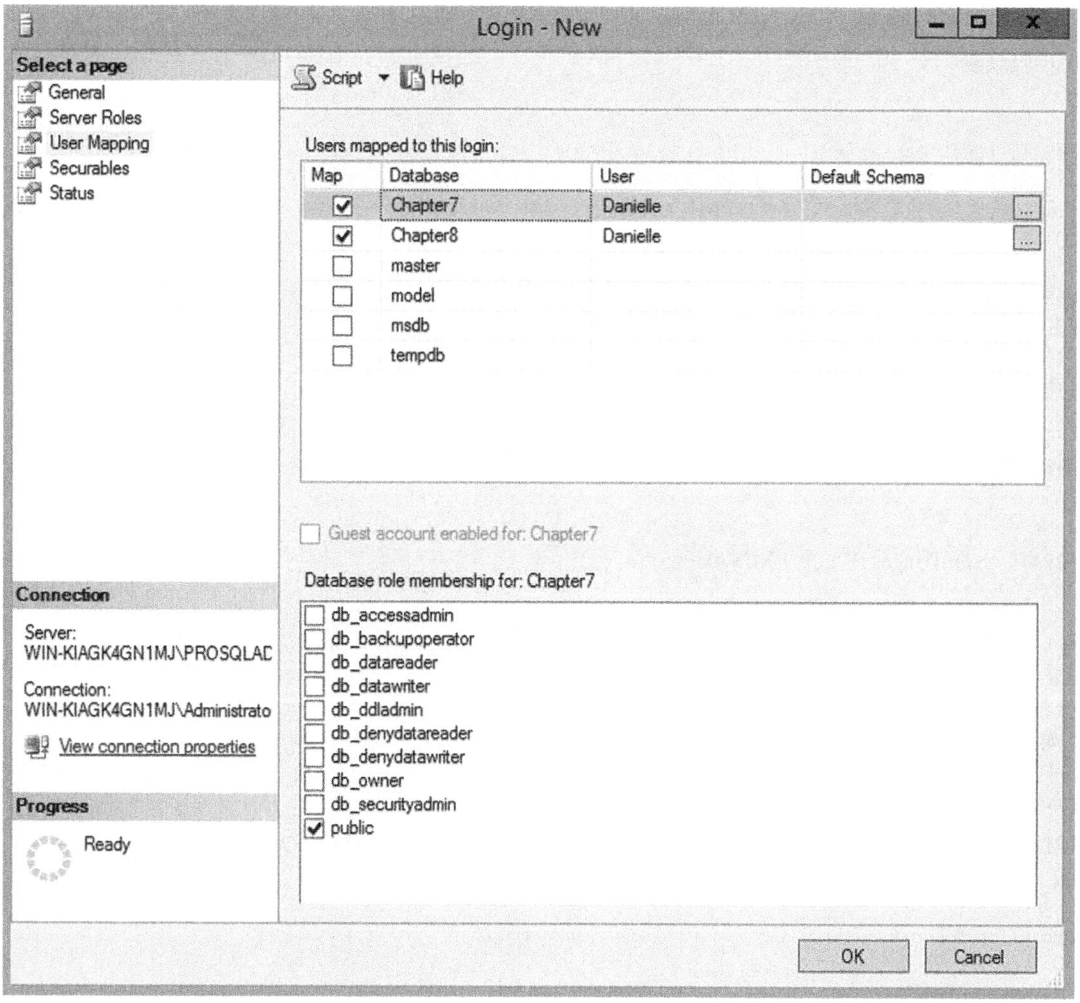

Figure 9-6. *The User Mapping tab*

On this screen, you can see that we have created a database user within the Chapter7 and Chapter8 databases. The name of the database user in each database has defaulted to the same name as the login. This is not mandatory, and you can change the names of the database users; however, it is good practice to keep the names consistent. Failure to do so only leads to confusion and increases the time you must spend managing your security principals. We have not added the users to any database roles at this point. Database roles are discussed later in this chapter.

On the Securables tab, we can search for specific instance-level objects on which to grant the login permissions. In the Status tab, we can grant or deny the login permissions to log in to the instance and enable or disable the login. Also, if the login has become locked out because an incorrect password has been entered too many times, we can unlock the user. The number of failed password attempts is based on the Group Policy settings for the Server, but the CHECK_POLICY option must be used on the login.

The same user can be created through T-SQL by running the script in Listing 9-4. You can see that in order to achieve the same results, multiple commands are required. The first creates the login and the others create database users that map to the login.

Listing 9-4. Creating a SQL Server Login

```
USE Master
GO

CREATE LOGIN Danielle
    WITH PASSWORD=N'Pa$$w0rd' MUST_CHANGE, DEFAULT_DATABASE=Chapter8,
    CHECK_EXPIRATION=ON, CHECK_POLICY=ON ;
GO

USE Chapter7
GO

CREATE USER Danielle FOR LOGIN Danielle ;
GO

USE Chapter8
GO

CREATE USER Danielle FOR LOGIN Danielle ;
GO
```

We can also use either the New Login dialog box or T-SQL to create Windows logins. If using the GUI, we can select the Windows login as opposed to the SQL Server login option and then search for the user or group that we want the login to map to. Listing 9-5 demonstrates how to create a Windows login using T-SQL. It maps the login to a domain user called Pete, with the same configuration as Danielle.

Listing 9-5. Creating a Windows Login

```
CREATE LOGIN [PROSQLADMIN\pete] FROM WINDOWS WITH DEFAULT_DATABASE=Chapter8 ;
GO

USE Chapter7
GO

CREATE USER [PROSQLADMIN\pete] FOR LOGIN [PROSQLADMIN\pete] ;

USE Chapter8
GO

CREATE USER [PROSQLADMIN\pete] FOR LOGIN [PROSQLADMIN\pete] ;
```

Granting Permissions

When assigning permissions to logins, you can use following actions:

- GRANT
- DENY
- REVOKE

GRANT gives principal permissions on a securable. You can use the WITH option with GRANT to also provide a principal with the ability to assign the same permission to other principals. DENY specifically denies login permissions on a securable; DENY overrules GRANT. Therefore, if a login is a member of a server role or roles that give the login permissions to alter an endpoint, but the principal was explicitly denied permissions to alter the same endpoint, then the principal is not able to manage the endpoint. REVOKE removes a permission association to a securable. This includes DENY associations as well as GRANT associations. If a login has been assigned permissions through a server role, however, then revoking the permissions to that securable, against the login itself, has no effect. In order to have an effect, you would need to use DENY, remove the permissions from the role, or change the permissions assigned to the role.

The command in Listing 9-6 grants Danielle permission to alter any login, but then it specifically denies her the permissions to alter the service account.

Listing 9-6. Granting and Denying Permissions

```
GRANT ALTER ANY LOGIN TO Danielle ;
GO

DENY ALTER ON LOGIN::[NT Service\MSSQL$PROSQLADMIN] TO Danielle ;
```

Note the difference in syntax between assigning permissions on a class of object, in this case, logins, and assigning permissions on a specific object. For an object type, the ANY [Object Type] syntax is used, but for a specific object, we use [Object Class]::[Securable].

We can add or remove logins from a server role by using the ALTER SERVER ROLE statement. Listing 9-7 demonstrates how to add Danielle to the sysadmin role and then remove her again.

Listing 9-7. Adding and Removing Server Roles

```
--Add Danielle to the sysadmin Role

ALTER SERVER ROLE sysadmin ADD MEMBER Danielle ;
GO

--Remove Danielle from the sysadmin role

ALTER SERVER ROLE sysadmin DROP MEMBER Danielle ;
GO
```

Implementing Database-Level Security

We have seen how security at the instance level is managed using logins and server roles. Security at the level of the individual database has a similar model, consisting of database users and database roles. The following sections describe this functionality.

Database Roles

Just as there are server roles at the instance level that help manage permissions, there are also database roles at the database level that can group principals together to assign common permissions. There are built-in database roles, but it is also possible to define your own, ones that meet the requirements of your specific data-tier application.

The built-in database roles that are available in SQL Server 2014 are described in Table 9-2.

Table 9-2. *Database Roles*

Database Role	Description
db_accessadmin	Members of this role can add and remove database users from the database.
db_backupoperator	The db_backupoperator role gives users the permissions they need to back up the database, natively. It may not work for third-party backup tools, such as CommVault or Backup Exec, since these tools often require sysadmin rights.
db_datareader	Members of the db_datareader role can run SELECT statements against any table in the database. It is possible to override this for specific tables by explicitly denying a user permissions to those tables. DENY overrides the GRANT.
db_datawriter	Members of the db_datawriter role can perform DML (Data Manipulation Language) statements against any table in the database. It is possible to override this for specific tables by specifically denying a user permissions against a table. The DENY will override the GRANT.
db_denydatareader	The db_denydatareader role denies the SELECT permission against every table in the database.
db_denydatawriter	The db_denydatawriter role denies its members the permissions to perform DLM statements against every table in the database.
db_ddladmin	Members of this role are given the ability to run CREATE, ALTER, and DROP statements against any object in the database. This role is rarely used, but I have seen a couple of examples or poorly written applications that create database objects on the fly. If you are responsible for administering an application such as this, then the ddl_admin role may be useful.
db_owner	Members of the db_owner role can perform any action within the database that has not been specifically denied.
db_securityadmin	Members of this role can grant, deny, and revoke a user's permissions to securables. They can also add or remove role memberships, with the exception of the db_owner role.

You can create your own database roles in SQL Server Management Studio by drilling down through Databases | Your Database | Security and then selected New Database Role from the context menu of database roles in Object Explorer. This displays the General tab of the Database Role - New dialog box, as shown in Figure 9-7.

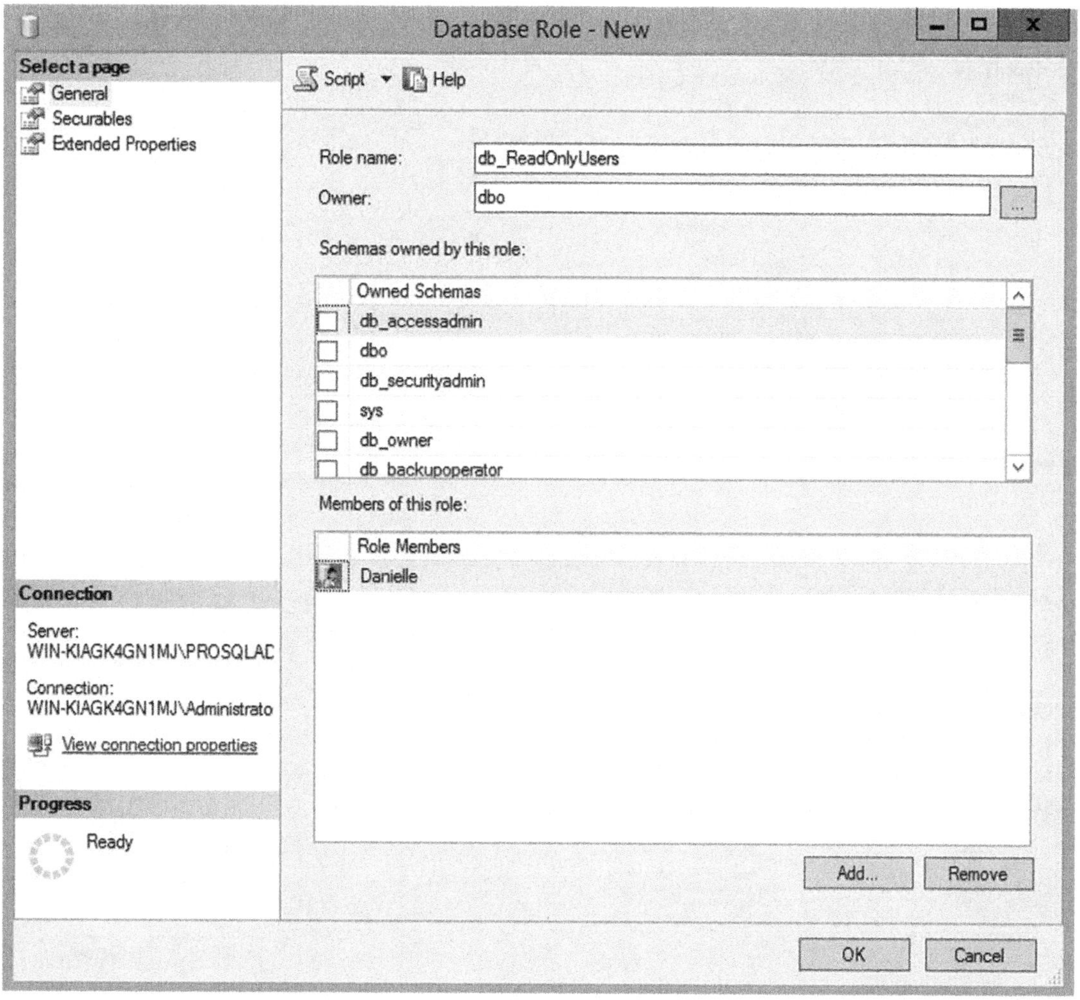

Figure 9-7. *The General tab*

You can see that we have specified db_ReadOnlyUsers as the name of our role and have stated that the role will be owned by dbo. dbo is system user that members of the sysadmin server role map to. We have then used the Add button to add Danielle to the role.

On the Securables tab, we can search for objects that we want to grant permissions on, and then we can select the appropriate permissions for the objects. Figure 9-8 illustrates the results of searching for objects that are part of the dbo schema. We have then selected that the role should have SELECT permissions against the SensitiveData table, but that DELETE, INSERT, and UPDATE permissions should be specifically denied.

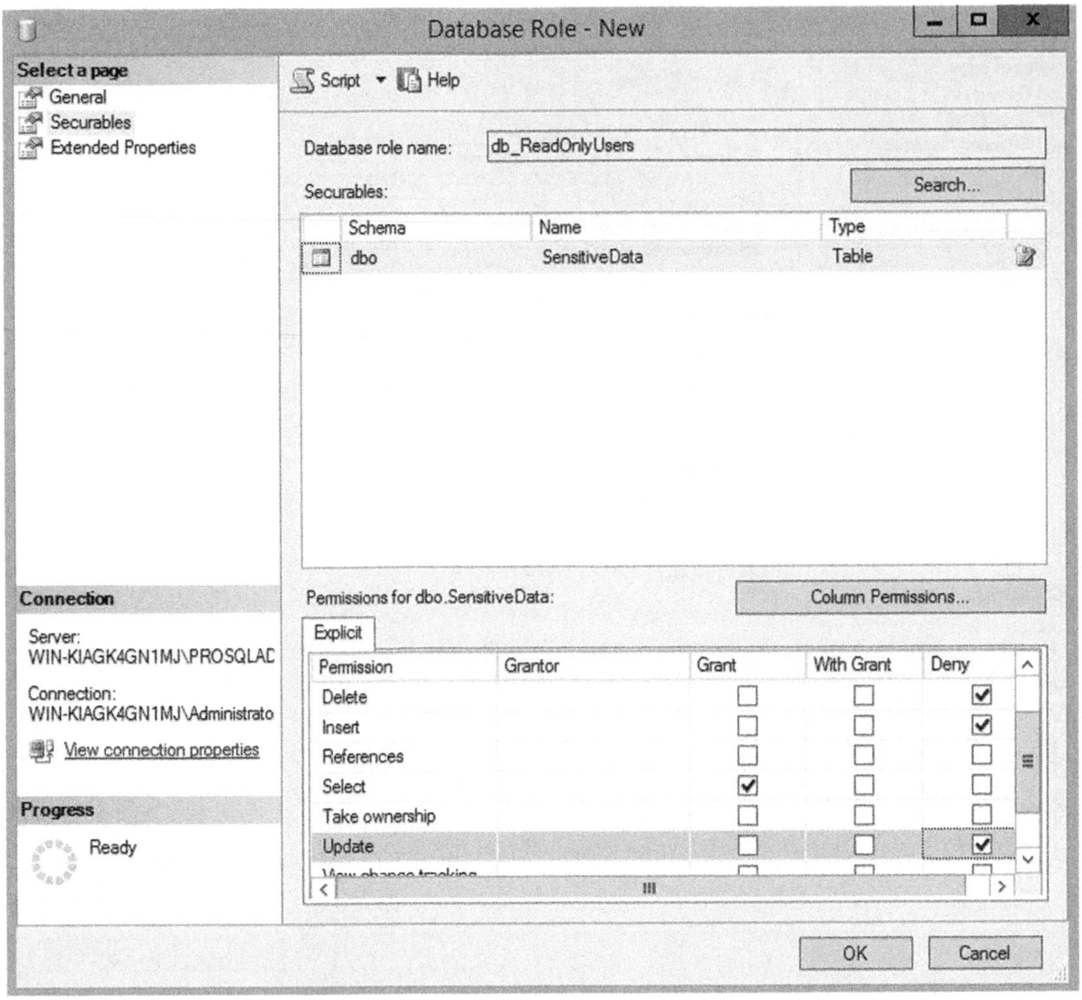

Figure 9-8. *The Securables tab*

Because there is currently only one table in our Chapter9 database, this role is functionally equivalent to adding Danielle to the db_datareader and db_denydatawriter built-in database roles. The big difference is that when we create new tables in our database, the permissions assigned to our db_ReadOnlyUsers role continue to apply only to the SensitiveData table. This is in contrast to the db_datareader and db_denydatawriter roles, which assign the same permission set to any new tables that are created.

An alternative way to create the db_ReadOnlyUsers role is to use the T-SQL script in Listing 9-8. You can see that we have had to use several commands to set up the role. The first command creates the role and uses the authorization clause to specify the owner. The second command adds Danielle as a member of the role, and the subsequent commands use GRANT and DENY keywords to assign the appropriate *permissions on the securable, to* the principal. Before we set up the roles and assign permissions, we first create the Chapter9 database.

Listing 9-8. Creating a Database Role

```
--Create Chapter9 database

CREATE DATABASE Chapter9 ;
GO

USE Chapter9
GO

--Create SensitiveData table

CREATE TABLE dbo.SensitiveData
(
ID      INT     PRIMARY KEY     IDENTITY,
SensitiveText           NVARCHAR(100)
) ;

--Populate SensitiveData table

DECLARE @Numbers TABLE
(
ID          INT
)

;WITH CTE(Num)
AS
(
SELECT 1 AS Num
UNION ALL
SELECT Num + 1
FROM CTE
WHERE Num < 100
)

INSERT INTO @Numbers
SELECT Num
FROM CTE ;

INSERT INTO dbo.SensitiveData
SELECT 'SampleData'
FROM @Numbers ;

--Set Up the Role

CREATE ROLE db_ReadOnlyUsers AUTHORIZATION dbo ;
GO

ALTER ROLE db_ReadOnlyUsers ADD MEMBER Danielle ;

GRANT SELECT ON dbo.SensitiveData TO db_ReadOnlyUsers ;
```

```
DENY DELETE ON dbo.SensitiveData TO db_ReadOnlyUsers ;

DENY INSERT ON dbo.SensitiveData TO db_ReadOnlyUsers ;

DENY UPDATE ON dbo.SensitiveData TO db_ReadOnlyUsers ;
GO
```

■ **Tip** Although DENY assignments can be helpful in some scenarios—for example, if you want to assign a securable permissions to all but one table—in a well-structured security hierarchy, use them with caution. DENY assignments can increase the complexity of managing security and you can enforce the principle of least privilege by exclusively using GRANT assignments in the majority of cases.

Schemas

Schemas provide a logical namespace for database objects while at the same time abstracting an object from its owner. Every object within a database must be owned by a database user. In much older versions of SQL Server, this ownership was direct. In other words, a user named Bob could have owned ten individual tables. From SQL Server 2005 onward, however, this model has changed so that Bob now owns a schema, and the ten tables are part of that schema.

This abstraction simplifies changing the ownership of database objects; in this example, to change the owner of the ten tables from Bob to Colin, you need to change the ownership in one single place (the schema) as opposed to changing it on all ten tables.

Well-defined schemas can also help simplify the management of permissions, because you can assign principal permissions on a schema, as opposed to the individual objects within that schema. For example, if you had five sales-related tables—OrdersHeaders, OrderDetails, StockList, PriceList, and Customers— putting all five tables within a single schema named Sales allows you to apply the SELECT, UPDATE, and INSERT permissions *on* the Sales schema, *to* the SalesUsers database role. Assigning permissions to an entire schema does not just affect tables, however. For example, granting SELECT on a schema also gives SELECT permissions to all views within the schema. Granting the EXECUTE permission on a schema grants EXECUTE on all procedures and functions within the schema.

For this reason, well-designed schemas group tables by business rules, as opposed to technical joins. Consider the entity relationship diagram in Figure 9-9.

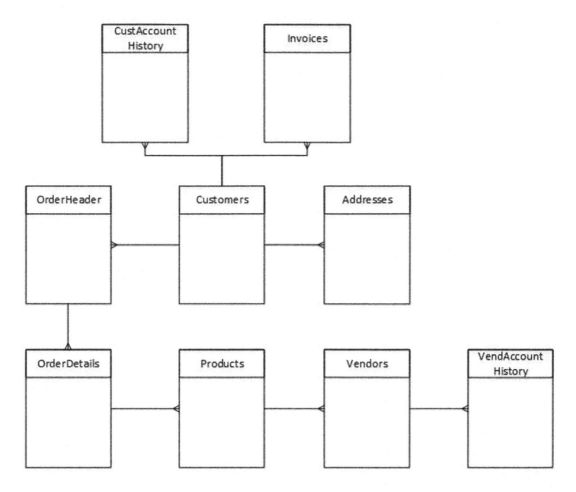

Figure 9-9. *Entity relationship diagram*

A good schema design for this example would involve three schemas, which are split by business responsibility—Sales, Procurement, and Accounts. Table 9-3 demonstrates how these tables can be split and permissions can then be assigned to the tables via database roles.

Table 9-3. *Schema Permissions*

Schema	Table	Database Role	Permissions
Sales	OrderHeader OrderDetails Customers Addresses	Sales Accounts	SELECT, INSERT, UPDATE SELECT
Procurement	Products Vendors	Purchasing Sales Accounts	SELECT, INSERT, UPDATE SELECT SELECT
Accounts	Invoices CustAccountHistory VendAccountHistory	Accounts	SELECT, INSERT, UPDATE

The command in Listing 9-9 creates a schema called CH9 and then grants the user Danielle SELECT permissions on the dbo schema. This will implicitly give her SELECT permissions on all tables within this schema, including new tables, which are yet to be created.

Listing 9-9. Granting Permissions on a Schema

```
CREATE SCHEMA CH9 ;
GO

GRANT SELECT ON SCHEMA::CH9 TO Danielle ;
```

To change a table's schema post creation, use the ALTER SCHEMA TRANSFER command, as demonstrated in Listing 9-10. This script creates a table without specifying a schema. This means that it is automatically placed in the dbo schema. It is then moved to the CH9 schema.

Listing 9-10. Transfering an Object Between Schemas

```
CREATE TABLE TransferTest
(
        ID int
) ;
GO

ALTER SCHEMA CH9 TRANSFER dbo.TransferTest ;
GO
```

Creating and Managing Contained Users

We have already seen how to create a database user, which maps to a login at the instance level in Listing 9-4 and Listing 9-5. It is also possible to create a database user, which does not map to a server principal, however. This is to support a technology called *contained databases*.

Contained databases allow you to reduce a database's dependency on the instance by isolating aspects such as security. This makes the database easier to move between instances and helps support technologies such as AlwaysOn Availability Groups, which are discussed in Chapter 13.

Currently, SQL Server supports the database containment levels of NONE, which is the default, and PARTIAL. PARTIAL indicates that the database supports contained database users and that metadata is stored inside the database using the same collation. However, the database can still interact with no-contained features, such as users mapped to logins at the instance level. There is currently no option for FULL containment, since there is no way to stop the database from interacting with objects outside its boundaries.

In order to use contained databases, you must enable them at both the instance and the database level. You can enable them at both levels by using the Server Properties and Database Properties dialog boxes in SQL Server Management Studio. Alternatively, you can enable them at the instance level by using sp_configure and at the database level by using the ALTER DATABASE statement. The script in Listing 9-11 demonstrates how to enable contained databases for the instance and the Chapter9 database using T-SQL. To use the ALTER DATABASE command, you need to disconnect users from the database.

Listing 9-11. Enabling Contained Databases

```
--Enable contained databases at the instance level

EXEC sp_configure 'show advanced options', 1 ;
GO


RECONFIGURE ;
GO


EXEC sp_configure 'contained database authentication', '1' ;
GO


RECONFIGURE WITH OVERRIDE ;
GO


--Set Chapter9 database to use partial containment

USE Master
GO


ALTER DATABASE [Chapter9] SET CONTAINMENT = PARTIAL WITH NO_WAIT ;
GO
```

Once you have enabled contained databases, you can create database users that are not associated with a login at the instance level. You can create a user from a Windows user or group by using the syntax demonstrated in Listing 9-12. This script creates a database user that maps to the Chapter9Users domain group. It specifies that dbo is the default schema.

Listing 9-12. Creating a Database User from a Windows Login

```
USE Chapter9
GO


CREATE USER [PROSQLADMIN\Chapter9Uusers] WITH DEFAULT_SCHEMA=dbo ;
GO
```

Alternatively, to create a database user who is not mapped to a login at the instance level but who still relies on second tier authentication, you can use the syntax in Listing 9-13. This script creates a user in the Chapter9 database called ContainedUser.

Listing 9-13. Creating a Database User with Second Tier Authentication

```
USE Chapter9
GO

CREATE USER ContainedUser WITH PASSWORD=N'Pa$$w0rd', DEFAULT_SCHEMA=dbo ;
GO
```

When you use contained database users, you need to take a number of additional security considerations into account. First, some applications may require that a user have permissions to multiple databases. If the user is mapped to a Windows user or group, then this is straightforward because the SID that is being authenticated is that of the Windows object. If the database user is using second tier authentication, however, then it is possible to duplicate the SID of the user from the first database. For example, we can create a user called ContainedUser in the Chapter9 database that will use second tier authentication. We can then duplicate this user in the Chapter8 database by specifying the SID, as demonstrated in Listing 9-14. Before duplicating the user, the script first configures the Chapter8 database to be contained.

Listing 9-14. Creating a Duplicate User

```
USE Master
GO

ALTER DATABASE Chapter8 SET CONTAINMENT = PARTIAL WITH NO_WAIT ;
GO

USE Chapter8
GO

CREATE USER ContainedUser WITH PASSWORD = 'Pa$$w0rd',
        SID = 0x0105000000000009030000009134B23303A7184590E152AE6A1197DF ;
```

We can determine the SID by querying the sys.database_principals catalog view from the Chapter9 database, as demonstrated in Listing 9-15.

Listing 9-15. Finding the User's SID

```
SELECT sid
FROM sys.database_principals
WHERE name = 'ContainedUser' ;
```

Once we have duplicated the user in the second database, we also need to turn on the TRUSTWORTHY property of the first database in order to allow cross database queries to take place. We can turn on TRUSTWORTHY in the Chapter9 database by using the command in Listing 9-16.

Listing 9-16. Turning on TRUSTWORTHY

```
ALTER DATABASE Chapter9 SET TRUSTWORTHY ON ;
```

Even if we do not create a duplicate user, it is still possible for a contained user to access other databases via the Guest account of another database if the Guest account is enabled. This is a technical requirement so that the contained user can access TempDB, but the Guest account in other databases should not be used.

DBAs should also be careful when they attach a contained database to an instance to ensure that they are not inadvertently granting permissions to users who are not meant to have access. This can happen when you are moving a database from a pre-production environment to a production instance and UAT (User Acceptance Testing) or development users were not removed from the database before the attach.

Implementing Object-Level Security

There are two variations of syntax for granting a database user permissions to an object. The first uses the OBJECT phrase whereas the second does not. For example, the two commands in Listing 9-17 are functionally equivalent.

Listing 9-17. Assigning Permissions

```
USE Chapter9
GO

--Grant with OBJECT notation

GRANT SELECT ON OBJECT::dbo.SensitiveData TO [PROSQLADMIN\Chapter9Users] ;
GO

--Grant without OBJECT notation

GRANT SELECT ON dbo.SensitiveData TO [PROSQLADMIN\Chapter9Users] ;
GO
```

Many permissions can be granted and not all permissions are relevant to each object. For example, the SELECT permission can be granted on a table or a view, but not to a stored procedure. The EXECUTE permission, on the other hand, can be granted on a stored procedure, but not to a table or view.

When granting permissions on a table, it is possible to grant permissions to specific columns, as opposed to the table itself. The script in Listing 9-18 gives the user ContainedUser SELECT permissions on the SensitiveData table in the Chapter9 database. Instead of being able to read the entire table, however, permissions are only granted on the SensitiveText column.

Listing 9-18. Granting Column-Level Permissions

```
GRANT SELECT ON dbo.SensitiveData ([SensitiveText]) TO ContainedUser ;
```

Ownership Chaining

Although it is possible to grant permissions at the column level, this can become very difficult and convoluted to manage. There is also no facility in SQL Server to grant permissions at the row level. To overcome these complexities and limitations, it is possible to use views or procedures to manage fine-grain security.

When multiple objects are called sequentially by a query, SQL Server regards them as a chain. When you are chaining objects together, the permissions are evaluated differently—for example, imagine that you have a view named View1 and the view is based on two tables: Table1 and Table2. If all three of these objects share the same owner, then when a SELECT statement is run against the view, the caller's permissions on the view are evaluated, but their permissions on the underlying tables are not.

This means that if you want to grant UserA SELECT permissions on Column1 and Column2 in TableA, or even on specific rows within TableA, then you need to create a view that stores the query that this user can run. At this point, the user can run a SELECT statement from the view, as opposed to the base table. As long as they have SELECT permission on the view and the view shares an owner with the base table, then their permissions on the underlying table are not checked, and the query succeeds.

The ownership chain is broken in the event that one of the objects that the view is based on does not have the same owner as the view. In this scenario, permissions on the underlying table are checked by SQL Server, and an error is returned if the user does not have appropriate permissions to the underlying table.

It is important to note that ownership chains actually lead to DENY assignments being bypassed. This is because neither the GRANT or DENY assignments of the user will be evaluated. This is demonstrated in Listing 9-19.

Listing 9-19. Ownership Chain Bypassing DENY Assignment

```
USE Chapter9
GO

CREATE TABLE dbo.ownershipChain
(
        OwnershipChainID int
) ;
GO

CREATE USER Colin WITH PASSWORD = 'Pa$$w0rd' ;
GO

DENY SELECT ON OwnershipChain TO Colin ;
GO

CREATE PROCEDURE OwnershipChainSelect
AS
SELET * FROM dbo.OwnershipChain ;
GO

GRANT EXECUTE ON OwnershipChainSelect TO Colin ;
GO

EXECUTE AS USER = 'Colin' ;
GO

--The following statement will fail, as Colin has been denied permissions to the table

SELECT *
FROM    dbo.OwnershipChain ;
GO
```

```
--The following statement will succeed, because ownership chaining will be used

EXECUTE dbo.OwnershipChainSelect ;
GO

REVERT
```

It is also possible to create ownership chains across multiple databases. For this to succeed, however, you must enable cross database ownership chaining either at the instance level or at the individual databases that will participate in the ownership chain. You should not turn on cross database ownership chaining at the instance level unless all databases within the instance will participate in the chaining. This is because the feature increases the risk of threats against your environment and needs to be managed. If you do wish to enable cross database ownership chaining at the instance level, do so by using the command in Listing 9-20.

Listing 9-20. Enabling Cross Database Ownership Chaining at the Instance

```
EXEC sys.sp_configure 'cross db ownership chaining', '1' ;
GO

RECONFIGURE WITH OVERRIDE ;
```

To enable cross database ownership chaining for a specific database, you can use the ALTER DATABASE command, as demonstrated in Listing 9-21.

Listing 9-21. Enabling Cross Database Ownership Chaining for a Database

```
ALTER DATABASE Chapter9 SET DB_CHAINING ON ;
```

Server Audit

SQL Server Audit provides DBAs with the ability to capture granular audits against instance- and database-level activity and save this activity to a file, the Windows Security log, or the Windows Application log. The location where the audit data is saved is known as the *target*. The SQL Server Audit object sits at the instance level and defines the properties of the audit and the target. You can have multiple server audits in each instance. This is useful if you have to audit many events in a busy environment, since you can distribute the IO by using a file as the target and placing each target file on a separate volume.

Choosing the correct target is important from a security perspective. If you choose the Windows Application log as a target, then any Windows user who is authenticated to the server is able to access it. The Security log is a lot more secure than the Application log but can also be more complex to configure for SQL Server Audit. The service account that is running the SQL Server service requires the Generate Security Audits user rights assignment within the server's local security policy. Application-generated auditing also needs to be enabled for success and failure within the audit policy. The other consideration for the target is size. If you decide to use the Application log or Security log, then it is important that you consider, and potentially increase, the size of these logs before you begin using them for your audit. Also, work with your Windows administration team to decide on how the log will be cycled when full and if you will be achieving the log by backing it up to tape.

The SQL Server Audit can then be associated with one or more server audit specifications and database audit specifications. These specifications define the activity that will be audited at the instance level and the database level, respectively. It is helpful to have multiple server or database audit specifications if you are auditing many actions, because you can categorize them to make management easier, while still associating them with the same server audit. Each database within the instance needs its own database audit specification if you plan to audit activity in multiple databases.

Creating a Server Audit

When you create a server audit, you can use the options detailed in Table 9-4.

Table 9-4. *Server Audit Options*

Option	Description
FILEPATH	Only applies if you choose a file target. Specifies the file path, where the audit logs will be generated.
MAXSIZE	Only applies if you choose a file target. Specifies the largest size that the audit file can grow to. The minimum size you can specify for this is 2MB.
MAX_ROLLOVER_FILES	Only applies if you choose a file target. When the audit file becomes full, you can either cycle that file, or generate a new file. The MAX_ROLLOVER_FILES setting controls how many new files can be generated before they begin to cycle. The default value is UNLIMITED, but specifying a number caps the number of files to this limit. If you set it to 0, then there will only ever be one file, and it will cycle every time it becomes full. Any value above 0 indicates the number of rollover files that will be permitted. So for example, if you specify 5, then there will be a maximum of six files in total.
MAX_FILES	Only applies if you choose a file target. As an alternative to MAX_ROLLOVER_FILES, the MAX_FILES setting specifies a limit for the number of audit files that can be generated, but when this number is reached, the logs will not cycle. Instead, the audit fails and events that cause an audit action to occur are handled based on the setting for ON_FAILURE.
RESERVE_DISK_SPACE	Only applies if you choose a file target. Pre-allocate space on the volume equal to the value set in MAXSIZE, as opposed to allowing the audit log to grow as required.
QUEUE_DELAY	Specify if audit events are written synchronously or asynchronously. If set to 0, events are written to the log synchronously. Otherwise, specify the duration in milliseconds that can elapse before events are forced to write. The default value is 1000 (1 second), which is also the minimum value.
ON_FAILURE	Specify what should happen if events that cause an audit action fail to be audited to the log. Acceptable values are CONTINUE, SHUTDOWN, or FAIL_OPERATION. When CONTINUE is specified, the operation is allowed to continue. This can lead to unaudited activity occurring. FAIL_OPERATION causes auditable events to fail, but allows other actions to continue. SHUTDOWN forces the instance to stop if auditable events cannot be written to the log.
AUDIT_GUID	Because server and database audit specifications link to the server audit through a GUID, there are occasions when an audit specification can become orphaned. These include when you attach a database to an instance, or when you implement technologies such as database mirroring. This option allows you to specify a specific GUID for the server audit, as opposed to having SQL Server generate a new one.

It is also possible to create a filter on the server audit. This can be useful when your audit specification captures activity against an entire class of object, but you are only interested in auditing a subset. For example, you may configure a server audit specification to log any member changes to server roles; however, you are only actually interested in members of the sysadmin server role being modified. In this scenario, you can filter on the sysadmin role.

You can create a server audit through the GUI in SQL Server Management Studio by drilling through Security in Object Explorer and choosing New Audit from the Audits node. Figure 9-10 illustrates the Create Audit dialog box.

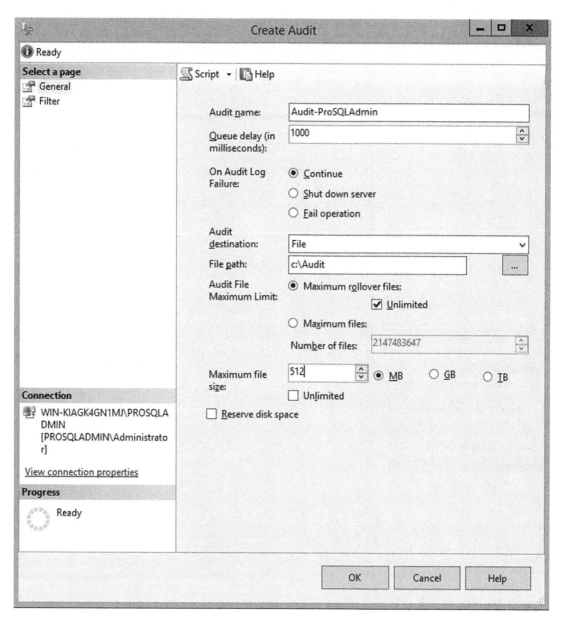

Figure 9-10. *The General tab*

You can see that we have decided to save our audit to a flat file, as opposed to a Windows log. Therefore, we need to specify the file-related parameters. We set our file to rollover and enforce the maximum size for any one file to be 512MB. We leave the default value of 1 second (1000 milliseconds) as a maximum duration before audit entries are forced to be written to the log and name the audit Audit-ProSQLAdmin.

On the Filter tab of the Create Audit dialog box, shown in Figure 9-11, we specify that we wish to filter on the object_name and only audit changes to the sysadmin role.

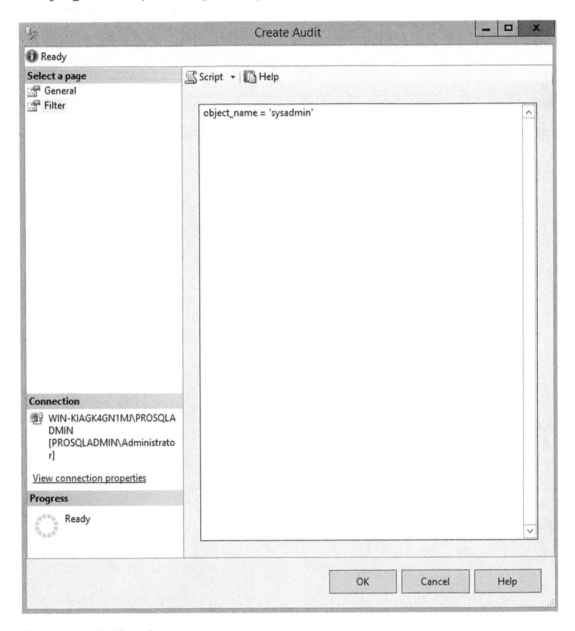

Figure 9-11. *The Filter tab*

Alternatively, we can use T-SQL to perform the same action. The script in Listing 9-22 creates the same server audit.

Listing 9-22. Creating a Server Audit

```
USE Master

GO

CREATE SERVER AUDIT [Audit-ProSQLAdmin]
TO FILE
(       FILEPATH = N'c:\audit'
        ,MAXSIZE = 512 MB
        ,MAX_ROLLOVER_FILES = 2147483647
        ,RESERVE_DISK_SPACE = OFF
)
WITH
(       QUEUE_DELAY = 1000
        ,ON_FAILURE = CONTINUE
)
WHERE object_name = 'sysadmin' ;
```

Creating a Server Audit Specification

To create the server audit specification through SSMS, we can drill through Security in Object Explorer and choose New Server Audit Specification from the Server Audit Specifications context menu. This will cause the Create Server Audit Specification dialog box to be displayed, as illustrated in Figure 9-12.

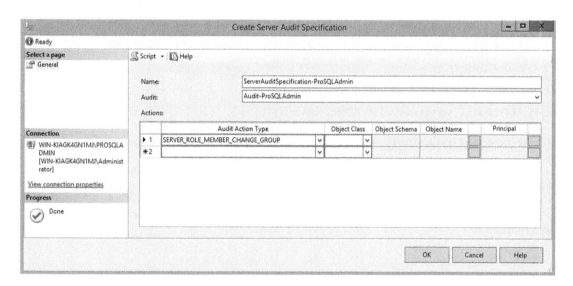

Figure 9-12. Server Audit Specification dialog box

You can see that we have selected the SERVER_ROLE_MEMBER_CHANGE_GROUP as the audit action type. This audits any additions or removals of the membership of server roles. Combined with the filter that we have put on the Server Audit object, however, the new result is that only changes to the sysadmin server role will be logged. We also selected the Audit-ProSQLAdmin audit from the Audit drop-down box to tie the objects together.

Alternatively, we can create the same server audit specification through T-SQL by running the command in Listing 9-23. In this command, we are using the FOR SERVER AUDIT clause to link the server audit specification to the Audit-ProSQLAdmin server audit, and the ADD clause to specify the audit action type to capture.

Listing 9-23. Creating the Server Audit Specification

```
CREATE SERVER AUDIT SPECIFICATION [ServerAuditSpecification-ProSQLAdmin]
FOR SERVER AUDIT [Audit-ProSQLAdmin]
ADD (SERVER_ROLE_MEMBER_CHANGE_GROUP) ;
```

Enabling and Invoking Audits

Even though we have created the server audit and server audit specification, we need to enable them before any data starts to be collected. We can achieve this by choosing Enable from the context menu of each of the objects in Object Explorer, or by altering the objects and setting their STATE = ON in T-SQL. This is demonstrated in Listing 9-24.

Listing 9-24. Enabling Auditing

```
ALTER SERVER AUDIT [Audit-ProSQLAdmin] WITH (STATE = ON) ;

ALTER SERVER AUDIT SPECIFICATION [ServerAuditSpecification-ProSQLAdmin]
WITH (STATE = ON) ;
```

We now add the Danielle login to the serveradmin and sysadmin server roles using the script in Listing 9-25 so that we can check that our audit is working.

Listing 9-25. Triggering the Audit

```
ALTER SERVER ROLE serveradmin ADD MEMBER Danielle ;

ALTER SERVER ROLE sysadmin ADD MEMBER Danielle ;
```

We expect that our server audit specification's definition has captured both actions, but that the WHERE clause has filtered out the first action we applied to the server audit. If we view the audit log by selecting View Audit Log from the context menu of the Audit-ProSQLAdmin server audit in Object Explorer, as illustrated in Figure 9-13, we can see that this is working as expected and review the audit entry that has been captured.

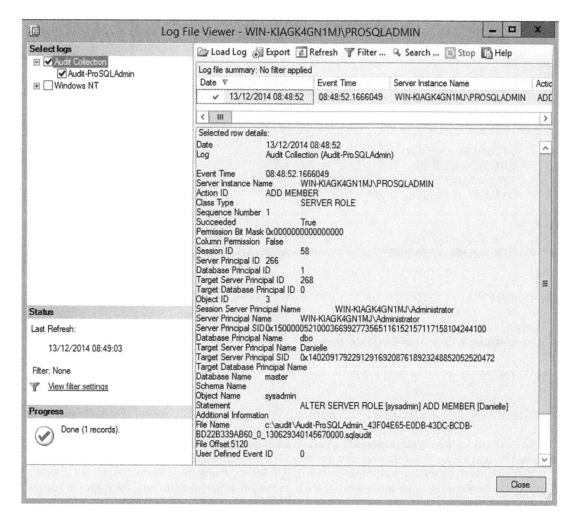

Figure 9-13. *Audit Log File Viewer*

We can see that a granular level of information has been captured. Most notably, this information includes the full statement that caused the audit to fire, the database and object involved, the target login, and the login that ran the statement.

Database Audit Specifications

A database audit specification is similar to a server audit specification but specifies audit requirements at the database level, as opposed to at the instance level. In order to demonstrate this functionality, we map the Danielle login to a user in this database and assign SELECT permissions to the SensitiveData table. We also create a new server audit, called Audit-Chapter9, which we use as the audit to which our database audit specification attaches. These actions are performed in Listing 9-26. Before executing the script, change the file path to match your own configuration.

Listing 9-26. Creating the Chapter9 Database

```
USE Master
GO

--Create Server Audit

CREATE SERVER AUDIT [Audit-Chapter9]
TO FILE
(        FILEPATH = N'C:\Audit'
        ,MAXSIZE = 512 MB
        ,MAX_ROLLOVER_FILES = 2147483647
        ,RESERVE_DISK_SPACE = OFF
)
WITH
(        QUEUE_DELAY = 1000
        ,ON_FAILURE = CONTINUE
) ;

USE Chapter9
GO

--Create database user from Danielle Login

CREATE USER Danielle FOR LOGIN Danielle WITH DEFAULT_SCHEMA=dbo ;
GO

GRANT SELECT ON dbo.SensitiveData TO Danielle ;
```

We now look to create a database audit specification that captures any INSERT statements made against the SensitiveData table by any user but also captures SELECT statements run specifically by Danielle.

We can create the database audit specification in SQL Server Management Studio by drilling through the Chapter9 database | Security and selecting New Database Audit Specification from the context menu of Database Audit Specifications. This invokes the Create Database Audit Specification dialog box, as illustrated in Figure 9-14.

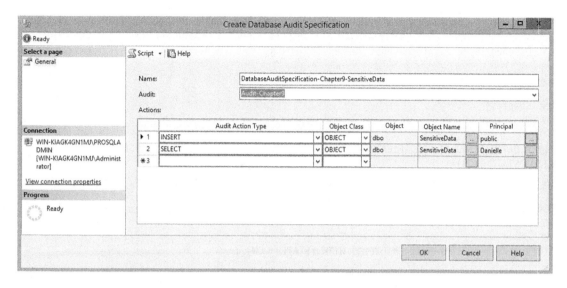

Figure 9-14. *Database Audit Specification dialog box*

You can see that we named the database audit specification `DatabaseAuditSpecification-Chapter9-SensitiveData` and linked it to the `Audit-Chapter9` server audit using the drop-down list. In the lower half of the screen, we specified two audit action types, `INSERT` and `SELECT`. Because we specified an object class of `OBJECT`, as opposed to the other available options of `DATABASE` or `SCHEMA`, we also need to specify the object name of the table that we want to audit. Because we only want Danielle's `SELECT` activity to be audited, we add this user to the Principal field for the `SELECT` action type, but we add the `Public` role as the principal for the `INSERT` action type. This is because all database users will be members of the `Public` role, and hence, all `INSERT` activity will be captured, regardless of the user.

■ **Tip** You can display a complete list of audit class types by running the query `SELECT * FROM sys.dm_audit_class_type_map`. You can find a complete list of auditable actions by running the query `SELECT * FROM sys.dm_audit_actions`.

We can create the same database audit specification in T-SQL by using the `CREATE DATABASE AUDIT SPECIFICATION` statement, as demonstrated in Listing 9-27.

Listing 9-27. Creating the Database Audit Specification

```
USE Chapter9
GO

CREATE DATABASE AUDIT SPECIFICATION [DatabaseAuditSpecification-Chapter9-SensitiveData]
FOR SERVER AUDIT [Audit-Chapter9]
ADD (INSERT ON OBJECT::dbo.SensitiveData BY public),
ADD (SELECT ON OBJECT::dbo.SensitiveData BY Danielle) ;
```

Just as we would with a server audit specification, we need to enable the database audit specification before any information starts to be collected. The script in Listing 9-28 enables both Audit-Chapter9 and DatabaseAuditSpecification-Chapter9-SensitiveData.

Listing 9-28. Enabling the Database Audit Specification

```
USE Chapter9
GO

ALTER DATABASE AUDIT SPECIFICATION [DatabaseAuditSpecification-Chapter9-SensitiveData]
WITH (STATE = ON) ;
GO

USE Master
GO

ALTER SERVER AUDIT [Audit-Chapter9] WITH (STATE = ON) ;
```

To test security, SQL Server allows you to impersonate a user. To do this, you must be a sysadmin or be granted the Impersonate permissions on the user in question. The script in Listing 9-29 impersonates the user Danielle in order to check that the auditing is successful. It does this by using the EXECUTE AS USER command. The REVERT command switches the security context back to the user who ran the script.

Listing 9-29. Testing Security with Impersonation

```
USE Chapter9
GO

GRANT INSERT, UPDATE ON dbo.sensitiveData TO Danielle ;
GO

INSERT INTO dbo.SensitiveData (SensitiveText)
VALUES ('testing') ;
GO

UPDATE dbo.SensitiveData
SET SensitiveText = 'Boo'
WHERE ID = 2 ;
GO

EXECUTE AS USER ='Danielle'
GO

INSERT dbo.SensitiveData (SensitiveText)
VALUES ('testing again') ;
GO

UPDATE dbo.SensitiveData
SET SensitiveText = 'Boo'
WHERE ID = 1 ;
GO

REVERT
```

Auditing the Audit

With the auditing that we have implemented up to this point, there is a security hole. If an administrator with the permissions to manage server audit has ill intent, then it is possible for them to change the audit specification before performing a malicious action and then finally reconfiguring the audit to its original state in order to remove reputability.

Server audit allows you to protect against this threat, however, by giving you the ability to audit the audit itself. It you add the AUDIT_CHANGE_GROUP to your server audit specification or database audit specification, then any changes to the specification are captured.

Using the Audit-Chapter9 server audit and the DatabaseAuditSpecification-Chapter9 database audit specification as an example, we are auditing any INSERT statements, by any user, to the SensitiveData table. To avoid a privileged user with ill intent inserting data into this table without traceability, we can use the script in Listing 9-30 to add the AUDIT_CHANGE_GROUP. Note that we have to disable the database audit specification before we make the change and then re-enable it.

Listing 9-30. Adding AUDIT_CHANGE_GROUP

```
USE Chapter9
GO

ALTER DATABASE AUDIT SPECIFICATION [DatabaseAuditSpecification-Chapter9-SensitiveData]
WITH (STATE=OFF) ;
GO

ALTER DATABASE AUDIT SPECIFICATION [DatabaseAuditSpecification-Chapter9-SensitiveData]
ADD (AUDIT_CHANGE_GROUP) ;
GO

ALTER DATABASE AUDIT SPECIFICATION [DatabaseAuditSpecification-Chapter9-SensitiveData]
WITH(STATE = ON) ;
GO
```

After executing this command, any changes we make to the auditing are captured, as shown in Figure 9-15. Here, you can see that the Administrator login has been audited, removing the INSERT audit on the SensitiveData table.

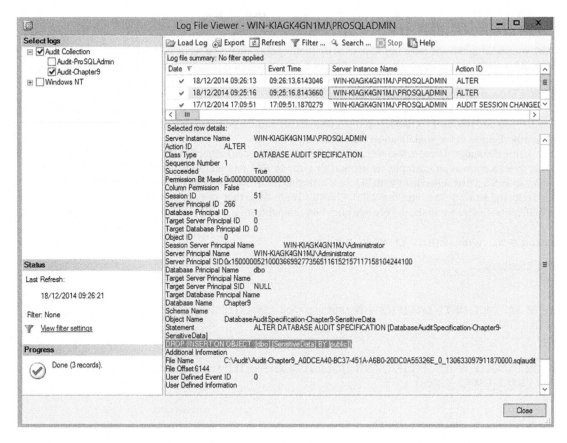

Figure 9-15. *Capture changes to the audit*

Summary

SQL Server offers a complex security framework for managing permissions that contains multiple, overlapping layers. At the instance level, you can create logins from Windows users or groups, or you can create them as second tier logins, with passwords stored inside the database engine. Second tier authentication requires that you enable mixed-mode authentication at the instance level.

Server roles allow logins to be grouped together so that you can assign them common permissions. This eases the administrative overhead of managing security. SQL Server provides built-in server roles for common scenarios, or you can create your own server roles that meet the needs of your data-tier applications.

At the database level, logins can map to database users. If you are using contained databases, then it is also possible to create database users that map directly to a Windows security principal or have their own second tier authentication credentials. This can help isolate the database from the instance by removing the dependency on an instance-level login. This can help you make the database more portable, but at the expense of additional security considerations.

Fine-grain permissions can become difficult to manage, especially when you need to secure data at the column level. SQL Server offers ownership chaining, which can reduce this complexity. With ownership chaining, it is possible to assign permissions on a view, as opposed to on the underlying tables. It is even possible to use ownership chasing across multiple databases. For ownership chaining to succeed, all of the objects in the chain must share the same owner. Otherwise the ownership chain is broken and permissions on the underlying objects are evaluated.

Server audit allows a fine-grain audit of activity at both the instance and database levels. It also includes the ability to audit the audit itself, thus removing the threat of a privileged user bypassing the audit with malicious intent. You can save audits to a file in the operating system and control permissions through NTFS. Alternatively, you can e save audits to the Windows Security log or Windows Application log.

## CHAPTER 10

Encryption

Encryption is a process of obfuscating data with an algorithm that uses keys and certificates so that if security is bypassed and data is accessed or stolen by unauthorized users, then it will be useless, unless the keys that were used to encrypt it are also obtained. This adds an additional layer of security over and above access control, but it does not replace the need for an access control implementation. Encrypting data also has the potential to considerably degrade performance, so you should use it on the basis of need, as opposed to implementing it on all data as a matter of routine.

In this chapter, we discuss the SQL Server encryption hierarchy before demonstrating how to implement Transparent Data Encryption (TDE) as well as cell-level encryption. We also discuss the management and performance implications of these technologies.

Encryption Hierarchy

SQL Server offers the ability to encrypt data through a hierarchy of keys and certificates. Each layer within the hierarchy encrypts the layer below it.

Encryption Concepts

Before we discuss the hierarchy in detail, it is important to understand the concepts that relate to encryption. The following sections provide an overview of the main artifacts that are involved in encryption.

Symmetric Keys

A *symmetric key* is an algorithm that you can use to encrypt data. It is the weakest form of encryption because it uses the same algorithm for both encrypting and decrypting the data. It is also the encryption method that has the least performance overhead. You can encrypt a symmetric key with a password or with another key or certificate.

Asymmetric Keys

In contrast to a symmetric key, which uses the same algorithm to both encrypt and decrypt data, an *asymmetric key* uses a pair of keys or algorithms. You can use one for encryption only and the other for decryption only. The key that is used to encrypt the data is called the *private key* and the key that is used to decrypt the data is known as the *public key*.

Certificates

A certificate is issued by a trusted source, known as a *certificate authority (CA)*. It uses an asymmetric key and provides a digitally signed statement, which binds the public key to a principal or device, which holds the corresponding private key.

Windows Data Protection API

The Windows Data Protection API (DPAPI) is a cryptographic application programming interface (API) that ships with the Windows operating system. It allows keys to be encrypted by using user or domain secret information. DPAPI is used to encrypt the Service Master Key, which is the top level of the SQL Server encryption hierarchy.

SQL Server Encryption Concepts

SQL Server's cryptography functionality relies on a hierarchy of keys and certificates, with the root level being the Service Master Key. The following sections describe the use of master keys, as well as SQL Server's encryption hierarchy.

Master Keys

The root level of the SQL Server encryption hierarchy is the Service Master Key. The Service Master Key is created automatically when the instance is built, and it is used to encrypt database master keys, credentials, and linked servers' passwords using the DPAPI. The Service Master Key is stored in the Master database and there is always precisely one per instance. In SQL Server 2012 and above, the Service Master Key is a symmetric key that is generated using the AES 256 algorithm. This is in contrast to older versions of SQL Server, which use the Triple DES algorithm.

Because of the new encryption algorithm used in SQL Server 2012 and above, when you upgrade an instance from SQL Server 2008 R2 or below, it is good practice to regenerate the key.

The issue with regenerating the Service Master Key, however, is that it involves decrypting and then re-encrypting every key and certificate that sits below it in the hierarchy. This is a very resource-intensive process and should only be attempted during a maintenance window.

You can regenerate the Service Master Key using the command in Listing 10-1. You should be aware, however, that if the process fails to decrypt and re-encrypt any key that is below it in the hierarchy, then the whole regeneration process fails. You can change this behavior by using the FORCE keyword. The FORCE keyword forces the process to continue, after errors. Be warned that this will leave any data that cannot be decrypted and re-encrypted unusable. You will have no way to regain access to this data.

Listing 10-1. Regenerating the Service Master Key

```
ALTER SERVICE MASTER KEY REGENERATE
```

Because the Service Master Key is so vital, you must take a backup of it after it has been created or regenerated and store it in a secure, offsite location for the purpose of disaster recovery. You can also restore the backup of this key if you are migrating an instance to a different server to avoid issues with the encryption hierarchy. The script in Listing 10-2 demonstrates how to back up and restore the Service Master Key. If the master key you restore is identical, then SQL Server lets you know and data does not need to be re-encrypted.

Listing 10-2. Backing Up and Restoring the Service Master Key

```
BACKUP SERVICE MASTER KEY
    TO FILE = 'c:\keys\service_master_key'
    ENCRYPTION BY PASSWORD = 'Pa$$w0rd'

RESTORE SERVICE MASTER KEY
    FROM FILE = 'c:\keys\service_master_key'
    DECRYPTION BY PASSWORD = 'Pa$$w0rd'
```

■ **Tip**   service_master_key is the name of the key file as opposed to a folder. By convention, it does not have an extension.

As when you are regenerating a Service Master Key, when you restore it, you can also use the FORCE keyword with the same consequences.

A Database Master Key is a symmetric key, encrypted using the AES 256 algorithm, that is used to encrypt the private keys and certificates that are stored within a database. It is encrypted using a password, but a copy is created that is encrypted using the Service Master Key. This allows the Database Master Key to be opened automatically when it is needed. If this copy does not exist, then you need to open it manually. This means that the key needs to be explicitly opened in order for you to use a key that has been encrypted by it. A copy of the Database Master Key is stored within the database and another copy is stored within the Master database. You can create a Database Master Key using the command in Listing 10-3.

Listing 10-3. Creating a Database Master Key

```
CREATE DATABASE Chapter10MasterKeyExample ;
GO

USE Chapter10MasterKeyExample
GO

CREATE MASTER KEY ENCRYPTION BY PASSWORD = 'Pa$$w0rd'
```

As with the Service Master Key, Database Master Keys should be backed up and stored in a secure offsite location. You can back up and restore a Database Master Key by using the commands in Listing 10-4.

Listing 10-4. Backing Up and Restoring a Database Master Key

```
BACKUP MASTER KEY TO FILE = 'c:\keys\Chapter10_master_key'
    ENCRYPTION BY PASSWORD = 'Pa$$w0rd';

RESTORE MASTER KEY
    FROM FILE = 'c:\keys\Chapter10_master_key'
    DECRYPTION BY PASSWORD = 'Pa$$w0rd' --The password in the backup file
    ENCRYPTION BY PASSWORD = 'Pa$$w0rd'; --The password it will be encrypted within the
database
```

As with the Service Master Key, if the restore is unable to decrypt and re-encrypt any of the keys below it in the hierarchy, the restore fails. You are able to use the FORCE keyword to force the restore to succeed, but when you do so, you permanently loose access to the data encrypted using the key(s) that could not be decrypted and re-encrypted.

Hierarchy

The SQL Server encryption hierarchy is illustrated in Figure 10-1.

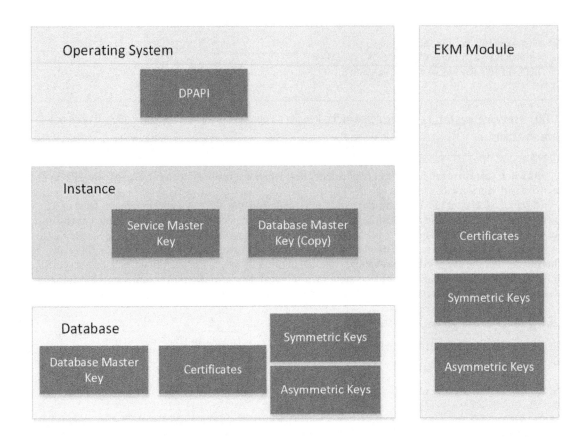

Figure 10-1. *Encryption hierarchy*

The diagram shows that the Service Master Key and a copy of the Database Master Key are stored at the instance level, with the Database Master Key also being stored within the database. The certificates, symmetric keys, and asymmetric keys that are encrypted using the Database Master Key are also stored within the database.

To the right of the diagram, you see a section called the EKM Module. An Extensible Key Management (EKM) module allows you to generate and manage keys and certificates used to secure SQL Server data in third-party hardware security modules, which interface with SQL Server using the Microsoft Cryptographic API (MSCAPI). This is more secure, because the key is not being stored with the data, but it also means that you can benefit from advanced features that may be offered by the third-party vendor, such as key rotation and secure key disposal.

Before you can use a third-party EKM module, you need to enable EKM at the instance level using sp_ configure, and you must register the EKM by importing the .dll into SQL Server. Many EKM providers are available, but the sample script in Listing 10-5 demonstrates how you might import the Thales EKM module after you install the database security pack.

Listing 10-5. Enabling EKM and Importing the EKM Module

```
--Enable EKM

sp_configure 'show advanced', 1
GO

RECONFIGURE
GO

sp_configure 'EKM provider enabled', 1
GO

RECONFIGURE
GO

--Register provider

CREATE CRYPTOGRAPHIC PROVIDER nCipher_Provider FROM FILE =
 'C:\Program Files\nCipher\nfast\bin\ncsqlekm64.dll'
```

■ **Note** A full discussion of EKM is beyond the scope of this book, but you can obtain further information from your cryptographic provider.

Transparent Data Encryption

When implementing a security strategy for your sensitive data, one important aspect to consider is the risk of data being stolen. Imagine a situation in which a privileged user with malicious intent uses detach/attach to move a database to a new instance in order to gain access to data they are not authorized to view. Alternatively, if a malicious user gains access to the database backups, they can restore the backups to a new server in order to gain access to the data.

Transparent Data Encryption (TDE) protects against these scenarios by encrypting the data pages and log file of a database and by storing the key, known as a Database Encryption Key, in the boot record of the database. Once you enable TDE on a database, pages are encrypted before they are written to disk and they are decrypted when they are read into memory.

TDE also provides several advantages over cell-level encryption, which will be discussed later in this chapter. First, it does not cause bloat. A database encrypted with TDE is the same size as it was before it was encrypted. Also, although there is a performance overhead, this is significantly less than the performance overhead associated with cell-level encryption. Another significant advantage is that the encryption is transparent to applications, meaning that developers do not need to modify their code to access the data.

When planning the implementation of TDE, be mindful of how it interacts with other technologies. For example, you are able to encrypt a database that uses In-Memory OLTP, but the data within the In-Memory filegroup is not encrypted because the data resides in memory, and TDE only encrypts data at rest, meaning when it is on disk. Even though the memory optimized data is not encrypted, log records associated with in-memory transactions are encrypted.

It is also possible to encrypt databases that use FILESTREAM, but again, data within a FILESTREAM filegroup is not encrypted. If you use full-text indexes, then new full-text indexes are encrypted. Existing full-text indexes are only encrypted after they are imported during an upgrade. It is regarded as bad practice to use full-text indexing with TDE, however. This is because data is written to disk in plain text during the full-text indexing scan operation, which leaves a window of opportunity for attackers to access sensitive data.

High availability and disaster recovery technologies such as database mirroring, AlwaysOn Availability Groups, and log shipping are supported with databases that have TDE enabled. Data on the replica database is also encrypted, and the data within the log is encrypted, meaning that it cannot be intercepted as it is being sent between the servers. Replication is also supported with TDE, but the data in the subscriber is not automatically encrypted. You must enable TDE manually on subscribers and the distributor.

■ **Caution**   Even if you enable TDE at the subscriber, data is still stored in plain text while it is in intermediate files. This, arguably, poses a greater risk than using FTE (Full-Text Indexes), so you should closely consider the risk/benefit scenario.

It is also important to note, that enabling TDE for any database within an instance causes TDE to be enabled on TempDB. The reason for this is that TempDB is used to store user data for intermediate results sets, during sort operations, spool operations, and so on. TempDB also stores user data when you are using Temp Tables, or row versioning operations occur. This can have the undesirable effect of decreasing the performance of other user databases that have not had TDE enabled. TDE performance considerations are further discussed later in this chapter.

It is also important to note, from the viewpoint of the performance of database maintenance, that TDE is incompatible with instant file initialization. Instant file initialization speeds up operations that create or expand files, as the files do not need to be zeroed out. If your instance is configured to use instant file initialization, then it no longer works for the files associated with any databases that you encrypt. It is a hard technical requirement that files are zeroed out when TDE is enabled.

Implementing TDE

To implement Transparent Data Encryption, you must first create a Database Master Key. Once this key is in place, you can create a certificate. You must use the Database Master Key to encrypt the certificate. If you attempt to encrypt the certificate using a password only, then it will be rejected when you attempt to use it to encrypt the Database Encryption Key. The Database Encryption Key is the next object that you need to create, and as implied earlier, you encrypt this using the certificate. Finally, you can alter the database to turn encryption on.

■ **Note**   It is possible to encrypt the Database Encryption Key using an asymmetric key as opposed to a server certificate, but only if the asymmetric key is protected using an EKM module.

When you enable TDE for a database, a background process moves through each page in every data file and encrypts it. This does not stop the database from being accessible, but it does take out locks, which stop maintenance operations from taking place. While the encryption scan is in progress, the following operations cannot be performed:

- Dropping a file
- Dropping a filegroup

- Dropping the database

- Detaching the database

- Taking the database offline

- Setting the database as read_only

It is also important to note that the operation to enable TDE will fail if any of the filegroups within a database are marked as read_only. This is because all pages within all files need to be encrypted when TDE is enabled, and this involves changing the data within the pages to obfuscate them.

The script in Listing 10-6 creates a database called Chapter10 Encrypted and then creates a table that is populated with data. Finally, it creates a Database Master Key and a server certificate.

Listing 10-6. Creating the Chapter10Encrypted Database

```
--Create the Database

CREATE DATABASE Chapter10Encrypted ;
GO

USE Chapter10Encrypted
GO

--Create the table

CREATE TABLE dbo.SensitiveData
(
ID                  INT                     PRIMARY KEY        IDENTITY,
FirstName           NVARCHAR(30),
LastName            NVARCHAR(30),
CreditCardNumber            VARBINARY(8000)
) ;
GO

--Populate the table

DECLARE @Numbers TABLE
(
        Number          INT
)

;WITH CTE(Number)
AS
(
        SELECT 1 Number
        UNION ALL
        SELECT Number + 1
        FROM CTE
        WHERE Number < 100
)
INSERT INTO @Numbers
SELECT Number FROM CTE ;
```

```
DECLARE @Names TABLE
(
        FirstName       VARCHAR(30),
        LastName        VARCHAR(30)
) ;

INSERT INTO @Names
VALUES('Peter', 'Carter'),
                ('Michael', 'Smith'),
                ('Danielle', 'Mead'),
                ('Reuben', 'Roberts'),
                ('Iris', 'Jones'),
                ('Sylvia', 'Davies'),
                ('Finola', 'Wright'),
                ('Edward', 'James'),
                ('Marie', 'Andrews'),
                ('Jennifer', 'Abraham'),
                ('Margaret', 'Jones') ;

INSERT INTO dbo.SensitiveData(Firstname, LastName, CreditCardNumber)
SELECT  FirstName, LastName, CreditCardNumber FROM
        (SELECT
                (SELECT TOP 1 FirstName FROM @Names ORDER BY NEWID()) FirstName
                ,(SELECT TOP 1 LastName FROM @Names ORDER BY NEWID()) LastName
                ,(SELECT CONVERT(VARBINARY(8000)
                ,(SELECT TOP 1 CAST(Number * 100 AS CHAR(4))
                  FROM @Numbers
                  WHERE Number BETWEEN 10 AND 99 ORDER BY NEWID()) + '-' +
                        (SELECT TOP 1 CAST(Number * 100 AS CHAR(4))
                          FROM @Numbers
                          WHERE Number BETWEEN 10 AND 99 ORDER BY NEWID()) + '-' +
                        (SELECT TOP 1 CAST(Number * 100 AS CHAR(4))
                          FROM @Numbers
                          WHERE Number BETWEEN 10 AND 99 ORDER BY NEWID()) + '-' +
                        (SELECT TOP 1 CAST(Number * 100 AS CHAR(4))
                          FROM @Numbers
                          WHERE Number BETWEEN 10 AND 99 ORDER BY NEWID()))))
CreditCardNumber
FROM @Numbers a
CROSS JOIN @Numbers b
CROSS JOIN @Numbers c
) d ;

USE Master
GO

--Ceate the Database Master Key (This will create the Service Master Key if it doesn't
already exist)

CREATE MASTER KEY ENCRYPTION BY PASSWORD = 'Pa$$w0rd';
GO
```

```
--Create the Server Certificate

CREATE CERTIFICATE TDECert WITH SUBJECT = 'Certificate For TDE';
GO
```

Now that we have created our database, along with the Database Master Key and certificate, we can now encrypt our database. To do this through SQL Server Management Studio, we can select Manage Database Encryption, from under Tasks, in the context menu of our database. This invokes the Manage Database Encryption wizard, illustrated in Figure 10-2.

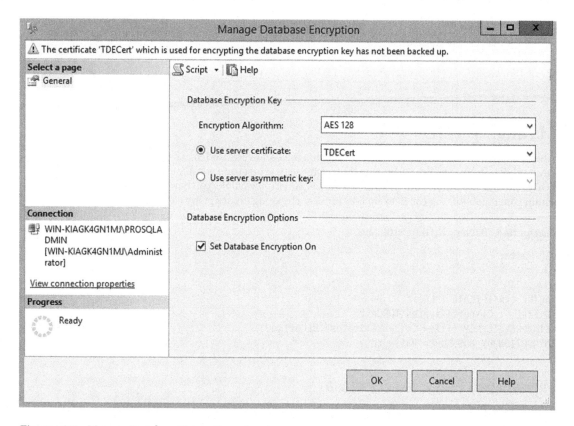

Figure 10-2. *Manage Database Encryption wizard*

You can see that we have selected our server certificate from the drop-down box and have chosen to enable database encryption. In the Encryption Algorithm drop-down box, we have selected AES 128, which is the default option.

■ **Note**   Choosing an algorithm is essentially a tradeoff between security and performance. Longer keys consume more CPU resources but are more difficult to crack.

Transparent Data Encryption can also be configured through T-SQL. We can achieve the same results via T-SQL by executing the script in Listing 10-7.

Listing 10-7. Enabling Transparent Data Encryption

```
USE CHAPTER10Encrypted
GO

--Create the Database Encryption Key

CREATE DATABASE ENCRYPTION KEY
WITH ALGORITHM = AES_128
ENCRYPTION BY SERVER CERTIFICATE TDECert ;
GO

--Enable TDE on the database

ALTER DATABASE CHAPTER10Encrypted SET ENCRYPTION ON ;
GO
```

Managing TDE

When configuring TDE, we are given a warning that the certificate used to encrypt the Database Encryption Key has not been backed up. Backing up this certificate is critical and you should do so before you configure TDE or immediately afterward. If the certificate becomes unavailable, you have no way to recover the data within your database. You can back up the certificate by using the script in Listing 10-8.

Listing 10-8. Backing Up the Certificate

```
USE Master
GO

BACKUP CERTIFICATE TDECert
TO FILE = 'C:\certificates\TDECert'
WITH PRIVATE KEY (file='C:\certificates\TDECertKey',
ENCRYPTION BY PASSWORD='Pa$$w0rd')
```

Migrating an Encrypted Database

By the very nature of TDE, if we attempt to move our Chapter10Encrypted database to a new instance, the operation fails, unless we take our cryptographic artifacts into account. Figure 10-3 illustrates the message we receive if we take a backup of the Chapter10Encrypted database and try to restore it on a new instance. You can find a full discussion of backups and restores in Chapter 15.

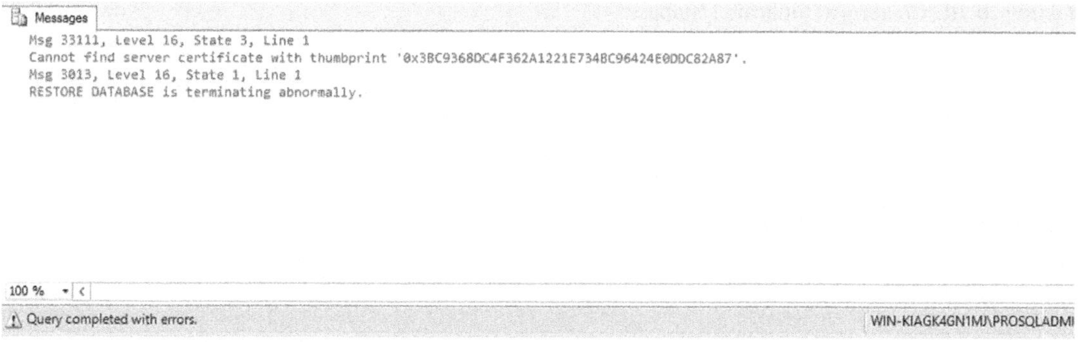

Figure 10-3. An attempt to restore an encrypted database on a new instance

We would receive the same error if we detached the database and attempted to attach it to the new instance. Instead, we must first create a Database Master Key with the same password and then restore the server certificate and private key to the new instance. We can restore the server certificate that we created earlier, using the script in Listing 10-9.

Listing 10-9. Restoring the Server Certificate

```
CREATE MASTER KEY ENCRYPTION BY PASSWORD = 'Pa$$w0rd' ;
GO

CREATE CERTIFICATE TDECert
FROM FILE = 'C:\Certificates\TDECert'
WITH PRIVATE KEY
(
    FILE = 'C:\Certificates\TDECertKey',
    DECRYPTION BY PASSWORD = 'Pa$$w0rd'
) ;
```

■ **Tip**   Make sure that the SQL Server service account has permissions to the certificate and key files in the operating system. Otherwise you will receive an error stating that the certificate is not valid, does not exist, or that you do not have permissions to it. This means that you should check the restore immediately and periodically repeat the test.

Performance Considerations for TDE

In order to observe the performance implications of Transparent Data Encryption, we create a duplicate of the Chapter10Encrypted database, and store it in plain text, as opposed to encrypting it. The code to create the Chapter10 database is in Listing 10-10.

Listing 10-10. Creating a Duplicate Database

```
--Create the duplicate Database

CREATE DATABASE Chapter10
GO

USE Chapter10
GO

--Create the table

CREATE TABLE dbo.SensitiveData
(
ID                INT                 PRIMARY KEY        IDENTITY,
FirstName        NVARCHAR(30),
LastName         NVARCHAR(30),
CreditCardNumber    VARBINARY(8000)
)
GO

--Populate the table

SET identity_insert dbo.SensitiveData ON

INSERT INTO dbo.SensitiveData(id, firstname, lastname, CreditCardNumber)
SELECT id
        ,firstname
        ,lastname
        ,CreditCardNumber
FROM  Chapter10Encrypted.dbo.SensitiveData

SET identity_insert dbo.SensitiveData OFF
```

We now run a SELECT statement and an INSERT statement against the Chapter10 database as a benchmark of performance. You can view this script in Listing 10-11.

Listing 10-11. Running a Performance Benchmark

```
--Drop the cache to ensure a fair result

DBCC DROPCLEANBUFFERS
DBCC FREEPROCCACHE

USE Chapter10
GO

--Turn on Time Statistics

SET STATISTICS TIME ON

--Run SELECT benchmark
```

```
SELECT *
FROM SensitiveData

--Run INSERT benchmark

DECLARE @Numbers TABLE
(
        Number          INT
)

;WITH CTE(Number)
AS
(
        SELECT 1 Number
        UNION ALL
        SELECT Number + 1
        FROM CTE
        WHERE Number < 100
)
INSERT INTO @Numbers
SELECT Number FROM CTE

DECLARE @Names TABLE
(
        FirstName       VARCHAR(30),
        LastName        VARCHAR(30)
)

INSERT INTO @Names
VALUES('Peter', 'Carter'),
               ('Michael', 'Smith'),
               ('Danielle', 'Mead'),
               ('Reuben', 'Roberts'),
               ('Iris', 'Jones'),
               ('Sylvia', 'Davies'),
               ('Finola', 'Wright'),
               ('Edward', 'James'),
               ('Marie', 'Andrews'),
               ('Jennifer', 'Abraham'),
               ('Margaret', 'Jones')

INSERT INTO SensitiveData(Firstname, LastName, CreditCardNumber)
SELECT          FirstName, LastName, CreditCardNumber FROM
        (SELECT
                (SELECT TOP 1 FirstName FROM @Names ORDER BY NEWID()) FirstName
               ,(SELECT TOP 1 LastName FROM @Names ORDER BY NEWID()) LastName
               ,(SELECT CONVERT(VARBINARY(8000)
               ,(SELECT TOP 1 CAST(Number * 100 AS CHAR(4))
                 FROM @Numbers
                 WHERE Number BETWEEN 10 AND 99 ORDER BY NEWID()) + '-' +
                        (SELECT TOP 1 CAST(Number * 100 AS CHAR(4))
                         FROM @Numbers WHERE Number BETWEEN 10 AND 99 ORDER BY NEWID()) + '-' +
```

329

```
                                    (SELECT TOP 1 CAST(Number * 100 AS CHAR(4))
                                     FROM @Numbers
                                     WHERE Number BETWEEN 10 AND 99 ORDER BY NEWID()) + '-' +
                                    (SELECT TOP 1 CAST(Number * 100 AS CHAR(4))
                                     FROM @Numbers
                                     WHERE Number BETWEEN 10 AND 99 ORDER BY NEWID())))
                                    CreditCardNumber
FROM @Numbers a
CROSS JOIN @Numbers b
) d

--Clean up inserted data

DELETE FROM SensitiveData
WHERE ID > 1000000
```

Figure 10-4 shows the results of the benchmark queries.

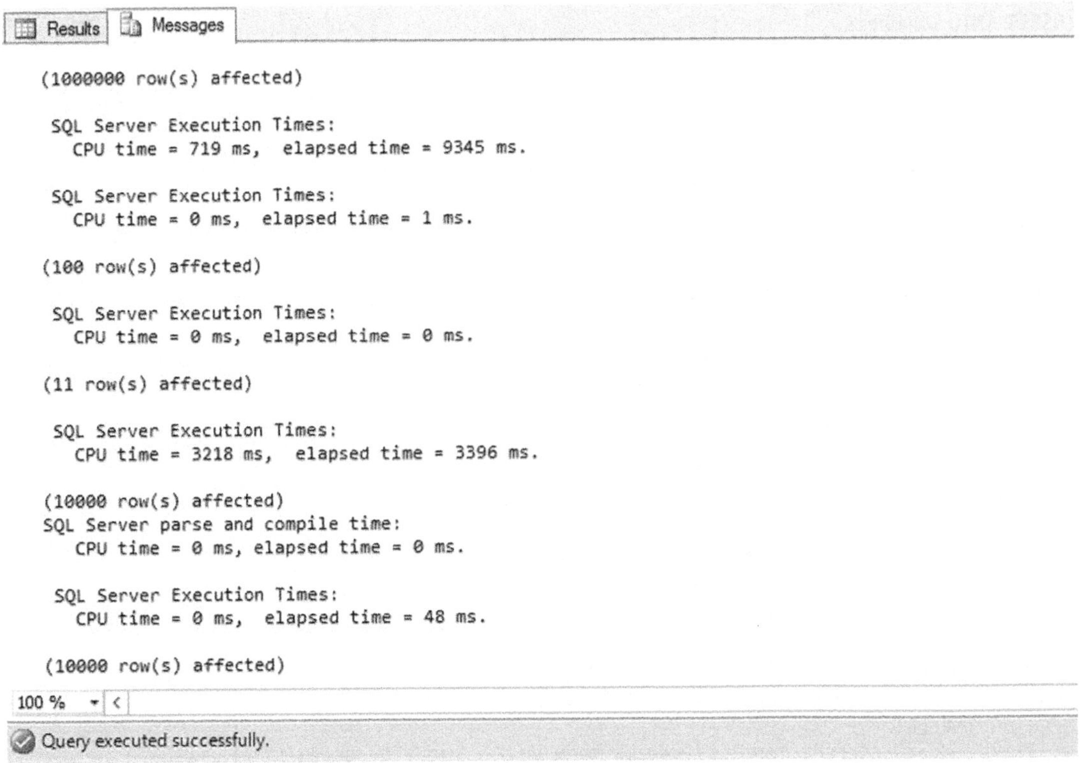

```
  Results    Messages

  (1000000 row(s) affected)

   SQL Server Execution Times:
     CPU time = 719 ms,  elapsed time = 9345 ms.

   SQL Server Execution Times:
     CPU time = 0 ms,  elapsed time = 1 ms.

  (100 row(s) affected)

   SQL Server Execution Times:
     CPU time = 0 ms,  elapsed time = 0 ms.

  (11 row(s) affected)

   SQL Server Execution Times:
     CPU time = 3218 ms,  elapsed time = 3396 ms.

  (10000 row(s) affected)
  SQL Server parse and compile time:
     CPU time = 0 ms, elapsed time = 0 ms.

   SQL Server Execution Times:
     CPU time = 0 ms,  elapsed time = 48 ms.

  (10000 row(s) affected)

100 %    ▾  <
  Query executed successfully.
```

Figure 10-4. *Results of benchmark queries against plain-text database*

We now repeat the benchmark against the Chapter10 Encrypted database so that we can compare the performance. Figure 10-5 shows the results of running the same script against the encrypted database.

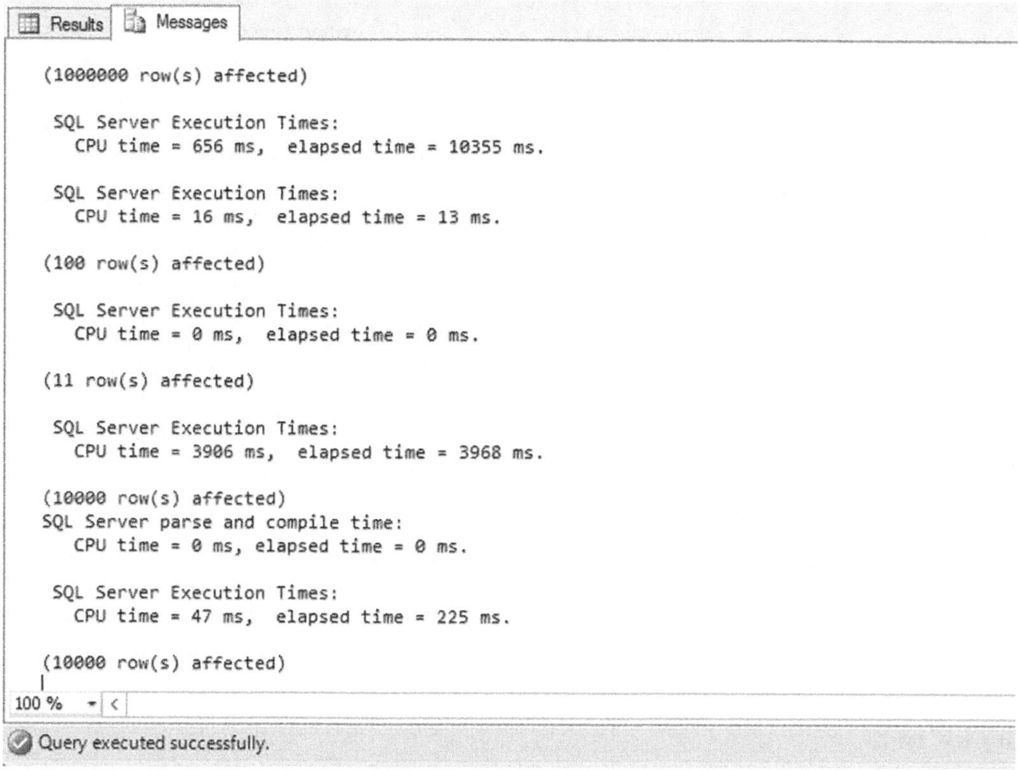

Figure 10-5. *Results of benchmark queries against encrypted database*

You can see that the SELECT query ran approximately 10 percent slower against the encrypted database. The INSERT statement ran approximately 15 percent slower than it did on the plain-text version of the database. This result depends on many factors including processor speed, disk speed, and server load.

Managing Cell-Level Encryption

Cell-level encryption allows you to encrypt a single column, or even specific cells from a column, using a symmetric key, an asymmetric key, a certificate, or a password. Although this can offer an extra layer of security for your data, it can also cause a significant performance impact and a large amount of bloat. *Bloat* means that the size of the data is much larger after the data has been encrypted than it was before. Additionally, implementing cell-level encryption is a manual process that requires you to make code changes to applications. Therefore, encrypting data should not be your default position, and you should only do it when you have a regulatory requirement or clear business justification.

Although it is common practice to encrypt data using a symmetric key, it is also possible to encrypt data using an asymmetric key, a certificate, or even a passphrase. If you encrypt data using a passphrase, then the TRIPLE DES algorithm is used to encrypt the data. Table 10-1 lists the cryptographic functions that you can use to encrypt or decrypt data using these methods.

Table 10-1. *Cryptographic Functions*

Encryption Method	Encryption Function	Decryption Function
Asymmetric key	ENCRYPTBYASYMKEY()	DECRYPTBYASYMKEY()
Certificate	ENCRYPTBYCERT()	DECRYPTBYCERT()
Passphrase	ENCRYPTBYPASSPHRASE()	DECRYPTBYPASSPHRASE()

When we created the SensitiveData table in our database, you may have noticed that we used the VARBINARY(8000) data type for the CreditCardNumber column when the obvious choice would have been a CHAR(19). This is because encrypted data must be stored as one of the binary data types. We have set the length to 8000 bytes, because this is the maximum length of the data that is returned from the function used to encrypt it.

The script in Listing 10-12 will create a duplicate of the Chapter10Encrypted database. The script then creates a Database Master Key for this database and a certificate. After that, it creates a symmetric key that will be encrypted using the certificate. Finally, it opens the symmetric key and uses it to encrypt the CreditCardNumber column in our SensitiveData table.

Listing 10-12. Encrypting a Column of Data

```
--Create the duplicate Database

CREATE DATABASE Chapter10CellEncrypted ;
GO

USE CHAPTER10CellEncrypted
GO

--Create the table

CREATE TABLE dbo.SensitiveData
(
ID              INT             PRIMARY KEY     IDENTITY,
FirstName       NVARCHAR(30),
LastName        NVARCHAR(30),
CreditCardNumber    VARBINARY(8000)
)
GO

--Populate the table

SET identity_insert dbo.SensitiveData ON

INSERT INTO dbo.SensitiveData(id, firstname, lastname, CreditCardNumber)
SELECT id
        ,firstname
        ,lastname
        ,CreditCardNumber
FROM  Chapter10Encrypted.dbo.SensitiveData
```

```
SET identity_insert dbo.SensitiveData OFF

--Create Database Master Key

CREATE MASTER KEY ENCRYPTION BY PASSWORD = 'Pa$$w0rd';
GO

--Create Certificate

CREATE CERTIFICATE CreditCardCert
    WITH SUBJECT = 'Credit Card Numbers';
GO

--Create Symmetric Key

CREATE SYMMETRIC KEY CreditCardKey
    WITH ALGORITHM = AES_128
    ENCRYPTION BY CERTIFICATE CreditCardCert;
GO

--Open Symmetric Key

OPEN SYMMETRIC KEY CreditCardKey
    DECRYPTION BY CERTIFICATE CreditCardCert;

--Encrypt the CreditCardNumber column

UPDATE SensitiveData
SET CreditCardNumber = EncryptByKey(Key_GUID('CreditCardKey'), CreditCardNumber);
GO

CLOSE SYMMETRIC KEY CreditCardKey --Close the key so it cannot be used again, unless reopened
```

Notice that the UPDATE statement that we used to encrypt the data uses a function called ENCRYPTBYKEY() to encrypt the data. Table 10-2 describes the parameters the ENCRYPTBYKEY() function accepts. If we wish only to encrypt a subset of cells, we can add a WHERE clause to the UPDATE statement.

Table 10-2. *EncryptByKey( ) Parameters*

Parameter	Description
Key_GUID	The GUID of the symmetric key that is used to encrypt the data
ClearText	The binary representation of the data that you wish to encrypt
Add_authenticator	A BIT parameter that indicates if an authenticator column should be added
Authenticator	A parameter that specifies the column that should be used as an authenticator

Also notice that before we use the key to encrypt the data, we issue a statement to open the key. The key must always be opened before it is used for either encrypting or decrypting data. To do this, the user must have permissions to open the key.

When you encrypt a column of data using the method shown in Listing 10-12, you still have a security risk caused by the deterministic nature of the algorithm used for for encryption, which means when you encrypt the same value, you get the same hash. Imagine a scenario in which a user has access to the SensitiveData table but is not authorized to view the credit card numbers. If that user is also a customer with a record in that table, they could update their own credit card number with the same hashed value as that of another customer in the table. They have then successfully stolen another customer's credit card number, without having to decrypt the data in the CreditCardNumber column. This is known as a *whole-value substitution attack*.

To protect against this scenario, you can add an authenticator column, which is also known as a *salt value*. This can be any column but is usually the primary key column of the table. When the data is encrypted, the authenticator column is encrypted along with the data. At the point of decryption, the authenticator value is then checked, and if it does not match, then the decryption fails.

■ **Caution**   It is very important that the values in the authenticator column are never updated. If they are, you may lose access to your sensitive data.

The script in Listing 10-13 shows how we can use an authenticator column to encrypt the CreditCardNumber column using the primary key of the table as an Authenticator column. Here, we use the HASHBYTES() function to create a hash value of the Authenticator column, and then we use the hash representation to encrypt the data. If you have already encrypted the column, the values are updated to include the salt.

■ **Tip**   This script is included as an example, but you should avoid running it at this point so you are able to follow later code examples.

Listing 10-13. Encrypting a Column Using an Authenticator

```
OPEN SYMMETRIC KEY CreditCardKey
   DECRYPTION BY CERTIFICATE CreditCardCert;

--Encrypt the CreditCardNumber column

UPDATE SensitiveData
SET CreditCardNumber = ENCRYPTBYKEY(Key_GUID('CreditCardKey')
                ,CreditCardNumber
                ,1
                ,HASHBYTES('SHA1', CONVERT(VARBINARY(8000), ID)));
GO

CLOSE SYMMETRIC KEY CreditCardKey ;
```

At the end of the script, we close the key. If we do not close it explicitly, then it remains open for the rest of the session. This can be useful if we are going to perform multiple activities using the same key, but it is good practice to explicitly close it immediately following its final usage within a session.

Even though it is possible to encrypt data using symmetric keys, asymmetric keys, or certificates for performance reasons, you will usually choose to use a symmetric key and then encrypt that key using either an asymmetric key or a certificate.

Accessing Encrypted Data

In order to read the data in the column encrypted using ENCRYPTBYKEY(), we need to decrypt it using the DECRYPTBYKEY() function. Table 10-3 describes the parameters for this function.

Table 10-3. *DecryptByKey Parameters*

Parameter	Description
Cyphertext	The encrypted data that you want to decrypt
AddAuthenticator	A BIT value specifying if an authenticator column is required
Authenticator	The column to be used as an authenticator

The script in Listing 10-14 demonstrates how to read the encrypted data in the CreditCardNumber column using the DECRYPTBYKEY() function after it has been encrypted without an authenticator.

Listing 10-14. Reading an Encrypted Column

```
--Open Key

OPEN SYMMETRIC KEY CreditCardKey
    DECRYPTION BY CERTIFICATE CreditCardCert;

--Read the Data using DECRYPTBYKEY()

SELECT
        FirstName
        ,LastName
        ,CreditCardNumber AS [Credit Card Number Encrypted]
        ,CONVERT(VARCHAR(30), DECRYPTBYKEY(CreditCardNumber)) AS [Credit Card Number
        Decrypted]
        ,CONVERT(VARCHAR(30), CreditCardNumber)
                                AS [Credit Card Number Converted Without Decryption]
FROM dbo.SensitiveData ;

--Close the Key

CLOSE SYMMETRIC KEY CreditCardKey ;
```

The sample of the results from the final query in this script is shown in Figure 10-6. You can see that querying the encrypted column directly returns the encrypted binary value. Querying the encrypted column with a straight conversion to the VARCHAR data type succeeds, but no data is returned. Querying the encrypted column using the DECRYPTBYKEY() function, however, returns the correct result when the value is converted to the VARCAH data type.

Figure 10-6. *Results of DECRYPTBYKEY( )*

Performance Considerations for Cell-Level Encryption

Cell-level encryption has implications for both the performance and the size of your database. The script in Listing 10-15 compares the size of the CreditCardNumber column in the Chapter10 and Chapter10CellEncrypted databases.

Listing 10-15. Encryption Bloat

```
USE Chapter10
GO


SELECT SUM(DATALENGTH(CreditCardNumber))/1024.0/1024.0 PlainTextLengthMB
FROM Chapter10.dbo.SensitiveData ;


USE Chapter10CellEncrypted
GO


SELECT SUM(DATALENGTH(CreditCardNumber))/1024.0/1024.0 EncryptedLengthMB
FROM Chapter10CellEncrypted.dbo.SensitiveData ;
```

You can see from the results in Figure 10-7 that the encrypted CreditCardNumber column consumes almost 65MB of space, compared to the 18MB of space consumed by the plain-text version of the column. If we had used a longer algorithm, then there would have been additional bloat.

Figure 10-7. *Encryption bloat results*

Let's now repeat the benchmark test that we performed against the TDE encrypted database earlier in this chapter. This time, we run the benchmark against the Chapter10CellEncrypted database to compare performance. Because we need to decrypt the data, we need to modify the benchmarking script. Listing 10-16 contains the modified version.

Listing 10-16. Benchmark Performance

```
 --Drop the cache to ensure a fair result

DBCC DROPCLEANBUFFERS
DBCC FREEPROCCACHE

USE Chapter10CellEncrypted
GO

--Open the CreditCardKey

OPEN SYMMETRIC KEY CreditCardKey
    DECRYPTION BY CERTIFICATE CreditCardCert;

--Turn on Time Statistics

SET STATISTICS TIME ON

--Run SELECT benchmark

SELECT
        ID
        ,FirstName
        ,LastName
        ,CONVERT(VARCHAR(30), DECRYPTBYKEY(CreditCardNumber)) CreditCardNumber
FROM dbo.SensitiveData ;

--Run INSERT benchmark

DECLARE @Numbers TABLE
(
        Number          INT
)

;WITH CTE(Number)
AS
(
        SELECT 1 Number
        UNION ALL
        SELECT Number + 1
        FROM CTE
        WHERE Number < 100
)
INSERT INTO @Numbers
SELECT Number FROM CTE
```

```
DECLARE @Names TABLE
(
        FirstName       VARCHAR(30),
        LastName        VARCHAR(30)
) ;

INSERT INTO @Names
VALUES('Peter', 'Carter'),
                ('Michael', 'Smith'),
                ('Danielle', 'Mead'),
                ('Reuben', 'Roberts'),
                ('Iris', 'Jones'),
                ('Sylvia', 'Davies'),
                ('Finola', 'Wright'),
                ('Edward', 'James'),
                ('Marie', 'Andrews'),
                ('Jennifer', 'Abraham'),
                ('Margaret', 'Jones') ;

INSERT INTO dbo.SensitiveData(Firstname, LastName, CreditCardNumber)
SELECT  FirstName, LastName, ENCRYPTBYKEY(KEY_GUID('CreditCardKey'), CreditCardNumber) FROM
        (SELECT
                (SELECT TOP 1 FirstName FROM @Names ORDER BY NEWID()) FirstName
                ,(SELECT TOP 1 LastName FROM @Names ORDER BY NEWID()) LastName
                ,(SELECT CONVERT(VARBINARY(8000)
                ,(SELECT TOP 1 CAST(Number * 100 AS CHAR(4))
                  FROM @Numbers
                  WHERE Number BETWEEN 10 AND 99 ORDER BY NEWID()) + '-' +
                        (SELECT TOP 1 CAST(Number * 100 AS CHAR(4))
                         FROM @Numbers
                         WHERE Number BETWEEN 10 AND 99 ORDER BY NEWID()) + '-' +
                        (SELECT TOP 1 CAST(Number * 100 AS CHAR(4))
                         FROM @Numbers
                         WHERE Number BETWEEN 10 AND 99 ORDER BY NEWID()) + '-' +
                        (SELECT TOP 1 CAST(Number * 100 AS CHAR(4))
                         FROM @Numbers
                         WHERE Number BETWEEN 10 AND 99 ORDER BY NEWID())))
CreditCardNumber
FROM @Numbers a
CROSS JOIN @Numbers b
) d ;

--Clean-up Inserted Data

DELETE FROM dbo.SensitiveData
WHERE ID > 1000000 ;

CLOSE SYMMETRIC KEY CreditCardKey ;
```

You can see from the results in Figure 10-8 that there are some drastic performance overheads. The SELECT statement took over eight times longer to execute and the INSERT was 34 percent slower.

```
    Results    Messages

    SQL Server Execution Times:
      CPU time = 4657 ms,  elapsed time = 75830 ms.

    SQL Server Execution Times:
      CPU time = 0 ms,  elapsed time = 1 ms.

  (100 row(s) affected)

    SQL Server Execution Times:
      CPU time = 0 ms,  elapsed time = 0 ms.

  (11 row(s) affected)

    SQL Server Execution Times:
      CPU time = 93 ms,  elapsed time = 4577 ms.

  (10000 row(s) affected)
  SQL Server parse and compile time:
      CPU time = 0 ms, elapsed time = 0 ms.

    SQL Server Execution Times:
      CPU time = 32 ms,  elapsed time = 71 ms.

  (10000 row(s) affected)

100 %   ▾  <

 ✓ Query executed successfully.
```

***Figure 10-8.** Performance benchmark results*

Summary

The SQL Server encryption hierarchy begins with the Service Master Key, which is encrypted using the Data Protection API (DPAPI) in the Windows operating system. You can then use this key to encrypt the Database Master Key. In turn, you can use this key to encrypt keys and certificates stored within the database. SQL Server also supports third-party Extensible Key Management (EKM) providers to allow for advanced key management of keys used to secure data.

Transparent Data Encryption (TDE) gives administrators the ability to encrypt an entire database with no bloat and an acceptable performance overhead. This offers protection against the theft of data by malicious users attaching a database to a new instance or stealing the backup media. TDE gives developers the advantage of not needing to modify their code in order to access the data.

Cell-level encryption is a technique used to encrypt data at the column level, or even the specific rows within a column, using a symmetric key, an asymmetric key, or a certificate. Although this functionality is very flexible, it is also very manual and causes a large amount of bloat and a large performance overhead. For this reason, I recommended that you only use cell-level encryption to secure the minimum amount of data you need in order to fulfill a regulatory requirement or that you have clear business justification for using it.

In order to mitigate the impact of bloat and performance degradation when using cell-level encryption, it is recommended that you encrypt data using a symmetric key. You can then encrypt the symmetric key using an asymmetric key or certificate.

CHAPTER 11

■ ■ ■

High Availability and Disaster Recovery Concepts

In today's 24×7 environments that are running mission critical applications, businesses rely heavily on the availability of their data. Although servers and their software are generally reliable, there is always the risk of a hardware failure or a software bug, each of which could bring a server down. To mitigate these risks, business-critical applications often rely on redundant hardware to provide fault tolerance. If the primary system fails, then the application can automatically fail over to the redundant system. This is the underlying principle of high availability (HA).

Even with the implementation of HA technologies, there is always a small risk of an event that causes the application to become unavailable. This could be due to a major incident, such as the loss of a data center, due to a natural disaster, or due to an act of terrorism. It could also be caused by data corruption or human error, resulting in the application's data becoming lost or damaged beyond repair.

In these situations, some applications may rely on restoring the latest backup to recover as much data as possible. However, more critical applications may require a redundant server to hold a synchronized copy of the data in a secondary location. This is the underpinning concept of disaster recovery (DR). This chapter discusses the concepts behind HA and DR before providing an overview of the technologies that are available to implement these concepts.

Availability Concepts

In order to analyze the HA and DR requirements of an application and implement the most appropriate solution, you need to understand various concepts. We discuss these concepts in the following sections.

Level of Availability

The amount of time that a solution is available to end users is known as the *level of availability*, or *uptime*. To provide a true picture of uptime, a company should measure the availability of a solution from a user's desktop. In other words, even if your SQL Server has been running uninterrupted for over a month, users may still experience outages to their solution caused by other factors. These factors can include network outages or an application server failure.

In some instances, however, you have no choice but to measure the level of availability at the SQL Server level. This may be because you lack holistic monitoring tools within the Enterprise. Most often, however, the requirement to measure the level of availability at the instance level is political, as opposed to technical. In the IT industry, it has become a trend to outsource the management of data centers to third-party providers. In such cases, the provider responsible for managing the SQL servers may not necessarily be the provider responsible for the network or application servers. In this scenario, you need to monitor uptime at the SQL Server level to accurately judge the performance of the service provider.

The level of availability is measured as a percentage of the time that the application or server is available. Companies often strive to achieve 99 percent, 99.9 percent, 99.99 percent, or 99.999 percent availability. As a result, the level of availability is often referred to in 9s. For example, five 9s of availability means 99.999 percent uptime and three 9s means 99.9 percent uptime.

Table 11-1 details the amount of acceptable downtime per week, per month, and per year for each level of availability.

Table 11-1. *Levels of Availability*

Level of Availability	Downtime per Week	Downtime per Month	Downtime per Year
99%	1 hour, 40 minutes, 48 seconds	7 hours, 18 minutes, 17 seconds	3 days, 15 hours, 39 minutes, 28 seconds
99.9%	10 minutes, 4 seconds	43 minutes, 49 seconds	8 hours, 45 minutes, 56 seconds
99.99%	1 minute	4 minutes, 23 seconds	52 minutes, 35 seconds
99.999%	6 seconds	26 seconds	5 minutes, 15 seconds

All values are rounded down to the nearest second.

To calculate other levels of availability, you can use the script in Listing 11-1. Before running this script, replace the value of @Uptime to represent the level of uptime that you wish to calculate. You should also replace the value of @UptimeInterval to reflect uptime per week, month, or year.

Listing 11-1. Calculating the Level of Availability

```
DECLARE @Uptime DECIMAL(5,3) ;

--Specify the uptime level to calculate

SET @Uptime = 99.9 ;

DECLARE @UptimeInterval VARCHAR(5) ;

--Specify WEEK, MONTH, or YEAR

SET @UptimeInterval = 'YEAR' ;

DECLARE @SecondsPerInterval FLOAT ;

--Calculate seconds per interval

SET @SecondsPerInterval =
(
SELECT CASE
        WHEN @UptimeInterval = 'YEAR'
                THEN 60*60*24*365.243
```

```
        WHEN @UptimeInterval = 'MONTH'
              THEN 60*60*24*30.437
        WHEN @UptimeInterval = 'WEEK'
              THEN 60*60*24*7
        END
) ;

DECLARE @UptimeSeconds DECIMAL(12,4) ;

--Calculate uptime

SET @UptimeSeconds = @SecondsPerInterval * (100-@Uptime) / 100 ;

--Format results
SELECT
    CONVERT(VARCHAR(12), FLOOR(@UptimeSeconds /60/60/24))   + ' Day(s), '
  + CONVERT(VARCHAR(12), FLOOR(@UptimeSeconds /60/60 % 24)) + ' Hour(s), '
  + CONVERT(VARCHAR(12),  FLOOR(@UptimeSeconds /60 % 60))   + ' Minute(s), '
  + CONVERT(VARCHAR(12),  FLOOR(@UptimeSeconds % 60))       + ' Second(s).' ;
```

Service-Level Agreements and Service-Level Objectives

When a third-party provider is responsible for managing servers, the contract usually includes service-level agreements(SLAs). These SLAs define many parameters, including how much downtime is acceptable, the maximum length of time a server can be down in the event of failure, and how much data loss is acceptable if failure occurs. Normally, there are financial penalties for the provider if these SLAs are not met.

In the event that servers are managed in-house, DBAs still have the concept of customers. These are usually the end users of the application, with the primary contact being the business owner. An application's business owner is the stakeholder within the business who commissioned the application and who is responsible for signing off on funding enhancements, among other things.

In an in-house scenario, it is still possible to define SLAs, and in such a case, the IT Infrastructure or Platform departments may be liable for charge-back to the business teams if these SLAs are not being met. However, in internal scenarios, it is much more common for IT departments to negotiate service-level objectives (SLOs) with the business teams, as opposed to SLAs. SLOs are very similar in nature to SLAs, but their use implies that the business do not impose financial penalties on the IT department in the event that they are not met.

Proactive Maintenance

It is important to remember that downtime is not only caused by failure, but also by proactive maintenance. For example, if you need to patch the operating system, or SQL Server itself, with the latest service pack, then you must have some downtime during installation.

Depending on the upgrade you are applying, the downtime in such a scenario could be substantial—several hours for a stand-alone server. In this situation, high availability is essential for many business-critical applications—not to protect against unplanned downtime, but to avoid prolonged outages during planned maintenance.

Recovery Point Objective and Recovery Time Objective

The recovery point objective (RPO) of an application indicates how much data loss is acceptable in the event of a failure. For a data warehouse that supports a reporting application, for example, this may be an extended period, such as 24 hours, given that it may only be updated once per day by an ETL process and all other activity is read-only reporting. For highly transactional systems, however, such as an OLTP database supporting trading platforms or web applications, the RPO will be zero. An RPO of zero means that no data loss is acceptable.

Applications may have different RPOs for high availability and for disaster recovery. For example, for reasons of cost or application performance, an RPO of zero may be required for a failover within the site. If the same application fails over to a DR data center, however, five or ten minutes of data loss may be acceptable. This is because of technology differences used to implement intra-site availability and inter-site recovery.

The recovery time objective (RTO) for an application specifies the maximum amount of time an application can be down before recovery is complete and users can reconnect. When calculating the achievable RTO for an application, you need to consider many aspects. For example, it may take less than a minute for a cluster to fail over from one node to another and for the SQL Server service to come back up; however it may take far longer for the databases to recover. The time it takes for databases to recover depends on many factors, including the size of the databases, the quantity of databases within an instance, and how many transactions were in-flight when the failover occurred. This is because all noncommitted transactions need to be rolled back.

Just like RPO, it is common for there to be different RTOs depending on whether you have an intra-site or inter-site failover. Again, this is primarily due to differences in technologies, but it also factors in the amount of time you need to bring up the entire estate in the DR data center if the primary data center is lost.

The RPO and RTO of an application may also vary in the event of data corruption. Depending on the nature of the corruption and the HA/DR technologies that have been implemented, data corruption may result in you needing to restore a database from a backup.

If you must restore a database, the worst-case scenario is that the achievable point of recovery may be the time of the last backup. This means that you must factor a hard business requirement for a specific RPO into you backup strategy. (Backups are discussed fully in Chapter 15.) If only part of the database is corrupt, however, you may be able to salvage some data from the live database and restore only the corrupt data from the restored database.

Data corruption is also likely to have an impact on the RTO. One of the biggest influencing factors is if backups are stored locally on the server, or if you need to retrieve them from tape. Retrieving backup files from tape, or even from off-site locations, is likely to add significant time to the recovery process.

Another influencing factor is what caused the corruption. If it is caused by a faulty IO subsystem, then you may need to factor in time for the Windows administrators to run the check disk command (CHKDSK) against the volume and potentially more time for disks to be replaced. If the corruption is caused by a user accidently truncating a table or deleting a data file, however, then this is not of concern.

Cost of Downtime

If you ask any business owners how much downtime is acceptable for their applications and how much data loss is acceptable, the answers invariably come back as zero and zero, respectively. Of course, it is never possible to guarantee zero downtime, and once you begin to explain the costs associated with the different levels of availability, it starts to get easier to negotiate a mutually acceptable level of service.

The key factor in deciding how many 9s you should try to achieve is the cost of downtime. Two categories of cost are associated with downtime: tangible costs and intangible costs. Tangible costs are usually fairly straightforward to calculate. Let's use a sales application as an example. In this case, the most obvious tangible cost is lost revenue because the sales staff cannot take orders. Intangible costs are more difficult to quantify but can be far more expensive. For example, if a customer is unable to place an order with your company, they may place their order with a rival company and never return. Other intangible costs can include loss of staff morale, which leads to higher staff turnover, or even loss of company reputation. Because intangible costs, by their very nature, can only be estimated, the industry rule of thumb is to multiply the tangible costs by three and use this figure to represent your intangible costs.

Once you have an hourly figure for the total cost of downtime for your application, you can scale this figure out, across the predicted lifecycle of your application, and compare the costs of implementing different availability levels. For example, imagine that you calculate that your total cost of downtime is $2,000/hour and the predicted lifecycle of your application is three years. Table 11-2 illustrates the cost of downtime for your application, comparing the costs that you have calculated for implementing each level of availability, after you have factored in hardware, licenses, power, cabling, additional storage, and additional supporting equipment, such as new racks, administrative costs, and so on. This is known as the total cost of ownership (TCO) of a solution.

Table 11-2. *Cost of Downtime*

Level of Availability	Cost of Downtime (Three Years)	Cost of Availability Solution
99%	$525,600	$108,000
99.9%	$52,560	$224,000
99.99%	$5,256	$462,000
99.999%	$526	$910,000

In this table, you can see that implementing five 9s of availability saves $525,474 over a two-9s solution, but the cost of implementing the solution is an additional $802,000, meaning that it is not economical to implement. Four 9s of availability saves $520,334 over a two-9s solution and only costs an additional $354,000 to implement. Therefore, for this particular application, a four-9s solution is the most appropriate level of service to design for.

Classification of Standby Servers

There are three classes of standby solution. You can implement each using different technologies, although you can use some technologies to implement multiple classes of standby server. Table 11-3 outlines the different classes of standby that you can implement.

Table 11-3. *Standby Classifications*

Class	Description	Example Technologies
Hot	A synchronized solution where failover can occur automatically or manually. Often used for high availability.	Clustering, AlwaysOn Availability Groups (Synchronous)
Warm	A synchronized solution where failover can only occur manually. Often used for disaster recovery.	Log Shipping, AlwaysOn Availability Groups (Asynchronous)
Cold	An unsynchronized solution where failover can only occur manually. This is only suitable for read-only data, which is never modified.	-

■ **Note**   Cold standby does not show an example technology because no synchronization is required and, thus, no technology implementation is required.

High Availability and Recovery Technologies

SQL Server provides a full suite of technologies for implementing high availability and disaster recovery. The following sections provide an overview of these technologies and discuss their most appropriate uses.

AlwaysOn Failover Clustering

A Windows cluster is a technology for providing high availability in which a group of up to 64 servers works together to provide redundancy. An AlwaysOn Failover Clustered Instance (FCI) is an instance of SQL Server that spans the servers within this group. If one of the servers within this group fails, another server takes ownership of the instance. Its most appropriate usage is for high availability scenarios where the databases are large or have high write profiles. This is because clustering relies on shared storage, meaning the data is only written to disk once. With SQL Server–level HA technologies, write operations occur on the primary database, and then again on all secondary databases, before the commit on the primary completes. This can cause performance issues. Even though it is possible to stretch a cluster across multiple sites, this involves SAN replication, which means that a cluster is normally configured within a single site.

Each server within a cluster is called a *node*. Therefore, if a cluster consists of three servers, it is known as a three-node cluster. Each node within a cluster has the SQL Server binaries installed, but the SQL Server service is only started on one of the nodes, which is known as the *active node*. Each node within the cluster also shares the same storage for the SQL Server data and log files. The storage, however, is only attached to the active node.

If the active node fails, then the SQL Server service is stopped and the storage is detached. The storage is then reattached to one of the other nodes in the cluster, and the SQL Server service is started on this node, which is now the active node. The instance is also assigned its own network name and IP address, which are also bound to the active node. This means that applications can connect seamlessly to the instance, regardless of which node has ownership.

The diagram in Figure 11-1 illustrates a two-node cluster. It shows that although the databases are stored on a shared storage array, each node still has a dedicated system volume. This volume contains the SQL Server binaries. It also illustrates how the shared storage, IP address, and network name are rebound to the passive node in the event of failover.

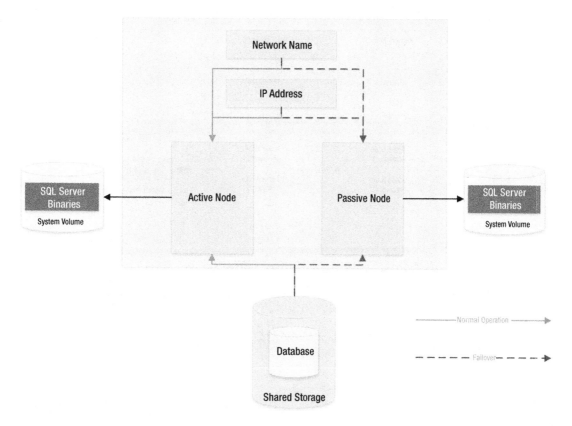

Figure 11-1. *Two-node cluster*

Active/Active Configuration

Although the diagram in Figure 11-1 illustrates an active/passive configuration, it is also possible to have an active/active configuration. Although it is not possible for more than one node at a time to own a single instance, and therefore it is not possible to implement load-balancing, it is possible to install multiple instances on a cluster, and a different node may own each instance. In this scenario, each node has its own unique network name and IP address. Each instance's shared storage also consists of a unique set of volumes.

Therefore, in an active/active configuration, during normal operations, Node1 may host Instance1 and Node2 may host Instance2. If Node1 fails, both instances are then hosted by Node2, and vice-versa. The diagram in Figure 11-2 illustrates a two-node active/active cluster.

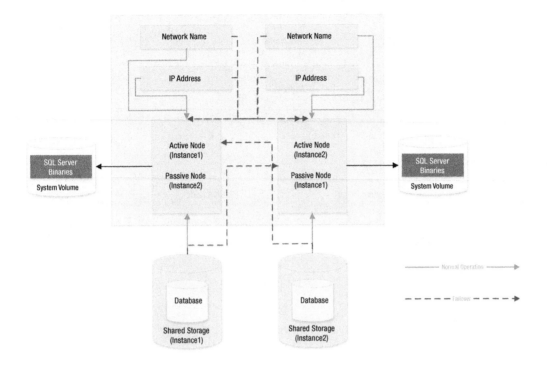

Figure 11-2. *Active/Active cluster*

■ **Caution**   In an active/active cluster, it is important to consider resources in the event of failover.
For example, if each node has 128GB of RAM and the instance hosted on each node is using 96GB of RAM and
locking pages in memory, then when one node fails over to the other node, this node fails as well, because it
does not have enough memory to allocate to both instances. Make sure you plan both memory and processor
requirements as if the two nodes are a single server. For this reason, active/active clusters are not generally
recommended for SQL Server.

Three-Plus Node Configurations

As previously mentioned, it is possible to have up to 64 nodes in a cluster. When you have 3 or more nodes,
it is unlikely that you will want to have a single active node and two redundant nodes, due to the associated
costs. Instead, you can choose to implement an N+1 or N+M configuration.

In an N+1 configuration, you have multiple active nodes and a single passive node. If a failure occurs on
any of the active nodes, they fail over to the passive node. The diagram in Figure 11-3 depicts a three-node
N+1 cluster.

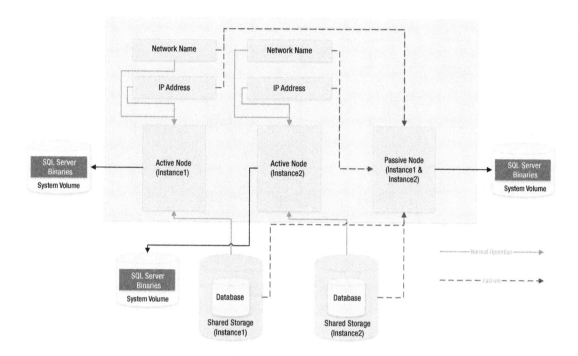

Figure 11-3. *Three-node N+1 configuration*

In an N+1 configuration, in a multifailure scenario, multiple nodes may fail over to the passive node. For this reason, you must be very careful when you plan resources to ensure that the passive node is able to support multiple instances. However, you can mitigate this issue by using an N+M configuration.

Whereas an N+1 configuration has multiple active nodes and a single passive node, an N+M cluster has multiple active nodes and multiple passive nodes, although there are usually fewer passive nodes than there are active nodes. The diagram in Figure 11-4 shows a five-node N+M configuration. The diagram shows that Instance3 is configured to always fail over to one of the passive nodes, whereas Instance1 and Instance2 are configured to always fail over to the other passive node. This gives you the flexibility to control resources on the passive nodes, but you can also configure the cluster to allow any of the active nodes to fail over to either of the passive nodes, if this is a more appropriate design for your environment.

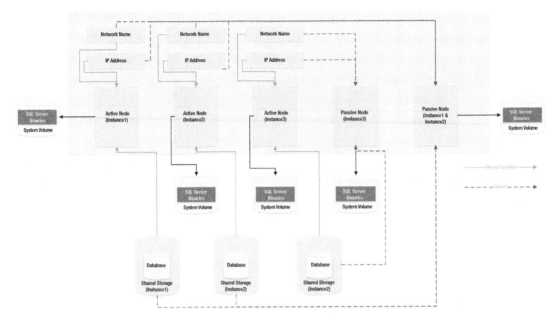

Figure 11-4. *Five-node N+M configuration*

Quorum

So that automatic failover can occur, the cluster service needs to know if a node goes down. In order to achieve this, you must form a quorum. The definition of a quorum is *"The minimum number of members required in order for business to be carried out."* In terms of high availability, this means that each node within a cluster, and optionally a witness device (which may be a cluster disk or a file share that is external to the cluster), receives a vote. If more than half of the voting members are unable to communicate with a node, then the cluster service knows that it has gone down and any cluster-aware applications on the server fail over to another node. The reason that more than half of the voting members need to be unable to communicate with the node is to avoid a situation known as a *split brain.*

To explain a split-brain scenario, imagine that you have three nodes in Data Center 1 and three nodes in Data Center 2. Now imagine that you lose network connectivity between the two data centers, yet all six nodes remain online. The three nodes in Data Center 1 believe that all of the nodes in Data Center 2 are unavailable. Conversely, the nodes in Data Center 2 believe that the nodes in Data Center 1 are unavailable. This leaves both sides (known as partitions) of the cluster thinking that they should take control. This can have unpredictable and undesirable consequences for any application that successfully connects to one or the other partition. *The Quorum = (Voting Members / 2) + 1* formula protects against this scenario.

■ **Tip**   If your cluster loses quorum, then you can force one partition online, by starting the cluster service using the /fq switch. If you are using Windows Server 2012 R2 or higher, then the partition that you force online is considered the *authoritative partition.* This means that other partitions can automatically rejoin the cluster when connectivity is reestablished.

Various quorum models are available and the most appropriate model depends on your environment. Table 11-4 lists the models that you can utilize and details the most appropriate way to use them.

Table 11-4. *Quorum Models*

Quorum Model	Appropriate Usage
Node Majority	When you have an odd number of nodes in the cluster
Node + Disk Witness Majority	When you have an even number of nodes in the cluster
Node + File Share Witness Majority	When you have nodes split across multiple sites or when you have an even number of nodes and are required to avoid shared disks*

*Reasons for needing to avoid shared disks due to virtualization are discussed later in this chapter.

Although the default option is one node, one vote, it is possibly to manually remove a nodes vote by changing the `NodeWeight` property to zero. This is useful if you have a *multi-subnet cluster* (a cluster in which the nodes are split across multiple sites). In this scenario, it is recommended that you use a file-share witness in a third site. This helps you avoid a cluster outage as a result of network failure between data centers. If you have an odd number of nodes in the quorum, however, then adding a file-share witness leaves you with an even number of votes, which is dangerous. Removing the vote from one of the nodes in the secondary data center eliminates this issue.

▪ **Caution**   A file-share witness does not store a full copy of the quorum database. This means that a two-node cluster with a file-share witness is vulnerable to a scenario know as *partition in time*. In this scenario, if one node fails while you are in the process of patching or altering the cluster service on the second node, then there is no up-to-date copy of the quorum database. This leaves you in a position in which you need to destroy and rebuild the cluster.

Windows Server 2012 R2 also introduces the concepts of Dynamic Quorum and Tie Breaker for 50% Node Split. When Dynamic Quorum is enabled, the the cluster service automatically decides whether or not to give the quorum witness a vote, depending on the number of nodes in the cluster. If you have an even number of nodes, then it is assigned a vote. If you have an odd number of nodes, it is not assigned a vote. Tie Breaker for 50% Node Split expands on this concept. If you have an even number of nodes and a witness and the witness fails, then the cluster service automatically removes a vote from one random node within the cluster. This maintains an odd number of votes in the quorum and reduces the risk of a cluster going offline, due to a witness failure.

▪ **Note**   Clustering is discussed in more depth in Chapter 12.

Database Mirroring

Database mirroring is a technology that can provide configurations for both high availability and disaster recovery. As opposed to relying on the Windows cluster service, Database Mirroring is implemented entirely within SQL Server and provides availability at the database level, as opposed to the instance level. It works by compressing transaction log records and sending them to the secondary server via a TCP endpoint. A database mirroring topology consists of precisely one primary server, precisely one secondary server, and an optional witness server.

Database mirroring is a deprecated technology, which means that it will be removed in a future version of SQL Server. In SQL Server 2014, however, it can still prove useful. For instance, if you are upgrading a data-tier application from SQL Server 2008, where AlwaysOn Availability Groups were not supported and database mirroring had been implemented, and also assuming your expectation is that the lifecycle of the application will end before the next major release of SQL Server, then you can continue to use database mirroring. Some organizations, especially where there is disconnect between the Windows administration team and the SQL Server DBA team, are also choosing not to implement AlwaysOn Availability Groups, especially for DR, until database mirroring has been removed; this is because of the relative complexity and multi-team effort involved in managing an AlwaysOn environment. Database mirroring can also be useful when you upgrade data-tier applications from older versions of SQL Server in a side-by-side migration. This is because you can synchronize the databases and fail them over with minimal downtime. If the upgrade is unsuccessful, then you can move them back to the original servers with minimal effort and downtime.

Database mirroring can be configured to run in three different modes: High Performance, High Safety, and High Safety with Automatic Failover. When running in High Performance mode, database mirroring works in an asynchronous manor. Data is committed on the primary database and is then sent to the secondary database, where it is subsequently committed. This means that it is possible to lose data in the event of a failure. If data is lost, the recovery point is the beginning of the oldest open transaction. This means that you cannot guarantee an RPO that relies on asynchronous mirroring for availability, since it will be nondeterministic. There is also no support for automatic failover in this configuration. Therefore, asynchronous mirroring offers a DR solution, as opposed to a high availability solution. The diagram in Figure 11-5 illustrates a mirroring topology, configured in High Performance mode.

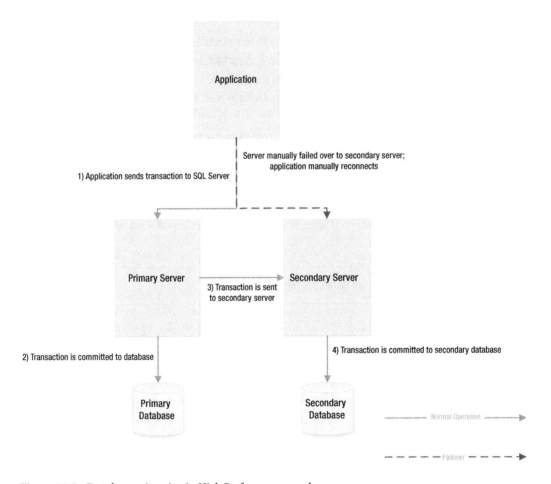

Figure 11-5. *Database mirroring in High Performance mode*

When running in High Safety with Automatic Failover mode, data is committed at the secondary server using a synchronous method, as opposed to an asynchronous method. This means that the data is committed on the secondary server before it is committed on the primary server. This can cause performance degradation and requires a fast network link between the two servers. The network latency should be less than 3 milliseconds.

In order to support automatic failover, the database mirroring topology needs to form a quorum. In order to achieve quorum, it needs a third server. This server is known as the witness server and it is used to arbitrate in the event that the primary and secondary servers loose network connectivity. For this reason, if the primary and secondary servers are in separate sites, it is good practice to place the witness server in the same data center as the primary server, as opposed to with the secondary server. This can reduce the likelihood of a failover caused by a network outage between the data centers, which makes them become isolated. The diagram in Figure 11-6 illustrates a database mirroring topology configured in High Protection with Automatic Failover mode.

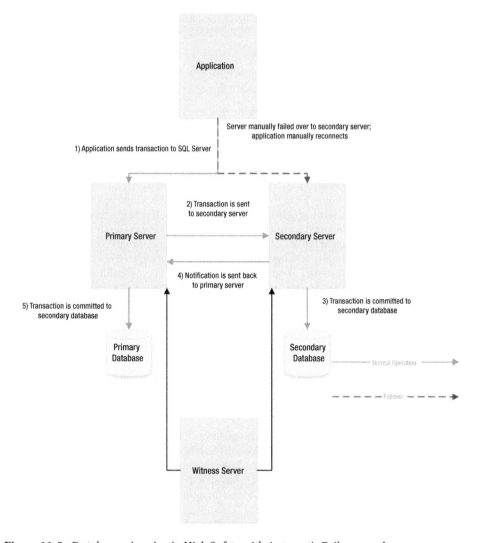

Figure 11-6. *Database mirroring in High Safety with Automatic Failover mode*

High Safety mode combines the negative aspects of the other two modes. You have the same performance degradation that you expect with High Safety with Automatic Failover, but you also have the manual server failover associated with High Performance mode. The benefit that High Safety mode offers is resilience in the event that the witness goes offline. If database mirroring loses the witness server, instead of suspending the mirroring session to avoid a split-brain scenario, it switches to High Safety mode. This means that database mirroring continues to function, but without automatic failover. High Safety mode is also useful in planned failover scenarios. If your primary server is online, but you need to fail over for maintenance, then you can change to High Safety mode. This essentially puts the database in a safe state, where there is no possibility of data loss, without you needing to configure a witness server. You can then fail over the database. After the maintenance work is complete and you have failed the database back, then you can revert to High Performance mode.

■ **Tip**   Database mirroring is not supported on databases that use In-Memory OLTP. You will be unable to configure database mirroring, if your database contains a memory-optimized filegroup.

AlwaysOn Availability Groups

AlwaysOn Availability Groups (AOAG) replaces database mirroring and is essentially a merger of database mirroring and clustering technologies. SQL Server is installed as a stand-alone instance (as opposed to an AlwaysOn Failover Clustered Instance) on each node of a cluster. A cluster-aware application, called an Availability Group Listener, is then installed on the cluster; it is used to direct traffic to the correct node. Instead of relying on shared disks, however, AOAG compresses the log stream and sends it to the other nodes, in a similar fashion to database mirroring.

AOAG is the most appropriate technology for high availability in scenarios where you have small databases with low write profiles. This is because, when used synchronously, it requires that the data is committed on all synchronous replicas before it is committed on the primary database. Unlike with database mirroring, however, you can have up to eight replicas, including two synchronous replicas. AOAG may also be the most appropriate technology for implementing high availability in a virtualized environment. This is because the shared disk required by clustering may not be compatible with some features of the virtual estate. As an example, VMware does not support the use of vMotion, which is used to manually move virtual machines (VMs) between physical servers, and the Distributed Resource Scheduler (DRS), which is used to automatically move VMs between physical servers, based on resource utilization, when the VMs use shared disks, presented over Fibre Channel.

■ **Tip**   The limitations surrounding shared disks with VMware features can be worked around by presenting the storage directly to the guest OS over an iSCSI connection at the expense of performance degradation.

AOAG is the most appropriate technology for DR when you have a proactive failover requirement but when you do not need to implement a load delay. AOAG may also be suitable for disaster recovery in scenarios where you wish to utilize your DR server for offloading reporting. When used for disaster recovery, AOAG works in an asynchronous mode. This means that it is possible to lose data in the event of a failover. The RPO is nondeterministic and is based on the time of the last uncommitted transaction.

When you use database mirroring, the secondary database is always offline. This means that you cannot use the secondary database to offload any reporting or other read-only activity. It is possible to work around this by creating a database snapshot against the secondary database and pointing read-only activity to the snapshot. This can still be complicated, however, because you must configure your application to issue read-only statements against a different network name and IP address. Availability Groups, on the other hand, allow you to configure one or more replicas as readable. The only limitation is that readable replicas and automatic failover cannot be configured on the same secondaries. The norm, however, would be to configure readable secondary replicas in asynchronous commit mode so that they do not impair performance.

To further simplify this, the Availability Group Replica checks for the read-only or read-intent properties in an applications connection string and points the application to the appropriate node. This means that you can easily scale reporting and database maintenance routines horizontally with very little development effort and with the applications being able to use a single connection string.

Because AOAG allows you to combine synchronous replicas (with or without automatic failover), asynchronous replicas, and replicas for read-only access, it allows you to satisfy high availability, disaster recovery, and reporting scale-out requirements using a single technology.

When you are using AOAG, failover does not occur at the database level, nor at the instance level. Instead, failover occurs at the level of the availability group. The availability group is a concept that allows you to group similar databases together so that they can fail over as an atomic unit. This is particularly useful in consolidated environments, because it allows you to group together the databases that map to a single application. You can then fail over this application to another replica for the purposes of DR testing, among other reasons, without having an impact on the other data-tier applications that are hosted on the instance.

No hard limits are imposed for the number of availability groups you can configure on an instance, nor are there any hard limits for the number of databases on an instance that can take part in AOAG. Microsoft, however, has tested up to, and officially recommends, a maximum of 100 databases and 10 availability groups per instance. The main limiting factor in scaling the number of databases is that AOAG uses a database mirroring endpoint and there can only be one per instance. This means that the log stream for all data modifications is sent over the same endpoint.

Figure 11-7 depicts how you can map data-tier applications to availability groups for independent failover. In this example, a single instance hosts two data-tier applications. Each application has been added to a separate availability group. The first availability group has failed over to Node2. Therefore, the availability group listeners point traffic for Application1 to Node2 and traffic for Application2 to Node1. Because each availability group has its own network name and IP address, and because these resources fail over with the AOAG, the application is able to seamlessly reconnect to the databases after failover.

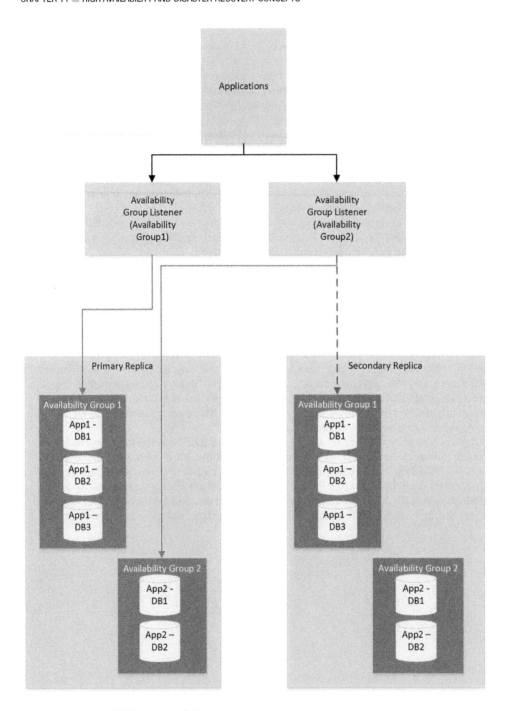

Figure 11-7. *Availability groups failover*

The diagram in Figure 11-8 depicts an AlwaysOn Availability Group topology. In this example, there are four nodes in the cluster and a disk witness. Node1 is hosting the primary replicas of the databases, Node2 is being used for automatic failover, Node3 is being used to offload reporting, and Node4 is being used for DR. Because the cluster is stretched across two data centers, multi-subnet clustering has been implemented. Because there is no shared storage, however, there is no need for SAN replication between the sites.

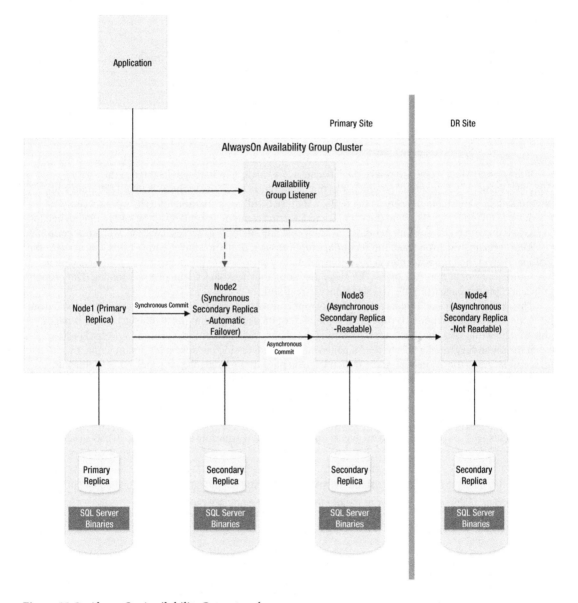

Figure 11-8. *AlwaysOn Availability Group topology*

▓ **Note**   AlwaysOn Availability Groups are discussed in more detail in Chapter 13 and Chapter 16.

Automatic Page Repair

If a page becomes corrupt in a database configured as a replica in an AlwaysOn Availability Group topology, then SQL Server attempts to fix the corruption by obtaining a copy of the pages from one of the secondary replicas. This means that a logical corruption can be resolved without you needing to perform a restore or for you to run DBCC CHECKDB with a repair option. However, automatic page repair does not work for the following page types:

- File Header page

- Database Boot page

- Allocation pages

  - GAM (Global Allocation Map)

  - SGAM (Shared Global Allocation Map)

  - PFS (Page Free Space)

If the primary replica fails to read a page because it is corrupt, it first logs the page in the MSDB.dbo.suspect_pages table. It then checks that at least one replica is in the SYNCHRONIZED state and that transactions are still being sent to the replica. If these conditions are met, then the primary sends a broadcast to all replicas, specifying the PageID and LSN (log sequence number) at the end of the flushed log. The page is then marked as restore pending, meaning that any attempts to access it will fail, with error code 829.

After receiving the broadcast, the secondary replicas wait, until they have redone transactions up to the LSN specified in the broadcast message. At this point, they try to access the page. If they cannot access it, they return an error. If they *can* access the page, they send the page back to the primary replica. The primary replica accepts the page from the first secondary to respond.

The primary replica will then replace the corrupt copy of the page with the version that it received from the secondary replica. When this process completes, it updates the page in the MSDB.dbo.suspect_pages table to reflect that it has been repaired by setting the event_type column to a value of 5 (Repaired).

If the secondary replica fails to read a page while redoing the log because it is corrupt, it places the secondary into the SUSPENDED state. It then logs the page in the MSDB.dbo.suspect_pages table and requests a copy of the page from the primary replica. The primary replica attempts to access the page. If it is inaccessible, then it returns an error and the secondary replica remains in the SUSPENDED state.

If it can access the page, then it sends it to the secondary replica that requested it. The secondary replica replaces the corrupt page with the version that it obtained from the primary replica. It then updates the MSDB.dbo.suspect_pages table with an event_id of 5. Finally, it attempts to resume the AOAG session.

▓ **Note**   It is possible to manually resume the session, but if you do, the corrupt page is hit again during the synchronization. Make sure you repair or restore the page on the primary replica first.

Log Shipping

Log shipping is a technology that you can use to implement disaster recovery. It works by backing up the transaction log on the principle server, copying it to the secondary server, and then restoring it. It is most appropriate to use log shipping in DR scenarios in which you require a load delay, because this is not possible with AOAG. As an example of where a load delay may be useful, consider a scenario in which a user accidently deletes all of the data from a table. If there is a delay before the database on the DR server is updated, then it is possible to recover the data for this table, from the DR server, and then repopulate the production server. This means that you do not need to restore a backup to recover the data. Log shipping is not appropriate for high availability, since there is no automatic failover functionality. The diagram in Figure 11-9 illustrates a log shipping topology.

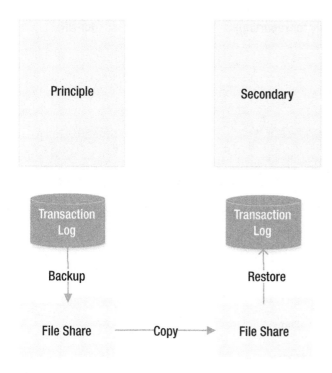

Figure 11-9. *Log Shipping topology*

Recovery Modes

In a log shipping topology, there is always exactly one principle server, which is the production server. It is possible to have multiple secondary servers, however, and these servers can be a mix of DR servers and servers used to offload reporting.

When you restore a transaction log, you can specify three recovery modes: Recovery, NoRecovery, and Standby. The Recovery mode brings the database online, which is not supported with Log Shipping. The NoRecovery mode keeps the database offline so that more backups can be restored. This is the normal configuration for log shipping and is the appropriate choice for DR scenarios.

The Standby option brings the database online, but in a read-only state so that you can restore further backups. This functionality works by maintaining a TUF (Transaction Undo File). The TUF file records any uncommitted transactions in the transaction log. This means that you can roll back these uncommitted transactions in the transaction log, which allows the database to be more accessible (although it is read-only). The next time a restore needs to be applied, you can reapply the uncommitted transaction in the TUF file to the log before the redo phase of the next log restore begins.

Figure 11-10 illustrates a log shipping topology that uses both a DR server and a reporting server.

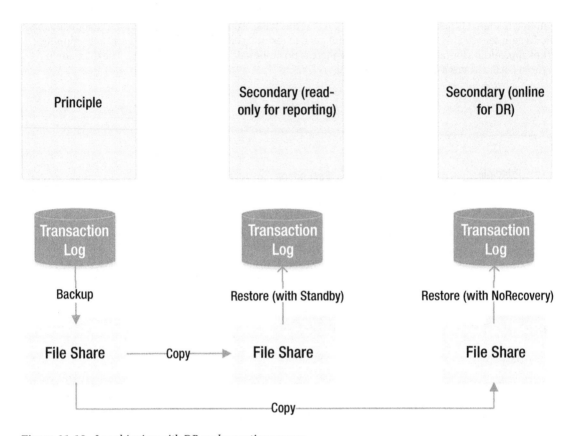

Figure 11-10. *Log shipping with DR and reporting servers*

Remote Monitor Server

Optionally, you can configure a monitor server in your log shipping topology. This helps you centralize monitoring and alerting. When you implement a monitor server, the history and status of all backup, copy, and restore operations are stored on the monitor server. A monitor server also allows you to have a single alert job, which is configured to monitor the backup, copy, and restore operations on all servers, as opposed to it needing separate alerts on each server in the topology.

■ **Caution**   If you wish to use a monitor server, it is important to configure it when you set up log shipping. After log shipping has been configured, the only way to add a monitor server is to tear down and reconfigure log shipping.

Failover

Unlike other high availability and disaster recovery technologies, an amount of administrative effort is associated with failing over log shipping. To fail over log shipping, you must back up the tail-end of the transaction log, and copy it, along with any other uncopied backup files, to the secondary server.

You now need to apply the remaining transaction log backups to the secondary server in sequence, finishing with the tail-log backup. You apply the final restore using the WITH RECOVERY option to bring the database back online in a consistent state. If you are not planning to fail back, you can reconfigure log shipping with the secondary server as the new primary server.

■ **Note**   Log shipping is discussed in further detail in Chapter 14. Backups and restores are discussed in further detail in Chapter 15.

Combining Technologies

To meet your business objectives and non-functional requirements (NFRs), you need to combine multiple high availability and disaster recovery technologies together to create a reliable, scalable platform. A classic example of this is the requirement to combine an AlwaysOn Failover Cluster with AlwaysOn Availability Groups.

The reason you may need to combine these technologies is that when you use AlwaysOn Availability Groups in synchronous mode, which you must do for automatic failover, it can cause a performance impediment. As discussed earlier in this chapter, the performance issue is caused by the transaction being committed on the secondary server before being committed on the primary server. Clustering does not suffer from this issue, however, because it relies on a shared disk resource, and therefore the transaction is only committed once.

Therefore, it is common practice to first use a cluster to achieve high availability and then use AlwaysOn Availability Groups to perform DR and/or offload reporting. The diagram in Figure 11-11 illustrates a HA/DR topology that combines clustering and AOAG to achieve high availability and disaster recovery, respectively.

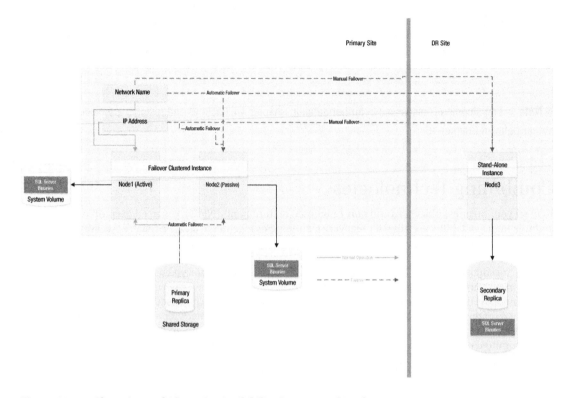

Figure 11-11. *Clustering and AlwaysOn Availability Groups combined*

The diagram in Figure 11-11 shows that the primary replica of the database is hosted on a two-node active/passive cluster. If the active node fails, the rules of clustering apply, and the shared storage, network name, and IP address are reattached to the passive node, which then becomes the active node. If both nodes are inaccessible, however, the availability group listener points the traffic to the third node of the cluster, which is situated in the DR site and is synchronized using log stream replication. Of course, when asynchronous mode is used, the database must be failed over manually by a DBA.

Another common scenario is the combination of a cluster and log shipping to achieve high availability and disaster recovery, respectively. This combination works in much the same way as clustering combined with AlwaysOn Availability Groups and is illustrated in Figure 11-12.

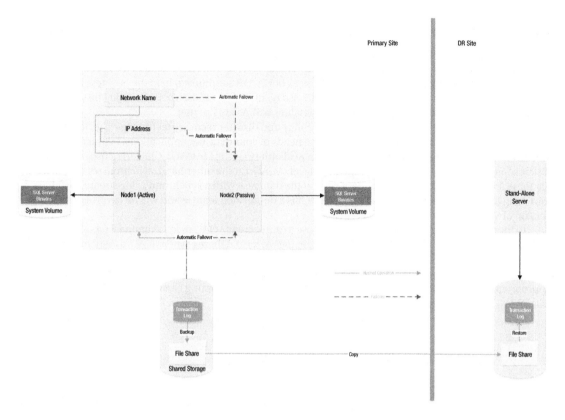

Figure 11-12. *Clustering combined with log shipping*

The diagram shows that a two-node active/passive cluster has been configured in the primary data center. The transaction log(s) of the database(s) hosted on this instance are then shipped to a stand-alone server in the DR data center. Because the cluster uses shared storage, you should also use shared storage for the backup volume and add the backup volume as a resource in the role. This means that when the instance fails over to the other node, the backup share also fails over, and log shipping continues to synchronize, uninterrupted.

■ **Caution**   If failover occurs while the log shipping backup or copy jobs are in progress, then log shipping may become unsynchronized and require manual intervention. This means that after a failover, you should check the health of your log shipping jobs.

Summary

Understanding the concepts of availability is key to making the correct implementation choices for your applications that require high availability and disaster recovery. You should calculate the cost of downtime and compare this to the cost of implementing choices of HA/DR solutions to help the business understand the cost/benefit profile of each option. You should also be mindful of SLAs when choosing the technology implementation, since there could be financial penalties if SLAs are not met.

SQL Server provides a full suite of high availability and disaster recovery technologies, giving you the flexibility to implement a solution that best fits the needs of your data-tier applications. For high availability, you can implement either clustering or AlwaysOn Availability Groups (AOAG). Clustering uses a shared disk resource and failover occurs at the instance level. AOAG, on the other hand, synchronizes data at the database level by maintaining a redundant copy of the database with a synchronous log stream. Database mirroring is also available in SQL Server 2014, but it is a deprecated feature and will be removed in a future version of SQL Server.

To implement disaster recovery, you can choose to implement AOAG or log shipping. Log shipping works by backing up, copying, and restoring the transaction logs of the databases, whereas AOAG synchronizes the data using an asynchronous log stream.

It is also possible to combine multiple HA and DR technologies together in order to implement the most appropriate availability strategy. Common examples of this are combining clustering for high availability with AOAG or log shipping to provide DR.

CHAPTER 12

■ ■ ■

Implementing Clustering

Engineers may find the process of building and configuring a cluster to be complex and that they can implement many variations of the pattern. Although DBAs may not always need to build a cluster themselves, they do need to be comfortable with the technology and often need to provide their input into the process. They may also take part in troubleshooting issues discovered with the cluster.

For these reasons, this chapter begins by looking at how to build a cluster at the Windows level and discusses some of the possible configurations. We then demonstrate how to build an AlwaysOn failover cluster instance (FCI). Finally, we explore managing a cluster, post implementation, including performing rolling patch upgrades and removing nodes from a cluster.

Building the Cluster

Before you install a SQL Server AlwaysOn failover cluster instance, you must prepare the servers that form the cluster (known as nodes) and build a Windows cluster across them. The following sections demonstrate how to perform these activities.

■ **Note** To support demonstrations in this chapter, we use a domain called PROSQLADMIN. The domain contains a domain controller, which is also configured to serve up five iSCSI disks (Data, Logs, TempDB, MSDTC, and Quorum). Two servers also act as cluster nodes named ClusterNode1 and ClusterNode2. Each server has two NICs (network interface cards) on different subnets; one will be used for data and the other for the cluster heartbeat.

Installing the Failover Cluster Feature

In order to build the cluster, the first thing we need to do is install the failover cluster feature on each of the nodes. To do this, we need to select the Add Roles And Features option in Server Manager. This causes the Add Roles And Features Wizard to display. The first page of this wizard offers guidance on prerequisites, as shown in Figure 12-1.

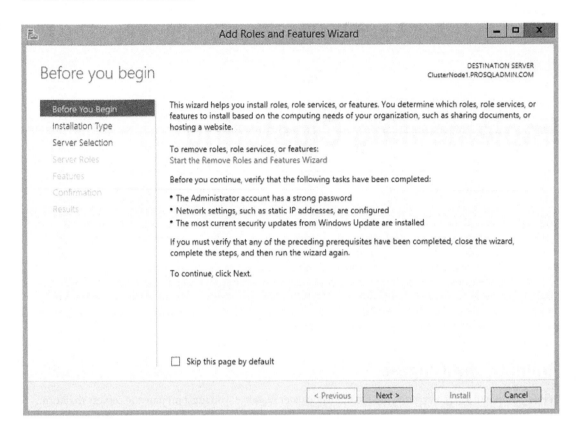

Figure 12-1. *The Before You Begin page*

On the Installation Type page, ensure that Role-Based Or Feature-Based Installation is selected, as illustrated in Figure 12-2.

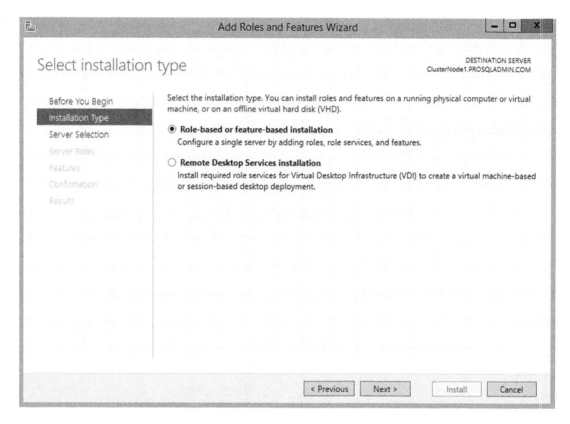

Figure 12-2. *The Installation Type page*

On the Server Selection page, ensure that the cluster node that you are currently configuring is selected. This is illustrated in Figure 12-3.

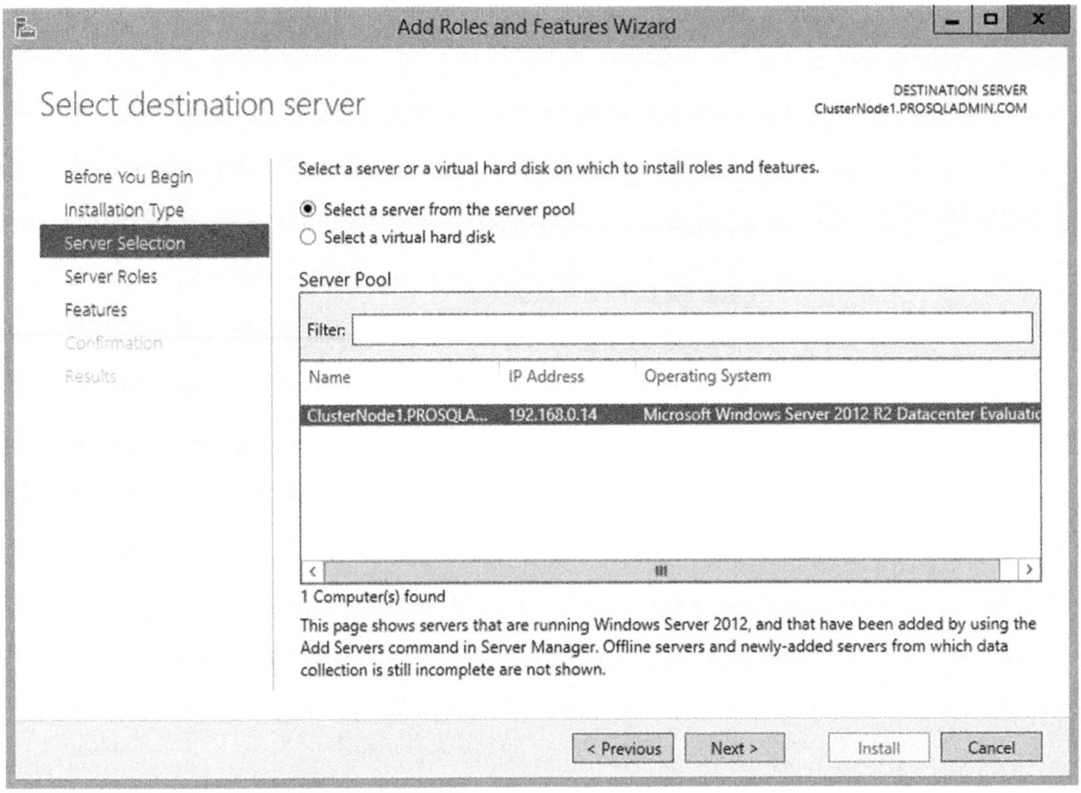

Figure 12-3. *The Server Selection page*

The Server Roles page of the wizard allows you to select any server roles that you want configured. As shown in Figure 12-4, this can include roles such as Application Server or DNS Server, but in our case, this is not appropriate, so we simply move to the next screen.

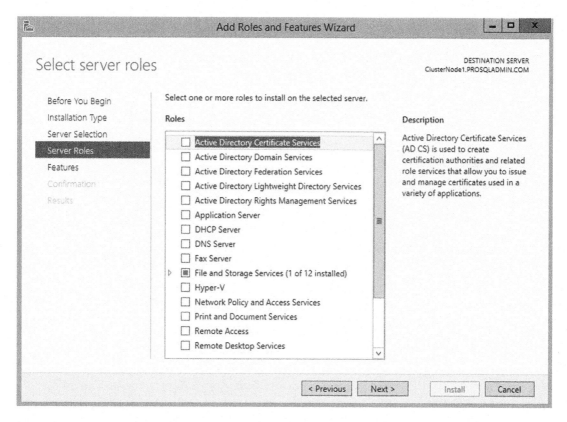

Figure 12-4. *The Server Roles page*

On the Features page of the wizard, we need to select both .NET Framework 3.5 Features and Failover Clustering, as shown in Figure 12-5. This satisfies the prerequisites for building the Windows cluster and also the AlwaysOn failover cluster instance.

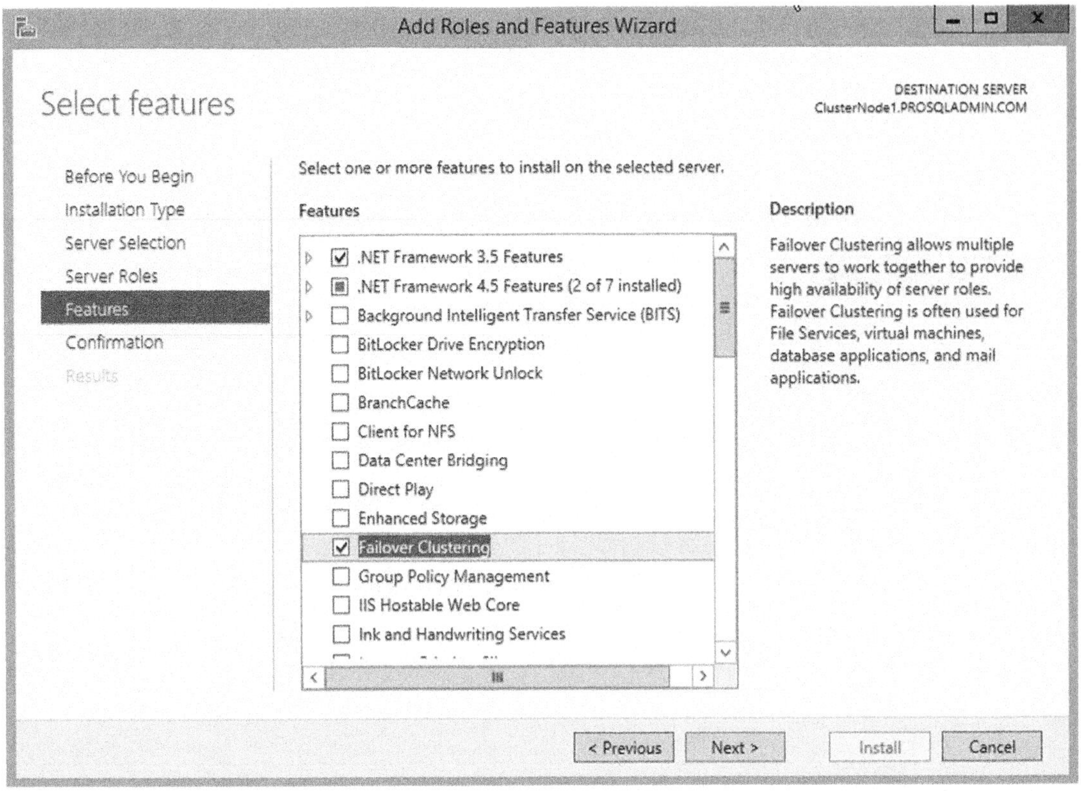

Figure 12-5. *The Features page*

When you select Failover Clustering, the wizard presents you with a screen (Figure 12-6) that asks if you want to install the management tools in the form of a checkbox. If you are managing the cluster directly from the nodes, check this option.

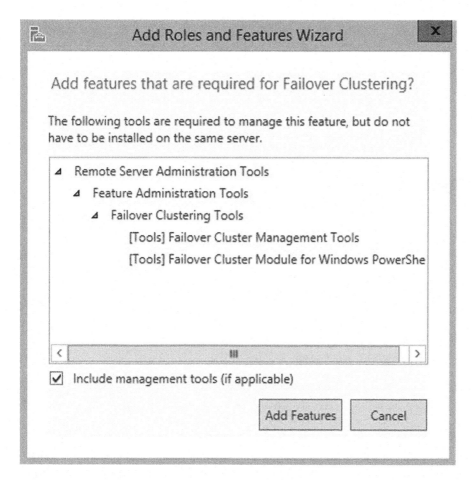

Figure 12-6. Selecting management tools

On the final page of the wizard, you see a summary of the features that are to be installed, as shown in Figure 12-7. Here, you can specify the location of the Windows media if you need to. You can also choose whether the server should automatically restart. If you are building out a new server, it makes sense to check this box. However, if the server is already in production when you add the feature, make sure you consider what is currently running on the box, and whether you should wait for a maintenance window to perform a restart if one is needed.

Figure 12-7. *The Confirmation page*

Instead of installing the cluster services through Server Manager, you can install them from PowerShell. The script in Listing 12-1 achieves the same results as the preceding steps.

Listing 12-1. Installing Cluster Services

```
Install-WindowsFeature –name NET-Framework-Core

Install-WindowsFeature -Name Failover-Clustering –IncludeManagementTools
```

Creating the Cluster

Once clustering has been installed on both nodes, you can begin building the cluster. To do this, connect to the server that you intended to be the active node using a domain account, and then run Failover Cluster Manager from Administrative Tools.

The Before You Begin page of the Create Cluster Wizard warns that the domain account you use to install the cluster must be an administrator of the cluster nodes and that Microsoft only supports clusters that pass all verification tests, as shown in Figure 12-8.

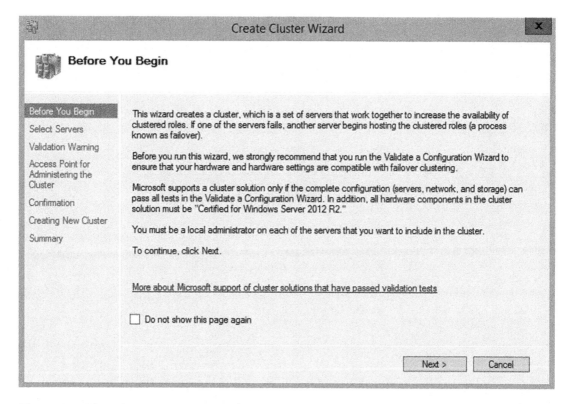

Figure 12-8. *The Before You Begin page*

On the Select Servers screen of the wizard, you need to enter the names of the cluster nodes. Even if you enter just the short names of the servers, they will be converted to fully qualified names in the format server.domain. This is illustrated in Figure 12-9. In our case, our cluster nodes are named ClusterNode1 and ClusterNode2, respectively.

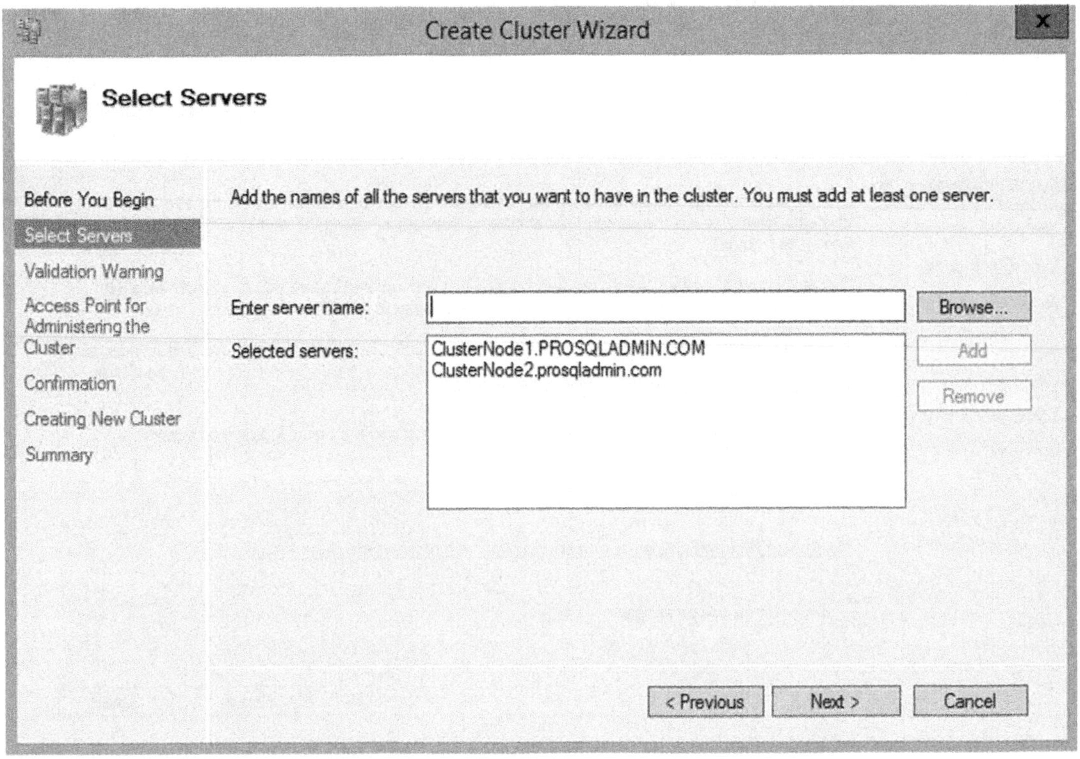

Figure 12-9. *The Select Servers page*

On the Validation Warnings page, you are asked if you wish to run the validation tests against the cluster. You should always choose to run this validation for production servers, because Microsoft will not offer support for the cluster unless it has been validated. Choosing to run the validation tests invokes the Validate A Configuration wizard. You can also run this wizard independently from the Management pane of Failover Cluster Manager. The Validation Warnings page is shown in Figure 12-10.

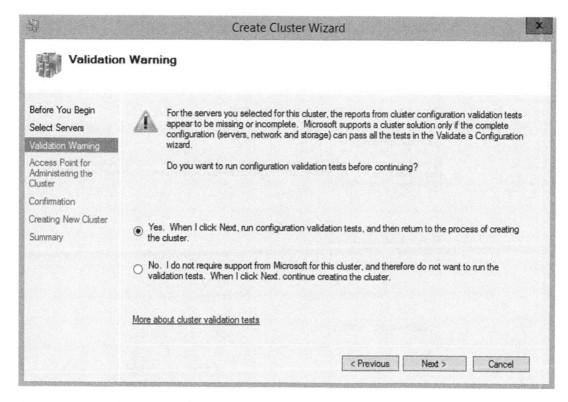

Figure 12-10. The Validation Warning page

■ **Tip**   There are some situations in which validation is not possible, and in these instances, you need to select the No, I Do Not Require Support… option. For example, some DBAs choose to install one-node clusters instead of stand-alone instances so that they can be scaled up to full clusters in the future, if need be. This approach can cause operational challenges for Windows administrators, however, so use it with extreme caution.

After you complete the Before You Begin page of the Validate A Configuration Wizard, you see the Testing Options page. Here, you are given the option of either running all validation tests or selecting a subset of tests to run, as illustrated in Figure 12-11. Normally when you are installing a new cluster, you want to run all validation tests, but it is useful to be able to select a subset of tests if you invoke the Validate A Configuration Wizard independently after you make a configuration change to the cluster.

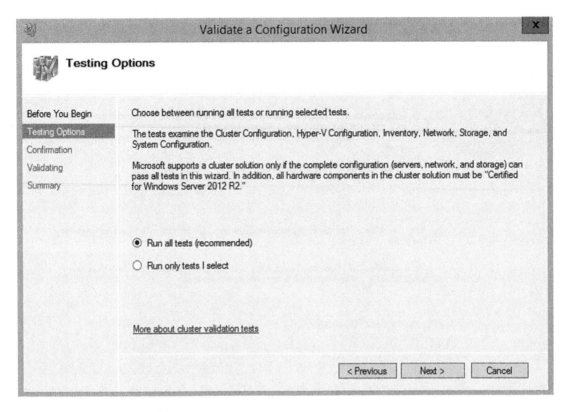

Figure 12-11. *The Testing Options page*

On the Confirmation page of the wizard, illustrated in Figure 12-12, you are presented with a summary of tests that will run and the cluster nodes that they will run against. The list of tests is comprehensive and includes the following categories:

- Inventory (such as identifying any unsigned drivers)

- Network (such as checking for a valid IP configuration)

- Storage (such as validating the ability to fail disks over, between nodes)

- System Configuration (such as validating the configuration of Active Directory)

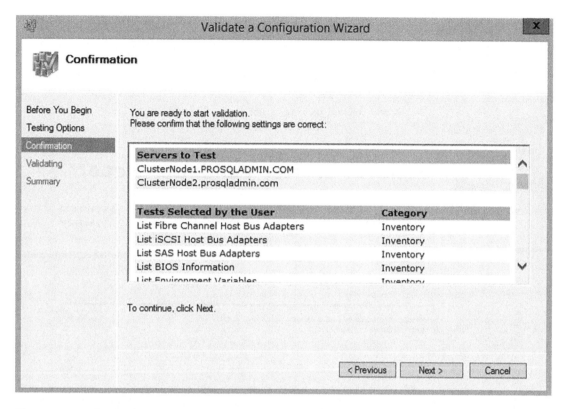

Figure 12-12. *The Confirmation page*

The Summary page, shown in Figure 12-13, provides the results of the tests and also a link to an HTML version of the report. Make sure to examine the results for any errors or warnings. You should always resolve errors before continuing, but some warnings may be acceptable. For example, if you are building your cluster to host AlwaysOn Availability Groups, you may not have any shared storage. This will generate a warning but is not an issue in this scenario. AlwaysOn Availability Groups are discussed in further detail in Chapter 13.

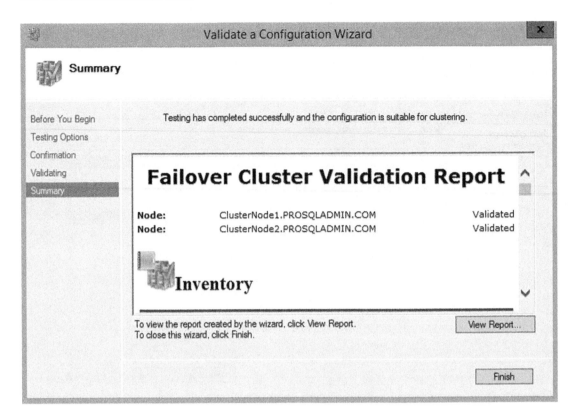

Figure 12-13. *The Summary page*

The View Report button displays the full version of the validation report, as shown in Figure 12-14. The hyperlinks take you to a specific category within the report, where further hyperlinks are available for each test. These allow you to drill down to messages generated for the specific test, making it easy to identify errors.

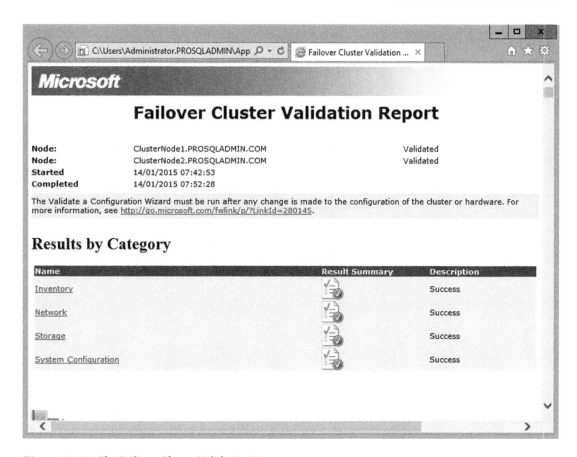

Figure 12-14. The Failover Cluster Validation Report

Clicking Finish on the Summary page returns you to the Create Cluster Wizard, where you are greeted with the Access Point For Administering The Cluster page. On this screen, illustrated in Figure 12-15, you need to enter the virtual name of your cluster and the IP address for administering the cluster. We name our cluster PROSQLADMIN-C and assign an IP address of 192.168.0.20.

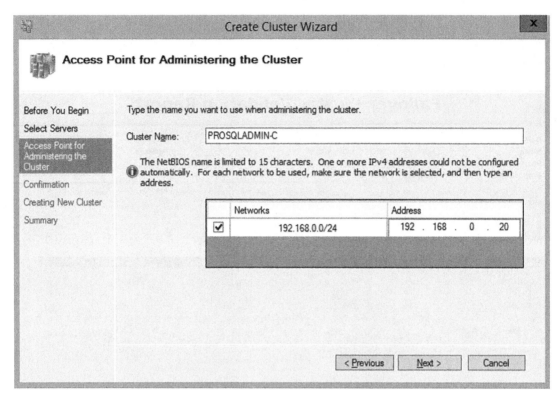

Figure 12-15. *The Access Point For Administering The Cluster page*

■ **Note**   The virtual name and IP address are bound to whichever node is active, meaning that the cluster is always accessible in the event of failover.

In our case, the cluster resides within a single site and single subnet, so only one network range is displayed. If you are configuring a multi-subnet cluster, however, then the wizard detects this, and multiple networks display. In this scenario, you need to enter an IP address for each subnet.

■ **Note**   Each of the two NICs within a node is configured on a separate subnet so that the heartbeat between the nodes is segregated from the public network. However, a cluster is only regarded as multi-subnet if the data NICs of the cluster nodes reside in different subnets.

■ **Tip**   If you do not have permissions to create AD (Active Directory) objects in the OU (organizational unit) that contains your cluster, then the VCO (virtual computer object) for the cluster must already exist and you must have the Full Control permission assigned.

The Confirmation page displays a summary of the cluster that is created. You can also use this screen to specify whether or not all eligible storage should be added to the cluster, which is generally a useful feature. This screen is displayed in Figure 12-16.

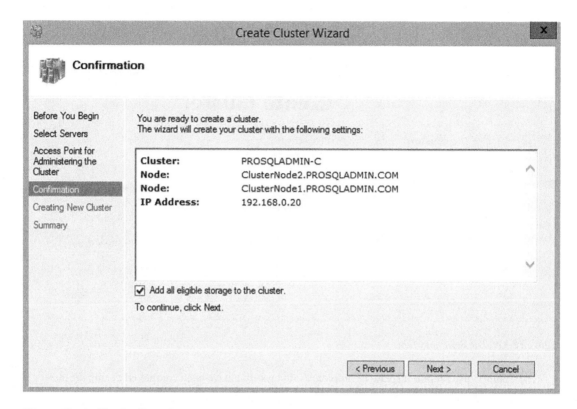

Figure 12-16. *The Confirmation page*

After the cluster has been built, the Summary page shown in Figure 12-17 displays. This screen summarizes the cluster name, IP address, nodes, and quorum model that have been configured. It also provides a link to an HTML (Hypertext Markup Language) version of the report.

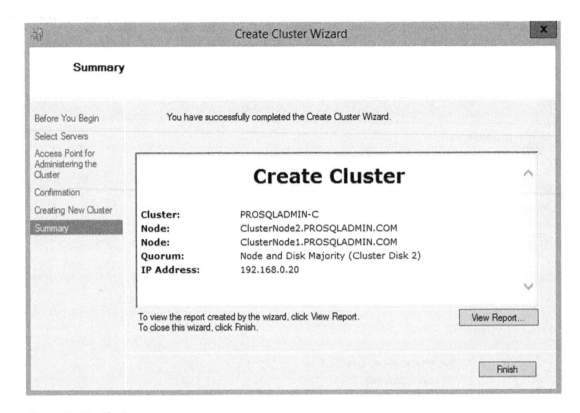

Figure 12-17. *The Summary page*

The Create Cluster report displays a complete list of tasks that have been completed during the cluster build, as shown in Figure 12-18.

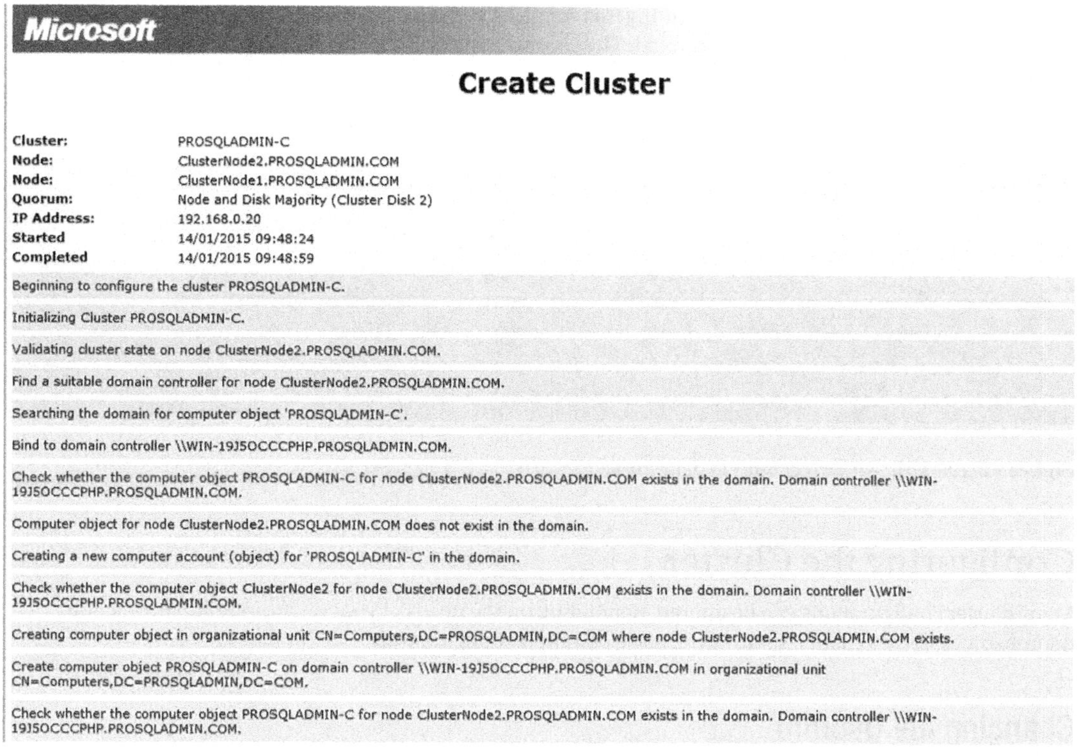

Microsoft

Create Cluster

Cluster:	PROSQLADMIN-C
Node:	ClusterNode2.PROSQLADMIN.COM
Node:	ClusterNode1.PROSQLADMIN.COM
Quorum:	Node and Disk Majority (Cluster Disk 2)
IP Address:	192.168.0.20
Started	14/01/2015 09:48:24
Completed	14/01/2015 09:48:59

Beginning to configure the cluster PROSQLADMIN-C.

Initializing Cluster PROSQLADMIN-C.

Validating cluster state on node ClusterNode2.PROSQLADMIN.COM.

Find a suitable domain controller for node ClusterNode2.PROSQLADMIN.COM.

Searching the domain for computer object 'PROSQLADMIN-C'.

Bind to domain controller \\WIN-19J5OCCCPHP.PROSQLADMIN.COM.

Check whether the computer object PROSQLADMIN-C for node ClusterNode2.PROSQLADMIN.COM exists in the domain. Domain controller \\WIN-19J5OCCCPHP.PROSQLADMIN.COM.

Computer object for node ClusterNode2.PROSQLADMIN.COM does not exist in the domain.

Creating a new computer account (object) for 'PROSQLADMIN-C' in the domain.

Check whether the computer object ClusterNode2 for node ClusterNode2.PROSQLADMIN.COM exists in the domain. Domain controller \\WIN-19J5OCCCPHP.PROSQLADMIN.COM.

Creating computer object in organizational unit CN=Computers,DC=PROSQLADMIN,DC=COM where node ClusterNode2.PROSQLADMIN.COM exists.

Create computer object PROSQLADMIN-C on domain controller \\WIN-19J5OCCCPHP.PROSQLADMIN.COM in organizational unit CN=Computers,DC=PROSQLADMIN,DC=COM.

Check whether the computer object PROSQLADMIN-C for node ClusterNode2.PROSQLADMIN.COM exists in the domain. Domain controller \\WIN-19J5OCCCPHP.PROSQLADMIN.COM.

Figure 12-18. *The Create Cluster report*

We could also have used PowerShell to create the cluster. The script in Listing 12-2 runs the cluster validation tests using the Test-Cluster cmdlet, before using the New-Cluster cmdlet to configure the cluster.

Listing 12-2. Validating and Creating the Cluster

```
#Run the validation tests

Test-Cluster -Node Clusternode1.prosqladmin.com,Clusternode2.prosqladmin.com

#Create the cluster

New-Cluster -Node ClusterNode1.prosqladmin.com,ClusterNode2.prosqladmin.com -StaticAddress
192.168.0.20 -Name PROSQLADMIN-C
```

Figure 12-19 shows the results of running this script. The first part of the output provides the details of the validation report that has been generated. The second part confirms the name of the cluster that has been created.

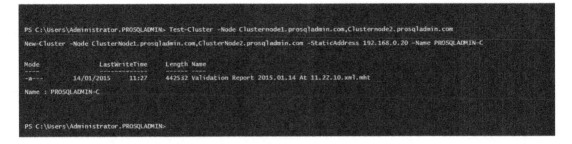

```
PS C:\Users\Administrator.PROSQLADMIN> Test-Cluster -Node Clusternode1.prosqladmin.com,Clusternode2.prosqladmin.com

New-Cluster -Node ClusterNode1.prosqladmin.com,ClusterNode2.prosqladmin.com -StaticAddress 192.168.0.20 -Name PROSQLADMIN-C

Mode              LastWriteTime      Length Name
----              -------------      ------ ----
-a---        14/01/2015     11:27    442532 Validation Report 2015.01.14 At 11.22.10.xml.mht

Name : PROSQLADMIN-C


PS C:\Users\Administrator.PROSQLADMIN>
```

Figure 12-19. *Validate and create cluster output*

Configuring the Cluster

Many cluster configurations can be altered, depending on the needs of your environment. This section demonstrates how to change some of the more common configurations.

Changing the Quorum

If we examine our cluster in the Failover Cluster Manager, we can instantly see one configuration change that we need to make. The cluster has chosen the Logs volume as the quorum drive, as shown in Figure 12-20.

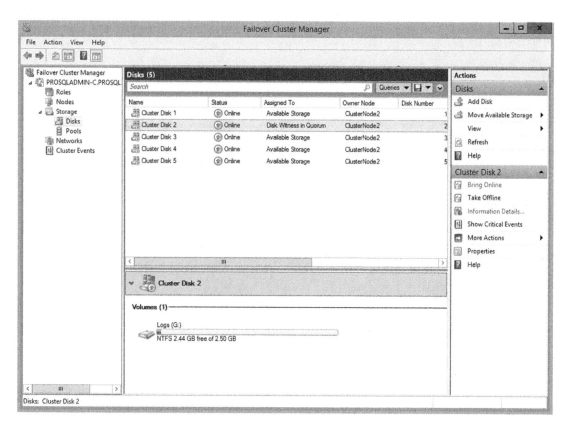

Figure 12-20. *Cluster disks*

We can modify this by entering the context menu of the cluster and by selecting More Actions | Configure Cluster Quorum Settings, which causes the Configure Cluster Quorum Wizard to be invoked. On the Select Quorum Configuration Option page, shown in Figure 12-21, we choose the Select The Quorum Witness option.

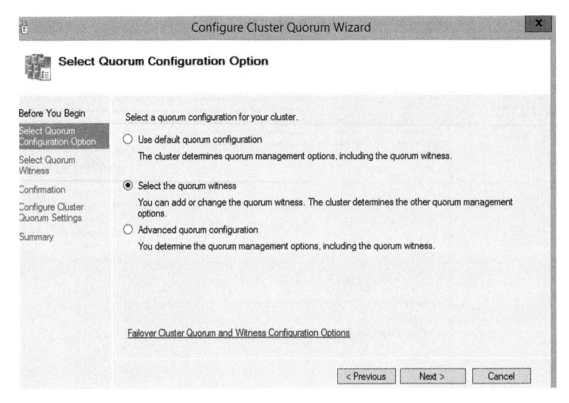

Figure 12-21. *The Select Quorum Configuration Option page*

On the Select Quorum Witness page, we select the option to configure a disk witness. This is illustrated in Figure 12-22.

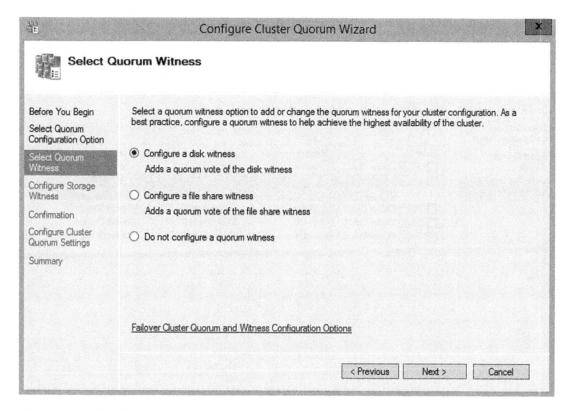

Figure 12-22. *The Select Quorum Witness page*

On the Configure Storage Witness page of the wizard, we can select the correct disk to use as a quorum. In our case, this is Disk 5, as illustrated in Figure 12-23.

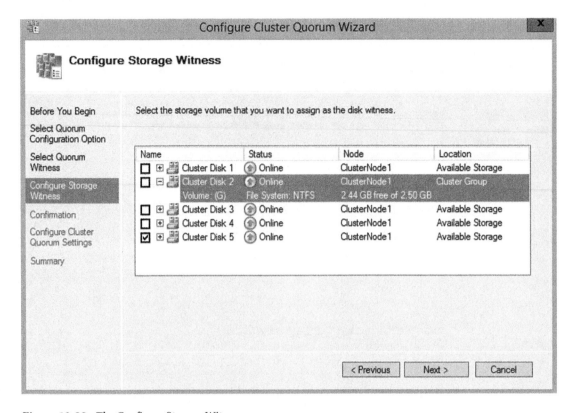

Figure 12-23. *The Configure Storage Witness page*

The Summary page of the wizard, shown in Figure 12-24, details the configuration changes that will be made to the cluster. It also highlights that dynamic quorum management is enabled and that all nodes, plus the quorum disk, have a vote in the quorum. Advanced quorum configurations are discussed in Chapter 13.

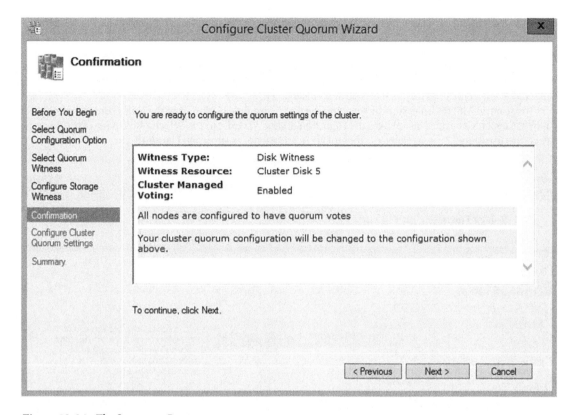

Figure 12-24. *The Summary Page*

We can also perform this configuration from the command line by using the PowerShell command in Listing 12-3. Here, we use the Set-ClusterQuorum cmdlet and pass in the name of the cluster, followed by the quorum type that we wish to configure. Because disk is included in this quorum type, we can also pass in the name of the cluster disk that we plan to use, and it is this aspect that allows us to change the quorum disk.

Listing 12-3. Configuring the Quorum Disk

```
Set-ClusterQuorum -Cluster PROSQLADMIN-C -NodeAndDiskMajority "Cluster Disk 5"
```

Configuring MSDTC

If your instance of SQL Server uses distributed transactions, or if you are installing SQL Server Integration Services (SSIS), then it relies on MSDTC (Microsoft Distributed Transaction Coordinator). If your instance will use MSDTC, then you need to ensure that it is properly configured. If it is not, then setup will succeed, but transactions that rely on it may fail.

When installed on a cluster, SQL Server automatically uses the instance of MSDTC that is installed in the same role, if one exists. If it does not, then it uses the instance of MSDTC to which it has been mapped (if this mapping has been performed). If there is no mapping, it uses the cluster's default instance of MSDTC, and if there is not one, it uses the local machine's instance of MSDTC.

Many DBAs choose to install MSDTC within the same role as SQL Server; however, this introduces a problem. If MSDTC fails, it can also bring down the instance of SQL Server. Of course, the cluster attempts to bring both of the applications up on a different node, but this still involves downtime, including the time it takes to recover the databases on the new node, which takes a non-deterministic duration. (Please refer to Chapter 11 for further details.) For this reason, I recommend installing MSDTC in a separate role. If you do, the SQL Server instance still utilizes MSDTC, since it is the cluster's default instance, and it removes the possibility of MSDTC causing an outage to SQL Server. This is also preferable to using a mapped instance or the local machine instance since it avoids unnecessary configuration, and the MSDTC instance should be clustered when a clustered instance of SQL Server is using it.

To create an MSDTC role, start by selecting the Configure Role option from the Roles context menu in Failover Cluster Manager. This invokes the High Availability Wizard. On the Select A Role page of the wizard, select the Distributed Transaction Coordinator (DTC) role type, as shown in Figure 12-25.

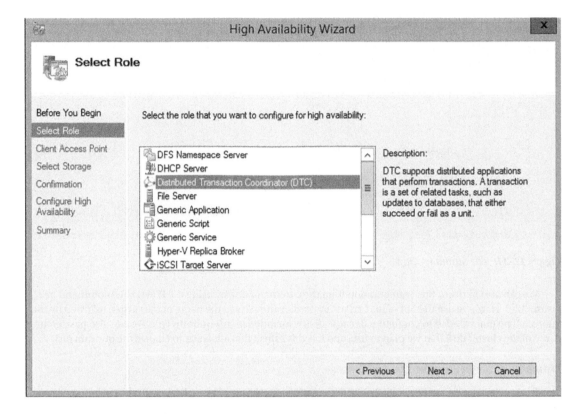

Figure 12-25. *The Select Role page*

On the Client Access Point page, illustrated in Figure 12-26, you need to enter a virtual name and IP address for MSDTC. In our case, we name it PROSQLMSDTC-C and assign 192.168.0.21 as the IP address. On a multi-subnet cluster, you need to provide an IP address for each network.

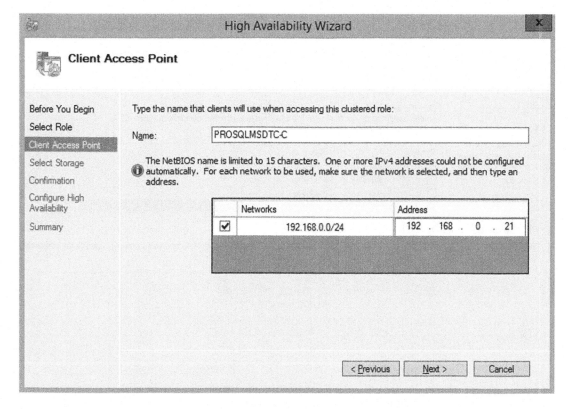

Figure 12-26. *The Client Access Point page*

On the Select Storage page of the wizard, select the cluster disk on which you plan to store the MSDTC files, as shown in Figure 12-27. In our case, this is Disk 4.

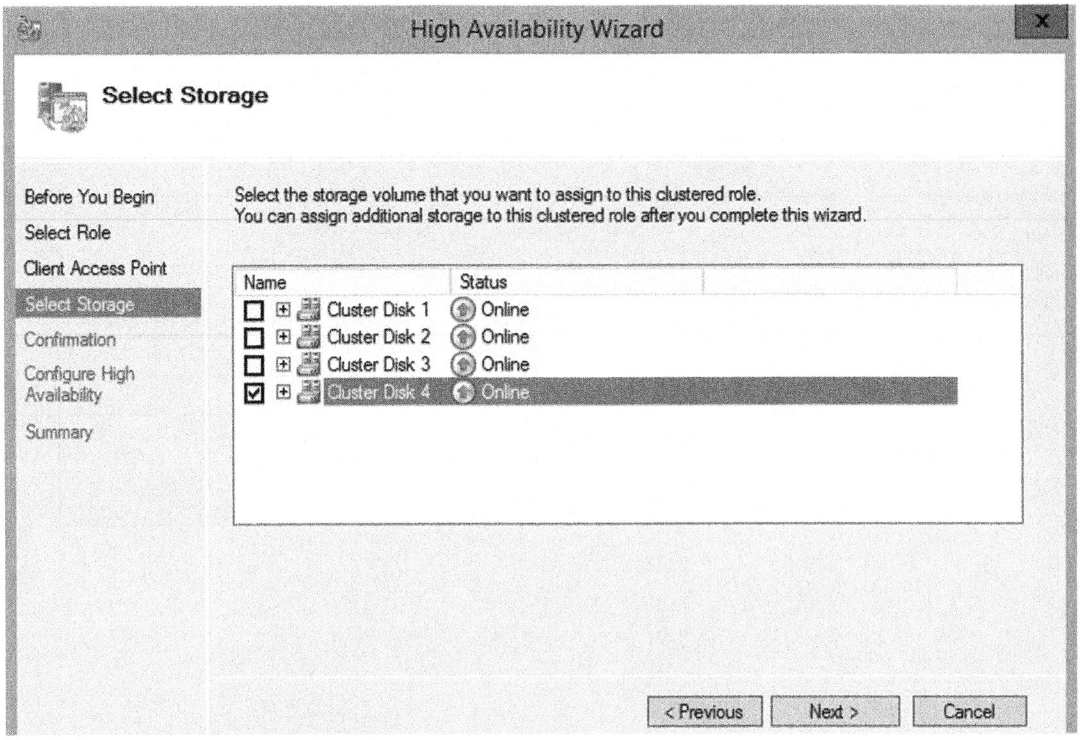

Figure 12-27. *The Select Storage page*

The Confirmation page displays an overview of the role that is about to be created, as shown in Figure 12-28.

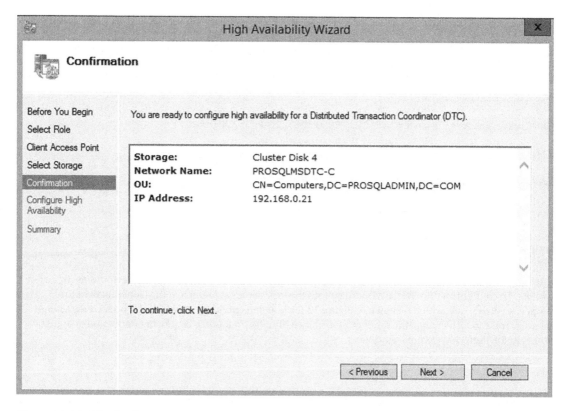

Figure 12-28. *The Confirmation page*

Alternatively, we could create this role in PowerShell. The script in Listing 12-4 first uses the
`Add-ClusterServerRole` cmdlet to create the role. We pass the virtual name to use for the role into the `Name`
parameter, the name of the cluster disk to use into the `Storage` parameter, and the IP address for the role
into the `StaticAddress` parameter.

We then use the `Add-ClusterResource` cmdlet to add the DTC resource. The `Name` parameter names
the resource and the `ResourceType` parameter specifies that it is a DTC resource. We then need to create the
dependencies between the resources within the role. We did not need to do this when using the GUI, as the
dependencies were created for us automatically. Resource dependencies specify the resource or resources
on which other resources depend. A resource failing propagates through the chain and could take a role
offline. For example, in the case of our `PROSQLMSDTC-C` role, if either the disk or the virtual name becomes
unavailable, the DTC resource goes offline. Windows Server supports multiple dependencies with both `AND`
and `OR` constraints. It is the `OR` constraints that make multi-subnet clustering possible, because a resource
can be dependent on IP address A OR IP address B. Finally, we need to bring the role online by using the
`Start-ClusterGroup` cmdlet.

Listing 12-4. Creating an MSDTC Role

```
#Create the Role

Add-ClusterServerRole -Name PROSQLMSDTC-C -Storage "Cluster Disk 4" -StaticAddress
192.168.0.21
```

```
#Create the DTC Resource

Add-ClusterResource -Name MSDTC-PROSQLMSDTC-C -ResourceType "Distributed Transaction
Coordinator" -Group PROSQLMSDTC-C

#Create the dependencies

Add-ClusterResourceDependency MSDTC-PROSQLMSDTC-C PROSQLMSDTC-C

Add-ClusterResourceDependency MSDTC-PROSQLMSDTC-C "Cluster Disk 4"

#Bring the Role online

Start-ClusterGroup PROSQLMSDTC-C
```

Configuring a Role

After creating a role, you may wish to configure it to alter the failover policy or configure nodes as preferred owners. To configure a role, select Properties from the role's context menu. On the General tab of the Properties dialog box, which is shown in Figure 12-29, you can configure a node as the preferred owner of the role. You can also change the order of precedence of node preference by moving nodes above or below others in the Preferred Owners window.

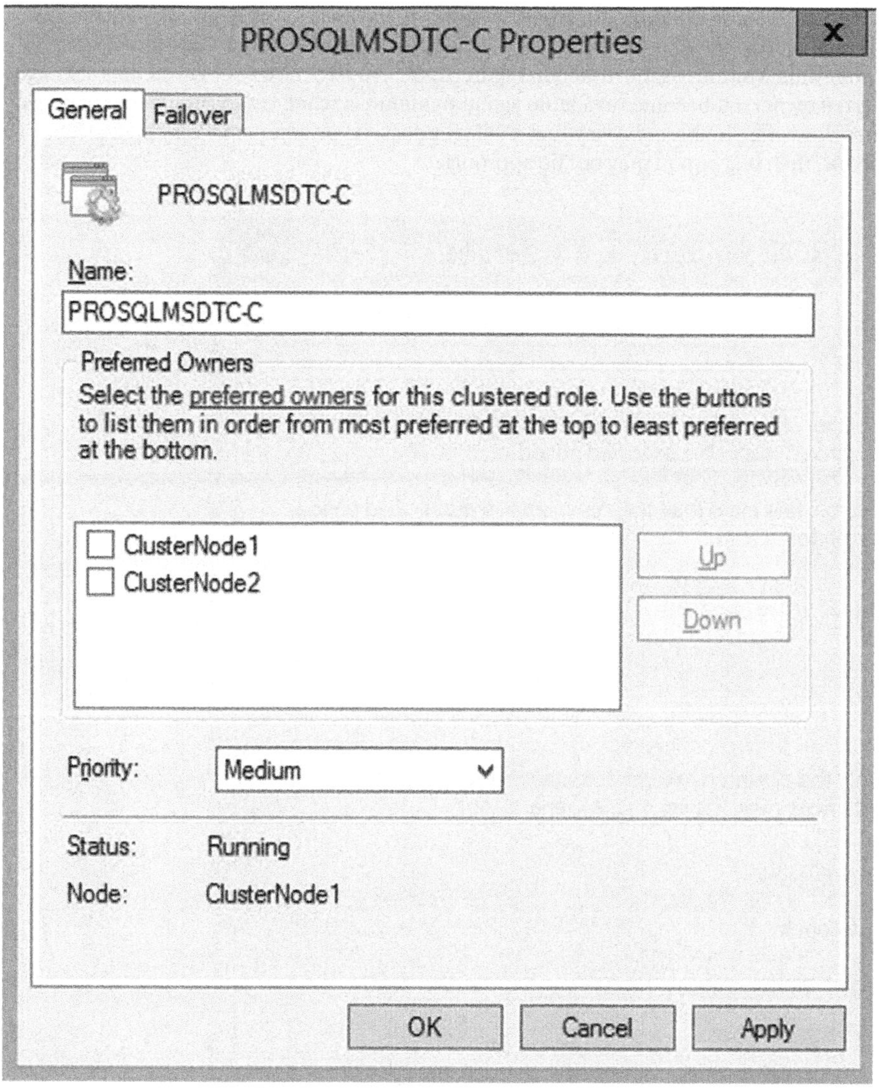

Figure 12-29. *The General tab*

You can also select the priority for the role in the event that multiple roles fail over to another node at the same time. The options for this setting are as follows:

- High

- Medium

- Low

- No Auto Start

On the Failover tab of the Properties dialog box, you can configure the number of times that the role can fail over within a given period before the role is left offline. The default value for this is one failure within 6 hours. The issue with this is that if a role fails over, and after you fix the issue on the original node, you fail the

395

role back, no more failovers are allowed within the 6-hour window. This is obviously a risk, and I generally advise that you change this setting. In our case, we have configured the role to allow a maximum of three failovers within a 24-hour time window, as illustrated in Figure 12-30. We have also configured the role to fail back to the most preferred owner if it becomes available again. Remember, when setting automatic failback, that failback also causes downtime in the same way that a failover does. If you aspire to a very high level of availability, such as five 9s, then this option may not be appropriate.

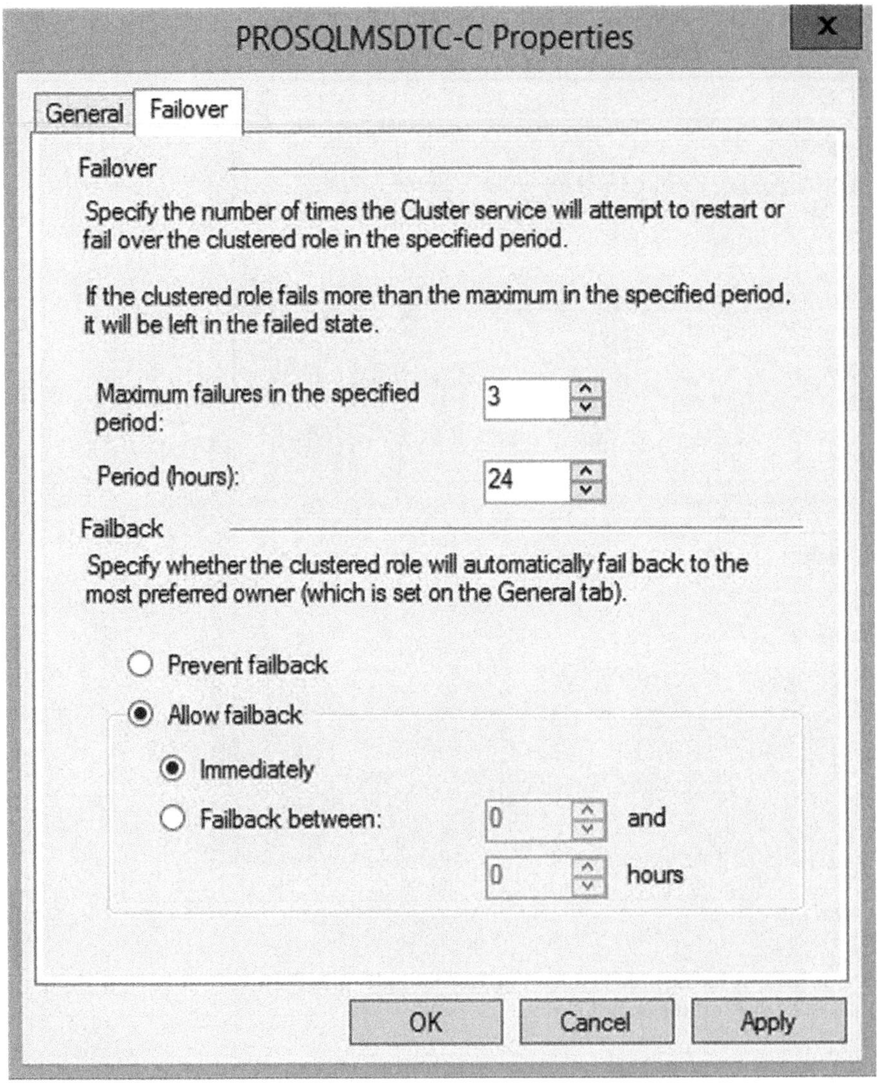

Figure 12-30. The Failover tab

Building the AlwaysOn Failover Cluster Instance

Once the cluster has been built and configured, it is time to install the AlwaysOn failover cluster instance of SQL Server. To do this, select the New SQL Server Failover Cluster Installation option from the Installation tab of the SQL Server Installation Center.

Preparation Steps

▪ **Note**   You can find further information on SQL Server Installation Center in Chapter 2.

When you select this option, you invoke the Install A SQL Server Failover Cluster Wizard. The majority of the pages in this wizard are identical to the pages in the SQL Server 2014 Setup Wizard. You can find details of these screens and discussions of the options in Chapter 2.

Cluster-Specific Steps

The first deviation from a stand-alone installation of SQL Server is the Instance Configuration page, which is illustrated in Figure 12-31. On this screen, you are prompted to enter the SQL Server Network Name as well as choose between a default instance and a named instance. The SQL Server Network Name is the virtual name, which is configured as a resource in the role. This allows client applications to connect to a server with a consistent name, regardless of the node that owns the instance.

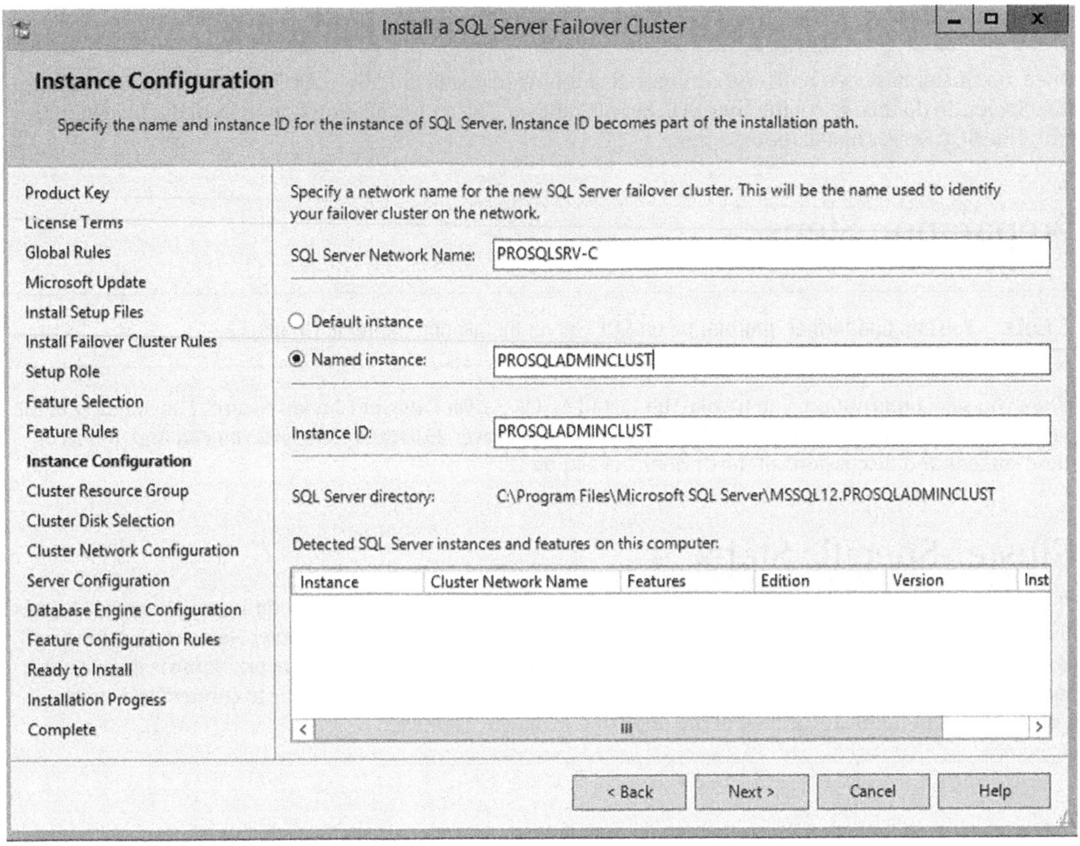

Figure 12-31. The Instance Configuration page

■ **Tip**   If you do not have permissions to create AD objects in the OU that contains your cluster, then the VCO for the instance must already exist, and you must have the Full Control permission assigned.

On the Cluster Resource Group page, displayed in Figure 12-32, a list of roles on the local cluster is displayed. It is possible to create an empty role prior to running the installation of the instance, and if you have done so, then you can select it from the list. Alternatively, you can modify the default name supplied in the SQL Server cluster resource group name box to create a new resource group. In this demonstration, we leave the default name.

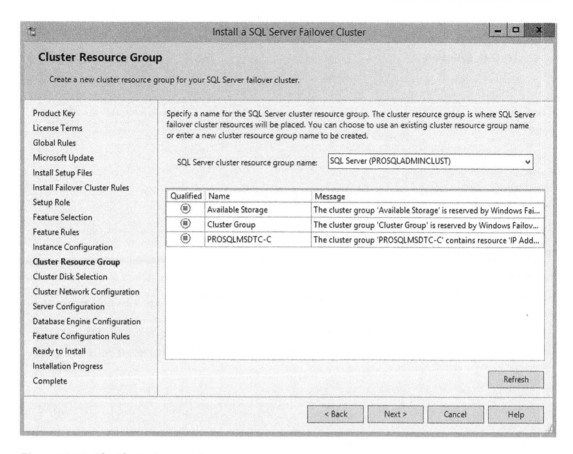

Figure 12-32. *The Cluster Resource Group page*

On the Cluster Disk Selection page of the wizard, shown in Figure 12-33, a list of cluster disks displays in the lower pane, with warnings next to any disks that you cannot select. In the top pane, you can check the disks that you want to add to the role. In our case, we select all of them, since there is one for data, one for logs, and one for TempDB.

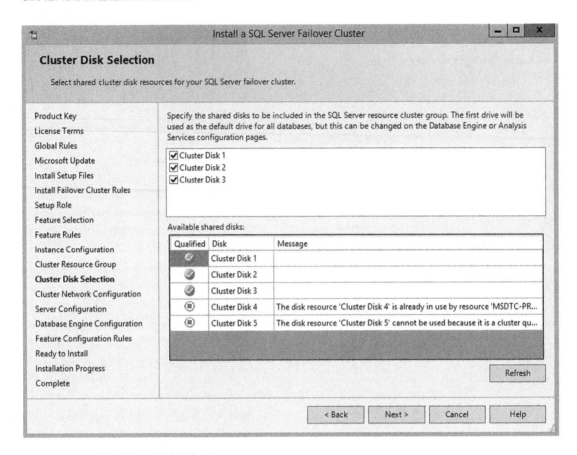

Figure 12-33. *The Cluster Disk Selection page*

On the Cluster Network Configuration page, we add an IP address for the role. In a multi-subnet cluster, we would add multiple IP addresses, one for each subnet. The Cluster Network Configuration page is illustrated in Figure 12-34.

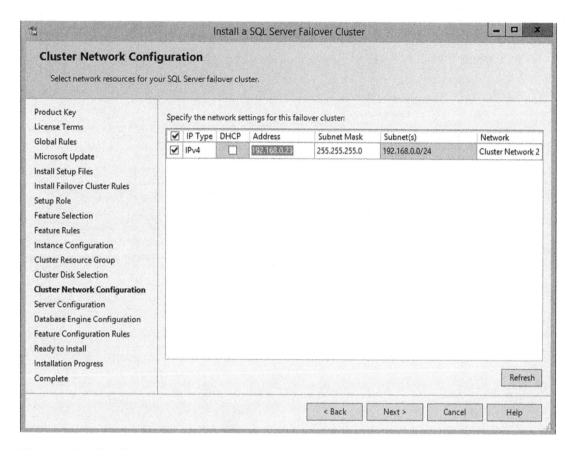

Figure 12-34. *The Cluster Network Configuration page*

On the Service Accounts tab of the Server Configuration page, the startup type for the SQL Server service and the Server Agent service can only be configured as manual, since startup is controlled by the cluster during failover. The other required service accounts are in a read-only display and cannot be configured, as shown in Figure 12-35.

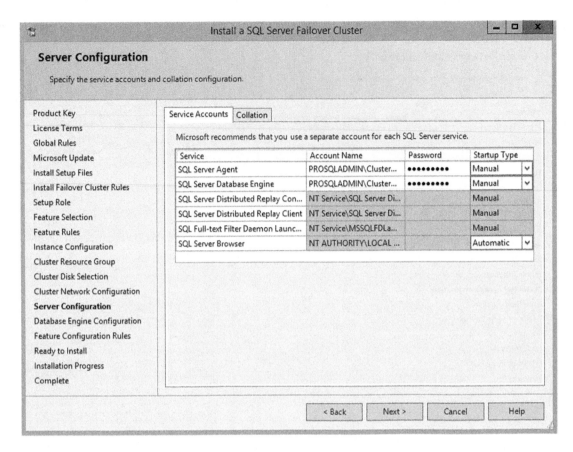

Figure 12-35. *The Sevice Account tab*

After instance installation is complete, the role is brought online and the instance is visible in Failover Cluster Manager, as shown in Figure 12-36.

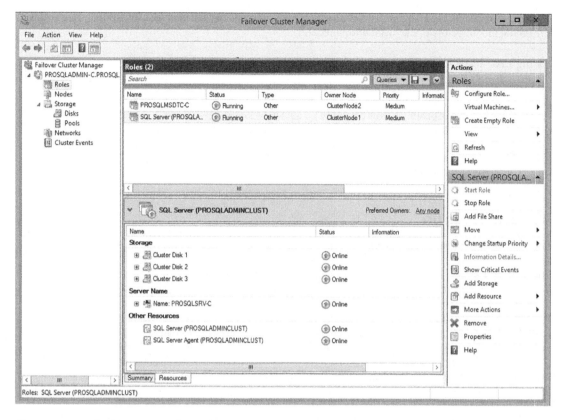

Figure 12-36. *The SQL Server role in Failover Cluster Manager*

Installing the Instance with PowerShell

Of course, we can use PowerShell to install the AlwaysOn failover cluster instance instead of using the GUI. To install an AlwaysOn failover cluster instance from PowerShell, we can use SQL Server's setup.exe application with the InstallFailoverCluster action specified.

When you perform a command-line installation of a clustered instance, you need the parameters in Table 12-1, in addition to the parameters that are mandatory when you install a stand-alone instance of SQL Server. For a complete description of mandatory parameters, please see Chapter 3.

Table 12-1. *Required Parameters for the Installation of a Clustered Instance*

Parameter	Usage
/FAILOVERCLUSTERIPADDRESSES	Specifies the IP address(s) to use for the instance in the format `<IP Type>;<address>;<network name>;<subnet mask>`. For multi-subnet clusters, the IP addresses are space delimited.
/FAILOVERCLUSTERNETWORKNAME	The virtual name of the clustered instance.
/INSTALLSQLDATADIR	The folder in which to place SQL Server data files. This must be a cluster disk.

The script in Listing 12-5 performs the same installation that has just been demonstrated when you run it from the root directory of the installation media.

Listing 12-5. Installing an AlwaysOn Failover Cluster Instance with PowerShell

```
.\SETUP.EXE /IACCEPTSQLSERVERLICENSETERMS /ACTION="InstallFailoverCluster"
/FEATURES=SQL,Conn,ADV_SSMS,DREPLAY_CTLR,DREPLAY_CLT /INSTANCENAME="PROSQLADMINCLUST"
/SQLSVCACCOUNT="PROSQLADMIN\ClusterAdmin" /SQLSVCPASSWORD="Pa$$w0rd"
/AGTSVCACCOUNT="PROSQLADMIN\ClusterAdmin" /AGTSVCPASSWORD="Pa$$w0rd"
/SQLSYSADMINACCOUNTS="PROSQLADMIN\SQLAdmin" /FAILOVERCLUSTERIPADDRESSES="IPv4;192.168.0.23;C
luster Network 2;255.255.255.0" /FAILOVERCLUSTERNETWORKNAME="PROSQLSRV-C"
/INSTALLSQLDATADIR="F:\" /qs
```

Adding a Node

The next step you should take when installing the cluster is to add the second node. Failure to add the second node results in the instance staying online, but with no high availability, since the second node is unable to take ownership of the role. To configure the second node, you need to log in to the passive cluster node and select the Add Node To SQL Server Failover Cluster option from the Installation tab of SQL Server Installation Center. This invokes the Add A Failover Cluster Node Wizard. The first page of this wizard is the Product Key page. Just like when you install an instance, you need to use this screen to provide the product key for SQL Server. Not specifying a product key only leaves you the option of installing the Evaluation Edition, and since this expires after 180 days, it's probably not the wisest choice for high availability.

The following License Terms page of the wizard asks you to read and accept the license terms of SQL Server. Additionally, you need to specify if you wish to participate in Microsoft's Customer Experience Improvement Program. As discussed in Chapter 2, if you select this option, then error reporting is captured and sent to Microsoft.

After you accept the license terms, a rules check runs to ensure that all of the conditions are met so you can continue with the installation. After the wizard checks for Microsoft updates and installing the setup files required for installation, another rules check is carried out to ensure that the rules for adding the node to the cluster are met.

■ **Note** For further discussion and illustrations of the preparation pages just described, please refer to Chapter 2.

On the Cluster Node Configuration page, illustrated in Figure 12-37, you are asked to confirm the instance name to which you are adding a node. If you have multiple instances on the cluster, then you can use the drop-down box to select the appropriate instance.

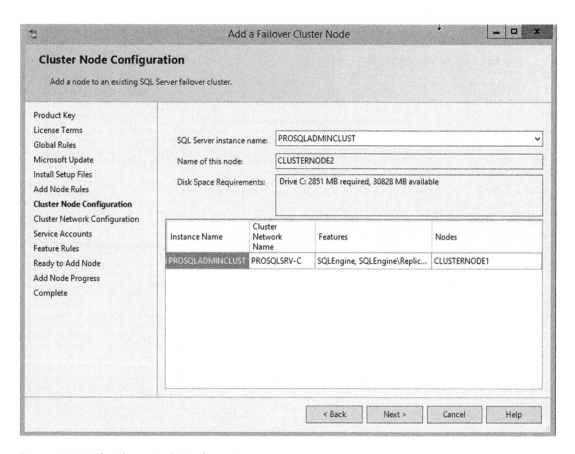

Figure 12-37. *The Cluster Node Configuration page*

On the Cluster Network Configuration page, shown in Figure 12-38, you confirm the network details. These should be identical to the first node in the cluster, including the same IP address, since this is, of course, shared between the two nodes.

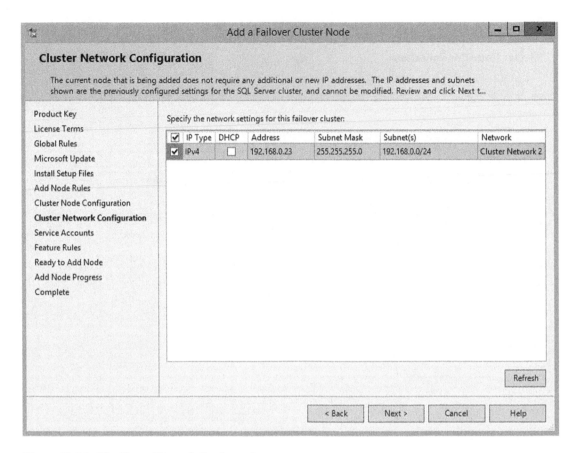

Figure 12-38. *The Cluster Network Configuration page*

On the Service Accounts page of the wizard, most of the information is in read-only mode and you are not able to modify it. This is because the service accounts you use must be the same for each node of the cluster. You need to re-enter the service account passwords, however. This page is shown in Figure 12-39.

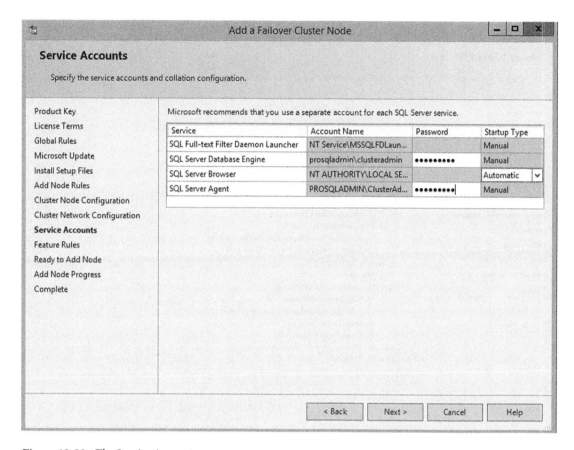

Figure 12-39. *The Service Accounts page*

Now that the wizard has all of the required information, an additional rules check is carried out before the summary page displays. The summary page, known as the Ready To Add Node page, is illustrated in Figure 12-40. It provides a summary of the activities that take place during the installation.

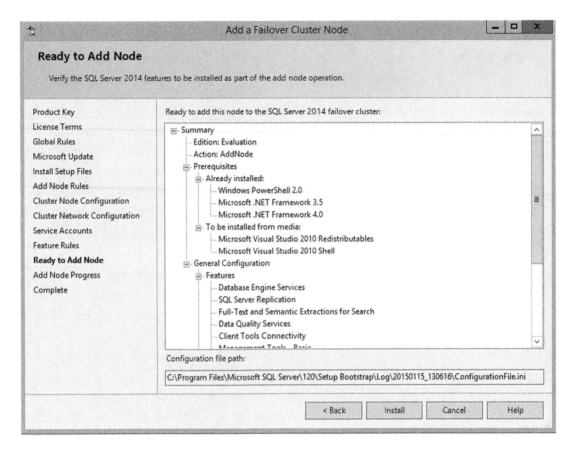

Figure 12-40. *The Read To Add Node page*

Adding a Node Using PowerShell

To add a node using PowerShell instead of the GUI, you can run SQL Server's setup.exe application with an AddNode action. When you add a node from the command line, the parameters detailed in Table 12-2 are mandatory.

Table 12-2. *Mandatory Parameters for the AddNode Action*

Parameter	Usage
/ACTION	Must be configured as AddNode.
/IACCEPTSQLSERVERLICENSETERMS	Mandatory when installing on Windows Server Core, since the /qs switch must be specified on Windows Server Core.
/INSTANCENAME	The instance that you are adding the extra node to support.
/CONFIRMIPDEPENDENCYCHANGE	Allows multiple IP addresses to be specified for multi-subnet clusters. Pass in a value of 1 for True or 0 for False.

(continued)

Table 12-2. (*continued*)

Parameter	Usage
/FAILOVERCLUSTERIPADDRESSES	Specifies the IP address(es) to use for the instance in the format `<IP Type>;<address>;<network name>;<subnet mask>`. For multi-subnet clusters, the IP addresses are space delimited.
/FAILOVERCLUSTERNETWORKNAME	The virtual name of the clustered instance.
/INSTALLSQLDATADIR	The folder in which to place SQL Server data files. This must be a cluster disk.
/SQLSVCACCOUNT	The service account that is used to run the Database Engine.
/SQLSVCPASSWORD	The password of the service account that is used to run the Database Engine.
/AGTSVCACCOUNT	The service account that issued to run SQL Server Agent.
/AGTSVCPASSWORD	The password of the service account that is used to run SQL Server Agent.

The script in Listing 12-6 adds `ClusterNode2` to the role when you run it from the root folder of the install media.

Listing 12-6. Adding a Node Using PowerShell

```
.\setup.exe /IACCEPTSQLSERVERLICENSETERMS /ACTION="AddNode" /INSTANCENAME="PROSQLADMINCLUST"
/SQLSVCACCOUNT="PROSQLADMIN\ClusterAdmin" /SQLSVCPASSWORD="Pa$$w0rd"
/AGTSVCACCOUNT="PROSQLADMIN\ClusterAdmin" /AGTSVCPASSWORD="Pa$$w0rd"
/FAILOVERCLUSTERIPADDRESSES="IPv4;192.168.0.23;Cluster Network 2;255.255.255.0"
/CONFIRMIPDEPENDENCYCHANGE=0 /qs
```

Managing a Cluster

Installing the cluster is not the end of the road from an administrative perspective. You still need to periodically perform maintenance tasks. The following sections describe some of the most common maintenance tasks.

Moving the Instance between Nodes

Other than protecting against unplanned outages, one of the benefits of implementing high availability technologies is that doing so significantly reduces downtime for maintenance tasks, such as patching. This can be at the operating system level or the SQL Server level.

If you have a two-node cluster, apply the patch to the passive node first. Once you are happy that the update was successful, fail over the instance and then apply the patch to the other node. At this point, you may or may not wish to fail back to the original node, depending on the needs of your environment. For example, if the overriding priority is the level of availability of the instance, then you will probably not wish to fail back, because this will incur another short outage.

On the other hand, if your instance is less critical and you have licensed SQL Server with Software Assurance, then you may not be paying for the SQL Server license on the passive node. In this scenario, you only have a limited time period in which to fail the instance back to avoid needing to purchase an additional license for the passive node.

■ **Note**   For versions of SQL Server prior to SQL Server 2014, Software Assurance is not required in order to have a passive node without a license.

To move an instance to a different node using Failover Cluster Manager, select Move | Select Node from the context menu of the role that contains the instance. This causes the Move Clustered Role dialog box to display. Here, you can select the node to which you wish to move the role, as illustrated in Figure 12-41.

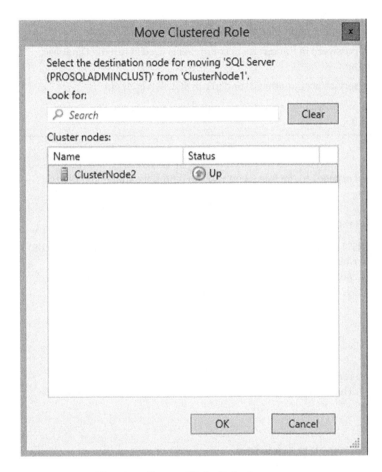

Figure 12-41.   *The Move Clustered Role dialog box*

The role is then moved to the new node. If you watch the role's resources window in Failover Cluster Manager, then you see each resource move through the states of Online ➤ Offline Pending ➤ Offline. The new node is now displayed as the owner before the resources move in turn through the states of Offline - Online Pending - Online, as illustrated in Figure 12-42. The resources are taken offline and placed back online in order of their dependencies.

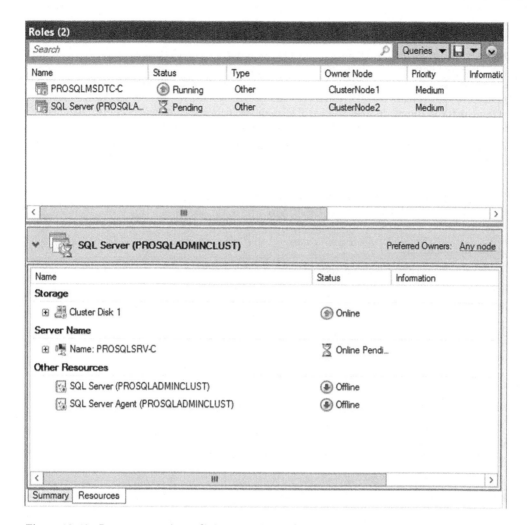

Figure 12-42. *Resources coming onlinie on passive node*

We can also fail over a role using PowerShell. To do this, we need to use the Move--ClusterGroup cmdlet. Listing 12-7 demonstrates this by using the cmdlet to fail back the instance to ClusterNode1. We use the -Name parameter to specify the role that we wish to move and the -Node parameter to specify the node to which we wish to move it.

Listing 12-7. Moving the Role Between Nodes

```
Move-ClusterGroup -Name "SQL Server (PROSQLADMINCLUST)" -Node ClusterNode1
```

Rolling Patch Upgrade

If you have a cluster with more than two nodes, then consider performing a rolling patch upgrade when you are applying updates for SQL Server. In this scenario, you mitigate the risk of having different nodes, which are possible owners of the role, running different versions or patch levels of SQL Server, which could lead to data corruption.

The first thing that you should do is make a list of all nodes that are possible owners of the role. Then select 50 percent of these nodes and remove them from the Possible Owners list. You can do this by selecting Properties from the context menu of the Name resource, and then, in the Advanced Policies tab, unchecking the nodes in the possible owners list, as illustrated in Figure 12-43.

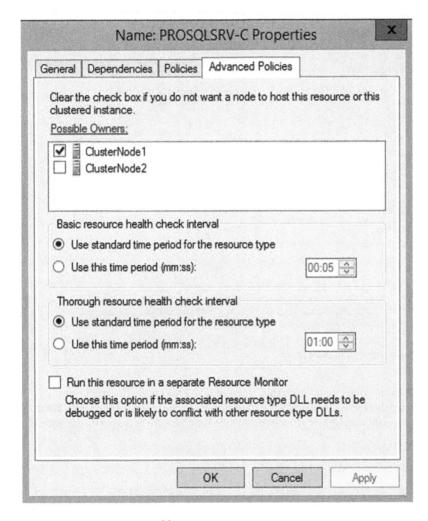

Figure 12-43. *Remove possible owners*

To achieve the same result using PowerShell, we can use the Get-Resource cmdlet to navigate to the name resource and then pipe in the Set-ClusterOwnerNode to configure the possible owners list. This is demonstrated in Listing 12-8. The possible owners list is comma separated in the event that you are configuring multiple possible owners.

Listing 12-8. Configuring Possible Owners

```
Get-ClusterResource "SQL Network Name (PROSQLSRV-C)" | Set-ClusterOwnerNode -Owners
clusternode1
```

Once 50 percent of the nodes have been removed as possible owners, you should apply the update to these nodes. After the update has been verified on this half of the nodes, you should reconfigure them to allow them to be possible owners once more.

The next step is to move the role to one of the nodes that you have upgraded. After failover has successfully completed, remove the other half of the nodes from the preferred owners list before applying the update to these nodes. Once the update has been verified on this half of the nodes, you can return them to the possible owners list.

■ **Tip**   The possible owners can only be set on a resource. If you run Set-ClusterOwnerNode against a role using the -Group parameter, then you are configuring preferred owners rather than possible owners.

Removing a Node from the Cluster

If you wish to uninstall an AlwaysOn failover cluster instance, then you cannot perform this action from Control Panel as you would a stand-alone instance. Instead, you must run the Remove Node Wizard on each of the nodes of the cluster. You can invoke this wizard by selecting Remove Node from a SQL Server Failover Cluster option from the Maintenance tab in SQL Server Installation Center.

The wizard starts by running a global rules check, followed by a rules check for removing a node. Then, on the Cluster Node Configuration page shown in Figure 12-44, you are asked to confirm the instance for which you wish to remove a node. If the cluster hosts multiple instances, you can select the appropriate instance from the drop-down box.

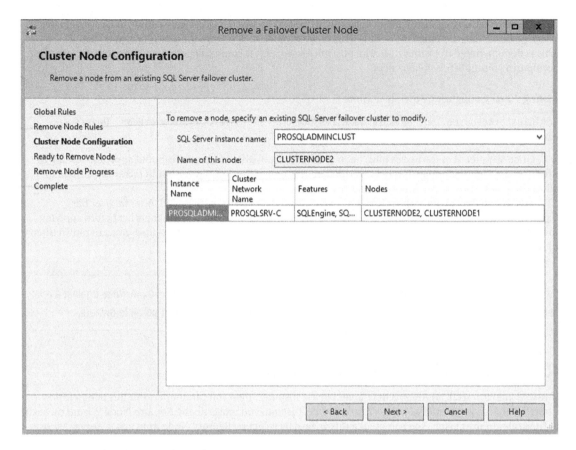

Figure 12-44. *The Cluster Node Configuration page*

On the Ready To Remove Node page, shown in Figure 12-45, you are given a summary of the tasks that will be performed. After confirming the details, the instance is removed. This process should be repeated on all passive nodes, and then finally on the active node. When the instance is removed from the final node, the cluster role is also removed.

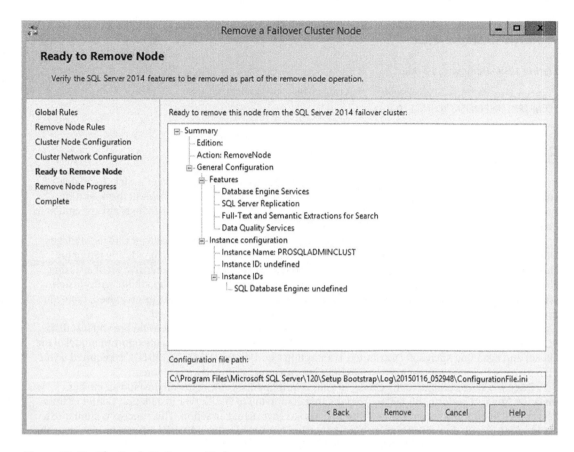

Figure 12-45. *The Ready To Remove Node page*

To remove a node using PowerShell, we need to run SQL Server's setup.exe application, with the action parameter configured as RemoveNode. When you use PowerShell to remove a node, the parameters in Table 12-3 are mandatory.

Table 12-3. *Mandatory Parameters When Removing a Node from a Cluster*

Parameter	Usage
/ACTION	Must be configured as AddNode.
/INSTANCENAME	The instance that you are adding the extra node to support.
/CONFIRMIPDEPENDENCYCHANGE	Allows multiple IP addresses to be specified for multi-subnet clusters. Pass in a value of 1 for True or 0 for False.

The script in Listing 12-9 removes a node from our cluster when we run it from the root directory of the SQL Server installation media.

Listing 12-9. Removing a Node

```
.\setup.exe /ACTION="RemoveNode" /INSTANCENAME="PROSQLADMINCLUST"
/CONFIRMIPDEPENDENCYCHANGE=0 /qs
```

Summary

Before you build a cluster, you must prepare the servers that will become the cluster nodes. To do this, you need to install the .NET Framework 3.5 features and the Failover Cluster features in the operating system. You can do this either through Server Manager or by using the `Install-WindowsFeature` cmdlet in PowerShell.

Once you have prepared the nodes, you need to build the cluster by using Failover Cluster Manager. During this process, you define the IP address and virtual name that will be used for administering the cluster. You also need to validate the cluster. This validation consists of a comprehensive set of tests that check the configuration of the network, the nodes, and the storage to ensure compatibility with clustering. Warnings raised by this validation may or may not indicate an issue, but if any errors are raised, then you must resolve them. Microsoft will not support clusters that have not been validated.

Once you have built the cluster, you may need to perform many configurations before you install the SQL Server failover cluster instance. These configurations may include changing the quorum model of the cluster and installing Microsoft Distributed Transaction Coordinator (MSDTC). MSTDC is required if you plan to use SQL Server Integration Services (SSIS) or run any distributed transactions.

Once you have configured the cluster to your requirements, you can install the failover cluster instance. You can perform this action from the Installation tab of SQL Server Installation Center or from PowerShell by running `setup.exe` with the `InstallFailoverCluster` action. This process is similar to a stand-alone installation of SQL Server, except that you need to supply additional information, such as the IP address and virtual name of the instance. This allows applications to connect, regardless of the node that owns the instance.

After the initial installation is complete, the instance is accessible, but there is no high availability. In order to allow the instance to fail over to other nodes, you must run the Add Node Wizard on each of the other nodes within the cluster.

One benefit of achieving high availability for SQL Server is that doing so allows you to minimize downtime during planned maintenance. On a two-node cluster, you can upgrade the passive node, fail over, and then upgrade the active node. For larger clusters, you can perform a rolling patch upgrade, which involves removing half of the nodes from the possible owners list and upgrading them. You then fail over the instance to one of the upgraded nodes and repeat the process for the remaining nodes. This mitigates the risk of mixed version, across the possible owners.

CHAPTER 13

■ ■ ■

Implementing AlwaysOn Availability Groups

AlwaysOn Availability Groups provide a flexible option for achieving high availability, recovering from disasters, and scaling out read-only workloads. The technology synchronizes data at the database level, but health monitoring and quorum are provided by a Windows cluster.

This chapter demonstrates how to build and configure availability groups for both high availability (HA) and disaster recovery (DR). We also discuss aspects such as performance considerations and maintenance. We discuss using availability groups to scale out read-only workloads in Chapter 16.

■ **Note**   For the demonstrations in this chapter, we use a domain that contains a domain controller and a two-node cluster. These servers are in a site called Site1. A second site, called Site2, contains a third server. During the course of the chapter, we add this as a node to the cluster. The cluster has no shared storage for data and there is no AlwaysOn failover clustered instance. Each node has a stand-alone instance of SQL Server installed on it named ClusterNode1\PrimaryReplica, ClusterNode2\SyncHA, and ClusterNode3\AsyncDR, respectively.

Implementing High Availability with AlwaysOn Availability Groups

Before implementing AlwaysOn Availability Groups, we first create three databases, which we will use during the demonstrations in this chapter. Two of the databases relate to the fictional application, App1, and the third database relates to the fictional application, App2. Each contains a single table, which we populate with data. Each database is configured with Recovery mode set to FULL. This is a hard requirement for a database to use AlwaysOn Availability Groups because data is synchronized via a log stream. The script in Listing 13-1 creates these databases.

Listing 13-1. Creating Databases

```
CREATE DATABASE Chapter13App1Customers ;
GO

ALTER DATABASE Chapter13App1Customers SET RECOVERY FULL ;
GO

USE Chapter13App1Customers
GO

CREATE TABLE App1Customers
(
ID                  INT                 PRIMARY KEY         IDENTITY,
FirstName           NVARCHAR(30),
LastName            NVARCHAR(30),
CreditCardNumber    VARBINARY(8000)
) ;
GO

--Populate the table

DECLARE @Numbers TABLE
(
        Number          INT
)

;WITH CTE(Number)
AS
(
        SELECT 1 Number
        UNION ALL
        SELECT Number + 1
        FROM CTE
        WHERE Number < 100
)
INSERT INTO @Numbers
SELECT Number FROM CTE

DECLARE @Names TABLE
(
        FirstName       VARCHAR(30),
        LastName        VARCHAR(30)
) ;

INSERT INTO @Names
VALUES('Peter', 'Carter'),
                ('Michael', 'Smith'),
                ('Danielle', 'Mead'),
                ('Reuben', 'Roberts'),
                ('Iris', 'Jones'),
                ('Sylvia', 'Davies'),
```

```
                   ('Finola', 'Wright'),
                   ('Edward', 'James'),
                   ('Marie', 'Andrews'),
                   ('Jennifer', 'Abraham'),
                   ('Margaret', 'Jones')

INSERT INTO App1Customers(Firstname, LastName, CreditCardNumber)
SELECT   FirstName, LastName, CreditCardNumber FROM
         (SELECT
                 (SELECT TOP 1 FirstName FROM @Names ORDER BY NEWID()) FirstName
                ,(SELECT TOP 1 LastName FROM @Names ORDER BY NEWID()) LastName
                ,(SELECT CONVERT(VARBINARY(8000)
                ,(SELECT TOP 1 CAST(Number * 100 AS CHAR(4))
                  FROM @Numbers
                  WHERE Number BETWEEN 10 AND 99 ORDER BY NEWID()) + '-' +
                        (SELECT TOP 1 CAST(Number * 100 AS CHAR(4))
                         FROM @Numbers
                         WHERE Number BETWEEN 10 AND 99 ORDER BY NEWID()) + '-' +
                        (SELECT TOP 1 CAST(Number * 100 AS CHAR(4))
                         FROM @Numbers
                         WHERE Number BETWEEN 10 AND 99 ORDER BY NEWID()) + '-' +
                        (SELECT TOP 1 CAST(Number * 100 AS CHAR(4))
                         FROM @Numbers
                         WHERE Number BETWEEN 10 AND 99 ORDER BY NEWID())))) CreditCardNumber
FROM @Numbers a
CROSS JOIN @Numbers b
CROSS JOIN @Numbers c
) d ;

CREATE DATABASE Chapter13App1Sales ;
GO

ALTER DATABASE Chapter13App1Sales SET RECOVERY FULL ;
GO

USE Chapter13App1Sales
GO

CREATE TABLE [dbo].[Orders](
        [OrderNumber] [int] IDENTITY(1,1) NOT NULL PRIMARY KEY CLUSTERED,
        [OrderDate] [date]  NOT NULL,
        [CustomerID] [int]  NOT NULL,
        [ProductID] [int]   NOT NULL,
        [Quantity] [int]    NOT NULL,
        [NetAmount] [money] NOT NULL,
        [TaxAmount] [money] NOT NULL,
        [InvoiceAddressID] [int] NOT NULL,
        [DeliveryAddressID] [int] NOT NULL,
        [DeliveryDate] [date] NULL,
) ;
```

```sql
DECLARE @Numbers TABLE
(
        Number          INT
)

;WITH CTE(Number)
AS
(
        SELECT 1 Number
        UNION ALL
        SELECT Number + 1
        FROM CTE
        WHERE Number < 100
)
INSERT INTO @Numbers
SELECT Number FROM CTE

--Populate ExistingOrders with data

INSERT INTO Orders
SELECT
        (SELECT CAST(DATEADD(dd,(SELECT TOP 1 Number
                              FROM @Numbers
                              ORDER BY NEWID()),getdate())as DATE)),
        (SELECT TOP 1 Number -10 FROM @Numbers ORDER BY NEWID()),
        (SELECT TOP 1 Number FROM @Numbers ORDER BY NEWID()),
        (SELECT TOP 1 Number FROM @Numbers ORDER BY NEWID()),
        500,
        100,
        (SELECT TOP 1 Number FROM @Numbers ORDER BY NEWID()),
        (SELECT TOP 1 Number FROM @Numbers ORDER BY NEWID()),
        (SELECT CAST(DATEADD(dd,(SELECT TOP 1 Number - 10
         FROM @Numbers
         ORDER BY NEWID()),getdate() as DATE))
FROM @Numbers a
CROSS JOIN @Numbers b
CROSS JOIN @Numbers c ;

CREATE DATABASE Chapter13App2Customers ;
GO

ALTER DATABASE Chapter13App2Customers SET RECOVERY FULL ;
GO

USE Chapter13App2Customers
GO
```

```
CREATE TABLE App2Customers
(
ID                  INT                  PRIMARY KEY        IDENTITY,
FirstName           NVARCHAR(30),
LastName            NVARCHAR(30),
CreditCardNumber    VARBINARY(8000)
) ;
GO

--Populate the table

DECLARE @Numbers TABLE
(
        Number          INT
) ;

;WITH CTE(Number)
AS
(
        SELECT 1 Number
        UNION ALL
        SELECT Number + 1
        FROM CTE
        WHERE Number < 100
)
INSERT INTO @Numbers
SELECT Number FROM CTE ;

DECLARE @Names TABLE
(
        FirstName          VARCHAR(30),
        LastName           VARCHAR(30)
) ;

INSERT INTO @Names
VALUES('Peter', 'Carter'),
                ('Michael', 'Smith'),
                ('Danielle', 'Mead'),
                ('Reuben', 'Roberts'),
                ('Iris', 'Jones'),
                ('Sylvia', 'Davies'),
                ('Finola', 'Wright'),
                ('Edward', 'James'),
                ('Marie', 'Andrews'),
                ('Jennifer', 'Abraham'),
                ('Margaret', 'Jones')
```

```
INSERT INTO App2Customers(Firstname, LastName, CreditCardNumber)
SELECT  FirstName, LastName, CreditCardNumber FROM
        (SELECT
               (SELECT TOP 1 FirstName FROM @Names ORDER BY NEWID()) FirstName
              ,(SELECT TOP 1 LastName FROM @Names ORDER BY NEWID()) LastName
              ,(SELECT CONVERT(VARBINARY(8000)
              ,(SELECT TOP 1 CAST(Number * 100 AS CHAR(4))
                FROM @Numbers
                WHERE Number BETWEEN 10 AND 99 ORDER BY NEWID()) + '-' +
                      (SELECT TOP 1 CAST(Number * 100 AS CHAR(4))
                       FROM @Numbers
                       WHERE Number BETWEEN 10 AND 99 ORDER BY NEWID()) + '-' +
                      (SELECT TOP 1 CAST(Number * 100 AS CHAR(4))
                       FROM @Numbers
                       WHERE Number BETWEEN 10 AND 99 ORDER BY NEWID()) + '-' +
                      (SELECT TOP 1 CAST(Number * 100 AS CHAR(4))
                       FROM @Numbers
                       WHERE Number BETWEEN 10 AND 99 ORDER BY NEWID())) CreditCardNumber
FROM @Numbers a
CROSS JOIN @Numbers b
CROSS JOIN @Numbers c
) d ;
```

Configuring SQL Server

The first step in configuring AlwaysOn Availability Groups is enabling this feature on the SQL Server service. To enable the feature from the GUI, we open SQL Server Configuration Manager, drill through SQL Server Services and select Properties from the context menu of the SQL Server service. When we do this, the service properties display and we navigate to the AlwaysOn High Availability tab, shown in Figure 13-1.

Figure 13-1. *The AlwaysOn High Avaiability tab*

On this tab, we check the Enable AlwaysOn Availability Groups box and ensure that the cluster name displayed in the Windows Failover Cluster Name box is correct. We then need to restart the SQL Server service. Because AlwaysOn Availability Groups uses stand-alone instances, which are installed locally on each cluster node, as opposed to a failover clustered instance, which spans multiple nodes, we need to repeat these steps for each stand-alone instance hosted on the cluster.

We can also use PowerShell to enable AlwaysOn Availability Groups. To do this, we use the PowerShell command in Listing 13-2. The script assumes that CLUSTERNODE1 is the name of the server and that PRIMARYREPLICA is the name of the SQL Server instance.

Listing 13-2. Enabling AlwaysOn Availability Groups

```
Enable-SqlAlwaysOn -Path SQLSERVER:\SQL\CLUSTERNODE1\PRIMARYREPLICA
```

The next step is to take a full backup of all databases that will be part of the availability group. We create separate availability groups for App1 and App2, respectively, so to create an availability group for App1, we need to back up the Chapter13App1Customers and Chapter13App1Sales databases. We do this by running the script in Listing 13-3.

Listing 13-3. Backing Up the Databases

```
BACKUP DATABASE Chapter13App1Customers
TO   DISK = N'C:\Backups\Chapter13App1Customers.bak'
WITH NAME = N'Chapter13App1Customers-Full Database Backup' ;
GO

BACKUP DATABASE Chapter13App1Sales
TO   DISK = N'C:\Backups\Chapter13App1Sales.bak'
WITH NAME = N'Chapter13App1Sales-Full Database Backup' ;
GO
```

■ **Note** Backups are discussed in Chapter 15.

Creating the Availability Group

You can create an availability group topology in SQL Server in several ways. It can be created manually, predominantly through dialog boxes, via T-SQL, or through a wizard. The following sections explore each of these options.

Using the New Availability Group Wizard

When the backups complete successfully, we invoke the New Availability Group wizard by drilling through AlwaysOn High Availability in Object Explorer and selecting the New Availability Group wizard from the context menu of the Availability Groups folder. The Introduction page of the wizard, displayed in Figure 13-2, now displays, giving us an overview of the steps that we need to undertake.

Figure 13-2. *The Introduction page*

On the Specify Name page (see Figure 13-3), we are prompted to enter a name for our availability group.

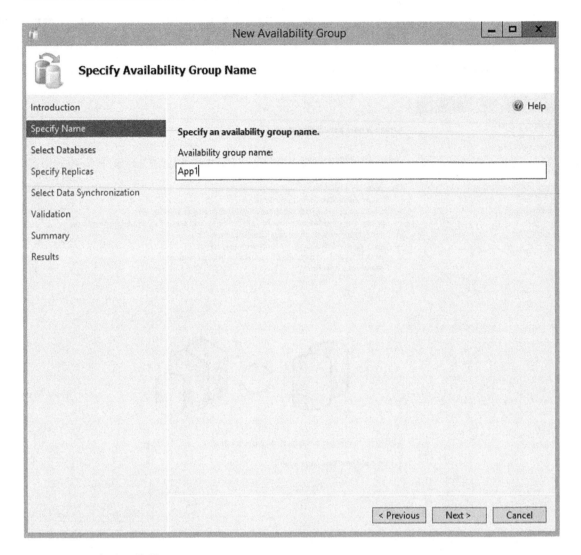

Figure 13-3. *The Specify Name page*

On the Select Databases page, we are prompted to select the database(s) that we wish to participate in the availability group, as illustrated in Figure 13-4. On this screen, notice that we cannot select the Chapter13App2Customers database, because we have not yet taken a full backup of the database.

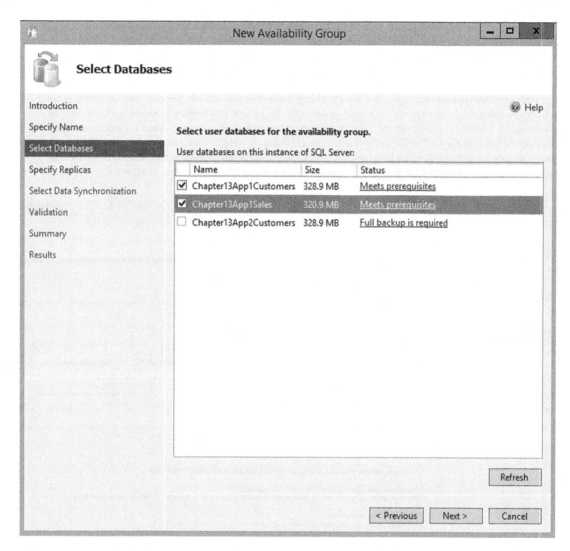

Figure 13-4. *The Select Database page*

The Specify Replicas page consists of four tabs. We use the first tab, Replicas, to add the secondary replicas to the topology. Checking the Synchronous Commit option causes data to be committed on the secondary replica before it is committed on the primary replica. (This is also referred to as *hardening the log* on the secondary before the primary.) This means that, in the event of a failover, data loss is not possible, meaning that we can meet an SLA (service level agreement) with an RPO (recovery point objective) of 0 (zero). It also means that there is a performance impediment, however. If we choose not to check the option for Synchronous Commit, then the replica operates in Asynchronous Commit mode. This means that data is committed on the primary replica before being committed on the secondary replica. This stops us from suffering a performance impediment, but it also means that, in the event of failover, the RPO is nondeterministic. Performance considerations for synchronous replicas are discussed later in this chapter.

When we check the Automatic Failover option, the Synchronous Commit option is also selected automatically if we have not already selected it. This is because automatic failover is only possible in Synchronous Commit mode. We can set the Readable Secondary drop-down to No, Yes, or Read-intent. When we set it to No, the database is not accessible on replicas that are in a secondary role. When we set it to read-intent, the Availability Group Listener is able to redirect read-only workloads to this secondary replica, but only if the application has specified Application Intent=Read-only in the connection string. Setting it to Yes enables the listener to redirect read-only traffic, regardless of whether the Application Intent parameter is present in the application's connection string. Although we can change the value of Readable Secondary through the GUI while at the same time configuring a replica for automatic failover without error, this is simply a quirk of the wizard. In fact, the replica is not accessible, since active secondaries are not supported when configured for automatic failover. The Replicas tab is illustrated in Figure 13-5.

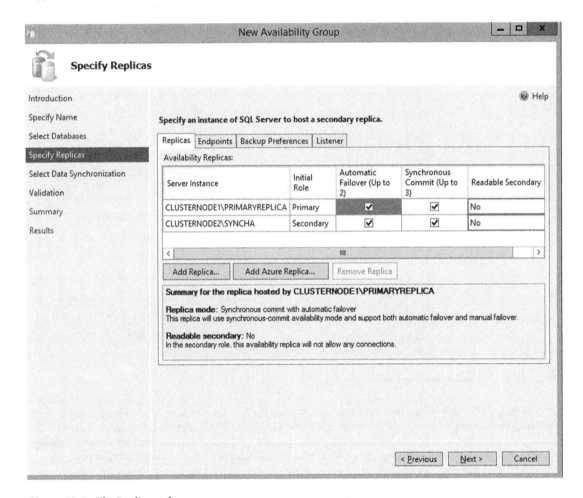

Figure 13-5. *The Replicas tab*

■ **Note**   Using secondary replicas for read-only workloads is discussed in more depth in Chapter 16.

On the Endpoints tab of the Specify Replicas page, illustrated in Figure 13-6, we specify the port number for each endpoint. The default port is 5022, but we can specify a different port if we need to. On this tab, we also specify if data should be encrypted when it is sent between the endpoints. It is usually a good idea to check this option, and if we do, then AES (Advanced Encryption Standard) is used as the encryption algorithm.

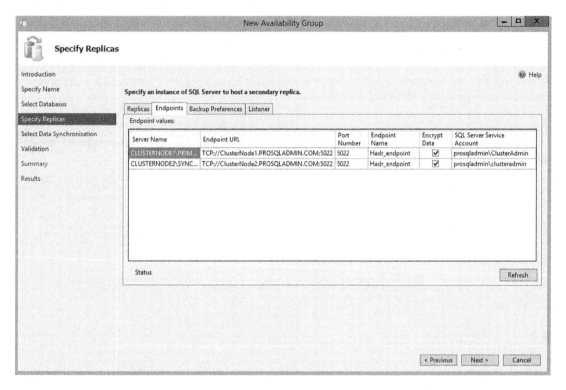

Figure 13-6. *The Endpoints tab*

Optionally, you can also change the name of the endpoint that is created. Because only one database mirroring endpoint is allowed per instance, however, and because the default name is fairly descriptive, there is not always a reason to change it. Some DBAs choose to rename it to include the name of the instance, since this can simplify the management of multiple servers. This is a good idea if your enterprise has many availability group clusters.

The service account each instance uses is displayed for informational purposes. It simplifies security administration if you ensure that the same service account is used by both instances. If you fail to do this, you will need to grant each instance permissions to each service account. This means that instead of reducing the security footprint of each service account by using it for one instance only, you simply push the footprint up to the SQL Server level instead of the Operating System level.

The endpoint URL specifies the URL of the endpoint that availability groups will use to communicate. The format of the URL is [Transport Protocol]://[Path]:[Port]. The transport protocol for a database mirroring endpoint is always TCP (Transmission Control Protocol). The path can either be the fully qualified domain name (FQDN) of the server, the server name on its own, or an IP address, which is unique across the network. I recommend using the FQDN of the server, because this is always guaranteed to work. It is also the default value populated. The port should match the port number that you specify for the endpoint.

■ **Note** Availability groups communicate with a database mirroring endpoint. Although database mirroring is deprecated, the endpoints are not.

On the Backup Preferences tab (see Figure 13-7), we can specify the replica on which automated backups will be taken. One of the big advantages of AlwaysOn Availability Groups is that when you use them, you can scale out maintenance tasks, such as backups, to secondary servers. Therefore, automated backups can seamlessly be directed to active secondaries. The possible options are Prefer Secondary, Secondary Only, Primary, or Any Replica. It is also possible to set priorities for each replica. When determining which replica to run the backup job against, SQL Server evaluates the backup priorities of each node and is more likely to choose the replica with the highest priority.

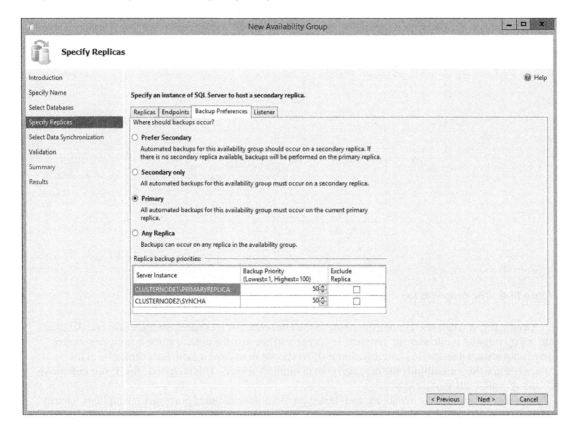

Figure 13-7. The Backup Preferences tab

Although the advantages of reducing IO on the primary replica are obvious, I, somewhat controversially, recommend against scaling automated backups to secondary replicas in many cases. This is especially the case when RTO (recovery time objective) is a priority for the application because of operational supportability issues. Imagine a scenario in which backups are being taken against a secondary replica and a user calls to say that they have accidently deleted all data from a critical table. You now need to restore a copy of the database and repopulate the table. The backup files, however, sit on the secondary replica. As a result, you need to copy the backup files over to the primary replica before you can begin to restore the database (or perform the restore over the network). This instantly increases your RTO.

Also, when configured to allow backups against multiple servers, SQL Server still only maintains the backup history on the instance where the backup was taken. This means that you may be scrambling between servers, trying to retrieve all of your backup files, not knowing where each one resides. This becomes even worse if one of the servers has a complete system outage. You can find yourself in a scenario in which you have a broken log chain.

The workaround for most of the issues that I just mentioned is to use a share on a file server and configure each instance to back up to the same share. The problem with this, however, is that by setting things up in this manner, you are now sending all of your backups across the network rather than backing them up locally. This can increase the duration of your backups as well as increase network traffic. The Backup Preferences tab is shown in Figure 13-7.

On the Listener tab, shown in Figure 13-8, we choose if we want to create an availability group listener or if we want to defer this task until later. If we choose to create the listener, then we need to specify the listener's name, the port that it should listen on, and the IP address(es) that it should use. We specify one address for each subnet, in multi-subnet clusters. The details provided here are used to create the client access point resource in the availability group's cluster role. You may notice that we have specified port 1433 for the listener, although our instance is also running on port 1433. This is a valid configuration, because the listener is configured on a different IP address than the SQL Server instance. It is also not mandatory to use the same port number, but it can be beneficial, if you are implementing AlwaysOn Availability Groups on an existing instance because applications that specify the port number to connect may need fewer application changes. Remember that the server name will still be different, however, because applications will be connecting to the virtual name of the listener, as opposed to the name of the physical server\instance. In our example, applications connect to APP1LISTEN\PRIMARYREPLICA instead of CLUSTERNODE1\PRIMARYREPLICA. Although connections via CLUSTERNODE1 are still permitted, they do not benefit from high availability or scale our reporting.

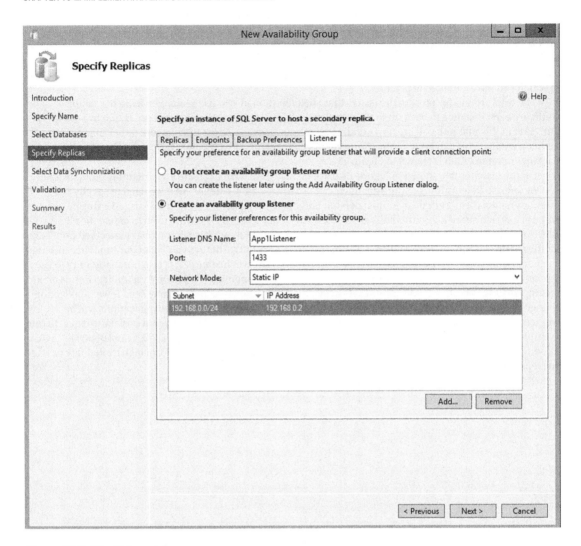

Figure 13-8. *The Listener tab*

■ **Tip** If you do not have Create Computer Objects permission within the OU, then the listener's VCO (virtual computer object) must be prestaged in AD and you must be assigned Full Control permissions on the object.

On the Select Initial Data Synchronization screen, shown in Figure 13-9, we choose how the initial data synchronization of the replicas is performed. If you choose Full, then each database that participates in the availability group is subject to a full backup, followed by a log backup. The backup files are backed up to a share, which you specify, before they are restored to the secondary servers. After the restore is complete, data synchronization, via log stream, commences.

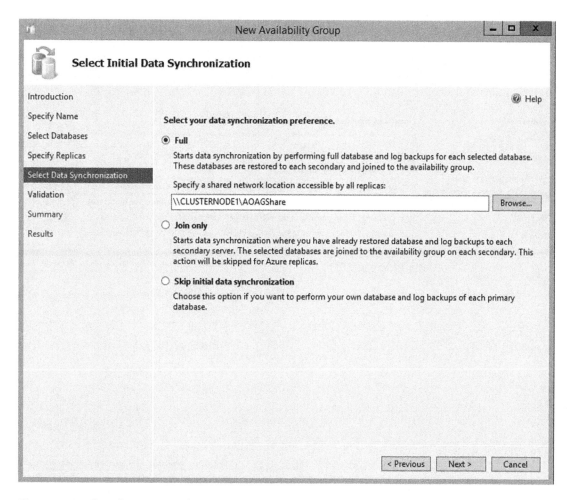

Figure 13-9. *The Select Data Synchronization page*

If you have already backed up your databases and restored them onto the secondaries, then you can select the Join Only option. This starts the data synchronization, via log stream, on the databases within the availability group. Selecting Skip Initial Data Synchronization allows you to back up and restore the databases yourself after you complete the setup.

■ **Tip**   If your availability group will contain many databases, then it may be best to perform the backup/restore yourself. This is because the inbuilt utility will perform the actions sequentially, and therefore, it may take a long time to complete.

On the Validation page, rules that may cause the setup to fail are checked, as illustrated in Figure 13-10. If any of the results come back as Failed, then you need to resolve them before you attempt to continue.

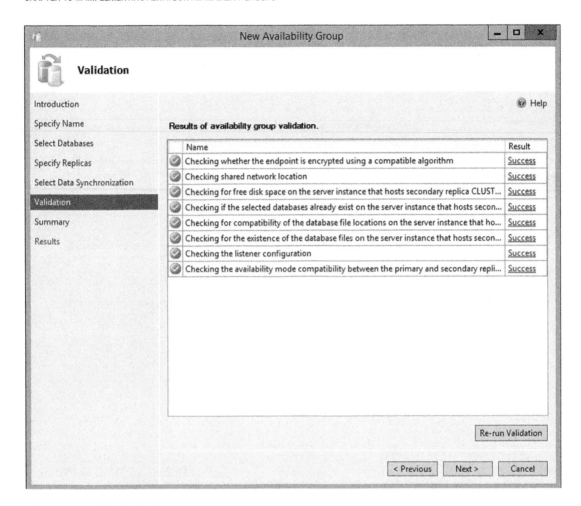

Figure 13-10. *The Validation page*

Once validation tests are complete and we move to the Summary page, we are presented with a list of the tasks that are to be carried out during the setup. This page is shown in Figure 13-11.

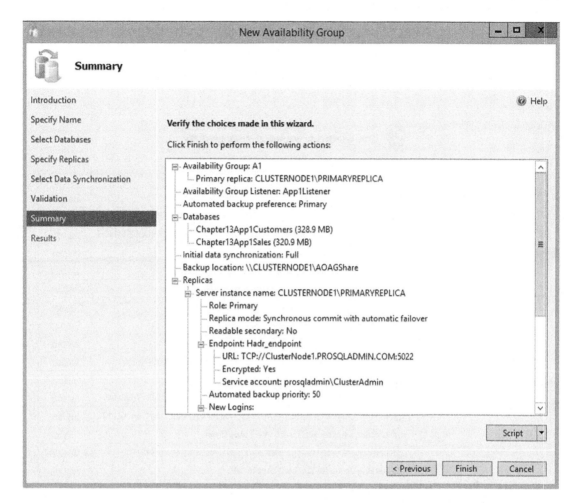

Figure 13-11. *The Summary page*

As setup progresses, the results of each configuration task display on the Results page, as shown in Figure 13-12. If any errors occur on this page, be sure to investigated them, but this does not necessarily mean that the entire availability group needs to be reconfigured. For example, if the creation of the availability group listener fails because the VCO had not been prestaged in AD, then you can re-create the listener without needing to re-create the entire availability group.

Figure 13-12. *The Results page*

As an alternative to using the New Availability Group wizard, you can perform the configuration of the availability group using the New Availability Group dialog box, followed by the Add Listener dialog box. This method of creating an availability group is examined later in this chapter.

Scripting the Availability Group

We can also script the activity by using the script in Listing 13-4. This script connects to both instances within the cluster, meaning that it can only be run in SQLCMD mode. First, the script creates a login for the service account on each instance. It then creates the TCP endpoint, assigns the connect permission to the service account, and starts the health trace for AlwaysOn Availability Groups (which we discuss later in this chapter). The script then creates the availability group on the primary and joins the secondary to the group. Next, we perform a full and log backup and a restore of each database that will participate in the availability group before we add the databases to the group. Note that the databases are backed up, restored, and added to the group in a serial manner. If you have many databases, then you may want to parallelize this process.

Listing 13-4. Creating Availability Group

```
--Create Logins for the Service Account,
--create Endpoints and assign Service Account permissions
--to the Endpoint on Primary Replica

:Connect CLUSTERNODE1\PRIMARYREPLICA

USE [master]
GO

CREATE LOGIN [prosqladmin\clusteradmin] FROM WINDOWS ;
GO

CREATE ENDPOINT [Hadr_endpoint]
       AS TCP (LISTENER_PORT = 5022)
       FOR DATA_MIRRORING (ROLE = ALL, ENCRYPTION = REQUIRED ALGORITHM AES) ;
GO

ALTER ENDPOINT [Hadr_endpoint] STATE = STARTED ;
GO

GRANT CONNECT ON ENDPOINT::[Hadr_endpoint] TO [prosqladmin\clusteradmin] ;
GO

IF EXISTS(SELECT * FROM sys.server_event_sessions WHERE name='AlwaysOn_health')
BEGIN
  ALTER EVENT SESSION [AlwaysOn_health] ON SERVER WITH (STARTUP_STATE=ON);
END
IF NOT EXISTS(SELECT * FROM sys.dm_xe_sessions WHERE name='AlwaysOn_health')
BEGIN
  ALTER EVENT SESSION [AlwaysOn_health] ON SERVER STATE=START;
END
GO

--Create Logins for the Service Account,
--create Endpoints and assign Service Account permissions
--to the Endpoint on Secondary Replica

:Connect CLUSTERNODE2\SYNCHA
```

```
USE [master]
GO

CREATE LOGIN [prosqladmin\ClusterAdmin] FROM WINDOWS ;
GO

CREATE ENDPOINT [Hadr_endpoint]
      AS TCP (LISTENER_PORT = 5022)
      FOR DATA_MIRRORING (ROLE = ALL, ENCRYPTION = REQUIRED ALGORITHM AES) ;
GO

ALTER ENDPOINT [Hadr_endpoint] STATE = STARTED ;
GO

GRANT CONNECT ON ENDPOINT::[Hadr_endpoint] TO [prosqladmin\ClusterAdmin] ;
GO

IF EXISTS(SELECT * FROM sys.server_event_sessions WHERE name='AlwaysOn_health')
BEGIN
  ALTER EVENT SESSION [AlwaysOn_health] ON SERVER WITH (STARTUP_STATE=ON);
END
IF NOT EXISTS(SELECT * FROM sys.dm_xe_sessions WHERE name='AlwaysOn_health')
BEGIN
  ALTER EVENT SESSION [AlwaysOn_health] ON SERVER STATE=START;
END
GO

--Create Avaiability Group

:Connect CLUSTERNODE1\PRIMARYREPLICA

USE [master]
GO

CREATE AVAILABILITY GROUP [App1]
WITH (AUTOMATED_BACKUP_PREFERENCE = PRIMARY)
FOR DATABASE [Chapter13App1Customers], [Chapter13App1Sales]
REPLICA ON N'CLUSTERNODE1\PRIMARYREPLICA'
WITH (ENDPOINT_URL = N'TCP://ClusterNode1.PROSQLADMIN.COM:5022',
FAILOVER_MODE = AUTOMATIC, AVAILABILITY_MODE = SYNCHRONOUS_COMMIT, BACKUP_PRIORITY = 50,
SECONDARY_ROLE(ALLOW_CONNECTIONS = NO)),
        N'CLUSTERNODE2\SYNCHA'
          WITH (ENDPOINT_URL = N'TCP://ClusterNode2.PROSQLADMIN.COM:5022',
          FAILOVER_MODE = AUTOMATIC, AVAILABILITY_MODE = SYNCHRONOUS_COMMIT,
          BACKUP_PRIORITY = 50, SECONDARY_ROLE(ALLOW_CONNECTIONS = NO));
GO
```

```
--Create the Listener (Use an IP Address applicable to your environment)

ALTER AVAILABILITY GROUP [App1]
ADD LISTENER N'App1Listen' (
WITH IP
((N'192.168.0.4', N'255.255.255.0')
)
, PORT=1433);
GO


--Join the Secondary Replica

:Connect CLUSTERNODE2\SYNCHA

ALTER AVAILABILITY GROUP [App1] JOIN;
GO


--Back Up Database and Log (First database)

:Connect CLUSTERNODE1\PRIMARYREPLICA

BACKUP DATABASE Chapter13App1Customers
TO  DISK = N'\\CLUSTERNODE1\AOAGShare\Chapter13App1Customers.bak'
WITH  COPY_ONLY, FORMAT, INIT, REWIND, COMPRESSION,  STATS = 5 ;
GO

BACKUP LOG Chapter13App1Customers
TO  DISK = N'\\CLUSTERNODE1\AOAGShare\Chapter13App1Customers.trn'
WITH NOSKIP, REWIND, COMPRESSION,  STATS = 5 ;
GO


--Restore Database and Log (First database)

:Connect CLUSTERNODE2\SYNCHA

RESTORE DATABASE Chapter13App1Customers
FROM  DISK = N'\\CLUSTERNODE1\AOAGShare\Chapter13App1Customers.bak'
WITH  NORECOVERY,  STATS = 5 ;
GO

RESTORE LOG Chapter13App1Customers
FROM  DISK = N'\\CLUSTERNODE1\AOAGShare\Chapter13App1Customers.trn'
WITH  NORECOVERY, STATS = 5 ;
GO


--Wait for replica to start communicating

DECLARE @connection BIT

DECLARE @replica_id UNIQUEIDENTIFIER
DECLARE @group_id UNIQUEIDENTIFIER
```

```
SET @connection = 0

WHILE @Connection = 0
BEGIN
        SET @group_id = (SELECT group_id
                         FROM Master.sys.availability_groups
                         WHERE name = N'App1')
        SET @replica_id = (SELECT replica_id
                           FROM Master.sys.availability_replicas
                           WHERE UPPER(replica_server_name COLLATE Latin1_General_CI_AS) =
                                  UPPER(@@SERVERNAME COLLATE Latin1_General_CI_AS)
                           AND group_id = @group_id)

        SET @connection = ISNULL((SELECT connected_state
                                  FROM Master.sys.dm_hadr_availability_replica_states
                                  WHERE replica_id = @replica_id), 1)

        WAITFOR DELAY '00:00:10'
END

--Add first Database to the Availability Group

ALTER DATABASE [Chapter13App1Customers] SET HADR AVAILABILITY GROUP = [App1];

GO

--Back Up Database and Log (Second database)

:Connect CLUSTERNODE1\PRIMARYREPLICA

BACKUP DATABASE [Chapter13App1Sales]
TO  DISK = N'\\CLUSTERNODE1\AOAGShare\Chapter13App1Sales.bak'
WITH  COPY_ONLY, FORMAT, INIT, REWIND, COMPRESSION,  STATS = 5 ;
GO

BACKUP LOG Chapter13App1Sales
TO  DISK = N'\\CLUSTERNODE1\AOAGShare\Chapter13App1Sales.trn'
WITH NOSKIP, REWIND, COMPRESSION,  STATS = 5 ;
GO

--Restore Database and Log (Second database)

:Connect CLUSTERNODE2\SYNCHA

RESTORE DATABASE [Chapter13App1Sales]
FROM  DISK = N'\\CLUSTERNODE1\AOAGShare\Chapter13App1Sales.bak'
WITH  NORECOVERY, STATS = 5 ;
GO
```

```
RESTORE LOG Chapter13App1Sales
FROM  DISK = N'\\CLUSTERNODE1\AOAGShare\Chapter13App1Sales.trn'
WITH  NORECOVERY,  STATS = 5 ;
GO


--Wait for replica to start communicating
DECLARE @connection BIT

DECLARE @replica_id UNIQUEIDENTIFIER
DECLARE @group_id UNIQUEIDENTIFIER


SET @connection = 0

WHILE @Connection = 0
BEGIN
        SET @group_id = (SELECT group_id
                            FROM Master.sys.availability_groups
                         WHERE name = N'App1')
        SET @replica_id = (SELECT replica_id
                             FROM Master.sys.availability_replicas
                             WHERE UPPER(replica_server_name COLLATE Latin1_General_CI_AS) =
                                     UPPER(@@SERVERNAME COLLATE Latin1_General_CI_AS)
                                 AND group_id = @group_id)

        SET @connection = ISNULL((SELECT connected_state
                                    FROM Master.sys.dm_hadr_availability_replica_states
                                    WHERE replica_id = @replica_id), 1)

        WAITFOR DELAY '00:00:10'
END

--Add Second database to the Availaility Group

ALTER DATABASE [Chapter13App1Sales] SET HADR AVAILABILITY GROUP = [App1];
GO
```

Creating the availability group via T-SQL gives you the most flexibility in terms of configuration. Table 13-1 contains a complete list of arguments, along with their explanation.

Table 13-1. *The CREATE AVAIABILITY GROUP Arguments*

Argument	Description	Acceptable Values
AUTOMATED_BACKUP_ PREFERENCE	Defines where backups run from automated jobs should be taken.	PRIMARY SECONDARY_ONLY SECONDARY NONE
FAILURE_CONDITION_LEVEL	Specifies how sensitive the failover will be. Further details in Table 13-2.	1 through 5
HEALTH_CHECK_TIMEOUT	Configures the amount of time, in milliseconds, that SQL Server has to return health check information to the cluster before the cluster assumes that the instance is not responding, which triggers a failover when FAILOVER_MODE is set to AUTOMATIC.	15000ms through 4294967295ms
DATABASE	A comma-separated list of databases that will join the availability group.	–
REPLICA ON	A comma-separated list of server\instance names that will be replicas within the group. The following arguments in this table form the WITH clause of the REPLICA ON argument.	–
ENDPOINT_URL	The URL of the TCP endpoint that the replica will use to communicate.	–
AVAILABILITY_MODE	Determines if the replica operates in synchronous or asynchronous mode.	SYNCHRONOUS_COMMIT ASYNCHRONOUS_COMMIT
FAILOVER_MODE	When the AVAILABILITY_MODE is set to synchronous, determines if automatic failover should be allowed.	AUTOMATIC MANUAL
BACKUP_PRIORITY	Gives the replica a weight when SQL Server is deciding where an automated backup job should run.	0 through 100
SECONDARY_ROLE	Specifies properties that only apply to the replica when it is in a secondary role. ALLOW_CONNECTIONS specifies if the replica is readable, and if so, by all read_only connections or only those that specify read-intent in the connection string. READ_ONLY_ ROUTING_URL specifies the URL for applications to connect to it, for read only operations, in the format: TCP://ServerName:Port.	–
PRIMARY_ROLE	Specifies properties that only apply to the replica when it is in the primary role. ALLOW_CONNECTIONS can be configured as All to allow any connection, or Read_Write, to disallow read-only connections. READ_ONLY_ROUTING_LIST is a comma-separated list of server\instance names that have been configured as read-only replicas.	–
SESSION_TIMEOUT	Specifies how long replicas can survive without receiving a ping before they enter the DISCONNECTED state.	5 to 2147483647 seconds

The FAILOVER_CONDITION_LEVEL argument determines the group's sensitivity to failover. Table 13-2 provides a description of each of the five levels.

Table 13-2. *The FAILOVER_CONDITION_LEVEL Arguement*

Level	Failover Triggered By
1	Instance down. AOAG lease expires.
2	Conditions of level 1 plus: HEALTH_CHECK_TIMEOUT is exceeded. The replica has a state of FAILED.
3 (Default)	Conditions of level 2 plus: SQL Server experiences critical internal errors.
4	Conditions of level 3 plus: SQL Server experiences moderate internal errors.
5	Failover initialed on any qualifying condition.

Using the New Availability Group Dialog Box

Now that we have successfully created our first availability group, let's create a second availability group for App2. This time, we use the New Availability Group and Add Listener Dialog boxes. We begin this process by backing up the Chapter13App2Customers database. Just like when we created the App1 availability group, the databases are not selectable until we perform the backup. Unlike when we used the wizard, however, we have no way to make SQL Server perform the initial database synchronization for us. Therefore, we back up the database to the share that we created during the previous demonstration and then restore the backup, along with a transaction log backup, to the secondary instance. We do this by using the script in Listing 13-5, which must be run in SQLCMD mode for it to work. This is because it connects to both instances.

Listing 13-5. Backing Up and Restoring the Database

```
--Back Up Database and Log

:Connect CLUSTERNODE1\PRIMARYREPLICA

BACKUP DATABASE [Chapter13App2Customers] TO  DISK = N'\\CLUSTERNODE1\AOAGShare\
Chapter13App2Customers.bak' WITH  COPY_ONLY, FORMAT, INIT, REWIND, COMPRESSION,  STATS = 5 ;
GO

BACKUP LOG [Chapter13App2Customers] TO  DISK = N'\\CLUSTERNODE1\AOAGShare\
Chapter13App2Customers.trn' WITH NOSKIP, REWIND, COMPRESSION,  STATS = 5 ;
GO

--Restore Database and Log

:Connect CLUSTERNODE2\SYNCHA
```

```
RESTORE DATABASE [Chapter13App2Customers] FROM  DISK = N'\\CLUSTERNODE1\AOAGShare\
Chapter13App2Customers.bak' WITH  NORECOVERY, STATS = 5 ;
GO

RESTORE LOG [Chapter13App2Customers] FROM  DISK = N'\\CLUSTERNODE1\AOAGShare\
Chapter13App2Customers.trn' WITH  NORECOVERY,  STATS = 5 ;
GO
```

If we had not already created an availability group, then our next job would be to create a TCP endpoint so the instances could communicate. We would then need to create a login for the service account on each instance and grant it the connect permissions on the endpoints. Because we can only ever have one database mirroring endpoint per instance, however, we are not required to create a new one, and obviously we have no reason to grant the service account additional privileges. Therefore, we continue by creating the availability group. To do this, we drill through AlwaysOn High Availability in Object Explorer and select New Availability Group from the context menu of availability groups.

This causes the General tab of the New Availability Group dialog box to display, as illustrated in Figure 13-13. On this screen, we type the name of the availability group in the first field. Then we click the Add button under the Availability Databases window before we type the name of the database that we wish to add to the group. We then need to click the Add button under the Availability Replicas window before we type the server\instance name of the secondary replica in the new row.

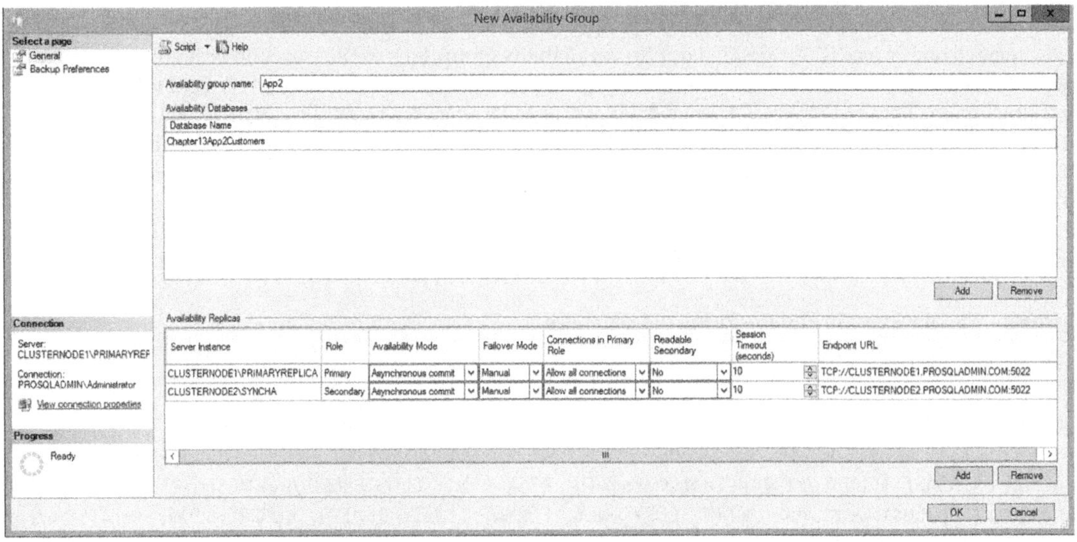

Figure 13-13. *The New Availability Group dialog box*

Now we can begin to set the replica properties. We discussed the Role, Availability Mode, Failover Mode, Readable Secondary, and Endpoint URL properties when we created the App1 availability group. The Connection In Primary Role property defines what connections can be made to the replica if the replica is in the primary role. You can configure this as either Allow All Connections, or allow Read/Write connections. When Read/Write is specified, applications using the Application Intent = Read only parameter in their connection string will not be able to connect to the replica.

The Session Timeout property sets how long the replicas can go without receiving a ping from one another before they enter the DISCONNECTED state and the session ends. Although it is possible to set this value to as low as 5 seconds, it is usually a good idea to keep the setting at or above 10 seconds, otherwise you run the risk of a false positive response, resulting in unnecessary failover. If a replica times out, it needs to be resynchronized, since transactions on the primary will no longer wait for the secondary, even if the secondary is running in Synchronous Commit mode.

■ **Note**   You may have noticed that we have configured the replica in Asynchronous Commit mode. This is for the benefit of a later demonstration. For HA, we would always configure Synchronous Commit mode, since otherwise, automatic failover is not possible.

On the Backup Preferences tab of the dialog box, we define the preferred replica to use for automated backup jobs, as shown in Figure 13-14. Just like when using the wizard, we can specify Primary, or we can choose between enforcing and preferring backups to occur on a secondary replica. We can also configure a weight, between 0 and 100 for each replica, and use the Exclude Replica check box to avoid backups being taken on a specific node.

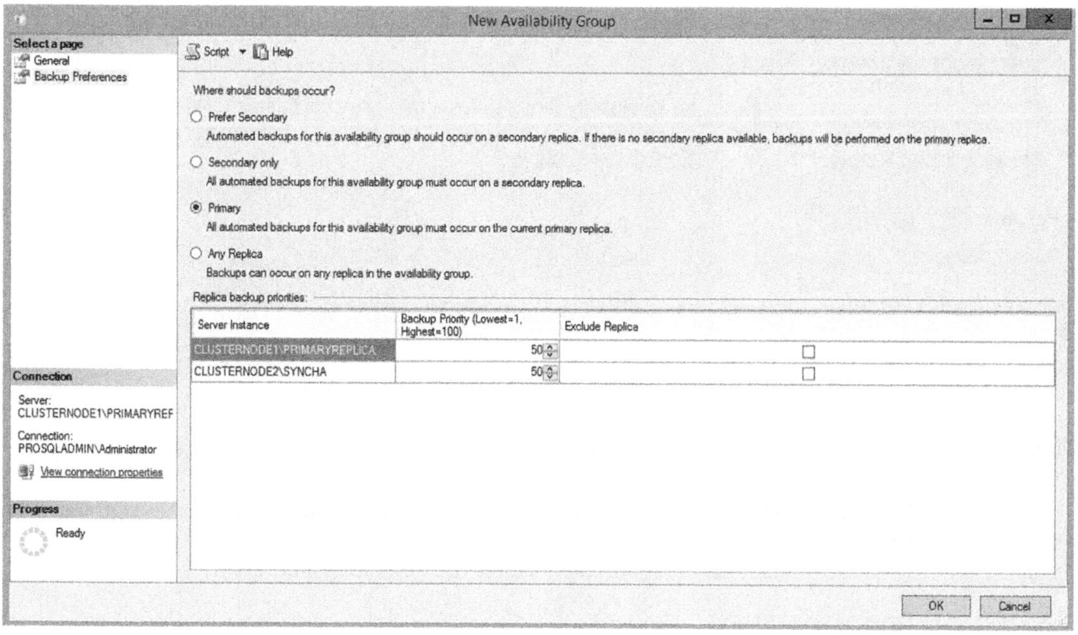

Figure 13-14.   *The Backup Preferences tab*

Once we have created the availability group, we need to create the availability group listener. To do this, we select New Listener from the context menu of the App2 availability group, which should now be visible in Object Explorer. This invokes the New Availability Group Listener dialog box, which can be seen in Figure 13-15.

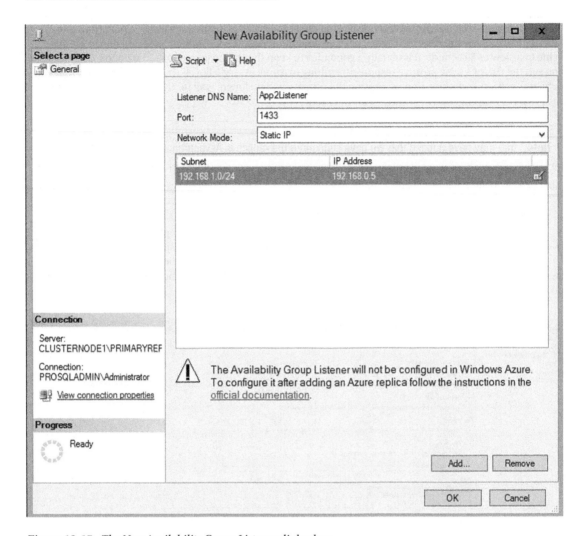

Figure 13-15. *The New Availability Group Listener dialog box*

In this dialog box, we start by entering the virtual name for the listener. We then define the port that it will listen on and the IP address that will be assigned to it. We are able to use the same port for both of the listeners, as well as the SQL Server instance, because all three use different IP addresses.

Performance Considerations for Synchronous Commit Mode

Unlike traditional clustering, Availability Group topology does not have any shared disk resources. Therefore, data must be replicated on two devices, which of course, has an overhead. This overhead varies depending on various aspects of your environment, such as network latency and disk performance, as well as the application profile. However, the script in Listing 13-6 runs some write-intensive tests against the Chapter13App2Customers database (which is in Asynchronous Commit mode) and then against the Chapter13App1Customers database (which is Synchronous Commit mode). This indicates the overhead that you can expect to witness.

■ **Tip**   It is important to remember that there is no overhead on read performance. Also, despite the overhead associated with writes, some of this is offset by distributing read-only workloads if you implement readable secondary replicas.

Listing 13-6. Performance Benchmark with Availability Groups

```
DBCC FREEPROCCACHE
DBCC DROPCLEANBUFFERS

SET STATISTICS TIME ON

PRINT 'Begin asynchronous commit benchmark'

USE Chapter13App2Customers
GO

PRINT 'Build a nonclustered index'

CREATE NONCLUSTERED INDEX NIX_FirstName_LastName ON App2Customers(FirstName, LastName) ;

PRINT 'Delete from table'

DELETE FROM [dbo].[App2Customers] ;

PRINT 'Insert into table'

DECLARE @Numbers TABLE
(
        Number          INT
)

;WITH CTE(Number)
AS
(
        SELECT 1 Number
        UNION ALL
        SELECT Number + 1
        FROM CTE
        WHERE Number < 100
)
INSERT INTO @Numbers
SELECT Number FROM CTE ;

DECLARE @Names TABLE
(
        FirstName       VARCHAR(30),
        LastName        VARCHAR(30)
) ;
```

```
INSERT INTO @Names
VALUES('Peter', 'Carter'),
                ('Michael', 'Smith'),
                ('Danielle', 'Mead'),
                ('Reuben', 'Roberts'),
                ('Iris', 'Jones'),
                ('Sylvia', 'Davies'),
                ('Finola', 'Wright'),
                ('Edward', 'James'),
                ('Marie', 'Andrews'),
                ('Jennifer', 'Abraham'),
                ('Margaret', 'Jones')

INSERT INTO App2Customers(Firstname, LastName, CreditCardNumber)
SELECT  FirstName, LastName, CreditCardNumber FROM
        (SELECT
                (SELECT TOP 1 FirstName FROM @Names ORDER BY NEWID()) FirstName
               ,(SELECT TOP 1 LastName FROM @Names ORDER BY NEWID()) LastName
               ,(SELECT CONVERT(VARBINARY(8000)
                 , (SELECT TOP 1 CAST(Number * 100 AS CHAR(4))
                    FROM @Numbers
                    WHERE Number BETWEEN 10 AND 99 ORDER BY NEWID()) + '-' +
                       (SELECT TOP 1 CAST(Number * 100 AS CHAR(4))
                        FROM @Numbers
                        WHERE Number BETWEEN 10 AND 99 ORDER BY NEWID()) + '-' +
                       (SELECT TOP 1 CAST(Number * 100 AS CHAR(4))
                        FROM @Numbers
                        WHERE Number BETWEEN 10 AND 99 ORDER BY NEWID()) + '-' +
                       (SELECT TOP 1 CAST(Number * 100 AS CHAR(4))
                        FROM @Numbers
                 WHERE Number BETWEEN 10 AND 99 ORDER BY NEWID()))) CreditCardNumber
FROM @Numbers a
CROSS JOIN @Numbers b
CROSS JOIN @Numbers c
) d ;
GO

PRINT 'Begin synchronous commit benchmark'

USE Chapter13App1Customers
GO

PRINT 'Build a nonclustered index'

CREATE NONCLUSTERED INDEX NIX_FirstName_LastName ON App1Customers(FirstName, LastName) ;

PRINT 'Delete from table'

DELETE FROM [dbo].[App1Customers] ;

PRINT 'Insert into table'
```

```
DECLARE @Numbers TABLE
(
        Number          INT
)

;WITH CTE(Number)
AS
(
        SELECT 1 Number
        UNION ALL
        SELECT Number + 1
        FROM CTE
        WHERE Number < 100
)
INSERT INTO @Numbers
SELECT Number FROM CTE ;

DECLARE @Names TABLE
(
        FirstName           VARCHAR(30),
        LastName            VARCHAR(30)
) ;

INSERT INTO @Names
VALUES('Peter', 'Carter'),
                ('Michael', 'Smith'),
                ('Danielle', 'Mead'),
                ('Reuben', 'Roberts'),
                ('Iris', 'Jones'),
                ('Sylvia', 'Davies'),
                ('Finola', 'Wright'),
                ('Edward', 'James'),
                ('Marie', 'Andrews'),
                ('Jennifer', 'Abraham'),
                ('Margaret', 'Jones') ;

INSERT INTO App1Customers(Firstname, LastName, CreditCardNumber)
SELECT  FirstName, LastName, CreditCardNumber FROM
        (SELECT
                (SELECT TOP 1 FirstName FROM @Names ORDER BY NEWID()) FirstName
               ,(SELECT TOP 1 LastName FROM @Names ORDER BY NEWID()) LastName
               ,(SELECT CONVERT(VARBINARY(8000)
               ,(SELECT TOP 1 CAST(Number * 100 AS CHAR(4))
                  FROM @Numbers
                  WHERE Number BETWEEN 10 AND 99 ORDER BY NEWID()) + '-' +
                        (SELECT TOP 1 CAST(Number * 100 AS CHAR(4))
                         FROM @Numbers
                         WHERE Number BETWEEN 10 AND 99 ORDER BY NEWID()) + '-' +
                        (SELECT TOP 1 CAST(Number * 100 AS CHAR(4))
                         FROM @Numbers
                         WHERE Number BETWEEN 10 AND 99 ORDER BY NEWID()) + '-' +
```

```
                              (SELECT TOP 1 CAST(Number * 100 AS CHAR(4))
                              FROM @Numbers
                              WHERE Number BETWEEN 10 AND 99 ORDER BY NEWID()))) CreditCardNumber
FROM @Numbers a
CROSS JOIN @Numbers b
CROSS JOIN @Numbers c
) d ;

GO


SET STATISTICS TIME OFF

GO
```

The relevant parts of the results of this query are displayed in Listing 13-7. You can see that the index rebuild was almost three times slower when the Availability Group was operating in Synchronous Commit mode, the insert was over six times slower, and the delete was also marginally slower. In productions environments in which I have implemented availability groups in Synchronous Commit mode, they have generally been around two times slower than in Asynchronous Commit mode.

Listing 13-7. Results of Performance Benchmark

```
Begin asynchronous commit benchmark

Build a nonclustered index
 SQL Server Execution Times:
   CPU time = 1109 ms,  elapsed time = 4316 ms.

Delete from table
 SQL Server Execution Times:
   CPU time = 6938 ms,  elapsed time = 69652 ms.
(1000000 row(s) affected)

Insert into table
 SQL Server Execution Times:
   CPU time = 13656 ms,  elapsed time = 61372 ms.
(1000000 row(s) affected)

Begin synchronous commit benchmark

Build a nonclustered index
 SQL Server Execution Times:
   CPU time = 1516 ms,  elapsed time = 12437 ms.

Delete from table
 SQL Server Execution Times:
   CPU time = 8563 ms,  elapsed time = 77273 ms.
(1000000 row(s) affected)

Insert into table
 SQL Server Execution Times:
   CPU time = 23141 ms,  elapsed time = 372161 ms.
(1000000 row(s) affected)
```

Because of the performance challenges associated with Synchronous Commit mode, many DBAs decide to implement high availability and disaster recovery by using a three-node cluster, with two nodes in the primary data center and one node in the DR data center. Instead of having two synchronous replicas within the primary data center, however, they stretch the primary replica across a failover clustered instance and configure the cluster to only be able to host the instance on these two nodes, and not on the third node in the DR data center. This is important, because it means that we don't need to implement SAN replication between the data centers. The DR node is synchronized using availability groups in Asynchronous Commit mode. If you combine an AlwaysOn failover clustered instance with AlwaysOn Availability Groups in this way, then automatic failover is not supported between the clustered instance and the replica. It can only be configured for manual failover. There is also no need for availability groups to fail over between the two nodes hosting the clustered instance, because this failover is managed by the cluster service. This configuration can prove to be a highly powerful and flexible way to achieve your continuity requirements.

Implementing Disaster Recovery with Availability Group

Now that we have successfully implemented high availability for the `Chapter13App1Customers` and `Chapter13App1Sales` databases through the `App1` availability group, we need to implement disaster recovery for these databases. To do this, we first need to build out a new server in our second site and install a stand-alone instance of SQL Server. Because the cluster now spans two sites, we need to reconfigure it as a multi-subnet cluster. We also need to reconfigure the quorum model to remove its dependency on the shared storage, which we currently have for the quorum. Once this is complete, we are able to add the instance on the new node to our availability group. The following sections assume that you have already built out a third server with a SQL Server instance called `CLUSTERNODE3\ASYNCDR`, and they demonstrate how to reconfigure the cluster as well as the availability group.

Configuring the Cluster

We need to perform several cluster configuration steps before we begin to alter our availability group. These include adding the new node, reconfiguring the quorum, and adding a new IP to the cluster's client access point.

Adding a Node

The first task in adding DR capability to our availability group is to add the third node to the cluster. To do this, we select Add Node from the context menu of nodes in Failover Cluster Manager. This causes the Add Node Wizard to be invoked. After passing through the Before You Begin page of this wizard, you are presented with the Select Servers page, which is illustrated in Figure 13-16. On this page, you need to enter the server name of the node that you plan to add to the cluster.

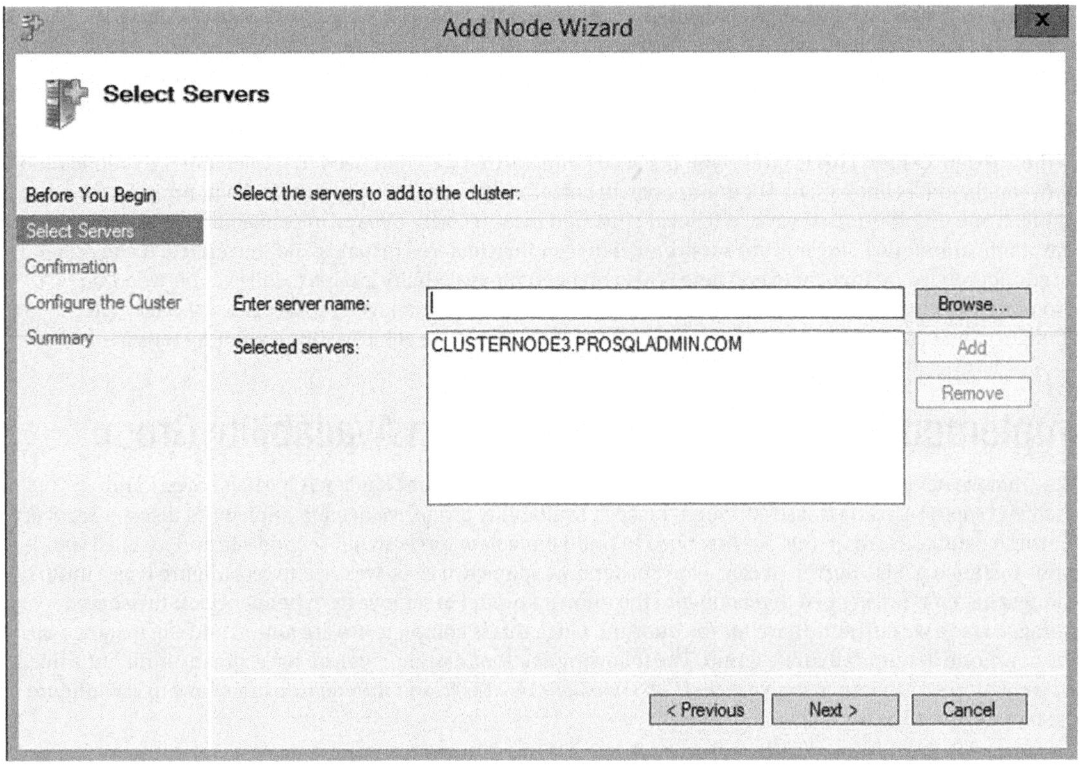

Figure 13-16. *The Select Servers page*

On the Validation Warning page, you are invited to run the Cluster Validation Wizard. You should always run this wizard in a production environment when making changes of this nature; otherwise, you will not be able to receive support from Microsoft for the cluster. Details of running the Cluster Validation wizard can be found in Chapter 12. Running the Cluster Validation wizard in our scenario is likely to throw up some warnings, which are detailed in Table 13-3.

Table 13-3. *Cluster Validation Warnings*

Warning	Reason	Resolution
This resource does not have all the nodes of the cluster listed as Possible Owners. The clustered role that this resource is a member of will not be able to start on any node that is not listed as a Possible Owner.	This warning has been displayed because we have not yet configured our availability group to use the new node.	Configuring the availability group to use the new node is discussed later in this chapter.
The `RegisterAllProvidersIP` property for network name `'Name: App1Listen'` is set to 1. For the current cluster configuration this value should be set to 0.	Setting the `RegisterAllProvidersIP` to 1 will cause all IP addresses to be registered, regardless of whether they are online or not. When we created the Availability Group Listener through SSMS, this setting was automatically configured to allow clients to fail over faster, and this warning should always be ignored. If we had created the Listener through Failover Cluster Manager, the property would have been set to 0 by default.	No resolution is required, but `RegisterAllProvidersIP` is discussed in more detail later in this chapter.

On the Confirmation page, we are given a summary of the tasks that will be performed. On this page, we deselect the option to add eligible storage, since one of our aims is to remove the dependency on shared storage. The Confirmation page is displayed in Figure 13-17.

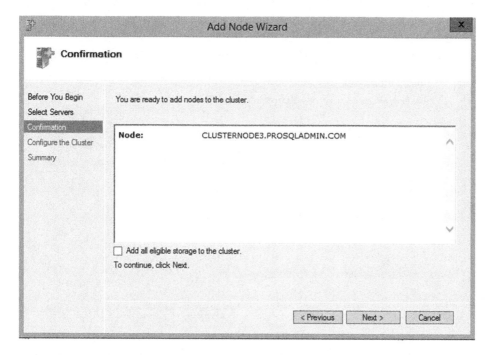

Figure 13-17. *Confirmation page*

On the Configure The Cluster page, the progress on the tasks displays until it is complete. The Summary page then displays, giving an overview of the actions and their success.

Modifying the Quorum

Our next step in configuring the cluster will be to modify the quorum. As mentioned earlier, we would like to remove our current dependency on shared storage. Therefore we need to make a choice. Since we now have three nodes in the cluster, one possibility is to remove the disk witness and form a node majority quorum. The issue with this is that one of our nodes is in a different location. Therefore, if we lose network connectivity between the two sites for an extended period, then we have no fault tolerance in our primary site. If one of the nodes goes down, we lose quorum and the cluster goes offline. On the other hand, if we have an additional witness in the primary location, then we are not maintaining best practice, since there are an even number of votes. Again, if we lose one voting member, we lose resilience.

Therefore, the approach that we take is to replace the disk witness with a file share witness, thus removing the shared disk dependency. We then remove the vote from the node in the DR site. This means that we have three voting members of the quorum, and all of them are within the same site. This mitigates the risk of an inter-site network issue causing loss of redundancy in our HA solution.

In order to invoke the Configure Cluster Quorum Wizard, we select Configure Cluster Quorum from the More Actions submenu within the context menu of our cluster in Failover Cluster Manager. After moving through the Before You Begin page of this wizard, you are asked to select the configuration that you wish to make on the Select Quorum Configuration Option page, which is shown in Figure 13-18. We select the Advanced Quorum Configuration option.

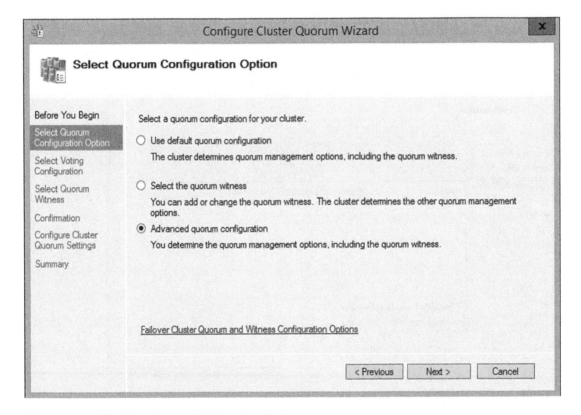

Figure 13-18. *The Select Quorum Configuration Option page*

On the Select Voting Configuration page, we choose to select nodes and remove the vote from CLUSTERNODE3. This is demonstrated in Figure 13-19.

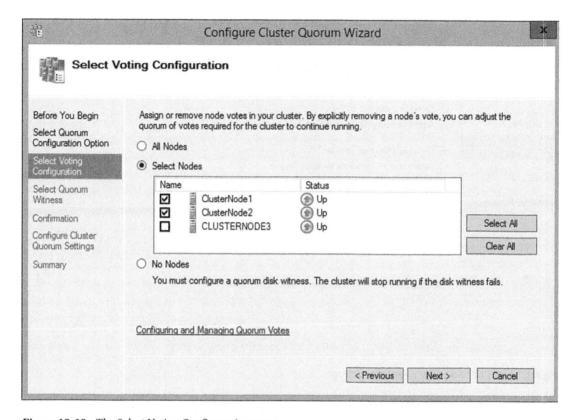

Figure 13-19. *The Select Voting Configuration page*

On the Select Quorum Witness page, we choose the Configure A File Share Witness option, as shown in Figure 13-20.

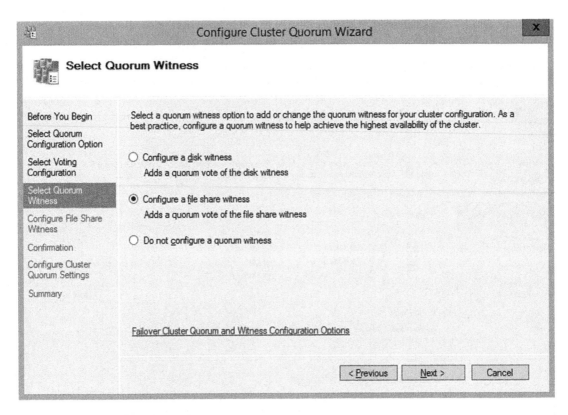

Figure 13-20. *The Select Quorum Witness page*

On the Configure File Share Witness page, which is illustrated in Figure 13-21, we enter the UNC of the share that we will use for the quorum. This file share must reside outside of the cluster and must be an SMB file share on a machine running Windows Server.

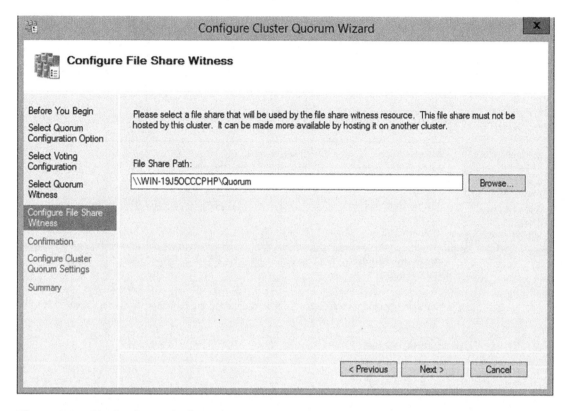

Figure 13-21. *The Configure File Share Witness page*

■ **Tip** Although many non-Windows–based NAS (network-attached storage) devices have support for SMB 3, I have experienced real-world implementations of a file share quorum on a NAS device work only intermittently, without resolution by either vendor.

■ **Caution** Remember that using a file share witness, with only two other voting nodes, can lead to a partition-in-time scenario. For more information, please refer to Chapter 11.

On the Confirmation page of the wizard, you are given a summary of the configuration changes that will be made, as shown in Figure 13-22.

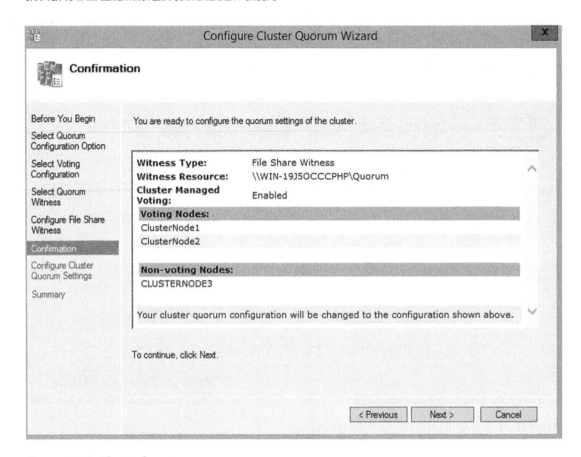

Figure 13-22. *The Confirmation page*

On the Configure Cluster Quorum Settings page, a progress bar displays. Once the configuration is complete, the Summary page appears. This page provides a summary of the configuration changes and a link to the report.

Adding an IP Address

Our next task is to add a second IP address to the cluster's client access point. We do not add an extra IP address for the Availability Group Listener yet. We perform this task in the "Configuring the Availability Group" section later in this chapter.

In order to add the second IP address, we select Properties from the context menu of Server Name in the Core Cluster Resources window of Failover Cluster Manager. On the General tab of the Cluster Properties dialog box, we add the IP address for administrative clients, following failover to DR, as illustrated in Figure 13-23.

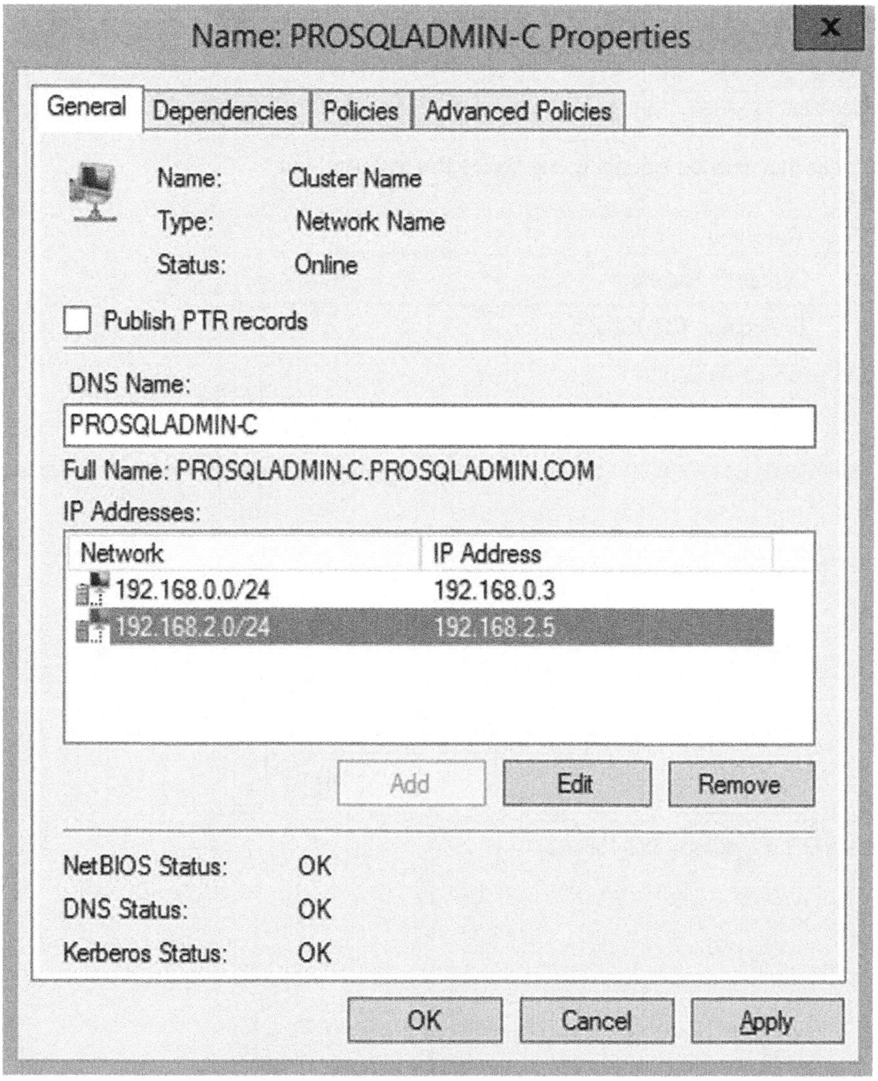

Figure 13-23. *The General tab*

When we apply the change, we receive a warning saying that administrative clients will temporarily be disconnected from the cluster. This does not include any clients connected to our availability group. If we choose to proceed, we then navigate to the Dependencies tab of the dialog box and ensure that an OR dependency has been created between our two IP addresses, as shown in Figure 13-24.

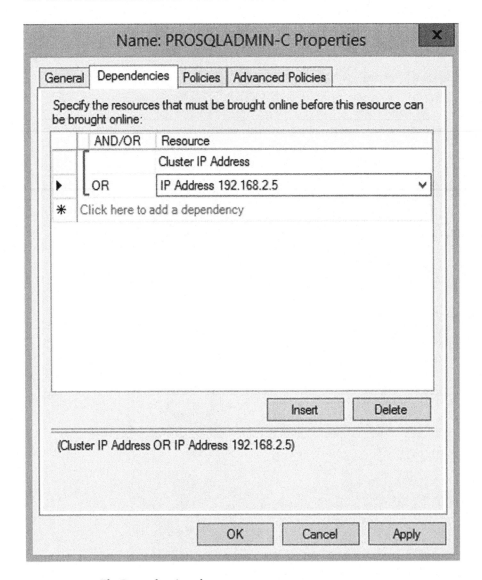

Figure 13-24. *The Dependencies tab*

After this process is complete, the second IP address resource in the Cluster Core Resources group shows up as offline. This is normal. In the event of failover to the server in the second subnet, this IP address comes online, and the IP address of the subnet in the primary site goes offline. This is why the OR dependency (as opposed to an AND dependency) is critical. Without it, the Server Name resource could never be online.

Configuring the Availability Group

To configure the availability group, we first have to add the new node as a replica and configure its properties. We then add a new IP address to our listener for the second subnet. Finally, we look at improving the connection times for clients.

Adding and Configuring a Replica

In SQL Server Management Studio (SSMS), on the primary replica, we drill through Availability Groups | App1 and select Add Replica from the context menu of the Availability Replicas node. This causes the Add Replica To Availability Group wizard to be displayed. After passing through the Introduction page of the wizard, you see the Connect To Replicas page, as displayed in Figure 13-25. On this page, you are invited to connect to the other replicas in the availability group.

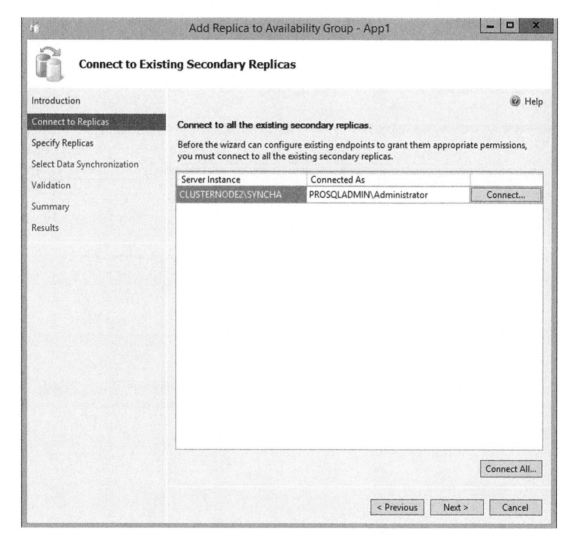

Figure 13-25. *The Connect To Replicas page*

On the Replicas tab of the Specify Replicas page, shown in Figure 13-26, we first use the Add Replica button to connect to the DR instance. After we have connected to the new replica, we specify the properties for that replica. In this case, we leave them as-is because it will be a DR replica. Therefore, we want it to be asynchronous and we do not want it to be readable.

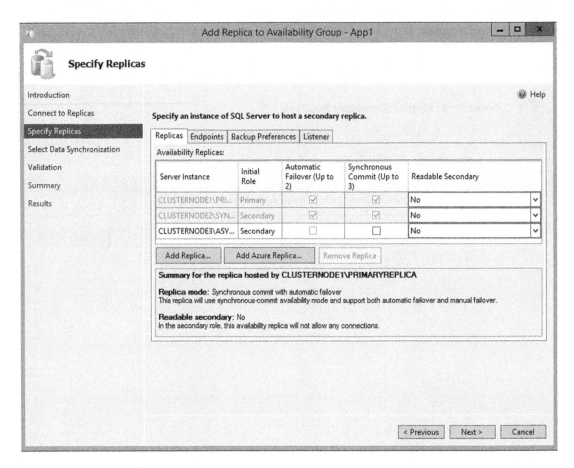

Figure 13-26. The Replicas tab

On the Endpoints tab, shown in Figure 13-27, we ensure that the default settings are correct and acceptable.

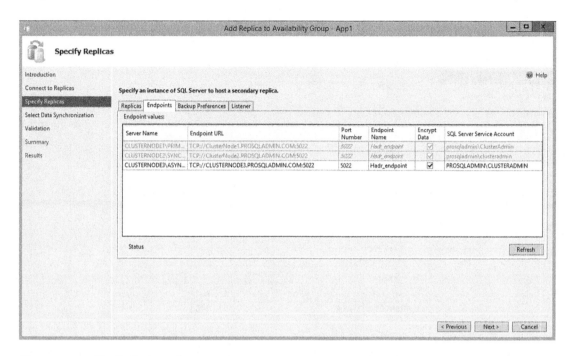

Figure 13-27. *The Endpoints tab*

On the Backup Preferences tab, the option for specifying the preferred backup replica is read-only. We are, however, able to specifically exclude our new replica as a candidate for backups or change its backup priority. This page is displayed in Figure 13-28.

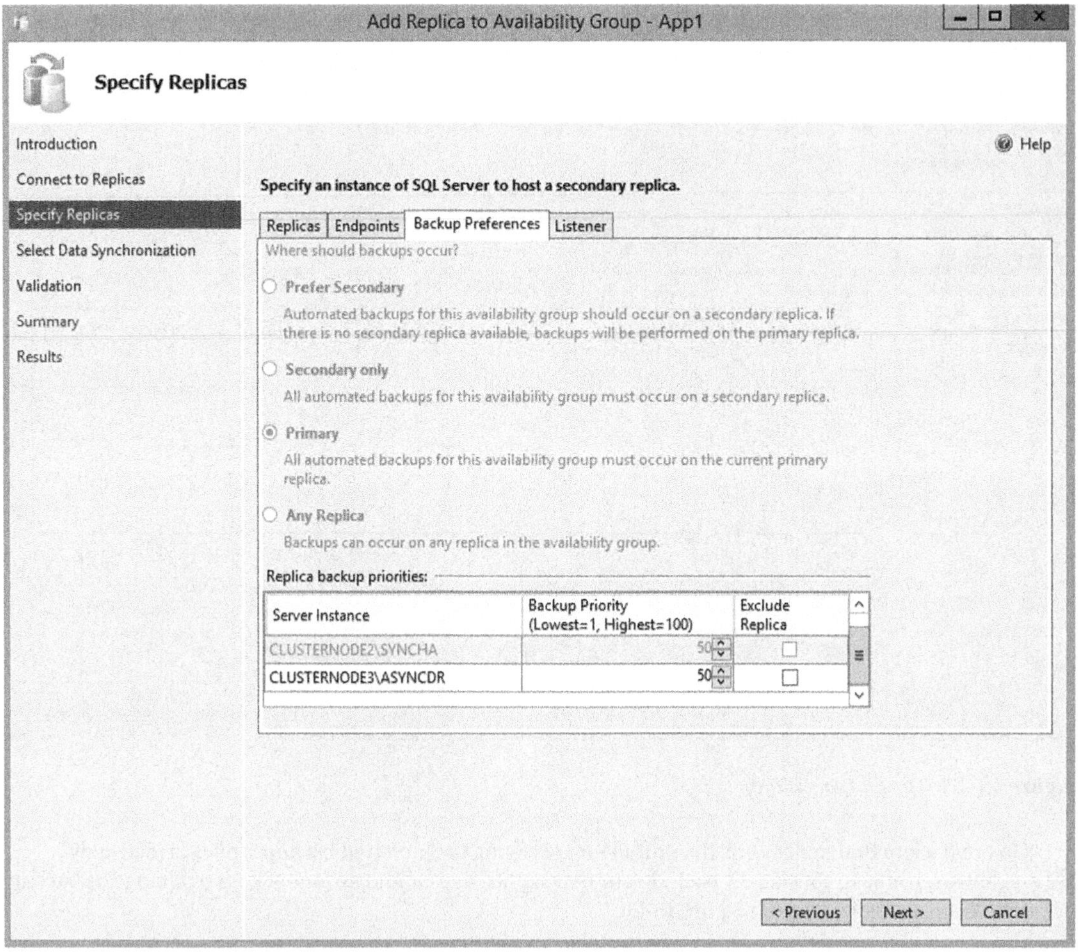

Figure 13-28. *The Backup Preferences tab*

On the Listener tab, illustrated in Figure 13-29, we can decide if we will create a new listener. This is a strange option, since SQL Server only allows us to create a single listener for an availability group, and we already have one. Therefore, we leave the default choice of Do Not Create An Availability Group Listener selected. It is possible to create a second listener, directly from Failover Cluster Manager, but you would only want a second listener for the same availability group in very rare, special cases, which we discuss later in this chapter.

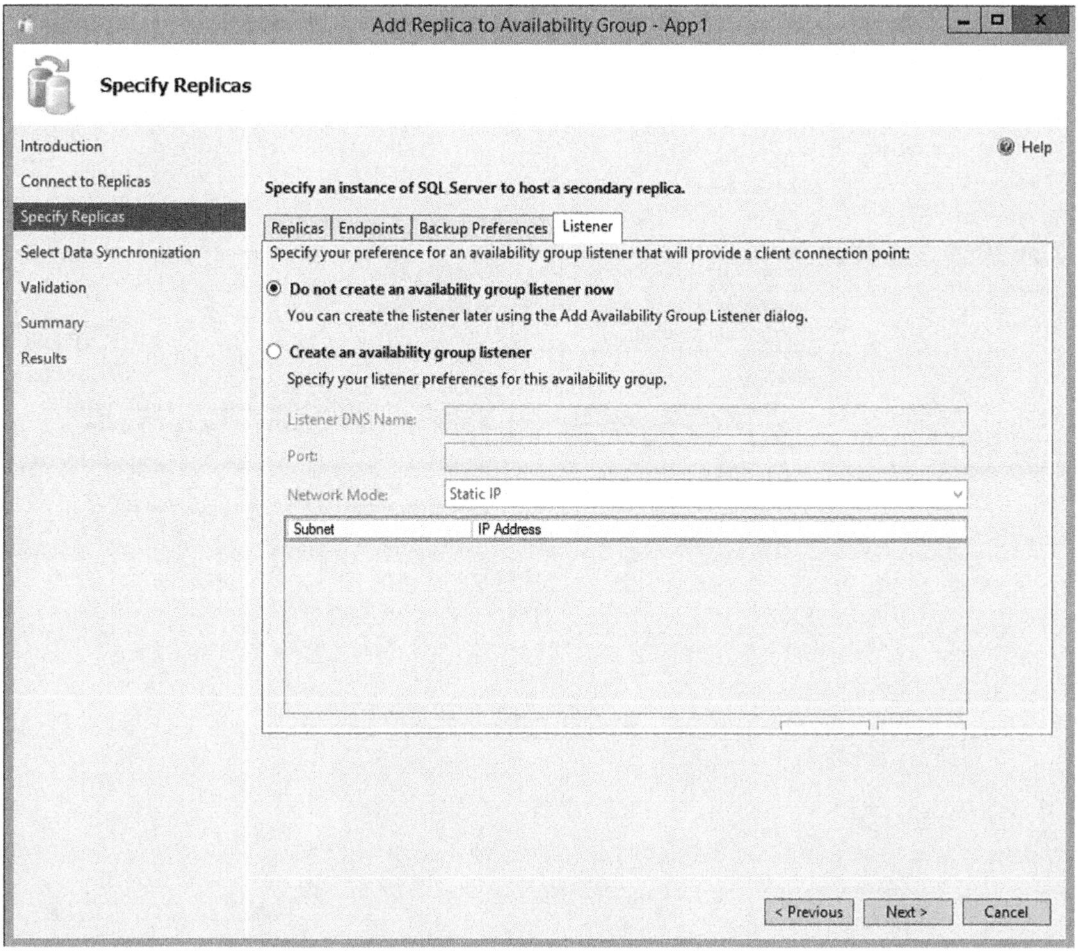

Figure 13-29. *The Listener tab*

On the Select Data Synchronization page, we choose how we want to perform the initial synchronization of the replica. The options are the same as they were when we created the availability group, except that the file share will be prepopulated, assuming that we choose the Full synchronization when creating the availability group. This screen is shown in Figure 13-30.

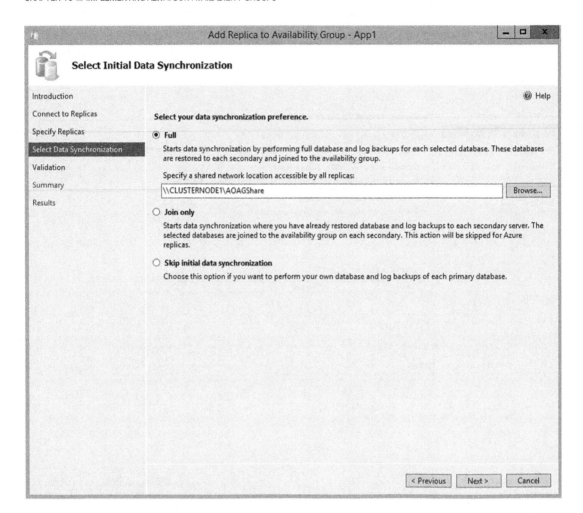

Figure 13-30. *The Select Data Synchronization page*

On the Validation page, which is illustrated in Figure 13-31, we should review any warnings or errors and resolve them before continuing.

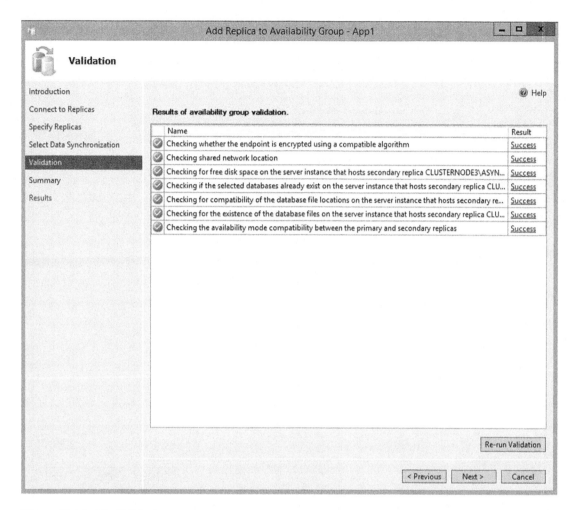

Figure 13-31. *The Validation page*

On the Summary page, displayed in Figure 13-32, we are presented with a summary of the configurations that will be carried out.

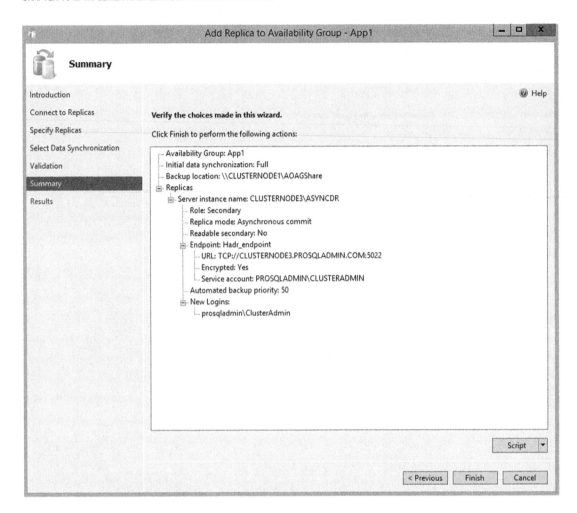

Figure 13-32. *The Summary page*

After the reconfiguration completes, our new replica is added to the cluster. We should then review the results and respond to any warnings or errors. We could also have used T-SQL to add the replica to the availability group. The script in Listing 13-8 performs the same actions just demonstrated. You must run this script in SQLCMD Mode since it connects to multiple instances.

Listing 13-8. Adding a Replica

```
:Connect CLUSTERNODE3\ASYNCDR

--Create Login for Service Account

USE [master]
GO

CREATE LOGIN [prosqladmin\ClusterAdmin] FROM WINDOWS ;
GO
```

```
--Create the Endpoint

CREATE ENDPOINT Hadr_endpoint
        AS TCP (LISTENER_PORT = 5022)
        FOR DATA_MIRRORING (ROLE = ALL, ENCRYPTION = REQUIRED ALGORITHM AES) ;
GO


ALTER ENDPOINT Hadr_endpoint STATE = STARTED ;
GO


--Grant the Service Account permissions to the Endpoint

GRANT CONNECT ON ENDPOINT::[Hadr_endpoint] TO [prosqladmin\ClusterAdmin] ;
GO


--Start the AOAG Health Trace

IF EXISTS(SELECT * FROM sys.server_event_sessions WHERE name='AlwaysOn_health')
BEGIN
  ALTER EVENT SESSION [AlwaysOn_health] ON SERVER WITH (STARTUP_STATE=ON);
END
IF NOT EXISTS(SELECT * FROM sys.dm_xe_sessions WHERE name='AlwaysOn_health')
BEGIN
  ALTER EVENT SESSION [AlwaysOn_health] ON SERVER STATE=START;
END
GO


:Connect CLUSTERNODE1\PRIMARYREPLICA

USE [master]
GO


--Add the replica to the Avaialability Group

ALTER AVAILABILITY GROUP [App1]
ADD REPLICA ON N'CLUSTERNODE3\ASYNCDR'
WITH (ENDPOINT_URL = N'TCP://CLUSTERNODE3.PROSQLADMIN.COM:5022',
      FAILOVER_MODE = MANUAL, AVAILABILITY_MODE = ASYNCHRONOUS_COMMIT, BACKUP_PRIORITY = 50,
      SECONDARY_ROLE(ALLOW_CONNECTIONS = NO));
GO


--Back up and restore the first database and log

BACKUP DATABASE Chapter13App1Customers TO  DISK = N'\\CLUSTERNODE1\AOAGShare\
Chapter13App1Customers.bak'
WITH  COPY_ONLY, FORMAT, INIT, REWIND, COMPRESSION,  STATS = 5 ;
GO


BACKUP LOG Chapter13App1Customers
TO  DISK = N'\\CLUSTERNODE1\AOAGShare\Chapter13App1Customers.trn'
WITH NOSKIP, REWIND, COMPRESSION,  STATS = 5 ;
GO
```

```
:Connect CLUSTERNODE3\ASYNCDR

ALTER AVAILABILITY GROUP [App1] JOIN;
GO

RESTORE DATABASE Chapter13App1Customers
FROM  DISK = N'\\CLUSTERNODE1\AOAGShare\Chapter13App1Customers.bak'
WITH  NORECOVERY,  STATS = 5 ;
GO

RESTORE LOG Chapter13App1Customers
FROM  DISK = N'\\CLUSTERNODE1\AOAGShare\Chapter13App1Customers.trn'
WITH  NORECOVERY, STATS = 5 ;
GO

-- Wait for the replica to start communicating
DECLARE @connection BIT

DECLARE @replica_id UNIQUEIDENTIFIER
DECLARE @group_id UNIQUEIDENTIFIER

SET @connection = 0

WHILE @Connection = 0
BEGIN
        SET @group_id = (SELECT group_id
                          FROM Master.sys.availability_groups
                          WHERE name = N'App1')
        SET @replica_id = (SELECT replica_id
                            FROM Master.sys.availability_replicas
                            WHERE UPPER(replica_server_name COLLATE Latin1_General_CI_AS) =
                                  UPPER(@@SERVERNAME COLLATE Latin1_General_CI_AS)
                              AND group_id = @group_id)

        SET @connection = ISNULL((SELECT connected_state
                                   FROM Master.sys.dm_hadr_availability_replica_states
                                   WHERE replica_id = @replica_id), 1)

        WAITFOR DELAY '00:00:10'
END

--Add the first Database to the Availability Group on the new replica

ALTER DATABASE Chapter13App1Customers SET HADR AVAILABILITY GROUP = [App1];
GO

--Back up and restore the second database and log

:Connect CLUSTERNODE1\PRIMARYREPLICA
```

```
BACKUP DATABASE Chapter13App1Sales
TO  DISK = N'\\CLUSTERNODE1\AOAGShare\Chapter13App1Sales.bak'
WITH  COPY_ONLY, FORMAT, INIT, REWIND, COMPRESSION,  STATS = 5 ;
GO


BACKUP LOG Chapter13App1Sales
TO  DISK = N'\\CLUSTERNODE1\AOAGShare\Chapter13App1Sales.trn'
WITH NOSKIP, REWIND, COMPRESSION,  STATS = 5 ;
GO


:Connect CLUSTERNODE3\ASYNCDR


ALTER AVAILABILITY GROUP [App1] JOIN;
GO


RESTORE DATABASE Chapter13App1Sales
FROM  DISK = N'\\CLUSTERNODE1\AOAGShare\Chapter13App1Sales.bak'
WITH  NORECOVERY,  STATS = 5 ;
GO


RESTORE LOG Chapter13App1Sales
FROM  DISK = N'\\CLUSTERNODE1\AOAGShare\Chapter13App1Sales.trn'
WITH  NORECOVERY, STATS = 5 ;
GO


-- Wait for the replica to start communicating
DECLARE @connection BIT

DECLARE @replica_id UNIQUEIDENTIFIER
DECLARE @group_id UNIQUEIDENTIFIER

SET @connection = 0

WHILE @Connection = 0
BEGIN
        SET @group_id = (SELECT group_id
                        FROM Master.sys.availability_groups
                      WHERE name = N'App1')
        SET @replica_id = (SELECT replica_id
                          FROM Master.sys.availability_replicas
                          WHERE UPPER(replica_server_name COLLATE Latin1_General_CI_AS) =
                                UPPER(@@SERVERNAME COLLATE Latin1_General_CI_AS)
                            AND group_id = @group_id)

        SET @connection = ISNULL((SELECT connected_state
                                FROM Master.sys.dm_hadr_availability_replica_states
                                WHERE replica_id = @replica_id), 1)

        WAITFOR DELAY '00:00:10'
END
```

```
--Add the second database to the Avaiability Group on the new replica

ALTER DATABASE Chapter13App1Sales SET HADR AVAILABILITY GROUP = [App1];
GO
```

Add an IP Address

Even though the replica has been added to the availability group and we are able to fail over to this replica, our clients are still not able to connect to it in the DR site using the Availability Group Listener. This is because we need to add an IP address resource, which resides in the second subnet. To do this, we can select Properties from the context menu of App1Listen in Object Explorer, which causes the Availability Group Listener Properties dialog box to be displayed, as in Figure 13-33. Here, we add the listener's second IP address.

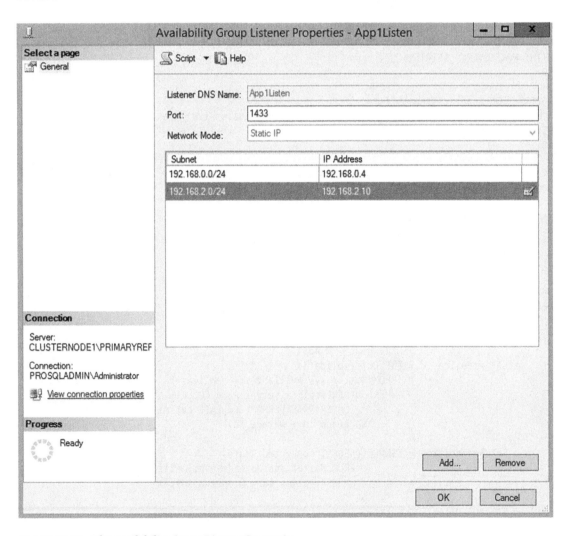

Figure 13-33. *The Availability Group Listener Properties*

We can also achieve this through T-SQL by running the script in Listing 13-9.

Listing 13-9. Adding an IP Address to the Listener

```
ALTER AVAILABILITY GROUP App1
MODIFY LISTENER 'App1Listen'
(ADD IP (N'192.168.2.10', N'255.255.255.0')) ;
```

SQL Server now adds the IP address as a resource in the App1 role, and also configures the OR dependency on the Name resource. You can view this by running the dependency report against the Name resource in Failover Cluster Manager, as illustrated in Figure 13-34.

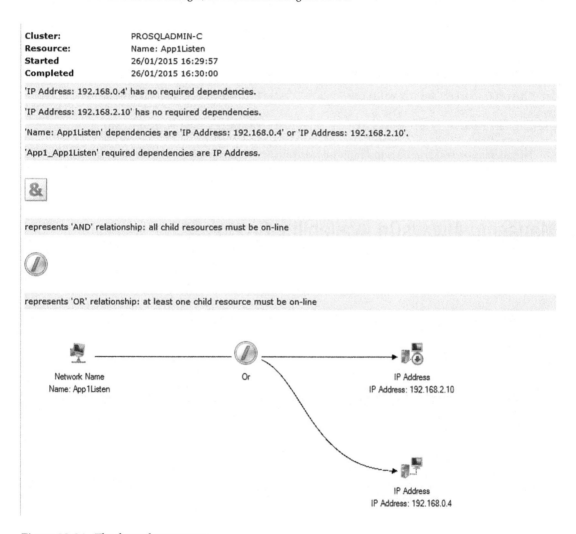

Figure 13-34. The dependency report

Improving Connection Times

Clients using .NET 4 or higher are able to specify the new `MultiSubnetFailover=True` property in their connecting strings when connecting to an AlwaysOn Availability Group. This improves connection times by retrying TCP connections more aggressively. If clients are using older versions of .NET, however, then there is a high risk of their connections timing out.

There are two workarounds for this issue. The first is to set the `RegisterAllProvidersIP` property to 0. This is the recommended approach, but the problem with it is that failover to the DR site can take up to 15 minutes. This is because the IP address resource for the second subnet is offline until failover occurs. It can then take up to 15 minutes for the PTR record to be published. In order to reduce this risk, it is recommended that you also lower the `HostRecordTTL`. This property defines how often the resource records for the cluster name are published.

The script in Listing 13-10 demonstrates how to disable `RegisterAllProvidersIP` and then reduce the `HostRecordTTL` to 300 seconds.

Listing 13-10. Configuring Connection Properties

```
Get-ClusterResource "App1_App1Listen" | Set-ClusterParameter RegisterAllProvidersIP 0

Get-ClusterResource "App1_App1Listen" | Set-ClusterParameter HostRecordTTL 300
```

The alternative workaround is to simply increase the time-out value for connections to 30 seconds. However, this solution accepts that a large volume of connections will take up to 30 seconds. This may not be acceptable to the business.

Managing AlwaysOn Availability Groups

Once the initial setup of your availability group is complete, you still need to perform administrative tasks. These include failing over the availability group, monitoring, and on rare occasions, adding additional listeners. These topics are discussed in the following sections.

Failover

If a replica is in Synchronous Commit mode and is configured for automatic failover, then the availability group automatically moves to a redundant replica in the event of an error condition being met on the primary replica. There are occasions, however, when you will want to manually fail over an availability group. This could be because of DR testing, proactive maintenance, or because you need to bring up an asynchronous replica following a failure of the primary replica or the primary data center.

Synchronous Failover

If you wish to fail over a replica that is in Synchronous Commit mode, launch the Failover Availability Group wizard by selecting Failover from the context menu of your availability group in Object Explorer. After moving past the Introduction page, you find the Select New Primary Replica page (see Figure 13-35). On this page, check the box of the replica to which you want to fail over. Before doing so, however, review the Failover Readiness column to ensure that the replicas are synchronized and that no data loss will occur.

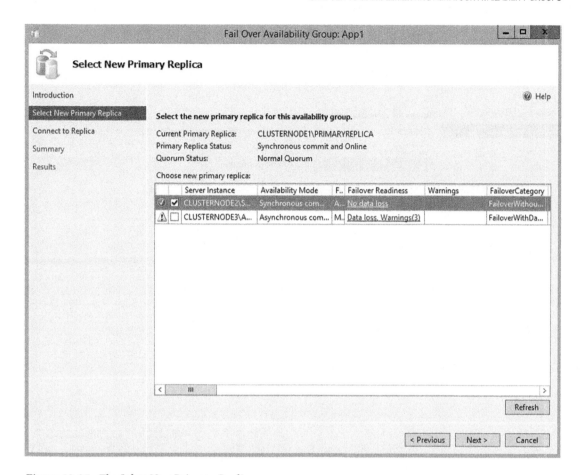

Figure 13-35. *The Select New Primary Replica page*

On the Connect To Replica page, illustrated in Figure 13-36, use the Connect button to establish a connection to the new primary replica.

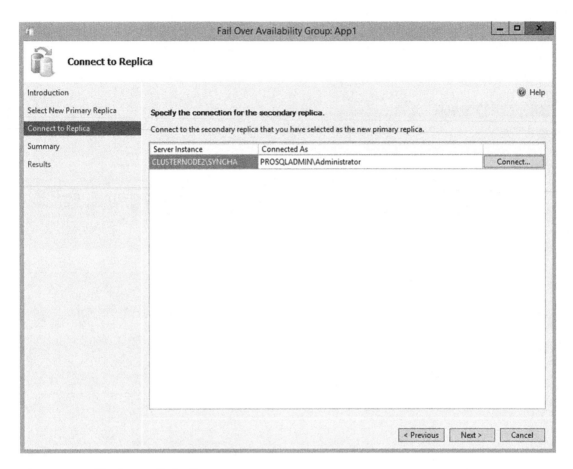

Figure 13-36. *The Connect To Replica page*

On the Summary page, you are given details of the task to be performed, followed by a progress indicator on the Results page. Once the failover completes, check that all tasks were successful, and investigate any errors or warnings that you receive.

We can also used T-SQL to fail over the availability group. The command in Listing 13-11 achieves the same results. Make sure to run this script from the replica that will be the new primary replica. If you run it from the current primary replica, use SQLCMD mode and connect to the new primary within the script.

Listing 13-11. Failing Over an Availability Group

```
ALTER AVAILABILITY GROUP App1 FAILOVER ;
GO
```

Asynchronous Failover

If your availability group is in Asynchronous Commit mode, then from a technical standpoint, you can fail over in a similar way to the way you can for a replica running in Synchronous Commit mode, except for the fact that you need to force the failover, thereby accepting the risk of data loss. You can force failover by using the command in Listing 13-12. You should run this script on the instance that will be the new primary.

For it to work, the cluster must have quorum. If it doesn't, then you need to force the cluster online before you force the availability group online.

Listing 13-12. Forcing Failover

```
ALTER AVAILABILITY GROUP App1 FORCE_FAILOVER_ALLOW_DATA_LOSS ;
```

From a process perspective, you should only ever do this if your primary site is completely unavailable. If this is not the case, first put the application into a safe state. This avoids any possibility of data loss. The way that I normally achieve this in a production environment is by performing the following steps:

1. Disable logins.

2. Change the mode of the replica to Synchronous Commit mode.

3. Fail over.

4. Change the replica back to Asynchronous Commit mode.

5. Enable the logins.

You can perform these steps with the script in Listing 13-13. When run from the DR instance, this script places the databases in App1 into a safe state before failing over, and then it reconfigures the application to work under normal operations.

Listing 13-13. Safe-stating an Application and Failing Over

```
--DISABLE LOGINS

DECLARE @AOAGDBs TABLE
(
DBName NVARCHAR(128)
) ;

INSERT INTO @AOAGDBs
SELECT database_name
FROM sys.availability_groups AG
INNER JOIN sys.availability_databases_cluster ADC
        ON AG.group_id = ADC.group_id
WHERE AG.name = 'App1' ;

DECLARE @Mappings TABLE
(
        LoginName NVARCHAR(128),
    DBname NVARCHAR(128),
    Username NVARCHAR(128),
    AliasName NVARCHAR(128)
) ;

INSERT INTO @Mappings
EXEC sp_msloginmappings ;

DECLARE @SQL NVARCHAR(MAX)
```

```sql
SELECT DISTINCT @SQL =
(
        SELECT 'ALTER LOGIN [' + LoginName + '] DISABLE; ' AS [data()]
        FROM @Mappings M
        INNER JOIN @AOAGDBs A
                ON M.DBname = A.DBName
        WHERE LoginName <> SUSER_NAME()
        FOR XML PATH ('')
)

EXEC(@SQL)
GO

--SWITCH TO SYNCHRONOUS COMMIT MODE

ALTER AVAILABILITY GROUP App1
MODIFY REPLICA ON N'CLUSTERNODE3\ASYNCDR' WITH (AVAILABILITY_MODE = SYNCHRONOUS_COMMIT) ;
GO

--FAIL OVER

ALTER AVAILABILITY GROUP App1 FAILOVER
GO

--SWITCH BACK TO ASYNCHRONOUS COMMIT MODE

ALTER AVAILABILITY GROUP App1
MODIFY REPLICA ON N'CLUSTERNODE3\ASYNCDR' WITH (AVAILABILITY_MODE = ASYNCHRONOUS_COMMIT) ;
GO

--ENABLE LOGINS

DECLARE @AOAGDBs TABLE
(
DBName NVARCHAR(128)
) ;

INSERT INTO @AOAGDBs
SELECT database_name
FROM sys.availability_groups AG
INNER JOIN sys.availability_databases_cluster ADC
        ON AG.group_id = ADC.group_id
WHERE AG.name = 'App1' ;

DECLARE @Mappings TABLE
(
        LoginName NVARCHAR(128),
    DBname NVARCHAR(128),
    Username NVARCHAR(128),
    AliasName NVARCHAR(128)
) ;
```

```
INSERT INTO @Mappings
EXEC sp_msloginmappings

DECLARE @SQL NVARCHAR(MAX)

SELECT DISTINCT @SQL =
(
        SELECT 'ALTER LOGIN [' + LoginName + '] ENABLE; ' AS [data()]
        FROM @Mappings M
        INNER JOIN @AOAGDBs A
                ON M.DBname = A.DBName
        WHERE LoginName <> SUSER_NAME()
        FOR XML PATH ('')
) ;

EXEC(@SQL)
```

Synchronizing Uncontained Objects

Regardless of the method you use to fail over, assuming that all of the databases within the availability group are not contained, then you need to ensure that instance-level objects are synchronized. The most straightforward way to keep your instance-level objects synchronized is by implementing an SSIS package, which is scheduled to run on a periodic basis.

Whether you choose to schedule a SSIS package to execute, or you choose a different approach, such as a SQL Server Agent job that scripts and re-creates the objects on the secondary servers, these are the objects that you should consider synchronizing:

- Logins

- Credentials

- SQL Server Agent jobs

- Custom error messages

- Linked servers

- Server-level event notifications

- Stored procedures in Master

- Server-level triggers

- Encryption keys and certificates

■ **Note** Details of how to create SSIS packages for administrative tasks, including synchronizing uncontained objects, are discussed in Chapter 21.

Monitoring

Once you have implemented availability groups, you need to monitor them and respond to any errors or warnings that could affect the availability of your data. If you have many availability groups implemented throughout the enterprise, then the only way to monitor them effectively and holistically is by using an enterprise monitoring tool, such as SOC (Systems Operations Center). If you only have a small number of availability groups, however, or if you are troubleshooting a specific issue, then SQL Server provides the AlwaysOn Dashboard and the AlwaysOn Health Trace. The following sections examine these two features.

AlwaysOn Dashboard

The AlwaysOn Dashboard is an interactive report that allows you to view the health of your AlwaysOn environment and drill through, or roll up elements within the topology. You can invoke the report from the context menu of the Availability Groups folder in Object Explorer, or from the context menu of the availability group itself. Figure 13-37 shows the report that is generated from the context menu of the App1 availability group. You can see that currently, synchronization of both replicas is in a healthy state.

Figure 13-37. *The availability group dashboard*

The three possible synchronization states that a database can be in are SYNCHRONIZED, SYNCRONIZING, and NOT SYNCHRONIZING. A synchronous replica should be in the SYNCHRONIZED state, and any other state is unhealthy. An asynchronous replica, however, will never be in the SYNCHRONIZED state, and a state of SYNCHRONIZING is considered healthy. Regardless of the mode, NOT SYNCHRONIZING indicates that the replica is not connected.

■ **Note** In addition to the synchronization states, a replica also has one of the following operational states: PENDING_FAILOVER, PENDING, ONLINE, OFFLINE, FAILED, FAILED_NO_QUORUM, and NULL (when the replica is disconnected). The operational state of a replica can be viewed using the sys.dm_hadr_availability_ replica_states DMV, which we discussed in Chapter 17.

At the top right of the report, there are links to the failover wizard, which we discussed earlier in this chapter; the AlwaysOn Health events, which we discussed in the next section; and also a link to view cluster quorum information. The Cluster Quorum Information screen, which is invoked by this link, is displayed in Figure 13-38. You can also drill through each replica in the Availability Replicas window to see replica-specific details.

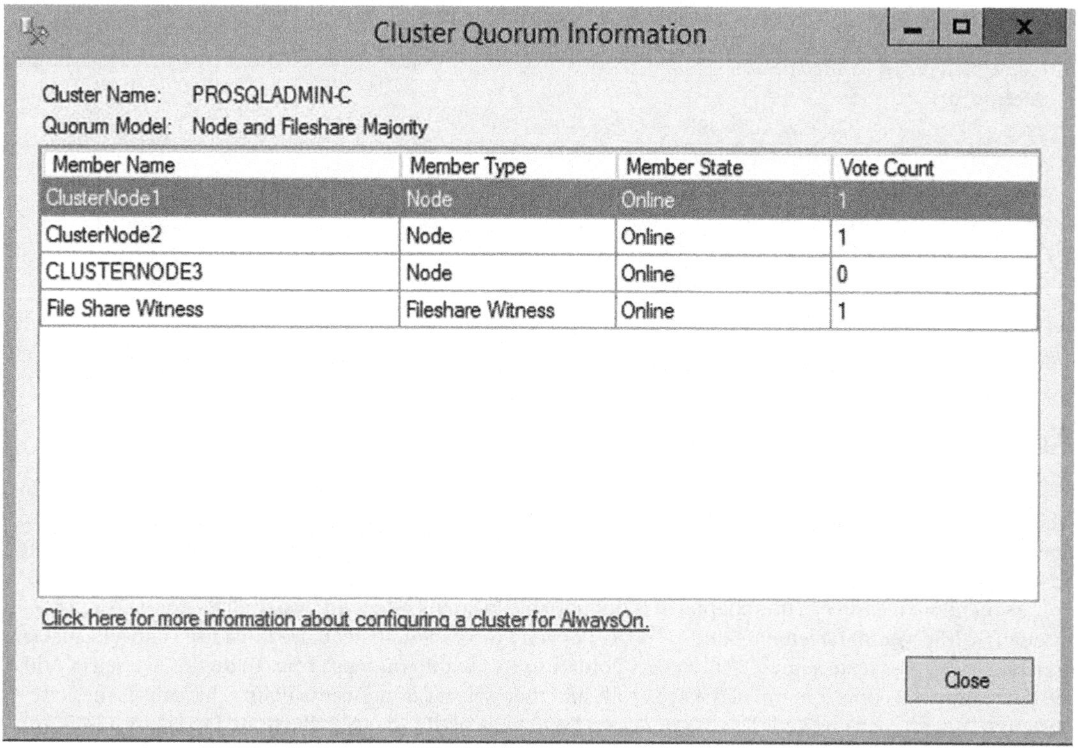

Cluster Name: PROSQLADMIN-C
Quorum Model: Node and Fileshare Majority

Member Name	Member Type	Member State	Vote Count
ClusterNode1	Node	Online	1
ClusterNode2	Node	Online	1
CLUSTERNODE3	Node	Online	0
File Share Witness	Fileshare Witness	Online	1

Click here for more information about configuring a cluster for AlwaysOn.

Figure 13-38. *The Cluster Quorum Information screen*

AlwaysOn Health Trace

The AlwaysOn Health Trace is an Extended Events session, which is created when you create you first availability group. It can be located in SQL Server Management Studio, under Extended Events | Sessions, and via its context menu, you can view live data that is being captured, or you can enter the session's properties to change the configuration of the events that are captured.

Drilling through the session exposes the session's package, and from the context menu of the package, you can view previously captured events. Figure 13-39 shows that the latest event captured, was Database 5 (which, in our case, is Chapter13App1Customers), was waiting for the log to be hardened on the synchronous replica. Extended Events is discussed in detail in Chapter 19.

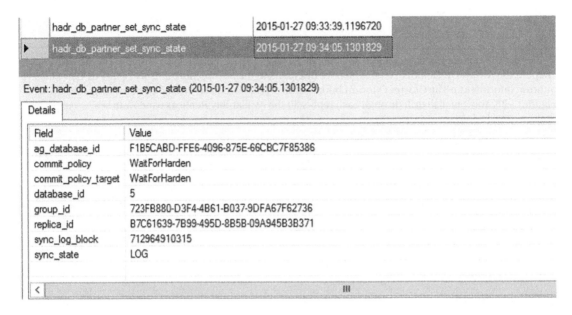

Figure 13-39. *The target data*

Adding Multiple Listeners

Usually, each availability group has a single Availability Group Listener, but there are some rare instances in which you may need to create multiple listeners for the same availability group. One scenario in which this may be required is if you have legacy applications with hard-coded connection strings. Here, you can create an extra listener with a client access point that matches the name of the hard-coded connection string.

As mentioned earlier in this chapter, it is not possible to create a second Availability Group Listener through SQL Server Management Studio, T-SQL, or even PowerShell. Instead, we must use Failover Cluster Manager. Here, we create a new Client Access Point resource within our App1 role. To do this, we select Add Resource from the context menu of the App1 role, and then select Client Access Point. This causes the New Resource Wizard to be invoked. The Client Access Point page of the wizard is illustrated in Figure 13-40. You can see that we have entered the DNS name for the client access point and specified an IP address from each subnet.

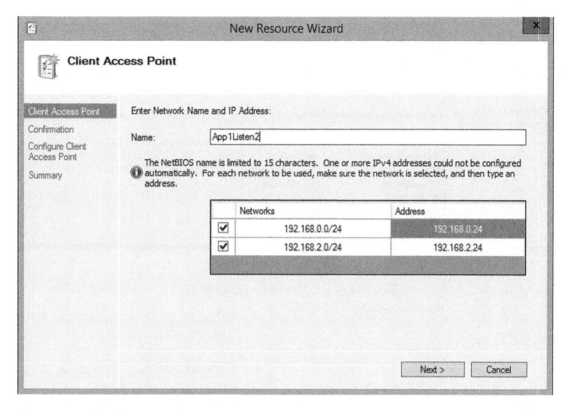

Figure 13-40. *The Client Access Point page*

On the Confirmation page, we are shown a summary of the configuration that will be performed. On the Configure Client Access Point page, we see a progress indicator, before we are finally shown a completion summary on the Summary page, which is illustrated in Figure 13-41.

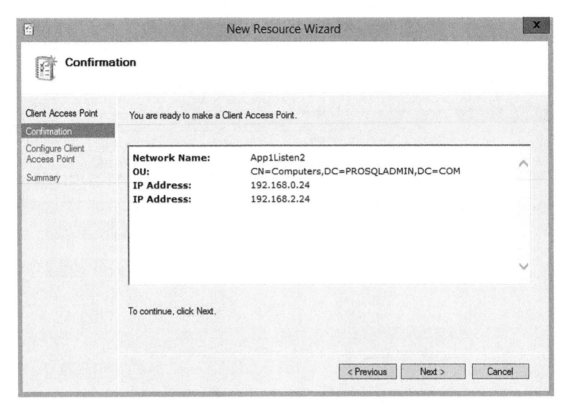

Figure 13-41. *The Confirmation page*

Now we need to configure the Availability Group resource to be dependent upon the new client access point. To do this, we select Properties from the context menu of the App1 resource and then navigate to the Dependencies tab. Here, we add the new client access point as a dependency and configure an OR constraint between the two listeners, as illustrated in Figure 13-42. Once we apply this change, clients are able to connect using either of the two listener names.

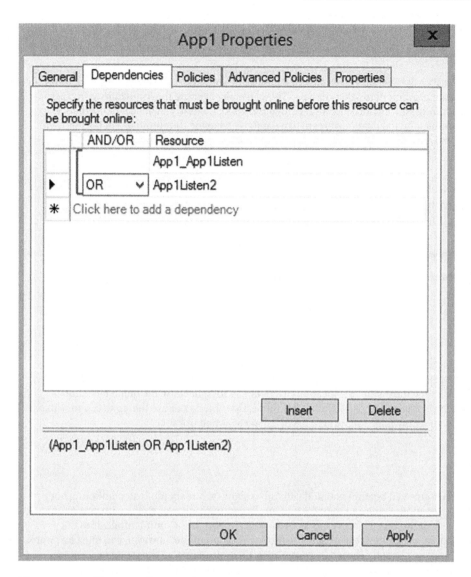

Figure 13-42. The Dependencies tab

Other Administrative Considerations

When databases are made highly available with AlwaysOn Availability Groups, several limitations are imposed. One of the most restrictive of these is that databases cannot be placed in single_user mode or be made read only. This can have an impact when you need to safe-state your application for maintenance. This is why, in the Failover section of this chapter, we disabled the logins that have users mapped to the databases. If you must place your database in single-user mode, then you must first remove it from the availability group.

A database can be removed from an availability group by running the command in Listing 13-14. This command removes the Chapter13App1Customers database from the availability group.

Listing 13-14. Removing a Database from an Availability Group

```
ALTER DATABASE Chapter13App1Customers SET HADR OFF ;
```

There may also be occasions in which you want a database to remain in an availability group, but you wish to suspend data movement to other replicas. This is usually because the availability group is in Synchronous Commit mode and you have a period of high utilization, where you need a performance improvement. You can suspend the data movement to a database by using the command in Listing 13-15, which suspends data movement for the Chapter13App1Sales database and then resumes it.

■ **Caution**   If you suspend data movement, the transaction log on the primary replica continues to grow, and you are not able to truncate it until data movement resumes and the databases are synchronized.

Listing 13-15. Suspending Data Movement

```
ALTER DATABASE Chapter13App1Customers SET HADR SUSPEND ;
GO


ALTER DATABASE Chapter13App1Customers SET HADR RESUME ;
GO
```

Another important consideration is the placement of database and log files. These files must be in the same location on each replica. This means that if you use named instances, it is a hard technical requirement that you change the default file locations for data and logs, because the default location includes the name of the instance. This is assuming, of course, that you do not use the same instance name on each node, which would defy many of the benefits of having a named instance.

Summary

AlwaysOn Availability Groups can be implemented with up to eight secondary replicas, combining both Synchronous and Asynchronous Commit modes. When implementing high availability with availability groups, you always use Synchronous Commit mode, because Asynchronous Commit mode does not support automatic failover. When implementing Synchronous Commit mode, however, you must be aware of the associated performance penalty caused by committing the transaction on the secondary replica before it is committed on the primary replica. For disaster recovery, you will normally choose to implement Asynchronous Commit mode.

The availability group can be created via the New Availability Group Wizard, though dialog boxes, through T-SQL, or even through PowerShell. If you create an availability group using dialog boxes, then some aspects, such as the endpoint and associated permissions, must be scripted using T-SQL or PowerShell.

If you implement disaster recovery with availability groups, then you need to configure a multi-subnet cluster. This does not mean that you must have SAN replication between the sites, however, since availability groups do not rely on shared storage. What you do need to do is add additional IP addresses for the administrative cluster access point and also for the Availability Group Listener. You also need to pay attention to the properties of the cluster that support client reconnection to ensure that clients do not experience a high number of timeouts.

Failover to a synchronous replica in the event of a failure of the primary replica is automatic. There are instances, however, in which you will also need to failover manually. This could be because of a disaster that requires failover to the DR site, or it could be for proactive maintenance. Although it is possible to failover to an asynchronous replica with the possibility of data loss, it is good practice to place the databases in a safe-state first. Because you cannot place a database in read only or single_user mode, if it is participating in an availability group, safe-stating usually consists of disabling the logins and then switching to Synchronous Commit mode before failover.

To monitor availability groups throughout the enterprise, you need to use a monitoring tool, such as Systems Operation Center. If you need to monitor a small number of availability groups or troubleshoot a specific issue, however, use one of the tools included with SQL Server, such as a dashboard for monitoring the health of the topology, and an extended events session, called the AlwaysOn Health Trace.

You should also consider other maintenance tasks. These include where to place database and log files, as they must have the same location on each replica, and removing a database from an availability group so that you can place it in single_user mode, for example. Changing to single_user mode may be due to a requirement to run DBCC CHECKDB in a repair mode, and suspend data movement. Suspending data movement allows you to remove the performance overhead during a period of high utilization, but be warned, it also causes the transaction log on the primary replica to grow, without an option to truncate it, until data movement has resumed and the databases are once again synchronized.

CHAPTER 14

■ ■ ■

Implementing Log Shipping

As discussed in Chapter 11, log shipping is a technology you can use to implement disaster recovery and the scale out of read-only reporting. It works by taking the transaction log backups of a database, copying them to one or more secondary servers, and then restoring them, in order to keep the secondary server(s) synchronized. This chapter demonstrates how to implement log shipping for disaster recovery (DR). You also discover how to monitor and fail over log shipping.

■ **Note**   For the purpose of the demonstrations in this chapter, we use a domain, consisting of a domain controller and four stand-alone servers, each with an instance of SQL Server installed. The server\instance names are PRIMARYSERVER\PROSQLADMIN, DRSERVER\PROSQLDR, REPORTSERVER\PROSQLREPORTS, and MONITORSERVER\PROSQLMONITOR, respectively.

Implementing Log Shipping for DR

Before we begin to implement log shipping for disaster recovery, we first create a database that we will use for the demonstrations in this chapter. The script in Listing 14-1 creates a database called Chapter14 with its recovery model set to FULL. We create one table within the database and populate it with data.

Listing 14-1. Creating the Database to Be Log Shipped

```
--Create the database

CREATE DATABASE Chapter14;
GO

ALTER DATABASE Chapter14 SET RECOVERY FULL;
GO

USE Chapter14
GO

--Create and populate numbers table
```

```
DECLARE @Numbers TABLE
(
        Number          INT
)

;WITH CTE(Number)
AS
(
        SELECT 1 Number
        UNION ALL
        SELECT Number + 1
        FROM CTE
        WHERE Number < 100
)
INSERT INTO @Numbers
SELECT Number FROM CTE;

--Create and populate name pieces

DECLARE @Names TABLE
(
        FirstName       VARCHAR(30),
        LastName        VARCHAR(30)
);

INSERT INTO @Names
VALUES('Peter', 'Carter'),
            ('Michael', 'Smith'),
            ('Danielle', 'Mead'),
            ('Reuben', 'Roberts'),
            ('Iris', 'Jones'),
            ('Sylvia', 'Davies'),
            ('Finola', 'Wright'),
            ('Edward', 'James'),
            ('Marie', 'Andrews'),
            ('Jennifer', 'Abraham') ;

--Create and populate Customers table

CREATE TABLE dbo.Customers
(
        CustomerID              INT           NOT NULL    IDENTITY    PRIMARY KEY,
        FirstName               VARCHAR(30)   NOT NULL,
        LastName                VARCHAR(30)   NOT NULL,
        BillingAddressID        INT           NOT NULL,
        DeliveryAddressID       INT           NOT NULL,
        CreditLimit             MONEY         NOT NULL,
        Balance                 MONEY         NOT NULL
);
```

```
SELECT * INTO #Customers
FROM
        (SELECT
                (SELECT TOP 1 FirstName FROM @Names ORDER BY NEWID()) FirstName,
                (SELECT TOP 1 LastName FROM @Names ORDER BY NEWID()) LastName,
                (SELECT TOP 1 Number FROM @Numbers ORDER BY NEWID()) BillingAddressID,
                (SELECT TOP 1 Number FROM @Numbers ORDER BY NEWID()) DeliveryAddressID,
                (SELECT TOP 1 CAST(RAND() * Number AS INT) * 10000
                    FROM @Numbers
                    ORDER BY NEWID()) CreditLimit,
                (SELECT TOP 1 CAST(RAND() * Number AS INT) * 9000
                    FROM @Numbers
                    ORDER BY NEWID()) Balance
        FROM @Numbers a
        CROSS JOIN @Numbers b
) a;

INSERT INTO dbo.Customers
SELECT * FROM #Customers;
GO
```

For the purpose of this demonstration, we would like to configure disaster recovery for the Chapter14 database so that we have an RPO (Recovery Point Objective) of 10 minutes. We will also implement a 10-minute load delay on the DR server. This means that if an application team notifies us immediately of an incident that has led to data loss—for example, a user accidently deletes rows from a table—then we are able to rectify the issue by using the data on the DR server before the log that contains the erroneous transaction is restored.

GUI Configuration

We can configure log shipping for our Chapter14 database through SQL Server Management Studio (SSMS). To do this, we select Properties from the context menu of the database and navigate to the Transaction Log Shipping page, which is displayed in Figure 14-1. The first task on this page is to check the Enable This As The Primary Database In A Log Shipping Configuration check box.

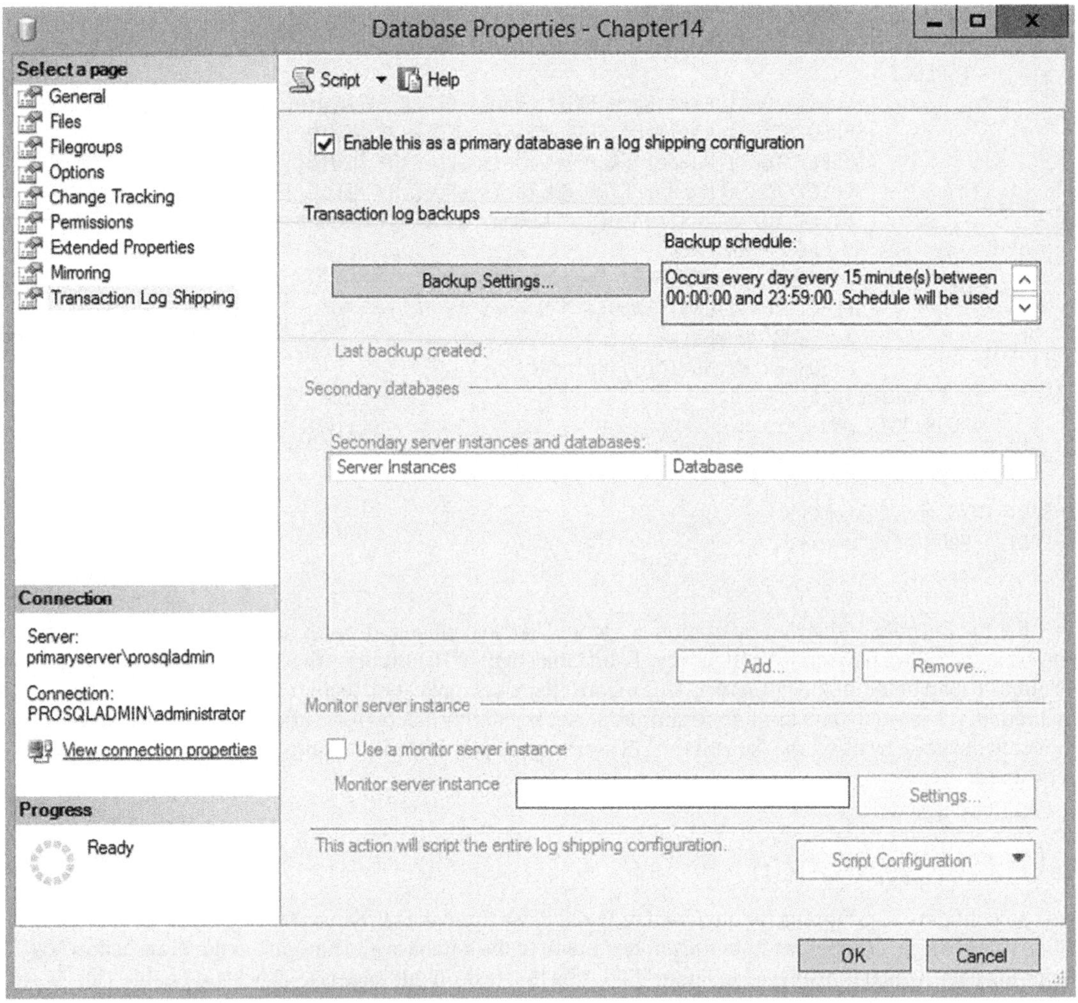

Figure 14-1. *The Transaction Log Shipping page*

We can now use the Backup Settings button to display the Transaction Log Backup Settings screen. On this screen, we enter the UNC (Universal Naming Convention) to the share that will be used for storing the log backups that log shipping takes. Because this share is actually configured on our primary server, we also enter the local path in the field below. The account that will be used to run the backup job needs to be granted read and change permissions on this share. By default, this will be the SQL Server service account, but for more granular security, it is possible to configure log shipping jobs to run under a proxy account. Proxy accounts are discussed in Chapter 21.

We then configure how long we want our backup files to be retained before they are deleted. The value that you select for this depends on your enterprise's requirements, but if your backup files are offloaded to tape, then you should make the files available long enough to allow the enterprise backup job to run, and you should potentially build in enough time for it to fail and then succeed on the following cycle. You should also consider your requirements for ad-hoc restores. For example, if a project notices a data issue and requests a restore, you want to be able to retrieve the relevant backups from local disk, if possible. Therefore, consider how long you should give projects to notice an issue and request a restore before SQL Server removes the local copy of the backups. Backup strategies are discussed further in Chapter 15.

You should also specify how soon you want an alert to be generated if no log backup occurs. To be notified of any backup failure, you can configure the value to be a minute longer than your backup schedule. In some environments, however, it may be acceptable to miss a few backups. In such an instance, you may set the value to a larger interval so that you are not flooded with failed backup alerts during maintenance windows and other such situations.

The Set Backup Compression drop-down determines if backup compression should be used. The default is to take the configuration from the instance, but you can override this by specifically choosing to use it, or not use it, for the backups taken by the log shipping job. The Transaction Log Backup Settings screen is illustrated in Figure 14-2.

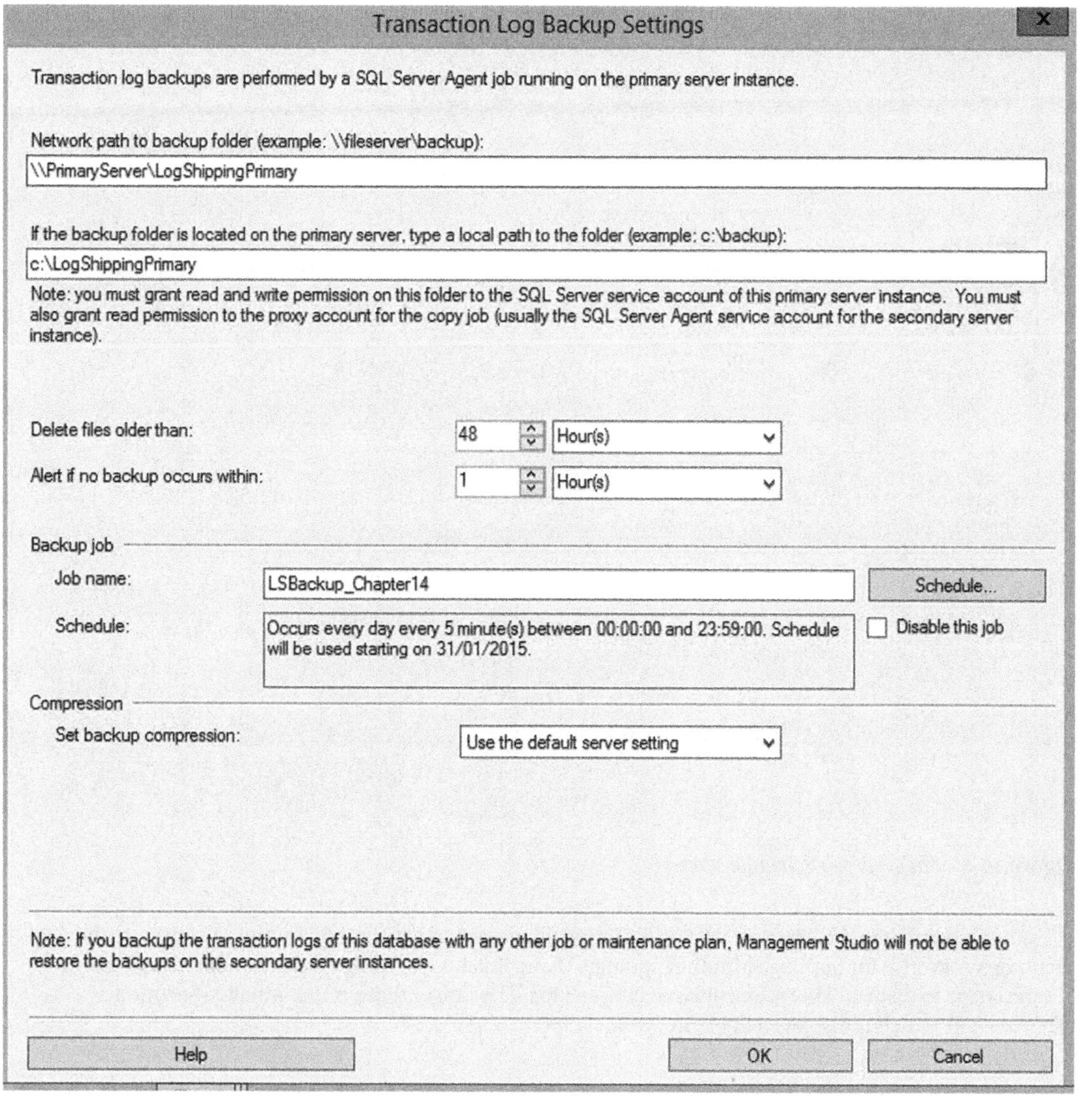

Figure 14-2. The Transaction Log Backup Settings screen

Clicking the Schedule button causes the New Job Schedule screen to be invoked. This screen, which is illustrated in Figure 14-3, is the standard SQL Server Agent screen used for creating job schedules, except that it has been prepopulated with the default name of the log shipping backup job. Because we are trying to achieve an RPO of 10 minutes, we configure the backup job to run every 5 minutes. This is because we also need to allow time for the copy job to run. In a DR planning, we cannot assume that the primary server will be available for retrieving our log backup.

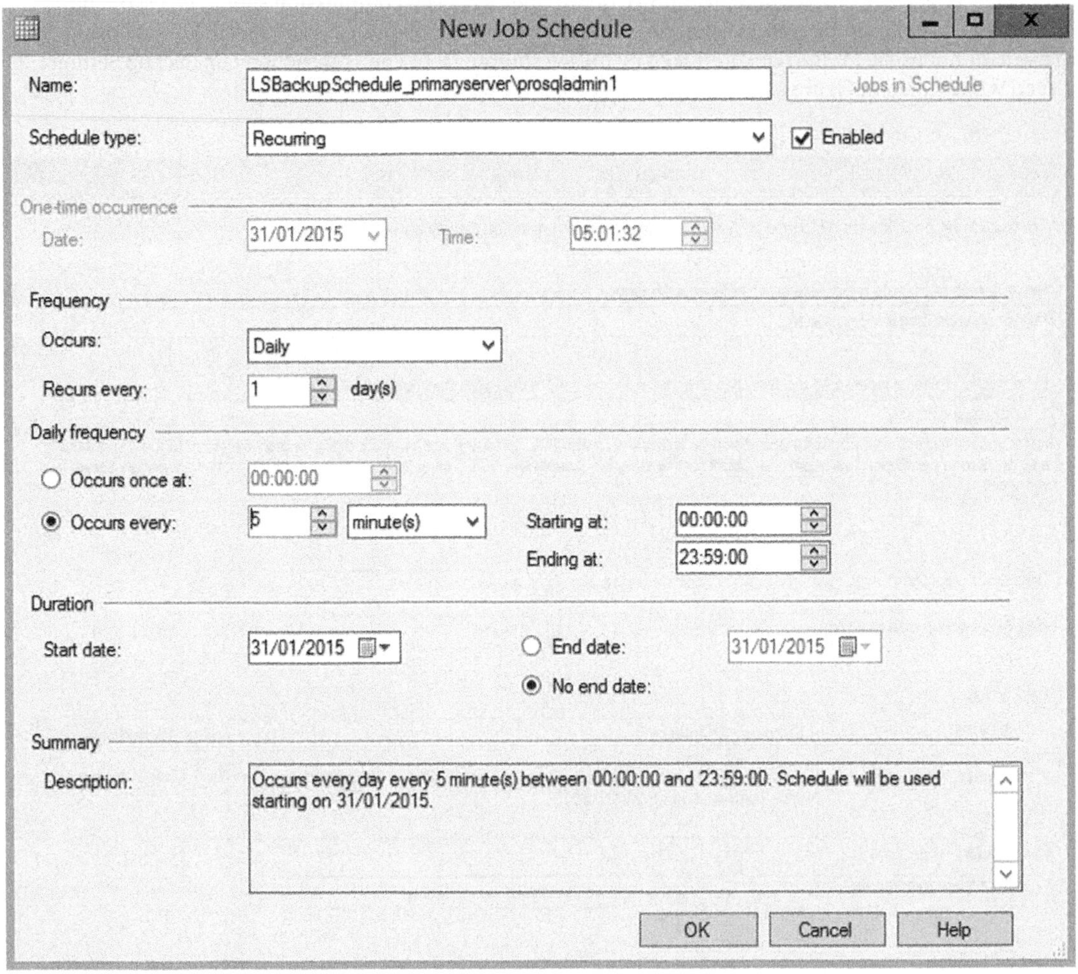

Figure 14-3. *The New Job Schedule screen*

After returning to the Transaction Log Shipping page, we can use the Add button to configure the secondary server(s) for our Log Shipping topology. Using this button causes the Secondary Database Settings page to display. This page consists of three tabs. The first of these is the Initialize Secondary Database tab, which is displayed in Figure 14-4.

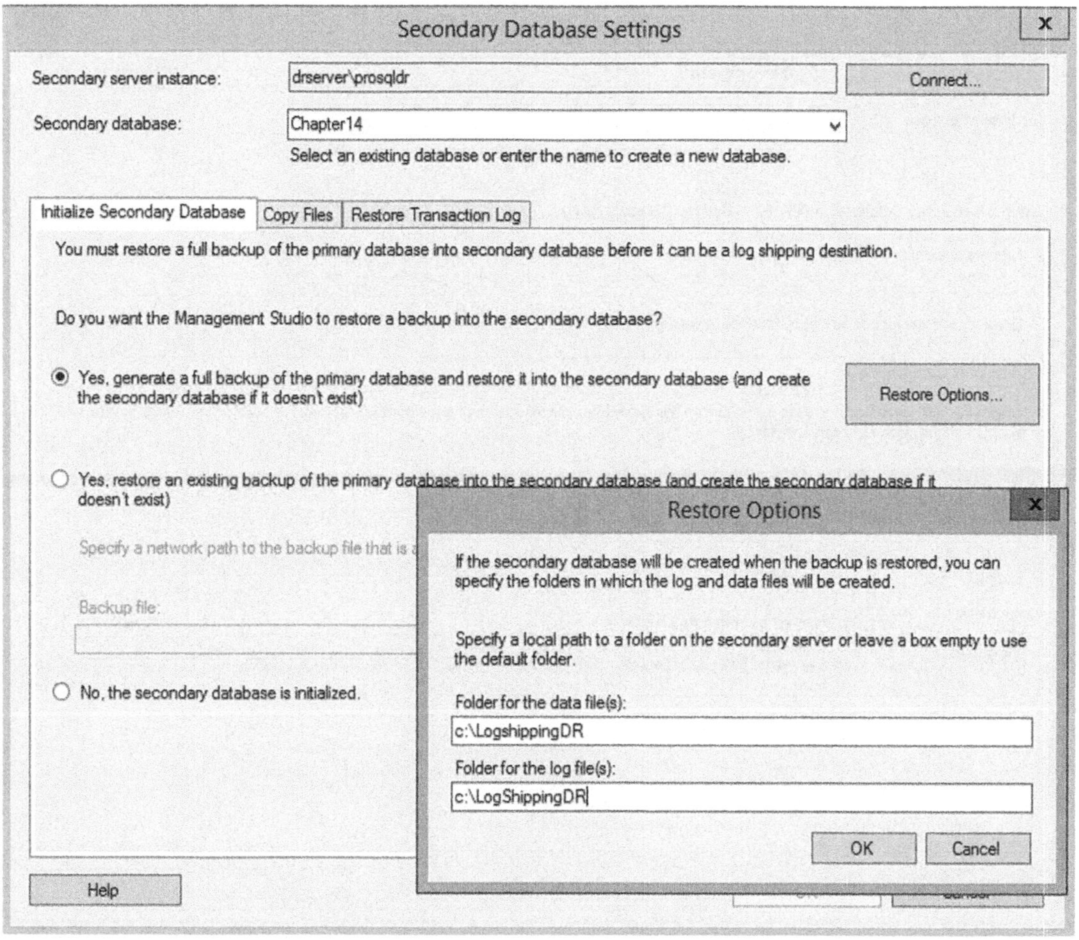

Figure 14-4. *The Initialize Secondary Database tab*

On this tab, we configure how we want to initialize our secondary database. We can preinitialize our databases by taking a full backup of the database and then manually restoring them to the secondary server using the NORECOVERY option. In this kind of instance, we would select the No, The Secondary Database Is Initialized option.

If we already have a full backup available, then we can place it in a file share that the SQL Server service account has read and modify permissions on, and then use the Yes, Restore An Existing Backup Of The Primary Database Into The Secondary Database option and specify the location of the backup file.

In our case, however, we do not have an existing full backup of the Chapter14 database, so we select the option to Yes, Generate A Full Backup Of The Primary Database And Restore It To The Secondary Database. This causes the Restore Options window to display; it is here where we enter the locations that we want the database and transaction log files to be created on the secondary server, as illustrated in Figure 14-4.

On the Copy Files tab, illustrated in Figure 14-5, we configure the job that is responsible for copying the transaction log files from the primary server to the secondary server(s). First, we specify the share on the secondary server to which we will copy the transaction logs. The account that runs the copy job must be configured with read and modify permissions on the share. Just like the backup job, this job defaults to running under the context of the SQL Server service account, but you can also configure it to run under a proxy account.

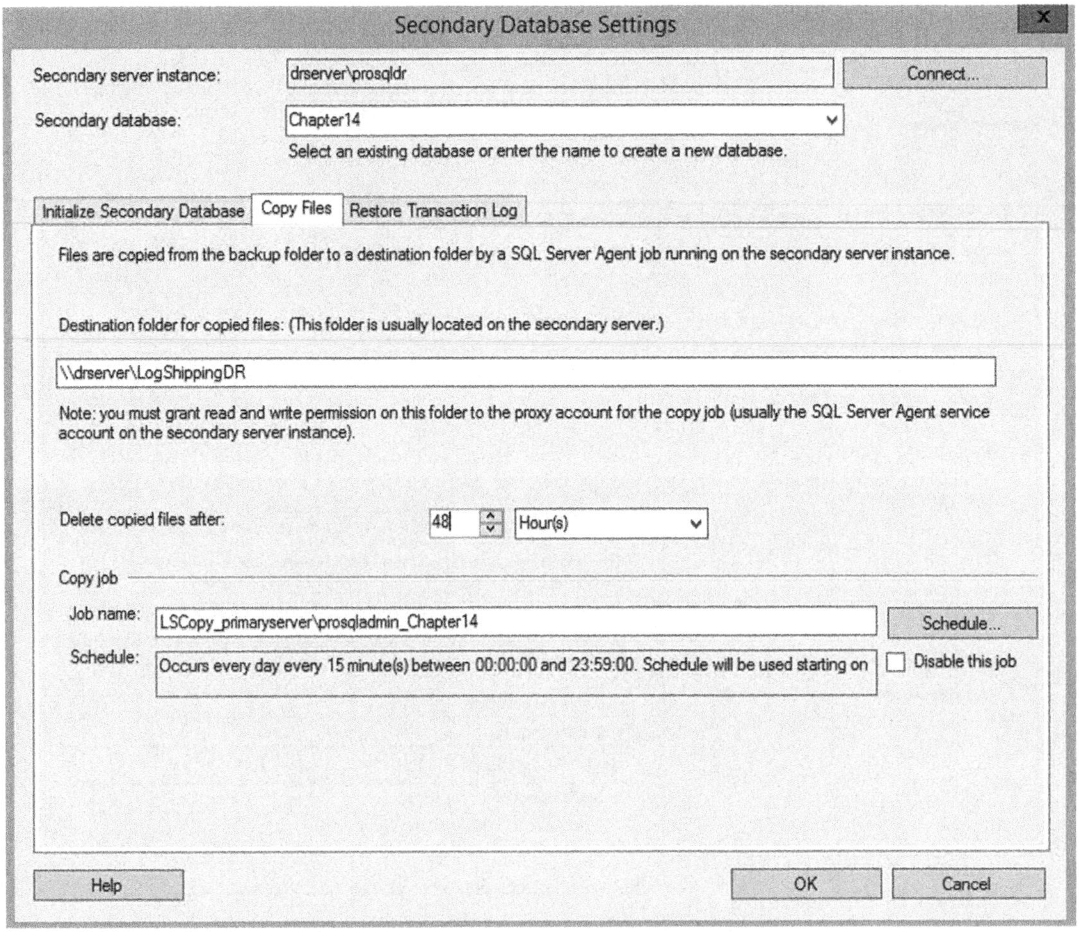

Figure 14-5. *The Copy Files tab*

We also use this tab to configure how long the backup files should be retained on the secondary server before they are deleted. I usually recommend keeping this value in line with the value that you specify for retaining the backups on the primary server for consistency.

The job Name field is automatically populated with the default name for a log shipping copy job, and, using the Schedule button, you can invoke the New Job Schedule screen, where you can configure the schedule for the copy job. As illustrated in Figure 14-6, we have configured this job to run every 5 minutes, which is in line with our RPO requirement of 10 minutes. It takes 5 minutes before the log is backed up, and then another 5 minutes before it is moved to the secondary sever. Once the file has been moved to the secondary server, we can be confident that, except in the most extreme circumstances, we will be able to retrieve the backup from either the primary or the secondary server, thus achieving our 10 minute RPO.

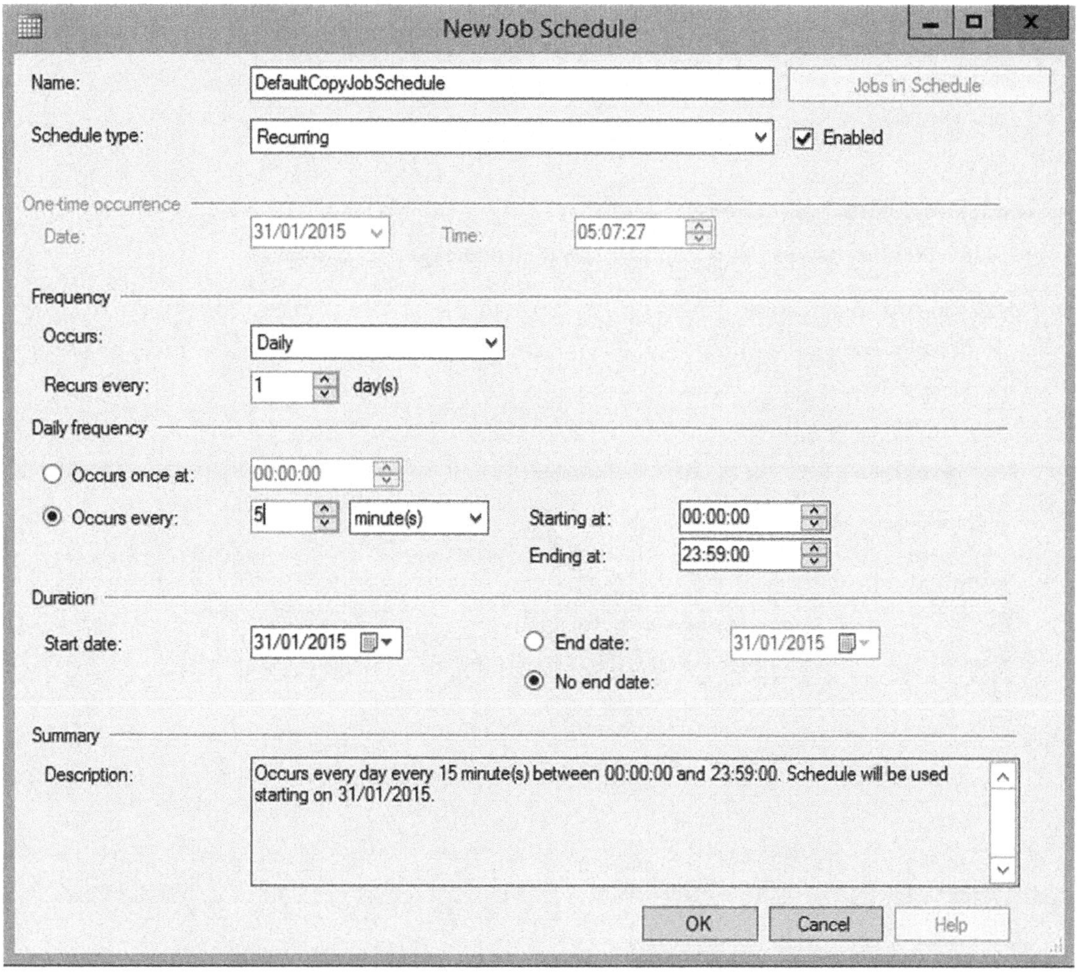

Figure 14-6. *The New Job Schedule screen*

On the Restore Transaction Log tab, we configure the job that is responsible for restoring the backups on the secondary server. The most important option on this screen is what database state we choose when restoring. Selecting the No Recovery Mode option is the applicable choice for a DR server. This is because if you choose Standby Mode, uncommitted transaction are saved to a Transaction Undo File, which means the database can be brought online in read-only mode (as discussed in Chapter 11). However, this action increases the recovery time, because these transactions then need to be reapplied before the redo phase of the next restore.

On this tab, we also use the Delay Restoring Backups For At Least option to apply the load delay, which gives users a chance to report data issues. We can also specify how long the delay should be before we are alerted that no restore operation has occurred. The Restore Transaction Log tab is illustrated in Figure 14-7.

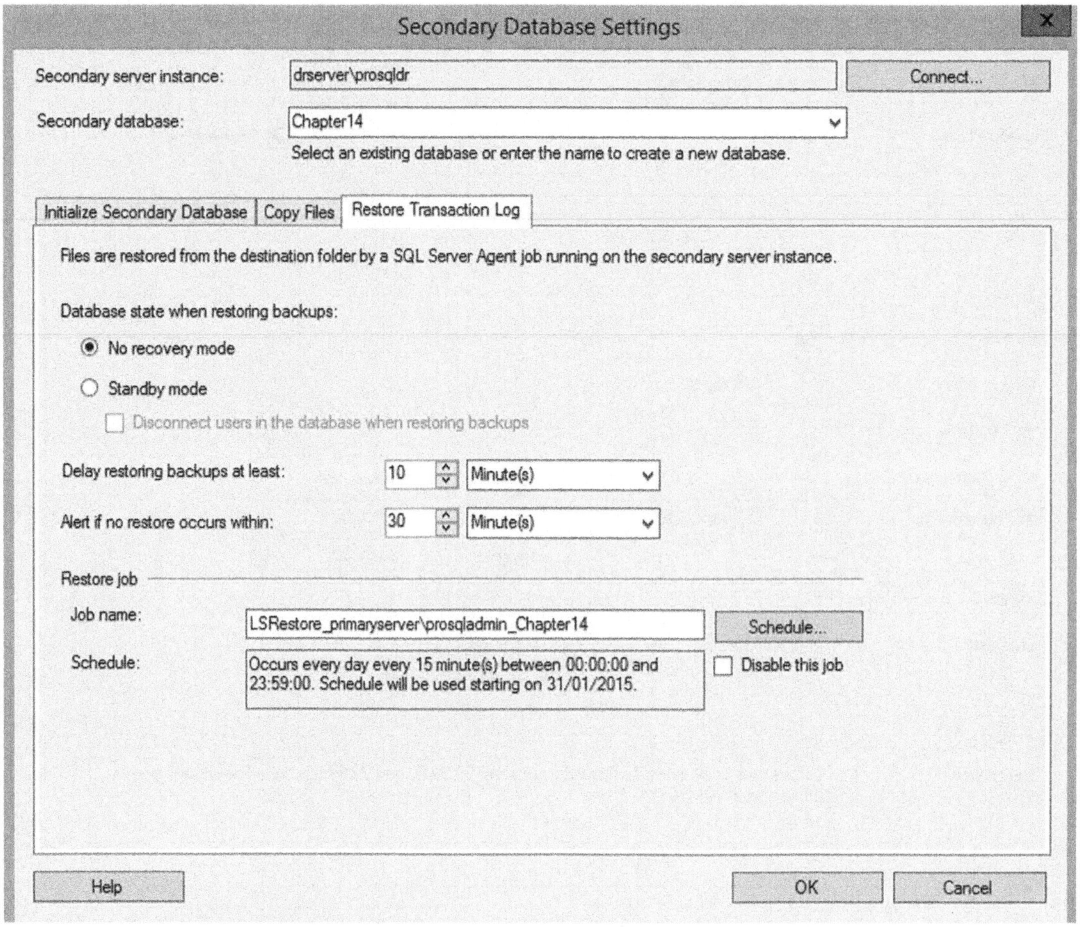

Figure 14-7. *The Restore Transaction Log tab*

The Schedule button invokes the New Job Schedule screen, displayed in Figure 14-8. On this screen, we can configure the job schedule for the restore of our transaction logs. Although doing so is not mandatory, for consistency, I usually recommend configuring this value so it is the same as the backup and copy jobs.

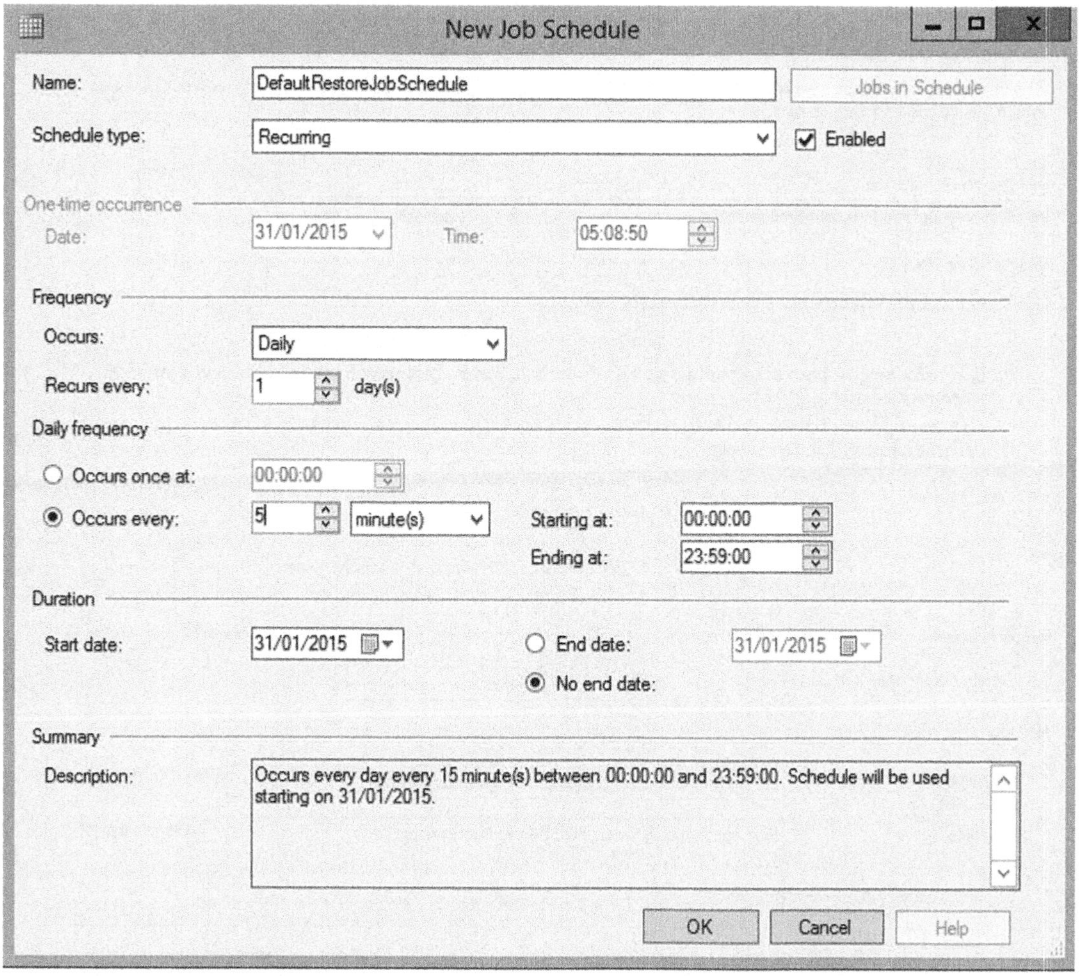

Figure 14-8. *New Job Schedule screen*

Once back on the Transaction Log Shipping page, we need to decide if we want to implement a monitor server. This option allows us to configure an instance, which acts as a centralized point for monitoring our Log Shipping topology. This is an important decision to make at this point, because after configuration is complete, there is no official way to add a monitor server to the topology without tearing down and reconfigured log shipping.

■ **Tip**   It is technically possible to force in a monitor server at a later time, but the process involves manually updating log shipping metadata tables in MSDB. Therefore, it is not recommended, or supported.

To add a monitor server, we check the option to Use A Monitor Server Instance and enter the server\instance name. Clicking the Settings button causes the Log Shipping Monitor Settings screen to display. We use this screen, shown in Figure 14-9, to configure how connections are made to the monitor server and the history retention settings.

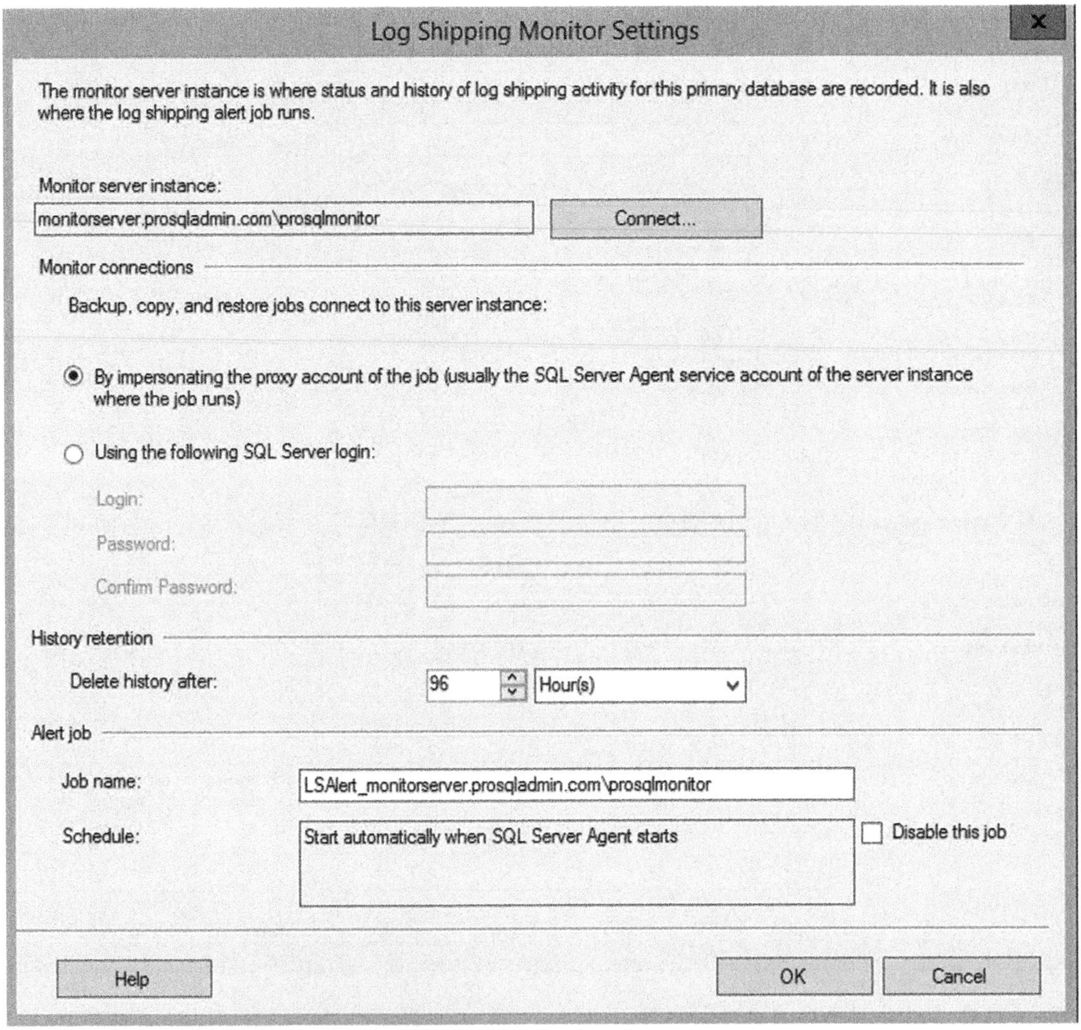

Figure 14-9. *The Log Shipping Monitor Settings screen*

Now that our Log Shipping topology is fully configured, we can choose to script the configuration, which can be helpful for the purposes of documentation and change control. We can then complete the configuration. The progress of the configuration displays in the Save Log Shipping Configuration window (see Figure 14-10). Once configuration is complete, we should check this window for any errors that may have occurred during configuration and resolve them as needed. The most common cause of issues with log shipping configuration tends to be permissions related, so we need to ensure that the SQL Server service account (or proxy account) has the correct permissions on the file shares and instances before we continue.

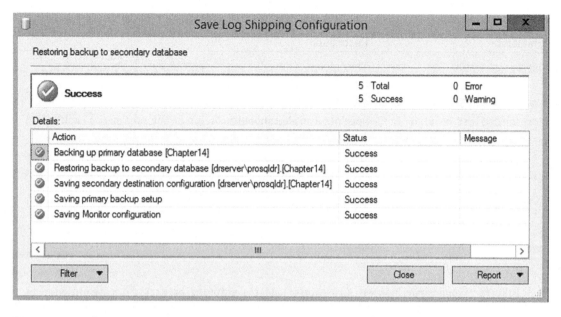

Figure 14-10. The Save Log Shipping Configuration page

T-SQL Configuration

To configure log shipping through T-SQL, we need to run a number of system stored procedures. The first of these procedures is sp_add_log_shipping_primary_database, which we use to configure the backup job and monitor the primary database. The parameters used by this procedure are described in Table 14-1.

Table 14-1. *sp_add_log_shipping_primary_database Parameters*

Parameter	Description
@database	The name of the database for which you are configuring log shipping.
@backup_directory	The local path to the backup folder.
@backup_share	The network path to the backup folder.
@backup_job_name	The name to use for the job that backs up the log.
@backup_retention_period	The duration that log backups should be kept for, specified in minutes.
@monitor_server	The server\instance name of the monitor server.
@monitor_server_Security_mode	The authentication mode to use to connect to the monitor server. 0 is SQL authentication and 1 is Windows authentication.
@monitor_server_login	The account used to connect to the monitor server (only use if SQL authentication is specified).
@monitor_server_password	The password of the account used to connect to the monitor server (only use if SQL authentication is specified).

(continued)

Table 14-1. (*continued*)

Parameter	Description
@backup_threshold	The amount of time that can elapse, without a log backup being taken, before an alert is triggered.
@threshold_alert	The alert to be raised if the backup threshold is exceeded.
@threshold_alert_enabled	Specifies if an alert should be fired. 0 disables the alert, 1 enables it.
@history_retention_period	The duration for which the log backup job history will be retained, specified in minutes.
@backup_job_id	An OUTPUT parameter that specifies the GUID of the backup job that is created by the procedure.
@primary_id	An OUTPUT parameter that specifies the ID of the primary database.
@backup_compression	Specifies if backup compression should be used. 0 means disabled, 1 means enabled, and 2 means use the instance's default configuration.

Listing 14-2 demonstrates how we can use the sp_add_log_shipping_primary_database procedure to configure Chapter14 for log shipping. This script uses the @backup_job_id output parameter to pass the job's GUID into the sp_update_job stored procedure. It also uses the sp_add_schedule and sp_attach_schedule system stored procedures to create the job schedule and attach it to the job. Because configuring log shipping involves connecting to multiple instances, we have added a connection to the primary instance. This means that we should run the script in SQLCMD mode.

■ **Note**   sp_update_job, sp_add_schedule, and sp_attach_schedule are system stored procedures used to manipulate SQL Server Agent objects. A full discussion of SQL Server Agent and its stored procedure can be found in Chapter 21.

Listing 14-2. Sp_add_log_shipping_primary_database

```
:connect primaryserver\prosqladmin

DECLARE @LS_BackupJobId        UNIQUEIDENTIFIER
DECLARE @LS_BackUpScheduleID    INT

--Configure Chapter14 database as the Primary for Log Shipping

EXEC master.dbo.sp_add_log_shipping_primary_database
            @database = N'Chapter14'
            ,@backup_directory = N'c:\logshippingprimary'
            ,@backup_share = N'\\primaryserver\logshippingprimary'
            ,@backup_job_name = N'LSBackup_Chapter14'
            ,@backup_retention_period = 2880
            ,@backup_compression = 2
            ,@monitor_server = N'monitorserver.prosqladmin.com\prosqlmonitor'
            ,@monitor_server_security_mode = 1
            ,@backup_threshold = 60
```

```
            ,@threshold_alert_enabled = 1
            ,@history_retention_period = 5760 ;
            ,@backup_job_id = @LS_BackupJobId OUTPUT ;
            --Create a job schedule for the backup job

EXEC msdb.dbo.sp_add_schedule
            @schedule_name =N'LSBackupSchedule_primaryserver\prosqladmin1'
            ,@enabled = 1
            ,@freq_type = 4
            ,@freq_interval = 1
            ,@freq_subday_type = 4
            ,@freq_subday_interval = 5
            ,@freq_recurrence_factor = 0
            ,@active_start_date = 20150201
            ,@active_end_date = 99991231
            ,@active_start_time = 0
            ,@active_end_time = 235900
            ,@schedule_id = @LS_BackUpScheduleID OUTPUT ;

--Attach the job schedule to the job

EXEC msdb.dbo.sp_attach_schedule
            @job_id = @LS_BackupJobId
            ,@schedule_id = @LS_BackUpScheduleID  ;

--Enable the backup job
EXEC msdb.dbo.sp_update_job
            @job_id = @LS_BackupJobId
            ,@enabled = 1 ;
```

We use the sp_add_log_shipping_primary_secondary system stored procedure to update the metadata on the primary server in order to add a record for each secondary server in the Log Shipping topology. The parameters that it accepts are described in Table 14-2.

Table 14-2. sp_add_log_shipping_primary_secondary Parameters

Parameter	Description
@primary_database	The name of the primary database
@secondary_server	The server/instance of the secondary server
@secondary_database	The name of the database on the secondary server

Listing 14-3 demonstrates how we can use the sp_add_log_shipping_primary_secondary procedure to add a record of our DRSERVER\PROSQLDR instance to our primary server. Again, we specifically connect to the primary server, meaning that the script should run in SQLCMS mode.

Listing 14-3. Sp_add_log_shipping_primary_secondary

```
:connect primaryserver\prosqladmin

EXEC master.dbo.sp_add_log_shipping_primary_secondary
                @primary_database = N'Chapter14'
                ,@secondary_server = N'drserver\prosqldr'
                ,@secondary_database = N'Chapter14'
```

We now need to configure our DR server. The first task in this process is to run the
sp_add_log_shipping_secondary_primary system stored procedure. This procedure creates the SQL
Server Agent jobs that copy the transaction logs to the secondary server and restore them. It also configures
monitoring. The parameters accepted by this stored procedure are detailed in Table 14-3.

Table 14-3. *sp_add_log_shipping_secondary_primary Parameters*

Parameter	Description
@primary_server	The server/instance name of the primary server.
@primary_database	The name of the primary database.
@backup_source_directory	The folder that the log backups are copied from.
@backup_destination_directory	The folder that the log backups are copied to.
@copy_job_name	The name that is given to the SQL Server Agent job used to copy the transaction logs.
@restore_job_name	The name that is given to the SQL Server Agent job used to restore the transaction logs.
@file_retention_period	The duration for which log backup history should be retained, specified in minutes.
@monitor_server	The server/instance name of the monitor server.
@monitor_server_security_mode	The authentication mode to be use to connect to the monitor server. 0 is SQL authentication and 1 is Windows authentication.
@monitor_server_login	The account used to connect to the monitor server (only use if SQL authentication is specified).
@monitor_server_password	The password of the account used to connect to the monitor server (only use if SQL authentication is specified).
@copy_job_id	OUTPUT parameter that specifies the GUID of the job that has been created to copy the transaction logs.
@restore_job_id	OUTPUT parameter that specifies the GUID of the job that has been created to restore the transaction logs.
@secondary_id	An OUTPUT parameter that specifies the ID of secondary database.

Listing 14-4 demonstrates how we can use the sp_add_log_shipping_secondary_primary stored
procedure to configure our DRSERVER\PROSQLDR instance as a secondary server in our Log Shipping topology.
The script connects explicitly to the DR instance, so we should run it in SQL command mode. Just as when
we set up the primary server, we use output parameters to pass to the SQL Server Agent stored procedures,
to create the job schedules and enable the jobs. SQL Server Agent, including its stored procedures, is
discussed in Chapter 21.

Listing 14-4. Sp_add_log_shipping_secondary_primary

```
:connect drserver\prosqldr

DECLARE @LS_Secondary__CopyJobId          AS uniqueidentifier
DECLARE @LS_Secondary__RestoreJobId       AS uniqueidentifier
DECLARE @LS_SecondaryCopyJobScheduleID       AS int
DECLARE @LS_SecondaryRestoreJobScheduleID       AS int


--Configure the secondary server

EXEC master.dbo.sp_add_log_shipping_secondary_primary
                @primary_server = N'primaryserver\prosqladmin'
                primary_database = N'Chapter14'
                ,@backup_source_directory = N'\\primaryserver\logshippingprimary'
                ,@backup_destination_directory = N'\\drserver\logshippingdr'
                ,@copy_job_name = N'LSCopy_primaryserver\prosqladmin_Chapter14'
                ,@restore_job_name = N'LSRestore_primaryserver\prosqladmin_Chapter14'
                ,@file_retention_period = 2880
                ,@monitor_server = N'monitorserver.prosqladmin.com\prosqlmonitor'
                ,@monitor_server_security_mode = 1
                ,@copy_job_id = @LS_Secondary__CopyJobId OUTPUT
                ,@restore_job_id = @LS_Secondary__RestoreJobId OUTPUT ;

--Create the schedule for the copy job

EXEC msdb.dbo.sp_add_schedule
                @schedule_name =N'DefaultCopyJobSchedule'
                ,@enabled = 1
                ,@freq_type = 4
                ,@freq_interval = 1
                ,@freq_subday_type = 4
                ,@freq_subday_interval = 15
                ,@freq_recurrence_factor = 0
                ,@active_start_date = 20150201
                ,@active_end_date = 99991231
                ,@active_start_time = 0
                ,@active_end_time = 235900
                ,@schedule_id = @LS_SecondaryCopyJobScheduleID OUTPUT ;

--Attach the schedule to the copy job

EXEC msdb.dbo.sp_attach_schedule
                @job_id = @LS_Secondary__CopyJobId
                ,@schedule_id = @LS_SecondaryCopyJobScheduleID  ;

--Create the job schedule for the restore job

EXEC msdb.dbo.sp_add_schedule
                @schedule_name =N'DefaultRestoreJobSchedule'
                ,@enabled = 1
                ,@freq_type = 4
```

```
                ,@freq_interval = 1
                ,@freq_subday_type = 4
                ,@freq_subday_interval = 15
                ,@freq_recurrence_factor = 0
                ,@active_start_date = 20150201
                ,@active_end_date = 99991231
                ,@active_start_time = 0
                ,@active_end_time = 235900
                ,@schedule_id = @LS_SecondaryRestoreJobScheduleID OUTPUT ;

--Attch the schedule to the restore job

EXEC msdb.dbo.sp_attach_schedule
                @job_id = @LS_Secondary__RestoreJobId
                ,@schedule_id = @LS_SecondaryRestoreJobScheduleID  ;

--Enable the jobs

EXEC msdb.dbo.sp_update_job
                @job_id = @LS_Secondary__CopyJobId
                ,@enabled = 1 ;

EXEC msdb.dbo.sp_update_job
                @job_id = @LS_Secondary__RestoreJobId
                ,@enabled = 1 ;
```

Our next step is to configure the secondary database. We can perform this task by using the sp_add_log_shipping_secondary_database stored procedure. The parameters accepted by this procedure are detailed in Table 14-4.

Table 14-4. *sp_add_log_shipping_secondary_database Paremeters*

Parameter	Description
@secondary_database	The name of the secondary database.
@primary_server	The server/instance of the primary server.
@primary_database	The name of the primary database.
@restore_delay	Specifies the load delay, in minutes.
@restore_all	When set to 1, the restore job restores all available log backups. When set to 0, the restore job only applies a single log backup.
@restore_mode	Specifies the backup mode for the restore job to use. 1 means STANDBY and 0 means NORECOVERY.
@disconnect_users	Determines if users should be disconnected from the database while transaction log backups are being applied. 1 means that they are and 0 means that they are not. Only applies when restoring logs in STANDBY mode.

(continued)

Table 14-4. (*continued*)

Parameter	Description
@block_size	Specifies the block size for the backup device, in bytes.
@buffer_count	Specifies the total number of memory buffers that can be used by a restore operation.
@max_transfer_size	Specifies the maximum size of the request that can be sent to the backup device, in bytes.
@restore_threshold	The amount of time that can elapse, without a restore being applied, before an alert is generated; specified in minutes.
@threshold_alert	The alert to be raised if the restore threshold is exceeded.
@threshold_alert_enabled	Specifies if the alert is enabled. 1 means that it is enabled and 0 means that it is disabled.
@history_retention_period	The retention period of the restore history, specified in minutes.
@Ignoreremotemonitor	An undocumented parameter that partially controls how the internal log shipping database journal is updated.

Listing 14-5 demonstrates how we can use the sp_add_log_shipping_secondary_database to configure our secondary database for log shipping. Since we are explicitly connecting to the DRSERVER\PROSQLDR instance, the script should run in SQLCMD mode.

Listing 14-5. Sp_add_log_shipping_secondary_database

```
:connect drserver\prosqldr

EXEC master.dbo.sp_add_log_shipping_secondary_database
                @secondary_database = N'Chapter14'
                ,@primary_server = N'primaryserver\prosqladmin'
                ,@primary_database = N'Chapter14'
                ,@restore_delay = 10
                ,@restore_mode = 0
                ,@disconnect_users = 0
                ,@restore_threshold = 30
                ,@threshold_alert_enabled = 1
                ,@history_retention_period = 5760
                ,@ignoreremotemonitor = 1
```

The final task is to synchronize the monitor server and the DR server. We do this by using the (surprisingly) undocumented stored procedure sp_processlogshippingmonitorsecondary. The parameters accepted by this procedure are detailed in Table 14-5.

Table 14-5. *sp_processlogshippingmonitorsecondary*

Parameter	Description
@mode	The recovery mode to use for the database. 0 indicates NORECOVERY and 1 indicates STANDBY.
@secondary_server	The server/instance of the secondary server.
@secondary_database	The name of the secondary database.
@secondary_id	The ID of the secondary server.
@primary_server	The server/instance of the primary server.
@monitor_server	The server/instance of the monitor server.
@monitor_server_security_mode	The authentication mode used to connect to the monitor server.
@primary_database	The name of the primary database.
@restore_threshold	The amount of time that can elapse without a restore being applied before an alert is triggered; specified in minutes.
@threshold_alert	The alert that fires if the alert restore threshold is exceeded.
@threshold_alert_enabled	Specifies if the alert is enabled or disabled.
@last_coppied_file	The file name of the last log backup to be copied to the secondary server.
@last_coppied_date	The date and time of the last time a log was copied to the secondary server.
@last_coppied_date_utc	The date and time of the last time a log was copied to the secondary server, converted to UTC (Coordinated Universal Time).
@last_restored_file	The file name of the last transaction log backup to be restored on the secondary server.
@last_restored_date	The date and time of the last time a log was restored on the secondary server.
@last_restored_date_utc	The date and time of the last time a log was restored on the secondary server, converted to UTC.
@last_restored_latency	The elapsed time between the last log backup on the primary and its corresponding restore operation completing on the secondary.
@history_rentention_period	The duration that the history is retained, specified in minutes.

The script in Listing 14-6 demonstrates how to use the sp_processlogshippingmonitorsecondary stored procedure to synchronize the information between our DR server and our monitor server. We should run the script against the monitor server, and since we are connecting explicitly to the MONITORSERVER\ PROSQLMONITOR instance, we should run the script in SQLCMD mode.

Listing 14-6. Sp_ processlogshippingmonitorsecondary

```
:connect monitorserver\prosqlmonitor

EXEC msdb.dbo.sp_processlogshippingmonitorsecondary
            @mode = 1
            ,@secondary_server = N'drserver\prosqldr'
```

```
,@secondary_database = N'Chapter14'
,@secondary_id = N''
,@primary_server = N'primaryserver\prosqladmin'
,@primary_database = N'Chapter14'
,@restore_threshold = 30
,@threshold_alert = 14420
,@threshold_alert_enabled = 1
,@history_retention_period = 5760
,@monitor_server = N'monitorserver.prosqladmin.com\prosqlmonitor'
,@monitor_server_security_mode = 1
```

Log Shipping Maintenance

After you configure log shipping, you still have ongoing maintenance tasks to perform, such as failing over to the secondary server, if you need to, and switching the primary and secondary roles. These topics are discussed in the following sections. We also discuss how to use the monitor server to monitor the log shipping environment.

Failing Over Log Shipping

If your primary server has an issue, or your primary site fails, you need to fail over to your secondary server. To do this, first back up the tail end of the log. We discuss this process fully in Chapter 15, but the process essentially involves backing up the transaction log without truncating it and with NORECOVERY. This stops users from being able to connect to the database, therefore avoiding any further data loss. Obviously, this is only possible if the primary database is accessible. You can perform this action for the Chapter14 database by using the script in Listing 14-7.

Listing 14-7. Backing Up the Tail End of the Log

```
BACKUP LOG Chapter14
TO  DISK = N'c:\logshippingprimary\Chapter14_tail.trn'
WITH  NO_TRUNCATE , NAME = N'Chapter14-Full Database Backup', NORECOVERY
GO
```

The next step is to manually copy the tail end of the log and any other logs that have not yet been copied to the secondary server. Once this is complete, you need to manually restore the outstanding transaction log backups to the secondary server, in sequence. You need to apply the backups with NORECOVERY until the final backup is reached. This final backup is applied with RECOVERY. This causes any uncommitted transactions to be rolled back and the database to be brought online. Listing 14-8 demonstrates applying the final two transaction logs to the secondary database.

Listing 14-8. Applying Transaction Logs

```
--Restore the first transaction log

RESTORE LOG Chapter14
FROM  DISK = N'C:\LogShippingDR\Chapter14.trn'
WITH  FILE = 1,  NORECOVERY,  STATS = 10 ;
GO
```

```
--Restore the tail end of the log

RESTORE LOG Chapter14
FROM  DISK = N'C:\LogShippingDR\Chapter14_tail.trn'
WITH  FILE = 1,  RECOVERY, STATS = 10 ;
GO
```

Switching Roles

After you have failed over log shipping to the secondary server, you may want to swap the server roles so that the secondary that you failed over to becomes the new primary server and the original primary server becomes the secondary. In order to achieve this, first you need to disable the backup job on the primary server and the copy and restore jobs on the secondary server. We can perform this task for our Log Shipping topology by using the script in Listing 14-9. Because we are connecting to multiple servers, we need to run this script in SQLCMD mode.

Listing 14-9. Disabling Log Shipping Jobs

```
:connect primaryserver\prosqladmin

USE [msdb]
GO

--Disable backup job

EXEC msdb.dbo.sp_update_job @job_name = 'LSBackup_Chapter14',
               @enabled=0 ;
GO

:connect drserver\prosqldr

USE [msdb]
GO

--Diable copy job

EXEC msdb.dbo.sp_update_job @job_name='LSCopy_primaryserver\prosqladmin_Chapter14',
               @enabled=0 ;
GO

--Disable restore job

EXEC msdb.dbo.sp_update_job @job_name='LSRestore_primaryserver\prosqladmin_Chapter14',
               @enabled=0 ;
GO
```

The next step is to reconfigure log shipping on the new primary server. When you do this, configure the following:

- Ensure that you use the same backup share that you used for the original primary server.

- Ensure that when you add the secondary database, you specify the database that was originally the primary database.

- Specify the synchronization No, The Secondary Database Is Initialized option.

The script in Listing 14-10, performs this action for our new secondary server. Since we are connecting to multiple servers, we should run the script in SQLCMD mode.

Listing 14-10. Reconfiguring Log Shipping

```
:connect drserver\prosqldr

DECLARE @LS_BackupJobId AS uniqueidentifier
DECLARE @SP_Add_RetCode As int
DECLARE @LS_BackUpScheduleID    AS int

EXEC @SP_Add_RetCode = master.dbo.sp_add_log_shipping_primary_database
                @database = N'Chapter14'
                ,@backup_directory = N'\\primaryserver\logshippingprimary'
                ,@backup_share = N'\\primaryserver\logshippingprimary'
                ,@backup_job_name = N'LSBackup_Chapter14'
                ,@backup_retention_period = 2880
                ,@backup_compression = 2
                ,@backup_threshold = 60
                ,@threshold_alert_enabled = 1
                ,@history_retention_period = 5760
                ,@backup_job_id = @LS_BackupJobId OUTPUT
                ,@overwrite = 1

EXEC msdb.dbo.sp_add_schedule
                @schedule_name =N'LSBackupSchedule_DRSERVER\PROSQLDR1'
                ,@enabled = 1
                ,@freq_type = 4
                ,@freq_interval = 1
                ,@freq_subday_type = 4
                ,@freq_subday_interval = 5
                ,@freq_recurrence_factor = 0
                ,@active_start_date = 20150203
                ,@active_end_date = 99991231
                ,@active_start_time = 0
                ,@active_end_time = 235900
                ,@schedule_id = @LS_BackUpScheduleID OUTPUT

EXEC msdb.dbo.sp_attach_schedule
                @job_id = @LS_BackupJobId
                ,@schedule_id = @LS_BackUpScheduleID
```

```
EXEC msdb.dbo.sp_update_job
            @job_id = @LS_BackupJobId
            ,@enabled = 1

EXEC master.dbo.sp_add_log_shipping_primary_secondary
            @primary_database = N'Chapter14'
            ,@secondary_server = N'primaryserver\prosqladmin'
            ,@secondary_database = N'Chapter14'
            ,@overwrite = 1

:connect primaryserver\prosqladmin

DECLARE @LS_Secondary__CopyJobId        AS uniqueidentifier
DECLARE @LS_Secondary__RestoreJobId       AS uniqueidentifier
DECLARE @LS_Add_RetCode         As int
DECLARE @LS_SecondaryCopyJobScheduleID         AS int
DECLARE @LS_SecondaryRestoreJobScheduleID         AS int

EXEC @LS_Add_RetCode = master.dbo.sp_add_log_shipping_secondary_primary
            @primary_server = N'DRSERVER\PROSQLDR'
            ,@primary_database = N'Chapter14'
            ,@backup_source_directory = N'\\primaryserver\logshippingprimary'
            ,@backup_destination_directory = N'\\primaryserver\logshippingprimary'
            ,@copy_job_name = N'LSCopy_DRSERVER\PROSQLDR_Chapter14'
            ,@restore_job_name = N'LSRestore_DRSERVER\PROSQLDR_Chapter14'
            ,@file_retention_period = 2880
            ,@overwrite = 1
            ,@copy_job_id = @LS_Secondary__CopyJobId OUTPUT
            ,@restore_job_id = @LS_Secondary__RestoreJobId OUTPUT

EXEC msdb.dbo.sp_add_schedule
            @schedule_name =N'DefaultCopyJobSchedule'
            ,@enabled = 1
            ,@freq_type = 4
            ,@freq_interval = 1
            ,@freq_subday_type = 4
            ,@freq_subday_interval = 5
            ,@freq_recurrence_factor = 0
            ,@active_start_date = 20150203
            ,@active_end_date = 99991231
            ,@active_start_time = 0
            ,@active_end_time = 235900
            ,@schedule_id = @LS_SecondaryCopyJobScheduleID OUTPUT

EXEC msdb.dbo.sp_attach_schedule
            @job_id = @LS_Secondary__CopyJobId
            ,@schedule_id = @LS_SecondaryCopyJobScheduleID

EXEC msdb.dbo.sp_add_schedule
            @schedule_name =N'DefaultRestoreJobSchedule'
            ,@enabled = 1
            ,@freq_type = 4
```

```
                 ,@freq_interval = 1
                 ,@freq_subday_type = 4
                 ,@freq_subday_interval = 5
                 ,@freq_recurrence_factor = 0
                 ,@active_start_date = 20150203
                 ,@active_end_date = 99991231
                 ,@active_start_time = 0
                 ,@active_end_time = 235900
                 ,@schedule_id = @LS_SecondaryRestoreJobScheduleID OUTPUT

EXEC msdb.dbo.sp_attach_schedule
                 @job_id = @LS_Secondary__RestoreJobId ,
                 ,@schedule_id = @LS_SecondaryRestoreJobScheduleID

EXEC master.dbo.sp_add_log_shipping_secondary_database
                 @secondary_database = N'Chapter14'
                 ,@primary_server = N'DRSERVER\PROSQLDR'
                 ,@primary_database = N'Chapter14'
                 ,@restore_delay = 10
                 ,@restore_mode = 0
                 ,@disconnect_users       = 0
                 ,@restore_threshold = 30
                 ,@threshold_alert_enabled = 1
                 ,@history_retention_period    = 5760
                 ,@overwrite = 1

EXEC msdb.dbo.sp_update_job
                 @job_id = @LS_Secondary__CopyJobId
                 ,@enabled = 1

EXEC msdb.dbo.sp_update_job
                 @job_id = @LS_Secondary__RestoreJobId
                 ,@enabled = 1
```

The final step is to reconfigure monitoring so it correctly monitors our new configuration. We can achieve this for our log shipping environment by using the script in Listing 14-11. This script connects to both the primary and secondary servers, so we should run it in SQLCMD mode.

Listing 14-11. Reconfiguring Monitoring

```
:connect drserver\prosqldr

USE msdb
GO

EXEC master.dbo.sp_change_log_shipping_secondary_database
        @secondary_database = N'database_name',
        @threshold_alert_enabled = 0 ;
GO

:connect primaryserver\prosqladmin
```

```
USE msdb
GO

EXEC master.dbo.sp_change_log_shipping_primary_database
        @database=N'database_name',
        @threshold_alert_enabled = 0 ;
GO
```

Because we have now created the backup, copy, and restore jobs on both servers, switching the roles after subsequent failovers is much more straight forward. From now on, after we have failed over, we can switch roles by simply disabling the backup job on the original primary server and the copy and restore jobs on the secondary server, and then enabling the backup job on the new primary server and the copy and restore jobs on the new secondary server.

Monitoring

The most important aspect of monitoring your Log Shipping topology is ensuring that the backups are occurring on the primary and being restored on the secondary. For this reason, when we configure log shipping in this chapter, we tweak the acceptable thresholds for backups and restores, and Server Agent Alerts are created on the monitor server. Before these alerts are useful, however, we need to configure them with an operator to notify.

On the monitor server, we have configured two alerts. The first is called Log Shipping Primary Server Alert, and when you view the General tab of this alert's properties, you see that it is configured to respond to Error 14420, as shown in Figure 14-11. Error 14420 indicates that a backup has not been taken of the primary database within the defined threshold.

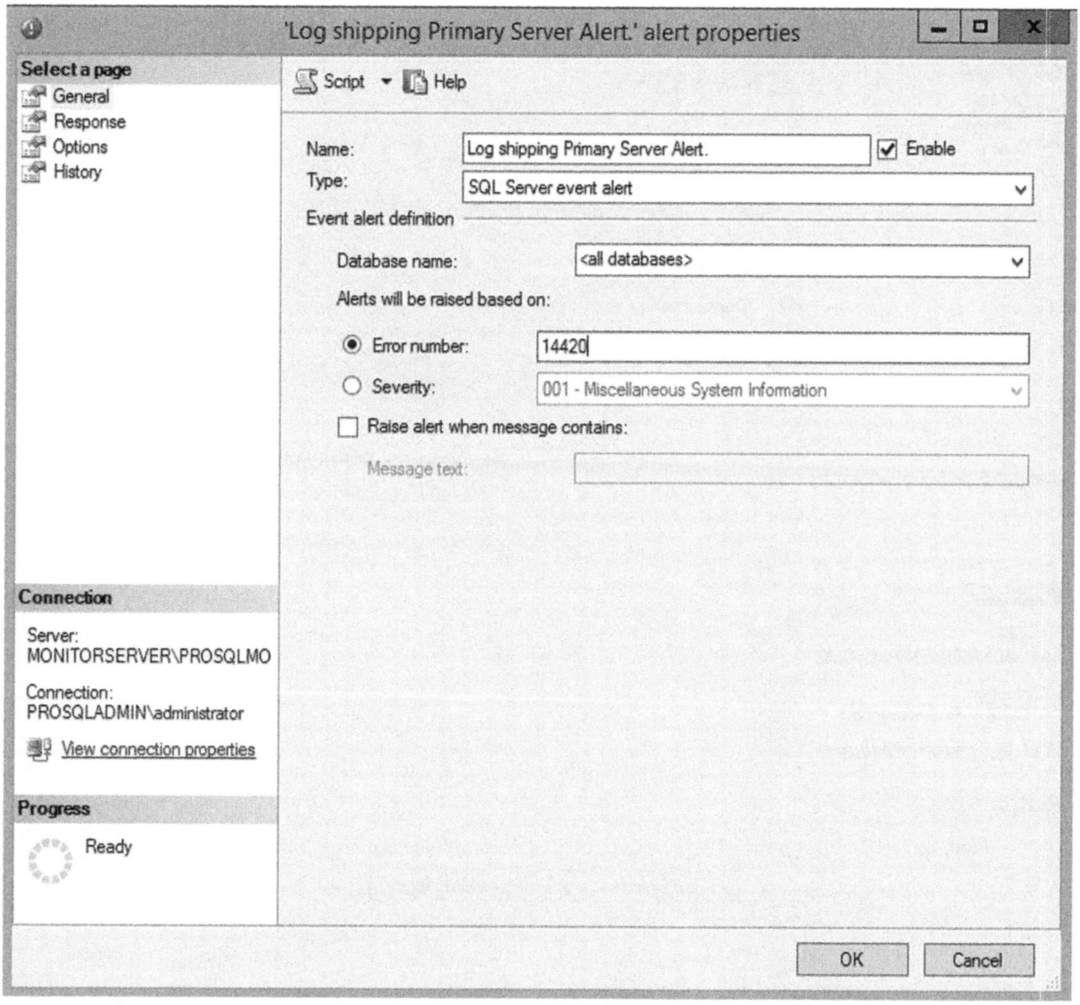

Figure 14-11. *The General tab*

On the Response tab, displayed in Figure 14-12, we need to configure an operator to receive the alerts. You can either use the New Operator button to configure a new operator, or as in our case, simply select the appropriate notification channel for the appropriate operator(s) in the list. You can also elect to run a SQL Server Agent job, which attempts to remediate the condition.

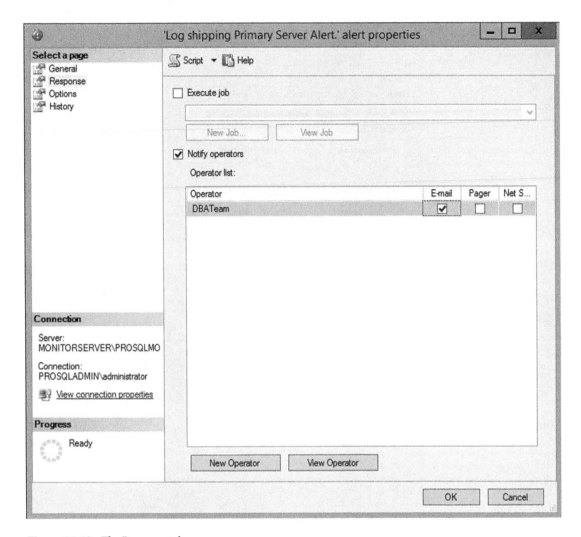

Figure 14-12. *The Response tab*

You should configure the Log Shipping Secondary Server Alert in the same way you configured the Log Shipping Primary Server Alert. The secondary server alert works in the same way, except that it is monitoring for Error 14421 instead of 14420. Error 14421 indicates that a transaction log has not been restored to the secondary server within the threshold period.

The log shipping report can be run from SQL Server Management Studio, and when you run it on the monitor server, it displays the status of the primary server and each secondary server. When run on the primary server, it shows the status of each database based on the backup jobs and includes a line for each secondary. When run on the DR server, it shows the status of each database based on the restore jobs. You can access the report by invoking the context menu of the instance and drilling through Reports | Standard Reports, before selecting the Transaction Log Shipping Status report.

Figure 14-13 illustrates the report when run against the primary server. You can see that the status of the backup jobs has been set to Alert and the text has been highlighted in red. This indicates that the threshold for a successful backup has been breached on the primary database. In our case, we simulated this by disabling the backup job. We could have obtained the same information by using the sp_help_log_shipping_monitor stored procedure.

Transaction Log Shipping Status
PRIMARYSERVER\PROSQLADMIN

Microsoft SQL Server 2014

This report shows the status of log shipping configurations for which this server instance is a primary, secondary, or monitor.

		Backup			Copy		Restore		
Status	Primary Database – Secondary Database	Time Since Last	Threshold	Alert Enabled	Time Since Last	Time Since Last	Latency of Last File	Threshold	Alert Enabled
Alert	[PRIMARYSERVER\PROSQLADMIN].[Chapter14]	190 min	60 min	True					
	– [DRSERVER\PROSQLDR].[Chapter14]								

■ - data in this column is not available or not applicable for this server instance.

Figure 14-13. *The Log Shipping report*

Summary

Log shipping is a technology that you can use to implement DR and offload reporting to secondary servers. It synchronizes data by backing up the transaction log of the primary database, copying it to a secondary server, and then restoring it. If the log is restored with STANDBY, then uncommitted transactions are stored in a Transaction Undo File and you can reapply them before subsequent backups. This means that you can bring the database online in read-only mode for reporting. If the logs are restored with NORECOVERY, however, then the servers are ready for a DR invocation, but the databases are in an offline state.

Failing over a database to a secondary server involves backing up the tail end of the transaction log and then applying any outstanding log backups to the secondary database, before finally bringing the database online by issuing the final restore with RECOVERY. If you wish to switch the server roles, then you need to disable the current log shipping jobs, reconfigure log shipping so that the secondary server is now the primary, and then reconfigure monitoring. After subsequent failovers, however, switching the roles becomes easier, because you are able to simply disable and enable the appropriate SQL Server Agent jobs used by log shipping.

To monitor the health of your Log Shipping topology, you should configure the log shipping alerts and add an operator who will be notified if the alert fires. The alert for the primary server is monitoring for Error 14420, which means that the backup threshold has been exceeded. The alert for the secondary server(s) monitors for Error 14421, which indicates that the restore threshold has been exceeded.

A log shipping report is available; it returns data about the primary databases, the secondary databases, or all servers in the topology, depending on whether it is invoked from the primary server, the secondary server, or the monitor server, respectively. The same information can be obtained from the sp_help_log_shipping_monitor stored procedure.

CHAPTER 15

■ ■ ■

Backups and Restores

Backing up a database is one of the most important tasks that a DBA can perform. Therefore, after discussing the principles of backups, we look at some of the backup strategies that you can implement for SQL Server databases. We then discuss how to perform the backup of a database before we finally look in-depth at restoring it, including restoring to a point in time, restoring individual files and pages, and performing piecemeal restores.

Backup Fundamentals

Depending on the recovery model you are using, you can take three types of backup within SQL Server: full, differential, and log. We discuss the recovery models in addition to each of the backup types in the following sections.

Recovery Models

As discussed in Chapter 5, you can configure a database in one of three recovery models: SIMPLE, FULL, and BULK LOGGED. These models are discussed in the following sections.

SIMPLE Recovery Model

When configured in SIMPLE recovery model, the transaction log (or to be more specific, VLFs [Virtual Log Files] within the transaction log that contain transactions that are no longer required) is truncated after each checkpoint operation. This means that usually you do not have to administer the transaction log. However, it also means that you can't take transaction log backups.

The SIMPLE recovery model can increase performance, for some operations, because transactions are minimally logged. Operations that can benefit from minimal logging are as follows:

- Bulk imports
- SELECT INTO
- UPDATE statements against large data types that use the .WRITE clause
- WRITETEXT
- UPDATETEXT
- Index creation
- Index rebuilds

The main disadvantage of the SIMPLE recovery model is that it is not possible to recover to a specific point in time; you can only restore to the end of a full backup. This disadvantage is amplified by the fact that full backups can have a performance impact, so you are unlikely to be able to take them as frequently as you would take a transaction log backup without causing an impact to users. Another disadvantage is that the SIMPLE recovery model is incompatible with some SQL Server HA/DR features, namely:

- AlwaysOn Availability Groups

- Database mirroring

- Log shipping

Therefore, in production environments, the most appropriate way to use the SIMPLE recovery model is for large data warehouse style applications where you have a nightly ETL load, followed by read-only reporting for the rest of the day. This is because this model provides the benefit of minimally logged transactions, while at the same time, it does not have an impact on recovery, since you can take a full backup after the nightly ETL run.

FULL Recovery Model

When a database is configured in FULL recovery model, the log truncation does not occur after a CHECKPOINT operation. Instead, it occurs after a transaction log backup, as long as a CHECKPOINT operation has occurred since the previous transaction log backup. This means that you must schedule transaction log backups to run on a frequent basis. Failing to do so not only leaves your database at risk of being unrecoverable in the event of a failure, but it also means that your transaction log continues to grow until it runs out of space and a 9002 error is thrown.

When a database is in FULL recovery model, many factors can cause the VLFs within a transaction log not to be truncated. This is known as *delayed truncation*. You can find the last reason for delayed truncation to occur in the log_reuse_wait_desc column of sys.databases; a full list of reasons for delayed truncation appears in Chapter 5.

The main advantage of the FULL recovery model is that point-in-time recovery is possible, which means that you can restore your database to a point in the middle of a transaction log backup, as opposed to only being able to restore it to the end of a backup. Point-in-time recovery is discussed in detail later in this chapter. Additionally, FULL recovery model is compatible with all SQL Server functionality. It is usually the best choice of recovery model for production databases.

■ **Tip**   If you switch from SIMPLE recovery model to FULL recovery model, you are not actually in FULL recovery model until after you take a transaction log backup. Therefore, make sure to back up your transaction log immediately.

BULK LOGGED Recovery Model

The BULK LOGGED recovery model is designed to be used on a short-term basis, while a bulk import operation takes place. The idea is that your normal model of operations is to use FULL recovery model, and then temporarily switch to the BULK LOGGED recovery model just before a bulk import takes place; you then switch back to FULL recovery model when the import completes. This may give you a performance benefit and also stop the transaction log from filling up, since bulk import operations are minimally logged.

Immediately before you switch to the BULK LOGGED recovery model, and immediately after you switch back to FULL recovery model, it is good practice to take a transaction log backup. This is because you cannot use any transaction log backups that contain minimally logged transactions for point-in-time recovery.

For the same reason, it is also good practice to safe-state your application before you switch to the BULK LOGGED recovery model. You normally achieve this by disabling any logins, except for the login that performs the bulk import and logins that are administrators, to ensure that no other data modifications take place. You should also ensure that the data you are importing is recoverable by a means other than a restore. Following these rules mitigates the risk of data loss in the event of a disaster.

Although the minimally logged inserts keep the transaction log small and reduce the amount of IO to the log, during the bulk import, the transaction log backup is more expensive than it is in FULL recovery model in terms of IO. This is because when you back up a transaction log that contains minimally logged transactions, SQL Server also backs up any data extents, which contain pages that have been altered using minimally logged transactions. SQL Server keeps track of these pages by using bitmap pages, called ML (minimally logged) pages. ML pages occur once in every 64,000 extents and use a flag to indicate if each extent in the corresponding block of extents contains minimally logged pages.

■ **Caution** BULK LOGGED recovery model may not be faster than FULL recovery model for bulk imports unless you have a very fast IO subsystem. This is because the BULK LOGGED recovery model forces data pages updated with minimally logged pages to flush to disk as soon as the operation completes instead of waiting for a checkpoint operation.

Changing the Recovery Model

Before we show you how to change the recovery model of a database, let's first create the Chapter15 database, which we use for demonstrations in this chapter. You can create this database using the script in Listing 15-1.

Listing 15-1. Creating the Chapter15 Database

```
CREATE DATABASE Chapter15
 ON  PRIMARY
( NAME = 'Chapter15', FILENAME = 'C:\MSSQL\DATA\Chapter15.mdf'),
 FILEGROUP FileGroupA
( NAME = 'Chapter15FileA', FILENAME = 'C:\MSSQL\DATA\Chapter15FileA.ndf' ),
 FILEGROUP FileGroupB
( NAME = 'Chapter15FileB', FILENAME = 'C:\MSSQL\DATA\Chapter15FileB.ndf' )
 LOG ON
( NAME = 'Chapter15_log', FILENAME = 'C:\MSSQL\DATA\Chapter15_log.ldf' ) ;
GO


ALTER DATABASE [Chapter15] SET RECOVERY FULL ;
GO


USE Chapter15
GO


CREATE TABLE dbo.Contacts
(
ContactID       INT        NOT NULL       IDENTITY       PRIMARY KEY,
FirstName       NVARCHAR(30),
LastName        NVARCHAR(30),
AddressID       INT
) ON FileGroupA ;
```

```
CREATE TABLE dbo.Addresses
(
AddressID        INT        NOT NULL        IDENTITY        PRIMARY KEY,
AddressLine1        NVARCHAR(50),
AddressLine2        NVARCHAR(50),
AddressLine3        NVARCHAR(50),
PostCode        NCHAR(8)
) ON FileGroupB ;
```

You can change the recovery model of a database from SQL Server Management Studio (SSMS) by selecting Properties from the context menu of the database and navigating to the Options page, as illustrated in Figure 15-1. You can then select the appropriate recovery model from the Recovery Model drop-down list.

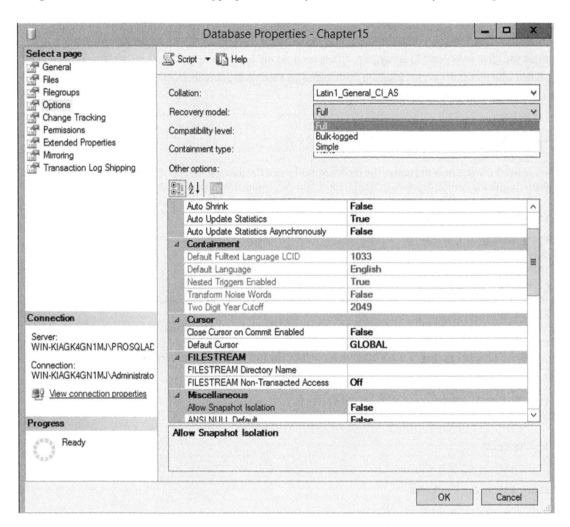

Figure 15-1. *The Options tab*

We can also use the script in Listing 15-2 to switch our Chapter15 database from the FULL recovery model to the SIMPLE recovery model and then back again.

Listing 15-2. Switching Recovery Models

```
ALTER DATABASE Chapter15 SET RECOVERY SIMPLE ;
GO

ALTER DATABASE Chapter15 SET RECOVERY FULL ;
GO
```

■ **Tip**   After changing the recovery model, refresh the database in Object Explorer to ensure that the correct recovery model displays.

Backup Types

You can take three types of backup in SQL Server: full, differential, and log. We discuss these backup types in the following sections.

Full Backup

You can take a full backup in any recovery model. When you issue a backup command, SQL Server first issues a CHECKPOINT, which causes any dirty pages to be written to disk. It then backs up every page within the database (this is known as the *data read phase*) before it finally backs up enough of the transaction log (this is known as the *log read phase*) to be able to guarantee transactional consistency. This ensures that you are able to restore your database to the most recent point, including any transactions that are committed during the data read phase of the backup.

Differential Backup

A differential backup backs up every page in the database that has been modified since the last full backup. SQL Server keeps track of these pages by using bitmap pages called DIFF pages, which occur once in every 64,000 extents. These pages use flags to indicate if each extent in their corresponding block of extents contains pages that have been updated since the last full backup.

The cumulative nature of differential backups means that your restore chain only ever needs to include one differential backup—the latest one. Only ever needing to restore one differential backup is very useful if there is a significant time lapse between full backups, but log backups are taken very frequently, because restoring the last differential can drastically decrease the number of transaction log backups you need to restore.

Log Backup

A transaction log backup can only be taken in the FULL or BULK LOGGED recovery models. When a transaction log backup is issued in the FULL recovery model, it backs up all transaction log records since the last backup. When it is performed in the BULK LOGGED recovery model, it also backs up any pages that include minimally logged transactions. When the backup is complete, SQL Server truncates VLFs within the transaction log until the first active VLF is reached.

Transaction log backups are especially important on databases that support OLTP (online transaction processing), since they allow a point-in-time recovery to the point immediately before the disaster occurred. They are also the least resource-intensive type of backup, meaning that you can perform them more frequently than you can perform a full or differential backup without having a significant impact on database performance.

Backup Media

Databases can be backed up to disk, tape, or URL. Tape backups are deprecated however, so you should avoid using them; their support will be removed in a future version of SQL Server. The terminology surrounding backup media consists of backup devices, logical backup devices, media sets, media families, and backup sets. The structure of a media set is depicted in Figure 15-2, and the concepts are discussed in the following sections.

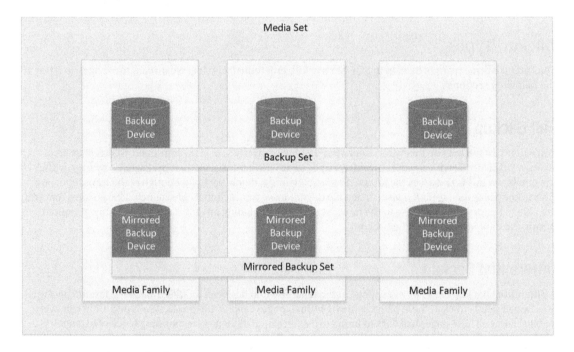

Figure 15-2. *Backup media diagram*

Backup Device

A *backup device* is a physical file on disk, a tape, or a Windows Azure Blob. When the device is a disk, the disk can reside locally on the server or on a backup share specified by a URL. A media set can contain a maximum of 64 backup devices, and data can be striped across the backup devices and can also be mirrored. In Figure 15-2, there are six backup devices, split into three mirrored pairs. This means that the backup set is striped across three of the devices and then mirrored to the other three.

■ **Note**   Windows Azure Blobs are discussed in Chapter 25.

Striping the backup can be useful for a large database, because doing so allows you to place each device on a different drive array to increase throughput. It can also pose administrative challenges, however; if one of the disks in the devices in the stripe becomes unavailable, you are unable to restore your backup. You can mitigate this by using a mirror. When you use a mirror, the contents of each device are duplicated to an additional device for redundancy. If one backup device in a media set is mirrored, then all devices within the media set must be mirrored. Each backup device or mirrored set of backup devices is known as a *media family*. Each device can have up to four mirrors.

Each backup device within a media set must be all disk or all tape. If they are mirrored, then the mirror devices must have similar properties; otherwise an error is thrown. For this reason, Microsoft recommends using the same make and model of device for mirrors.

It is also possible to create logical backup devices, which abstract a physical backup device. Using logical devices can simplify administration, especially if you are planning to use many backup devices in the same physical location. A *logical backup device* is an instance-level object and can be created in SSMS by choosing New Backup Device from the context menu of Server Objects | Backup Devices; this causes the Backup Device dialog box to be displayed, as illustrated in Figure 15-3.

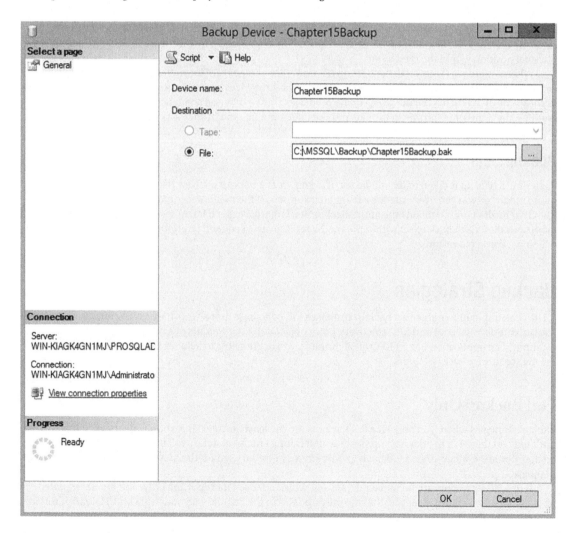

Figure 15-3. *Backup Device dialog box*

Alternatively, you can create the same logical backup device via T-SQL using the `sp_addumpdevice` system stored procedure. The command in Listing 15-3 uses the `sp_addumpdevice` procedure to create the `Chapter15Backup` logical backup device. In this example, we use the `@devtype` parameter to pass in the type of the device, in our case, disk. We then pass the abstracted name of the device into the `@logicalname` parameter and the physical file into the `@physicalname` parameter.

Listing 15-3. Creating a Logical Backup Device

```
EXEC sp_addumpdevice   @devtype = 'disk',
                       @logicalname = 'Chapter15Backup',
                       @physicalname = 'C:\MSSQL\Backup\Chapter15Backup.bak' ;
GO
```

Media Sets

A media set contains the backup devices to which the backup is written. Each media family within a media set is assigned a sequential number based upon their position in the media set. This is called the *family sequence number*. Additionally, each physical device is allocated a *physical sequence number* to identify its physical position within the media set.

When a media set is created, the backup devices (files or tapes) are formatted, and a media header is written to each device. This media header remains until the devices are formatted and contains details, such as the name of the media set, the GUID of the media set, the GUIDs and sequence numbers of the media families, the number of mirrors in the set, and the date/time that the header was written.

Backup Sets

Each time a backup is taken to the media set, it is known as a *backup set*. New backup sets can be appended to the media, or you can overwrite the existing backup sets. If the media set contains only one media family, then that media family contains the entire backup set. Otherwise, the backup set is distributed across the media families. Each backup set within the media set is given a sequential number; this allows you to select which backup set to restore.

Backup Strategies

A DBA can implement numerous backup strategies for a database, but always base your strategy on the RTO (recovery time objective) and RPO (recovery point objective) requirements of a data-tier application. For example, if an application has an RPO of 60 minutes, you are not able to achieve this goal if you only back up the database once every 24 hours.

Full Backup Only

Backup strategies where you only take full backups are the least flexible. If databases are infrequently updated and there is a regular backup window that is long enough to take a full backup, then this may be an appropriate strategy. Also, a full backup only strategy is often used for the Master and MSDB system databases.

It may also be appropriate for user databases, which are used for reporting only, and are not updated by users. In this scenario, it may be that the only updates to the database are made via an ETL load. If this is the case, then your backup only needs to be as frequent as this load. You should, however, consider adding a dependency between the ETL load and the full backup, such as putting them in the same SQL Server

Agent job. This is because, if your backup takes place halfway through an ETL load, it may render the backup useless when you come to restore. At least, not without unpicking the transactions performed in the ETL load, that were included in the backup before finally re-running the ETL load.

Using a full backup–only strategy also limits your flexibility for restores. If you only take full backups, then your only restore option is to restore the database from the point of the last full backup. This can pose two issues. The first is that if you take nightly backups at midnight every night and your database becomes corrupt at 23:00, then you lose 23 hours of data modifications.

The second issue occurs if a user accidently truncates a table at 23:00. The earliest restore point for the database is midnight the previous night. In this scenario, once again, your RPO for the incident is 23 hours, meaning 23 hours of data modifications are lost.

Full and Transaction Log Backups

If your database is in FULL recovery model, then you are able to take transaction log backups, as well as the full backups. This means that you can take much more frequent backups, since the transaction log backup is quicker than the full backup and uses fewer resources. This is appropriate for databases that are updated throughout the day, and it also offers more flexible restores, since you are able to restore to a point in time just before a disaster occurred.

If you are taking transaction log backups, then you schedule your log backups to be in line with your RPO. For example, if you have an RPO of one hour, then you can schedule your log backups to occur every 60 minutes, because this means that you can never lose more than one hour of data. (This is true as long as you have a complete log chain, none of your backups are corrupt, and the share or folder where the backups are stored is accessible when you need it.)

When you use this strategy, you should also consider your RTO. Imagine that you have an RPO of 30 minutes, so you are taking transaction log backups every half hour, but you are only taking a full backup once per week, at 01:00 on a Saturday. If your database becomes corrupt on Friday night at 23:00, you need to restore 330 backups. This is perfectly feasible from a technical view point, but if you have an RTO of 1 hour, then you may not be able to restore the database within the allotted time.

Full, Differential, and Transaction Log Backups

To overcome the issue just described, you may choose to add differential backups to your strategy. Because a differential backup is cumulative, as opposed to incremental in the way that log backups are, if you took a differential backup on a nightly basis at 01:00, then you only need to restore 43 backups to recover your database to the point just before the failure. This restore sequence consists of the full backup, the differential backup taken on the Friday morning at 01:00, and then the transaction logs, in sequence, between 01:30 and 23:00.

Filegroup Backups

For very large databases, it may not be possible to find a maintenance window that is large enough to take a full backup of the entire database. In this scenario, you may be able to split your data across filegroups and back up half of the filegroups on alternate nights. When you come to a restore scenario, you are able to restore only the filegroup that contains the corrupt data, providing that you have a complete log chain from the time the filegroup was backed up to the end of the log.

■ **Tip** Although it is possible to back up individual files as well as a whole filegroup, I find this less helpful, because tables are spread across all files within a filegroup. Therefore, if a table is corrupted, you need to restore all files within the filegroup, or if you only have a handful of corrupt pages, then you can restore just these pages.

Partial Backup

A partial backup involves backing up all read/write filegroups, but not backing up any read-only filegroups. This can be very helpful if you have a large amount of archive data in the database. The BACKUP DATABASE command in T-SQL also supports the READ_WRITE_FILEGROUP option. This means that you can easily perform a partial backup of a database without having to list out the read/write filegroups, which of course, can leave you prone to human error if you have many filegroups.

Backing Up a Database

A database can be backed up through SSMS or via T-SQL. We examine these techniques in the following sections. Usually, regular backups are scheduled to run with SQL Server Agent or are incorporated into a maintenance plan. These topics are discussed in Chapter 21.

Backing Up in SQL Server Management Studio

You can back up a database through SSMS by selecting Tasks | Backup from the context menu of the database; this causes the General page of the Backup Database dialog box to display, as shown in Figure 15-4.

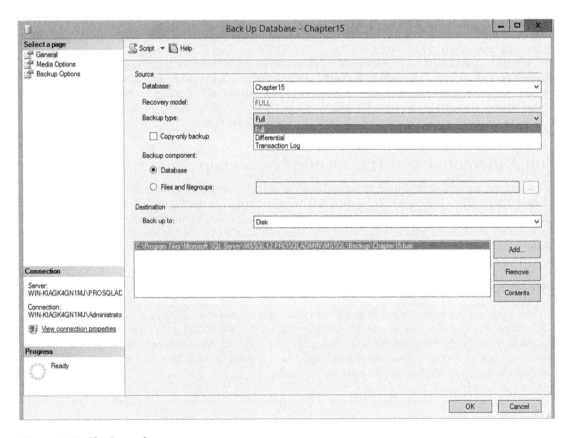

Figure 15-4. *The General page*

In the Database drop-down list, select the database that you wish to back up, and in the Backup Type drop-down, choose to perform either a Full, a Differential, or a Transaction Log backup. The Copy-Only Backup check box allows you to perform a backup that does not affect the restore sequence. Therefore, if you take a copy-only full backup, it does not affect the differential base. Under the covers, this means that the DIFF pages are not reset. Taking a copy-only log backup does not affect the log archive point, and therefore the log is not truncated. Taking a copy-only log backup can be helpful in some online restore scenarios. It is not possible to take a copy-only differential backup.

If you have selected a full or differential backup in the Backup Component section, choose if you want to back up the entire database, or specific files and filegroups. Selecting the Files And Filegroups radio button causes the Select File And Filegroups dialog box to display, as illustrated in Figure 15-5. Here, you can select individual files or entire filegroups to back up.

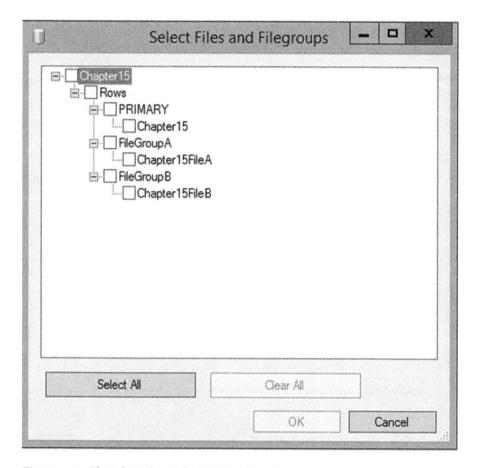

Figure 15-5. *The Select Files And Filegroups dialog box*

In the Back Up To section of the screen, you can select either Disk, Tape, or URL from the drop-down list before you use the Add and Remove buttons to specify the backup devices that form the definition of the media set. You can specify a maximum of 64 backup devices. The backup device may contain multiple backups (backup sets), and when you click the Contents button, the details of each backup set contained within the backup device will be displayed. Figure 15-6 illustrates the contents of a backup file that contains multiple backups.

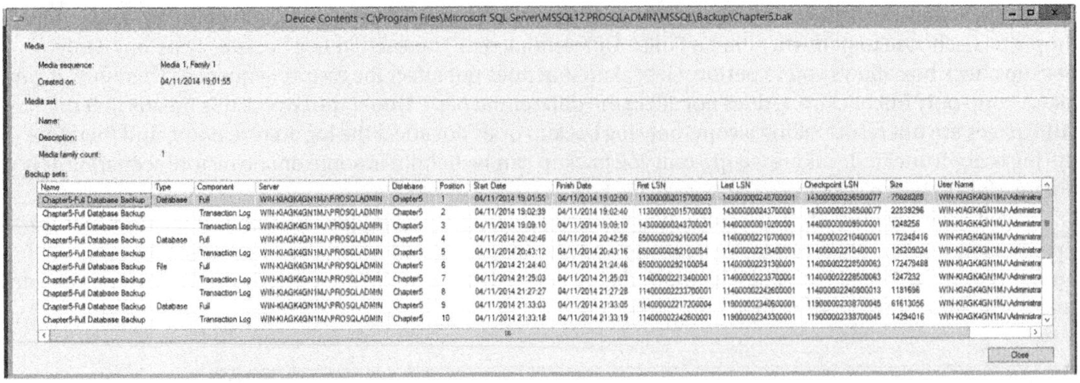

Figure 15-6. *The Backup file contents*

On the Media Option page, shown in Figure 15-7, you can specify if you want to use an existing media set or create a new one. If you choose to use an existing media set, then specify if you want to overwrite the content of the media set or append a new backup set to the media set. If you choose to create a new media set, then you can specify the name, and optionally, a description for the media set. If you use an existing media set, you can verify the date and time that the media set and backup set expire. These checks may cause the backup set to be appended to the existing backup device, instead of overwriting the backup sets.

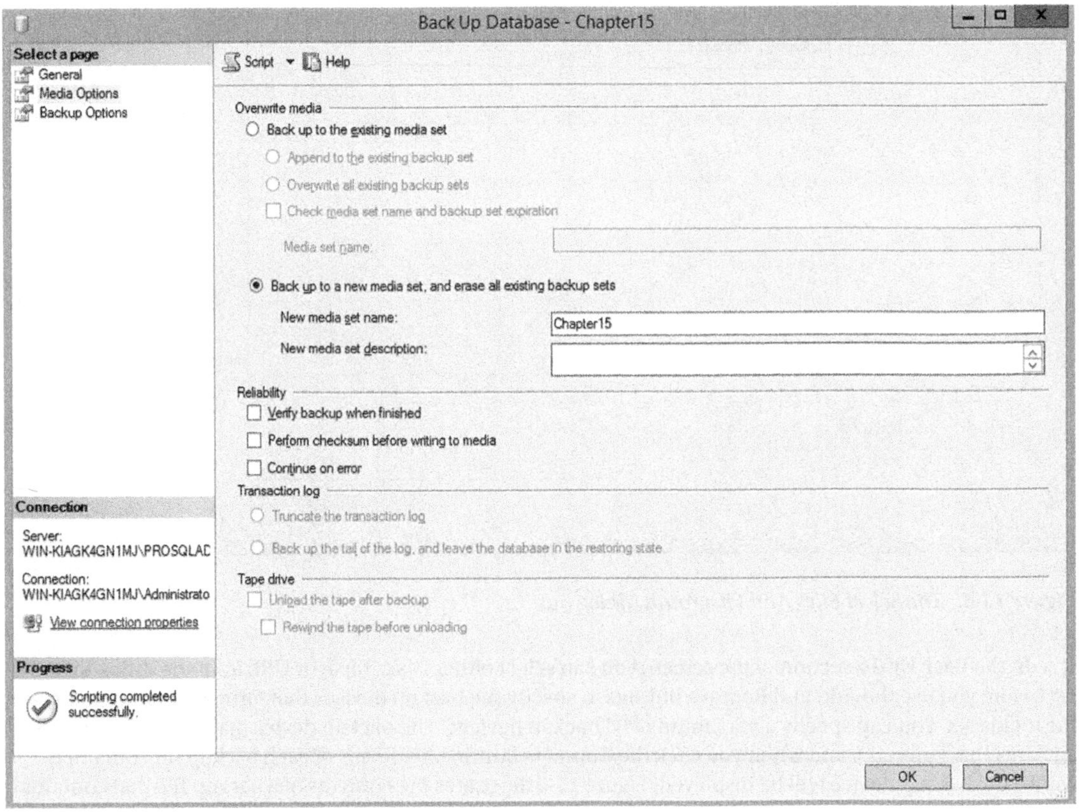

Figure 15-7. *The Media Options page*

Under the Reliability section, specify if the backup should be verified after completion. This is usually a good idea, especially if you are backing up to a URL, since backups across the network are prone to corruption. Choosing the Perform Checksum Before Writing To Media option causes the page checksum of each page of the database to be verified before it is written to the backup device. This causes the backup operation to use additional resources, but if you are not running DBCC CHECKDB as frequently as you take backups, then this option may give you an early warning of any database corruption. (Please see Chapter 8 for more details.) The Continue On Error option causes the backup to continue, even if a bad checksum is discovered during verification of the pages.

On the Backup Options page, illustrated in Figure 15-8, you are able to set the expiration date of the backup set as well as select if you want the backup set to be compressed or encrypted. For compression, you can choose to use the instance default setting, or you can override this setting by specifically choosing to compress, or not compress, the backup.

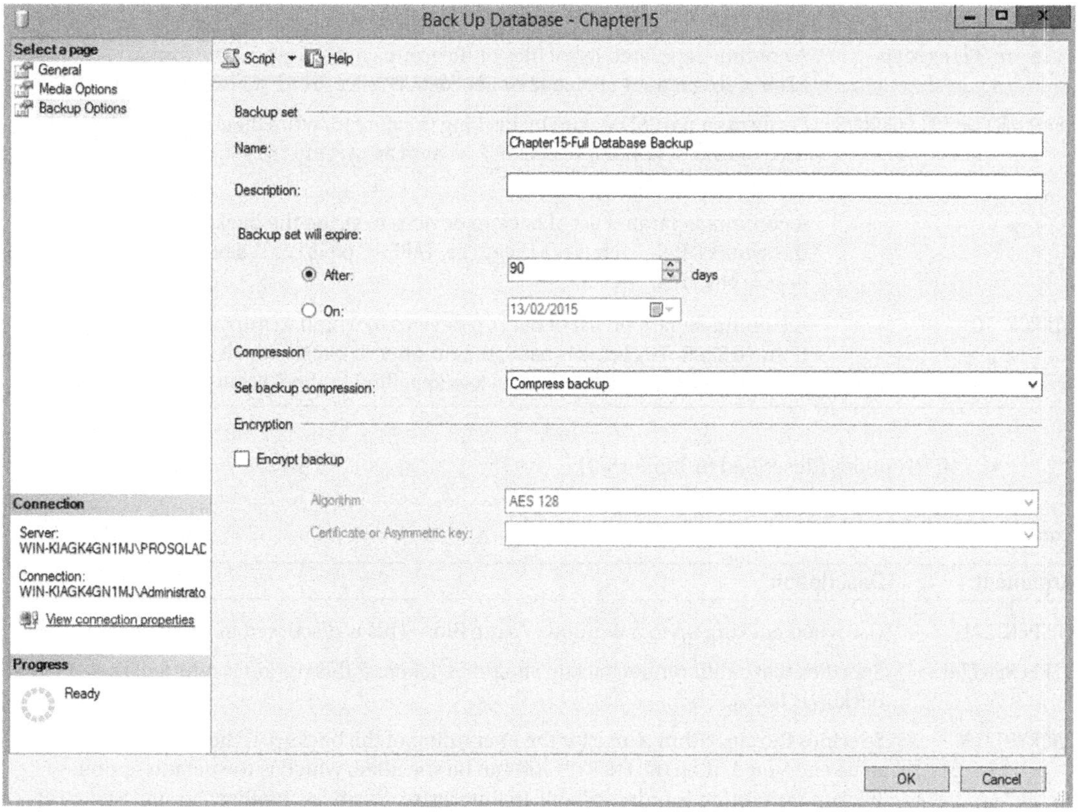

Figure 15-8. *The Backup Options page*

If you choose to encrypt the backup, then you need to select a preexisting certificate. (You can find details of how to create a certificate in Chapter 10.) You then need to select the algorithm that you wish to use to encrypt the backup. Available algorithms in SQL Server 2014 are AES 128, AES 192, AES 256, or 3DES. You should usually select an AES algorithm, because support for 3DES will be removed in a future version of SQL Server.

Backing Up via T-SQL

When you back up a database or log via T-SQL, you can specify many arguments. These can be broken down into the following categories:

- Backup options (described in Table 15-1)

Table 15-1. *Backup Options*

Argument	Description
DATABASE/LOG	Specify DATABASE to perform a full or differential backup. Specify LOG to perform a transaction log backup.
database_name	The name of the database to perform the backup operation against. Can also be a variable containing the name of the database.
file_or_filegroup	A comma-separated list of files or filegroups to back up, in the format FILE = logical file name or FILEGROUP = Logical filegroup name.
READ_WRITE_FILEGROUPS	Performs a partial backup by backing up all read/write filegroups. Optionally, use comma-separated FILEGROUP = syntax after this clause to add read-only filegroups.
TO	A comma-separated list of backup devices to stripe the backup set over, with the syntax DISK = physical device, TAPE = physical device, or URL = physical device.
MIRROR TO	A comma-separated list of backup devices to which to mirror the backup set. If the MIRROR TO clause is used, the number of backup devices specified must equal the number of backup devices specified in the TO clause.

- WITH options (described in Table 15-2)

Table 15-2. *WITH Options*

Argument	Description
CREDENTIAL	Use when backing up to a Windows Azure Blob. This is discussed in Chapter 25.
DIFFERENTIAL	Specifies that a differential backup should be taken. If this option is omitted, then a full backup is taken.
ENCRYPTION	Specifies the algorithm to use for the encryption of the backup. If the backup is not to be encrypted, then NO_ENCRYPTION can be specified, which is the default option. Backup encryption is only available in Enterprise, Business Intelligence, and Standard Editions of SQL Server.
encryptor_name	The name of the encryptor in the format SERVER CERTIFICATE = encryptor name or SERVER ASYMETRIC KEY = encryptor name.

- Backup set options (described in Table 15-3)

Table 15-3. *Backup Set Options*

Argument	Description
COPY_ONLY	Specifies that a copy_only backup of the database or log should be taken. This option is ignored if you perform a differential backup.
COMPRESSION/NO COMPRESSION	By default, SQL Server decides if the backup should be compressed based on the instance-level setting. You can override this setting, however, by specifying COMPRESSION or NO COMPRESSION, as appropriate. Backup compression is only available in Enterprise, Business Intelligence, and Standard Editions of SQL Server.
NAME	Specifies a name for the backup set.
DESCRIPTION	Adds a description to the backup set.
EXPIRYDATE/RETAINEDDAYS	Use EXPIRYDATE = datetime to specify a precise date and time that the backup set expires. After this date, the backup set can be overwritten. Specify RETAINDAYS = int to specify a number of days before the backup set expires.

- Media set options (described in Table 15-4)

Table 15-4. *Media Set Options*

Argument	Description
INIT/NOINIT	INIT attempts to overwrite the existing backup sets in the media set but leaves the media header intact. It first checks the name and expiry date of the backup set, unless SKIP is specified. NOINIT appends the backup set to the media set, which is the default behavior.
SKIP/NOSKIP	SKIP causes the INIT checks of backup set name and expiration date to be skipped. NOSKIP enforces them, which is the default behavior.
FORMAT/NOFORMAT	FORMAT causes the media header to be overwritten, leaving any backup sets within the media set unusable. This essentially creates a new media set. The backup set names and expiry dates are not checked. NOFORMAT preserves the existing media header, which is the default behavior.
MEDIANAME	Specifies the name of the media set.
MEDIADESCRIPTION	Adds a description of the media set.
BLOCKSIZE	Specifies the block size in bytes that will be used for the backup. The BLOCKSIZE defaults to 512 for disk and URL and defaults to 65,536 for tape.

- Error management options (described in Table 15-5)

Table 15-5. *Error Management Options*

Argument	Description
CHECKSUM/NO_CHECKSUM	Specifies if the page checksum of each page should be validated before the page is written to the media set.
CONTINUE_AFTER_ERROR/ STOP_ON_ERROR	STOP_ON_ERROR is the default behavior and causes the backup to fail if a bad checksum is discovered when verifying the page checksum. CONTINUE_AFTER_ERROR allows the backup to continue if a bad checksum is discovered.

- Tape options (described in Table 15-6)

Table 15-6. *Tape Options*

Argument	Description
UNLOAD/NOUNLOAD	NOUNLOAD specifies that the tape remains loaded on the tape drive after the backup operation completes. UNLOAD specifies that the tape is rewound and unloaded, which is the default behavior.
REWIND/NOREWIND	NOREWIND can improve performance when you are performing multiple backup operations by keeping the tape open after the backup completes. NOREWIND implicitly implies NOUNLOAD as well. REWIND releases the tape and rewinds it, which is the default behavior.

* Tape options are ignored unless the backup device is a tape.

- Log-specific options (described in Table 15-7)

Table 15-7. *Log-Specific Options*

Argument	Description
NORECOVERY/STANDBY	NORECOVERY causes the database to be left in a restoring state when the backup completes, making it inaccessible to users. STANDBY leaves the database in a read-only state when the backup completes. STANDBY requires that you specify the path and file name of the transaction undo file, so it should be used with the format STANDBY = transaction_undo_file. If neither option is specified, then the database remains online when the backup completes.
NO_TRUNCATE	Specifies that the log backup should be attempted, even if the database is not in a healthy state. It also does not attempt to truncate an inactive portion of the log. Taking a tail-log backup involves backing up the log with NORECOVERY and NO_TRUNCATE specified.

- Miscellaneous options (described in Table 15-8)

Table 15-8. *Miscellaneous Options*

Argument	Description
BUFFERCOUNT	The total number of IO buffers used for the backup operation.
MAXTRANSFERSIZE	The largest possible unit of transfer between SQL Server and the backup media, specified in bytes.
STATS	Specifies how often progress messages should be displayed. The default is to display a progress message in 10-percent increments.

To perform the full database backup of the Chapter15 database, which we demonstrate through the GUI, we can use the command in Listing 15-4. Before running this script, modify the path of the backup device to meet your system's configuration.

Listing 15-4. Performing a Full Backup

```
BACKUP DATABASE Chapter15
      TO  DISK = 'H:\MSSQL\Backup\Chapter15.bak'
      WITH  RETAINDAYS = 90
      , FORMAT
      , INIT
      , MEDIANAME = 'Chapter15'
      , NAME = 'Chapter15-Full Database Backup'
      , COMPRESSION ;
GO
```

If we want to perform a differential backup of the Chapter15 database and append the backup to the same media set, we can add the WITH DIFFERENTIAL option to our statement, as demonstrated in Listing 15-5. Before running this script, modify the path of the backup device to meet your system's configuration.

Listing 15-5. Performing a Differential Backup

```
BACKUP DATABASE Chapter15
      TO  DISK = 'H:\MSSQL\Backup\Chapter15.bak'
      WITH  DIFFERENTIAL
      , RETAINDAYS = 90
      , NOINIT
      , MEDIANAME = 'Chapter15'
      , NAME = 'Chapter15-Diff Database Backup'
      , COMPRESSION ;
GO
```

If we want to back up the transaction log of the Chapter15 database, again appending the backup set to the same media set, we can use the command in Listing 15-6. Before running this script, modify the path of the backup device to meet your system's configuration.

Listing 15-6. Performing a Transaction Log Backup

```
BACKUP LOG Chapter15
      TO  DISK = 'H: \MSSQL\Backup\Chapter15.bak'
      WITH  RETAINDAYS = 90
      , NOINIT
```

```
        , MEDIANAME = 'Chapter15'
        , NAME = 'Chapter15-Log Backup'
        , COMPRESSION ;
GO
```

■ **Note**   In enterprise scenarios, you may wish to store full, differential, and log backups in different folders.

If we are implementing a filegroup backup strategy and want to back up only FileGroupA, we can use the command in Listing 15-7. We create a new media set for this backup set. Before running this script, modify the path of the backup device to meet your system's configuration.

Listing 15-7. Performing a Filegroup Backup

```
BACKUP DATABASE Chapter15 FILEGROUP = 'FileGroupA'
        TO  DISK = 'H:\MSSQL\Backup\Chapter15FGA.bak'
        WITH  RETAINDAYS = 90
        , FORMAT
        , INIT
        , MEDIANAME = 'Chapter15FG'
        , NAME = 'Chapter15-Full Database Backup-FilegroupA'
        , COMPRESSION ;
GO
```

To repeat the full backup of the Chapter15 but stripe the backup set across two backup devices, we can use the command in Listing 15-8. This helps increase the throughput of the backup. Before running this script, you should modify the paths of the backup devices to meet your system's configuration.

Listing 15-8. Using Multiple Backup Devices

```
BACKUP DATABASE Chapter15
        TO  DISK = 'H:\MSSQL\Backup\Chapter15Stripe1.bak',
                   'G:\MSSQL\Backup\Chapter15Stripe2.bak'
        WITH  RETAINDAYS = 90
        , FORMAT
        , INIT
        , MEDIANAME = 'Chapter15Stripe'
        , NAME = 'Chapter15-Full Database Backup-Stripe'
        , COMPRESSION ;
GO
```

For increased redundancy, we can create a mirrored media set by using the command in Listing 15-9. Before running this script, modify the paths of the backup devices to meet your system's configuration.

Listing 15-9. Using a Mirrored Media Set

```
BACKUP DATABASE Chapter15
        TO  DISK = 'H:\MSSQL\Backup\Chapter15Stripe1.bak',
                   'G:\MSSQL\Backup\Chapter15Stripe2.bak'
        MIRROR TO = 'J:\MSSQL\Backup\Chapter15Mirror1.bak',
                    'K:\MSSQL\Backup\Chapter15Mirror2.bak'
```

```
        WITH  RETAINDAYS = 90
        , FORMAT
        , INIT
        , MEDIANAME = 'Chapter15Mirror'
        , NAME = 'Chapter15-Full Database Backup-Mirror'
        , COMPRESSION ;
GO
```

Restoring a Database

You can restore a database either through SSMS or via T-SQL. We explore both of these options in the following sections.

Restoring in SQL Server Management Studio

To begin a restore in SSMS, select Restore Database from the context menu of Databases in Object Explorer. This causes the General page of the Restore Database dialog box to display, as illustrated in Figure 15-9. Selecting the database to be restored from the drop-down list causes the rest of the tab to be automatically populated.

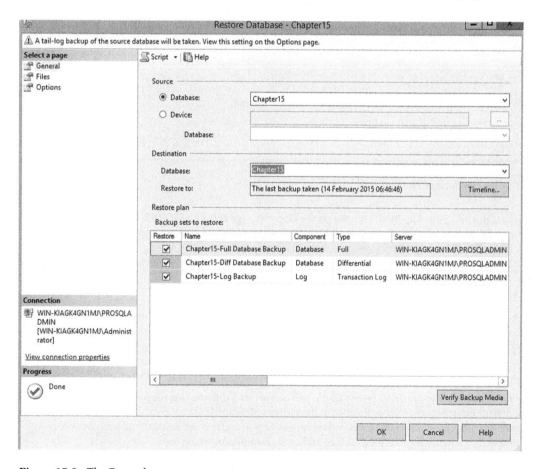

Figure 15-9. *The General page*

You can see that the contents of the Chapter15 media set are displayed in the Backup Sets To Restore pane of the page. In this case, we can see the contents of the Chapter15 media set. The Restore check boxes allow you to select the backup sets that you wish to restore.

The Timeline button provides a graphical illustration of when each backup set was created, as illustrated in Figure 15-10. This allows you to easily see how much data loss exposure you have, depending on the backup sets that you choose to restore. In the Timeline window, you can also specify if you want to recover to the end of the log, or if you wish to restore to a specific date/time.

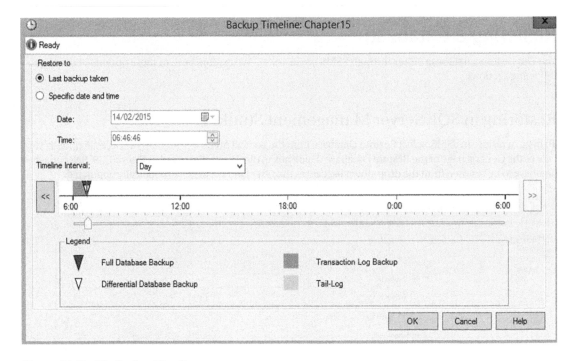

Figure 15-10. *The Backup Timeline page*

Clicking the Verify Backup Media button on the General page causes a RESTORE WITH VERIFYONLY operation to be carried out. This operation verifies the backup media without attempting to restore it. In order to do this, it performs the following checks:

- The backup set is complete.

- All backup devices are readable.

- The CHECKSUM is valid (only applies if WITH CHECKSUM was specified during the backup operation).

- Page headers are verified.

- There is enough space on the target restore volume for the backups to be restored.

On the Files page, illustrated in Figure 15-11, you can select a different location to which to restore each file. The default behavior is to restore the files to the current location. You can use the ellipses, next to each file, to specify a different location for each individual file, or you can use the Relocate All Files To Folder option to specify a single folder for all data files and a single folder for all log files.

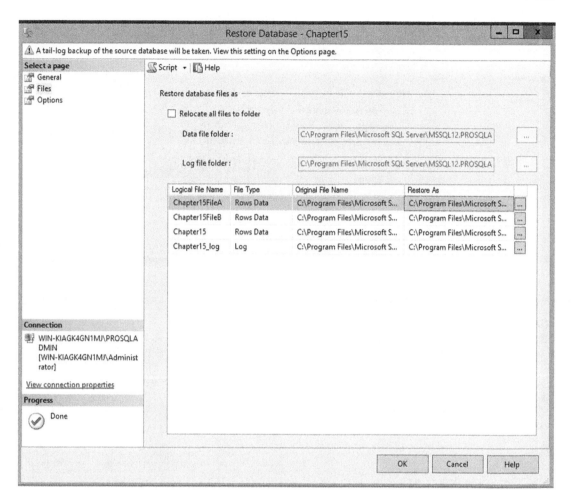

Figure 15-11. *The File page*

On the Options page, shown in Figure 15-12, you are able to specify the restore options that you plan to use. In the Restore Options section of the page, you can specify that you want to overwrite an existing database, preserve the replication settings within the database (which you should use if you are configuring log shipping to work with replication), and restore the database with restricted access. This last option makes the database accessible only to administrators and members of the db_owner and db_creator roles after the restore completes. This can be helpful if you want to verify the data, or perform any data repairs, before you make the database accessible to users.

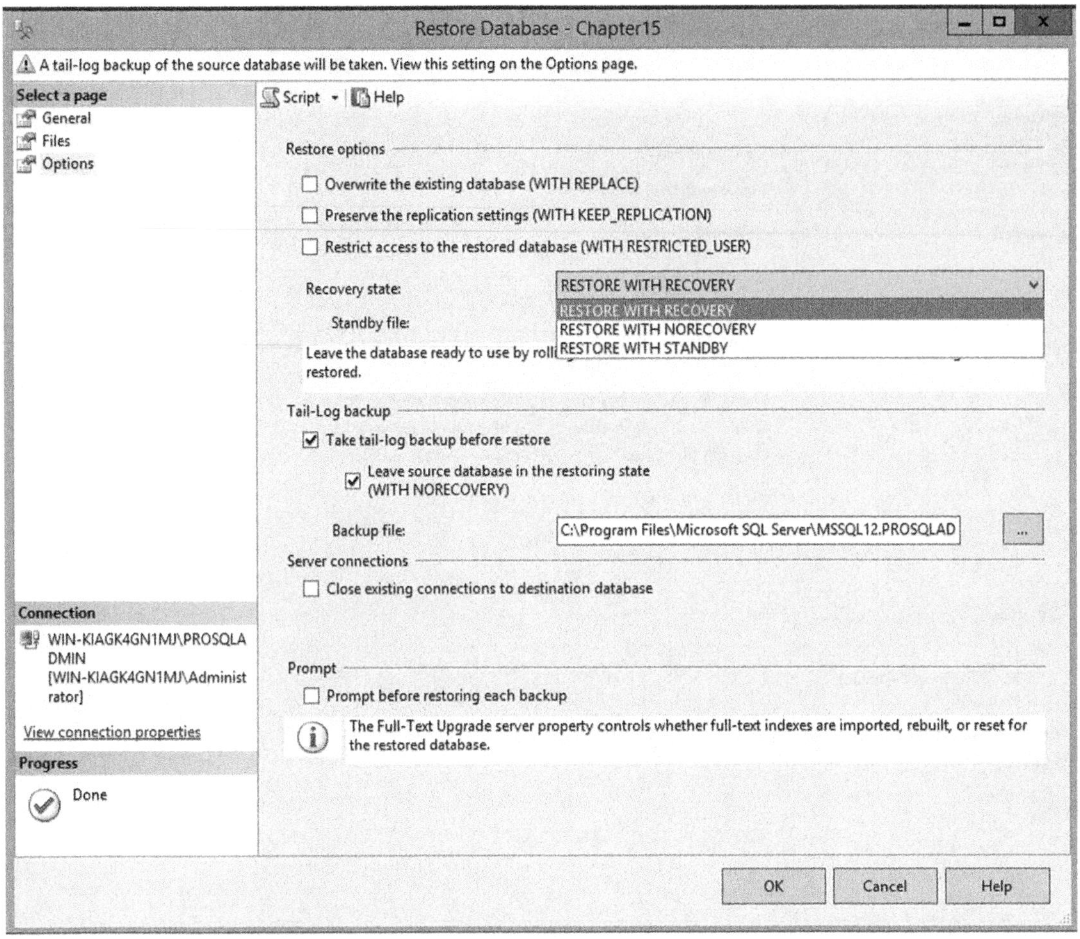

Figure 15-12. *The Options page*

In the Restore Options section, you can also specify the recovery state of the database. Restoring the database with RECOVERY brings the database online when the restore completes. NORECOVERY leaves the database in a restoring state, which means that further backups can be applied. STANDBY brings the database online but leaves it in a read-only state. This option can be helpful if you are failing over to a secondary server. If you choose this option, you are also able to specify the location of the Transaction Undo file.

■ **Tip** If you specify WITH PARTIAL during the restore of the first backup file, you are able to apply additional backups, even if you restore WITH RECOVERY. There is no GUI support for piecemeal restores, however. Performing piecemeal restores via T-SQL is discussed later in this chapter.

In the Tail-Log Backup section of the screen, you can choose to attempt a tail-log backup before the restore operation begins, and if you choose to do so, you can choose to leave the database in a restoring state. A tail-log backup may be possible even if the database is damaged. Leaving the source database in a restoring state essentially safe-states it to mitigate the risk of data loss. If you choose to take a tail-log backup, you can also specify the file path for the backup device to use. You can also specify if you want to close existing connections to the destination database before the restore begins and if you want to be prompted before restoring each individual backup set.

Restoring via T-SQL

When using the RESTORE command in T-SQL, in addition to restoring a database, the following options are available.

Table 15-9. *Restore Options*

Restore Option	Description
RESTORE FILELISTONLY	Returns a list of all files in the backup device.
RESTORE HEADERONLY	Returns the backup headers for all backup sets within a backup device.
RESTORE LABELONLY	Returns information regarding the media set and media family to which the backup device belongs.
RESTORE REWINDONLY	Closes and rewinds the tape. Only works if the backup device is a tape.
RESTORE VERIFYONLY	Checks that all backup devices exist and are readable. Also performs other high-level verification checks, such as ensuring there is enough space of the destination drive, checking the CHECKSUM (providing the backup was taken with CHECKSUM) and checking key Page Header fields.

When using the RESTORE command to perform a restore, you can use many arguments to allow many restore scenarios to take place. These arguments can be categorized as follows:

- Restore arguments (described in Table 15-10)

Table 15-10. *Restore Arguments*

Argument	Description
DATABASE/LOG	Specify DATABASE to which to restore all or some of the files that constitute the database. Specify LOG to restore a transaction log backup.
database_name	Specifies the name of the target database that will be restored.
file_or_filegroup_or_pages	Specifies a comma-separated list of the files, filegroups, or pages to be restored. If restoring pages, use the format PAGE = FileID:PageID. In simple recovery model, files and filegroups can only be specified if they are read-only or if you are performing a partial restore using WITH PARTIAL.
READ_WRITE_FILEGROUPS	Restores all read/write filegroups but no read-only filegroups.
FROM	A comma-separated list of backup devices that contains the backup set to restore or the name of the database snapshot from which you wish to restore. Database snapshots are discussed in Chapter 16.

- WITH options (described in Table 15-11)

Table 15-11. *WITH Options*

Argument	Description
PARTIAL	Indicates that this is the first restore in a piecemeal restore, which is discussed later in this chapter.
RECOVERY/NORECOVERY/STANDBY	Specifies the state that the database should be left in when the restore operation completes. RECOVERY indicates that the database will be brought online. NORECOVERY indicates that the database will remain in a restoring state so that subsequent restores can be applied. STANDBY indicates that the database will be brought online in read-only mode.
MOVE	Used to specify the file system location that the files should be restored to if this is different from the original location.
CREDENTIAL	Used when performing a restore from a Windows Azure Blob, which will be discussed in Chapter 25.
REPLACE	If a database already exists on the instance with the target database name that you have specified in the restore statement, or if the files already exist in the operating system with the same name or location, then REPLACE indicates that the database or files should be overwritten.
RESTART	Indicates that if the restore operation is interrupted, it should be restarted from that point.
RESTRICTED_USER	Indicates that only administrators and members of the db_owner and db_creator roles should have access to the database after the restore operation completes.

- Backup set options (described in Table 15-12)

Table 15-12. *Backup Set Options*

Argument	Description
FILE	Indicates the sequential number of the backup set, within the media set, to be used.
PASSWORD	If you are restoring a backup that was taken in SQL Server 2008 or earlier where a password was specified during the backup operation, then you need to use this argument to be able to restore the backup.

- Media set options (described in Table 15-13)

Table 15-13. *Media Set Options*

Argument	Description
MEDIANAME	If you use this argument, then the MEDIANAME must match the name of the media set allocated during the creation of the media set.
MEDIAPASSWORD	If you are restoring from a media set created using SQL Server 2008 or earlier and a password was specified for the media set, then you must use this argument during the restore operation.
BLOCKSIZE	Specifies the block size to use for the restore operation, in bytes, to override the default value of 65,536 for tape and 512 for disk or URL.

- Error management options (described in Table 15-14)

Table 15-14. *Error Management Options*

Argument	Description
CHECKSUM/NOCHECKSUM	If CHECKSUM was specified during the backup operation, then specifying CHECKSUM during the restore operation will verify page integrity during the restore operation. Specifying NOCKECKSUM disables this verification.
CONTINUE_AFTER_ERROR/STOP_ON_ERROR	STOP_ON_ERROR causes the restore operation to terminate if any damaged pages are discovered. CONTINUE_AFTER_ERROR causes the restore operation to continue, even if damaged pages are discovered.

- Tape options (described in Table 15-15)

Table 15-15. *Tape Options*

Argument	Description
UNLOAD/NOUNLOAD	NOUNLOAD specifies that the tape will remain loaded on the tape drive after the backup operation completes. UNLOAD specifies that the tape will be rewound and unloaded, which is the default behavior.
REWIND/NOREWIND	NOREWIND can improve performance when you are performing multiple backup operations by keeping the tape open after the backup completes. NOREWIND implicitly implies NOUNLOAD as well. REWIND releases the tape and rewinds it, which is the default behavior.

* Tape options are ignored unless the backup device is a tape.

- Miscellaneous options (described in Table 15-16)

Table 15-16. *Miscillaneous Options*

Argument	Description
BUFFERCOUNT	The total number of IO buffers used for the restore operation.
MAXTRANSFERSIZE	The largest possible unit of transfer between SQL Server and the backup media, specified in bytes.
STATS	Specifies how often progress messages should be displayed. The default is to display a progress message in 5-percent increments.
FILESTREAM (DIRECTORY_NAME)	Specifies the name of the folder to which FILESTREAM data should be restored.
KEEP_REPLICATION	Preserves the replication settings. Use this option when configuring log shipping with replication.
KEEP_CDC	Preserves the Change Data Capture (CDC) settings of a database when it is being restored. Only relevant if CDC was enabled at the time of the backup operation.
ENABLE_BROKER/ ERROR_BROKER_CONVERSATIONS/NEW BROKER	ENABLE_BROKER specifies that service broker message delivery will be enabled after the restore operation completes so that messages can immediately be sent. ERROR_BROKER_CONVERSATIONS specifies that all conversations will be terminated with an error message before message delivery is enabled. NEW_BROKER specifies that conversations will be removed without throwing an error and the database will be assigned a new Service Broker identifier. Only relevant if Service Broker was enabled when the backup was created.
STOPAT/STOPATMARK/STOPBEFOREMARK	Used for point-in-time recovery and only supported in FULL recovery model. STOPAT specifies a datetime value, which will determine the time of the last transaction to restore. STOPATMARK specifies either an LSN (log sequence number) to restore to, or the name of a marked transaction, which will be the final transaction that is restored. STOPBEFOREMARK restores up to the transaction prior to the LSN or marked transaction specified.

To perform the same restore operation that we performed through SSMS, we use the command in Listing 15-10. Before running the script, change the path of the backup devices to match your own configuration.

Listing 15-10. Restoring a Database

```
USE master
GO

--Back Up the tail of the log

BACKUP LOG Chapter15
TO  DISK = N'H:\MSSQL\Backup\Chapter15_LogBackup_2015-02-16_12-17-49.bak'
        WITH NOFORMAT,
             NAME = N'Chapter15_LogBackup_2015-02-16_12-17-49',
             NORECOVERY ,
             STATS = 5 ;

--Restore the full backup

RESTORE DATABASE Chapter15
FROM  DISK = N'H:\MSSQL\Backup\Chapter15.bak'
         WITH  FILE = 1,
               NORECOVERY,
               STATS = 5 ;

--Restore the differential

RESTORE DATABASE Chapter15
FROM  DISK = N'H:\MSSQL\Backup\Chapter15.bak'
         WITH  FILE = 2,
               NORECOVERY,
               STATS = 5 ;

--Restore the transaction log

RESTORE LOG Chapter15
FROM  DISK = N'H:\MSSQL\Backup\Chapter15.bak'
         WITH  FILE = 3,
               STATS = 5 ;

GO
```

Restoring to a Point in Time

In order to demonstrate restoring a database to a point in time, we first take a series of backups, manipulating data between each one. The script in Listing 15-11 first creates a base full backup of the Chapter15 database. It then inserts some rows into the Addresses table before it takes a transaction log backup. It then inserts some further rows into the Addresses table before truncating the table; and then finally, it takes another transaction log backup.

Listing 15-11. Preparing the Chapter15 Database

```
USE Chapter15
GO

BACKUP DATABASE Chapter15
        TO  DISK = 'H:\MSSQL\Backup\Chapter15PointinTime.bak'
        WITH  RETAINDAYS = 90
        , FORMAT
        , INIT, SKIP
        , MEDIANAME = 'Chapter15Point-in-time'
        , NAME = 'Chapter15-Full Database Backup'
        , COMPRESSION ;

INSERT INTO dbo.Addresses
VALUES('1 Carter Drive', 'Hedge End', 'Southampton', 'SO32 6GH')
        ,('10 Apress Way', NULL, 'London', 'WC10 2FG') ;

BACKUP LOG Chapter15
        TO  DISK = 'H:\MSSQL\Backup\Chapter15PointinTime.bak'
        WITH  RETAINDAYS = 90
        , NOINIT
        , MEDIANAME = 'Chapter15Point-in-time'
        , NAME = 'Chapter15-Log Backup'
        , COMPRESSION ;

INSERT INTO dbo.Addresses
VALUES('12 SQL Street', 'Botley', 'Southampton', 'SO32 8RT')
        ,('19 Springer Way', NULL, 'London', 'EC1 5GG') ;

TRUNCATE TABLE dbo.Addresses ;

BACKUP LOG Chapter15
        TO  DISK = 'H:\MSSQL\Backup\Chapter15PointinTime.bak'
        WITH  RETAINDAYS = 90
        , NOINIT
        , MEDIANAME = 'Chapter15Point-in-time'
        , NAME = 'Chapter15-Log Backup'
        , COMPRESSION ;
GO
```

Imagine that after the series of events that occurred in this script, we discover that the Addresses table was truncated in error and we need to restore to the point immediately before this truncation occurred. To do this, we either need to know the exact time of the truncation and need to restore to the date/time immediately before, or to be more accurate, we need to discover the LSN of the transaction where the truncation occurred and restore up to this transaction. In this demonstration, we choose the latter option.

We can use a system function called sys.fn_dump_dblog() to display the contents of the final log backup that includes the second insert statement and the table truncation. The procedure accepts a massive 68 parameters, and none of them can be omitted!

The first and second parameters allow you to specify a beginning and end LSN with which to filter the results. These parameters can both be set to NULL to return all entries in the backup. The third parameter specifies if the backup set is disk or tape, whereas the fourth parameter specifies the sequential ID of the backup set within the device. The next 64 parameters accept the names of the backup devices within the media set. If the media set contains less than 64 devices, then you should use the value DEFAULT for any parameters that are not required.

The script in Listing 15-12 uses fn_dump_dblog() to identify the starting LSN of the autocommit transaction in which the truncation occurred. The issue with this function is that it does not return the LSN in the same format required by the RESTORE command. Therefore, the calculated column, ConvertedLSN, converts each of the three sections of the LSN from binary to decimal, pads them out with zeros as required, and finally concatenates them back together to produce an LSN that can be passed into the RESTORE operation.

Listing 15-12. Finding the LSN of the Truncation

```
SELECT
        CAST(
            CAST(
                CONVERT(VARBINARY, '0x'
                        + RIGHT(REPLICATE('0', 8)
                        + SUBSTRING([Current LSN], 1, 8), 8), 1
                ) AS INT
            ) AS VARCHAR(11)
        ) +
        RIGHT(REPLICATE('0', 10) +
        CAST(
            CAST(
                CONVERT(VARBINARY, '0x'
                        + RIGHT(REPLICATE('0', 8)
                        + SUBSTRING([Current LSN], 10, 8), 8), 1
                ) AS INT
            ) AS VARCHAR(10)), 10) +
        RIGHT(REPLICATE('0',5) +
        CAST(
            CAST(CONVERT(VARBINARY, '0x'
                        + RIGHT(REPLICATE('0', 8)
                        + SUBSTRING([Current LSN], 19, 4), 8), 1
                ) AS INT
            ) AS VARCHAR
        ), 5) AS ConvertedLSN
        ,*
FROM
    sys.fn_dump_dblog (
        NULL, NULL, N'DISK', 3, N'H:\MSSQL\Backup\Chapter15PointinTime.bak'
        DEFAULT, DEFAULT, DEFAULT, DEFAULT, DEFAULT, DEFAULT, DEFAULT,
        DEFAULT, DEFAULT, DEFAULT, DEFAULT, DEFAULT, DEFAULT, DEFAULT,
        DEFAULT, DEFAULT, DEFAULT, DEFAULT, DEFAULT, DEFAULT, DEFAULT,
        DEFAULT, DEFAULT, DEFAULT, DEFAULT, DEFAULT, DEFAULT, DEFAULT,
        DEFAULT, DEFAULT, DEFAULT, DEFAULT, DEFAULT, DEFAULT, DEFAULT,
        DEFAULT, DEFAULT, DEFAULT, DEFAULT, DEFAULT, DEFAULT, DEFAULT,
        DEFAULT, DEFAULT, DEFAULT, DEFAULT, DEFAULT, DEFAULT, DEFAULT,
        DEFAULT, DEFAULT, DEFAULT, DEFAULT, DEFAULT, DEFAULT, DEFAULT,
        DEFAULT, DEFAULT, DEFAULT, DEFAULT, DEFAULT, DEFAULT, DEFAULT,
        DEFAULT, DEFAULT, DEFAULT, DEFAULT, DEFAULT, DEFAULT, DEFAULT)
WHERE [Transaction Name] = 'TRUNCATE TABLE' ;
```

Now that we have discovered the LSN of the transaction that truncated the Addresses table, we can restore the Chapter15 database to this point. The script in Listing 15-13 restores the full and first transaction log backups in their entirety. It then restores the final transaction log but uses the STOPBEFOREMARK argument to specify the first LSN that should not be restored. Before running the script, change the locations of the backup devices, as per your own configuration. You should also replace the LSN with the LSN that you generated using sys.fn_dump_dblog().

Listing 15-13. Restorimg to a Point in Time

```
USE master
GO

RESTORE DATABASE Chapter15
        FROM  DISK = N'H:\MSSQL\Backup\Chapter15PointinTime.bak'
        WITH  FILE = 1
        ,   NORECOVERY
        ,   STATS = 5
        , REPLACE ;

RESTORE LOG Chapter15
        FROM  DISK = N'H:\MSSQL\Backup\Chapter15PointinTime.bak'
        WITH  FILE = 2
        ,   NORECOVERY
        ,   STATS = 5
        , REPLACE ;

RESTORE LOG Chapter15
        FROM  DISK = N'H:\MSSQL\Backup\Chapter15PointinTime.bak'
        WITH  FILE = 3
        ,   STATS = 5
        , STOPBEFOREMARK = 'lsn:35000000036000001'
        , RECOVERY
        , REPLACE ;
```

Restoring Files and Pages

The ability to restore a filegroup, a file, or even a page, gives you great control and flexibility in disaster recovery scenarios. The following sections demonstrate how to perform a file restore and a page restore.

Restoring a File

You may come across situations in which only some files or filegroups within the database are corrupt. If this is the case, then it is possible to restore just the corrupt file, assuming you have the complete log chain available, between the point when you took the file or filegroup backup and the end of the log. In order to demonstrate this functionality, we first insert some rows into the Contacts table of the Chapter15 database before we back up the primary filegroup and FileGroupA. We then insert some rows into the Addresses table, which resides on FileGroupB before we take a transaction log backup. These tasks are performed by the script in Listing 15-14.

Listing 15-14. Preparing the Database

```
INSERT INTO dbo.Contacts
VALUES('Peter', 'Carter', 1),
       ('Danielle', 'Carter', 1) ;

BACKUP DATABASE Chapter15 FILEGROUP = N'PRIMARY',  FILEGROUP = N'FileGroupA'
       TO  DISK = N'H:\MSSQL\Backup\Chapter15FileRestore.bak'
       WITH FORMAT
       , NAME = N'Chapter15-Filegroup Backup'
       , STATS = 10 ;

INSERT INTO dbo.Addresses
VALUES('SQL House', 'Server Buildings', NULL, 'SQ42 4BY'),
       ('Carter Mansions', 'Admin Road', 'London', 'E3 3GJ') ;

BACKUP LOG Chapter15
       TO  DISK = N'H:\MSSQL\Backup\Chapter15FileRestore.bak'
       WITH NOFORMAT
       , NOINIT
       ,  NAME = N'Chapter15-Log Backup'
       , NOSKIP
       , STATS = 10 ;
```

If we imagine that Chapter15FileA has become corrupt, we are able to restore this file, even though we do not have a corresponding backup for Chapter15FileB, and recover to the latest point in time by using the script in Listing 15-15. This script performs a file restore on the file Chapter15FileA before taking a tail-log backup of the transaction log and then finally applying all transaction logs in sequence. Before running this script, change the location of the backup devices to reflect your own configuration.

■ **Caution**　If we had not taken the tail-log backup, then we would no longer have been able to access the Contacts table (In FileGroupB), unless we had also been able to restore the Chapter15FileB file.

Listing 15-15. Restoring a File

```
USE master
GO

RESTORE DATABASE Chapter15 FILE = N'Chapter15FileA'
       FROM  DISK = N'H:\MSSQL\Backup\Chapter15FileRestore.bak'
       WITH  FILE = 1
       , NORECOVERY
       , STATS = 10
       , REPLACE ;
GO

BACKUP LOG Chapter15
       TO  DISK = N'H:\MSSQL\Backup\Chapter15_LogBackup_2015-02-17_15-26-09.bak'
       WITH NOFORMAT
       , NOINIT
       ,  NAME = N'Chapter15_LogBackup_2015-02-17_15-26-09'
```

```
        , NOSKIP
        , NORECOVERY
              ,   STATS = 5 ;

RESTORE LOG Chapter15
        FROM  DISK = N'H:\MSSQL\Backup\Chapter15FileRestore.bak'
        WITH  FILE = 2
        , STATS = 10
        , NORECOVERY ;

RESTORE LOG Chapter15
        FROM  DISK = N'H:\MSSQL\Backup\Chapter15_LogBackup_2015-02-17_15-26-09.bak'
        WITH FILE = 1
        , STATS = 10
        , RECOVERY ;
GO
```

Restoring a Page

If a page becomes corrupt, then it is possible to restore this page instead of restoring the complete file or even the database. This can significantly reduce downtime in a minor DR scenario. In order to demonstrate this functionality, we take a full backup of the Chapter15 database and then use the undocumented DBCC WRITEPAGE to cause a corruption in one of the pages of our Contacts table. These steps are performed in Listing 15-16.

■ **Caution**   DBCC WRITEPAGE is used here for educational purposes only. It is undocumented, but also extremely dangerous. It should not ever be used on a production system and should only ever be used on any database with extreme caution.

Listing 15-16. Preparing the Database

```
--Back up the database

BACKUP DATABASE Chapter15
        TO  DISK = N'H:\MSSQL\Backup\Chapter15PageRestore.bak'
        WITH FORMAT
        , NAME = N'Chapter15-Full Backup'
        , STATS = 10 ;

--Corrupt a page in the Contacts table

ALTER DATABASE Chapter15 SET SINGLE_USER WITH NO_WAIT ;
GO

DECLARE @SQL NVARCHAR(MAX)
```

```
SELECT @SQL = 'DBCC WRITEPAGE(' +
(
        SELECT CAST(DB_ID('Chapter15') AS NVARCHAR)
) +
', ' +
(
        SELECT TOP 1 CAST(file_id AS NVARCHAR)
        FROM dbo.Contacts
        CROSS APPLY sys.fn_PhysLocCracker(%%physloc%%)
) +
 ', ' +
(
        SELECT TOP 1 CAST(page_id AS NVARCHAR)
        FROM dbo.Contacts
        CROSS APPLY sys.fn_PhysLocCracker(%%physloc%%)
) +
', 2000, 1, 0x61, 1)' ;

EXEC(@SQL) ;

ALTER DATABASE Chapter15 SET MULTI_USER ;
GO
```

If we attempt to access the Contacts table after running the script, we receive the error message warning us of a logical consistency-based I/O error, and the statement fails. The error message also provides details of the page that is corrupt, which we can use in our RESTORE statement. To resolve this, we can run the script in Listing 15-17. The script restores the corrupt page before taking a tail-log backup, and then finally it applies the tail of the log. Before running the script, modify the location of the backup devices to reflect you configuration. You should also update the PageID to reflect the page that is corrupt in your version of the Chapter15 database. Specify the page to be restored in the format FileID:PageID.

■ **Tip**   The details of the corrupt page can also be found in MSDB.dbo.suspect_pages.

Listing 15-17. Restoring a Page

```
USE Master
GO

RESTORE DATABASE Chapter15 PAGE='3:8'
        FROM  DISK = N'H:\MSSQL\Backup\Chapter15PageRestore.bak'
        WITH  FILE = 1
        , NORECOVERY
        ,  STATS = 5 ;

BACKUP LOG Chapter15
        TO  DISK = N'H:\MSSQL\Backup\Chapter15_LogBackup_2015-02-17_16-47-46.bak'
        WITH NOFORMAT, NOINIT
        , NAME = N'Chapter15_LogBackup_2015-02-17_16-32-46'
        , NOSKIP
        , STATS = 5 ;
```

```
RESTORE LOG Chapter15
        FROM  DISK = N'H:\MSSQL\Backup\Chapter15_LogBackup_2015-02-17_16-47-46.bak'
        WITH  STATS = 5
              , RECOVERY ;
GO
```

Piecemeal Restores

A piecemeal restore involves bringing the filegroups of a database online one by one. This can offer a big benefit for a large database, since you can make some data accessible, while other data is still being restored. In order to demonstrate this technique, we first take filegroup backups of all filegroups in the Chapter15 database and follow this with a transaction log backup. The script in Listing 15-18 performs this task. Before running the script, modify the locations of the backup devices to reflect your own configurations.

Listing 15-18. Filegroup Backup

```
BACKUP DATABASE Chapter15
        FILEGROUP = N'PRIMARY',  FILEGROUP = N'FileGroupA',  FILEGROUP = N'FileGroupB'
        TO  DISK = N'H:\MSSQL\Backup\Chapter15Piecemeal.bak'
        WITH FORMAT
        , NAME = N'Chapter15-Fiegroup Backup'
        , STATS = 10 ;

BACKUP LOG Chapter15
        TO  DISK = N'H:\MSSQL\Backup\Chapter15Piecemeal.bak'
        WITH NOFORMAT, NOINIT
        , NAME = N'Chapter15-Full Database Backup'
        ,  STATS = 10 ;
```

The script in Listing 15-19 now brings the filegroups online, one by one, starting with the primary filegroup, followed by FileGroupA, and finally, FileGroupB. Before beginning the restore, we back up the tail of the log. This backup is restored WITH RECOVERY after each filegroup is restored. This brings the restored databases back online. It is possible to restore further backups because we specify the PARTIAL option on the first restore operation.

Listing 15-19. Piecemeal Restore

```
USE master
GO

BACKUP LOG Chapter15
        TO  DISK = N'H:\MSSQL\Backup\Chapter15_LogBackup_2015-02-17_27-29-46.bak'
        WITH NOFORMAT, NOINIT
        , NAME = N'Chapter15_LogBackup_2015-02-17_17-29-46'
        , NOSKIP
        , NORECOVERY
        , NO_TRUNCATE
        , STATS = 5 ;

RESTORE DATABASE Chapter15
        FILEGROUP = N'PRIMARY'
        FROM  DISK = N'H:\MSSQL\Backup\Chapter15Piecemeal.bak'
```

```
        WITH  FILE = 1
        , NORECOVERY
        , PARTIAL
        , STATS = 10 ;

RESTORE LOG Chapter15
        FROM  DISK = N'H:\MSSQL\Backup\Chapter15Piecemeal.bak'
        WITH  FILE = 2
        , NORECOVERY
        , STATS = 10 ;

RESTORE LOG Chapter15
        FROM  DISK = N'H:\MSSQL\Backup\Chapter15_LogBackup_2015-02-17_27-29-46.bak'
        WITH  FILE = 1
        , STATS = 10
        , RECOVERY ;

-----------------The PRIMARY Filegroup is now online--------------------

RESTORE DATABASE Chapter15
        FILEGROUP = N'FileGroupA'
        FROM  DISK = N'H:\MSSQL\Backup\Chapter15Piecemeal.bak'
        WITH  FILE = 1
        , NORECOVERY
        , STATS = 10 ;

RESTORE LOG Chapter15
        FROM  DISK = N'H:\MSSQL\Backup\Chapter15Piecemeal.bak'
        WITH  FILE = 2
        , NORECOVERY
        , STATS = 10 ;

RESTORE LOG Chapter15
        FROM  DISK = N'H:\MSSQL\Backup\Chapter15_LogBackup_2015-02-17_27-29-46.bak'
        WITH  FILE = 1
        , STATS = 10
        , RECOVERY ;

-----------------The FilegroupA Filegroup is now online--------------------

RESTORE DATABASE Chapter15
        FILEGROUP = N'FileGroupB'
        FROM  DISK = N'H:\MSSQL\Backup\Chapter15Piecemeal.bak'
        WITH  FILE = 1
        , NORECOVERY
        , STATS = 10 ;

RESTORE LOG Chapter15
        FROM  DISK = N'H:\MSSQL\Backup\Chapter15Piecemeal.bak'
        WITH  FILE = 2
        , NORECOVERY
        , STATS = 10 ;
```

```
RESTORE LOG Chapter15
        FROM  DISK = N'H:\MSSQL\Backup\Chapter15_LogBackup_2015-02-17_27-29-46.bak'
        WITH  FILE = 1
        , STATS = 10
        , RECOVERY ;
```

```
-----------------The database is now fully online--------------------
```

Summary

A SQL Server database can operate in three recovery models. The SIMPLE recovery model automatically truncates the transaction log after CHECKPOINT operations occur. This means that log backups cannot be taken and, therefore, point-in-time restores are not available. In FULL recovery model, the transaction log is only truncated after a log backup operation. This means that you must take transaction log backups for both disaster recovery and log space. The BULK LOGGED recovery model is meant to be used only while a bulk insert operation is happening. In this case, you switch to this model if you normally use the FULL recovery model.

SQL Server supports three types of backup. A full backup copies all database pages to the backup device. A differential backup copies all database pages that have been modified since the last full backup to the backup device. A transaction log backup copies the contents of the transaction log to the backup device.

A DBA can adopt many backup strategies to provide the best possible RTO and RPO in the event of a disaster that requires a database to be restored. These include taking full backups only, which is applicable to SIMPLE recovery model; scheduling full backups along with transaction log backups; or scheduling full, differential, and transaction log backups. Scheduling differential backups can help improve the RTO of a database if frequent log backups are taken. DBAs may also elect to implement a filegroup backup strategy; this allows them to stager their backups into more manageable windows or perform a partial backup, which involves backing up only read/write filegroups.

Ad-hoc backups can be taken via T-SQL or SQL Server Management Studio (SSMS). In production environments, you invariably want to schedule the backups to run periodically, and we discuss how to automate this action in Chapter 21.

You can also perform restores either through SSMS or with T-SQL. However, you can only perform complex restore scenarios, such as piecemeal restores, via T-SQL. SQL Server also provides you with the ability to restore a single page or file. You can restore a corrupt page as an online operation, and doing so usually provides a better alternative to fixing small scale corruption than either restoring a whole database or using DBCC CHECKDB with the ALLOW_DATA_LOSS option. More details on DBCC CHECKDB can be found in Chapter 8.

■ **Tip**   Many other restore scenarios are beyond the scope of this book, because a full description of every possible scenario would be worthy of a volume in its own right. I encourage you to explore various restore scenarios in a sandpit environment before you need to use them for real!

CHAPTER 16

■ ■ ■

Scaling Workloads

SQL Server provides multiple technologies that allow DBAs to horizontally scale their workloads between multiple databases to avoid lock contention or to scale them horizontally between servers to spread resource utilization. These technologies include database snapshots, replication, and AlwaysOn Availability Groups. This chapter discusses the considerations for these technologies and demonstrates how to implement them.

Database Snapshots

A *database snapshot* is a point-in-time view of a database that never changes after it is generated. It works using copy-on-write technology; this means that if a page is modified in the source database, the original version of the page is copied to an NTFS sparse file, which is used by the database snapshot. A *sparse file* is a file that starts off empty, with no disk space allocated. As pages are updated in the source database and these pages are copied to the sparse file, it grows to accommodate them. This process is illustrated in Figure 16-1.

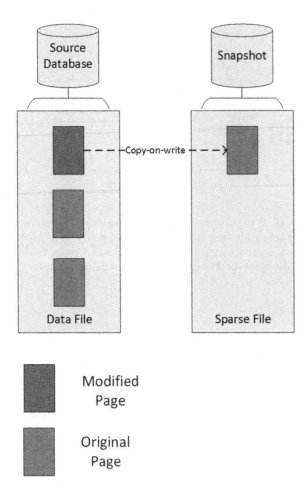

Figure 16-1. *Database snapshots*

If a user runs a query against the database snapshot, SQL Server checks to see if the required pages exist in the database snapshot. Any pages that do exist are returned from the database snapshot, whereas any other pages are retrieved from the source database, as illustrated in Figure 16-2. In this example, to satisfy the query, SQL Server needs to return Page 1:100 and Page 1:101. Page 1:100 has been modified in the source database since the snapshot was taken. Therefore, the original version of the page has been copied to the sparse file and SQL Server retrieves it from there. Page 1:101, on the other hand, has not been modified in the source database since the snapshot was created. Therefore it does not exist in the sparse file, and SQL Server retrieves it from the source database.

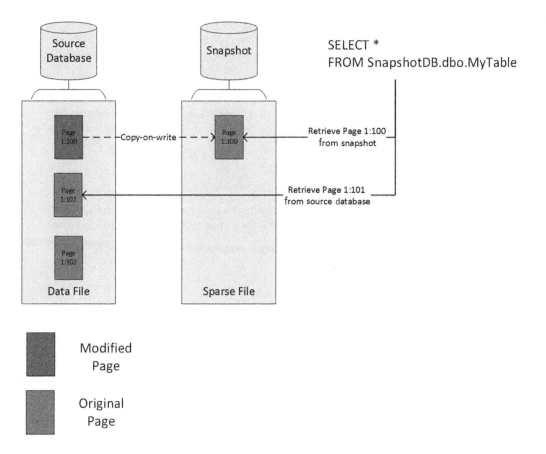

Figure 16-2. *Querying a database snapshot*

If your data-tier application is suffering from contention caused by locking, then you can scale-out reporting to a database snapshot. It is important to note, however, that because a database snapshot must reside on the same instance as the source database, it does not help overcome resource utilization issues. In fact, the opposite is true. Because any modified pages must be copied to the sparse file, the IO overhead increases. The memory footprint also increases, since pages are duplicated in the buffer cache for each database.

■ **Tip** It may not be appropriate to have a database snapshot present while IO-intensive tasks are carried out. I have seen a couple of scenarios—one involving index rebuilds on a VLDB and the other involving a snapshot on the Subscriber database in a Replication topology—where the copy-on-write thread and the ghost clean-up thread have blocked each other so badly that processes never complete. If you encounter this scenario and you must have a snapshot present during IO-intensive tasks, then the only workaround is to disable the ghost clean-up task using Trace Flag 661. Be warned, however, that if you take this approach, deleted rows are never automatically removed, and you must clean them up in another way, such as by rebuilding all indexes.

In addition to the resource overhead of database snapshots, another issue you encounter when you use them to reduce contention for reporting is that data becomes stale as pages in the source database are modified. To overcome this, you can create a metadata-driven script to periodically refresh the snapshot. This is demonstrated in Chapter 17.

The issue of data becoming stale can also be an advantage however, because it gives you two benefits: first, it means that you can use snapshots for historic reporting purposes; and second, it means that you can use database snapshots to recover data after user error has occurred. Be warned, however, that these snapshots provide no resilience against IO errors or database failures, and you cannot use them to replace database backups.

Implementing Database Snapshots

Before demonstrating how to create a database snapshot, we first create the Chapter16 database, which we use for demonstrations throughout this chapter. The script in Listing 16-1 creates this database and populates it with data.

Listing 16-1. Creating the Chapter16 Database

```
CREATE DATABASE Chapter16 ;
GO

USE Chapter16
GO

CREATE TABLE Customers
(
ID                 INT             PRIMARY KEY        IDENTITY,
FirstName          NVARCHAR(30),
LastName           NVARCHAR(30),
CreditCardNumber   VARBINARY(8000)
) ;
GO

--Populate the table

DECLARE @Numbers TABLE
(
        Number        INT
)

;WITH CTE(Number)
AS
(
        SELECT 1 Number
        UNION ALL
        SELECT Number + 1
        FROM CTE
        WHERE Number < 100
)
```

```
INSERT INTO @Numbers
SELECT Number FROM CTE ;

DECLARE @Names TABLE
(
        FirstName       VARCHAR(30),
        LastName        VARCHAR(30)
) ;

INSERT INTO @Names
VALUES('Peter', 'Carter'),
                ('Michael', 'Smith'),
                ('Danielle', 'Mead'),
                ('Reuben', 'Roberts'),
                ('Iris', 'Jones'),
                ('Sylvia', 'Davies'),
                ('Finola', 'Wright'),
                ('Edward', 'James'),
                ('Marie', 'Andrews'),
                ('Jennifer', 'Abraham'),
                ('Margaret', 'Jones') ;

INSERT INTO Customers(Firstname, LastName, CreditCardNumber)
SELECT  FirstName, LastName, CreditCardNumber FROM
        (SELECT
                (SELECT TOP 1 FirstName FROM @Names ORDER BY NEWID()) FirstName
               ,(SELECT TOP 1 LastName FROM @Names ORDER BY NEWID()) LastName
               ,(SELECT CONVERT(VARBINARY(8000)
               ,(SELECT TOP 1 CAST(Number * 100 AS CHAR(4))
                 FROM @Numbers
                 WHERE Number BETWEEN 10 AND 99
                 ORDER BY NEWID()) + '-' +
                        (SELECT TOP 1 CAST(Number * 100 AS CHAR(4))
                         FROM @Numbers
                         WHERE Number BETWEEN 10 AND 99
                         ORDER BY NEWID()) + '-' +
                        (SELECT TOP 1 CAST(Number * 100 AS CHAR(4))
                         FROM @Numbers
                         WHERE Number BETWEEN 10 AND 99
                         ORDER BY NEWID()) + '-' +
                        (SELECT TOP 1 CAST(Number * 100 AS CHAR(4))
                         FROM @Numbers
                         WHERE Number BETWEEN 10 AND 99
                         ORDER BY NEWID())))) CreditCardNumber
FROM @Numbers a
CROSS JOIN @Numbers b
) d ;
```

559

To create a database snapshot on the Chapter16 database, we use the CREATE DATABASE syntax, adding the AS SNAPSHOT OF clause, as demonstrated in Listing 16-2. The number of files must match the number of files of the source database, and the snapshot must be created with a unique name. The .ss file extension is standard, but not mandatory. I have known some DBAs to use an .ndf extension if they cannot gain an antivirus exception for an additional file extension. I recommend using the .ss extension if possible, however, because this clearly identifies the file as being associated with a snapshot.

Listing 16-2. Creating a Database Snapshot

```
CREATE DATABASE Chapter16_ss_0630
ON PRIMARY
( NAME = N'Chapter16', FILENAME = N'F:\MSSQL\DATA\Chapter16_ss_0630.ss' )
AS SNAPSHOT OF Chapter16 ;
```

The fact that each database snapshot must have a unique name can cause an issue for connecting applications if you plan to use multiple snapshots; this is because the applications do not know the name of the database to which they should connect. You can resolve this issue by programmatically pointing applications to the latest database snapshot. You can find an example of how to do this in Listing 16-3. This script creates and runs a procedure that returns all data from the Contacts table. It first dynamically checks the name of the most recent snapshot that is based on the Chapter16 database, which means that the data will always be returned from the most recent snapshot.

Listing 16-3. Directing Clients to Latest Snapshot

```
USE Chapter16
GO

CREATE PROCEDURE dbo.usp_Dynamic_Snapshot_Query
AS
BEGIN
        DECLARE @LatestSnashot NVARCHAR(128)
        DECLARE @SQL NVARCHAR(MAX)

        SET @LatestSnashot = (
            SELECT TOP 1 name from sys.databases
            WHERE source_database_id = DB_ID('Chapter16')
            ORDER BY create_date DESC ) ;

        SET @SQL = 'SELECT * FROM ' + @LatestSnashot + '.dbo.Customers' ;

        EXEC(@SQL) ;
END

EXEC dbo.usp_Dynamic_Snapshot_Query ;
```

Recovering Data from a Snapshot

If user error leads to data loss, then a database snapshot can allow a DBA to recover data without needing to restore a database from a backup, which can reduce the RTO for resolving the issue. Imagine that a user accidently truncates the Contacts table in the Chapter16 database; we can recover this data by reinserting it from the snapshot, as demonstrated in Listing 16-4.

Listing 16-4. Recovering Lost Data

```
--Truncate the table

TRUNCATE TABLE Chapter16.dbo.Customers ;

--Allow Identity values to be re-inserted

SET IDENTITY_INSERT Chapter16.dbo.Customers ON ;

--Insert the data

INSERT INTO Chapter16.dbo.Customers(ID, FirstName, LastName, CreditCardNumber)
SELECT *
        FROM Chapter16_ss_0630.dbo.Customers ;

--Turn off IDENTITY_INSERT

SET IDENTITY_INSERT Chapter16.dbo.Customers OFF ;
```

If a large portion of the source database has been damaged by user error, then instead of fixing each data issue individually, it may be quicker to recover the entire database from the snapshot. You can do this using the RESTORE command with the FROM DATABASE_SNAPSHOT syntax, as demonstrated in Listing 16-5.

Listing 16-5. Recovering from a Database Snapshot

```
USE Master
GO

RESTORE DATABASE Chapter16
        FROM DATABASE_SNAPSHOT = 'Chapter16_ss_0630' ;
```

■ **Note** If more than one snapshot of the database that you wish to recover exists, then you must drop all the snapshots but the one you are going to restore from before you run this script.

Replication

SQL Server provides a suite of replication technologies, which you can use to disperse data between instances. You can use replication for many purposes, including offloading reporting, integrating data from multiple sites, supporting data warehousing, and exchanging data with mobile users.

Replication Concepts

Replication draws its terminology from the publishing industry. The components of a Replication topology are described in Table 16-1.

Table 16-1. *Replication Components*

Component	Description
Publisher	The publisher is the instance that makes data available to other locations. This is essentially the primary server.
Subscriber	The subscriber is the instance that receives data from the publisher. This is essentially the secondary server. A Replication topology can have multiple subscribers.
Distributor	The distributor is the instance that stores the metadata for the replication technology and may also take the workload of processing. This instance may be the same instance as the publisher.
Article	An article is a database object that is replicated, such as a table or a view. The article can be filtered to reduce the amount of data that needs to be replicated.
Publication	A publication is a collection of articles from a database that is replicated as a single unit.
Subscription	A subscription is a request from a subscriber to receive publications. It defines which publications are received by the subscriber. There are two types of subscription: push and pull. In a pull subscription model, the distribution or merge agent that is responsible for moving the data runs on each subscriber. In a push model, the distribution or merge agent runs on the distributor.
Replication Agents	Replication agents are applications that sit outside of SQL Server that are used to perform various tasks. The agents that are used depend on the type of replication that you implement.

Figure 16-3 illustrates how the replication components fit together within a Replication topology. In this example, two subscribers each receiving the same publication and the distributor has been separated from the publisher. This is known as a *remote distributor*. If the publisher and distributor shared an instance, then it is known as a *local distributor*.

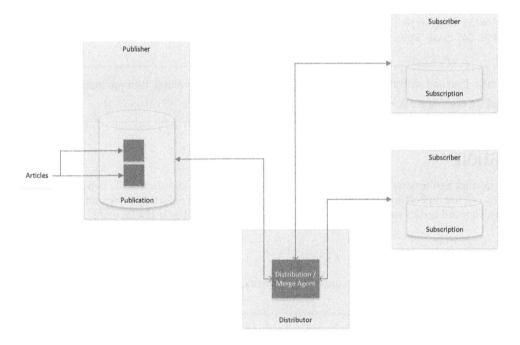

Figure 16-3. *Replication component overview*

Types of Replication

SQL Server offers three broad types of replication: snapshot, transactional, and merge. These replication technologies are introduced in the following sections.

Snapshot

Snapshot replication works by taking a complete copy of all articles at the point when synchronizations occurs; therefore, it does not need to track data changes between synchronizations. If you have defined a filter on the article, then only the filtered data is copied. This means that snapshot replication has no overhead, except when synchronization is occurring. When synchronization does occur, however, the resource overhead can be very high if there is a large amount of data to replicate.

The Snapshot Agent creates a system view and system stored procedure for each article in the publication. It uses these objects to generate the contents of the articles. It also creates schema files, which it applies to the subscription database before it uses BCP (Bulk Copy Program) to bulk copy the data.

Because of the resource utilization profile, snapshot replication is most suited to situations in which the dataset being replicated is small and changes infrequently, or in cases in which many changes happen in a short time period. (An example of this may include a price list, which is updated monthly.) Additionally, snapshot replication is the default mechanism you use to perform the initial synchronization for transactional and merge replication.

When you are using snapshot replication, the Snapshot Agent runs on the publisher to generate the publication. The Distribution Agent (which runs either on the distributor or on each subscriber) then applies the publication to the subscribers. Snapshot replication always works in a single direction only, meaning that the subscribers can never update the publisher.

Transactional

Transactional replication works by reading transactions from the transaction log on the publisher and then sending these transactions to be reapplied on the subscribers. The Log Reader Agent, which runs at the publisher, reads the transactions, and a VLF is not truncated until all log records marked for replication have been processed. This means that if there is a long period between synchronizations and many data modifications occur, there is a risk that your transaction log will grow or even run out of space. After the transactions have been read from the log, the Distribution Agent applies the transactions to the subscribers. This agent runs at the distributor in a push subscription model or at each of the subscribers in a pull subscription model. Synchronization is scheduled by SQL Server Agent jobs, which are configured to run the replication agents, and you can configure synchronization so it happens continuously or periodically, depending on your requirements. The initial data synchronization is performed using the Snapshot Agent by default.

Transactional replication is normally used in server-to-server scenarios where there is a high volume of data modifications at the publisher and there is a reliable network connection between the publisher and subscriber. A global data warehouse is an example of this, having subsets of data replicated to regional data warehouses.

Standard transactional replication always works in a single direction only, which means that it is not possible for the subscribers to update the publisher. SQL Server also offers peer-to-peer transactional replication, however. In a Peer-to-Peer topology, each server acts as a publisher and a subscriber to the other servers in the topology. This means that changes you make on any server are replicated to all other servers in the topology.

Because all servers can accept updates, it is possible for conflicts to occur. For this reason, peer-to-peer replication is most suitable when each peer accepts updates on a differ partition of data. If a conflict does occur, you can configure SQL Server to apply the transaction with the highest OriginatorID (a unique integer that is assigned to each node in the topology), or you can choose to resolve the conflict manually, which is the recommended approach.

■ **Tip** If you are unable to partition the updateable data between nodes, and conflicts are likely, you may find merge replication to be a better choice of technology.

Merge

Merge replication allows you to update both the publisher and the subscribers. This is a good choice for client-server scenarios, such as mobile sales persons who can enter orders on their laptops and then have them sync with the main sales database. It can also be useful in some server-server scenarios—for example, regional data warehouses that are updated via ETL processes and then rolled up into a global data warehouse.

Merge replication works by maintaining a rowguid on every table that is an article within the publication. If the table does not have a uniquiidentifier column with the ROWGUID property set, then merge replication adds one. When a data modification is made to a table, a trigger fires, which maintains a series of change-tracking tables. When the Merge Agent runs, it applies only the latest version of the row. This means that resource utilization is high for tracking changes that occur, but the tradeoff is that merge replication has the lowest overhead for actually synchronizing the changes.

Because the subscribers, as well as the publisher, can be updated, there is a risk that conflicts between rows will occur. You manage these using conflict resolvers. Merge replication offers 12 conflict resolvers out of the box, including earliest wins, latest wins, and subscriber always wins. You can also program your own COM-based conflict resolvers or choose to resolve conflicts manually.

Because you can use merge replication in client-server scenarios, it offers you a technology called Web synchronization for updating subscribers. When you use Web synchronization, after extracting the changes, the Merge Agent makes an HTTPS request to IIS and sends the data changes to the subscribers in the form of an XML message. Replication Listener and Merge Replication Reconciler, which are processes running on the subscriber, process the data changes, after sending any data modifications made at the subscriber back to the publisher.

Implementing Transactional Replication

The most appropriate type of replication for scaling workloads is standard transactional replication. We discuss how to implement this technology in the following sections.

■ **Note** For the demonstrations in this section, we use two instances: WIN-KIAGK4GN1MJ\PROSQLADMIN and WIN-KIAGK4GN1MJ\PROSQLADMIN2.

Implementing the Distributor and Publisher with SSMS

To begin configuring transaction replication for the Chapter16 database, we select New Publication from the context menu of Replication | Local Publications in Object Explorer, within the PROSQLADMIN instance. This causes the New Publication Wizard to be invoked. After passing through the welcome screen, we see the Distributor page of the wizard, as illustrated in Figure 16-4. On this page, we can choose to use the publisher instance as the distributor or specify a different instance. If you specify a different instance, then you must already have configured the instance as a distributor, but in our case, we use the same instance, thereby configuring a local distributor.

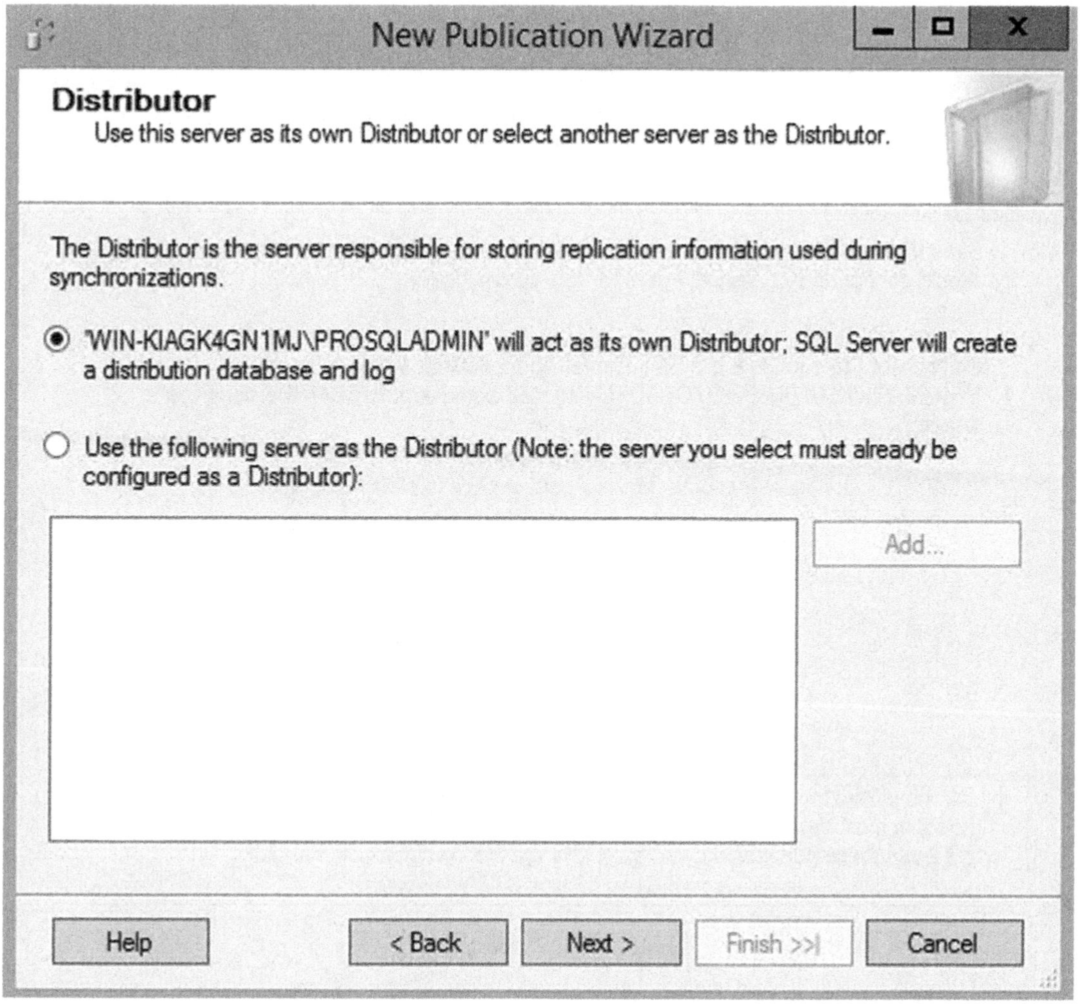

Figure 16-4. The Distributor page

Because our instance is not currently configured for SQL Server Agent service to start automatically, we now see the SQL Server Agent Start page, which warns us of this situation. This is because replication agents rely on SQL Server Agent to be scheduled and run. We choose the option for SQL Server Agent to be configured to start automatically, as shown in Figure 16-5.

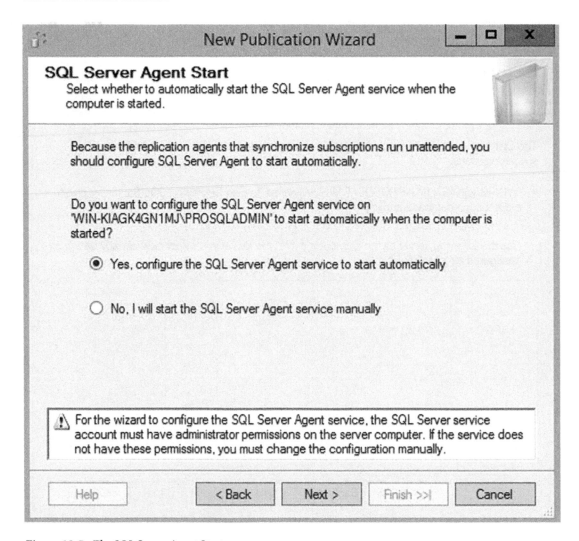

Figure 16-5. *The SQL Server Agent Start page*

On the Snapshot Folder page of the wizard, we select the location the Snapshot Agent will use to store the initial data for synchronization. This can be a local folder or a network share, but if you specify a local folder, then pull subscriptions are not supported, since the subscribers are unable to access it. In our case, we use a network share. The Snapshot Folder page is illustrated in Figure 16-6.

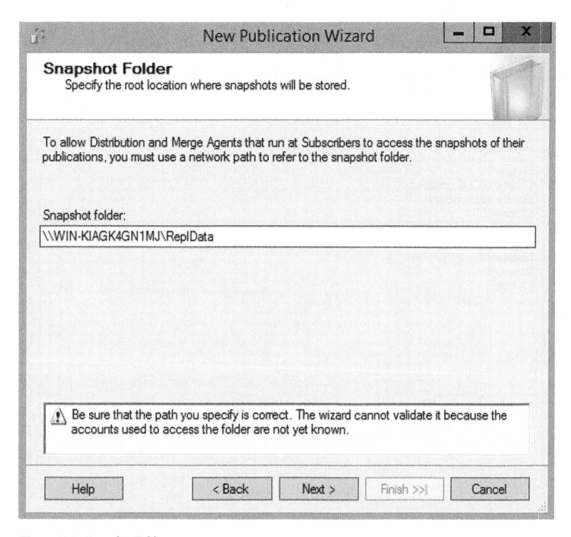

Figure 16-6. Snapshot Folder page

On the Publication Database page, shown in Figure 16-7, we select the database that contains the objects that we wish to use as articles in our publication. All articles within a publication must reside in the same database, so we can only select one database on this screen. To replicate articles from multiple databases, we must have multiple publications.

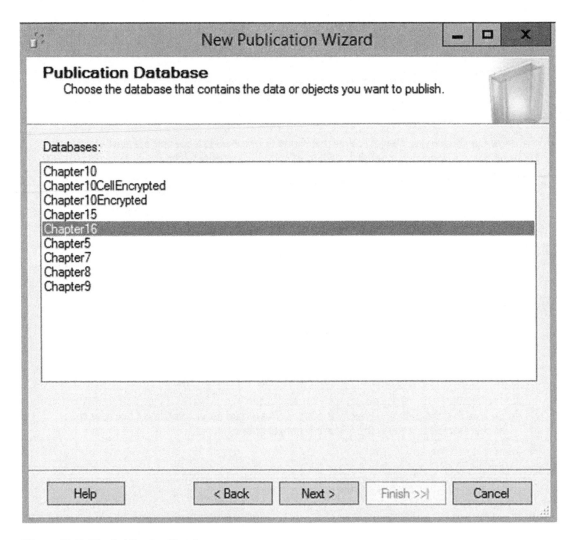

Figure 16-7. *The Publication Database page*

On the Publication Type page, shown in Figure 16-8, we select the type of replication we wish to use for the publication—in our case, transactional.

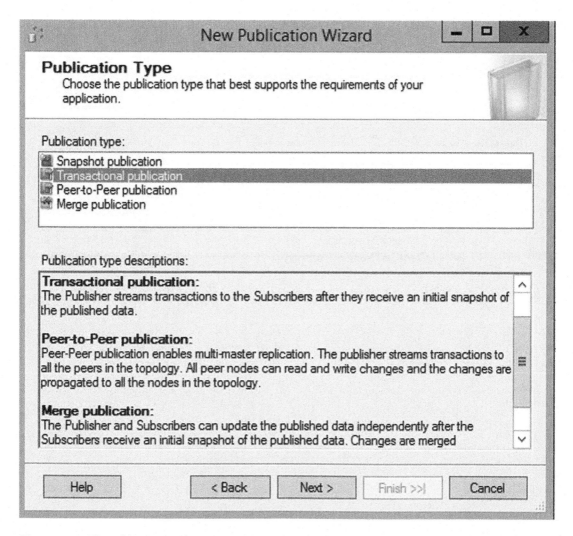

Figure 16-8. *The Publication Type page*

On the Articles page of the wizard, illustrated in Figure 16-9, we select the objects that we wish to include in our publication. All tables that you wish to publish must have a primary key, or you are not able to select them. Within a table, you can also select individual columns to replicate, if you need to.

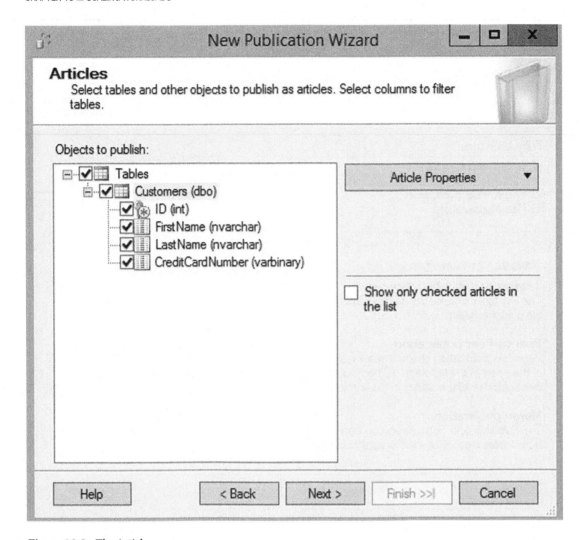

Figure 16-9. *The Articles page*

The Article Properties button allows us to alter the properties, either for the selected article or for all articles within the Article Properties dialog box, which is shown in Figure 16-10. You should usually leave most properties as the default unless you have a specific reason to change them. However, you should pay particular attention to some properties.

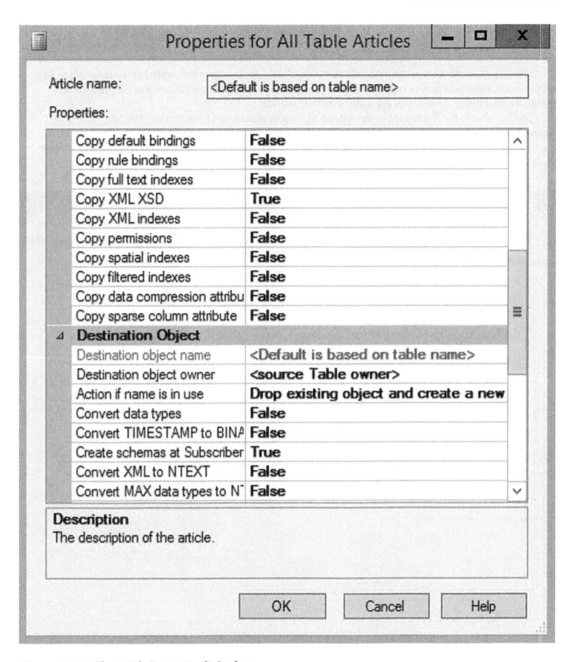

Figure 16-10. *The Article Properties dialog box*

You use the Action If Name Is In Use property to determine the behavior if a table with the same name already exists in the subscriber database. The possible options are as follows:

- Keep the existing object unchanged.

- Drop the existing object and create a new one.

- Delete data. If the article has a row filter, delete only the data that matches the filter.

- Truncate all data in the existing object.

The Copy Permissions property demines if object-level permissions are copied to the subscriber. This is important, since you may or may not want to configure the permissions the same as they are for the publisher depending on how you are using the environment.

On the Filter Table Rows page of the wizard, shown in Figure 16-11, we can use the Add, Edit, and Delete buttons to manage filters. Filters essentially add a WHERE clause to the article so that you can limit the number of rows that are replicated. You'll find this is especially useful for partitioning the data across multiple subscribers.

Figure 16-11. *The Filter Table Rows page*

Figure 16-12 illustrates the Add Filter dialog box. In our case, we are creating a filter so that only customers with an ID > 500 are replicated. The ways you can use this in production scenarios include filtering based on region, account status, and so on.

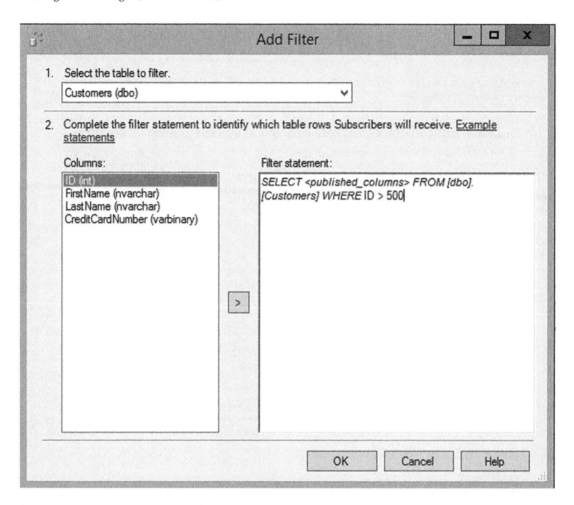

Figure 16-12. *The Add Filter dialog box*

On the Snapshot Agent page, illustrated in Figure 16-13, you can configure the initial snapshot to be created immediately, as we have done here, or you can schedule the Snapshot Agent to run at a specific time.

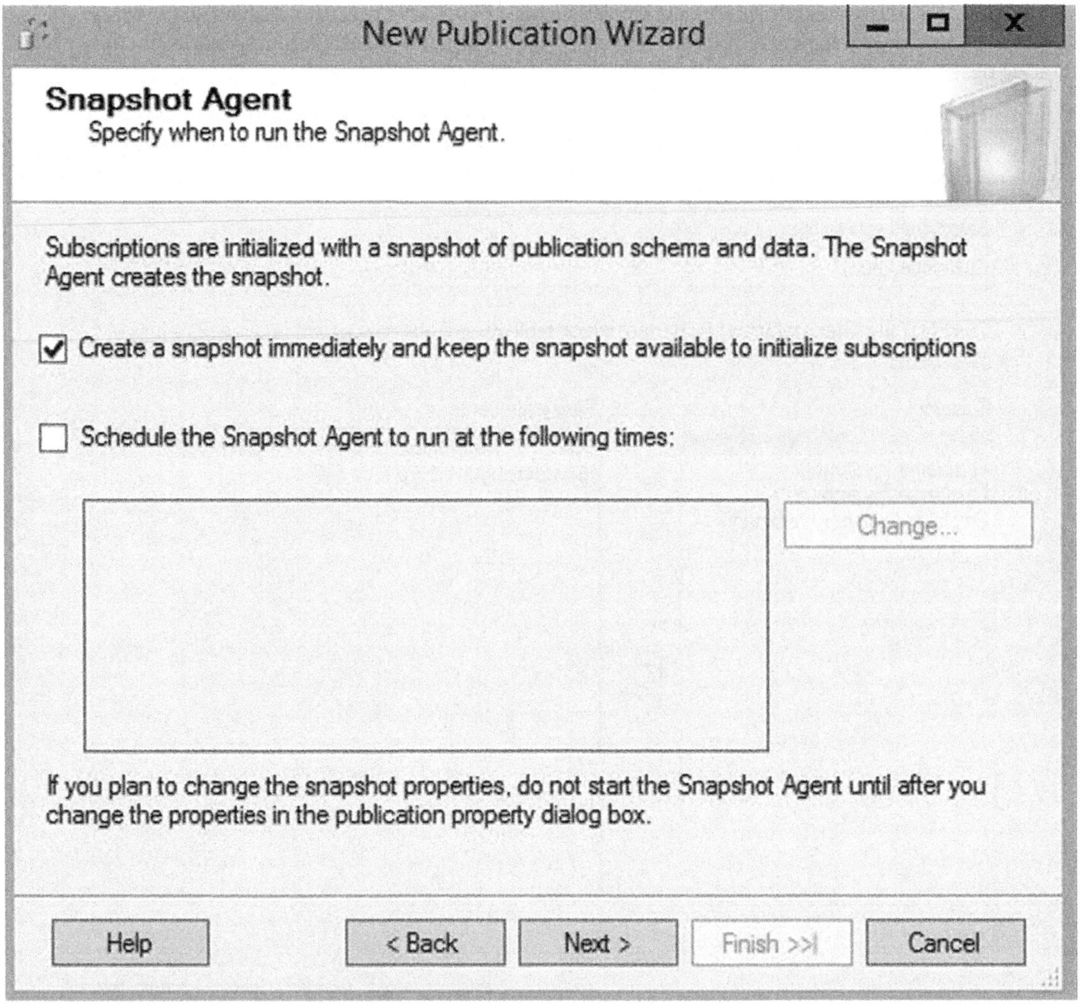

Figure 16-13. *The Snapshot Agent page*

On the Agent Security page, illustrated in Figure 16-14, you are invited to configure the accounts that are used for running each of the replication agents. At a minimum, the account that runs the Snapshot Agent should have the following permissions:

- Be a member of the db_owner database role in the distribution database
- Have read, write, and modify permissions on the share that contains the snapshot

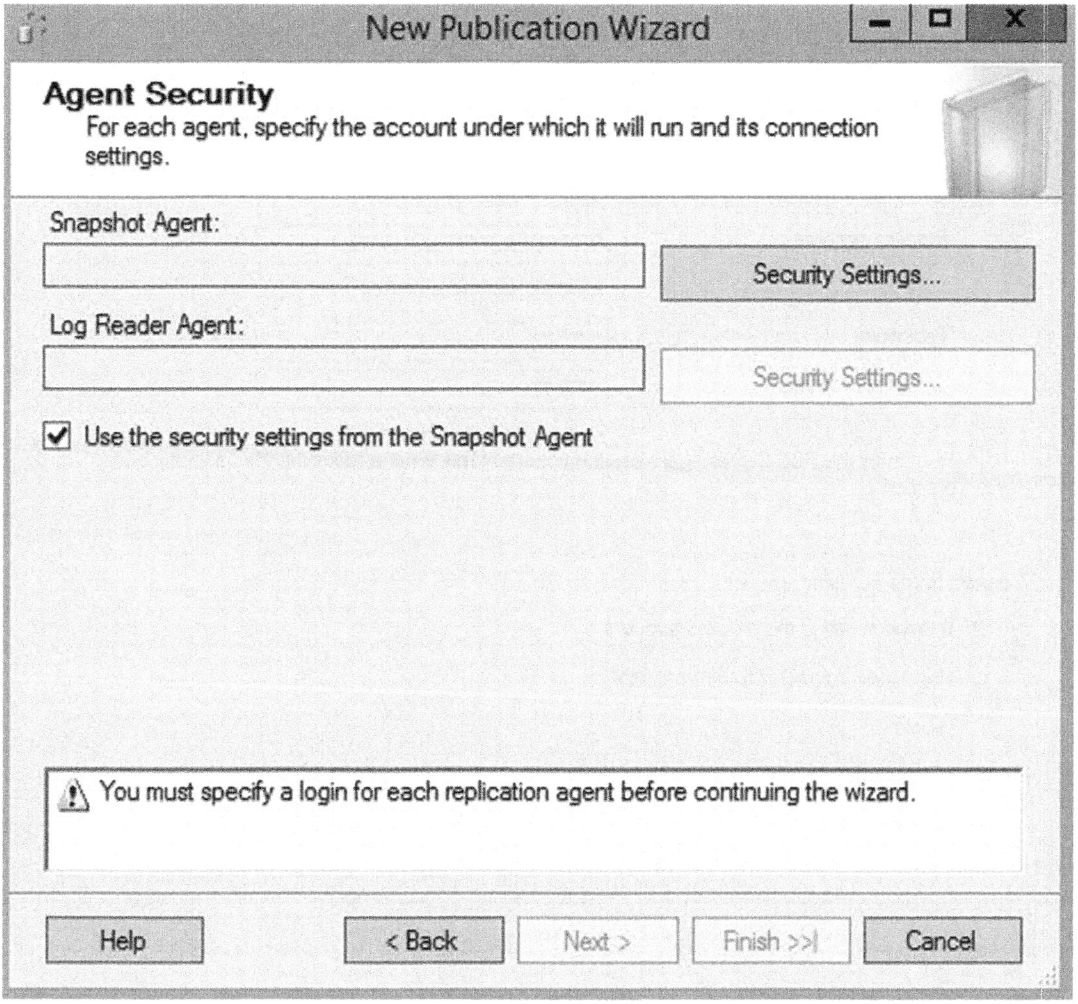

Figure 16-14. *The Agent Security page*

At a minimum, the account that runs the Log Reader Agent must have the following permissions:

- Be a member of the db_owner database role in the distribution database

When you create the subscription, choose the sync_type. This configuration choice affects the Log Reader account's required permissions in the following ways:

- Automatic—No additional permissions required

- Anything else—sysadmin on the distributor

Clicking the Security Settings button for the Snapshot Agent causes the Snapshot Agent Security dialog box to display, as shown in Figure 16-15. In this dialog box, you can choose to run the Snapshot Agent under the context of the Server Agent service account, or you can specify a different Windows account to use. To follow the principle of least privilege, you should use a separate account. It is also possible to specify a different account from which to make connections to the publisher instance. In our case though, we specify that the same account should make all the connections.

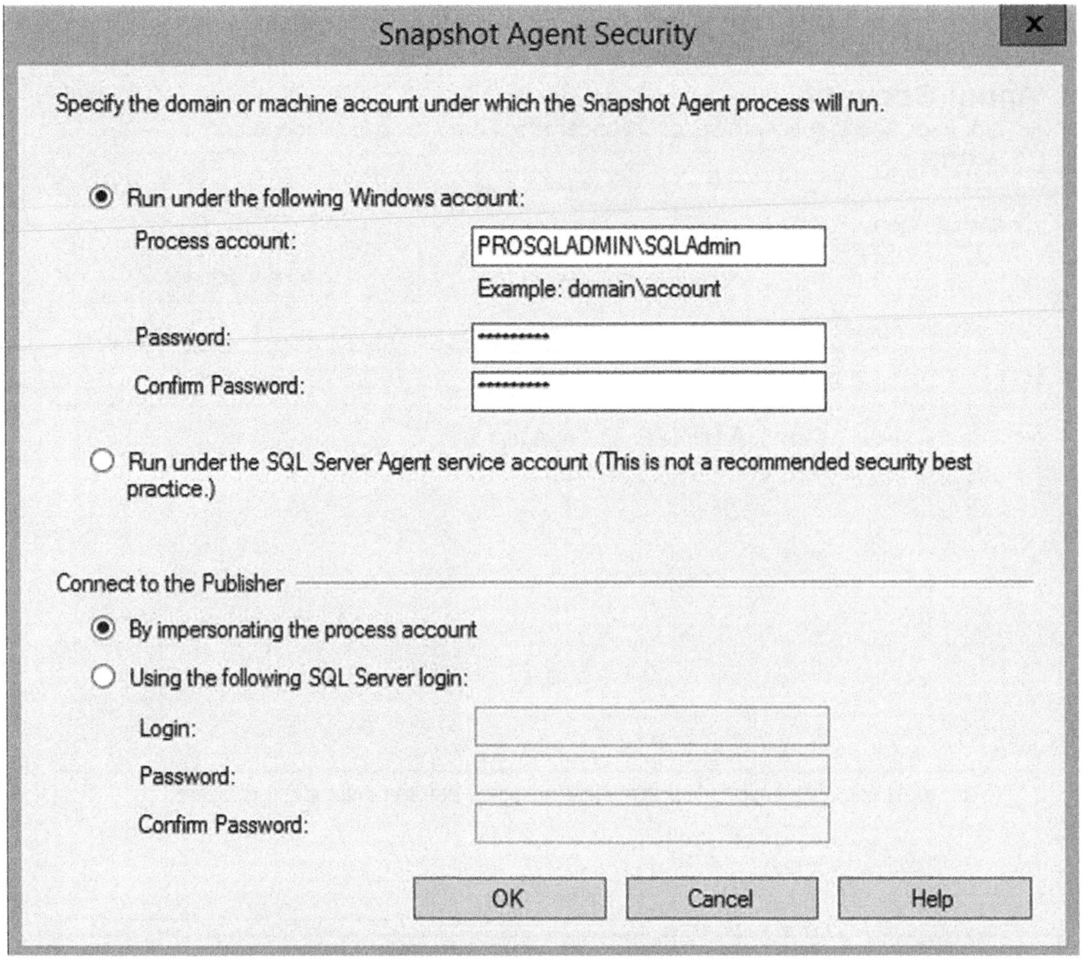

Figure 16-15. *The Snapshot Agent Security dialog box*

Back on the Agent Security page, you can elect to either specify the details for the account that will run the Log Reader Agent, or you can clone the information you have already entered for the account that will run the Snapshot Agent.

On the Wizard Actions page, you can elect to either generate the publication, as we have done, script the generation of the publication, or both. This page is illustrated in Figure 16-16.

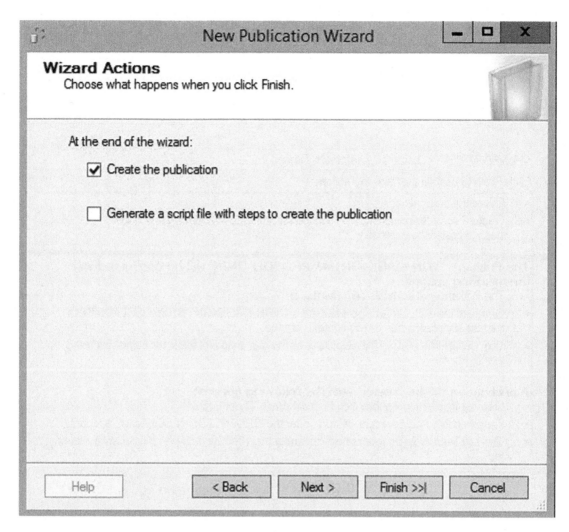

Figure 16-16. *The Wizard Actions page*

Finally, on the Complete The Wizard page, shown in Figure 16-17, a summary of the actions that the wizard will perform displays. You also need to enter a name for the publication on this screen.

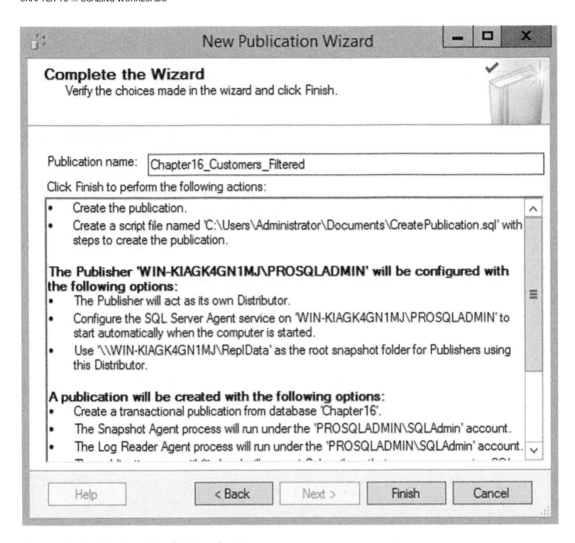

Figure 16-17. *The Complete The Wizard page*

Implementing the Distributor and Publisher with T-SQL

It is important that, as a DBA, you master the ability to script a Replication topology, because at times, you need to tear down and rebuild the environment, such as when you are performing a major code deployment. Also, not all options are available when you are adding replication from the wizard. To perform the same actions via T-SQL, we first need to configure the instance as a distributor. The first step in this process is to register and mark the instance as a distributor. You can do this using the sp_adddistributor system stored procedure, which accepts the parameters described in Table 16-2.

Table 16-2. *sp_adddistributor Parameters*

Parameter	Description
@distributor	Specifies the server\instance that you are configuring as a distributor.
@heartbeat_interval	Specifies the maximum amount of time that can elapse without a running agent reporting a progress message, in minutes. The default is 10 minutes.
@password	Used to specify the password for the distributor_Admin login. Because we are using a local distributor, we can pass a NULL value, and a random password is generated. We do not need to configure a password unless we are configuring a remote distributor.

▪ **Note** Replication parameters that are no longer supported, such as those that are used for implementing updating subscribers, have been omitted from the tables within the Replication section of this chapter.

We can run the procedure in our scenario by using the command in Listing 16-6.

Listing 16-6. sp_adddistributor

```
USE MASTER
GO

EXEC sp_adddistributor @distributor = N'WIN-KIAGK4GN1MJ\PROSQLADMIN', @password = NULL ;
```

Our next step is to create the Distribution database. We can perform this task by running the sp_adddistributiondb system stored procedure. This procedure accepts the parameters detailed in Table 16-3.

Table 16-3. *sp_adddistributiondb Parameters*

Parameter	Description
@database	Specifies the name of the Distribution database.
@data_folder	Specifies the folder in which the data file of the Distribution database is created.
@data_file	Specifies the name of the data file that is created.
@data_file_size	Specifies the initial size of the data file, in megabytes.
@log_folder	Specifies the folder in which the transaction log of the Distribution database is created.
@log_file	Specifies the name of the transaction log file that is created.
@log_file_size	Specifies the initial size of the transaction log file, in megabytes.
@min_distretention	Specifies the minimum period of time that transactions are held in the Distribution database, before they are deleted, in hours.
@max_distretention	Specifies the maximum period of time that transactions are held in the Distribution database before they are deleted, in hours. The default is 72 hours.
@history_retention	Specifies the duration for which the performance history is retained in the Distribution database, in hours. The default is 48 hours.

(continued)

Table 16-3. (*continued*)

Parameter	Description
@security_mode	Specifies the authentication mode used to connect to the distributor to create the Distribution database. • 0 specifies SQL authentication. • 1 specifies Windows authentication, which is the default behavior.
@login	Specifies the name of the login used to connect to the distributor.
@password	Specifies the password of the login used to connect to the distributor.
@createmode	• The default value of 1 indicates that the database will be created or that the existing database will be reused and that the instaldist.sql file will be used to create the replication objects. • The other possible values of 0 or 2 are undocumented and should not be used.

We can use the command in Listing 16-7 to run the sp_adddistributiondb stored procedure for our configuration. Before running the script, be sure to change the file paths to match your own configuration.

Listing 16-7. sp_adddistributiondb

```
EXEC sp_adddistributiondb @database = N'Distribution'
        , @data_folder = N'C:\MSSQL\Data'
        , @log_folder = N'C:\MSSQL\Data'
        , @log_file_size = 2
        , @min_distretention = 0
        , @max_distretention = 72
        , @history_retention = 48
        , @security_mode = 1 ;
GO
```

We now need to register our instance as a publisher within the Distribution database. We can achieve this using the sp_adddistpublisher system stored procedure. This procedure accepts the parameters described in Table 16-4.

Table 16-4. *sp_adddistpublisher Parameters*

Parameter	Description
@publisher	Specifies the server\instance of the publisher.
@distribution_db	Specifies the name of the Distribution database.
@security_mode	Used for heterogeneous replication, which is beyond the scope of this book. • 0 specifies that agents connect to the publisher via SQL authentication. • 1 specifies the agents connect to the publisher using Windows authentication.
@login	Specifies the login that is used to connect to the publisher.
@password	Specifies the password of the login that is used to connect to the publisher.

(*continued*)

Table 16-4. (*continued*)

Parameter	Description
@working_directory	Specifies the folder that stores the snapshot.
@thirdparty_flag	Specifies if the publisher is a SQL Server instance.
	• 0 indicates that it is.
	• 1 indicates that the publisher is a third-party instance.
@publisher_type	Specifies the type of heterogeneous publisher. These are acceptable values:
	• ORACLE
	• ORACLE GATEWAY
	• MSSQLSERVER (The default value, which indicates a homogeneous publisher.)

For our environment, we can run the sp_adddistpublisher by using the command in Listing 16-8.

Listing 16-8. sp_adddistpublisher

```
EXEC sp_adddistpublisher
        @publisher = N'WIN-KIAGK4GN1MJ\PROSQLADMIN'
        , @distribution_db = N'Distribution'
        , @working_directory = N'\\WIN-KIAGK4GN1MJ\ReplData'
        , @thirdparty_flag = 0 ;
```

We now need to enable the Chapter16 database for replication. We do this using the sp_replicationdboption system stored procedure, which accepts the parameters detailed in Table 16-5.

Table 16-5. sp_replicationdboption Parameters

Parameter	Description
@dbname	The name of the database from which the publication is generated.
@optname	The option that is enabled or disabled. These are the possible values:
	• Merge Publish (which configures a database as a publisher in merge replication)
	• Publish (which configures a database as publisher for other replication types)
	• Subscribe (which configures a database as a subscription database)
	• Sync with backup (which enables coordinated backups)
	• Coordinated backups (which enforce that, in the event of a backup at the publisher, the transaction log will not be truncated until the transaction has been received by the distributor and the Distribution database has been backed up. This option only applies to transactional replication.)
@value	Specifies true or false to determine if the option is being turned on or off.
@ignore_distributor	Specifies if the procedure can execute without being connected to the distributor and update its status.
	• 0 means that it must be connected.
	• 1 specifies that it does not have to connect. 1 should only be used in exceptional circumstances in which the distributor is not available.

581

The sp_replicationdboption procedure can be run to achieve our goals by using the script in Listing 16-9.

Listing 16-9. sp_replicationdboption

```
USE Chapter16
GO

EXEC sp_replicationdboption
        @dbname = N'Chapter16'
      , @optname = 'publish'
      , @value = 'true' ;
```

Our next step is to configure the Log Reader Agent. We can do this using the sys.sp_addlogreader_agent system stored procedure. This procedure accepts the parameters detailed in Table 16-6.

Table 16-6. sp_addlogreader_agent Parameters

Parameter	Description
@job_login	The name of the Windows account that runs the Log Reader Agent.
@job_password	The password of the Windows account that runs the Log Reader Agent.
@job_name	The name of the SQL Server Agent job that runs the agent. You should only use this parameter if the SQL Server Agent job already exists.
@publisher_security_mode	Specifies how the agent authenticates to the publisher. • 0 indicates SQL authentication. • 1 indicates Windows authentication, which is the default behavior.
@publisher_login	Specifies the login that connects to the publisher. If the @publisher_security_mode parameter is set to 1 and this parameter is not supplied, then the agent connects under the account specified in @job_login.
@publisher_password	The password of the login that is used to connect to the publisher.
@publisher	The name of the publisher. Should only be specified for a heterogeneous publisher.

For the purpose of configuring our environment, we can use the command in Listing 16-10 to execute the sp_addlogreader_agent procedure.

Listing 16-10. sp_addlogreader_agent

```
EXEC Chapter16.sys.sp_addlogreader_agent
        @job_login = N'PROSQLADMIN\SQLAdmin'
      , @job_password = 'Pa$$w0rd'
      , @publisher_security_mode = 1
      , @job_name = NULL ;
```

■ **Caution** Do not store the password in your script, because this is an obvious security vulnerability. Either enter the password at runtime or store the password in an encrypted table and create a script to decrypt the password and add it to the script dynamically. This advice applies to all scripts, so please heed the same caution for other scripts within this chapter.

Our next step in configuring replication is to add the publisher. You can perform this task using the sp_addpublication system stored procedure. sp_addpublication accepts the parameters described in Table 16-7.

Table 16-7. *sp_addpublication Parameters*

Parameter	Description
@publication	Specifies the name of the publication that is being created.
@sync_method	Specifies how the publication is synchronized. Use this parameter to configure what BCP output is generated. For example, native produces native mode BCP output, while character produces character mode BCP output, and concurrent produces native mode BCP output without locking tables. Passing concurrent_c produces character mode BCP output without locking tables, databasesnapshot produces the native mode BCP output from a database snapshot, and databasesnapshotcharacter produces character mode BCP output from a database snapshot. The default is to use native.
@repl_freq	Specifies if replication should happen continuously by passing continuous, which is the default behavior, or by using pass snapshot to specify that synchronization events should be scheduled.
@description	Specifies a description for the publication.
@status	Specifies if publication data is made immediately available to subscribers. Specify active to make the data available immediately, or inactive to allow subscribers to connect, but without processing the subscription, which is the default behavior.
@independent_agent	Specifies if the publication uses a dedicated distribution agent. The default is false, which means that all publication/subscription pairs on the publisher share a distribution agent.
@immediate_sync	Specifies if the subscribers resynchronize with the snapshot every time the Snapshot Agent runs. • If this is set to true, then you must use an independent distribution agent for the publication. • If set to false, which is the default behavior, only new subscriptions are automatically synchronized with the latest snapshot.
@enabled_for_internet	Specifies that you can use FTP to transfer snapshot data to the subscriber.
@allow_push	Specifies if push subscriptions can be configured against the publication.
@allow_pull	Specifies if pull subscriptions can be configured against the publication.
@allow_anonymous	Specifies if anonymous subscriptions are permitted. If set to true, you must use an independent distribution agent.

(continued)

Table 16-7. (*continued*)

Parameter	Description
@retention	Specifies the duration for which subscription activity is retained, in hours. If a subscription has not become active after this period of time, it is removed. The default is 336 hours (2 weeks).
@snapshot_in_ defaultfolder	<ul><li>If set to true, snapshots are stored in the default location.</li><li>If set to false, snapshots are stored in the location specified in @alt_snapshot_folder.</li><li>If set to true and a value is specified for @alt_snapshot_folder, the snapshot is stored in both locations.</li></ul>
@alt_snapshot_folder	Specifies an alternate file location for snapshots. This can be a folder, a network location, or even an FTP site.
@pre_snapshot_script	Specifies the location of a .sql file that you should run before you take the snapshot. This can be useful if you want to add custom logic to the process—such as checking to see if a specific process is running and looping until it is complete—before you take the snapshot.
@post_snapshot_script	Specifies the location of a .sql file that you should run immediately after you take the snapshot. This can be useful if you are implementing custom logic, such as logging custom details about the snapshot execution.
@compress_snapshot	Specifies that the copy of the snapshot written to the alternate snapshot location will be compressed into a CAB file. Snapshot files are uncompressed at the location at which the Distribution Agent runs.
@ftp_address	If the publication is enabled for FTP, specify the FTP service where the snapshot files are located for the Distribution Agent.
@ftp_port	Specifies the FTP port to use. The default is 21.
@ftp_subdirectory	Specifies the folder path of the FTP service for the snapshot files.
@ftp_login	Specifies the login to use to connect to the FTP service.
@ftp_password	Specifies the password of the login used to connect to the FTP service.
@allow_dts	When creating the subscription, it is possible to specify an SSIS package to perform data transformations on the data. If this is required, you should specify true for this parameter. To enable this option, you must configure the sync_method as character or concurrent_c.
@allow_subscription_copy	Specifies if copies of the Subscription database should be allowed.
@logreader_job_name	Specifies the name of the SQL Server Agent job that runs the Log Reader Agent. You should only use this parameter if the job already exists.
@publisher	Specifies the name of a heterogeneous publisher. Do not use this parameter for homogeneous replication.
@allow_initialize_from_ backup	Specifies if subscriptions are allowed to be initialized from a backup, as opposed to from the Snapshot Agent.
@replicate_ddl	Specifies if the publication supports schema replication.
@enabled_for_p2p	Specifies if the publication can be used for peer-to-peer replication.

(*continued*)

Table 16-7. (*continued*)

Parameter	Description
@enabled_for_het_sub	Specifies if heterogeneous subscriptions are allowed for the publication.
@p2p_conflictdetection	Specifies if conflict resolution is enabled for the publication. This is only appropriate if @enabled_for_p2p if set to true.
@p2p_originator_id	The unique integer that identifies the publication in a peer-to-peer topology. This is only appropriate if @enabled_for_p2p is set to true.
@p2p_continue_onconflict	When set to true, the publication with the highest OriginatorID wins in the event of a conflict. This is only appropriate if @enabled_for_p2p is set to true.
@allow_partition_switch	Specifies if you can perform partition switching on the publication database. Please see Chapter 6 for more details on partition switching.
@replicate_partition_switch	Specifies if Partition Switch statements should be replicated to the subscriber.

To add the publication to our topology using the sp_addpublication procedure, we could run the command in Listing 16-11.

Listing 16-11. sp_addpublication

```
USE Chapter16
GO

EXEC sp_addpublication
        @publication = 'Chapter16_Customers_Filtered'
        , @description = 'Transactional publication of database ''Chapter16'' from Publisher
        ''WIN-KIAGK4GN1MJ\PROSQLADMIN''.'
        , @sync_method = N'concurrent'
        , @retention = 0
        , @allow_push = N'true'
        , @allow_pull = N'true'
        , @allow_anonymous = N'true'
        , @enabled_for_internet = N'false'
        , @snapshot_in_defaultfolder = N'true'
        , @allow_subscription_copy = N'false'
        , @repl_freq = N'continuous'
        , @status = N'active'
        , @independent_agent = N'true'
        , @immediate_sync = N'true'
        , @allow_sync_tran = N'false'
        , @allow_dts = N'false'
        , @replicate_ddl = 1
        , @allow_initialize_from_backup = N'false'
        , @enabled_for_p2p = N'false'
        , @enabled_for_het_sub = N'false' ;
```

Our next task is to configure the Snapshot Agent for the publication. We can perform this task by using the sp_addpublication_snapshot system stored procedure. This procedure accepts the parameters detailed in Table 16-8.

Table 16-8. *sp_addpublication_snapshot Parameters*

Parameter	Description
@publication	Specifies the name of the publication.
@frequency_type	Specifies the type of schedule to use.
	• 1 indicates it should be run once.
	• 4 indicates it should be run daily.
	• 8 indicates weekly.
	• 16 indicates monthly.
	• 32 indicates it should run on a specific day of the month.
	• 64 indicates it should run when SQL Server Agent starts.
	• 128 indicates that it should run when the server is idle.
@frequency_interval	Specifies when the schedule should run, relative to the type of schedule used. Details of how to calculate this value can be found in Table 16-9.
@frequency_subday	Specifies how @frequently_type, within a day, the schedule should run in relation to the subday interval.
	• 1 indicates once.
	• 2 indicates seconds.
	• 4 indicates minutes.
	• 8 indicates hours.
@frequency_subday_interval	The frequency, within a day, that the schedule should run. For example, if @frequency_subday is configure as hours and @frequency_subday_interval is configured as 2, then the schedule runs every two hours.
@active_start_date	Specifies the date that the agent is first scheduled to run.
@active_end_date	Specifies the date that the agent stops being scheduled.
@active_start_time_of_day	Specifies the time that the agent is first scheduled to run.
@active_end_time_of_day	Specifies the time that the agent stops being scheduled.
@snapshot_job_name	Specifies the name for the SQL Server Agent job that runs the Snapshot Agent.
@publisher_security_mode	Specifies the authentication mechanism that the Snapshot Agent uses when connecting to the publisher.
	• 0 specifies SQL authentication.
	• 1 specifies Windows authentication.
@publisher_login	Specifies the name of the login that the Snapshot Agent uses to connect to the publisher.
@publisher_password	Specifies the password of the login that the Snapshot Agent uses to connect to the publisher.
@job_login	Specifies the name of the Windows account that runs the SQL Server Agent job that schedules the Snapshot Agent.
@job_password	Specifies the password of the account that runs the SQL Server Agent job that schedules the Snapshot Agent.
@publisher	Specifies the name of a heterogeneous publisher. You should not use this parameter for a homogeneous publisher.

Table 16-9 describes how to calculate the correct value for @frequency_interval based on the value specified for @frequency_type.

Table 16-9. @frequency_interval Values

@frequency_type value	Usage of @frequency_interval
1	Unused.
4	Specifies the number of days that should elapse before the schedule repeats. For example, 10 would mean the schedule runs every ten days.
8	Specifies: • 1 for Sunday • 2 for Monday • 4 for Tuesday • 8 for Wednesday • 16 for Thursday • 32 for Friday • 64 for Saturday The value is a bitmask, converted to an int, so if you need multiple days of the week, combine the values with a bitwise OR operator. For example, if you want it to run every weekday, the value would be 62.
16	The day of the month.
32	Specify: • 1 for Sunday • 2 for Monday • 3 for Tuesday • 4 for Wednesday • 5 for Thursday • 6 for Friday • 7 for Saturday • 8 for day • 9 for weekday • 10 for weekend day
4	Unused.
128	Unused.

To use the sp_addpublication_snapshot procedure to create the Snapshot Agent for our environment, we can use the command in Listing 16-12.

Listing 16-12. sp_addpublication_snapshot

```
EXEC sp_addpublication_snapshot
        @publication = 'Chapter16_Customers_Filtered'
      , @frequency_type = 1
      , @frequency_interval = 1
      , @frequency_subday = 8
      , @frequency_subday_interval = 1
      , @active_start_time_of_day = 0
      , @active_end_time_of_day = 235959
      , @active_start_date = 0
      , @active_end_date = 0
      , @job_login = N'PROSQLADMIN\SQLAdmin'
      , @job_password = 'Pa$$w0rd'
      , @publisher_security_mode = 1 ;
```

Our next step is to add the Customers article to our publication. To do this, we use the sp_addarticle system stored procedure. This procedure accepts the parameters described in Table 16-10.

Table 16-10. *sp_addarticle Parameters*

Parameter	Description
@publication	Specifies the name of the publication that contains the article.
@article	Specifies a name for the article.
@source_table	Specifies the table in the Publication database on which the article is based.
@destination_table	Specifies the name of the subscription table to which the article is replicated.
@vertical_partition	Specifies if filtering is enabled on the article.
@type	Specifies the type of article. Possible values are described in Table 16-11.
@filter	Specifies the name of the stored procedure that is used to filter the rows.
@sync_object	Specifies the name of the view that is used to generate the data file for this article, in the snapshot.
@ins_cmd	Specifies the command that is used to insert data on the subscriber. By default, this uses CALL to run a stored procedure on the subscriber, with the name format sp_MSIns_Table, where Table is the name of the table on which the article is based. You can configure it to use CALL to run a custom stored procedure, implementing your own logic, or you can specify SQL to replicate an INSERT statement.
@del_cmd	Specifies the command that is used to delete data on the subscriber. By default, this uses CALL to run a stored procedure on the subscriber, with the name format sp_MSDel_Table, where Table is the name of the table on which the article is based. You can configure it to use CALL to run a custom stored procedure, implementing your own logic, or you can use XCALL syntax instead. You can also specify SQL to replicate a DELETE statement.

(continued)

Table 16-10. (*continued*)

Parameter	Description
@upd_cmd	Specifies the command that is used to update data on the subscriber. By default, this uses SCALL to run a procedure on the subscriber with the name format sp_MSUpd_Table, where Table is the name of the table on which the article is based. You can also configure it to use SCALL to run a custom stored procedure implementing your own logic, or you can use CALL, MCALL, or XCALL syntax.
@creation_script	Specifies the name and file path to the .sch file, which is used to create the article at the subscriber.
@description	Specifies a description of the article.
@pre_creation_cmd	Specifies what action you should take if a table with the same name already exists in the Subscription database. • DELETE deletes all data in the table before applying the snapshot; if there is a filter, only data that matches the filter is deleted. • TRUNCATE truncates the table before applying the snapshot. • DROP removes the table, which is the default behavior.
@filter_clause	Specifies the WHERE clause to apply to the filter.
@schema_option	A bitmask that is used to specify the properties of the article. If you pass NULL for this parameter, then a bitmask is generated based on the other property options that you have specified.
@destination_owner	Specifies the owner of the object in the Subscription database.
@status	Specifies the status of the article and how changes are propagated. • 0 indicates that the article is inactive. • 1 indicates the article is active. • 8 indicates that column names should be included in INSERT statements. • 16 indicates parameterized statements should be used. All settings, with the exception of 0, can be added together to specify multiple values. For example, a value of 24 indicates that parameterized statements should be used and that column names should be included in INSERT statements.
@source_owner	Specifies the owner of the object in the Publication database. This parameter applies to heterogeneous publishers.
@sync_object_owner	Specifies the owner of the view that is created for the published article.
@filter_owner	Specifies the owner of the filter.
@source_object	Specifies the name of the table that will be published through this article.
@identityrange managementoption	Specifies how identity ranges should be managed. • MANUAL indicates that the identity column is marked as NOT FOR REPLICATION. • AUTO indicates that ranges are handled automatically.

(*continued*)

Table 16-10. (*continued*)

Parameter	Description
@pub_identity_range	Specifies the range size at the publisher. Only valid if @identityrangemanagementoption is set to AUTO.
@identity_range	Specifies the range size at the subscriber. Only valid if @identityrangemanagementoption is set to AUTO.
@threshold	Specifies a percentage value that defines when a new identity range is assigned by the Distribution Agent.
@force_invalidate_snapshot	Specifies if existing snapshots will be invalidated. • 0 indicates that they are still valid. • 1 indicates they will be invalidated.
@use_default_datatypes	Controls the data type mappings for heterogeneous replication.
@publisher	Specifies the name of the publisher. This parameter should only be used for heterogeneous replication.
@fire_triggers_on_snapshot	Specifies if replicated triggers should fire when the snapshot is applied.
@artid	An OUTPUT parameter that specifies the ID of the article that is created.

When you use CALL syntax to update a subscriber, all values for inserted and updated columns are passed. When you use SCALL, which is valid for updates, only values for updated columns are passed, along with the original primary key values. When you use XCALL syntax, which you can use for updates or deletes, both the old value and the new value for every column are passed. When you use MCALL syntax, which is valid for updates, the update values are passed, along with the original primary key values.

Possible values for the article type are described in Table 16-11.

Table 16-11. *Article Types*

Type	Description
Aggregate schema only	Replicates the schema of an aggregate function.
Func schema only	Replicates the schema of a function.
Indexed view logbased	Replicates an indexed view based on log records.
Indexed view logbased manualboth	Replicates an indexed view based on a view and a filter.
Indexed view logbased manualfilter	Replicates an indexed view based on a filter.
Indexed view logbased manualview	Replicates an indexed view based on a view.
Indexed view schema only	Replicates the schema of an indexed view.
Logbased	Replicates a table based on log records, which is the default behavior.
Logbased manualboth	Replicates a table based on log records with a filter and a view.
Logbased manualfilter	Replicates a table based on log records with a filter.
Logbased manualview	Replicates a table based on log records with a view.
Proc exec	Replicates the execution of a stored procedure.

(*continued*)

Table 16-11. (*continued*)

Type	Description
Proc schema only	Replicates the schema of a stored procedure.
Serializable proc exec	Replicates the execution of a stored procedure, but only if that execution happened within the context of a serializable transaction. Full details of isolation levels can be found in Chapter 18.
View schema only	Replicates the schema of a view.

To use sp_addarticle to create an article for the Customers table with the same filter that we created through the GUI, we can use the command in Listing 16-13.

Listing 16-13. Sp_addaticle

```
EXEC sp_addarticle
        @publication = 'Chapter16_Customers_Filtered'
        , @article = 'Customers'
        , @source_owner = 'dbo'
        , @source_object = 'Customers'
        , @type = 'logbased'
        , @pre_creation_cmd = 'drop'
        , @schema_option = NULL
        , @identityrangemanagementoption = 'manual'
        , @destination_table = 'Customers'
        , @destination_owner = 'dbo'
        , @ins_cmd = 'CALL sp_MSins_dboCustomers'
        , @del_cmd = 'CALL sp_MSdel_dboCustomers'
        , @upd_cmd = 'SCALL sp_MSupd_dboCustomers'
        , @filter_clause = 'ID > 500' ;
```

Our next step is to add the filter to the article, which we do by using the sp_articlefilter system stored procedure. This procedure accepts the parameters detailed in Table 16-12.

Table 16-12. *sp_articlefilter Parameters*

Parameter	Description
@publication	Specifies the publication that contains the article.
@article	Specifies the article to which the filter will be applied.
@filter_name	Specifies a name for the filter.
@filter_clause	Specifies the WHERE clause that defines the filter.
@force_invalidate_snapshot	Specifies if adding the filter invalidates existing snapshots. • 1 indicates that it invalidates snapshots. • 0 indicates that it does not.
@force_reinit_subscription	Specifies if adding the filter causes existing subscriptions to be reinitialized. • 1 indicates that they do. • 0 indicates that they do not.
@publisher	Specifies the name of the publisher. Only use this parameter for heterogeneous replication.

To use the sp_articlefilter to add the filter to our Chapter16 article, we can use the command in Listing 16-14.

Listing 16-14. Sp_articlefilter

```
EXEC sp_articlefilter
        @publication = 'Chapter16_Customers_Filtered'
        , @article = 'Customers'
        , @filter_name = 'FLTR_Customers_1__54'
        , @filter_clause = 'ID > 500'
        , @force_invalidate_snapshot = 1
        , @force_reinit_subscription = 1 ;
```

Finally, we need to create the view that we use to synchronize the article. We can achieve this with the sp_articleview system stored procedure. This procedure accepts the parameters detailed in Table 16-13.

Table 16-13. *sp_articleview Parameters*

Parameter	Description
@publication	Specifies the publication that contains the article.
@article	Specifies the name of the article that the view supports.
@view_name	Specifies a name for the view.
@filter_clause	Specifies a WHERE clause that defines a filter for the view.
@change_active	Specifies if changes to the view's schema are permitted when there are active subscriptions. • 1 indicates that views can be created or re-created. • 0 indicates that they cannot, which is the default behavior.

(continued)

Table 16-13. (*continued*)

Parameter	Description
@force_invalidate_snapshot	Specifies if adding the view invalidates existing snapshots.
	• 1 indicates that it invalidates snapshots.
	• 0 indicates that it does not.
@force_reinit_subscription	Specifies if adding the view causes existing subscriptions to be reinitialized.
	• 1 indicates that they do.
	• 0 indicates that they do not.
@publisher	Specifies the name of the publisher. Only use this parameter for heterogeneous replication.
@refreshsynctranprocs	Specifies if the procedures used to synchronize replication will be re-created.
	• 1 indicates that they will, which is the default behavior.
	• 0 indicates that they will not.

We can use the sp_articleview procedure to create a view for our article by using the command demonstrated in Listing 16-15.

Listing 16-15. sp_articleview

```
EXEC sp_articleview
        @publication = 'Chapter16_Customers_Filtered'
        , @article = 'Customers'
        , @view_name = 'SYNC_Customers_1__54'
        , @filter_clause = 'ID > 500'
        , @force_invalidate_snapshot = 1
        , @force_reinit_subscription = 1 ;
```

Implementing the Subscriber with SSMS

Now that the PROSQLADMIN instance is configured as a distributor and publisher and our publication has been created, we need to configure our PROSQLADMIN2 instance as a subscriber. We can perform this task from either the publisher or from the subscriber. From the subscriber, we perform this task by connecting to the PROSQLADMIN2 instance and then by drilling through replication and selecting New Subscription from the context menu of Local Subscriptions. This causes the New Subscription Wizard to be invoked. After passing through the Welcome page of this wizard, you are presented with the Publication page, as illustrated in Figure 16-18. On this page, you use the Publisher drop-down box to connect to the instance that is configured as the publisher, and then you select the appropriate publication from the Databases And Publications area of the screen.

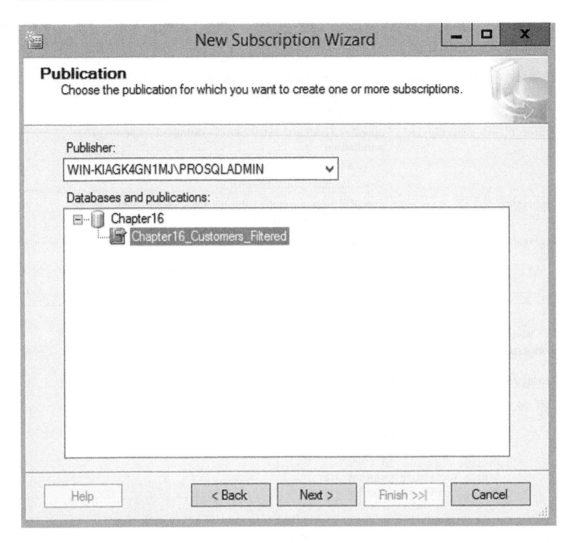

Figure 16-18. *The Publication page*

On the Distribution Agent Location page, you choose if you want to use push subscriptions or pull subscriptions. The appropriate choice here depends on your topology. If you have many subscribers, then you may choose to implement a remote distributor. If this is the case, then it is likely that you will use push subscriptions so that the server configured as the distributor has the impact of agents running. If you have many subscribers and you are using a local distributor, however, then it is likely that you will use pull subscriptions so that you can spread the cost of the agents between the subscribers. In our case, we have a local distributor, but we also only have a single subscriber, so from a performance perspective, it is an obvious choice of which server is most equipped to deal with the workload. We also have to consider security when we place the distribution agent, however; we discuss this later in this section. For this demonstration, we use push subscriptions. The Distribution Agent Location page is illustrated in Figure 16-19.

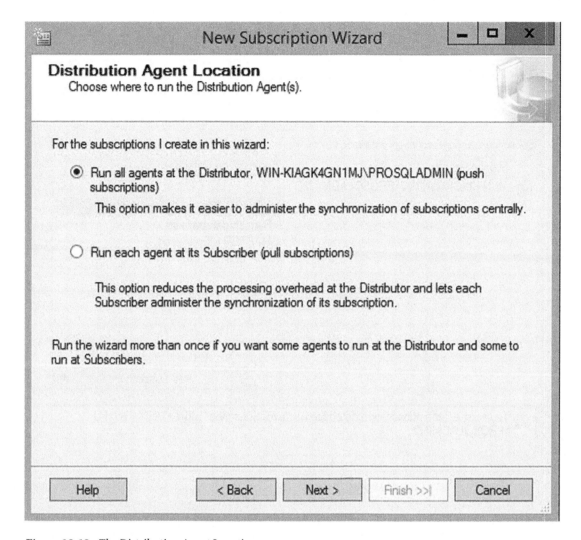

Figure 16-19. *The Distribution Agent Location page*

On the Subscribers page, we can select the name of our subscription database from the drop-down list. Because our subscription database doesn't already exist, however, we select New Database, as shown in Figure 16-20, which causes the New Database dialog box to be invoked.

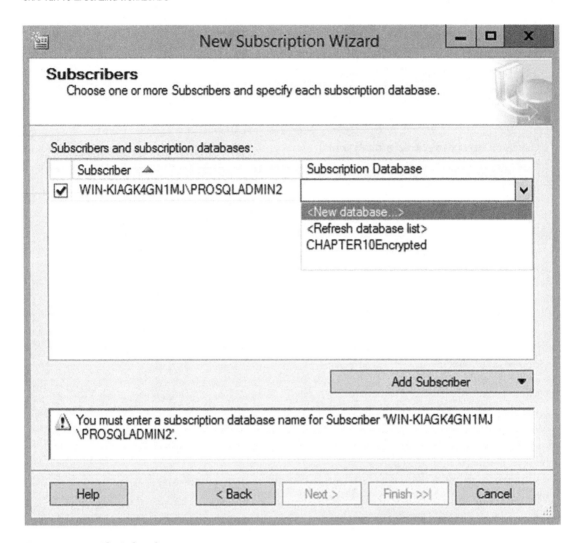

Figure 16-20. *The Subscribers page*

On the General page of the New Database dialog box, shown in Figure 16-21, you need to enter appropriate settings for the subscription database based upon its planned usage. If you need to, you can configure many of the database properties on the Options page.

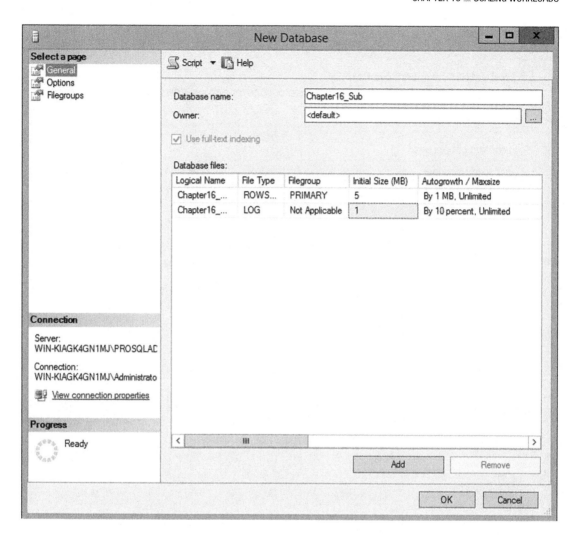

Figure 16-21. *The General page*

On the Distribution Agent Security page, illustrated in Figure 16-22, click the ellipses to invoke the Distribution Agent Security dialog box.

Figure 16-22. *The Distribution Agent Security page*

In the Distribution Agent Security dialog box, illustrated in Figure 16-23, specify the details of the account that runs the Distribution Agent. When you are using push subscription, at a minimum, the account that runs the Distribution Agent should have the following permissions:

- Be a member of the db_owner role on the Distribution database

- Be a member of the publication access list (We discuss configuring publication access later in this chapter.)

- Have read permissions on the share where the snapshot is located

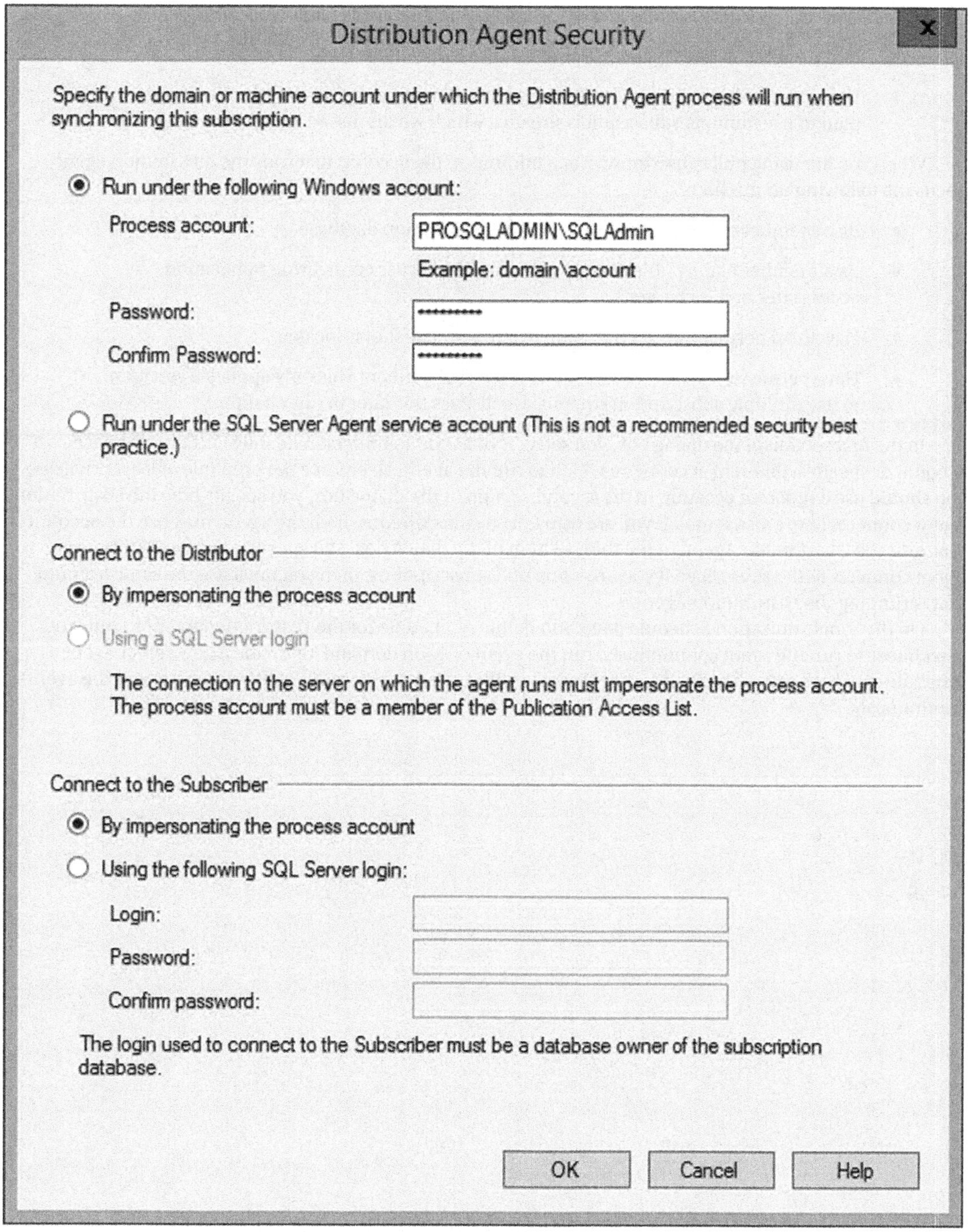

Figure 16-23. *The Distribution Agent Security dialog box*

The account that is used to connect to the subscriber must have the following permissions:

- Be a member of the db_owner role in the subscription database

- Have permissions to view server state on the subscribers (This only applies if you plan to use multiple subscription streams, which we discussed later in this chapter.)

When you are using pull subscriptions, at a minimum, the account that runs the distribution agent needs the following permissions:

- Be a member of the db_owner role on the subscription database

- Be a member of the publication access list (We discuss configuring publication access later in this chapter.)

- Have read permissions on the share where the snapshot is located

- Have permissions to view server state on the subscriber (This only applies if you plan to use multiple subscription streams; we discuss this later in this chapter.)

In the first section of the dialog box, you select if you want to impersonate the SQL Server service account or specify a different account on which to run the agent. To enforce the principle of least privilege, you should use a different account. In the second section of the dialog box, you specify how the Distribution Agent connects to the distributor. If you are using push subscriptions, then the agent must use the account that runs the Distribution Agent. In the third section of the dialog box, you specify how the Distribution Agent connects to the subscriber. If you are using pull subscriptions, then you must use the same account that is running the Distribution Agent.

On the Synchronization Schedule page, you define a schedule for the Distribution Agent to run. You can choose to run the agent continuously, run the agent only on demand, or define a new server agent schedule on which to run the Distribution Agent, as illustrated in Figure 16-24. We choose to run the agent continuously.

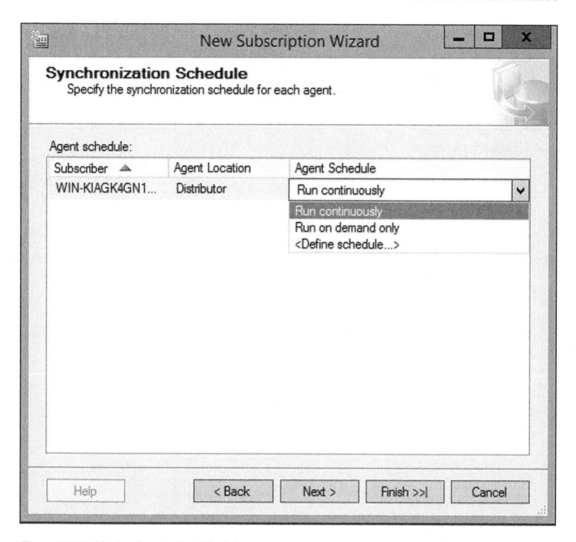

Figure 16-24. *The Synchronization Schedule page*

On the Initialize Subscriptions page, depicted in Figure 16-25, you choose if you want the subscription to be initialized immediately, or if you want to wait for the first synchronization, and then initialize it from the snapshot at that point. For this demonstration, we initialize the subscription immediately.

Figure 16-25. *The Initialize Subscriptions page*

On the Wizard Actions page, you need to choose between whether you want to create the subscription immediately or if you want to script the process. We choose to create the subscription immediately. This page is shown in Figure 16-26.

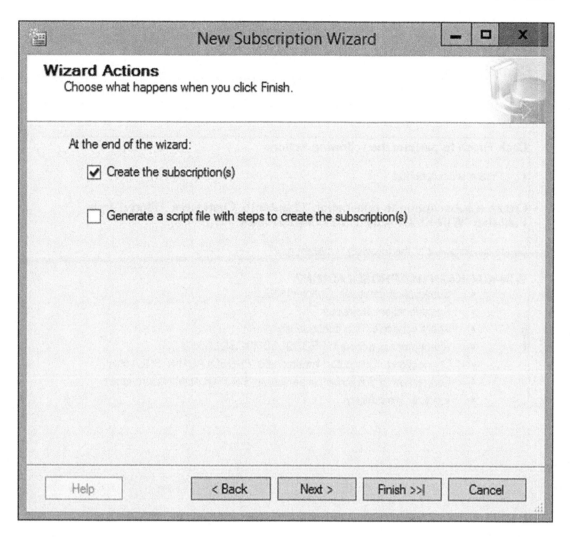

Figure 16-26. *The Wizard Actions page*

Finally, on the Complete The Wizard page, illustrated in Figure 16-27, you are given a summary of the actions that the wizard performs.

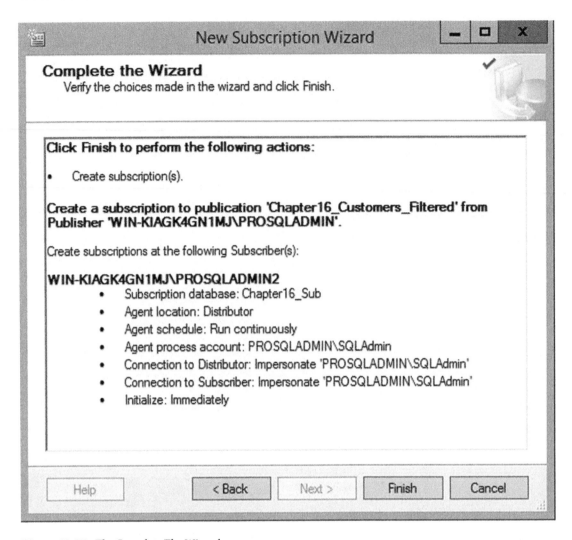

Figure 16-27. *The Complete The Wizard page*

Implementing the Subscriber with T-SQL

When you are implementing the subscriber with T-SQL, as opposed to with the GUI, your first task is to add the subscription to the publication and set its status. We perform this task by using the sp_addsubscriber system stored procedure. This procedure accepts the parameters describer in Table 16-14.

Table 16-14. *sp_addsubscription Parameters*

Parameter	Description
@publication	Specifies the name of the publication to which the subscription is linked.
@article	Specifies the name of an article to which the subscriber is linked. Pass a value of all to indicate that it is linked to all articles in the publication.
@subscriber	Specifies the name of the subscriber.
@destination_db	Specifies the name of the subscription database.
@sync_type	Specifies how the subscriber is initialized. • Automatic (default) indicates that the schema and data is synchronized using a snapshot; replication support only indicates that procedures required at the subscriber are created, but it assumes that the data is already synchronized. • Initialize with backup indicates that the subscriber is initialized with a backup of the publication database, as opposed to with the Snapshot Agent. • Initialize from LSN can be used with peer-to-peer replication.
@status	Specifies the status of the subscription. • Active indicates that the subscription is initialized and ready to accept changes. • Subscribed indicates that the subscription has yet to be initialized.
@subscription_type	Specifies if the subscription is a push subscription or a pull subscription.
@frequency_type	Specifies the frequency type for the Distribution Agent's schedule. Please see Table 16-8 for further details.
@frequency_interval	Specifies the frequency interval for the Distribution Agent's schedule. Please see Table 16-8 for further details.
@frequency_subday	Specifies the subday frequency for the Distribution Agent's schedule. Please see Table 16-8 for further details.
@frequency_subday_interval	Specifies the subday frequency interval for the Distribution Agent's schedule. Please see Table 16-8 for further details.
@active_start_date	Specifies the date that the agent is first scheduled to run.
@active_end_date	Specifies the date that the agent stops being scheduled.
@active_start_time_of_day	Specifies the time that the agent is first scheduled to run.
@active_end_time_of_day	Specifies the time that the agent stops being scheduled.
@optional_command_line	Optionally, use this parameter to specify a command-line command that should be executed.
@enabled_for_syncmgr	Specifies if the subscription can be synchronized using Windows Synchronization Manager.
@dts_package_name	When creating the subscription, it is possible to specify an SSIS package that performs data transformations on the data. If you have enabled this for the publication, then you can specify the name of the SSIS package in this parameter.

(continued)

Table 16-14. (*continued*)

Parameter	Description
@dts_package_password	Specifies the password that has been used to encrypt the SSIS package.
@dts_package_location	Specifies the file path to the SSIS package.
@publisher	Specifies the name of the publisher. Only use this parameter for heterogeneous replication.
@backupdevicetype	If you are initializing a subscription from a backup, then use this parameter to specify the type of backup device: DISK or TAPE.
@backupdevicename	If you are initializing a subscription from a backup, then use this parameter to specify the name of the backup device.
@password	If you are initializing a subscription from a backup, then use this parameter to specify the password of the backup device, if it has one.
@fileidhint	If you are initializing a subscription from a backup, then use this parameter to specify the number of the backup set within the media set to be restored.
@unload	If you are initializing a subscription from a backup and the backup device type is TAPE, then use this parameter to specify that the tape should be unloaded.
@subscriptionlsn	Used for peer-to-peer replication.
@subscriptionstreams	Specifies the number of connections allowed to the subscriber by the Distribution Agent for applying batches. This is discussed in more detail later in this chapter.
@subscriber_type	Specifies the type of subscriber for heterogeneous subscriptions. • 0 indicates SQL Server, which is the default behavior. • 1 indicates an ODBC Data Source. • 2 indicates Microsoft Jet Engine. • 3 indicates OLEDB Provider.

To use the sp_addsubscription procedure to add the subscriber as we did through the GUI, we can use the command in Listing 16-16. This command should be run on the publisher. We do not specify the details for the SQL Server Agent job, because we configure this job in the next step.

Listing 16-16. sp_ addsubscription

```
USE Chapter16
GO

EXEC sp_addsubscription
      @publication = N'Chapter16_Customers_Filtered'
    , @subscriber = N'WIN-KIAGK4GN1MJ\PROSQLADMIN2'
    , @destination_db = N'Chapter16_Sub'
    , @subscription_type = N'Push'
    , @sync_type = N'automatic'
    , @article = N'all' ;
```

Finally, we need to configure the SQL Server Agent job that runs the Distribution Agent. We can do this using the `sp_addpushsubscription_agent` system stored procedure, which accepts the parameters detailed in Table 16-15.

Table 16-15. *sp_addpushsubscription_agent Parameters*

Parameter	Description
@publication	Specifies the name of the publication to which the subscription is linked.
@subscriber	Specifies the name of the subscriber.
@subscriber_db	Specifies the name of the subscription database.
@subscriber_security_mode	Specifies the authentication method for connecting to the subscriber. • 0 indicates SQL authentication. • 1 indicates Windows authentication.
@subscriber_login	Specifies the name of the login to use when connecting to the subscriber.
@subscriber_password	Specifies the password of the login that is used for connecting to the subscriber.
@job_login	Specifies the Windows account that runs the SQL Server Agent job that is used to schedule the Distribution Agent.
@job_password	Specifies the password of the Windows account that is used to schedule the Distribution Agent.
@job_name	Specifies the name of the SQL Server Agent job that is used to schedule the Distribution Agent. Only use this parameter if the job already exists.
@frequency_type	Specifies the frequency type for the Distribution Agent's schedule. Please see Table 16-8 for further details.
@frequency_interval	Specifies the frequency interval for the Distribution Agent's schedule. Please see Table 16-8 for further details.
@frequency_subday	Specifies the subday frequency for the Distribution Agent's schedule. Please see Table 16-8 for further details.
@frequency_subday_interval	Specifies the subday frequency interval for the Distribution Agent's schedule. Please see Table 16-8 for further details.
@active_start_time_of_day	Specifies the date that the agent is first scheduled to run.
@active_end_time_of_day	Specifies the date that the agent stops being scheduled.
@active_start_date	Specifies the time that the agent is first scheduled to run.
@active_end_date	Specifies the time that the agent stops being scheduled.
@dts_package_name	When creating the subscription, it is possible to specify a SSIS package to perform data transformations on the data. If you have enabled this for the publication, then you can specify the name of the SSIS package in this parameter.
@dts_package_password	Specifies the password that has been used to encrypt the SSIS package.
@dts_package_location	Specifies the file path to the SSIS package.
@enabled_for_syncmgr	Specifies if the subscription can be synchronized using Windows Synchronization Manager.

(continued)

Table 16-15. (*continued*)

Parameter	Description
@publisher	Specifies the name of the publisher. Only use this parameter for heterogeneous replication.
@subscriber_provider	Specifies the PROGID of the OLEDB provider. Only used for heterogeneous subscribers.
@subscriber_datasrc	Specifies the name of the data source used by the OLEDB provider. Only used for heterogeneous subscriptions.
@subscriber_location	Specifies the location of the subscriber database used by the OLEDB provider. Only used for heterogeneous subscribers.
@subscriber_provider_string	Specifies the OLEDB provider–specific connection string. Only used for heterogeneous subscribers.
@subscriber_catalog	The catalog to be used when connecting to the OLEDB provider. Only used for heterogeneous subscriptions.

To use the sp_addpushsubscription_agent procedure to configure the SQL Server Agent job, which runs the Distribution Agent in our environment, we can use the command in Listing 16-17.

Listing 16-17. sp_addpushsubscription_agent

```
EXEC sp_addpushsubscription_agent
      @publication = 'Chapter16_Customers_Filtered'
      , @subscriber = N'WIN-KIAGK4GN1MJ\PROSQLADMIN2'
      , @subscriber_db = 'Chapter16_Sub'
      , @job_login = N'PROSQLADMIN\SQLAdmin'
      , @job_password = Pa$$w0rd
      , @subscriber_security_mode = 1
      , @frequency_type = 64
      , @frequency_interval = 0
      , @frequency_subday = 0
      , @frequency_subday_interval = 0
      , @active_start_time_of_day = 0
      , @active_end_time_of_day = 235959
      , @active_start_date = 20150223
      , @active_end_date = 99991231
      , @enabled_for_syncmgr = N'False' ;
```

Replicating to Memory-Optimized Tables

Transactional replication is the only form of replication that supports memory-optimized tables. It does not allow memory-optimized tables to be used as articles in the publication, but it does allow data to be replicated to memory-optimized tables in the subscription database.

In order to demonstrate the configuration of this functionality, we first create a copy of the Chapter16 database, called Chapter16MemOpt, and populate the table with the data from the Chapter16 database. We then create a new publication with an independent agent and generate the snapshot. These tasks are performed in Listing 6-18.

Listing 16-18. Preparing the Database and Publication

```
--Create the database

CREATE DATABASE Chapter16MemOpt ;
GO

USE Chapter16MemOpt
GO

--Create and populate the table

CREATE TABLE dbo.Customers
(
        ID              INT             IDENTITY        PRIMARY KEY
        , FirstName     NVARCHAR(30)
        , LastName      NVARCHAR(30)
) ;
GO

INSERT INTO Chapter16MemOpt.dbo.Customers
SELECT
        FirstName
        , LastName
FROM Chapter16.dbo.Customers ;
GO

--Add the Publication

EXEC sp_replicationdboption
        @dbname = N'Chapter16MemOpt'
        , @optname = N'publish'
        , @value = N'true' ;
GO

EXEC Chapter16MemOpt.sys.sp_addlogreader_agent
        @job_login = N'PROSQLADMIN\SQLAdmin'
        , @job_password = Pa$$w0rd
        , @publisher_security_mode = 1
        , @job_name = NULL ;
GO

EXEC sp_addpublication
        @publication = N'Chapter16_MemOpt'
        , @description = N'Transactional publication of database ''Chapter16MemOpt'' from
        Publisher ''WIN-KIAGK4GN1MJ\PROSQLADMIN''.'
        , @sync_method = N'concurrent'
        , @retention = 0
        , @allow_push = N'true'
        , @allow_pull = N'true'
        , @allow_anonymous = N'true'
        , @enabled_for_internet = N'false'
```

```
        , @snapshot_in_defaultfolder = N'true'
        , @allow_subscription_copy = N'false'
        , @repl_freq = N'continuous'
        , @status = N'active'
        , @independent_agent = N'true'
        , @immediate_sync = N'true'
        , @allow_sync_tran = N'false'
        , @allow_dts = N'false'
        , @replicate_ddl = 1
        , @allow_initialize_from_backup = N'false'
        , @enabled_for_p2p = N'false'
        , @enabled_for_het_sub = N'false' ;
GO

EXEC sp_addpublication_snapshot
        @publication = N'Chapter16_MemOpt'
        , @frequency_type = 1
        , @frequency_interval = 1
        , @frequency_subday = 8
        , @frequency_subday_interval = 1
        , @active_start_time_of_day = 0
        , @active_end_time_of_day = 235959
        , @active_start_date = 0
        , @active_end_date = 0
        , @job_login = N'PROSQLADMIN\SQLAdmin'
        , @job_password = Pa$$w0rd
        , @publisher_security_mode = 1 ;
GO

EXEC sp_addarticle
        @publication = N'Chapter16_MemOpt'
        , @article = N'Customers'
        , @source_owner = N'dbo'
        , @source_object = N'Customers'
        , @type = N'logbased'
        , @pre_creation_cmd = N'drop'
        , @schema_option = 0x000000000803509F
        , @identityrangemanagementoption = N'manual'
        , @destination_table = N'Customers'
        , @destination_owner = N'dbo'
        , @ins_cmd = N'CALL sp_MSins_dboCustomers'
        , @del_cmd = N'CALL sp_MSdel_dboCustomers'
        , @upd_cmd = N'SCALL sp_MSupd_dboCustomers' ;
GO

EXEC sp_startpublication_snapshot @publication = N'Chapter16_MemOpt' ;
```

Instead of immediately adding the subscriber, we first need to perform some manual configuration. This involves manually creating the subscription database and then modifying the .SCH file for the article. The script in Listing 16-19 creates the database when run on the subscriber. In the script, we configure the database collation to be Kana sensitive and Width sensitive, as well as Case and Accent sensitive. We also configure the database to default to the SNAPSHOT isolation level for transactions involving memory-optimized tables. Transaction isolation levels are discussed in Chapter 18. The script also manually creates the table in the subscription database.

Listing 16-19. Creating the Subscription Database

```
CREATE DATABASE Chapter16MmemOpt_Sub
ON PRIMARY ( NAME = PRIMARY, FILENAME = [C:\MSSQL\DATA\Chapter16MemOpt_Sub.mdf]),
FILEGROUP MemoryOptimized
        CONTAINS MEMORY_OPTIMIZED_DATA ( NAME = MemoryOptimized, FILENAME =
        [C:\MSSQL\DATA\Sub])
LOG ON ( NAME = [Chapter16MemOpt_Sub_Log], FILENAME = [C:\MSSQL\LOG\Sub.ldf])
COLLATE Latin1_General_CS_AS_KS_WS;

ALTER DATABASE Chapter16MmemOpt_Sub SET MEMORY_OPTIMIZED_ELEVATE_TO_SNAPSHOT = ON;
GO

USE Chapter16MemOpt_Sub
GO

CREATE TABLE dbo.Customers(
        ID int IDENTITY(1,1) NOT FOR REPLICATION NOT NULL
                            PRIMARY KEY NONCLUSTERED HASH WITH (BUCKET_COUNT = 2000),
        FirstName nvarchar(30) COLLATE Latin1_General_BIN2 NULL,
        LastName nvarchar(30) COLLATE Latin1_General_BIN2 NULL
) WITH (MEMORY_OPTIMIZED = ON, DURABILITY = SCHEMA_AND_DATA) ;
```

We now manually synchronize the data between the publication and subscription databases. It is important to ensure that no further data changes are made in the publication database from this point until replication is fully configured and synchronizing the data. The script in Listing 16-20 uses BCP to synchronize the data, so run it from the command line.

Listing 16-20. Synchronizing Data

```
BCP Chapter16MemOpt.dbo.Customers out c:\Customers.dat -S WIN-KIAGK4GN1MJ\PROSQLADMIN -T -c

BCP Chapter16MmemOpt_Sub.dbo.Customers in C:\Customers.dat -S WIN-KIAGK4GN1MJ\PROSQLADMIN2 -T -c
```

Our next task is to reconfigure the article in order to avoid schema changes. This is because we are not able to use a snapshot to regenerate the schema. We can achieve this using the sp_changearticle system stored procedure, which accepts the parameters detailed in Table 16-16.

Table 16-16. *sp_changearticle Parameters*

Parameter	Description
@publication	Specifies the name of the publication that contains the article.
@article	Specifies the name of the article to modify.
@property	Specifies which property of the article you wish to change.
@value	Specifies the value that you wish to configure for the property.
@force_invalidate_snapshot	Specifies if existing snapshots are invalidated. • 0 indicates that they are still valid. • 1 indicates they are invalidated.
@force_reinit_subscription	Specifies if adding the filter causes existing subscriptions to be reinitialized. • 1 indicates that they are. • 0 indicates that they are not.
@publisher	Specify the name of the publisher. Only use this parameter for heterogeneous publishers.

Therefore, to use the sp_changearticle procedure to stop schema changes from being made to our article, we can use the command in Listing 16-21.

Listing 16-21. sp_changearticle

```
USE Chapter16MemOpt
GO

EXEC sp_changearticle
    @publication = N'Chapter16_MemOpt',
    @article = N'Customers',
    @property = N'schema_option',
    @value = 0,
    @force_invalidate_snapshot = 1,
    @force_reinit_subscription = 1;
GO
```

Finally, we can create a subscription, which is configured to not be synchronized with a snapshot, along with the SQL Server Agent job to run the independent Distribution Agent. We do this using the sp_addsubscription and sp_addpushsubscription_agent system stored procedures as demonstrated in Listing 16-22.

Listing 16-22. Sp_addsubscription

```
USE Chapter16MemOpt
GO

EXEC sp_addsubscription
    @publication = N'Chapter16_MemOpt',
    @subscriber = N'WIN-KIAGK4GN1MJ\PROSQLADMIN2',
    @destination_db = N'Chapter16MemOpt_Sub',
```

```
    @subscription_type = N'Push',
    @sync_type = N'replication support only',
    @article = N'all',
    @update_mode = N'read only',
    @subscriber_type = 0;
GO

EXEC sp_addpushsubscription_agent
        @publication = 'Chapter16_MemOpt'
        , @subscriber = N'WIN-KIAGK4GN1MJ\PROSQLADMIN2'
        , @subscriber_db = 'Chapter16MemOpt_Sub'
        , @job_login = N'PROSQLADMIN\SQLAdmin'
        , @job_password = Pa$$w0rd
        , @subscriber_security_mode = 1
        , @frequency_type = 64
        , @frequency_interval = 0
        , @frequency_subday = 0
        , @frequency_subday_interval = 0
        , @active_start_time_of_day = 0
        , @active_end_time_of_day = 235959
        , @active_start_date = 20150223
        , @active_end_date = 99991231
        , @enabled_for_syncmgr = N'False' ;
```

Configuring Replication

After replication has been set up, a DBA may need to perform various maintenance activities. Two of the most common tasks are modifying the permissions of the PAL (publication access list) and optimizing the performance of replication. These topics are covered in the following sections.

Modifying the PAL

The PAL is used to control access security to the publication. When agents connect to the publication, their credentials are compared to the PAL to ensure they have the correct permissions. The benefit of the PAL is that it abstracts security from the publication database and prevents client applications from needing to modify it directly.

To view the PAL of the Chapter16_Customers_Filtered publication in SSMS and add a login called ReplicationAdmin, you must drill through Replication | Local Publishers and select Properties from the context menu of the Chapter16_Customers_Filtered publication. This causes the Properties dialog box to be invoked, and you should navigate to the Publication Access List page, which is illustrated in Figure 16-28.

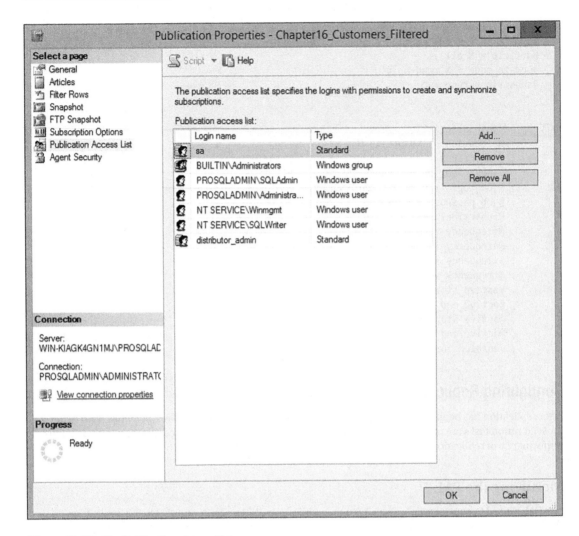

Figure 16-28. *The Publication Access List page*

You can now use the Add button to display a list of logins that do not have current access to the publication. You should select the appropriate login from the list to add it to the PAL, as shown in Figure 16-29.

Figure 16-29. *Add Publication Access*

To view the PAL via T-SQL, you can use the sp_help_publication_access system stored procedure. This parameter accepts the parameters describer in Table 16-17.

Table 16-17. *sp_help_publication_access Parameters*

Parameter	Description
@publication	Specifies the name of the publication.
@return_granted	Specifies if logins with or without access should be returned. • 0 indicates logins without access. • 1 indicates logins with access, which is the default behavior.
@login	Specifies a specific login name to check. By default, a wildcard is used.
@initial_list	Specifies if all logins should be returned or only those that originally had access.

We can run this stored procedure, passing in the name of the publication, to retrieve a list of logins with access, as demonstrated in Listing 16-23.

Listing 16-23. sp_help_publication_access_list

```
EXEC sp_help_publication_access @publication = 'Chapter16_Customers_Filtered'
```

To add the ReplicationAdmin login to the PAL using T-SQL, we can use the sp_grant_publication_ access system stored procedure, passing the name of the publication and the name of the login, which are the only two parameters accepted by this procedure. This is demonstrated in Listing 16-24.

Listing 16-24. sp_grant_publication_access

```
EXEC sp_grant_publication_access
        @publication = 'Chapter16_Customers_Filtered',
        @Login = 'DistributionAdmin'
```

Optimizing Performance

Out of the box, the performance of transaction replication is not always optimal. You can view the current performance of your topology by using Replication Monitor. To invoke Replication Monitor, select Launch Replication Monitor from the Replication context menu in Object Explorer.

In Replication Monitor, drill through the publisher and select the appropriate publication from the list to display the All Subscriptions tab, illustrated in Figure 16-30. In this tab, the status of each subscription displays, along with the average latency and the current performance level, based on predefined thresholds. The date and time of the last synchronization also display.

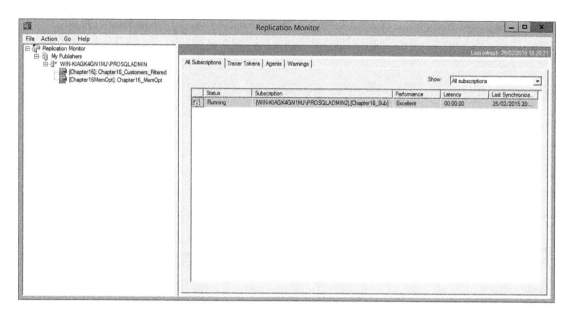

Figure 16-30. *The All Subscriptions tab*

To check the latency for a single packet between the publication and distribution database, and between the distribution database and the subscription database, you can insert a tracer token by navigating to the Tracer Tokens tab and selecting Insert Tracer, as shown in Figure 16-31. This causes a special token to be sent through the topology, and the time it takes to reach each component is recorded.

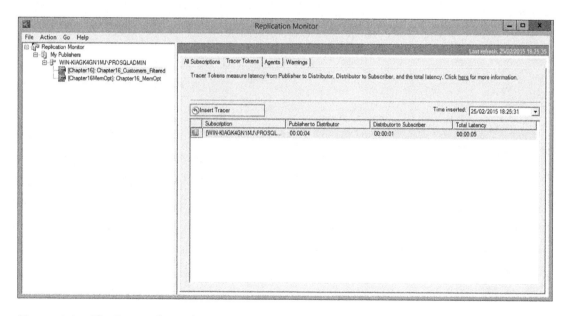

Figure 16-31. *The Tracer Tokens tab*

To configure the latency threshold, as well alerts, navigate to the Warnings tab, as illustrated in Figure 16-32. Here, you can alter the thresholds of the default warnings, or select the Alert check box, to create a SQL Server Agent alert.

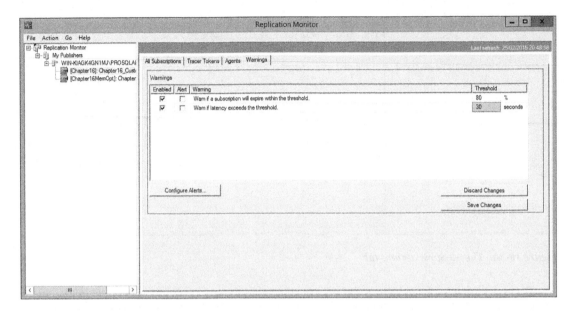

Figure 16-32. *Warnings tab*

SQL Server Agent alerts can be configured by using the Configure Alerts button and then by selecting the appropriate alert from the list, as illustrated in Figure 16-33.

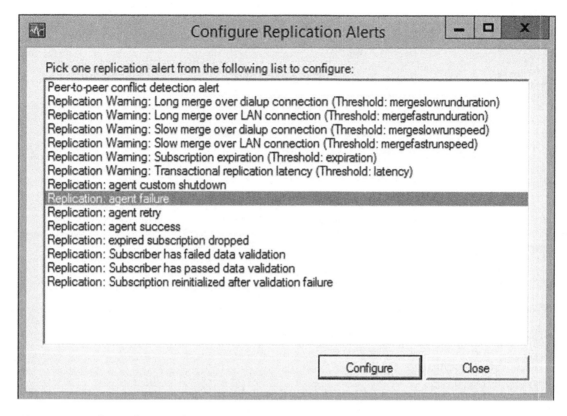

Figure 16-33. *The Configure Replication Alerts dialog box*

The Alerts Properties dialog box is now invoked, prepopulated with relevant information. Figure 16-34 illustrates the General page of the Alert Properties dialog box, which is prepopulated with an appropriate name and the correct error number.

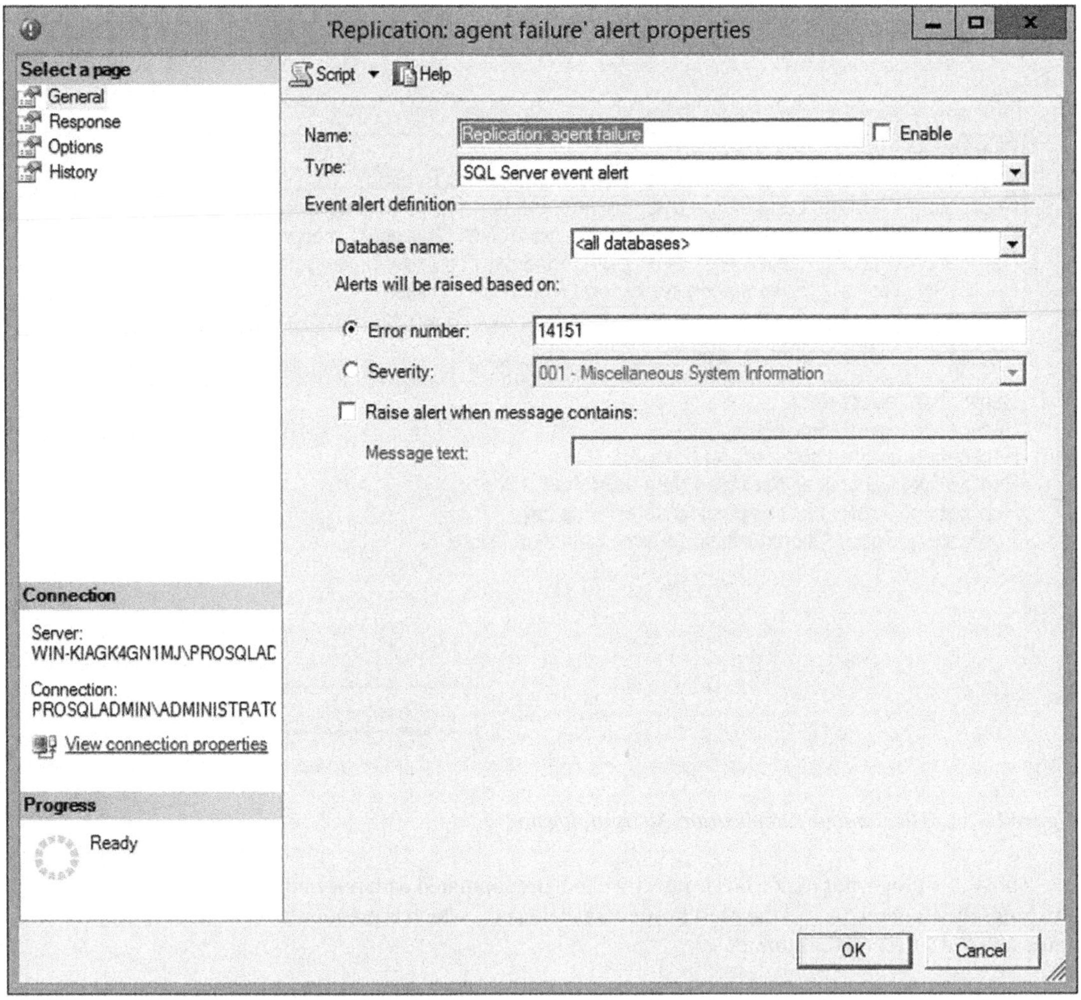

Figure 16-34. The General page

On the Response page of the dialog box, shown in Figure 16-35, you are able to configure a SQL Server Agent job, which is fired in response to the failure. You can also configure which operators are notified of the condition. In this case, they are notified of the agent failure.

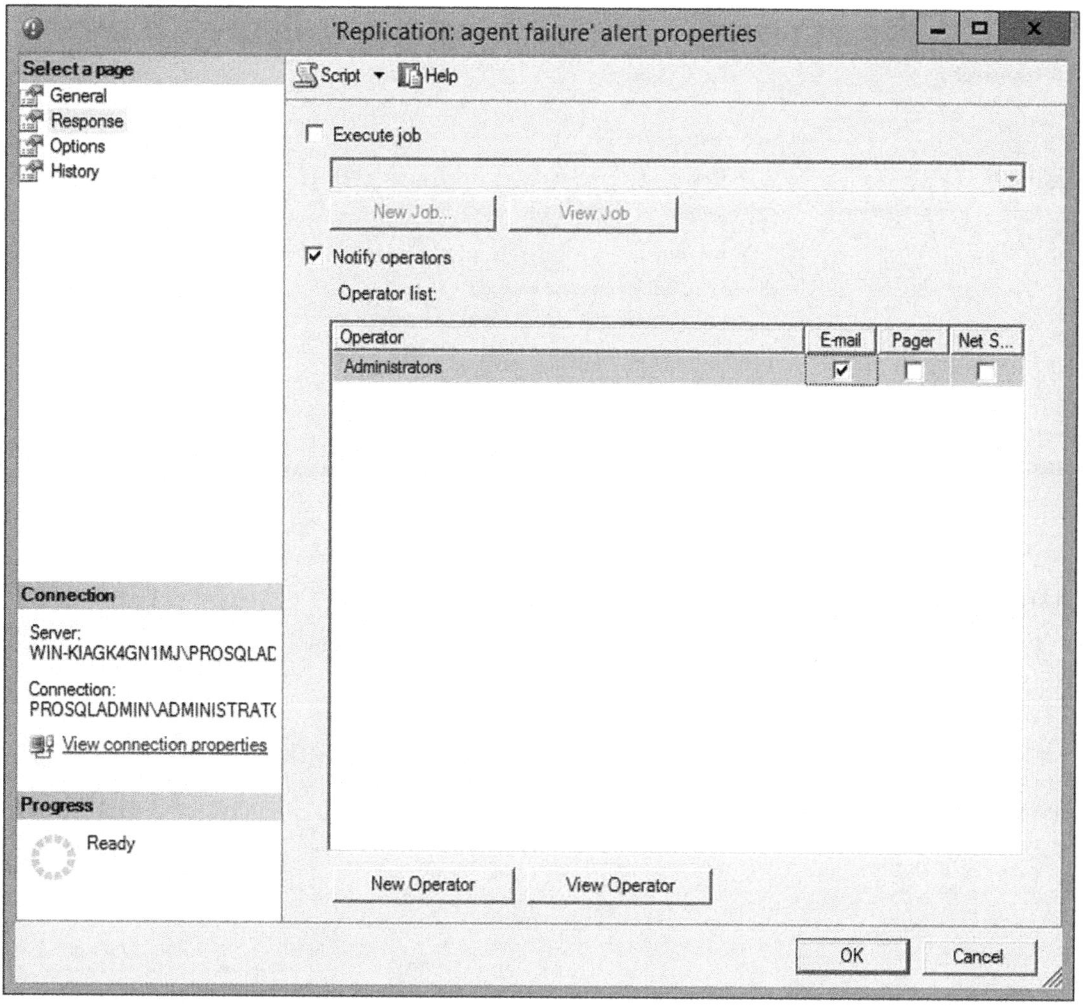

Figure 16-35. *The Response page*

On the Options page, illustrated in Figure 16-36, you can specify if you want the error message to be included in the text of the alert; you can specify any other information that you want to appear in the text. You can also configure a delay between invocations of the response to avoid multiple alerts from being triggered for the same event.

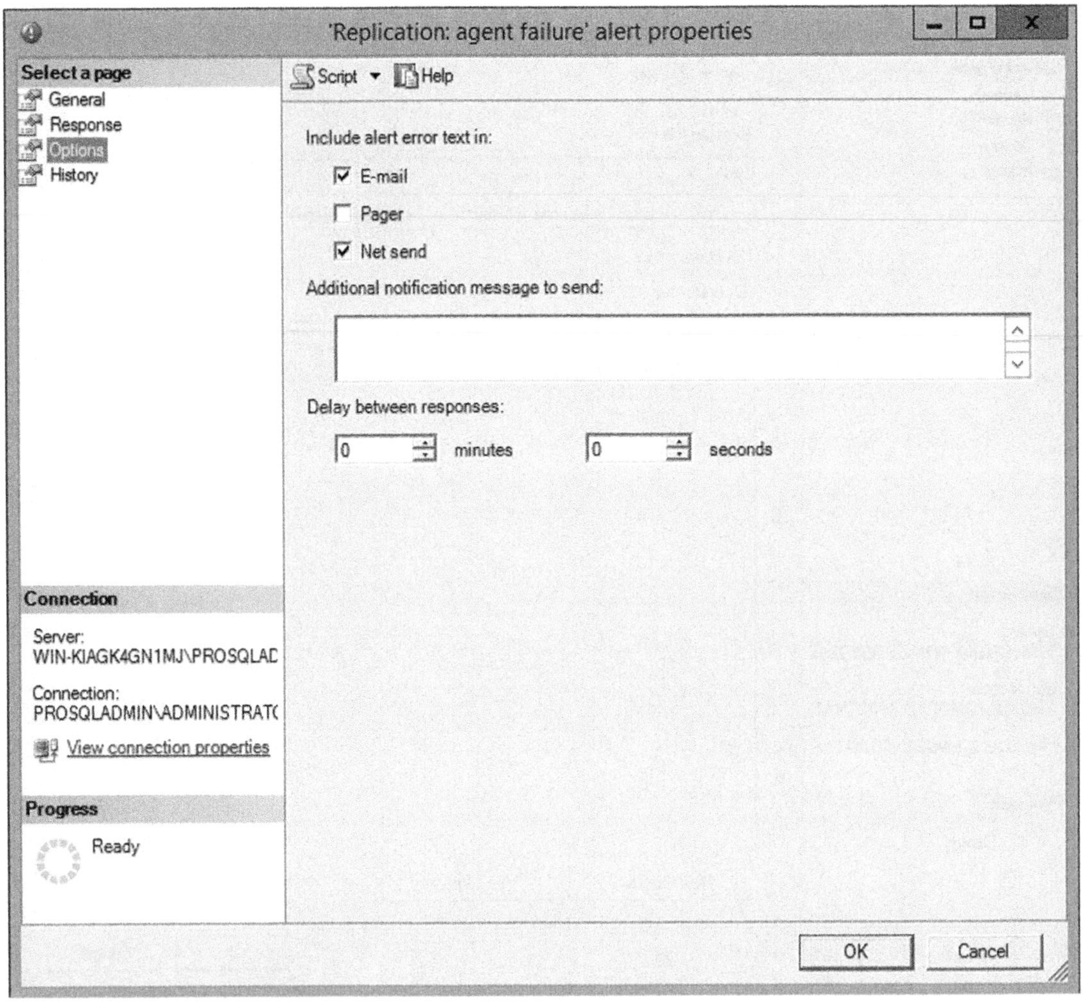

Figure 16-36. *The Options page*

For troubleshooting performance-related issues, it can help to turn on verbose logging for the Distribution Agent. To do this, select Agent Profile from the subscriber's context menu in the All Subscriptions tab of Replication Monitor before you select VerboseHistoryAgentProfile from the Agent Profile dialog box, as illustrated in Figure 16-37.

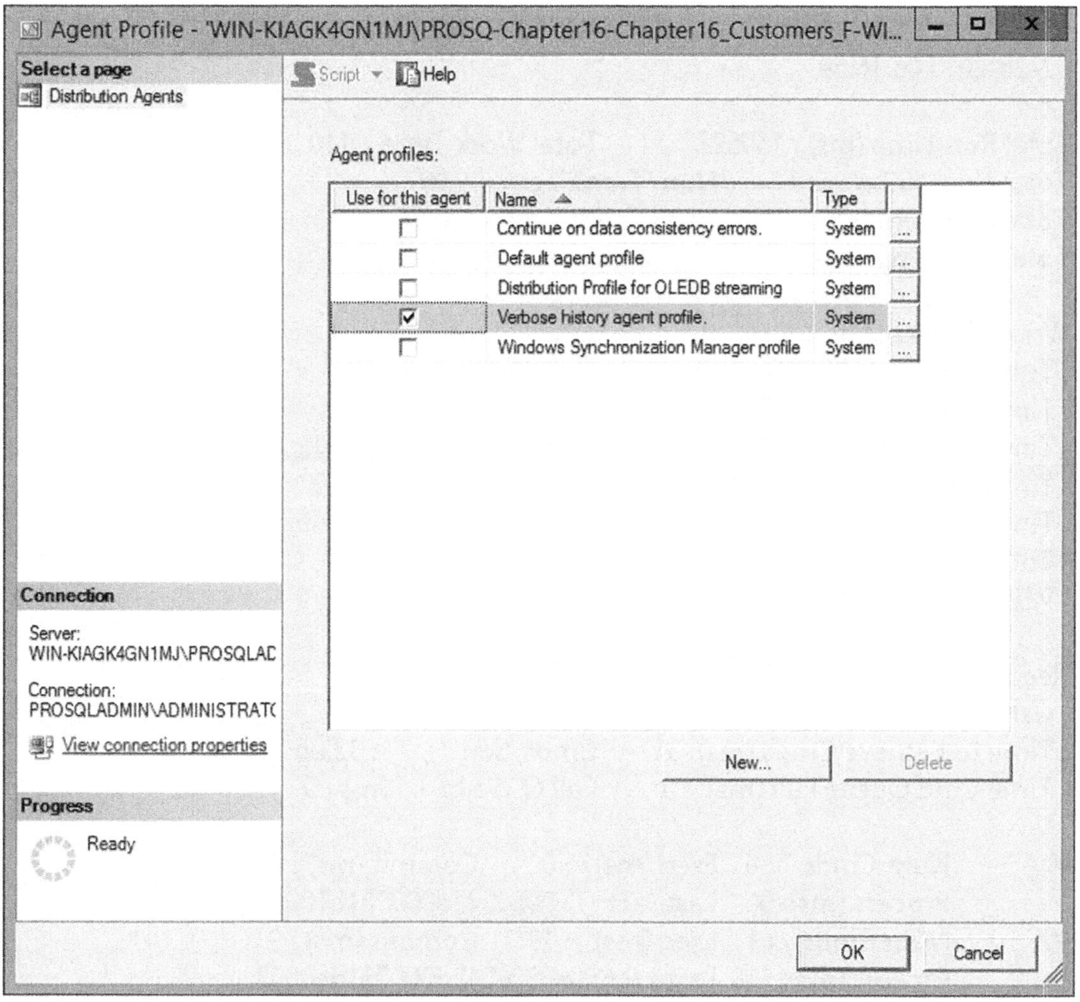

Figure 16-37. *Enable verbose logging*

Now, after restarting the Distribution Agent, take a look at the Distributor To Subscriber History in Replication Monitor; this exposes a row that gives you the statistics since the agent last started. Hovering over the row shows the complete message, similar to what appears in the illustration in Figure 16-38.

```
*********************** STATISTICS SINCE AGENT STARTED ***********************
02-26-2015 05:16:59

Total Run Time (ms) : 150593        Total Work Time : 110
Total Num Trans   : 1      Num Trans/Sec   : 9.09
Total Num Cmds    : 1      Num Cmds/Sec    : 9.09
Total Idle Time   : 149545

Writer Thread Stats
 Total Number of Retries  : 0
 Time Spent on Exec       : 0
 Time Spent on Commits (ms): 438  Commits/Sec      : 218.18
 Time to Apply Cmds (ms)  : 110   Cmds/Sec         : 9.09
 Time Cmd Queue Empty (ms) : 658           Empty Q Waits > 10ms: 2
 Total Time Request Blk(ms): 150203
 P2P Work Time (ms)       : 0        P2P Cmds Skipped   : 0

Reader Thread Stats
 Calls to Retrieve Cmds   : 31
 Time to Retrieve Cmds (ms): 31     Cmds/Sec         : 32.26
 Time Cmd Queue Full (ms) : 0       Full Q Waits > 10ms : 0

#1      Num Cmds  : 0  Exec (ms)  : 0     Commit (ms) : 438
        Process (ms): 0    Last xact : 0x0000042d000001b10004
#2      Num Cmds  : 1  Exec (ms)  : 79    Commit (ms) : 0
        Process (ms): 110  Last xact : 0x0000042d000001de0003
#3      Num Cmds  : 0  Exec (ms)  : 0     Commit (ms) : 0
        Process (ms): 0    Last xact : 0x0000042d000001b10004
#4      Num Cmds  : 0  Exec (ms)  : 0     Commit (ms) : 0
        Process (ms): 0    Last xact : 0x0000042d000001b10004
Last global update to sub xact : 0x0000042d000001de0003
```

Figure 16-38. *Verbose statistics*

If you discover that the performance of your Transactional Replication topology is poor, you can improve performance in various ways. Two of the most effective ways are to optimize the Log Reader Agent by increasing the size of batches that the agent reads, and to optimize the Distribution Agent by increasing the size of batches that are committed and parallelizing the update of the subscribers.

By default, the Log Reader Agent reads 500 transactions at a time. If your publication has a high transactional throughput, but only a smaller subset of those transactions are being replicated, then you can improve the performance of the Log Reader Agent by increasing the batch size of transactions read. You can do this by configuring the -ReadBatchSize property.

You can change the -ReadBatchSize of the Log Reader Agent by adding the switch to the command that runs the Log Reader Agent in the second job step of the SQL Server Agent job that runs the Log Reader Agent. If we want to change the -ReadBatchSize of our Log Reader Agent to 1000, we change the command being executed to be the same as the command in Listing 16-25.

Listing 16-25. Configuring ReadBatchSize

```
-Publisher [WIN-KIAGK4GN1MJ\PROSQLADMIN] -PublisherDB [Chapter16] -Distributor
[WIN-KIAGK4GN1MJ\PROSQLADMIN] -DistributorSecurityMode 1  -Continuous -ReadBatchSize 1000
```

Applying a set of transactions on the subscriber has a fixed overhead. Therefore, if you increase the number of transactions being committed in a single batch, you can improve the overall performance of the synchronization. By default, 100 transactions are committed as a single batch. We can increase this value by using the -CommitBatchSize property of the Distribution Agent.

You can change the -CommitBatchSize of the Distribution Agent. To do so, we add the -CommitBatchSize switch to the command in the second job step of the SQL Server Agent job that runs the Distribution Agent. If we want to change the –CommitBatchSize switch of the Distribution Agent that we are using to synchronize the Chapter16_Customers_Filtered publication so that 250 transactions are grouped together, we can change the command being executed to match the command in Listing 16-26.

Listing 16-26. Configuring CommitBatchSize

```
-Subscriber [WIN-KIAGK4GN1MJ\PROSQLADMIN2] -SubscriberDB [Chapter16_Sub] -Publisher
[WIN-KIAGK4GN1MJ\PROSQLADMIN] -Distributor [WIN-KIAGK4GN1MJ\PROSQLADMIN]
-DistributorSecurityMode 1 -Publication [Chapter16_Customers_Filtered] -PublisherDB
[Chapter16]    -Continuous -CommitBatchSize 250
```

We can further improve the performance of the Distribution Agent by allowing the subscriptions to be updated in parallel. By default, only a single connection is made to the subscriber, in order to apply changes. If we allow multiple connections, however, then we can greatly increase throughput.

To enable parallel updates, we need to set the -SubscriptionStreams parameter of the Distribution Agent. If we want to allow four parallel connections, for example, we can update the command run by the second job step of the SQL Server Agent job running the Distribution Agent to mirror the command in Listing 16-27.

Listing 16-27. Configuring SubscriptionStreams

```
-Subscriber [WIN-KIAGK4GN1MJ\PROSQLADMIN2] -SubscriberDB [Chapter16_Sub] -Publisher
[WIN-KIAGK4GN1MJ\PROSQLADMIN] -Distributor [WIN-KIAGK4GN1MJ\PROSQLADMIN]
-DistributorSecurityMode 1 -Publication [Chapter16_Customers_Filtered] -PublisherDB
[Chapter16]    -Continuous -CommitBatchSize 250 -SubscriptionStreams 4
```

■ **Caution** Over-optimizing the throughput to the subscribers can lead to timeouts if the subscriber cannot keep up. Therefore, when applying optimizations to the Distribution Agent, you should move up in small increments, and stop, when the performance begins to level off.

Adding AlwaysOn Readable Secondary Replicas

■ **Note**   For the demonstrations in this chapter, we use the AlwaysOn topology, which we built in Chapter 13.

It can be very useful to add readable secondary replicas to an AlwaysOn Availability Group topology in order to implement vertically scaled reporting. When you use this strategy, the databases are kept synchronized, with variable, but typically low latency, using log streaming. The additional advantage of readable secondary replicas from SQL Server 2014 onward is that they stay online, even if the primary replica is offline. The limitation here, however, is that users must connect directly to the instance, as opposed to the Availability Group Listener.

You can further improve read performance in readable secondary replicas by using temporary statistics, which you can also use to optimize read-only workloads. Also, snapshot isolation is also used exclusively on readable secondary replicas, even if other isolation levels or locking hints are explicitly requested. This helps avoid contention, but it also means that TempDB should be suitably scaled and on a fast disk array.

The main risk of using readable secondary replicas is that implementing snapshot isolation on the secondary replica can actually cause deleted records not to be cleaned up on the primary replica. This is because the ghost record cleanup task only remove rows from the primary once they are no longer required at the secondary. In this scenario, log truncation is also delayed on the primary replica. This means that you potentially risk having to kill long-running queries that are being satisfied against the readable secondary. This issue can also occur if the secondary replica becomes disconnected from the primary. Therefore, there is a risk that you may need to remove the secondary replica from the Availability Group and subsequently re-add it.

To make a secondary replica readable, you need to perform three tasks. First configure the secondary replica to allow read-only connections. Second, specify a read-only URL for reporting. The Availability Group Listener then directs appropriate traffic to this URL. The final task is to update the read-only routing list on the primary replica. These tasks are performed by the script in Listing 16-28.

Listing 16-28.   Configuring Read-only Routing

```
--Configure the ASYNCDR Replica to allow read-only connections

ALTER AVAILABILITY GROUP App1
 MODIFY REPLICA ON N'CLUSTERNODE3\ASYNCDR' WITH
(SECONDARY_ROLE (ALLOW_CONNECTIONS = READ_ONLY)) ;

--Configure the read-only URL for the ASYNCDR Replica

ALTER AVAILABILITY GROUP App1
 MODIFY REPLICA ON N'CLUSTERNODE3\ASYNCDR' WITH
(SECONDARY_ROLE (READ_ONLY_ROUTING_URL = N'TCP://CLUSTERNODE3.PROSQLADMIN.com:1433')) ;

--Configure the read-only routing list on the Primary Replica

ALTER AVAILABILITY GROUP App1
MODIFY REPLICA ON N'CLUSTERNODE1\PRIMARYREPLICA' WITH
(PRIMARY_ROLE (READ_ONLY_ROUTING_LIST=('CLUSTERNODE3\ASYNCDR'))) ;
```

Summary

Database snapshots use copy-on-write technology to create a point-in-time copy of a database. The snapshot must exist on the same instance as the source database, so although you cannot use them to distribute load between servers, you can use them to reduce contention between read and write operations.

Snapshots can be used to recover data that has been lost due to human error as well as for reporting purposes. You can either copy the data back to the source database, or you can restore the source database from a snapshot, as long as it is the only snapshot linked with the source database. Snapshots do not offer a protection against failure or corruption, however, and they are not a suitable alternative to backups.

Replication is a suite of technologies, offered by SQL Server, that allow you to distribute data between systems. For the purpose of scaling workloads, transactional replication is the most appropriate choice. Transactional replication can be implemented by configuring a distributor, which will hold replication metadata and potentially take the weight off the synchronization; a publisher, which hosts the data that is synchronized; and subscribers, which are the targets for synchronization. Replication is a complex technology, and as a DBA, you should understand how to implement it using T-SQL, as well as the GUI, since you will encounter situations in which you need to tear down and rebuild replication. Replication also exposes the RMO (Replication Management Objects) API, which is a replication programming interface for .NET.

You can configure readable secondary replicas within an AlwaysOn Availability Group topology; these allow for vertical scaling of read-only workloads. From SQL Server 2014 on, readable secondary replicas stay online even if the primary replica goes offline. The caveat here is that connections must be made directly to the instance.

In order to implement readable secondary replicas, you must configure read-only routing. This involves giving the secondary a URL for read-only reporting and then updating the read-only routing list on the primary replica. The risk of using this strategy for scale-out reporting is that long-running transactions at the secondary, or the secondary becoming disconnected, can lead to log truncation delays and delays in ghost records being cleaned up.

## PART IV

Monitoring and Maintenance

CHAPTER 17

■ ■ ■

SQL Server Metadata

Metadata is data that describes other data. SQL Server exposes a vast array of metadata including structural metadata, which describes every object, and descriptive metadata, which described the data itself. Metadata is exposed through a series of catalog views; information schema views; dynamic management views; and functions, system functions, and stored procedures.

Introducing Metadata Objects

Catalog views reside in the sys schema. There are many catalog views, some of the most useful of which, such as sys.master_files, are explored in this chapter. Listing 17-1 shows an example of how to use a catalog view to produce a list of databases that are in FULL recovery model.

Listing 17-1. Using Catalog Views

```
SELECT name
FROM sys.databases
WHERE recovery_model_desc = 'FULL' ;
```

Information schema views reside in the INFORMATION_SCHEMA schema. They return less detail than catalog views but are based on the ISO standards. This means that you can port your queries between RDBMS (Relational Database Management Systems). Listing 17-2 shows an example of using information schema views to produce a list of principals that have been granted SELECT access to the Chapter9.dbo. SensitiveData table.

Listing 17-2. Using Information Schema Views

```
USE Chapter9
GO

SELECT GRANTEE, PRIVILEGE_TYPE
FROM INFORMATION_SCHEMA.TABLE_PRIVILEGES
WHERE TABLE_SCHEMA = 'dbo'
        AND TABLE_NAME = 'SensitiveData'
        AND PRIVILEGE_TYPE = 'SELECT' ;
```

Many dynamic management views and functions available in SQL Server. Collectively, they are known as DMVs and they provide information about the current state of the instance, which you can use for troubleshooting and tuning performance. The following categories of DMV are exposed in SQL Server 2014:

- AlwaysOn Availability Groups

- Change data capture

- Change tracking

- Common language runtime (CLR)

- Database mirroring

- Databases

- Execution

- Extended events

- FILESTREAM and FileTable

- Full-text search and semantic search

- Indexes

- I/O

- Memory-optimized tables

- Objects

- Query notifications

- Replication

- Resource Governor

- Security

- Service broker

- SQL Server operating system

- Transactions

We demonstrate and discuss how to use DMVs many times throughout this chapter. DMVs always begin with a dm_ prefix, followed by two to four characters that describe the category of the object—for example, os_ for operating system, db_ for database, and exec_ for execution. This is followed by the name of the object. In Listing 17-3, you can see two things: an example of how to use a dynamic management view to find a list of logins that are currently connected to the Chapter16 database, and a dynamic management function you can use to produce details of the pages that store the data relating to the Chapter16.dbo. Customers table.

Listing 17-3. Using Dynamic Management Views and Functions

```
USE Chapter16
GO

--Find logins connected to the Chapter16 database

SELECT login_name
FROM sys.dm_exec_sessions
WHERE database_id = DB_ID('Chapter16') ;

--Return details of the data pages storing the Chapter16.dbo.Customers table

SELECT *
FROM sys.dm_db_database_page_allocations(DB_ID('Chapter16'),
                                         OBJECT_ID('dbo.Customers'),
                                         NULL,
                                         NULL,
                                         'DETAILED') ;
```

SQL Server also offers many metadata-related system functions, such as DB_ID() and OBJET_ID(), which we used in the Listing 17-3. Another example of a metadata-related system function is DATALENGTH, which we use in Listing 17-4 to return the length of each value in the LastName column of the Chapter16. dbo.Customers table.

Listing 17-4. Using System Functions

```
USE Chapter16
GO

SELECT DATALENGTH(LastName)
FROM dbo.Customers ;
```

Server- and Instance-Level Metadata

Many forms of metadata are available for the server and instance. Server-level metadata can be very useful for DBAs who need to find configuration information or troubleshoot an issue when they do not have access to the underlying operating system. For example, the dm_server category of DMVs offers views that allow you to check the status of server audits, view SQL Server's Registry keys, find the location of memory dump files, and find details of the instance's services. In the following sections, we discuss how to view the Registry keys associated with the instance, expose details of SQL Server's services, and view the contents of the buffer cache.

Exposing Registry Values

The sys.dm_server_registry DMV exposes key registry entries pertaining to the instance. The view returns three columns, which are detailed in Table 17-1.

Table 17-1. *sys.dm_server_registry Columns*

Column	Description
Regstry_key	The name of the Registry key
Value_name	The name of the key's value
Value_data	The data contained within the value

A very useful piece of information that you can find in the sys.dm_server_registry DMV is the port number on which SQL Server is currently listening. The query in Listing 17-5 uses the sys.dm_server_registry DMV to return the port on which the instance is listening, assuming the instance is configured to listen on all IP addresses.

Listing 17-5. Finding the Port Number

```
SELECT *
FROM (
        SELECT
        CASE
                WHEN value_name = 'tcport' AND value_data <> ''
                        THEN value_data
                WHEN value_name = 'tcpport' AND value_data = ''
                        THEN (
                                SELECT value_data
                                FROM sys.dm_server_registry
                                WHERE registry_key LIKE '%ipall'
                                        AND value_name = 'tcpdynamicports' )
        END PortNumber
        FROM sys.dm_server_registry
        WHERE registry_key LIKE '%IPAll' ) a
WHERE a.PortNumber IS NOT NULL ;
```

Another useful feature of this DMV is its ability to return the startup parameters of the SQL Server service. This is particularly useful if you want to find out if switches such as -E have been configured for the instance. The -E switch increases the number of extents that are allocated to each file in the round-robin algorithm. The query in Listing 17-6 displays the startup parameters configured for the instance.

Listing 17-6. Finding Startup Parameters

```
SELECT *
FROM sys.dm_server_registry
WHERE value_name LIKE 'SQLArg%' ;
```

Exposing Service Details

Another useful DMV within the dm_server category is sys.dm_server_services, which exposes details of the services the instance is using. Table 17-2 describes the columns returned.

Table 17-2. sys.dm_server_services Columns

Column	Description
Servicename	The name of the service.
Startup_type	An integer representing the startup type of the service.
Startup_desc	A textual description of the startup type of the service.
Status	An integer representing the current status of the service.
Status_desc	A textual description of the current service state.
Process_id	The process ID of the service.
Last_startup_time	The date and time that the service last started.
Service_account	The account used to run the service.
Filename	The file name of the service, including the full file path.
Is_clustered	1 indicates that the service is clustered, 0 indicates that it is standalone.
Clusternodename	If the service is clustered, this column indicates the name of the node on which the service is running.

The query in Listing 17-7 returns the name of each service, its startup type, its current status, and the name of the service account that runs the service.

Listing 17-7. Exposing Service Details

```
SELECT servicename
       ,startup_type_desc
       ,status_desc
       ,service_account
FROM sys.dm_server_services ;
```

Analyzing Buffer Cache Usage

The dm_os category of DMV exposes 41 objects that contain information about the current status of SQLOS, although only 31 of these are documented. A particularly useful DMV in the dm_os category, which exposes the contents of the buffer cache, is sys.dm_os_buffer_descriptors. When queried, this object returns the columns detailed in Table 17-3.

Table 17-3. sys.dm_os_buffer_descriptors Columns

Column	Description
Database_id	The ID of the database that the page is from
File_id	The ID of the file that the page is from
Page_id	The ID of the page
Page_level	The index level of the page
Allocation_unit_id	The ID of the allocation unit that the page is from
Page_type	The type of page, for example, DATA_PAGE, INDEX_PAGE, IAM_PAGE, or PFS_PAGE

(continued)

Table 17-3. (*continued*)

Column	Description
Row_count	The number of rows stored on the page
Free_space_in_bytes	The amount of free space on the page
Is_modified	A flag that indicates if the page is dirty
Numa_node	The NUMA node for the buffer
Read_microset	The amount of time taken to read the page into cache, specified in microseconds

The script in Listing 17-8 demonstrates how we can use the sys.dm_os_buffer_descriptors DMV to determine the percentage of the buffer cache each database is using on the instance. This can help you during performance tuning, as well as give you valuable insights that you can use during capacity planning or consolidation planning.

Listing 17-8. Determining Buffer Cache Usage per Database

```
DECLARE @DB_PageTotals TABLE
(
CachedPages INT,
Database_name NVARCHAR(128),
database_id INT
) ;

INSERT INTO @DB_PageTotals
SELECT COUNT(*) CachedPages
        ,CASE
                WHEN database_id = 32767
                        THEN 'ResourceDb'
                ELSE DB_NAME(database_id)
        END Database_name
        ,database_id
FROM sys.dm_os_buffer_descriptors a
GROUP BY DB_NAME(database_id)
                ,database_id ;

DECLARE @Total FLOAT = (SELECT SUM(CachedPages) FROM @DB_PageTotals) ;

SELECT     Database_name,
           CachedPages,
           SUM(cachedpages) over(partition by database_name)
                   / @total * 100 AS RunningPercentage
FROM       @DB_PageTotals a
ORDER BY   CachedPages DESC ;
```

■ **Note**　More DMVs within the dm_os category are discussed in the "Metadata for Troubleshooting and Performance Tuning" section of this chapter.

Metadata for Capacity Planning

One of the most useful ways you can use metadata is during your pursuit of proactive capacity management. SQL Server exposes metadata that provides you with information about the current size and usage of your database files, and you can use this information to plan ahead and arrange additional capacity, before your enterprise monitoring software starts generating critical alerts.

Exposing File Stats

The sys.dm_db_file_space_usage DMV returns details of the space used within each data file of the database in which it is run. Before SQL Server 2012, it could only be used against TempDB, but it is now supported against any database. The columns returned by this object are detailed in Table 17-4.

Table 17-4. *sys.dm_db_file_space_usage Columns*

Column	Description
database_id	The ID of the database to which the file belongs.
file_id	The ID of the file within the database. These IDs are repeated between databases. For example, the primary file always has an ID of 1, and the first log file always has an ID of 2.
filegroup_id	The ID of the filegroup in which the file resides.
total_page_count	The total number of pages within the file.
allocated_extent_page_count	The number of pages within the file that are in extents that have been allocated.
unallocated_extent_page_count	The number of pages within the file that are in extents that have not been allocated.
version_store_reserved_page_count	The number of pages reserved to support transactions using snapshot isolation. Only applicable to TempDB.
user_object_reserved_page_count	The number of pages reserved for user objects. Only applicable to TempDB.
internal_object_reserved_page_count	The number of pages reserved for internal objects. Only applicable to TempDB.
mixed_extent_page_count	The number of extents that have pages allocated to different objects.

The sys.dm_io_virtual_file_stats DMV returns IO statistics for the database and log files of the database. This can help you determine the amount of data being written to each file and warn you of high IO stalls. The object accepts database_id and file_id as parameters and returns the columns detailed in Table 17-5.

Table 17-5. *sys.dm_io_virtual_file_stats Columns*

Column	Description
database_id	The ID of the database to which the file belongs.
file_id	The ID of the file within the database. These IDs are repeated between databases. For example, the primary file always has an ID of 1 and the first log file always has an ID of 2.
sample_ms	The number of milliseconds since the computer started.
num_of_reads	The total number of reads against the file.
num_of_bytes_read	The total number of bytes read from the file.
io_stall_read_ms	The total time waiting for reads to be issued against the file, specified in milliseconds.
num_of_writes	The total number of write operations performed against the file.
num_of_bytes_written	The total number of bytes written to the file.
io_stall_write_ms	The total time waiting for writes to complete against the file, specified in milliseconds.
io_stall	The total time waiting for all IO requests against the file to be completed, specified in milliseconds.
size_on_disk_bytes	The total space used by the file on disk, specified in bytes.
file_handle	The Windows file handle.
io_stall_queued_read_ms	Total IO latency for read operations against the file, caused by Resource Governor. Resource Governor is discussed in Chapter 23.
io_stall_queued_write_ms	Total IO latency for write operations against the file, caused by Resource Governor. Resource Governor is discussed in Chapter 23.

■ **Tip** *IO stalls* are the amount of time it takes the IO subsystem to respond to SQL Server.

Unlike the previous two DMVs discussed in this section, the sys.master_files catalog view is a system-wide view, meaning that it returns a record for every file within every database on the instance. The columns returned by this view are described in Table 17-6.

Table 17-6. *sys.master_files Columns*

Column	Description
database_id	The ID of the database to which the file belongs.
file_id	The ID of the file within the database. These IDs are repeated between databases. For example, the primary file always has an ID of 1 and the first log file always has an ID of 2.
file_guid	The GUID of the file.
type	An integer representing the file type.
type_desc	A textual description of the file type.

(*continued*)

Table 17-6. (*continued*)

Column	Description
data_space_id	The ID of the filegroup in which the file resides.
name	The logical name of the file.
physical_name	The physical path and name of the file.
state	An integer indicating the current state of the file.
state_desc	A textual description of the current state of the file.
size	The current size of the file, specified as a count of pages.
max_size	The maximum size of the file, specified as a count of pages.
growth	The growth setting of the file. 0 indicates autogrowth is disabled. If is_percent_growth is 0, then the value indicates the growth increment as a count of pages. If is_percent_growth is 1, then the value indicates a whole number percentage increment.
is_media_read_only	Specifies if the media on which the file resides is read only.
is_read_only	Specifies if the file is in a read-only filegroup.
is_sparse	Specifies that the file belongs to a database snapshot.
is_percent_growth	Indicates if the growth output is a percentage or a fixed rate.
is_name_reserved	Specifies if the filename is reusable.
create_lsn	The LSN (Log Sequence Number) at which the file was created.
drop_lsn	The LSN at which the file was dropped (if applicable).
read_only_lsn	The most recent LSN at which the filegroup was marked read only.
read_write_lsn	The most recent LSN at which the filegroup was marked read/write.
differential_base_lsn	The LSN at which changes in the file started being marked in the DIFF pages.
differential_base_guid	The GUID of the full backup on which differential backups for the file are made.
differential_base_time	The time of the full backup on which differential backups for the file are made.
redo_start_lsn	The LSN at which the next roll forward will start.
redo_start_fork_guid	The GUID of the recovery fork.
redo_target_lsn	The LSN at which an online roll forward for the file can stop.
redo_target_fork_guid	The GUID of the recovery fork.
backup_lsn	The most recent LSN at which a full or differential backup was taken.

Using File Stats for Capacity Analysis

When combined together, you can use the three metadata objects described in the previous section to produce powerful reports that can help you with capacity planning and diagnosing performance issues. For example, the query in Listing 17-9 provides the file size, amount of free space remaining, and IO stalls for each file in the database. Because sys.dm_io_virtual_file_stats is a function as opposed to a view, we CROSS APPLY the function to the results set, passing in the database_id and the file_id of each row as parameters.

Listing 17-9. File Capacity Details

```
SELECT m.name
        ,m.physical_name
        ,CAST(fsu.total_page_count / 128. AS NUMERIC(12,4)) [Fie Size (MB)]
        ,CAST(fsu.unallocated_extent_page_count / 128. AS NUMERIC(12,4)) [Free Space (MB)]
        ,vfs.io_stall_read_ms
        ,vfs.io_stall_write_ms
FROM sys.dm_db_file_space_usage fsu
CROSS APPLY sys.dm_io_virtual_file_stats(fsu.database_id, fsu.file_id) vfs
INNER JOIN sys.master_files m
        ON fsu.database_id = m.database_id
                AND fsu.file_id = m.file_id ;
```

The script in Listing 17-10 demonstrates how you can use sys.master_files to analyze drive capacity for each volume by detailing the current size of each file, the amount each file will grow by the next time it grows, and the current free capacity of the drive. You can obtain the free space on the drive by using the xp_fixeddrives stored procedure.

Listing 17-10. Analyzing Drive Space with xp_fixeddrives

```
DECLARE @fixeddrives TABLE
(
Drive          CHAR(1),
MBFree         BIGINT
) ;

INSERT INTO @fixeddrives
EXEC xp_fixeddrives ;

SELECT
    Drive
    ,SUM([File Space Used (MB)]) TotalSpaceUsed
    , SUM([Next Growth Amount (MB)]) TotalNextGrowth
    , SpaceLeftOnVolume
FROM (
SELECT Drive
        ,size * 1.0 / 128 [File Space Used (MB)]
        ,CASE
                WHEN is_percent_growth = 0
                        THEN growth * 1.0 / 128
                WHEN is_percent_growth = 1
                        THEN (size * 1.0 / 128 * growth / 100)
                END [Next Growth Amount (MB)]
        ,f.MBFree SpaceLeftOnVolume
FROM sys.master_files m
INNER JOIN @fixeddrives f
        ON LEFT(m.physical_name, 1) = f.Drive ) a
GROUP BY Drive, SpaceLeftOnVolume
ORDER BY drive ;
```

The issue with xp_fixeddrives is that it cannot see mapped drives. Therefore, as an alternative, you can employ the script in Listing 17-11, which uses PowerShell to return the information.

▨ **Caution**   The drawback of this approach is that it requires xp_cmdshell to be enabled, which is against security best practice.

Listing 17-11. Analyzing Drive Space with PowerShell

```
USE [master];

DECLARE @t TABLE
(
        name varchar(150),
        minimum tinyint,
        maximum tinyint ,
        config_value tinyint ,
        run_value tinyint
)

DECLARE @psinfo TABLE(data  NVARCHAR(100)) ;

INSERT INTO @psinfo
EXEC xp_cmdshell 'Powershell.exe "Get-WMIObject Win32_LogicalDisk -filter "DriveType=3"|
Format-Table DeviceID, FreeSpace, Size"'  ;

DELETE FROM @psinfo WHERE data IS NULL  OR data LIKE '%DeviceID%' OR data LIKE '%----%';
UPDATE @psinfo SET data = REPLACE(data,' ',',');

;WITH DriveSpace AS
(
        SELECT LEFT(data,2)  as [Drive],
        REPLACE((LEFT((SUBSTRING(data,(PATINDEX('%[0-9]%',data))
                , LEN(data))),CHARINDEX(',',
         (SUBSTRING(data,(PATINDEX('%[0-9]%',data))
                , LEN(data))))-1)),',','') AS FreeSpace
        ,
        REPLACE(RIGHT((SUBSTRING(data,(PATINDEX('%[0-9]%',data))
                , LEN(data))),PATINDEX('%,%',
         (SUBSTRING(data,(PATINDEX('%[0-9]%',data)) , LEN(data)))))) ,',','')
        AS [Size]
        FROM @psinfo
)
SELECT
    mf.Drive
    ,CAST(sizeMB as numeric(18,2)) as [File Space Used (MB)]
    ,CAST(growth as numeric(18,2)) as [Next Growth Amount (MB)]
    ,CAST((CAST(FreeSpace as numeric(18,2))
                    /(POWER(1024., 3))) as numeric(6,2)) AS FreeSpaceGB
    ,CAST((CAST(size as numeric(18,2))/(POWER(1024., 3))) as numeric(6,2)) AS TotalSizeGB
```

```
        ,CAST(CAST((CAST(FreeSpace as numeric(18,2))/(POWER(1024., 3))) as numeric(6,2))
                    / CAST((CAST(size as numeric(18,2))/(POWER(1024., 3))) as numeric(6,2))
                    * 100 AS numeric(5,2)) [Percent Remaining]
FROM DriveSpace
        JOIN
        (       SELECT DISTINCT  LEFT(physical_name, 2) Drive, SUM(size / 128.0) sizeMB
                ,SUM(CASE
                        WHEN is_percent_growth = 0
                                THEN growth / 128.
                        WHEN is_percent_growth = 1
                                THEN (size / 128. * growth / 100)
                        END) growth
                FROM master.sys.master_files
                WHERE db_name(database_id) NOT IN('master','model','msdb')
                GROUP BY LEFT(physical_name, 2)
        )               mf ON DriveSpace.Drive = mf.drive ;
```

Metadata for Troubleshooting and Performance Tuning

You can use many metadata objects to tune performance and troubleshoot issues within SQL Server. In the following sections, we explore how to capture performance counters from within SQL Server, how to analyze waits, and how to use DMVs to troubleshoot issues with expensive queries.

Retrieving Perfmon Counters

Perfmon is a Windows tool that captures performance counters for the operating system, plus many SQL Server-specific counters. DBAs who are trying to diagnose performance issues find this very useful. The problem is that many DBAs do not have administrative access to the underlying operating system, which makes them reliant on Windows Administrators to assist with the troubleshooting process. A workaround for this issue is the sys_dm_os_performance_counters DMV, which exposes the SQL Server Perfmon counters within SQL Server. The columns returned by sys.dm_os_performance_counters are described in Table 17-7.

Table 17-7. *sys.dm_os_performance_counters Columns*

Column	Description
object_name	The category of the counter.
counter_name	The name of the counter.
instance_name	The instance of the counter. For example, database-related counters have an instance for each database.
cntr_value	The value of the counter.
cntr_type	The type of counter. Counter types are described in Table 17-8.

The sys.dm_os_performance_counters DMV exposes different types of counters that can be identified by the cntr_type column, which relates to the underlying WMI performance counter type. You need to handle different counter types in different ways. The counter types exposed are described in Table 17-8.

Table 17-8. *Counter Types*

Counter Type	Description
1073939712	You will use PERF_LARGE_RAW_BASE as a base value in conjunction with the PERF_LARGE_RAW_FRACTION type to calculate a counter percentage, or with PERF_AVERAGE_BULK to calculate an average.
537003264	Use PERF_LARGE_RAW_FRACTION as a fractional value in conjunction with PERF_LARGE_RAW_BASE to calculate a counter percentage.
1073874176	PERF_AVERAGE_BULK is a cumulative average that you use in conjunction with PERF_LARGE_RAW_BASE to calculate a counter average. The counter, along with the base, is sampled twice to calculate the metric over a period of time.
272696320	PERF_COUNTER_COUNTER is a 32-bit cumulative rate counter. The value should be sampled twice to calculate the metric over a period of time.
272696576	PERF_COUNTER_BULK_COUNT is a 64-bit cumulative rate counter. The value should be sampled twice to calculate the metric over a period of time.
65792	PERF_COUNTER_LARGE_RAWCOUNT returns the last sampled result for the counter.

The query in Listing 17-12 demonstrates how to use sys.dm_os_performance_counters to capture metrics of the PERF_COUNTER_LARGE_RAWCOUNT type, which is the simplest form of counter to capture. The query returns the number of memory grants that are currently pending.

Listing 17-12. Using Counter Type 65792

```
SELECT *
FROM sys.dm_os_performance_counters
WHERE counter_name = 'Memory Grants Pending' ;
```

The script in Listing 17-13 demonstrates capturing the number of lock requests that are occurring per second over the space of one minute. The lock requests/sec counter uses the PERF_COUNTER_BULK_COUNT counter type, but the same method applies to capturing counters relating to In-Memory OLTP, which uses the PERF_COUNTER_COUNTER counter type.

Listing 17-13. Using Counter Types 272696576 and 272696320

```
DECLARE @cntr_value1 BIGINT = (
SELECT cntr_value
FROM sys.dm_os_performance_counters
WHERE counter_name = 'Lock Requests/sec'
        AND instance_name = '_Total') ;

WAITFOR DELAY '00:01:00'

DECLARE @cntr_value2 BIGINT = (
SELECT cntr_value
FROM sys.dm_os_performance_counters
WHERE counter_name = 'Lock Requests/sec'
        AND instance_name = '_Total') ;

SELECT (@cntr_value2 - @cntr_value1) / 60 'Lock Requests/sec' ;
```

The script in Listing 17-14 demonstrates capturing the plan cache hit ratio for the instance. The Plan Cache Hit Ratio counter is counter type 537003264. Therefore, we need to multiply the value by 100 and then divide by the base counter to calculate the percentage. Before running the script, you should change the instance name to match your own.

Listing 17-14. Using Counter Type 537003264

```
SELECT
        100 *
         (
        SELECT cntr_value
        FROM sys.dm_os_performance_counters
        WHERE object_name = 'MSSQL$PROSQLADMIN:Plan Cache'
                AND counter_name = 'Cache hit ratio'
                AND instance_name = '_Total')
        /
         (
        SELECT cntr_value
        FROM sys.dm_os_performance_counters
        WHERE object_name = 'MSSQL$PROSQLADMIN:Plan Cache'
                AND counter_name = 'Cache hit ratio base'
                AND instance_name = '_Total') [Plan cache hit ratio %] ;
```

The script in Listing 17-15 demonstrates how to capture the Average Latch Wait Time (ms) counter. Because this counter is of type PERF_AVERAGE_BULK, we need to capture the value and its corresponding base counter twice. We then need to deduct the first capture of the counter from the second capture, deduct the first capture of the base counter from the second capture, and then divide the fractional counter value by its base value to calculate the average over the time period. Because it is possible that no latches will be requested within the time period, we have wrapped the SELECT statement in an IF/ELSE block to avoid the possibility of a divide-by-0 error being thrown.

Listing 17-15. Using Counter Type 1073874176

```
DECLARE @cntr TABLE
(
ID          INT          IDENTITY,
counter_name NVARCHAR(256),
counter_value BIGINT,
[Time] DATETIME
) ;

INSERT INTO @cntr
SELECT
        counter_name
        ,cntr_value
        ,GETDATE()
        FROM sys.dm_os_performance_counters
        WHERE counter_name IN('Average Latch Wait Time (ms)',
                             'Average Latch Wait Time base') ;
        WAITFOR DELAY '00:01:00' ;
```

```
INSERT INTO @cntr
SELECT
        counter_name
        ,cntr_value
        ,GETDATE()
        FROM sys.dm_os_performance_counters
        WHERE counter_name IN('Average Latch Wait Time (ms)',
                                'Average Latch Wait Time base') ;

IF (SELECT COUNT(DISTINCT counter_value)
    FROM @cntr
    WHERE counter_name = 'Average Latch Wait Time (ms)') > 2
BEGIN
SELECT
        (
                (
                SELECT TOP 1 counter_value
                FROM @cntr
                WHERE counter_name = 'Average Latch Wait Time (ms)'
                ORDER BY [Time] DESC
                )
                -
                (
                SELECT TOP 1 counter_value
                FROM @cntr
                WHERE counter_name = 'Average Latch Wait Time (ms)'
                ORDER BY [Time] ASC
                )
        )
        /
        (
                (
                SELECT TOP 1 counter_value
                FROM @cntr
                WHERE counter_name = 'Average Latch Wait Time base'
                ORDER BY [Time] DESC
                )
                -
                (
                SELECT TOP 1 counter_value
                FROM @cntr
                WHERE counter_name = 'Average Latch Wait Time base'
                ORDER BY [Time] ASC
                )
        ) [Average Latch Wait Time (ms)] ;
END
ELSE
BEGIN
        SELECT 0 [Average Latch Wait Time (ms)] ;
END
```

Analyzing Waits

Waits are a natural aspect of any RDBMS, but they can also indicate a performance bottleneck. A full explanation of all wait types can be found at msdn.microsoft.com, but all wait types break down into three categories: resource waits, queue waits, and external waits.

Resource waits occur when a thread requires access to an object, but that object is already in use, and therefore, the thread has to wait. This can include the thread waiting to take a lock out on an object or waiting for a disk resource to respond. *Queue waits* occur when a thread is idle and is waiting for a task to be assigned. This does not necessarily indicate a performance bottleneck, since it is often a background task, such as the Deadlock Monitor or Lazy Writer waiting until it is needed. *External waits* occur when a thread is waiting for an external resource, such as a linked server. The hidden gotcha here is that an external wait does not always mean that the thread is actually waiting. It could be performing an operation external to SQL Server, such as an extended stored procedure running external code.

Any task that has been issued is in one of three states: running, runnable, or suspended. If a task is in the running state, then it is actually being executed on a processor. When a task is in the runnable state, it sits on the processor queue, awaiting its turn to run. This is known as a *signal wait*. When a task is suspended, it means that the task is waiting for any reason other than a signal wait. In other words, it is experiencing a resource wait, a queue wait, or an external wait. Each query is likely to alternate between the three states as it progresses.

The sys.dm_os_wait_stats returns details of the cumulative waits for each wait type, since the instance started, or since the statistics exposed by the DMV were reset. You can reset the statistics by running the command in Listing 17-16.

Listing 17-16. Resetting Wait Stats

```
DBCC SQLPERF ('sys.dm_os_wait_stats', CLEAR) ;
```

The columns returned by sys.dm_os_wait_stats are detailed in Table 17-9.

Table 17-9. *sys.dm_os_wait_stats Columns*

Column	Description
wait_type	The name of the wait type that has occurred.
waiting_tasks_count	The number of tasks that have occurred on this wait type.
wait_time_ms	The cumulative time of all waits against this wait type, displayed in milliseconds. This includes signal wait times.
max_wait_time_ms	The maximum duration of a single wait against this wait type.
signal_wait_time_ms	The cumulative time for all signal waits against this wait type.

To find the wait types that are responsible for the highest cumulative wait time, run the query in Listing 17-17. This query adds a calculated column to the result set, which deducts the signal wait time from the overall wait time to avoid CPU pressure from skewing the results.

Listing 17-17. Finding the Highest Waits

```
SELECT *
      , wait_time_ms - signal_wait_time_ms ResourceWaits
FROM sys.dm_os_wait_stats
ORDER BY wait_time_ms - signal_wait_time_ms DESC ;
```

Of course, signal wait time can be a cause for concern in its own right, potentially identifying the processor as a bottleneck, and you should analyze it. Therefore, use the query in Listing 17-18 to calculate the percentage of overall waits, which are due to a task waiting for its turn on the processor. The value is displayed for each wait type and it is followed by a row that displays the overall percentage for all wait types.

Listing 17-18. Calculating Signal Waits

```
SELECT ISNULL(wait_type, 'Overal Percentage:') wait_type
        ,PercentageSignalWait
FROM (
                SELECT wait_type
                        ,CAST(100. * SUM(signal_wait_time_ms)
                            / SUM(wait_time_ms) AS NUMERIC(20,2)) PercentageSignalWait
                FROM sys.dm_os_wait_stats
                WHERE wait_time_ms > 0
                GROUP BY wait_type WITH ROLLUP) a ;
```

To find the highest waits over a defined period, you need to sample the data twice and then deduct the first sample from the second sample. The script in Listing 17-19 samples the data twice with a ten-minute interval and then displays the details of the five highest waits within that interval.

Listing 17-19. Calculating the Highest Waits over a Defined Period

```
DECLARE @Waits1 TABLE
(
wait_type NVARCHAR(128),
wait_time_ms BIGINT
) ;

DECLARE @Waits2 TABLE
(
wait_type NVARCHAR(128),
wait_time_ms BIGINT
) ;

INSERT INTO @waits1
SELECT wait_type
        ,wait_time_ms
FROM sys.dm_os_wait_stats ;

WAITFOR DELAY '00:10:00' ;

INSERT INTO @Waits2
SELECT wait_type
        ,wait_time_ms
FROM sys.dm_os_wait_stats ;

SELECT TOP 5
        w2.wait_type
        ,w2.wait_time_ms - w1.wait_time_ms
```

```
FROM @Waits1 w1
INNER JOIN @Waits2 w2
        ON w1.wait_type = w2.wait_type
ORDER BY w2.wait_time_ms - w1.wait_time_ms DESC ;
```

Finding and Tuning Expensive Queries

Although poor performance can be the sign of a hardware bottleneck, more often than not, you can achieve larger performance gains from tuning queries than from throwing hardware at the problem. If developers have written queries using cursors or other suboptimal techniques, then you may need to pass the queries back to the development or technical support team; but in other cases, the DBA may be able to resolve the issue—by adding a missing index, for example.

The first step in the query troubleshooting process is to find the most expensive queries, which are frequently being run. You can achieve this by using the sys.dm_exec_query_stats DMV in conjunction with the sys.dm_exec_sql_text and sys.dm_exec_query_plan DMVs. The columns returned by the sys.dm_exec_query_plan dynamic management view are detailed in Table 17-10.

Table 17-10. *sys.dm_exec_query_stats Columns*

Column	Description
sql_handle	A token that identifies the parent procedure or batch of the query.
statement_start_offset	A zero-based offset, denoting the start of the query within the parent batch or procedure.
statement_end_offset	A zero-based offset, denoting the start of the query within the parent batch or procedure. If statement_end_offset is -1, then this denotes the end of the parent batch or procedure.
plan_generation_num	Identifies the instance of a query plan following a recompile.
plan_handle	A token that identifies the query plan, which contains the query.
creation_time	The time that the query plan was compiled.
last_execution_time	The time that the plan last started to execute. This does not include invocations that are currently running.
execution_count	The number of times the plan has been executed. This does not include invocations that are currently running.
total_worker_time	The cumulative amount of CPU time that has been used by all executions of the plan, specified in microseconds.
last_worker_time	The amount of CPU time used by the plan the last time it was executed, specified in microseconds.
min_worker_time	The minimum amount of CPU time used by any single execution of the plan, specified in microseconds.
max_worker_time	The maximum amount of CPU time used by any single execution of the plan, specified in microseconds.
total_physical_reads	The cumulative number of reads made from disk during executions of the plan.

(continued)

Table 17-10. (*continued*)

Column	Description
last_physical_reads	The number of reads from disk made the last time the query was executed.
min_physical_reads	The minimum number of reads from disk made for any single execution of the plan.
max_physical_reads	The maximum number of reads from disk made for any single execution of the plan.
total_logical_writes	The cumulative number of writes made to the buffer cache during all executions of the plan.
last_logical_writes	The number of writes made to the buffer cache the last time the plan was executed.
min_logical_writes	The minimum number of writes made to the buffer cache on any single execution of the plan.
max_logical_writes	The maximum number of writes made to the buffer cache on any single execution of the plan.
total_logical_reads	The cumulative number of reads made to the buffer cache during all executions of the plan.
last_logical_reads	The number of reads made to the buffer cache the last time the plan was executed.
min_logical_reads	The minimum number of reads made to the buffer cache on any single execution of the plan.
max_logical_reads	The maximum number of reads made to the buffer cache on any single execution of the plan.
total_clr_time	The cumulative total amount of CPU time used within CLR objects for all executions of the plan, specified in microseconds.
last_clr_time	The amount of CPU time used inside CLR objects the last time that the plan was executed, specified in microseconds.
min_clr_time	The minimum amount of CPU time used within CLR objects for a single execution of the plan, specified in microseconds.
max_clr_time	The maximum amount of CPU time used within CLR objects for a single execution of the plan, specified in microseconds.
total_elapsed_time	The cumulative total execution time for all executions of the plan, specified in microseconds.
last_elapsed_time	The total execution time for the plan the last time it was run, specified in microseconds.
min_elapsed_time	The minimum execution time for any single execution of the plan, specified in microseconds.
max_elapsed_time	The maximum execution time for any single execution of the plan, specified in microseconds.
query_hash	A binary hash representation of the query that is used by the optimizer to identify similar queries.

(*continued*)

Table 17-10. (*continued*)

Column	Description
query_plan_hash	A binary hash representation of the execution plan that is used by the optimizer to identify similar plans.
total_rows	The cumulative total number of rows returned by all executions of the plan.
last_rows	The number of rows that was returned the last time that the plan was executed.
min_rows	The minimum number of rows that have been returned by a single execution of the plan.
max_rows	The maximum number of rows that have been returned by a single execution of the plan.

The sys.dm_exec_sql_text dynamic management function accepts a single parameter, which is the sql_handle. This means that the function can be cross-applied to the sys.dm_exec_query_stats results. The function returns the text of the batch or procedure, of which the query is a part. The sys.dm_exec_query_plan accepts a single parameter, which is the plan_handle. This means that it can also be cross-applied to the results of sys.dm_exec_query_stats. It returns the XML representation of the query plan.

Before we demonstrate how to use sys.dm_exec_query_stats, we first create the Chapter17 database, which includes two tables that we populate with data. These tasks are performed in Listing 17-20.

Listing 17-20. Creating the Chapter17 Database

```
--Create the database

CREATE DATABASE Chapter17;
GO

ALTER DATABASE Chapter17 SET RECOVERY FULL;
GO

USE Chapter17
GO

--Create and populate numbers table

DECLARE @Numbers TABLE
(
        Number          INT
)

;WITH CTE(Number)
AS
(
        SELECT 1 Number
        UNION ALL
        SELECT Number + 1
        FROM CTE
        WHERE Number < 100
)
```

650

```
INSERT INTO @Numbers
SELECT Number FROM CTE;

--Create and populate name pieces

DECLARE @Names TABLE
(
        FirstName           VARCHAR(30),
        LastName            VARCHAR(30)
);

INSERT INTO @Names
VALUES('Peter', 'Carter'),
                ('Michael', 'Smith'),
                ('Danielle', 'Mead'),
                ('Reuben', 'Roberts'),
                ('Iris', 'Jones'),
                ('Sylvia', 'Davies'),
                ('Finola', 'Wright'),
                ('Edward', 'James'),
                ('Marie', 'Andrews'),
                ('Jennifer', 'Abraham');

--Create and populate Customers table

CREATE TABLE dbo.Customers
(
        CustomerID          INT             NOT NULL    IDENTITY    PRIMARY KEY,
        FirstName           VARCHAR(30)     NOT NULL,
        LastName            VARCHAR(30)     NOT NULL,
        BillingAddressID    INT             NOT NULL,
        DeliveryAddressID   INT             NOT NULL,
        CreditLimit         MONEY               NOT NULL,
        Balance             MONEY               NOT NULL
);

SELECT * INTO #Customers
FROM
        (SELECT
                (SELECT TOP 1 FirstName FROM @Names ORDER BY NEWID()) FirstName,
                (SELECT TOP 1 LastName FROM @Names ORDER BY NEWID()) LastName,
                (SELECT TOP 1 Number FROM @Numbers ORDER BY NEWID()) BillingAddressID,
                (SELECT TOP 1 Number FROM @Numbers ORDER BY NEWID()) DeliveryAddressID,
                (SELECT TOP 1 CAST(RAND() * Number AS INT) * 10000
                        FROM @Numbers ORDER BY NEWID()) CreditLimit,
                (SELECT TOP 1 CAST(RAND() * Number AS INT) * 9000
                        FROM @Numbers ORDER BY NEWID()) Balance
        FROM @Numbers a
        CROSS JOIN @Numbers b
) a;

INSERT INTO dbo.Customers
SELECT * FROM #Customers;
```

651

In Listing 17-21, we tear down the plan cache and run some queries against the Customers table in our Chapter17 database before we use the sys.dm_exec_query_stats object to view details of our longest running queries. Because we have reset the plan cache, we know that our queries against the Customers table will be returned. In a production scenario, you may choose to filter the results by execution count, since you may not be interested in ad-hoc queries that have only run once or twice. You may also choose to filter by last execution time to avoid returning information for old queries that are no longer run.

Listing 17-21. Finding Longest Running Queries

```
DBCC FREEPROCCACHE
GO

SELECT *
FROM dbo.Customers ;

SELECT *
FROM dbo.Customers
WHERE CreditLimit > 100000 ;
GO

SELECT SUM(Balance) TotalExposure
FROM dbo.Customers ;
GO

SELECT Duplicates.CustomerID
       ,Customers.FirstName
       ,Customers.LastName
       ,Duplicates.DuplicateMarker
FROM
(
       SELECT CustomerID
               ,ROW_NUMBER() OVER(PARTITION BY FirstName, LastName ORDER BY FirstName,
LastName) DuplicateMarker
       FROM dbo.Customers
) Duplicates
INNER JOIN dbo.Customers Customers
       ON Duplicates.CustomerID = Customers.CustomerID
WHERE Duplicates.DuplicateMarker > 1 ;
GO

SELECT TOP 5
       execution_count
       ,total_elapsed_time
       ,total_worker_time
       ,total_physical_reads
       ,total_logical_reads
       ,total_logical_writes
       ,qp.dbid
       ,SUBSTRING(ST.text, (QS.statement_start_offset/2) + 1,
```

```
     ((CASE statement_end_offset
          WHEN -1 THEN DATALENGTH(st.text)
          ELSE QS.statement_end_offset END
              - QS.statement_start_offset)/2) + 1) Query
          ,qp.query_plan
FROM sys.dm_exec_query_stats qs
CROSS APPLY sys.dm_exec_sql_text(qs.sql_handle) st
CROSS APPLY sys.dm_exec_query_plan(qs.plan_handle) qp
ORDER BY total_elapsed_time DESC ;
```

The results of the query against sys.dm_exec_query_stats are displayed in Figure 17-1. You can see that, unsurprisingly, the query to identify duplicates was the longest running query, as well as the most expensive in terms of CPU time and IO.

	execution_count	total_elapsed_time	total_worker_time	total_physical_reads	total_logical_reads	total_logical_writes	dbid	Query	query_plan
1	1	115364	51346	0	142	0	18	SELECT Duplicates.CustomerID Customers.First	<ShowPlanXML xmlns="http://schemas.microsoft.com...
2	1	110170	5922	0	71	0	18	SELECT * FROM dbo.Customers	<ShowPlanXML xmlns="http://schemas.microsoft.com...
3	1	1243	1243	0	71	0	18	SELECT SUM(Balance) TotalExposure FROM dbo...	<ShowPlanXML xmlns="http://schemas.microsoft.com...

Query executed successfully.   WIN-KJAGK4GN1MA\PROSQLADMIN...   PROSQLADMIN\Administra...   Chapter17   00:00:00   19904 ro

Figure 17-1. *Longest running query results*

The right-most column in the results displays the XML execution plan. Clicking this execution plan in SQL Server Management Studio displays the graphical representation of the execution plan. The execution plan for the most expensive query is shown in Figure 17-2.

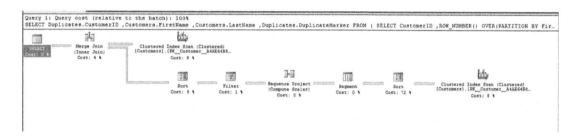

Figure 17-2. *Execution plan*

The query optimizer is very clever, and the vast majority of the time, it chooses the best plan for a query, unless statistics are out of date or indexes are fragmented. Occasionally, however, when troubleshooting a performance issue with a query, you may notice that the optimizer has chosen a suboptimal plan. In the case of our query to identify duplicate names, the optimizer chose a Merge join, which requires the data to be sorted first. The Nested Loop algorithm is likely to perform better for this query, because although using it involves increasing the reads because the data pages of the table are warm, the elapsed time is likely to still be less. We can resolve this issue by asking the development team to add a query hint, but this is not always possible either because of third-party code or delays caused by change control. Therefore, you can resolve the issue by using plan freezing.

Plan Freezing

Plan freezing involves creating an object called a plan guide, which influences the optimizer by attaching query hints to a specific query or programmable object. When the optimizer is passed a query, it checks to see if there is a plan guide that matches the query pattern stored in the sys.plan_guides table. If there is, it modifies the query to incorporate the hints before compiling it.

You can create a plan guide by using the sp_create_plan_guide stored procedure, which accepts the parameters detailed in Table 17-11.

Table 17-11. sp_create_plan_guide Parameters

Parameter	Description
@name	The name of the plan guide that you are creating.
@stmt	The test of the SQL statement that the plan guide is matched against.
@type	Acceptable values are OBJECT, SQL, or TEMPLATE. If OBJECT is specified, the statement must form part of a programmable object, such as a stored procedure or function. If SQL is specified, then the statement must be in an ad-hoc batch. If TEMPLATE is specified, then the statement must match the query after it has been parameterized. For example, WHERE Col1 = @0. TEMPLATE is only compatible with the PARAMETERIZATION query hint.
@module_or_batch	Specifies the name of the programmable object in the format schema.object if the type is object. This needs to be set to the exact text of the batch if the type is SQL. If NULL is passed, the statement supplied in the @stmt parameter is used.
@params	Specifies the definitions of all parameters that are embedded in the statement.
@hints	Specifies either the hint to use by using N'OPTION(), the query plan to use by using XML_SHOWPLAN, or that hints embedded within the statement should be ignored by passing NULL.

■ **Caution** The batch in the plan guide to the batch must be identical to the batch being executed, or the plan guide will not be used. This includes white space, case, and accents. However, EXEC, EXECUTE, and execute are all considered identical.

The command in Listing 17-22 creates a plan guide that forces our duplicate identifying query to use a Loop join, as opposed to a Merge join.

Listing 17-22. Creating a Plan Guide

```
USE Chapter17
GO

EXEC sp_create_plan_guide
        @name = N'[PlanGuide-FindDuplicates]'
        , @stmt = N'SELECT Duplicates.CustomerID
        ,Customers.FirstName
        ,Customers.LastName
        ,Duplicates.DuplicateMarker
```

```
FROM
(
        SELECT CustomerID
                ,ROW_NUMBER() OVER(PARTITION BY FirstName, LastName ORDER BY FirstName,
LastName) DuplicateMarker
        FROM dbo.Customers
) Duplicates
INNER JOIN dbo.Customers Customers
        ON Duplicates.CustomerID = Customers.CustomerID
WHERE Duplicates.DuplicateMarker > 1'
, @type = N'SQL'
, @hints = N'OPTION(LOOP JOIN)' ;
GO
```

After running the duplicates query again, you have two plans in the plan cache. We can run the query in Listing 17-23 to find the details.

Listing 17-23. Finding the Plans for a Specifc Statement

```
SELECT
        execution_count
        ,total_elapsed_time
        ,total_worker_time
        ,total_physical_reads
        ,total_logical_reads
        ,total_logical_writes
        ,qp.dbid
        ,SUBSTRING(ST.text, (QS.statement_start_offset/2) + 1,
    ((CASE statement_end_offset
        WHEN -1 THEN DATALENGTH(st.text)
        ELSE QS.statement_end_offset END
            - QS.statement_start_offset)/2) + 1) Query
        ,qp.query_plan
FROM sys.dm_exec_query_stats qs
CROSS APPLY sys.dm_exec_sql_text(qs.sql_handle) st
CROSS APPLY sys.dm_exec_query_plan(qs.plan_handle) qp
WHERE SUBSTRING(ST.text, (QS.statement_start_offset/2) + 1,
    ((CASE statement_end_offset
        WHEN -1 THEN DATALENGTH(st.text)
        ELSE QS.statement_end_offset END
            - QS.statement_start_offset)/2) + 1) = 'SELECT Duplicates.CustomerID
        ,Customers.FirstName
        ,Customers.LastName
        ,Duplicates.DuplicateMarker
FROM
(
        SELECT CustomerID
                ,ROW_NUMBER() OVER(PARTITION BY FirstName, LastName ORDER BY FirstName,
LastName) DuplicateMarker
        FROM dbo.Customers
) Duplicates
```

```
INNER JOIN dbo.Customers Customers
        ON Duplicates.CustomerID = Customers.CustomerID
WHERE Duplicates.DuplicateMarker > 1'
ORDER BY total_elapsed_time DESC ;'
```

■ **Caution**   Because of the string function in the WHERE clause, this query may not perform well on systems with a large volume of cached plans.

The results of this query are displayed in Figure 17-3. Notice that there are two plans and that each has been executed once. Although the logical reads for the second plan are substantially higher, the elapsed time of the query is shorter.

	execution_count	total_elapsed_time	total_worker_time	total_physical_reads	total_logical_reads	total_logical_writes	dbid	Query	query_plan
1	1	115364	51346	0	142	0	18	SELECT Duplicates.CustomerID ,Customers.First...	<ShowPlanXML xmlns='http://schemas.microsoft.com...
2	1	110930	55559	0	21125	0	18	SELECT Duplicates.CustomerID ,Customers.First...	<ShowPlanXML xmlns='http://schemas.microsoft.com...

Figure 17-3. Find the plan for specific query results

If we view the graphical execution plan of the faster plan shown in Figure 17-4, we can see that a Nested Loop operator was used to join the results set, as per the instruction in our plan guide.

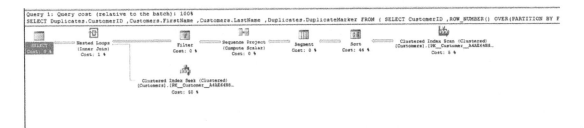

Figure 17-4. Query plan with nested loops

■ **Caution**   Exercise caution when using query hints or plan guides. If the distribution of values changes, your hints may no longer be optimal. Also, the Optimizer is smart, so it is best to work with it rather than against it. For example, if you know that a Loop join is always a poor choice, then instead of using OPTION(HASH JOIN), use OPTION(HASH JOIN, MERGE JOIN). This gives the Optimizer the choice of using any join algorithm, except Loop join, and gives you the best chance of generating the most optimal plan.

Metadata Driven Automation

You can use metadata to drive intelligent scripts that you can use to automate routine DBA maintenance tasks, while at the same time incorporating business logic. In the following sections, you see how you can use metadata to generate rolling database snapshots and also to rebuild only those indexes that are fragmented.

Dynamically Cycling Database Snapshots

As discussed in Chapter 16, we can use database snapshots to create a read-only copy of the database that can reduce contention for read-only reporting. The issue is that the data becomes stale, as data in the source database is modified. For this reason, a useful tool for managing snapshots is a stored procedure, which dynamically creates a new snapshot and drops the oldest existing snapshot. You can then schedule this procedure to run periodically, using SQL Server Agent. (SQL Server Agent is discussed in Chapter 21.) The script in Listing 17-24 creates a stored procedure that, when passed the name of the source database, drops the oldest snapshot and creates a new one.

The procedure accepts two parameters. The first specifies the name of the database that should be used to generate the snapshot. The second parameter specifies how many snapshots you should have at any one time. For example, if you pass in a value of Chapter17 to the @DBName parameter and a value of 2 to the @RequiredSnapshots parameter, the procedure creates a snapshot against the Chapter17 database but only removes the oldest snapshot if at least two snapshots already exist against the Chapter17 database.

The procedure builds up the CREATE DATABASE script in three parts (see Listing 17-24). The first part contains the initial CREATE DATABASE statement. The second part creates the file list, based on the files that are recorded as being part of the database in sys.master_files. The third part contains the AS SNAPSHOT OF statement. The three strings are then concatenated together before being executed. The script appends a sequence number to the name of the snapshot, and the name of each file within the snapshot, to ensure uniqueness.

Listing 17-24. Dynamically Cycling Database Snapshots

```
CREATE PROCEDURE dbo.DynamicSnapshot @DBName NVARCHAR(128), @RequiredSnapshots INT
AS
BEGIN

        DECLARE @SQL NVARCHAR(MAX)
        DECLARE @SQLStart NVARCHAR(MAX)
        DECLARE @SQLEnd NVARCHAR(MAX)
        DECLARE @SQLFileList NVARCHAR(MAX)
        DECLARE @DBID INT
        DECLARE @SS_Seq_No INT
        DECLARE @SQLDrop NVARCHAR(MAX)

        SET @DBID = (SELECT DB_ID(@DBName)) ;

        --Generate sequence number

        IF (SELECT COUNT(*) FROM sys.databases WHERE source_database_id = @DBID) > 0
                SET @SS_Seq_No = (SELECT TOP 1 CAST(SUBSTRING(name, LEN(Name), 1) AS INT)
                                FROM sys.databases
                                WHERE source_database_id = @DBID
                                ORDER BY create_date DESC) + 1
```

657

```
    ELSE
            SET @SS_Seq_No = 1
            --Generate the first part of the CREATE DATABASE statement

    SET @SQLStart = 'CREATE DATABASE '
                    + QUOTENAME(@DBName + CAST(CAST(GETDATE() AS DATE) AS NCHAR(10))
                    + '_ss' + CAST(@SS_Seq_No AS NVARCHAR(4))) + ' ON ' ;

    --Generate the file list for the CREATE DATABASE statement

    SELECT @SQLFileList =
     (
            SELECT
                    '(NAME = N''' + mf.name + ''', FILENAME = N'''
                    + SUBSTRING(mf.physical_name, 1, LEN(mf.physical_name) - 4)
                    + CAST(@SS_Seq_No AS NVARCHAR(4)) + '.ss' + '''),' AS [data()]
            FROM  sys.master_files mf
            WHERE mf.database_id = @DBID
                    AND mf.type = 0
            FOR XML PATH ('')
     ) ;

    --Remove the extra comma from the end of the file list

    SET @SQLFileList = SUBSTRING(@SQLFileList, 1, LEN(@SQLFileList) - 2) ;

    --Generate the final part of the CREATE DATABASE statement

    SET @SQLEnd = ') AS SNAPSHOT OF ' + @DBName ;

    --Concatenate the strings and run the completed statement

    SET @SQL = @SQLStart + @SQLFileList + @SQLEnd ;

    EXEC(@SQL) ;

    --Check to see if the requird number of snapshots exists for the database,
    --and if so, delete the oldest

    IF (SELECT COUNT(*)
            FROM sys.databases
            WHERE source_database_id = @DBID) > @RequiredSnapshots
    BEGIN
            SET @SQLDrop = 'DROP DATABASE ' + (
            SELECT TOP 1
                    QUOTENAME(name)
            FROM sys.databases
            WHERE source_database_id = @DBID
            ORDER BY create_date ASC )
                    EXEC(@SQLDrop)
    END ;

END
```

The command in Listing 17-25 runs the `DynamicSnapshot` procedure against the `Chapter17` database specifying that two snapshots should exist at any one time.

Listing 17-25. Running the DynamicSnapshot Procedure

```
EXEC dbo.DynamicSnapshot 'Chapter17', 2 ;
```

Rebuilding Only Fragmented Indexes

When you rebuilds all indexes with a maintenance plan, which we discuss in Chapter 21, SQL Server supplies no intelligent logic out of the box. Therefore, all indexes are rebuilt, regardless of their fragmentation level, which requires unnecessary time and resource utilization. A workaround for this issue is to write a custom script that rebuilds indexes only if they are fragmented.

The script in Listing 17-26 demonstrates how you can use SQLCMD to identify indexes that have more than 25-percent fragmentation and then rebuild them dynamically. The reason that the code is in a SQLCMD script, as opposed to a stored procedure, is because `sys.dm_db_index_physical_stats` must be called from within the database that you wish to run it against. Therefore, when you run it via SQLCMD, you can use a scripting variable to specify the database you require; doing so makes the script reusable for all databases. When you run the script from the command line, you can simply pass in the name of the database as a variable.

Listing 17-26. Rebuilding Only Required Indexes

```
USE $(DBName)
GO

DECLARE @SQL NVARCHAR(MAX)

SET @SQL =
(
        SELECT 'ALTER INDEX '
                + i.name
                + ' ON ' + s.name
                + '.'
                + OBJECT_NAME(i.object_id)
                + ' REBUILD ; '
        FROM sys.dm_db_index_physical_stats(DB_ID('$(DBName)'),NULL,NULL,NULL,'DETAILED') ps
        INNER JOIN sys.indexes i
                ON ps.object_id = i.object_id
                        AND ps.index_id = i.index_id
        INNER JOIN sys.objects o
                ON ps.object_id = o.object_id
                INNER JOIN sys.schemas s
                        ON o.schema_id = s.schema_id
        WHERE index_level = 0
                AND avg_fragmentation_in_percent > 25
                FOR XML PATH('')
) ;

EXEC(@SQL) ;
```

When this script is saved as in the root of C:\ as RebuildIndexes.sql, it can be run from the command line. The command in Listing 17-27 demonstrates running it against the Chapter17 database.

Listing 17-27. Running RebuildIndexes.sql

```
Sqlcmd -v DBName="Chapter17" -I c:\RebuildIndexes.sql -S ./PROSQLADMIN
```

Summary

SQL Server exposes a vast array of metadata, which describes the data structures within SQL Server as well as the data itself. Metadata is exposed through a series of catalog views, dynamic management views and functions, system functions, and the INFORMATION_SCHEMA. Normally you only use the INFORMATION_SCHEMA if you need your scripts to be transferable to other RDBMS products. This is because it provides less detail than SQL Server–specific metadata but conforms to ISO standards, and therefore, it works on all major RDBMS.

This chapter also covered much useful information about the underlying operating system, as well as SQLOS. For example, you can use the dm_server category of DMV to find details of the instance's Registry keys and expose details of the instance's services. You can use the dm_os category of DMV to expose many internal details regarding the SQLOS, including the current contents of the buffer cache.

SQL Server also exposes metadata that you can use for capacity planning, such as the usage statistics for all files within a database (for example, IO stalls) and the amount of free space remaining. You can use this information to proactively plan additional capacity requirements before alerts start being triggered and applications are put at risk.

Metadata can also help in the pursuit of troubleshooting and performance tuning. The sys.dm_os_performance_counters DMV allows DBAs to retrieve Perfmon counters, even if they do not have access to the operating system. This can remove inter-team dependencies. You can use sys.dm_os_wait_stats to identify the most common cause of waits within the instance, which can in turn help diagnose hardware bottlenecks, such as memory or CPU pressure. The dm_exec category of DMV can help identify expensive queries, which may be tuned, to improve performance.

DBAs can also use metadata to create intelligent scripts, which can reduce their workload by adding business rules to common maintenance tasks. For example, a DBA can use metadata for tasks such as dynamically rebuilding only indexes that have become fragmented, or dynamically managing the cycling of database snapshots. I encourage you to explore the possibilities of metadata-driven automation further; the possibilities are endless.

CHAPTER 18

■ ■ ■

Locking and Blocking

Locking is an essential aspect of any RDBMS, because it allows concurrent users to access the same data, without the risk of their updates conflicting and causing data integrity issues. This chapter discusses how locking, deadlocks, and transactions work in SQL Server; it then moves on to discuss how transactions impact SQL Server 2014's new In-Memory transaction functionality and how the DBA can observe lock metadata regarding transactions and contention.

Understanding Locking

The following sections discuss how processes can take locks at various levels of granularity, which types of lock are compatible with others, and SQL Server 2014's new features for controlling lock behavior during online maintenance operations and lock partitioning, which can improve performance on large systems.

Lock Granularity

Processes can take out locks at many different levels of granularity, depending on the nature of the operation requesting the lock. To reduce the impact of operations blocking each other, it is sensible to take out a lock at the lowest possible level of granularity. The tradeoff, however, is that taking out locks uses system resources, so if an operation requires acquiring millions of locks at the lowest level of granularity, then this is highly inefficient, and locking at a higher level is a more suitable choice. Table 18-1 describes the levels of granularity at which locks can be taken out.

Table 18-1. *Locking Granularity*

Level	Description
RID/KEY	A row identifier on a heap or an index key. Use locks on index keys in serializable transactions to lock ranges of rows. Serializable transactions are discussed later in this chapter.
PAGE	A data or index page.
EXTENT	Eight continuous pages.
HoBT	A heap of a single index (B-Tree).
TABLE	An entire table, including all indexes.
FILE	A file within a database.

(continued)

Table 18-1. (*continued*)

Level	Description
METADATA	A metadata resource.
ALLOCTION_UNIT	Tables are split into three allocation units: row data, row overflow data, and LOB (Large Object Block) data. A lock on an allocation unit locks one of the three allocation units of a table.
DATABASE	The entire database.

When SQL Server locks a resource within a table, it takes out what is known as an *intent lock* on the resource directly above it in the hierarchy. For example, if SQL Server needs to lock a RID or KEY, it also takes out an intent lock on the page containing the row. If the Lock Manager decides that it is more efficient to lock at a higher level of the hierarchy, then it escalates the lock to a higher level. It is worth noting, however, that row locks are not escalated to page locks; they are escalated directly to table locks. If the table is partitioned, then SQL Server can lock the partition as opposed to the whole table. The thresholds that SQL Server uses for lock escalation are as follows:

- An operation requires more than 5000 locks on a table, or a partition, if the table is partitioned.

- The number of locks acquired within the instance causes memory thresholds to be exceeded.

You can change this behavior for specific tables, however, by using the LOCK_ESCALATION option of a table. This option has three possible values, as described in Table 18-2.

Table 18-2. *LOCK_ESCALATION Values*

Value	Description
TABLE	Locks escalate to the table level, even when you are using partitioned tables.
AUTO	This value allows locks to escalate to a partition, rather than the table, on partitioned tables.
DISABLE	The value disables locks being escalated to the table level except when a table lock is required to protect data integrity.

Locking Behaviors for Online Maintenance

New in SQL Server 2014, you can also control the behavior of locking for online index rebuilds and partition SWITCH operations. The available options are described in Table 18-3.

Table 18-3. *Blocking Behaviors*

Option	Description
MAX_DURATION	The duration, specified in minutes, that an online index rebuild or SWITCH operation waits before the ABORT_AFTER_WAIT action is triggered.
ABORT_AFTER_WAIT	These are the available actions: • NONE specifies that the operation will continue to wait, with normal priority. • SELF means that the operation will be terminated. • BLOCKERS means that all user transactions that are currently blocking the operation will be killed.
WAIT_AT_LOW_PRIORITY	Functionally equivalent to MAX_DURATION = 0, ABORT_AFTER_WAIT = NONE.

The script in Listing 18-1 creates the Chapter18 database, which includes a table called Customers that is populated with data. The script then demonstrates configuring LOCK_ESCALATION before rebuilding the nonclustered index on dbo.customers, specifying that any operations should be killed if they are blocking the rebuild for more than one minute.

Listing 18-1. Configuring Table Locking Options

```
--Create the database

CREATE DATABASE Chapter18
ON  PRIMARY
( NAME = N'Chapter18', FILENAME = 'F:\MSSQL\DATA\Chapter18.mdf' ),
 FILEGROUP MemOpt CONTAINS MEMORY_OPTIMIZED_DATA  DEFAULT
( NAME = N'MemOpt', FILENAME = 'F:\MSSQL\DATA\MemOpt' )
 LOG ON
( NAME = N'Chapter18_log', FILENAME = 'E:\MSSQL\DATA\Chapter18_log.ldf' ) ;
GO

USE Chapter18
GO

--Create and populate numbers table

DECLARE @Numbers TABLE
(
	Number		INT
)

;WITH CTE(Number)
AS
(
	SELECT 1 Number
	UNION ALL
	SELECT Number + 1
	FROM CTE
	WHERE Number < 100
)
```

```
INSERT INTO @Numbers
SELECT Number FROM CTE;

--Create and populate name pieces

DECLARE @Names TABLE
(
        FirstName          VARCHAR(30),
        LastName           VARCHAR(30)
);

INSERT INTO @Names
VALUES('Peter', 'Carter'),
               ('Michael', 'Smith'),
               ('Danielle', 'Mead'),
               ('Reuben', 'Roberts'),
               ('Iris', 'Jones'),
               ('Sylvia', 'Davies'),
               ('Finola', 'Wright'),
               ('Edward', 'James'),
               ('Marie', 'Andrews'),
               ('Jennifer', 'Abraham');

--Create and populate Addresses table

CREATE TABLE dbo.Addresses
(
AddressID          INT              NOT NULL        IDENTITY        PRIMARY KEY,
AddressLine1       NVARCHAR(50),
AddressLine2       NVARCHAR(50),
AddressLine3       NVARCHAR(50),
PostCode           NCHAR(8)
) ;

INSERT INTO dbo.Addresses
VALUES('1 Carter Drive', 'Hedge End', 'Southampton', 'SO32 6GH')
        ,('10 Apress Way', NULL, 'London', 'WC10 2FG')
        ,('12 SQL Street', 'Botley', 'Southampton', 'SO32 8RT')
        ,('19 Springer Way', NULL, 'London', 'EC1 5GG') ;

--Create and populate Customers table

CREATE TABLE dbo.Customers
(
        CustomerID           INT          NOT NULL        IDENTITY        PRIMARY KEY,
        FirstName            VARCHAR(30)  NOT NULL,
        LastName             VARCHAR(30)  NOT NULL,
        BillingAddressID     INT          NOT NULL,
        DeliveryAddressID    INT          NOT NULL,
        CreditLimit          MONEY        NOT NULL,
        Balance              MONEY        NOT NULL
);
```

```
SELECT * INTO #Customers
FROM
        (SELECT
                (SELECT TOP 1 FirstName FROM @Names ORDER BY NEWID()) FirstName,
                (SELECT TOP 1 LastName FROM @Names ORDER BY NEWID()) LastName,
                (SELECT TOP 1 Number FROM @Numbers ORDER BY NEWID()) BillingAddressID,
                (SELECT TOP 1 Number FROM @Numbers ORDER BY NEWID()) DeliveryAddressID,
                (SELECT TOP 1 CAST(RAND() * Number AS INT) * 10000
                    FROM @Numbers
                    ORDER BY NEWID()) CreditLimit,
                (SELECT TOP 1 CAST(RAND() * Number AS INT) * 9000
                    FROM @Numbers
                    ORDER BY NEWID()) Balance
        FROM @Numbers a
        CROSS JOIN @Numbers b
) a;

INSERT INTO dbo.Customers
SELECT * FROM #Customers;
GO

CREATE TABLE dbo.CustomersMem
(
        CustomerID              INT             NOT NULL    IDENTITY
                                PRIMARY KEY NONCLUSTERED HASH WITH(BUCKET_COUNT = 20000),
        FirstName           VARCHAR(30)     NOT NULL,
        LastName            VARCHAR(30)     NOT NULL,
        BillingAddressID    INT             NOT NULL,
        DeliveryAddressID   INT             NOT NULL,
        CreditLimit         MONEY           NOT NULL,
        Balance             MONEY           NOT NULL
) WITH(MEMORY_OPTIMIZED = ON) ;

INSERT INTO dbo.CustomersMem
SELECT
        FirstName
        , LastName
        , BillingAddressID
        , DeliveryAddressID
        , CreditLimit
        , Balance
FROM dbo.Customers ;
GO

CREATE INDEX idx_LastName ON dbo.Customers(LastName)

--Set LOCK_ESCALATION to AUTO

ALTER TABLE dbo.Customers SET (LOCK_ESCALATION = AUTO) ;
```

```
--Set WAIT_AT_LOW_PRIORITY

ALTER INDEX idx_LastName ON dbo.Customers REBUILD
WITH
(ONLINE = ON (WAIT_AT_LOW_PRIORITY (MAX_DURATION = 1 MINUTES, ABORT_AFTER_WAIT = BLOCKERS))) ;
```

Lock Compatibility

A process can acquire different types of locks. These lock types are described in Table 18-4.

Table 18-4. *Lock Types*

Type	Description
Shared (S)	Used for read operations.
Update (U)	Taken out on resources that may be updated.
Exclusive (X)	Used when data is modified.
Schema Modification (Sch-M) / Schema Stability (Sch-S)	Schema modification locks are taken out when DDL statements are being run against a table. Schema stability locks are taken out while queries are being compiled and executed. Stability locks only block operations that require a schema modification lock, whereas schema modification locks block all access to a table.
Bulk Update (BU)	Bulk update locks are used during bulk load operations to allow multiple threads to parallel load data to a table while blocking other processes.
Key-range	Key-range locks are taken on a range of rows when using pessimistic isolation levels. Isolation levels are discussed later in this chapter.
Intent	Intent locks are used to protect resources lower in the lock hierarchy by signaling their intent to acquire a shared or exclusive lock.

Intent locks improve performance, because they are only examined at the table level, which negates the need to examine every row or page before another operation acquires a lock. The types of intent lock that can be acquired are described in Table 18-5.

Table 18-5. *Intent Lock Types*

Type	Description
Intent shared (IS)	Protects shared locks on some resources at the lower level of the hierarchy
Intent exclusive (IX)	Protects shared and exclusive locks on some resources at the lower level of the hierarchy
Shared with intent exclusive (SIX)	Protects shared locks on all resources and exclusive locks on some resources at the lower level of the hierarchy
Intent update (IU)	Protects update locks on all resources at the lower level of the hierarchy
Shared intent update (SIU)	The resultant set of S and IU locks
Update intent exclusive (UIX)	The resultant set of X and IU locks

The matrix in Figure 18-1 shows basic lock compatibility. You can find a complete matrix of lock compatibility at msdn.micrososft.com.

	Shared	Update	Exclusive
Shared	Yes	Yes	No
Update	Yes	No	No
Exclusive	No	No	No

Figure 18-1. *Lock compatability matrix*

Lock Partitioning

It is possible for locks on frequently accessed resources to become a bottleneck. For this reason, SQL Server automatically applies a feature called *lock partitioning* for any instance that has affinity with more than 16 cores. Lock partitioning reduces contention by dividing a single lock resource into multiple resources. This means that contention is reduced on shared resources such as the memory used by the lock resource structure.

Understanding Deadlocks

Because of the very nature of locking, operations need to wait until a lock has been released before they can acquire their own lock on a resource. A problem can occur, however, if two separate processes have taken out locks on different resources, but both are blocked, waiting for the other to complete. This is known as a *deadlock*.

How Deadlocks Occur

To see how this issue can arise, examine Table 18-6.

Table 18-6. *Deadlock Chronology*

Process A	Process B
Acquires a lock on Row1 in Table1	
	Acquires a lock on Row2 in Table2
Attempts to acquire a lock on Row2 in Table2 but is blocked by Process B	
	Attempts to acquire a lock on Row1 in Table1 but is blocked by Process A

In the sequence described here, neither Process A nor Process B can continue, which means a deadlock has occurred. SQL Server detects deadlocks via an internal process called the deadlock monitor. When the deadlock monitor encounters a deadlock, it checks to see if the processes have been assigned a transaction priority. If the processes have different transaction priorities, it kills the process with the lowest priority. If they have the same priority, then it kills the least expensive process in terms of resource utilization. If both processes have the same cost, it picks a process at random and kills it.

The scripts in Listing 18-2 generates a deadlock. You must run the first and third parts of the script in a different query window than the second and fourth parts. You must run each section of the script in sequence.

Listing 18-2. Generating a Deadlock

```
--Part 1 - Run in 1st query window

BEGIN TRANSACTION

UPDATE dbo.Customers
SET LastName = 'Andrews'
WHERE CustomerID = 1

--Part 2 - Run in 2nd query window

BEGIN TRANSACTION

UPDATE dbo.Addresses
SET PostCode = 'SA12 9BD'
WHERE AddressID = 2

--Part 3 - Run in 1st query window

UPDATE dbo.Addresses
SET PostCode = 'SA12 9BD'
WHERE AddressID = 2

--Part 4 - Run in 2nd query window

UPDATE dbo.Customers
SET LastName = 'Colins'
WHERE CustomerID = 1
```

SQL Server chooses one of the processes as a deadlock victim and kills it. This leads to an error message being thrown in the victim's query window, as illustrated in Figure 18-2.

Figure 18-2. *Deadlock victim error*

Minimizing Deadlocks

Your developers can take various steps to minimize the risk of deadlocks. Because it is you (the DBA) who is responsible for supporting the instance in production, it is prudent to check to make sure the development team's code meets standards for minimizing deadlocks before you release the code to production.

When reviewing code, prior to code release, you should look to ensure that the following guidelines are being followed:

- Optimistic isolation levels are being used where appropriate (You should also consider the tradeoffs regarding TempDB usage, disk overhead, etc.).

- There should be no user interaction within transactions (this can avoid locks being held for extended periods).

- Transactions are as short as possible and within the same batch (this can avoid long-running transactions, which hold locks for longer than necessary).

- All programmable objects access objects in the same order (this can offset the likelihood of deadlocks and replace at the expense of contention on the first table).

Understanding Transactions

Every action that causes data or objects to be modified happens within the context of a transaction. SQL Server supports three types of transaction: autocommit, explicit, and implicit. *Autocommit transactions* are the default behavior and mean that each statement is performed in the context of its own transaction. *Explicit transactions* are started and ended manually. They start with a BEGIN TRANSACTION statement and end with either a COMMIT TRANSACTION statement, which causes the associated log records to be hardened to disk; or a ROLLBACK statement, which causes all actions within the transaction to be undone. If *implicit transactions* are turned on for a connection, then the default autocommit behavior no longer works for that connection. Instead, transactions are started automatically, and then committed manually, using a COMMIT TRANSACTION statement.

Transactional Properties

Transactions exhibit properties known as ACID (atomic, consistent, isolated, and durable). Each of these is discussed in the following sections.

Atomic

For a transaction to be atomic, all actions within a transaction must either commit together or roll back together. It is not possible for only part of a transaction to commit. SQL Server's implementation of this property is slightly more flexible, however, through the implementation of Savepoints.

A *Savepoint* is a marker within a transaction where, in the event of a rollback, everything before the Savepoint is committed, and everything after the Savepoint can be either committed or rolled back. This can be helpful in trapping occasional errors that may occur. For example, the script in Listing 18-3 performs a large insert into the Customers table before performing a small insert into the Addresses table. If the insert into the Addresses table fails, the large insert into the Customers table is still committed.

Listing 18-3. Savepoints

```
SELECT COUNT(*) InitialCustomerCount FROM dbo.Customers ;

SELECT COUNT(*) InitialAddressesCount FROM dbo.Addresses ;

BEGIN TRANSACTION

DECLARE @Numbers TABLE
(
        Number          INT
)

;WITH CTE(Number)
AS
(
        SELECT 1 Number
        UNION ALL
        SELECT Number + 1
        FROM CTE
        WHERE Number < 100
)
INSERT INTO @Numbers
SELECT Number FROM CTE;

--Create and populate name pieces

DECLARE @Names TABLE
(
        FirstName       VARCHAR(30),
        LastName        VARCHAR(30)
);

INSERT INTO @Names
VALUES('Peter', 'Carter'),
              ('Michael', 'Smith'),
              ('Danielle', 'Mead'),
              ('Reuben', 'Roberts'),
              ('Iris', 'Jones'),
              ('Sylvia', 'Davies'),
              ('Finola', 'Wright'),
              ('Edward', 'James'),
              ('Marie', 'Andrews'),
              ('Jennifer', 'Abraham');

--Populate Customers table
```

```
SELECT * INTO #Customers
FROM
        (SELECT
                (SELECT TOP 1 FirstName FROM @Names ORDER BY NEWID()) FirstName,
                (SELECT TOP 1 LastName FROM @Names ORDER BY NEWID()) LastName,
                (SELECT TOP 1 Number FROM @Numbers ORDER BY NEWID()) BillingAddressID,
                (SELECT TOP 1 Number FROM @Numbers ORDER BY NEWID()) DeliveryAddressID,
                (SELECT TOP 1 CAST(RAND() * Number AS INT) * 10000
                 FROM @Numbers
                 ORDER BY NEWID()) CreditLimit,
                (SELECT TOP 1 CAST(RAND() * Number AS INT) * 9000
                 FROM @Numbers
                 ORDER BY NEWID()) Balance
        FROM @Numbers a
        CROSS JOIN @Numbers b
) a;

INSERT INTO dbo.Customers
SELECT * FROM #Customers;

SAVE TRANSACTION CustomerInsert

BEGIN TRY
--Populate Addresses table - Will fail, due to length of Post Code

INSERT INTO dbo.Addresses
VALUES('1 Apress Towers', 'Hedge End', 'Southampton', 'SA206 2BQ') ;
END TRY
BEGIN CATCH
        ROLLBACK TRANSACTION CustomerInsert
END CATCH

COMMIT TRANSACTION

SELECT COUNT(*) FinalCustomerCount FROM dbo.Customers ;

SELECT COUNT(*) FinalAddressesCount FROM dbo.Addresses ;
```

The results of the row counts, illustrated in Figure 18-3, show that the insert to the Customers table committed, while the insert to the Addresses table rolled back. It is also possible to create multiple Savepoints within a single transaction and then roll back to the most appropriate point.

Figure 18-3. Row counts

Consistent

The consistent property means that the transaction moves the database from one consistent state to another; at the end of the transaction, all data must conform to all data rules, which are enforced with constraints, data types, and so on.

SQL Server fully enforces this property, but there are workarounds. For example, if you have a check constraint, or a foreign key on a table, and you wish to perform a large bulk insert, you can disable the constraint, insert the data, and then re-enable the constraint with NOCHECK. When you use NOCHECK, the constraint enforces the rules for new data modification, but it does not enforce the rule for data that already exists in the table. When you do this, however, SQL Server marks the constraint as not trusted, and the Query Optimizer ignores the constraint until you have validated the existing data in the table using an ALTER TABLE MyTable WITH CHECK CHECK CONSTRAINT ALL command.

Isolated

Isolation refers to the concurrent transaction's ability to see data modifications made by a transaction before they are committed. Isolating transactions avoids transactional anomalies and is enforced by either acquiring locks or maintaining multiple versions of rows. Each transaction runs with a defined isolation level. Before we discuss available isolation levels, however, we first need to examine the transactional anomalies that can occur.

Transactional Anomalies

Transactional anomalies can cause queries to return unpredictable results. Three types of transaction anomalies are possible within SQL Server: dirty reads, nonrepeatable reads, and phantom reads. These are discussed in the following sections.

Dirty Reads

A *dirty read* occurs when a transaction reads data that never existed in the database. An example of how this anomaly can occur is outlined in Table 18-7.

Table 18-7. *A Dirty Read*

Transaction1	Transaction2
Inserts row1 into Table1	
	Reads row1 from Table1
Rolls back	

In this example, because Transaction1 rolled back, Transaction2 read a row that never existed in the database. This anomaly can occur if shared locks are not acquired for reads, since there is no lock to conflict with the exclusive lock taken out by Transaction1.

Nonrepeatable Read

A nonrepeatable read occurs when a transaction reads the same row twice but receives different results each time. An example of how this anomaly can occur is outlined in Table 18-8.

Table 18-8. *A Nonrepeatable Read*

Transaction1	Transaction2
Reads row1 from Table1	
	Updates row1 in Table1
	Commits
Reads row1 from Table1	

In this example, you can see that Transaction1 has read row1 from Table1 twice. The second time, however, it receives a different result, because Transaction2 has updated the row. This anomaly can occur if Transaction1 takes out shared locks but does not hold them for the duration of the transaction.

Phantom Read

A phantom read occurs when a transaction reads a range of rows twice but receives a different number of rows the second time it reads the range. An example of how this anomaly can occur is outlined in Table 18-9.

Table 18-9. *Phantom Reads*

Transaction1	Transaction2
Reads all rows from Table1	
	Inserts ten rows into Table1
	Commits
Reads all rows from Table1	

In this example, you can see that Transaction1 has read all rows from Table1 twice. The second time, however, it reads an extra ten rows, because Transaction2 has inserted ten rows into the table. This anomaly can occur when Transaction1 does not acquire a key-range lock and hold it for the duration of the transaction.

Isolation Levels

SQL Server provides four pessimistic and two optimistic transaction isolation levels for transactions that involve disk-based tables. Pessimistic isolation levels use locks to protect against transactional anomalies and optimistic isolation levels use row versioning.

Pessimistic Isolation Levels

Read Uncommitted is the least restrictive isolation level. It works by acquiring locks for write operations but not acquiring any locks for read operations. This means that under this isolation level, read operations do not block other readers or writers. The result is that all transactional anomalies described in the previous sections are possible.

Read Committed is the default isolation level. It works by acquiring shared locks for read operations as well as locks for write operations. The shared locks are only held during the read phase of a specific row, and the lock is released as soon as the record has been read. This results in protection against dirty reads, but nonrepeatable reads and phantom reads are still possible.

■ **Tip** In some circumstances, shared locks may be held until the end of the statement. This occurs when a physical operator is required to spool data to disk.

In addition to acquiring locks for write operations, Repeatable Read acquires shared locks on all rows that it touches and then it holds these locks until the end of the transaction. The result is that dirty reads and nonrepeatable reads are not possible, although phantom reads can still occur. Because the reads are held for the duration of the transaction, deadlocks are more likely to occur than when you are using Read Committed or Read Uncommitted isolation levels.

Serializable is the most restrictive isolation level, and the level where deadlocks are most likely to occur. It works by not only acquiring locks for write operations, but also by acquiring key-range locks for read operations, and then holding them for the duration of the transaction. Because key-range locks are held in this manner, no transactional anomalies are possible, including phantom reads.

Optimistic Isolation Levels

Optimistic isolation levels work without acquiring any locks for either read or write operations. Instead, they use a technique called *row versioning*. Row versioning works by maintaining a new copy of a row in TempDB for uncommitted transactions every time the row is updated. This means that there is always a consistent copy of the data that transactions can refer to. This can dramatically reduce contention on highly concurrent systems. The tradeoff is that you need to scale TempDB appropriately, in terms of both size and throughput capacity, since the extra IO can have a negative impact on performance.

Snapshot isolation uses optimistic concurrency for both read and write operations. It works by assigning each transaction a transaction sequence number at the point the transaction begins. It is then able to read the version of the row from TempDB that was current at the start of the transaction by looking for the closest sequence number that is lower than the transaction's own sequence number. This means that although other versions of the row may exist with modifications, it cannot see them, since the sequence numbers are higher. If two transactions try to update the same row at the same time, instead of a deadlock occurring, the second transaction throws error 3960 and the transaction is rolled back. The result of this behavior is that dirty reads, nonrepeatable reads, and phantom reads are not possible.

The Read Committed Snapshot uses pessimistic concurrency for write operations and optimistic concurrency for read operations. For read operations, it uses the version of the row that is current at the beginning of each statement within the transaction, as opposed to the version that was current at the beginning of the transaction. This means that you achieve the same level of isolation as you would by using the pessimistic Read Committed isolation level.

Unlike the pessimistic isolation levels, you need to turn on optimistic isolation levels at the database level. When you turn on Read Committed Snapshot, this replaces the functionality of Read Committed. This is important to bear in mind, because Read Committed Snapshot becomes your default isolation level and is used for all transactions that do not specifically set an isolation level. The script in Listing 18-4 demonstrates how to turn on Snapshot isolation and Read Committed Snapshot isolation for the Chapter18 database. The script first checks to make sure that Read Committed and Read Committed Snapshot are not already enabled. If they are not, it kills any sessions that are currently connected to the Chapter18 database before finally running the ALETER DATABASE statements.

Listing 18-4. Turning On Optimistic Isolation

```
--Check if already enabled

IF EXISTS (
        SELECT name
                ,snapshot_isolation_state_desc
                ,is_read_committed_snapshot_on
        FROM sys.databases
        WHERE name = 'Chapter18'
                AND snapshot_isolation_state_desc = 'OFF'
                AND is_read_committed_snapshot_on = 0 )
BEGIN
        --Kill any existing sessions

        IF EXISTS(
        SELECT * FROM sys.dm_exec_sessions where database_id = DB_id('Chapter18')
        )
        BEGIN
                PRINT 'Killing Sessions to Chapter18 database'
                DECLARE @SQL NVARCHAR(MAX)
                SET @SQL = (SELECT 'KILL ' + CAST(Session_id AS NVARCHAR(3)) + '; ' [data()]
                                    FROM sys.dm_exec_sessions
                                    WHERE database_id = DB_id('Chapter18')
                                    FOR XML PATH('')
                                    )
                EXEC(@SQL)
        END

        PRINT 'Enabling Snapshot and Read Committed Sanpshot Isolation'

        ALTER DATABASE Chapter18
        SET ALLOW_SNAPSHOT_ISOLATION ON ;

        ALTER DATABASE Chapter18
        SET READ_COMMITTED_SNAPSHOT ON ;
END
ELSE
        PRINT 'Snapshot Isolation already enabled'
```

Durable

For a transaction to be durable, after it has been committed, it stays committed, even in a catastrophic event. This means that the change must be written to disk, since the change within memory will not withstand a power failure, a restart of the instance, and so on. SQL Server achieves this by using a process called write-ahead logging (WAL). This process flushes the log cache to disk at the point the transaction commits, and the commit only completes once this flush finishes.

SQL Server 2014 relaxes these rules, however, by introducing a feature called delayed durability. This feature works by delaying the flush of the log cache to disk until one of the following events occurs:

- The log cache becomes full and automatically flushes to disk.

- A fully durable transaction in the same database commits.

- The sp_flush_log system stored procedure is run against the database.

When delayed durability is used, the data is visible to other transaction as soon as the transaction commits; however, the data committed within the transaction could potentially be lost, if the instance goes down or is restarted, until the log records have been flushed. Support for delayed durability is configured at the database level, using one of the three options detailed in Table 18-10.

Table 18-10. *Support Levels for Delayed Durability*

Support Level	Description
ALLOWED	Delayed durability is supported within the database and specified on a transaction level basis.
FORCED	All transactions within the database will use delayed durability.
DISBALED	The default setting. No transactions within the database are permitted to use delayed durability.

The command in Listing 18-5 shows how to allow delayed durability in the Chapter 18 database.

Listing 18-5. Allowing Delayed Durability

```
ALTER DATABASE Chapter18
SET DELAYED_DURABILITY  = ALLOWED ;
```

If a database is configured to allow delayed durability, then Full or Delayed durability is configured at the transaction level, in the COMMIT statement. The script in Listing 18-6 demonstrates how to commit a transaction with delayed durability.

Listing 18-6. Commiting with Delayed Durability

```
USE Chapter18
GO

BEGIN TRANSACTION
        UPDATE dbo.Customers
        SET DeliveryAddressID = 1
        WHERE CustomerID = 10 ;
COMMIT WITH (DELAYED_DURABILITY = ON)
```

■ **Caution** The most important thing to remember, when using delayed durability, is the potential for data loss. If any transactions have committed but the associated log records have not been flushed to disk when the instance goes down, this data is lost.

In the event of an issue, such as an IO error, is possible for uncommitted transactions to enter a state where they cannot be committed or rolled back. This occurs when you are bringing a database back online and it fails during both the redo phase and the undo phase. This is called a *deferred transaction*. Deferred transactions stop the VLF that they are in from being truncated, meaning that the transaction log continues to grow.

Resolving the issue depends on the cause of the problem. If the problem is caused by a corrupt page, then you may be able to restore this page from a backup. If the issue is caused because a filegroup was offline, then you must either restore the filegroup or mark the filegroup as defunct. If you mark a filegroup as defunct, you cannot recover it.

Transaction with In-Memory OLTP

Memory-optimized tables do not support locks; this changes the way isolation levels can work, since pessimistic concurrency is no longer an option. We discuss isolation levels supported for In-Memory OLTP, along with considerations for cross-container queries, in the following sections.

Isolation Levels

Because all isolation levels used with In-Memory OLTP must be optimistic, each isolation level implements row versioning. Unlike row versioning for disk-based tables, however, row versions for memory-optimized tables are not maintained in TempDB. Instead, they are maintained in the memory-optimized table that they relate to.

Read Committed

The Read Committed isolation level is supported against memory-optimized tables, but only if you are using autocommit transactions. It is not possible to use Read Committed in explicit or implicit transactions. It is also not possible to use Read Committed in the ATOMIC block of a natively compiled stored procedure. Because Read Committed is the default isolation level for SQL Server, you must either ensure that all transactions involving memory-optimized tables explicitly state an isolation level, or you must set the MEMORY_OPTIMIZED_ELEVATE_TO_SNAPSHOT database property. This option elevates all transactions that involve memory-optimized tables but do not specify an isolation level to Snapshot isolation, the least restrictive isolation level, which is fully supported for In-Memory OLTP.

The command in Listing 18-7 shows how to set the MEMORY_OPTIMIZED_ELEVATE_TO_SNAPSHOT property for the Chapter17 database.

Listing 18-7. Elevating to Snapshot

```
ALTER DATABASE Chapter18
SET MEMORY_OPTIMIZED_ELEVATE_TO_SNAPSHOT = ON ;
```

Read Committed Snapshot

The Read Committed Snapshot isolation level is supported for memory-optimized tables, but only when you are using autocommit transactions. This isolation level is not supported when the transaction accesses disk-based tables.

Snapshot

The Snapshot isolation level uses row versioning to guarantee that a transaction always sees the data, as it was at the start of the transaction. Snapshot isolation is only supported against memory-optimized tables when you use interpreted SQL if it is specified as a query hint as opposed to at the transaction level. It is fully supported in the ATOMIC block of natively compiled stored procedures.

If a transaction attempts to modify a row that has already been updated by another transaction, then the conflict detection mechanism rolls back the transaction, and Error 41302 is thrown. If a transaction attempts to insert a row that has the same primary key value as a row that has been inserted by another transaction, then conflict detection rolls back the transaction and Error 41352 is thrown. If a transaction attempts to modify the data in a table that has been dropped by another transaction, then Error 41305 is thrown, and the transaction is rolled back.

Repeatable Read

The Repeatable Read isolation level provides the same protection as Snapshot, but additionally, it guarantees that rows read by the transaction have not been modified by other rows since the start of the transaction. If the transaction attempts to read a row that has been modified by another transaction, then Error 41305 is thrown and the transaction is rolled back. The Repeatable Read isolation is not supported against memory-optimized tables when using interpreted SQL, however. It is only supported in the ATOMIC block of natively compiled stored procedures.

Serializable

The Serializable isolation level offers the same protection that is offered by Repeatable Read, but in addition, it guarantees that no rows have been inserted within the range of rows being accessed by queries within the transaction. If a transaction using the Serializable isolation level cannot meet its guarantees, then the conflict detection mechanism rolls back the transaction and Error 41325 is thrown. Serializable isolation is not supported against memory-optimized tables when using interpreted SQL, however. It is only supported in the ATOMIC block of natively compiled stored procedures.

Cross-Container Transactions

Because isolations levels' use is restricted, when a transaction accesses both memory-optimized tables and disk-based tables, you may need to specify a combination of isolation levels and query hints. The query in Listing 18-8 joins together the Customers and CustomersMem tables. It succeeds only because we have turned on MEMORY_OPTIMIZED_ELEVATE_TO_SNAPSHOT. This means that the query uses the default Read Committed Snapshot isolation level to access the disk-based table and automatically upgrades the read of the CustomersMem table to use Snapshot isolation.

Listing 18-8. Joining Disk and Memory Tables with Automatic Elevation

```
BEGIN TRANSACTION
        SELECT *
        FROM dbo.Customers C
        INNER JOIN dbo.CustomersMem CM
                ON C.CustomerID = CM.CustomerID ;
COMMIT TRANSACTION
```

However, if we now turn off MEMORY_OPTIMIZED_ELEVATE_TO_SNAPSHOT, which you can do using the script in Listing 18-9, the same transaction now fails with the error message shown in Figure 18-4.

Listing 18-9. Turning Off MEMORY_OPTIMIZED_ELEVATE_TO_SNAPSHOT

```
ALTER DATABASE Chapter18
SET MEMORY_OPTIMIZED_ELEVATE_TO_SNAPSHOT=OFF
GO
```

Figure 18-4. *Join disc and memory tables without automatic elevation*

The query in Listing 18-10 demonstrates how we can join the Customers table with the CustomersMem table using the Snapshot isolation level for the memory-optimized table and the Serializable isolation level for the disk-based table. Because we are using interpreted SQL, the Snapshot isolation level is the only level we can use to access the memory-optimized table, and we must specify this as a query hint. If we specify it at the transaction level instead of at serializable the transaction fails.

Listing 18-10. Joining Disk and Memory-Optimized Tables Using Query Hints

```
BEGIN TRANSACTION
SET TRANSACTION ISOLATION LEVEL SERIALIZABLE
        SELECT *
        FROM dbo.Customers C
        INNER JOIN dbo.CustomersMem CM (SNAPSHOT)
                ON C.CustomerID = CM.CustomerID ;
COMMIT TRANSACTION
```

If we use a natively compiled stored procedure instead of interpreted SQL, we add the required transaction isolation level to the ATOMIC block of the procedure definition. The script in Listing 18-11 demonstrates creating a natively compiled stored procedure that updates the CustomersMem table using the Serializable isolation level. Because natively compiled stored procedures are not able to access disk-based tables, you do not need to be concerned with locking hints to support cross-container transactions.

Listing 18-11. Using Serializable Isolation in a Nativley Compiled Stored Procedure

```
CREATE PROCEDURE dbo.UpdateCreditLimit
WITH native_compilation, schemabinding, execute as owner
AS
BEGIN ATOMIC
        WITH(TRANSACTION ISOLATION LEVEL = SERIALIZABLE, LANGUAGE = 'English')
                UPDATE dbo.CustomersMem
                SET CreditLimit = CreditLimit * 1.1
                WHERE Balance < CreditLimit / 4 ;
```

679

```
            UPDATE dbo.CustomersMem
            SET CreditLimit = CreditLimit * 1.05
            WHERE Balance < CreditLimit / 2 ;
END
```

Retry Logic

Whether you are using interpreted SQL or a natively compiled stored procedure, always ensure that you use retry logic when you are running transactions against memory-optimized tables. This is because of the optimistic concurrency model, which means that the conflict detection mechanism rolls transactions back, as opposed to managing concurrency with locking. It is also important to remember that SQL Server even rolls back read-only transactions if the required level of isolation cannot be guaranteed. For example, if you are using serializable isolation in a read-only transaction, and another transaction inserts rows that match your query filters, the transaction is rolled back.

The script in Listing 18-12 creates a wrapper-stored procedure for the UpdateCreditLimit procedure, which retries the procedure up to ten times should the procedure fail, with a one-second gap between each iteration. You should change this delay to match the average duration of conflicting transactions.

Listing 18-12. Retry Logic for Memory-Optimized Tables

```
CREATE PROCEDURE UpdateCreditLimitWrapper
AS
BEGIN
        DECLARE @Retries INT = 1 ;

        WHILE @Retries <= 10
        BEGIN
                BEGIN TRY
                        EXEC dbo.UpdateCreditLimit ;
                END TRY
                BEGIN CATCH
                        WAITFOR DELAY '00:00:01' ;
                        SET @Retries = @Retries + 1 ;
                END CATCH
        END
END
```

Observing Transactions, Locks, and Deadlocks

SQL Server provides a set of DMVs that expose information about current transactions and locks. The following sections explore the metadata available.

Observing Transactions

The sys.dm_tran_active_transactions DMV details the current transactions within the instance. This DMV returns the columns described in Table 18-11.

Table 18-11. *Columns Returned by sys.dm_tran_active_transactions*

Column	Description
transaction_id	The unique ID of the transaction.
name	The name of the transaction. If the transaction has not been marked with a name, then the default name is displayed—for example, "user_transaction".
transaction_begin_time	The date and time that the transaction started.
transaction_type	An integer value depicting the type of transaction. • 1 indicates a read/write transaction. • 2 indicates a read-only transaction. • 3 indicates a system transaction. • 4 indicates a distributed transaction.
transaction_uow	A unit of work ID that MSDTC uses to work with distributed transactions.
transaction_state	The current status of the transaction. • 0 indicates that the transaction is still initializing. • 1 indicates that the transaction is initialized but has not yet started. • 2 indicates that the transaction is active. • 3 indicates that the transaction has ended. This status is only applicable to read-only transactions. • 4 indicates that the commit has been initiated. This status is only applicable to distributed transactions. • 5 indicates that the transaction is prepared and awaiting resolution. • 6 indicates that the transaction has been committed. • 7 indicates that the transaction is being rolled back. • 8 indicates that the rollback of a transaction has finished.
dtc_state	Indicates the state of a transaction on an Azure database. • 1 indicates that the transaction is active. • 2 indicates that the transaction is prepared. • 3 indicates that the transaction is committed. • 4 indicates that the transaction is aborted. • 5 indicates that the transaction is recovered.

■ **Note** Undocumented columns have been omitted from DVMs in this chapter.

The script in Listing 18-13 indicates how to use sys.dm_tran_active_transactions to find details of long-running transactions. The query looks for transactions that have been running for longer than ten minutes and returns information including their current state, the amount of resources they are consuming, and the login that is executing them.

■ **Tip**   In a test environment, begin a transaction but do not commit it ten minutes before running this query.

Listing 18-13. Long-Running Transactions

```
SELECT
         name
         ,transaction_begin_time
         ,CASE transaction_type
         WHEN 1 THEN 'Read/Write'
         WHEN 2 THEN 'Read-Only'
         WHEN 3 THEN 'System'
         WHEN 4 THEN 'Distributed'
         END TransactionType,
         CASE transaction_state
         WHEN 0 THEN 'Initializing'
         WHEN 1 THEN 'Initialized But Not Started'
         WHEN 2 THEN 'Active'
         WHEN 3 THEN 'Ended'
         WHEN 4 THEN 'Committing'
         WHEN 5 THEN 'Prepared'
         WHEN 6 THEN 'Committed'
         WHEN 7 THEN 'Rolling Back'
         WHEN 8 THEN 'Rolled Back'
     END State
         ,SUSER_SNAME(es.security_id) LoginRunningTransaction
         ,es.memory_usage * 8 MemUsageKB
         ,es.reads
         ,es.writes
         ,es.cpu_time
 FROM sys.dm_tran_active_transactions at
         INNER JOIN sys.dm_tran_session_transactions st
                 ON at.transaction_id = st.transaction_id
                 INNER JOIN sys.dm_exec_sessions es
                         ON st.session_id = es.session_id
 WHERE st.is_user_transaction = 1
 AND at.transaction_begin_time < DATEADD(MINUTE,-10,GETDATE()) ;
```

The query works by joining to sys.dm_exec_sessions via sys.dm_tran_session transactions. This DMV can be used to correlate transactions with sessions and it returns the columns described in Table 18-12.

Table 18-12. *sys.dm_tran_session_transactions Columns*

Column	Description
session_id	The ID of the session in which the transaction is running.
transaction_id	The unique ID of the transaction.
transaction_descriptor	The ID used to communicate with the client driver.
enlist_count	The number of active requests in the session.
is_user_transaction	Indicates if the transaction is a user or a system transaction. 0 indicates a system transaction and 1 indicates a user transaction.
is_local	Indicates if the transaction is distributed. 0 indicates a distributed transaction and 1 indicates a local transaction.
is_enlisted	Indicates that a distributed transaction is enlisted.
is_bound	Indicates if the transaction is running in a bound session.
open_transaction_count	A count of open transactions within the session.

Observing Locks and Contention

Details of current locks on the instance are exposed through a DMV called sys.dm_tran_locks. This DMV returns the columns detailed in Table 18-13.

Table 18-13. *sys.dm_tran_locks*

Column	Description
resource_type	The resource type on which the lock has been placed.
resource_subtype	The subtype of the resource type that has a lock placed on it. For example, if you are updating the properties of a database, then the resource_type is METADATA and the resource_subtype is DATABASE.
resource_database_id	The ID of the database that contains the resource that has a lock placed on it.
resource_description	Additional information about the resource that is not contained in other columns.
resource_associated_entity_id	The ID of the database entity with which the resource is associated.
resource_lock_partition	The partition number of the lock, if lock partitioning is being used.
request_mode	The locking mode that has been requested or acquired. For example, S for a shared lock, or X for an exclusive lock.
request_type	The request_type is always LOCK.
request_status	The current status of the lock request. Possible values are ABORT_BLOCKERS, CONVERT, GRANTED, LOW_PRIORITY_CONVERT, LOW_PRIORITY_WAIT, and WAIT.
request_reference_count	The number of times that the requestor has requested a lock on the same resource.

(continued)

Table 18-13. (*continued*)

Column	Description
request_session_id	The session ID that currently owns the request. It is possible for the session ID to change if the transaction is distributed.
request_exec_context_id	The execution ID of the process that requested the lock.
request_request_id	The Batch ID of the batch that currently owns the request. This ID can change if Multiple Active Result Sets (MARS) are being used by the application.
request_owner_type	The type of the owner of the lock request. Possible vales are TRANSACTION, SESSION, and CURSOR for user operations. Values can also be SHARED_TRANSACTION_WORKSPACE and EXCLUSIVE_TRANSACTION_WORKSPACE, which are used internally to hold locks for enlisted transactions; or NOTIFICATION_OBJECT, which is used by internal SQL Server operations.
request_owner_id	The ID of the transaction that owns the lock request, unless the request was made by a FileTable, in which case -3 indicates a table lock, -4 indicates a database lock, and other values indicate the file handle of the file.
request_owner_guid	A GUID identifying the request owner. Only applicable to distributed transactions.
lock_owner_address	Memory address of the request's internal data structure.

The sys.dm_os_waiting_tasks DMV returns information about tasks that are waiting on resources, including locks. The columns returned by this DMV are detailed in Table 18-14. This DMV can be used with sys.dm_tran_locks to find the details of processes that are blocked and blocking, due to locks.

Table 18-14. sys.dm_os_waiting_tasks Columns

Column	Description
waiting_task_address	The address of the task that is waiting.
session_id	The ID of the session in which the waiting task is running.
exec_context_id	The ID of the thread and subthread that is running the task.
wait_duration_ms	The duration of the wait, specified in milliseconds.
wait_type	The type of wait that is being experienced. Waits are discussed in Chapter 17.
resource_address	The address of the resource the task is waiting for.
blocking_task_address	Indicates the address of the task that is currently consuming the resource.
blocking_session_id	The Session ID of the task that is currently consuming the resource.
blocking_exec_context_id	The ID of the thread and subthread of the task that is currently consuming the resource.
resource_description	Additional information about the resource, which is not contained in other columns, including the lock resource owner.

The script in Listing 18-14 demonstrates how to use sys.dm_tran_locks and sys.dm_os_waiting_tasks to identify blocking on the instance. The script contains three parts, each of which you should run in a separate query window. The first two parts of the script cause contention. The third part identifies the source of the contention.

Listing 18-14. Using sys.dm_tran_locks

```
--Part 1 - Run in 1st query window

BEGIN TRANSACTION
UPDATE Customers
SET CreditLimit = CreditLimit ;

--Part 2 - Run in 2nd query window

SELECT creditlimit
FROM dbo.Customers (SERIALIZABLE) ;

--Part 3 - Run in 3rd query window

SELECT
        DB_NAME(tl.resource_database_id) DatabaseName
        ,tl.resource_type
        ,tl.resource_subtype
        ,tl.resource_description
        ,tl.request_mode
        ,tl.request_status
        ,os.session_id BlockedSession
        ,os.blocking_session_id BlockingSession
        ,os.resource_description
        ,OBJECT_NAME(
                CAST(
                    SUBSTRING(os.resource_description,
                            CHARINDEX('objid=',os.resource_description,0)+6,9)
                    AS INT)
            ) LockedTable
FROM sys.dm_os_waiting_tasks os
INNER JOIN sys.dm_tran_locks tl
        ON os.session_id = tl.request_session_id
WHERE tl.request_owner_type IN ('TRANSACTION', 'SESSION', 'CURSOR') ;
```

■ **Tip** To stop the blocking, run ROLLBACK in the first query window.

The results in Figure 18-5 show that the second part of our script is being blocked by the first part of the script. The final column pulls the Object ID out of the resource_description column and identifies the table on which the contention is occurring.

Figure 18-5. *sys.dm_tran_locks results*

Observing Deadlocks

You can capture details of deadlocks and have them written to the error log by turning on trace flags 1204 and 1222. Trace flag 1204 captures details of the resources and types of lock involved in a deadlock. It contains a section for each node involved in the deadlock, followed by a section detailing the deadlock victim. Trace flag 1222 returns three sections. The first gives details of the deadlock victim; the second gives details of the processes involved in the deadlock; and the final section describes the resources that are involved in the deadlock.

In the modern world of SQL Server, it is often not necessary to turn on these trace flags, since you can find details of deadlocks retrospectively, by looking at the system health session, which is an extended event session enabled by default on every instance of SQL Server. Among other important details, the system health session captures details of any deadlocks that occur. You can access the System Health Session by drilling through Management | Extended Events | Sessions | system_health in SQL Server Management Studio, and then by selecting View Target Data from the context menu of Package0.eventfile. If you search for xml:deadlock_report in the name column, you will expose details of deadlock incidents that have occurred. The Details tab provides the full deadlock report, including information about the deadlock victim, and the processes, resources, and owners involved in the deadlock. The Deadlock tab displays the Deadlock Graph, as shown in Figure 18-6, for the deadlock that we generated in Listing 18-2.

Figure 18-6. *Deadlock Graph*

Summary

Locks can be taken at different levels of granularity. Locking at a lower level reduces contention but uses additional resources for internal lock memory structures. Locking at a higher level can increase the wait time of other processes and increase the likelihood of deadlocks. SQL Server 2014 introduces new features that give DBAs the ability to control locking behaviors for online maintenance operations, such as index rebuilds and partition switching operations. On large systems with 16 or more cores available to the instance, SQL Server automatically implements lock partitioning, which can reduce contention by splitting a single lock resource into multiple resources.

Transactions have ACID properties, making them atomic, consistent, isolated, and durable. SQL Server offers the functionality to relax some of these rules, however, in order to improve performance and make coding easier. Six isolation levels are available against disk tables, two of which are optimistic, and the others are pessimistic. Pessimistic isolation levels work by acquiring locks to avoid transactional anomalies, whereas optimistic concurrency relies on row versioning.

Because memory-optimized tables do not support locks, all transactions against memory-optimized tables use optimistic concurrency. SQL Server has implemented optimistic isolation levels, which can only be used against memory-optimized tables. Because of the optimistic nature of the transactions, you should implement retry logic for both read-only and read/write transactions.

SQL Server offers a wide array of metadata that can help you, as a DBA, observe transactions, locks, contention, and deadlocks. Sys.dm_tran_active_transactions show details of transactions that are currently active on the instance. Sys.dm_tran_locks exposes information about locks that have currently been requested or granted within the instance. You can capture deadlock information in the SQL Server error log by enabling trace flags 1204 and 1222, but the system health trace also captures deadlock information by default. This means that you can retrieve deadlock information after the fact, without having to perform upfront configuration or tracing.

CHAPTER 19

■ ■ ■

Extended Events

Extended Events are a lightweight monitoring system offered by SQL Server. Because the architecture uses so few system resources, they scale very well and allow you to monitor their instances, with minimal impact on user activity. They are also highly configurable, which gives you in your role as a DBA a wide range of options for capturing details from a very fine grain, such as page splits, to higher-level detail, such as CPU utilization. You can also correlate Extended Events with operating system data to provide a holistic picture when troubleshooting issues. The predecessor to Extended Events was SQL Trace, and its GUI, called Profiler. This is now deprecated for use with the Database Engine, and it is recommended that you only use it for tracing Analysis Service activity.

Extended Events Concepts

Extended Events have a rich architecture, which consists of events, targets, actions, types, predicates, and maps. These artifacts are stored within a package, which is, in turn, stored within a module, which can be either a .dll or an executable. We discuss these concepts in the following sections.

Packages

A *package* is a container for the objects used within Extended Events. Here are the four types of SQL Server package:

- Package0: The default package, used for Extended Events system objects.
- Sqlserver: Used for SQL Server–related objects.
- Sqlos: Used for SQLOS-related objects.
- SecAudit: Used by SQL Audit; however, its objects are not exposed.

Events

An *event* is an occurrence of interest that you can trace. It may be a SQL batch completing, a cache miss, or a page split, or virtually anything else that can happen within the Database Engine, depending on the nature of the trace that you are configuring. Each event is categorized by channel and keyword (also known as category). A *channel* is a high-level categorization, and all events in SQL Server 2014 fall into one of the channels described in Table 19-1.

Table 19-1. *Channels*

Channel	Description
Admin	Well-known events with well-known resolutions. For example, deadlocks, server starts, CPU thresholds being exceeded, and the use of deprecated features.
Operational	Used for troubleshooting issues. For example, bad memory being detected, an AlwaysOn Availability Group replica changing its state, and a long IO being detected, are all events that fall within the Operational channel.
Analytic	High-volume events that you can use for troubleshooting issues such as performance. For example, a transaction beginning, a lock being acquired, and a file read completing are all events that fall within the Analytic channel.
Debug	Used by developers to diagnose issues by returning internal data. The events in the Debug channel are subject to change in future versions of SQL Server, so you should avoid them when possible.

Keywords, or categories, are much more fine grain. There are 47 categories within SQL Server 2014, which are detailed in Table 19-2.

Table 19-2. *Categories*

Category	Description
access_methods	Events related to parallel scans with IO affinity.
alwayson | hadr	Events related to AlwaysOn Availability Groups.
broker	Events related to Service Broker communications.
cdc_logscan	Events related to Change Data Capture errors and sessions.
change_tracking	Events related to Change Tracking cleanup operations.
checkpoint | ckpt_trace | ckptworker_trace	Events related to memory-optimized checkpoints.
clr	Events related to the Common Language Runtime—for example, when an assembly is loaded.
cursor	Events related to cursors, such as a cursor being opened or recompiled.
database	Database-level events, such as checkpoints beginning and databases starting, as well as page splits and Ghost Cleanup operations (used to physically remove deleted records from a page).
deadlock_monitor	Events related to deadlocks.
deploy	Events related to memory-optimized table internals.
errors	Events related to errors within the Database Engine.
exception	Events related to exceptions within the Database Engine, such as a memory dump or a stack trace occurring.
execution	Events related to query execution, such as statements starting and plan cache hits.
filetable	Events related to the use of FileTables, such as IO requests to FileTables.

(continued)

Table 19-2. (*continued*)

Category	Description
fulltext	Events related to full-text search operations.
garbage_collection | gc	Events related to garbage collection internals, such as when a garbage collection cycle completes.
index	Events related to index operations, such as an index scan occurring or a full-text index crawl starting.
init	The CLR initialization failure event.
io	Events related to IO, such as physical page reads and writes.
latch	Events related to latching, such as latch promotion and demotion.
lock	Events related to locking, such as locks being acquired or lock timeouts occurring.
memory	Events related to memory, such as bad memory being detected by the operating system or pages being allocated to the buffer pool.
merge_trace	Events related to internal SQL Server operations.
oledb	Events related to distributed queries using an OLEDB provider.
optimization	Events related to the Query Optimizer's cardinality estimation.
process	Events related to CPU management internals, such as CPU configuration changes.
query_store	Events related to the Query Store, which is a feature that will be available in the next major release of SQL Server.
replication	Events related to the Log Reader Agent in a Replication topology.
scheduling	Events related to SQLIO's task scheduler, including wait information.
security	Events related to authentication performance.
server	Instance level events, such as reads and writes to a buffer pool extension and trace flags being changed.
session	Events related to the user session. For example, login, logout, and when a Resource Governor classifier function fires. Resource Governor is discussed in Chapter 23.
storage_management	Events related to storage, such as page and extent allocation and deallocation.
synchronization	Events related to spinlocks.
task	Events related to subroutine initialization internals.
transaction | transactions	Events related to transactions, such as when a transaction begins and when a memory-optimized OLTP operation generates a log record.
transmitter | transport | ucs	Events related to the unified communications stack.
warnings	Events related to warnings in the Database Engine, such as Query Optimizer timeouts and missing column statistics.
xtp	Events related to In-Memory OLTP.

Targets

A *target* is the consumer of the events; essentially, it is the device to which the trace data will be written. The targets available within SQL Server 2014 are detailed in Table 19-3.

Table 19-3. *Targets*

Target	Synchronous/ Asynchronous	Description
Event counter	Synchronous	Counts the number of events that occur during a session
Event file	Asynchronous	Writes the event output to memory buffers and then flushes them to disk
Event pairing	Asynchronous	Determines if a paired event occurs without its matching event, for example, if a statement started but never completed
ETW*	Synchronous	Used to correlate Extended Events with operating system data
Histogram	Asynchronous	Counts the number of events that occur during a session, based on an action or event column
Ring buffer	Asynchronous	Stores data in a memory buffer, using First In First Out (FIFO) methodology

Event Tracking for Windows

Actions

Actions are commands that allow additional information to be captured when an event fires. An action is fired synchronously when an event occurs and the event is unaware of the action. There are 50 actions available in SQL Server 2014 that allow you to capture a rich array of information, including the statement that caused the event to fire, the login that ran this statement, the transaction ID, the CPU ID, and the call stack.

Predicates

Predicates are filter conditions that you can apply before the system sends events to the target. It is possible to create simple predicates, such as filtering statements completing based on a database ID, but you can also create more complex predicates, such as only capturing a long IO that has a duration greater than five seconds, or only capturing the role change of an AlwaysOn Availability Group replica if it happens more than twice.

Predicates also fully support short-circuiting. This means that if you use multiple conditions within a predicate, then the order of predicates is important, because if the evaluation of the first predicate fails, the second predicate will not be evaluated. Because predicates are evaluated synchronously, this can have an impact on performance. Therefore, it is prudent to design you predicates in such a way that predicates that are least likely to evaluate to true come before predicates that are very likely to evaluate to true. For example, imagine that you are planning to filter on a specific database (with a database ID of 6) that is the target of a high percentage of the activity on the instance, but you also plan to filter on a specific user ID (MyUser), which is responsible for a lower percentage of the activity. In this scenario, you would use the WHERE ((([sqlserver].[username]=N'MyUser') AND ([sqlserver].[database_id]=(6))) predicate to first filter out activity that does not relate to MyUser and then filter out activity that does not relate to database ID 6.

Types and Maps

All objects within a package are assigned a type. This type is used to interpret the data stored within the byte collection of an object. Objects are assigned one of the following types:

- Action

- Event

- Pred_compare (retrieve data from events)

- Pred_source (compare data types)

- Target

- Type

You can find a list of predicate comparators and predicate sources by executing the queries in Listing 19-1.

Listing 19-1. Retrieving Predicate Comparators and Sources

```
--Retrieve list of predicate comparators

SELECT name
        ,description,
    (SELECT name
                FROM sys.dm_xe_packages
                WHERE guid = xo.package_guid) Package
FROM sys.dm_xe_objects xo
WHERE object_type = 'pred_compare'
ORDER BY name ;

--Retrieve list of predicate sources

SELECT name
        ,description,
    (SELECT name
                FROM sys.dm_xe_packages
                WHERE guid = xo.package_guid) Package
FROM sys.dm_xe_objects xo
WHERE object_type = 'pred_source'
ORDER BY name ;
```

A *map* is a dictionary that maps internal ID vales to strings that DBAs can understand. Map keys are only unique within their context and are repeated between contexts. For example, within the statement_recompile_cause context, a map_key of 1 relates to a map_value of Schema Changed. Within the context of a database_sql_statement type, however, a map_key of 1 relates to a map_value of CREATE DATABASE. You can find a complete list of mappings by using the sys.dm_xe_map_values DMV, as demonstrated in Listing 19-2. To check the mappings for a specific context, filter on the name column.

Listing 19-2. Sys.dm_xe_map_values

```
SELECT
        map_key
        , map_value
        , name
FROM sys.dm_xe_map_values ;
```

Sessions

A *session* is essentially a trace. It can contain events from multiple packages, actions, targets, and predicates. When you start or stop a session, you are turning the trace on or off. When a session starts, events are written to memory buffers and have predicates applied before they are sent to the target. Therefore, when creating a session, you need to configure properties, such as how much memory the session can use for buffering, what events can be dropped if the session experiences memory pressure, and the maximum latency before the events are sent to the target.

Creating an Event Session

You can create an event session using either the New Session Wizard, the New Session Dialog Box, or via T-SQL. We explore each of these options in the following sections. Before creating any event sessions, however, we first create the Chapter19 database, populate it with data, and create stored procedures, which we use in later examples. Listing 19-3 contains the script to do this.

Listing 19-3. Creating the Chapter19 Database

```
--Create the database

CREATE DATABASE Chapter19 ;
GO

USE Chapter19
GO

--Create and populate numbers table

DECLARE @Numbers TABLE
(
        Number          INT
)

;WITH CTE(Number)
AS
(
        SELECT 1 Number
        UNION ALL
        SELECT Number + 1
        FROM CTE
        WHERE Number < 100
)
```

```
INSERT INTO @Numbers
SELECT Number FROM CTE;

--Create and populate name pieces

DECLARE @Names TABLE
(
        FirstName       VARCHAR(30),
        LastName        VARCHAR(30)
);

INSERT INTO @Names
VALUES('Peter', 'Carter'),
                ('Michael', 'Smith'),
                ('Danielle', 'Mead'),
                ('Reuben', 'Roberts'),
                ('Iris', 'Jones'),
                ('Sylvia', 'Davies'),
                ('Finola', 'Wright'),
                ('Edward', 'James'),
                ('Marie', 'Andrews'),
                ('Jennifer', 'Abraham');

--Create and populate Customers table

CREATE TABLE dbo.Customers
(
        CustomerID          INT             NOT NULL        IDENTITY        PRIMARY KEY,
        FirstName           VARCHAR(30)     NOT NULL,
        LastName            VARCHAR(30)     NOT NULL,
        BillingAddressID    INT             NOT NULL,
        DeliveryAddressID   INT             NOT NULL,
        CreditLimit         MONEY           NOT NULL,
        Balance             MONEY           NOT NULL
);

SELECT * INTO #Customers
FROM
        (SELECT
                (SELECT TOP 1 FirstName FROM @Names ORDER BY NEWID()) FirstName,
                (SELECT TOP 1 LastName FROM @Names ORDER  BY NEWID()) LastName,
                (SELECT TOP 1 Number FROM @Numbers ORDER  BY NEWID()) BillingAddressID,
                (SELECT TOP 1 Number FROM @Numbers ORDER  BY NEWID()) DeliveryAddressID,
                (SELECT TOP 1 CAST(RAND() * Number AS INT) * 10000
                 FROM @Numbers
                 ORDER BY NEWID()) CreditLimit,
                (SELECT TOP 1 CAST(RAND() * Number AS INT) * 9000
                 FROM @Numbers
                 ORDER BY NEWID()) Balance
        FROM @Numbers a
        CROSS JOIN @Numbers b
) a;
```

695

```
INSERT INTO dbo.Customers
SELECT * FROM #Customers;
GO

CREATE INDEX idx_LastName ON dbo.Customers(LastName)
GO

CREATE PROCEDURE UpdateCustomerWithPageSplits
AS
BEGIN
        UPDATE dbo.Customers
        SET FirstName = cast(FirstName + replicate(FirstName,10) as varchar(30))
        ,LastName = cast(LastName + replicate(LastName,10) as varchar(30)) ;
END ;
GO

CREATE PROCEDURE UpdateCustomersWithoutPageSplits
AS
BEGIN
        UPDATE dbo.Customers
        SET CreditLimit = CreditLimit * 1.5
        WHERE Balance < CreditLimit - 10000 ;
END ;
GO
```

Using the New Session Wizard

You can invoke the New Session Wizard from SQL Server Management Studio by drilling through
Management | Extended Events in Object Explorer and selecting New Session Wizard from the Sessions
context menu. After you pass through the Introduction page of the wizard, the Set Session Properties page
displays, as illustrated in Figure 19-1. Use this page to specify a name for the session and to indicate if the
session should start automatically each time the instance starts. We use the session to track log file IO, so we
configure it to start when the instance starts and name it LogFileIO.

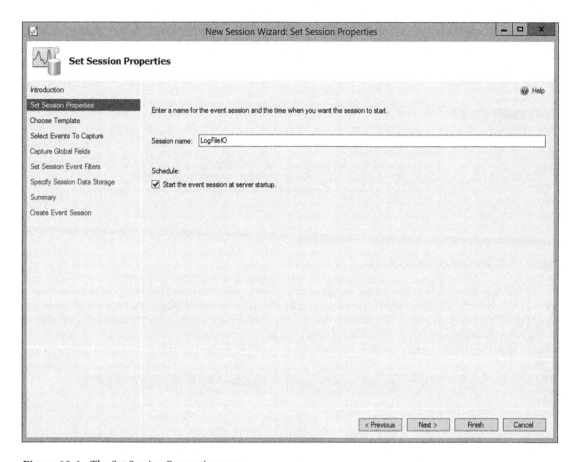

Figure 19-1. *The Set Session Properties page*

On the Choose Template page of the wizard, you can select a predefined template from the drop-down list. Predefined templates are configured with sets of events and predicates that are useful for DBAs in common scenarios. After you select a template, you are able to refine it to suit your individual requirements, or alternatively, you can choose to not use a template. This option configures an empty session into which you can add all events and predicates manually. The Choose Template page is illustrated in Figure 19-2. Because we plan to monitor log file IO, unsurprisingly, we select the Database Log File IO Tracing template.

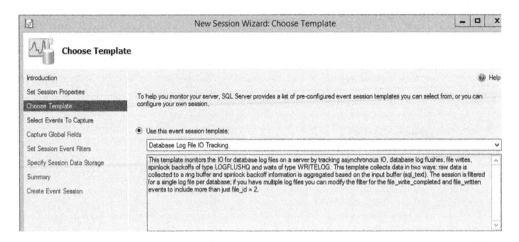

Figure 19-2. *The Choose Template page*

On the Select Events To Capture page, we can add or remove events we would like captured in the session. You can search the Event Library for a keyword, or filter by channel or category. When you highlight an event, a description displays, along with the Event fields. You can then select the event by using the right pointing arrow, or you can remove an event by selecting it in the right hand pane and using the left pointing arrow. In our case, we have filtered on the IO category and added the `database_log_flush_wait` event, as shown in Figure 19-3.

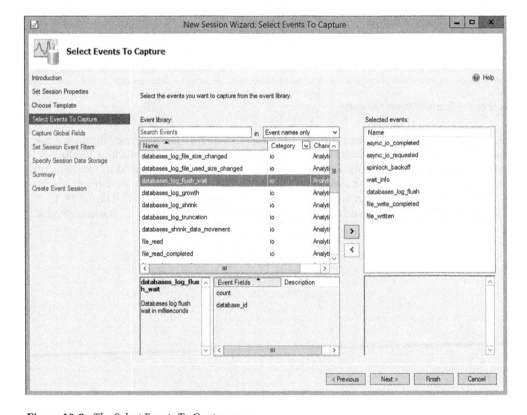

Figure 19-3. *The Select Events To Capture page*

On the Capture Global Fields page, we can specify any actions that we need. In our scenario, in addition to the preselected actions, we choose to capture the database_name, as demonstrated in Figure 19-4. Actions are known as global fields, because they are available to all events as opposed to event fields, which are local to their specific event.

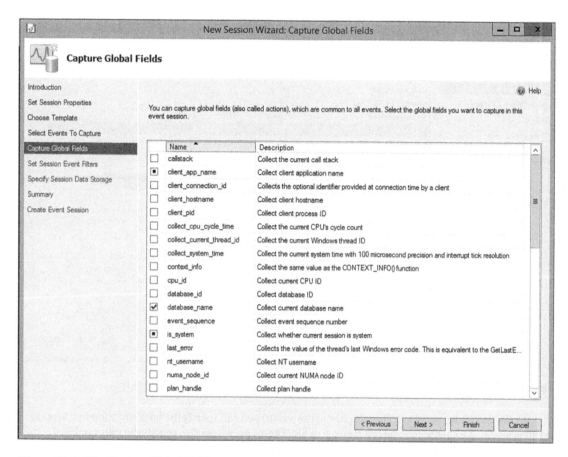

Figure 19-4. *The Capture Global Fields page*

On the Set Session Event Filters page, you can review the filters that have been applied to the template in the top pane. In the bottom pane, you can add additional predicates to target the trace to your specific needs. Figure 19-5 illustrates adding a predicate that filters on the database_name global field so that only events from this database are captured.

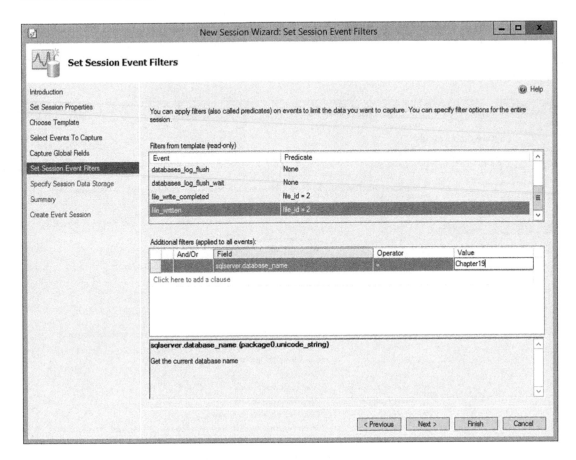

Figure 19-5. *The Set Session Event Filters page*

On the Specify Session Data Storage page of the wizard you can specify the target for the event session. In our scenario, we choose to write the events to a file. Therefore, we need to specify the fully qualified filename for the trace file on the server. The default file extension is .XEL. We also specify the maximum file size for the capture, and if we want new files to be created when this maximum size is reached, we also need to specify a value for the maximum number of files, as shown in Figure 19-6.

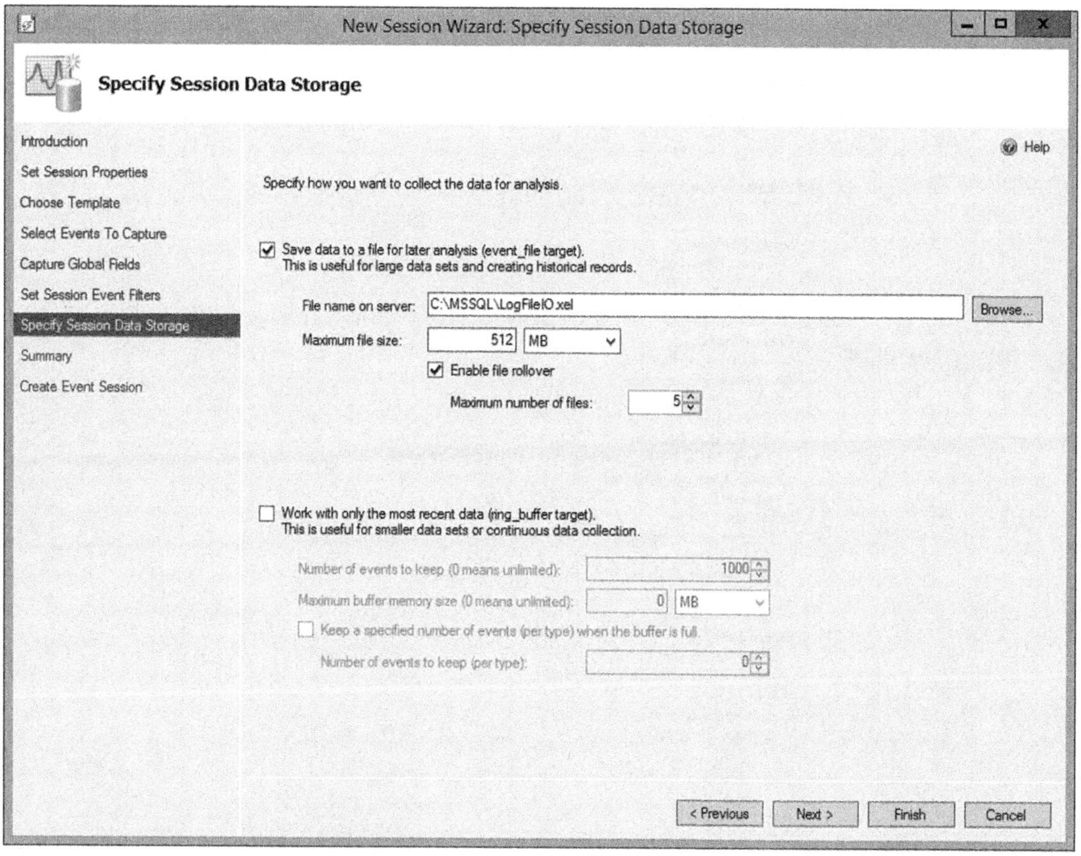

Figure 19-6. *Specify Session Data Storage*

The Summary page, displayed in Figure 19-7, summarizes how the Event Session will be configured; it also gives us the option of scripting the configuration, which is highly recommended for documentation, change control, and code reusability.

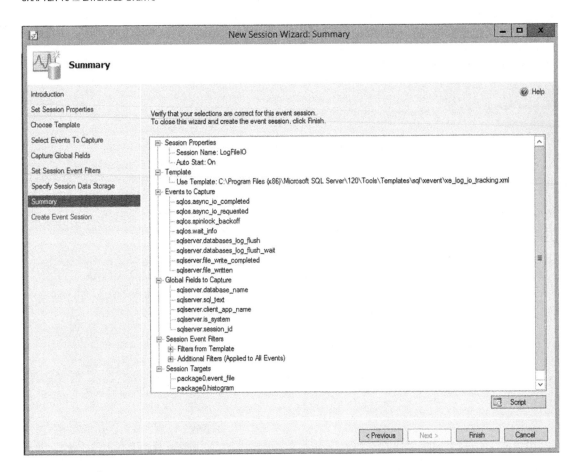

Figure 19-7. *TheSummary page*

Finally, the Create Event Session page informs us of the status of the Event Session creation (see Figure 19-8). On this page, we specify whether we want the session to start immediately, and if we select this option, we are also given the opportunity of immediately launching the live data viewer, which we discuss later in this chapter.

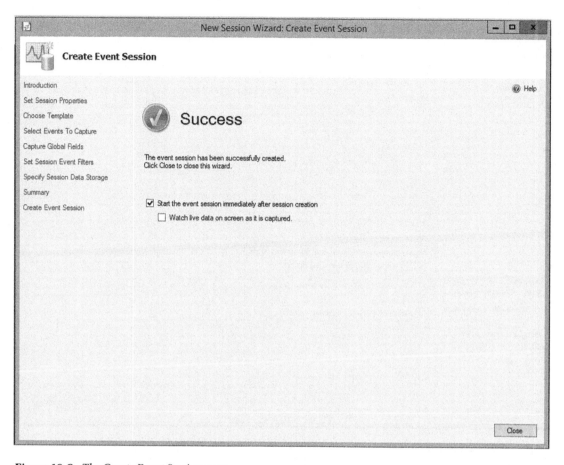

Figure 19-8. *The Create Event Session page*

Using the New Session Dialog Box

You can access the New Session dialog box from SQL Server Management Studio by first drilling through Management | Extended Events in Object Explorer, and then by selecting New Session from the Sessions context menu. We use the New Session dialog box to create a session that monitors page splits and correlates them with the stored procedures that caused them to occur. To allow this, we need to enable causality tracking, which gives each event an additional GUID value, called an `ActivityID`, and a sequence number; together, these allow the events to be correlated.

When you invoke the dialog box, the General page displays, as illustrated in Figure 19-9. On this page, you can specify a name for the session, choose whether or not it should start automatically after it is completed and automatically when the instance starts, whether the live data view launches after the session completes, and if causality tracking should be enabled.

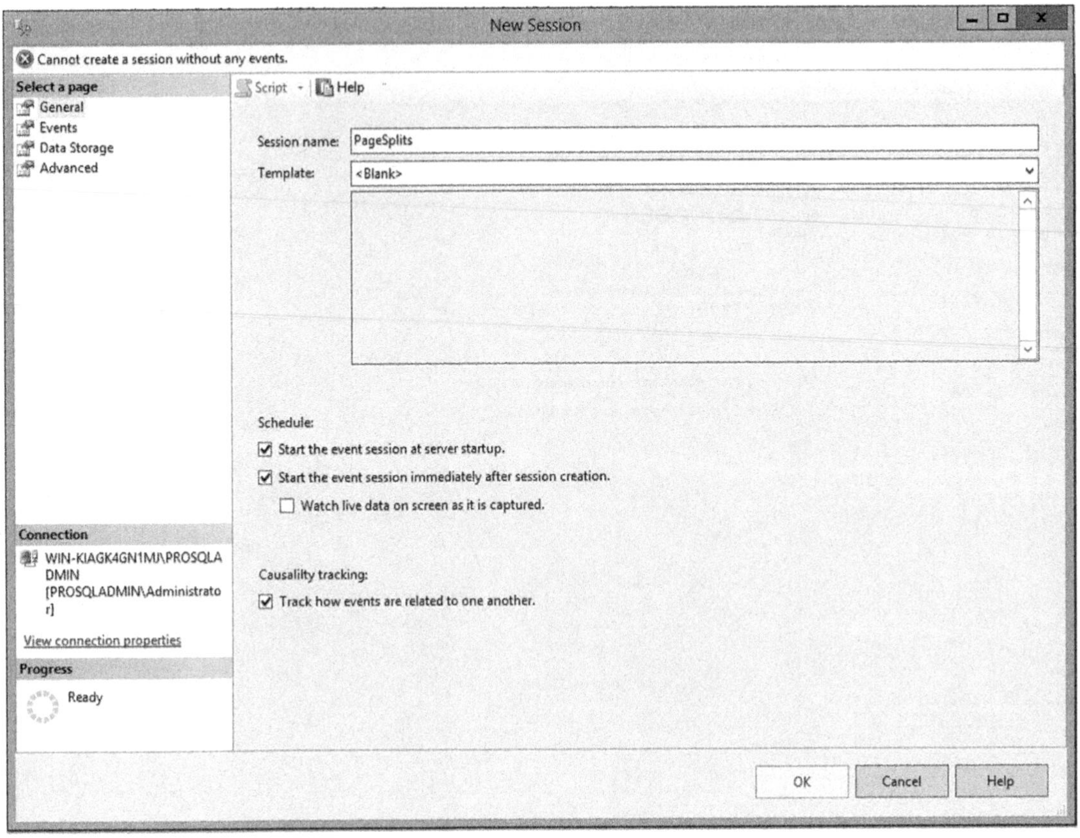

Figure 19-9. *The General page*

Because we are going to monitor page splits, we name the session PageSplits and specify that the session should start automatically, both after creation and also when the instance starts. We also turn on causality tracking.

On the Events page, we first search for and select the page_splits and module_start events, as shown in Figure 19-10. The module_start event is triggered every time a programmable object fires.

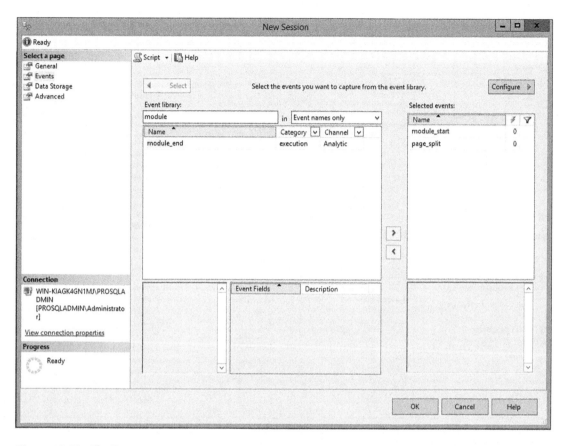

Figure 19-10. *The Events page*

We now need to use the Configure button to configure each of the events. In the Global Fields (Actions) tab of the Configure screen, we select the nt_username and database_name actions for the module_start event, as illustrated in Figure 19-11.

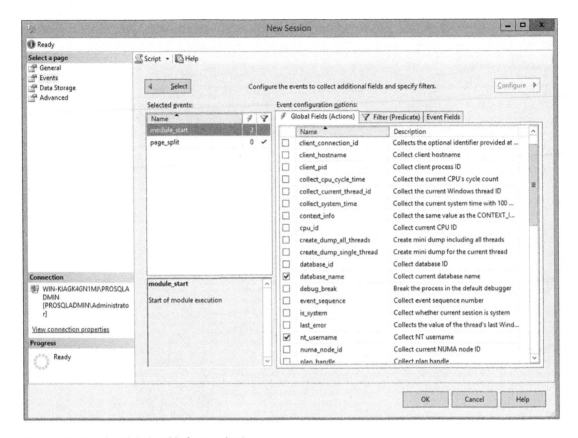

Figure 19-11. *The Global Fields (Actions) tab*

■ **Tip**   If you need to configure the same actions for multiple events, you can multiselect the events.

On the Filter (Predicates) tab, we configure the page_splits event to be filtered on the database_name, which is Chapter19 in this case, as show in Figure 19-12. This means that only page splits relating to this database are captured. We do not filter the module_start event on the database_name, because the procedure that caused the page splits could, in theory, have been fired from any database.

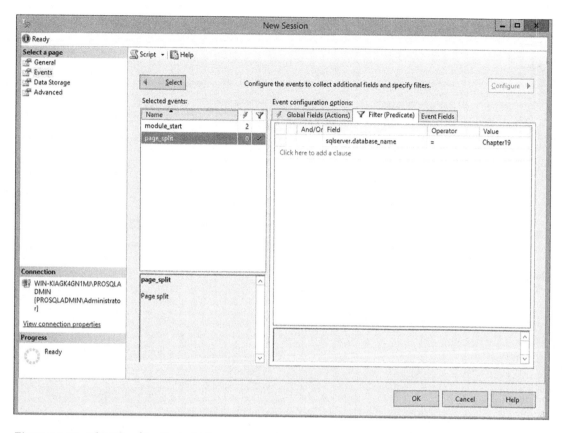

Figure 19-12. *The Filter (Predicates) tab*

In the Event Fields tab of the Configure screen, the fields that relate to the event are displayed. If there are any optional fields, then we are able to select them. Figure 19-13 shows that we have selected the statement field for the module_start event.

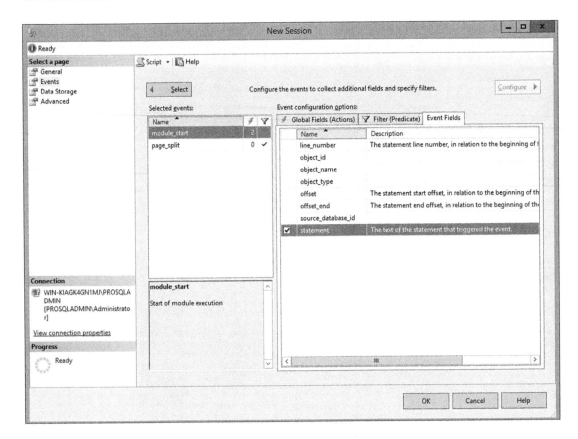

Figure 19-13. *The Event Fields tab*

On the Data Storage page of the New Session dialog box, we configure the target(s). For our scenario, we configure a single event file target, as demonstrated in Figure 19-14. The parameters are context sensitive, depending on the type of target that you select. Because we have selected a file target, we need to configure the location and maximum size of the file. We also need to specify if we want new files to be created if the initial file becomes full, and if so, how many times this should happen.

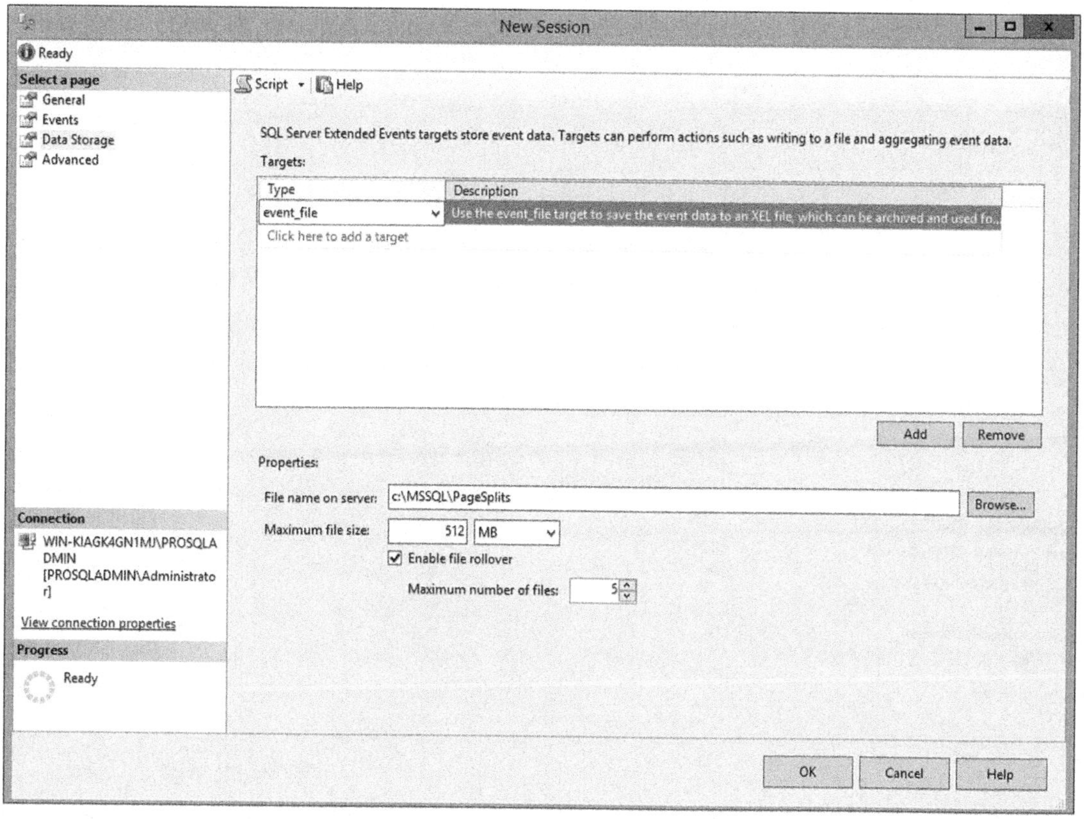

Figure 19-14. *The Data Storage page*

On the Advanced page, shown in Figure 19-15, we can specify the desired behavior in the event of memory pressure: whether single-event loss is acceptable, whether multiple-event loss is acceptable, or whether there should be no event loss at all. We can also set the minimum and maximum size for events and how memory partitioning should be applied. This is discussed in more detail in the following section. Additionally, we can configure dispatch latency. This indicates the maximum amount of time that an event remains in the buffers before it is flushed to disk.

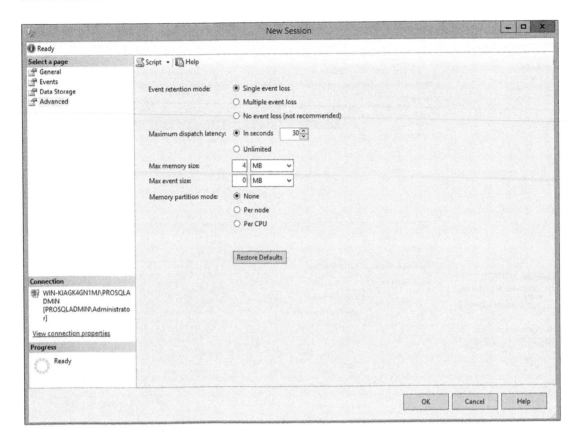

Figure 19-15. *The Advanced tab*

Using T-SQL

You can also create event sessions via T-SQL using the CREATE EVENT SESSION DDL statement. The command accepts the arguments detailed in Table 19-4.

Table 19-4. *Create Event Session Arguments*

Argument	Description
event_session_name	The name of the event session that you are creating.
ADD EVENT | SET	Specified for every event that is added to the session, followed by the name of the event, in the format package.event. You can use the SET statement to set event-specific customizations, such as including non-mandatory event fields.
ACTION	Specified after each ADD EVENT argument if global fields should be captured for that event.
WHERE	Specified after each ADD EVENT argument if the event should be filtered.
ADD TARGET | SET	Specified for each target that will be added to the session. You can use the SET statement to populate target-specific parameters, such as the filename parameter for the event_file target.

The statement also accepts the WITH options, detailed in Table 19-5. The WITH statement is specified once, at the end of the CREATE EVENT SESSION statement.

Table 19-5. *Create Event Session WITH Options*

Option	Description
MAX_MEMORY	The maximum amount of memory that the event session can use for buffering events before dispatching them to the target(s).
EVENT_RETENTION_MODE	Specifies the behavior if the buffers become full. Acceptable values are ALLOW_SINGLE_EVENT_LOSS, which indicates that a single event can be can be dropped if all buffers are full; ALLOW_MULTIPLE_EVENT_LOSS, which indicates that an entire buffer can be dropped if all buffers are full; and NO_EVENT_LOSS, which indicates that tasks that cause events to fire are to wait until there is space in the buffer.
MAX_DISPATCH_LATENCY	The maximum amount of time that events can reside in the sessions buffers before being flushed to the target(s), specified in seconds.
MAX_EVENT_SIZE	The maximum possible size for event data from any single event. It can be specified in kilobytes or megabytes and should only be configured to allow events that are larger than the MAX_MEMORY setting.
MEMORY_PARTITION_MODE	Specifies where vent buffers are created. Acceptable values are NONE, which indicates that the buffers will be created within the instance; PER_NODE, which indicates that the buffers will be created for each NUMA node; and PER_CPU, which means that buffers will be created for each CPU.
TRACK_CAUSALITY	Specifies that an additional GUID and sequence number will be stored with each event so that events can be correlated.
STARTUP_STATE	Specifies if the session automatically starts when the instance starts. ON indicates it does, OFF indicates it does not.

■ **Caution** Using the NO_EVENT_LOSS option for EVENT_RETENTION_MODE can cause performance issues on your instance, because tasks may have to wait to complete until there is space in the event session's buffers to hold the event data.

The script in Listing 19-4 demonstrates how you can use T-SQL to create the PageSplits session that we created in the previous section.

Listing 19-4. Creating an Event Session

```
CREATE EVENT SESSION PageSplits
ON SERVER
--Add the module_start event
ADD EVENT sqlserver.module_start(SET collect_statement=(1)
--Add actions to the module_start event
    ACTION(sqlserver.database_name,sqlserver.nt_username)),
```

```
--Add the page_split event
ADD EVENT sqlserver.page_split(
--Create the predicate to filter on the database name
    WHERE ([sqlserver].[database_name]=N'Chapter19'))
--Add the event_file target
ADD TARGET package0.event_file(SET filename=N'c:\MSSQL\PageSplits',max_file_size=(512))
WITH (MAX_MEMORY=4096 KB, EVENT_RETENTION_MODE=ALLOW_SINGLE_EVENT_LOSS,
        MAX_DISPATCH_LATENCY=30 SECONDS, MAX_EVENT_SIZE=0 KB, MEMORY_PARTITION_MODE=NONE,
        TRACK_CAUSALITY=ON, STARTUP_STATE=ON);
GO

--Start the session
ALTER EVENT SESSION PageSplits
ON SERVER
STATE = start;
```

Viewing the Collected Data

SQL Server provides a data viewer that you can use for basic analysis of event data from a file or live data from the buffers. For more complex analysis, however, you can access and manipulate the event data via T-SQL. The following sections discuss each of these methods of analysis.

Analyzing Data with Data Viewer

You can use the data viewer to watch live data as it hits the buffers by drilling through Management | Extended Events | Sessions in Object Explorer and selecting Watch Live Data from the Session context menu. Alternatively, you can use it to view data in the target by drilling through the session and selecting View Target Data from the Target context menu.

■ **Tip** The data viewer does not support the ring buffer or ETW target types.

The script in Listing 19-5 inserts data into the Customers table in the Chapter19 database, which causes IO activity for the transaction log, which is captured by our LogFileIO session.

Listing 19-5. Inserting into Customers

```
USE Chapter19
GO

--Create and populate numbers table

DECLARE @Numbers TABLE
(
        Number          INT
)
```

```
;WITH CTE(Number)
AS
(
        SELECT 1 Number
        UNION ALL
        SELECT Number + 1
        FROM CTE
        WHERE Number < 100
)
INSERT INTO @Numbers
SELECT Number FROM CTE;

--Create and populate name pieces

DECLARE @Names TABLE
(
        FirstName        VARCHAR(30),
        LastName         VARCHAR(30)
);

INSERT INTO @Names
VALUES('Peter', 'Carter'),
                ('Michael', 'Smith'),
                ('Danielle', 'Mead'),
                ('Reuben', 'Roberts'),
                ('Iris', 'Jones'),
                v('Sylvia', 'Davies'),
                ('Finola', 'Wright'),
                ('Edward', 'James'),
                ('Marie', 'Andrews'),
                ('Jennifer', 'Abraham');

--Insert to Customers

SELECT * INTO #Customers
FROM
        (SELECT
                (SELECT TOP 1 FirstName FROM @Names ORDER BY NEWID()) FirstName,
                (SELECT TOP 1 LastName FROM @Names ORDER BY NEWID()) LastName,
                (SELECT TOP 1 Number FROM @Numbers ORDER BY NEWID()) BillingAddressID,
                (SELECT TOP 1 Number FROM @Numbers ORDER BY NEWID()) DeliveryAddressID,
                (SELECT TOP 1 CAST(RAND() * Number AS INT) * 10000
                 FROM @Numbers
                 ORDER BY NEWID()) CreditLimit,
                (SELECT TOP 1 CAST(RAND() * Number AS INT) * 9000
                 FROM @Numbers
                 ORDER BY NEWID()) Balance
        FROM @Numbers a
        CROSS JOIN @Numbers b
        CROSS JOIN @Numbers c
) a;
```

```
INSERT INTO dbo.Customers
SELECT * FROM #Customers;
GO
```

If we now open the data viewer for the event_file target under the LogFileIO session in Object Explorer, we see the results illustrated in Figure 19-16. The viewer shows each event and timestamp in a grid; selecting an event exposes the Details pane for that event.

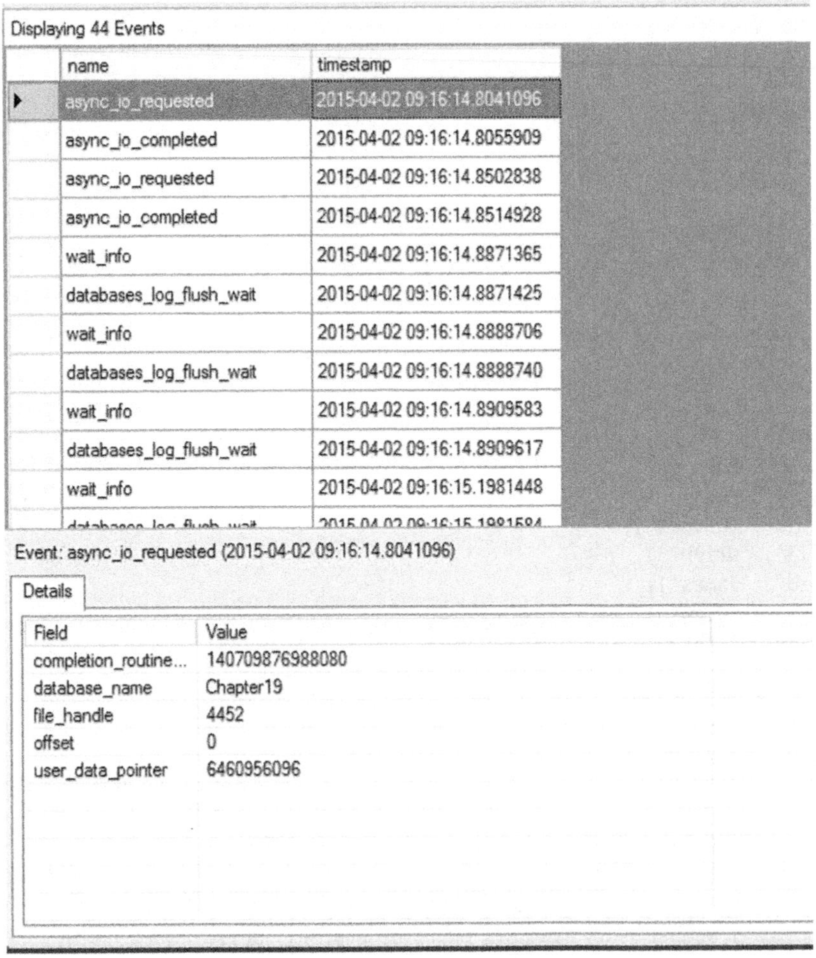

Displaying 44 Events

	name	timestamp
▶	async_io_requested	2015-04-02 09:16:14.8041096
	async_io_completed	2015-04-02 09:16:14.8055909
	async_io_requested	2015-04-02 09:16:14.8502838
	async_io_completed	2015-04-02 09:16:14.8514928
	wait_info	2015-04-02 09:16:14.8871365
	databases_log_flush_wait	2015-04-02 09:16:14.8871425
	wait_info	2015-04-02 09:16:14.8888706
	databases_log_flush_wait	2015-04-02 09:16:14.8888740
	wait_info	2015-04-02 09:16:14.8909583
	databases_log_flush_wait	2015-04-02 09:16:14.8909617
	wait_info	2015-04-02 09:16:15.1981448
	databases_log_flush_wait	2015-04-02 09:16:15.1981584

Event: async_io_requested (2015-04-02 09:16:14.8041096)

Details

Field	Value
completion_routine...	140709876988080
database_name	Chapter19
file_handle	4452
offset	0
user_data_pointer	6460956096

Figure 19-16. *Data view on event_file target*

Notice that a data viewer toolbar is displayed in SQL Server Management Studio, as illustrated in Figure 19-17. You can use this toolbar to add or remove columns from the grid, as well as to perform grouping and aggregation operations.

Figure 19-17. *Data viewer toolbar*

Clicking the Choose Columns button invokes the Choose Columns dialog box. We use this dialog box to add the duration and wait_type columns to the grid, as shown in Figure 19-18.

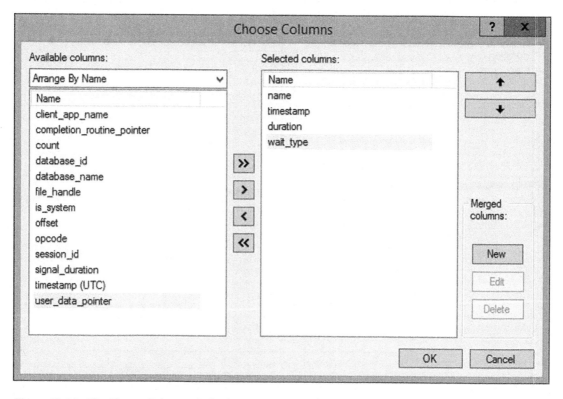

Figure 19-18. *The Choose Columns dialog box*

We can now use the Grouping button to invoke the Grouping dialog box. In this dialog box, we choose to group the events by their name, as shown in Figure 19-19.

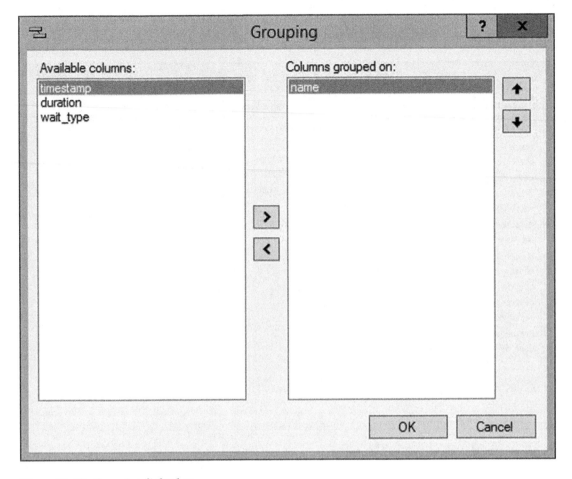

Figure 19-19. *Grouping dialog box*

We can now use the Aggregation button to invoke the Aggregation dialog box. We can use this dialog box to apply aggregate functions, such as SUM, AVG, or COUNT to the data. It is also possible to sort the data by an aggregated value. Figure 19-20 shows that we are using this dialog box to add a SUM of the wait durations.

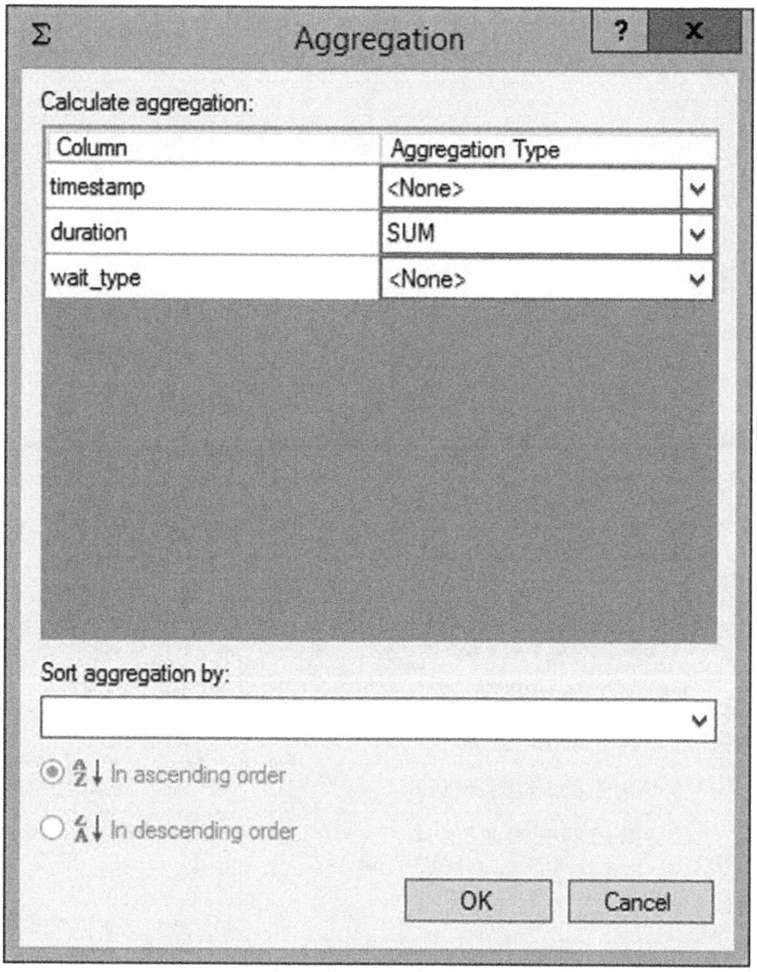

Figure 19-20. *The Aggregation dialog box*

In the data viewer grid, we are now able to see a SUM of the duration column for the wait_info events, and if we expand this group, it displays the granular details, as shown in Figure 19-21. We see N/A as the subtotal for groups, which do not have a duration field.

name	timestamp	duration	wait_type
⊟ **name: wait_info (16)**			
		SUM: 517	
wait_info	2015-04-02 09:16:14.8871365	1	WRITELOG
wait_info	2015-04-02 09:16:14.8888706	0	WRITELOG
wait_info	2015-04-02 09:16:14.8909583	0	WRITELOG
wait_info	2015-04-02 09:16:15.1981448	243	WRITELOG
wait_info	2015-04-02 09:16:15.2960307	0	WRITELOG
wait_info	2015-04-02 09:16:15.3600921	61	WRITELOG
wait_info	2015-04-02 09:16:15.3878682	23	WRITELOG
wait_info	2015-04-02 09:16:15.4201550	27	WRITELOG
wait_info	2015-04-02 09:16:15.4230253	0	WRITELOG
wait_info	2015-04-02 09:16:15.4312739	5	WRITELOG
wait_info	2015-04-02 09:16:15.5204259	87	WRITELOG
wait_info	2015-04-02 09:16:15.5437243	20	WRITELOG
wait_info	2015-04-02 09:16:15.5982117	7	WRITELOG
wait_info	2015-04-02 09:16:15.6350999	0	WRITELOG
wait_info	2015-04-02 09:16:15.8588104	41	WRITELOG

Figure 19-21. *The Data viewer grid*

Analyzing Data with T-SQL

If you require more complex analysis of the data, then you can achieve this via T-SQL. The sys.fn_xe_file_target_read_file function makes this possible by reading the target file and returning one row per event in XML format. The sys.fn_xe_file_target_read_file accepts the parameters detailed in Table 19-6.

Table 19-6. *sys.fn_xe_file_target_read_file Parameters*

Parameter	Description
path	The file path and file name of the .XEL file. This can contain the * wildcard so that rollover files can be included.
mdpath	The file path and name of the metadata file. This is not required for SQL Server 2012 and above but is for backward compatibility only, so you should always pass NULL.
initial_file_name	The first file in the path to read. If this parameter is not NULL, then you must also specify initial_offset.
initial_offset	Specifies the last offset that was read so that all events prior are skipped. If specified, then you must also specify initial_file_name.

The sys.fn_xe_file_target_read_file procedure returns the columns detailed in Table 19-7.

Table 19-7. *sys.fn_xe_file_target_read_file Results*

Column	Description
module_guid	The GUID of the module that contains the package
package_guid	The GUID of the package that contains the event
object_name	The name of the event
event_data	The event data, in XML format
file_name	The name of the XEL file that contains the event
file_offset	The offset of the block within the file that contains the event

Because the event data is returned in XML format, we need to use XQuery to shred the nodes into relational data. A full description of XQuery is beyond the scope of this book, but Microsoft provides an XQuery language reference on msdn.microsoft.com.

The script in Listing 19-6 runs the UpdateCustomersWithPageSplits and UpdateCustomersWithoutPageSplits procedures in the Chapter19 database before extracting the event data using the sys.fn_xe_file_target_read_file. We then use the XQuery Value method to extract relational values from the XML results. Finally, because we have turned on causality tracking, we group the data by the correlation GUID to see how many page splits each stored procedure caused. UpdateWithoutPageSplits provides a contrast.

■ **Tip**   Remember to update filepaths to match your own configuration before running the query.

Listing 19-6. Analyzing Event Data with T-SQL

```
--Run the update procedures

EXEC UpdateCustomersWithoutPageSplits ;
GO

EXEC UpdateCustomerWithPageSplits ;
GO

--Wait 30 seconds to allow for the XE buffers to be flushed to the target

WAITFOR DELAY '00:00:30' ;

--Query the XE Target

SELECT c.procedurename, d.pagesplits
 FROM
 (
        SELECT
                correlationid,
                COUNT(*) -1 PageSplits -- -1 to remove the count of the module_start event
        FROM
```

```
        (
                SELECT CapturedEvent,
                        xml:data.value('(/event/data[@name=''object_name'']/value)[1]',
                        'nvarchar(max)') procedurename,   --extract procedure name
                        xml:data.value('(/event/action[@name=''attach_activity_id'']/value)
                        [1]', 'uniqueidentifier') correlationid --extract Correlation ID
                FROM
                    (
--Query the fn_xe_file_target_read_file function, to extract the raw XML
                            SELECT
                            OBJECT_NAME CapturedEvent,
                            CAST(event_data AS XML) xml:data
                            FROM
sys.fn_xe_file_target_read_file('C:\mssql\pagesplits*.xel', NULL , NULL, NULL) as XE ) a
                    ) b
                GROUP BY correlationid
        ) d
INNER JOIN --Self join, to allow the count of page splits
(
        SELECT CapturedEvent,
                xml:data.value('(/event/data[@name=''object_name'']/value)[1]',
                'nvarchar(max)') procedurename,
                xml:data.value('(/event/action[@name=''attach_activity_id'']/value)[1]',
                'uniqueidentifier') correlationid
        FROM
         (
                SELECT object_name CapturedEvent,
                CAST(event_data AS XML) xml:data
                FROM
                sys.fn_xe_file_target_read_file('C:\mssql\pagesplits*.xel', NULL , NULL,
                NULL) as XE ) a
        ) c
ON c.correlationid = d.correlationid
        AND c.procedurename IS NOT NULL ;
```

■ **Tip** Using XQuery allows you to query on every event field and action that is captured within your trace, so you can create very complex queries, providing rich and powerful analysis of the activity within your instance.

Correlating Extended Events with Operating System Data

Extended Events offer the capability to integrate with operating system–level data. The following sections discuss how to correlate SQL Server events with Perfmon data and other operating system–level events.

Correlating Events with Perfmon Data

Before Extended Events were introduced, DBAs used a tool called SQL Trace and its GUI, Profiler, to capture traces from SQL Server; it was possible to correlate this data with data from Perfmon. With Extended Events, you do not often need to make this correlation, because Extended Events include Perfmon counters for processor, logical disk, and system performance objects, such as context switches and file writes. Therefore, you can correlate SQL Server events with operating system counters by adding these objects to the session and by following the T-SQL analysis techniques discussed in the previous section.

■ **Tip** Perfmon counters are in the Analytic channel but have no category.

The script in Listing 19-7 demonstrates creating an event session that captures statements executed within the instance, alongside processor counters. Processor counters are captured every 15 seconds for each processor in the system. The results are saved to an event file target and an ETW target.

Listing 19-7. Creating an Event Session with Perfmon Counters

```
CREATE EVENT SESSION Statements_with_Perf_Counters
ON SERVER
--Add the Events and Actions relating to each Event
ADD EVENT sqlserver.error_reported(
    ACTION(sqlserver.client_app_name,sqlserver.database_id,sqlserver.query_hash,
    sqlserver.session_id)
    WHERE ([package0].[greater_than_uint64]([sqlserver].[database_id],(4)) AND
[package0].[equal_boolean]([sqlserver].[is_system],(0)))),
ADD EVENT sqlserver.module_end(SET collect_statement=(1)
    ACTION(sqlserver.client_app_name,sqlserver.database_id,sqlserver.query_hash,
    sqlserver.session_id)
    WHERE ([package0].[greater_than_uint64]([sqlserver].[database_id],(4)) AND
[package0].[equal_boolean]([sqlserver].[is_system],(0)))),
ADD EVENT sqlserver.perfobject_processor,
ADD EVENT sqlserver.rpc_completed(
    ACTION(sqlserver.client_app_name,sqlserver.database_id,sqlserver.query_hash,
    sqlserver.session_id)
    WHERE ([package0].[greater_than_uint64]([sqlserver].[database_id],(4)) AND
[package0].[equal_boolean]([sqlserver].[is_system],(0)))),
ADD EVENT sqlserver.sp_statement_completed(SET collect_object_name=(1)
    ACTION(sqlserver.client_app_name,sqlserver.database_id,sqlserver.query_hash,
    sqlserver.query_plan_hash,sqlserver.session_id)
    WHERE ([package0].[greater_than_uint64]([sqlserver].[database_id],(4)) AND
[package0].[equal_boolean]([sqlserver].[is_system],(0)))),
```

```
ADD EVENT sqlserver.sql_batch_completed(
    ACTION(sqlserver.client_app_name,sqlserver.database_id,sqlserver.query_hash,
    sqlserver.session_id)
    WHERE ([package0].[greater_than_uint64]([sqlserver].[database_id],(4)) AND
[package0].[equal_boolean]([sqlserver].[is_system],(0)))),
ADD EVENT sqlserver.sql_statement_completed(
    ACTION(sqlserver.client_app_name,sqlserver.database_id,sqlserver.query_hash,
    sqlserver.query_plan_hash,sqlserver.session_id)
    WHERE ([package0].[greater_than_uint64]([sqlserver].[database_id],(4)) AND
[package0].[equal_boolean]([sqlserver].[is_system],(0))))
--Add the Targets
ADD TARGET package0.event_file(SET filename=N'C:\MSSQL\StatementsAndProcessorUtilization.xel'),
ADD TARGET package0.etw_classic_sync_target(SET default_etw_session_logfile_path=
N'C:\MSSQL\StatementsWithPerfCounters.etl')
WITH (MAX_MEMORY=4096 KB,EVENT_RETENTION_MODE=ALLOW_SINGLE_EVENT_LOSS,MAX_
DISPATCH_LATENCY=30 SECONDS,MAX_EVENT_SIZE=0 KB,MEMORY_PARTITION_MODE=NONE,TRACK_
CAUSALITY=ON,STARTUP_STATE=OFF) ;

GO


--Start the instance
ALTER EVENT SESSION Statements_with_Perf_Counters
ON SERVER
STATE = start;
```

■ **Tip**   The SQL Server service account must be in the Performance Log Users group, or an error is thrown.

Integrating Event Sessions with Operating System–Level Events

---

■ **Note**   To follow the demonstrations in this section, you need to install Windows Performance Toolkit, which you can download from `msdn.microsoft.com` as part of the Windows Deployment and Assessment Toolkit.

There are instances in which you may need to integrate event session data with operating system data other than Perfmon counters that SQL Server provides. For example, imagine a scenario in which you have an application that exports SQL Server data to flat files in the operating system so that a middleware product, such as BizTalk, can pick them up. You are having trouble generating some files and you need to view the process flow—from SQL statement being run through to the WMI events being triggered in the operating system. For this, you need to merge event session data with a trace of WMI events. You can achieve this through the ETW (Event Tracking for Windows) architecture.

To demonstrate this, we first create an event trace session in Performance Monitor using the WMI provider, and then we integrate it with the event session that we created in the previous section. (You can find Performance Monitor in Administrative Tools in Windows.) After we open Performance Monitor, we select New | Data Collector Set from the Event Trace Sessions context menu, which causes the Create New Data Collector Set wizard to be invoked. On the first page of the wizard, specify a name for the Collector Set, as illustrated in Figure 19-22, and specify if the Data Collector set should be configured manually or based on a template. In our scenario, we choose to configure it manually.

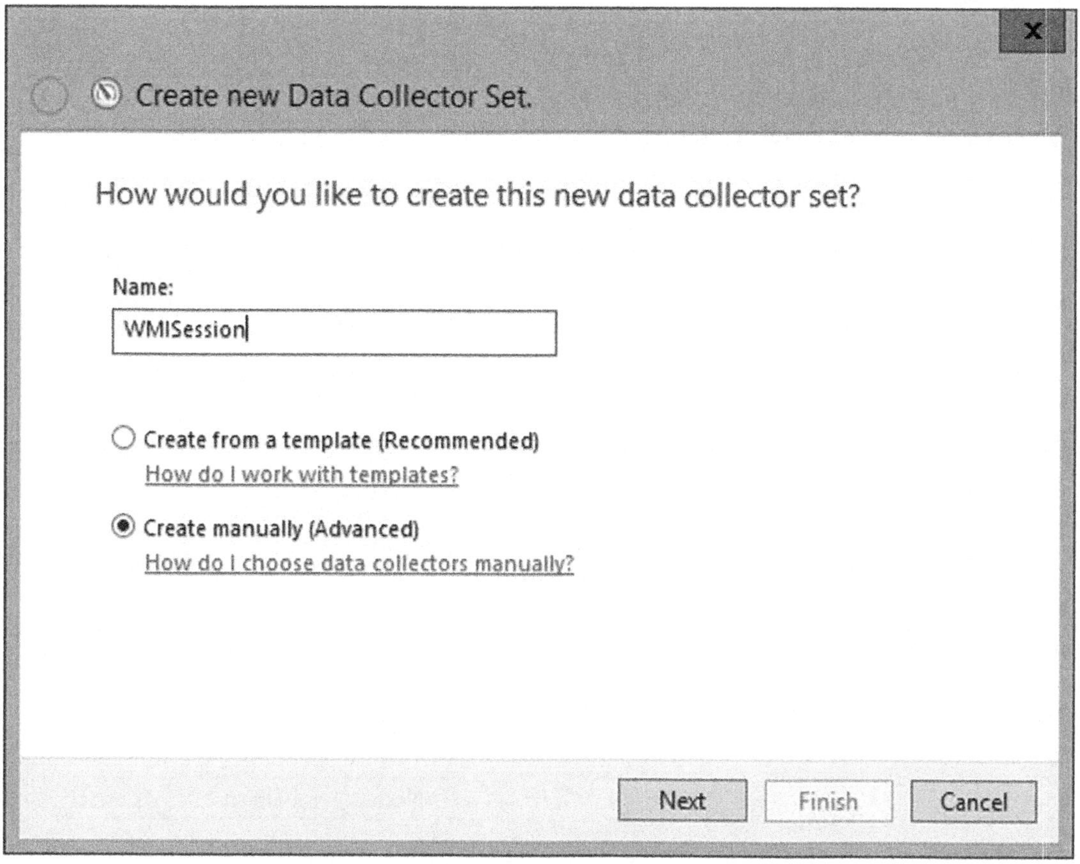

Figure 19-22. *The Create New Data Collector Set wizard*

On the page for enabling event trace providers, we can use the Add button to add the WMI-Activity provider, as illustrated in Figure 19-23.

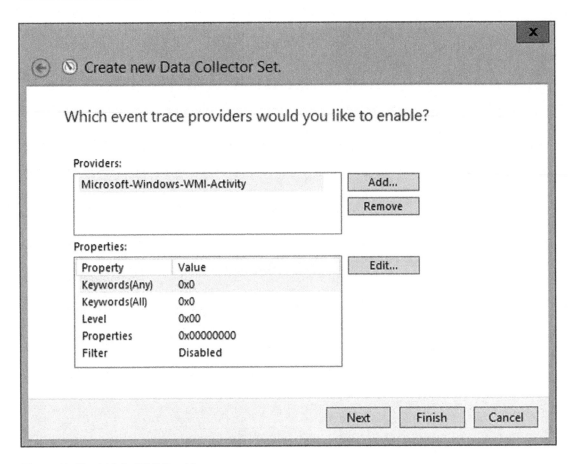

Figure 19-23. *Add the WMI Provider*

We now use the Edit button to invoke the Properties dialog box. Here, we add the Trace and Operational categories by using the check boxes, as shown in Figure 19-24.

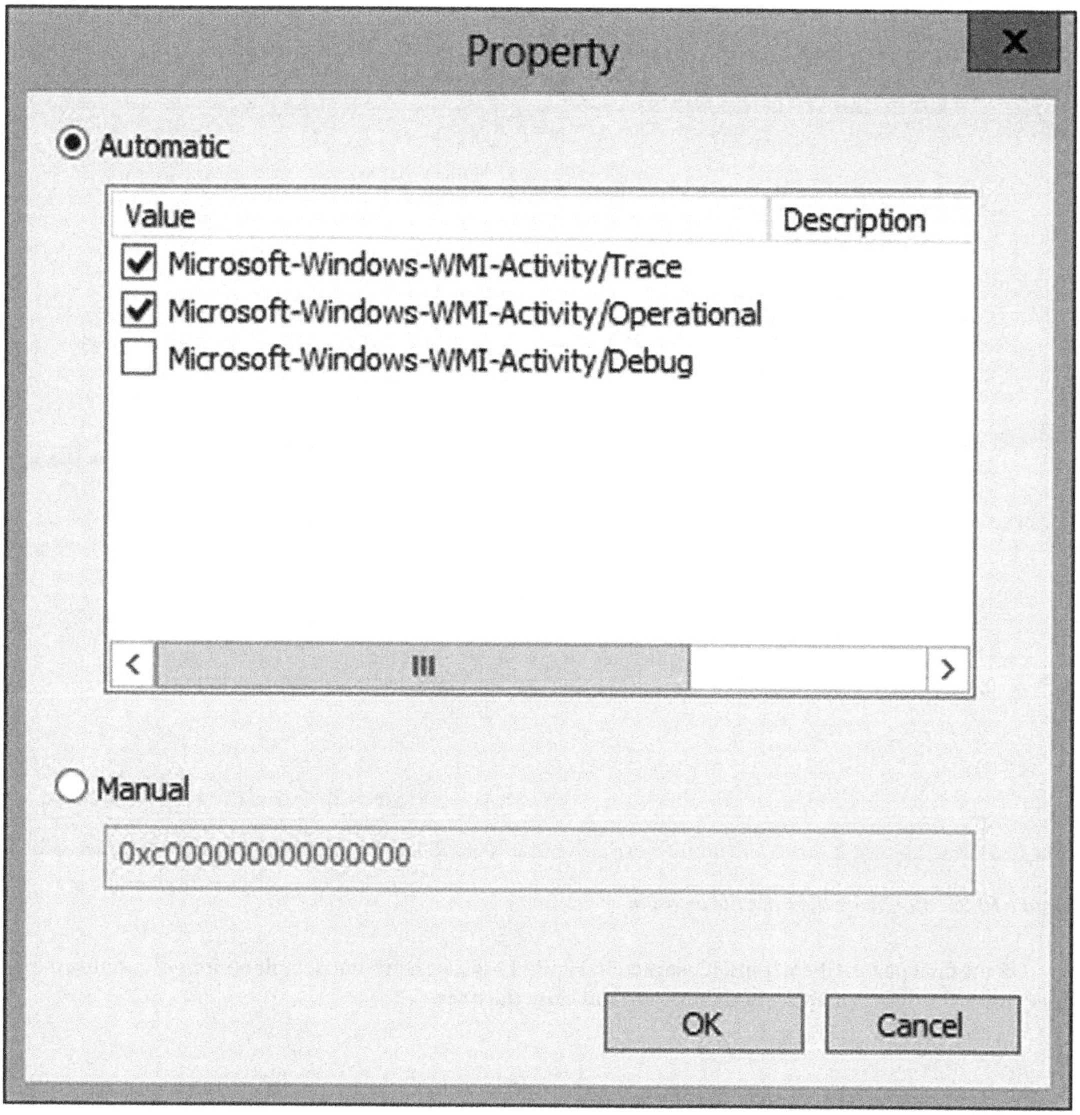

Figure 19-24. *Properties dialog box*

After exiting the Properties dialog box, we move to the next page of the wizard, where we can configure the location where the trace file is stored. We configure the trace file to be saved to the same location as our event session trace, as shown in Figure 19-25.

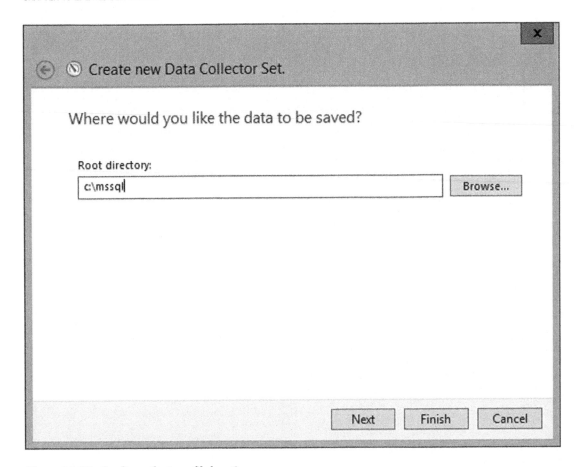

Figure 19-25. *Configure the trace file location*

On the final page of the wizard, illustrated in Figure 19-26, we leave the default options of running the trace under the default account and then save and close the trace.

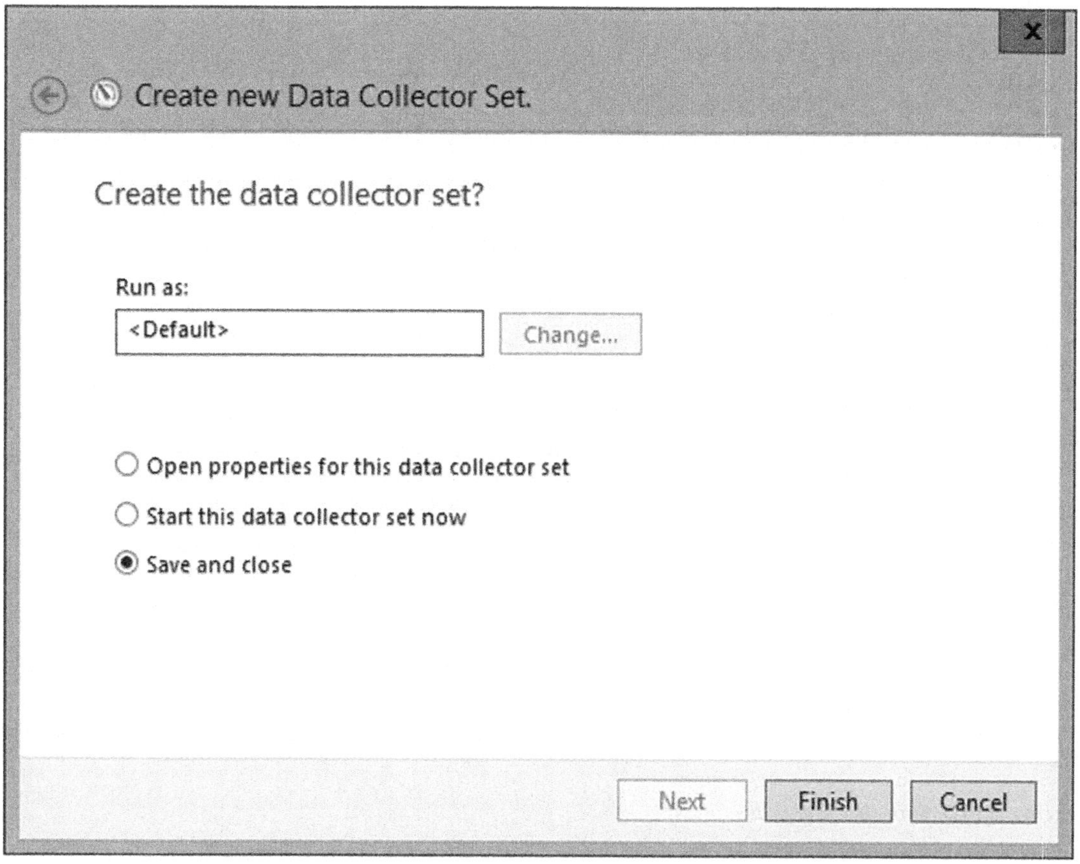

Figure 19-26. *Save the trace*

In Performance Monitor, our trace is now visible in the Event Trace Sessions folder, but showing as stopped. We can use the context menu of the trace to start the Data Collector Set, as shown in Figure 19-27. Also notice that there is a Data Collector Set called XE_DEFAULT_ETW_SESSION. Our extended event session created this because we created an ETW target. This session is required for integrating the data.

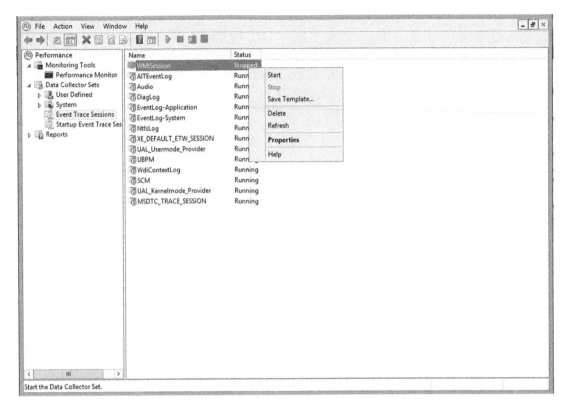

Figure 19-27. *Start the Data Collector Set*

Now that both the WMISession and Statements_with_Perf_Counters sessions are started, we use the BCP command in Listing 19-8 to generate activity, which causes events to fire in both sessions.

Listing 19-8. Generating Activity

```
bcp chapter19.dbo.customers out c:\mssql\dump.dat -S .\PROSQLADMIN -T -c
```

We now need to ensure that the buffers of both sessions are flushed to disk. We do this by stopping both sessions. After stopping the Statements_with_Perf_Counters session, we also need to stop the XE_DEFAULT_ETW_SESSION ETW session in Performance Monitor. You can stop the Statements_with_Perf_Counters session by using the T-SQL command in Listing 19-9.

Listing 19-9. Stopping the Event Session

```
ALTER EVENT SESSION Statements_with_Perf_Counters
ON SERVER
STATE = stop;
```

You can stop the WMISession and XE_DEFAULT_ETW_SESSION by selecting Stop from their respective context menus in Performance Monitor.

The next step is to merge the two trace files together. You can achieve this from the command line by using the XPERF utility with the -Merge switch (demonstrated in Listing 19-10). This command merges the files together, with StatementsWithPerfCounters.etl being the target file. You should navigate to the C:\Program Files (x86)\Windows Kits\8.1\Windows Performance Toolkit folder, before running the script.

Listing 19-10. Merging Trace Files

```
xperf -merge c:\mssql\wmisession.etl C:\MSSQL\StatementsWithPerfCounters.etl
```

Now that all events are in the same file, you can open and analyze this .etl file with Windows Performance Analyzer, which is available as part of the Windows Performance Toolkit, as shown in Figure 19-28. Once installed, you can access Windows Performance Analyzer via the Windows Start menu. A full discussion of Windows Performance Analyzer is beyond the scope of this book, but you can find it in Administrative Tools in Windows after it's installed. You will find full documentation on msdn.microsoft.com.

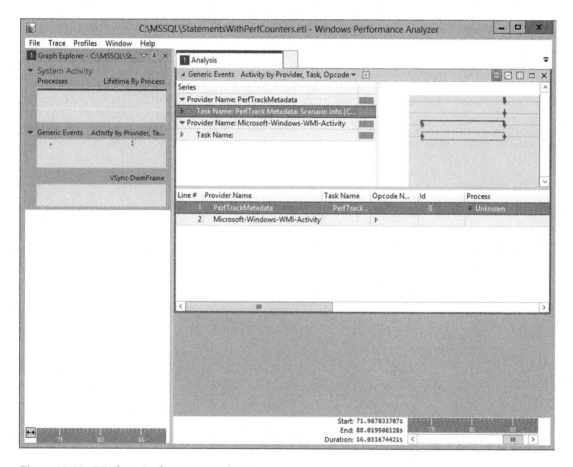

Figure 19-28. *Windows Performance Analyzer*

729

Summary

Extended Events introduce new concepts that you must understand in order to fully harness their power. Events are points of interest that are captured in a trace, whereas actions provide extended information, in addition to the event columns. Predicates allow you to filter events in order to provide a more targeted trace, and targets define how the data is stored. A session is the trace object itself, and it can be configured to include multiple events, actions, predicates, and targets.

You can create an event session through the New Session Wizard, an easy and quick method that exposes Templates; via the New Session dialog box; or of course, via T-SQL. When creating a session via T-SQL, you use the CREATE EVENT SESSION DDL statement to configure all aspects of the trace.

Each Extended Event artifact is contained within one of four packages: Package0, Sqlserver, Sqlos, and SecAudit. The contents of SecAudit are not exposed, however, since these are used internally to support SQL Audit functionality, which is discussed in Chapter 9.

You can view data using the data viewer. The data viewer allows you to watch live data in the session's buffers, and it also supports viewing target data from the Event File, Event Count, and Histogram Target types. The data viewer provides basic data analysis capability, including grouping and aggregating data.

For more complex data analysis, you can open targets in T-SQL. To open an Event File target, use the sys. fn_xe_file_target_read_file results system stored procedure. You then have the power of T-SQL at your disposal for complex analysis requirements.

You can correlate events by turning on causality tracking within the session. This adds a GUID and a sequence number to each event so that you can identify relationships. You can also easily correlate SQL events with Perfmon data, because Extended Events expose processor, logical disk, and system performance counters. To correlate events with other operating system–level events, event sessions can use the ETW target, which you can then merge with other data collector sets to map Extended Events to events from other providers in the ETW architecture.

CHAPTER 20

■ ■ ■

Distributed Replay

Distributed Replay is a utility supplied with SQL Server that offers you the ability to replay traces on one or more clients and dispatch the events to a target server. This is useful for scenarios in which you are testing the impact of software updates, such as OS-level and SQL Server–level service packs; testing performance tuning; load testing; and consolidation planning.

In older versions of SQL Server, SQL Trace and its GUI, Profiler, were commonly used to both generate traces and replay them. This had limitations, however, such as the overhead to capture the trace and the inability to replay the trace on multiple servers. For this reason, SQL Trace and Profiler have been deprecated for the Database Engine, and it is recommended that you only use Profiler for tracing Analysis Services activity. Instead, the recommendation is that you use Extended Events (discussed in Chapter 19) to capture traces with less overhead and then use Distributed Replay to replay them.

■ **Note**　For the demonstrations in this chapter, we will be using four servers, named Controller, Client1, Client2, and Target. Each server has a default instance of SQL Server installed, and all servers are part of the PROSQLADMIN domain. The Distributed Replay Controller feature is installed on the controller instance and the Distributed Replay Client is installed on the Client1 and Client2 instances. Although the Distributed Replay Client should be installed on the target instance for application compatibility testing, in our scenarios, we look at performance testing, while simulating concurrent activity, and therefore the Distributed Replay Client is not installed on the target, since it is not recommended for these purposes. The Distributed Replay Administration Tool is installed as part of the Management Tools feature, so this feature has been installed on the controller.

Distributed Replay Concepts

To harness the power of Distributed Replay, it is important that you understand its concepts, such as the controller, the clients, and the target servers. It is also important to understand the architecture of Distributed Replay. These topics are discussed in the following sections.

Distributed Replay Components

The Distributed Replay Controller sits at the heart of the Distributed Replay infrastructure and is used to orchestrate the activity on each of the Distributed Replay clients. When the Distributed Replay Controller service starts, it pulls its settings from the DReplayController.config file, so you may need to edit this file to configure logging options. We discuss this later in the chapter. There is only one controller in a Distributed Relay topology.

The Distributed Replay client(s) are the server(s) you use to replay the workloads. When the Distributed Replay Client service starts, it pulls its configuration from the DReplayClient.config file, so you may need to edit this file to configure the logging options and folders where the trace results and intermediate files will be stored. This is discussed later in the chapter. You can configure multiple clients in a Distributed Replay topology with support for a maximum of 16 clients.

The target is the instance in which the trace is replayed. There is always one target in a Distributed Replay topology. Because you can have a ratio of multiple clients to one target, you can use Distributed Replay as a tool for load testing with commodity hardware or to simulate concurrent workloads.

The Distributed Replay Administration Tool is a command-line tool that allows you to prepare and replay traces. The executable is called DReplay.exe; it relies on the DReplay.exe.preprocess.config file to obtain the configuration it needs to process intermediate trace files and the DReplay.exe.replay.config file to obtain the configuration it needs to replay the trace. This means that you may need to edit each of these configuration files to specify settings, such as whether or not system activity should be included and specify query timeout values, which we discussed later in this chapter.

Distributed Replay Architecture

The diagram in Figure 20-1 gives you an overview of the Distributed Replay components and how the replay process works across the preprocess and replay phases. In the preprocess phase, an intermediate file is created in the working directory of the controller. In the Replay phase, dispatch files are created at the clients before the events are dispatched to the target.

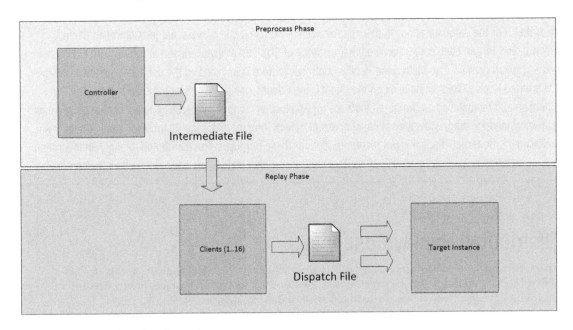

Figure 20-1. *Distributed Replay architecture*

Configuring the Environment

Before we begin to replay traces, we need to configure the Distributed Replay controller, the Distributed Replay clients and the Distributed Replay Administration Tool. These activities are discussed in the following sections.

Configuring the Controller

You can find the DReplayController.config file within the Tools\DReplayController folder, which resides in the 32-bit shared directory of SQL Server. Therefore, if SQL Server is installed with default paths, the fully qualified path is C:\Program Files (x86)\Microsoft SQL Server\120\Tools\DReplayController\ DReplayController.config. You can use this configuration file to control the logging level. These are the possible options:

- INFORMATIONAL—Logs all messages to the controller log.

- WARNINGS—Filters out informational messages, but logs all errors and warnings.

- CRITICAL—Logs only critical errors. This is the default value.

The default contents of the DReplayController.config file are shown in Listing 20-1.

Listing 20-1. DReplayController.config

```
<?xml version='1.0'?>
<Options>
    <LoggingLevel>CRITICAL</LoggingLevel>
</Options>
```

Because the service pulls this logging level from the configuration file at the point when the service starts, if you change the logging level after starting the service, then you need to restart the service. The log itself is created when the service starts, and it include startup information, such as the service account being used. You can find the log in the \DReplayController\Log folder named DReplay Controller Log_<Uniquifier>. A new log is generated each time the service starts.

If you are running the Distributed Replay Client service under a different service account than the Distributed Replay Controller service, then you also need to configure DCOM (Distributed Component Object Model) permissions on the Distributed Replay Controller service. You can do this via Component Services, which can be found in Administrative Tools in Windows.

Once Component Services has been invoked, you need to drill through Console Root | Component Services | Computers | My Computer | DCOM Config and then select Properties from the DReplayController context menu. This causes the Properties dialog box to be invoked. From here, you should navigate to the Security tab, which is shown in Figure 20-2.

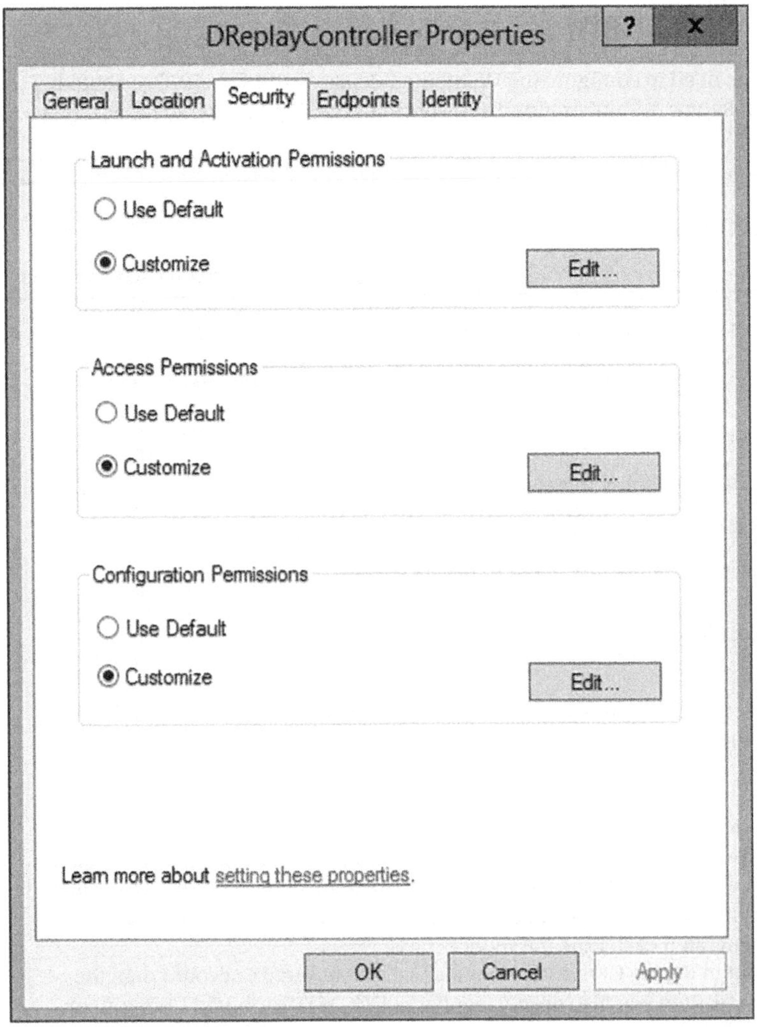

Figure 20-2. *The Security tab*

Now use the Edit button in the Launch And Activation Permissions section to launch the Permissions dialog box. Here, use the Add button to add the service account of the Distributed Replay Client service before granting it the Local Activation and Remote Activation privileges, as illustrated in Figure 20-3.

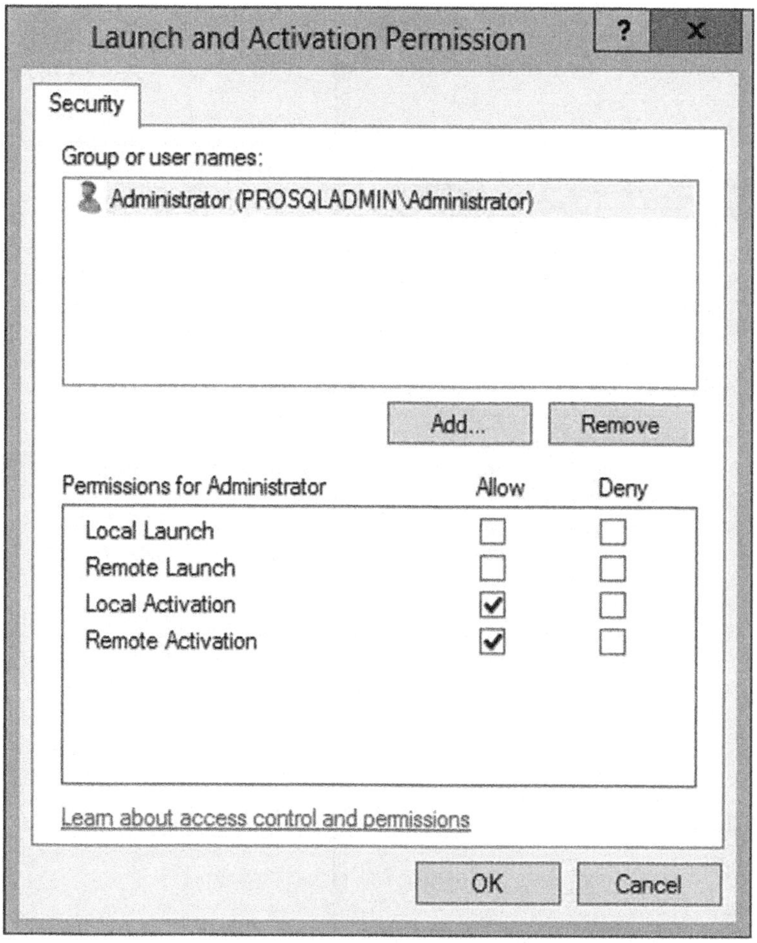

Figure 20-3. *The Permissions dialog box (Launch and Activation permissions)*

You now need to repeat this process in the Access Permissions section to grant the service account the Local Access and Remote Access privileges, as shown in Figure 20-4.

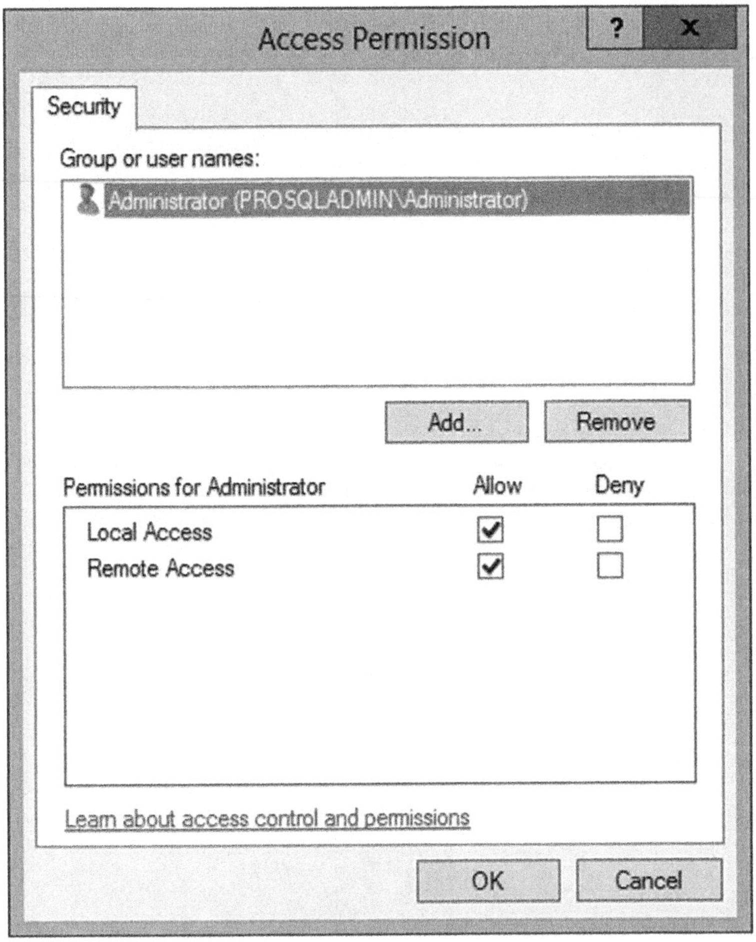

Figure 20-4. *The Permissions dialog box (Access Permissions)*

You also need to ensure that the Distributed Replay Client service account is added to the Distributed COM Users Windows Group on the server running the Distributed Replay Controller. Once you have applied these changes, you need to restart both the Distributed Replay Controller service and the Distributed Replay Client service(s) for the changes to take effect.

■ **Tip**   In regard to firewall configuration, the controller and the client communicate using port 135 and dynamic ports; therefore, you must ensure that these are open between the servers. Opening the dynamic port range can violate some organization's security best practice, however. The workaround is to configure Windows Firewall so it allows the Distributed Replay executables to communicate through any port. This poses its own issues, however, because some corporate firewalls are not configured to offer this functionality, meaning that even though Windows Firewall does allow the traffic through, the packets may be dropped at the corporate firewall level. For more information on configuring Windows Firewall, please refer to Chapter 4.

Configuring Clients

You can find the DReplayClient.config file in the Tools\DReplayClient folder, which resides in the 32-bit shared directory of SQL Server. Therefore, if SQL Server is installed with default paths, the fully qualified path would be C:\Program Files (x86)\Microsoft SQL Server\120\Tools\DReplayController\ DReplayClient.config. You can use this configuration file to configure the settings detailed in Table 20-1.

Table 20-1. *DReplayClient.config Options*

Option	Description
Controller	The name of the server hosting the Distributed Replay Controller. It is important to note that this is the server name, not the server\instance name.
WorkingDirectory	The location on the client where dispatch files are stored. If this option is not included in the configuration file, then the folder where the configuration file is stored is used.
ResultsDirectory	The location where the results file from the replay is stored. If this option is not specified in the configuration file, then the folder that the configuration file is stored in is used.
Logging	Use this option to control the logging level. The possible options are: • INFORMATIONAL, which logs all messages to the controller log. • WARNINGS, which filters out informational messages, but logs all errors and warnings. • CRITICAL, which logs only critical errors. This is the default value.

Listing 20-2 displays an edited version of the DReplayClient.config file, which has been configured to point to our controller server and the Working and Results folders.

Listing 20-2. DReplayClient.config

```xml
<?xml version="1.0" encoding="utf-8"?>
<Options>
  <Controller>controller</Controller>
  <WorkingDirectory>C:\DistributedReplay\WorkingDir\</WorkingDirectory>
  <ResultDirectory>C:\DistributedReplay\ResultDir\</ResultDirectory>
  <LoggingLevel>CRITICAL</LoggingLevel>
</Options>
```

■ **Tip**   You must start the Distributed Replay Controller service before you start the Distributed Replay Client service on each client.

Because we are using two clients, we need to repeat these activities on each. In our environment, these clients are the servers, Client1 and Client2.

■ **Tip**   In regards to firewall configuration, the client and the target communicate using the SQL Server ports. In a standard configuration, this means using TCP 1433 and UDP 1434 for the browser service, if you are using a named instance. If you are using nonstandard ports, configure the firewall accordingly.

Configuring the Replay

The replay is started using the Administration tool, which relies on two configuration files, DReplay.exe. preprocess.config and DReplay.exe.replay.config. The first of these configuration files controls the building of the intermediate files and the second controls replay options and output options. Both files are located within the 32-bit shared directory, so with a default installation, the fully qualified paths are C:\Program Files (x86)\Microsoft SQL Server\120\Tools\Binn\DReplay.exe.preprocess.config and C:\Program Files (x86)\Microsoft SQL Server\120\Tools\Binn\DReplay.exe.replay.config, respectively. Table 20-2 details the options you can configure in DReplay.exe.preprocess.config.

Table 20-2. *DReplay.exe.preprocess.config Options*

Option	Description
IncSystemSession	Specifies if activity captured from system sessions should be included in the replay.
MaxIdleTime	Specifies a limit for the amount of idle time in seconds.
	• -1 specifies that the idle time between activities should be the same as the original trace.
	• 0 specifies that there should be no idle time between activities.

The default contents of the DReplay.exe.preprocess.config file are shown in Listing 20-3.

Listing 20-3. *DReplay.exe.preprocess.config*

```xml
<?xml version="1.0" encoding="utf-8"?>
<Options>
    <PreprocessModifiers>
        <IncSystemSession>No</IncSystemSession>
        <MaxIdleTime>-1</MaxIdleTime>
    </PreprocessModifiers>
</Options>
```

Table 20-3 details the options you can configure within DReplay.exe.replay.config.

Table 20-3. *DReplay.exe.replay.config Options*

Option	Category	Description
Server	Replay options	The server\instance name of the target server.
SequencingMode	Replay options	Specifies the mode to be used for scheduling events. The possible options are • Synchronization, which indicates that the order of transactions is subject to time-based synchronization, across the clients, which is useful for performance testing. • Stress, which is the default option, indicates that transactions are fired as quickly as possible, without time-based synchronization. This is useful for load testing.
StressScaleGranularity	Replay options	When the SequenceMode is set to Stress, StressScaleGranularity determines how to scale activity on a SPID. • SPID indicates that connections on a single SPID should be scaled as if they were a single SPID. • Connection indicates that connections on a single SPID should be scaled as if they were separate connections.
ConnectTimeScale	Replay options	A percentage value that indicates if connection time should be reduced during the replay when the SequenceMode is Stress. 100 indicates 100 percent of connection time is included. Lower values reduce the simulated connection times accordingly.
ThinkTimeScale	Replay options	A percentage value that indicates if the user thinks time should be reduced during the replay when SequenceMode is Stress. 100 indicates 100 percent of think time is included, so transactions replay at the speed they were captured. Specifying lower values reduces the interval.
UseConnectionPooling	Replay options	Specifies if connection pooling should be used on the clients. A *connection pool* is a cache of connections that subsequent connection can reuse.
HealthmonInterval	Replay options	When SequenceMode is set to Synchronization, HealthmonInterval determines how often the health monitor runs, specified in seconds. -1 indicates that the health monitor is disabled.
QueryTimeout	Replay options	Specifies the query timeout value in seconds. -1 indicates that it is disabled.
ThreadsPerClient	Replay Options	Specifies the number of threads to use for the replay on each client.
RecordRowCount	Output Options	Specifies if you should include a row count for each results set.
RecordResultSet	Output Options	Specifies if you should save the contents of each record set.

Listing 20-4 shows an example of the `DReplay.exe.replay.config` file, which has been modified for our environment to allow us to perform a performance test by simulating multiple connections.

Listing 20-4. DReplay.exe.replay.config

```xml
<?xml version="1.0" encoding="utf-8"?>
<Options>
    <ReplayOptions>
        <Server>Target</Server>
        <SequencingMode>synchronization</SequencingMode>
        <HealthmonInterval>60</HealthmonInterval>
        <QueryTimeout>3600</QueryTimeout>
        <ThreadsPerClient>255</ThreadsPerClient>
        <EnableConnectionPooling>No</EnableConnectionPooling>
     </ReplayOptions>
    <OutputOptions>
        <ResultTrace>
            <RecordRowCount>Yes</RecordRowCount>
            <RecordResultSet>No</RecordResultSet>
        </ResultTrace>
    </OutputOptions>
</Options>
```

Working with Distributed Replay

Now that the Distributed Replay utility is configured, we create a trace using Extended Events before we synchronize the target. We then use Distributed Replay to replay the trace in order to test performance tweaks, simulating concurrent activity on the two clients. Before we do this, however, we create the Chapter20 database on the controller using the script in Listing 20-5.

Listing 20-5. Creating the Chapter20 Database

```sql
--Create the database

CREATE DATABASE Chapter20 ;
GO

USE Chapter20
GO

--Create and populate numbers table

DECLARE @Numbers TABLE
(
        Number          INT
)
```

```
;WITH CTE(Number)
AS
(
        SELECT 1 Number
        UNION ALL
        SELECT Number + 1
        FROM CTE
        WHERE Number < 100
)
INSERT INTO @Numbers
SELECT Number FROM CTE;

--Create and populate name pieces

DECLARE @Names TABLE
(
        FirstName        VARCHAR(30),
        LastName         VARCHAR(30)
);

INSERT INTO @Names
VALUES('Peter', 'Carter'),
                ('Michael', 'Smith'),
                ('Danielle', 'Mead'),
                ('Reuben', 'Roberts'),
                ('Iris', 'Jones'),
                ('Sylvia', 'Davies'),
                ('Finola', 'Wright'),
                ('Edward', 'James'),
                ('Marie', 'Andrews'),
                ('Jennifer', 'Abraham');

--Create and populate Addresses table

CREATE TABLE dbo.Addresses
(
AddressID        INT        NOT NULL        IDENTITY        PRIMARY KEY,
AddressLine1        NVARCHAR(50),
AddressLine2        NVARCHAR(50),
AddressLine3        NVARCHAR(50),
PostCode        NCHAR(8)
) ;

INSERT INTO dbo.Addresses
VALUES('1 Carter Drive', 'Hedge End', 'Southampton', 'SO32 6GH')
        ,('10 Apress Way', NULL, 'London', 'WC10 2FG')
        ,('12 SQL Street', 'Botley', 'Southampton', 'SO32 8RT')
        ,('19 Springer Way', NULL, 'London', 'EC1 5GG') ;
```

```
--Create and populate Customers table

CREATE TABLE dbo.Customers
(
        CustomerID              INT             NOT NULL        IDENTITY            PRIMARY KEY,
        FirstName               VARCHAR(30)     NOT NULL,
        LastName                VARCHAR(30)     NOT NULL,
        BillingAddressID        INT             NOT NULL,
        DeliveryAddressID       INT             NOT NULL,
        CreditLimit             MONEY           NOT NULL,
        Balance                 MONEY           NOT NULL
);

SELECT * INTO #Customers
FROM
        (SELECT
                (SELECT TOP 1 FirstName FROM @Names ORDER BY NEWID()) FirstName,
                (SELECT TOP 1 LastName FROM @Names ORDER BY NEWID()) LastName,
                (SELECT TOP 1 Number FROM @Numbers ORDER BY NEWID()) BillingAddressID,
                (SELECT TOP 1 Number FROM @Numbers ORDER BY NEWID()) DeliveryAddressID,
                (SELECT TOP 1 CAST(RAND() * Number AS INT) * 10000
                  FROM @Numbers ORDER BY NEWID()) CreditLimit,
                (SELECT TOP 1 CAST(RAND() * Number AS INT) * 9000
                  FROM @Numbers ORDER BY NEWID()) Balance
        FROM @Numbers a
        CROSS JOIN @Numbers b
        CROSS JOIN @Numbers c
) a;

INSERT INTO dbo.Customers
SELECT * FROM #Customers;
GO
```

Synchronizing the Target

Because we replay a trace that includes DML statements, we need to synchronize our target database immediately before we start capturing the trace to ensure that the IDs align. We perform this task by backing up the Chapter20 database on the controller and restoring it on the target. We can achieve this by using the script in Listing 20-6.

■ **Tip**   Remember to change the file locations to match your own configuration before running the script.

Listing 20-6. Synchronizing the Chapter20 Database

```
--Part 1 - To be run on the controller

BACKUP DATABASE Chapter20
TO  DISK = N'F:\MSSQL\Backup\Chapter20.bak'
WITH NOFORMAT, NOINIT,  NAME = N'Chapter20-Full Database Backup', SKIP,  STATS = 10
GO


--Part 2 - To be run on the client, after moving the backup file across

RESTORE DATABASE Chapter20
FROM  DISK = N'F:\MSSQL\Backup\Chapter20.bak'
WITH  FILE = 1, STATS = 5
GO
```

Ideally, the database should have the same DatabaseID on each server, but if this is not feasible, then ensure that the Database_name action is captured in the event session for mapping purposes. You should also ensure that any logins contained within the trace are created on the Target server, with the same permissions and the same default database. If you fail to do this, you get replay errors.

Since our demonstration is for testing performance enhancements, you may wish to take this opportunity to create appropriate indexes on the Customers and Addresses tables in the synchronized database. You can find a script including index suggestions that are appropriate for our trace workload in Listing 20-7.

Listing 20-7. Index Suggestions

```
USE Chapter20
GO

CREATE INDEX IDX_Customers_LastName ON dbo.Customers(LastName) INCLUDE(FirstName) ;
GO

CREATE INDEX IDX_Customers_AddressID ON dbo.Customers(DeliveryAddressID) ;
GO

CREATE INDEX IDX_Addresses_AddressID ON dbo.Addresses(AddressID) ;
GO

CREATE INDEX IDX_Customers_LastName_CustomerID ON dbo.Customers(LastName, CustomerID) ;
GO
```

Creating a Trace

Let's now create our Extended Event session and start the trace. You should configure the Event session to capture the events, event fields, and actions detailed in Table 20-4.

Table 20-4. *Events and Event Fields*

Event	Event Fields	Actions
assembly_load	-	• collect_current_thread_id • event_sequence • cpu_id • scheduler_id • system_thread_id • task_address • worker_address • database_id • database_name • is_system • plan_handle • request_id • session_id • transaction_id
attention	-	• event_sequence • database_id • database_name • is_system • request_id • session_id
begin_tran_completed	statement	• collect_current_thread_id • event_sequence • cpu_id • scheduler_id • system_thread_id • task_address • worker_address • database_id • database_name • is_system • plan_handle • request_id • session_id • transaction_id

(*continued*)

CHAPTER 20 ■ DISTRIBUTED REPLAY

Table 20-4. (*continued*)

Event	Event Fields	Actions
begin_tran_starting	statement	• collect_current_thread_id • event_sequence • cpu_id • scheduler_id • system_thread_id • task_address • worker_address • database_id • database_name • is_system • plan_handle • request_id • session_id • transaction_id
commit_tran_completed	statement	• collect_current_thread_id • event_sequence • cpu_id • scheduler_id • system_thread_id • task_address • worker_address • database_id • database_name • is_system • plan_handle • request_id • session_id • transaction_id

(*continued*)

Table 20-4. (*continued*)

Event	Event Fields	Actions
commit_tran_starting	statement	• collect_current_thread_id • event_sequence • cpu_id • scheduler_id • system_thread_id • task_address • worker_address • database_id • database_name • is_system • plan_handle • request_id • session_id • transaction_id
cursor_close	-	• collect_current_thread_id • event_sequence • cpu_id • scheduler_id • system_thread_id • task_address • worker_address • database_id • database_name • is_system • plan_handle • request_id • session_id • sql_text • transaction_id

(*continued*)

Table 20-4. (*continued*)

Event	Event Fields	Actions
cursor_execute	-	• collect_current_thread_id • event_sequence • cpu_id • scheduler_id • system_thread_id • task_address • worker_address • database_id • database_name • is_system • plan_handle • request_id • session_id • sql_text • transaction_id
cursor_implicit_conversion	-	• collect_current_thread_id • event_sequence • cpu_id • scheduler_id • system_thread_id • task_address • worker_address • database_id • database_name • is_system • plan_handle • request_id • session_id • sql_text • transaction_id

(*continued*)

Table 20-4. (*continued*)

Event	Event Fields	Actions
cursor_open	-	• collect_current_thread_id • event_sequence • cpu_id • scheduler_id • system_thread_id • task_address • worker_address • database_id • database_name • is_system • plan_handle • request_id • session_id • sql_text • transaction_id
cursor_prepare	-	• collect_current_thread_id • event_sequence • cpu_id • scheduler_id • system_thread_id • task_address • worker_address • database_id • database_name • is_system • plan_handle • request_id • session_id • sql_text • transaction_id

(*continued*)

Table 20-4. (*continued*)

Event	Event Fields	Actions
cursor_recompile	-	<ul><li>collect_current_thread_id</li><li>event_sequence</li><li>cpu_id</li><li>scheduler_id</li><li>system_thread_id</li><li>task_address</li><li>worker_address</li><li>database_id</li><li>database_name</li><li>is_system</li><li>plan_handle</li><li>request_id</li><li>session_id</li><li>sql_text</li><li>transaction_id</li></ul>
cursor_unprepare	-	<ul><li>collect_current_thread_id</li><li>event_sequence</li><li>cpu_id</li><li>scheduler_id</li><li>system_thread_id</li><li>task_address</li><li>worker_address</li><li>database_id</li><li>database_name</li><li>is_system</li><li>plan_handle</li><li>request_id</li><li>session_id</li><li>sql_text</li><li>transaction_id</li></ul>

(*continued*)

Table 20-4. (*continued*)

Event	Event Fields	Actions
database_file_size_change	database_name	• collect_current_thread_id • event_sequence • cpu_id • scheduler_id • system_thread_id • task_address • worker_address • database_id • database_name • is_system • plan_handle • request_id • session_id • transaction_id
dtc_transaction	-	• collect_current_thread_id • event_sequence • cpu_id • scheduler_id • system_thread_id • task_address • worker_address • database_id • database_name • is_system • plan_handle • request_id • session_id • transaction_id

(*continued*)

Table 20-4. (*continued*)

Event	Event Fields	Actions
exec_prepared_sql	-	• collect_current_thread_id • event_sequence • cpu_id • scheduler_id • system_thread_id • task_address • worker_address • database_id • database_name • is_system • plan_handle • request_id • session_id • transaction_id
existing_connection	• database_name • option_text	• event_sequence • client_app_name • client_hostname • client_pid • database_id • database_name • is_system • nt_username • request_id • server_instance_name • server_principal_name • session_id • session_nt_username • session_resource_group_id • session_resource_pool_id • session_server_principal_name • username

(*continued*)

Table 20-4. (*continued*)

Event	Event Fields	Actions
login	• database_name • option_text	• collect_current_thread_id • event_sequence • cpu_id • scheduler_id • system_thread_id • task_address • worker_address • client_app_name • client_hostname • client_pid • database_id • database_name • is_system • nt_username • plan_handle • request_id • server_instance_name • server_principal_name • session_id • session_nt_username • session_resource_group_id • session_resource_pool_id • session_server_principal_name • transaction_id • username

(*continued*)

Table 20-4. (*continued*)

Event	Event Fields	Actions
logout	-	• collect_current_thread_id • event_sequence • cpu_id • scheduler_id • system_thread_id • task_address • worker_address • client_app_name • client_hostname • client_pid • database_id • database_name • is_system • nt_username • plan_handle • request_id • server_instance_name • server_principal_name • session_id • session_nt_username • session_resource_group_id • session_resource_pool_id • session_server_principal_name • transaction_id • username

(*continued*)

Table 20-4. (*continued*)

Event	Event Fields	Actions
prepare_sql	-	• collect_current_thread_id • event_sequence • cpu_id • scheduler_id • system_thread_id • task_address • worker_address • database_id • database_name • is_system • plan_handle • request_id • session_id • transaction_id
promote_tran_completed	-	• collect_current_thread_id • event_sequence • cpu_id • scheduler_id • system_thread_id • task_address • worker_address • database_id • database_name • is_system • plan_handle • request_id • session_id • transaction_id

(*continued*)

Table 20-4. (*continued*)

Event	Event Fields	Actions
promote_tran_started	-	• collect_current_thread_id • event_sequence • cpu_id • scheduler_id • system_thread_id • task_address • worker_address • database_id • database_name • is_system • plan_handle • request_id • session_id • transaction_id
rollback_tran_completed	statement	• collect_current_thread_id • event_sequence • cpu_id • scheduler_id • system_thread_id • task_address • worker_address • database_id • database_name • is_system • plan_handle • request_id • session_id • transaction_id

(*continued*)

Table 20-4. (*continued*)

Event	Event Fields	Actions
rollback_tran_started	statement	• collect_current_thread_id • event_sequence • cpu_id • scheduler_id • system_thread_id • task_address • worker_address • database_id • database_name • is_system • plan_handle • request_id • session_id • transaction_id
rpc_completed	• data_stream • output_parameters	• collect_current_thread_id • event_sequence • cpu_id • scheduler_id • system_thread_id • task_address • worker_address • database_id • database_name • is_system • plan_handle • request_id • session_id • transaction_id

(*continued*)

Table 20-4. (*continued*)

Event	Event Fields	Actions
rpc_starting	data_stream	• collect_current_thread_id • event_sequence • cpu_id • scheduler_id • system_thread_id • task_address • worker_address • database_id • database_name • is_system • plan_handle • request_id • session_id • transaction_id
save_tran_completed	statement	• collect_current_thread_id • event_sequence • cpu_id • scheduler_id • system_thread_id • task_address • worker_address • database_id • database_name • is_system • plan_handle • request_id • session_id • transaction_id

(*continued*)

Table 20-4. (*continued*)

Event	Event Fields	Actions
save_tran_started	statement	• collect_current_thread_id • event_sequence • cpu_id • scheduler_id • system_thread_id • task_address • worker_address • database_id • database_name • is_system • plan_handle • request_id • session_id • transaction_id
server_memory_change	-	• collect_current_thread_id • event_sequence • cpu_id • scheduler_id • system_thread_id • task_address • worker_address • database_id • database_name • is_system • plan_handle • request_id • session_id • transaction_id

(*continued*)

Table 20-4. (*continued*)

Event	Event Fields	Actions
sql_batch_completed	batch_text	• collect_current_thread_id • event_sequence • cpu_id • scheduler_id • system_thread_id • task_address • worker_address • database_id • database_name • is_system • plan_handle • request_id • session_id • transaction_id
sql_batch_starting	batch_text	• collect_current_thread_id • event_sequence • cpu_id • scheduler_id • system_thread_id • task_address • worker_address • database_id • database_name • is_system • plan_handle • request_id • session_id • transaction_id

(*continued*)

Table 20-4. (*continued*)

Event	Event Fields	Actions
sql_transaction	-	• collect_current_thread_id • event_sequence • cpu_id • scheduler_id • system_thread_id • task_address • worker_address • database_id • database_name • is_system • plan_handle • request_id • session_id • transaction_id
trace_flag_changed	-	• collect_current_thread_id • event_sequence • cpu_id • scheduler_id • system_thread_id • task_address • worker_address • database_id • database_name • is_system • plan_handle • request_id • session_id • transaction_id

(*continued*)

Table 20-4. (*continued*)

Event	Event Fields	Actions
unprepare_sql	-	• collect_current_thread_id
		• event_sequence
		• cpu_id
		• scheduler_id
		• system_thread_id
		• task_address
		• worker_address
		• database_id
		• database_name
		• is_system
		• plan_handle
		• request_id
		• session_id
		• transaction_id

So these are the events, event fields, and actions that we include in our session definition (see Listing 20-8).

■ **Tip**   If you do not include all recommended events, event fields, and actions, then errors may be thrown when you convert the .xel file to a .trc file. A workaround here is to use trace flag -T28 when running ReadTrace in order to ignore the RML requirements. This can lead to unpredictable results, however, and is not advised.

Listing 20-8. Creating the Extended Event Session and Starting the Trace

```
CREATE EVENT SESSION DReplay
ON SERVER
ADD EVENT sqlserver.assembly_load(

    ACTION(package0.collect_current_thread_id,package0.event_sequence,sqlos.cpu_id,
    sqlos.scheduler_id,sqlos.system_thread_id,sqlos.task_address,sqlos.worker_address,
    sqlserver.database_id,sqlserver.database_name,sqlserver.is_system,sqlserver.plan_handle,
    sqlserver.request_id,sqlserver.session_id,sqlserver.transaction_id)),

ADD EVENT sqlserver.attention(

    ACTION(package0.event_sequence,sqlserver.database_id,sqlserver.database_name,
    sqlserver.is_system,sqlserver.request_id,sqlserver.session_id)),

ADD EVENT sqlserver.begin_tran_completed(SET collect_statement=(1)

    ACTION(package0.collect_current_thread_id,package0.event_sequence,sqlos.cpu_id,
    sqlos.scheduler_id,sqlos.system_thread_id,sqlos.task_address,sqlos.worker_address,
    sqlserver.database_id,sqlserver.database_name,sqlserver.is_system,sqlserver.plan_handle,
    sqlserver.request_id,sqlserver.session_id,sqlserver.transaction_id)),
```

```
ADD EVENT sqlserver.begin_tran_starting(SET collect_statement=(1)

    ACTION(package0.collect_current_thread_id,package0.event_sequence,sqlos.cpu_id,
    sqlos.scheduler_id,sqlos.system_thread_id,sqlos.task_address,sqlos.worker_address,
    sqlserver.database_id,sqlserver.database_name,sqlserver.is_system,sqlserver.plan_handle,
    sqlserver.request_id,sqlserver.session_id,sqlserver.transaction_id)),

ADD EVENT sqlserver.commit_tran_completed(SET collect_statement=(1)

    ACTION(package0.collect_current_thread_id,package0.event_sequence,sqlos.cpu_id,
    sqlos.scheduler_id,sqlos.system_thread_id,sqlos.task_address,sqlos.worker_address,
    sqlserver.database_id,sqlserver.database_name,sqlserver.is_system,sqlserver.plan_handle,
    sqlserver.request_id,sqlserver.session_id,sqlserver.transaction_id)),

ADD EVENT sqlserver.commit_tran_starting(SET collect_statement=(1)

    ACTION(package0.collect_current_thread_id,package0.event_sequence,sqlos.cpu_id,
    sqlos.scheduler_id,sqlos.system_thread_id,sqlos.task_address,sqlos.worker_address,
    sqlserver.database_id,sqlserver.database_name,sqlserver.is_system,sqlserver.plan_handle,
    sqlserver.request_id,sqlserver.session_id,sqlserver.transaction_id)),

ADD EVENT sqlserver.cursor_close(

    ACTION(package0.collect_current_thread_id,package0.event_sequence,sqlos.cpu_id,sqlos.
    scheduler_id,sqlos.system_thread_id,sqlos.task_address,sqlos.worker_address,sqlserver.
    database_id,sqlserver.database_name,sqlserver.is_system,sqlserver.plan_handle,sqlserver.
    request_id,sqlserver.session_id,sqlserver.sql_text,sqlserver.transaction_id)),

ADD EVENT sqlserver.cursor_execute(

    ACTION(package0.collect_current_thread_id,package0.event_sequence,sqlos.cpu_id,
    sqlos.scheduler_id,sqlos.system_thread_id,sqlos.task_address,sqlos.worker_address,
    sqlserver.database_id,sqlserver.database_name,sqlserver.is_system,sqlserver.plan_handle,
    sqlserver.request_id,sqlserver.session_id,sqlserver.sql_text,sqlserver.transaction_id)),

ADD EVENT sqlserver.cursor_implicit_conversion(

    ACTION(package0.collect_current_thread_id,package0.event_sequence,sqlos.cpu_id,
    sqlos.scheduler_id,sqlos.system_thread_id,sqlos.task_address,sqlos.worker_address,
    sqlserver.database_id,sqlserver.database_name,sqlserver.is_system,sqlserver.plan_handle,
    sqlserver.request_id,sqlserver.session_id,sqlserver.sql_text,sqlserver.transaction_id)),

ADD EVENT sqlserver.cursor_open(

    ACTION(package0.collect_current_thread_id,package0.event_sequence,sqlos.cpu_id,
    sqlos.scheduler_id,sqlos.system_thread_id,sqlos.task_address,sqlos.worker_address,
    sqlserver.database_id,sqlserver.database_name,sqlserver.is_system,sqlserver.plan_handle,
    sqlserver.request_id,sqlserver.session_id,sqlserver.sql_text,sqlserver.transaction_id)),

ADD EVENT sqlserver.cursor_prepare(

    ACTION(package0.collect_current_thread_id,package0.event_sequence,sqlos.cpu_id,
    sqlos.scheduler_id,sqlos.system_thread_id,sqlos.task_address,sqlos.worker_address,
    sqlserver.database_id,sqlserver.database_name,sqlserver.is_system,sqlserver.plan_handle,
    sqlserver.request_id,sqlserver.session_id,sqlserver.sql_text,sqlserver.transaction_id)),
```

```
ADD EVENT sqlserver.cursor_recompile(

    ACTION(package0.collect_current_thread_id,package0.event_sequence,sqlos.cpu_id,
    sqlos.scheduler_id,sqlos.system_thread_id,sqlos.task_address,sqlos.worker_address,
    sqlserver.database_id,sqlserver.database_name,sqlserver.is_system,sqlserver.plan_handle,
    sqlserver.request_id,sqlserver.session_id,sqlserver.sql_text,sqlserver.transaction_id)),

ADD EVENT sqlserver.cursor_unprepare(

    ACTION(package0.collect_current_thread_id,package0.event_sequence,sqlos.cpu_id,
    sqlos.scheduler_id,sqlos.system_thread_id,sqlos.task_address,sqlos.worker_address,
    sqlserver.database_id,sqlserver.database_name,sqlserver.is_system,sqlserver.plan_handle,
    sqlserver.request_id,sqlserver.session_id,sqlserver.sql_text,sqlserver.transaction_id)),

ADD EVENT sqlserver.database_file_size_change(SET collect_database_name=(1)

    ACTION(package0.collect_current_thread_id,package0.event_sequence,sqlos.cpu_id,
    sqlos.scheduler_id,sqlos.system_thread_id,sqlos.task_address,sqlos.worker_address,
    sqlserver.database_id,sqlserver.database_name,sqlserver.is_system,sqlserver.plan_handle,
    sqlserver.request_id,sqlserver.session_id,sqlserver.transaction_id)),

ADD EVENT sqlserver.dtc_transaction(

    ACTION(package0.collect_current_thread_id,package0.event_sequence,sqlos.cpu_id,
    sqlos.scheduler_id,sqlos.system_thread_id,sqlos.task_address,sqlos.worker_address,
    sqlserver.database_id,sqlserver.database_name,sqlserver.is_system,sqlserver.plan_handle,
    sqlserver.request_id,sqlserver.session_id,sqlserver.transaction_id)),

ADD EVENT sqlserver.exec_prepared_sql(

    ACTION(package0.collect_current_thread_id,package0.event_sequence,sqlos.cpu_id,
    sqlos.scheduler_id,sqlos.system_thread_id,sqlos.task_address,sqlos.worker_address,
    sqlserver.database_id,sqlserver.database_name,sqlserver.is_system,sqlserver.plan_handle,
    sqlserver.request_id,sqlserver.session_id,sqlserver.transaction_id)),

ADD EVENT sqlserver.existing_connection(SET collect_database_name=(1),collect_options_
text=(1)

    ACTION(package0.event_sequence,sqlserver.client_app_name,sqlserver.client_hostname,
    sqlserver.client_pid,sqlserver.database_id,sqlserver.database_name,sqlserver.is_system,
    sqlserver.nt_username,sqlserver.request_id,sqlserver.server_instance_name,sqlserver.
    server_principal_name,sqlserver.session_id,sqlserver.session_nt_username,sqlserver.
    session_resource_group_id,sqlserver.session_resource_pool_id,sqlserver.session_server_
    principal_name,sqlserver.username)),

ADD EVENT sqlserver.login(SET collect_database_name=(1),collect_options_text=(1)

    ACTION(package0.collect_current_thread_id,package0.event_sequence,sqlos.cpu_id,
    sqlos.scheduler_id,sqlos.system_thread_id,sqlos.task_address,sqlos.worker_address,
    sqlserver.client_app_name,sqlserver.client_hostname,sqlserver.client_pid,sqlserver.
    database_id,sqlserver.database_name,sqlserver.is_system,sqlserver.nt_username,
    sqlserver.plan_handle,sqlserver.request_id,sqlserver.server_instance_name,sqlserver.
    server_principal_name,sqlserver.session_id,sqlserver.session_nt_username,sqlserver.
    session_resource_group_id,sqlserver.session_resource_pool_id,sqlserver.session_server_
    principal_name,sqlserver.transaction_id,sqlserver.username)),
```

```
ADD EVENT sqlserver.logout(

    ACTION(package0.collect_current_thread_id,package0.event_sequence,sqlos.cpu_id,sqlos.
    scheduler_id,sqlos.system_thread_id,sqlos.task_address,sqlos.worker_address,sqlserver.
    client_app_name,sqlserver.client_hostname,sqlserver.client_pid,sqlserver.database_
    id,sqlserver.database_name,sqlserver.is_system,sqlserver.nt_username,sqlserver.
    plan_handle,sqlserver.request_id,sqlserver.server_instance_name,sqlserver.server_
    principal_name,sqlserver.session_id,sqlserver.session_nt_username,sqlserver.session_
    resource_group_id,sqlserver.session_resource_pool_id,sqlserver.session_server_principal_
    name,sqlserver.transaction_id,sqlserver.username)),

ADD EVENT sqlserver.prepare_sql(

    ACTION(package0.collect_current_thread_id,package0.event_sequence,sqlos.cpu_id,sqlos.
    scheduler_id,sqlos.system_thread_id,sqlos.task_address,sqlos.worker_address,sqlserver.
    database_id,sqlserver.database_name,sqlserver.is_system,sqlserver.plan_handle,sqlserver.
    request_id,sqlserver.session_id,sqlserver.transaction_id)),

ADD EVENT sqlserver.promote_tran_completed(

    ACTION(package0.collect_current_thread_id,package0.event_sequence,sqlos.cpu_id,sqlos.
    scheduler_id,sqlos.system_thread_id,sqlos.task_address,sqlos.worker_address,sqlserver.
    database_id,sqlserver.database_name,sqlserver.is_system,sqlserver.plan_handle,sqlserver.
    request_id,sqlserver.session_id,sqlserver.transaction_id)),

ADD EVENT sqlserver.promote_tran_starting(

    ACTION(package0.collect_current_thread_id,package0.event_sequence,sqlos.cpu_id,sqlos.
    scheduler_id,sqlos.system_thread_id,sqlos.task_address,sqlos.worker_address,sqlserver.
    database_id,sqlserver.database_name,sqlserver.is_system,sqlserver.plan_handle,sqlserver.
    request_id,sqlserver.session_id,sqlserver.transaction_id)),

ADD EVENT sqlserver.rollback_tran_completed(SET collect_statement=(1)

    ACTION(package0.collect_current_thread_id,package0.event_sequence,sqlos.cpu_id,sqlos.
    scheduler_id,sqlos.system_thread_id,sqlos.task_address,sqlos.worker_address,sqlserver.
    database_id,sqlserver.database_name,sqlserver.is_system,sqlserver.plan_handle,sqlserver.
    request_id,sqlserver.session_id,sqlserver.transaction_id)),

ADD EVENT sqlserver.rollback_tran_starting(SET collect_statement=(1)

    ACTION(package0.collect_current_thread_id,package0.event_sequence,sqlos.cpu_id,sqlos.
    scheduler_id,sqlos.system_thread_id,sqlos.task_address,sqlos.worker_address,sqlserver.
    database_id,sqlserver.database_name,sqlserver.is_system,sqlserver.plan_handle,sqlserver.
    request_id,sqlserver.session_id,sqlserver.transaction_id)),

ADD EVENT sqlserver.rpc_completed(SET collect_data_stream=(1),collect_output_
parameters=(1),collect_statement=(0)

    ACTION(package0.collect_current_thread_id,package0.event_sequence,sqlos.cpu_id,sqlos.
    scheduler_id,sqlos.system_thread_id,sqlos.task_address,sqlos.worker_address,sqlserver.
    database_id,sqlserver.database_name,sqlserver.is_system,sqlserver.plan_handle,sqlserver.
    request_id,sqlserver.session_id,sqlserver.transaction_id)),
```

```
ADD EVENT sqlserver.rpc_starting(SET collect_data_stream=(1),collect_statement=(0)

    ACTION(package0.collect_current_thread_id,package0.event_sequence,sqlos.cpu_id,
    sqlos.scheduler_id,sqlos.system_thread_id,sqlos.task_address,sqlos.worker_address,
    sqlserver.database_id,sqlserver.database_name,sqlserver.is_system,sqlserver.plan_handle,
    sqlserver.request_id,sqlserver.session_id,sqlserver.transaction_id)),

ADD EVENT sqlserver.save_tran_completed(SET collect_statement=(1)

    ACTION(package0.collect_current_thread_id,package0.event_sequence,sqlos.cpu_id,sqlos.
    scheduler_id,sqlos.system_thread_id,sqlos.task_address,sqlos.worker_address,sqlserver.
    database_id,sqlserver.database_name,sqlserver.is_system,sqlserver.plan_handle,sqlserver.
    request_id,sqlserver.session_id,sqlserver.transaction_id)),

ADD EVENT sqlserver.save_tran_starting(SET collect_statement=(1)

    ACTION(package0.collect_current_thread_id,package0.event_sequence,sqlos.cpu_id,sqlos.
    scheduler_id,sqlos.system_thread_id,sqlos.task_address,sqlos.worker_address,sqlserver.
    database_id,sqlserver.database_name,sqlserver.is_system,sqlserver.plan_handle,sqlserver.
    request_id,sqlserver.session_id,sqlserver.transaction_id)),

ADD EVENT sqlserver.server_memory_change(

    ACTION(package0.collect_current_thread_id,package0.event_sequence,sqlos.cpu_id,sqlos.
    scheduler_id,sqlos.system_thread_id,sqlos.task_address,sqlos.worker_address,sqlserver.
    database_id,sqlserver.database_name,sqlserver.is_system,sqlserver.plan_handle,sqlserver.
    request_id,sqlserver.session_id,sqlserver.transaction_id)),

ADD EVENT sqlserver.sql_batch_completed(SET collect_batch_text=(1)

    ACTION(package0.collect_current_thread_id,package0.event_sequence,sqlos.cpu_id,sqlos.
    scheduler_id,sqlos.system_thread_id,sqlos.task_address,sqlos.worker_address,sqlserver.
    database_id,sqlserver.database_name,sqlserver.is_system,sqlserver.plan_handle,sqlserver.
    request_id,sqlserver.session_id,sqlserver.transaction_id)),

ADD EVENT sqlserver.sql_batch_starting(SET collect_batch_text=(1)

    ACTION(package0.collect_current_thread_id,package0.event_sequence,sqlos.cpu_id,sqlos.
    scheduler_id,sqlos.system_thread_id,sqlos.task_address,sqlos.worker_address,sqlserver.
    database_id,sqlserver.database_name,sqlserver.is_system,sqlserver.plan_handle,sqlserver.
    request_id,sqlserver.session_id,sqlserver.transaction_id)),

ADD EVENT sqlserver.sql_transaction(

    ACTION(package0.collect_current_thread_id,package0.event_sequence,sqlos.cpu_id,sqlos.
    scheduler_id,sqlos.system_thread_id,sqlos.task_address,sqlos.worker_address,sqlserver.
    database_id,sqlserver.database_name,sqlserver.is_system,sqlserver.plan_handle,sqlserver.
    request_id,sqlserver.session_id,sqlserver.transaction_id)),

ADD EVENT sqlserver.trace_flag_changed(

    ACTION(package0.collect_current_thread_id,package0.event_sequence,sqlos.cpu_id,sqlos.
    scheduler_id,sqlos.system_thread_id,sqlos.task_address,sqlos.worker_address,sqlserver.
    database_id,sqlserver.database_name,sqlserver.is_system,sqlserver.plan_handle,sqlserver.
    request_id,sqlserver.session_id,sqlserver.transaction_id)),
```

```
ADD EVENT sqlserver.unprepare_sql(

    ACTION(package0.collect_current_thread_id,package0.event_sequence,sqlos.cpu_id,sqlos.
    scheduler_id,sqlos.system_thread_id,sqlos.task_address,sqlos.worker_address,sqlserver.
    database_id,sqlserver.database_name,sqlserver.is_system,sqlserver.plan_handle,sqlserver.
    request_id,sqlserver.session_id,sqlserver.transaction_id))

ADD TARGET package0.event_file(SET filename=N'C:\MSSQL\DReplay.xel')

WITH (MAX_MEMORY=4096 KB,EVENT_RETENTION_MODE=ALLOW_SINGLE_EVENT_LOSS,MAX_
DISPATCH_LATENCY=30 SECONDS,MAX_EVENT_SIZE=0 KB,MEMORY_PARTITION_MODE=NONE,TRACK_
CAUSALITY=ON,STARTUP_STATE=ON) ;
GO

ALTER EVENT SESSION DReplay
ON SERVER
STATE = start;
GO
```

To generate activity to be traced, depending on your scenario, you may wish to capture real user activity; to do so, you need to use a tool, such as SQLStress, or script activity. In our case, we script activity to be traced (see Listing 20-9).

Listing 20-9. Generating Activity

```
USE Chapter20
GO

DECLARE @Numbers TABLE
(
        Number          INT
)

;WITH CTE(Number)
AS
(
        SELECT 1 Number
        UNION ALL
        SELECT Number + 1
        FROM CTE
        WHERE Number < 100
)
INSERT INTO @Numbers
SELECT Number FROM CTE;

DECLARE @Names TABLE
(
        FirstName       VARCHAR(30),
        LastName        VARCHAR(30)
);
```

```
INSERT INTO @Names
VALUES('Peter', 'Carter'),
                ('Michael', 'Smith'),
                ('Danielle', 'Mead'),
                ('Reuben', 'Roberts'),
                ('Iris', 'Jones'),
                ('Sylvia', 'Davies'),
                ('Finola', 'Wright'),
                ('Edward', 'James'),
                ('Marie', 'Andrews'),
                ('Jennifer', 'Abraham');

SELECT * INTO #Customers
FROM
        (SELECT
                (SELECT TOP 1 FirstName FROM @Names ORDER BY NEWID()) FirstName,
                (SELECT TOP 1 LastName FROM @Names ORDER BY NEWID()) LastName,
                (SELECT TOP 1 Number FROM @Numbers ORDER BY NEWID()) BillingAddressID,
                (SELECT TOP 1 Number FROM @Numbers ORDER BY NEWID()) DeliveryAddressID,
                (SELECT TOP 1 CAST(RAND() * Number AS INT) * 10000
                 FROM @Numbers
                 ORDER BY NEWID()) CreditLimit,
                (SELECT TOP 1 CAST(RAND() * Number AS INT) * 9000
                 FROM @Numbers
                 ORDER BY NEWID()) Balance
        FROM @Numbers a
) a;

INSERT INTO dbo.Customers
SELECT * FROM #Customers ;

DROP TABLE #Customers
GO 10

SELECT FirstName, LastName
FROM dbo.Customers
WHERE LastName = 'Carter'
GO 100

SELECT COUNT(*)
FROM dbo.Customers c
INNER JOIN dbo.Addresses a
ON c.DeliveryAddressID = a.AddressID
GO 100

SELECT *
FROM dbo.Addresses
GO 100
```

```
DELETE FROM dbo.Customers
WHERE LastName = 'Mead'
        OR CustomerID > 1000000
GO 50

SELECT TOP 10 PERCENT *
FROM dbo.Customers
GO 100
```

We can now stop our trace by using the command in Listing 20-10.

Listing 20-10. Stopping the Trace

```
ALTER EVENT SESSION DReplay
ON SERVER
STATE = stop;
GO
```

Replaying the Trace

Now that we have captured a trace, we convert it to a .trc file and then preprocess it before replaying it by using the Distributed Replay Administration Tool from the command line.

Converting the Trace File

In order to use our .xel file with Distributed Replay, we first need to convert it to a .trc file. We do this with the help of the readtrace.exe command-line tool, which uses RML (Replay Markup Language) to convert the data. ReadTrace ships as part of Microsoft's RML Utilities for SQL Server toolset, which you can download from www.microsoft.com/en-gb/download/details.aspx?id=4511. The following example assumes that you have installed this toolkit.

Here, we convert our trace file by navigating to the C:\Program Files\Microsoft Corporation\ RMLUtils folder and running ReadTrace.exe with the arguments detailed in Table 20-5.

Table 20-5. ReadTrace Arguments

Argument	Description
-I	The fully qualified file name of the .xel file to convert.
-O	The folder to output the results to. This includes the log file as well as the .trc file.
-a	Prevent analytical processing.
-MS	Mirror to a single .trc file, as opposed to separate files for each SPID.

> ■ **Tip** You can find a full description of all ReadTrace arguments in the RML Utilities for SQL Server help file.

We run ReadTrace by using the command in Listing 20-11.

■ **Tip**   Remember to change the filename and path of the input and output files before running this script. Even if you have used the same location, your .xel file name will include a different uniquifier.

Listing 20-11. Converting to .trc Using ReadTrace

```
readtrace.exe -I"C:\MSSQL\DReplay_0_130737313343740000.xel" -O"C:\MSSQL\DReplayTraceFile"
-a -MS
```

Preprocessing the Trace Data

The Administration Tool is a command line utility, which can be run with the options detailed in Table 20-6.

Table 20-6. *Administration Tool Options*

Option	Description
Preprocess	Prepares the trace data by creating the intermediate files
Replay	Dispatches the trace to the clients and begins the replay
Status	Displays the controller's current status
Cancel	Cancels the current operation

When run with the preprocess option, the Administration Tool accepts the arguments detailed in Table 20-7.

Table 20-7. *Preprocess Arguments*

Argument	Full Name	Description
-m	Controller	The name of the server hosting the Distributed Replay Controller.
-i	input_trace_file	The fully qualified file name of the trace file. If there are rollover files, then specify a comma-separated list.
-d	controller_working_dir	The folder where intermediate files are stored.
-c	config_file	The fully qualified file name of the DReplay.exe.preprocess. config configuration file.
-f	status_interval	The frequency with which status messages are displayed, specified in milliseconds.

To preprocess our trace file, we can use the command in Listing 20-12. This process creates an intermediate file, which can then be dispatched to the clients, ready for replay.

■ **Tip**   Change the file paths to match your configuration before you run this script.

Listing 20-12. Preprocessing the Trace

```
dreplay preprocess -m controller  -i "C:\MSSQL\DReplayTraceFile\SPID00000.trc" -d "c:\
Distributed Replay\WorkingDir" -c "C:\Program Files (x86)\Microsoft SQL Server\120\Tools\
Binn\DReplay.exe.preprocess.config"
```

Starting the Replay

You can start the replay using the Distributed Replay Administration Tool. The arguments accepted when the tool is used with the replay option are detailed in Table 20-8.

Table 20-8. Replay Arguments

Argument	Full Name	Description
-m	Controller	The name of the server hosting the Distributed Replay Controller.
-d	controller_working_dir	The folder where intermediate files are stored.
-o	output	Specifies that client's replay activity should be captured and saved to the Results directory.
-s	target_server	The server\instance name of the Target server.
-w	clients	A comma-separated list of clients.
-c	config_file	The fully qualified name of the DReplay.exe.replay.config configuration file.
-f	status_interval	The frequency at which to display the status, specified in seconds.

Therefore, to replay the trace, using Client1 and Client2, against our Target server, we use the command in Listing 20-13.

Listing 20-13. Replaying the Trace

```
dreplay replay -m controller -d "c:\Distributed Replay\WorkingDir" -s Target -o -w Client1,
Client2 -c "C:\Program Files (x86)\Microsoft SQL Server\120\Tools\Binn\DReplay.Exe.Replay.
config"
```

■ **Tip** The first line of the output may indicate that no events have been dispatched. This is not an issue—it just means that the event dispatch has not yet started.

Summary

Distributed Replay provides a mechanism to replay traces captured with either Profiler or Extended Events. Unlike its predecessor, Profiler, which is deprecated for use with the Database Engine, Distributed Replay can replay the workload from multiple servers, which allows you to perform load testing and simulate multiple concurrent connections.

The controller is the server running the Distributed Replay Controller service, which synchronize the replay and can be configured to work in two different modes; stress and synchronization. In stress mode, the controller fires the events as quickly as possible, while in synchronization mode, it fires the events in the order in which they were captured.

The clients are the servers running the Distributed Replay Client service, which replays the trace. Distributed Replay supports a maximum of 16 clients. The target is the instance to which the events are dispatched by the clients.

Although it is possible to replay a trace captured in Profiler, Extended Events use less resources and provide more flexibility. Therefore, consider using this method to capture the trace. In order to replay an Extended Event session with Distributed Replay, however, you first need to convert the `.xel` file to a `.trc` file. You can do this using RML Utilities, which are available for download at `www.microsoft.com`.

The Distributed Replay Administration Tool is a command-line tool that is used to both preprocess and run the trace. When run in preprocess mode, it creates an intermediate file. When run in replay mode, it generates dispatch files on the clients and uses these files to dispatch the events to the target.

■ ■ ■

## CHAPTER 21

Automating Maintenance Routines

Automation is a critical part of database administration because it reduces the total cost of ownership (TCO) of the enterprise by allowing repeatable tasks to be carried out with little or no human intervention. SQL Server provides a rich set of functionality for automating routine DBA activity, including a scheduling engine, decision-tree logic, and a comprehensive security model. In this chapter, we discuss how you can harness SQL Server Agent, maintenance plans, and SSIS (SQL Server Integration Services) to reduce the maintenance burden on your time. We also look at how you can reduce effort by using multiserver jobs, which allow you to operate a consistent set of routines across the enterprise.

SQL Server Agent

SQL Server Agent is a service that provides the ability to create automated routines with decision-based logic and schedule them to run one time only, on a reoccurring basis, when the SQL Server Agent service starts or when a CPU idle condition occurs.

SQL Server Agent also controls alerts, which allow you to respond to a wide range of conditions, including errors, performance conditions, or WMI (Windows Management Instrumentation) events. Responses can include sending e-mails or running tasks.

After introducing you to the concepts surrounding SQL Server Agent, the following sections discuss the SQL Server Agent security model, how to create and manage jobs, and how to create alerts.

SQL Server Agent Concepts

SQL Server Agent is implemented using jobs, which orchestrate the tasks that are run; schedules, which define when the tasks run; alerts, which can respond to events that occur within SQL Server; and operators, which are users (usually DBAs) who are notified of occurrences, such as job status or alerts that have been triggered. The following sections introduce you to each of these concepts.

Schedules

A *schedule* defines the time or condition that triggers a job to start running. A schedule can be defined as follows:

> **One time:** Allows you to specify a specific date and time.

> **Start automatically when SQL Server Agent starts:** Useful if a set of tasks should run when the instance starts, assuming that the SQL Server Agent service is configured to start automatically.

Start when CPU becomes idle: Useful if you have resource-intensive jobs that you do not wish to impact user activity.

Recurring: Allows you to define a complex schedule, with start and end dates, that can reoccur daily, weekly, or monthly. If you schedule a job to run weekly, then you can also define multiple days on which it should run. If you define the schedule as daily, you can opt to have the trigger occur once daily, on an hourly basis, every minute, or even as frequently as every ten seconds. If the schedule is reoccurring based on second, minute, or hour, then it is possible to define start and stop times within a day. This means that you can schedule a job to run every minute, between 18:00 and 20:00, for example.

▪ **Tip**   A recurring daily schedule is actually used to define a schedule that runs daily, hourly, every minute, or every seconds.

You can create individual schedules for each job, or you can choose to define a schedule and use this to trigger multiple jobs that you need to run at the same times—for example, when you have multiple maintenance jobs you want to run when the CPU is idle. In this case, you use the same schedule for all of these jobs. Another example is when you have multiple ETL runs against different databases. If you have a small ETL window, you may want all of these jobs to run at the same time. Here again, you can define a single schedule and use it for all of the ETL jobs. This approach can reduce administration; if, for example, the ETL window moves, you can change a single schedule rather than many schedules.

Operators

An *operator* is an individual or team that is configured to receive a notification of job status or when an alert is triggered. You can confine operators to be notified via e-mail, NET SEND, or the pager. It is worth noting, however, that the pager and NET SEND options are deprecated and you should avoid using them.

If you choose to configure operators so they are notified through e-mail, then you must also configure Database Mail, discussed later in this chapter, specifying the address and port of the SMTP Replay server that delivers the messages. If you configure operators to be notified via NET SEND, then the SQL Server Agent Windows service is dependent on the NET SEND service, as well as the SQL Server service, in order to start. If you configure operators to be notified by pager, then you must use Database Mail to relay the messages to the e-mail to pager service.

▪ **Caution**   You increase your operational risk by introducing reliance on the NET SEND service.

When using pager alerts, you can configure each operator with days and times that they are on duty. You can configure this in 24/7 organizations that run support shifts or "follow the sun" support models for operational support, which see shifts being passed to support teams in different global regions. This functionality also allows you to configure each operator with different shift patterns on weekdays, Saturdays, and Sundays.

Jobs

A job is comprised of a series of actions that you should perform. Each action is known as a *job step*. You can configure each job step to perform an action within one of the following categories:

- SSIS packages

- T-SQL commands

- PowerShell scripts

- ActiveX scripts

- Operating system commands

- Replication Distributor tasks

- Replication Merge Agent tasks

- Replication Queue Reader Agent tasks

- Replication Snapshot Agent tasks

- Replication Transaction Log Reader tasks

- Analysis Services commands

- Analysis Services queries

You can configure each job step, with the exception of T-SQL commands, to run under the context of the service account running the SQL Server Agent service or to run under a proxy account, which is linked to a credential. You can also configure each step to retry a specific number of times, with an interval between each retry.

Additionally, you can configure On Success and On Failure actions individually for each job step. This allows DBAs to implement decision-based logic and error handling, as outlined in Figure 21-1.

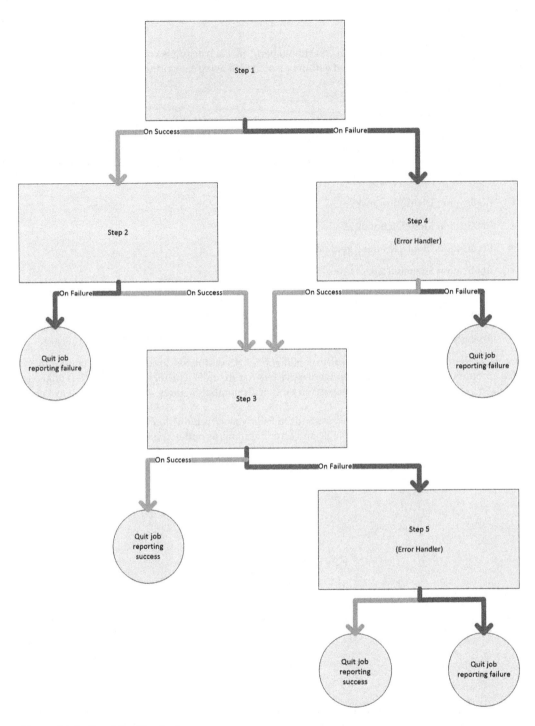

Figure 21-1. *Descision-Tree logic*

You can run each job on a schedule that you can create specifically for the job that you are configuring, or share between multiple jobs, which should all run on the same schedule.

You can also configure notifications for each job. A notification alerts an operator to the success or failure of a job, but you can also configure it to write entries to the Windows Application Event Log or even delete the job.

Alerts

Alerts respond to events that occur in SQL Server and have been written to the Windows application event log. Alerts can respond to the following categories of activity:

- SQL Server events

- SQL Server performance conditions

- WMI events

When you create an alert against a SQL Server events category, you can configure it to respond to a specific error message or to a specific error severity level that occurs. You can also filter alerts so that they only fire if the error or warning contains specific text. They can also be filtered by the specific database in which they occur.

When you create alerts against the SQL Server performance conditions category, they are configured so they are triggered if a counter falls below, becomes equal to, or rises above a specified value. When configuring such an alert, you need to select the performance object that is essentially the category of performance condition, the counter within that performance object, and the instance of the counter that you wish to alert against. So, for example, to trigger an alert in the event that the Percentage Log Used for the Chapter21 database rises above 70 percent, you would select the Databases object, the Percent Log Used counter, and the Chapter21 instance, and configure the alert to be triggered if this counter rises above 70. A complete list of performance objects available to alerts is detailed here:

- Access methods

- Availability replica

- Batch Resp statistics

- Broker activation

- Broker statistics

- Broker TO statistics

- Broker/DBM transport

- Buffer manager

- Buffer node

- Catalog metadata

- CLR

- Cursor manager by type

- Cursor manager total

- Database replica

- Databases

- Deprecated features

- Exec statistics

- FileTable
- General statistics
- HTTP storage
- Latches
- Locks
- Memory broker clerks
- Memory manager
- Memory node
- Plan cache
- Resource pool stats
- SQL errors
- SQL statistics
- Transactions
- User settable
- Wait statistics
- Workload group stats
- XTP cursors
- XTP garbage collection
- XTP phantom processor
- XTP storage
- XTP transaction log
- XTP transactions

SQL Server Agent Security

You control access to SQL Server Agent via database roles and you can run job steps under the context of the SQL Server Agent service account or by using separate proxy accounts that map to credentials. Both of these concepts are explored in the following sections.

SQL Server Agent Database Roles

Other than members of the sysadmin server role, who have full access to SQL Server Agent, access can be granted to SQL Server Agent using fixed database roles within the MSDB database. The following roles are provided:

- SQLAgentUserRole
- SQLAgentReaderRole
- SQLAgentOperatorRole

The permissions provided by the roles are detailed in Table 21-1. Members of the sysadmin role are granted all permissions to SQL Server Agent. This includes permissions that are not provided by any of the SQL Server Agent roles, such as editing multiserver job properties. Actions that are not possible through SQL Server Agent role membership can only be actioned by members of the sysadmin role.

Table 21-1. *SQL Server Agent Permissions Matrix*

Permission	SQLAgentUserRole	SQLAgentReaderRole	SQLAgentOperatorRole
CREATE/ALTER/DROP operator	No	No	No
CREATE/ALTER/DROP local job	Yes (Owned only)	Yes (Owned only)	Yes (Owned only)
CREATE/ALTER/DROP multiserver job	No	No	No
CREATE/ALTER/DROP schedule	Yes (Owned only)	Yes (Owned only)	Yes (Owned only)
CREATE/ALTER/DROP proxy	No	No	No
CREATE/ALTER/DROP alerts	No	No	No
View list of operators	Yes	Yes	Yes
View list of local jobs	Yes (Owned only)	Yes	Yes
View list of multiserver jobs	No	Yes	Yes
View list of schedules	Yes (Owned only)	Yes	Yes
View list of proxies	Yes	Yes	Yes
View list of alerts	No	No	No
Enable/disable operators	No	No	No
Enable/disable local jobs	Yes (Owned only)	Yes (Owned only)	Yes
Enable/disable multiserver jobs	No	No	No
Enable/disable schedules	Yes (Owned only)	Yes (Owned only)	Yes
Enable/disable alerts	No	No	No
View operator properties	No	No	Yes
View local job properties	Yes (Owned only)	Yes	Yes
View multiserver job properties	No	Yes	Yes
View schedule properties	Yes (Owned only)	Yes	Yes
View proxy properties	No	No	Yes
View alert properties	No	No	Yes
Edit operator properties	No	No	No
Edit local job properties	No	Yes (Owned only)	Yes (Owned only)
Edit multiserver job properties	No	No	No
Edit schedule properties	No	Yes (Owned only)	Yes (Owned only)
Edit proxy properties	No	No	No
Edit alert properties	No	No	No
Start/stop local jobs	Yes (Owned only)	Yes (Owned only)	Yes

(continued)

Table 21-1. (*continued*)

Permission	SQLAgentUserRole	SQLAgentReaderRole	SQLAgentOperatorRole
Start/stop multiserver jobs	No	No	No
View local job history	Yes (Owned only)	Yes	Yes
View multiserver job history	No	Yes	Yes
Delete local job history	No	No	Yes
Delete multiserver job history	No	No	No
Attach/detach schedules	Yes (Owned only)	Yes (Owned only)	Yes (Owned only)

SQL Server Agent Proxy Accounts

By default, all job steps run under the context of the SQL Server Agent service account. Adopting this approach, however, can be a security risk, since you may need to grant the service account a large number of permissions to the instance and objects within the operating system. The amount of permissions you need to grant the service account is especially important for jobs that require cross-server access.

To mitigate this risk and follow the principle of least privilege, you should instead consider using proxy accounts. Proxies are mapped to credentials within the instance level and you can configure them to run only a subset of step types. For example, you can configure one proxy to be able to run operating system commands, while configuring another to be able to run only PowerShell scripts. This means that you can reduce the permissions that each proxy requires.

For job steps with the Transact-SQL (T-SQL) script step type, it is not possible to select a proxy account. Instead, the Run As User option allows you to select a database user to use as the security context to run the script. This option uses the EXECUTE AS functionality in T-SQL to change the security context.

Creating SQL Server Agent Jobs

In the following sections, we create a simple SQL Server Agent job, which runs an operating system command to delete old backup files. We then create a more complex SQL Server Agent job, which backs up a database and runs a PowerShell script to ensure the SQL Server Browser service is running. Before creating the SQL Server Agent jobs, however, we first create the Chapter21 database, as well as security principles that we use in the following sections.

You can find the script to perform these tasks in Listing 21-1. The script uses PowerShell to create two domain users: SQLUser and WinUser. It then uses SQLCMD to create the Chapter21 database, before creating a login for SQLUser and mapping it to the Chapter21 database with backup permissions. You can run the script from the PowerShell ISE (Integrated Scripting Environment) or from the PowerShell command prompt. You should run the script on a Windows Server operating system; if you are running it on a different operating system, you need to prepare the environment manually.

■ **Note**   For demonstrations in this section, I use an instance called SQLSERVER\MASTERSERVER, which is part of the PROSQLADMIN.COM domain.

Listing 21-1. Preparing the Environment

```
Set-ExecutionPolicy Unrestricted

import-module SQLPS
import-module servermanager

Add-WindowsFeature -Name "RSAT-AD-PowerShell" -IncludeAllSubFeature

New-ADUser SQLUser -AccountPassword (ConvertTo-SecureString -AsPlainText "Pa$$w0rd" -Force)
-Server "PROSQLADMIN.COM"
Enable-ADAccount -Identity SQLUser

New-ADUser WinUser -AccountPassword (ConvertTo-SecureString -AsPlainText "Pa$$w0rd" -Force)
-Server "PROSQLADMIN.COM"
Enable-ADAccount -Identity WinUser

$perm = [ADSI]"WinNT://SQLServer/Administrators,group"
$perm.psbase.Invoke("Add",([ADSI]"WinNT://PROSQLADMIN/WinUser").path)

invoke-sqlcmd -ServerInstance .\MasterServer -Query "--Create the database

CREATE DATABASE Chapter21 ;
GO

USE Chapter21
GO


--Create and populate numbers table

DECLARE @Numbers TABLE
(
        Number          INT
)

;WITH CTE(Number)
AS
(
        SELECT 1 Number
        UNION ALL
        SELECT Number + 1
        FROM CTE
        WHERE Number < 100
)
INSERT INTO @Numbers
SELECT Number FROM CTE;

--Create and populate name pieces
```

```
DECLARE @Names TABLE
(
        FirstName       VARCHAR(30),
        LastName        VARCHAR(30)
);

INSERT INTO @Names
VALUES('Peter', 'Carter'),
      ('Michael', 'Smith'),
      ('Danielle', 'Mead'),
      ('Reuben', 'Roberts'),
      ('Iris', 'Jones'),
      ('Sylvia', 'Davies'),
      ('Finola', 'Wright'),
      ('Edward', 'James'),
      ('Marie', 'Andrews'),
  ('Jennifer', 'Abraham');

--Create and populate Customers table

CREATE TABLE dbo.Customers
(
        CustomerID          INT             NOT NULL    IDENTITY    PRIMARY KEY,
        FirstName           VARCHAR(30)     NOT NULL,
        LastName            VARCHAR(30)     NOT NULL,
        BillingAddressID    INT             NOT NULL,
        DeliveryAddressID   INT             NOT NULL,
        CreditLimit         MONEY           NOT NULL,
        Balance             MONEY           NOT NULL
);

SELECT * INTO #Customers
FROM
        (SELECT
                (SELECT TOP 1 FirstName FROM @Names ORDER BY NEWID()) FirstName,
                (SELECT TOP 1 LastName FROM @Names ORDER BY NEWID()) LastName,
                (SELECT TOP 1 Number FROM @Numbers ORDER BY NEWID()) BillingAddressID,
                (SELECT TOP 1 Number FROM @Numbers ORDER BY NEWID()) DeliveryAddressID,
                (SELECT TOP 1 CAST(RAND() * Number AS INT) * 10000
                 FROM @Numbers
                 ORDER BY NEWID()) CreditLimit,
                (SELECT TOP 1 CAST(RAND() * Number AS INT) * 9000
                 FROM @Numbers
                 ORDER BY NEWID()) Balance
        FROM @Numbers a
) a;

--Create the SQLUser Login and DB User

USE Master
GO
```

```
CREATE LOGIN [PROSQLADMIN\sqluser] FROM WINDOWS WITH DEFAULT_DATABASE=Chapter21 ;
GO

USE Chapter21
GO

CREATE USER [PROSQLADMIN\sqluser] FOR LOGIN [PROSQLADMIN\sqluser] ;
GO

--Add the SQLUser to the db_backupoperator group

ALTER ROLE db_backupoperator ADD MEMBER [PROSQLADMIN\sqluser] ;
GO"
```

Creating a Simple SQL Server Agent Job

We start by creating a simple Server Agent job, which uses an operating system command to delete backup files that are older than 30 days, and schedule this job to run on a monthly basis. We create the SQL Server Agent artifacts using the New Job dialog box. To invoke this dialog box, drill through SQL Server Agent in Object Explorer, and select New Job from the Jobs context menu. Figure 21-2 illustrates the General page of the New Job dialog box.

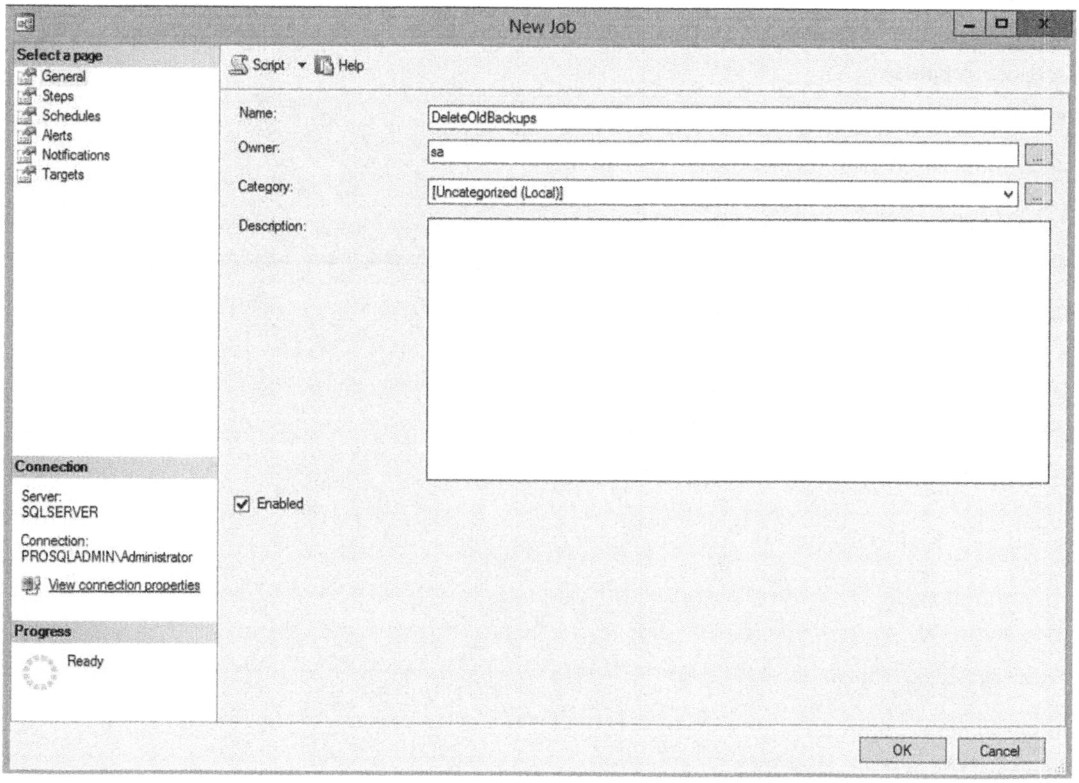

Figure 21-2. *The General page*

On this page, we name our job DeleteOldBackups and change the job owner to be the sa account. We can also optionally add a description for the job and choose a category.

On the Steps page, illustrated in Figure 21-3, we use the New button to invoke the New Job Step dialog box. The General tab of this dialog box is illustrated in Figure 21-4.

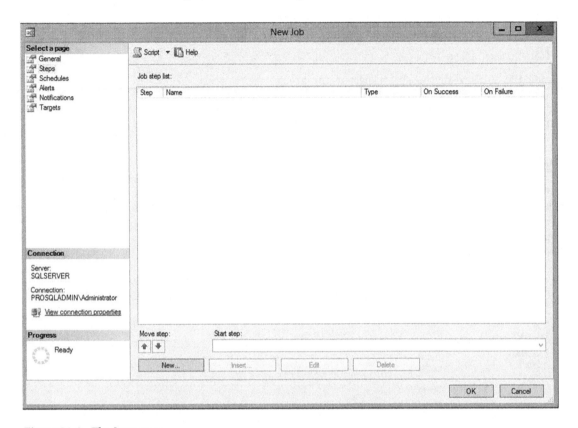

Figure 21-3. The Steps page

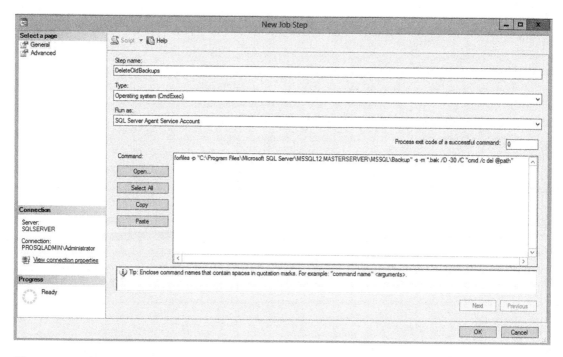

Figure 21-4. *The General page*

On this page, we give our job step a name, specify that the step is an operating system command in the Type drop-down, and confirm in the Run As drop-down that the step runs under the security context of the SQL Server Agent service account. In the Command section, we enter a batch command, which deletes all files from our default backup location that are older than 30 days and have a file extension of .bak. You can find this batch command in Listing 21-2.

Listing 21-2. Removing Old Backups

```
forfiles -p "C:\Program Files\Microsoft SQL Server\MSSQL12.MASTERSERVER\MSSQL\Backup"
-s -m *.bak /D -30 /C "cmd /c del @path"
```

On the Advanced page of the New Job Step dialog box, shown in Figure 21-5, we leave the default settings. We could use this page, however, in more complex scenarios, to configure logging and to control decision tree logic. We discuss this in the next section.

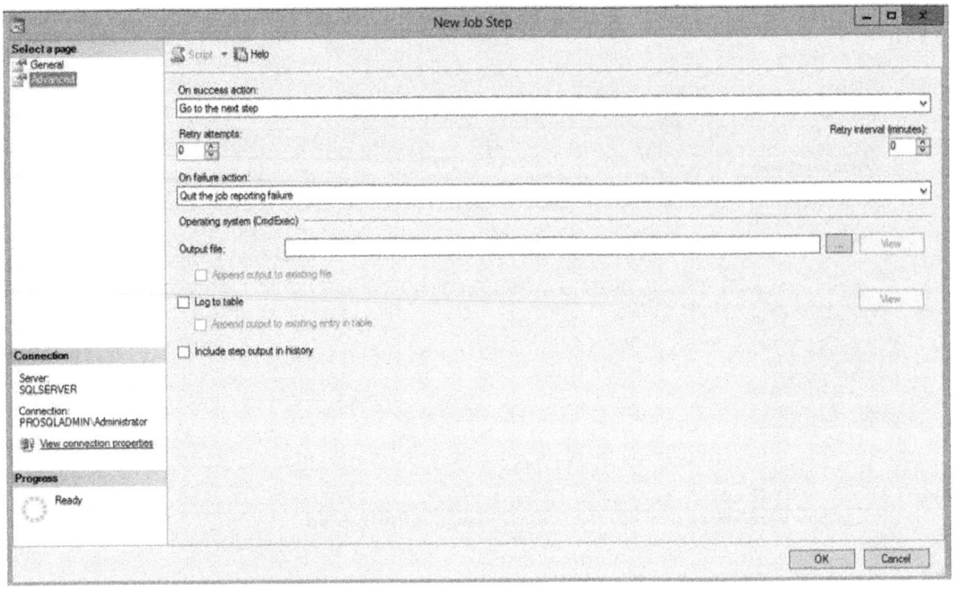

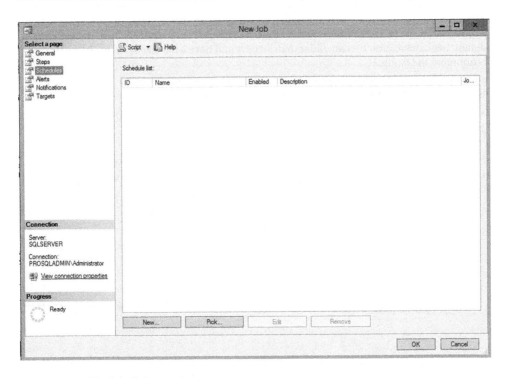

Figure 21-5. *The Advanced page*

Once we have configured our job step, we can exit out of the New Job Step dialog box and return to the New Job dialog box. Here, we now move to the Schedules page, illustrated in Figure 21-6. On this page, we use the New button to invoke the New Job Schedule dialog box, illustrated in Figure 21-7.

Figure 21-6. *The Schedules page*

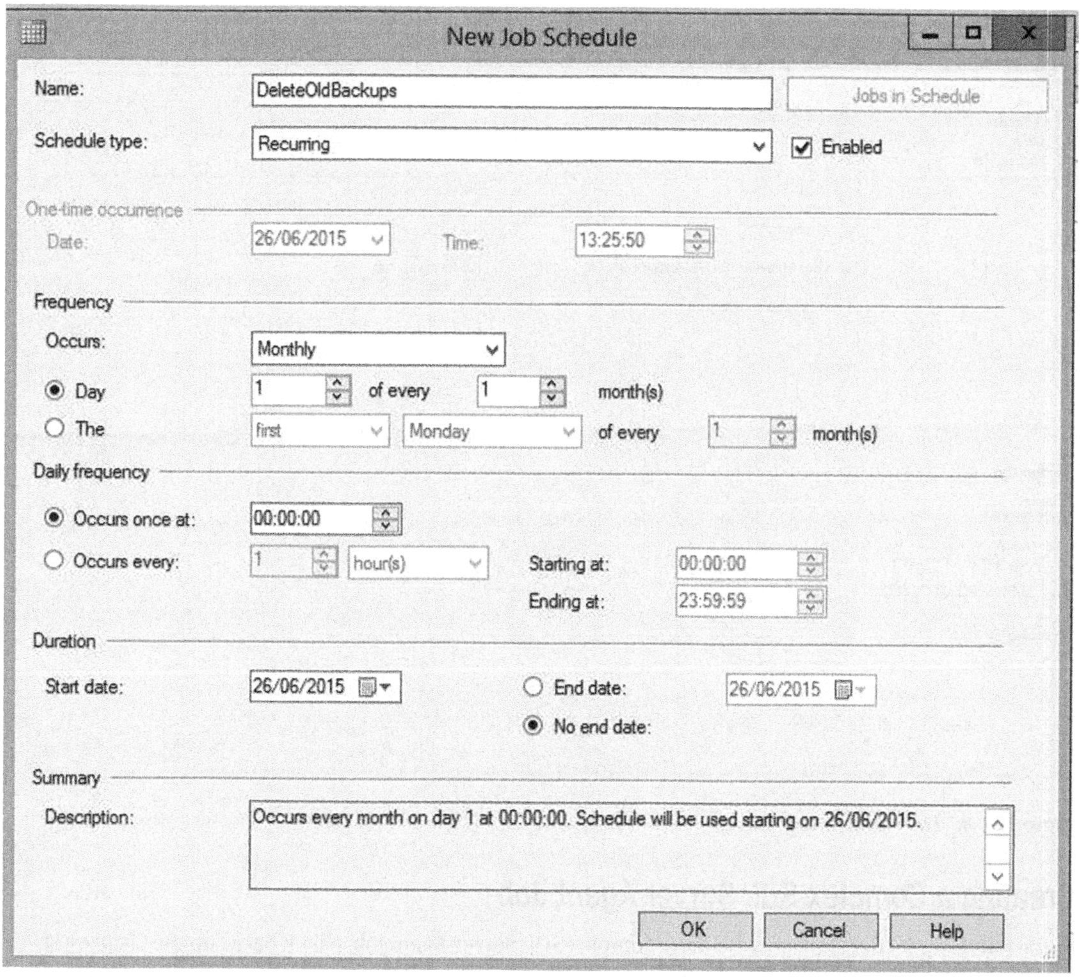

Figure 21-7. *The New Job Schedule dialog box*

In the New Job Schedule dialog box, we first enter a name for our schedule. The default schedule type is Recurring, but the screen changes dynamically if we choose other options. In the Frequency section of the screen, we select Monthly. Again, the screen changes dynamically if we select weekly or daily in this drop-down.

We can now configure the date and time that we would like the schedule to invoke job execution. In our scenario, we leave the default option of midnight, on the first day of each month.

On the Notifications page of the New Job dialog box, we configure any actions that we want to occur when the job completes. As illustrated in Figure 21-8, we configure an entry to write to the Windows Application Log if the job fails. This is an especially useful option if your enterprise is managed by a monitoring tool such as SCOM, because you can configure SCOM to monitor for a failure entry in the Windows application log and send an alert to the DBA team. In the next section, we discuss how to configure e-mail notifications directly from SQL Server Agent.

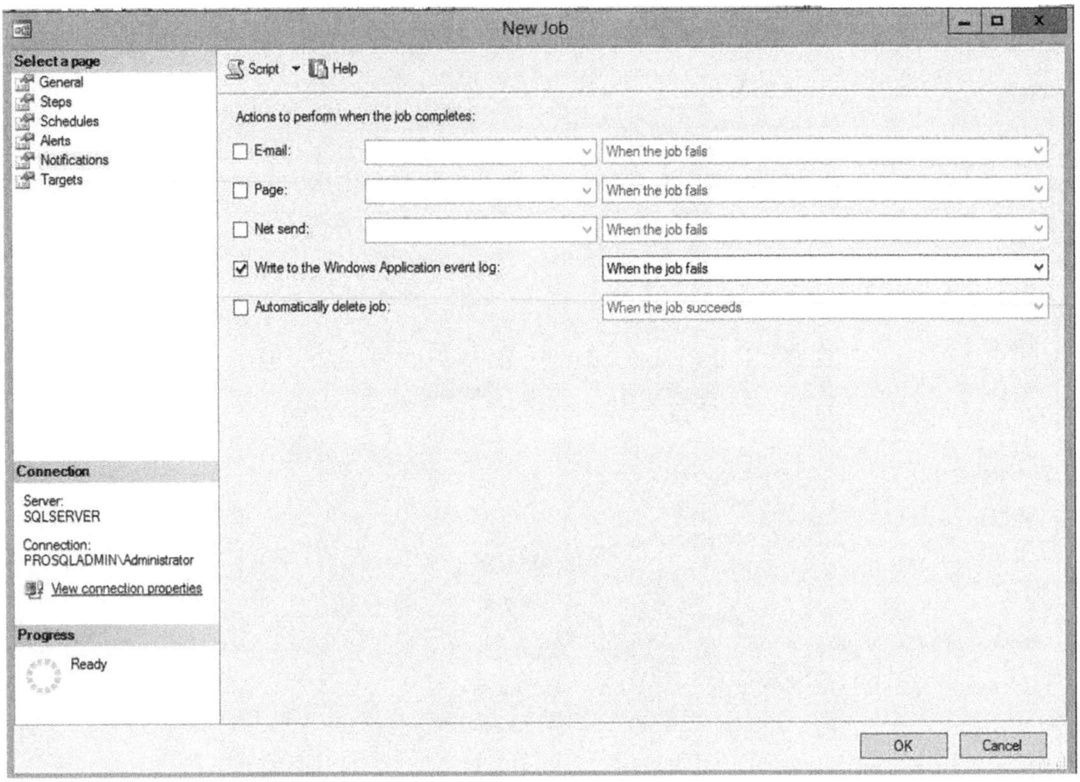

Figure 21-8. *The Notifications page*

Creating a Complex SQL Server Agent Job

In the following sections, we create a more complex SQL Server Agent job, which backs up the Chapter21 database. The job then checks that the SQL Server Browser service is running. We use Run As to set the context under which the T-SQL job step runs and a proxy to run the PowerShell job step. We also configure Database Mail so that an operator can be notified of the success or failure of the job and schedule the job to run periodically. You can also see how to create the SQL Server Agent artifacts using T-SQL, which may prove useful when you are working in Server Core environments.

Creating the Credential

Now that our environment is prepared, we create a SQL Server Agent job, which first backs up the Chapter21 database. The job then checks to ensure that the SQL Server Browser service is running. Checking that the browser service is running is a useful practice, because if it stops, then applications are only able to connect to the instance if they specify the port number of the instance in their connection strings. We run the backup as a T-SQL command under the context of SQL User, and we use PowerShell to check that the browser service is running by using the WinUser account. Therefore, our first step is to create a credential, which uses the WinUser account. We can achieve this in SQL Server Management Studio by drilling through Security and selecting New Credential from the Credentials context menu. This causes the New Credential dialog box to be invoked, as shown in Figure 21-9.

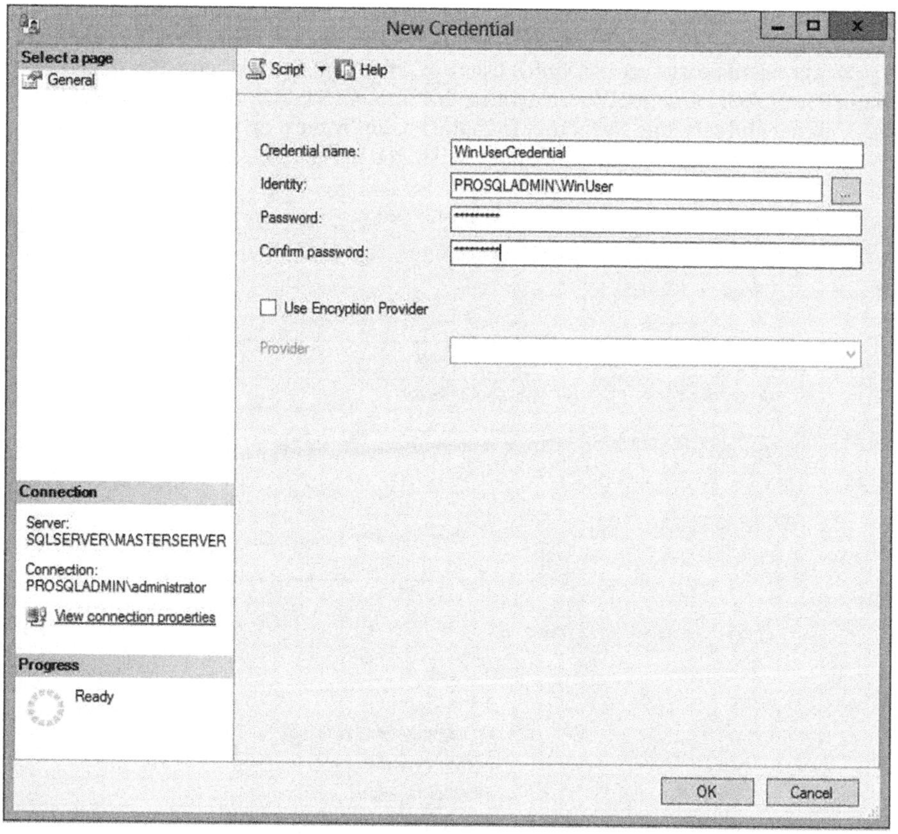

Figure 21-9. *The New Credential dialog box*

In this dialog box, use the Credential Name field to specify a name for your new credential. In the Identity field, specify the name of the Windows security principle that you wish to use and then type the Windows password in the Password and Confirm Password fields. You can also link the credential to an EKM provider. If you wish to do this, check Use Encryption Provider and select your provider from the drop-down list. EKM is discussed further in Chapter 10.

You can create the same credential in T-SQL by using the CREATE CREDENTIAL DDL command. The command in Listing 21-3 achieves the same result.

Listing 21-3. Creating a Credential with T-SQL

```
USE Master
GO

CREATE CREDENTIAL WinUserCredential
        WITH IDENTITY = 'PROSQLADMIN\WinUser', SECRET = 'Pa$$w0rd' ;
GO
```

Creating the Proxy

Next, let's create a SQL Server Agent proxy account, which uses this credential. We configure this proxy account to be able to run PowerShell job steps. We can achieve this through SSMS by drilling through SQL Server Agent in Object Explorer and selecting New Proxy from the Proxies context menu. This causes the General page of the New Proxy Account dialog box to display, illustrated in Figure 21-10.

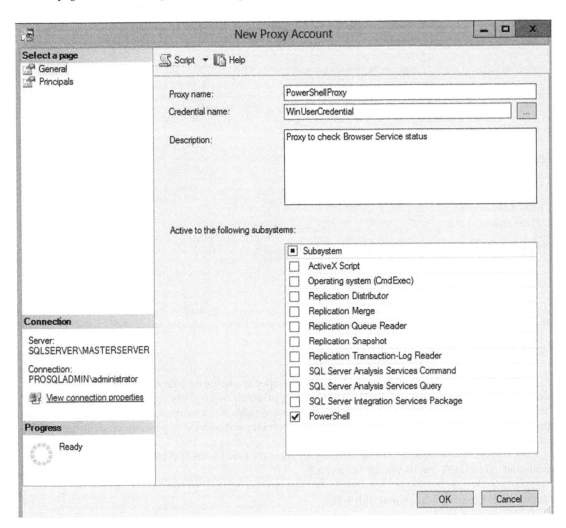

Figure 21-10. *The New Proxy Account dialog box*

On this page, we specify a name for our proxy account and give it a description. We use the Credential Name field to select our WinUserCredential credential and then use the Active To The Following Subsystems section to authorize the proxy to run PowerShell job steps.

■ **Tip** If you enter the new proxy account from the node of the relevant subsystem located under the Proxies node in Object Explorer, the relevant subsystem is automatically selected within the dialog box.

On the Principles page, we can add logins or server roles that have permissions to use the proxy. In our case, this is not required, because we are using SQL Server with an administrator account, and administrators automatically have permissions to proxy accounts.

To create the proxy account using T-SQL, we use the sp_add_proxy and sp_grant_proxy_to_subsystem system stored procedures. The sp_add_proxy procedure accepts the parameters detailed in Table 21-2.

Table 21-2. *sp_add_proxy Parameters*

Parameter	Description
@proxy_name	Specifies a name for the proxy.
@enabled	Specifies if the proxy should be enabled on creation.
	• 0 indicates disabled.
	• 1 indicates enabled.
@description	A textual description of the proxy account.
@credential_name	The name of the credential to which the proxy maps. If NULL, then @credential_id must be specified.
@credential_id	The ID of the credential to which the proxy maps. If NULL, then the @credential_name parameter must be specified.
@proxy_id	An OUTPUT parameter that returns the ID of the proxy account.

■ **Note** Deprecated and undocumented parameters are omitted from this chapter.

The sp_grant_proxy_to_subsystem stored procedure is used to add the new proxy account to the relevant subsystem(s) that it should be able to execute. The procedure accepts the parameters detailed in Table 21-3.

Table 21-3. *sp_grant_proxy_to_subsystem Parameters*

Parameter	Description
@proxy_id	The ID of the proxy. If this is NULL, then @proxy_name must be specified.
@proxy_name	The name of the proxy. If this is NULL, then the proxy_id must be specified.
@subsystem_id	The ID of the subsystem that the proxy is allowed to run. Table 21-4 contains a list of mappings.
@subsystem_name	The name of the subsystem that the proxy is allowed to run. Table 21-4 contains a list of mappings.

Table 21-4 provides a list of mappings between subsystem IDs and names.

Table 21-4. Sybsystem Mappings

Subsystem ID	Subsystem Name	Description
3	CmdExec	Operating system commands
4	Snapshot	Replication Snapshot Agent tasks
5	LogReader	Replication Transaction Log Reader tasks
6	Distribution	Replication Distributor tasks
7	Merge	Replication Merge Agent tasks
8	QueueReader	Replication Queue Reader Agent tasks
9	ANALYSISQUERY	Analysis Services queries
10	ANALYSISCOMMAND	Analysis Services commands
11	Dts	SSIS packages
12	PowerShell	PowerShell scripts

The script in Listing 21-4 demonstrates how we can create the same proxy using T-SQL.

Listing 21-4. Creating the Proxy

```
USE MSDB
GO

--Create the Proxy

EXEC msdb.dbo.sp_add_proxy
        @proxy_name='PowerShellProxy'
        ,@credential_name='WinUserCredential'
        ,@enabled=1
        ,@description='Proxy to check Browser Service status' ;
GO

--Grant the Proxy access to the PowerShell subsystem

EXEC msdb.dbo.sp_grant_proxy_to_subsystem
        @proxy_name='PowerShellProxy'
        ,@subsystem_name='PowerShell' ;
GO
```

Creating the Schedule

Now that our proxy account is configured, we create the schedule to be used by our job. We need our maintenance job to run on a nightly basis, so we configure the schedule to run at 1 AM every morning. To invoke the New Job Schedule dialog box from SSMS, we select New | Schedule from the SQL Server Agent context menu in Object Explorer. This dialog box is shown in Figure 21-11.

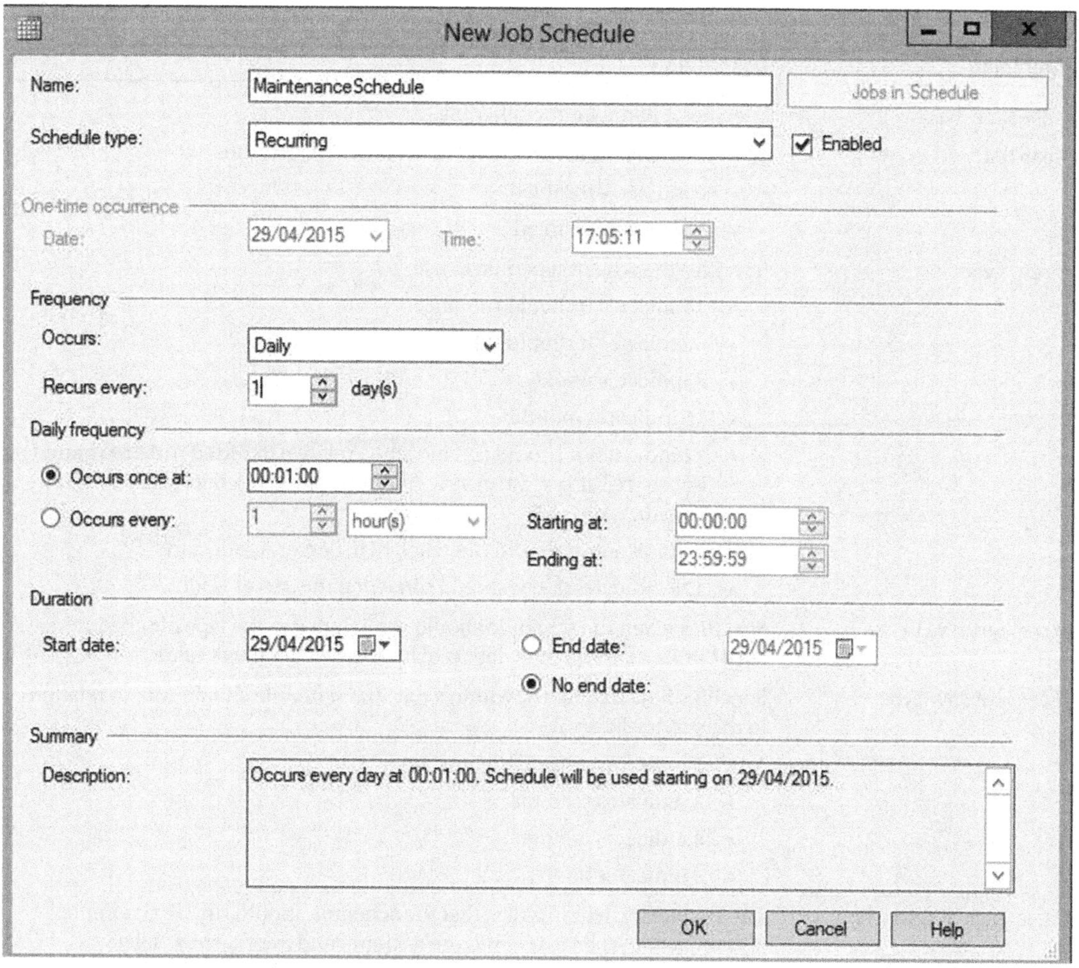

Figure 21-11. *The New Job Schedule dialog box*

In this dialog box, we specify a name for the schedule in the Name field and select the condition for the schedule in the Schedule Type field. Selecting any condition other than Recurring causes the Frequency and Duration sections to become unavailable. Selecting any condition other than One Time causes the One-Time Occurrence section to become unavailable. We also ensure that the Enabled box is checked so that the schedule can be used.

In the Frequency section, we select Daily in the Occurs drop-down list. Our selection in this field causes the options within the Frequency and Daily Frequency sections to be altered dynamically to suit our selection. Since we want our schedule to run daily at 1 AM, we ensure that 1 is specified in the Recurs Every field and change the Occurs Once At field to be 1 AM. Because we want our job to start running immediately and never expire, we do not need to edit the fields in the Duration section.

To create a Schedule using T-SQL, we use the sp_add_schedule system stored procedure. This procedure accepts the parameters detailed in Table 21-5.

Table 21-5. *sp_add_schedule Parameters*

Parameter	Description
@schedule_name	Specifies a name for the schedule.
@enabled	Specifies if the schedule should be enabled on creation. • 0 indicates disabled. • 1 indicates enabled.
@freq_type	Specifies the type of schedule to use. • 1 indicates it should run once. • 4 indicates it should run daily. • 8 indicates weekly. • 16 indicates monthly. • 32 indicates it should run monthly, relative to @freq_interval and @freq_relative_interval—for example, every first Tuesday of the month. • 64 indicates it should run when SQL Server Agent starts. • 128 indicates that it should run when the server is idle.
@freq_interval	Specifies when the schedule should run relative to the type of schedule used. Table 21-6 contains details of how to calculate this value.
@freq_subday_type	Specifies how frequently, within a day, the schedule should run, in relation to the subday interval. • 1 indicates a specified time. • 2 indicates seconds. • 4 indicates minutes. • 8 indicates hours.
@freq_subday_interval	The frequency, within a day, that the schedule should run. For example, if @frequency_subday is configure as hours and @frequency_subday_interval is configured as 2, then the schedule will run every two hours.
@freq_relative_interval	When a schedule is monthly, relative (32), this parameter is used in conjunction with @freq_interval to calculate the day of the month that it runs. • 1 indicates the first day of the month. • 2 indicates the second. • 4 indicates the third. • 8 indicates the fourth. • 16 indicates the last. For example, if @freq_type is 32, @freq_relative_interval is 1, and @freq_interval is 4, then the schedule runs on the first Tuesday of the month. This is because 1 for @freq_relative_interval implies "the first" and 4 for @freq_interval implies Tuesday.
@freq_recurrence_factor	For schedules that run weekly and monthly (relative to frequency interval), this specifies the number of weeks or months between executions.

(continued)

Table 21-5. (*continued*)

Parameter	Description
@active_start_date	Specifies the date that the job is first scheduled to run.
@active_end_date	Specifies the date that the job stops being scheduled.
@active_start_time	Specifies the time that the job is first scheduled to run.
@active_end_time	Specifies the time that the job stops being scheduled.
@owner_login_name	Specifies the name of the principle that owns the schedule.
@schedule_uid	An OUTPUT parameter that returns the GUID of the schedule.
@schedule_id	An OUTPUT parameter that returns the ID of the schedule.

Table 21-6 describes how to calculate the correct value for @frequency_interval based on the value specified for @frequency_type.

Table 21-6. *@frequency_interval Values*

@frequency_type value	Usage of @frequency_interval
1	Unused.
4	Specifies the number of days that should elapse before the schedule repeats. For example, 10 would mean the schedule runs every ten days.
8	Specifies • 1 for Sunday • 2 for Monday • 4 for Tuesday • 8 for Wednesday • 16 for Thursday • 32 for Friday • 64 for Saturday The value is a bitmask, converted to an int, so if multiple days of the week are required, combine the values with a bitwise OR operator. For example, to run every weekday, the value would be 62. The math here is 2 (Mon) + 4 (Tue) + 8 (Wed) + 16 (Thur) + 32 (Fri) = 62.
16	The day of the month.

(continued)

Table 21-6. (*continued*)

@frequency_type value	Usage of @frequency_interval
32	Specifies • 1 for Sunday • 2 for Monday • 3 for Tuesday • 4 for Wednesday • 5 for Thursday • 6 for Friday • 7 for Saturday • 8 for day • 9 for weekday • 10 for weekend day
64	Unused.
128	Unused.

To create our schedule using T-SQL, we can use the command in Listing 21-5.

Listing 21-5. Creating a Schedule

```
EXEC msdb.dbo.sp_add_schedule
                @schedule_name=N'Maintenance Schedule',
                @enabled=1,
                @freq_type=4,
                @freq_interval=1,
                @freq_subday_type=1,
                @freq_subday_interval=0,
                @freq_relative_interval=0,
                @freq_recurrence_factor=1,
                @active_start_time=100 ;
GO
```

Configuring Database Mail

We would like our DBA's distribution list to be notified if our job fails. Therefore, we need to create an operator. Before we do this, however, we need to configure the Database Mail on the instance so that the notifications can be delivered. Our first step is to enable the Database Mail extended stored procedures, which are disabled by default. We can activate these using sp_configure, as demonstrated in Listing 21-6.

■ **Note**   If you do not have access to an SMTP Replay server, then the examples in this section will still work, but you will not receive e-mail.

Listing 21-6. Enabling Database Mail XPs

```
EXEC sp_configure 'show advanced options', 1 ;
GO

RECONFIGURE
GO

EXEC sp_configure 'Database Mail XPs', 1 ;
GO
RECONFIGURE
GO
```

We can now launch the Database Mail Configuration Wizard by drilling through Management in Object Explorer and selecting Database Mail. After passing through the Welcome page, we see the Select Configuration Task page shown in Figure 21-12.

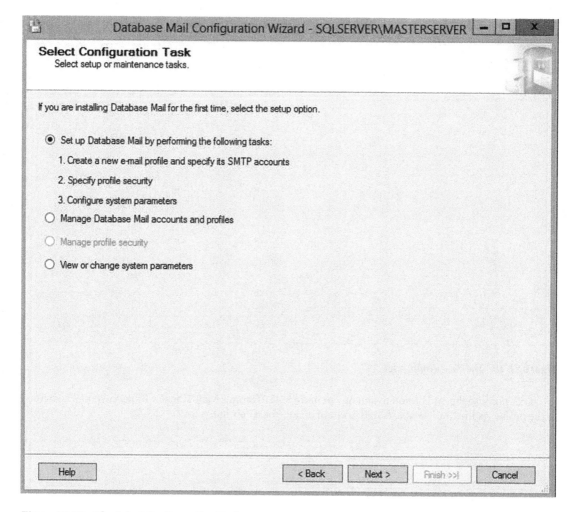

Figure 21-12. *The Select Configuration Task page*

On this page, we should ensure that the Set Up Database Mail By Performing The Following Tasks option is selected. On the new Profile page, we specify a name for our profile. A profile is an alias for one or more mail accounts, which are used to send the notification to the operator. It is good practice to add multiple accounts to a profile; that way, if one account fails, you can use a different one. This page is illustrated in Figure 21-13.

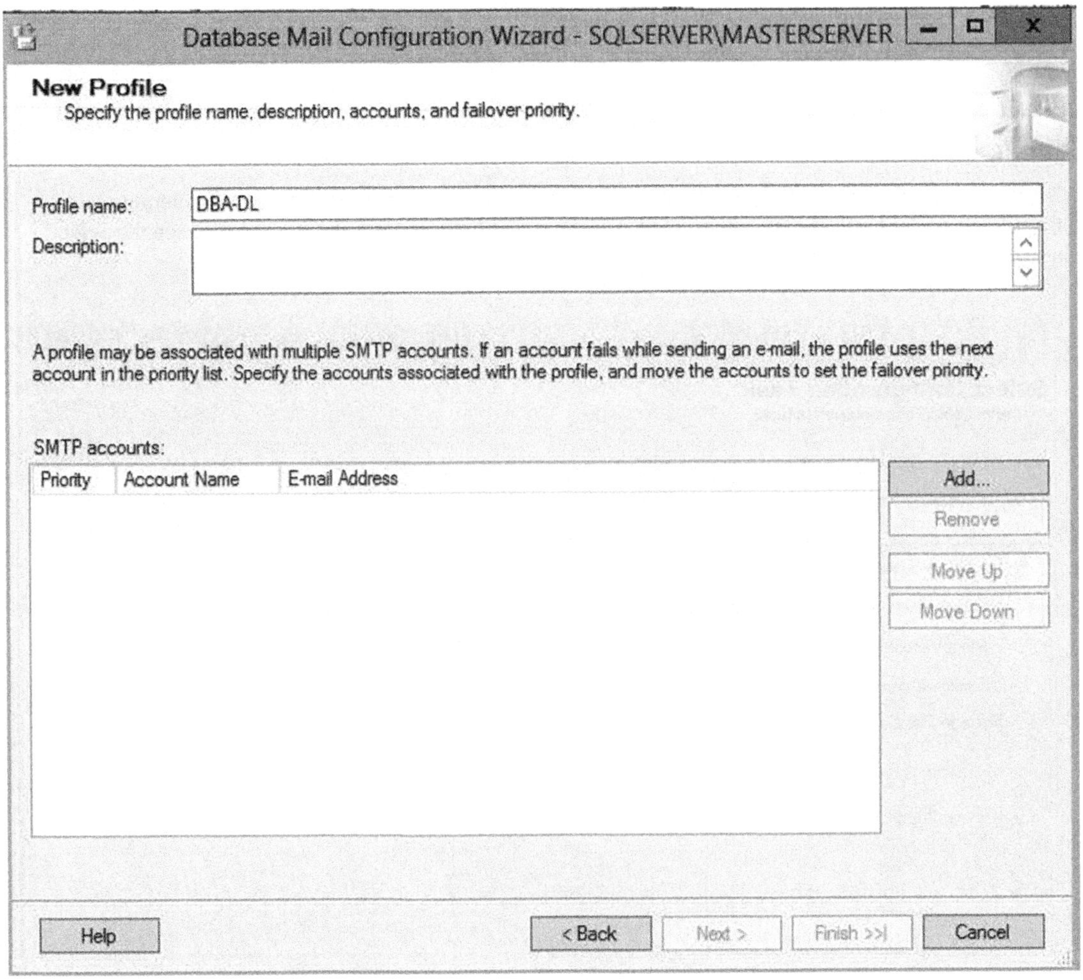

Figure 21-13. *The New Profile page*

Let's now use the Add button to add one or more SMTP (Simple Mail Transfer Protocol) email accounts to the profile via the New Database Mail Account dialog box, show in Figure 21-14.

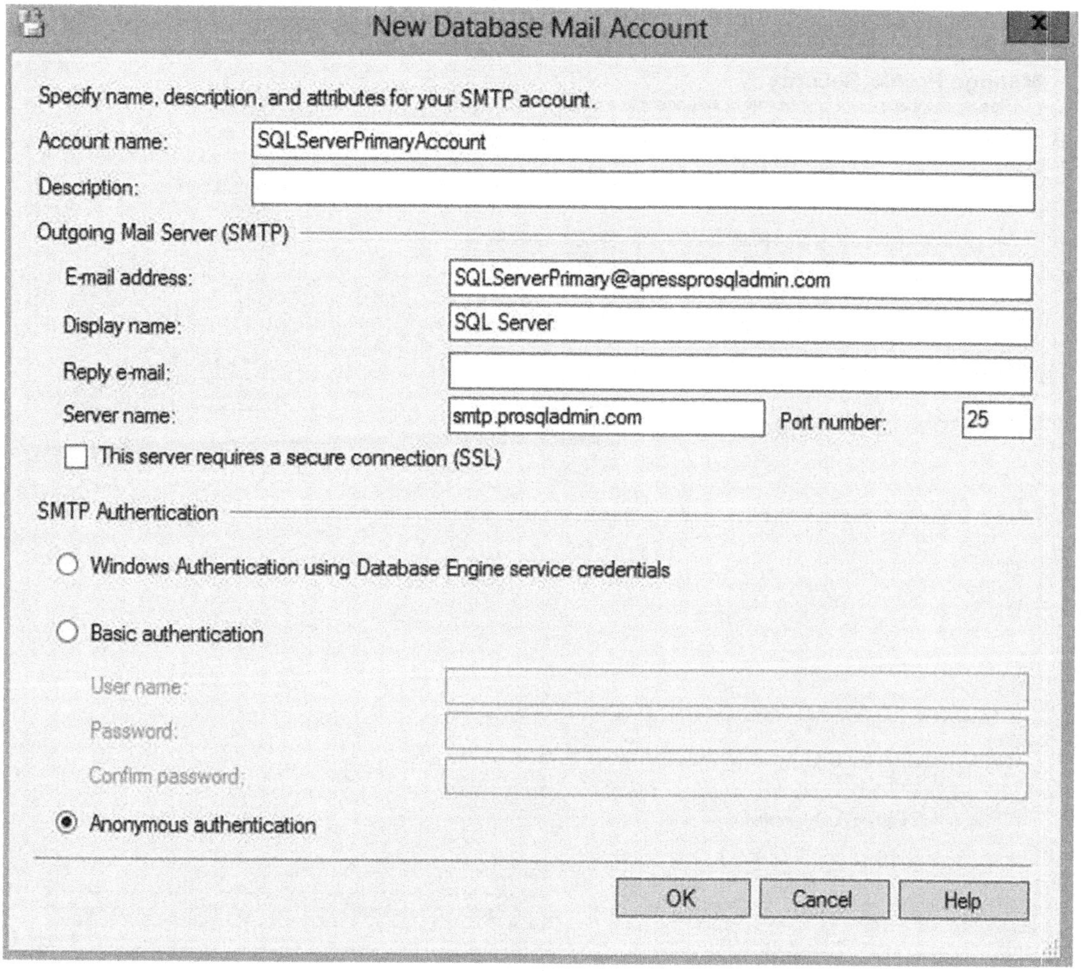

Figure 21-14. *The New Database Mail Account dialog box*

In this dialog box, we specify a name for the account and, optionally, a description. We then need to specify the email address that we will use to send mails, along with the name and port of the SMTP server that will deliver the messages. You can also specify a display name for when the e-mails are received. For DBAs who receive the notification, it helps if the display name includes the server/instance from which the notification was generated.

After adding the account, we can move to the Manage Profile Security page of the wizard. This page has two tabs: Public Profiles and Private Profiles. We configure our profile as public and also mark it as the default profile. Making the profile public means that any user with access to the MSDB database can send e-mail from that profile. If we make the profile private, then we need to specify a list of users or roles who may use the profile for sending e-mail. Marking the profile as default makes the profile default for the user or role. Each user or role can have one default profile. The Public Profiles tab is displayed in Figure 21-15.

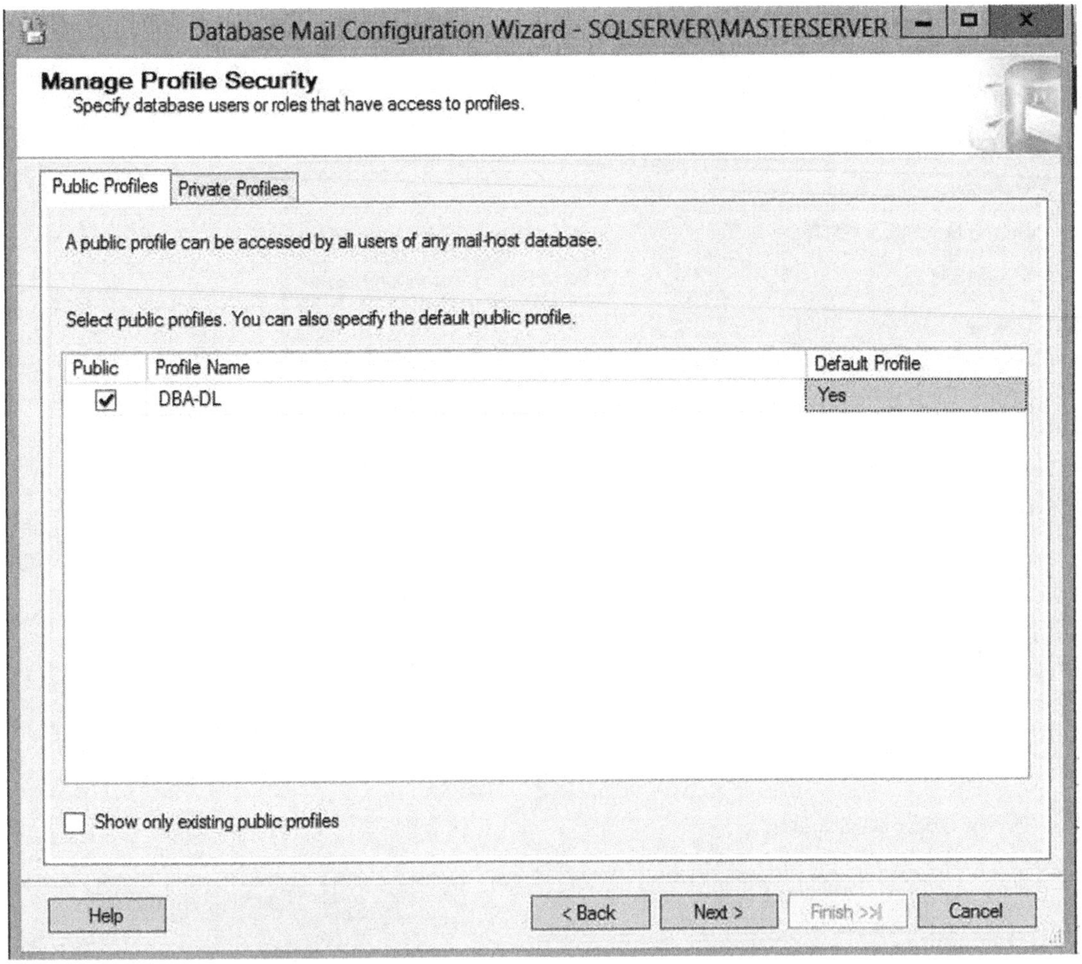

Figure 21-15. *The Public Profiles tab*

On the Configure System Parameters page of the wizard, illustrated in Figure 21-16, you can alter the default system properties, which control how mail is handled. This includes specifying the number of times an account should be retried and the time lapse between retries. It also involves setting the maximum allowable size of an e-mail and configuring a blacklist of extensions. The Database Mail Executable Minimum Lifetime (Seconds) setting configures how long the Database Mail process should remain active when there are no e-mails in the queue waiting to be sent. The Logging Level can be configured with the following settings:

> **Normal:** Logs errors
>
> **Extended:** Logs errors, warnings, and informational messages
>
> **Verbose:** Logs errors, warnings, informational messages, success messages, and internal messages

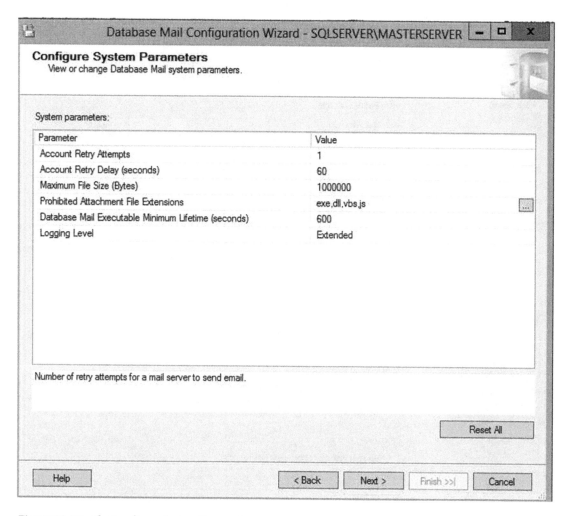

Figure 21-16. *The Configure System Parameters page*

■ **Caution** Unfortunately, attachment exclusions are implemented as a blacklist, as opposed to a whitelist. This means that to achieve the best balance of security and operational support, you should give time and thought to the file types that should be excluded.

On the Complete The Wizard page, you are provided with a summary of the tasks that will be performed. In our scenario, this includes creating a new account, creating a new profile, adding the account to the profile, and configuring the profile's security.

We now need to configure SQL Server Agent to use our mail profile. To do this, we select Properties from the SQL Server Agent context menu in Object Explorer to invoke the SQL Server Agent Properties dialog box and navigate to the Alert System page, shown in Figure 21-17.

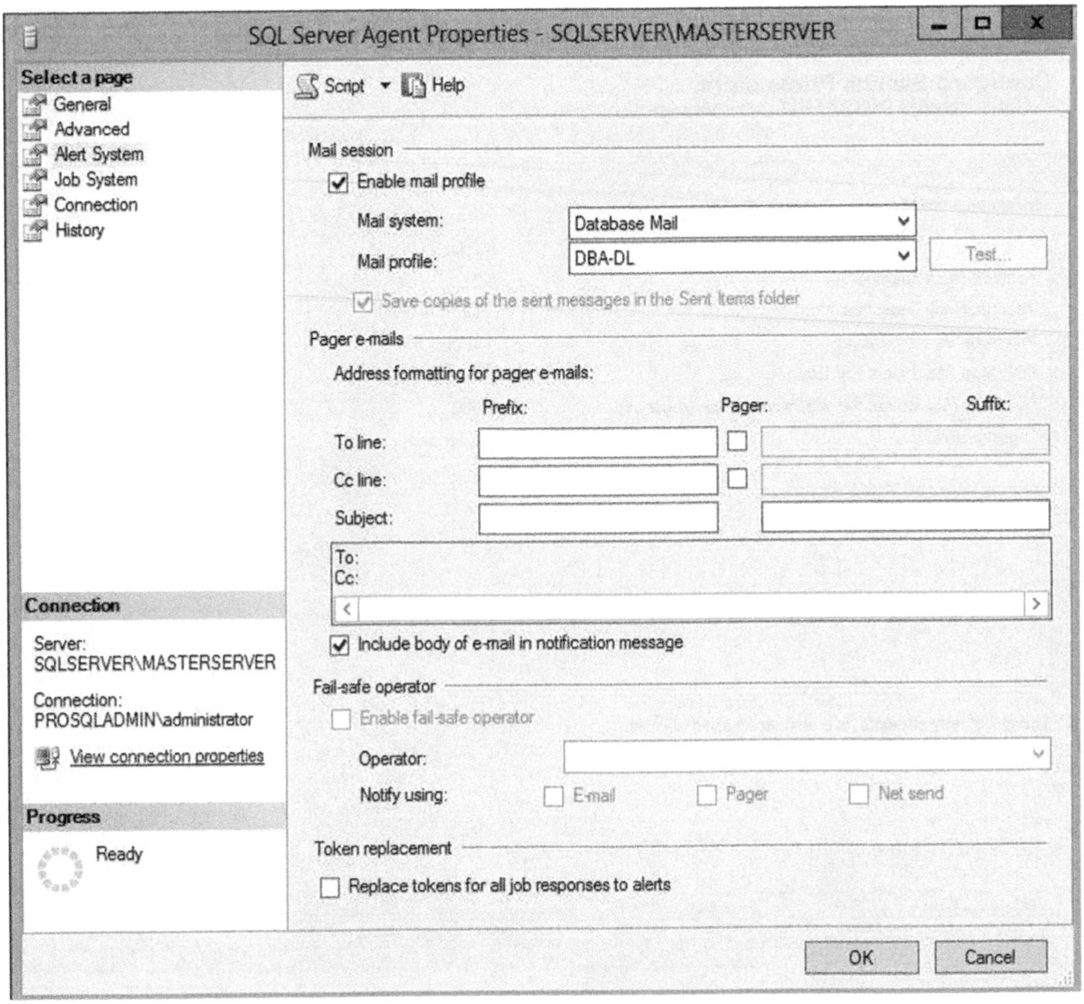

Figure 21-17. *The Alert System page*

On this page, we check the Enable Mail Profile check box before selecting the DBA-DL profile from the drop-down list. After we exit the dialog box, operators are able to use Database Mail.

Creating the Operator

Now that Database Mail has been configured, we need to create an operator that will receive e-mails in the event that our job fails. We can access the New Operator dialog box by drilling through SQL Server Agent in Object Explorer and by selecting New Operator from the Operators context menu. The General page of the New Operator dialog box is shown in Figure 21-18.

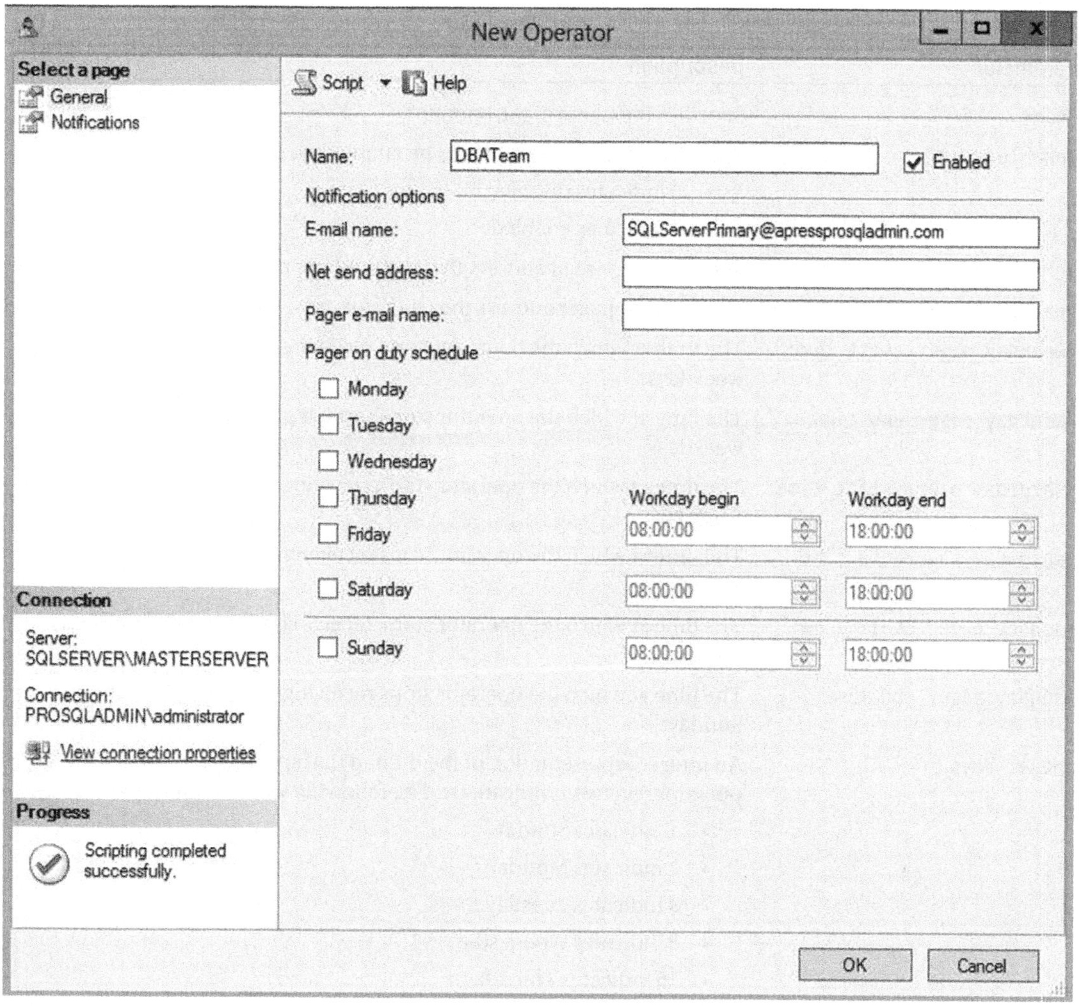

Figure 21-18. *The General page*

On this page, we specify a name for the operator and also add the e-mail address that the operator will be using. This must match the e-mail address that has been configured within Database Mail. The Notifications page displays details of the alerts and notifications that are already configured for the operator, so it is irrelevant to us at this point.

To create the operator using T-SQL, we need to use the sp_add_operator system stored procedure. This procedure accepts the parameters detailed in Table 21-7.

Table 21-7. *sp_add_operator Parameters*

Parameter	Description
@name	Specifies the name of the operator.
@enabled	Specifies if the operator should be enabled on creation. • 0 indicates disabled. • 1 indicates enabled.
@email_address	Specifies the e-mail address that the operator uses.
@pager_address	Specifies the pager address the Operator uses.
@weekday_pager_start_time	The time at which the operator starts receiving pager notifications on weekdays.
@weekday_pager_end_time	The time at which the operator stops receiving pager notifications on weekdays.
@saturday_pager_start_time	The time at which the operator starts receiving pager notifications on Saturdays.
@saturday_pager_end_time	The time at which the operator stops receiving pager notifications on Saturdays.
@sunday_pager_start_time	The time at which the operator starts receiving pager notifications on Sundays.
@sunday_pager_end_time	The time at which the operator stops receiving pager notifications on Sundays.
@pager_days	An integer representation of the bitmap that specifies which days the operator receives notifications. The following values represent each day: • 1 indicates Sunday. • 2 indicates Monday. • 4 indicates Tuesday. • 8 indicates Wednesday. • 16 indicates Thursday. • 32 indicates Friday. • 64 indicates Saturday. When an operator is active for multiple days, then these values should be added together. For example, if an operator should only receive notifications on Saturdays and Sundays, then the value 96 should be passed to this parameter.
@netsend_address	The network address used by the operator.
@category_name	Optimally specifies a category to which the operator belongs.

■ **Note**   For completeness, `pager` and `netsend` options are included in Table 21-7 despite being deprecated.

To create our operator using the `sp_add_operator` system stored procedure, we can use the command in Listing 21-7.

Listing 21-7. Creating an Operator

```
USE MSDB
GO

EXEC msdb.dbo.sp_add_operator
                @name=N'DBATeam',
                @enabled=1,
                @email_address=N'SQLServerPrimary@apressprosqladmin.com' ;
GO
```

■ **Tip**   You can modify operators using the `sp_update_operator` system stored procedure.

Creating the Job

Now that all of the prerequisites are in place, we can create the SQL Server Agent job. We can achieve this in SQL Server Management Studio by drilling through SQL Server Agent in Object Explorer and choosing New Job from the Jobs context menu. This causes the General page of the New Job dialog box to display, as illustrated in Figure 21-19.

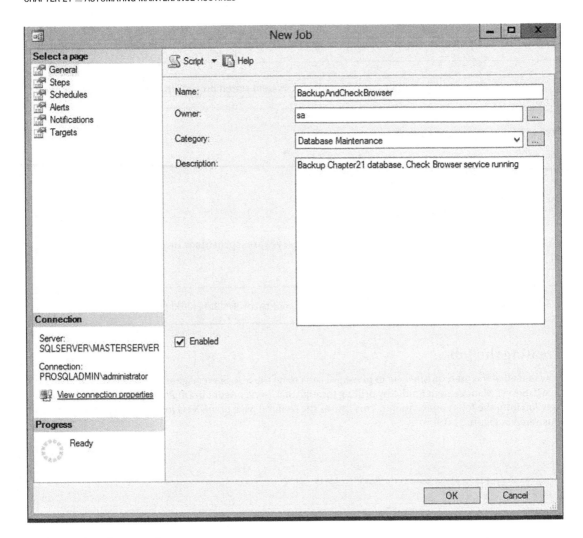

Figure 21-19. *The General page*

On this page, we use the Name field to specify a name for our job and, optionally, add a description in the Description field. It's also optional to add the job to a category; in our instance, we have added the job to the Database Maintenance category by selecting it from the drop-down list. We also check the Enabled box so that the job will be active as soon as it is created.

We also specify that the job owner will be sa. This is a controversial topic, but I generally recommend this approach for the following reason: job ownership does not matter much. No matter who owns the job, it functions in the same way. If the owner's account is dropped, however, then the job no longer functions. If you make sa the owner, then there is no chance of this situation occurring. If you are using the Windows Authentication model as opposed to mixed-mode authentication, however, then it is reasonable to use the SQL Server Agent service account as an alternative. This is because, although it is possible that you will change the service account and drop the associated login, it is more unlikely than dropping other user's logins, such as a DBAs' login, when he leaves the company.

On the Steps page of the dialog box, we use the New button to add our first step—backing up the Chapter21 database. The General page of the New Job Step dialog box is illustrated in Figure 21-20.

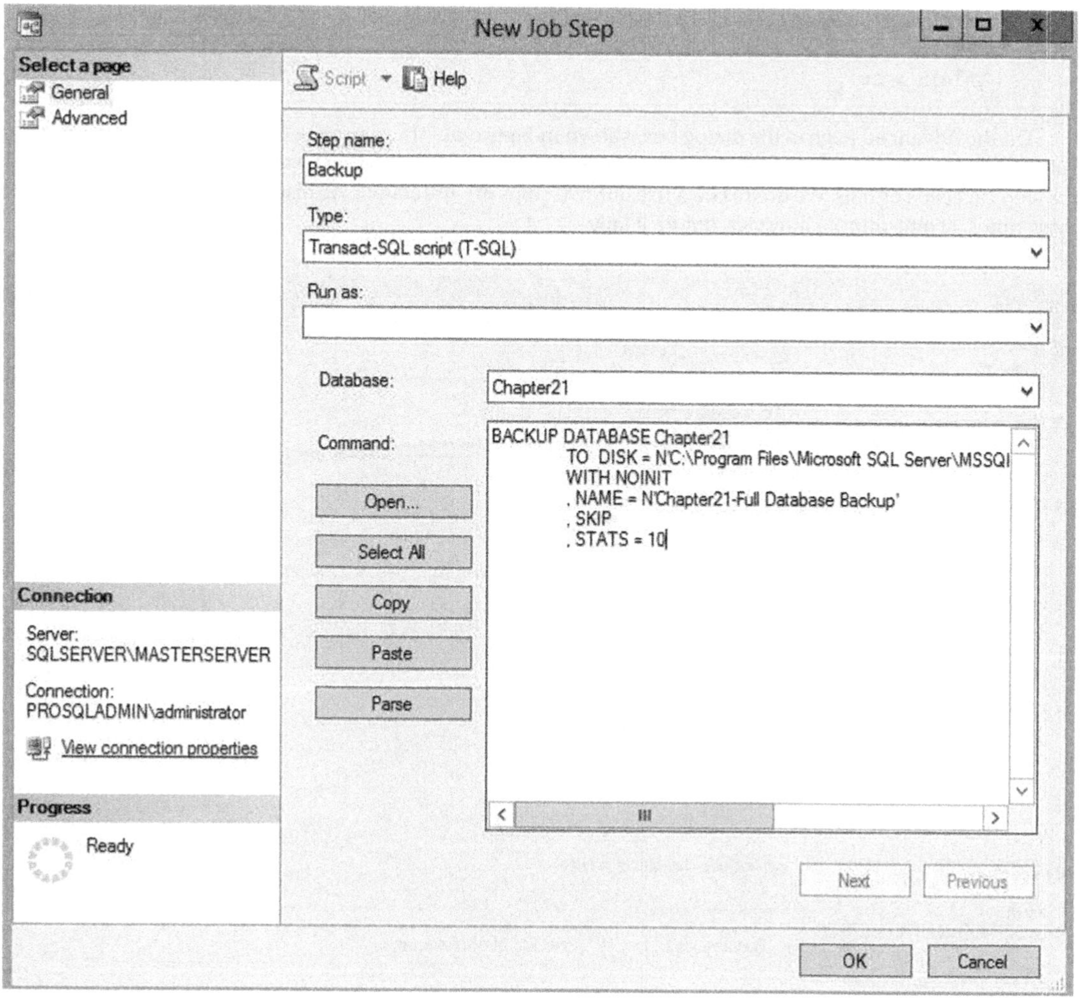

Figure 21-20. *The General page of the New Job Step dialog box*

On this page, we enter Backup as the name of the job step and type the `BACKUP DATABASE` command in the Command field. The Type field allows us to select the subsystem to use, but it defaults to T-SQL, so we do not need to alter this. Listing 21-8 contains the backup script.

■ **Tip**   Make sure to always test scripts before you add them to your jobs.

Listing 21-8. Backup Script

```
BACKUP DATABASE Chapter21
      TO DISK =
          N'C:\ Program Files\Microsoft SQL Server\MSSQL12.MASTERSERVER\MSSQL\Backup\
          Chapter21.bak'
      WITH NOINIT
```

```
,NAME = N'Chapter21-Full Database Backup'
,SKIP
,STATS = 10 ;
```

On the Advanced page of the dialog box, shown in Figure 21-21, we use the On Success Action and On Failure Action drop-down boxes to configure the step so that it moves to the next step, regardless of whether the step succeeds or fails. We do this because our two steps are unrelated. We also configure the step to retry three times, at one-minute intervals, before it fails.

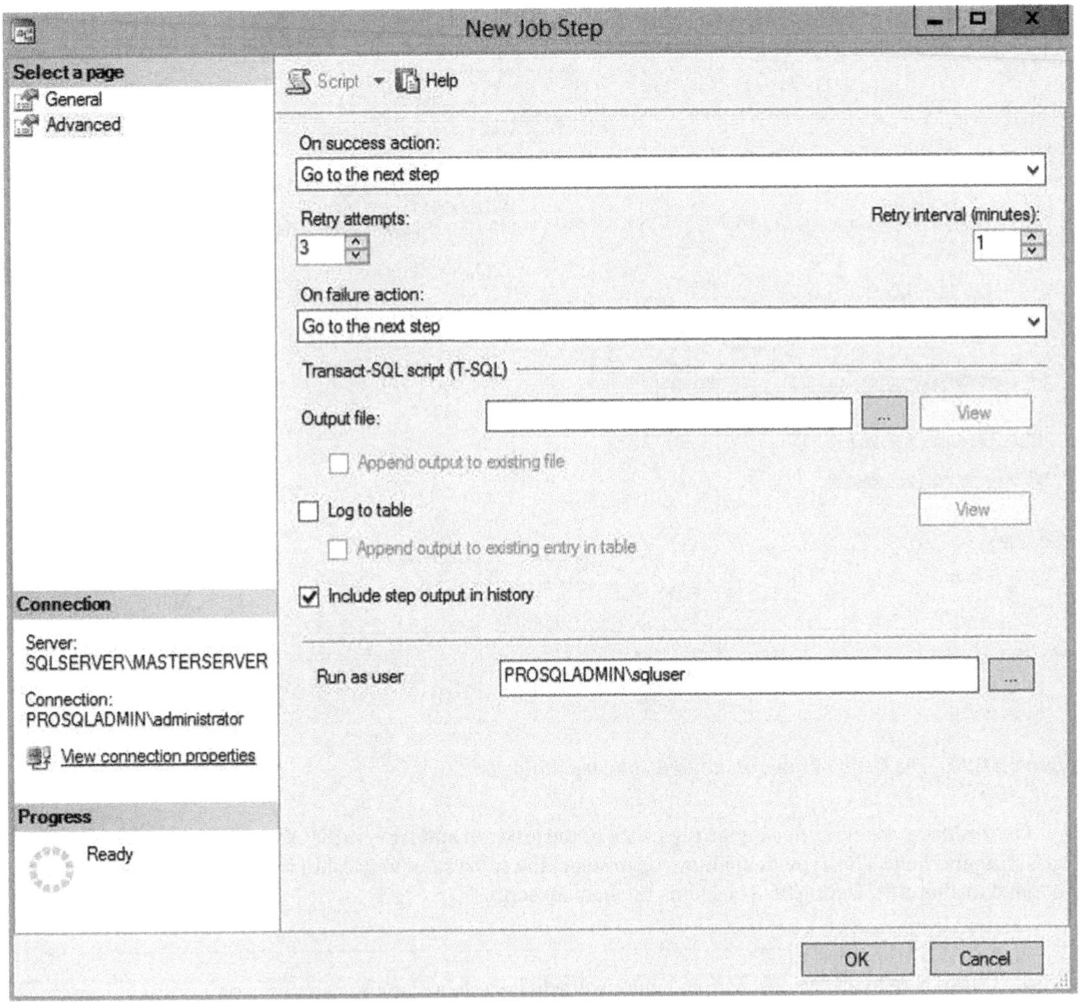

Figure 21-21. *The Advanced page*

We check the Include Step Output In History box so that the step output is included in the job history (doing so helps DBAs troubleshoot any issues) and configure the step to run as the SQLUser user. We configure the Run as user option because, as previously discussed, job steps of the T-SQL type use EXECUTE AS technology, instead of a proxy account, to implement security.

Once we exit the dialog box, we need to use the New button, on the Steps page of the New Job dialog box again to add our second job step. This time, on the General page, we specify the PowerShell type and enter the PowerShell script that checks the status of the SQL Server Browser service. We also use the Run As box to specify that the step runs under the context of the PowerShellProxy proxy. This is demonstrated in Figure 21-22. Listing 21-9 shows the command that we use.

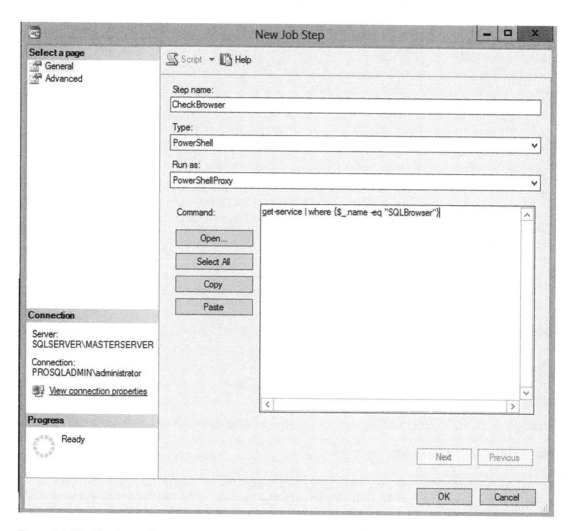

Figure 21-22. *The General page*

Listing 21-9. Checking Browser Service

```
Get-Service | Where {$_.name -eq "SQLBrowser"}
```

On the Advanced page, shown in Figure 21-23, we choose to include the step output in the job history. We can leave all other options with their default values.

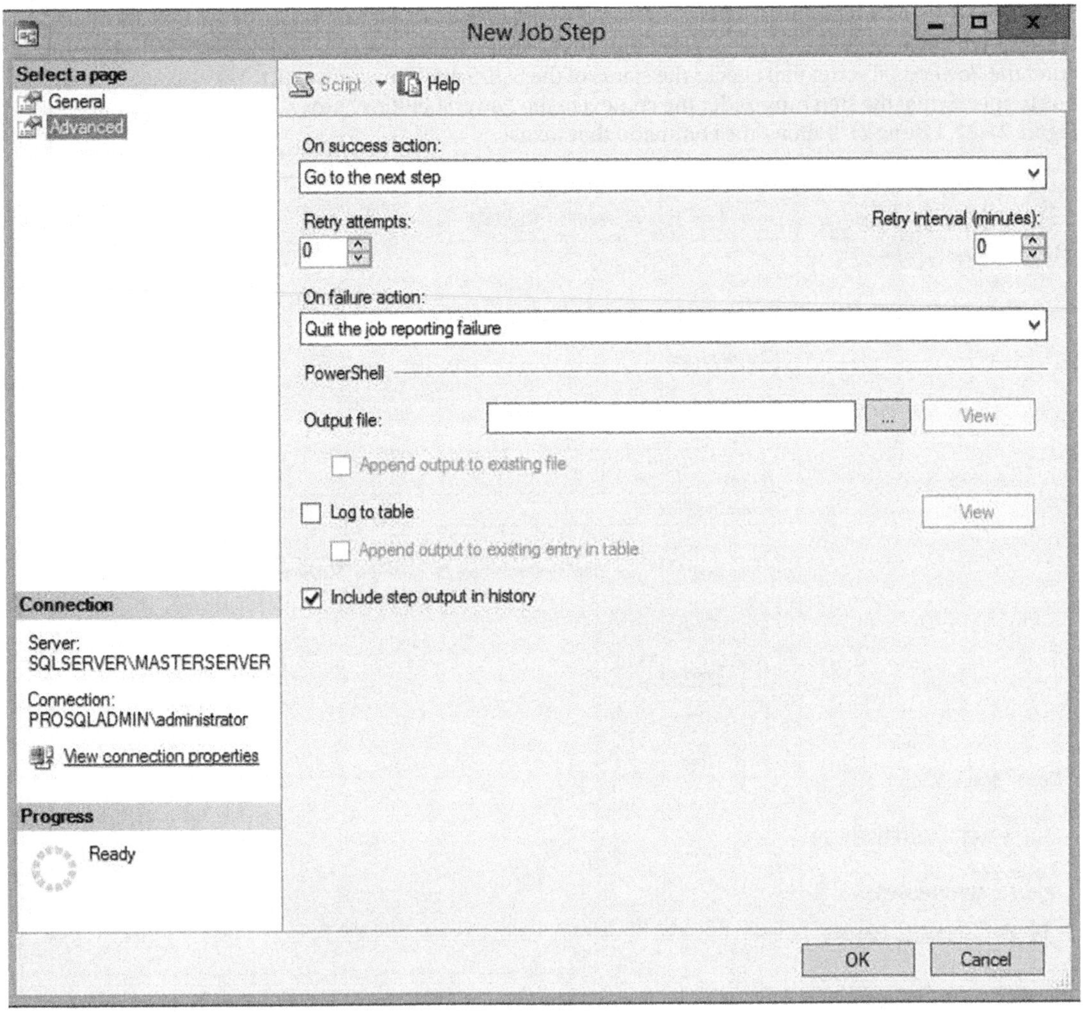

Figure 21-23. *The Advanced page*

When we return to the Steps page of the New Job dialog box, we see both of our steps listed in the correct order, as shown in Figure 21-24. If we wish to change the order of the steps, however, we can use the up and down arrows in the Move Step section. We can also bypass early steps by selecting to start the job at a later step using the Start Step drop-down list.

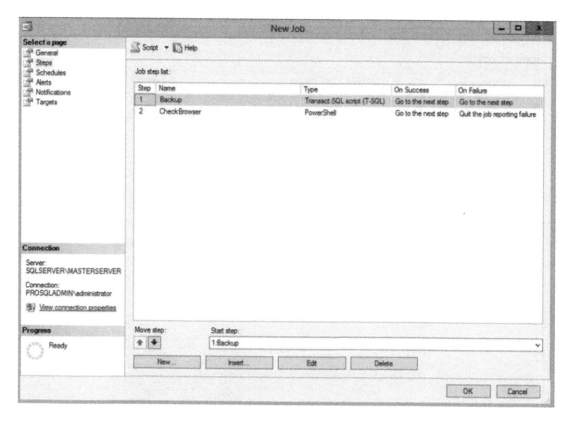

Figure 21-24. *The Steps page*

On the Schedules page of the wizard, we click the Pick button; doing so displays a list of existing schedules in the Pick Schedule For Job dialog box (see Figure 21-25). We use this dialog box to select our maintenance schedule.

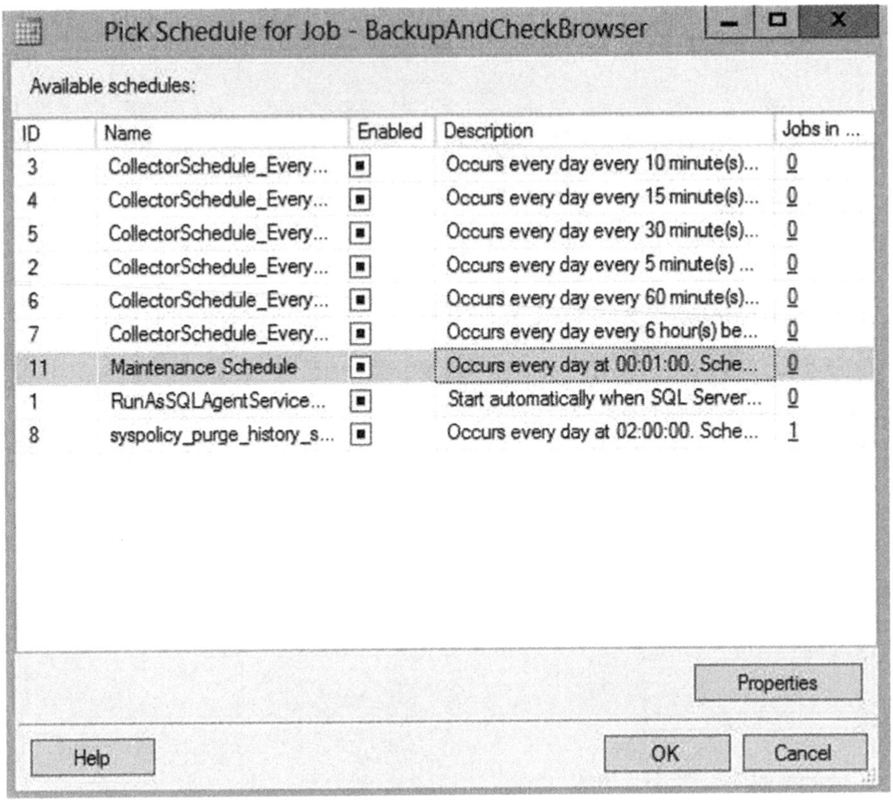

Figure 21-25. *The Pick Schedule For Job dialog box*

After we exit the dialog box, the Schedule displays on the Schedules page of the Job Properties dialog box, as shown in Figure 21-26.

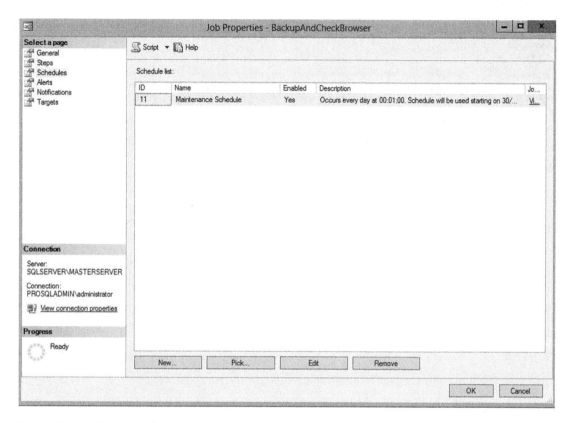

Figure 21-26. *The Schedules page*

You can use the Alerts page to organize alerts for the job. This is not relevant to our scenario right now, but alerts are discussed later in the chapter.

On the Notifications page, we configure the DBATeam operator we want notified by e-mail in the event that the job fails. We do this by checking the E-mail check box and selecting our DBATeam operator from the drop-down list, as shown in Figure 21-27.

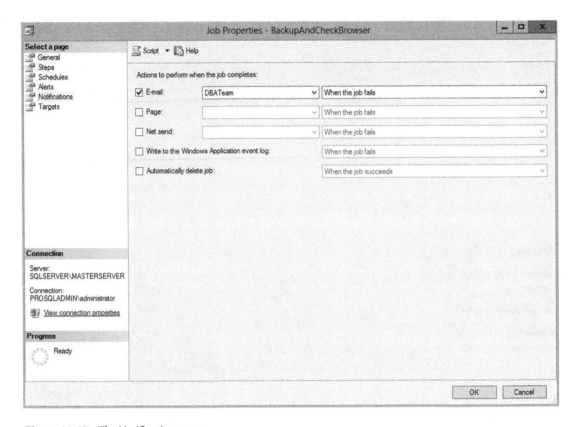

Figure 21-27. *The Notifications page*

You can use the Targets page to configure multiserver jobs, which are not relevant to our current scenario, but we do discuss them later in this chapter.

To create a job using T-SQL, we first run the sp_add_job system stored procedure to create the shell of the job. The sp_add_job procedure accepts the parameters detailed in Table 21-8.

Table 21-8. *sp_add_job Parameters*

Parameter	Description
@job_name	Specifies a name for the job.
@enabled	Specifies if the job should be enabled on creation.
	• 0 indicates disabled.
	• 1 indicates enabled.
@description	A textual description of the job.
@start_step_id	The job step ID of the step that should be the first step executed.
@category_name	Specifies the name of the category in which the job should be included.
@category_id	Specifies the ID of the category in which the job should be included.
@owner_login_name	Specifies the login that will own the job.

(continued)

Table 21-8. (*continued*)

Parameter	Description
@notify_level_eventlog	Specifies when the job status should be written to the Windows Application Event Log. • 0 indicates Never. • 1 indicates On Success. • 2 indicates On Failure. • 3 indicates Always.
@notify_level_email	Specifies when the job status should be sent as an e-mail notification. • 0 indicates Never. • 1 indicates On Success. • 2 indicates On Failure. • 3 indicates Always.
@notify_level_netsend	Specifies when the job status should be sent as a NET SEND notification. • 0 indicates Never. • 1 indicates On Success. • 2 indicates On Failure. • 3 indicates Always.
@notify_level_page	Specifies when the job status should be sent as a pager notification. • 0 indicates Never. • 1 indicates On Success. • 2 indicates On Failure. • 3 indicates Always.
@notify_email_operator_name	The name of the operator that should be notified via e-mail.
@notify_netsend_operator_name	The name of the operator that should be notified via NETSEND.
@notify_page_operator_name	The name of the operator that should be notified via pager.
@delete_level	Specifies what status should result in the job being deleted. • 0 indicates Never. • 1 indicates On Success. • 2 indicates On Failure. • 3 indicates Always.
@job_id	An OUTPUT parameter that returns the ID of the job.

To create the shell of the job in our scenario, we use the command in Listing 21-10.

Listing 21-10. Creating a Job

```
USE MSDB
GO

EXEC sp_add_job @job_name=N'BackupAndCheckBrowser',
                @enabled=1,
                @notify_level_eventlog=0,
                @notify_level_email=2,
                @notify_level_netsend=0,
                @notify_level_page=0,
                @delete_level=0,
                @description=N'Backup Chapter21 database, Check Browser service running',
                @category_name=N'Database Maintenance',
                @owner_login_name=N'sa',
                @notify_email_operator_name=N'DBATeam' ;
GO
```

We now need to add the job steps to the job by using the sp_add_jobstep system stored procedure. This procedure accepts the parameters detailed in Table 21-9.

Table 21-9. *sp_add_jobstep Paremeters*

Parameter	Description
@job_id	Specifies the GUID of the job. If omitted, then the @job_name parameter must be specified.
@job_name	Specifies the name of the job. If omitted, then the @job_id parameter must be specified.
@step_id	The sequential ID of the job step within the job. Used to define the order of the steps.
@step_name	Specifies a name for the job step.
@subsystem	Specifies the subsystem to use for the job step. Table 21-4 lists the acceptable values.
@command	The command that should be executed.
@cmdexec_success_code	The success code expected to be returned from the operating system.
@on_success_action	Specifies the action that should be performed if the step succeeds. • 1 indicates Quit With Success. • 2 indicates Quit With Failure. • 3 indicates Go To Next Step. • 4 indicates that the next step to be executed is specified by @on_success_step_id.
@on_success_step_id	The step ID of the next step to be executed if a value of 4 has been passed to @on_success_action.

(continued)

Table 21-9. (*continued*)

Parameter	Description
@on_fail_action	Specifies the action that should be performed if the step fails. • 1 indicates Quit With Success. • 2 indicates Quit With Failure. • 3 indicates Go To Next Step. • 4 indicates that the next step to be executed is specified by @on_success_step_id.
@on_fail_step_id	The step ID of the next step to be executed, if a value of 4 has been passed to @on_fail_action.
@database_name	If the subsystem is T-SQL, specifies the database name in which to execute the command.
@database_user_name	If the subsystem is T-SQL, specifies the database user to use as the security context for executing the command.
@retry_attempts	Specifies how many times the step should be retried in the event of failure.
@retry_interval	Specifies an interval between retries in the event of failure.
@output_file_name	Specifies the fully qualified file name of a file where the output of the step should be saved.
@flags	Controls the behavior of the step output. • 0 indicates that the output file should be overwritten. • 2 indicates that the output should be appended to the output file. • 4 indicates that T-SQL job step output should be written to the step history. • 8 indicates that the log should be written to a table and overwrite existing entries. • 16 indicates that the log should be appended to the log table. • 32 indicates that all output should be written to the job history. • 64 indicates that a Windows event should be created to use as an abort signal when the subsystem is cmdexec.
@proxy_id	The ID of the proxy that should run the job step.
@proxy_name	The name of the proxy that should run the job step.

In our scenario, we use the script in Listing 21-11 to add our two job steps to the job.

Listing 21-11. Adding Job Steps

```
USE MSDB
GO

EXEC sp_add_jobstep
                @job_name=N'BackupAndCheckBrowser',
                @step_name=N'Backup',
                @step_id=1,
                @cmdexec_success_code=0,
```

```
                @on_success_action=3,
                @on_success_step_id=0,
                @on_fail_action=3,
                @on_fail_step_id=0,
                @retry_attempts=3,
                @retry_interval=1,
                @os_run_priority=0, @subsystem=N'TSQL',
                @command=N'BACKUP DATABASE Chapter21 TO  DISK =
N''C:\Program Files\Microsoft SQL Server\MSSQL12.MASTERSERVER\MSSQL\Backup\Chapter21.bak''
     WITH NOINIT
     , NAME = N''Chapter21-Full Database Backup''
     , SKIP
     , STATS = 10',
                @database_name=N'Chapter21',
                @database_user_name=N'PROSQLADMIN\sqluser',
                @flags=4 ;

EXEC sp_add_jobstep @job_name=N'BackupAndCheckBrowser', @step_name=N'CheckBrowser',
                @step_id=2,
                @cmdexec_success_code=0,
                @on_success_action=1,
                @on_success_step_id=0,
                @on_fail_action=2,
                @on_fail_step_id=0,
                @retry_attempts=0,
                @retry_interval=0,
                @os_run_priority=0, @subsystem=N'PowerShell',
                @command=N'get-service | where {$_.name -eq "SQLBrowser"}',
                @database_name=N'master',
                @flags=32,
                @proxy_name=N'PowerShellProxy' ;
GO
```

Next, we need to attach our schedule to the job; to do so, we use the sp_attach_schedule system stored procedure. This procedure accepts the parameters detailed in Table 21-10.

Table 21-10. sp_attach_schedule Parameters

Parameter	Description
@job_id	The GUID of the job. If omitted, then @job_name must be specified.
@job_name	The name of the job. If omitted then @job_id must be specified.
@schedule_id	The ID of the schedule. If omitted, then @schedule_name must be specified.
@schedule_name	The name of the schedule. If omitted, then @schedule_id must be specified.

To attach our schedule, we use the command in Listing 21-12.

Listing 21-12. Attaching the Schedule

```
USE MSDB
GO

EXEC sp_attach_schedule
            @job_name='BackupAndCheckBrowser',
            @schedule_name='Maintenance Schedule' ;
GO
```

Finally, we need to register the job on our instance. To do this, we use the sp_add_jobserver system stored procedure. This procedure accepts the parameters detailed in Table 21-11.

Table 21-11. *sy_add_jobserver Parameters*

Parameter	Description
@job_id	The GUID of the job. If omitted, then @job_name must be specified.
@job_name	The name of the job. If omitted then @job_id must be specified.
@server_name	The name of the server on which you are registering the job.

To register the job on our instance, we use the command in Listing 21-13. This targets our job against the local instance.

Listing 21-13. Registering the Job

```
USE MSDB
GO

EXEC sp_add_jobserver
        @job_name=N'BackupAndCheckBrowser',
        @server_name = N'SQLSERVER\MASTERSERVER' ;
GO
```

Monitoring and Managing Jobs

Although jobs are usually scheduled to run automatically, you still encounter monitoring and maintenance requirements, such as executing jobs manually and viewing job history. These tasks are discussed in the following sections.

Executing Jobs

Even if a job is scheduled to run automatically, at times you may wish to execute a job on an ad-hoc basis. For example, if you have a job that is scheduled to run nightly to take full backups of the databases within your instance, you may wish to execute it manually just before a code release or software upgrade.

A job can be executed manually in SQL Server Management Studio by drilling through SQL Server Agent | Jobs in Object Explorer and then selecting Start Job At Step from the Job's context menu; doing this invokes the Start Job dialog box. Figure 21-28 displays the Start Job dialog box for the BackupAndCheckBrowser job. In this dialog box, you can select the first step of the job you want to run before you use the Start button to execute the job.

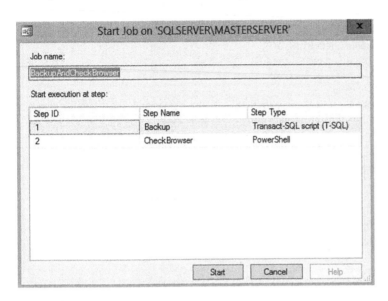

Figure 21-28. *Start Job dialog box*

To execute a job using T-SQL, you can use the sp_start_job system stored procedure. This procedure accepts the parameters detailed in Table 21-12.

Table 21-12. *sp_start_job Parameters*

Parameter	Description
@job_name	The name of the job to execute. If NULL, then the @job_name parameter must be specified.
@job_id	The ID of the job to execute. If NULL, then the @job_name parameter must be specified.
@server_name	Used for multiserver jobs. Specifies the target server on which to run the job.
@step_name	The name of the job step where execution should begin.

To run our BackupAndCheckBrowser job, we execute the command in Listing 21-14. Once a job has been executed, it cannot be executed again until it has completed.

Listing 21-14. Executing a Job

```
EXEC sp_start_job @job_name=N'BackupAndCheckBrowser' ;
```

If we wanted the job to start executing at a later step, we can use the @step_name parameter. For example, in our scenario, imagine that we want to execute our job in order to check that the SQL Server Browser service is running, but do not want the database backup to occur beforehand. To achieve this, we execute the command in Listing 21-15.

Listing 21-15. Starting a Job from a Specific Step

```
EXEC sp_start_job @job_name=N'BackupAndCheckBrowser', @step_name = 'CheckBrowser' ;
```

Viewing Job History

You can view the job history for a specific job by selecting View History from the Job context menu in SQL Server Agent | Jobs within Object Explorer, or for all jobs by opening Job Activity Monitor, which you can find under the SQL Server Agent node in Object Explorer. Figure 21-29 shows what the job history of our BackupAndCheckBrowser job looks like after a single execution.

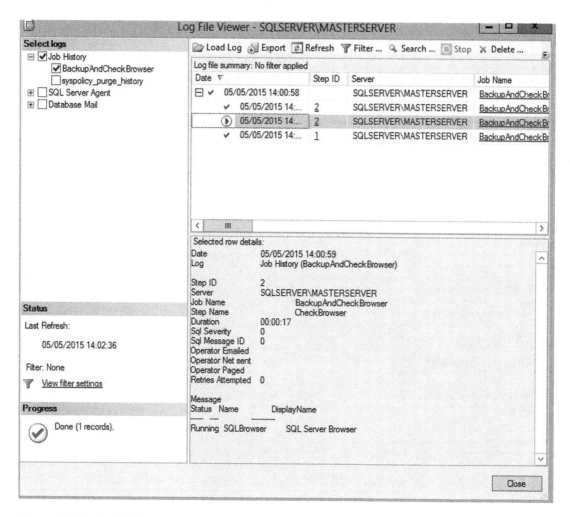

Figure 21-29. *The job history*

Here, you can see that we have drilled through Job History to see the history of each individual step. After highlighting the Step 2 progress entry, we can see that the results of the PowerShell script have been written to the step history and they show us that the SQL Server Browser service is running, as expected.

Creating Alerts

Creating an alert allows you to proactively respond to conditions that occur within your instance by either notifying an operator, running a job, or both. On our instance, we want to notify the DBATeam operator in the event that our Chapter21 log file becomes more than 75 percent full.

To create this alert in SQL Server Management Studio, we drill through SQL Server Agent in Object Explorer and select New Alert from the Alerts context menu. This causes the General page of the New Alert dialog box to display. This page is shown in Figure 21-30.

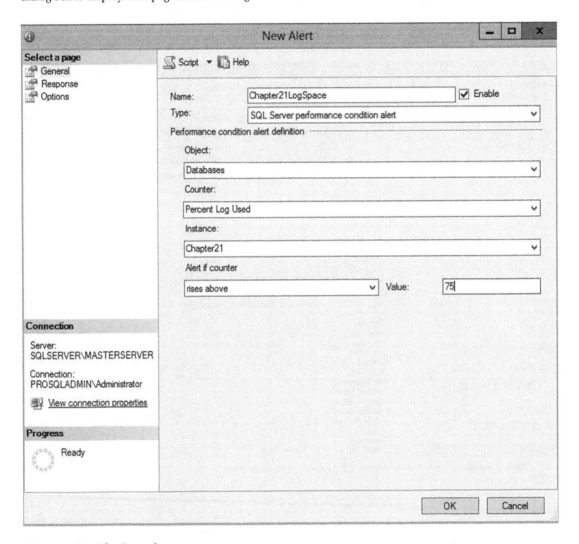

Figure 21-30. The General page

On this page of the dialog box, we use the Name field to specify a name for our alert and select SQL Server Performance Condition Alert from the Type drop-down list. This causes the options within the page to dynamically update. We then select the Percent Log Used counter from the Databases object and specify that we are interested in the Chapter21 instance of our object. (There is an instance of this counter for each database that resides on the instance). Finally, we specify that the alert should be triggered if the value of this counter rises above 75 within the Alert If Counter section of the page.

On the Response page of the dialog box, shown in Figure 21-31, we check the Notify Operators box if the condition is met, and then select an e-mail notification for our DBATeam operator.

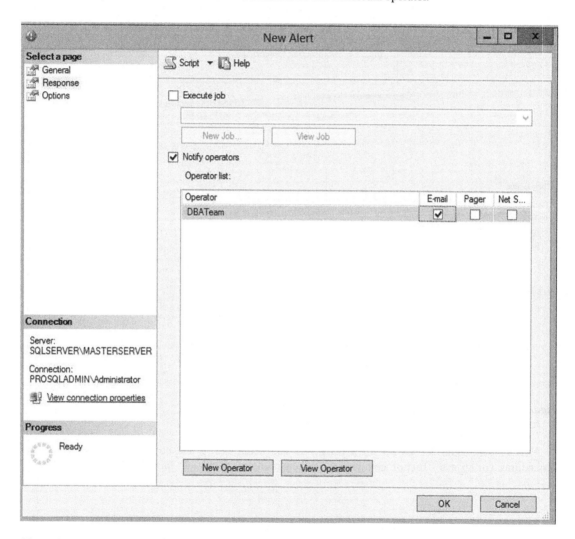

Figure 21-31. *Response page*

On the Options page of the dialog box, you can specify if alert error text should be included in the notification and also additional information to include. You can also configure a delay to occur between occurrences of the response being triggered. This can help you avoid duplicate notifications or needlessly running a job to fix an issue that is already being resolved. Figure 21-32 shows that we included the server/ instance name in our notification to assist the DBAs in identifying the source of the alert.

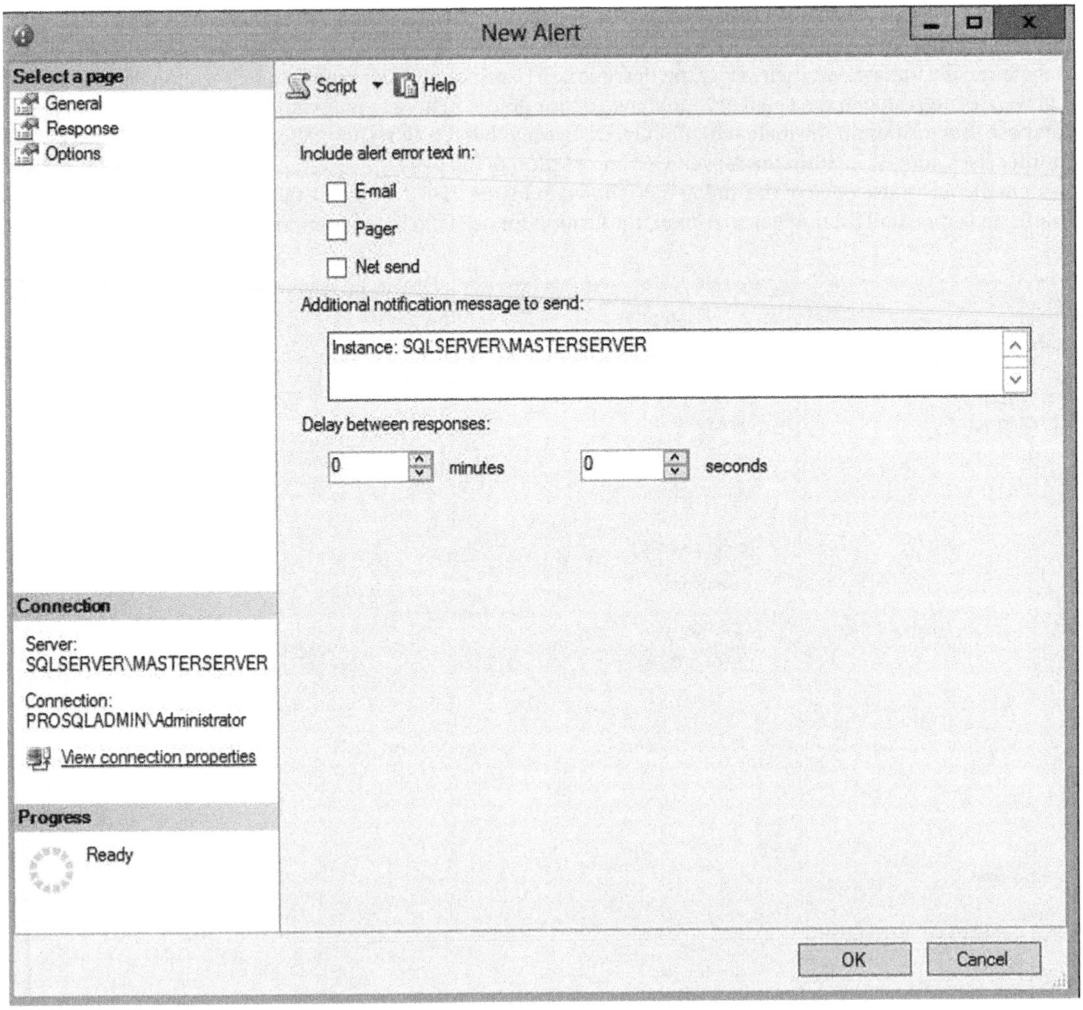

Figure 21-32. *The Options page*

To create the same alert via T-SQL, we use the `sp_add_alert` and `sp_add_notification` system stored procedures. The `sp_add_alert` procedure accepts the parameters detailed in Table 21-13.

Table 21-13. sp_add_alert Parameters

Parameter	Description
@name	Specifies a name for the alert.
@message_id	When the alert is triggered by a SQL Server event, this parameter specifies the error number that causes the alert to fire.
@severity	When the alert is triggered by a SQL Server event, this parameter specifies the error severity level that causes the alert to fire.
@enabled	Specifies if the alert should be enabled on creation. • 0 indicates disabled. • 1 indicates enabled.
@delay_between_responses	If there should be a delay between the responses being triggered, then this specifies the duration of the delay, in seconds.
@notification_message	Optionally specifies a message that should be included in the notification.
@include_event_description_in	Specifies when the alert error message should be included in the notification. • 0 indicates never. • 1 indicates when operators are notified by e-mail. • 2 indicates when operators are notified by the pager. • 4 indicates when operators are notified by NET SEND. To send the error text in multiple instances, add these values together. For example, if the error text should always be sent, then you would pass a value of 7.
@database_name	When the alert is triggered by a SQL Server event, specifies the name of the database in which the error must occur in order for the alert to fire.
@event_description_keyword	When the alert is triggered by a SQL Server event, specifies a string of characters that must appear in the error message in order for the alert to fire.
@job_id	If the response should include running a SQL Server Agent job, then either the job ID or name must be specified. Use this parameter to specify the ID.
@job_name	If the response should include running a SQL Server Agent job, then either the Job ID or name must be specified. Use this parameter to specify the name.
@performance_condition	When responding to a performance condition, specify the condition in the following format: Object | Counter | Target | Comparator | Value.
@category_name	Specifies the name of the alert category.
@wmi_namespace	When responding to a WMI event, specifies the WMI namespace.
@wmi_query	When responding to a WMI event, specifies the WMI Query that will run.

In our scenario, we can create the alert by using the script in Listing 21-16.

Listing 21-16. Adding an Alert

```
USE MSDB
GO

EXEC sp_add_alert
                @name=N'Chapter21LogSpace',
                @enabled=1,
                @delay_between_responses=0,
                @include_event_description_in=0,
                @notification_message=N'Instance: SQLSERVER\MASTERSERVER',
                @performance_condition=N'Databases|Percent Log Used|Chapter21|>|75' ;
GO
```

We now need to add the notification. The sp_add_notification system stored procedure accepts the parameters detailed in Table 21-14.

Table 21-14. *sp_add_notification Parameters*

Parameter	Description
@alert_name	The name of the alert to which the notification is attached.
@operator_name	The name of the operator that is notified.
@notification_method	Specifies how the operator is notified.* • 1 indicates e-mail. • 2 indicates pager. • 4 indicates NETSEND. You can combine these values using the logical OR operator.

* *Option 2 (pager) and 4 (NETSEND) are deprecated.*

To add our notification, we use the script in Listing 21-17.

Listing 21-17. Adding a Notification

```
USE msdb
GO

EXEC sp_add_notification
                @alert_name=N'Chapter21LogSpace',
                @operator_name=N'DBATeam',
                @notification_method = 1 ;
GO
```

Multiserver Jobs

Administration can be drastically simplified when you use multiserver administration. In a multiserver environment, you can configure one instance as a master server (MSX) and then other servers as target servers (TSX). You can then create a set of maintenance jobs on the MSX and configure them to run on the TSXs, or a subset of the TSXs.

Configuring the MSX and TSX Servers

Before creating multiserver jobs, you must first prepare the environment. The first step is to edit the Registry on the MSX and set the value of the AllowDownloadedJobsToMatchProxyName REG_DWORD to 1, which allows jobs to match the proxy name. You can find this value under the SQL Server Agent key, which is located under the Software\Microsoft\Microsoft SQL Server\[YOUR INSTANCE NAME] key in the Registry. You also need to ensure that the TSXs have a proxy account configured with the same name as the proxy account on the MSX that will be running the job.

We also need to configure how the TSXs encrypt the data when they communicate with the MSX. We achieve this using the MsxEncryptChannelOptions Registry key for the TSX. You can find this key in the SQL Server Agent key, which is located under the Software\Microsoft\Microsoft SQL Server\[YOUR INSTANCE NAME] key in the Registry. A value of 0 means that encryption is not used. 1 indicates that encryption is used, but the certificate is not validated, and an option of 2 indicates that full SSL encryption and certificate validation is used. In our environment, since all instances are on the same physical box, we disable encryption.

Therefore, to prepare our SQLSERVER\MASTERSERVER instance to be an MSX, and to prepare our SQLSERVER\TARGETSERVER1 and SQLSERVER\TARGETSERVER2 instances to be TSXs, we run the script in Listing 21-18 to update the Registry.

■ **Note**   The demonstrations in this section use three instances named SQLSERVER\MASTERSERVER, which we configure as an MSX, and SQLSERVER\TARGETSERVER1 and SQLSERVER\TARGETSERVER2, both of which we configure as TSXs.

Listing 21-18. Updating the Registry

```
USE Master
GO

EXEC xp_regwrite
  @rootkey = N'HKEY_LOCAL_MACHINE'
 ,@key = N'Software\Microsoft\Microsoft SQL Server\MasterServer\SQL Server Agent'
 ,@value_name = N'AllowDownloadedJobsToMatchProxyName'
 ,@type = N'REG_DWORD'
 ,@value = 1 ;

EXEC xp_regwrite
  @rootkey='HKEY_LOCAL_MACHINE',
  @key='SOFTWARE\Microsoft\Microsoft SQL Server\MSSQL12.TARGETSERVER1\SQLServerAgent',
  @value_name='MsxEncryptChannelOptions',
  @type='REG_SZ',
  @value='0' ;

EXEC xp_regwrite
  @rootkey='HKEY_LOCAL_MACHINE',
  @key='SOFTWARE\Microsoft\Microsoft SQL Server\MSSQL12.TARGETSERVER2\SQLServerAgent',
  @value_name='MsxEncryptChannelOptions',
  @type='REG_SZ',
  @value='0' ;

GO
```

■ **Tip** Because all of our instances reside on the same server, this script can be run from any of the three instances. If your instances are on different servers, then the first command will run on the MSX and the other two commands should run against their corresponding TSX.

We now use the SQLCMD script in Listing 21-19 to create the PowerShell proxy account on TARGETSERVER1 and TARGETSERVER2. The script must be run in SQLCMD mode to work because it connects to multiple instances.

Listing 21-19. Creating a Proxy

```
:connect sqlserver\targetserver1

CREATE CREDENTIAL WinUserCredential
        WITH IDENTITY = N'PROSQLADMIN\WinUser', SECRET = N'Pa$$w0rd' ;
GO

EXEC msdb.dbo.sp_add_proxy
                @proxy_name=N'PowerShellProxy',
                @credential_name=N'WinUserCredential',
                @enabled=1,
                @description=N'Proxy to check Browser Service status' ;
GO

EXEC msdb.dbo.sp_grant_proxy_to_subsystem
                @proxy_name=N'PowerShellProxy',
                @subsystem_id=12 ;
GO


:connect sqlserver\targetserver2

CREATE CREDENTIAL WinUserCredential
        WITH IDENTITY = N'PROSQLADMIN\WinUser', SECRET = N'Pa$$w0rd' ;
GO

EXEC msdb.dbo.sp_add_proxy
                @proxy_name=N'PowerShellProxy',
                @credential_name=N'WinUserCredential',
                @enabled=1,
                @description=N'Proxy to check Browser Service status' ;
GO

EXEC msdb.dbo.sp_grant_proxy_to_subsystem
                @proxy_name=N'PowerShellProxy',
                @subsystem_id=12 ;
GO
```

We can now begin to configure our SQLSERVER\MASTERSERVER instance as an MSX. To do this through SQL Server Management Studio, we invoke the Master Server Wizard by opening the SQL Server Agent context menu in Object Explorer and selecting Multi Server Administration | Make This A Master.

After passing through the Welcome page of the wizard, we find the Master Server Operator page (see Figure 21-33). On this page, we enter the details of an operator who will be notified of the status of multiserver jobs.

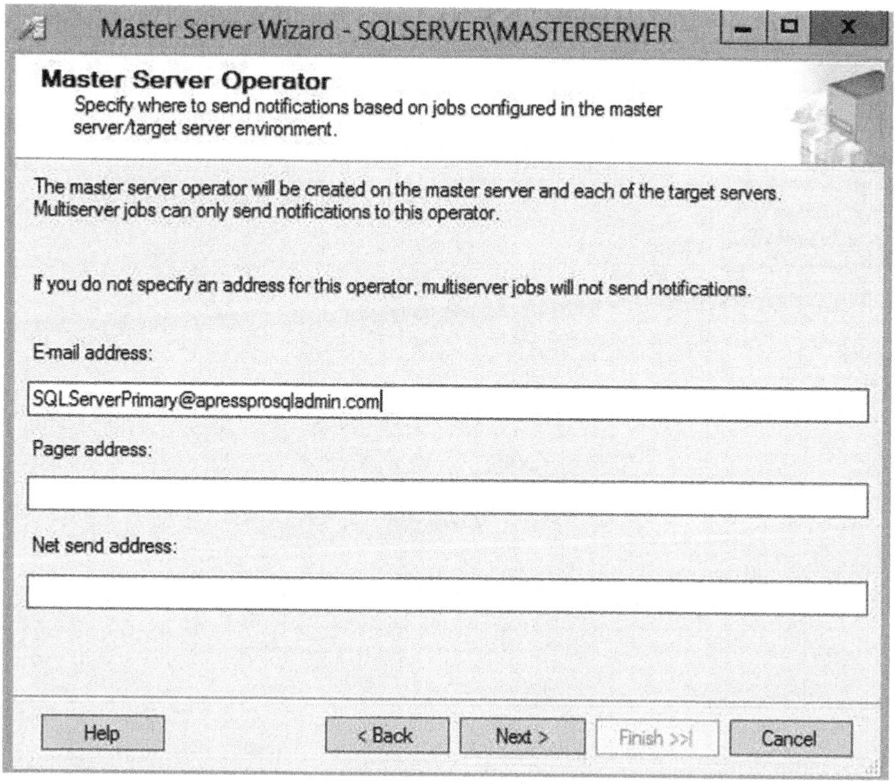

Figure 21-33. *The Master Server Operator page*

On the Target Servers page of the wizard, shown in Figure 21-34, we select our target servers from the list of registered servers in the Registered Servers pane and move them to the Target Servers pane using the arrows. After highlighting a server in the Target Servers pane, we can use the Connection button to ensure connectivity.

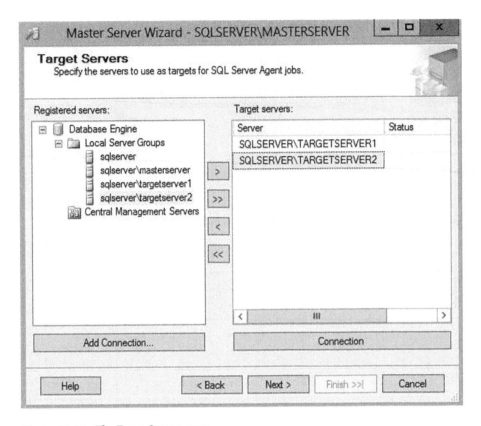

Figure 21-34. *The Target Servers page*

■ **Tip** All of our instances appear in the Local Server Groups node of the Registered Servers pane because they are all on the same server. If the instances that you wish to be target servers are not local, you can register servers by using the Registered Servers window, which you can access from the View menu in SQL Server Management Studio. This is discussed further in Chapter 22.

On the Master Server Login Credentials page of the wizard, displayed in Figure 21-35, we are asked if a New Login should be created if required. This is the login that the TSXs use to connect to the MSX and download the jobs that they should run. If the instances of SQL Server Agent share the same service account as the MSX, then this is not required.

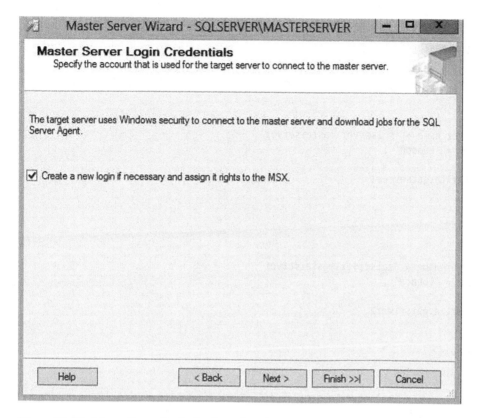

Figure 21-35. *Master Server Login Credentials page*

Now we see a summary of the actions that will be performed on the Completion page of the wizard before we are presented with a progress window, which informs us of the success or failure of each task.

To configure the environment using T-SQL, we use the `sp_msx_enlist` system stored procedure. This procedure accepts the parameters detailed in Table 21-15.

Table 21-15. *sp_msx_enlist Parameters*

Parameter	Description
@msx_server_name	The name of the MSX
@location	A textual description of the server's location

We need to run this procedure on our MSX first and then subsequently on each of the TSXs. Listing 21-20 contains the script to achieve this. Because the script connects to multiple instances, we must run it in SQLCMD mode.

Listing 21-20. Enlisting Servers

```
:connect sqlserver\masterserver

USE MSDB
GO

sp_msx_enlist
        @msx_server_name = 'sqlserver\masterserver',
        @location = 'London' ;

:connect sqlserver\targetserver1

USE MSDB
GO

sp_msx_enlist
        @msx_server_name = 'sqlserver\masterserver',
        @location = 'London' ;

:connect sqlserver\targetserver2

USE MSDB
GO

sp_msx_enlist
        @msx_server_name = 'sqlserver\masterserver',
        @location = 'London' ;
```

Creating Master Jobs

You can create a master job in the same way as a local job, with the exception of specifying the target servers on which it should run. However, a limitation of using multiserver jobs is that T-SQL job steps cannot run under the context of another user; they must run under the context of the service account. Therefore, before we convert our BackupAndCheckBrowser job to be a multiserver job, we must edit it to remove the Run As Account. We can do this by using the sp_update_jobstep procedure, as demonstrated in Listing 21-21.

Listing 21-21. Updating Job Step

```
USE MSDB
GO

EXEC msdb.dbo.sp_update_jobstep
                @job_name=N'BackupAndCheckBrowser',
                @step_id=1 ,
                @database_user_name=N'' ;
GO
```

Another limitation of multiserver jobs is that the only allowable operator is the MSXOperator, who receives all notifications for multiserver jobs. Therefore, we also need to change the DBATeam operator to the MSXOperator operator before continuing. We can use the sp_update_job procedure to achieve this with the script in Listing 21-22.

Listing 21-22. Updating a Job

```
USE msdb
GO

EXEC msdb.dbo.sp_update_job
            @job_name=N'BackupAndCheckBrowser',
            @notify_email_operator_name=N'MSXOperator' ;
GO
```

We can now proceed to convert our BackupAndCheckBrowser job to a multiserver job from Management Studio by opening the Job Properties dialog box and navigating to the Targets page. As illustrated in Figure 21-36, we can use this page to change the job to a multiserver job and specify the target servers that it should run against from a list of target servers that have been enlisted using the sp_msx_enlist stored procedure. After closing the properties dialog box, the job runs against the TargetServer1 and TargetServer2 instances instead of the MASTERSERVER instance.

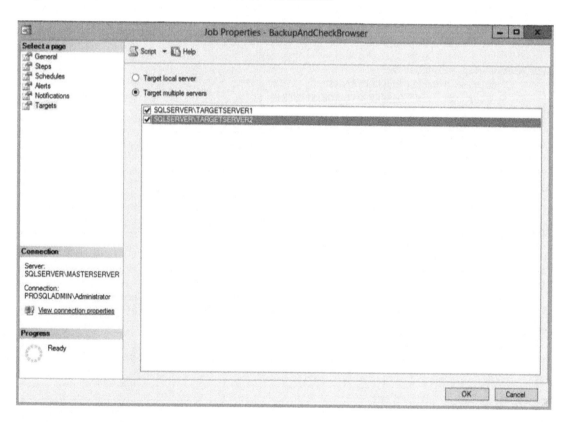

Figure 21-36. *Convert to multiserver job*

To achieve the same results via T-SQL, we use the sp_delete_jobserver system stored procedure to stop the job from running against the MSX and the sp_add_jobserver system stored procedure to configure the job to run against the TSXs. Both of these procedures accept the parameters detailed in Table 21-16.

Table 21-16. *sp_delete_jobserver and sp_add_jobserver Parameters*

Parameter	Description
@job_id	The GUID of the job that you are converting to a multiserver job. If NULL, then the @job_name parameter must be specified.
@job_name	The name of the job that you are converting to a multiserver job. If NULL, then the @job_id parameter must be specified.
@server_name	The server/instance name that you want the job to run against.

In our scenario, we can use the script in Listing 21-23 to convert the job.

Listing 21-23. Converting to a Multiserver Job

```
EXEC msdb.dbo.sp_delete_jobserver
     @job_name=N'BackupAndCheckBrowser',
     @server_name = N'SQLSERVER\MASTERSERVER' ;
GO

EXEC msdb.dbo.sp_add_jobserver
     @job_name=N'BackupAndCheckBrowser',
     @server_name = N'SQLSERVER\TARGETSERVER1' ;
GO

EXEC msdb.dbo.sp_add_jobserver
     @job_name=N'BackupAndCheckBrowser',
     @server_name = N'SQLSERVER\TARGETSERVER2' ;
GO
```

Managing Target Servers

When you configure your MSX, make sure you consider various maintenance activities against the TSXs. These include polling the TSXs, synchronizing time across the servers, running ad-hoc jobs, and defecting (delisting) TSXs.

We can achieve these tasks in the Target Server Status dialog box, which we can invoked from the context menu of SQL Server Agent on the MSX by selecting Multi Server Administration | Manage Target Servers. The Target Server Status tab of this dialog box is shown in Figure 21-37.

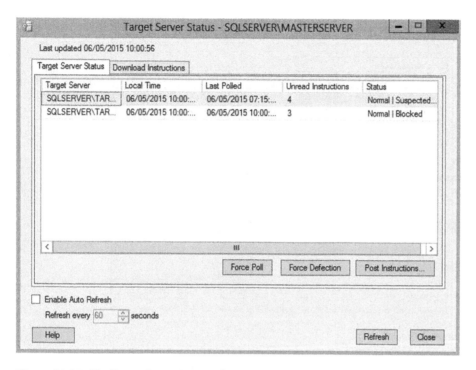

Figure 21-37. *The Target Server Status tab*

On this tab, we can use the Force Poll button to make the Target Servers Poll the MSX. When a TSX polls the MSX, we are forcing it to download the latest copy of the jobs that it is configured to run. This is useful if you have updated the master job.

The Force Defection button causes the highlighted TSX to be delisted from the MSX. After it is delisted, the selected TSX no longer polls for or runs multiserver jobs.

The Post Instructions button invokes the Post Download Instructions dialog box, where you are able to send one of the following instructions to TSXs:

- Defect

- Set Polling Interval

- Synchronize Clocks

- Start Job

To synchronize the time on all servers, you would choose the Synchronize Clocks instruction type and ensure that All Target Servers is selected in the Recipients section, as illustrated in Figure 21-38. The clocks are then synchronized when the targets next poll the master.

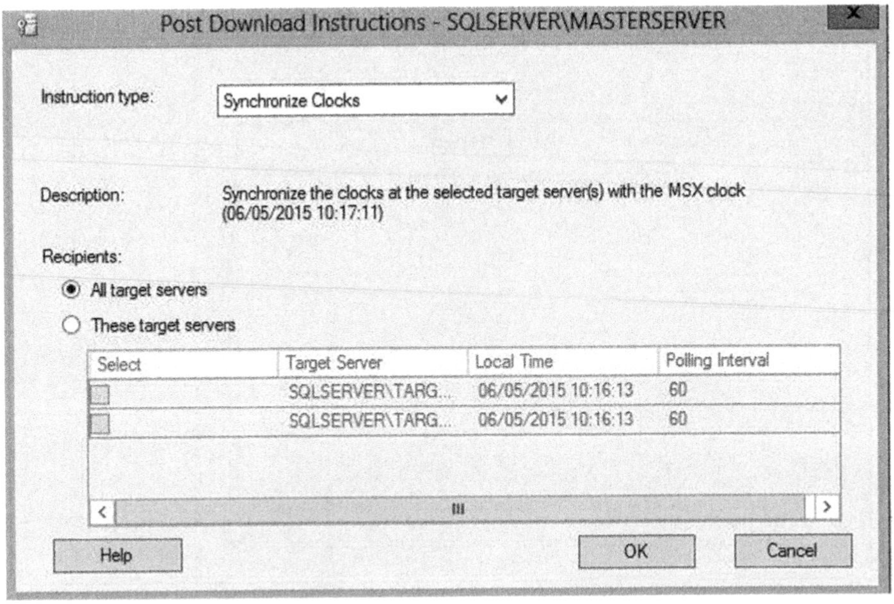

Figure 21-38. *Synchronize Clocks*

In another scenario, there may be a time when we wish to perform an ad-hoc run of our BackupAndCheckBrowser job against TARGETSERVER1. We can do this by selecting Start Job as the Instruction Type and then choosing our job from the Job Name drop-down list. We then use the Recipients section of the screen to select TARGETSERVER1. This is illustrated in Figure 21-39.

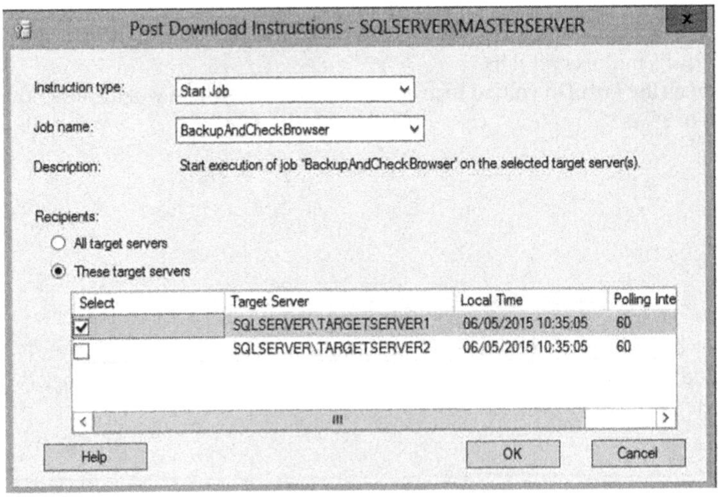

Figure 21-39. *Start a job on TARGETSERVER1*

On the Download Instructions tab of the Target Server Status dialog box, which is illustrated in Figure 21-40, we see a list of instructions that have been sent to targets. We can use the drop-down lists at the top of the screen to filter the instructions by job or by target server.

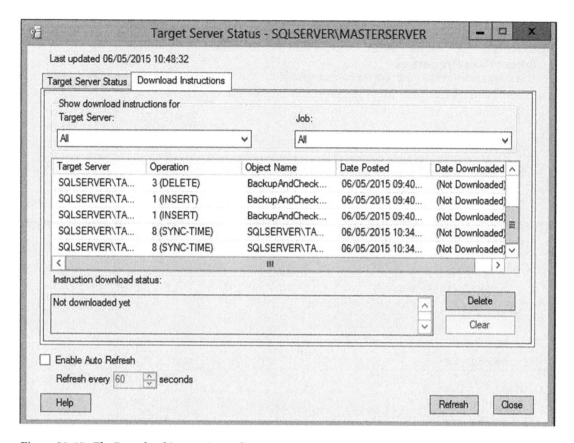

Figure 21-40. *The Download Instructions tab*

Maintenance Plans

Maintenance plans use SSIS to provide a graphical surface for automating common maintenance tasks that are then scheduled to run with SQL Server Agent. You can create them via a wizard or manually on a graphical design surface. The following sections discuss each of these options.

Creating a Maintenance Plan with the Wizard

We can invoke the New Maintenance Plan Wizard by drilling through Management in Object Explorer and selecting Maintenance Plan Wizard from the Maintenance Plans context menu. After passing through the Welcome page, the Select Plan Properties page displays, as shown in Figure 21-41.

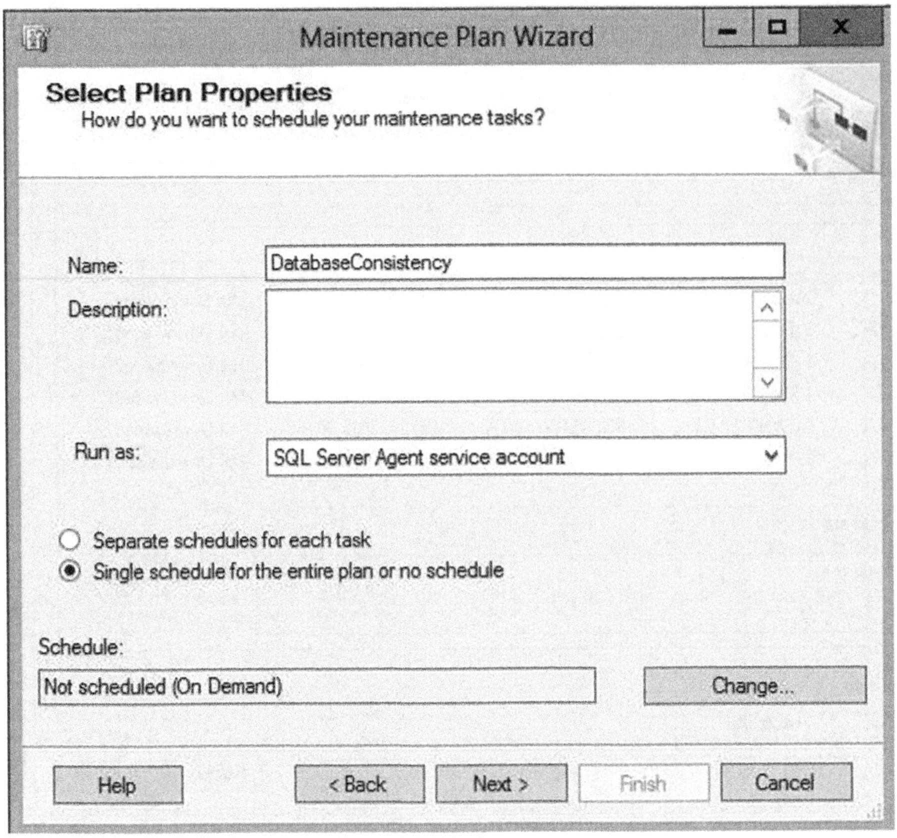

Figure 21-41. *Select Plan Properties page*

On this page, we specify a name for our maintenance plan. We will use this plan to run DBCC CHECKDB, so we name it DatabaseConsistency. For our purposes, we allow it to run under the context of the SQL Server Agent service account and specify a single schedule for the whole plan.

Using separate schedules for each task helps in scenarios such as backups, where you want to have Full, Differential, and Log backups in a single plan but running on different schedules. Using the Change button, we invoke the New Job Schedule dialog box, which we discussed earlier in this chapter. In this demonstration, we schedule the plan to run daily at 7 AM.

Because our SQLSERVER\MASTERSERVER instance is configured as an MSX, the Select Target Servers page allows us to control if the plan is run locally, or against our TSXs, as shown in Figure 21-42. We choose to run the plan against our local instance.

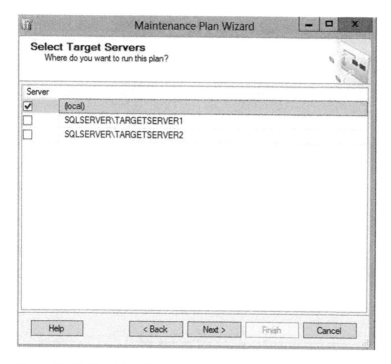

Figure 21-42. *The Select Target Servers page*

On the Select Maintenance Tasks page, shown in Figure 21-43, we use the check boxes to indicate which maintenance tasks we would like included in the plan. Because we wish to run DBCC CHECKDB, we choose the Check Database Integrity task.

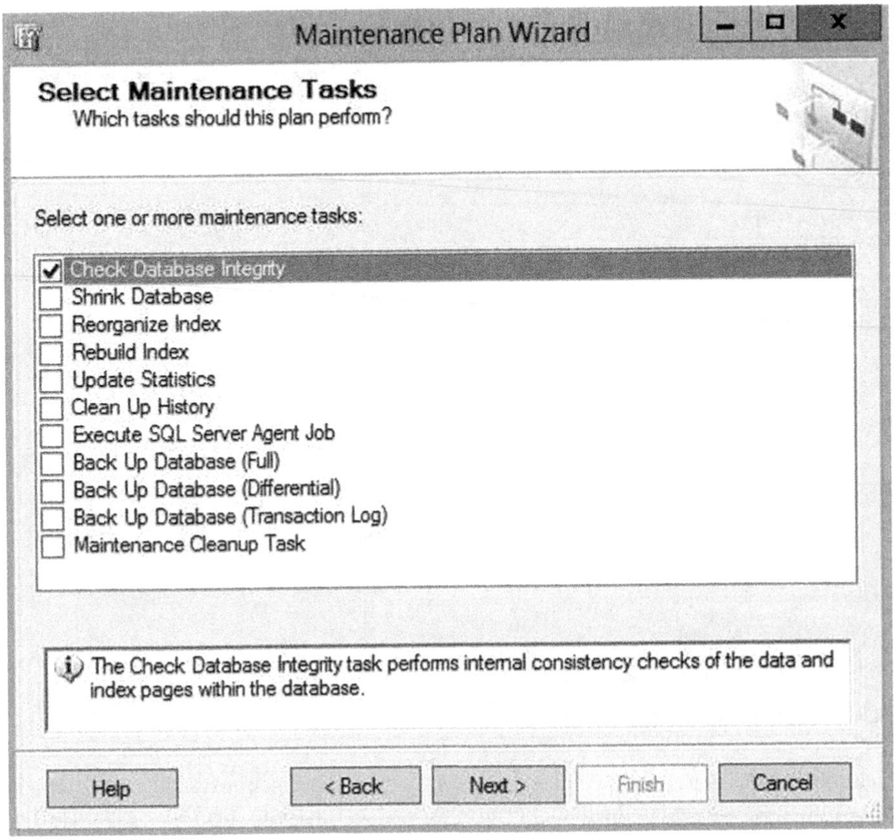

Figure 21-43. *The Select Maintenance Tasks page*

If we had selected multiple maintenance tasks, then we would be able to use the Select Maintenance Task Order page to choose the order in which the tasks execute. To do this, select a task and use the Move Up and Move Down buttons. This page is illustrated in Figure 21-44.

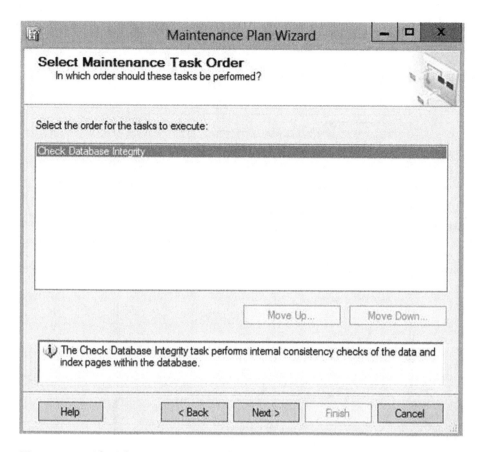

Figure 21-44. *The Select Maintenance Task Order page*

The following pages change dynamically based on the maintenance tasks that we chose to include in our plan, with one configuration page per task selected. Because we have chosen the Check Database Integrity task, we see the Define Database Check Integrity Task page, as shown in Figure 21-45. On this screen, we specify that the task should run against all databases on the instance by using the Databases drop-down. We also leave the Include Indexes option checked.

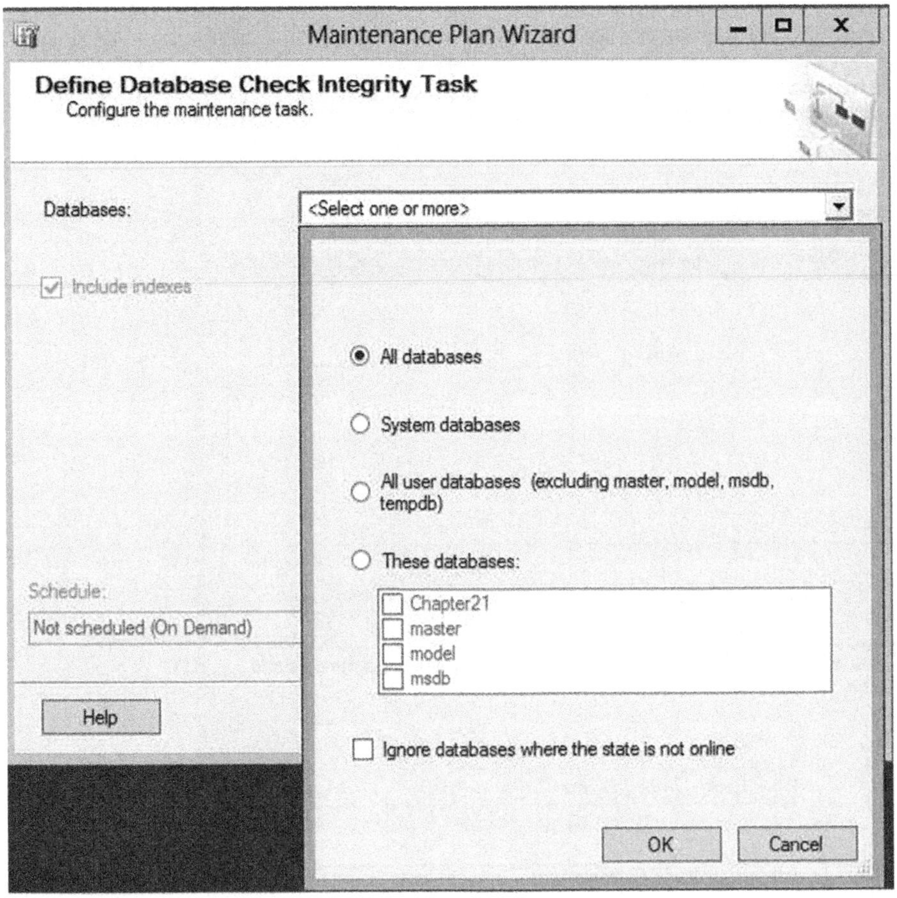

Figure 21-45. *The Define Database Check Integrity Task page*

On the Select Report Options page, we can choose to have the maintenance plan actions report written to a text file or have it sent to an operator. As illustrated in Figure 21-46, we have configured it so our DBATeam operator is sent the report.

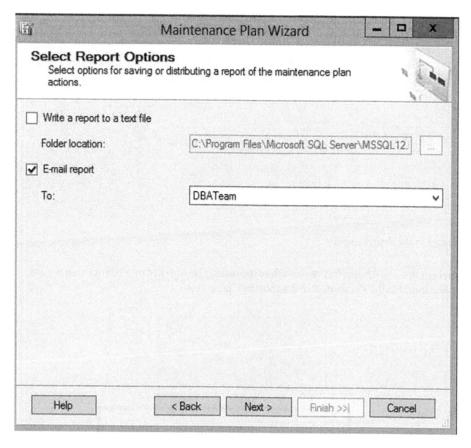

Figure 21-46. *The Select Report Options page*

On the Completion page of the wizard, we are given a summary of the tasks that the wizard will perform. This happens before the Progress dialog box displays, which indicates the success or failure of each task performed by the wizard. Once the plan has been created, a new SQL Server Agent job becomes visible under the SQL Server Agent | Local Jobs node in Object Explorer.

Creating a Maintenance Plan Manually

You can also create maintenance plans manually using a graphical design surface. You can invoke the Maintenance Plan designer by drilling through Management in Object Explorer and selecting New Maintenance Plan from the Maintenance Plans context menu. Creating a maintenance plan manually gives you more flexibility and the ability to create success and failure precedence constraints between tasks.

Once the design surface is open, you can drag and drop tasks from the toolbox onto the surface. In Figure 21-47, you can see that we have dragged the Database Integrity Check, Backup Database, and Maintenance Cleanup tasks onto the design surface, since we will create a plan for checking database consistency and backing up databases on the local instance. We have also added two Notify Operator tasks.

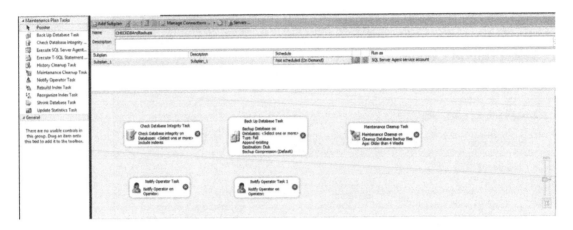

Figure 21-47. *Drag tasks to the design surface*

Let's now add precedence constraints between each of the tasks. The order of precedence that we are looking to achieve is illustrated in the decision-tree diagram in Figure 21-48.

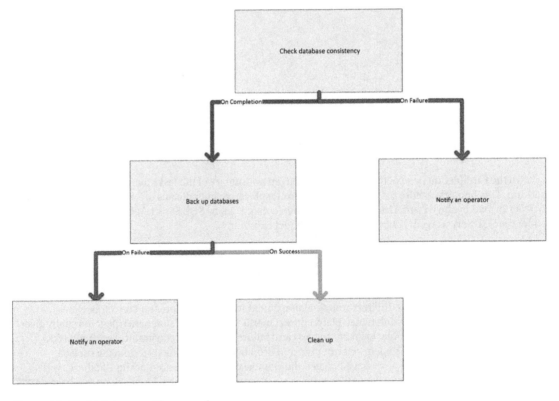

Figure 21-48. *Maintenance Plan precedence*

To control the order of precedence, we need to highlight each task in turn and then drag the arrow that appears to the next task that should be executed. This creates success precedence constraints. Once the constraints are attached, we can enter their context menu and select Success, Failure, or Completion as appropriate. If there are no constraints between tasks, then they execute in parallel. The correct precedence constraints for our scenario are illustrated in Figure 21-49.

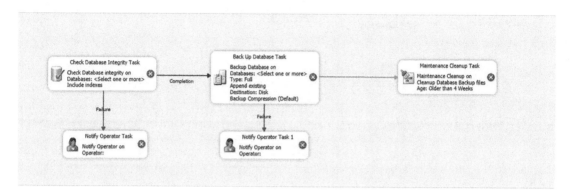

Figure 21-49. *Add precedence constraints*

We now need to configure each of the tasks. We can do this by double clicking each task in turn to enter its Properties dialog box. Figure 21-50 shows the Check Database Integrity Task properties dialog box. Here, we use the Databases drop-down to configure the task to run against all databases. We can examine the T-SQL that will execute by using the View T-SQL button.

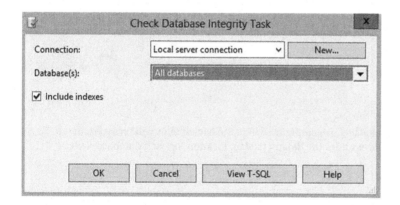

Figure 21-50. *Check Database Integrity Task properties dialog box*

■ **Tip** Some of the dialog boxes within this section have changed in SQL Server 2014. Therefore, if you are using an older version of SQL Server Management Studio, they may look different, even if the instance is 2014.

Figure 21-51 shows General tab the Back Up Database Task properties dialog box. On this page, we select a Backup Type of Full for all databases on the instance and ensure that Disk is specified as the Back Up To option.

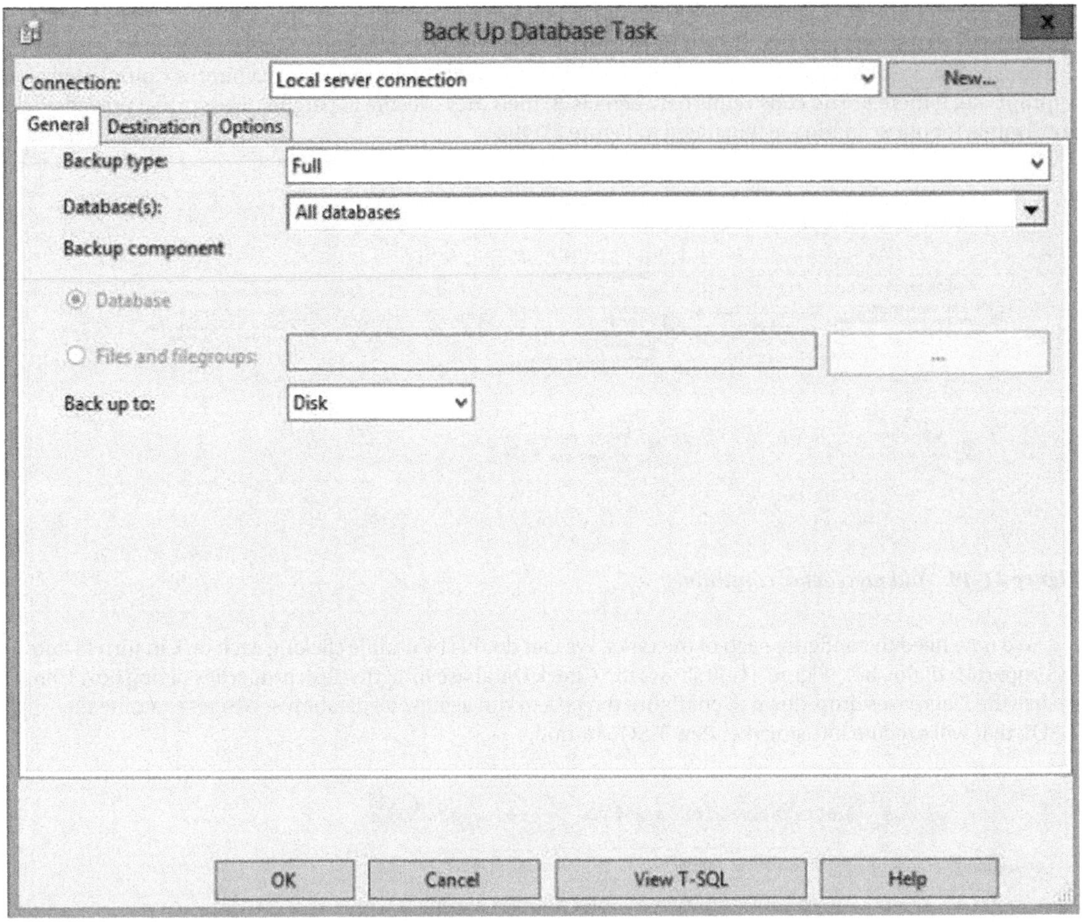

Figure 21-51. *The General tab*

On the Destination tab of the dialog box, we configure where the backup files will be saved. In our scenario, we choose to create a subfolder under the default backup location for each database. This is illustrated in Figure 21-52.

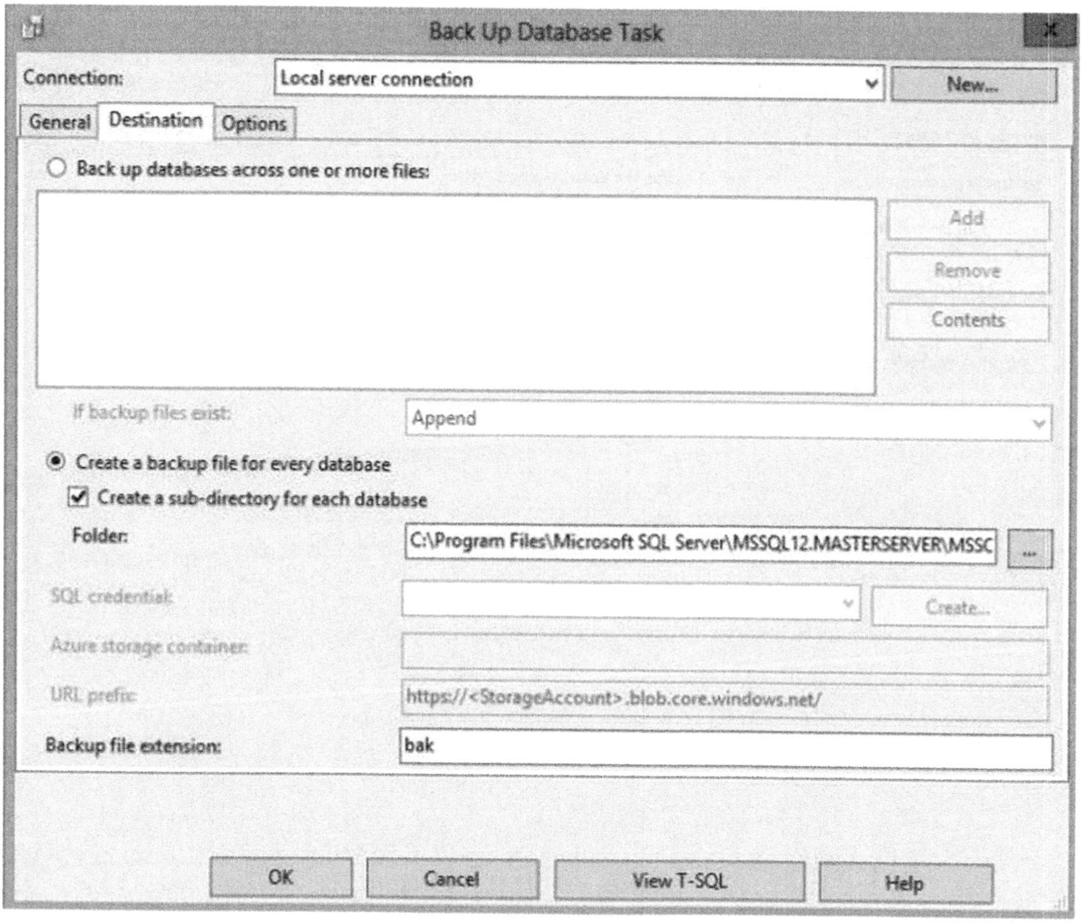

Figure 21-52. *The Destination tab*

On the Options tab, we can select our compression and encryption options, as well as choose when the backup set should expire, if the backup should be verified and the backup should be taken as a copy-only backup. This tab is illustrated in Figure 21-53.

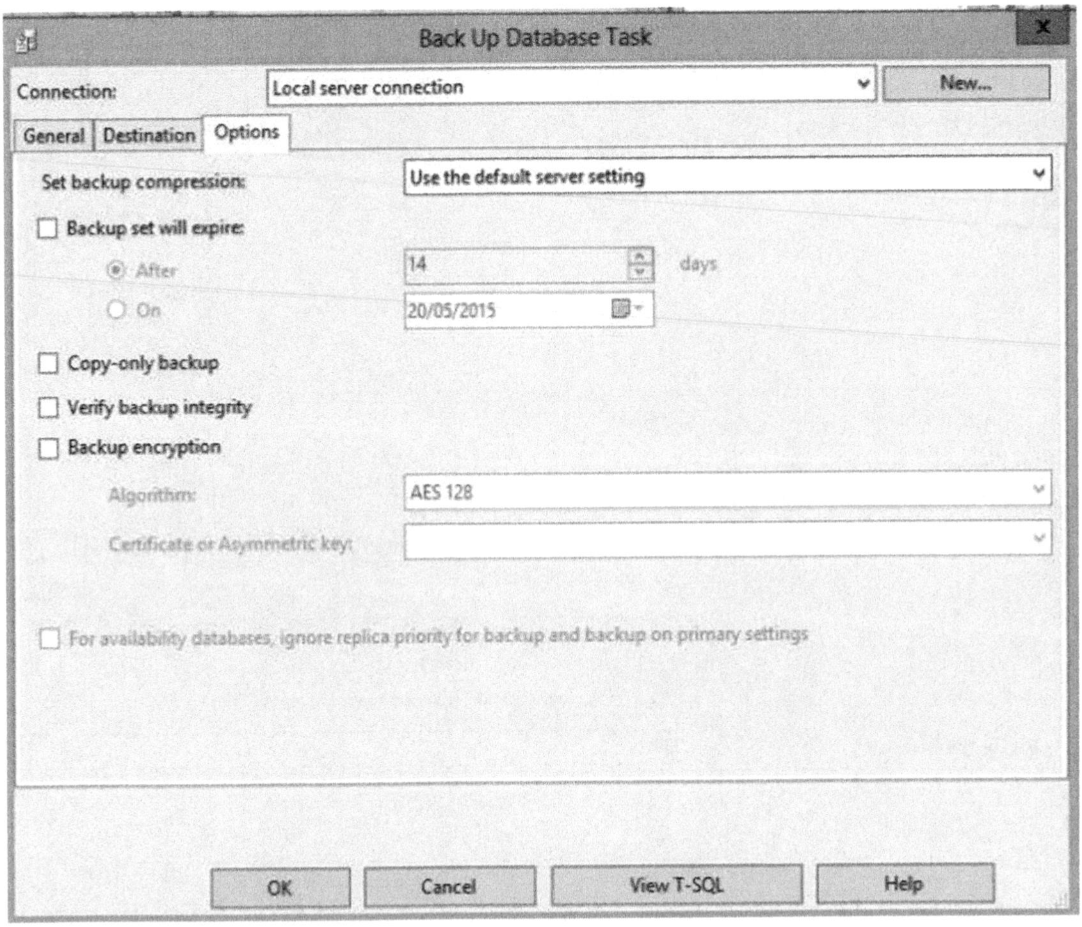

Figure 21-53. The Options tab

■ **Note**   For more information on backups and backup options, please see Chapter 15.

Figure 21-54 shows the Maintenance Cleanup Task properties dialog box. We use this dialog box to configure the folder where our backup files are stored and to specify that first-level subfolders should also be searched. This is important, because in the properties of the Back Up Database Task, we specify that a subfolder should be created for each database. We also specify that backups with a .bak file extension should be deleted and indicate that backup files should be older than four weeks before they are removed.

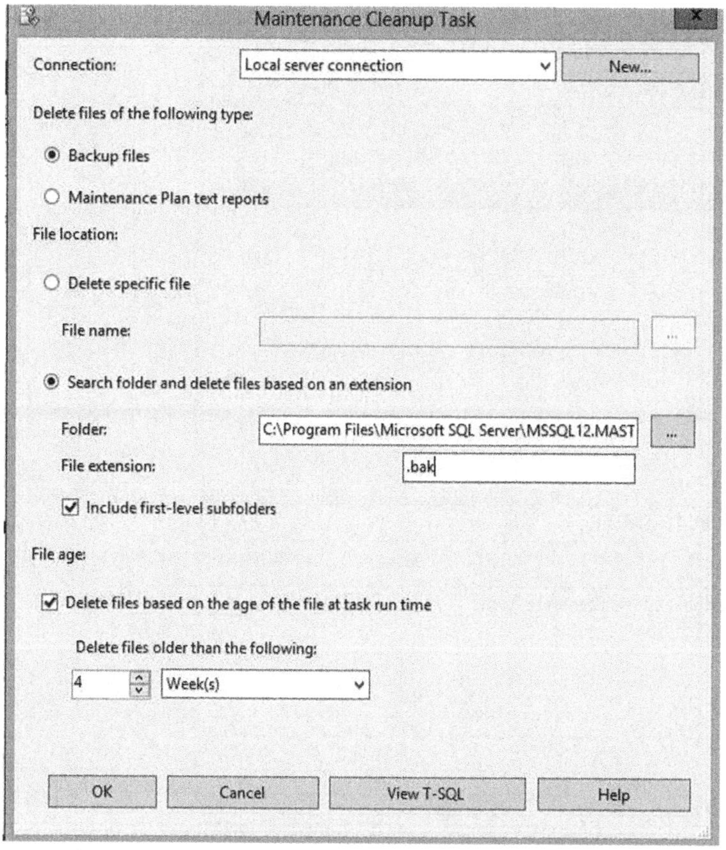

Figure 21-54. *Maintenance Cleanup Task properties dialog box*

Figure 21-55 illustrates the Notify Operator Task properties dialog box. In this dialog box, we need to specify the operator(s) that the notification will be sent to, along with the subject and body of the e-mail. In this example, we configure the Notify Operator task, which is attached to the Check Database Consistency task, to inform the DBATeam operator that the DBCC CHECKDB task failed and configure the Notify Operator task, which is attached to the Database Backup task, to inform the DBATeam operator that the backups failed.

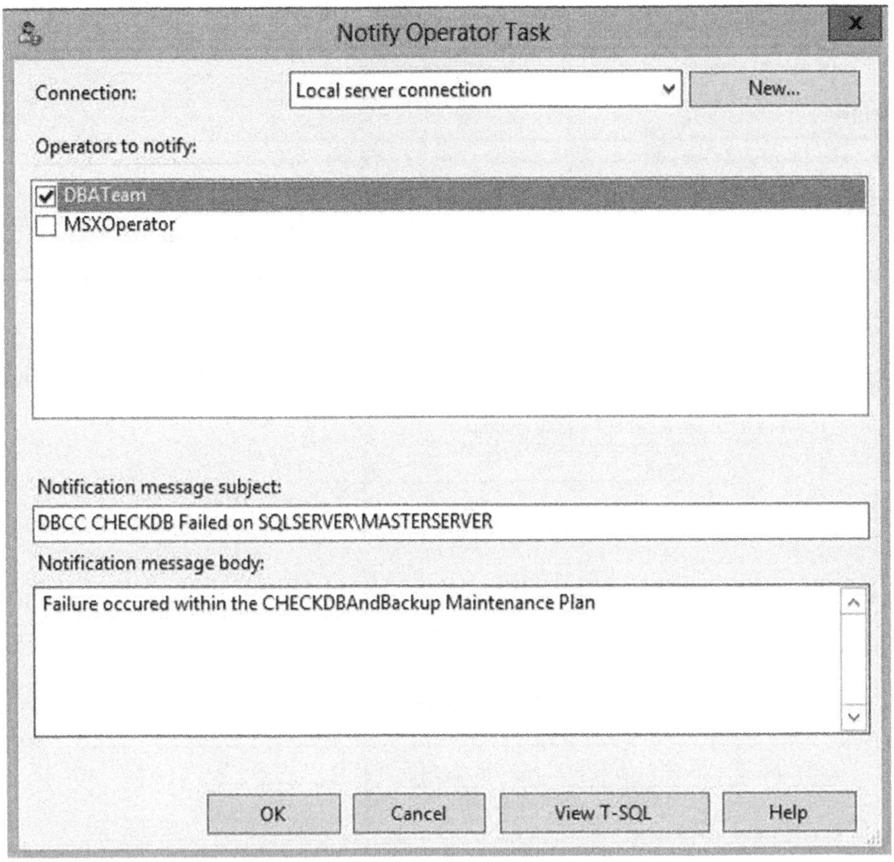

Figure 21-55. *The Notify Operator Task properties dialog box*

Now that all of the tasks are configured, we double-click the subplan, to enter the Subplan Properties dialog box, which is displayed in Figure 21-56. We give the subplan a descriptive name and a description and then use the calendar icon to enter the New Schedule dialog box, where we configure the subplan to run at midnight every Sunday. We can also use this dialog box to configure the account that the subplan will run under. We use the SQL Server Agent service account, but to use a proxy, we would need to create a proxy with access to the Integration Services subsystem. This is because maintenance plans are SSIS packages.

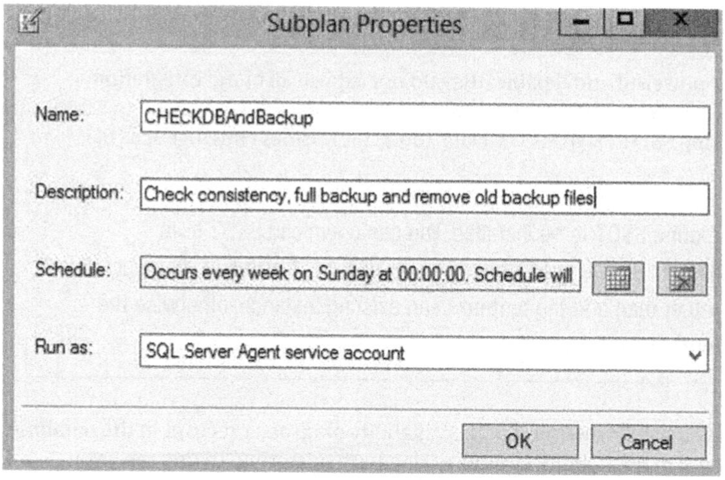

Figure 21-56. *The Subplan Properties dialog box*

For each subplan in the maintenance plan a new SSIS package is created, along with a new SQL Server Agent job. Having a separate set of artifacts for each subplan gives you the flexibility to run each subplan with a different security context and on a different schedule.

We would like our maintenance plan to also include differential backups on a daily schedule, as opposed to the weekly schedule of the full backups. Therefore, we create a new subplan within our maintenance plan by using the Add Subplan button in the maintenance plan toolbar. This causes a new Subplan Properties dialog box to be invoked and we use this dialog box to specify a name, description, and schedule for the subplan. We also have the option of configuring a proxy to run the SSIS package.

After this is complete, an additional subplan is listed in the Subplans section of the screen, as illustrated in Figure 21-57. You can move between the subplan design surfaces by highlighting the appropriate subplan in the Subplans section.

Subplan	Description	Schedule	Run as
CHECKDBAndBackup	Check consistency, full backup and remove old ...	Occurs every week on Sunday at 00:00:0...	SQL Server Agent service account
DifferentialBackup	Run Differential Backup on all DBs	Occurs every day at 00:01:00. Schedule ...	SQL Server Agent service account

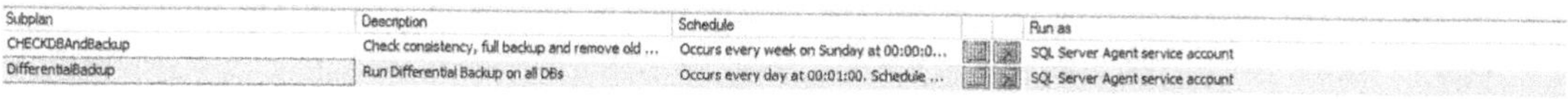

Figure 21-57. *Subplans*

Within the DifferentialBackup subplan, we can now drag a Database Backup task onto the design surface and configure it to perform differential backups of all databases on the instance. We may also wish to add another Notify Operator task and attach it to the Database Backup task with a failure precedence constraint.

Once we have finished configuring the task, we can save our maintenance plan. After the maintenance plan has been saved, we return to the SQL Server Agent | Local Jobs node in Object Explorer, which exposes two new SQL Server Agent jobs named with the convention `MaintenancePlan.Subplan`.

■ **Tip**   It is possible to create a maintenance plan using the Maintenance Plan Wizard and then modify that plan in the designer, to failure or completion precedence constraints, or make other advanced configuration changes.

Automating Administration with SSIS

Although maintenance plans are very powerful and flexible, they do not expose all of the Integration Services tasks that a DBA finds useful. Therefore, for some administrative scenarios, DBAs need to create their own SSIS Packages manually, using SSDT (SQL Server Data Tools) for business intelligence (BI).

■ **Tip** The examples in this section require SSDT to be installed. You can download SSDT from www.microsoft.com. In order to install SSDT BI, you must already have .NET 4.5.1 installed. You must also choose to perform a new installation, rather than add the feature to an existing instance, otherwise the installation fails on the Same Architecture Validation rule.

An example of this occurs when you are maintaining high availability or disaster recover at the database level, using a technology such as AlwaysOn Availability Groups or database mirroring. In this case, you need to find a way to synchronize instance-level objects, such as logins, stored procedures from the Master database, SQL Server Agent jobs, custom error messages, and so on. In this section, we create a SSIS package, which synchronizes logins and SQL Server Agent jobs between TARGETSERVER1 and TARGETSERVER2.

First, upon opening SQL Server Data Tools, we choose New | Project from the File menu and then select the Integration Services template and name the solution SyncInstanceLevelObjects, as shown in Figure 21-58.

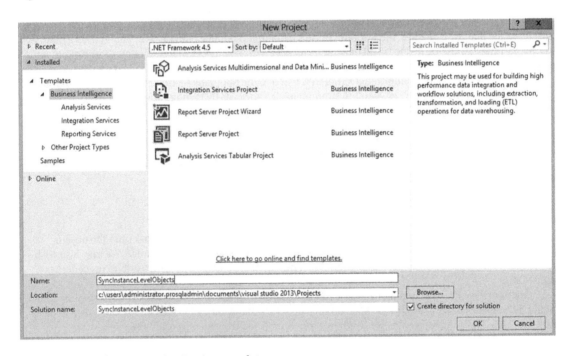

Figure 21-58. *Select Integration Services template*

Once the solution is open, the toolbox offers numerous control flow tasks, which we can drag to the design surface. Under the Other Tasks node of this toolbox, you will find many tasks that are useful to DBAs, including the maintenance plan tasks. This is illustrated in Figure 21-59.

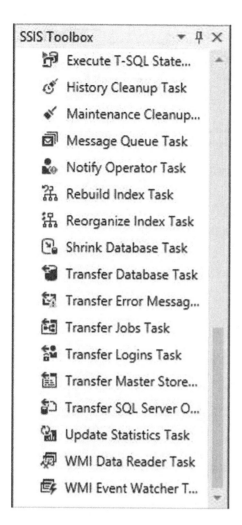

Figure 21-59. *The toolbox*

For our purposes, we drag the Transfer Logins task and Transfer Jobs task to the design surface. At this point, our design surface looks similar to Figure 21-60.

Figure 21-60. *Design Surface*

We then double click the Transfer Logins task to enter the Properties dialog box. The first page to display is the General page, illustrated in Figure 21-61. Here we have the option of modifying the name and description of the task.

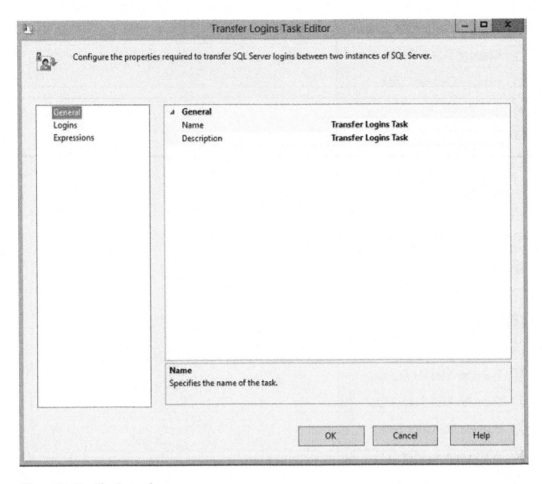

Figure 21-61. *The General page*

On the Logins page, we use the SourceConnection drop-down to invoke the SMO Connection Manager Editor, which is illustrated in Figure 21-62. We use this window to specify the name of our instance and then test the connection using the Test Connection button.

Figure 21-62. *The SMO Connection Manager Editor*

We then repeat this process for the DestinationConnection drop-down, adding the details for our SQLSERVERTARGETSERVER2 instance. Also on the Logins page, which is illustrated in Figure 21-63, we specify AllLogins from the LoginsToTransfer drop-down and specify that if a login exists, it should be skipped. Other options here include failing the task and overwriting the login. We also use the CopySids option to ensure that the SIDs are aligned between instances for SQL layer Logins.

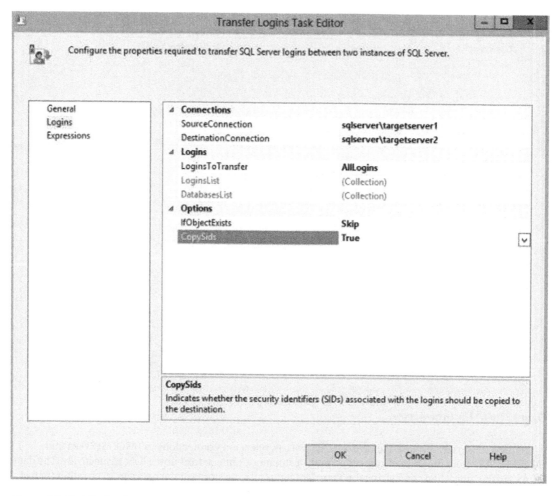

Figure 21-63. *The Logins page*

On the Expressions page, we have the option of populating task properties dynamically, at run time, based on expressions. This can be very useful in scenarios in which you want dynamic logic to be incorporated into your package. An example of this is if you need to specify a dynamic list of logins to transfer, depending on the name of the destination connection. This allows you to create a reusable package that you can use to transfer all logins between production machines but only a subset of logins between an OAT (Operational Acceptance Testing) environment and production.

Now that the Transfer Logins task has been configured, we modify the properties of the Transfer Jobs task. The first page of this dialog box is the General page, as illustrated in Figure 21-64. We can use this page to enter a custom name and description for the task.

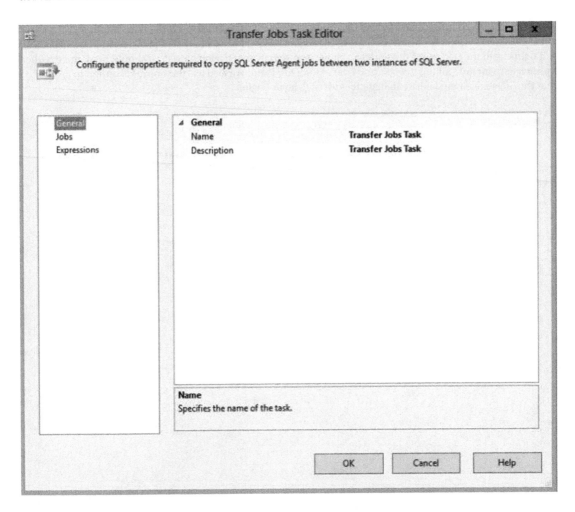

Figure 21-64. The General page

On the Jobs page, displayed in Figure 21-65, we can select our connections to TARGETSERVER1 and TARGETSERVER2 from the SourceConnection and DestinationConnect drop-down lists, respectively. The data sources we created when configuring the Transfer Logins task are stored at the package level, rather than at the task level, and therefore we can reuse them, rather than having to create new connections.

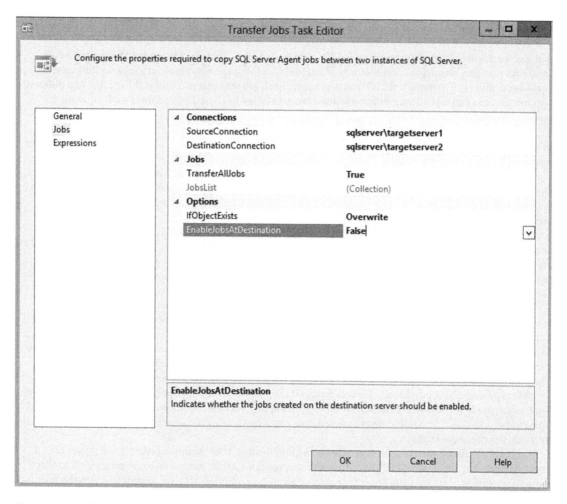

Figure 21-65. *The Jobs page*

We then specify that all jobs should be transferred and that if they already exist on the destination instance, they should be overwritten. This is useful because any changes we make to jobs on TARGETSERVER1 are propagated to TARGETSERVER2. We can also choose to enable or disable jobs on the destination instance. In most scenarios, such as synchronizing for disaster recovery (DR), we want them to be deleted and then we re-enable them manually in the event of a failover.

Unlike the maintenance plan that we created earlier in this chapter, we do not add any precedence constraints between the tasks. This means that they execute in parallel and the package completes faster. We can test our package in Debug mode by clicking the Play button on the task bar. Each task is given a spinning wheel during its execution and then either a green tick or a red cross at the end. Debug Windows also displays at the bottom of the screen. We can now schedule our package to run with SQL Server Agent on a periodic basis.

Summary

SQL Server Agent is a scheduling engine for SQL Server that allows you to create powerful maintenance jobs, with decision-based logic, on a variety of schedules. A job is the container for the tasks that should be performed, and each of these tasks is known as a step. Each job step can run under the context of a different account and can run tasks under different subsystems, or types, such as T-SQL, PowerShell, operating system command, or SSIS package.

A schedule is attached to a job and can be triggered at a specific date and time, when the CPU is idle, or on a reoccurring schedule, such as daily, weekly, or monthly. A schedule can also reoccur on an intraday basis, such as hourly, every minute, or even as frequently as every ten seconds.

An operator is an individual or team who is notified of the success or failure of jobs and if an alert fires. Operators can be notified of job status via e-mail, pager, or NET SEND; however, support for NETSEND and pager are deprecated. For an operator to be notified by e-mail, Database Mail must be configured so that e-mails can be sent via your SMTP Replay server.

By default, jobs run under the context of the SQL Server Agent service account. However, for good security practice, you should consider using proxy accounts to run the job steps. Proxy accounts map to credentials at the instance level, which in turn map to a Windows-level security principle. Proxies can be used for all subsystems, except T-SQL. T-SQL job steps use EXECUTE AS to execute the commands under the context of a database user. This is configured using the Run As property.

Alerts can be triggered when an error or warning is fired within the Database Engine, when a WMI event occurs, or in response to a performance condition being met. When an alert fires, responses include notifying an operator or running a job to resolve an issue.

Multiserver jobs allow DBAs to run jobs consistently across their enterprise. In a multiserver scenario, there is a master server (MSX), in which jobs are created and modified, and multiple target servers (TSXs). The TSXs periodically poll the MSX and retrieve a list of jobs that they should be running.

Maintenance plans provide a graphical design surface on which DBAs can build maintenance routines. They allow you to incorporate decision-based logic using precedence constraints and to run different tasks on different schedules. You implement maintenance plans by creating SSIS packages and SQL Server Agent jobs that run those packages.

Although maintenance plans are very powerful and flexible, they do not expose the full power of SQL Server Integration Services (SSIS). Therefore, for some routines, DBAs may need to create an SSIS package manually, using SQL Server Data Tools for business intelligence (SSDT BI). This approach offers the full functionality of SSIS, including tasks for synchronizing instance-level objects. This can be very helpful for synchronizing disaster recovery (DR) environments, or for promoting and demoting data-tier applications between production and test environments.

CHAPTER 22

■ ■ ■

Policy-Based Management

Policy-Based Management (PBM) is a system DBAs can use to report on or enforce standards across the enterprise. This chapter first introduces you to the concepts used by PBM and then demonstrates how to use PBM to effectively manage an estate through the GUI and with PowerShell.

PBM Concepts

Policy-Based Management uses the concepts of targets, facets, conditions, and policies. *Targets* are entities PBM manages, such as databases or tables. *Facets* are collections of properties that relate to a target. For example, the database facet includes a property relating to the name of the database. *Conditions* are Boolean expressions that can be evaluated against a property. A binds conditions to targets. The following sections discuss each of these concepts.

Facets

A facet is a collection of properties that relate to a type of target, such as View, which has properties including IsSchemaBound, HasIndex, and HasAfterTrigger; Database Role, which has properties including Name Owner and IsFixedRole; and Index, which has properties including IsClustered, IsPartitioned, and IsUnique. The Index facet also exposes properties relating to geospatial indexes, memory-optimized indexes, XML indexes, and full-text indexes. Other notable facets include Database, StoredProcedure, SurfaceAreaConfiguration, LinkedServer, and Audit. SQL Server provides 93 facets in all, and you can find a complete list within the "Evaluation Modes" section of this chapter. You can also access a list of facets by running the command in Listing 22-1.

Listing 22-1. Finding a List of Facets

```
SELECT name
FROM msdb.dbo.syspolicy_management_facets ;
```

Conditions

A condition is a Boolean expression that is evaluated against an object property to determine whether or not it matches your requirement. Each facet contains multiple properties that you can create conditions against, but each condition can only access properties from a single facet. Conditions can be evaluated against the following operators:

- =
- !=
- LIKE
- NOT LIKE
- IN
- NOT IN

For example, you can use the LIKE operator to ensure that all database names begin with Chapter by using the following expression Database.Name LIKE 'Chapter%'.

Targets

A target is an entity to which a policy can be applied. This can be a table, a database, an entire instance, or most other objects within SQL Server. When adding targets to a policy, you can use conditions to limit the number of targets. This means, for example, if you create a policy to enforce database naming conventions on an instance, you can use a condition to avoid checking the policy against database names that contain the words "SharePoint," "bdc," or "wss," since these are your SharePoint databases and they may contain GUIDs that may be disallowed under your standard naming conventions.

Policies

A policy contains one condition and binds it to one or more targets (targets may also be filtered by separate conditions) and an evaluation mode. Depending on the evaluation mode you select, the policy may also contain a schedule on which you would like the policy to be checked. Policies support four evaluation modes, which are discussed in the following section.

Evaluation Modes

Policies support between one and four evaluation modes, depending on which facet you use within the condition. The following are the evaluation modes:

- On Demand
- On Schedule
- On Change: Log Only
- On Change: Prevent

If the evaluation mode is configured as On Demand, then the policies are only evaluated when you (the DBA) manually evaluate them. If the evaluation mode is configured as On Schedule, then you create a schedule when you create the policy; this causes the policy to be evaluated periodically.

■ **Tip** A policy can be evaluated On Demand even if it has been configured with a different evaluation mode.

If you select the On Change: Log Only evaluation mode, then whenever the relevant property of a target changes, the result of the policy validation is logged to the SQL Server log. In the event that the policy is fired but not validated, a message is generated in the log. This occurs when a target has been configured in such a way that one of your policies is violated. If the policy is violated, then Error 34053 is thrown with a severity level of 16.

■ **Tip** When you create an object, this causes the properties to be evaluated in the same way that they are when an existing object's properties are altered.

If you choose On Change: Prevent as the evaluation mode, then when a property is changed, SQL Server evaluates the property, and if there is a violation, an error message is thrown and the statement that caused the policy violation is rolled back.

Because policies work based on DDL events being fired, depending on the properties within the facet, not all evaluation modes can be implemented for all facets. The rules for working out the evaluation modes supported by a specific facet are rather opaque, so Table 22-1 provides a list of facets and the evaluation modes each supports.

Table 22-1. *Evaluation Mode Compatability*

Facet	On Demand	On Schedule	On Change: Log Only	On Change: Prevent
ApplicationRole	Yes	Yes	Yes	Yes
AsymmetricKey	Yes	Yes	Yes	Yes
Audit	Yes	Yes	No	No
AvailabilityDatabase	Yes	Yes	No	No
AvailabilityGroup	Yes	Yes	No	No
AvailabilityReplica	Yes	Yes	No	No
BackupDevice	Yes	Yes	No	No
BrokerPriority	Yes	Yes	No	No
BrokerService	Yes	Yes	No	No
Certificate	Yes	Yes	No	No
Computer	Yes	Yes	No	No
Credential	Yes	Yes	No	No
CryptographicProvider	Yes	Yes	No	No
Database	Yes	Yes	No	No
DatabaseAuditSpecification	Yes	Yes	No	No
DatabaseDdlTrigger	Yes	Yes	No	No

(continued)

Table 22-1. (*continued*)

Facet	On Demand	On Schedule	On Change: Log Only	On Change: Prevent
DatabaseReplicaState	Yes	Yes	No	No
DatabaseRole	Yes	Yes	Yes	Yes
DataFile	Yes	Yes	No	No
Default	Yes	Yes	No	No
DeployedDac	Yes	Yes	No	No
Endpoint	Yes	Yes	Yes	Yes
FileGroup	Yes	Yes	No	No
FullTextCatalog	Yes	Yes	No	No
FullTextIndex	Yes	Yes	No	No
FullTextStopList	Yes	Yes	No	No
IAvailabilityGroupState	Yes	Yes	No	No
IDatabaseMaintenanceFacet	Yes	Yes	No	No
IDatabaseOptions	Yes	Yes	Yes	No
IDatabasePerformanceFacet	Yes	Yes	No	No
IDatabaseSecurityFacet	Yes	Yes	No	No
IDataFilePerformanceFacet	Yes	Yes	No	No
ILogFilePerformanceFacet	Yes	Yes	No	No
ILoginOptions	Yes	Yes	Yes	Yes
IMultipartNameFacet	Yes	Yes	Yes	Yes
INameFacet	Yes	Yes	No	No
Index	Yes	Yes	No	No
IServerAuditFacet	Yes	Yes	No	No
IServerConfigurationFacet	Yes	Yes	Yes	No
IServerInformation	Yes	Yes	No	No
IServerPerformanceFacet	Yes	Yes	No	No
IServerProtocolSettingsFacet	Yes	Yes	No	No
IServerSecurityFacet	Yes	Yes	No	No
IServerSelectionFacet	Yes	No	No	No
IServerSettings	Yes	Yes	No	No
IServerSetupFacet	Yes	Yes	No	No
ISmartAdminState	Yes	Yes	No	No
ISurfaceAreaConfigurationForAnalysisServer	Yes	No	No	No

(*continued*)

Table 22-1. (*continued*)

Facet	On Demand	On Schedule	On Change: Log Only	On Change: Prevent
ISurfaceAreaConfigurationForReportingServices	Yes	No	No	No
ISurfaceAreaFacet	Yes	Yes	Yes	No
ITableOptions	Yes	Yes	Yes	Yes
IUserOptions	Yes	Yes	Yes	Yes
IViewOptions	Yes	Yes	Yes	Yes
LinkedServer	Yes	Yes	No	No
LogFile	Yes	Yes	No	No
Login	Yes	Yes	No	No
MessageType	Yes	Yes	No	No
PartitionFunction	Yes	Yes	No	No
PartitionScheme	Yes	Yes	No	No
PlanGuide	Yes	Yes	No	No
Processor	Yes	Yes	No	No
RemoteServiceBinding	Yes	Yes	No	No
ResourceGovernor	Yes	Yes	No	No
ResourcePool	Yes	Yes	Yes	Yes
Rule	Yes	Yes	No	No
Schema	Yes	Yes	Yes	Yes
SearchPropertyList	Yes	Yes	Yes	No
Sequence	Yes	Yes	Yes	Yes
Server	Yes	Yes	No	No
ServerAuditSpecification	Yes	Yes	No	No
ServerDdlTrigger	Yes	Yes	No	No
ServerRole	Yes	Yes	Yes	Yes
ServiceContract	Yes	Yes	No	No
ServiceQueue	Yes	Yes	No	No
ServiceRoute	Yes	Yes	No	No
SmartAdmin	Yes	Yes	No	No
Statistic	Yes	Yes	No	No
StoredProcedure	Yes	Yes	Yes	Yes
SymmetricKey	Yes	Yes	No	No
Synonym	Yes	Yes	No	No
Table	Yes	Yes	No	No

(*continued*)

Table 22-1. (*continued*)

Facet	On Demand	On Schedule	On Change: Log Only	On Change: Prevent
Trigger	Yes	Yes	No	No
User	Yes	Yes	No	No
UserDefinedAggregate	Yes	Yes	No	No
UserDefinedDataType	Yes	Yes	No	No
UserDefinedFunction	Yes	Yes	Yes	Yes
UserDefinedTableType	Yes	Yes	No	No
UserDefinedType	Yes	Yes	No	No
Utility	Yes	Yes	No	No
View	Yes	Yes	No	No
Volume	Yes	Yes	No	No
WorkloadGroup	Yes	Yes	Yes	Yes
XmlSchemaCollection	Yes	Yes	No	No

You can reproduce this list in SQL Server by running the query in Listing 22-2.

Listing 22-2. Listing Supported Execution Types per Facet

```
SELECT
      name ,
          'Yes' AS on_demand,
      CASE
          WHEN (CONVERT(BIT, execution_mode & 4)) = 1
          THEN 'Yes'
          ELSE 'No'
          END  AS on_schedule,
          CASE
          WHEN (CONVERT(BIT, execution_mode & 2)) = 1
          THEN 'Yes'
          ELSE 'No'
          END  AS on_change_log,
      CASE
          WHEN (CONVERT(BIT, execution_mode & 1)) = 1
          THEN 'Yes'
          ELSE 'No'
          END  AS on_change_prevent
FROM msdb.dbo.syspolicy_management_facets ;
```

Central Management Servers

SQL Server Management Studio provides a feature called a central management server. This feature allows you to register an instance as a central management server and then register other instances as registered servers of this central management server. Once you have registered servers under a central management server, you can run queries against all servers in the group or run policies against all servers within a group.

To register a central management server, select Registered Servers from the View menu in SQL Server Management Studio. This causes the Registered Servers window to appear, which is illustrated in Figure 22-1.

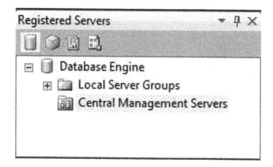

Figure 22-1. *The Registered Servers window*

Let's register our SQLSERVER\MASTERSERVER instance (which is the server\instance name we use in the demonstrations within this section) as a central management server by selecting Register Central Management Server from the context menu of Central Management Servers. This causes the General tab of the New Server Registration dialog box to display, as illustrated in Figure 22-2.

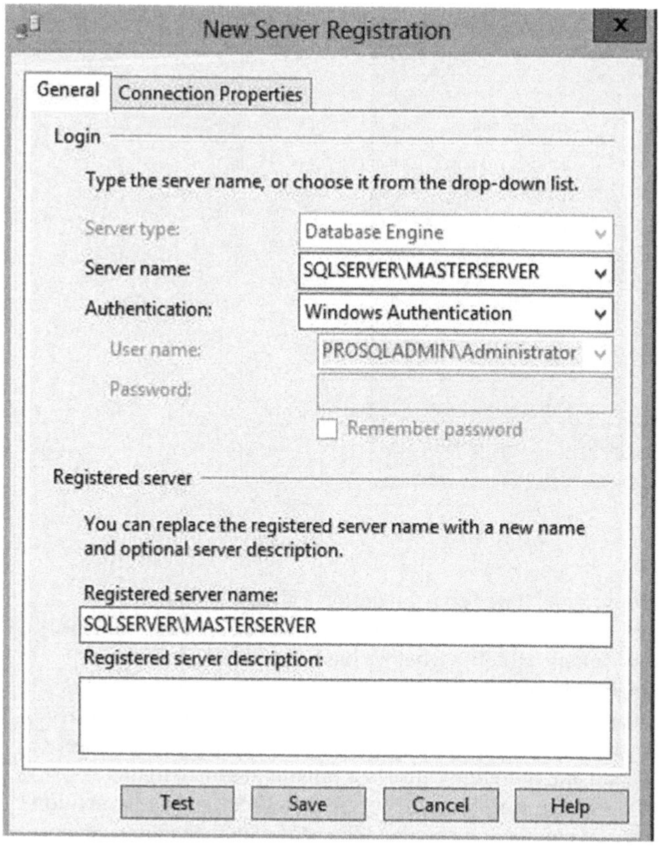

Figure 22-2. *The General tab*

On this tab, we enter the Server\Instance name of the central management server in the Server Name box. This causes the Registered Server Name field to update, but you can edit this manually to give it a new name if you wish. Optionally, you can also add a description for the instance.

On the Connection Properties tab, displayed in Figure 22-3, we specify our preferences for connecting to the instance.

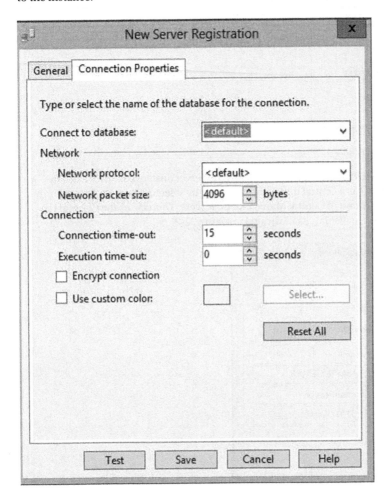

Figure 22-3. *The Connection Properties tab*

On this tab, we enter a database as a landing zone. If we leave the option as Default, then the connection is made to our default database. In the Network section of the tab, you can specify a specific network protocol to use, or leave the setting as Default, which is what we have done here. Leaving this as Default causes the connection to use the highest priority protocol specified in the instance's network configuration. Although changing the network packet size is not normally advised, doing so can improve performance in atypical scenarios by allowing the connection to benefit from jumbo frames, which are Ethernet frames that can support a larger payload and therefore cause less fragmentation of traffic.

In the Connection section of the screen, we specify durations for connection time-outs and execution time-outs. You can also specify whether to encrypt connections made to the central management server. If you are managing multiple instances within a single instance of SQL Server Management Studio, the Use Custom Color option is very useful for color coding the instance. Checking this option and specifying a color helps avoid queries accidently being run against an incorrect server. I find color coding instances particularly useful when I'm troubleshooting failed code releases, since I don't want to accidently run Dev/Test code against production! Clicking the Test button at the bottom of the New Server Registration window allows you to test the connection to the instance before you save it. This is always a good idea because it helps you avoid unnecessary troubleshooting at a later date.

Once we have registered the central management server, we can choose to either register servers directly below the central management server, or create server groups below the central management server. Base the strategy you choose here on the requirements of your environment. For example, if all servers that the central management server manages should have the same policies applied, it is probably sufficient to register the servers directly below the central management server. If your central management server will manage servers from different environments, however, such as Prod and Dev/Test, then you probably want to enforce different sets of policies against different environments; in such cases, it makes sense to create different server groups. Selecting New Server Group from the context menu of your newly created central management server invokes the New Server Group Properties dialog box, as illustrated in Figure 22-4.

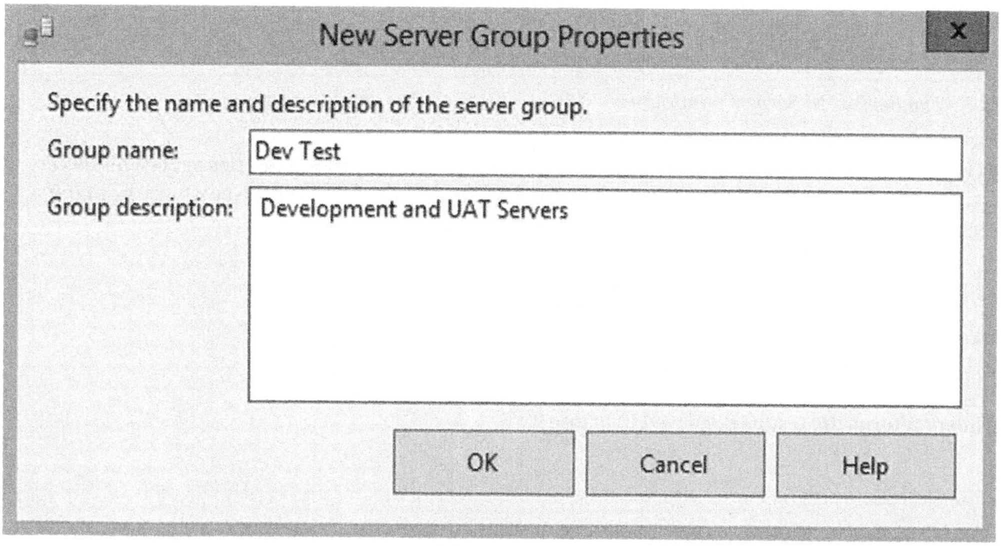

Figure 22-4. *New Server Group Properties dialog box*

You can see that we are using this dialog box to enter the name and description of the server group that will group our Dev/Test servers together. After exiting the dialog box, we repeat the process to create a server group for our production servers, which we name Prod.

■ **Tip** You can also nest server groups. Therefore, in more complex topologies, you can have a server group for each geographical region, which contains a server group for each environment.

Now let's choose the New Server Registration option from the context menu of each server group to add our instances to the appropriate groups. We add SQLSERVER\TARGETSERVER1 and SQLSERVER\TARGETSERVER2 to the Prod group and add the default instance of SQLSERVER to the DevTest group. You can add the servers using the same New Server Registration dialog box that you used to register the central management server. Figure 22-5 shows the Registered Servers screen after the servers have been added.

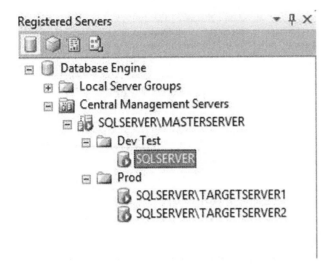

Figure 22-5. *The Registered Servers window*

One very useful feature of central management servers is their ability to run queries against all servers within a server group or against all servers they manage. For example, we can select New Query from the context menu of the Prod Server Group and run the query in Listing 22-3.

Listing 22-3. Listing All Database in the Server Group

```
SELECT name
FROM sys.Databases ;
```

This query returns the results displayed in Figure 22-6.

	Server Name	Name
1	SQLSERVER\TARGETSERVER1	master
2	SQLSERVER\TARGETSERVER1	tempdb
3	SQLSERVER\TARGETSERVER1	model
4	SQLSERVER\TARGETSERVER1	msdb
5	SQLSERVER\TARGETSERVER2	master
6	SQLSERVER\TARGETSERVER2	tempdb
7	SQLSERVER\TARGETSERVER2	model
8	SQLSERVER\TARGETSERVER2	msdb

Query executed successfully. Prod PROSQLADMIN\Administrator master 00:00:00 8 rows

Figure 22-6. *Results of listing all servers in the server group*

The first thing you notice is that the status bar below the query results is pink instead of yellow. This indicates that the query has been run against multiple servers. Second, instead of displaying an instance name, the status bar displays the server group that the query has been run against; in our case, this is Prod. Finally, notice that an additional column has been added to the result set. This column is called Server Name, and it indicates which instance within the server group the row returned from. Because no user databases exist on SQLSERVER\TARGETSERVER1 or SQLSERVER\TARGETSERVER2, the four system databases have been returned from each instance.

Creating Policies

You can create policies using either SQL Server Management Studio or T-SQL. The following sections discuss how to create a simple static policy, before they go on to discuss how to create advanced, dynamic policies.

■ **Tip**   SQL Server provides 50 predefined policies; you can find these in the `C:\Program Files (x86)\` `Microsoft SQL Server\120\Tools\Policies\DatabaseEngine\1033` folder, assuming you have installed the instance using the default installation directory. You can import these polices to your instance and evaluated them to ensure that your configuration is in line with Microsoft's recommended best practices.

Creating Simple Policies

PBM offers a great deal of flexibility within its predefined facets, properties, and conditions. You can use this flexibility to create a comprehensive set of policies for your enterprise. The following sections discuss how to use PBM's built-in functionality to create simple policies.

Creating a Policy That You Can Manually Evaluate

As you've probably noticed, example databases in this book use the name format of `Chapter<ChapterNumber>`. Therefore, here we create a policy that enforces this naming convention by causing any policy that violates this policy to roll back and generate an error. To do this, we invoke the Create New Policy dialog box by drilling through Management | Policy Management in Object Explorer on the Master server and then selecting New Policy from the Policies context menu. Figure 22-7 displays the General page of the dialog box.

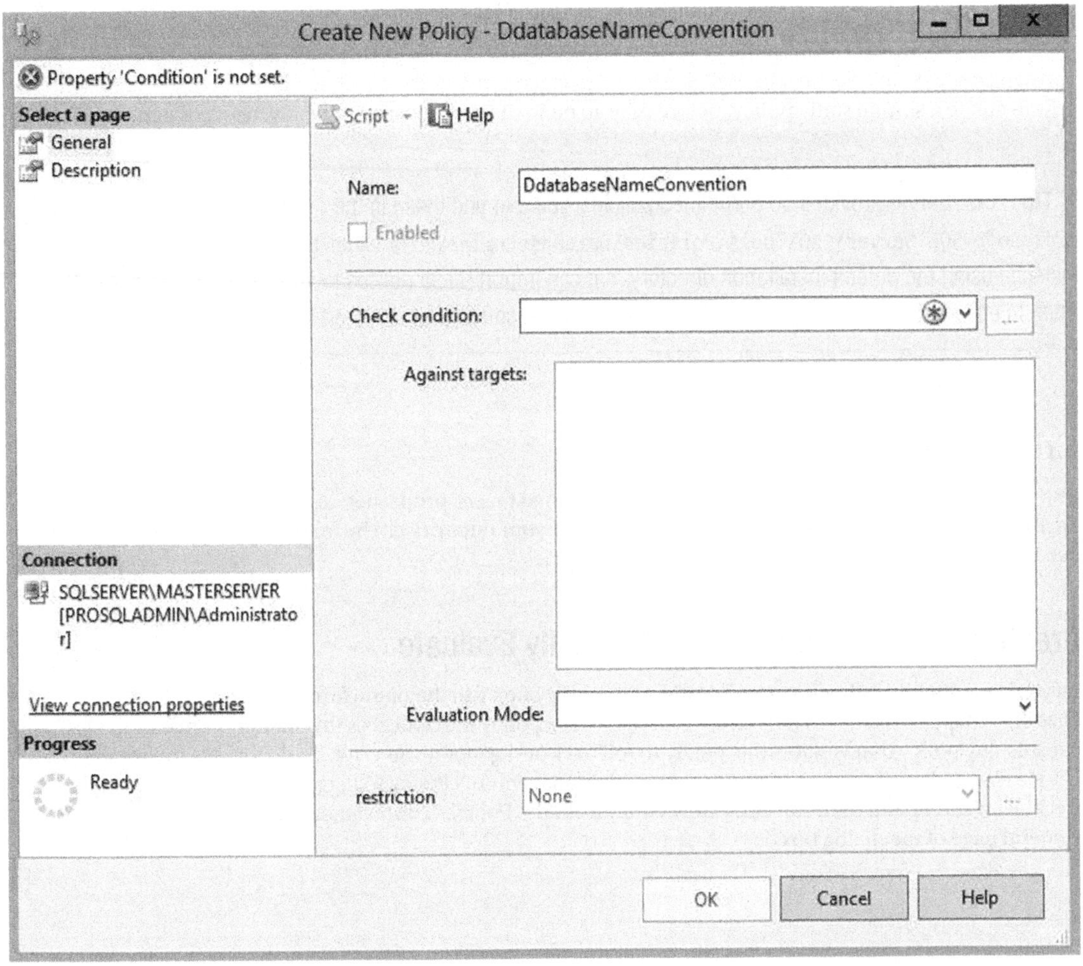

Figure 22-7. *New Policy Dialog box, General page*

On this page, we give the policy a name but find that the Against Targets and Evaluation Mode options are not accessible. This is because we have not yet created a condition. Therefore, our next step is to use the Check Condition drop-down box to select New Condition. This causes the General page of the Create New Condition dialog box to display, illustrated in Figure 22-8.

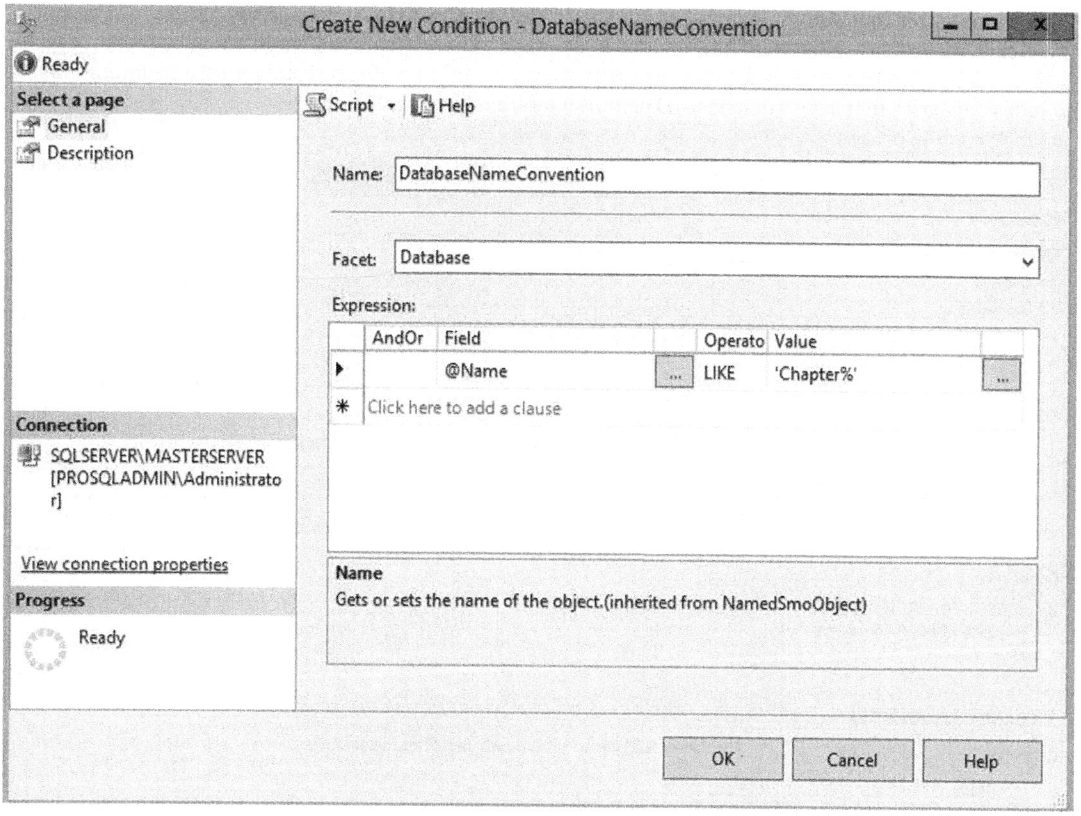

Figure 22-8. *Create New Condition dialog box, General page*

On this page, we give the condition a name and select the Database facet. In the Expression area of the screen, we select that the @Name field should be LIKE 'Chapter%', where % is a zero-or-more-character wildcard. On the Description page, we are optionally able to specify a textual description for the condition.

Back on the General page of the Create New Policy dialog box, we ensure that the Evaluation Mode drop-down is set to select On Demand, which means that the policy is not evaluated unless we explicitly evaluate it. The only other option available is to schedule the evaluation. This is because the Database facet does not support the On Change: Log Only or On Change: Prevent evaluation modes.

■ **Note**   Please refer back to Table 22-1 for a complete list of facets and the evaluation mode each supports.

Our policy obviously does not apply to system databases. This matters because we can use our policy to check existing databases as well as new databases we create. Therefore, in the Against Targets section of the page, we use the drop-down box to enter the Create New Condition dialog box and create a condition that excludes databases that have a database ID of four or less, as shown in Figure 22-9.

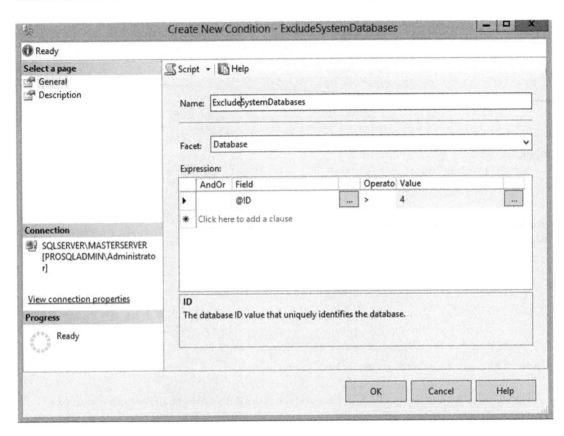

Figure 22-9. *Create an ExcludeSystemDatabases condition*

Back in the Create New Policy dialog box, we can create a condition to enforce a server restriction, which filters the instances that the policy is evaluated against. Because we are only evaluating the policy against our SQLSERVER\MASTERSERVER instance, however, we do not need to do this. Instead, we navigate to the Description page, illustrated in Figure 22-10.

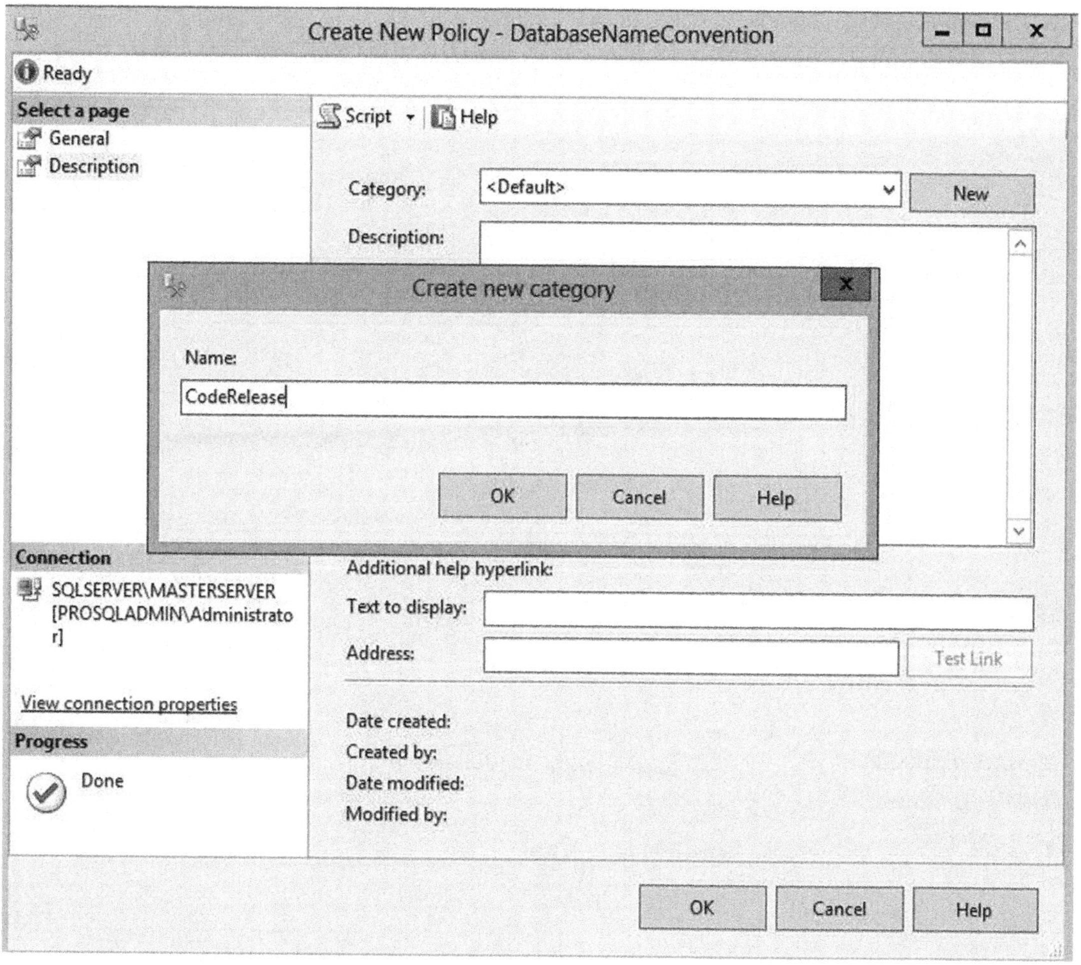

Figure 22-10. *The Description page*

On this page, we use the New button to create a new category, CodeRelease, which help us check code quality in a UAT (user acceptance testing) or OAT (operational acceptance testing) environment before the code is promoted to production. Optionally, we can also add a free text description of the policy and a help hyperlink, alongside a website address or e-mail link.

The final view of the policy is illustrated in Figure 22-11.

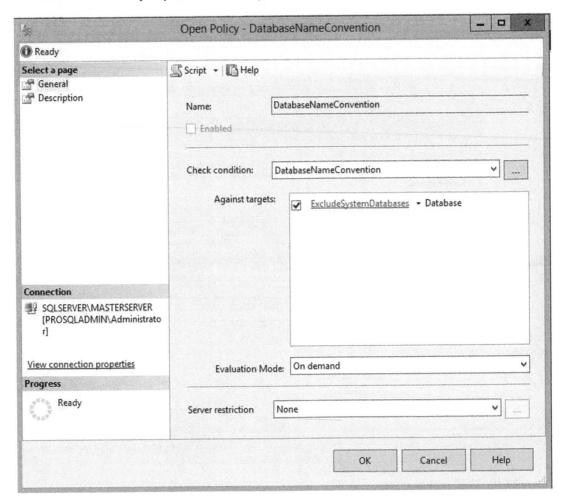

Figure 22-11. *Final view of policy*

Manually Evaluating a Policy

Before evaluating our policy, we first create a database that does not match our naming convention by executing the command in Listing 22-4.

Listing 22-4. Creating a BrokenPolicy Database

```
CREATE DATABASE BrokenPolicy ;
```

We can evaluate our new policy against our instance by using the Evaluate Policies dialog box, which we can invoke by drilling through Management | Policy Management | Policies and by selecting Evaluate from the context menu of our policy.

■ **Tip**   You can manually evaluate the policy even if it is disabled.

In the Evaluate Policies dialog box, shown in Figure 22-12, you see a list of policies that have been evaluated in the top half of the window; a status indicator informs you if any policies have been broken. In the bottom half of the window, you see a list of targets that the highlighted policy was evaluated against; here a status indicator informs you of the policy's status on a target-by-target basis.

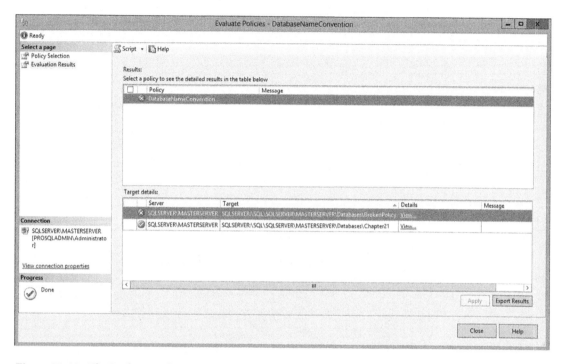

Figure 22-12.   *The Evaluate Policies dialog box*

■ **Tip**   If you wish to evaluate multiple polices, select Evaluate from the context menu of the Policies folder in Object Explorer, and then select which policies you would like to evaluate. All selected policies are then evaluated and displayed in the Evaluation Results page.

We created the Chapter21 database in Chapter 21 of this book. If you do not have a Chapter21 database, you can create it using the statement CREATE DATABASE Chapter21 ;.

Click the View link in the Details column to invoke the Results Detailed View dialog box, as illustrated in Figure 22-13. This information is useful for failed policy evaluations because it provides the details of the actual value that did not meet the policy's condition.

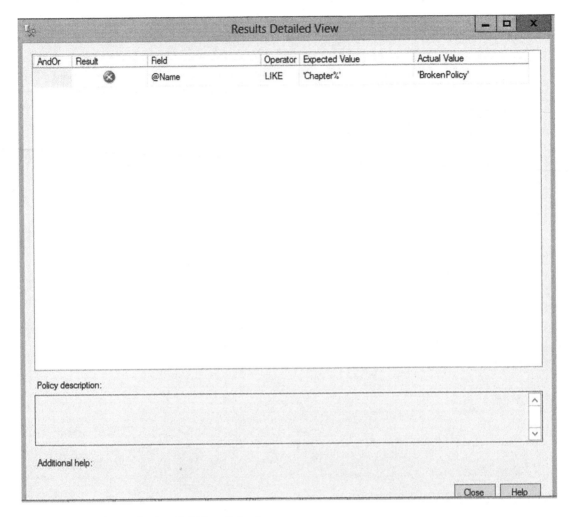

Figure 22-13. *The Results Detailed View dialog box*

Creating a Policy That Prevents Unwanted Activity

Another very useful simple policy is one that helps you prevent developers from using NOLOCK in their stored procedures as a perceived performance enhancement. In this instance, rather than just evaluating the policy on an ad-hoc basis, we want to prevent stored procedures that contain NOLOCK from being created. If this succeeds, during code releases, you do not need to review every stored procedure for the NOLOCK or READUNCOMMITTED syntax. Instead, you can expect the policy to be evaluated and the CREATE PROCEDURE statement to be rolled back.

Before we create this policy, we need to ensure that nested triggers are enabled on the instance. This is because the policy will be enforced using DDL triggers, which we discuss in Chapter 24, and nested triggers are a hard technical requirement for this functionality. You can enable nested triggers using sp_configure, with the script in Listing 22-5; however, they are turned on by default.

Listing 22-5. Enabling Nested Triggers

```
EXEC sp_configure 'nested triggers', 1 ;
RECONFIGURE
```

After creating the policy, you need to create a condition. When creating the condition, as illustrated in Figure 22-14, we use the UPPER function to convert the @MethodName property of the StoredProcedure facet to uppercase. We do this so that it can be evaluated to see if it contains the strings NOLOCK or READUNCOMMITTED, which when specified as a query hint, have the same effect as each other. By converting the @MethodName property to uppercase before the evaluation, we avoid issues with case-sensitivity if our instance is running a case-sensitive collation.

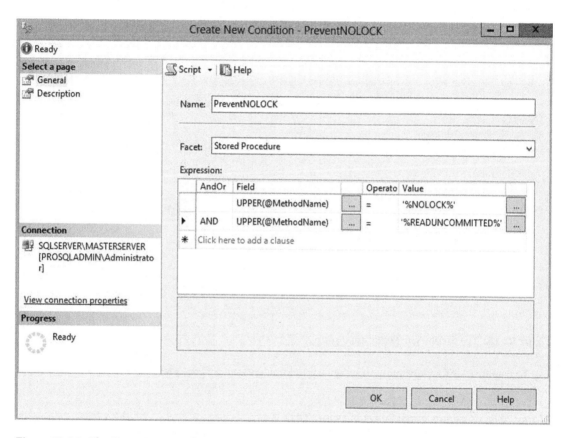

Figure 22-14. *The Create New Condition dialog box*

In the Create New Policy dialog box, illustrated in Figure 22-15, we use the Against Targets area to configure which targets should be evaluated by the policy; the settings default to Every Stored Procedure In Every Database. This suits our needs, so we do not need to create a condition. In the Evaluation Mode drop-down, we select On Change: Prevent; this makes it so it is not possible to create stored procedures on our SQLSERVER\MASTERSERVER instance if the definition contains the words NOLOCK or READUNCOMMITTED. We also make sure to check the Enabled box so that the policy is enabled when it is created.

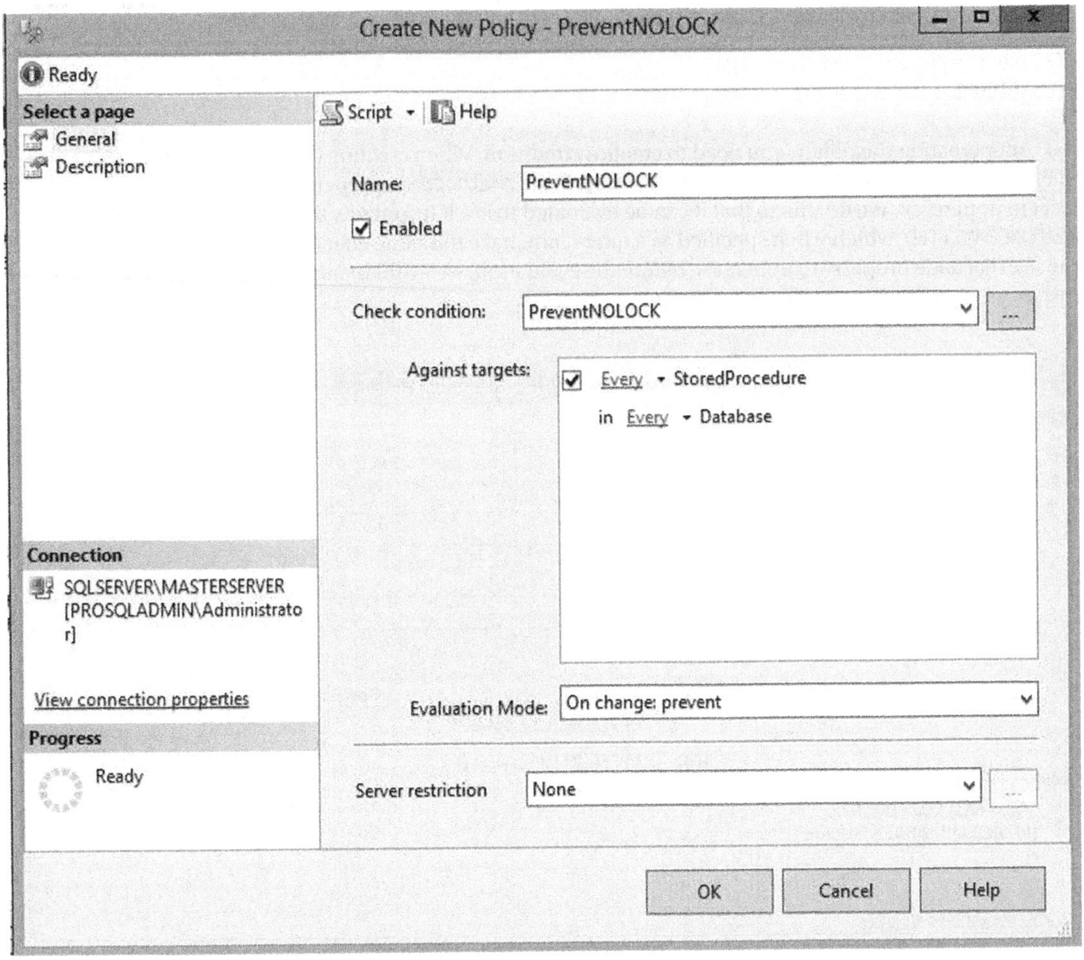

Figure 22-15. *The Create New Policy dialog box*

To demonstrate the prevention in action, we attempt to create a stored procedure using the script in Listing 22-6.

Listing 22-6. Creating a Stored Procedure with NOLOCK

```
CREATE PROCEDURE ReadWithNOLOCK
AS
BEGIN
        SELECT *
        FROM sys.tables WITH (NOLOCK)
END
```

Figure 22-16 shows the error that is thrown when we attempt to run this CREATE PROCEDURE statement.

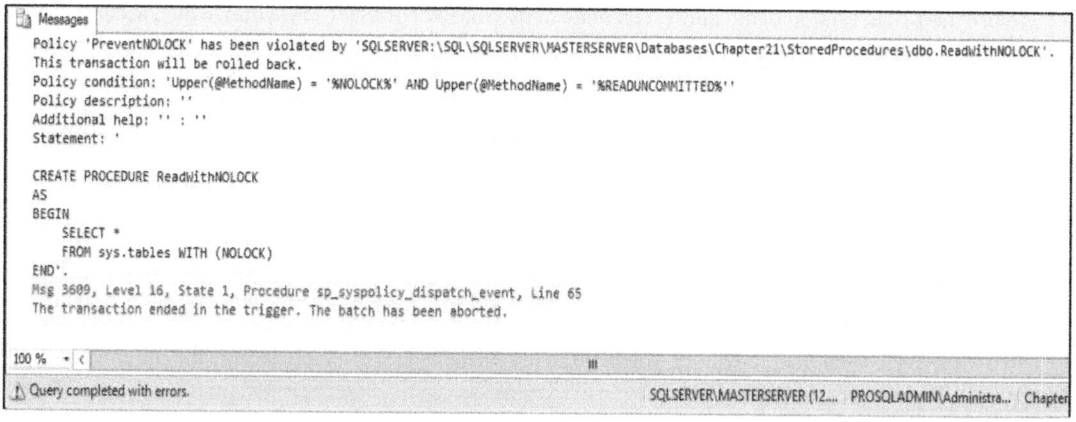
Messages
Policy 'PreventNOLOCK' has been violated by 'SQLSERVER:\SQL\SQLSERVER\MASTERSERVER\Databases\Chapter21\StoredProcedures\dbo.ReadWithNOLOCK'.
This transaction will be rolled back.
Policy condition: 'Upper(@MethodName) = '%NOLOCK%' AND Upper(@MethodName) = '%READUNCOMMITTED%''
Policy description: ''
Additional help: '' : ''
Statement: '
CREATE PROCEDURE ReadWithNOLOCK
AS
BEGIN
SELECT *
FROM sys.tables WITH (NOLOCK)
END'.
Msg 3609, Level 16, State 1, Procedure sp_syspolicy_dispatch_event, Line 65
The transaction ended in the trigger. The batch has been aborted.
100 %
Query completed with errors.
SQLSERVER\MASTERSERVER (12.... PROSQLADMIN\Administra... Chapter

Figure 22-16. *The error thrown by the policy trigger*

Creating an Advanced Policy

PBM is extensible, and if you can't create the required condition using the built-in facet properties, the Expression Advanced Editor allows you to use a wide range of functions. These functions include `ExecuteSql()` and `ExecuteWql()`, which allow you to build your own SQL and WQL (Windows Query Language), respectively. The `ExecuteSql()` and `ExecuteWql()` functions are not T-SQL functions. They are part of the PBM framework.

You can use these functions to write queries against either the Database Engine or Windows and evaluate the result. The functions are called once for each target. So, for example, if they are used with the `Server` facet, they only run once, but if they are used against the `Table` facet, they are evaluated for every target table. If multiple columns are returned when you are using `ExecuteSql()`, then the first column of the first row is evaluated. If multiple columns are returned when you are using `ExecuteWql()`, then an error is thrown. For example, imagine that you want to ensure that the SQL Server Agent service starts. You can achieve this in T-SQL by running the query in Listing 22-7. This query uses the `LIKE` operator because the `servicename` column also includes the name of the service, and the `LIKE` operator makes the query generic so that it can be run on any instance, without needing to be modified.

Listing 22-7. Checking to Make Sure SQL Server Agent Is Running with T-SQL

```
SELECT status_desc
FROM sys.dm_server_services
WHERE servicename LIKE 'SQL Server Agent%' ;
```

Or alternatively, you can achieve the same result by using the WQL query in Listing 22-8.

■ **Note** You can find an WQL reference at `https://msdn.microsoft.com/en-us/library/aa394606(v=vs.85).aspx`.

Listing 22-8. Checking That SQL Server Agent Is Running with WQL

```
SELECT State FROM Win32_Service  WHERE Name ="SQLSERVERAGENT$MASTERSERVER"
```

To use the T-SQL version of the query, you need to use the ExecuteSql() function, which accepts the parameters in Table 22-2.

Table 22-2. *ExecuteSQL() Parameters*

Parameter	Description
returnType	Specifies the return type expected from the query. Acceptable values are Numeric, String, Bool, DateTime, Array, and GUID.
sqlQuery	Specifies the query that should run.

To use the WQL version of the query, you need to use ExecuteWql(), which accepts the parameters described in Table 22-3.

Table 22-3. *ExecuteWQL() Parameters*

Parameter	Description
returnType	Specifies the return type expected from the query. Acceptable values are Numeric, String, Bool, DateTime, Array, and GUID.
namespace	Specifies the WQL namespace that the query should be executed against.
wqlQuery	Specifies the query that should run.

Therefore, if you are using the T-SQL approach, your condition would use the script in Listing 22-9.

Listing 22-9. ExecuteSQL()

```
ExecuteSql('string', 'SELECT status_desc FROM sys.dm_server_services WHERE servicename LIKE
''SQL Server Agent%''')
```

■ **Tip**   It is important to note here that we had to escape the single quotes in our query, to ensure that they are recognised during execution.

If you use the WQL approach, your condition needs to use the script in Listing 22-10.

Listing 22-10. ExecuteWQL()

```
ExecuteWql('String', 'root\CIMV2', 'SELECT State FROM Win32_Service  WHERE Name ="SQLSERVERA
GENT$MASTERSERVER"')
```

Figure 22-17 shows how we would create the condition using the WQL approach.

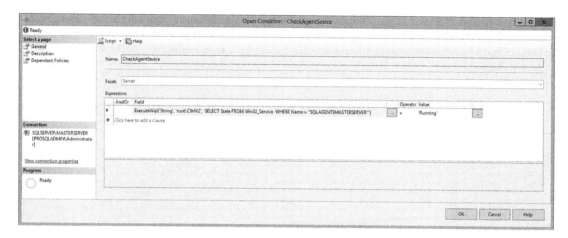

Figure 22-17. *Creating the condition with ExecuteWql()*

■ **Caution**   Because of the power and flexibility of the `ExecuteWql()` and `ExecuteSql()` functions, it is possible that they will be abused to create security holes. Therefore, make sure you carefully control who has permissions to create policies.

Managing Policies

Policies are installed on an instance of SQL Server, but you can export them to XML files, which in turn allows them to be ported to other servers or to central management servers so that they can be evaluated against multiple instances at the same time. The following sections discuss how to import and export policies, as well as how to use policies in conjunction with central management servers. We also discuss how to manage policies with PowerShell.

Importing and Exporting Policies

SQL Server provides a folder structure for storing policies under the 32-bit installation path. Assuming that you have installed SQL Server using the default installation directory, the full path would be `C:\Program Files (x86)\Microsoft SQL Server\120\Tools\Policies`. In this folder, you will find three additional folders; `DatabaseEngine`, `AnalysisServices`, and `ReportingServices`.

If we want to export our DatabaseNameConvention policy to the DatabaseEngine folder, we select Export Policy from the context menu of the DatabaseNameConvention policy in Object Explorer and navigate to the DatabaseEngine folder in the Export Policy dialog box before we choose a name for the file and click Save, as shown in Figure 22-18.

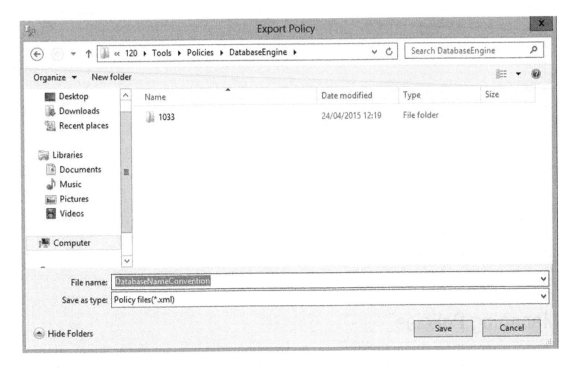

Figure 22-18. *The Export Policy dialog box*

We now import the policy into our SQLSERVER\TARGETSERVER1 instance. To do this, we connect to the TARGETSERVER1 instance in Object Explorer and then drill through Management | Policy Based Management, before selecting Import Policy from the Policies context menu. This invokes the Import dialog box, as displayed in Figure 22-19.

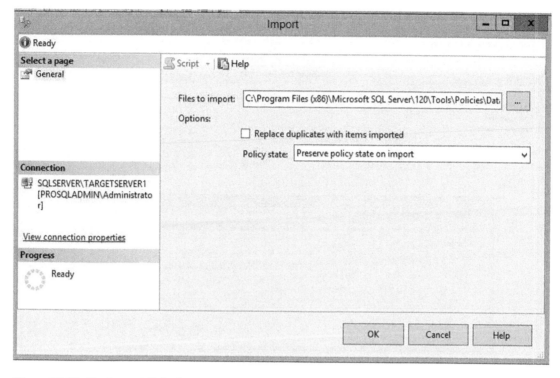

Figure 22-19. *The Import dialog box*

In this dialog box, we use the Files To Import ellipses button to select our DatabaseNameConvention policy. We can also choose the state of the policy after it is imported from the Policy State drop-down and specify whether policies that already exist on the instance with the same name should be overwritten.

Enterprise Management with Policies

Although being able to evaluate a policy against a single instance of SQL Server is useful, to maximize the power of PBM, you can combine policies with central management servers so that the policy can be evaluated against the SQL Server Enterprise in a single execution.

For example, imagine that we want to evaluate the DatabaseNameConvention policy against all servers within the Prod group that we created when we registered the SQLSERVER\MASTERSERVER instance as a central management server. To do this, we drill through Central Management Servers | SQLSERVER\MASTERSERVER in the Registered Servers window before we select Evaluate Policies from the Prod context menu.

This invokes the Evaluate Policies dialog box. Here, you can use the Source ellipses button to invoke the Select Source dialog box and choose the policy or policies that you would like to evaluate against the group, as shown in Figure 22-20.

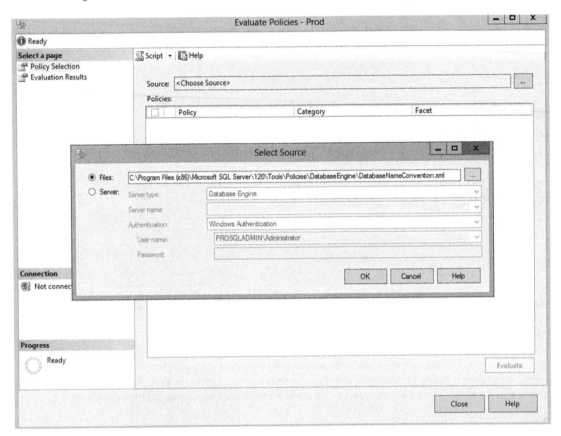

Figure 22-20. *The Evaluate Policies dialog box*

In the Select Source dialog box, either select policies stored as XML files from the file system, or specify the connection details of an instance where the policy is installed. In our case, we select the DatabaseNameConvention by clicking the Files ellipses button.

Selected policies then display in the Policies section of the screen, as shown in Figure 22-21. If you selected a source with multiple policies, you can use the check boxes to define which policies to evaluate. Clicking the Evaluate button causes the selected policies to be evaluated against all servers in the group.

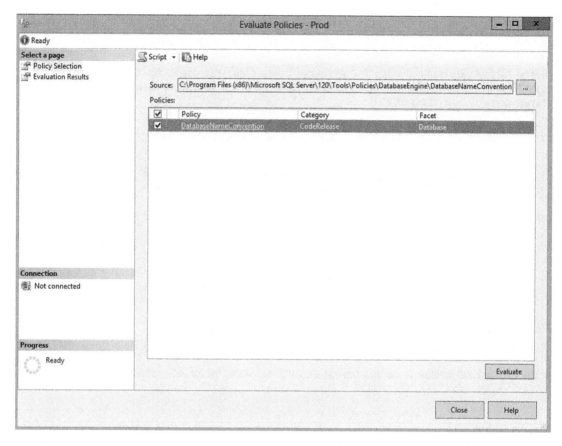

Figure 22-21. *The Evaluate Policies dialog box*

Evaluating Policies with PowerShell

When policies are installed on an instance, they can be evaluated using the methods already described
in this chapter. If your policies are stored as XML files, however, then you can still evaluate them using
PowerShell. This can be helpful if your SQL Server enterprise includes SQL Server 2000 or 2005 instances, as
many still do. Because PBM was only introduced in SQL Server 2008, policies cannot be imported into older
instances, but PowerShell offers a useful workaround for this issue.

To evaluate our DatabaseNameConvention policy against our SQLSERVER\MASTERSERVER instance, from
the XML file using PowerShell, we need to run the script in Listing 22-11. The first line of this script changes
the path to the folder where the policy is stored. The second line actually evaluates the policy.

If the property we were configuring was settable and deterministic (which ours is not), then we could
add the -AdHocPolicyExecutionMode parameter and set it to "Configure". This would cause the setting to
change to fall inline with our policy.

Listing 22-11. Evaluating a Policy with PowerShell

```
sl "C:\Program Files (x86)\Microsoft SQL Server\120\Tools\Policies\DatabaseEngine"

Invoke-PolicyEvaluation -Policy " C:\Program Files (x86)\Microsoft SQL Server
\120\Tools\Policies\DatabaseEngine\DatabaseNameConvention.xml DatabaseNameConvention.xml"
-TargetServer" .\MASTERSERVER"
```

The output of this policy evaluation is shown in Figure 22-22.

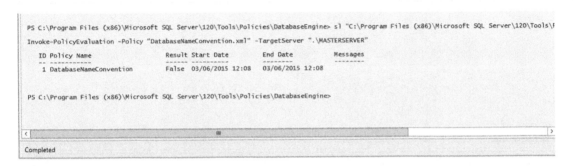

Figure 22-22. *Results of policy evaluation*

■ **Tip** To evaluate multiple properties, provide a comma-separated list for the -Policy parameter.

Summary

Policy-Based Management (PBM) offers a powerful and flexible method for ensuring coding standards and hosting standards are met across your enterprise. A target is an entity managed by PBM. A condition is a Boolean expression that the policy evaluates against the targets, and a facet is a collection of properties that relate to a specific type of target.

Depending on the facet you use, a policy offers up to four policy evaluation modes: On Demand, On Schedule, On Change: Log Only, and On Change: Prevent. On Demand, On Schedule, and On Change: Log Only can be thought of as reactive, whereas On Change: Prevent can be thought of as proactive, since it actively stops a configuration from being made, which violates a policy. Because On Change modes rely on DDL triggers, you must enable nested triggers at the instance level, and they are not available for all facets.

Policies are extensible, through the use of the ExecuteSql() and ExecuteWql() functions, which allow you to evaluate the results of T-SQL or WQL queries. These functions offer massive flexibility, but their power can also cause security holes to be opened, so exercise caution when granting permissions to create policies.

An instance can be registered as a central management server, and other servers can be registered underneath it, either directly, or in groups. This gives DBAs the ability to run a query across multiple instances at the same time, and it also offers them the ability to evaluate policies against multiple servers at the same time. This means that you can use Policy-Based Management at the Enterprise level to enforce standards.

You can evaluate policies from within SQL Server or using PowerShell with the -InvokePolicyEvaluation cmdlet. This offers you increased flexibility for managing estates that have older SQL Server instances, such as 2000 or 2005. This is because PowerShell allows DBAs to evaluate the policies from XML files, instead of only being able to evaluate them after importing them to MSDB.

CHAPTER 23

Resource Governor

Resource Governor provides a method for throttling applications at the SQL Server layer by imposing limits on CPU, memory, and physical IO on different classifications of connection. This chapter discusses the concepts the Resource Governor uses before demonstrating how to implement it. We then look at how to monitor the effect that Resource Governor has on resource utilization.

Resource Governor Concepts

Resource Governor uses resource pools to define a subset of server resources, workload groups as logical containers for similar session requests, and a classifier function to determine to which workload group a specific request should be assigned. The following sections discuss each of these concepts.

Resource Pool

A *resource pool* defines a subset of server resources that sessions can utilize. When Resource Governor is enabled, two pools are automatically created: the internal pool and the default pool. The *internal pool* represents the server resources the instance uses. This pool cannot be modified. The *default pool* is designed as a catch-all pool and is used to assign resources to any session that is not assigned to a user-defined resource pool. You cannot remove this pool; however, you can modify its settings.

Resource pools allow you to configure the minimum and maximum amount of resources (CPU, memory, and in SQL Server 2014 onward, physical IO) that will be available to sessions that are assigned to that pool. As you add additional pools, maximum values of existing pools are transparently adjusted so they do not conflict with the minimum resource percentages assigned to all pools. For example, imagine that you have configured the resource pools, which are represented in Table 23-1, to throttle CPU usage.

Table 23-1. *Resource Pools Simple Effective Maximum Percentages*

Resource Pool*	Min CPU %	Max CPU %	Effective Max CPU %	Calculation
Default	0	100	75	Smallest(75,(100-25)) = 75
SalesApplication	25	75	75	Smallest(75,(100-0)) = 75

The internal resource pool is not mentioned here since it is not configurable either directly, or implicitly. Instead, it can consume whatever resources it requires and has a minimum CPU of 0; therefore, it does not impact the effective maximum CPU calculation for other pools.

In this example, the actually Max CPU % settings will be as you configured them. However, imagine that you now add an additional resource pool, called `AccountsApplication`, which is configured with a Min CPU % of 50 percent and a Max CPU % of 80 percent. The sum of the minimum CPU percentages is now greater than the sum of the maximum CPU percentages. This means that the effective maximum CPU percentage for each resource pool is reduced accordingly. The formula for this calculation is `Smallest( Default(Max), Default(Max) - SUM(Other Min CPU))`, which is reflected in Table 23-2.

Table 23-2. *Resource Pools Effective Maximum Percentages after Implicit Reductions*

Resource Pool*	Min CPU %	Max CPU %	Effective Max CPU %	Calculation
Default	0	100	25	`Smallest((100,(100-sum(25,50)) = 25`
SalesApplication	25	75	50	`Smallest((75,(100-50)) = 50`
AccountsApplication	50	80	75	`Smallest((80,(100-25)) = 75`

* *The internal resource pool is not mentioned here since it is not configurable either directly, or implicitly. Instead, it can consume whatever resources it requires and has a minimum CPU of 0; therefore, it does not impact the effective maximum CPU calculation for other pools.*

Workload Group

A resource pool can contain one or more workload groups. A *workload group* represents a logical container for similar sessions that have been classified as similar by executing a classifier function, which is covered in the next section. For example, in the `SalesApplication` resource pool mentioned earlier, we can create two workload groups. We can use one of these workload groups as a container for normal user sessions, while using the second as a container for reporting sessions.

This approach allows us to monitor the groups of sessions separately. It also allows us to define separate policies for each set of sessions. For example, we may choose to specify that sessions used for reporting have a lower `MAXDOP` (Maximum Degree Of Parallelization) setting than the sessions used for standard users, or that sessions used for reporting should only be able to specify a limited number of concurrent requests. These settings are in addition to the settings we can configure at the resource pool level.

Classifier Function

A *classifier function* is a scalar function, created in the Master database. It is used to determine which workload group each session should be assigned to. Every new session is classified using a single classifier function, with the exception of DACs (dedicated administrator connections), which are not subject to Resource Governor. The classifier function can group sessions based on virtually any attribute that it is possible to code within interpreted SQL. For example, you may choose to classify requests based upon user name, role membership, application name, host name, login property, connection property, or even time.

Implementing Resource Governor

To configure Resource Governor on an instance, you must create and configure one or more resource pools, each with one or more workload groups. In addition, you must also create a classifier function. Finally, you need to enable Resource Governor, which results in all subsequent sessions being classified. These topics are discussed in the following sections.

Creating Resource Pools

From SQL Server 2012 on, it is possible to create a maximum of 64 resource pools per instance. Let's create a resource pool through SQL Server Management Studio, drill through Management | Resource Governor in Object Explorer, and then select New Resource Pool from the Resource Pools context menu. This causes the Resource Governor Properties dialog box to be invoked, as illustrated in Figure 23-1.

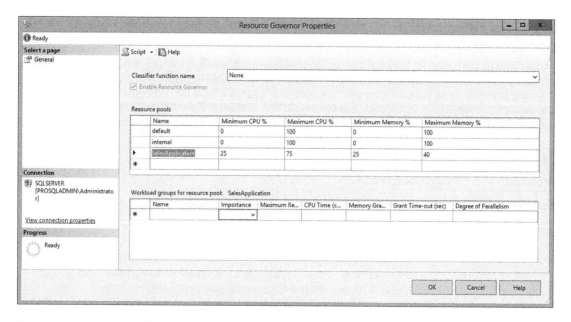

Figure 23-1. *The Resorce Governor Properties dialog box*

In the Resource Pools section of this dialog box, we create a new row in the grid and populate it with the information we need to create our new resource pool. In our case, we add the details for a resource pool named SalesApplication, which has a Minimum CPU % of 25, a Maximum CPU % of 75, a Minimum Memory % of 25, and a Maximum Memory % of 40.

■ **Tip**　Highlighting a resource pool causes the workload groups associated with that resource pool to display in the Workload Groups For Resource Pool section of the screen. Here, you can add, amend, or remove resource pools at the same time. However, you can also access this dialog box by drilling through Management | Resource Governor | [*Resource Pool name*] and then selecting New Workload Group from the Workload Groups context menu.

In this scenario, the maximum memory limit is a hard limit. This means that no more than 40 percent of the memory available to this instance is ever allocated to this resource pool. Also, even if no sessions are using this resource pool, 25 percent of the memory available to the instance is still allocated to this resource pool and is unavailable to other resource pools.

In contrast, the maximum CPU limit is soft, or opportunistic. This means that if more CPU is available, the resource pool utilizes it. The cap only kicks in when there is contention on the processor.

> **■ Tip** From SQL Server 2012 on, it is possible to configure a hard cap on CPU usage. This is helpful in PaaS (Platform as a Service) or DaaS (Database as a Service) environments where clients are charged based on CPU usage and you need to ensure consistent billing for their applications. A client can easily dispute a bill if they have agreed to pay for 40 percent of a core, but the soft cap allows them to reach 50 percent, resulting in a higher charge automatically being applied. Implementing this is discussed later in this section.

You can also create resource pools via T-SQL. When you do so, you have access to more functionality than you do through the GUI, which allows you to configure minimum and maximum IOPS (Input/Output per second), set hard caps on CPU usage, and affinitize a resource pool with specific CPUs or NUMA nodes. Creating an affinity between a resource pool and a subset of CPUs, means that the resource pool will only use the CPUs, to which it is aligned. You can use the CREATE RESOURCE POOL DDL statement to create a resource pool in T-SQL. The settings you can configure on a resource pool are detailed in Table 23-3.

Table 23-3. *CREATE RESOURCE POOL Arguments*

Argument	Description
pool_name	The name that you assign to the resource pool.
MIN_CPU_PERCENT	Specifies the guaranteed average minimum CPU resource available to the resource pool as a percentage of the CPU bandwidth available to the instance.
MAX_CPU_PERCENT	Specifies the average maximum CPU resource available to the resource pool as a percentage of the CPU bandwidth available to the instance. This is a soft limit that applies when there is contention for the CPU resource.
CAP_CPU_PERCENT	Specifies a hard limit on the amount of CPU resource available to the resource pool as a percentage of the CPU bandwidth available to the instance.
MIN_MEMORY_PERCENT	Specifies the minimum amount of memory that is reserved for the resource pool as a percentage of the memory available to the instance.
MAX_MEMORY_PERCENT	Specifies the maximum amount of memory that the resource pool can use as a percentage of the memory available to the instance.
MIN_IOPS_PER_VOLUME	Specifies the number of IOPS per volume that is reserved for the resource pool. Unlike CPU and memory thresholds, IOPS are expressed as an absolute value, as opposed to a percentage.
MAX_IOPS_PER_VOLUME	Specifies the maximum number of IOPS per volume that the resource pool can use. Like the minimum IOPS threshold, this is expressed as an absolute number, as opposed to a percentage.
AFFINITY SCHEDULER*	Specifies that the resource pool should be bound to specific SQLOS (SQL operating system) schedulers, which in turn map to specific virtual cores within the server. Cannot be used with AFFINITY NUMANODE. • Specify AUTO to allow SQL Server to manage the schedulers that are used by the resource pool. • Specify the range of scheduler IDs. For example (0, 1, 32 TO 64).
AFFINITY NUMANODE*	Specifies that the resource pool should be bound to a specific range of NUMA nodes. For example (1 TO 4). Cannot be used with AFFINITY SCHEDULER.

*For further details of CPU and NUMA affinity, refer to Chapter 4.

When we are working with minimum- and maximum-IOPS-per-volume thresholds, we need to take a few things into account. First, if we do not set a maximum IOPS limit, SQL Server does not govern the IOPS for the resource pool at all. This means that if you configure minimum IOPS limits for other resource pools, they are not respected. Therefore, if you want Resource Governor to govern IO, always set a maximum IOPS threshold for every resource pool.

It is also worth noting that the majority of IO that you can control through Resource Governor is read operations. This is because write operations, such as Lazy Writer and Log Flush operations, occur as system operations and fall inside the scope of the internal resource pool. Because you cannot alter the internal resource pool, you cannot govern the majority of write operations. This means that using Resource Governor to limit IO operations is most appropriate when you have a reporting application or another application with a high ratio of reads to writes.

Finally, you should be aware that Resource Governor can only control the number of IOPS; it cannot control the size of the IOPS. This means that you cannot use Resource Governor to control the amount of bandwidth into a SAN an application is using.

If you want to create a resource pool called ReportingApp that sets a minimum CPU percentage of 50, a maximum CPU percentage of 80, a minimum IOPS reservation of 20, and a maximum IOPS reservation of 100, you can use the script in Listing 23-1. The final statement of the script uses ALTER RESOURCE GOVERNOR to apply the new configuration. You should also run this statement after you create workload groups or apply a classifier function.

Listing 23-1. Creating a Resource Pool

```
CREATE RESOURCE POOL ReportingApp
    WITH(
        MIN_CPU_PERCENT=50,
        MAX_CPU_PERCENT=80,
        MIN_IOPS_PER_VOLUME = 20,
        MAX_IOPS_PER_VOLUME = 100
        ) ;

GO

ALTER RESOURCE GOVERNOR RECONFIGURE ;

GO
```

Creating Workload Groups

Each resource pool can contain multiple workload groups. To begin creating a workload group for our SalesApplication resource pool, we drill though Management | Resource Governor | Resource Pools. We then drill through our SalesApplication resource pool and select New Workload Group from the Workload Groups context menu. This invokes the Resource Governor Properties dialog box, which is displayed in Figure 23-2.

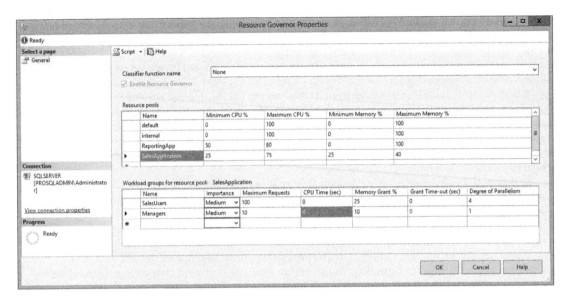

Figure 23-2. *The Resource Governor Properties dialog box*

You can see that with the SalesApplication resource pool highlighted in the Resource Pools section of the dialog box, we have created two rows within the Workload Groups section of the screen. Each of these rows represents a workload group that is associated with the SalesApplication resource pool.

We have configured the SalesUsers workload group to allow a maximum of 100 simultaneous requests and a MAXDOP of 4, meaning that requests classified under this workload group are able to use a maximum of four schedulers.

We have configured the Managers workload group to allow a maximum of 10 simultaneous requests and use a maximum of 1 scheduler. We have also configured this workload group to be able to use a maximum of 10 percent of the memory that the resource pool can reserve, as opposed to the default of 25 percent.

If the Memory Grant % setting is set to 0, then any requests classified under that workload group are blocked from running any operations that require a SORT or HASH JOIN physical operator. If queries need more than the specified amount of RAM, then SQL Server reduces the DOP for that query in an attempt to reduce the memory requirement. If the DOP reaches 1 and there is still not enough memory, then Error 8657 is thrown.

To create a resource pool via T-SQL, use the CREATE WORKLOAD GROUP DDL statement. This statement accepts the arguments detailed in Table 23-4.

Table 23-4. *CREATE WORKLOAD GROUP Arguments*

Argument	Description
group_name	Specifies the name of the workload group.
IMPORTANCE	Can be configured to HIGH, MEDIUM, or LOW, and allows you to prioritize requests in one workload group above another.
REQUEST_MAX_MEMORY_GRANT_PERCENT	Specifies the maximum amount of memory that any one query can use from the resource pool expressed as a percentage of the memory available to the resource pool.
REQUEST_MAX_CPU_TIME_SEC	Specifies the amount of CPU time, in seconds, that any one query can use. It is important to note that if the threshold is exceeded, then an event is generated that can be captured with Extended Events. The query is not cancelled, however.
REQUEST_MEMORY_GRANT_TIMEOUT_SEC	Specifies the maximum amount of time that a query can wait for a work buffer memory to become available before it times out. The query only times out under memory contention, however. Otherwise, the query receives the minimum memory grant. This results in performance degradation for the query. The maximum wait time is expressed in seconds.
MAX_DOP	The maximum number of processors that a single parallel query can use. The MAXDOP for a query can be further restrained by using query hints, by changing the MAXDOP setting for the instance, or when the relational engine chooses a serial plan.
GROUP_MAX_REQUESTS	Specifies the maximum number of concurrent requests that can be executed within the workload group. If the number of concurrent requests reaches this value, then further queries are placed in a waiting state until the number of concurrent queries falls below the threshold.
USING	Specifies the resource pool with which the workload group is associated. If not specified, then the group is associated with the default pool.

■ **Caution** Workload group names must be unique, even if they are associated with different pools. This is so they can be returned by the classifier function.

If we create two workload groups we want associated with our ReportingApp resource pool—one named InternalReports with a MAXDOP of 4 and a 25-percent maximum memory grant and the other named ExternalReports with a MAXDOP of 8 and a maximum memory grant percentage of 75 percent—we could use the script in Listing 23-2.

Listing 23-2. Creating Workload Groups

```
CREATE WORKLOAD GROUP InternalReports
    WITH(
        GROUP_MAX_REQUESTS=100,
        IMPORTANCE=Medium,
        REQUEST_MAX_CPU_TIME_SEC=0,
        REQUEST_MAX_MEMORY_GRANT_PERCENT=25,
        REQUEST_MEMORY_GRANT_TIMEOUT_SEC=0,
        MAX_DOP=4
                ) USING ReportingApp ;

GO

CREATE WORKLOAD GROUP ExternalReports
    WITH(
        GROUP_MAX_REQUESTS=100,
        IMPORTANCE=Medium,
        REQUEST_MAX_CPU_TIME_SEC=0,
        REQUEST_MAX_MEMORY_GRANT_PERCENT=75,
        REQUEST_MEMORY_GRANT_TIMEOUT_SEC=0,
        MAX_DOP=8
        ) USING ReportingApp ;

GO

ALTER RESOURCE GOVERNOR RECONFIGURE;

GO
```

Creating a Classifier Function

A classifier function is a scalar UDF (user-defined function) that resides in the Master database. It returns a value of type SYSNAME, which is a system-defined type equivalent to NVARCHAR(128). The value returned by the function corresponds to the name of the workload group into which each request should fall. The logic within the function determines which workload group name is returned. You only ever have one classifier function per instance, so you need to modify the function if you add additional workload groups.

Now let's create a classifier function using the Resource Governor environment that we have built in this chapter. This function will classify each request made against our instance using the following rules:

1. If the request is made under the context of the SalesUser login, then the request should fall under the SalesUsers workload group.

2. If the request is made by the SalesManager login, then requests should be placed in the Managers workload group.

3. If the request is made by the ReportsUser login and the request was made from a server named ReportsApp, then the request should fall into the InternalReports workload group.

4. If the request is made by the ReportsUser login but did not originate from the ReportsApp server, then it should fall into the ExternalReports workload group.

5. All other requests should be placed into the default workload group.

Before creating our classifier function, we prepare the instance. To do this, we first create the Chapter23 database. We then create the SalesUser, ReportsUser, and SalesManager logins, with Users mapped to the Chapter23 database. (Further detail on security principles can be found in Chapter 9.) Listing 23-3 contains the code we need to prepare the instance.

■ **Note** The users are mapped to the Chapter23 database for the purpose of this example, but you can make the queries against any database in the instance.

Listing 23-3. Preparing the Instance

```
--Create the database

USE [master]
GO

CREATE DATABASE Chapter23 ;

--Create the Logins and Users

CREATE LOGIN SalesUser
    WITH PASSWORD=N'Pa$$w0rd', DEFAULT_DATABASE=Chapter23,
        CHECK_EXPIRATION=OFF, CHECK_POLICY=OFF ;
GO

CREATE LOGIN ReportsUser
    WITH PASSWORD=N'Pa$$w0rd', DEFAULT_DATABASE=Chapter23,
        CHECK_EXPIRATION=OFF, CHECK_POLICY=OFF ;
GO

CREATE LOGIN SalesManager
    WITH PASSWORD=N'Pa$$w0rd', DEFAULT_DATABASE=Chapter23,
        CHECK_EXPIRATION=OFF, CHECK_POLICY=OFF ;
GO

USE Chapter23
GO

CREATE USER SalesUser FOR LOGIN SalesUser ;
GO

CREATE USER ReportsUser FOR LOGIN ReportsUser ;
GO

CREATE USER SalesManager FOR LOGIN SalesManager ;
GO
```

In order to implement the business rules pertaining to which workload group each request should be placed into, we use the system functions detailed in Table 23-5.

Table 23-5. *System Functions for Implementing Business Rules*

Function	Description	Business Rule(s)
SUSER_SNAME()	Returns the name of a login	1, 2, 3, 4
HOST_NAME()	Returns the name of the host from which the request was issued	3, 4

When we create a classifier function, it must follow specific rules. First, the function must be *schema-bound*. This means that any underlying objects that are referenced by the function cannot be altered without the function first being dropped. The function must also return the SYSNAME data type and have no parameters.

It is worth noting that the requirement for the function to be schema-bound is significant, and it poses limitations on the flexibility of Resource Governor. For example, it would be very useful if you were able to delegate workloads based upon database role membership; however, this is not possible, because schema-bound functions cannot access objects in other databases, either directly or indirectly. Because the classifier function must reside in the Master database, you cannot access information regarding database roles in other databases.

As with all things, there are workarounds for this issue. For example, you can create a table in the Master database that maintains role membership from user databases. You can even keep this table updated automatically by using a combination of views and triggers in the user database. The view would be based on the sys.sysusers catalog view and the trigger would be based on the view that you created. This would be a complex design, however, which would pose operational challenges to maintain.

The script within Listing 23-4 creates the classifier function, which implements our business rules before associating the function with Resource Governor. As always, Resource Governor is then reconfigured so that our changes take effect.

Listing 23-4. Creating the Classifier Function

```
USE Master
GO

CREATE FUNCTION dbo.Classifier()
RETURNS SYSNAME
WITH SCHEMABINDING
AS
BEGIN
        --Declare variables

        DECLARE @WorkloadGroup        SYSNAME ;
        SET @WorkloadGroup = 'Not Assigned' ;

        --Implement business rule 1

        IF (SUSER_NAME() = 'SalesUser')
        BEGIN
                SET @WorkloadGroup = 'SalesUsers' ;
        END
```

```
        --Implement business rule 2

        ELSE IF (SUSER_NAME() = 'SalesManager')
        BEGIN
                SET @WorkloadGroup = 'Managers' ;
        END
                --Implement business rules 3 & 4
        ELSE IF (SUSER_SNAME() = 'ReportsUser')
        BEGIN
                IF (HOST_NAME() = 'ReportsApp')
                BEGIN
                        SET @WorkloadGroup = 'InternalReports'
                END
                ELSE
                BEGIN
                        SET @WorkloadGroup = 'ExternalReports'
                END
        END

        --Implement business rule 5 (Put all other requests into the default workload group)

        ELSE IF @WorkloadGroup = 'Not Assigned'
        BEGIN
                SET @WorkloadGroup = 'default'
        END

        --Return the apropriate Workload Group name

        RETURN @WorkloadGroup
END

GO

--Associate the Classifier Function with Resource Governor

ALTER RESOURCE GOVERNOR WITH (CLASSIFIER_FUNCTION = dbo.Classifier) ;

ALTER RESOURCE GOVERNOR RECONFIGURE ;
```

Testing the Classifier Function

After we create the classifier function, we want to test that it works. We can test business rules 1 and 2 by using the EXECUTE AS statement to change our system context and then call the classifier function. This is demonstrated in Listing 23-5. The script temporarily allows all logins to access the classifier function directly, which allows the queries to work. It implements this by granting the Public role the EXECUTE permission before revoking this permission at the end of the script.

Listing 23-5. Testing Business Rules 1 and 2

```
USE MASTER
GO

GRANT EXECUTE ON dbo.Classifier TO public ;
GO

EXECUTE AS LOGIN = 'SalesUser' ;
SELECT dbo.Classifier() AS 'Workload Group' ;
REVERT

EXECUTE AS LOGIN = 'SalesManager' ;
SELECT dbo.Classifier() as 'Workload Group' ;
REVERT

REVOKE EXECUTE ON dbo.Classifier TO public ;
GO
```

The result of running these two queries is shown in Figure 23-3; it shows that business rules 1 and 2 are working as expected.

Figure 23-3. *Results of testing business rules 1 and 2*

To test business rule 4, we can use the same process we used to validate business rules 1 and 2. The only difference is that we change the execution context to ReportsUser. In order to validate rule 3, we use the same process, but this time, we invoke the query from a server named ReportsApp.

■ **Tip**   If you do not have access to a server named ReportsApp, then update the function definition to use a server name that you do have access to.

Monitoring Resource Governor

SQL Server exposes dynamic management views (DMVs) that you can use to return statistics relating to resource pools and workload groups. You can also monitor Resource Governor's usage using Windows' Performance Monitor tool, however, and this gives you the advantage of a graphical representation. The following sections discuss both of these approaches to monitoring Resource Governor.

Monitoring with Performance Monitor

DBAs can monitor how resource pools and their associated workload groups are being utilized by using Performance Monitor, which is built into Windows. You can access Performance Monitor from Control Panel | Administrative Tools or by searching for Perfmon in the Start menu.

■ **Note** To follow the demonstrations in this section, you should be running a Windows Server operating system.

Two categories are available to Performance Monitor that relate to Resource Governor. The first is `MSSQL$[INSTANCE NME]:Resource Pool Stats`. This contains counters that relate to the consumption of resources, which have been made available to resource groups. An instance of each counter is available for each resource group that has been configured on the instance.

The second category is `MSSQL$[INSTANCE NAME]:Workload Group Stats`, which contains counters that relate to the utilization of each workload group that has been configured on the instance. Figure 23-4 illustrates how we can add the `InternalReports`, `ExternalReports`, `SalesUsers`, and `Managers` instances of the CPU Usage % counter from within the Workload Group Stats category. After highlighting the instances, we will use the Add button, to move them to the Added Counters section. We can invoke the Add Counters dialog box by selecting Monitoring Tools | Performance Monitor from the left pane and then using the Plus (+) symbol on the toolbar in the right hand pane.

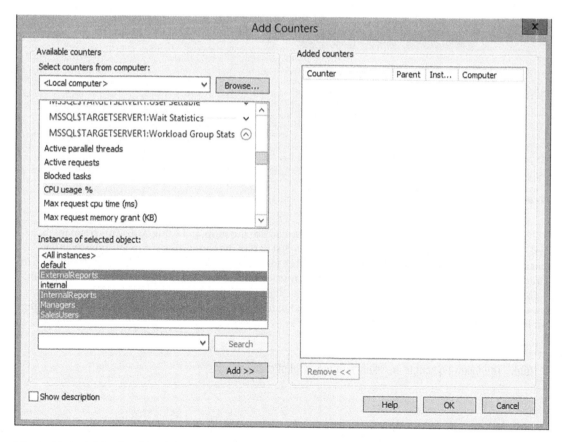

Figure 23-4. *Adding Workload Group Stats*

Now that we have added this counter, we also need to add the `ReportingApp` and `SalesApplication` app instances of the Active Memory Grant Amount (KB) counter from within the Resource Pool Stats category, as illustrated in Figure 23-5.

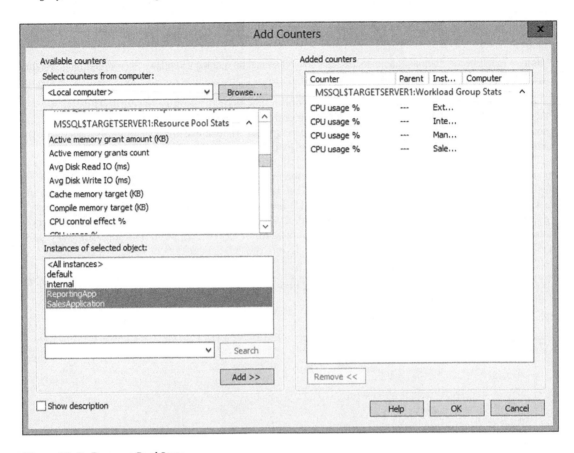

Figure 23-5. *Resource Pool Stats*

To test our Resource Governor configuration, we can use the script in Listing 23-6. This script is designed to run in two separate query windows. The first part of the script should run in a query window that is connected to your instance using the `SalesUser` login, and the second part of the script should run in a query window that is connected to your instance by using the `SalesManager` login. The two scripts should run simultaneously and cause Performance Monitor to generate a graph similar to the one Figure 23-6. Although the scripts do not cause the classifier function to be called, they act as an interactive way of testing our logic.

■ **Note**   The following scripts are likely to return a lot of data.

Listing 23-6. Generating Load against the SalesUsers and Managers Workload Groups

```
--Script Part 1 - To be run in a query windows that is connected using the SalesManager Login

EXECUTE AS LOGIN = 'SalesManager'

DECLARE @i INT = 0 ;

WHILE (@i < 10000)
BEGIN
SELECT DBName = (
        SELECT Name AS [data()]
        FROM sys.databases
        FOR XML PATH('')
) ;

SET @i = @i + 1 ;

END


--Script Part 2 - To be run in a query windows that is connected using the SalesUser Login

EXECUTE AS LOGIN = 'SalesUser'

DECLARE @i INT = 0 ;

WHILE (@i < 10000)
BEGIN
SELECT DBName = (
        SELECT Name AS [data()]
        FROM sys.databases
        FOR XML PATH('')
) ;

SET @i = @i + 1 ;

END
```

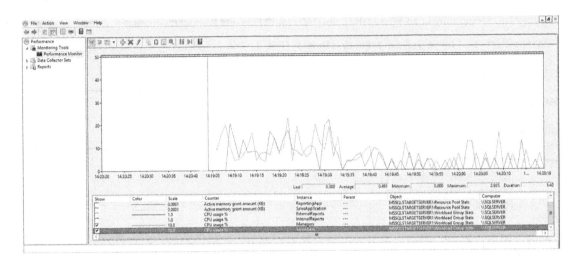

Figure 23-6. *Viewing CPU utilization*

You can see that the CPU usage for the SalesUsers and Managers workload groups is almost identical, which means that the Resource Governor implementation is working as expected.

Monitoring with DMVs

SQL Server provides the sys.dm_resource_governor_resource_pools and sys.dm_resource_governor_workload_groups DMVs that DBAs can use to examine Resource Governor statistics. The sys.dm_resource_governor_resource_pools DMV returns the columns detailed in Table 23-6.

Table 23-6. *Columns Returned by sys.dm_resource_governor_resource_pools*

Column	Description
pool_id	The unique ID of the resource pool
name	The name of the resource pool
statistics_start_time	The date/time of the last time the resource pool's statistics were reset
total_cpu_usage_ms	The total CPU time used by the resource pool since the statistics last reset
cache_memory_kb	The total cache memory currently being used by the resource pool
compile_memory_kb	The total memory the resource pool is currently using for compilation and optimization
used_memgrant_kb	The total memory the resource pool is using for memory grants
total_memgrant_count	A count of memory grants in the resource pool since the statistics were reset
total_memgrant_timeout_count	A count of memory grant timeouts in the resource pool since the statistics were last reset
active_memgrant_count	A count of current memory grants within the resource pool

(continued)

Table 23-6. (*continued*)

Column	Description
active_memgrant_kb	The total amount of memory currently being used for memory grants in the resource pool
memgrant_waiter_count	A count of queries currently pending, waiting for memory grants within the resource pool
max_memory_kb	The maximum amount of memory the resource pool can reserve
used_memory_kb	The amount of memory the resource pool currently has reserved
target_memory_kb	The amount of memory that the resource pool is currently trying to maintain
out_of_memory_count	A count of failed memory allocations for the resource pool
min_cpu_percent	The guaranteed average minimum CPU % for the resource pool
max_cpu_percent	The average maximum CPU % for the resource pool
min_memory_percent	The guaranteed minimum amount of memory that is available to the resource pool during periods of memory contention
max_memory_percent	The maximum percentage of server memory that can be allocated to the resource pool
cap_cpu_percent	The hard limit on the maximum CPU % available to the resource pool

The sys.dm_resource_governor_workload_groups DMV returns the columns detailed in Table 23-7.

Table 23-7. *Columns Returned by sys.dm_resource_governor_workload_groups*

Column	Description
group_id	The unique ID of the workload group.
name	The name of the workload group.
pool_id	The unique ID of the resource pool with which the workload group is associated.
statistics_start_time	The date/time of the last time the workload group's statistics were reset.
total_request_count	A count of the number of requests in the workload group since the statistics were last reset.
total_queued_request_count	The number of requests within the workload group that have been queued as a result of the GROUP_MAX_REQUESTS threshold being reached since the statistics were last reset.
active_request_count	A count of requests that are currently active within the workload group.
queued_request_count	The number of requests within the workload group that are currently queued as a result of the GROUP_MAX_REQUESTS threshold being reached.

(*continued*)

Table 23-7. (*continued*)

Column	Description
total_cpu_limit_violation_count	A count of requests in the workload group that have exceeded the CPU limit since the statistics were last reset.
total_cpu_usage_ms	The total CPU time used by requests within the workload group since the statistics were last reset.
max_request_cpu_time_ms	The maximum CPU time used by any request within the workload group since the last time the statistics were reset.
blocked_task_count	A count of tasks within the workload group that are currently blocked.
total_lock_wait_count	A count of all lock waits that have occurred for requests within the workload group since the last time the statistics were reset.
total_lock_wait_time_ms	A sum of time that locks have been held by requests within the workload group since statistics were last reset.
total_query_optimization_count	A count of all query optimizations that have occurred within the workload group since the statistics were reset.
total_suboptimal_plan_ generation_count	A count of all suboptimal plans that have been generated within the workload group, since the last time the statistics were reset. These suboptimal plans indicate that the workload group was experiencing memory pressure.
total_reduced_memgrant_count	A count of all memory grants that have reached the maximum size limit within the workload group since the last time the statistics were reset.
max_request_grant_memory_kb	The size of the largest single memory grant that has occurred within the workload group since the last time the statistics were reset.
active_parallel_thread_count	A count of how many parallel threads are currently in use within the workload group.
importance	The current value specified for the workload group's importance setting.
request_max_memory_grant_ percent	The current value specified for the workload group's maximum memory grant percentage.
request_max_cpu_time_sec	The current value specified for the workload group's CPU limit.
request_memory_grant_timeout_ sec	The current value specified for the workload group's memory grant timeout.
group_max_requests	The current value specified for the workload group's maximum concurrent requests.
max_dop	The current value specified for the workload group's MAXDOP.

You can join the sys.dm_resource_governor_resource_pools and sys.dm_resource_governor_ workload_groups DMVs, using the pool_id column in each view. The script in Listing 23-7 demonstrates how you can achieve this so you can return a report of CPU usage across the workload groups as compared to the overall CPU usage of the resource pool.

Listing 23-7. Reporting on CPU Usage

```
SELECT
        rp.name ResourcePoolName
        ,wg.name WorkgroupName
        ,rp.total_cpu_usage_ms ResourcePoolCPUUsage
        ,wg.total_cpu_usage_ms WorkloadGroupCPUUsage
        ,CAST(ROUND(CASE
                WHEN rp.total_cpu_usage_ms = 0
                        THEN 100
                ELSE (wg.total_cpu_usage_ms * 1.)
                        / (rp.total_cpu_usage_ms * 1.) * 100 Percentage
                END, 3) AS FLOAT) WorkloadGroupPercentageOfResourcePool
FROM sys.dm_resource_governor_resource_pools rp
INNER JOIN sys.dm_resource_governor_workload_groups wg
        ON rp.pool_id = wg.pool_id
ORDER BY rp.pool_id ;
```

You can reset the cumulative statistics exposed by the sys.resource_governor_resource_pools and sys.dm_resource_governor_workload_groups DMVs using the command in Listing 23-8.

Listing 23-8. Resetting Resource Governor Statistics

```
ALTER RESOURCE GOVERNOR RESET STATISTICS ;
```

From SQL Server 2012 on, SQL Server exposes a third DMV named sys.dm_resource_governor_ resource_pool_affinity, which returns the columns detailed in Table 23-8.

Table 23-8. Columns Returned by sys.dm_resource_governor_resource_pool_affinity

Column	Description
pool_id	The unique ID of the resource pool.
processor_group	The ID of the logical processor group.
scheduler_mask	The binary mask, which represents the schedulers that are affinitized with the resource pool. For further details on interpreting this binary mask, please refer to Chapter 4.

You can join the sys.dm_resource_governor_resource_pool_affinity DMV to the sys.resource_ governor_resource_pools DMV using the pool_id column in each view. Listing 23-9 demonstrates this; it first alters the default resource pool so that it only uses processor 0 before it displays the scheduler binary mask for each resource pool that has processor affinity configured.

Listing 23-9. Scheduling a Binary Mask for Each Resource Pool

```
ALTER RESOURCE POOL [Default] WITH(AFFINITY SCHEDULER = (0)) ;

ALTER RESOURCE GOVERNOR RECONFIGURE ;

SELECT
        rp.name ResourcePoolName
        ,pa.scheduler_mask
FROM sys.dm_resource_governor_resource_pool_affinity pa
INNER JOIN sys.dm_resource_governor_resource_pools rp
        ON pa.pool_id = rp.pool_id ;
```

In SQL Server 2014, an additional DMV, called sys.dm_resource_governor_resource_pool_volumes was also introduced. This DMV returns details of the IO statistics for each resource pool. This DMV's columns are described in Table 23-9.

Table 23-9. *Columns Returned by sys.dm_resource_governor_resource_pool_volumes*

Column	Description
pool_id	The unique ID of the resource pool
volume_name	The name of the disk volume
min_iops_per_volume	The current configuration for the minimum number of IOPS per volume for the resource pool
max_iops_per_volume	The current configuration for the maximum number of IOPS per volume for the resource pool
read_ios_queued_total	The total read IOs queued for the resource pool against this volume since the last time the statistics were reset
read_ios_issued_total	The total read IOs issued for the resource pool against this volume since the last time the statistics were reset
read_ios_completed_total	The total read IOs completed for the resource pool against this volume since the last time the statistics were reset
read_bytes_total	The total bytes read for the resource pool against this volume since the last time the statistics were reset
read_io_stall_total_ms	The cumulative time between read IO operations being issued and completed for the resource pool against this volume since the last time the statistics were reset
read_io_stall_queued_ms	The cumulative time between read IO operations arriving and being completed for the resource pool against this volume since the last time the statistics were reset
write_ios_queued_total	The total write IOs queued for the resource pool against this volume since the last time the statistics were reset
write_ios_issued_total	The total write IOs issued for the resource pool against this volume since the last time the statistics were reset
write_ios_completed_total	The total write IOs completed for the resource pool against this volume since the last time the statistics were reset

(*continued*)

Table 23-9. (*continued*)

Column	Description
write_bytes_total	The total bytes written for the resource pool against this volume since the last time the statistics were reset
write_io_stall_total_ms	The cumulative time between write IO operations being issued and completed for the resource pool against this volume since the last time the statistics were reset
write_io_stall_queued_ms	The cumulative time between write IO operations arriving and being completed for the resource pool against this volume since the last time the statistics were reset
io_issue_violations_total	The total number of times that more IO operations were performed against the resource pool and volume than are allowed by the configuration
io_issue_delay_total_ms	The total time between when IO operations were scheduled to be issued and when they were actually issued

You can use the sys.dm_resource_governor_resource_pool_volumes DMV to determine if your resource pool configuration is causing latency by adding the read_io_stall_queued_ms and write_io_stall_queued_ms and then subtracting this value from the total of read_io_stall_total_ms added to write_io_stall_total_ms, as shown in Listing 23-10. This script first alters the default resource pool so that IOPS are governed before subsequently reporting on IO stalls.

▪ **Tip** Remember that you are likely to see far fewer write operations than read operations in user-defined resource pools. This is because the vast majority of write operations are system operations and therefore, they take place within the internal resource pool.

Listing 23-10. Discovering If Resource Pool Configuration Is Causing Disk Latency

```
ALTER RESOURCE POOL [default] WITH(
            min_iops_per_volume=50,
            max_iops_per_volume=100) ;

ALTER RESOURCE GOVERNOR RECONFIGURE ;

SELECT
       rp.name ResourcePoolName
      ,pv.volume_name
      ,pv.read_io_stall_total_ms
      ,pv.write_io_stall_total_ms
      ,pv.read_io_stall_queued_ms
      ,pv.write_io_stall_queued_ms
      ,(pv.read_io_stall_total_ms + pv.write_io_stall_total_ms)
          - (pv.read_io_stall_queued_ms + pv.write_io_stall_queued_ms) GovernorLatency
FROM sys.dm_resource_governor_resource_pool_volumes pv
RIGHT JOIN sys.dm_resource_governor_resource_pools rp
       ON pv.pool_id = rp.pool_id ;
```

■ **Tip** If you do not see any IO stalls, create a database on a low-performance drive and run some intensive queries against it before you rerun the query in Listing 23-10.

Summary

Resource Governor allows you to throttle applications at the SQL Server instance level. You can use it to limit a request's memory, CPU, and disk usage. You can also use it to affinitize a category of requests with specific scheduler or NUMA ranges, or to reduce the MAXDOP for a category of requests.

A resource pool represents a set of server resources and a workload group is a logical container for similar requests that have been classified in the same way. Resource Governor provides an internal resource pool and workload group for system requests and a default resource pool and workload group as a catch-all for any requests that have not been classified. Although the internal resource pool cannot be modified, user-defined resource pools have a one-to-many relationship with workload groups.

Requests made to SQL Server are classified using a user-defined function, which the DBA must create. This function must be a scalar function that returns the sysname data type. It must also be schema-bound and reside in the Master database. DBAs can use system functions, such as USER_SNAME(), IS_MEMBER(), and HOST_NAME() to assist them with the classification.

SQL Server provides four dynamic management views (DMVs) that DBAs can use to help monitor Resource Governor configuration and usage. DBAs can also monitor Resource Governor usage using Performance Monitor, however, and this gives them the advantage of a visual representation of the data. When taking this approach, you will find that Performance Monitor exposes counter categories for resource pools and workload groups for each instance that resides on the server. The counters within these categories have one instance for each resource pool or workload group, respectively, that is currently configured on the instance.

CHAPTER 24

■ ■ ■

Triggers

SQL Server supports three types of triggers. The first type is made up of DDL (data definition language) triggers, which fire in response to a DDL statement being executed, such as CREATE, ALTER, or DROP. You can use DDL triggers for auditing or for limiting DBA activity. The second type, logon triggers, fire when a session to the instance is established. You can use these triggers to stop a user from establishing a connection to an instance. The final type, DML triggers, fire as a result of a DML (data manipulation language) statement being executed, such as an INSERT, UPDATE, or DELETE statement. Developers use DML triggers to maintain complex logic and data integrity rules. This type of trigger is rarely used for administrative purposes, however, and is therefore beyond the scope of this book.

Triggers are code modules, similar to stored procedures. The difference is that triggers fire automatically when an event occurs in the instance, as opposed to being executed manually or via a script. This chapter discusses how DBAs can implement DDL and logon triggers to improve security and regulate administrative tasks.

■ **Note**   You can create triggers using T-SQL or in a .NET language. If you write them in a .NET language, you can then import them into assemblies in SQL Server through CLR (Common Language Runtime) integration. CLR triggers are beyond the scope of this book, since they are seldom used for administrative purposes.

DDL Triggers

The following sections first help you understand the concepts behind DDL triggers before moving on to discuss appropriate implementations.

Understanding DDL Triggers

You can create DDL triggers at either the instance level or the database level. When created at the instance level, they are said to be server scoped and can be used to respond to events such as new objects or logins being created. When triggers are scoped at the database level, they can respond to events such as tables being altered or dropped. You can also create triggers that respond to all database-level events at the server level so that they respond to events in all databases.

DDL triggers can provide you with a mechanism for auditing or limiting DBA activity, which can be very useful in environments where development or support teams need elevated permissions to instances or databases. You can use DLL triggers to limit the activity DBAs carry out, which can also prove useful if you have inexperienced or junior DBAs and want to ensure their actions are audited.

DDL triggers always execute after the event that caused them to fire, but within the context of the same transaction. This means that you can use a ROLLBACK statement within the body of the trigger to undo the actions the original statement performed. So, for example, if you implement a trigger at the instance level to restrict users from creating new databases, when a user runs a CREATE DTABASE statement, a ROLLBACK statement within the trigger undoes the action before it is committed.

■ **Warning**   Note, however, that you should not use triggers as a substitute for security. For example, imagine that a user runs a series of statements inside a transaction, which takes an hour to execute, just to have all their changes rolled back by a trigger. For a detailed discussion of transactions, please refer to Chapter 18.

While a trigger is executing, you have access to a system function called EVENTDATA(). This function returns a well-formed XML document, which conforms to the Event_Schema XSD schema. You can find full details of this schema at http://schemas.microsoft.com/sqlserver/2006/11/eventdata/events.xsd. The data included within this XML result set includes the SPID of the user who executed the original statement, when the event began, and the statement itself. This means that you can interrogate the XML result set using XQuery and insert the results into an audit table to ensure full reputability.

As well to respond to individual DDL events, you can also configure triggers to respond to DDL event groups. For example, the DDL_SERVER_LEVEL_EVENTS event group contains all events that occur only at the instance level. You can generate a list of the event groups available in SQL Server by running the query in Listing 24-1. This query returns each event name, along with the event group that contains it.

Listing 24-1. Generating a List of Event Groups

```
SELECT
        b.type_name GroupName
      , a.type_name EventName
FROM sys.trigger_event_types a
INNER JOIN sys.trigger_event_types b
        ON a.parent_type = b.type
ORDER BY b.type_name ;
```

You can modify this query so that it returns a list of events within a specific event group. You do this by having it return all type names from the instance of the table aliased as a and filter on the type_name column of the table aliased as b. For example, the query in Listing 24-2 returns all events captured by the DDL_TABLE_EVENTS event group, as shown in Figure 24-1.

Listing 24-2. Determining Events within an Event Group

```
SELECT a.type_name
FROM sys.trigger_event_types a
INNER JOIN sys.trigger_event_types b
        ON a.parent_type = b.type
WHERE b.type_name = 'DDL_TABLE_EVENTS' ;
```

Figure 24-1. *Events included within the DDL_TABLE_EVENTS event group*

You can use the script in Listing 24-3 to view the complete event group hierarchy of an event. In this instance, we again focus on the CREATE, ALTER, and DROP TABLE events.

Listing 24-3. Viewing Event Hierarchy

```
;WITH EventsHierarchy
AS
(
        SELECT
                type
                , type_name
                , CAST(type_name as NVARCHAR(4000)) AS type_hierarchy
                , parent_type
        FROM sys.trigger_event_types
        WHERE parent_type IS NULL

        UNION ALL

        SELECT
                TET.type
                , TET.type_name
                , CONCAT(TE.type_hierarchy,' \ ' , TET.type_name)
                , TET.parent_type
        FROM    sys.trigger_event_types TET
                    INNER JOIN EventsHierarchy TE
                            ON TET.parent_type = TE.type
)

-- Select results from CTE

SELECT
        type_name
        , type_hierarchy
FROM EventsHierarchy
WHERE type_name IN ('CREATE_TABLE', 'ALTER_TABLE', 'DROP_TABLE')
ORDER BY type_name ; --type_hierarchy
```

The results of this query are displayed in Figure 24-2.

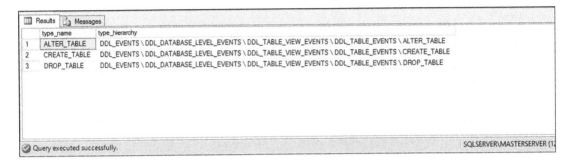

Figure 24-2. *TABLE DDL event hierarchy*

■ **Tip** You can find a complete list of DDL events at `https://technet.microsoft.com/en-us/library/` `bb522542(v=sql.120).aspx`.

Implementing DDL Triggers

DDL triggers can respond to the following statements being issued:

- CREATE
- ALTER
- DROP
- GRANT
- DENY
- REVOKE
- UPDATE STATISTICS

To create DDL triggers, use the `CREATE TRIGGER` DDL statement. This statement has the basic structure shown in Listing 24-4.

Listing 24-4. Structure of the CREATE TRIGGER Statement

```
CREATE TRIGGER <Name>
ON <Scope>
WITH <Options>
AFTER
AS
<code>
```

This statement accepts the arguments detailed in Table 24-1.

Table 24-1. *CREATE TRIGGER Arguments*

Argument	Description
ON	Specifies the scope of the DDL trigger. • `ALL SERVER` specifies that the trigger is created at the instance level. • `DATABASE` specifies that the trigger is created at the database level.
WITH	`ENCRYPTION` and `EXECUTE AS` are acceptable options for the `WITH` clause and have the following uses: • `ENCRYPTION` obfuscates the definition of the trigger so that it cannot be discovered, even via system tables. The obfuscation process is not supported by Microsoft, so you should ensure your original code is kept within source control, or you will not be able to alter the definition. • `EXECUTE AS` changes the security context of the trigger. This allows you to elevate the permissions that the trigger has, while minimizing the impact on the security footprint of the user executing the code. These are the possible values: 　• `LOGIN`, which is followed by the name of a login to impersonate 　• `USER`, which is followed by the name of a user, within the same database, who should be impersonated 　• `SELF`, which executes under the context that either created, or last altered, the code 　• `OWNER`, which executes under the context that owns the schema in which the module resides 　• `CALLER` the default behavior; executes under the context that executed the module
FOR | AFTER	`FOR` and `AFTER` are interchangeable in the context of DDL triggers. This argument specifies that the trigger will fire after the original statement completes (but before it commits). This is the only valid option for a DDL trigger. This keyword is followed by a comma-separated list of events to which the trigger will respond. For example `CREATE_DATABASE` or `ALTER_TABLE, DROP_TABLE`.
AS	Specifies either the SQL statements that define the code body of the trigger or the `EXTERNAL NAME` clause to point to a CLR trigger.

Implementing Server Scope DDL Triggers

Imagine a scenario in which development teams are creating test databases on an instance without seeking necessary approval. This kind of issue is surprisingly common and can make an environment very challenging to manage. We can resolve this issue by creating a server-scoped DDL trigger with a definition matching that of Listing 24-5. In this script, we create a trigger called `PreventDatabaseCreation`. In the body of the trigger, we declare a variable named `@Message` and populate this message with the login name of the user who ran the `CREATE DATABASE` statement, followed by a message informing the user that they are not following the correct process. We finally roll back the transaction. Because the trigger fires in the context of the same transaction as the original statement (even if the statement runs in autocommit mode as opposed to as an explicit transaction) the `CREATE DATABASE` statement is rolled back.

Listing 24-5. Creating a Server Scoped Trigger

```
USE MASTER
GO

CREATE TRIGGER PreventDatabaseCreation
ON ALL SERVER
AFTER CREATE_DATABASE
AS
BEGIN
        DECLARE @Message NVARCHAR(256) ;
        SET @Message =
            (SELECT SUSER_SNAME()
                + ', you must follow due process in order to create Databases in this
environment. Pleae contact the DBA Team') ;
        PRINT @Message ;
        ROLLBACK ;
END
```

If we use the statement in Listing 24-6 to attempt to create the Chapter24 database, we see the result illustrated in Figure 24-3. This result indicates that the transaction has been rolled back and it also displays our custom message to the user.

Listing 24-6. Attempting to Create a Database

```
CREATE DATABASE Chapter24 ;
```

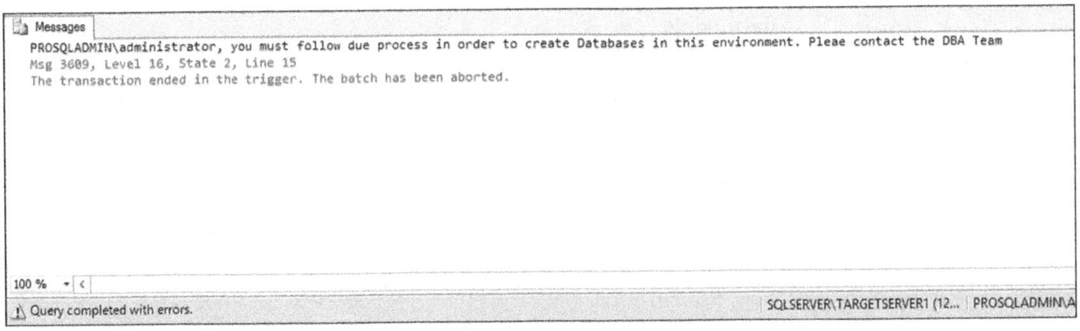

Figure 24-3. *Result of attempting to create a database*

After implementing such a trigger, you obviously need to change your process for creating new databases so that your team still has the ability to create databases in a controlled fashion. The easiest way to do this is to ensure that all CREATE DATABASE statements are preceded by a statement to disable the trigger and succeeded by a statement to reenable the trigger. You can achieve this by using the DISABLE TRIGGER and ENABLE TRIGGER statements, as demonstrated in Listing 24-7.

Listing 24-7. Creating a Database Following Due Process

```
--Disable the trigger

DISABLE TRIGGER PreventDatabaseCreation ON ALL SERVER ;

--Create the database

CREATE DATABASE Chapter24 ;

--Enable the trigger

ENABLE TRIGGER PreventDatabaseCreation ON ALL SERVER ;
```

To enable or disable all triggers at a particular scope, you can use the ALL keyword. For example, the command in Listing 24-8 disables all triggers at the server scope before reenabling them.

Listing 24-8. Disabling and Enabling All Triggers at the Server Scope

```
--Disable all triggers at the server scope

DISABLE TRIGGER ALL ON ALL SERVER ;


--Enable all triggers at the server scope

ENABLE TRIGGER ALL ON ALL SERVER ;
```

Implementing Database Scope DDL Triggers

Imagine a scenario in which you require an audit on any changes to programmable object definitions within the Chapter24 database. You should not prevent the changes from occurring, but you want all changes logged to an audit table. The first step in implementing a solution for this scenario is to create an audit table in the Chapter24 database. We can do this using the script in Listing 24-9.

Listing 24-9. Creating an Audit Table

```
USE Chapter24
GO

CREATE TABLE dbo.Audit
(
ID              INT             IDENTITY        PRIMARY KEY,
PostTime        DATETIME2       NOT NULL,
LoginName       NVARCHAR(128)   NOT NULL,
DatabaseName    NVARCHAR(128)   NOT NULL,
EventType       NVARCHAR(128)   NOT NULL,
SchemaName      NVARCHAR(128)   NULL,
ObjectName      NVARCHAR(128)   NOT NULL,
CommandText     NVARCHAR(MAX)   NOT NULL
) ;
```

Next, we need to create the trigger itself. Listing 24-10 demonstrates how to create this trigger. We name the trigger `DDLAudit` and define it to fire after any programmable objects, or other objects that contain code, are created, altered, or dropped. The `WITH EXECUTE AS SELF` clause means that the trigger executes under the security context of the user who created the trigger. This is beneficial, because it means we do not have to grant permissions to the `Audit` table to all users who issue DDL statements. This is possible because both objects are owned by the same user, within the same database.

■ **Tip**   Types, rules (which are now deprecated), and defaults do not have a corresponding `ALTER` statement. To change them, you must first create them and then drop them. Therefore, there are no corresponding event types for these statements.

In the body of the trigger, we use the XQuery Value method, which returns scalar values from XML, to pull data from the results of the `EVENTDATA()` function. We then use this data to populate the `Audit` table.

Listing 24-10. Creating the DDLAudit Trigger

```
USE Chapter24
GO

CREATE TRIGGER DDLAudit
ON DATABASE
WITH EXECUTE AS SELF
AFTER CREATE_PROCEDURE, CREATE_FUNCTION, CREATE_TRIGGER, CREATE_ASSEMBLY, CREATE_TYPE,
CREATE_RULE, CREATE_DEFAULT, CREATE_PLAN_GUIDE, CREATE_SEQUENCE, ALTER_PROCEDURE,
ALTER_FUNCTION, ALTER_TRIGGER, ALTER_ASSEMBLY, ALTER_PLAN_GUIDE, ALTER_SEQUENCE,
DROP_PROCEDURE, DROP_FUNCTION, DROP_TRIGGER, DROP_ASSEMBLY, DROP_TYPE, DROP_RULE,
DROP_DEFAULT, DROP_PLAN_GUIDE, DROP_SEQUENCE
AS
BEGIN
        INSERT INTO dbo.Audit
        SELECT EVENTDATA().value('(/EVENT_INSTANCE/PostTime)[1]','datetime2'),
                EVENTDATA().value('(/EVENT_INSTANCE/LoginName)[1]','nvarchar(128)'),
                EVENTDATA().value('(/EVENT_INSTANCE/DatabaseName)[1]','nvarchar(128)'),
                EVENTDATA().value('(/EVENT_INSTANCE/EventType)[1]','nvarchar(128)'),
                EVENTDATA().value('(/EVENT_INSTANCE/SchemaName)[1]','nvarchar(128)'),
                EVENTDATA().value('(/EVENT_INSTANCE/ObjectName)[1]','nvarchar(128)'),
                EVENTDATA().value('(/EVENT_INSTANCE/TSQLCommand/CommandText)
                [1]','nvarchar(max)') ;
END
```

In order to test our trigger, we create a simple stored procedure called TestTrigger in the Chapter24 database. We can do this using the script in Listing 24-11.

Listing 24-11. Creating Test Stored Procedure

```
USE Chapter24
GO

CREATE PROCEDURE TestTrigger
AS
BEGIN
        SELECT 1 ;
END
```

If you run a SELECT * statement against our dbo.Audit table, you see results similar to those in Figure 24-4.

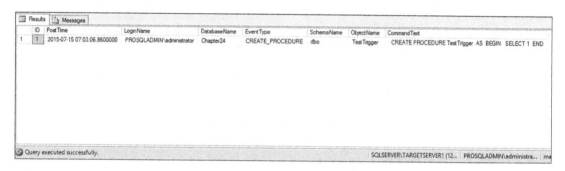

Figure 24-4. Entry in dbo.Audit

Trigger Metadata

You can find metadata regarding server-scoped DDL triggers in the sys.server_triggers catalog view. This view returns the columns detailed in Table 24-2.

Table 24-2. *Columns Returned by sys.server_triggers*

Column	Description
name	The name of the trigger.
object_id	The unique object ID that has been assigned to the trigger.
parent_class	The parent class of the trigger. As the trigger is defined at the server scope, the parent class is always 100, which means server.
parent_class_desc	A textual description of the parent class of the trigger. Since the trigger is defined at the server scope, the parent class description is always server.
parent_id	The parent ID is always 0 for server-scoped triggers.
type	The value for type can be one of the following: • TA—CLR trigger • TR—T-SQL trigger
type_desc	A textual description of the type. Values can be one of these: • CLR_TRIGGER • SQL_TRIGGER
create_date	The date and time that the trigger was created.
modify_date	The data and time that the trigger was last modified using an ALTER TRIGGER statement.
is_ms_shipped	Specifies if the trigger is a system trigger or user defined. • 0—User-defined trigger • 1—System trigger
is_disabled	Specifies if the trigger is currently enabled. • 0—Enabled • 1—Disabled

You can use the sys.triggers catalog view to find details of triggers defined within the scope of a database. Table 24-3 describes the columns that this catalog view returns.

Table 24-3. *Columns Returned by sys.triggers*

Column	Description
name	The name of the trigger.
object_id	The unique object ID that has been assigned to the trigger.
parent_class	The parent class of the trigger. • This value is always 0 for DDL triggers. • This catalog view also contains details of DML triggers; therefore, a value of 1 indicates a table or column.
parent_class_desc	The description of the parent class of the trigger. • This value is always DATABASE for DDL triggers. • DML triggers have a parent_class_description of OBJECT_OR_COLUMN.
parent_id	The ID of the parent object. • This is always 0 for DDL triggers. • For DML triggers, this is the object ID of the table or view on which they are defined.
type	The value for type can be one of the following: • TA—CLR trigger • TR—T-SQL trigger
type_desc	A textual description of the type. Values can be one of the following: • CLR_TRIGGER • SQL_TRIGGER
create_date	The date and time that the trigger was created.
modify_date	The data and time that the trigger was last modified.
is_ms_shipped	Specifies if the trigger is a system trigger or user defined. • 0—User-defined trigger • 1—System trigger
is_disabled	Specifies if the trigger is currently enabled. • 0—Enabled • 1—Disabled
is_not_for_replication	Only applies to DML triggers, since DDL triggers cannot be replicated. Specifies if the trigger is marked NOT_FOR_REPLICATION. • 0 indicates it will be replicated. • 1 indicates it will not be replicated.

is_instead_of_trigger	Specifies if the trigger is defined as INSTEAD OF or AFTER.
	
	• DDL triggers can only be defined as AFTER triggers and therefore always have a value of 0, meaning AFTER.
	
	• DML triggers can have the following values:
	
	  • 1, indicating INSTEAD OF
	
	  • 0, indicating AFTER

You can use the sys.triggers and sys.server_triggers catalog views together to produce a query that returns a list of all user-defined DDL triggers within the instance, along with their scope. The script in Listing 24-12 achieves this by inserting the names of the server-scoped triggers into a global temporary table before using the XML data() function to insert the triggers for each database into the global temporary table. You can then access the temporary table with a simple SELECT statement. Finally, this script cleans up the temporary table, which makes the script rerunnable.

Listing 24-12. Generating a List of DDL Triggers

```
CREATE TABLE #Triggers
(name          NVARCHAR(128),
scope          NVARCHAR(128)) ;

INSERT INTO #Triggers
SELECT
        name
        ,'Server'
FROM sys.server_triggers ;

DECLARE @SQL          NVARCHAR(MAX) ;

SET @SQL = (SELECT 'INSERT INTO #Triggers SELECT name, '''
                            + d.name
                            + ''' FROM '
                            + d.name
                            + '.sys.triggers WHERE parent_class = 0 AND
                            is_ms_shipped = 0 ; ' AS [data()]

                  FROM sys.databases d
                  FOR XML PATH ('')) ;

EXEC (@SQL) ;

SELECT *
FROM #Triggers ;

DROP TABLE #Triggers ;
```

Logon Triggers

Logon triggers are very similar to DDL triggers, except that instead of firing in response to DDL events, they fire in response to a LOGON event occurring on the instance. This is the same event as the AUDIT_LOGON trace event. The advantage that a logon trigger offers over tracing and auditing is its ability to actually stop a user from establishing a connection. This is because the trigger fires synchronously with the event, as opposed to asynchronously.

Logon triggers prove most useful when you need to limit connections to the instance. For example, imagine that you have a reporting application that has a complex ETL process that runs between 8PM and 11PM every evening; however, you have an issue with staff accessing the application between these times and seeing an inconsistent version of the data. In this scenario, you may wish to use a logon trigger to stop any users, other than the service account that runs the ETL processes, from accessing the instance.

■ **Note**   If any connections exist at the start of the ETL window, you need to kill them using a separate process, since the trigger only fires at the point of login.

The script in Listing 24-13 creates a logon trigger, called PreventingLoginDuringETL, to avoid any users establishing sessions between 8PM and 11PM, with the exception of the service account that runs the ETL loads. The script uses the time portion of the GETDATE() system function to establish the current server time and the ORIGINAL_NAME() system function to determine the login.

Listing 24-13. Creating a Logon Trigger to Prevent Activity during ETL Window

```
CREATE TRIGGER PreventLoginDuringETL
ON ALL SERVER
FOR LOGON
AS
BEGIN
        IF (CAST(GETDATE() AS TIME) >= CAST('20:00:00' AS TIME)
                AND CAST(GETDATE() AS TIME) <= CAST('23:00:00' AS TIME)
                AND UPPER(ORIGINAL_LOGIN()) <> 'ETLSVCACC')
        ROLLBACK ;
END
```

Another example of when a logon trigger is useful for limiting connections is a scenario in which you are hosting a data-tier application that has a limited number of user licenses associated with it, and you need to ensure that the number of concurrent users accessing the database does not exceed this limit. For example, if our instance is hosting a data-tier application with a license for a maximum of 100 concurrent users, then we can use the script in Listing 24-14 to create a trigger called EnforceLicensing. This trigger performs a count of the concurrent logins to the instance and if this exceeds 100, then subsequent connections fail to establish a connection until the number of concurrent users drops below the threshold.

Listing 24-14. Creating a Trigger to Enforce Licensing

```
CREATE TRIGGER EnforceLicensing
ON ALL SERVER
FOR LOGON
AS
BEGIN
        IF (SELECT COUNT(DISTINCT login_name)
                FROM sys.dm_exec_sessions
                WHERE is_user_process = 1) > 100
        ROLLBACK ;
END
```

If a connection is rolled back due to trigger execution, then the user receives a message similar to the one illustrated in Figure 24-5.

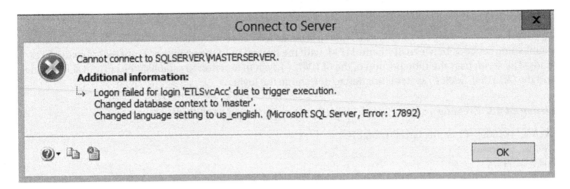

Figure 24-5. *Error received if logon fails due to trigger execution*

Controlling Trigger Order

It is possible to create multiple DDL (and logon) triggers that respond to the same event. If you create multiple triggers that are triggered by the same transaction, then you have some, but not complete, control over the order in which they fire.

■ **Tip**   Controlling the order in which triggers fire is particularly useful if you have one trigger that consumes significantly fewer resources than another trigger that responds to the same event, and setting an order may negate the need for the resource intensive trigger to fire. For example, imagine that you have two triggers created against the CREATE TABLE event. If one of these triggers audits every DDL statement and the other trigger rolls back unauthorized table creations, then it is very sensible to fire the trigger that may perform the rollback first. This means that there will be instances where you roll back the transaction and do not need the audit trigger, which requires you to invoke disk activity.

You can exercise this control by using the sp_settriggerorder system stored procedure. This procedure allows you to control the first and the last trigger that are fired. If you have more than three triggers that respond to the same event, then you have no way to guarantee the order of the triggers that are not marked as the first trigger or the last trigger. The sp_settriggerorder procedure accepts the parameters detailed in Table 24-4.

Table 24-4. *sp_settriggerorder Parameters*

Parameter	Description
@triggername	The name of the trigger that you wish to mark as first or last.
@order	Acceptable values are First, Last, and None. If triggers exist that are marked as First or Last, then None indicates that the trigger is not the first or the last trigger.
@stmttype	The type of statement that causes the trigger to fire. For logon triggers, this is the LOGON event. For DDL triggers, this can be any DDL event; however, specifying an event class is not permitted. For DML triggers, the value can be INSERT, UPDATE, or DELETE.
@namespace	Specifies the scope of the trigger. This can be specified as SERVER, DATABASE, or NULL. If NULL is passed, then it indicates that the trigger is a DML trigger.

It is important to note that it is possible to mark triggers as First and Last for both the server scope and the database scope. The limitation here, however, is that the server trigger marked as First will fire before the database trigger marked as First. This is because all server-level triggers fire before any database-level triggers fire.

The script in Listing 24-15 configures our EnforceLicensing logon trigger to fire before our PreventLoginDuringETL trigger. If we subsequently create any further logon triggers on the instance, then they fire after the EnforceLicensing trigger but before the PreventLoginTrigger trigger.

> ▪ **Note**   If we alter a trigger that is marked as First or Last, then its Order property reverts back to None. This means that your change control processes should take this into account and that you should follow any ALTER TRIGGER statement immediately by calling sp_settriggerorder to remark it as the first or last trigger.

Listing 24-15. Configuring First and Last Logon Triggers

```
USE Master
GO

EXEC sp_settriggerorder @triggername='EnforceLicensing', @order='First', @stmttype='LOGON',
@namespace='SERVER' ;

EXEC sp_settriggerorder @triggername='PreventLogindURINGetl', @order='Last', @
stmttype='LOGON', @namespace='SERVER' ;
```

> ▪ **Caution**   Creating multiple triggers on the same event is often not a good idea for performance reasons. However, it is important to understand how to control the order in case you discover them in third-party applications.

Summary

You can use DDL triggers to restrict changes to objects or audit user activity. They always fire after the event that caused them to fire, but within the context of the same transaction. This means that you can always roll back the action that caused the trigger to fire if you need to. You can scope DDL triggers at the instance level or at the database level, and you can configure them to respond to specific events or groups of events.

Within the context of a DDL trigger, you have access to the EVENTDATA() function, which contains information about the action that caused the trigger to fire. This information includes the time that the event occurred, the user that executed the event, and the statement itself. This data is provided in XML format, so it can be interrogated using XML and can be used for auditing purposes.

Logon triggers are always scoped at the instance level and fire when a connection is made to the instance. Logon triggers fire synchronously with the logon, and thus you can use them to prevent a connection from being established. This can be useful in circumstances in which you want to impose a limit on the number of concurrent users.

You can find metadata regarding server-scoped triggers in the sys.server_triggers catalog view and metadata regarding database-scoped triggers in the sys.triggers catalog view from within the context of the relevant database. To a limited extent, you can control the order in which triggers fire by using the sp_settrigger order system stored procedure. This procedure allows you to mark a trigger as either first or last. When more than three triggers fire in response to the same event, it is not possible to control the order of the other triggers.

PART V

Managing a Hybrid Cloud Environment

CHAPTER 25

■ ■ ■

Cloud Backups and Restores

Traditionally, enterprise environments rely on backups taken either directly to tape, or first to disk, and then offloaded to tape by an enterprise-level backup tool. These tapes are often sent to an offsite location where they are retained for a period of time before they are recycled. However, this practice can cause issues related to the cost of secure offsite storage and the length of time it can take to restore a backup if you must retrieve the backup from an offsite location.

In SQL Server 2014, Microsoft has introduced the ability to back up your SQL Server databases to Windows Azure. This solution can offer many benefits, including cost savings and the rapid availability of backups. SQL Server lets you manually take or schedule backups that you want taken to Windows Azure, but it also supplies you with the functionality to simplify and automate the process. On the flip side, retrieving large backup files from the Internet is likely to be slower than retrieving the files from on-premises disks.

After discussing the fundamentals behind cloud backups, this chapter demonstrates how you can manually back up databases to Windows Azure and how to automate the backup process.

Understanding Cloud Backups

In order to perform backups to Windows Azure, you must first have a Windows Azure account and a Windows Azure storage account. The Windows Azure storage account includes an account name and two access keys. This means that if you have an issue with your primary access key, you can still access your account using the secondary access key. You can create a Windows Azure account by visiting https://account.windowsazure.com, and then you can go on to create a Windows Azure storage account by subsequently visiting the Windows Azure management portal.

A *container* is a group that contains files. Each Windows Azure storage account must have at least one container, and there is no upper limit on the number of containers an account can have. The files stored within a container are known as *blobs*. Windows Azure supports two types of blob: one is known as a block blob and the other as a page blob. A *block blob* is optimized for efficient uploads, whereas a *page blob* is optimized for efficient read/write activity.

■ **Caution** SQL Server only supports page blobs. If you create your backup as a block blob, you will be unable to restore it.

Each container can contain multiple blobs, and no upper limits are imposed on the number of blobs you can store within a container. However, there is a maximum file size of 1TB for each individual page blob. This means that if your database is larger than 1TB, you need to maintain a file or filegroup backup strategy. You can access blobs via a URL by using the following URL format: https://MyStorageAccount.blob.core.windows.net/MyContainer/MyBlob. SQL Server uses credentials to access the URL, because it is, of course, an external resource to SQL Server. The credential uses the storage account name and access key to connect to the URL.

■ **Note** The demonstrations in this chapter assume that you have created a Windows Azure account and a Windows Azure storage account. These demonstrations use a storage account named `prosqladmin`.

Simple Back Up and Restore to Windows Azure

The following sections discuss how to create a container, how to back up a database to Windows Azure, how to view your backups from SQL Server Management Studio, and how to restore a database that has been backed up to Windows Azure.

Creating a Container

The first step in enabling backups to Windows Azure is to create your storage container. To do this, navigate to the Storage pane and then drill through your storage account in the Windows Azure management portal, which you can find at `https://manage.windowsazure.com`. You should then select the Containers tab, displayed in Figure 25-1.

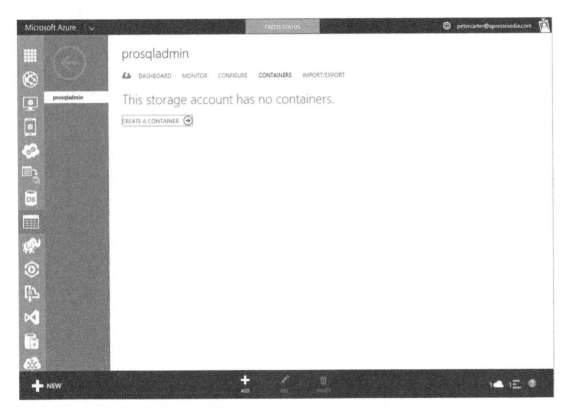

Figure 25-1. The Containers tab

Next, choose the Create A Container option. This invokes the New Container dialog box (see Figure 25-2). Here, enter a name for your container and select the access level. We call our container chapter25 and select the access level of Private. This means that only our account can view the container or its contents. Other access levels that you can choose include Public, which makes the container and its contents accessible to anybody who knows the URL; and Public Blob, which keeps the container metadata private but makes the blobs it contains public.

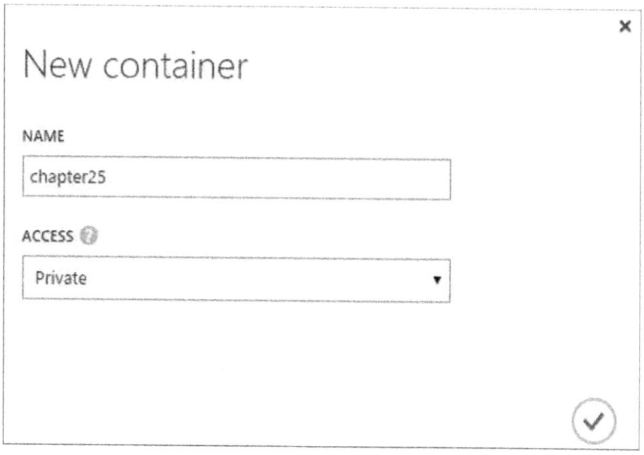

Figure 25-2. *The New Container dialog box*

■ **Tip**   When choosing a name for your container, be aware that it can consist of letters and numbers, but all letters must be lowercase. The only special character allowed is a hyphen, but you are not permitted to use two consecutive hyphens. A hyphen is also not permitted as the first character.

■ **Caution**   For the security of your data, you should know that Private is the only appropriate access level for SQL Server backups.

Our container now displays under our account, along with the URL that we can use to access it, as illustrated in Figure 25-3.

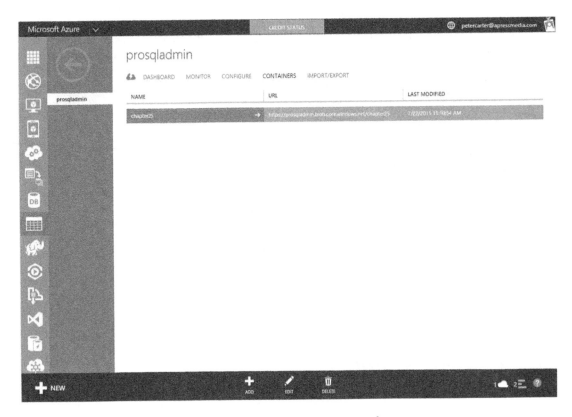

Figure 25-3. *Container displayed in Windows Azure management portal*

■ **Tip** Windows Azure Storage does not support container hierarchies. All containers are stored at the same level.

Backing Up a Database

Now that our container is ready, we need to prepare our instance of SQL Server. To do this, we create a database called Chapter25. We then create a SQL Login called URLBackupOperator, which is a member of the db_backupoperator for the Chapter25 database, and also grant it permission to alter any credential. This is the minimum set of permissions that allows the account to perform the backup to a URL. The script in Listing 25-1 performs these activities.

■ **Tip** ALTER ANY CREDENTIAL permissions are a technical requirement for the login that takes the backups. If you have multiple credentials, however, you can explicitly deny the login ALTER permissions to those credentials.

Listing 25-1. Preparing the Instance

```
USE Master
GO


CREATE DATABASE Chapter25 ;
GO


CREATE LOGIN URLBackupOperator
        WITH PASSWORD=N'Pa$$w0rd', DEFAULT_DATABASE=master,
            CHECK_EXPIRATION=OFF, CHECK_POLICY=OFF ;
GO


GRANT ALTER ANY CREDENTIAL TO URLBackupOperator ;
GO


USE Chapter25
GO


CREATE USER URLBackupOperator FOR LOGIN URLBackupOperator ;
GO


ALTER ROLE db_backupoperator ADD MEMBER URLBackupOperator ;
GO
```

Our next task is to create the credential that SQL Server uses to connect to the URL. When we create the credential, we use the name of our storage account as the identity for the credential, and we should use our primary access key as the secret to secure the credential. The command in Listing 25-2 creates a credential for the prosqladmin Windows Azure account. If you are following the demonstration, change the script to use your own Windows Azure account name and access key. You can find your access key by navigating to Storage in the Windows Azure management portal and selecting the Manage Keys option.

■ **Tip**   You can find more details regarding credentials in Chapter 21.

Listing 25-2. Creating a Credential

```
CREATE CREDENTIAL URLBackupCredential
WITH IDENTITY = 'prosqladmin'
             ,SECRET
='/Md/eNZs8HtJNpVFl992sBaPO54v7Bp1gyL61I33wNrTMSC5uDp6JRvi59FeY2/IjxyqsuLU2xrkrNNvmIBAGT==' ;
```

We can now take a backup of our Chapter25 database. Be aware that with SQL Server 2014, it is only possible to back up to a single URL. It is not possible to stripe a backup in the same way that you can stripe a backup to disk or tape. We will need to specify the credential we just created. The command in Listing 25-3 l performs the backup. You can also place this statement within a T-SQL job step of a SQL Server Agent job to schedule the backup process. If you are following the demonstrations, remember to change the URL to match your own configuration.

■ **Tip** When deciding upon a name for your backup file, bear in mind that the maximum number of characters allowed for the entire URL is 259. The uniform aspects of the URL consume 36 characters and, in our case, the account name consumes another 11. This means that the maximum length of the filename is 212 characters.

Listing 25-3. Backing Up the Chapter25 Database

```
BACKUP DATABASE Chapter25
TO URL = 'https://prosqladmin.blob.core.windows.net/chapter25/chapter25.bak'
WITH CREDENTIAL = 'URLBackupCredential';

GO
```

■ **Note** You must create the container *before* you back up the database or a 404 Error is thrown.

Chapter 15 discusses the syntax of the BACKUP command completely. You should know, however, that when you are backing up to URL, specifying the BLOCKSIZE, MAXTRANSFERSIZE, RETAINDAYS, and EXPIRYDAYS options is not supported. Creating a logical device name is also not supported.

INIT and NOINIT are valid syntax for a backup operation to a URL; however, they will be ignored. This is because you cannot append a backup to a blob. If you specify a URL that includes a blob that already exists, the operation fails, unless you specify FORMAT, which causes the blob to be overwritten.

Viewing Backup Files from SQL Server Management Studio

As long as you are using the 2014 version of SQL Server Management Studio, it is possible to connect to Azure Storage and view the backups that you have taken to the cloud. To do this, use the Connect drop-down in Object Explorer to connect to Azure Storage, as illustrated in Figure 25-4.

Figure 25-4. Using the Object Explorer to connect to Azure Storage

Following these steps causes the Connect To Windows Azure Storage dialog box to display, as illustrated in Figure 25-5. In this dialog box, you should enter your storage account name and access key. You can also choose whether the connection should be made with HTTPS, which is not required, but highly recommended. You can also specify if the access key should be saved. Saving it can save time, but it can also widen the security footprint of the solution, and if a malicious user gained access to the DBA's desktop, they could potentially access the backup files.

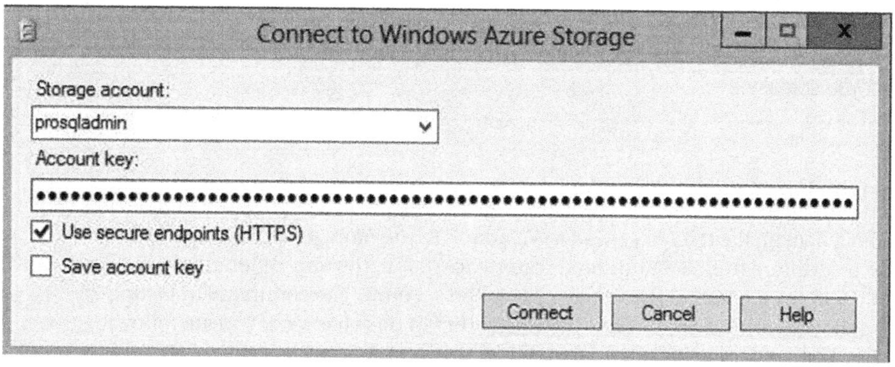

Figure 25-5. *The Connect To Windows Azure Storage dialog box*

Now that you have connected to Windows Azure Storage, you can browse the account in Object Explorer. This allows you to drill down through your containers and see the blobs that you have stored in them, as shown in Figure 25-6. It is also possible to delete a blob, or even an entire container, from the object's context menu.

Figure 25-6. *Browse Windows Azure Storage*

■ **Tip** Your backup files are also visible in the Windows Azure management portal. To see them, drill through your account and then you container.

Restoring from a Backup

When you restore from a backup file that you saved to Windows Azure Storage, all restore options are valid. If you choose to restore from a disk or tape restore operation, the only difference is that you must specify FROM URL and the credential that has access to the account. The command in Listing 25-4 restores the Chapter25 database from the backup we took earlier in this chapter. If you are following the demonstrations, remember to change the URL to match your own configuration.

Listing 25-4. Restoring from a Backup

```
USE Master
GO

RESTORE DATABASE Chapter25
FROM URL = 'https://prosqladmin.blob.core.windows.net/chapter25/chapter25.bak'
WITH CREDENTIAL = 'URLBackupCredential', REPLACE ;

GO
```

SQL Server Managed Backup to Windows Azure

SQL Server 2014 introduces Managed Backup to Windows Azure to ease the burden of configuring schedules on DBAs and to lessen the risk that they would lose date when they were baking up to Windows Azure Storage. When DBAs use Managed Backup, they only need to configure a retention period—SQL Server does everything else. This means that DBAs do not need to spend their time creating maintenance plans or SQL Server Agent jobs to manage backup routines.

The following sections discuss the concepts of SQL Server Managed Backup to Windows Azure before they demonstrate how to configure this feature for an individual database and for the instance. Finally, you see how to perform advanced configuration of Managed Backup.

■ **Note** If you are using a version of SQL Server older than SQL Server 2014, Microsoft provides a tool named SQL Server Backup to Windows Azure Tool, which you can download from http://www.microsoft.com/en-gb/download/details.aspx?id=40740 and use to help simplify the process of managing backups to the cloud.

Understanding Managed Backup to Windows Azure

You can configure Managed Backup for an individual database or at the instance level. When you configure Managed Backup at the instance level, you get an additional advantage: any new databases created on the instance automatically fall under the management of Managed Backups. This reduces the risk of losing data when you accidentally forget to configure backups for a new database.

■ **Caution** If you enable Managed Backup to Windows Azure at the instance level, all new databases are managed automatically; however, you must configure Managed Backup for any existing databases manually.

The primary limitation of Managed Backup to Windows Azure is that the SIMPLE recovery model is not supported. Databases can only be managed if they are configured to use the FULL recovery model or are temporarily using the BULK LOGGED recovery model. This means that the feature is more suitable for OLTP databases than it is for data warehouses or VLDBs. For more information of the recovery models, please refer to Chapter 15.

When you configure Managed Backup to Windows Azure, the database(s) managed by the tool all share the same backup strategy both for full backups and for transaction log backups. For full backups, the rules of this strategy are as follows:

- A backup will be taken when Managed Backup to Windows Azure is enabled for the database or instance

- A backup will be taken when the transaction log has grown by 1GB since the last full backup was taken

- A backup will be taken when one week has elapsed since the last full backup was taken

- A backup will be taken if the log chain becomes broken

For transaction log backups, these are the rules of the strategy:

- A backup will be taken when no log backup history can be found

- A backup will be taken when 5MB of transaction log space has been used since the last time a transaction log backup was taken

- A backup will be taken when two hours have elapsed since the last transaction log backup was taken

- A backup will be taken when there has been a full backup since the last transaction log backup

For stand-alone databases, Managed Backup to Windows Azure creates a container based upon the name of the server name and SQL Server instance name. It creates the blobs using the convention <First 40 characters of database name>_<Database GUID>_<Timestamp>.bak for full backups and <First 40 characters of database name>_<Database GUID>_<Timestamp>.log for transaction log backups.

When you want to enable Managed Backup to Windows Azure for a database that participates in an AlwaysOn Availability Group, Managed Backup to Windows Azure creates a container based upon the GUID of the availability group. It creates the blobs using the convention <First 40 characters of database name>_<Availability Group GUID>_<Database GUID>_<Timestamp>.bak for full backups and <First 40 characters of database name>_<Availability Group GUID>_<Database GUID>_<Timestamp>.log for transaction log backups.

Configuring Managed Backup to Windows Azure for an Individual Database

You can use the msdb.smart_admin.sp_set_db_backup system stored procedure to enable Managed Backup to Windows Azure for an individual database. This procedure accepts the parameters detailed in Table 25-1.

Table 25-1. *msdb. smart_admin.sp_set_db_backup Parameters*

Parameter	Description
@database_name	The name of the database to be managed by Managed Backup to Windows Azure.
@enable_backup	Specifies if the feature should be enabled for the database. • 0 indicates disabled. • 1 indicates enabled.
@retention_days	Specifies the number of days for which backups should be retained. This value should be between 1 and 30.
@credential_name	Specifies the name of the credential used to access the URL.
@encryption_algorithm	Specifies the encryption algorithm that you should use to encrypt the backup. The following are acceptable values: • AES_128 • AES_192 • AES_256 • TRIPLE_DES_3KEY • NO_ENCRYPTION
@encryptor_type	Specifies the type of encryptor used to encrypt the backup. The following are acceptable values: • CERTIFICATE • ASYMMETRIC KEY Asymmetric keys are only supported when stored in an EKM (Extensible Key Management) provider.
@encryptor_name	Specifies the name of the certificate or asymmetric key used to encrypt the backup.

■ **Tip** Full details of keys and certificates can be found in Chapter 10.

The command in Listing 25-5 demonstrates how to configure the Chapter25 database so it is backed up using Managed Backup to Windows Azure without being encrypted.

■ **Tip** Make sure SQL Server Agent is running before you perform this procedure, otherwise it will fail.

Listing 25-5. Configuring a Database for Managed Backup

```
USE msdb;
GO

EXEC smart_admin.sp_set_db_backup
            @database_name='Chapter25'
            ,@enable_backup=1
```

```
            ,@retention_days =30
            ,@credential_name ='URLBackupCredential'
            ,@encryption_algorithm ='NO_ENCRYPTION' ;
GO
```

■ **Tip** Retention settings you specify at the database level override retention settings you specify at the instance level.

After we configure the Managed Backup to Windows Azure for the Chapter25 database, when we connect to Windows Azure Storage in Object Explorer, we see that a new container has been created and that both a full backup and a transaction log backup of the Chapter25 database have been taken, as shown in Figure 25-7. The full backup was taken because of the rule that states that a full backup is taken when Managed Backup to Windows Azure is enabled for the database or instance. The transaction log backup was taken because of the following two rules:

- A transaction log backup is taken when no log backup history can be found.

- A transaction log backup is taken when a full backup has been performed since the last transaction log backup.

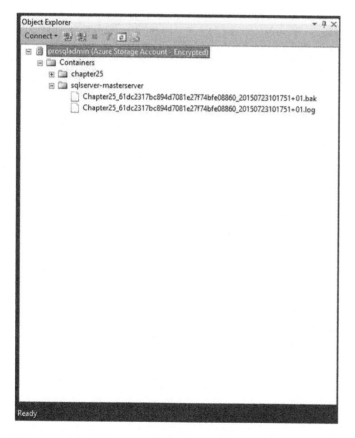

Figure 25-7. *Backups displayed in Object Explorer*

■ **Tip** If you are configuring Managed Backup to Windows Azure for databases that participate in an Availability Group, you should configure the feature on all replicas using the `msdb.smart-admin.sp_set_db_backup` procedure. Managed Backup uses the preferred backup replica settings to determine from which replica to take the backup.

Configuring Managed Backup to Windows Azure for an Instance

You can configuring Managed Backup to Windows Azure at the instance level either through the GUI or by using T-SQL. To configure the feature using the GUI, drill through Management in Object Explorer and select Configure from the Managed Backup context menu. This invokes the Managed Backup dialog box, as illustrated in Figure 25-8.

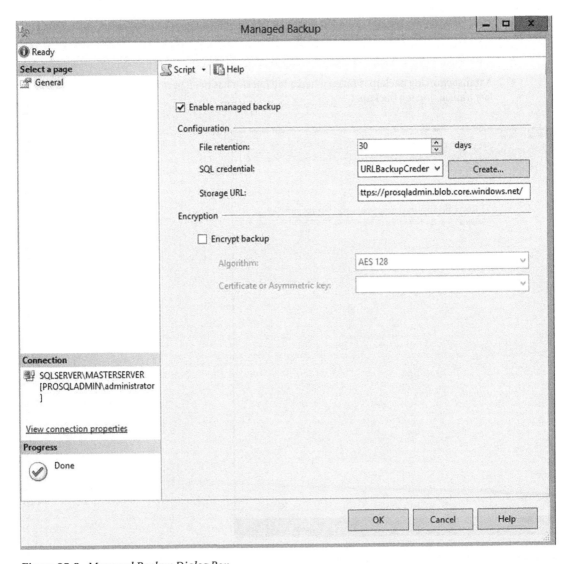

Figure 25-8. Managed Backup Dialog Box

In this dialog box, we enable Managed Backup using the check box at the top of the screen. We then configure the feature by specifying a file retention and selecting our URLBackupCredential credential from the drop-down list. If we have not already created a credential, then we can use the Create button to invoke the Create Credential - Authenticate To Azure Storage dialog box. We also need to make sure the Storage URL box is populated with the URL to our Windows Azure storage account. The URL should not include the container name since this is created by SQL Server. Optionally, we can also use this dialog box to configure encryption for our backups by checking the Encrypt Backup check box before specifying the appropriate algorithm and encryptor to use.

To configure Managed Backup to Windows Azure at the instance level by using T-SQL, you need to use the msdb.smart_admin.sp_set_instance_backup system stored procedure. This procedure accepts the parameters detailed in Table 25-2.

Table 25-2. *msdb.smart_admin.sp_set_instance_backup Parameters*

Parameter	Description
@enable_backup	Specifies if the feature should be enabled for the instance. • 0 indicates disabled. • 1 indicates enabled.
@storage_url	The URL of the Windows Azure storage account. This should not include the container name, since the container is created automatically.
@retention_days	Specifies the number of days for which backups should be retained. This value should be between 1 and 30.
@credential_name	Specifies the name of the credential used to access the URL.
@encryption_algorithm	Specifies the encryption algorithm that you should use to encrypt the backup. These are acceptable values: • AES_128 • AES_192 • AES_256 • TRIPLE_DES_3KEY • NO_ENCRYPTION
@encryptor_type	Specifies the type of encryptor used to encrypt the backup. These are acceptable values: • CERTIFICATE • ASYMMETRIC KEY Asymmetric keys are only supported when stored in an EKM (Extensible Key Management) provider.
@encryptor_name	Specifies the name of the certificate or asymmetric key used to encrypt the backup.

The command in Listing 25-6 enables Managed Backup for our instance without using encryption.

Listing 25-6. Enabling Managed Backup for the Instance

```
EXEC smart_admin.sp_set_instance_backup
                        @enable_backup = 1,
                        @retention_days = 30,
                        @credential_name = N'URLBackupCredential',
                        @storage_url = N'https://prosqladmin.blob.core.windows.net/',
                        @encryption_algorithm = N'NO_ENCRYPTION' ;

GO
```

Let's now create a new database on the instance, called NewDB, by using the command in Listing 25-7.

Listing 25-7. Creating a New Database

```
CREATE DATABASE NewDB ;
GO
```

Now that we have created a new database, we can connect to Windows Azure Storage in Object Explorer to make sure that a backup of the new database has been taken. In Figure 25-9, you can see that Managed Backup has used the container we created when we configured Managed Backup for the Chapter25 database and taken a full backup and transaction log backup of the NewDB database to this location.

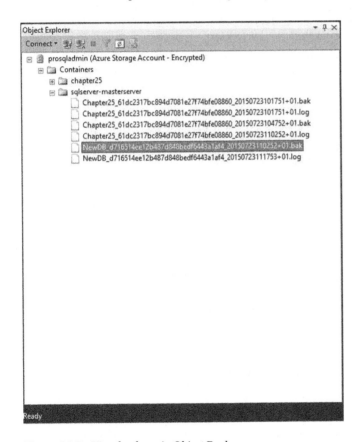

Figure 25-9. *View backups in Object Explorer*

■ **Tip** If your database is not backed up instantly, it is because the default setting for how often the instance is scanned for new databases is every 15 minutes. We discuss changing this value in the following section.

Managed Backup to Windows Azure Advanced Configuration

SQL Server supplies a system stored procedure named msdb.smart_admin.sp_set_parameter that allows you to configure advanced aspects of Managed Backup to Windows Azure. The procedure accepts the parameters detailed in Table 25-3.

Table 25-3. *msdb.smart_admin.sp_set_parameter Parameters*

Parameter	Description
@parameter_name	The name of the parameter that you wish to configure
@parameter_value	The value that you would like to configure for the parameter

The parameters that you can configure using this system stored procedure are described in Table 25-4.

Table 25-4. *Managed Backup Parameters*

Parameter	Description
SSMBackup2WANotificationEmailId	Specifies a semicolon-delimited list of e-mail addresses to which errors and warnings should be sent.
FileRetentionDebugXevent	Specifies if file retention debug events should be captured. The value can be True or False.
FileRetentionOperationalXevent	Specifies if file retention operational events should be captured. The value can be True or False.
StorageOperationDebugXevent	Specifies if the storage operation debug events should be captured. The value can be True or False.
SSMBackup2WAFrequency	This is an undocumented parameter that allows you to configure how often Managed Backup scans the instance for new databases. The value is specified in seconds.

■ **Caution** The SSMBackup2WAFrequency parameter is undocumented and, therefore, unsupported by Microsoft.

Listing 25-8 demonstrates how to use the msdb.smart_admin.sp_set_parameter procedure to make Managed Backup to Windows Azure scan for new databases more frequently (every five minutes).

Listing 25-8. Using msdb.smart_admin.sp_set_parameter

```
USE MSDB
GO

EXEC smart_admin.sp_set_parameter
            @parameter_name = 'SSMBackup2WAFrequency',
            @parameter_value = 300 ;
```

Currently you can view configured settings by using the `msdb.smart_admin.fn_get_parameter()` system function, as demonstrated in Listing 25-9. This function accepts one parameter that specifies the name of the parameter that you wish to view the configuration of. If you want to view all configured values, pass `NULL`.

Listing 25-9. Viewing Managed Backup to Windows Azure Parameters

```
USE MSDB
GO

SELECT *
FROM smart_admin.fn_get_parameter (NULL) ;
```

■ **Note**   If a setting has never been configured, it will not appear in the results.

Disabling Managed Backup to Windows Azure

You can disable Managed Backup to Windows Azure for a specific database or for any new databases created on the instance. To do so for a specific database, use the `MSDB.smart_admin.sp_set_db_backup` system stored procedure. The command in Listing 25-10 disables Managed Backup to Windows Azure for the Chapter25 database.

Listing 25-10. Disabling Managed Backup to Windows Azure for a Specific Database

```
EXEC MSDB.smart_admin.sp_set_db_backup
            @database_name='Chapter25'
            ,@enable_backup=0;
GO
```

To disable Managed Backup to Windows Azure so it is not the default setting for any new databases created on the instance, use the `MSDB.smart_admin.sp_set_instance_backup` system stored procedure. The command in Listing 25-11 disables Managed Backup to Windows Azure for any new databases.

Listing 25-11. Disabling Managed Backup to Windows Azure for New Databases

```
EXEC MSDB.smart_admin.sp_set_instance_backup
            @enable_backup=0;
GO
```

Summary

Cloud backups can provide a highly available and cost-effective alternative to disk or tape backups. In order to harness backups to Windows Azure, you must first have a Windows Azure account and a Windows Azure storage account. Once you have created these accounts, you must create a container, which is a grouping for blobs. Blobs are the files that you store within Windows Azure.

Within SQL Server, you must create a credential so that the instance can connect to the URL, where the backup will be stored. This credential should use your Windows Azure storage account name as the identity, and the access key as the secret for securing the Credential. When you take the backup, this credential is used to authenticate to Windows Azure.

SQL Server also allows backups to be managed automatically with the Managed Backup to Windows Azure feature. You can configure this feature for specific databases or for an entire instance. This feature reduces pressure on DBAs by backing up databases using a predefined strategy. This way the only thing that a DBA has to configure is the retention period and, optionally, encryption. The retention period at the database level overrides the retention period at the instance level.

CHAPTER 26

■ ■ ■

SQL Data Files in Windows Azure

SQL Server offers you the ability to natively store SQL Server data files and log files as page blobs in Windows Azure, which in turn helps you increase the portability of your databases—for example, if you need to move databases between on-premises instances, or between an on-premises instance and a Windows Azure SQL virtual machine (VM). This chapter discusses the concepts of this functionality before demonstrating how to implement it.

Understanding SQL Data Files in Windows Azure

SQL Server Data Files in Windows Azure is a new feature of SQL Server 2014 that allows you to store data and log files in the cloud, while maintaining on-premises compute nodes. This hybrid cloud functionality can offer advantages in many business cases. For example, it offers limitless storage without the overheads of SAN (Storage Area Network) management. It can also help you improve the availability of your systems because it is possible for the database to be attached to more than one server at a time. It is important to note, however, that the database must be offline on all but one node. This is because SQL Server Data Files in Windows Azure does not support connections from multiple servers, and if you accidently bring the database online on both servers at the same time, queries fail. However, this means that if your primary server crashes, you can bring the database online on your secondary server and the data becomes immediately accessible.

■ **Tip**   If you have a database attached to multiple instances, then the database must be offline on one of the instances.

The ability to attach a database to multiple servers also makes your databases very portable. If you need to migrate a database between servers, or even migrate from an on-premises server to a Windows Azure VM, you can do so with a very small amount of downtime.

One of the most interesting benefits of storing data files in Windows Azure, however, is a security enhancement. It is possible to use TDE (Transparent Data Encryption) with SQL Data Files in Windows Azure. When you combine these technologies, the data is encrypted at rest, in the cloud. When data is accessed, it is decrypted at the on-premises compute node. Because the certificates are stored on the compute node, in the unlikely event that your account is compromised, your data is still safe.

Another very interesting hybrid solution that SQL Server Data Files in Windows Azure makes available to you is the ability to store some data files on premises and others in the cloud. For example, imagine that you have a large database comprised of 20 percent live data and 80 percent historical data. You need maximum performance for the live data, but you are reaching your maximum on-premises storage capacity. In this scenario, you can implement a solution in which the live data is stored in data files on premises and the historic data is stored in files that are hosted in Windows Azure. A sliding-windows implementation of partitioning, which is discussed in Chapter 6, allows you to maintain this data split with minimal effort.

SQL Server Data Files in Windows Azure also has its limitations, however. One of the most notable limitations is that FILESTREAM, FileTable, and In-Memory OLTP are not supported.

Additionally, if you use this feature, then your Windows Azure storage account will not support the use of geo-replication. This is because of the risk of data corruption in the event that a geo-failover is invoked. The 1TB max blob size limit within Windows Azure also applies. This means that if your database is larger than 1TB, you need to split it down into multiple files.

In order to use SQL Server Data Files in Windows Azure, you must have a Windows Azure account and a Windows Azure storage account. Once these are in place, you must create a container that you will use to store you data files. I highly recommend using the Private access level for this container, meaning that no anonymous authentication is permitted to the URL of you container or the blobs within it.

■ **Note**   Demonstrations in this chapter assume that you have created a Windows Azure account and a Windows Azure storage account.

In order to use SQL Data Files in Windows Azure, you must generate a SAS (shared access signature) on the container where your data files will be stored. A SAS is a URI (uniform resource indicator) that is generated on the server side and provides a mechanism for granting a limited set of permissions against your container to the clients who use them. Clients can then access the container without needing to know your Windows Azure storage access key. When you generate a SAS, you specify the start time and end time and also the granular permissions that the client needs. SQL Server then requires that you create a credential within the instance, which allows SQL Server to connect to the URL using the signature, as opposed to the standard URL.

Implementing SQL Data Files in Windows Azure

The following sections first discuss how to prepare Windows Azure Storage to support SQL Server Data Files in Windows Azure. They then go on to discuss how to prepare the SQL Server instance, and finally, they demonstrate how to create and manage data files in Windows Azure.

■ **Note**   Demonstrations in this section use the Windows Azure management portal. This portal is occasionally updated by Microsoft and, therefore, subject to change.

Preparing Windows Azure

The first step in implementing SQL Server Data Files in Windows Azure is to create a container in which to store the files. This is a different container than the one we created in Chapter 25. To do this, we navigate to the Storage pane and drill through our storage account in the Windows Azure management portal. We then select the Containers tab, which is displayed in Figure 26-1.

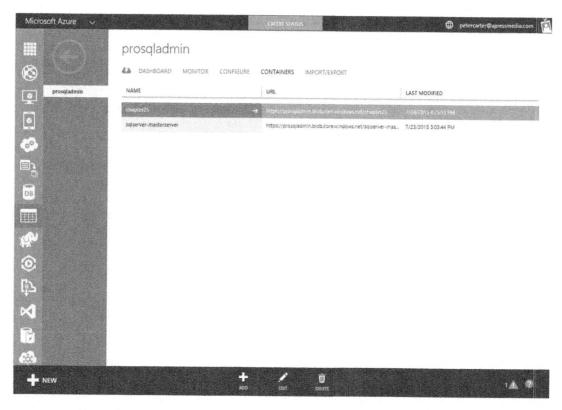

Figure 26-1. *The Containers tab*

We then choose the option to create a new container, which invokes the New Container dialog box, displayed in Figure 26-2. This is where you can enter a name for your container and select the access level. We have called our container chapter26 and have selected the access level of Private. This means that only our account can view the container or its contents.

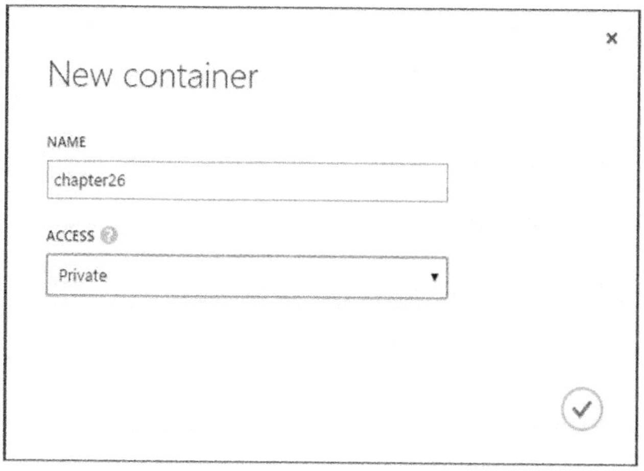

Figure 26-2. *The New Container dialog box*

The next task is to generate a SAS for the chapter26 container. Unfortunately, at the time of writing, this functionality has not been implemented within the Windows Azure management portal. Instead, you must either write custom code to generate the key by using the CloudBlobContainer.GetSharedAccessSignature method in the Windows Azure SDK, or by using the Create Container, Set Container ACL, and Get Container ACL Window Azure REST APIs.

Alternatively you can use a third-party Windows Azure Storage management tool. You can find a list of third-party management tools at http://blogs.msdn.com/b/windowsazurestorage/archive/2010/04/17/windows-azure-storage-explorers.aspx.

■ **Note** Demonstrations in this section use the Azure Management Studio tool, which you can downloaded from http://www.cerebrata.com.

In the Connection Group windows of Azure Management Studio, we select the Add Storage Account Connection hyperlink, which causes the Add Storage Account Connection dialog box to display, as illustrated in Figure 26-3.

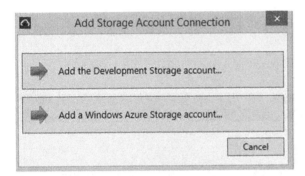

Figure 26-3. *The Add Storage Account Connection dialog box*

Here, we choose Add A Windows Azure Storage Account, which invokes the Add Storage Account Connection dialog box, illustrated in Figure 26-4. If you are following the demonstrations, please substitute the account name for your own account.

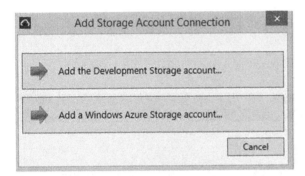

Figure 26-4. *The Add Storage Account Connection dialog box*

In this dialog box, we enter the name of our Windows Azure storage account and copy the primary access key of the account into the Storage Account Key field. We now need to specify the type of account that we have, which in our case is a Standard Local Redundant account. (Remember that Windows Azure geo-replication is not compatible with SQL Server Data Files in Windows Azure.) Optionally, you can specify your preferences for the account within Azure Management Studio. In our case, we have left the default settings.

In the Connection Group window of Windows Azure Management Studio, we drill through Storage Accounts | [Your Account] | Blob Containers and select Access Policies from the context menu of the chapter26 container. This invokes the Access Policies dialog box. Here, you should use the plus (+) icon on the right of the screen to create a new access policy. You can then give the policy a name and specify the start time and end time of the policy as well as use the check boxes to define the permissions that it should be given, as shown in Figure 26-5.

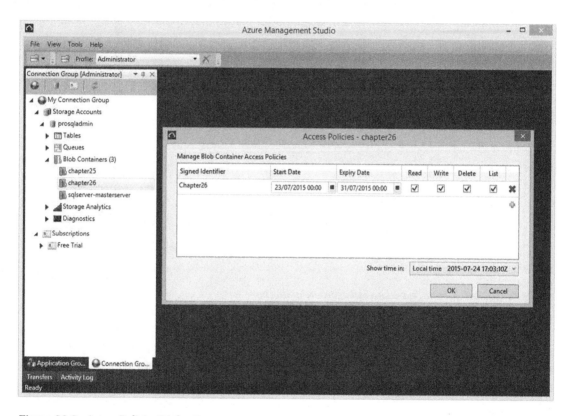

Figure 26-5. *Access Policies Dialog Box*

You can see that we have named our policy Chapter26 and have assign Read, Write, Delete, and List permissions. MSDN documentation currently states that only Read, Write, and List permissions are required to use SQL Server Data Files in Windows Azure. This is true until you need to drop a database. At this point, Delete permissions are also required.

Now that we have created the access policy, we need to generate the shared access signature. To do this, we select Generate Signed URL from the context menu of the chapter26 container. This invokes the Generate Shared Access Signature dialog box, as illustrated in Figure 26-6.

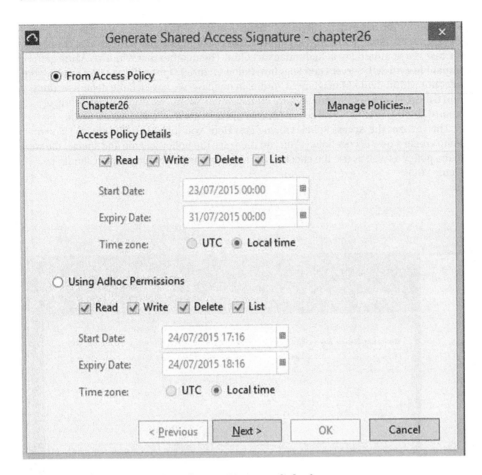

Figure 26-6. *The Generate Shared Access Signature dialog box*

■ **Tip**   I highly recommend generating the signed URL from an access policy as opposed to using ad-hoc permissions. This is because if you use ad-hoc permissions, then you need to alter the credential in SQL Server every time you update the expiry date, because when you use this approach, the expiry date is included in the query string.

On this tab, we select the radio button to generate the signature from an access policy and then selected our policy from the drop-down list. We then click the next button to generate the signature. On the next page of the dialog box, shown in Figure 26-7, we see three boxes. The first displays the entire URL, the second displays the query string, which is made up of the components listed in Table 26-1, and the third box displays a C# code sample for using the signature. Each box has a copy to clipboard button next to it, and we use this button to copy the URL to a file, which can be stored securely.

Figure 26-7. The Generate Shared Access Signature dialog box

Table 26-1. *Query String Components*

Component	Description	Example From Our URL

Entire URL	The entire URL	`https://prosqladmin.blob.core.`
		`windows.net/chapter26?sr=c&sv=2015-`
		`02-21&si=Chapter26&sig=VwyIjeonRnu`
		`ItpjDKgtle2V%2B%2F4ja%2BO%2FZkJcDJ`
		`GLLrrM%3D`

Container URI	The address of the container	`https://prosqladmin.blob.core.` `windows.net/chapter26`
Query String	Designates the beginning of the query string	`?`
Parameter Separator	Delimitates parameters	`&`
Resource	Defines the resource that has been secured—in our case, a container	`sr=c`
Storage Services Version	Indicates the version of storage services to use	`sv=2015-02-21`
Access Policy	Defines the policy used to create the signature	`si=Chapter26`

Signature	The key, generated on the server side, that is used to authenticate to the URL	`si=Chapter26&sig=VwyIjeonRnuItpjD`
		`Kgtle2V%2B%2F4ja%2BO%2FZkJcDJGLLr`
		`rM%3D`

If you were to generate an ad-hoc SAS as opposed to create one from an access policy, then the Access Policies properties would not be inherited; therefore, the query string components detailed in Table 26-2 would replace the Access Policy component.

Table 26-2. *Ad-hoc Query String Components*

Component	Description
Start Time	The start time of the SAS, specified in ISO 8061 format. Begins `st=`.
Expiry Time	The expiry time of the SAS, specified in ISO 8061 format. Begins `se=`.
Permissions	The permissions assigned to the signature. R indicates read, w indicate write, l indicates list, and d indicates delete. Begins `sp=`. For example, if read, write, and list permissions are granted, then the component reads `sp=rwl`.

■ **Tip** The security best practice for shared access signatures is to create them for a short time period and then regenerate them; it is usually recommended to specify an expiry date (which avoids making an infinite lease). However, the more frequently SASs are regenerated, the higher the administrative overhead, since you will need to change the credential every time the signature expires. Therefore, make sure to balance security against manageability when you are choosing an appropriate expiry date. Personally, I tend to recommend a lease of one year. It is important that you set a reminder to update the credential with a new signature before the lease expires, however, or your database will be inaccessible until the issue is resolved.

Preparing the SQL Server Instance

Now that our Windows Azure storage is ready for SQL Server Data Files in Windows Azure, we need to prepare our SQL Server instance. This preparation consists of creating a credential that uses the SAS to authenticate to our storage account. The advantage of the credential using a SAS is that we do not need to store our access key within the instance.

When we create the credential, we need to use the URL of our container as the name. We use an arbitrary string, 'SHARED ACCESS SIGNATURE', as the identity, and we use the query string (excluding the leading question mark) that we generated as the secret. Therefore, to create a certificate that can authenticate to our container, we use the command in Listing 26-1. If you are following the demonstration, remember to change the values for name and secret to match your own environment.

Listing 26-1. Creating the Credential

```
USE Master
GO


CREATE CREDENTIAL [https://prosqladmin.blob.core.windows.net/chapter26]
WITH IDENTITY = 'SHARED ACCESS SIGNATURE',
SECRET =
'sr=c&sv=2015-02-21&si=Chapter26&sig=VwyIjeonRnuItpjDKgtle2V%2B%2P4ja%2BO%2FYdJcDJGGPrrM%3D' ;
```

Creating a Database

Once we have created the credential, we can create a database the way we would create any other, and SQL Server automatically uses the credential to authenticate to our container. For example, the script in Listing 26-2 creates a database called Chapter26, which resides in the cloud. The database contains one table, called Title, which we populate with data.

Listing 26-2. Creating a Database

```
CREATE DATABASE Chapter26
    ON (NAME = 'Chapter26Data',
        FILENAME = 'https://prosqladmin.blob.core.windows.net/chapter26/Chapter26.mdf'),
        (NAME = 'Chapter26Log',
        FILENAME = 'https://prosqladmin.blob.core.windows.net/chapter26/Chapter26.ldf') ;
GO


USE Chapter26
GO


CREATE TABLE dbo.Title
(ID        INT           NOT NULL    IDENTITY    PRIMARY KEY,
 Title     NVARCHAR(8)
) ;
GO


INSERT INTO dbo.Title
VALUES('Mr'),('Mrs'),('Miss'),('Dr'),('Master'),('Ms'),('Lord'),('Lady') ;
GO
```

Next we create a hybrid database, called Chapter26Hybrid. This database contain a table called Orders, and we configure partitioning so that orders taken before 1st Jan 2015 are stored on premises and historic orders are stored in Windows Azure. For further details of implementing partitioning, please see Chapter 6.

First, we create the database, with two filegroups, using the script in Listing 26-3. If you are following the demonstrations, remember to change the file locations to match your own configuration.

Listing 26-3. Creating the Chapter26Hybrid Database

```
CREATE DATABASE Chapter26Hybrid
ON  PRIMARY
( NAME = N'Chapter26Hybrid',
  FILENAME = N'F:\MSSQL12.MASTERSERVER\MSSQL\Chapter26Hybrid.mdf' ),
FILEGROUP HistoricData
( NAME = N'HistoricData',
  FILENAME =
  'https://prosqladmin.blob.core.windows.net/chapter26/Chapter26HybridHistoricData.ndf')
LOG ON
( NAME = N'Chapter26Hybrid_log',
  FILENAME = N'G:\MSSQL12.MASTERSERVER\MSSQL\DATA\Chapter26Hybrid_log.ldf') ;

GO
```

We now create the partitioning objects that are required to implement our solution. Listing 26-4 contains a script to achieve this.

Listing 26-4. Creating the Partitioning Objects

```
USE Chapter26Hybrid
GO

CREATE PARTITION FUNCTION HybridPartFunc(datetime2)
AS RANGE LEFT
FOR VALUES('2014-12-31') ;
GO

CREATE PARTITION SCHEME HybridPartScheme
AS PARTITION HybridPartFunc
TO ([PRIMARY], HistoricData) ;
GO
```

Finally, we create the Orders table by using the script in Listing 26-5.

Listing 26-5. Creating the Orders Table

```
USE Chapter26Hybrid
GO

CREATE TABLE dbo.Orders
      (
      OrderID      INT          NOT NULL,
      OrderDate    DATETIME2    NOT NULL,
      ProductID    INT          NOT NULL,
      OrderQty     INT          NOT NULL,
```

```
        ItemPrice       MONEY        NOT NULL,
        SubTotal        MONEY        NOT NULL,
        CustomerID      INT          NOT NULL
        ) ;
GO

ALTER TABLE dbo.Orders ADD CONSTRAINT
        PK_Orders PRIMARY KEY CLUSTERED
        (
          OrderID,
          OrderDate
        ) ON HybridPartScheme(OrderDate) ;
GO
```

Now that we have created the database, we can optionally encrypt it using TDE. The script in Listing 26-6 encrypts the Chapter26Hybrid database. As discussed earlier in this chapter, because the certificate is stored in the Master database, which is on premises, using TDE protects your data, even in the event that your Windows Azure storage account is compromised. If you are following the demonstrations, remember to change the file locations to match your own configuration.

■ **Note**   Chapter 10 discusses TDE in detail.

Listing 26-6. Implementing TDE

```
USE Master
GO

--Create the master Key

CREATE MASTER KEY ENCRYPTION BY PASSWORD = 'Pa$$w0rd';
GO

--Create the Certificate

CREATE CERTIFICATE TDECert WITH SUBJECT = 'SQL Server Data Files Certificate'
GO

USE Chapter26Hybrid;
GO

--Create the encryption key

CREATE DATABASE ENCRYPTION KEY
WITH ALGORITHM = AES_256
ENCRYPTION BY SERVER CERTIFICATE TDECert ;
GO

--Turn on encryption

ALTER DATABASE Chapter26Hybrid
SET ENCRYPTION ON ;
GO
```

■ **Caution**   After creating the certificate, back it up; failing to do so may result in data loss. You can find details on how to do this in Chapter 10.

Monitoring and Managing SQL Server Data Files in Windows Azure

After implementing SQL Data Files for Windows Azure, DBAs need to monitor and manage the solution. This is because, in addition to existing on-premises monitoring and management, DBAs need to monitor the performance of their Windows Azure blobs and renew the SAS keys when they expire. The following sections discuss how to monitor the feature before going on to discuss common maintenance scenarios.

Monitoring SQL Server Data File in Windows Azure

A new performance object has been added to allow DBAs to monitor the performance of SQL Server Data Files in Windows Azure. This object is called HTTPS Storage and it contains the following counters:

- Read Bytes/Sec
- Write Bytes/Sec
- Total Bytes/Sec
- Reads/Sec
- Writes/Sec
- Transfers/Sec
- Avg. Bytes/Read
- Avg. Bytes/Write
- Avg. Bytes/Transfer
- Avg. microsec/Read—(The average amount of time for each read in microseconds)
- Avg. microsec/Write—(The average amount of time for each write in microseconds)
- Avg. microsec/Transfer—(The average amount of time for each transfer in microseconds)
- Outstanding HTTP Storage IO
- HTTP Storage IO retry/sec

These counters are exposed through Perfmon and also through the DMV sys.dm_os_performance_counters. You can find full details of how to query sys.dm_os_performance_counters in Chapter 17. An instance of each counter is available for each Windows Azure storage account and a _Total instance of each counter is also available. The query in Listing 26-7 demonstrates how to obtain the current number of outstanding IOs against the prosqladmin Windows Azure storage account.

Listing 26-7. Querying sys.dm_os_performance_counters

```
SELECT
        counter_name
        ,cntr_value
FROM sys.dm_os_performance_counters
WHERE counter_name = 'Outstanding HTTP Storage IO'
AND instance_name = 'prosqladmin.blob.core.windows.net' ;
```

■ **Tip**   If you remove the filter on instance_name, then you can view totals across all of your storage accounts.

Managing SQL Server Data Files in Windows Azure

When your SAS is reaching its expiry date, alter the access policy to extend the end date. To do this using the Azure Management Studio tool (from Cerebrata), drill through My Connection Group | Storage Accounts | [Storage Account Name] | Blob Containers in Azure Management Studio, and then select Access Policies from the context menu of the chapter26 container. This invokes the Access Policies dialog box. Here, you can change the end date of the policy, as illustrated in Figure 26-8.

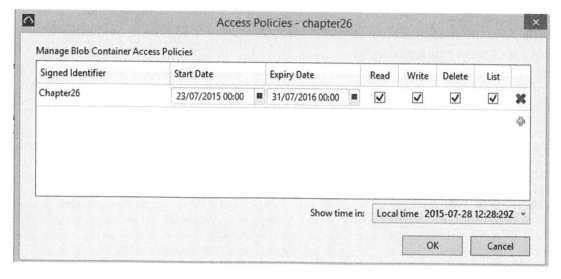

Figure 26-8. *Access Policies dialog box*

■ **Note**   If you generated an ad-hoc signed URL, as opposed to using an access policy, then you also need to update the credential. This is because the query string includes the end date and time.

If you do not change the end date of the access policy before it expires, then any databases that use the SAS are placed in Recovery Pending mode, and any attempt to access them will receive the error message shown in Figure 26-9. This error message is thrown in response to the query in Listing 26-8.

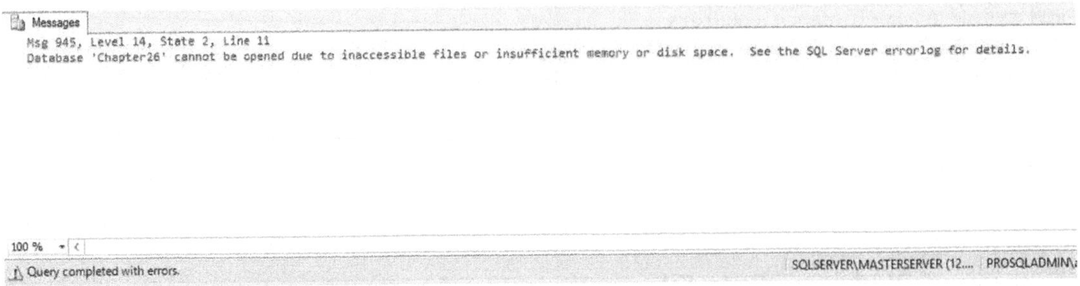

Figure 26-9. Error if access policy expires

Listing 26-8. Querying to Generate Error

```
SELECT *
FROM Chapter26.dbo.Title ;
```

■ **Tip**   This error message can have multiple causes, but if you are using SQL Data Files in Windows Azure, first check that your lease has not expired.

If this situation occurs, then after you change the expiry date of the SAS, you need to take the affected database(s) offline and then bring them back online. You can achieve this for the Chapter26 database by using the script in Listing 26-9 or by restarting the SQL Server service.

Listing 26-9. Fixing the Access Policy Expiry Issue

```
ALTER DATABASE Chapter26
SET OFFLINE
WITH ROLLBACK IMMEDIATE ;
GO

ALTER DATABASE Chapter26
SET ONLINE ;
GO
```

Summary

You can use the SQL Server Data Files in Windows Azure feature to store your database data and log files in Windows Azure while keeping the compute node on premises. It is also possible to keep some data files on premises while moving other data files to Windows Azure. This gives you the flexibility of a hybrid database, where some data, such as historical data, is stored in the cloud, while the most frequently accessed data remains on premises.

In order to implement SQL Server Data Files in Windows Azure, you must first have a Windows Azure account and a Windows Azure storage account. You must then create a container that you will use for your data files and generate a shared access key for this container. Unfortunately, Windows Azure management portal does not allow you to create a SAS (shared access signature) natively, so you must either write custom code, or use a third-party Windows Azure management tool, such as Windows Azure Management Studio. The SAS is a way of providing a limited set of permissions to a client without needing to expose your Windows Azure storage access key.

Once Windows Azure Storage has been configured for SQL Server Data Files in Windows Azure, you need to create a credential within the instance. You use this credential to access the blob container via the SAS. You should create the credential using the URL of the container as the name. The credential's identity should be the arbitrary string "SHARED ACCESS SIGNATURE" and the credential's secret should be configured as the query string generated when you are creating the SAS.

A new performance object, HTTP Storage, has been created to help DBAs monitor SQL Server Data Files in Windows Azure. This performance object is exposed through Performance Monitor and the sys.dm_os_performance_counters dynamic management view (DMV). An instance of the object is exposed for each Windows Azure storage account, and a _Total object is also exposed.

Make sure to extend the expiry date of the access policy you use to create the SAS before it is due to expire. If you do not, the databases(s) you access using the SAS are placed in Recovery Pending and all your attempts to access them will fail. To resolve this issue, update the expiry date of the access policy and then take the database(s) offline before you bring them back online.

CHAPTER 27

■ ■ ■

Migrating to the Cloud

Windows Azure offers you the ability to host SQL Server databases to the cloud using either Windows Azure SQL Server virtual machines (VMs), which offer an IaaS (Infrastructure as a Service), or Azure SQL Database, which offers DaaS (Database as a Service).

When migrating to an IaaS offering, you remove the overheads associated with managing a physical or virtual infrastructure on premises. Instead, the infrastructure is contained and managed in Microsoft data centers. Your company only needs to manage the platforms used by the VMs. In the case of SQL Server VMs, this means Windows Server and SQL Server.

When migrating to a DaaS offering, your company no longer needs to manage the infrastructure or the platform. Not only does Microsoft manage the hardware platform, it also manages the operating system and SQL Server instance as part of the offering. In fact, you only need staff to maintain the databases themselves. Although the latest versions of Azure SQL Database are very mature, they do not completely overlap with on-premises SQL Server offerings. This means that you should be careful not to try to migrate any databases that use functionality not offered by Azure SQL Database. Take a look at https://azure.microsoft.com/en-gb/documentation/articles/sql-database-transact-sql-information/ to find features that are not supported, or that are only partially supported by Azure SQL Database.

This chapter discusses how to work with databases in Azure, which offers DaaS, and how to work with Azure SQL VMs, which offer IaaS.

■ **Note**   Demonstrations in this chapter use the Windows Azure management portal. This portal is subject to updates from Microsoft and may change, although it is likely that concepts will change more slowly than the GUI.

Working with Azure SQL Database

The following sections describe how to work with DaaS by creating an Azure SQL Database and by migrating an existing database to it; how to deploy a new database to Azure SQL Database; and how to migrate an existing database to Azure SQL Database.

Creating an Azure SQL Database

When creating your first Azure SQL Database, you will also need to configure the SQL instance with a login name and password. To create the database, navigate to SQL Databases in the Azure management portal and choose the option to create a new database. This invokes the New SQL Database dialog box, as displayed in Figure 27-1. You can find the Azure management portal at manage.windowsazure.com.

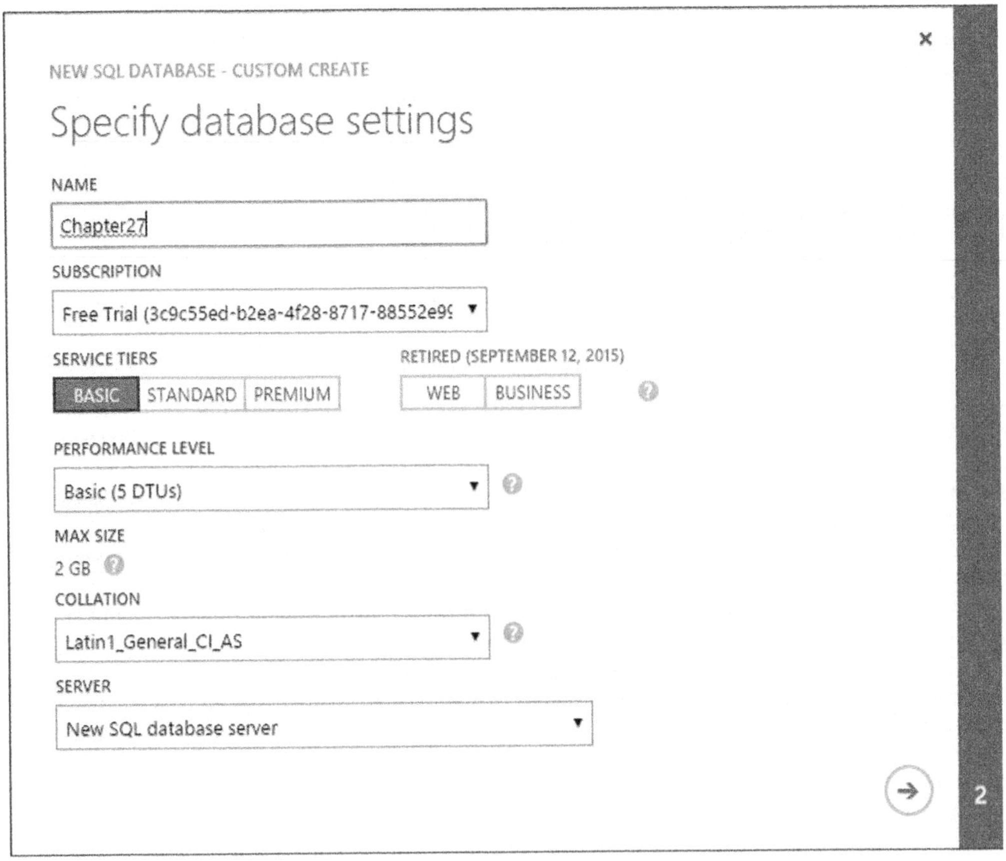

Figure 27-1. *The New SQL Database dialog box*

In this dialog box, we first specify a name for our database before going on to define the subscription that we plan to use (if we have multiple subscriptions). We then need to choose the service tier that we need for our database. In Figure 27-1, we select the Basic tier, since this is the recommended level for development and test environments. You can find details of the available service tiers in Chapter 1; however, these tiers are subject to change.

The performance level you select depends on the service tier that you choose. Performance levels are defined in DTUs (database throughput units). This measure represents the overall power of the database engine based on CPU, memory, and IO rates. The performance levels are subject to change, but Table 27-1 details the current performance level for the Basic service tier.

Table 27-1. *Basic Tier Performance Level*

Configuration	Basic Level
DTU (database throughput unit)	5
Max DB size	2GB
Max concurrent requests	30
Max concurrent logins	30
Max sessions	300
Benchmark transaction rate	16,600 transactions/hour
Predictability	Good

If you select the Standard tier, then the performance levels detailed in Table 27-2 are available.

Table 27-2. *Standard Tier Performance Levels*

Configuration	Std/S0 Level	Std/S1 Level	Std/S2 Level	Std/S3 Level
DTU (database throughput unit)	10	20	50	100
Max DB size	250GB	250GB	250GB	250GB
Max concurrent requests	60	90	120	200
Max concurrent logins	60	90	120	200
Max sessions	600	900	1200	2400
Benchmark transaction rate	521 transactions/min	934 transactions/min	2570 transactions/min	5100 transactions/min
Predictability	Better	Better	Better	Better

If you select the Premium tier, then the performance levels detailed in Table 27-3 are available.

Table 27-3. *Premium Performance Levels*

Configuration	Premium/P1 Level	Premium/P2 levels	Premium/P6 Level
DTU (database throughput unit)	125	250	1000
Max DB size	500GB	500GB	500GB
Max concurrent requests	200	400	1600
Max concurrent logins	200	400	1600
Max sessions	2400	4800	19200
Benchmark transaction rate	105 transactions/sec	228 transactions/sec	735 transactions/sec
Predictability	Best	Best	Best

■ **Note**   Service levels are subject to alteration. They are also meant to be representative and indicative benchmarks, as opposed to guaranteed performance levels.

We also need to specify a collation for our database. If the database is part of a hybrid solution, then you should ensure, where possible, that the collation matches your on-premises collation. In this scenario, the collation is configured as Latin1_General_CI_AS, although if possible, you should consider configuring your collation globally to Latin1_General_100_CI_AS, since this newer collation handles all Unicode characters correctly. For more information on collations, please refer to Chapter 2. Finally, you need to choose whether the database should be created on a new database server, or on an existing server, if you already have one configured.

Because we are choosing the option to create a new server, a second page of the dialog box becomes available, as illustrated in Figure 27-2.

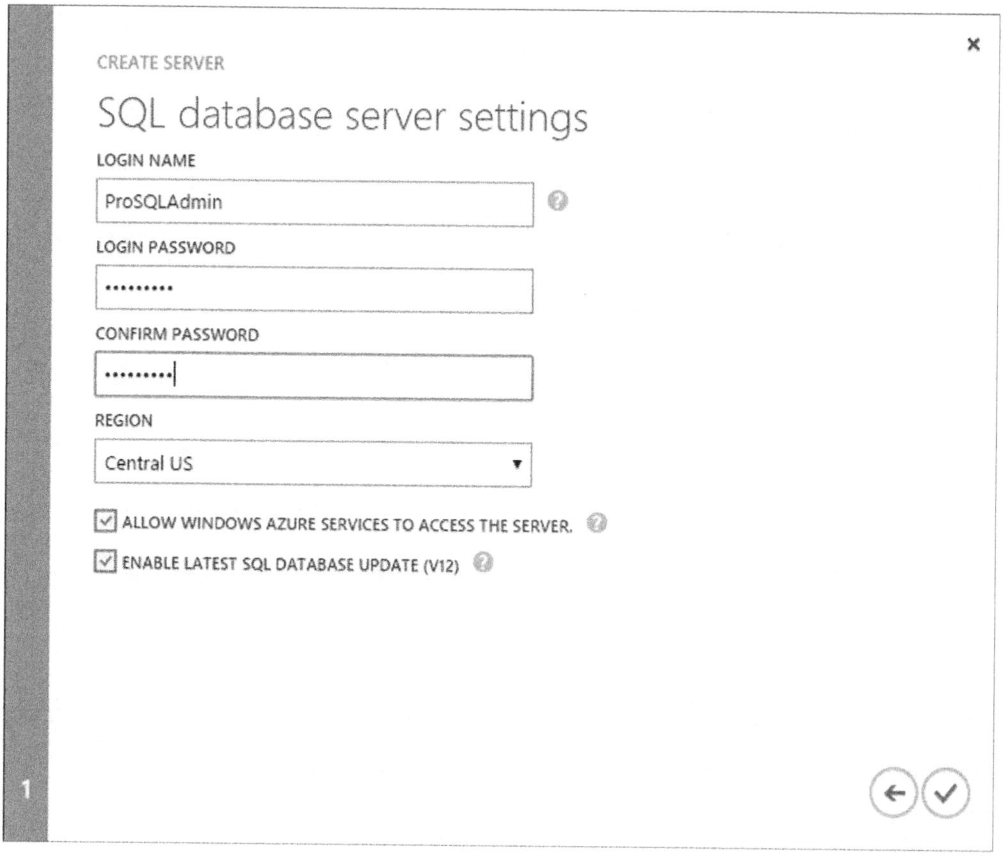

Figure 27-2. *The Create Server dialog box*

On this page, we specify a login name and password for authenticating to the server. We also choose the most appropriate region for the server to be hosted. The Allow Windows Azure Service To Access The Server check box determines whether other Azure services are able to access the database server, and the Enable Latest SQL Database Update option specifies if the server should be configured with the latest version of Azure SQL Database. At the time of writing, this is Version 12. Checking this box is generally a good idea, unless you have a specific compatibility issue.

■ **Note**　After you click the check at the bottom right, the database starts being created. This may take a few minutes, and during this time, you may receive pop-ups. I suggest that you select Not Now to any pop-ups that appear if you are following this demonstration, as they may change the flow of your work.

Once the database has been created, it displays in the SQL Databases tab of Azure management portal. Drilling through the database causes the Quick Start menu for the database to display, which is shown in Figure 27-3. Here, you can see the full connection string for the database server.

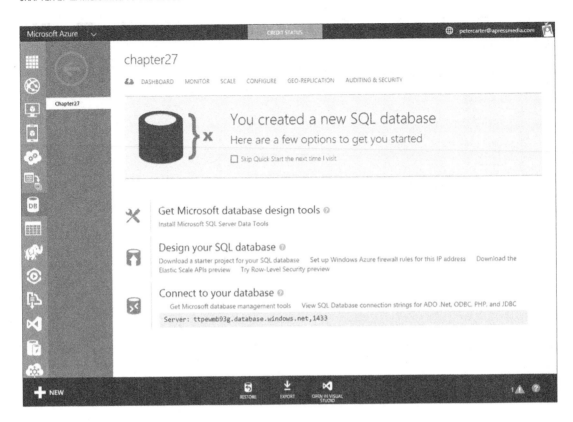

Figure 27-3. *SQL Database Quick Start page*

We can use this page to configure the firewall rules for this server by clicking Set Up Windows Azure Firewall Rules For This IP Address under Design Your SQL Database. Clicking this causes us to be prompted to add the current IP address of the server into the firewall rule, as displayed in Figure 27-4. We select Yes to make the server accessible.

Figure 27-4. *Add the firewall rules*

We now need to configure the firewall to allow clients to access this server. To do this, we navigate to the Servers tab of the SQL Databases page in Azure management portal. We then drill through our server and navigate to the Configure tab, as shown in Figure 27-5. Here, we use the Add To Allowed IP Addresses button in the Current Client IP Address section to create a rule for our current workstation. Alternatively, we can use the text boxes in the lower section of the screen to enter a rule name and an IP Address range manually.

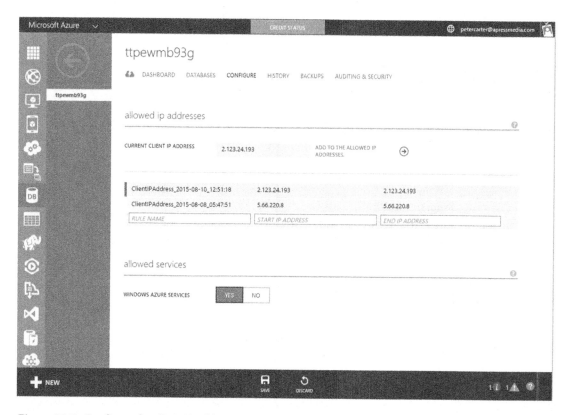

Figure 27-5. *Configure the client IP address*

Now that the firewall has been configured for our server, we can open the new database in SQL Server Management Studio (SSMS), or SSQL Server Data Tools (SSDT), from any client for which a firewall rule has been created. To connect to the server in SSMS, use the connection string, which is displayed on the Home tab of the Chapter27 database, and specify SQL Server authentication using the login name and password you created when you set up the server.

Figure 27-6 shows the server open in SSMS. In Object Explorer, you can see that logins are the only instance-level feature available. This is by design, because the Chapter27 database uses a DaaS model. Also, notice that Extended Events are available, but they are displayed at the database level, as opposed to the instance level. You may also notice a node in Object Explorer for Federation—this feature is being retired and you should not use it. By the time you are reading this book, it may not even appear in Object Explorer. Instead, use Azure SQL Database's elastic database tools to scale your database. A full discussion of elastic database tools is beyond the scope of this book, but you can find further information at https://azure.microsoft.com/en-gb/documentation/articles/sql-database-elastic-scale-get-started/.

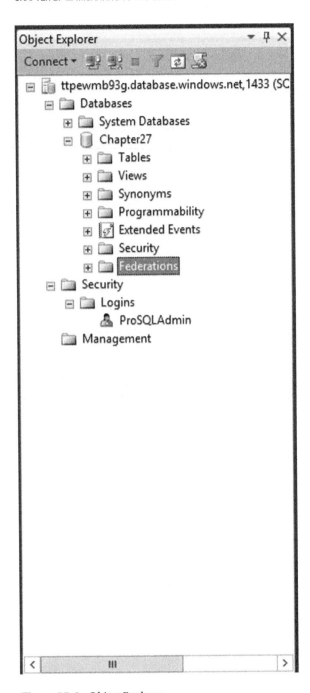

Figure 27-6. *Object Explorer*

Migrating a Database to Azure SQL Database

If you have an existing database that you would like to migrate to the cloud, you can use the wizard SQL Server Management Studio provides to simplify this process. Before we discuss how to use the wizard, let's first use the script in Listing 27-1 to create the Chapter27Migrate database. Make sure you run this script on an on-premises instance of SQL Server.

Listing 27-1. Creating the Database

```
CREATE DATABASE Chapter27Migrate ;
GO

USE Chapter27Migrate
GO

CREATE TABLE dbo.Contacts

        ID              INT              PRIMARY KEY        IDENTITY        NOT NULL,
        FirstName       NVARCHAR(128)      NOT NULL,
        LastName        NVARCHAR(128)      NOT NULL
) ;


INSERT INTO dbo.Contacts(FirstName, LastName)
VALUES('Peter', 'Carter'),
              ('Michael', 'Smith'),
              ('Danielle', 'Mead'),
              ('Reuben', 'Roberts'),
              ('Iris', 'Jones'),
              ('Sylvia', 'Davies'),
              ('Finola', 'Wright'),
              ('Edward', 'James'),
              ('Marie', 'Andrews'),
              ('Jennifer', 'Abraham'),
              ('Margaret', 'Jones') ;
```

Now that we've created the Chapter27Migrate database, we can access the wizard by selecting Tasks | Deploy Database To Windows Azure SQL Database from the context menu of the Chapter27Migrate database in Object Explorer. This invokes the Introduction page of the Deploy Database Wizard. This wizard copies the database to the cloud, while maintaining the original copy on-premises. When you pass through this page, you will see the Deployment Settings page, which is illustrated in Figure 27-7.

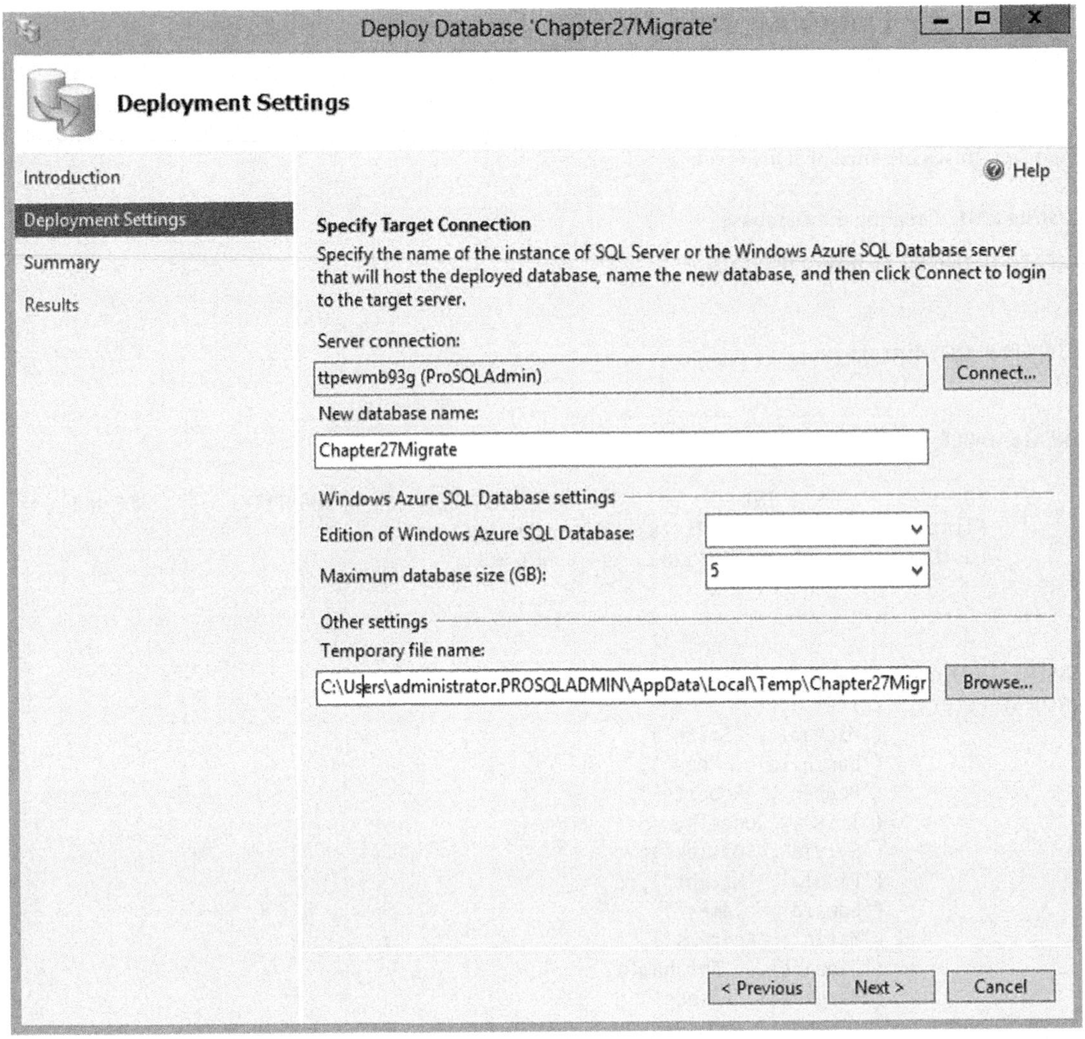

Figure 27-7. *The Deployment Settings page*

■ **Tip** For the wizard to work, you must have Management Tools CU (Cumulative Update) 4 or higher installed for SQL Server 2014 RTM (Release to Manufacture), or SP1. If you do not have this CU level, then you are only able to see the Web and Business editions of Azure SQL Database, neither of which are under continued support. Choosing one of these options will cause the deployment to fail. You can find CU 4 for SQL Server 2014 RTM at https://support.microsoft.com/en-us/kb/2999197. To check your current build version, run SELECT @@VERSION. This returns the build number, which you can check against Microsoft's list of build versions, which is published for SQL Server 2014 at https://support.microsoft.com/en-us/kb/2936603.

On this page of the wizard, you can use the Connect button to connect to the database server. You do this using the connection string provided on the Home page of the Azure SQL Database and the login name and password that you used when you created the server. You then specify a name for your database in the New Database Name field. This field defaults to the name of the existing database, but you can change this if you need to.

In the Windows Azure SQL Database Settings section, specify a maximum size for your Azure SQL Database; when choosing this, make sure to consider the service tier you plan to use. Depending on the version of Management Tools you have installed, you may or may not see a complete list of tiers in the Edition Of Windows Azure SQL Database drop-down box. If you see the tier you wish to use, select it. If the tier that you wish to use is not listed, leave the field blank. You can change this setting at a later date in the Windows Azure Management Portal.

You can use the Temporary File Name field to specify a location for the intermediate .bacpac file that will be created on the local machine. This intermediate file is created because the wizard uses SQL Server's Data-Tier Application feature to extract the database. Data tier applications are beyond the scope of this book.

Figure 27-8 shows the Summary page of the wizard. You should use this page to review the actions that are performed by the wizard.

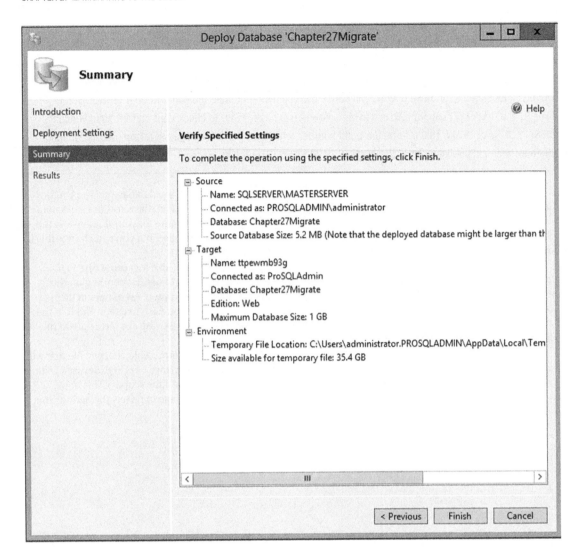

Figure 27-8. The Summary page

The Results page of the wizard, illustrated in Figure 27-9, displays the progress of the deployment. You should review this page for any issues that may have occurred and respond appropriately.

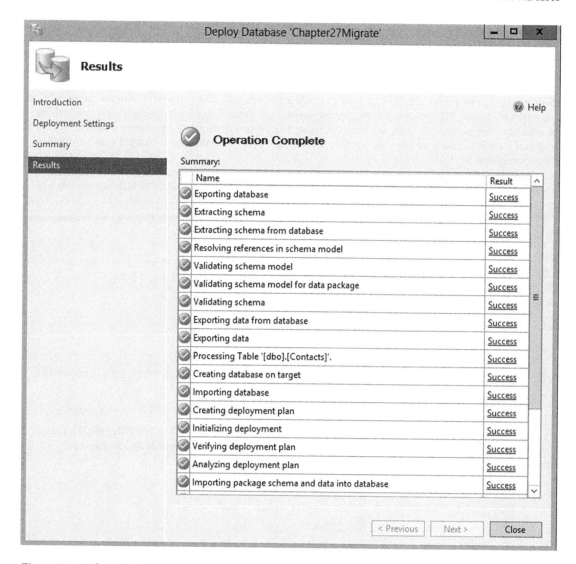

Figure 27-9. *The Results page*

Managing Azure SQL Database

Azure management portal provides tools for monitoring and managing your Azure SQL Databases. The following sections discuss how to monitor your Azure SQL Databases, how to audit them, and how to restore one from a backup.

Monitoring Azure SQL Databases

Azure provides tools for monitoring key metrics on Azure SQL Databases. These metrics include data and log file IO, CPU usage, and database size. This section demonstrates how to use this monitoring capability.

When you drill through the Chapter27Migrate database in the Azure SQL Databases page of Windows Azure Management Studio and then navigate to the Monitor tab, you cause an overview of the database's utilization to display. The lower half of the tab displays the minimum, maximum, average, and total values for each currently selected counter, whereas the upper half of the tab displays the counter values in a graphical format. Because we have not used the Chapter27Migrate database since we uploaded, the values are currently static.

Before we fully explore Azure SQL Database's monitoring functionality, let's first generate some activity in the database by running the script in Listing 27-2 from a query windows in SSMS, which is connected to the Chapter27Migrate database.

Listing 27-2. Generating Activity

```
SELECT *
FROM dbo.Contacts a
CROSS JOIN dbo.Contacts b
CROSS JOIN dbo.Contacts c
CROSS JOIN dbo.Contacts d
CROSS JOIN dbo.Contacts e ;
```

■ **Tip** USE statements are not supported against Azure SQL Database, since it is not possible to connect to, or reference, multiple databases.

To show activity against the database, navigate to the Monitor tab of the Chapter27Migrate database. Figure 27-10 illustrates this activity after the Duration drop-down on the top right of the tab has been changed to 1 Hour. This change causes the graph to rescale.

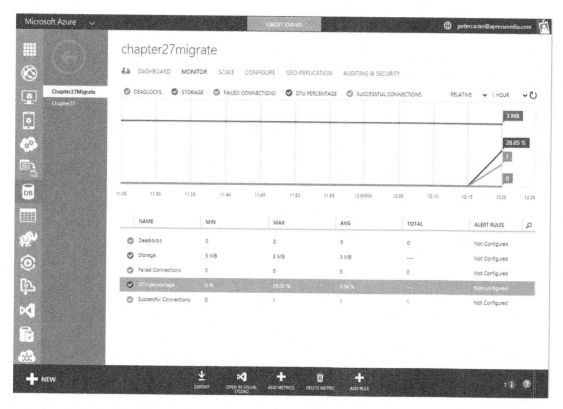

Figure 27-10. *Chapter27Migrate performance metrics*

Imagine that we are interested in analyzing the CPU usage and IO that is generated from our load. We can add these metrics to the output using the Add Metrics button at the bottom of the tab. This causes the Choose Metrics dialog box to display, as illustrated in Figure 27-11.

Figure 27-11. *The Choose Metrics dialog box*

In this dialog box, we check the Log IO Percentage, Data IO Percentage, and CPU Percentage metrics before we return to the Monitor tab. The other selected items are checked by default.

Once we have navigated back to the Monitor tab, we can uncheck the metrics that we do not need in the lower half of the screen. This causes the graph to update, as shown in Figure 27-12.

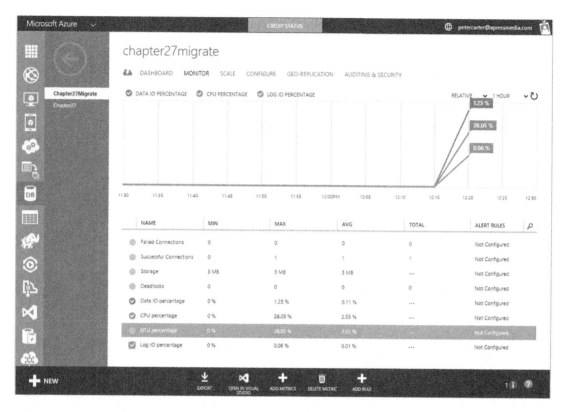

Figure 27-12. *Updated metrics*

When using Windows Azure Management Studio, you can also issue alerts based on specific metrics, by emailing administrators, or by emailing other specific users that you choose. For example, imagine that we want to create an alert if the CPU usage rises above 75 percent of our limit. This is useful in that it warns us that we may need to upgrade our service level to a higher DTU. We can achieve this by highlighting the CPU Percentage metric in the lower half of the screen and then by clicking the Add Rule button. This invokes the Create Alert Rule dialog box, as shown in Figure 27-13.

Figure 27-13. *The Create Alert Rule dialog box*

On the first page of this dialog box, we define a name and a description for the rule. The alert name and description may only contain letters, number, commas, spaces, and periods.

On the second page of the dialog box, illustrated in Figure 27-14, we define the conditions that cause the alert to be fired and the actions that should be taken if it does fire.

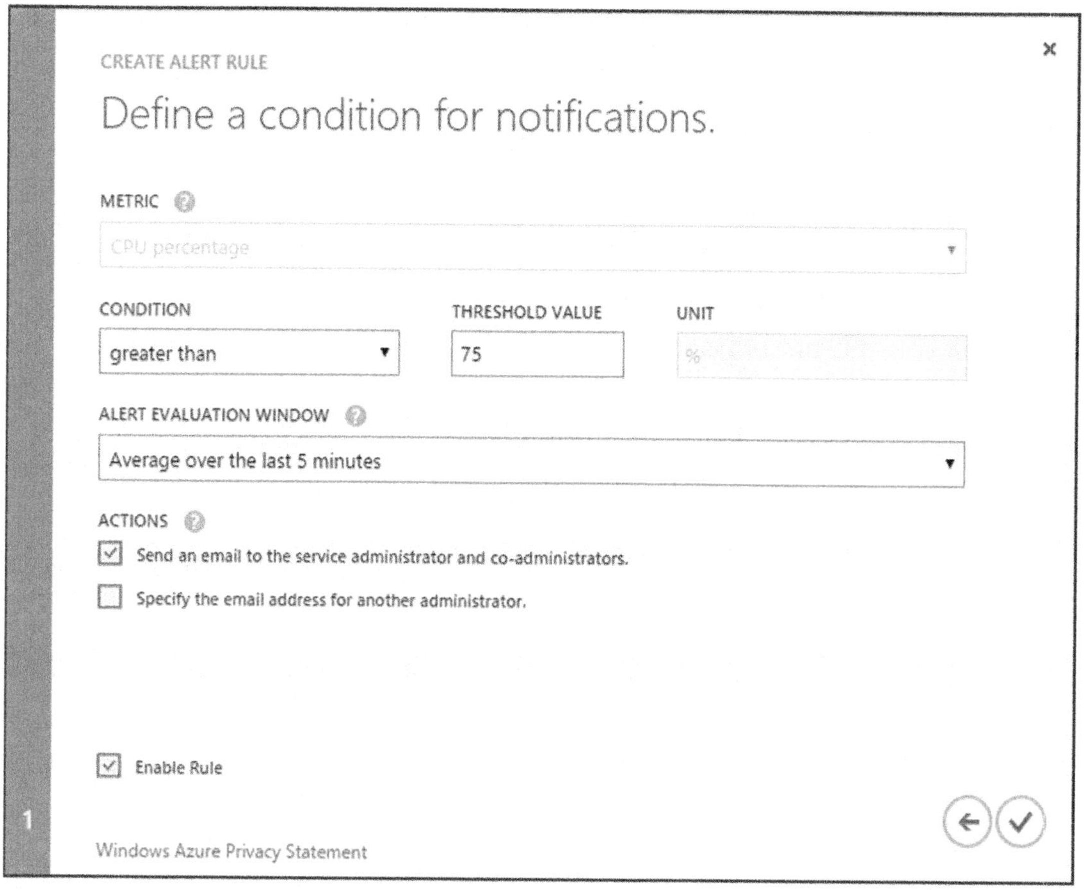

Figure 27-14. *Defining alert conditions and actions*

The Metric field is automatically set to the metric that you selected in the Monitor tab. You can configure the Condition drop-down with the following operators, depending on your requirements:

- Greater Than

- Greater Than Or Equal To

- Less Than

- Less Than Or Equal To

In our case, Greater Than is the logical choice, since we want to be alerted if CPU usage rises above 75 percent.

In the Threshold Value field, we specify the value that will be used in conjunction with the operator. In our case, that is 75. Because the CPU Usage metric is a percentage, percent (%) is the only unit of measurement available. For some other metrics, you can specify an absolute value.

The Average Evaluation Window field specifies the duration that should be used for averaging the metric. Evaluating the average is very useful, because it avoid alerts being raised by temporary spikes. Longer periods of high utilization are more likely to be what you will be concerned with. We want SQL

Server to use 100 percent of the CPU to respond to queries more quickly, but if we are constantly using large amounts of CPU, it could mean we need to do some optimization or consider increasing our DTUs. The Alert Evaluation Window field can be configured as one of the following:

- Average Over The Last 5 Minutes

- Average Over The Last 10 Minutes

- Average Over The Last 15 Minutes

- Average Over The Last 30 Minutes

- Average Over The Last 45 Minutes

- Average Over The Last Hour

Configuring Auditing for Azure SQL Databases

You can configure auditing for the Azure SQL Database by navigating to the Auditing & Security tab of the database in Azure management portal. On this tab, you can enable auditing for the database by setting Auditing to Enabled. This causes the events that can be logged to display in the Auditing section of the tab, followed by configuration options for how you would like your audit logs to be stored, as displayed in Figure 27-15.

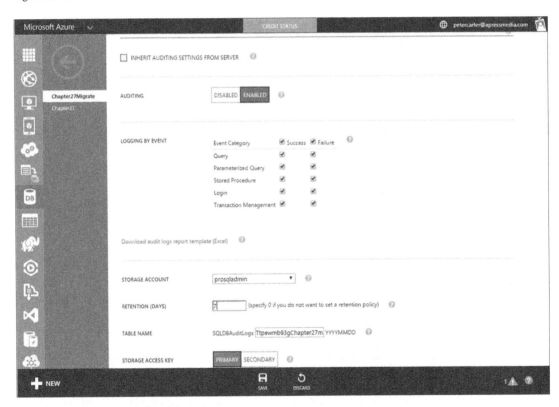

Figure 27-15. *Configuring auditing*

■ **Tip**   You can also configure auditing from the Auditing & Security tab of the database server. In this case, you can use the Inherit Auditing Settings From Server check box to help ensure consistent auditing for your Azure SQL Databases.

In this dialog box, we can first use the check boxes, next to the event categories, to define what success criteria and what failure criteria will be audited. In the lower section of the screen, we need to specify a storage account to use to store the audit logs, since they will be stored in Azure tables. We can also specify the retention period for the logs. It is worth noting that the retention period specified is the minimum retention period; logs may be stored for up to 30 days longer than that threshold. The table name defaults to the configurable part of the name of the server, followed by the name of the database. This is prefixed with SQLDBAuditLogs and is given a suffix relating to the date that the log was created if you specify retention. The name is important, because you use this to access the log. The tables are cycled between 10 and 30 days, depending on the retention period you specify. Finally, specify if the logs should be updated using the primary or secondary storage access key. The reason this feature is helpful is because if you need to regenerate your storage access keys, you can switch to use you secondary access key, regenerate the primary access key, switch back to the primary key and then finally regenerate your secondary access key.

■ **Tip**   Please refer to Chapter 25 for further details on the storage access key.

Once audit data has been captured, you can view the audit logs by using the Azure SQL DB Audit Logs Report template, which you can downloaded from the Auditing & Security tab of the database in Azure Management Studio. This Excel workbook provides a rich template for analyzing audit data.

Restoring Azure SQL Databases

Azure SQL Databases are automatically subject to geo-redundant backups. If you need to restore a database, navigate to the Servers tab within the SQL Databases area of Azure Management Studio before you drill through your server and navigate to the Backups tab, which is displayed in Figure 27-16.

Figure 27-16. *The Backups tab*

On this tab, select the database that you want to restore, and use the Restore button at the bottom of the screen to invoke the Restore dialog box. This dialog box is illustrated in Figure 27-17.

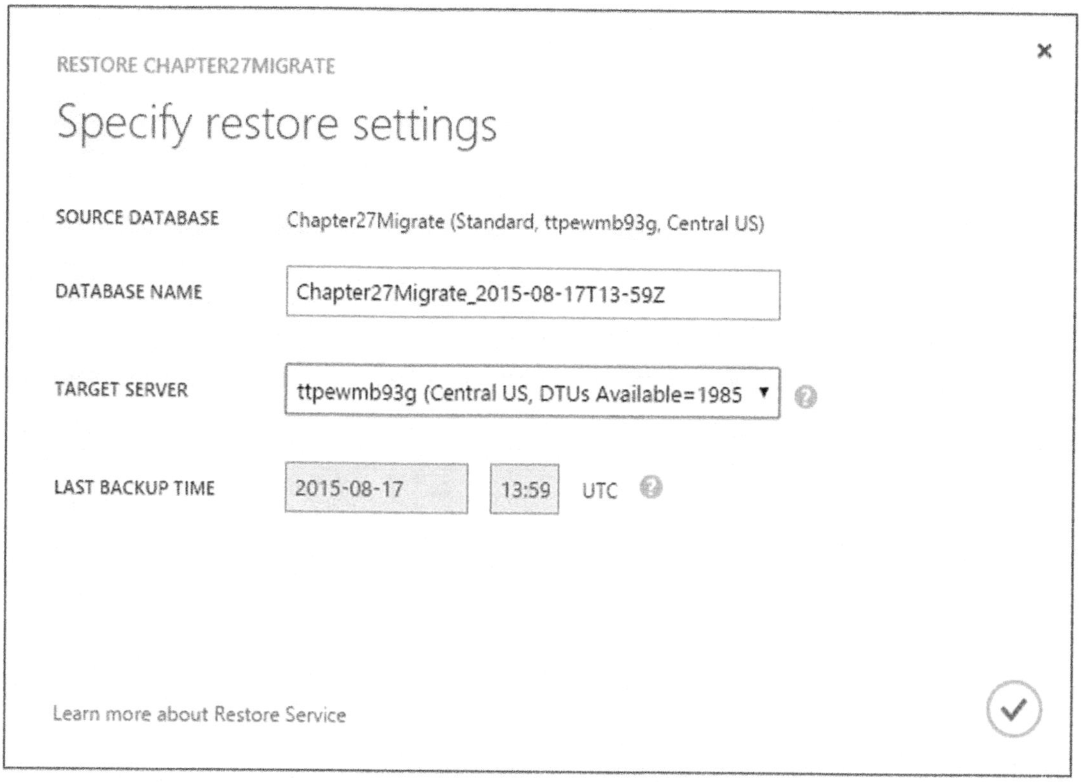

Figure 27-17. *The Restore dialog box*

In this dialog box, you first need to specify a name for the restored database. Because Azure SQL Database is a DaaS offering, you will not be restoring your database due to a hardware or platform failure or for DR invocation. Instead, you will most likely be restoring your database to resolve a data corruption. Therefore, the name of the database to be restored defaults to the database name followed by the timestamp. This allows you to restore your database side by side with the original and merge the two datasets appropriately.

You then select your server from the list of target servers that are available. You also have the option of creating a new server for the restore, if you need to. When you exit the dialog box using the check mark at the bottom right, your database is restored.

Migrating to an Azure VM

To migrate a database to an Azure VM, you first need to create the VM and then run the Deploy Database To Windows Azure VM Wizard from SSMS. The following sections discuss these activities.

Creating a VM

If you plan to migrate your databases to an Azure VM, you first need to create the VM. You can achieve this by navigating to the VM page of Azure Management Studio and selecting the Create New Virtual Machine option. This cause the New | Compute | VM menu to open. Here, choose the From Gallery option. This invokes the Choose An Image page of the Create A Virtual Machine dialog box, as shown in Figure 27-18.

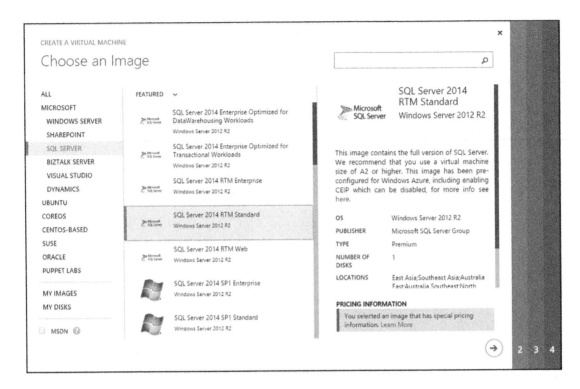

Figure 27-18. *The Choose An Image page*

On this page, you navigate to the SQL Server branch and then select the most appropriate image for your needs. In this example, we choose the SQL Server 2014 RTM Standard image. After you make your choice, you then navigate to the Virtual Machine Configuration page, which is displayed in Figure 27-19.

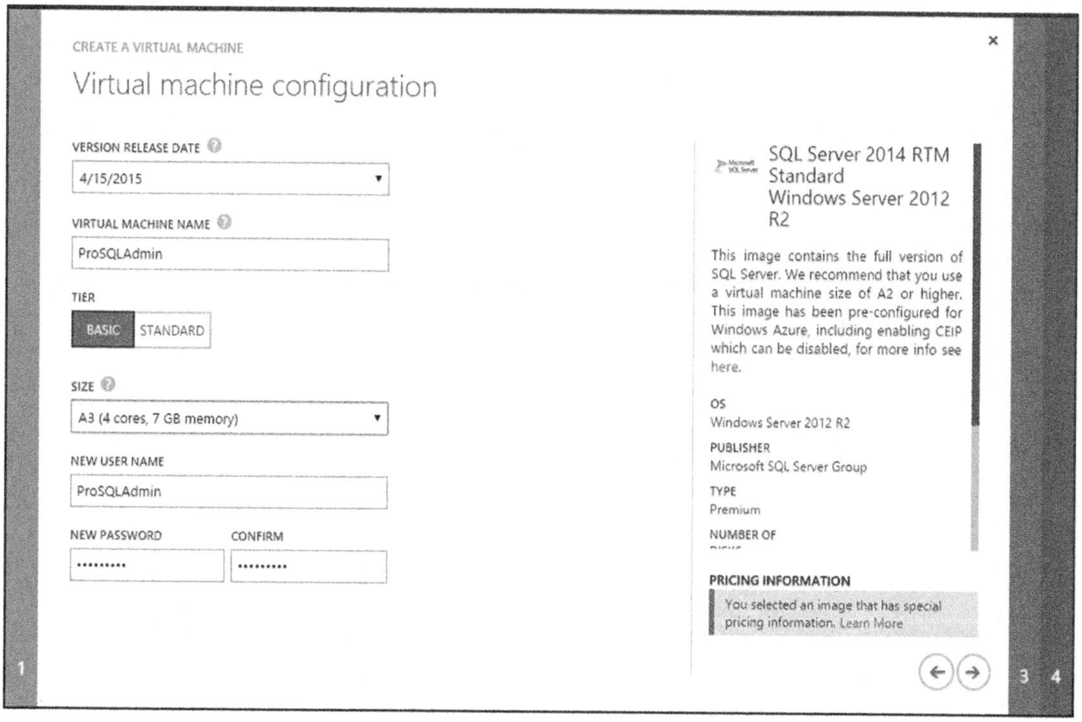

Figure 27-19. The Virtual Machine Configuration page

■ **Tip**　We have chosen the RTM version for consistency with other builds in this book. Unless you have a specific reason to choose the RTM edition, however, you will probably choose to select the version with the highest service pack level.

On this page, we first choose the version of the image that we would like to use to build our machine. The best practice here is to use the most recent version. We also need to give our VM a descriptive name. The options that are available for the size of the VM depend on the service tier that you select; the Standard tier allows higher spec VMs than the Basic tier allows. We also need to provide a user name and password, which are created during the setup of the VM.

■ **Tip**　The minimum size that Microsoft recommends for a production workload is A1, or A3 if you are running SQL Server Enterprise Edition.

Figure 27-20 shows the second Virtual Machine Configuration page. On this page, you first choose if you want to create a new cloud service or use an existing one. A *cloud service* is a container for one or more VMs. If you place multiple VMs inside a cloud service, the traffic can be load-balanced between them. You also need to choose a name for your VM, which is added to the cloudapp.net domain. This computer name must, of course, be unique. You should also choose the region that the VM should reside in and either select an existing storage account to use, or specify that a new one should be created. If you choose Create An Availability Set, then the VM is placed in a fault domain and there is no single point of failure. Finally, enter the details of the ports that you need opened for the VM. The RDP (Remote Desktop Protocol) and PowerShell ports are listed automatically, but here, we have also added the port 11435. This allows the Deploy Database To A Windows Azure VM to connect the virtual machine.

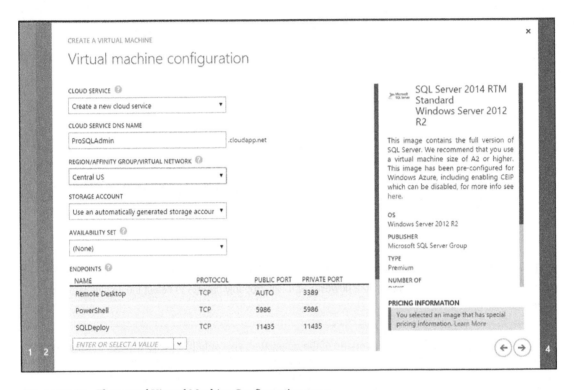

Figure 27-20. *The second Virtual Machine Configuration page*

On the third Virtual Machine Configuration page, illustrated in Figure 27-21, you are able to select extensions that you can install on the VM. The VM Agent is the tool you need to use to install and manage extensions, so it makes sense to install this tool, even if you do not need any extensions immediately.

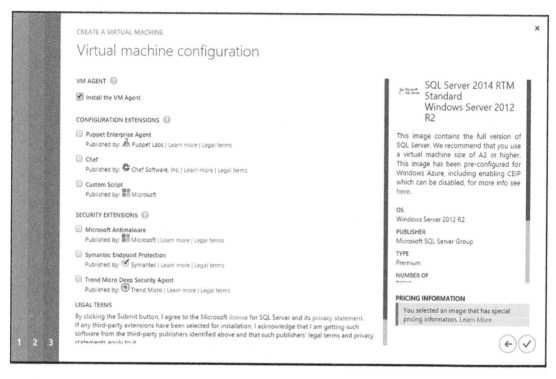

Figure 27-21. *The third Virtual Machine Configuration page*

Once the Virtual Machine has been created, you can use the Connect button in Azure Management Studio to download the RDP file, which allows you to remote onto the server, or (because you opened the SQL port publicly), you are able to connect to the instance via your local SSMS. This may take a few minutes to complete.

Deploying a Database

Before deploying a database, you need a management certificate. You can either create a certificate using Visual Studio before you save this certificate to your local certificate store and upload it to Azure, or you need to generate a publishing profile in Azure. For demonstrations in this section, we work with a publishing profile. This profile is generated and downloaded automatically when you are logged into Windows Azure and visit https://manage.windowsazure.com/publishsettings/index?client=powershell.

■ **Note**   To use the Deploy Database To A Windows Azure VM wizard, ensure that you are running SQL Server 2012 SP1 CU2 or higher. Otherwise the wizard may not recognize your virtual machine size.

Now that you have your publishing profile, you can use the Deploy Database To A Windows Azure VM wizard to deploy your database. In this section, we deploy our Chapter27Migrate database to the VM we created in the previous section. You can access this wizard by drilling through Databases in SSMS and selecting Tasks | Deploy Database To A Windows Azure VM, from the context menu of the database that you wish to migrate. After you pass through the Introduction page, the Source Settings page displays, as illustrated in Figure 27-22.

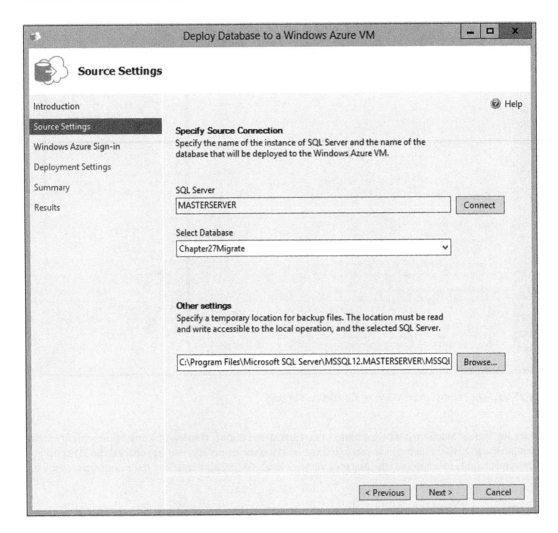

Figure 27-22. *The Source Settings page*

On this page, specify the name of the instance that the database currently resides in, as well as the name of the database itself. In the Other Settings section of the screen, specify a directory where backup files can temporarily be stored, since this is how the wizard moves the data. A sensible location to choose is the instance backup folder.

On the Windows Azure Sign-In page, shown in Figure 27-23, either select a certificate or browse to the file location of your publishing profile. Because we are using a publishing profile, the certificate and field are automatically populated and the Subscription field is populated with a list of active Subscription IDs that are linked to the account.

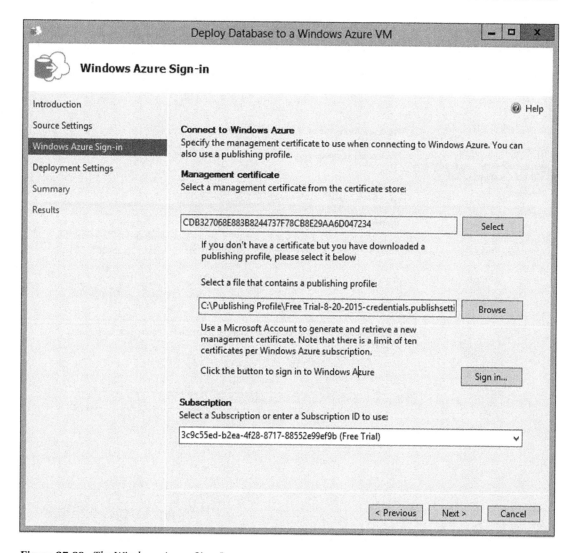

Figure 27-23. *The Windows Azure Sign-In page*

■ **Tip** If you have not generated a publishing profile, you can use the Sign In button to sign into Azure and download a publishing profile.

On the Deployment Settings page of the wizard, illustrated in Figure 27-24, specify the name of the cloud service you created or selected when you created the VM. This populates the Virtual Machine Name field with a list of VMs within that cloud service and the Storage Account field with a list of possible storage accounts that can be used. Then use the Settings button to specify the user name and password that will be used to access the VM. After successfully connecting to the VM, the SQL Instance Name and Database Name fields are automatically populated. You can amend these, however, if you have multiple instances installed on the VM or if you wish the database to have a different name post migration.

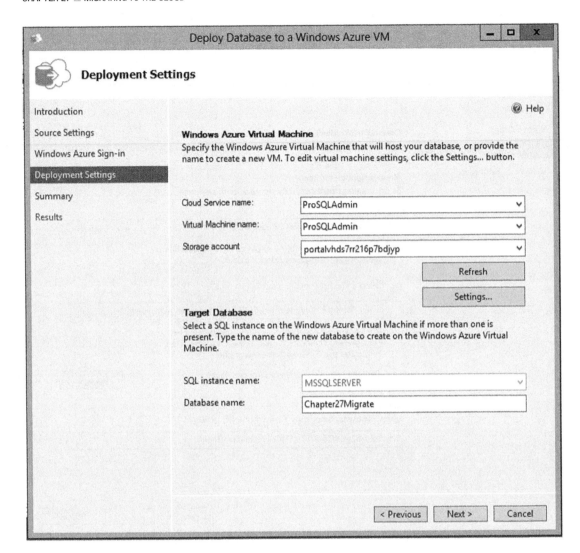

Figure 27-24. *The Deployment Settings page*

After you review the actions that are performed on the Summary page of the wizard, the database is migrated to the VM.

■ **Tip**   If you have not already created your VM, then the Settings button provides you with the opportunity to create one, as opposed to connecting to your existing VM.

Summary

You can create an empty database in Azure management portal. If you do this, you are prompted to create a server at the same time. This provides you with an instance on which to host your database. You can then connect to this server using SQL Server Management Studio (SSMS). Alternatively, you can deploy a Greenfield database to an Azure SQL Database directly from SQL Server Data Tools.

■ **Tip** A Greenfield database implies a new project, where you are not bound by the constraints of upgrading an existing database

---

If you wish to migrate an existing database from an on-premises instance of SQL Server to an Azure SQL Database, then SSMS provides a wizard to assist you. This wizard packages the database as a data tier application before deploying it to the cloud.

Azure management portal provides you with tools for managing Azure SQL Databases. This functionality allows you to monitor key performance metrics and configure endpoints. Because Azure SQL Database offers DaaS, all databases are backed up automatically and you can easily restore these backup files from the Azure management portal.

If you plan to migrate databases to a Windows Azure VM, you have multiple SQL Server VM images and sizing options to choose from.

Once you have created you virtual machine, you can use the Deploy A Database To A Windows Azure VM wizard in SSMS to deploy your database. This wizard uses a backup and restore to migrate the data to the cloud. Before running the wizard, ensure that you have generated a management certificate. You can do this by either creating a certificate in Visual Studio and importing this to your certificate store, or alternatively, by downloading a publishing profile from Azure.

Index

■ R

Get the eBook for only $5!

Why limit yourself?

Now you can take the weightless companion with you wherever you go and access your content on your PC, phone, tablet, or reader.

Since you've purchased this print book, we're happy to offer you the eBook in all 3 formats for just $5.

Convenient and fully searchable, the PDF version enables you to easily find and copy code—or perform examples by quickly toggling between instructions and applications. The MOBI format is ideal for your Kindle, while the ePUB can be utilized on a variety of mobile devices.

To learn more, go to www.apress.com/companion or contact support@apress.com.

CPSIA information can be obtained at www.ICGtesting.com
Printed in the USA
BVOW09s0727141115

427139BV00012B/97/P